Maeve Binchy

LIGHT
A PENNY
CANDLE

ECHOES

This edition published in 1999 by Cresset Editions,
an imprint of Random House UK Ltd,
20 Vauxhall Bridge Road, London SW1V 2SA

Printed and bound in Germany

ISBN 0 0918 7280 4

LIGHT
A PENNY
CANDLE

For dearest Gordon with all my love

It had been very dull and matter-of-fact in the coroner's court. No great raised bench with wigged judges, no dock, no uniformed police calling down the corridors for the next person to appear. It was actually quite like an ordinary office; there were books in glassfronted cases, and lino on the floor – at one corner it had definitely been nibbled or chewed by something.

Outside, the world was going on normally. Buses passed by, no one stopped to see them. A man in a taxi read his newspaper and didn't even raise his eyes as the little group came out on to the street.

Both the women wore black, but then they would have worn black anyway if they had been going somewhere formal. Aisling wore a black velvet blazer over a grey dress. It was an outfit that made her copper hair look even more coppery than usual. Elizabeth wore her good black coat. She had bought it at a January sale two years before for half price and the sales woman had said it was the only genuine bargain in the store. 'It'll take you anywhere, my dear,' she had said, and Elizabeth had liked the sound of that . . . it reminded her of a magic carpet.

Although the rest of the world took no notice, the little group watched them for a moment. Elizabeth, putting her hand up over her eyes as she turned the corner, came out on to the steps leading down into the street. Aisling stood on the steps already. They looked at each other for a long time – probably only seconds, but that can be a long time. . . .

PART ONE

1940–1945

I

Violet finished the library book and closed it with a snap. Yet again, a self-doubting, fluttery, bird-brain heroine had been swept away by a masterful man. He would silence her protests with kisses, the urgency of his passion would express itself in all sorts of positive ways. . . . *He* would organise the elopement or the wedding plans or the emigration to his South American estates. The heroine would never have to make all the arrangements herself, standing in queues at the travel agency, the ticket office, the passport office. Violet had to do everything herself. She had come back from an endless morning of standing in shops to beat the shortages. Other women seemed to enjoy it, to think of it as a game of hunt-the-thimble. 'I'll tell you where there's bread if you tell me how you got those carrots.'

Violet had been to the school and had a highly unsatisfactory discussion with Miss James. Miss James was not going to organise any evacuation for her class. All the parents so far had friends or relations in the country. There was no question of the whole class decamping and continuing their education in some rural setting with safety from bombs and plenty of good country food. Miss James had said quite tartly that she was certain Mr and Mrs White must have friends outside London. Violet wondered suddenly whether they had friends anywhere, city or country. She felt very dissatisfied with Miss James for forcing her to face this possibility. George did have some cousins in Somerset, near Wells. But they had lost touch. Oh yes, she'd read all the heart-warming stories of long-lost families having been brought together over the evacuation of children . . . but somehow she didn't think it would happen to George. Violet had no relations to speak of. Her father and his

3

second wife were in Liverpool, separated from her by a feud too long-lasting to dream of mending. To heal would be to open the wound, examine it and forgive. It was so long ago it was almost forgotten. Let it stay that way.

Elizabeth was so timid, so unsure of herself, she would not be an easy evacuee. She had inherited her father's awkwardness, Violet thought regretfully. She seemed to expect the worst from every situation. Well, perhaps it was better than having expected great things and having got so little. Violet suspected that Elizabeth and George might be the lucky ones; to expect defeat and conflict and being relegated to second best meant freedom from shock when it happened.

It was no use whatsoever discussing it with George. These days George had only one thing he could discuss – the kind of country which would accept a man for military service who hadn't a brain in his head, and refuse a man like George who could have been of some real assistance in the war. . . . It had been bad enough to see all those younger, brainless men do well in the bank, move into different aspects, get preferment, buy motor cars, even – that had been galling. But now, when their land was threatened and their nation was in danger, George had been told that some services were essential to the country and that banking was one of them.

They had found no terminal disease at his medical examination, just a series of inadequacies. He had flat feet, he had a whistling chest, he had sinus trouble, he had varicose veins, he was slightly deaf in one ear. His offer to lay down his life for his country had been met with a series of insults.

From time to time, Violet felt an old, familiar surge of affection for him, a sharing in his outrage, but mainly she felt he brought a lot of it on himself. Not his deafness, not his veins, but his rejection and his disappointment. He went out half-way to invite it.

So the problem of what they were to do with Elizabeth would, of course, be Violet's and Violet's alone. As were so many of the problems.

Violet stood up and examined her face in the mirror. It

was a perfectly acceptable face. It had nice colouring, according to what the magazines advised; and her hair was blonde, naturally blonde. Her figure had always been good. Even before the drawing in of belts that had become associated with patriotism and this dreadful war, Violet used to watch what she ate. Why, then, did her face have no sparkle? It wasn't a lively face. It looked flat somehow.

Of course it looked flat, Violet thought with a surge of resentment. Anyone's face would look flat had they been dealt such a poor hand in everything. The chap that had said her eyes were violet like her name had turned out to be a confidence trickster, and had swindled everyone in the neighbourhood. The fellow who had said she should sing professionally had only meant her to sing to him in the bath while he poured her sparkling wine. The eager young banker who told her that together they would rise in London society so that everyone would know her name and envy her distinguished husband his luck, was at this moment with his flat feet and varicose veins, picking his teeth and making excuses down at the local branch of the bank where he would stay forever.

It had all been so different, so dull. It had all been so unfair and so flat. No wonder her features had blended into the background.

She looked at the cover of the library book. Under the transparent library binding a masterful man leaned on an old gnarled apple tree with his riding crop in his hand. Violet wondered whether people should be prosecuted for writing novels like that.

Elizabeth came home from school slowly. Miss James had said that Mother had been in to discuss things. She had said not to look so anxious, there was nothing to worry about. Elizabeth had looked doubtful. No, really, Miss James had assured her, Elizabeth's Mummy had only come in to discuss what would happen when the children all went off to the country to stay in quiet places by the seaside or on farms. Elizabeth wasn't fooled by Miss James's way of describing what lay ahead. She knew it was something dreadful,

5

something spoken of with dread by parents . . . as if it were torture. They tried to make light of it, but it was no use.

Elizabeth had thought it was 'vaccination' when she had heard of it first. It was another long word with dangerous associations. Father had laughed and put his arms around her, and Mother had smiled too. No, they assured her, evacuation was being sent to the country in case bombs fell and hurt children. But why couldn't parents come to the country too, Elizabeth had wanted to know. Father had said he had to work in the bank, and Mother had sniffed; and suddenly the nice smiling bit, the short happy bit when she had mixed up the words was gone. Father said Mother could go to the country, as she had no job. Mother had replied that if she had a job she wouldn't have remained on the bottom rung of it for fifteen years.

Elizabeth had run off pretending that she had to do her homework, but she just took out an old doll and unpicked it, stitch by stitch, while she cried and wondered what she could do to make them smile more, and what she had done that made them so angry all the time.

Today she had another fear in her heart. She wondered if Mother had fought with Miss James about something. Mother had thought Miss James was silly before, when she had taught them to sing nursery rhymes in harmony. 'Big girls, ten years old, singing silly nursery rhymes,' Mother had said, and Miss James had answered her pleasantly. But a lot of the fun went out of it after that. . . .

Elizabeth found it hard to know when Mother would be happy. Sometimes she was happy for days on end, like the time they had gone to the music hall, and Mother had met an old friend and he had said that Mother used to sing better than anyone on the stage in London. Father had been a bit put out, but what with Mother being so cheerful, and even suggesting they all have a fish supper, he cheered up. Mother didn't usually suggest anything so common as a fish supper. When they had fish at home, it was little bits of fish, with lots of bones and funny knives that weren't really knives to eat it with. Mother loved those knives. They had been a wedding present and she warned everyone not to let their handles go

6

into the water when the washing-up was being done. Elizabeth didn't like the fish that Mother cooked, with the bones and little bits of egg and parsley on it, but she was glad to see it because the knives always made Mother so good-humoured.

And sometimes when she came home from school, Mother would be singing: that was always a very good omen indeed. Other times, Mother would come and sit on Elizabeth's bed and stroke her fine, fair hair and tell her about her childhood and how she had read books about men who did brave deeds for beautiful women. Sometimes she told Elizabeth funny stories about the nuns in the extraordinary convent school where everyone had been Roman Catholics and believed the most amazing things, but Mother had been allowed to go for walks during the religious instruction classes because it had all been quite so amazing.

The terrible thing was that you never knew when Mother would be happy or when she would not.

Today she was writing a letter, which was unusual. Elizabeth thought that it was a complaint letter, and she prayed that it wasn't about Miss James. She approached nervously.

'Are you busy, Mother?' she asked.

'Mm,' said Mother.

She stood there, a thin little ten-year-old; her short, fair hair – almost white it was so fair – was pulled back from her face with an Alice band, but when she was fussed – like now – little wisps of it escaped, standing up like spikes. Her face was red and white at the same time; the parts around her eyes and nose ashen, while the crimson high up on her cheeks moved like a red shadow.

'Oh,' she said.

'I'm going to send you to Eileen.'

Eileen was a name on a Christmas card, it was a name associated with a small, cheap toy on her birthday. Last year, Mother had said she wished Eileen would drop the birthday gifts, it was silly to keep it up and *she* couldn't possibly be expected to remember all the birthdays of Eileen's dozens of children.

'It seems the only possible solution.'

Elizabeth's eyes filled with tears. She wished she knew what she could do to be allowed to stay. She wished hard that she could be the kind of girl that parents didn't send away, or that they'd come with her.

'Will you come with me?' She looked at the carpet hard.

'Oh, heavens, no dear.'

'I was just hoping. . . .'

'Elizabeth, don't be so silly. I can't possibly go to Eileen's, to the O'Connors, with you. . . . Darling, they live in Ireland. Who would go to Ireland, Elizabeth, for heaven's sake? It's out of the question.'

Thursday was always a busy day because the farmers coming in for the market brought their lists into the shop. Sean employed a boy, Jemmy, who wasn't 'all there', to help carry out the supplies from the yard. He didn't want the children cluttering up the shop on a Thursday, he had said so a dozen times. He wiped a weary forehead with a dusty hand in annoyance when he saw Aisling and Eamonn escaping from the ineffectual grabs and shouts of Peggy and running into the shop.

'Where's Mammy, Da, where's Mammy?' shouted Aisling.

'Where's Mammy, where's Mammy?' repeated Eamonn.

Peggy, running and giggling, was just as bad.

'Will ya come here, you brats,' she laughed. 'I'll tan the backside offa you, Aisling, when I catch you. Your father's after saying a hundred times, he'll have yez locked up if you come in here on a Thursday.'

The farmers, busy men who hated having to take any time at all away from their deals and discussions on beasts, laughed at the sideshow. Peggy, hair escaping from a bun, filthy apron stained with the last twenty meals she had served, was loving the sensation she knew she was causing. Sean looked at her helplessly as she darted here and there, making even more of a game of it than the children were, with her bold winks at the farmers and the come-on glance giving encouragement to any of them that might want to come back and find her at the end of the market when the pubs were making them feel like powerful men. Johnny stood open-mouthed and delighted, with the planks in his hands that should have been loaded on a trailer.

'Get those bloody bits of wood outside and come back in here,' roared Sean. 'Now, Michael, ignore these antics, I'll deal with that lot later. How much are you going to need for the plastering? Are you doing all the outhouses now? No, no, of course you're not. Far too much to take on at one time.'

Eileen had heard the commotion, and in small quick steps she came out of her little office and down to the shop. Her office, with its mahogany surrounds and glass windows on all sides, looked like a little closed-in pulpit, Young Sean had said to her once. She should really preach a sermon to everyone in the shop, rather than fill in books and ledgers. But if Eileen didn't fill books and ledgers, there would be no shop, no house, no luxuries like Peggy, and Jemmy, who got a few shillings on a Thursday which made him important again in his family.

Her face was set in a hard line when she met the excited children and the flushed Peggy. Taking each child in a most uncomfortable place, just under the shoulder, she marched them firmly out of the shop; and after one glance from the Mistress, Peggy lost a lot of her bounce and followed quickly with her eyes down. Sean sighed with relief and got back to what he knew about.

Up the stairs of the house in the square, the children squealing and wriggling, Eileen was unwavering.

'Put on some tea, please, Peggy,' she said, her voice cold.

'But Mammy, we just wanted to show you the letter.'

'With the picture of a man on it.'

'It came by the afternoon post. . . .'

'And Johnny said when he was giving it that it was from England. . . .'

'And the man was the King of England. . . .'

Eileen ignored them. She put them sitting on two dining chairs opposite her and faced them.

'If I've told you once, I've told you a million times, on

9

Thursday, on market day, your father doesn't want to see hide nor hair of you in that shop and neither do I. As it is, he's over there waiting on me to come back and do the bills, and write up the books for the farmers. Have you no idea at all of obedience? Aisling, a great, big girl of ten years of age? Do you hear me?'

Aisling hadn't heard a word. She wanted her mother to open the letter, which she vaguely thought was from the King of England because of what the postman had said.

'Aisling, listen to me!' shouted Eileen, and seeing that she was getting nowhere, she reached out and slapped the bare legs of the two of them. Hard. Both began to cry. At the sound, Niamh woke up and began to cry in the cot in the corner of the living room.

'I only wanted to give you the letter,' wailed Aisling. 'I hate you, I hate you.'

'I hate you too,' echoed Eamonn.

Eileen marched to the door. 'Well, you can sit here and hate me.' She tried not to raise her voice, since she knew that little Donal would be sitting up in bed, listening to every sound. Just thinking of his little face made her heart move suddenly, so she decided to run upstairs and see him just for a few seconds. If she went in and said something cheerful he would smile and go back to his book. Otherwise she might see his face pressed anxiously to the bedroom window as he watched her crossing from the house to the shop. She peeped in at his door, knowing well that he was awake.

'You're to try and sleep, pet, you know that.'

'Why is there shouting?' he asked.

'Because that bold sister and brother of yours came into the shop caterwauling on a Thursday, that's why,' she said, adjusting the bedclothes.

'Have they said sorry?' he asked, begging to be reassured.

'No, they haven't – yet,' said Eileen.

'What's going to happen now?'

'Nothing too bad,' she said, and kissed him.

Back in the living room, Aisling and Eamonn were still mutinous.

'Peggy called us for tea, but we're not going,' said Aisling.

'As you wish. You can certainly have my permission to sit here for as long as you like. In fact you can sit here for a long time. Because neither of you two will get to have a lemonade this Thursday evening after your behaviour.'

The faces were round-eyed with disbelief and disappointment. Always on a Thursday, with his order-book full and his cash-box bursting, Sean O'Connor took his wife and children down to Maher's. It was a quiet place. There would be no farmers with manure on their boots sealing bargains in there. Maher's was the drapery as well as having a pub and Eileen liked looking at the new jackets or boxes of cardigans with Mrs Maher. Young Sean and Maureen liked sitting up on high stools reading the notices behind the bar and looking like grown-ups; Aisling and Eamonn loved the way the fizzy red lemonade went up their noses, and how Mr Maher would give them a biscuit with icing on it, and their father would say they were spoiled. The Mahers had a cat which had just had kittens. Last Thursday the kittens' eyes hadn't been open, so this week, for the first time, they would be allowed to play with them.

And now it was all cancelled.

'Please, Mammy, please, I'll be good, I'll be very good. . . .'

'I thought you hated me?'

'I don't really hate you,' said Eamonn hopefully.

'I mean, nobody could hate their mother?' added Aisling.

'That's what I thought,' said Eileen. 'That's why I was so surprised you both forgot that, the way you forgot about coming to the shop. . . .' She gave in. It was the only time in the week when Sean relaxed properly, that hour in Maher's with the children nicely scrubbed and neat playing peacefully with cats or rabbits or caged birds. She picked up the letter and went into the kitchen.

'I've the tea wet, Mam,' said Peggy nervously.

'Pour me the large mug, please. Keep those children in the living room and see to the baby.' In a moment, she had her tea and, letter in her pocket, was striding back to the shop. It was an hour before she had time to open the letter.

In Maher's that night, Eileen passed it to Sean to read.

11

'My eyes are so tired I can hardly see it,' he said. 'Anyway, that writing's like a spider half-drunk getting out of an ink-pot.'

'That's italic script, you ignoramus, that's the way the nuns in St Mark's taught us to write. Violet remembers it, I don't, that's all.'

'That Violet has little else to remember,' said Sean. 'Life of ease over there, she has.'

'Not since the war started,' Eileen pointed out.

'No,' Sean agreed into his pint. 'No. Is her man out in the trenches? I suppose he'd be an officer, being in the bank and all. That's the way the British Empire does things. If men have good accents they get good jobs and they get to be officers.'

'No, George isn't in the army at all, he had something wrong. I don't know what, anyway he was medically unfit.'

'Too cushy a life in the bank, I suppose he didn't want to leave,' said Sean.

'Sean, it's the child, it's Violet's child, Elizabeth. They're all being sent out of London for fear of the bombs . . . you know, we read it in the papers. Violet wants to know will we have her here?'

'This isn't the country . . . they're not evacuating them to Ireland, this is our country. They can't make us join their bloody war by sending us all their children and old people . . . haven't they done bloody enough already . . . ?'

'Sean, will you *listen* to me!' Eileen snapped. 'Violet would like to know whether we would take Elizabeth for a few months. The little school she's in is closing down because all the children are being evacuated. George has relations, and so has Violet, but they . . . they asked if she could come here. What do you think?'

'I think it's a bloody liberty, a bloody cheek and typical of the British Empire. Unless you can be of some use to them they've no time for you, they don't want to know you, not a letter, barely a Christmas card. Then when they get themselves into this stupid war they're fawning all over you. That's what I think.'

'Violet is not the British Empire, she's my friend from

school. She was never a letter-writer, even this one is jerky and full of . . . I don't know, brackets and inverted commas. She's not used to writing to people, not twenty or thirty letters a day, like I am. That's not the point. The point is will you have the child in the house?'

'That's not the point, the point is she's got a bloody neck to ask.'

'Shall I say no, then? Will I write tonight and say I'm sorry, no. Reason? Because Sean says the British Empire has a bloody neck. Will that do?'

'Don't be all bitter. . . .'

'I'm not being all bitter. I've had just as exhausting a day as you have. All right. Of course I think Violet has a bloody neck. Of course I'm insulted when I think she hasn't much time for me, if she doesn't bother to write unless she wants something. That goes without saying. The point is, do we have the child or not? She's Aisling's age, *she* didn't declare war on Germany, or invade Ireland, or attack De Valera or whatever. . . . She's only ten, she's probably lying there at night wondering will a bomb fall on her and blow her to bits. Now, do we have her or don't we?'

Sean looked surprised. Eileen didn't usually make speeches. And it was even more unusual for her to admit to a hurt or an insult from her precious friend of schooldays.

'Will she be too much trouble for you?' he asked.

'No, she might even be a friend for Aisling. And what can one child eat more than we all eat already?'

Sean called for another pint, a port for Eileen and more lemonades. He looked at Eileen, smart now in her white blouse with the brooch at the neck, her brown-red hair pulled up at the sides with combs. She was a handsome woman, he thought, and a strong partner in everything he did. Few people, seeing her in her navy office coat, working out the credit and the cash for a growing business, would know what she was like underneath. A passionate wife – he had always been amazed that she should respond to him as eagerly as he turned to her – and a loving mother too. He looked at her warmly. She had such a heart it could include more children than she had herself.

'Send for her, it's the least we can do to try and keep a child away from all the madness that's going on,' he announced. And Eileen patted him on the arm in a rare display of public affection.

The letter from Eileen arrived so quickly that Violet believed it was a refusal. In her experience, people who were about to make excuses and justify their actions always wrote quickly and at length. With a heavy sigh she picked it up from the mat.

'Well I expect we'll have to smoke out your father's relations after all,' she sighed as she brought it back to the breakfast table.

'Does this mean she says no . . . ?' began Elizabeth. 'Maybe she says yes inside. . . .'

'Don't speak with your mouth full. Pick up your serviette and *try* to behave properly, Elizabeth, *please*,' said Violet mechanically as she slit the envelope with a paper knife. George had already gone to work and there were just the two of them. Violet thought that if you let standards fall you were on the way to destruction, so the toast was served with the crusts cut off in a small china toast rack, and all three of them had their napkin rings into which the folded napkin must be replaced after every meal.

Elizabeth nearly burst waiting for Violet to read the news. It couldn't have been more irritating. She would read bits aloud and then mutter.

'My dear Violet . . . delighted to hear from you . . . emm . . . umm . . . very concerned about you and George and Elizabeth . . . emm . . . umm . . . many people here think that we should be in the war too . . . do anything we can . . . children very pleased and excited. . . .'

Elizabeth knew she had to wait. She screwed her table napkin very tightly into a little ball. She didn't know what she wanted to hear: it would be a relief not to have to go across the sea to another country, a place that Father seemed to think was just as dangerous as London and a place that Mother dismissed as somewhere you couldn't go except in dire circumstances. She didn't want to go and stay in *an awful dump with dozens of children, and in a town full of*

14

animal droppings and drunkards which was how Mother had remembered Kilgarret. Elizabeth didn't want to be in a dirty place somewhere that Mother disapproved of. But still, Mother had said this was the best place for her to go. Perhaps it had got better. It had been years since Mother had visited it, long before she had married Father. She had said she would never go back again – she couldn't understand how Eileen had been able to stand it.

But it was this place with all its dangers and dirt, or else it was more trouble and anxiety and looking for Father's cousins.

After a long time, and two pages, Violet spoke.

'They're going to take you.'

Elizabeth's face went its bright red and white colour. Violet was irritated; she hated it when Elizabeth flushed in this vivid way over nothing at all.

'When am I to go?'

'Whenever we like. It will take time, of course. We have to pack, and I have to write to Eileen about school books . . . what you need. She's full of welcomes but little practical advice about what to take with you and what you'll need. Oh, and there's this note for you. . . .'

Elizabeth took the single sheet of paper. It was the first letter she had ever got from anyone. She read it slowly to savour it.

Dear Elizabeth,
We are all so glad that your Mummy is lending you to us for a little while, and we hope you'll be happy here. Kilgarret is very different from London but everyone is looking forward to meeting you and making you feel at home. You will share a room with Aisling, who is exactly the same age as you, there is only one week in the difference so we hope you'll be great friends. Sister Mary at the school says you'll probably know far more than all the class put together. Bring any toys or dolls or books you want, we've plenty of room here, and we're counting the days till you come.

Auntie Eileen

At the bottom of the page in a section where someone had ruled lines to keep the writing straight, there was another note.

Dear Elizabeth,
I have left all the shelves on the left side of the room for you and half the press and half the dressing table. Be sure to come for Eamonn's birthday, there will be a party. The Mahers's kittens are sweet they have their eyes open. Mammy is going to get one for you and me to share.
Love, Aisling.

'A kitten to share,' said Elizabeth, her eyes shining.

'And nothing about school fees, uniforms, anything,' said Violet.

Donal's cough was worse, but Doctor Lynch said there was no need to worry. Keep him warm, no draughts but plenty of fresh air all the same. How on earth did people manage that, Eileen wondered. He was finding the excitement about the girl from England almost too much for him.

'When will she be here?' he would ask a dozen times a day.

'She's going to be my friend, not yours,' Aisling said.

'Mam said she'd be *everyone's* friend,' he replied, his face clouding.

'Yes, but mainly mine. After all, she wrote to me,' said Aisling. This was undeniable. There had been a letter which Aisling had read out several times. It was very formal. It was the first proper letter Elizabeth had ever written. It had words like 'grateful' and 'appreciate' in it.

'They must have a better educational system altogether over there,' commented Eileen, reading it.

'Why wouldn't they? With all the wealth they made off the backs of other people,' said Sean. It was Saturday lunchtime. He had come in for his bacon and cabbage lunch. The shop closed on Saturdays at half past one, and the afternoon was spent making up orders in the back yard, but at least it was his own time and he didn't have to be in and out every time the door clanged open and the bell over the doorframe rang.

'Now, I hope you won't be going on with that kind of thing when the child arrives,' said Eileen. 'Isn't it hard enough for her going to another country without having you running her down?'

'And it isn't even true either, Da,' said Young Sean.

'It is bloody true,' said his father. 'But your mother is right. When the child comes we'll all hold our tongues and put our real thoughts out of our minds for a bit. It's only fair on the little one.'

'I don't have to put my real thoughts anywhere out of sight,' said Young Sean. 'I don't have any of this constant bellyaching about the British to make me feel good.'

Sean laid down his knife and fork and pointed across the table. Eileen interrupted quickly.

'Will you listen to me, please. I was just about to say that when she comes it might be the opportunity for this family to improve its table manners. Like a lot of puppies you are, slopping food on the table cloth and speaking with your mouths full.'

'Puppies don't speak with their mouths full,' said Eamonn. Donal laughed and, hearing the laughter, Niamh cooed and gurgled in the pram beside the table.

'I'm sure she'll think we're very rude,' said Aisling. Eileen was surprised to have support from this source.

'We all talk at the same time and no one listens to anyone else,' continued Aisling disapprovingly. Something in the way she said it, something schoolmistressish about her tone, made everyone laugh. She didn't know why they were laughing and looked annoyed.

'What's so funny?' she said, 'what's funny?'

Donal was sitting beside her. 'They're laughing because it's true,' he said. Aisling felt better and laughed a little herself.

They would have to be at the station early to look for someone reliable to look after Elizabeth on the journey. It had been thought that Violet might go with her as far as

Holyhead, but it seemed a waste because she would have had to turn around and come back again, and the trains took hours and hours with all the delays and the shortage of fuel, and then of course there was the whole matter of the fare – it seemed senseless to throw money away in these hard times. . . .

George had wondered whether they should pay the O'Connors for Elizabeth's board; but Violet had said no. Evacuees in England didn't pay the host families, it was all part of the war effort. George had pointed out that Ireland wasn't part of the war effort; Violet had sniffed and said they should be, they jolly well should be, and anyway, the principle was the same. She had given Elizabeth five pounds and told her to spend it *intelligently*.

At Euston, Violet looked around for respectable middle-aged women to whom Elizabeth might be entrusted. She wanted someone travelling alone. A woman chatting might forget to look after her charge. She had several failures. One was only going to Crewe. One was waiting for her gentleman friend, one was coughing so much that Elizabeth would surely catch some disease from her. Finally, Violet settled on a woman who walked with a stick. She offered Elizabeth's services as a runner of errands and a helper with luggage on the trip. The woman was pleased with the arrangement and promised to deliver Elizabeth into the hands of a young man called Sean O'Connor at Dunlaoghaire when the boat docked. The woman settled herself into a corner and said she would leave Elizabeth to say goodbye to her parents alone.

Mother gave her a kiss on the cheek and said to *try* to be a good girl and not to cause Mrs O'Connor too much trouble. Father said goodbye very formally. Elizabeth looked up at him.

'Goodbye, Father,' she said gravely. He bent to hug her; he hugged her for a long time. She felt her arms clasping round his neck, but looked at Mother and detected those early signs of impatience. She released him.

'You'll write lots of letters, write and tell us everything,' he said.

'Yes, but you're not to go asking Eileen for letter-paper and stamps, those things cost money.'

'I have money! I have five pounds!' cried Elizabeth.

'Hush! Don't let everyone in the station hear you! That's the way to get robbed,' said Violet warningly.

Elizabeth's face went red and white again, her heart started beating and she heard the train doors slamming.

'It'll be fine, it'll be fine,' she said.

'Good girl,' said Mother.

'Don't cry, now, you're a big girl,' said Father.

Two big tears ran down Elizabeth's face.

'She had no intention of crying until you mentioned it,' said Violet. 'Now look what you've started.'

The train moved out, and among all the other people waving on the platform stood Mother and Father. Stiffly. Elizabeth shook her head to clear away the tears and as the blur went she saw them standing as if each of them was holding their elbows close in to their sides for fear of touching the other.

II

Donal wanted to know had all Elizabeth's brothers and sisters died. Were they killed dead?

'Don't be silly,' Peggy had said. 'Of course they didn't die.'

'Then where are they? Why aren't they coming?' Donal was feeling left out because Aisling had appropriated the coming guest so firmly. It was a question of 'my friend Elizabeth won't like that' and 'when my friend Elizabeth arrives'. Donal hoped that there might be a secret cache of brothers and sisters he could adopt himself.

'There was only one of her,' said Peggy.

'There's never only one of people,' complained Donal. 'There's families. What happened to them?'

Eileen couldn't manage to elicit similar enthusiasm from the rest of them. Only Aisling and Donal were excited. Young Sean never noticed who was in the house anyway; Maureen said that it was going to be painful having someone else as silly as Aisling around. Eamonn said he was not going to wash himself for some awful girl he had never met, and anyway he *did* wash . . . enough. Niamh, cutting a tooth, was red-faced and angry and cried in long, sharp bouts. Eileen herself had a few moments' worry about Violet's little girl. The letter had been very stilted, the girl was used to a much more gracious way of living. If Violet's short, sharp and unhelpful glimpses into her life were accurate. . . .

She hoped the child wouldn't be a frightened pickaheen of a thing, afraid to open her mouth. Then it would really be out of the frying pan and into the fire for the girl . . . the blitz of London or the noisy O'Connors in full cry. It would be hard to know which was worse.

In any event, the child might bring her closer to Violet again, after all these years. Eileen wished they could have kept in touch more. She had tried, Lord knows, writing often and giving little details about life in Kilgarret and sending Violet's only child little gifts on birthdays – but Violet only scribbled a card from time to time. It annoyed Eileen that their closeness had seemed to vanish into the air, because it had been a very real closeness based on the fact that they had both been in that convent school on a false premise. Violet, because her family (wrongly) thought that a convent school might give their girl a little polish; Eileen, because her family thought that a convent school in England would be a cut above any kind of a Catholic education in the homeland.

Still, she was going to be brought back into Eileen's life again and Eileen was glad of it. Perhaps, in a year or two, when this terrible war was over, George and Violet might even come to stay in Donnelly's Hotel on the other side of the square, and thank Eileen from the bottom of their hearts for putting roses back into the cheeks of their daughter. The friendship would blossom all over again, and Eileen would have someone to remember those long-gone days in St Mark's which she couldn't talk to anyone else about because they all said she was uppity to have been at an English school at all. . . .

She would like to have gone up on the bus herself to meet the little girl. A day in Dublin would cheer her. No squinting over books and bills, she could collect Elizabeth in Dunlaoghaire when the boat got in – or Kingstown, as some people still called it, just to get a rise out of Sean – and then they could take a tram into Dublin. She could take Elizabeth to see the sights, maybe even climb Nelson's Pillar, something else she had never done. But this was fanciful. . . . She couldn't go, Young Sean must collect the girl. He had been so restless and ready to fight with his father over anything, Eileen thought a day off from the shop would be no harm. He was to go off that Tuesday after work, on the evening bus. He could stay with her cousin, who ran a small boarding house in Dunlaoghaire – half a dozen eggs would pay the compliment for giving him a bed in the sitting room for the night. He had strict instructions to be on the pier before the boat even berthed so that the child wouldn't fear that no one had come to meet her. He was to tell her his name when he saw a ten-year-old in a green coat, with blonde hair, and carrying a brown suitcase and wearing a brown shoulder bag. He was to be welcoming, and give her some buttered brack and a bottle of orange squash while they waited for the bus home. On no account was he to dawdle so they would miss the bus. Eileen knew well Sean's interest in collecting a ten-year-old girl from a mail-boat was minimal, but if he were to meet any group of young lads about to enlist in the British army, as he had done the last time he was in Dublin, his excitement would be enormous.

Eileen arranged with the Mahers to collect the new kitten on the afternoon Elizabeth arrived; she wanted to have plenty of distract everyone if the arrival was not a success. She also wanted them all to think of the coming of Elizabeth with that of a new, black and white furry bundle, which was guaranteed to be a success.

Mrs Moriarty was a very kind woman. She had a picnic of her own and shared some cold tinned peas with Elizabeth; they spooned them together out of the tin.

'I didn't know you were allowed to eat them cold,' said Elizabeth. Elizabeth's own little picnic was very dull in comparison; six small, neat sandwiches with the crusts all cut off, very little cheese in three and even less tomato in the other three. There was an apple and two biscuits, all wrapped in white paper – even a folded paper napkin as well.

'Mother said I must make two meals of this, supper and breakfast,' she said gravely. 'But please do have a sandwich now in exchange for the peas.'

Mrs Moriarty took one and pronounced it excellent.

'Aren't you a lucky little girl to have a Mammy make all that for you now?' she said.

'Well, I made it myself really, but Mother wrapped it,' said Elizabeth.

Mrs Moriarty told Elizabeth that she was going home to live with her son and his scald of a wife in County Limerick. She had lived since she was a widow in England, and she loved the place, the bigness of London did your heart good. She had worked in a vegetable shop and everyone had been very pleasant and friendly, but now, what with her arthritis, and the blitz and everything, they insisted she came home. Mrs Moriarty didn't like it a bit. She wouldn't feel the same when the war was over, the others in the shop would think she had run away. But there was nothing she could do, her son and his brazen strap of a wife had been writing every week – they had even come over to plead with her. Everyone in their street said they were heartless to let a mother be roasted alive by bombs in London, so they had demanded that she come back.

Elizabeth agreed that it was hard to make a journey when you didn't want to, and as Mrs Moriarty spooned out some tinned pears she told her about Mother's friends, the O'Connors, who lived in a dirty town in a house where everything was untidy and in a square where animals came and soiled the place. Mrs Moriarty said thoughtfully that maybe Elizabeth should keep her worries about the town being dirty to herself, that perhaps she shouldn't pass on her mother's views until she had had time to form an opinion of her own. Elizabeth flushed and said that she wouldn't dream of saying anything like that when she got to Mrs O'Connor's – it was only because Mrs Moriarty was a friend and had told her about the awful daughter-in-law. . . .

They ate a tin of condensed milk to seal their conspiracy, and Elizabeth fell asleep with her head on Mrs Moriarty's shoulder and didn't stir until they were all woken up and turned out into the cold night air in Holyhead, with porters shouting to each other in Welsh and great confusion as they waited to be called into line for the mail-boat.

'Will they speak like that in Ireland?' asked Elizabeth nervously. The place seemed to be very unsafe with people shouting and laughing in a foreign language. Mother would have said something very putting down about it; Elizabeth tried to imagine what it might have been, but failed.

'No,' said Mrs Moriarty. 'In Ireland we speak English, we've thrown out anything that was any good to us, like our language and our way of going on.'

'And our mothers-in-law,' said Elizabeth seriously.

'That's it,' laughed Mrs Moriarty. 'Well, if they're bringing back mothers-in-law, Lord knows what else they might revive,' and she leaned on Elizabeth's shoulder as the line started to shuffle off slowly to the mail-boat, which stood large and awesome in the night.

Sean hated people like Mrs Moriarty, people who clutched at your arm and whispered you confidences out of the side of their mouths as if you were in the know, and they were in the know, but somebody else was not in the know. He pulled away slightly as she started to hiss at him that the little girl was very tired and sick from the journey, and that her mother had a hard mouth, and that he and his family shouldn't mind too much what she said.

'I think those people are waving at you,' he said eventually, in order to escape. A middle-aged man and woman were shouting, 'Mam, Mam, we're here!'

Elizabeth looked up for the first time since she had agreed to Sean identifying who she was. She stared long and hard at Mrs Moriarty's daughter-in-law, who had a smile of welcome nailed on her face.

'She doesn't look scalded any more,' she said clearly. 'Perhaps the burns have healed now.'

Sean offered Elizabeth brack and lemonade as they walked in the early morning sunlight towards the bus stop.

'Mam said you were to have this if you were hungry,' he said ungraciously.

'Do I have to?' she asked. Her face was paler than her hair, her eyes were red and her legs were like sticks. He thought she was a miserable specimen.

'No, indeed you don't, it was only Mam being nice. I'll eat it myself, I love brack,' he said, loyalty to his mother coming unexpectedly to the fore.

'I didn't mean. . . .' she said.

'No matter.' He unwrapped two huge doorsteps of brack

with a lump of butter spread unevenly between them, and began to demolish them.

'Is it cake?' Elizabeth asked.

'It's brack, I told you it was brack, you said you didn't want it.'

'I didn't know what it was.'

'Why didn't you ask me?' He wondered what kind of child would never have heard of brack.

'I don't know.'

They walked in silence to the stop for the Bray bus. Her suitcase was heavy and it dragged her down; she wore her shoulder bag criss-crossed over her thin chest. She looked the picture of an orphan.

Sean's mind was full of the boy he had met last night in the guesthouse. Terry was seventeen, too young to join up, but he said that you could always say your birth certificate went up in the Customs House fire. Nobody in England knew when that was. Terry was off on the very same mail-boat when it turned around. He'd go to the nearest recruitment centre and he'd be in uniform in a couple of weeks. Sean couldn't sleep a wink from envy. Terry had spoken of other friends who had gone a month ago. Earning proper salaries, real wages, training, drilling, handling weapons, learning all the skill needed; going across the sea soon, but it was all hush-hush. Terry, too, worked for his father, on a small farm. He knew what it was like to get no real money, only pocket money, and a so-called training. He knew what it was like not to be allowed to grow up, your mam asking if you had been to confession, your da asking you to do a bit around the house to help your mam. No life. No chance to get into a uniform. . . .

'What kind of uniform does your da wear?' he asked Elizabeth suddenly.

Her little white face became all flushed, as if someone had hit her with a strong hand and left the marks of a slap.

'He . . . isn't . . . doesn't . . . you see he didn't have to go to the war. He's at home.'

'Why was that?' demanded Sean, his slight and marginal interest in this new girl waning as she couldn't even provide him with information about the day to day business of war.

'He had to stay in the bank, I think ... I think they needed. ...' And Elizabeth's face was working with the effort of trying to explain honestly something she had never understood, but which she knew was something that made Mother and Father prickly with each other.

'I think they had to keep senior men with bad chests,' she said eventually.

Sean looked at her without interest, his mind back with Terry and enlistment. They waited in Bray for the Wicklow bus.

'Do you want to go to the lavatory before the bus comes?' he asked suddenly. In all her ten years, Elizabeth had never been asked such a direct and embarrassing question.

'Er, yes, please,' she said.

Young Sean indicated two public conveniences with a jerk of his head.

'Over there, don't be all day and all night, the bus'll be here in five minutes.'

Elizabeth scampered up to the two low buildings. But there was no 'Ladies' or 'Gents' written on them. She had found it adventurous enough to use a public toilet in London with Mother, who had always insisted that she use lots of lavatory paper to guard her from all the infections which lay in the seat, but here the problem was monumental. There only seemed to be sets of initials over the doors, no names. One had MNA, the other FIR. Elizabeth gave it some thought. She looked back at Sean. He already thought she was silly, what would he think if she ran back to ask him which convenience she should use? Think hard. M must be for males, F for females. Courageously, she walked into the Fir.

Four men stood with their backs to her as she walked in. She wondered whether they were painting the wall in front of them, or doing some kind of repairs, and hesitated before going past them to seek the entry to the Ladies'.

One of the men turned around and, to her horror, his trousers were undone. He was an old man, without many teeth, and his cap was on back to front.

'Get on out of here, girlie, go on home and don't be a bold little girl,' he shouted. The other men turned around.

'Get on off with you . . . you'll see plenty of it when you're older!' shouted a young man, and the others laughed.

Scarlet, her heart pounding, Elizabeth ran out to where Sean was shouting at her to hurry as the bus had just come around the corner.

'Holy God, did you go into the Men's?' he asked, and before she could say anything he added warningly, 'Don't tell that to Mam or she'll beat the bottom off you.' Elizabeth's brown case was snatched and thrown on the roof rack of the bus.

'It says Cill Maintain!' she cried. 'It doesn't say Wicklow, this is the wrong bus!'

'Oh, Jesus, Mary and Joseph, will you get in,' said Young Sean, who had found it hard enough to have to travel with a normal ten-year-old, but one who was obviously mentally disturbed was proving even worse.

It began to rain just then, as the bus headed off, passing by the fields of green, each surrounded by a hedge of darker green; and Elizabeth stared hard out of the window willing the tears back into her head. She was also willing herself to hold on until the bus stopped at another convenience where someone might tell her the significance of all these initials. It seemed like weeks since she had left London, and she realised to her horror that it was less than twenty-four hours.

Eileen had left the shop early, just in case the bus arrived sooner than expected. She wanted to be sure that she was there to welcome the child. Peggy was screeching, Aisling tongue-tied, Eamonn truculent, Donal unintelligible. . . . This would be no way to start a new life in the country. She smoothed her skirt and tidied stray wisps of hair, wondering how Violet looked now: she had always had fine hair and a milk-white face. Perhaps the little girl would be the same, not covered with freckles like all the O'Connors.

The table had been laid with more than usual care. Eileen had sent back a cloth which was badly stained – Peggy was annoyed that standards were seeming to be raised. Aisling ran in.

'Since you're home, Mammy, will we go on up to Maher's and get the kitten now and have it ready for your one when she arrives?'

'Her name is Elizabeth, not your one,' snapped Eileen. 'No, the kitten is for both of you to share.'

'I know,' said Aisling unconvincingly. Eamonn had bounded in behind her.

'Two paws each,' he giggled. 'One lot for you and one lot for her.'

'I'll have the front paws,' said Aisling thoughtfully.

'That's not fair, then she'd only get the bottom!' Eamonn snorted at his own audacity.

'Don't say "bottom", Mammy will belt you,' retorted Aisling, looking sideways at her mother like a trouble-maker.

Eileen wasn't paying attention. 'Come here to me now Aisling and I'll brush your hair. It's like a furze bush. Stand still now.' The brush was always on the mantelpiece of the breakfast room by the clock and it was taken down on Saturday nights for a weekly assault. Maureen and Aisling hated it and squirmed away – the boys were usually able to rely on their father for rescue.

'Stop titivating them, Eileen,' he would say, 'sure aren't they men? Their hair is fine. Leave them alone now.' But he never had any salvation for the long curly hair of his daughters. Aisling pulled and resisted.

'It's worse than getting ready for mass,' she complained.

'Don't say anything bad about mass, that's a sin,' said Eamonn, delighted to have caught her out in a crime equal to his own. 'Mammy, she said she hated getting ready for mass.'

'No, she didn't, she said she hated having her hair brushed. Aisling wouldn't say anything bad about God's Holy Mass, would you, Aisling?'

'No, Mammy,' said Aisling, eyes lowered. Eamonn was annoyed. Usually any question of insulting Holy God brought great retribution on the head of the culprit.

Peggy was still in a bad humour and she felt that times were about to change for the worse.

'Will I get Donal up, Mam? He says he's mad to be down here when the one arrives and he knows there's a fire. He says he doesn't want the one to think he's. . . .'

'Peggy, Elizabeth White is called Elizabeth. She is not *the one*. Do you hear me?'

'Yes, Mam. I know, Mam,' said Peggy, alarmed.

The hair brush was put away.

'I'll go up for him now.' Eileen crossed the room, but as she did so she looked automatically out on to the square. The bus must have arrived. There were straggles of people coming across the square from Donnelly's Hotel, where the Dublin bus drew up each day. And there was Sean, walking ahead, kicking moodily at a stone. Her big, handsome, restless son, worried and unhappy about something. Eileen's heart skipped with worry about him, as it so often did.

And behind him, dragging her own heavy case, was a white-faced little girl. Smaller and thinner than Aisling with hair so pale that it didn't look like hair at all. The green coat made her look more pale and wan than ever. She had a school hat with elastic under her chin and one of her gloves, attached by elastic to her sleeve, flapped about.

There, in the square in Kilgarret, her eyes like two big holes burned in a blanket, stood Elizabeth.

Just as she had predicted, Eileen noticed that Aisling had become awkward and tongue-tied.

'No, you go down, Mammy,' she said.

'Is she there? What's she like?' cried Eamonn. He rushed to the window and saw the little figure.

'Is that her?' he cried in disbelief. Stung to hear her new friend attacked before she had even laid eyes on her, Aisling moved to the window. But she couldn't see her. Elizabeth and her case had moved into the house. There was a scream up the stairs from Peggy.

'Mam, she's here, Donal's after opening the door for her. He came out of his bed and we never saw. . . .'

Eileen ran down the stairs from the breakfast room on the first floor. In the big, shabby door, silhouetted against the light, was the frail shape of Violet's daughter. Donal had helped her drag her suitcase into the hall. He looked at her with delight. A new thing come into the house. A new person coming to live.

'They're getting the kitten because you came,' he said to Elizabeth.

Eileen opened her arms out wide.

'Come here to me and tell me all about the terrible journey,' she said.

Close up, Elizabeth's eyes were even more enormous than ever. 'I wet my knickers,' she said. 'I'm very sorry.'

Eileen tightened her grip on the bony little frame.

'It doesn't matter, love, we'll have that sorted out in no time.'

Elizabeth started to cry.

'No, it's terrible. The back of my coat is wet and it's gone on my shoes. I'm so ashamed, Mrs O'Connor. I didn't . . . I didn't know . . . I couldn't. . . .' Her shoulders heaved.

'Listen to me, child, this is a house where people are always wetting their knickers, come on upstairs with me, there there. . . .' and Eileen stroked the fine hair and brushed away the tears, taking Elizabeth's hand away from her eyes. 'Sure, aren't you here now, home safe and sound. Come on with me. . . .'

Sean came in. 'Hello, Ma. Ma, I met a man in Dublin, this fellow Terry. . . .'

Eileen turned on him. 'Carry that suitcase upstairs at once you big useless lump. Get a move on now. Shut your mouth about who you met. You couldn't carry the child's luggage for her, you couldn't get a sick child down here safely and with some kindness. You hadn't a brain in your head to ask her did she need a lavatory.'

'I did!' Sean was enraged by the injustice of it. 'I did and do you know, she went into the men's.'

'You're a big, ignorant lump,' Eileen said, and didn't even notice the tears of rage and misunderstanding well up in his eyes. Tight-lipped, he picked up the case and carried it upstairs. He opened the door of Aisling's room and flung the case in hard. He had suspected that this girl was going to cause trouble. He was right.

It only took Eileen ten minutes to get Elizabeth ready for her first meal in her new home. There was a rapid unpack to unearth clean clothes. The contents of the case were flung on the bed with an abandon that would never have been known back in London. Mother didn't do things like that. Mother would have gone away and let Elizabeth cope by herself but Mrs O'Connor didn't seem to understand.

'Step out of these wet things, come on now, sure we'll throw them in the wash with everything else. Come on, now, there's a good girl, and into the bathroom there with you. Give yourself a bit of a quick wash and you'll feel fresh all over. I'll hang up these. Come on, now, that's it.'

Mrs O'Connor actually expected Elizabeth to go across the corridor in just her vest and carrying a towel. She couldn't mean it. Never in her whole life had Elizabeth left her bedroom without being fully dressed or wearing a dressing-gown. She made an ineffectual stab at her suitcase.

'Could I please take. . . .'

'Yes, pet?'

'My . . . er . . . dressing-gown. . . .' Elizabeth was scarlet.

'Surely. Aren't you a funny little thing.'

And then there was no escape. She had to meet the family. If they were all as horrible as the one on the bus it would be very frightening. But Mrs O'Connor was . . . well . . . very friendly, Elizabeth supposed. Not like Mother, not like anyone's mother but very . . . busy and easy-going. The bathroom was enormous, not like the one at home. It had plaster falling off, and the geyser over the bath was all rusty. There were a lot of face flannels all screwed up, not on neat hooks. There were two mugs full of toothbrushes – how did they know which belonged to which person, Elizabeth wondered. There was a knock at the door. Elizabeth held on to the basin for a moment. Right. She did feel clean and comfortable again, and hungry – a bit travel-sick but definitely hungry. Bravely she unlocked the door and came out. Eileen took Violet's child by the hand and led her down the stairs to the breakfast room.

Donal was sitting by the fire, wrapped in a blanket that Peggy had found for him. He jumped up at once and the blanket nearly went into the grate. Eamonn was playing with two china dogs, making them bark at each other. Young Sean was standing moodily at the window. Maureen had come in, as instructed, in time for lunch; she had a mirror and was examining her nose without much enthusiasm. Peggy was hovering, not knowing whether to bring in the pot of soup or wait until the mistress called for it. The master of the house was sitting in his shirt-sleeves reading the *Irish Independent*. Aisling was at a drawing book, writing furiously; she barely looked up when the door opened.

'This-is-Elizabeth-and-will-you-mind-that-blanket,' Eileen said in one breath. Eamonn rushed and rescued it before it caught the flame. Sean put his paper down.

'You're very welcome in this house, child,' he said. Elizabeth shook hands with him gravely. Maureen nodded and Eamonn giggled. There was a gurgle from Niamh in her pram. Young Sean's eyes never left the square, where the bus, now loaded with passengers and provisions, had just left again.

'Aisling, come here and say hello to Elizabeth – what are you doing?' asked Eileen crossly.

'I was making a notice,' said Aisling, with one of her huge enveloping smiles. 'For our door. It's very important.' In big, uneven letters, she had written:

AISLING AND ELIZABETH. PLEASE KNOCK. NO ADMITTANCE.

She showed it to Elizabeth proudly.

'Who'd want to go into your silly old room, anyway,' said Eamonn.

'I don't think anyone is seeking admittance,' said Maureen.

'Better to have it there all the same,' said Aisling, seeking approval from Elizabeth. It was an important moment.

'Much better, I think,' said Elizabeth as she took the notice. 'Aisling and Elizabeth. Please Knock. No Admittance. Super.'

III

Eileen was beginning her letter to Violet. Somehow the presence of Elizabeth in the house made Violet seem further away rather than nearer. For three days she had been with them with her pinched little face flushing when anyone addressed her directly, trying to answer and be polite and often finding the wrong words. If Eileen hadn't known better she might have thought the child had been reared in an institution.

'How will I explain all about Sister Bonaventure?' she asked.

'What?' Sean shuffled the paper. He was sitting by the fire with his socks almost in the grate.

'You know how bad Violet is at writing, she mightn't reply for a month and we'd be in all kinds of trouble.'

'Huh,' said Sean, hardly attending to her. Violet and her ways interested him hardly at all.

'Of course, years back in St Mark's, Violet never went to religious knowledge classes. We used to see her out of the window walking round the hockey pitch.'

'Well, then?' grunted Sean.

Young Sean was sitting by the window. He always sat by the window nowadays, as if he hoped to see some other kind of life through it, or so Eileen imagined.

'What do you think, son?' she called to him. He hadn't been listening, but he thought that Elizabeth should go to the catechism classes, or whatever else was on offer. No point in making her more different than she was already. Eileen was about to agree, when her husband rattled the paper at the fireside and said that the English people were atheists, and that the one thing they feared most in the world was the domination of the Roman Catholic Church. Better not give them any more grounds for complaint.

33

'I suppose I'll have to make up my own mind as usual,' sighed Eileen and took up her pen.

Dear Sister Bonaventure,
I have been in touch with Elizabeth's parents, both devout Anglicans, and they would prefer it if she spent the time reading her Bible while the rest of the children are having their religious instruction lessons. They are very grateful to the convent for making this arrangement.

She read it out to them, and both men laughed.

'I hope God will forgive me,' she said seriously.

'*I* hope someone will be able to find the child a Bible – you know, the one she's supposed to be reading,' said Young Sean, and for a moment, there was real family laughter between them.

The kitten had been named Monica after endless arguments between Aisling, Eamonn and Donal. Elizabeth had not joined in. As the battle had reached a crescendo, Aisling had turned to Elizabeth and demanded to know who her best friend at school in England had been.

'I didn't have a best friend,' stammered poor Elizabeth.

'Well, who did you like best?' shouted Aisling.

'At school . . . um . . . Miss James,' was the honest reply.

'You can't call a cat Miss James!' Aisling tried once more. 'Who did you sit beside?'

'Monica. . . .' Elizabeth began.

'Monica!' exclaimed Aisling. 'That's it!'

They all said the name. None of them knew anyone called Monica. Elizabeth was a little disappointed. She had never liked Monica Hart – a bossy girl who used to laugh at Elizabeth and pinch her sometimes just to make her jump. She wished the beautiful furry kitten were not called that. Something like Blackie or Sooty – names that kittens were called in books – but the O'Connors seemed to think entirely in terms of people's names; they had been debating Oliver and Seamus before Monica had been settled on.

And now it was Monica's eternal future that was

34

worrying. Aisling had been very anxious to baptise the new kitten, but Eileen had arrived in time to halt the ceremony.

'But, God couldn't send Monica to limbo, could he?' Aisling had persisted.

'No, of course not,' said Eileen, who often got weary of filling in the gaps that appeared after the daily religious instruction classes.

'What's limbo?' Elizabeth asked fearfully. It sounded bad.

'Oh, it's full of babies – you know, dead babies that didn't get baptised.'

'There are no cats in limbo,' said Eileen firmly. She had noticed the large eyes in the small anxious face becoming even rounder and darker at the mention of a place full of dead babies. It seemed so natural in the convent, with Sister Mary and Sister Bonaventure, to talk of unbaptised babies going to limbo because they didn't have the sanctifying grace that would let them look at God. It seemed unnatural and macabre trying to explain this to Elizabeth, who knew nothing of the rules.

'You never see pictures of them in heaven, mind,' said Eamonn, trying to disrupt the calm.

'They're all round the other side,' cut in Eileen. Then, as she saw the question forming on all their faces, 'You know, the bit they don't show in the pictures of heaven where all the animals and birds and all the creatures St Francis loved are all gathered.' As she spoke, she wondered did all other parents have to interpret religion so wildly for their children, and whether the Lord approved of her efforts.

Violet opened the letter eagerly. The house had been far emptier without Elizabeth than she would have believed possible. Already she had forgotten her constant irritation with the little face that reddened and whitened like the colours mixing in a painting box. She hoped that Elizabeth was not being too timid amid the undoubtedly boisterous family in Kilgarret. She had forgotten to warn her about keeping her money safely hidden or giving it to Eileen for safe-keeping in case the rough boys and girls took it from her. Two letters fell out. Violet picked up Elizabeth's first. Lines had been ruled on a page for her. More lines than were used.

Dear Mother and Father,
I am very well I hope you are very well. We have got a new kitten called Monica, it is only for Aisling and me. Its not for Eamonn but we are going to let Donal play with it. Aisling is not like Aisling it's like Ashleen. It's an Irish name. I start school next week. Aunt Eileen has borrowed a big Bible from some people who are Protestants and I will take it to the school to read when the others are reading about the Virgin and the Saints. Peggy tells us stories every night.
Love from
    Elizabeth

A wave of anti-climax flowed over Violet. Who was Peggy? What was all this about a Bible, a kitten, the Virgin? Was all this rubbish about Aisling to do with how you pronounced her name? Violet read the little note again. It seemed happy and preoccupied, she thought, that much at least was good. But no question about home, no hint of missing anyone. Of course, this was only the second letter that Elizabeth had written in her life. There had been no reason for her to write letters home before.

Sighing slightly, Violet picked up the other paper. Normally Eileen's correspondence was so long and flowery that she skimmed through, but this time she was eager to read every word. But Eileen had decided to be brief too.

My dear Violet,
Just a word to tell you how delighted we are to have Elizabeth with us. She is a lovely child, very gentle and eager to please. I hope she doesn't find our brood too much for her. She was pale and weary after the long journey but has cheered up greatly and is eating well and bouncing around. I thought you would prefer her not to have Christian Doctrine lessons so I arranged a Bible for

her from some of Sean's customers who are C. of I. It's the right one, it has Authorised Version on it, I looked.

We'll encourage her to write to you every week and she can post these letters herself in the square and she can say what she likes so you needn't think they come through us. The same when you write to her. Nobody but Elizabeth will see it.

I hope you are all managing over there all right. Our thoughts are with you in this awful time.
As always,
Eileen

What *did* Eileen mean about Elizabeth 'bouncing around?' Elizabeth didn't *bounce*. And why all the fuss about Bibles and authorised versions? The Irish were indeed obsessed with religion.

Violet put the letters on the hall table so that George could see them, then she put her headscarf on and went out to join the lengthening queues in the shops. . . .

Young Sean was being even more of a trial than usual in the shop and his father's patience was extremely limited. Eileen could remember a time when they had all looked forward to Sean's serving his time in O'Connor's shop. Sean more than anyone. He had begged to be allowed to leave school after his Intermediate Certificate when he was fifteen, but his parents would hear none of it. The eldest of the family, he had to put the stamp of education on them all by doing his Leaving Certificate.

Now the examination was done and the results expected any day, but the promised excitement and manliness of joining his father in the family business had not materialised. Young Sean was moody and would flare up on any subject. 'Ah, leave him alone,' Eileen would sometimes say to her husband across the supper table when another list of complaints about the day's work began. 'Can't you see the boy's worried sick about his exam results . . . ?'

Sean Senior would grunt. 'Can't imagine that any piece of

paper will make him any more use in the shop, only more arrogant if he gets it.'

Young Sean, stung by the sudden and unfair lack of interest in all school work, would retaliate. 'Well, you had me working like a black man all the last years saying it was the most important thing on earth – why?'

'Don't speak to me in that tone of voice. . . .' the master of the house would say.

And, 'I won't speak to you at all then,' the son of the house would reply; and a scraping of the chair and a bang of the door and he would be gone. A second bang of the door and he would be out in the square and across to the library where he would sit and read the newspapers for hours on end with everything they had to say about the world where there was war.

He would be seventeen on 7 September. Eileen remembered so well the year he was born, with the Civil War still all around them, and how she had written to Violet about her hopes that her son would grow up in a land that would never go to war again. She couldn't remember what, if anything, Violet had replied. But now it was happening, in a distorted way, her son was grown-up and his land was not at war – and that *was* the problem. . . .

She had thought of having a party of some kind on his birthday. It would be the day the school reopened and so the horror would be taken out of it for little Elizabeth.

Eileen found herself more and more drawn to this odd little girl. There was something more gracious, less rude and heavy and rough about her than there was in any of Eileen's own children. It was as if the polish which St Mark's was meant to confer had skipped Violet and Eileen and landed on Violet's child. She was so willing to please, and so unlike any of the O'Connors in this that Eileen felt somehow wistful. Why hadn't she been able to give any of this gentleness to her own family? Only Donal had any trace of it and that was because he was delicate and not able to tear through the house, shove and push, shout and grab.

Yes, a bit of a party might cheer up her restless son. He might lose his strained look and even Sean Senior might mellow a bit in the light of birthday candles. She began to make a list, then felt a pang of guilt about the birthday parties in England where no child would have cakes or cream – but it passed. And perhaps he would bring over a few of his friends from school; that young Murray boy, or one of the Healys, or whoever it was he was friendly with these days. Funny that she didn't know. There was a time when he used to have the house full of his friends.

When he came back from the library and crept into the kitchen to eat something from the meat safe, she would talk to him about the party. It would cheer him up. Cheer them all up.

7 September. Donal was waved off to school – he didn't want to be accompanied any further, not by his mother and *two girls*; and he ran off on spindly legs, like a leaf, Eileen thought, comparing him to the stout twigs of boys who were already pummelling each other cheerfully in the yard of the boys' preparatory. Then, with a smile, she deposited Aisling and Elizabeth, trying not to notice Elizabeth's fearful glance at the huge statue pointing to its exposed and open heart . . .

She returned to the house in the square. Peggy, who hadn't expected the mistress back so soon, was half-heartedly fending off the gropings of Johnny O'Hara, the postman. Johnny was drinking tea and eating bacon on his soda bread, and that annoyed Eileen more than the fumblings. She had ruled that it was extravagant to have bacon for breakfast, and here it was being handed out to the postman. She took the letter from the speechless Johnny, brushed aside the protests and explanations from Peggy with a curt request that Niamh should be restored to her cot.

Then she read that Sean had failed his Leaving Certificate examination.

She decided that she would tell her husband before anyone else.

Then she found that Eamonn had already gone to the school when the list was being read out and had galloped back to the shop with the news.

Then she heard on the wireless that an almighty blitz had

begun on London, and that people were huddling down in the Underground to avoid the bombs and the falling buildings.

Then a message was sent from the school to say that Elizabeth had been sick and that Aisling was being sent home with her.

And as she sat down to try to cope with all the day had brought, she realised that she had not had her period since the middle of July and that she was probably pregnant. Pregnant at the age of forty.

Most things had sorted themselves out, as most things do, after two weeks. Most, not all.

Donal seemed stronger and happier at school than he had been during the summer term. He came home with names of friends and stories of what Sister Maureen had said. And plans for the Christmas play, where he would be playing an angel.

Elizabeth was not quite so fearful, and seemed to clutch at Aisling for safety. Aisling, in turn, was pleased and proud to have a new responsibility. It was better than a sister if not quite as good as a best friend. She was now an object of great interest in her class. An English Protestant refugee from the war over there *and* a kitten called Monica.

Peggy was so contrite about the episode with the postman that she took it on herself to make amends. She scrubbed floors unasked, and even tidied out cupboards, unearthing the most extraordinary things.

Young Sean got over the disappointment of his failure. Several other boys had failed too. The Brothers couldn't understand it, although one told Eileen quietly that he thought a few of the lads had their heads stuffed with all this nonsense about going over and fighting a war, and they hadn't given their work or their books enough attention.

Sean O'Connor had taken his eldest son's failure much better than Eileen had hoped. He had had a man-to-man talk and told him that life was full of failures and problems, that Irish history had been one crisis after another . . . all had to be met, faced and solved. He arranged a regular wage and regular hours of work for Young Sean in the store, and saw that he had a smart dun-coloured coat to wear, which lifted him into a different category.

News from London was bad. Every night the bombers were coming over. Every night the Underground stations were full. There were stories of people leaving London again for another evacuation, but not nearly as many went as had gone before, the previous year. A message came from George and Violet, that they were managing. They had taken their beds down to the cellar and lined the walls with mattresses and padding. Eileen shuddered to think what it would be like, and managed to explain it all to Elizabeth in terms of fun. Elizabeth found it hard to think of her parents doing anything in a spirit of fun.

Eileen's period resumed before she had told anyone of its delay. For four evenings she had had very hot baths and a glass of gin. It was just a relaxing thing to do after a day's work. She didn't even think she would worry Father Kenny by telling him about it in confession. It wasn't a sin or anything, it was just something women did to get their bodies back to normal when they were a bit overstrained.

Maureen had seen pictures of nurses bending low over fevered brows and holding the hands of brave young men while reading temperatures and noting pulses and being generally indispensable. She had started writing to Dublin hospitals for details of training. She thought that there would be more brave young men languishing in Dublin than there were likely to be in the local county hospital which they visited whenever Grannie was taken in, which was every winter. Or when Donal had been there for his asthma.

Sometimes Young Sean discussed it with her, which pleased her. It made her feel grown-up to be talking about careers and futures with her elder brother.

He had tried to persuade her to train for war nursing; then they could both go together. There wouldn't be so much fuss if they both said they thought it would be a great opportunity. He had changed his approach: he had begun to realise that his father really didn't see the cause of Good and

Honour being with Britain. He now brought the subject up in a purely practical way. . . .

'What other chance would ever be half so good . . . the pay alone is terrific . . . they'll train you, you know, for a career or a trade. I'd be a skilled man when I came out . . . I'd have a whole set of qualifications I'd never be able to get anywhere else. . . . Did you not hear there's fellows already from Dublin, fellows with hardly any education doing great out there, learning and getting qualified. . . .'

It wasn't any better than other lines of persuasion. Ones about duty and wishing to defend our way of life. But at least when he and his father argued now it was about points of fact and not blazing ideological rows which Young Sean didn't really understand and always lost. . . .

'Tell me, boy, why we should lift one finger to help them, let alone lose our young men for them in their fight? Yes, it's their fight. What ever did they do for us except bring us torture and humiliation for eight hundred years. . . . Yes, and leave our country when they had to leave it . . . leave it in the state it's in . . . half the land still bitter about the Civil War and a good quarter of it they're still hanging on to. . . . When they give us back the North, which belongs to us by right, when they make some compensation for all they did, then I'd consider fighting in their wars. . . .'

Maureen tried out her hair in different ways with her friend, Berna Lynch, and wore lipstick and powder when she was out of the house. Sixteen was a tiresome age to be in Kilgarret. There was nothing for young people: instead they were watched with suspicion, as if they were on probation from the age of sixteen to twenty – and even longer if, by then, they hadn't settled into the role of 'walking out' decorously with a suitable person. There were no social occasions. Maureen and Berna were considered too respectable to go to the local dance, where messenger boys and maids went. Peggy went to the dance on Saturday nights, but she hated to be asked about it. It wasn't for the likes of Berna and Maureen, she kept saying. They'd hate it even if they managed to get there. They were too well born for the fun and glitter of a hot dance hall, but they weren't well born enough for the tennis parties and supper parties of the people in the big houses. There were the Wests and the Grays and the Kents, all with young people of Maureen and Berna's age, but they never met them. The children had been in boarding schools in Dublin; they came home at the end of term to the railway station three miles away, sometimes they arrived on the bus in the square with their lacrosse sticks and suitcases and blazers. Families in station-wagons met them with cries of excitement, but they never mixed in the life of the town.

Berna, as a doctor's daughter, could have been their social equal . . . but for all their gentility, it was known that her father had a problem with the drink. It was well hidden, but well known at the same time. So Berna missed her chance. Sweet little thing – such a pity about her father. Awfully good doctor, of course, but inclined to go off on his own and mixing with all kinds of rough people. Then into a nursing home in Dublin and after that he wouldn't touch the stuff for about eight months. . . .

They were bored at the convent, they thought the other girls silly and parochial. The time passed very slowly while they waited for Maureen to be called for interview to the hospital and for Berna to go to secretarial college in Dublin. Meanwhile, they sorted out their hair and their skin . . . and hoped that they would have *some* experience of something before they got to Dublin and everyone considered them real eejits.

Eamonn was having an unexpectedly bad term. He had looked forward to going back to school, for it held no terrors for a big strong eleven-year-old able to defend himself. But this term, everything was different. Brother John kept rapping him over the fingers.

'Concentrate, young Eamonn O'Connor . . . we don't want you flopping your exams like that big brother of yours. . . .' And Brother Kevin, one of the kindest Brothers who never said a hard word to anyone, was also coming at him and being annoying.

'Now, listen to me, Eamonn, like a good boy. Remember next year you'll have little Donal here, after he makes his first communion, please God. Now, he's not a strong little lad and you'll have to take care of him, you know, you'll have to keep an eye on him. . . .'

And at home, things weren't any better. Peggy was no fun; she was forever cleaning and looking nervously over her shoulder, as if she and Ma had had a row. But there had been no row. He couldn't understand it.

Niamh had begun to cut teeth, and oh janey, what an awful noise she made. She had a bright red boiled face and her mouth was always open and dribbling. Eamonn thought she looked revolting and couldn't understand why they were always picking her up and soothing her. Everyone cut teeth, he thought savagely. When he had lost his and got new ones there was no fuss and roaring.

And Father was in a bad humour, he'd fight with Sean at the drop of a hat. And then Ma would get upset and look away; she was very tired every evening and had no time to talk to him about school or anything. Even Maureen was never there any more, she was always up at Berna's house.

But the worst of all was Aisling. Aisling used to be all right. Someone to play with. A girl, of course, and a sister, but only a year younger, so not too bad. But since the arrival of this Elizabeth, there was no fun to be had out of her. When the two of them came home from school, it was a glass of milk and a bit of soda cake with currants in it and then up the stairs with the kitten. Stupid name, Monica. Up the stairs and the door with their silly notice on it would close with a bang. Aisling and Elizabeth. Eizabeth and Aisling. It would sicken you.

IV

Aisling had taken her responsibilities about Elizabeth very seriously indeed. Not everyone was given a foreigner of their own to look after at the age of ten. Admittedly there were compensations like the beautiful Monica who had a white front and a purr like an engine and an endless capacity for running after bits of string and rubber balls. And another was that she could get away with lots of things by 'having to help Elizabeth'. She never had to help with the clearing of the table at home nor the washing-up on Peggy's half day. At school she could get out of extra homework.

'I can't Sister, I really can't, I have to show Elizabeth how we do things. Honestly Sister.'

And she thought she was doing a good job. Day by day Elizabeth began to appear more confident. That anxious upturned look was getting less frequent. Aisling noticed that she didn't say sorry so much. She still wasn't very forthcoming about secrets and confidences and though Aisling pressed her about a whole variety of subjects she seemed withdrawn.

'But go on tell me about school . . . tell me about Monica . . . the first Monica.'

'There's nothing to tell,' Elizabeth would say.

'Oh go on, go on. I tell you everything.'

'Well, she was Monica Hart. She used to sit near me, that's all.'

'That's *all*?' Aisling was not only disappointed, she felt that Elizabeth was holding out on her. There must have been more.

Or about birthdays. What did Elizabeth do, who came to the house, what did she get as presents?

Elizabeth had got a cardigan last May when she had been ten, and a box of paints. Yes, that was all. No, no party. Yes, perhaps some of the girls at school had parties. No, not Monica Hart. Who did she miss most? Well Miss James. Miss James was very nice. Nicer than Sister Mary? Well different. Nicer in a way because she wasn't a Holy Sister. You know, more a real person. Yes, she missed Miss James most.

'Apart from your Mam and Dad,' Aisling added just to have the record straight.

'Oh yes. You said at school. Of course I miss my Mum and Dad.'

Aisling used to include Elizabeth's parents in her prayers.

'God bless me and make me good, and God bless Mam and Dad, and Peggy and Sean and Maureen and Eamonn and Donal and Niamh, and Sister Mary, and everyone in Kilgarret, and everyone in Wicklow, and in Ireland, and in the world. And God bless Elizabeth and make sure that her parents, Auntie Violet and Uncle George, are safe during all the things that are happening in London.'

Elizabeth used to say thank you at the end of these prayers which were chanted from the end of Aisling's bed. But Aisling pointed out that she wasn't saying them to Elizabeth, just to God.

Sometimes Elizabeth wondered what Mother would do if Aisling ran up to her and called her Auntie Violet. She was sure that Mother would think Aisling and all the O'Connors very rough. Which, of course, they were. But she hoped that Mother wouldn't come over and see them just yet anyway. If Mother came now she might take Elizabeth away. Mother hated dirt, and really sometimes the house was very dirty.

Nobody ever cleaned the bathroom, and the kitchen had bits of food all over it, not just under nice food covers like Mother had. Mother would never understand sitting at a table where the cloth was full of stains, where nobody had their own napkin ring, where if something fell on the floor it was picked up and eaten as often as not. Mother had been here years and years ago and only remembered that it had been dirty. Elizabeth feared that it might have got even worse since those days.

Even in a few short weeks Elizabeth had become very

defensive about her new home; she would hate to hear Mother criticise it, or Father to make a disparaging remark about the way they lived. When Sister Mary had corrected Aisling in class the other day Elizabeth's face had burned.

'Sit up straight child and tie that carroty hair back. Now do you hear me, Aisling O'Connor, don't come into this classroom tomorrow without a bow on all that streelish hair.'

Elizabeth had been offended on Aisling's behalf. To call her beautiful hair 'carroty'. It was a great insult. Miss James would never have said anything about a pupil's appearance. It just wasn't done. But funnily, Aisling hadn't minded at all; she had just shaken it back, giggled at Elizabeth and, when Sister Mary's back was turned, made a face at her retreating presence which made all the other girls stuff their hands into their mouths to prevent a squeak escaping.

The other girls were from farms near Kilgarret, or else their parents had small businesses in the town. It was all so different here from home. Hardly anyone's father went out to work at a place and then came home from it in the evening. There *was* a bank but there only seemed to be two people in it, not like Father's bank. Eileen had pointed it out to her one day, as she pointed out lots of things which had some kind of link with home.

The pupils in the convent welcomed Elizabeth as a novelty but because she was so shy and timid some of them lost interest in her fairly quickly. This in itself was a relief, as she hated being the object of their attention. Aisling, as her self-appointed knight-in-armour, was often more of a menace than a help.

When the girls asked her about her other school, Aisling would intervene on her behalf. . . .

'She doesn't know much about it. It was bombed, you see, in the blitz. Everyone dead and buried in the rubble. . . .'

Sometimes Elizabeth would protest afterwards.

'Honestly Aisling . . . you shouldn't say that, I don't think the school is all in rubble . . . it's not true.'

'Oh, it might be,' Aisling would say airily. 'Anyway, you talk so little about your life in London people think it's funny. It's better to have an excuse.'

47

Did she talk very little? Possibly. Mother hadn't encouraged long tales with no middles or ends like Aisling, Eamonn and Donal related about their doings . . . Mother hadn't been interested to enquire about the other girls at school and had even been bored when she talked about Miss James. It was all so *different*.

Nothing had led Elizabeth to expect their passionate interest in her soul. It had been explained to the class that since she was of the Protestant faith she would read her Bible during catechism classes. Green with envy for a lifestyle that didn't include five hard questions of catechism each evening, the others pestered Elizabeth about her own particular route to God.

'But you don't go to church, not even the Protestant church,' Joannie Murray persisted.

'No. I . . . Auntie Eileen said she would take me . . . but, no. It's a bit different you see,' Elizabeth stammered.

'But don't you have to go to some church even if it's only a Protestant church?' Joannie Murray hated things to be inconclusive.

'Well . . . yes if you can. I think.'

'Why don't you to to the Protestant church then? It's just beside you . . . it's nearer than our church and we all go up the hill to our church. Every Sunday and holidays of obligation. Otherwise we'd go to hell. Why won't you have to go to hell?'

Aisling was usually at hand.

'It's different for her. She didn't have the gift of faith.'

This satisfied some of them but not all.

'The gift of faith is only hearing about God, she's heard about God from us now.'

Aisling found this a hard one to deal with.

'Sister Mary said that Reverend Mother knows all about Elizabeth not going to church and says that for her brand of Protestant religion that's all right. Not all of the types of Protestants have to go to church you know.' This was greeted with some doubt so she went on triumphantly, 'After all, for all we know she mightn't have been baptised.'

'Weren't you baptised?' Joannie Murray examined

Elizabeth like a possible leper. 'Oh you *must* have been baptised, mustn't you?'

'Um,' said Elizabeth.

'Well were you?' Aisling the Defender lost her patience and forgot her role momentarily. Really there were times when Elizabeth was very vague. Imagine not knowing whether you were baptised or not.

'Christened do you mean?'

'Yes, of course. Baptism.'

'I did have a christening robe,' Elizabeth recalled. It was in a box between layers of paper, and smelling of moth balls. That seemed to settle it. She had been baptised. Now the knotty problem. As a baptised Christian, shouldn't she be going to a church of some kind? Aisling was at a loss. But only for a while.

'We have no way of knowing whether she was baptised properly,' she said firmly. 'If not, then it doesn't count.'

'We could do it ourselves,' said Joannie Murray. 'You know, pour the water and say the words at the same time.'

Elizabeth looked around like a rabbit caught in a trap. Her eyes pleaded with Aisling. Mutely she begged to be rescued. She was disappointed.

'Not now,' Aisling said authoritatively, 'she has to have instruction first. When she's been instructed in the faith then we'll do it. We'll do it at break in the cloakroom.'

'How long will it take to instruct her?' They were eager now, anxious for the adventure of baptising someone. Elizabeth was the first possibly unbaptised person they had met.

'She's full of original sin of course,' said one of the girls. 'If she died the way she is she'd have to go to limbo.'

'Wouldn't it be better for her to go to limbo than risk hell? I mean if we baptised her now and she didn't know what she should do she might go to hell. She's better off as she is until she knows the rules,' Aisling insisted.

'But how long will instructing her take?' Elizabeth too looked trustingly at Aisling. Instruction might only take ten minutes. It was hard to know with matters of faith.

'About six months I think,' Aisling said. They were

disappointed and prepared to query her. 'Sure she doesn't even know a word of catechism. Not a word. There'd be no point in her being baptised until she knows it as well as the rest of us. It was just her bad luck that they didn't do a proper job on her when she was a baby.'

'Of course, they might have done it properly,' Elizabeth piped up without very much hope.

'Not a chance,' said Aisling.

'Probably didn't get the water pouring and the words being said at the same time,' Joannie said sagely. 'That's the important thing.'

Her first Christmas in Kilgarret approached and Elizabeth was a much stronger and healthier child than the one who had crept across the square. Her skirt was even a little too tight around the waist and the pale face looked stronger and seemed less like Dresden china. Her voice was louder too. You now knew whether or not she was in the house.

Each week she wrote a letter home; Eileen added a note and then gave the child the envelope to post. None of them knew whether the sparse replies were due to the terrible chaos of London during the blitz or to the normal inertia of Violet. The newspapers had been filled with stories of the blitz. The Emergency, as the trouble continued to be called, had reached very serious proportions. An average of 200 tons of bombs fell on London an hour. One night in October the bombing had been so intense that it was almost impossible to imagine that any kind of normal life could go on.

Eileen said repeatedly that Violet was welcome to come to Kilgarret herself, and each time she wrote it she said a small prayer that she would not come. Not now, with everything so unsettled between Young Sean and his father. Not until they had time to do up the house in the spring. Not until she had a chance to put some manners on her own pack. She hadn't realised how uncouth they must all be until she watched the dainty manners and considerate behaviour of Elizabeth. The child stood up politely when an adult came into the room, she offered her chair, she held doors open.

Eileen sighed. It would take a large bomb to get any of hers out of their chairs unless they felt like getting up. She didn't question Elizabeth's decision to come to mass on Sunday, regarding it as a further part of belonging. It meant that she had to join the Saturday night inspection of clean shoes, clean socks. Berets, hats, gloves and missals laid out. Hair washed, clean necks, clean nails. It was the one day in the week when Sean and Eileen O'Connor could see some sense in what they were doing, working until their bodies ached. To admire five shining children at mass, a kind of reward.

Elizabeth tried to remember whether she had known any church-going on this scale at home, but she could not recall it. Mr and Mrs Flint were 'church types', Mother had said, but she hadn't known that it meant all this washing and shoe polishing and great masses of people walking to and from a building where you knew everyone.

The crib had been put up in the beginning of December. Great life-size figures of the Family in the stable and real straw. Aisling went to pray in front of it when mass was over, and put a penny into a big collection box which was covered in melted wax. This allowed you to light a candle and stick it with all the other lighted candles; apparently, if you did this you got a wish.

'Do you get a wish even if you haven't got the gift of faith?' Elizabeth whispered on one occasion. Her wish would have been to receive a long cheerful letter from Mother and Father.

'I don't think so.' Aisling considered the matter seriously. 'No, I've never heard that you do. Better not waste the penny, keep it for sweets in Mangans.'

Christmas Day, for Elizabeth, had always been an anti-climax; so much looked forward to, so much talked about, but when it came it always seemed to bring some dis-approval, or some other cause for complaint which she would pretend not to notice. Last year it had been one long discussion about rationing and arguments about how they could possibly manage. Elizabeth thought that the Day with the O'Connors would be utterly perfect. She expected a storybook Christmas for the first time in her life.

For weeks they had all been making each other presents, and the cry of 'Don't come in!' arose whenever you went into a room unexpectedly. To Elizabeth's great surprise, Aisling talked enthusiastically about Santa Claus. Once or twice, Elizabeth had ventured a small doubt about him.

'Do you think that there actually might not be a Santa Claus, you know, the gifts might come from . . . somewhere else?'

'Don't be daft,' Aisling said. 'Sure, where else would they come from?' She had lit several candles asking God to remind Santa Claus of her requests.

Elizabeth had changed a great deal in her four months with the O'Connors. Once upon a time, she would have said nothing and just hoped that things would turn out for the best. Now, however, she felt able to intervene.

'Auntie Eileen?'

'Yes, darling?' Eileen was writing in the big household book she filled in every Saturday.

'I don't want to interfere but . . . you see, Aisling is praying to the Holy Family people in the church and asking them to tell Santa Claus that she wants a bicycle . . . and, you know . . . just . . . I thought you should know as well, if you see what I mean, just in case she doesn't tell you.'

Eileen pulled the child towards her affectionately. 'Now, that's very kind of you to tell me that,' she said.

'It's not that I'm asking you to buy expensive things like that, it's just that Aisling believes very strongly that what you tell Santa Claus should be a secret, and she mightn't tell you.'

'Well, I'll keep that information very carefully in my mind,' said Eileen solemnly. 'Run off with you, now.'

Christmas Eve was like a combination of Saturday nights with all the shoe polishing and neck washing, and the day of the Christmas play at school, all feverish excitement. Even grown-up people like Maureen and her friend Berna were giggling, and Young Sean was happy and wrapping up parcels.

During the night Elizabeth heard the door open. She glanced worriedly over at Aisling's bed but the red hair out on the pillow never stirred. Through half-closed eyes Elizabeth saw Sean place the bicycle, wrapped in brown paper and holly sprigs, at the end of Aisling's bed. And to her amazement she saw a similar shape coming to the end of her own bed. Two sharp trickles of tears began in her eyes. They were such a kind family, she would never be able to thank them. She must really try to explain to Mother in her next letter how kind they were. Please could she find words that wouldn't irritate Mother and make Mother feel that she was being criticised.

Then it was morning and there were screams of excitement as Aisling in pyjamas tore off the wrapping paper. As Elizabeth swung her legs out of bed, Aisling, her face flushed with happiness, came over and gave her a great hug. She forced herself to put her arms around Aisling too. Though this was a new experience and she was always nervous of something new. Up to now they had only linked arms when coming home from school. That had been the closest contact. But now it was a sea of affection and excitement and it almost drowned Elizabeth with its unfamiliarity.

But in no time there were shouts and calls, and squeaks and hoots on a trumpet, and more shouts. . . .

'Down here in two minutes or Christmas or no Christmas you'll feel the palm of my hand!'

It was still dark as they went up the hill to the church calling and wishing people Happy Christmas. Several people asked Elizabeth what she got in her stocking . . . and Doctor Lynch, Berna's father, pinched her cheek and asked her was an Irish Christmas better than an English one. His wife pulled him away crossly.

There were sausages and eggs for breakfast, paper table napkins on the table. Niamh sat up in her high chair and gurgled at them. There was more suppressed excitement since presents were going to be given afterwards beside the fire. The big things had come in the night but the individual ones would come now, and then the girls could go out in the square with their bicycles, Maureen could parade with her new jacket and matching beret, Eamonn with his football and boots, Donal with his scooter. Then it would

53

be in again for the huge goose that was already cooking in the range.

There were oohs and aahs over the presents, the pincushions, the bookmarks, the dish painted as an ashtray for Da, the necklace made of carefully threaded beads. But there was the greatest applause for the presents that Maureen gave. For Mam there was beautiful soap, and for Da there was a proper man's scarf. For Aisling and Elizabeth big bangles with coloured glass in them; for Eamonn a big light for his bicycle; for Donal a funny furry hat, and even for the baby a rattle. She had given her elder brother two matching hair brushes like gentlemen used in picture books, and for Peggy she had a sparkling brooch.

Maureen had been the last to do the distributing. She had asked if she could be and it seemed a glorious end to the present-giving. The air was so full of gratitude and re-examination of gifts that none of them except Elizabeth noted the anxious glances exchanged between Auntie Eileen and Uncle Sean. She couldn't interpret them – it was as if they alone had seen some hidden disaster. Uncle Sean evidently had decided to let Auntie deal with it, whatever it was. Elizabeth's face was reddening with anxiety, she knew it was.

'Right everyone, clear up all the mess, paper into this box, string into that, and *don't lose anything*!' Eileen supervised a huge sweep on the room. 'Now all of you out in the square, yes, you too, Sean, get a bit of exercise . . . and Donal, of course you can child . . . wrap up well. No, leave your furry hat here, that's the boy.'

In minutes she had the room cleared of people and presents. Elizabeth's heart pounded because she knew something was very wrong. She went into the kitchen with Peggy and helped to fold the paper up into squares. Peggy kept up a monologue about how much there was to be done for the meal and how little help anyone gave . . . but she was only muttering, and didn't expect any answer.

The voices came clearly from the next room.

'No, Maureen, sit down. Come on sit down. . . .'

'I don't know what you mean Ma, what is it?'

54

'Maureen, where did you get the money to pay for these things . . . where?'

'Ma, I don't know what you mean. I saved up my pocket money like everyone else. . . . Of course I did Ma.'

'We're not fools Maureen . . . look at these things. They cost a fortune. That soap you bought your mother . . . it's fifteen shillings. I saw it myself in the chemist.'

'But Da, I didn't. . . .'

'Just tell us where you got the money child, that's all your father and I want to know. Tell us quickly and don't ruin the day for all the rest of them.'

'I never took any of your money Mam, you can look in your desk, I didn't take a penny. . . .'

'I didn't miss anything Sean.'

'And I didn't touch anything in your pocket, Da. . . .'

'Come on, Maureen, you get a shilling a week, you have pounds' worth of stuff here. Pounds and pounds. Can't you see your mother and I are heart-scalded over it. . . .'

'Is this the thanks I get for giving you nice Christmas presents. . . .' Maureen had begun to cry. 'Is this . . . all . . . you . . . say, accuse me of stealing from you?'

'Well, the only other alternative . . . is that you stole them from the shops.' Eileen's voice was shaking as she voiced the suspicion.

'I *bought* them,' persisted Maureen.

'God almighty, those hair brushes you gave Sean, they're over two pounds!' roared Sean. 'You're not leaving this room till we know. Christmas dinner or no Christmas dinner . . . if I have to shake every bone out of your body, I'll find out. Don't treat us like fools. *Bought* them indeed. . . .'

'You'll have to tell us soon or later, your father is right. Tell us now.'

'I bought you Christmas presents to please you and this is all you say. . . .'

'I'm going to go up to Doctor Lynch's house and see whether their family got fine presents from that Berna of theirs. Maybe the two of you were in this together. Maybe Berna will tell us if you won't. . . .'

'No!' It was a scream. 'No Da, don't go. Please don't go.'

There were sobs from Eileen, and shocked noises and wailings from Maureen as well as her mother. There was the sound of great slappings and a chair turning over. Elizabeth heard Aunt Eileen pleading with Uncle Sean not to be so hard.

'Leave her, Sean, leave her till you calm down.'

'Calm down. Stealing from every other trader in the town. Into their shops with that brat of a Lynch girl. Five shops, five families who've done business with us for years and this brat goes in and steals from them. Jesus Christ, what's there to be calm about . . . you're going in to every one of them when the shops open. Every single one of them do you hear, every item will be returned. And the Lynches will be told too, mind that. They're not going to live in innocence over the pair of thieves we have stalking the town. . . .'

Elizabeth exchanged a fearful glance with Peggy as they heard another blow and another scream.

'Don't you be minding all that now,' said Peggy. 'Better not to poke your nose into others' affairs. Better to hear nothing and say nothing.'

'I know,' said Elizabeth. 'But it's going to spoil Christmas.'

'Not at all,' said Peggy. 'We'll have a grand Christmas.'

'Ah, Da you can't hit a girl like that, stop it, Da, stop it!'

'Go away, Sean, I don't want you here, get out, it's my business.'

'Da, you can't hit Maureen like that, Ma stop him, he's hit her on the head. Stop it, Da, stop it, you're too big, you'll kill her.'

Elizabeth fled from the kitchen and got her new bicycle. Round and round the square she cycled, trying to brush the tears out of her eyes. She didn't want the others to ask her what was wrong. She had no hope that they would even get together for the goose now. Aunt Eileen had probably gone to the bedroom, Sean gone off out after the row with his father. Uncle Sean might have taken the keys and gone back into the store, and Maureen – heaven knew what would happen to Maureen. It was all turning out badly like everything always did. It was so unfair.

56

Other children who lived in the square had bicycles too and tricycles and scooters; there were marvellous tales about how Martin Ryan had seen the leg of Santa disappearing up a chimney and Maire Kennedy had heard the reindeer coming into the square. Aisling had already learned how to do tricks on her new bicycle . . . she was swooping around where the bus would stop on a normal day with both hands spread out wide and her red hair flying behind her. She saw Elizabeth looking at her and pedalled over.

'What's wrong, you look sad?' she asked.

'No, I'm fine.'

'Are you thinking of your own family and being a bit lonely?' Sometimes Aisling got great fits of concern over Elizabeth's temporary orphan status.

'Well, a bit,' Elizabeth lied.

'You have our family now, and we'll have a grand Christmas,' she said firmly.

At that moment, the O'Connors were called from the top of the steps by Eileen.

'Come on my four. Wash hands and ready for Christmas Feast. . . .'

She looked quite calm again, Elizabeth thought, and then felt a little lift at being called one of her four. Unwillingly, Eamonn, Donal and Aisling gathered their gifts and left their friends. A cursory hand wash was done and all hands dried simultaneously on a wet towel. The table was all set and Christmas crackers criss-crossed between each plate. As they slid to their places, Aunt Eileen said almost casually, 'Oh, by the way, there's been a mistake about some of the presents, could you give Maureen back what she gave you; there was a mistake about some of the prices. It has to be sorted out.' There was a bit of a grumble, a demand for reassurance that he would still get his bicycle light back from Eamonn. But it was over. The crisis was somehow finished. Maureen's eyes were very red, and so were Young Sean's. But no comment was made, and they pulled crackers with everyone else.

And afterwards when there were records on the gramophone there was dancing. Everyone danced except Eamonn who said it was silly, but he was in charge of winding up the gramophone which was a great help.

And as Elizabeth saw Uncle Sean dance a waltz with Maureen and noticed her lean her head against his jacket and cry, she thought she would never understand them in a million years.

The new term began with cold weather and Sister Mary in a very bad humour. She had chilblains and wore mittens, her fingers seemed swollen and purple and she had a racking cough. Donal was wheezing again, and Eileen kept him at home.

Maureen had gone to each of the shops where the Christmas gifts had been 'bought'. In front of Eileen she had handed them back, saying that she had taken them by mistake during her Christmas shopping. Nowhere was she met with anything but kindness. As soon as she left the shop, face burning with shame, the shopkeepers softened the humiliation for Eileen by saying that it was all that young Berna Lynch's doing, a wild bold strap if ever there was one; of course, with all the trouble the poor mother had with the doctor it was hard to know who to blame. They said that poor Maureen had had enough punishment by having to face them and told Eileen to forget it.

Sean had asked the convent what time Maureen's classes ended each day and insisted that she be home fifteen minutes later. He asked her to come into the shop and present herself to him and then to return to the house and begin her homework. Berna Lynch was not to come inside their home again, and Maureen was not to enter hers.

Young Sean read that in England an Air Training Corps had been started for boys between the ages of sixteen and eighteen. He read it out to his father as proof that seventeen was a man's age already. His father said that he didn't care if the British Empire reached into playpens and took their own boys out to fight at the age of four, no son of his, no Irishman of any decency was going to go and fight with them in further attempts to conquer the globe.

Aisling, annoyed by all the efforts to make her less giddy

and to extract more work from her, decided that she would organise a baptism for Elizabeth to liven up the term. They fixed the date for 2 February, the Feast of the Purification. Aisling had an instinct that they should keep the baptism a secret. This instinct was shared by the other girls in the class.

It took place on the stone floor of the Junior Girls' cloakroom, less attractive than the River Jordan where Jesus had his baptism, according to the nice picture in the school corridor. Water from four holy water fonts had been poured into a school mug. Joannie Murray and Aisling had the words of the ceremony written out in case they forgot them . . . which Elizabeth thought added to the importance and magic of it all. She knelt, and then in front of all the class they poured the water and said, 'I baptise thee in the name of the Father and the Son and the Holy Ghost, Amen!' There was a silence; then they all clapped.

Elizabeth stood up. Her pale hair was stuck to her head, her shoulders were dripping. She didn't like to rub away the water, as it was holy water and was special. She squeezed Aisling's hand.

'Thank you,' she said.

Aisling put her arm around her.

'You'll find it all a lot easier now,' she said.

Her letters from Mother did not arrive every week. Aunt Eileen's explanation was always the terrible postal system.

'The poor woman is demented posting you letters, it's just that things are so bad over there it could take days to clear a post box.' And later there was the excuse of Violet's work. 'Now your mother must be worn out from all that war work. We've no idea here at all how desperate things must be for them.'

Violet had written just after Christmas to say that she had volunteered for the WAAFs but the ridiculous people were only taking single people or childless people or people under thirty. It was so foolish of them since Violet would have been much more suitable than these silly girls only interested in face powder and wearing a smart uniform. It was the same apparently with the Army and the Navy so Violet wasn't going to keep on offering. She was doing her bit with the WVS of course and it was fairly harrowing.

None of these initials meant anything to Elizabeth but she discovered an unexpected ally in Aisling's elder brother, Sean. He used to read the letters with her and explain what WAAFs were. It wasn't the same as being in the *real* Air Force, he assured her, but it was the best women could be. Her mother would wear a uniform, he told her, and do drilling and training and have her kit examined every day. This didn't seem at all likely. Elizabeth couldn't imagine Mother in a dark uniform like a policeman or a bus conductor. Mother wore cardigans and skirts. She couldn't get into rough clothes could she?

Sean, in his conversations with her, told her far more about London than Mother's letters did. He said that the Women's Voluntary Service wasn't just a lot of ladies doing charity things like Aunt Eileen had thought; they didn't make cakes and have coffee mornings, they were down there in the rubble on the streets finding bodies and feeding poor people and clothing them. He showed her articles in the papers about the evacuation and the finding of foster homes. He read to her that some families had turned out to be so poor and badly looked after that the children had slept on the floor and had lice all over them. Women in the WVS who had never seen such poverty were having to cope with it.

Sean's eyes almost shone as he talked about the heroism. Elizabeth didn't like to tell him that she felt sure her mother could not possibly have got caught up in such earthy work as delousing children. It was so unusual and unexpected to see him talkative that she listened and felt flattered.

His father would grunt when he heard the tales his son would tell. 'There's plenty of charity work goes on in this country too you know. . . .' When he heard of women training for war he laughed. 'Oh, we had women soldiers here long before they had them over in England . . . what do you think Countess Markievicz was doing?'

When Sean told Elizabeth about boys of his own age and younger joining an Air Corps recruiting scheme by the hundred every day ... thousands within weeks ... his father lost his temper.

'God, it would be a relief if you joined them some day, I tell you that, instead of all this bellyaching about what a great lot they are over there.'

Eileen the peacemaker, darning from the huge bag that was always beside her chair, looked up mildly.

'Ah, Sean, leave the boy alone, isn't he just praising the people for doing so much to defend their country ... wouldn't we do the same here but thank God we don't have to. That's all he's saying.'

'That's all he'd better be saying,' Sean said.

On the first day of May Sister Bonaventure toured the classrooms in the convent to inspect the altars for Our Lady. May was Our Lady's special month and it was an act of love and daughterly respect to our heavenly mother to decorate a little altar in front of her statue. Children who lived out in the country had brought bluebells and primroses, fresh white cloths and clean vases everywhere. Sister Bonaventure was very pleased. As she was leaving the classroom that nice little English refugee who was staying with the O'Connors held the door open for her.

'Settling in all right child?' she asked.

'Oh yes, Sister.' The child flushed politely.

Sister Bonaventure patted her on the head.

It had been no trouble at all taking in a non-Catholic, she thought with pleasure, she was very glad she agreed.

On the first day of May, Eileen opened a letter from Violet which had a ten-shilling note pinned to it. It was to buy birthday presents for Elizabeth and Aisling – there was only ten days' difference between them. Eileen thought ruefully of all the years that she had parcelled up some little trinket for Violet's daughter in England and that this was the first time that Aisling had ever been remembered. It must have been through Elizabeth's letters. Eileen hoped that the child hadn't asked too openly for a present. 'It's impossible to buy anything here, will you do it?' Violet wrote.

Everything is in chaos. I'm glad now that I wasn't accepted into the WAAFs, they've passed laws to stop you getting out . . . it's in for the duration like men. We've all had to register for mobilisation. I could be sent off to some munitions factory in the country, the Lord knows where. George is an ARP and he's out every night with the other wards . . . I think they quite enjoy it – they behave like schoolboys, and he brings the most extraordinary people back to breakfast sometimes. Really rough men.

This week the cheese ration goes down to one ounce . . . think of it, one ounce a week. Nobody has any clothes and we are living like paupers because everything is in short supply.

You are awfully good to look after Elizabeth for us. And to get her to write all those letters. It's very expensive on stamps for you . . . so I shan't mind if she misses a week now and then. George says to thank you too . . . he's very impressed that you should take in a total stranger . . . but then he doesn't understand the bloodbrothership of St Mark's and all we went through.

Thank you again my dear. As ever, Violet

Yes, as ever remembering bloodbrothership to relieve her conscience but not remembering a card or a letter to the child. Eileen knew that this was it as far as the birthday was concerned. Her only child was going to be eleven years of age in a foreign country with no acknowledgement from her home.

On that first day of May, young Sister Helen, Donal's teacher, wrote a note to his mother saying that the little boy was flushed and became overexcited and wheezed whenever he was asked a question. Perhaps his asthma hadn't entirely cleared? Should she talk to the doctor again, because it might be something in the classroom that brought it on? Sister Helen said that the child was so eager to learn it was very distressing to see him held back by his wheezing attacks. She put the note in an envelope and packed it in his schoolbag.

'Is it about me, Sister?' he asked with his face reddening.

'There's not a bad word in it, Donal,' she said. 'I'm telling your mother that you're one of the hardest-working boys in the class.'

He reddened even more with pleasure and bit his lips with excitement over it all.

On that first day of May, Maureen got the letter from the hospital which said that if her examination results were satisfactory she could have a place in the hospital in Dublin. She wrote a note about it to Berna Lynch, since the two girls did not meet. But Berna had new friends now and didn't reply. Maureen decided that it didn't matter. She must work like a demon for the next six weeks and pass her exams.

And on that first day of May, Aisling and Elizabeth went into the shop after school to deliver a message. Da was to come home please for a minute, Mam wanted to talk to him.

'Well, how can I come home?' Sean asked crossly. 'Who'll look after the place? That lout of a son of mine is too good to be in here apparently ... he hasn't been seen since lunchtime. . . .'

'Mam said to bring you.' Aisling was swinging out on the handles of the door that led to the back yard. 'She said no matter what.'

'Is she sick or something?' Sean was irritated. He pulled Aisling off the door and she shied away.

'No, Uncle Sean, she's not ill, she's sitting at her desk up in the sitting room, but she said it was important.'

'Well, tell her to come down to me if it's that important,' he said, about to turn away. . . .

'She *said* no matter what.' Aisling put on a baby voice.

In one movement Sean pulled off his dun-coloured coat, picked up his jacket from a nail, and strode to the door calling over his shoulder, 'Come on you two, outa there. We've enough annoyance without the two of you breaking the tools in here.' He put the 'Back in Five Minutes' notice on the door. He had no one but poor Jemmy to help him today. Jemmy looked at him with dulled eyes. It never occurred to him that the master would let him look after the shop. He came out and stood in the street patiently.

The girls trotted home after Sean, arriving in time to hear the news. Young Sean had gone to Dublin on the lunchtime bus. He was taking the boat to Holyhead tonight. He had said to Mam that if they brought him back he'd just go again. They couldn't keep him from doing what everyone wanted to do, fight in the war.

'Let him go!' roared Sean. 'Let him go, God damn him and blast him to hell forever!'

V

Elizabeth never told Violet about Sean's leaving. She didn't
know why. It seemed somehow disloyal to describe any
unhappiness, any scenes in the household. It was as if she
were telling tales. Anyway there weren't any words.
Nothing could tell anyone who wasn't there what it was
like, even if anyone wanted to tell. About the weeks when
Uncle Sean had gone down three or four nights a week to
Maher's and had come home very late banging doors and
singing bits of 'The Soldier's Song'. Or other times when
things seemed to be going calmly and someone mentioned
the war or rations or the time when Germany invaded
Russia. Then Uncle Sean would laugh; a horrible kind of
sound that only looked like a laugh when you saw his face
grinning but didn't sound like one; and he would say, 'Ah
sure, they've no trouble nowadays, the Allies. Haven't they
got bould Sean O'Connor from Kilgarret on their side and
he's a big man. He'll be eighteen next authumn, mind. He'll
be helping them plan their strategies out there. . . .'

There was no news, no word. Bit by bit Eileen stopped
looking out the window in case he was getting off the bus in
the square. Bit by bit Peggy stopped setting places for him at
table and even moved a chair out of the room. Bit by bit his
bedroom became a boxroom. Things that weren't needed
ended up in Sean's room. Once Peggy called it a boxroom,
and that day Eileen went up and cleared it out, distributing
things all around the house and saying loudly that it was
Sean's room and she'd thank everyone to remember that.

But soon it went back to being a boxroom again. People
didn't ask for news any more. Elizabeth begged Aunt Eileen
not to worry about having a party for her birthday, she
never had one at home, anyway, she explained. Auntie

65

Eileen had hugged her and cried and cried into her hair. 'You're a lovely little girl,' she had said over and over. 'That's what you are, a lovely little girl.'

Aisling's birthday, ten days later, was firmly celebrated. It was now four full weeks since Sean had left. Aisling had said to Dad that she was going to invite six girls from the class to tea, Mam had said she could. There would be a cake and games and if Da was going to spoil everything and make them all ashamed of him like Berna Lynch's father had done at one of her birthday parties then could he go off to Maher's early and not come back till they were finished. Elizabeth trembled when she heard this ultimatum but it turned out to be the right action. Uncle Sean didn't stop being bitter, and laughing those imitation laughs but he did stop shouting and banging doors and smelling like the smell you got when you went into Maher's through the back door.

By the time that Maureen had got her Leaving Certificate things had become normal enough for a real family celebration. Everyone ignored Sean's remarks about Maureen now being his eldest child. Nobody picked him up on it, not even Donal who had a very literal mind. They all went to Dublin to settle Maureen into her new life. All except Peggy and Niamh, and they had been given so many instructions and warnings by Eileen that even Sean had to laugh.

'You've set so many spies on her that she'll be unable to move.'

'She's a desperate eejit, you know,' Eileen had said unguardedly. 'She'd lie down on our bed for half of Kilgarret if I hadn't put the fear of God into her. Haven't we got enough to occupy us without Peggy producing another baby for us by spring?' This comment mystified Aisling and Elizabeth.

They went to Dublin in the back of a lorry which had seats put in it and rugs over the seats. Donal sat in the driving compartment with Da and Mr Moriarty who was giving them the lift. He had to go to Dublin to get medical supplies for the chemist so he got his petrol easily. There was rationing in Ireland too but not nearly as bad as back in

London; even milk and eggs were rationed there, Elizabeth learned in her letters from home. Mother had got a job now as a book-keeper in a munitions factory. She couldn't say where the factory was in case any Germans read the letter and came and dropped bombs on it. Elizabeth wished she could have shown Sean the letter. He would have been very excited about it.

They bumped along the road from Wicklow, past the sea on their right.

'Your home is just over there, Elizabeth,' Eileen said once. She noticed that Elizabeth didn't respond as she normally did when someone brought her into the conversation. 'I mean your other home,' Eileen added hastily, and this time Elizabeth smiled.

Mrs Moriarty, all wrapped up, sat in the back of the truck with her two daughters, who were going to the same hospital. Tonight they would all see the three girls off into their nurses' home and meet the nuns who ran it; then the Moriartys would go to their relations in Blackrock and the O'Connors to stay in the guesthouse in Dunlaoghaire where Eileen's cousin, Gretta, did a good business. They had eggs, and butter for her, ham and a chicken. It would more than pay for the night for the six of them in two rooms. Gretta would be delighted with the country food; she had hinted more than once that they could even sell her food and make a handsome profit since so many people getting on the boat were anxious to bring a little extra across the water. Big turkeys had been known to travel to England plucked and well wrapped up in blankets and cooed over as if they were babies. Customs men didn't poke their noses too deeply into shawls containing babies.

But Eileen didn't want to get involved in the black market. She was happy to use the food to pay for the outing.

Maureen's hospital looked very forbidding. Elizabeth thought it looked a frightening place, Aisling said it was worse than school. But they were told to straighten themselves up and behave nicely and not to make a show of themselves.

The goodbyes were said; Maureen was to write every single week. Eileen had given her eleven stamped envelopes.

That would see her up to the Christmas holidays. The two Moriarty girls were saying goodbye too. Donal looked as if he might cry, Eamonn looked as if he couldn't get out quick enough. Sean ended it with a formal note.

'It's always hard to see the first bird leave the nest but it's the way things are.'

The nuns and everyone else seemed to like this and it got people moving.

'Yes, this is our first *girl* to leave the nest,' said Eileen firmly to the nun who ran the students' home. And then they were out and getting back into the truck.

Mrs Moriarty was crying and sniffing into her handkerchief. Suddenly Elizabeth leaned over to her.

'Do you have any relations in Cork, Mrs Moriarty?' she asked. This was such an odd event that the tears ceased almost at once.

'No, child . . . no, why do you ask?'

'It's just that . . . oh, about a year ago when I was coming to live here, I met a Mrs Moriarty on the train, and she was going to her son and daughter-in-law in Cork . . . and you know I hadn't heard the name before . . . and I wondered, since everyone in Ireland seems to be related. . . .'

Elizabeth stopped. Everyone was looking at her. She had never spoken like that before.

'You talk like us now,' said Aisling, laughing.

'God help us, we'll have to get that out of you fast before the war is over,' said Eileen.

Violet got out of bed just as the hall door closed, and George came in from his night's work. Sleepily, she put on her lilac dressing-gown, brushed her hair and padded down the stairs to put on the kettle.

'What kind of a night was it?' she asked him. He looked very drawn and old. He looked fifteen years older than his forty-two-years.

'All right, really,' he said.

'George, what does that mean? Does it mean that you were fire watching and there were no fires, or that you put them out?'

68

'No, I was shelter attendant,' he said wearily.

'But what did you do?' Violet leaned against the sink. 'You never tell me what it's like, what happens.'

'Well. It's like when we went to the shelters, you know, and they sort of took charge.'

'Do you mean just shepherding people in and out . . . ?'

'Yes, in a way. . . .'

'Like a porter in a station . . . ?' Her voice had a high cracked disappointed note about it.

'It's much more dangerous,' he said, hurt.

Suddenly her tense body seemed to soften and she looked at him with real concern. An old, tired man, just finished a night of fear. He could have stayed in their own 'shelter', a cellar which had always been considered a nuisance and now was padded with cushions and mattresses. But two nights a week he spent with a torch and a round tin hat guiding people, people with no shelters, up and down stairs, trying to sound authoritative and trying to sound calming.

Tears came to Violet's eyes and poured down her cheeks. George raised his tired head and half stood up . . .

'What is it Violet . . . what did I say?' he began.

Her shoulders heaved.

'I didn't say *anything*. . . .'

'Oh, the pity of it . . . the stupid pity . . . if someone up in the sky were looking down at this pathetic house in this pathetic stupid life, what would they say? You've had no sleep, I've only had a little sleep. Other people are dead. There's nowhere to rest, no food to eat, you have to go to that silly stupid bank and I have to go off to this dreary, dull endless factory. Two buses there, two buses back, four sets of queuing . . . and what's it all for?'

The kettle whistled behind her and she took no notice.

'What are we doing it for, George, what on earth is the point? There's going to be nothing afterwards. It's going to be just as bad after the war. . . .'

'Oh no . . . after the war. . . .'

'Yes, after the war. Tell me, what will be so wonderful?'

'Elizabeth will be back,' he said simply.

'Yes.' She stopped crying. 'That will be something.'

George got up and turned off the kettle; he made a pot of tea slowly.

Violet wiped her eyes.

'I must write to Elizabeth today,' she said. 'I might do it at my break at work.'

Aisling and Elizabeth were now the senior members of the family. It was even suggested that they might have separate rooms, since Maureen would not be needing hers, except for the holidays. Sean's room, boxroom or not, would never be offered to them. But the girls didn't want to change their ways, finding first one excuse and then another. Maureen's room didn't get such good light for homework. It was further up the stairs and away from the bathroom. Aisling clinched it, in a fit of kindness, when she said that it would be sad for Maureen if she didn't think her room would be there to come back to.

Eileen let it go. It would be nice to have a guest room in case they ever had any guests. She had often hoped, over the years, that Violet would come to stay. There had been that visit a long time ago . . . before Violet had married . . . it hadn't been a success. Probably because Sean had been a baby and Violet had been full of the bright young flappers and all the excitement of the twenties in London. Nobody had ever said that it was a failure, but deep down Eileen almost wished that it had never taken place. Now? Well, now, of course, anything would be a treat for Violet and George after the miseries of Britain, the long queues, the black market, the endless waiting at night for the bombs to fall. . . . In fact she should really write and suggest it. . . .

Elizabeth was distressed to hear that Eileen had asked Mother to come over to Kilgarret. She wished the invitation had never been sent. She remembered Mother saying the place was dirty – sudden visions of Mother's nose wrinkled up in horror at some of the habits in the O'Connor household made Elizabeth almost faint. If Mother did come, she wouldn't fit in and Elizabeth would be running from one side to the other. It would be like old times, when Miss James said one thing and Mother misunderstood, and then

Mother would say something and Miss James would be offended. Here in this house, people didn't brood and wonder what other people had meant, they asked them, and they shouted at them and often they thumped them. Elizabeth's heart lurched again when she thought how Mother might react when she saw Aunt Eileen slapping things out of Eamonn's hands if he had picked up some food that he wasn't meant to have taken. Mother would be appalled at Niamh's nappies trailing as she toddled round, and at Donal's stained dressing-gown, which he wore as much around the house as he did in his bedroom. Elizabeth couldn't even bear to think of what Mother would make of Peggy and whether she would ever bring herself to eat anything that Peggy had touched. . . .

The prayers that were muttered kneeling in the bathroom – she didn't want Aisling to know what she was praying for – were answered. Violet wrote to say that it was quite impossible. She did envy everyone in Ireland eating butter and cream and meat. She thought that it sounded like a kind of paradise. There was little gratitude for the invitation, but much on how everyone in Kilgarret was faring better than those in London. Eileen showed the letter to Sean.

'You can't say she isn't making much of us now. She says it sounds like heaven here compared to what they have to endure.'

'Well, you can write back and tell her that Ireland doesn't have to endure all that because Ireland didn't go on like the British Empire, shadow-boxing and fighting other European people instead of minding its own business.' Eileen had no intention of telling her anything of the sort. She went back to the letter. It sounded more interested in Elizabeth than any of the previous notes and scribbles had been.

I suppose she's much taller now. They do grow between ten and eleven. A woman beside me at work asked me if I had children, and when I said I had a daughter of eleven she couldn't believe me. I told her I hadn't married until I was twenty-eight and she couldn't believe that either, but she said I didn't look like anyone who had children.

Suddenly, right in the middle of work, I felt very lonely and I started to cry. I've been doing a lot of that lately – it's war nerves, people say. They tell me to take these nerve tonics – everyone takes them – but they're worse than useless. I think of Elizabeth a lot these nights. I'm glad she's well and out of reach of the blitz. But sometimes, when I've had a long day, I wonder whether there was any point to all we learnt at school. It means nothing now. There's no point in being able to run a gracious home with nothing to run it on. And all that history. They never told us that wars just went on and on. . . .

Maureen's letters arrived every week. Sometimes they had blots on them, and the lines were crooked, but neither Sean nor Eileen seemed to mind a bit, and read them out cheerfully to everyone. Una Moriarty, who was eleven months younger than Norah, was doing very well, but Norah was being homesick and silly. They had been given a late pass and they all went to the pictures in O'Connell Street, but it was the one night when the projector broke down and there was half an hour's delay, so they'd had to go home without knowing the end of the picture. There was an awful lot of bed-making. The way the beds are made at home is all wrong, they have no corners. Staff Sister Margaret is like a devil but Sister Tutor is very beautiful and glides around, seeming not to walk like other people. They'd all be home on the bus the day before Christmas Eve. Maureen was looking forward to sleeping on and on and on.

Doctor Lynch went on one of his batters the day the Japanese bombed Pearl Harbor. It had nothing to do with the event, in fact he didn't even hear of it until five days later when he was discovered by the Guarda in a sailors' public house in Cork, slumped over a table. This time the return home was less dignified and discreet than on previous occasions. This time, Doctor Lynch was handed unceremoniously to a Guarda van going to Dublin, and then to another on its way to County Wicklow. The family had been told to expect him. The Guarda left him in the square. Their custody of him had been entirely informal; they had abuse from him all the way to Kilgarret. . . . He was now sobering, but in deadly need of another drink. He ranted that he had their numbers and they would all be demoted for this. Unshaven, without his coat – which had been abandoned somewhere on his joyous journey south to Cork – his eyes narrowed at the sight of the O'Connor house. That was the bloody family which had dared to insult his position by refusing to let their red-haired brat play with Berna. Tears of self-pity came into his eyes. That thick, ignorant Sean O'Connor with his builder's yard and dirty shop, with his tinker's brood of children, had dared to forbid Berna his house. Had dared to apologise on *his* daughter's behalf for something . . . which had never been proved, mind you.

Doctor Lynch came slowly up the steps. Peggy let him in and stood back fearfully as he climbed the stairs. Donal, running down to see who was the visitor, met him on the landing between the kitchen and the sitting room.

'Doctor Lynch.'

'Yes. Which one of them are you? Which of Sean O'Connor's brats are you? You're in your dressing-gown. Are you sick? Have you been sick, boy, come on?'

Flattened against the wall, Donal stared up at him with huge eyes.

'I'm Donal,' he said. 'I'm seven. I've a touch of asthma. It's not bad. I'll grow out of it.'

'Who told you that?'

'Everyone says it. Mam says it.'

'What does your Mam know about it? Does she deign to take you to a doctor at all, or does she have medical skills herself?'

Aisling and Elizabeth heard the shouting and rushed to protect Donal.

'Well, has she?' Doctor Lynch was roaring.

'Go to the shop and get Mam,' hissed Aisling, and Elizabeth, round-eyed, slipped down the stairs.

'Who are you?' The man smelt awful and had stubble all over his face.

'I'm just visiting,' said Elizabeth, backing away. She didn't stop to get her coat, though it was freezing outside.

'Nice to know the O'Connors are still allowed some visitors. Who's her father, then – a duke? A doctor's child isn't good enough for Sean O'Connor. . . .'

'Her father works in a bank in England,' said Donal helpfully.

Doctor Lynch gazed at him. 'You've more than a touch of asthma, young fella, you have a chest that whistles like a kettle. A great pity your mother never took you to a doctor. I don't like the sound of it. . . .'

Aisling's face blazed. 'There isn't a thing wrong with Donal, not a thing. He's a touch of asthma, that's all, it gets worse in the bad weather. And Mam has taken him to a doctor, to Doctor MacMahon. And the hospital. And everything. So you're all wrong. You're not a proper doctor anyway.'

'Oh, Aisling.' Donal looked at her nervously, afraid that she had gone too far. People didn't say things like that. . . . Doctor Lynch drew himself up. Aisling's mind churned, but she saw that she had to go on. If she stopped now, Donal's faith would go. He would always believe he had a terrible disease if she backed down in front of Berna Lynch's awful father. Taking a big breath and putting her arm around her brother's shoulder, she continued.

'I know what I'm talking about. My father and mother don't approve of you, Doctor Lynch. They think you're unreliable. That's why none of us go to you when we're sick. We go right out to Doctor MacMahon's house.'

She didn't hear her mother bounding lightly up the stairs, summoned by Elizabeth in a few short sentences.

'Doctor Lynch . . . Aisling. . . .' She saw that Donal was terrified as the two faced each other – the shaggy, unkempt doctor and Aisling, her eyes bright and her red curls bouncing.

'You'll answer for this, you impudent little brat,' he said, moving towards her. Donal, standing in the corner, raised his voice, but only a thin squeak came out.

'No, she didn't mean. . . .'

'But I did,' cried Aisling. 'It's wrong to come here, to come here all dirty and shabby and start frightening Donal and telling him he's not well. He's only got a touch of asthma, do you hear me? Everyone knows it . . . everyone. . . .'

Eileen stepped in. It was to Aisling she moved, and she put a hand on a trembling shoulder.

'Come on, Matthew,' she said calmly. 'Go home with you at once. If you want to call on us, come back when you're in better shape. I can't imagine why you want to come here bringing yourself down to the level of children. Come on, shoo.'

Her voice brought relief to Donal's face. She was treating the doctor like a bold child.

'High and mighty Eileen O'Connor,' he said venomously, looking around him. 'Too good for this town . . . educated in England . . . what did it get you? A house falling down for want of a coat of paint, a husband covered with dirt over in a yard and a lean-to, a crowd of children one more wild than the next. . . .'

'We have the best children in town,' said Eileen. 'Are you going now or shall I send one of them over for your wife?'

'The best,' he laughed. 'This one will be in the churchyard before much longer, you sent that Maureen away before she disgraced you, and what about young fellow-me-lad strutting about in a Tommy's uniform?'

Eileen forced herself to laugh. Once she heard the sound of it it encouraged her and her second attempt was almost a peal.

'My God, Matthew Lynch, isn't it true what they say about drunks! They weave more fairy tales and have more imagination than the people who write books. Listen, will you get out of here before my Sean comes back and kicks you out. . . .' She wiped her eyes at the amusement of it all. The children looked at her amazed. Even Peggy, who had come to stand at the door with Niamh in her arms, smiled without quite knowing why. The doctor, deflated and unexpectedly defeated, began to leave. Eileen's laughter annoyed him more than he could believe. He had only said what was true, why was she laughing? The door slammed and Eileen sat down. Her mirth hadn't subsided. Cautiously the children moved towards her and Peggy advanced into the room. When the door downstairs banged, Eileen leapt up and looked out of the window.

'Look at him, the poor buffoon, heading for a few quick ones now to give him the courage to face the wife. Oh dear, there's nothing so desperate as a drunk man – whatever you two girls do, and you too, Peggy, and you Niamh little heart, for God's sake don't marry a drunk. . . .'

Donal felt excluded. 'Doesn't he know what he's saying? Is he really unreliable?' he asked anxiously.

'When he's like that he's only got old potatoes rattling around in his head, not brains. Poor fool.' His insults burned into her like a hot rod pushed down the back of her throat. But she was winning, she was managing to make him ridiculous. She didn't have to deny what he'd said about Donal if she laughed at everything he said. She watched him pick up a newspaper from a bench near the bus stop, and then he shouted something to her. The window was closed so she couldn't hear.

'He's saying something, Mam,' said Peggy.

'I'm sure he is.' She shivered. 'Come on, Peggy, since I'm home anyway let's all have a cup of tea.'

'He keeps pointing to the paper,' said Donal.

'Come on away and we'll close the curtains, it's dark almost.' Peggy scuttled out to the kitchen as Eileen opened the window slightly.

'That's cooked your goose . . . America's in the war now. . . . Your snot-nosed boy'll be sent to fight . . . it's getting worse, not better . . . you'll lose two sons you cackling old hen . . . your big Tommy of a son'll be mincemeat in no time now.'

Eileen closed the window quickly and joined the little group by the fire.

'What's he saying, Mam?' Donal, worried still.

'Oh, more rubbishing and rawmaishing out of him . . . the man doesn't know what day it is . . . he just goes on and on and on. . . .'

*

There were, of course, other mothers who didn't know if their sons lived or died, but Eileen got no comfort from thinking about them. For some reason which she couldn't quite explain to herself she had pretended to other people that she heard from him. When a well-meaning or even just curious friend or neighbour would ask, 'Any word at all from Sean in England?' she would nod brightly and say yes, she heard from him, he was fine. She said it with quick darting looks in the direction her husband might come from . . . just brief letters, you know, and people thought that the boy wrote to his mother but had fought with his father. In some convoluted way, Eileen thought that this made things more *right*.

At times she wondered should she write to Violet and enquire about how to trace a missing boy who had gone to sign up. How did you set the machinery in motion to get him back? Show his birth certificate? Prove he was neither British nor eighteen? Then she knew she would never do that; but she was still tempted to hunt him out, just so that she could write to him. She could even get him to write to her at the chemist's. The Moriartys were unusual in Kilgarret, in that they were able to keep secrets. She had also read somewhere that you could contact missing persons through the Salvation Army, but it made it very final, in a way, if you asked an organisation like that to hunt for him. While you left it, and hoped and hoped, it didn't seem too bad. It didn't actually define him as a runaway son, a missing person. Sean was still going to write some time soon. . . .

She read the paper on her desk and tried to work out from the reports in the *Irish Independent* whether her son might have been trained by now, or if he were still too young. She went dutifully through accounts of what Stafford Cripps had said, and Churchill had said and Beaverbrook had said and Harold Nicolson had said; but none of them ever said what happened to young Irish boys who went off on boats to join the war. And the paper always referred to it as the Emergency, which seemed less frightening. She followed the progress of events as they moved out to the Far East, and of simpler matters nearer home. She read of the austerity measures, gasping at the idea of onions being so precious they were offered as raffle prizes. She read these things privately and without discussing them with Sean, though she didn't hide her interest either.

She was utterly unprepared for young Sean's letter when it did arrive, ten months after he had left home. It was from Liverpool. It was very short. He hadn't wanted to write at all, he said, or at least not until he was properly in the army and couldn't be got out of it. But there was this woman, his friend's mam, she was very nice and she said he should write just a word to his own mam becaue she'd be grieving. *He* had said that there were plenty more at home to keep his mam busy, but Gerry's mam, Mrs Sparks, had said he should still write. So. He was fine and he was meeting a whole lot of very nice people. He had done this and that until September, because they wanted to know what age was he and they wouldn't take him until he was actually eighteen. He had sent to Ireland for his birth certificate. He got a copy from the Customs House. He was in a camp now doing basic training. It was very interesting. He often spent time off with Gerry Sparks who was his mate and with Gerry's mam who was very nice and used to cook very well before the war because nowadays you couldn't get anything.

He sent her no love, no enquiries, no excuses, no pleas for understanding. His writing was bad and his grammar and spelling poor. Eileen thought of the years with the Brothers; she remembered how she and Sean had always thought he was very bright because he was their eldest son; but this was the letter of a near illiterate. She read it again and again, the birth certificate and Customs House and the basic training, and the tears fell slowly down her cheeks.

She didn't tell anyone about the letter. She kept it folded in her handbag, and she kept the next one and the next, and the fourth one in November when El Alamein was won. She replied almost lightly, raking her letters before she posted them for any hint of anxiety or grievance. She even found funny little things to tell him, about the day the goat got into the shop and knocked down all the boxes; about Maureen coming home from nursing school and practising bandaging so enthusiastically that she stopped the circulation in Eamonn's arms for ages and ages; about the play that Aisling, Elizabeth and the little Murray girl wrote and performed, which was meant to be a serious and inspirational account of St Bernadette, and was such high comedy that the audience was convulsed. She sent cheerful greetings to Gerry Sparks's mother and wished there was some way of sending her a few things; but perhaps some time if Sean came home on leave he might be able to take her back a couple of chickens and some butter and eggs?

The life-line to her son was so gossamer thin she didn't dare to break it. Even telling someone might put it in danger. . . .

Sean knew that there were letters, but he never mentioned them. He grew more silent in the shop; he worked just as hard as ever, but he smiled less and had no time for a chat on Fair Day. Sometimes, Eileen would look at him, bending down in the yard and trying to take the strain out of his back, and she would fill with pity for him. Since the Emergency, coal was almost impossible to get, so they had to fill their outhouses with turf instead. Turf took so much room to store; even the rooms over the shop which had been stacked with brooms and potato baskets, boxes of globes and wicks for the lamps, brushes for whitewash and distemper . . . they were now all full of turf. Eileen felt she was breathing it through her pores as it billowed out of the grate and covered everything with its flakes.

Sean looked older than a man in his forties should look. Perhaps, Eileen thought, he had the worst of all worlds: living in the country but without the countryside's healthy life; a father of six without a father's hope and pride in his eldest son taking over the business. He had always been the one with energy and drive; he had saved and hoarded to buy this small place . . . the year of the Treaty. It had all been so symbolic. A new nation, a new business; and there they were, twenty years later and their son out fighting for that same country from which they had won their freedom. . . . And Sean himself, who had seen this shop as a life's dream

79

come true, was out in the cold yard, rooting around behind the road signs for some spare plough-shares. It was raining, and his head was getting very wet. Eileen left her little glass cage and, a bag over her head, went out to help him.

She held the huge black and yellow road signs, which had been taken down during the Emergency to confuse any invaders, and made room for him to find the bits of machinery.

'We'll do a great tidy-up on this lot, one day,' he said, gratitude in his tone if not in his words.

'I know we will,' she said. She wondered, as she spoke, whether he knew or cared that his son was spending springtime fighting in North Africa. The excitement had been so great when his call-up papers had arrived that even Gerry Sparks had added a few more words to the letter. Gerry was going with him. Eileen still didn't know whether Sean ever read his son's letters. She often left her bag open so that he would see them; but he never made any mention of it and they never seemed to have been disturbed when she returned.

Donal had eventually moved to the Brothers', having been persuaded to spend another year at the convent after he had made his first communion. It wasn't usual for a boy to stay there until he was eight, but Sister Maureen had managed to convey that it was perfectly reasonable. She had said, privately, that they should give him one more year before he had to face the rough and tumble of the school yard down at the Brothers'. Another year might make his breathing easier, his anxieties less. Eileen, who would have been happy for Donal to be educated for the rest of his life with the kind Sister Maureen, agreed readily. But the day had had to come, and now her delicate child was coming home every day, clothes torn, face terrorised, lips sealed. 'I fell,' he said, every day. Eamonn was worn out defending him.

'You see, Mam,' Eamonn explained, 'the fellows pick on Donal because he's nearly nine, fellows of just eight, and they're too tough and then I have to go an' clout them, and then the other fellows come up to me and say what am I doing clouting fellows of only eight for when I'm fourteen. It's desperate, Mam. That's why my coat's torn again.'

Aisling and Elizabeth, cycling home from school – arms touching, dangerously sophisticated thirteen-year-olds, with no time for the bold rough lads from the Brothers' – saw a crowd gathered around someone lying at the side of the road. Together, they slowed down and curiosity made them get off the bikes to see what had happened. At almost the same moment they recognised Donal's scarf, a long multi-coloured one that Peggy had knitted from bits of spare wool. Peggy loved wrapping him up in it every morning and would turn him like a top until he was under three layers at least. At exactly the same moment they dropped their bicycles in the middle of the road and ran to him. The other boys were looking frightened.

'He's only putting it on,' muttered one.

'Look at his eyes,' said another. . . .

Donal lay on the side of the road gasping for breath, his hands flailing in the air; his scarf lay trailing in the mud, one end of it still caught in the top button of his coat. Aisling was on her knees beside him in a flash. Just as she had seen her mother do a dozen times, she loosened his coat and his shirt collar with a wrench, at the same time raising his head on her arm.

'Take your time, Donal, you've got all the time in the world. As slowly as you like. Don't fight it,' she murmured. Elizabeth was on her knees at the other side, helping with the support. Her pale hair was in her eyes, her lisle stockings wet and torn from kneeling on the ground, her up-turned bicycle forgotten.

'Your breath is coming, that's it, in, out, in, out, that's it, you've got it again. . . .'

Aisling stood up and faced the seven boys, who were all just as shocked by the sudden swoop the girls had made as by the whites of Donal O'Connor's eyes.

'We didn't do anything,' said one.

'No, nothing, we were only playing, we never touched him,' and there was a gabble of voices all trying to be freed of blame and guilt and involvement.

'You listen to me,' Aisling shouted. She glanced over at Elizabeth; they understood each other well enough. Elizabeth started to whisper to Donal. She still had her arm around his shoulder and she bent closer to his cold ear.

Aisling was formidable. 'I know every one of your names. I know you all. Tonight my Mam and Dad will be down to the school. Brother Kevin will know who you all are and Brother Thomas and Brother John. All of them. They'll deal with you. You know Donal has asthma. You could have killed him. You could all have been standing down in the courthouse if we hadn't come along. You could have been young murderers. You hit him, or you knocked him down. . . .'

'We only pulled his scarf off him.'

'Yes, and nearly choked him. The worst thing you could do. Choke him and stop air getting into his chest. You stupid, thick murderer, Johnny Walsh, if Donal isn't well you're the cause.'

'She's only letting them think that, she's only frightening them,' Elizabeth muttered urgently to Donal. 'She doesn't mean it, but just look at them!'

Donal looked. They did indeed look frightened of Aisling.

'Don't say anything. . . .' Johnny Walsh began in a whimper.

'Don't be such a coward! Don't be such a murdering coward! I'll not keep quiet and let you get away with it, murdering a boy with a bad heart and a bad chest!' Aisling had the taste of power and loved it.

'You haven't a bad heart,' hissed Elizabeth. 'It's for show.' In the darkening evening, under the light drizzle, seven young lads were terrified.

'He's older than us, he's fourteen months older than me. . . .' began Eddie Moriarty, white with fear at the thought of what his parents would do to him when this came out.

'Yes, and Jemmy in our shop is older than you and Paddy Hickey, the blind man, is older than you and you don't torment them, you great eejit!' shouted Aisling.

'What are you going to do?' asked Johnny Walsh fearfully. Aisling had been thinking.

'Pick up those bicycles. Now,' she ordered. 'Pick them up and wheel them back to town. Johnny and Eddie and you, Michael, come into my Da's shop and tell him what's happened. And tell him that from now on you're going to look after Donal. No need to mention his heart, just tell him that Donal had a fall and that you seven are going to look after him and protect him until his chest gets better.'

It seemed like a glorious escape, but Johnny wanted to make sure he wasn't walking into a trap.

'What do we have to tell your father?'

'That you're going to see no harm comes to Donal. And you'd all better pray on your knees that Donal's heart doesn't give out during the night.'

Magnificent, like the leader of a procession, she marched in front of them back to the town and into the square, while Elizabeth and Donal followed. Donal's face was wrapped up again in the scarf so no one else would see the giggles, and Elizabeth had one hand over her face. The other was holding Donal's hand.

It was the only high spot in what was otherwise a very long, very dull term. Aisling thought it would never end. She was as defiant as she dared be, staying just within the limits, and she gave no time at all to her work. She fell behind in her marks and slipped from seventh to eighteenth in class in three weeks. Elizabeth had managed a steady average of tenth or eleventh – which was considered very good for a child who had never studied the basics. There was an element of suspicion that outside an Irish convent very little could have been taught; and that any child who had emerged fairly educated through a non-Irish, non-Catholic system must be a very diligent child indeed. She now joined in the religious knowledge classes; it had seemed silly to sit in the library reading a big Bible full of words she didn't understand, when she could hear marvellous stories of apparitions and angels and sins and Jesus being so good to his mother. . . .

There had been some more worrying conversations about Elizabeth's conversion. Some of the class wondered whether they should arrange for her first communion, so that she should have the chance to confess all her sins and get forgiveness at confession.

'I don't have all that many sins,' Elizabeth had said innocently once, and everyone was horrified. She was riddled with sin, they all were, but Elizabeth was particularly bad because of all that original sin, as well.

'But I thought that the original sin had been washed away after all the baptisms?' Elizabeth had now been baptised four times. There had been doubt about the validity of the first one on the cloakroom floor. There had been an accusation that the water might not have flowed at exactly the same time as the words were being said. Then there was a long and bitter debate about whether the words should be said in Latin or English; one school of thought was convinced that lay baptisms were conducted in the vernacular. . . .

For no reason that was ever voiced, Elizabeth's conversion had never been made public. There was an unspoken feeling that, for all the nuns were exhorting them to go and convert all races and spend their pocket money contributing to the conversion of little black babies, there might be a different attitude taken to doing the job on Elizabeth. It was also feared that if Elizabeth's parents in England were to hear about it there might be great trouble.

Her mother's letters seemed to come from another world, not just another country. Elizabeth was pleased that she wrote more often and that her letters did not consist of a list of instructions: be sure to take your medicine, wear your gloves, thank everyone. . . . As the war went on, Mother seemed to have cheered up, despite the complaints. There was no soap – the ration was three ounces every month: fancy trying to live a normal healthy life on three ounces of soap a month. There was no white bread – Mother had forgotten what it tasted like. She had friends in the munitions factory where she worked and very often she stayed overnight with Lily because it was such a long journey home and somehow in this depressing war, it was nice to have a friend to laugh with. Mother had changed her hair-style, she had a victory roll now; it looked funny at first but people said it suited her. Once or twice she said that she missed Elizabeth. She always ended her letters saying she hoped Elizabeth was well and happy and that it wouldn't be long now until she could come home and they could all lead a nice normal life again.

Mother said very little about Father in her letters. And when she sent a pound for her birthday present, just before she was fourteen, Elizabeth realised with horror that she hadn't mentioned Father for months.

Eileen was at her desk when Elizabeth came to talk to her.

'Are you busy?' she asked.

Eileen smiled. None of her own family would dream of asking such a question; they all assumed that she was always ready and willing to listen, to help, to act.

'I'm not busy,' she said, pulling up a chair. On her desk she had a shoe box filled with the shop accounts, the bills overdue that had to be sent out with a personal note. No firm reminders on a printed form could be sent to a farmer who might take offence and buy from the next town. She had a letter she now knew by heart from Mrs Sparks in Liverpool, an awkward, stunted little letter from a lonely widow whose son was away and who felt she had an ally in Sean's mother. She wrote of her loneliness and her hopes that they'd be back soon, and how she hadn't heard anything for six weeks and how she wondered whether Mrs O'Connor might have. She had a letter to a specialist in Dublin, and she had to plan which day to take Donal. She had a note from Sister Margaret saying that it was time they had young Niamh at school as she was nearly five now and could they bring her down towards the end of term so that it wouldn't be so strange to her when she started in September. And, Sister Margaret said, wasn't it the blessings of God how well young Donal had settled in at the Brothers'? She had heard from all sides how the youngest young hooligans were all a great support to him instead of picking on him. The Lord worked in mysterious ways. There was a letter from Maureen wondering would Da ever let her have three pounds for a gorgeous dance dress and she'd pay him back out of her allowance, when they started to get an allowance in summer. She had a letter from the County Home that said that Sean's father was sinking fast and was very anxious to see them. They mustn't be put off by the fact that he might not recognise them; he kept saying that he wanted to see his son and his family.

'No, I'm not busy, child,' said Eileen.

'It's just that, I don't know how to say it, but, you know, there wouldn't be any danger, could there, that my father is dead?'

'*Dead*? Oh, God forbid it should be true – what makes you say that, child? Where did you get such an idea?'

Elizabeth produced a large envelope with a little sticker on it saying 'Mother's letters'. There were over fifty letters, each with the date they had arrived. She laid them out, picking up one from August 1943.

'This is the last time Mother said anything about Father. She says he was upset because of women striking for equal pay with men, that they shouldn't do that when there's a war on. And then not ever again. Not even at Christmas. She doesn't say Father sends his love. She doesn't say anything about his ARP work. . . .' Elizabeth's eyes filled with tears. 'Do you think something's happened and she's protecting me?'

Eileen rocked her in her arms, the soothing words and the denials, the positive statements tumbling out. Of course he was fine, of course they'd have heard, of course they would, it was that things had changed so much in England, and since Mother was going out to work she now had a much broader life and she didn't just write about home. And men were hopeless at writing letters, sure just look at Uncle Sean now, he was most concerned to know how Maureen was getting on up in Dublin, but did he ever put pen to paper to write to her? Never. And then people don't always keep mentioning the same things, after all when Eileen wrote to Sean she often made no mention of his father. . . .

It had slipped out.

'Do you write to Sean? Oh, I didn't know. Where is he?'

'He's in Africa, he's grand, he's got a lovely English friend called Gerry Sparks. He often asks after you in his letters . . .

now to go back to you and your worries. We'll go and ring up home for you on your birthday. We'll go into the shop tomorrow night and make a three-minute call. We'll even book it tonight. And you can tell them that it's their big, fourteen-year-old girl talking. How about that?'

'Will it be very expensive?' Elizabeth wondered.

'Not at all, and isn't it a birthday?'

'Thank you very much,' said Elizabeth, wiping her eyes on the back of her hand and her nose on a sleeve.

'Oh, Elizabeth, there's just one thing. . . .'

'I know, Auntie Eileen, they're your business, the letters to Sean. I know.'

The next letter that came said that Sean and Gerry had left North Africa. They had been in the Anzio landings and now were well into Italy. Sean wrote that the Italian countryside was beautiful and bits of it would remind you of County Wicklow. There was even less life in his words and he wished for the fighting to end. He was glad that everything was well at home. Gerry's mum had written about how you wouldn't recognise Liverpool after all the raids. It was strange to think that nothing had happened in Ireland. He wrote that they might well see Rome. When he thought of all he had learned about the Holy City at the Brothers' and now he was going to see it! He was telling Gerry about it but Gerry hadn't heard of anything and didn't know about the Vatican and St Peter's. He'd write a letter from Rome, a proper letter and Mam could take it down to Brother John and show him that a boy didn't need a Leaving Certificate to get to the Holy City.

But Sean and Gerry didn't get to the Holy City with the rest of the allies. A minefield in the Italian countryside that looked a bit like County Wicklow took both legs off Gerry Sparks from Liverpool, aged twenty-one; and twenty yards away killed outright his friend Sean O'Connor from Kilgarret who still had four months to go before he was twenty-one.

Private S. O'Connor had listed his address as the small terraced house in Liverpool where Amy Sparks received the news. She sat in her dark kitchen and thought of her only son. She read the telegram over and over again, thinking that she should react more. Then she prepared herself to tell the mother of Gerry's mate that Sean O'Connor would not be coming back to Kilgarret.

The call came through to the shop, and Eileen took it in her little eyrie. She listened without tears as Mrs Sparks explained. She waited calmly until the sobbing of the woman she had never met ceased. She sympathised in a low voice over Gerry, she said she was glad to hear that he would recover. She agreed that it was a blessing that Sean had been killed outright, but that it was great that Mrs Sparks would be able to look after Gerry.

'You sound such a wonderful woman,' Amy Sparks sobbed. 'Sean always did say "My Mam is grand". That's what he called you, *grand*.'

'He didn't mean it in the English sense, like a grand lady,' said Eileen. 'I was at school in England, I remember it was used differently.'

'Perhaps, if you ever came over to see your old school, perhaps you could come and stay with me. Perhaps you could come and see Gerry when they bring him back. . . .' The longing in her voice was clear. 'There'd be no restrictions on you travelling.'

Eileen didn't even pause.

'I'll come very soon. If Gerry is coming back the week after next I'll come too.' She heard Amy Sparks gasp down the telephone. 'If there had been a funeral for Sean I'd have come.'

For some reason that she couldn't explain to herself afterwards, Eileen didn't tell anyone for four days. In that time she went mechanically around her daily jobs, doing them with almost superhuman energy. It was as if she had made up a game with rules: she mustn't cry. If she let herself go and cried it would be worse for Sean. She had to be strong. Otherwise his whole life had no meaning, going out to that terrible place and being blown up. It would just be meaningless if people at home just wept great tears for him.

She was very methodical. She left Peggy a great list of

things to do; she arranged for Eamonn to work in the shop. She extracted a promise from Donal that he would rest and keep warm. She arranged for Maureen to come to Dunlaoghaire and meet her in a hotel.

Then she told them why she was going to be away.

She told Sean on a sunny June evening. She sat on an upturned drum and told him that their son was dead. She told him of Gerry and how his legs were gone and of the telephone call from his mother. She talked about the countryside in Italy and how they had been on the way to Rome. The noises of the shop came up from time to time as Sean tried to take it in.

They never touched each other or held each other as she spoke of the telegram that had come to the house in Liverpool, and of the details that would follow later about the grave. She spoke the way Amy Sparks had done, in slightly halting sentences about how it had been very quick, and Sean must have known nothing.

Then she listened. She listened while he ranted, she listened, still sitting on the upturned drum, while he sobbed. She couldn't hear what he said into his big blue handkerchief. She waited while the sobbing ended and was replaced by sighs.

'Would you like me to come to Liverpool with you? It's a kind of pilgrimage, isn't it? A sort of funeral?'

She looked at him gratefully. He had understood, after all.

'No, he'd prefer you to be here.'

And then she called the children together and told them their brother was dead. She made the telling full of words like 'peaceful' and 'heaven' and 'what he wanted to do'. She used words like 'brave' and 'strong' and 'proud' . . . then she said that they could help her and help Sean by being very strong.

The tears were coursing down Elizabeth's face and Aisling's was working in disbelief. He couldn't be. . . . How did you. . . . It's not fair. . . . Maybe. . . . What if. . . . Then she ran out of words and cried on Elizabeth's shoulder and Elizabeth patted her head and said that they must be brave.

Eamonn rushed back to the shop, his big innocent face stained and red. Donal protested that Sean couldn't be happy in heaven, he hadn't intended to go there, it was the bloody Germans and Italians that had sent him there. He had never said the word bloody before.

And Eileen told Maureen in the chilly lounge of a Dunlaoghaire hotel, where Maureen cried like a baby and rocked backwards and forwards in Eileen's arms until the manageress came and asked would they like to go somewhere more private. So they walked up and down the pier for two hours while Maureen cried while she thought of all the things that Sean would never do.

Then the pilgrimage began.

It passed in a blur; the rubble in the streets of Liverpool, the blackout, the queues outside every shop. There was the visit to the hospital, where Gerry had cried. She had been very strong and she had smiled. Then she had asked a young priest with an Irish accent to say a mass for Sean. It was at seven in the morning and Amy Sparks had been there. Eileen had worn her black hat and gloves and carried a bunch of flowers which she was going to leave in the church. It was as near as she could manage to a wreath.

But she cried as she sat on the boat back to Ireland and the tears ran down her face while she made no attempt to wipe them away. Her coat was stained with them as she sat looking out to the dark sea and crying at the waste. She stood up, the tears still falling and her shoulders heaving and walked to the rail of the ship. As she held onto the bar, her hat was whipped away by the night wind. It flew up in the air, hit the deck and was borne off. But the other passengers saw that the handsome woman in the black coat didn't even seem to notice it had gone. She was saying something over and over again. Praying, possibly.

PART TWO

1945–1954

VI

Violet had never understood why they had agreed to Elizabeth finishing her summer term at that convent school. It meant she missed VE Day; she missed all the celebrations, the turning on of lights, the tearing down of the blackout curtains and the scenes of wild excitement, where American soldiers swung passing girls into crazy dances, where crowds marched back and forth up Regent Street and round Piccadilly mad with happiness, hooting on car horns and singing 'Bless 'Em All' with tears running down their faces. It had been a heady day, but Violet had felt very left out. She didn't have a man with a kit-bag coming home triumphantly with tales of battles won; she had George, moodier and more nervy than ever. He had taken now to muttering to himself about fellows with medals and ribbons coming back to civvy street for promotion and praise. She had no daughter to clutch proudly to herself like other women had; nobody she could hold and urge to remember this day for the rest of her life. Her daughter was finishing some exam and singing in a concert carrying an image of the Virgin Mary and wouldn't be able to travel until the holidays – or that's what Eileen's letter had seemed to say. Violet hoped with a great sigh that they had not done the wrong thing in sending Elizabeth away for the duration.

Her own work in the munitions factory was over now. There had been a chance to work in a tobacco factory – so great was the shortage of cigarettes that there were unheard-of working conditions now, with shifts around the clock. But Violet didn't want to get involved. It was one thing doing important war work, which had to be done; it was another sitting at a factory bench making cigarettes with hundreds of factory workers. A few of the girls from the munitions factory said they would try it – anything was better than sitting around at home all day, or standing in never-ending queues. But Violet did not agree. After all those years of early-morning buses and late-night buses; of standing in whatever the weather and of bending low and straining to see . . . she thought she deserved a rest.

Anyway, her fifteen-year-old daughter was coming home.

Anyway, her friend, Mr Elton – Harry – said that she should pamper herself a bit. Harry Elton knew instinctively how women felt at the end of this long war. They felt dull and grey and drab and they needed a little . . . well, pampering. Mr Elton had been marvellous about getting silly little things, like small bags of sugar and a few ounces of knitting wool. She had been a little worried when he had got her four pairs of silk stockings. To accept a pair of silk stockings meant you had to give something in return, however small. But Harry Elton had laughed and told Violet he only wanted to see her smile. So she had taken them and told George that everyone in the factory had been given stockings as a bonus.

Everyone had been given a month's notice in the ARP on 1 May, but George seemed reluctant to accept it. He still went around to the Wardens' Post and the First Aid Post, and so did one or two of the others. Together they shook their heads over the situation. Irresponsible decisions like closing the Tube stations at night! Suppose it happened again? How were people to trust the Germans – how could anyone trust anyone in the war? So long had George worried and so often had he muttered that Violet had begun to wonder whether he were right. After all, he had been out there at night. Perhaps he did know what he was talking about.

'Silly old buffers – not your husband, mind – but those folk who don't want to believe it's over,' Harry Elton had said. 'Can't bear to think that it's all behind us and the fun and laughter are all ahead. . . .'

Violet always felt better when she talked to Harry Elton; he had visited the munitions factory a lot – he was something to do with installing radios and loudspeakers for them all to hear *Music While You Work*. And then he had

had something to do with organising transport. Always something new, something different. Harry Elton had nothing but praise for the brave boys in the forces, he didn't run them down like George did. He didn't complain, or make excuses about why he wasn't at the front; he just followed their progress all the time as if he were cheering on his local football team. Harry Elton made everyone feel good. Violet was pleased that he liked her so much.

There was so much noise and bustle at Euston that Elizabeth was momentarily worried that something was wrong. What, she wondered, could have gathered so many people together? But then, she had thought that at Crewe, too, and it was only the normal business of a big railway station. All around there were greetings and welcomings. People stood in groups, waving to a young couple who were going off on honeymoon. The bride's little hat was perched at a dangerous angle and she waved enthusiastically until she and the train were gone from view. Elizabeth paused and changed her suitcases to the other hands. She always liked looking at weddings; she and Aisling used to go to the church to observe the brides and comment on them, usually unfavourably, to each other. None of them had looked as, well, as ordinary as this little girl in her navy serge suit and her red and navy hat.

Elizabeth was glad of the distraction as she walked towards the barrier. She was afraid. Afraid that they might not want her back, despite their letters. Afraid that she wouldn't know what to say. Afraid that there might be nothing to say.

She was apprehensive about the days and weeks ahead. Back in Kilgarret they had seen the newsreels showing some of the blitz in London, but the reality was still quite different. Here it looked as if everything had been destroyed. She had seen from the train, particularly during the last, halting approaches to Euston, whole blocks with wooden planks nailed across windows. Twice she had been able to read the words 'Danger – Unexploded Bomb', which had made her heart leap; but the other passengers had said it didn't mean much, just that the authorities were still working on clearing the site. They seemed so unconcerned.

She walked up the platform with the crowd, wondering which side Mother would be. Would she be pressed up against the railings, or standing on a porter's trolley peering down? Perhaps she was late? Suppose Mother wasn't there – should she go home, back to Clarence Gardens? Or wait? Perhaps she should wait a while and see.

She smiled at her silliness, and her smile broadened as she imagined what Aunt Eileen would say. 'Always facing a thousand worries, my poor Elizabeth, long before one has come on the horizon.' She had added that the perfect state of mind was half-way between Aisling and Elizabeth; Aisling never saw worries or responsibilities even when she was surrounded by them. A perfect state of mind . . . what a funny phrase. . . . And as she smiled, she met the eyes of a woman smiling back. A woman much younger than she remembered, with shining fair hair, and a smart suit and a little hat with three feathers in it. The woman was waving and calling 'Elizabeth!' Her lipstick was very red. 'Elizabeth!'

It was Mother.

She smelled lovely as they hugged each other awkwardly, though some of the powder from her cheeks brushed off on to Elizabeth, who couldn't say anything for a while.

'You look like an advertisement, Mother, you look so young and . . . everything,' she managed at last. 'I thought you'd have got different.'

Violet had been going to say that she could hardly believe she had a grown-up daughter – a daughter with a waist and a small bosom; a tall girl instead of a trembling ten-year-old . . . but she was so taken aback by the compliment to herself that she tinkled a little laugh and said the first thing that came into her head. Sadly, it was a negative thing.

'Oh, darling, what a nonsense, and what *have* they done to your hair, your lovely hair? Did they cut it with a knife and fork? We'll have to see to that before we do anything else.'

She picked up one of Elizabeth's suitcases and they

walked out into the late June sunshine. Election posters stared at them as Churchill and Attlee still sought the people's support. Elizabeth was fascinated; in Kilgarret there had only been ordinary notices describing dances or fairs or pilgrimages. Not instructions to keep mum. . . .

'Look, Mother,' she giggled, pointing to a big picture. Violet looked, wondering what had happened. 'Keep Mum . . . it's a pun. . . .' Her voice trailed away. 'Is your journey really necessary?' 'Careless talk costs lives.' Some of them flyblown and torn. Some newer and shiny. But none of them were new to Mother. Elizabeth could have spent hours reading them – what fun she would have had with Aisling. Together they would have memorised the phrases and recited them to each other. With a pang, Elizabeth realised she would be sleeping in a room by herself from now on and have no Aisling to talk to.

Outside the station some rebuilding had begun, but the street was still full of debris. Heaps of rubble on both sides of the road told Elizabeth more about the blitz than a hundred letters or a hundred newsreels had done. These had been houses and offices. Now they were bits of buildings. Odd, awkward-looking bits jutted up, doorways remained standing in isolation.

Yet Mother walked past it all on the way to the bus stop, unperturbed, giving the little laugh she used to give when she was impatient.

As they scrambled on the bus, Elizabeth staring to see a woman conductor, Mother said, 'Your father's very excited about your homecoming – he's bought gulls' eggs. They were one and three each. We're going to have them tonight as a celebration. And a nice friend of mine, a Mr Elton, has got us some real cake. You know, with sugar and butter in it.'

Elizabeth looked at Mother with affection. She seemed so like a girl, more like Maureen and her friends than Aunt Eileen. And she did look lovely. Her belted, dark green jacket had big, military shoulders – she had such a tiny waist. Elizabeth touched her hair. It had been cut a week ago in Kilgarret by Maisie O'Reilly who ran the La Bella hair salon. Only very smart people went there, but Aunt Eileen had said that she must have a nice style and set before they sent her back to England. It had cost quite a lot but Aunt Eileen had said not to think about that; they couldn't send her back looking like a tinker. Aisling had tossed her own mop of red curls around in the salon and discussed long and loud what fashionable people would do if they had been unlucky enough to have been born with this dreadful colour of hair. It had been another funny-sad day with the end of her stay in sight. Aisling had said twice that maybe Elizabeth should make her home in Ireland and abandon the idea of going back to London. Aunt Eileen had been very short-tempered and said this was a selfish and infantile suggestion and she didn't want to hear it again.

Elizabeth looked out of the window; everywhere there seemed to be queues, and there were lots of people in uniform. It was all very crowded. She thought of Kilgarret. Aunt Eileen might at this very moment be writing a letter to her. She said she would write every week for a while, that Aisling would promise to write but would never put pen to paper. Aunt Eileen wouldn't promise that she'd come over to London, but said she'd think about it.

'Child, when you get back there you might be of a different mind,' she had said. 'I don't mean that you wouldn't want me, or any of us, but we're part of a separate life. Remember that you weren't at all displeased when your own mother didn't come over here. People have to have compartments in their lives.'

Mother was smiling at her. 'I can't tell you how good it is to have you home,' she said unexpectedly. 'It was a good long war. It's hard to have lost all those years of you growing up. But you've grown up very nicely. I hope I did the right thing. . . . I've always hoped that.'

'I liked it there, very much. It was different, but they were all very kind, all of them. . . .'

'I know, you always said that in your letters. That's another thing. You were a good letter-writer. Your father and I were delighted.'

'How is Father?' asked Elizabeth with her hands clenched tight until the knuckles stood out.

'He's very well, of course he is. I told you he got us some gulls' eggs, didn't I? He's been looking forward to your coming back for ages.'

Violet laughed again, and Elizabeth felt a flood of relief. It wasn't a cruel laugh, she wasn't thinking of Father as someone who was going to make her impatient and purse her lips. She squeezed her mother's arm happily.

'It's great to be back,' she said.

George had been looking at fifteen-year-old girls for three months. He wondered if Elizabeth would look like young Miss Ellison might have looked two years ago. Miss Ellison who came into the bank with her father was seventeen. He wondered whether she might look like the little princesses. He hoped that she would not have picked up too many Irish ways. The Irish were very unreliable, and from their irresponsible attitude towards the war which Mr Churchill had severely trounced them about, to their smuggling and black market tricks they were very devious and knavish. He had wished that Elizabeth had never been sent there.

Admittedly she had written regularly and these friends of Violet's had been very kind to her. They had been remarkably generous, too, for people with no great income and a large family. It had all gone on far too long and he felt cheated of his child's youth. She would now be a grown-up girl, silly and female and wanting to talk about film stars and make-up. He would never be able to talk with her and show her things and explain how things worked. She would never come to him for advice or believe that he knew everything which is what daughters always did to their fathers.

This war had robbed everyone of what was their right. It had robbed him of his wife, too. Violet hardly knew whether he breathed or not. She was perfectly agreeable most of the time, but she seemed to live on a different planet. It was as if she didn't even notice him. That's what the war had done to people like Violet, taken away their normal family feeling, taken away a sense of home. Violet didn't even cook or take a pride in what she could get from the shops like other women did. Everyone at the bank talked about the

99

rationing, the shortages, and joked that if you stopped to talk to a friend in the street people would think it was a queue and would line up behind you.

But Violet barely cared, she read novels and she saw friends from the munitions factory from time to time. She was getting thinner too, all skin and bone, he thought.

'Mrs Simpson always said that you can never be too thin or too rich,' Violet would laugh if he said anything about it.

She hadn't even planned a special meal for Elizabeth's return. If he hadn't been able to get out yesterday and queue for gulls' eggs there would have been the usual powdered egg omelette or a tin of corned beef.

He hoped that Elizabeth would not have become very distant and giggly. He hoped she would be glad to see him and want to talk to him and ask him his views about things. He wanted to tell her about the war – properly, not the way the Irish would see it. He wanted to show her his maps of the world, and the charts he had made, with all the armies in different colours. She would question him about tactics and strategy, and he would look thoughtful and give her his considered opinion.

The gate clicked and they were there. Violet carrying one suitcase, the tall girl with the shining fair hair clasping the other. He cleared his throat as he opened the hall door. She was going to be a tall blonde stranger.

Aunt Eileen had said that she would probably find Clarence Gardens had got smaller when she got back; it was something that happened to everyone; they thought the places they knew when they were young were huge. Elizabeth had laughed at this, she remembered Clarence Gardens very well, she said, the blue and beige carpet, the hall stand, the front room where they only sat on *occasions*. This was the room which had the little corner cabinets with ornaments and where Mother used to sit and write her letters or read in the afternoons.

But how odd, the house itself hadn't got smaller, just the stairs, and the distance from the hall door to the stairs. She had thought it was quite a big hall, but in fact it was only a small passage. She hung up her brown coat, draping it over a peg, and moved quickly to take stock of her surroundings. Father went into the kitchen ahead of her. . . .

He was fussing now, touching things, patting them, like an old woman, not like Father. He seemed flustered as if she was a visitor. Which of course she was in a way.

'Well well,' he said rubbing his hands, 'Well well well.'

'It's amazing to be back again Father,' she said.

'Heavens,' he said, smiling at her happily.

'Did you miss me a lot, it must have been a bit empty . . . I mean lonely or quiet. Quiet without me,' she said. She stumbled over the words, knowing that 'empty' was wrong, but not being sure why.

'Oh I missed you, all the time, a child growing up in a different country . . . very odd . . . very peculiar. . . .'

'Yes.' She wished Father had said something more extravagant. 'Of course I wrote a lot,' she said.

'Yes yes, but it's not the same.'

He was trying to be polite to her, trying to tell her how much he missed her, yet it sounded as if he was complaining.

'Well, I didn't start the war,' she said, laughing.

'No, no, and you were so good, no complaints from you all that time . . . such cheery letters,' he said hastily.

'You never wrote Father, I wish you had.'

'I can't write letters, your mother is the letter-writer in this house.'

Elizabeth wondered why he couldn't write letters, he must have been taught to write them like everyone else. She said nothing.

'It's been so strange,' Father said, struggling. 'So strange, and now having you back, that's strange too.'

He echoed Elizabeth's own thoughts . . . but she wished he could have found a nicer word than strange. . . .

'Yes, you'll have to start getting used to me again,' she said, hoping that it might make him smile to hear her talking in that grown-up voice. But he must have missed the jokey note in her tone.

He seemed more anxious than ever to please her . . . he

waved towards the oven . . . a big expansive wave taking in the whole kitchen. . . .

'We have a special supper tonight . . . great treat in your honour. . . .' he said. In the little hall, Mother was carefully rehanging her coat, fishing out the little loop at the top which Elizabeth had hardly ever done since she had got the coat. The O'Connors were not great for hanging clothes on hangers or using the little loop.

'It's all just the same,' Elizabeth marvelled. She did wonder whether they had not a new and smaller range, but no, it seemed exactly the same as the one that had been there. She saw the garden changed through the windows, the remains of the Anderson shelter . . . she remembered Mother had written about that. . . . She walked into the front room, it smelled cold and musty. Mother's little desk was still there, but there were a lot of boxes on top of it with a permanent look. The room felt damp and Elizabeth gave a little shiver. The antimacassars, the linen backs on the dark red sofa and chairs, seemed crumpled and the room looked as if it hadn't been used for a long time.

Father was behind her.

'Perhaps we should have a cup of tea in here in your honour?' he said, eager to please and hoping that she wasn't disappointed for some reason.

Elizabeth shivered slightly again. 'Heavens no, Father, let's go back to the kitchen, it's just grand in there.'

'It's not really *grand*. . . .' began Father.

'In Ireland they say "grand" when they mean good,' she said, linking him into the kitchen.

'What do they say when they mean grand?' Violet asked, bringing up the rear.

'I think they still say "grand",' said Elizabeth, and they all laughed and it felt like being at home.

There was so much that was new, so much to absorb and remember. Of course, Violet had written about the points system and rationing and the endless queues; but the reality was so mean and shabby, it was all so dispiriting. Sixteen points for this, two for that – and even when you had sorted out points and coupons, and queued for ages, there were still shortages. 'Waiting for further orders,' Elizabeth would be told, and then, from force of habit, 'Don't you know there's a war on?'

'Do you remember Monica Hart?' Violet wanted to know. 'She was at school with you. . . .'

'I remember,' laughed Elizabeth. 'Aisling and I called our cat after her. It's still there you know, a huge black cat called Monica. Niamh sort of thinks she owns it now, but it was Aisling's and mine for a long time. . . .'

Violet noted the dreamy note that came into Elizabeth's voice when she spoke all the strange Irish names of Eileen's family. She had never said she had missed them nor hinted that she was lonely. But Violet realised that it must be a huge shock, coming back to a house that was silent all day from one where there was constant companionship and apparently half the town passing through on some errand or other.

'They live just down the road now, the Harts,' she went on. 'I see Monica sometimes on her bicycle. Perhaps you could be friends. It would be nice for you to have a friend.'

'Yes.' Elizabeth was unenthusiastic.

'Before you go to school. Monica is at the grammar school, she can tell you what it's like and give you hints. . . .'

'Whatever you like,' said Elizabeth. She didn't like the thought of meeting Monica again, bossy Monica who used to pinch her during Miss James's class. Miss James was in hospital she had heard, she suffered from war nerves. Mother had met someone who had gone to visit her and Miss James was smoking a cigarette and making a basket and didn't want to talk.

'Good.' Violet was brisk. Elizabeth had been home for five days. She was very content to sit around, reading and writing an interminable letter to Ireland. She would stand placidly in queues, and once she had understood coupons and points had been very helpful with the shopping. But Violet wanted her to live a more normal life and not behave like a visitor in her own home.

Monica had become much less bossy, though, or at any

rate she showed no desire to pinch Elizabeth any more. She was polite and rather silent when she came to tea. Elizabeth had to do most of the questioning. Violet seemed to think it was all going quite successfully.

'I'll leave you two to talk over old times,' she said, putting on her hat. 'I have to meet people from the munitions factory. We're going for a little drive.'

'Do the factory ladies have a car?' asked Monica with interest.

'Oh Monica, you'd be surprised what we factory ladies have these days,' said Violet with a tinkle and she was gone.

'Your mother's like a film star,' said Monica.

'Yes, I suppose so,' shrugged Elizabeth. Suddenly she remembered saying to Aisling, 'You've got the loveliest mother in the world, she's so strong,' and Aisling had shrugged too. Perhaps people don't ever appreciate their own mothers properly, she decided.

'What's your mother like?' she asked Monica.

'She's all right,' said Monica unhelpfully.

Elizabeth sighed. It was uphill work. Aunt Eileen would have known how to get the conversation going, and Aisling wouldn't have cared, she would have just chattered on happily about whatever interested her, and it would be up to Monica to join in or not as she wished. . . .

But Elizabeth wasn't able to do either of these things.

'Do you collect stamps?' she asked Monica desperately.

'No,' said Monica.

'Neither do I,' said Elizabeth, and for some reason that seemed funny to both of them, and they laughed until they had pains in their sides.

Monica was an avid film-goer. She knew all the details of the film stars' lives and was anxious to fill Elizabeth in on all she had been missing.

'Of course, you were away for all of this,' she would say forgivingly, as if Elizabeth had actually lost out on being part of the Hollywood scene because of her five years in Ireland. Monica had no time for Shirley Temple who had just had her first screen kiss with much publicity . . . Shirley

Temple was strictly for adults to go ooh and aah over. No, Monica liked Deanna Durbin, and Hedy Lamar and Lana Turner and Ava Gardner, and she admired Judy Garland and Bette Davis though she didn't actually want to imitate them. She knew all about their marriages, their romances and which child was by which marriage to whom.

Monica suggested that Elizabeth wear her hair like Veronica Lake hiding her face, but it didn't work. The shock of blonde, almost white, hair looked odd and untidy when Elizabeth tried it. Elizabeth wondered what it would be like to kiss Clark Gable as she studied his photograph. Would his moustache tickle her nose and make her sneeze?

'I expect it would be just like kissing anyone with a moustache,' Monica said sagely.

'I expect it would,' Elizabeth agreed emptily. She felt so ignorant about the world of films; now she was going to be a non-starter in the world of kissing too. The only field where she had any superiority was having come from a land of plenty. From a place where there was as much to eat as you could ever want, and where nobody stood in queues for anything.

'What used they to eat on Sundays, tell me again,' Monica would beg.

Elizabeth described the Sunday lunch; soup and home-made soda bread. Then a boiled chicken with white sauce and boiled bacon, and potatoes in their jackets, and cabbage cooked in the same water as the bacon so it tastes all flavoury. And apple tart and the top of the milk. And sometimes they had red lemonade and sometimes they had glasses of milk. Monica listened in a dream of gluttony, her mouth watering at the thought of it.

'And teas, tell me about their teas.'

Sometimes Elizabeth wished she wouldn't go on so about food because it made them all feel deprived. She told of the apple cake which Peggy made, and how it was like bread but there were bits of apple and sugar baked in it, or when they had black pudding spread on bread.

Monica said enviously, 'They must have had very good connections.'

'No, they didn't have any connections . . . you see there wasn't a war there.'

'Of course there was a war there, there was a war everywhere, and what about the Enniskillens and all those, they're Irish aren't they?'

'Yes, but it's a different part of Ireland. There was a war up in the North but not . . . not where I was. That's why I was there.'

Monica dismissed it.

'You missed lots of fun not being here, I tell you. You could see all kinds of famous people . . . they were all round the place keeping up people's spirits. I even spoke to Sarah Churchill once. You must know Sarah Churchill, she's famous. She has gorgeous red hair.'

With a pang Elizabeth thought of Aisling and how her face would light up if she heard someone talking about gorgeous red hair. She wished again and again that it was easy to write what you felt. Her letters to Aisling seemed so dull and Aisling's were very off-hand and breezy. If it weren't for Aunt Eileen she would think that nobody in Kilgarret even remembered her.

Violet wondered whether they should send some gift to Eileen's family to thank them for all they had done for Elizabeth. She had discussed it with George.

'You were the one who said that they wouldn't notice an extra mouth at the table,' he had grumbled. 'Anyway, where are we going to get some kind of proper present as you call it?'

Violet reflected.

'They were very generous, you know, they bought her a bike, and when she left they told her to sell it and keep the money because it was hers not theirs. They bought her clothes, you know, underwear too.'

'I thought we sent money for clothes.'

'We did, but not enough. I mean, Eileen always wrote to say she'd bought Elizabeth a new winter coat with the money we sent, but Elizabeth tells me that she got everything the other children did, you know, and Sean used to give them all money for the cinema or whatever. I suppose I'm just a little worried in case we took it all too casually.'

'You wrote and thanked them, didn't you?' George said in an aggrieved tone.

'Oh certainly, I wrote and thanked . . . but you know they did a marvellous job on Elizabeth. She's so grown-up and yet not changed at all. Did you know that she's going to be in a form with sixteen-year-olds? She's far ahead of what we had expected.'

'She's read quite a lot,' George said, pleased. 'She was telling me yesterday that she and Aisling used to read Wilkie Collins to each other at night. Only one of them could have the torch so they took it in turns to do the reading aloud.' He laughed at the thought of it.

Violet smiled too. 'I don't think she's lonely or anything, but it would be nice to keep in contact. The trouble is there's nothing for us to buy here. They're the ones who can buy things. I wonder if they realise it?'

'Why don't you write again and say when rationing's over we'll send them a gift to say thank you.'

'I'll need to say it tactfully,' Violet mused. Eileen was always full of pride, and stubborn. She was very much her own person, and you had to go fairly carefully not to offend her.

'Elizabeth was very fond of her. She doesn't say much about her husband, though,' George said.

'I suppose he was busy and not home much, he was always a very hard worker. Rather uncouth but a lot of get-up-and-go.'

'Not like some you could mention, I suppose.'

Violet looked at him. 'Oh George, my dear,' she had said gently. 'I wasn't thinking of comparing him with you. You've got all the get-up-and-go you want . . . or any of us wants. Really, I wasn't making a point. You must know that.'

George looked surprised and pleased. He grunted and left her sitting at her desk. She had decided then that she would ask Harry Elton what he thought. Harry always knew exactly what to do. He had a feel for that sort of thing.

Harry indeed had given it all some cheerful thought when he met Violet for a Saturday drink by the river.

'Let's treat it as a serious problem of state,' he had laughed. He had been delighted at the defeat of Winston Churchill in the election the month before. Labour had said they would build five million houses and they were the boys to have in power. Harry was as sunny about this as he was about everything else.

'Sorry for Churchill? Never. He was a great old geezer when we needed a bit of puffing and blowing. But now we need houses and jobs.'

He took everything that Violet said as being important and worth discussing. Harry Elton never grunted. He probably didn't know how to.

The classrooms were only a little like the convent class-rooms. They had bigger and better blackboards and good maps on the wall, but there were no statues, no holy pictures, no little altar to the Sacred Heart or the Little Flower which someone would be in charge of each week.

Elizabeth found it very strange that classes did not begin with a prayer. She used to stand waiting for this to be said each time and then sit down quickly and shamefacedly.

'You mean they prayed before every class?' Monica was disbelieving.

'Well yes, a short prayer.'

'Before maths and history as well as RK?'

'Oh yes, just a quick Hail Mary for an intention.'

'What kind of intention?' Monica was fascinated.

'A sick nun, perhaps, or a happy death, or the conversion of China. . . .' Elizabeth said, feeling a hopeless interpreter of the ways of the convent.

She found the smell of chalk and disinfectant, the long dirty-cream-coloured corridors, more like a hospital than a school. It was a million miles from the incense-filled corridors around the chapel in the convent, the chapel where they dropped in almost every day to pray that Sister wouldn't ask for their history essays today, or that they'd know the answer if the bishop came and asked a catechism question.

'Was this Aisling more or less clever than you?' asked Monica as they walked home from school. Monica was very anxious to be allowed to go up West to see the crowds and the royal family going into the Royal Variety Command Performance. It was going to be the first for seven years. Her mother had agreed only if her school work improved, so now she had a serious interest in it.

'Aisling was much more clever, but she was very . . . I don't know . . . the nuns said lazy or careless. I think she was just bored by it . . . she hadn't time for it. It got in the way of all the fun. . . .'

'And did she get higher marks than you?' Monica was very annoyed at Elizabeth's success at school. Her years in a foreign land had not hindered her; in fact they had made her forge ahead. All Sister Catherine's patient work in the mathematics class had paid off, and she was top of her weekly tests in geography and grammar too. History and French were a little weak, but Elizabeth seemed to believe that if you were given homework you did it, if you were told you must learn a poem you learned it. . . .

'If she tried, Aisling could be top at anything. Sometimes we used to make a bargain. If she would learn her work for school I would go and make us midnight feasts. I had to do that because Aunt Eileen never minded if I came down to the kitchen for food, but she always said Aisling was up to no good.'

Monica walked moodily, kicking the heaps of leaves into the gutter. 'I don't know what my mother means by improve. I know more than she does already. How's she going to know whether I improve or not. . . .'

'I think you should just let her see you working . . . you know, have your school books out more than your magazines or film annuals. That would let her see you were improving.'

Monica screamed with laughter. 'Ooh you are deceitful Elizabeth White . . . I always thought you were really good. But you only pretend. . . .'

Elizabeth wasn't upset.

'No, I do work hard, I've nothing else to do . . . and in Kilgarret I worked hard because I didn't want to let Aunt Eileen down. But Aisling used to do that, she always pretended that she was working and she got away with it . . . she liked laughing really.'

Monica said gloomily, 'That's not a bad thing. Lots of people like a good laugh.'

Elizabeth thought suddenly of her mother with her head thrown back. She never looked as young and happy as when she was having a good laugh. She seemed to be having more good laughs nowadays. And Aisling didn't appreciate all Aunt Eileen did . . . not even a little. Wasn't it funny how people often got the wrong mothers? Or the wrong daughters.

In December the good news was announced that the beef content of sausages was going to be increased from thirty-seven per cent to forty per cent.

'It doesn't seem very much,' Elizabeth commented to Father as they went for one of their Saturday rambles.

'Oh, you should have tasted a sausage when the rationing was at its height,' Father said. He loved telling Elizabeth about things she didn't know.

They had fallen into the habit of taking a Saturday stroll when Father would point out the various bombed sites, the condemned buildings and the streets which had had direct hits during the blitz. It was a catalogue of sadness, of disasters and near-disasters. Stories of Old Charlie, and Mr This and Mr That. There had been no laughter to remember, nothing very funny had happened. Nothing very dramatic had happened, like when Uncle Sean remembered things, where men were mighty and lads were brave. There were no tales of kindnesses, or how well people had behaved to other people, like Aunt Eileen always remembered. . . . With Father it was all defeat, and opportunities missed, and good deeds being misunderstood.

'They must have been awful times Dad,' she said as they were coming home down the street. The afternoon was dark and it was nice to think of a cup of soup in the warm kitchen. Mother might be back too, she usually met her friends from the munitions factory on Saturdays, which made it a good time to go for a walk with Father. Or Dad. Sometimes she called him Dad, he seemed to like it. It was what the O'Connors used to call Uncle Sean. They used to laugh when she had mentioned Mother and Father. Fother! Fother! they had pealed, as if it was an odd form of address.

But Elizabeth felt she could never call Violet 'Mum' or 'Mummy'. That was what you called rounder, older people. She was Mother – or nothing.

'Perhaps Mother will be home,' she said as an attempt to cheer him up. His face had grown sombre in the telling of another gloomy story.

'No, Mother's going out, there's a reunion party for all her munitions people . . . or some war workers, anyway. In a hotel. She said she wouldn't bother coming back, she'd go straight on.'

'Oh,' said Elizabeth. She didn't particularly mind. She was going to read anyway for the evening, and then when *Saturday Night Theatre* came on the radio she would make some sardines on toast and cocoa. Mother had done some washing that morning, it would dry near the fire and they would have to sit close in for warmth.

'We could play draughts,' Father said.

Elizabeth found draughts very boring. She wished that Father would learn to play chess. But chess and bridge were for intellectuals, he said. How could she convince him that it had only taken her half an hour to learn the pieces and the moves and then you knew it for life. She and Aisling used to play but Aisling was too impatient, she never cared about strategy or plans, she just exchanged pieces mercilessly until they were both left with hardly anything on the board. Elizabeth used to play with Donal – out of kindness because Donal wasn't really any good. He kept walking into awful trouble without seeing it coming. But she had played with him to be kind. Now she was playing draughts with Father to be kind. She wondered if Aunt Eileen would pat her on the head and say she was a great child if she were to see her playing draughts with Father.

The play turned out to be a historical one and Father said he couldn't bear all those play-acting ways of going on, calling people Thee and Thou, so when they had finished the sardines, he brought out the draughts board.

'Shall we take it in turns to be Black?' he asked, his face anxious.

'Do you mind Mother going out with Mr Elton and all the munitions people, Dad?' she said.

Father was very surprised.

'Mind?' he repeated. 'Mind? It's not a matter of minding. It's not a matter of going out with Mr Elton . . . it's all of them going to a reunion.'

'I know Dad, but you know, that's all Mother likes doing. Don't you want her to like being at home, and being with us . . . ?'

'Heavens above, what are you saying? Of course Mother likes being at home with us, she's just gone out to one reunion party tonight. Just one night and you start saying that she's always out.'

Elizabeth looked down. She felt she had gone too far, but retreating was going to be just as bad. He would keep asking her what on earth she had meant, and he would go over and over the comforting clichés as if repetition made them more true.

'She's entitled to her night out like anyone is. She worked very hard during the war. Naturally she likes to meet her friends and talk about the times they had. . . .'

Elizabeth gritted her teeth. 'But you know what I mean, Dad, you do. You must notice that Mother only has half of her attention here with us . . . she's not really thinking about you and me. No Dad, it's true. We don't make the place fun enough for Mother, we're very boring you and I, we don't laugh and make jokes, I just read books and you read the paper, and I say "What did you say?" and you say "What's that?" when she speaks. We've got no bit of . . . I don't know . . . no bit of excitement in us.' She stopped. He was silent for a moment. His face worked slightly as if he were about to speak but was afraid he might cry.

Please, please God may he not cry. Please good kind Lord may I not have made him cry.

'Well. Em . . . well,' he mumbled.

Oh please God, I'll never bring the subject up again. I'm so sorry God, Elizabeth prayed. In her mind she saw the statue of the Sacret Heart on the landing in Kilgarret. The statue where Aisling would close her eyes and say, 'Please Kind Sacred Heart I'll give you anything if we don't have a test at school today.'

'No, you're right. I've got very little excitement in me. In fact I never had. But your mother always knew this. She wasn't misled, you know. She wants reliability and a nice safe harbour as well as a laugh and . . . what you call a little excitement. So everyone is what they are . . . you understand. Some of us are hard-working and reliable and provide the home and the hearth, other people provide the fun and excitement. That's the way the world is. Do you understand?'

'Yes, Father,' whispered Elizabeth. 'I see.'

'No, there's no need to apologise,' Father said, not noticing that she hadn't. 'No, you were quite right to say what you did. A person should be honest. You're a very good girl, Elizabeth. You are a great joy to me, and to your mother. We often talk about how lucky we are to have such a responsible little girl. Don't think we don't appreciate you.'

There was a hint of a snuffle in his voice. Elizabeth decided it must be headed off.

'Oh I'm not all that great,' she said. 'Come on, let me be Black first and we'll start the game.'

There was a present from every one of the O'Connors for Elizabeth at Christmas and a beret that Peggy had knitted, and holy pictures from four of the nuns, a calendar from Sister Catherine, and half a dozen Christmas cards from other people in the town.

Elizabeth was amazed as she unwrapped each gift. 'Look

Mother, this is from Eamonn. Imagine Eamonn writing a card, and two butterfly hairslides. Aren't they lovely Mother, imagine Eamonn doing that! Do you think he went into the shop himself and asked Mrs McAllister? Oh, no, he couldn't have. Perhaps Aunt Eileen got them.'

Violet was sitting at the table helping her to open them and flattening out the paper and untying the string.

'Oh they are frightfully gaudy . . . but how sweet. Is Eamonn the delicate one, the invalid?'

'No Mother, that's Donal, Eamonn's the eldest boy, well, eldest now. I told you, he's going to work in the shop with Uncle Sean, he's nearly seventeen. . . .'

Every card had a proper message . . . and Aisling's enclosed a six-page letter which Elizabeth slipped into her pocket and read later.

'They're all frightfully holy, the cards. . . .' Violet said, fingering them.

'Well, you see, that's what Christmas is all about there . . . you know cribs and mangers . . . they go on about it a lot,' Elizabeth said. She felt a twinge of guilt now and then about having Lost Her Faith so easily on her return to England. She had tried to find the nearest Roman Catholic church, and visited it, but it was cold and damp, and very uninviting. But she felt sure that God (and Aisling's class at school) would understand, and regard it as a temporary lapse. Later she would take it all up again.

'What's this one?' A card in babyish writing fell from the pack.

'That's Niamh, she's sweet Mother, she's six. Were you not able to have any more children after me or did you just not want to? Or did they not turn up?'

'How funny you are, dear, er, there were complications and so that meant you couldn't have a sister.'

'But it didn't stop you sleeping in the same bed as Father? I mean could you still go on having . . . er . . . ?' Elizabeth stopped uncertainly.

Violet looked taken aback. 'Eileen wrote to me that she had . . . explained all about . . . the facts of life and everything to you, she said she told you at the same time as

Aisling . . . and that as far as she could see you seemed to have grasped everything satisfactorily. Now I'm not so sure.'

'What haven't I grasped?' Elizabeth wanted to know.

'Elizabeth, now I'm all for frankness, but there are some things you do not ask. People just don't talk about it. It's intimate, it's between the two people themselves. Eileen wouldn't tell you about her activities.'

'But it was different with Aunt Eileen, Mother,' said Elizabeth thoughtlessly. 'I mean, everyone knew that she and Uncle Sean loved each other anyway. Despite all the things they said, they were obviously very fond of each other . . .' her voice trailed away again as she looked at her mother's face.

Violet said nothing.

'Oh Mother, what have I said?' Elizabeth cried, stricken.

'Nothing, dear.' Violet stood up. 'Nothing at all. Now, do they know in Kilgarret that there's been a war here, and that we can't go around getting them gifts like this . . . ?' her voice was brittle.

'Oh they know,' said Elizabeth. She had sent a letter to Aunt Eileen five weeks ago enclosing four pounds and a lot of ready-written Christmas cards asking her to buy things in Mrs McAllister's.

'That's all right then,' said Violet briskly.

'Mother I didn't mean. . . .'

'Gather up those things and tidy them away, won't you dear?' Violet said and she walked out of the room looking like people in films who've been deeply wounded and don't want other people to know.

Dear Elizabeth,
This is meant to be a happy Christmas letter, but I've never felt so fed up in my life. Mam's after saying that I should tell you all the news, but honestly there's nothing to tell. The place is so boring and I look so awful, I look so ugly, and there's nothing to do and everyone's in bad tempers like weasels. Sister Catherine's really a devil. I know you wouldn't hear a word against her, and she had a soft spot for you because you understood all those

awful things, trains coming into a station and the platform half a mile long . . . but really she's the end. She has it in for me.

She called to the shop. *To the shop*. A nun coming all the way to talk to Mam at work. She said to Mam and Dad that I would have to be taken away from the school because I was a distraction and a bad influence on the rest of the class. I was getting one last chance.

Honestly it's not fair. I don't do nearly as much to disrupt her stupid classes as others I could mention. It's only because she never liked me, it's only because she can see me easily because of my hair. I wish you were here. You used to be able to make them see that things weren't serious. She said that as a favour, and *one last chance* I'll be taken back next term, but I'll be watched like a hawk. What's so new about that, I wonder? I'm watched like a hawk anyway.

I wish you could come here for Christmas and cheer us up. We never seemed to fight so much when you were here, or maybe we fight much more nowadays and it would still go on if you came back. But I don't think so. Mam said after the vicious, evil Sister Catherine left that you had the right attitude about work, you just put your head down and did it. I wish I could. I wish I could put my head down but it's so pointless. Seems so useless.

Maureen's doing a line with that stupid Brendan Daly, you remember him, they live in that place with the huge falling-down barn we used to pass cycling to school when we went round by the river. We used to say it was more of a barn than a farm. Anyway, he's serving his time in some food firm in Dublin and he met Maureen at a dance, and now they're going out together. Imagine going all the way to Dublin and having a life of your own and meeting someone from Kilgarret! Joanie and I say that when we leave and go into the world the first question we'll ask every single person is, 'Are you from Kilgarret?' Then we won't be in any danger of falling for someone from here.

Maureen's all silly and giggly and she actually calls him

'my Brendan'. You'd die laughing if you heard her. Daddy was asking her would she get the ring for Christmas, and Maureen got all annoyed and said she was twenty-one and could do what she liked. Daddy said he was only asking a civil question and when Maureen had gone off in floods of tears, Mam said to Dad that he should be more gentle because Maureen was obviously hoping for the ring but didn't dare to let us know that in case it didn't happen.

Honestly imagine marrying Brendan Daly and his awful sticky-out teeth! Imagine going to bed in the same bed as him and imagine being stuck with him forever and ever for the rest of your life.

Joannie thinks it's very funny, she keeps calling Brendan my 'brother-in-law' and whenever we're going to school she says, 'Will we ride past your in-laws' barn?' Joannie's very funny now, you'd like her more than we did last term, she's got more lively.

It's funny in your letters when you mention Monica. I always think of the cat. I never heard of anyone else called Monica. When you said you went to *Brief Encounter* with Monica I thought for a moment that you had taken a cat to the cinema. I saw it too, it came here two weeks ago for three nights. Everyone cried except me. I thought they were stupid not to go away together. I mean in England they can do that, there's divorce and everything and it's not against the religion. There was no reason for them to stay with their awful husbands and wives, except just to make a plot.

I said that to Mam and she said I had a lot to learn about loyalty and making a bargain and keeping it. Whatever I say or do it appears I have a lot to learn.

I have awful spots, on my forehead and on my chin. Joannie says that you can't see them much but when I asked Eamonn he said they were like lighthouses and that if people got lost they could see their way home by the red glares on my face.

Can you think of one single piece of cheering news to tell me? Like that you'll come and stay, or come back and live here. Or what am I to do to get that rotten, bad, half-mad Sister Catherine off my trail?

Happy Christmas to you all, we couldn't get over that picture of you and your mother. Mam has it in her bedroom on the dressing table. Your mother looks like a beauty queen. Do you get on well with her these days? It must be funny going back and finding a new mother in a way.

Love from a very miserable
Aisling

Mother developed a bad flu just before Christmas. The doctor came and said she must build herself up more, that she had gone to skin and bone. Father and Elizabeth tried to give the doctor a picture of what Mother normally ate during an average day. She had no bread, no potatoes, no puddings. She just picked at things. She looked very pale and listless.

'I'm sorry to be such a trouble,' she kept saying. Father and Elizabeth had been preparing for Christmas in their own ways, making chains of paper, gathering greenery, holly and ivy from the common, making fancy place cards for the table, reading recipes for novel seasonal punches. Now Mother was ill and it would all be in vain. She refused to have her bed taken downstairs to where the one fire burned.

'That's out of the question,' she said faintly. 'Only invalids and old people have their beds taken down to the living room. I shall stay here until it's gone.'

Elizabeth offered to have the chimney in the bedroom swept and light a fire there, but Mother wouldn't hear of it. She wore mittens and had two hot-water bottles and that was fine. She lay uncomplainingly, her hair lank on the pillow. Father was totally unable to cope with it all. In the bedroom he stood wringing his hands saying, 'Violet, is there anything we can do?' in a hushed, death-chamber voice that obviously drove Violet to the limits of her patience with him. Downstairs he would rail senselessly at anything from current dieting fads, to the shortages in the war, to Mother getting colds going to meet friends from the munitions factory.

Monica's mother taught Elizabeth how to make broths and hot drinks and how to make a cold compress without drowning the patient and saturating the bed. On Christmas Eve the doctor assured them that there was no danger of pneumonia and that it was just a matter of a slow return to her old energy and her old self. Elizabeth, cheered greatly by the pronouncement, became impatient with Father who was still grumbling and muttering about doctors being know-alls and knowing nothing when it came to it.

'Father, do you never see any good in anything? Can you never see light at the end of the tunnel?' she snapped.

'Not really,' he said.

'But that's a dreadful way to live,' she said.

'In my experience, lights at the end of the tunnel tend to flicker out,' said Father.

Elizabeth thought of last Christmas as she prepared Mother's beef tea. Last Christmas Day, walking in the frost and early-morning darkness up to mass, shouting greetings at everyone, full of anticipation for the day ahead. Little Niamh had fallen and cut her knee. There had been enormous sympathy, dabbing with clean white handkerchiefs, taking her to a street lamp to examine the wound, but Niamh, more frightened than hurt, was roaring in great bellows.

'Oh Niamh, for goodness' sake stop crying,' Aisling had said. 'Your leg isn't going to fall off. Don't spoil Christmas Day.'

'You can't spoil Christmas Day,' Donal had said.

Eileen had lifted the hefty five-year-old up in her arms. 'Tie a bandage on it Sean,' she had said briskly. 'Poor old warrior Niamh. But Donal's right, of course it won't spoil Christmas Day, nothing can spoil Christmas Day.'

Mother's hand was very thin. The soup spoon looked big and heavy when she held it.

'I'm sorry you're having such an awful Christmas, my darling,' she said to Elizabeth.

Elizabeth sat like a guard watching that she finished every mouthful.

'You can't spoil Christmas Day,' she said like an echo.

Violet looked at her. There was not a trace of irony in what Elizabeth had said.

Downstairs George was huffing and puffing with damp sticks to light a fire that wouldn't catch.

Tears came down Violet's pale face.

'It's all such a dreadful mess,' she sobbed. 'It wasn't meant to be like this. It's all such a hopeless mess. . . .'

'Mother, it's all going to be fine.' Elizabeth was distraught to see Mother's shoulders heaving like this. With her foot she closed the bedroom door in case Father should hear and come up to make things worse.

'No, it's all turned out wrong. There's no point in any of it. I couldn't be more sorry, but I can't think what else I could do . . . I tried my best, but I'm just not a good little housewife . . . I can't stand polishing up a house and cooking meals for nothing. . . .'

'But Mother, it's not for nothing, its for *us*,' cried Elizabeth. 'And we're very grateful, and when you're better we'll help you much more. I was saying to Father that we don't do enough for you. . . .'

Violet looked at her with swimming eyes. 'You still don't understand, you'll never understand. Oh God, it's such a hopeless mess.'

She turned her head on the pillow, and Elizabeth decided not to force any more beef tea on her. She sat there for a while but Mother said no more; her breathing became less agitated and then she slept or pretended to sleep. Elizabeth crept out.

Father looked like a big eager dog as he knelt by the fire with a newspaper hoping the draught would catch the flames. 'How is she?' he whispered.

Elizabeth paused. 'She's fine Dad, she's having a little sleep.'

She went back to the kitchen table which had been set for the festive meal. There were drawings of robins on cards, with holly in their beaks; Elizabeth had cut them out as shapes. There were three home-made Santa Claus figures propping up the table napkins. Bits of ivy and greenery had been criss-crossed across the table. Elizabeth sat down and looked at the plate of corned beef, and the three pieces of chicken. She had stood in a queue for four hours to get the chicken pieces; the corned beef was from a tin.

She felt fifty as she prepared the Christmas dinner.

Dear Aisling,

I meant to write, but everything was so confused and awful here, I couldn't take my mind away from it all. First about you . . . now remember the way you used to get away with everything by looking as if you were doing something? It worked before, why won't it work now; or is there any point in saying to Sister Catherine, let's have a truce? Or what about actually doing what they say and forgetting everything else except work for two terms? Then you'll be top of the class and they'll all be delighted and they'll leave you alone.

I don't think the first will work. Maybe we're all too old now to get away with things, or maybe the nuns are worried about exam results. In your place I would make a truce with Old Catherine. Honestly, she was nice, but you'll never believe it. She was very lonely, she's much older than the other nuns. She lives for the pupils, and she'd feel so happy if you had a man-to-man talk, or a girl-to-nun talk. But you won't I suppose. So that leaves the last solution, work yourself to the bone as they say. You could regard it as a kind of a competition. You'll show them, you'll prove them wrong about you. I honestly think you could wipe the floor with the rest of the class. Monica (not the cat!) was asking me about you and I told her you were brighter than anyone here in Weston High, and she couldn't believe it, because she actually thinks I'm bright. And I'm not, I just put my fingers in my ears and learn.

Please let me know what happens. I wish you would write every day. I wish *I* could write every day. It all seems so far away sometimes, and then when I was reading your letter about Maureen and Brendan Daly — of course I remember him, he was awful — it all comes back. Did she get engaged, are they really in-laws now? I suppose we'll all have to be very polite and not say anything bad about them in case they become Maureen's nearest and dearest. Isn't it funny though that she likes him! You'd think Maureen could have anyone. . . .

I keep rambling on and on about Maureen because I want to put off writing the next part.

Everything is so frightening here at home. Mother was very ill over Christmas. She was in bed for ten days, it was a chest cold and flu but she was very weak, and she lay there like a ghost. But she worried all the time about something, and I think that she's thinking about leaving us and going away. Now please, please, please, don't tell Aunt Eileen this, I may be wrong, it may have been just because she was so ill. But she kept apologising for things not turning out right, as if something was over.

I think Dad knows it too and won't admit it. Whenever I say that we might all do something, you know something cheerful that would please Mother, he just asks what's the point. If you knew how awful it is. They are both moving around the house apologising if they come into the same room as each other. No, don't laugh, that's what it's like. It seems impossible to try to place it in Kilgarret, with everyone running in and out of rooms all the time, but here there's only the three of us, and I sit reading and pretending not to be watching them.

Could you pray that it will be all right? I suppose you must know that I sort of gave up my faith. I never knew if I really had the faith anyway, since you wouldn't let me go to communion and confession, but whatever I had of it is gone. Just pray that Mother won't go away with Mr Elton, please Aisling, and ask people at school to pray for a special intention. I know you won't tell anyone. Mr Elton's very nice, it was he who took that silly picture, the present to you all, and he's always laughing and making jokes. And now that Mother's better and everything, she meets him a lot, and I'm so afraid he and she might be thinking of going off together. Sometimes when I come in from school and there's a note from Mother on the table saying she may be late, I'm almost afraid to read it in case it's saying more than that.

I may be wrong. Remember the time we all thought that Eamonn was drowned in the river, and he'd just gone home the other way? Well, that's the kind of fear I have now.

Love from
Elizabeth

Harry had said that no good came out of lies. Harry had said that there was nothing evil and wrong about falling in love, and now Violet must take the deception out of it by telling them. She must say it fair and square to George, she must tell Elizabeth. She must explain that there was no need for hurt or blame.

Violet wished it was as easy as that. Harry's wife, long gone from anyone's life and living in the west of England with her new husband, presented no problem. Harry had no children. He would be very happy to include Elizabeth in their household if she wanted to come. He was starting a new business, they would have a flat over the premises. There would be plenty of room for the girl.

Violet decided to tell them the day before Elizabeth's sixteenth birthday. But she knew that they both had seen it coming. The May sunshine fell on the table and on Violet's restless thin hands, which twisted and turned as she spoke.

Father didn't answer. He just sat there with his head bent.

'George, please say something,' Violet said.

'What is there to say? You've made up your mind.'

'Daddy, don't let it happen, say something to show Mother you want her to stay,' begged Elizabeth.

'Mother knows I want her to stay,' said George.

'Oh don't be so weak Daddy, do something,' Elizabeth cried.

George lifted his head.

'Why am *I* the one who is weak, why am *I* the one who must say something, do something? *I've* done nothing. *I've* just done what anyone else does, plod along. This is what happens.'

123

'But George, we have to talk, we have to talk about arrangements.'

'Make whatever arrangements you like.'

Elizabeth stood up.

'If you have to talk about arrangements, like for a battle, you won't want me here. I'll go upstairs and I'll come down when you've finished.'

George had stood up also.

'No, there's no talk about arrangements. Do what you like Violet, set up whatever you want. I presume you want me to divorce you, you're not suggesting that I give you evidence or anything. . . .'

'No, of course. . . .'

'Fine, then whenever it's to be done get some solicitor to write a letter. . . .'

'But George. . . .'

'That's all, isn't it? I'm going out for a walk now. I'll be back at teatime.'

'But Daddy, you can't walk out now, you can't just go out of the room and not discuss it. . . .'

'George, what about Elizabeth, what will we do? Will you . . . ? I mean . . . .'

'Elizabeth is a grown-up girl, she's almost sixteen years of age. She can go with you or stay here, or move between both houses . . . I presume you will have a house. Your friend isn't going to expect you to live in his van is he . . . ?' George had reached the door. 'I'll be back for tea,' he said and closed it behind him.

Violet and Elizabeth looked at each other.

'I'm sorry Daddy was so weak, he's a bit afraid of you, that's it,' Elizabeth said.

'Oh . . .' Violet began to speak but she was choked with emotion. She moved over and held Elizabeth's hand. 'Do you understand, do you have any understanding?'

Elizabeth sighed. 'Yes Mother, I do, I think I do. It's awful, but I think I do understand. And you'd better cheer up because if the point of going off with Mr Elton is to have more life and fun and zing and everything, there's no point in feeling guilty and wretched. . . .'

'It's not going off, it's only half a mile away. Will you come? Harry wants you to, and I do. Very much.'

'No Mother, I can't, who'd look after Father? But I'll come often to see you, honestly and I . . .' Her voice broke.

'What darling?' Violet looked at her, trying to help out the words.

'I was . . . I was wondering, if it happened because I went away? If I had been here during the war, would you and Dad have been more of a family, you know? More to keep you together.'

'Oh my poor child.' Violet put both her arms around Elizabeth, she hugged her, and swayed as her voice was saying soothingly into Elizabeth's hair, 'My poor child, in all the useless years that your father and I have been pretending to get along like normal people, you were the one thing that made any sense out of it all. You've always been the only thing that made sense of seventeen years of wrong turnings, and George thinks that too. If you were to blame yourself that would be the last straw.'

Mother sat and talked for another hour, about loneliness and age and the fear that you might go to the grave not knowing any spark. She talked about the war and the blitz and about people making fresh starts. She said lamely that George might find a nice lady who shared his interests. And then to Elizabeth's horror she went upstairs to pack.

'You're going now, Mother!' she cried.

'Darling, you don't expect me to serve beans on toast and talk to your father normally when I've told him that I've committed adultery and am leaving him?'

'No of course not,' said Elizabeth.

VII

... Oh do stop apologising for blots and lines being crooked and not knowing what to say. I just want you to say *something*. You were always the one who told me that the important thing was to say *something*, not to wait until I knew what to say, and thought it was right. I've started doing it. But *you* must continue to do it.

If you knew what it was like here. If you had even just a small idea, I think you would be so stunned that even you would be speechless. It's very kind of you to write and say perhaps they'll get over it, but it's not like that. It's not a bit like Uncle Sean and Auntie Eileen shouting at each other, because that was only for the evening at most. And anyway they always talked immediately afterwards, and then there was the whole family . . . there were all of you, and the house, and the shop, and everything. Here there's nothing, there's only the two of them, and they keep telling me I'm grown-up.

I wish I wish so much I could have stayed in Kilgarret. Suppose I had got a job after school there, or helped Aunt Eileen with the accounts or in the house or something. Then they might have had to hold off until I came back. They could have said they couldn't have done anything serious until I was home. But, you see, the awful thing is that they both say to me that I'm so sensible and I'm so understanding . . . but I don't understand anything. I'm *not* grown-up. I wish they could see that. Mr Elton keeps saying to me that he'd like me to call him Uncle Harry. I told him I was no relation and that, without wishing to be difficult, it was a bit artificial. That's what I said.

He said, 'You called those people in Ireland Uncle and Auntie and you'd never met them, and look at how well that worked out.' I said to him that that was totally different, that I had gone to live with you, I was part of the family. I told him I lived there for over a third of my life. (I just worked it out). And then Mr Elton said, 'Well, Elizabeth, your mother and I hope you'll live with us a lot of the time, even most of the time too, so don't you think it's a bit formal to have all this "Mr" business? I don't call you Miss White, now, do I?'

I didn't know what to say, so I said nothing.

'Right, that's a good girl,' he said. He thought I was considering it. But I feel that if I *did* call him Uncle Harry it would be letting Father down somehow. Giving in or something, letting Father see that the other side had won.

Father always calls him 'Your-mother's-friend-Mr-Elton'. She went to live in a boarding house. Well she calls it living there, but it's so odd. She only pays a little because she helps the woman run the place. I went in there on Tuesday and she was in this awful room with all kinds of dirty sheets with a frightful smell and Mother was sorting them for the laundry. It really smelled foul. I said to Mother I couldn't believe she was doing this, and she said that a woman had to have dignity, and that she couldn't sit at home and wait for Father to make up his mind about the divorce, while eating his food and living in lodgings he had paid for; she had to make her own way.

I said, why didn't she go and move in with Mr Elton if that's what she was going to do eventually? She said it was to do with disgrace and reputation. I said that Monica's mother knew all about it already and I hadn't said anything to Monica. She said there were legal terms like reputation and disgrace which I didn't understand.

Sometimes she talks as if her mind was gone, like poor Jemmy in the shop. But mainly she sounds like someone much younger than she is setting out on some kind of dangerous mission. I don't blame Father for thinking it will blow over, but it won't. Please write, I'll go mad if I make any more dreadful silent suppers for Father with nothing else to think about.

127

What does Aunt Eileen say?
Love,
Elizabeth

Dear Elizabeth,
I got your letter this morning. Mam gave it to me on my
way downstairs. You won't believe it but the postman
still goes in to the kitchen to start messing with Peggy. I
mean, they're nearly a hundred, both of them, and he still
thinks it's great fun. Mam keeps a beady eye on them.
Anyway, she said, why not take this stamped envelope,
I've a bit of a note for Elizabeth myself in it. Mam must be
like the fortune tellers, she couldn't have known you said
write back really quick.

I think you should call him Harry. Very suddenly. Cut
out all the nonsense about Uncles and Misses, if they're
making out you're so grown-up, act grown-up. That's
one thing.

Secondly, you'll have to stop worrying about the two
of them, they were never happy. Honestly, even when
you were here you used to tell me about them going all
cold and prickly with each other. It would have happened
anyway. Dad was reading in the paper about half the
English population getting separations and divorces
because of the war.

And another thing, it's not even a sin for them. They
were never properly married in a Catholic church or
anything, so there's nothing to be undoing or rending
apart.

And if your mother is looking and acting all young,
well isn't that great! Isn't that what people are trying to
do all the time? Whenever Mam says she feels like a girl
again it's always over something nice like a picnic or a
run up a hill.

And, I know Mam said it in her letter because she
didn't seal it so I know I was allowed to read it, why don't
you come over here for a bit? We could chat about it, and
it'll be the holidays soon, and I'd love to know you were
coming. It's dead lonely here without you. I'm very

friendly with Joannie of course, and she's much nicer than we thought last year. But it's not the same as when you were here, it's not living with someone and being able to say anything you like.

What about your friend Monica (I still think it's Niamh's cat)? Is she able to laugh like we did? I don't think she can be, otherwise you'd have told her and her mother all about the business at home.

Listen, try to cheer up. I mean in a way they're right. You are grown-up. We're sixteen and a bit, and if people aren't grown-up then when will they be?

Can you talk to your Da about other things? Like we do with Dad here when he starts complaining about things. No, I don't suppose that's really a good example. At least he doesn't complain about Mam going off with another man. It's kind of unbelievable.

But it must have been desperate. I'm very sorry. I'm not good at writing it, but it's awful and I can't find words to tell you how I wish and pray that it will somehow be all right.

In the meantime you should go right up to him and call him Harry. Be sure to tell me what he says.

Love,
Aisling

Dear Aisling,
This is just a short letter. Calling him Harry was marvellous. He said 'What?' I said, 'I said, no thank you, Harry.' 'Oh,' he said. 'You asked me not to be so formal,' I said.

'Quite correct my dear,' he said. But he was knocked sideways. Then I called him Harry in front of Father, and Father laughed. He said I was right, that's exactly what Mother's-gentleman-friend was: a real Flash Harry.

Mother is pleased too. She says that she always knew I'd get round to liking him.

It's the first day of holidays, I'm going to stay with Monica for a week. Aunt Eileen suggested that maybe they might find it easier to talk if I wasn't there. She said that there wasn't much hope they'd get back together but they might be able to get formal things worked out if they didn't have to keep looking at me. I think she's right.

Monica has this awful boyfriend, well he's sort of unsuitable but she's delighted. I'm coming to stay because it means we can all go out together and her mother thinks she's only going out with me.

Love to all of you. I'm sorry to hear from Auntie Eileen that Donal was worse, I hope he's all right.

Love,
   Elizabeth

Dear Elizabeth,
Donal's fine again, he had extreme unction, do you remember what that was? Annointing the hands and feet with holy oil, you only do it when people are dying. But he turned a corner. Sometimes it cures people. It cured Donal, he's fine, he's sitting up again and laughing. He has a fire in his room even though it's July.

Joannie has a boyfriend too, he's David Gray, one of the Grays, a Protestant. He's super-looking, but nobody's meant to know. He writes her notes and says he thinks he'll be able to take us both to Wexford next week in his cousin's car. Wexford! In a car! With the Grays!

Aren't you sorry you didn't come to stay with us instead of with Monica down the road? Why didn't you come by the way?

Love,
   Aisling

When Elizabeth came back to the house in Clarence Gardens after her week with Monica, the first thing she noticed was how dirty it had become. All around the little rubbish pail in the kitchen there were bits of food, and the cooker was stained and crusted with old food that had been allowed to burn into the enamel. There was a smell of sour milk. The ashes in the sitting room had not been cleared and there was a trail of dirt around the front of the fireplace as if they had been very carelessly cleared on a previous occasion. The linen basket in the bathroom was open and clothes tumbled out on the floor. There was a sour smell in the bathroom too, and damp towels were rolled up in the corner.

A tray with the remains of a breakfast was beside Father's bed. Wasps buzzed around the jam and the milk had soured in the jug.

Out the window Elizabeth saw the garden overgrown and unwelcoming; nettles and briars choked the plants that she had helped to plant in the spring. This was to be the first year that flowers were acceptable. Up to now only vegetables had had a right to grow in a garden.

Elizabeth looked at Father's pyjamas thrown on the floor. He had left her a note saying that he had gone to have a consultation with the firm of solicitors who did work for the bank. He said in the note that the manager had told him he must feel free to call on them in his personal capacity.

Imagine. Father had sat down at this filthy table in the kitchen, leaving the house like a shipwreck and written about solicitors and personal capacity. He hadn't put the dishes under the tap, he hadn't said he was glad to have Elizabeth back.

No wonder there was no light in his life nowadays.

A wave of irritation about Mother came over Elizabeth suddenly. It wasn't fair. It just wasn't fair. People had to stay where they were. Aunt Eileen didn't like a lot of things, but there was no question of her running off. She did not like the way Uncle Sean talked about the British and the war, she didn't like Eamonn's 'rough friends', as they were called. She didn't like the way Aisling answered back, or Maureen brought all her dirty clothes down in a bag from Dublin to be washed at weekends. She didn't like Peggy's hair falling into her eyes or the postman coming in to neck with Peggy when everyone was out. She didn't like Niamh acting the baby to get her own way. Aunt Eileen got very cross if Donal went out without his coat or scarf, or if anyone ever mentioned the folly of Irishmen who had joined up during the war. But Aunt Eileen was able to cope. Her mouth would go into a tight line, and she would just get busier and busier. And even Monica Hart's mother who was meant to have 'nerves' coped with things when they went wrong. There had been some trouble when Mr Hart came back but Mrs Hart hadn't just packed her bag and left. And remember that poor Mrs Lynch, Berna's mother, *her* husband was awful, really awful, he had come around to the house in the square and nearly frightened them to death and he had been found drunk in bus shelters and everything. And Mrs Lynch didn't get on the next bus out of town.

Mother was behaving very badly, and it was silly. Suppose things went wrong with Harry Elton? She couldn't keep running away all the time. She really should face up to things. The nuns had always said that life was not meant to be easy. God had implanted in us a sense of restlessness so that when we got to heaven in the end, we'd calm down, and know the meaning of peace. That might well be true, certainly the restless bit was, everyone had it. Why did Mother give in to it when other people were able to damp it down?

Elizabeth sighed and just as she was about to boil a saucepan of water and start to cope with the mess an even greater wave of irritation came over her. He didn't love her, any more than he loved Mother. Father was incapable of loving people, he had become so wrapped up in himself and his worries he didn't even seem able to see the fact that there were other people around.

Elizabeth put down the saucepan again. For months she had worried about him, she had tried to console him, she had played draughts with him, kept away from subjects that might upset him, steered away from danger areas and tried to keep an atmosphere of normality in the house. Things were not normal. He and Mother didn't even like each other any more. They both said they loved Elizabeth, and presumably they both wished her well, and were sorry that things hadn't turned out the way that people always hoped they would turn out when they were young and had a baby girl.

And if things weren't normal and if Father and Mother

had actually spent the week deciding something so utterly non-normal as whether Father should divorce Mother for adultery and desertion or whether Mother should want Father to be a gentleman and go off to Brighton with a lady and pretend to spend the night with her so that a detective could say that Father was committing adultery, then that was about as non-normal as things could get.

Elizabeth stood up full of resolution. So why on earth should she, Elizabeth, pretend that things were normal? Why should she be the only one of the three of them acting as if nothing had happened? She was going to please herself now. Everyone else seemed to be acting as if they lived as individuals. So, what did *she* want to do, because whatever it was she was jolly well going to do it.

She didn't want to run away to Kilgarret. First there would be too much trouble, too much upset. Auntie Eileen would have to cope with Mother and Father, both writing and telephoning and perhaps even coming over to Kilgarret. Anyway, Aisling might not want her now, Aisling seemed very busy for the summer with her friend Joannie Murray and all these friends of Joannie's, the Grays who lived in a big house with stables outside the town. Perhaps it wouldn't be the same with Aisling, and she'd be in the way. It would be hard at the convent too. Sister Catherine would want to know why she was back, the nuns wouldn't understand about divorce and Mother going off with Harry Elton, and even less about Elizabeth running away. Uncle Sean? He always liked her, perhaps he would just say that it was a further sign of the decaying English empire that their marriages couldn't even hold together. But would it be fair to ask them to pay for her? It would cost money to have her. And perhaps Father would be so cross he wouldn't send any.

No, going to Kilgarret would hurt too many people. And it wouldn't work. She couldn't go and live with the Harts; they wouldn't agree, it would be too strange to move a few streets away. It would cause too much talk. She didn't want to live with Mother and Harry because that would be saying she approved of what they were doing, and she did not. Anyway they giggled too much and made jokes that left her out and then said, 'Sorry Darling'. But she would not live in this house clearing up dirt and rubbish and trying to look after Father and cheer him up, getting no thanks and no love in return.

Elizabeth went to her desk and got a pad of paper. Then, very carefully, she wrote three letters.

Mother, Father and Harry

You have all said that you want the best for me. Thank you. I want the best for you all too.

I do not think that coming back to a cold, dirty house with no explanations from any of you is the best for me. I do not think it is even half-way towards the best.

I am going back to the Harts. I shall tell them that you would like another week to make up your minds about the future. I shall return again next Saturday to see what you have all worked out.

I am about to begin my last two years at school; at the end of these holidays I will need somewhere to live where I can study and have peace and freedom from worry. I would prefer to live here in Clarence Gardens with Father, but I am not going to clean the place up so that it will be fit for us. It is like a pig-sty. If you decide that this is where I shall live please make arrangements to have it cleaned, and tell me what you intend to do about laundry from now on. I do not mind doing the cooking for Father and myself, but if I am going to study hard I will not have time to stand in queues for things, so there should be some other arrangement made about shopping.

I am sorry to sound so business-like about this, but I have been shocked and hurt, sitting here realising that nobody is giving any thought to what is going to happen next.

You will all say that I am upset. I am. I have taken fifteen shillings from the piggy bank because I think if I am going to ask the Harts if I may stay another week I should give them a present. That's something nobody ever thinks of either.

When I come back next Saturday around three o'clock, it would be nice if you were all here. It will not help matters, it will only make them worse, if you come to Mrs Hart's house to discuss it there.

It's been going on for months. It can wait another week.

Elizabeth

She found three envelopes, and addressed one to Father. She left it propped beside the dirty milk bottle.

Then she walked to the lodging house where Mother still stayed and dropped it in the door. Then she squeezed the third envelope in through a slit between the door and the side of Harry Elton's van which she saw parked near the lodging house. It fell on the floor where he would see it. Hitching her bag up on her shoulder she headed towards the Harts' house. Monica saw her coming and ran to the door, delighted. With a wry sort of a smile Elizabeth thought that Aisling would be proud of her.

Elizabeth woke the following Saturday with the taste of dread in her mouth. There had been a message, a note slipped into the Harts' house late on Sunday night. Nobody had seen who delivered it. It had been as brusque as Elizabeth's own letter.

You are perfectly right, nobody has been business-like, and it has taken you to show us. George, Harry and I will be happy to make plans with you next Saturday. You can reassure the Harts that it will all be solved by then.

Violet

Elizabeth thought with a pang, as she read and reread the note, that she must indeed have grown up suddenly if Mother was referring to Father as George and to herself as Violet.

Throughout the week she had accompanied Monica

135

absentmindedly on various outings with the unsuitable boyfriend; they went to the cinema a great deal and Monica and Colin kissed while Elizabeth stared at the screen. Monica had said that Elizabeth should say her parents had sent the fifteen shillings for entertainment money for the girls. Mrs Hart had thought this very reasonable, and indeed generous. Mr Hart had grunted and warned them not to stay out too late and not to injure their eyes by being too close to the flickering screen.

Now it was time to go home and face what had to be faced. Elizabeth washed her hair and sat in the garden while it dried.

'You have a beautiful head of hair,' Mrs Hart said approvingly, 'it's like silk.'

'That's very nice of you, I think it's a bit wishy-washy,' Elizabeth said.

'No, in fact women try to dye their hair your colour, flaxen, you're very lucky.'

Mrs Hart was shelling peas. Elizabeth started to help her. 'You're very helpful,' Mrs Hart said. Monica was up in her room reading a movie magazine and working out a complicated method of meeting Colin next week.

'I always get on with other people's mothers better than with my own,' said Elizabeth sadly.

'Everyone does,' Mrs Hart said cheerfully. 'It's the law of averages, isn't it? If you see someone too much you learn to hate them. Monica hates me, Mr Hart would hate me if he didn't go out so much. People shouldn't see each other too much. It leads to trouble.'

'That's a bit depressing isn't it?' Elizabeth stopped with the peas in the pod open and ready to fall. 'I mean, there's not much point in love and families and friends if you're going to get tired of people when you see a lot of them. . . .'

'It may be depressing,' Mrs Hart said, 'but it's the truth. Look dear, haven't you got the living proof of it in your own house this afternoon?'

Even the front garden looked neater as Elizabeth crossed the road to 29 Clarence Gardens. She had her own key, but lest she catch people unawares she decided to ring at the door. It was just ten past three, she had dawdled on the way in case it looked *too* business-like to arrive spot on time. With a lurch of her heart she noticed Harry Elton's van parked outside the gate.

Father answered the door.

'Welcome home, dear,' he said. 'How are all the Harts?'

'Oh, they're fine,' Elizabeth said. She left her case in the hall, hung her school blazer on the hall stand, and noticed with a quick glance that the place had been cleaned. The carpet was swept, and the paintwork had been wiped. So far, so good.

In the kitchen, Mother and Harry sat at the table rather awkwardly and stagily; for the first time since the whole business had begun they seemed ill at ease and self-conscious.

'Here you are,' boomed Harry in a falsely cheerful voice.

Mother stood up. She was twisting a handkerchief in the way she did when she was upset.

'How nice you look darling, your hair is lovely.'

'Thank you Mother, hello Harry.' Elizabeth was so accustomed to jollying everyone along and pretending that nothing was amiss that she almost fell into the role again. She had to steel herself to remain aloof rather than creating some bustle and air of business to tide over the awkwardness around her. She stood very deliberately waiting for the next move.

It came from Mother.

'We've made some tea. It's cooling a little, shall we make some more?' She was awkward. It wasn't her kitchen any more. She looked to her husband. 'George? What do you think?'

'I don't know. Would you care for some tea Elizabeth?' he asked politely.

'No thank you, we had a late lunch at the Harts',' Elizabeth said, bouncing the ball right back to them. Time could not be spent with kettles, artificial activity could not be generated.

'Well, it's not my place really, but won't you sit down, my

girl,' said Harry. Mother darted him a nervous glance and Father a resentful one.

'Thank you, Harry,' said Elizabeth and took the proffered chair.

There was a silence.

'Monica all right is she?' Mother asked.

'Oh fine,' said Elizabeth.

Father cleared his throat. 'We did have discussions during the week . . . er . . . we faced the things that had to be faced, and . . . er . . . as you requested we are all here. You see.'

George stopped. Elizabeth looked at him levelly. 'Yes Father.'

'And it's only fair that you should be brought into the discussion and your views . . . sought . . . on aspects of what we discussed.'

Elizabeth remained silent.

Mother took over. 'It hasn't been easy, you'll know yourself some day that the big things in life are not easy to discuss, and they cloud everything else. But as you pointed out, we were all ignoring the little things as well. So, what it boiled down to is this. . . . Your father is very generously going to give me evidence, let me divorce him. He will agree to do this because it is a courteous thing to do, and a gentleman's attitude. I do not deserve it, since as you know I am the one who is at fault. In return I shall ask your father for no allowance of course, no settlement. Harry and I will start again as if I were a girl with no stake, no belongings. I shall keep my clothes and some small pieces of china and furniture. Your father will employ a woman, whom I shall find, to come twice a week to do the laundry and cleaning. I have already cleaned out the entire kitchen and cupboards and listed what brands we buy . . . used to buy. It's all there.'

Elizabeth raised her eyes and looked approvingly at the cupboards, which had even had a new coat of paint.

'Harry has dug the back garden. From now on if your father doesn't like working it himself he could give some as an allotment. Plenty of people do that. There is a back entrance so you would not be disturbed. . . .'

'We should wait and see how it turns out, perhaps you

might enjoy doing it now that the basic stuff has been done.'
Elizabeth stood up and looked out at the tidied squares and
the cut-back briars and thorns. Harry must have worked all
week on it.

Harry spoke. 'I've been able to get you a stove, an oil stove
for your room. Vi was saying you would want a place to
study on your own so that George could have the wireless
on.'

'That's nice,' Elizabeth said.

'And I got a bookcase, a small bookcase at the second-
hand shop, it fits in nicely under your window,' Father said
eagerly.

'Thank you.'

'There are new curtains too. Very luckily exactly the same
size – they were changing curtains in the family hotel where
I'm staying so I took the opportunity. They're blue, like the
bedspread. . . .'

'Thank you very much.'

A silence.

Mother said, 'Does all that seem suitable darling? I mean,
I know we're talking about inessentials, but you know, for
the moment, the sort of nuts and bolts.'

'Yes, Mother, I think that's fine.'

'Your mother wants to know whether you will go on
living here with me or whether you want to tell us what you
would prefer.'

'I'll go on living with you Father, if that's all right. And if
we're both fairly tidy and don't make demands on each
other I'm sure we'll get along just fine. I think you should go
out more, Father, in the evenings. Go to meet people, or to
play cards. I won't be much company in the evenings, I'm
going to study, and it would be dull for you if you didn't go
out a bit.'

'Yes, yes, of course, of course.'

'Mother, will you and Harry be nearby, will you want to
come around and see us?'

'Well, no dear, that's what I was going to say, darling.
Actually, your Uncle Harry and I . . . I mean Harry and I, are
thinking of going north. It won't affect your visiting us in the

slightest. If there's a chance that you'll come to see us you'll have the train fare right away. . . .'

'Even sooner,' said Harry.

'And our home will be your home. But for a lot of reasons, if it doesn't seem too harsh we thought. . . .'

Elizabeth looked at Mother helpfully, but did not finish the sentence for her.

'We thought a new start . . . and a clean sheet . . . a fresh start. . . .' Her voice trailed away.

Harry butted in. 'And, as I said, you only have to ask – you don't even have to ask – once we get settled you just turn up, any day any night. It's as much your place as this is.'

Father gave a kind of snort – it might have been a cough.

'Thank you,' Elizabeth said.

'So that's about it, I suppose,' Father said. 'Unless there's anything else you want to discuss.'

Elizabeth's voice was very calm. 'No, that's fine, really. I think that covers everything. Have you all discussed everything, I mean, there's nothing more you have to clear up about arrangements and money and divorces and everything . . . ?' She sounded as if she were talking about a shopping list. Detached, anxious to help, efficient.

'No, I think that side of things is all. . . .'

'Sorted out . . .' Father finished for Mother. She gave him a little smile and he half-smiled back. Elizabeth's heart nearly burst. Why couldn't they make the smiles last, and maybe they would all burst out laughing and Harry Elton would go out and drive away with a wave and it would all be perfect.

But that didn't happen. Mother picked up her bag and gloves, looked proudly around the kitchen that she had decorated in order to leave it with a clear heart. Harry pinched the small geranium on the window sill.

'Give that a lot to drink, Elizabeth, thirsty little devils, geraniums.'

Father stood politely holding the door open for the man who was taking his wife away. Elizabeth walked out to the van.

'I'll write in a week,' Mother said.

'Great,' Elizabeth said.

'I mean it, you know, whatever home we get will have a room for you, Elizabeth, we'll put blue curtains in that too,' said Harry.

'I know you will, thank you, Harry.' Elizabeth shook his hand. He gripped her around the elbow as well as shaking hands; he was very eager to give her a hug but didn't dare. . . .

Mother didn't look to see whether Father was at the door or not.

'Oh, I wish things were different.' Her eyes were full of tears, she looked very lost and young somehow. 'Oh if you knew how . . . how I wished that things could be different.'

Elizabeth sighed. Mother blinked away the tears.

'I'll say no more now. I'll say it all in the letter. Bless you my dear, dear Elizabeth.'

'Goodbye Mother.' Elizabeth touched Mother's thin cheek with hers, Violet held on to her, shaking.

'Say it in a letter, that's best,' Elizabeth said. Wordlessly, Mother got into the van and waved.

They were gone.

Father was standing at the kitchen table. 'We'll take it in turns to wash up after meals,' Elizabeth said. 'You do this one, I'll do supper. I'm going up to my room now.' She managed to get out without breaking down. She grabbed the bag she had brought back from the Harts' and ran up the stairs. She closed the door and threw herself on the bed with its new blue bedspread. She stuffed the pillowcase with its new blue frill into her mouth to muffle the sobs. She cried until her throat was sore, her ribs ached and her nose was so stuffed up she could hardly breathe. If she had taken the pillowcase away from her face the sound that came out would have been like a long, lonely wail.

Aisling thought that Elizabeth was extraordinary to have been so worried, in case something would happen to her Mam and Dad, and then when it did happen she turned out to be as cool as cucumber. She had written a very unworried kind of letter which had been more about new curtains and fresh painting in the kitchen than it was about what it felt like to be in the middle of a broken marriage. Mam had been very insistent that Aisling did not talk about it.

'Can't I tell Joannie? Please?' Aisling had begged. 'You see I've told her up as far as the bit where she got to calling Mr Elton "Harry", like I suggested, and Joannie will want to know what happened next. It's not fair to tell someone the story and then leave them hanging without knowing the end.'

Mam had laughed and said all right, but not to broadcast it around the town. If Elizabeth came back to see them she mightn't like to hear that everyone in the place knew of her private family matters.

'Do you think she'll ever come back?' Aisling wished she would. But she wished she'd come soon, otherwise there would be too much to catch up on, too many things to explain.

'Would she come back here, do you think, and start school again here in September?'

Mam thought not; she said she had written to Elizabeth and suggested it as a possibility; but Elizabeth had replied that bad and all as things were she would feel worse if she deserted her father entirely.

'I don't know why she writes such things to you,' grumbled Aisling, 'she only told me about the blue curtains.'

'She told me about those too.' Eileen looked worried. 'I think she was very upset by the whole business. . . . You know all of them doing up the house but for the wrong reasons.'

'Um.' Aisling was vague. 'Mam, would Mrs White, you know, Elizabeth's mother . . . would she technically be in mortal sin and everything, living with Mr Elton? I know she's not a Catholic, but she was at a Catholic school with you . . . and she was baptised . . . and it could be a sin.'

Mam ran after her with the tea towel she happened to have in her hands and started to belt her around the legs. . . . 'Will you go away you stupid idiotic child and stop bothering me about sin! Sin, sin and more sin . . . what nonsense you all talk.'

142

But Mam was laughing. Laughing at somebody breaking their marriage vows. . . . Mam was hard to fathom sometimes. . . .

'I wonder where they did it?' Joannie speculated as they both rubbed Vaseline on to their eyelashes with the narrow bits of combs, flicking them upwards.

'Did what? Who?' Aisling concentrated intensely but the lash wouldn't bend. 'The best I can do is to make these look like spikes. Why do yours bend? Are they made of weaker fibre or what?'

'I think they're naturally curly, I have a feeling they might be.' Joannie examined her eyelashes, pleased. 'No, I was talking about the couple, you know. Elizabeth's mother and that man . . . where did they make love?'

'I never thought of that. His house maybe?'

'But he didn't have a house remember, always in lodging houses. They couldn't go there. Maybe they went to hotel rooms for the afternoons.'

Aisling thought about that. 'I think you have to stay in a hotel once you book in. I don't think you can leave at teatime and say that's enough. Maybe they didn't do it at all, maybe they only held hands and necked.'

'Oh, don't be silly!' Joannie was very cross. 'Of course they did it, wasn't adultery mentioned and all? I mean, necking isn't adultery. Anyway you'd never leave one man and go off with another unless you'd done it with the other. Stands to reason.'

Aisling didn't agree with this. She put down her mirror and hugged her knees as she sat on Joannie's bed. She looked around the big room with its windows down to the floor. The Murrays' house was one of the best houses of Kilgarret. Eamonn always said, 'Off to your friends the Rockefellers?' when she went to Joannie's house.

'I think you've got it all wrong, Joannie,' she said seriously. 'I think you think that most of the world is much more interested in doing it than they really are. Elizabeth and I used to say we'd never mind if we never did it as long as we lived. . . .'

'Ah, but that was ages ago . . . I bet you feel different now.'

'No I don't,' said Aisling with spirit. 'I really mean this. I think it's something everyone goes on about and makes a big thing out of and nobody likes it at all. It's love people want. That's different to doing it.'

'They're meant to be the same.' Joannie's round face was puzzled. 'Didn't you listen when Sister Catherine said that love was the highest expression of doing it – or was it doing it was the highest expression of love? Remember, we nearly choked trying to keep straight faces in class? It was a scream.'

'Sister Catherine never talked about doing it!' Aisling was amazed at the very idea.

'No, she didn't use those words . . . she said something about the high something of married love resulting in the creation of children . . . if that's not doing it what is?'

'Yes, I remember. But, honestly, I think it's the love bit that people want, that's what all the songs are about and the films and the poems, not all this other thing.'

'But the other thing is lovely!' Joannie said.

'How do you know, you're only going on what people say.'

'Well, David's done it.'

'He never has.'

'He says he has.'

This was electrifying news.

'What did he say it was like?' Aisling was so excited she nearly fell off the bed.

'He says it was perfect pleasure . . . and that I'd love it,' Joannie said smugly.

'That's no description. *Perfect pleasure*, sure that's no help at all, and of course he wants you to think you'd love it, then you would go all the way with him. . . .'

'Well, then we'd know anyway . . . we'd not be sitting round and talking about it and guessing,' said Joannie mutinously.

'That's true mind you,' said Aisling. 'But would you mind?'

'I'd love it,' said Joannie.

They both whooped with laughter.

'Then you must. That's definite,' said Aisling.

'Well, why won't you?' Joannie was anxious at being thrust into the role of trail-blazer.

'Well, use your head! How can I? You can't go off and knock at someone's door. Hallo I'm Aisling O'Connor and my friend Joannie Murray would like me to sample sexual intercourse with someone to give her courage before she does it with David Gray, so may I come in and shall we take our clothes off now?'

'I didn't mean that.'

'But what else could I do? *You're* the one who has a fellow and *you're* the one whose fellow says it would be pure pleasure for you, and *you're* the one who's mad to try it. I'm only just being a supporter that's all.'

'I'd never do it, I'm only talking about it. I'd be terrified of having a baby. Anyway, David's only asking me because he expects me to say no. Nobody with any sense would say yes.'

'Because he'd leave you once he had got his way do you mean?'

'Well, yes, and anyway he wouldn't be able to trust me would he? You see if I did it with him, then what's to stop him thinking I'd do it with anyone else?'

'There has to be a flaw in that, somewhere,' said Aisling. 'How does anyone ever get together with anyone else if that's what they all think?'

'They get married first silly, then it's all right,' said Joannie confidently.

'But what about the *pure pleasure* one, the one who did go the whole way?'

'That was in south Gloucestershire, when he was on holiday. They all do, there, apparently it's a different kind of way of going on, it's not like here.'

'Well, why didn't he do it with lots of people if it was going on all around him?'

'Aisling O'Connor, you deliberately pick holes in what people say. It's impossible to talk to you,' said Joannie.

'I'm just interested, that's all,' said Aisling. 'Everyone else seems to think being interested in things is unhealthy. I'll never know why.'

Joannie's famlily liked having Aisling around the house; she was so bright and funny, they thought. Everything Aisling said seemed witty and entertaining when she said it at the Murrays' table. It seemed self-centred and showing-off according to Mam, Eamonn and Maureen when she said it at home. For the first time, she began to realise that in the Murrays' house she was a treat, but at home they had had enough of her. Perhaps that was why everyone liked Elizabeth so much in Kilgarret. Because she was a treat. When she went back to her own place it had been awful. Anyway it was just as well that the Murrays did like her because things at home were very depressing. Donal's illness had left a shadow of terror on Mam. Every time he coughed she would glance at him, while pretending not to.

The day that Father Kearney had come with the extreme unction had been dreadful. One of the nuns had come first to prepare the room and Donal for the sacrament. Da had been very annoyed at that and said that nuns were interfering busybodies and how could a child like Donal need to be prepared for anything? Mam had held Donal's hand all the time and smiled. Peggy had been crying at the door and Mam had thought she had a cold and said she should go down and sit at the fire rather than stand there in the draught. Father Kearney said that the sacrament worked in one of two ways: it brought back health and strength, or it gave comfort to the sick person to make a happy death. Eamonn had said something under his breath about covering your bets and Mam had nearly murdered him afterwards. Told him to keep his heathen beliefs out of a sick child's bedroom.

Anyway, Donal was better; he had to be careful never to catch pneumonia again and Mam seemed to think that pneumonia was like an enemy outside the door waiting to come in. Aisling felt it was very peculiar of God to keep sending bad fortune to people who could bear it least. After all, Sean hadn't been a bad person, he had been a good person who had believed in a cause, and God had let him be blown up, and Donal was by far the nicest of the whole family and God kept giving him whistling chests and bouts of pneumonia on top of his weak lungs. Maureen and Eamonn were awful and they were both as healthy as bullocks. God had no sense of fair play. Mam worked hard and was up till all hours and did she get any holiday or nice clothes? No, she didn't. Aisling herself had worked like a slave at school this year and what had she got? Any reward? Any thanks? Just a grudging admission that she had come to her senses at last and made an attempt to catch up on lost time. Mrs Murray said that there was a line about 'Whom the Lord loveth He persecuteth'. They found it eventually and Aisling said that the Lord must be simply mad about her because He persecuted her from morning to night with awful hair, straight eyelashes and demon nuns. Mrs Murray and John, who was Joannie's brother, a clerical student, thought that was very funny. Aisling repeated the remark at home in case Mam might find it funny and it would make her laugh. Mam said it was blasphemous and that there was great danger that Aisling was becoming a show-off.

Aisling liked talking to John Murray when he was home on occasional weekends from the seminary. He told them things about their trainings which were meant to be secrets. He told the enthralled Joannie and Aisling that sometimes they had lessons in manners so that when they were priests they wouldn't make eejits of themselves and bring down the respect of the clergy by eating with their knives and shovelling the food into their mouths with their hands. Aisling thought this was uproarious, but as usual got no enthusiasm when she told the tales at home.

'If that young Murray is cracked enough to go joining the priests when he has all that big family business to have a share in then he's even more cracked to be telling tales about how daft they're all inside there,' said Dad.

Mam was naturally annoyed at the disrespect Dad showed for the church, but she was also annoyed with John

Murray. 'That place is like his family now, you don't go round telling secrets about the family. It's disloyal.'

Aisling remembered a few small acts of disloyalty when she had made the Murrays rock with laughter by imitating Dad coming in from work and being like a sultan asking for water to wash himself, a clean towel, his slippers, and the best chair . . . without words. He didn't have to speak, so well were his little impatient gestures known; and whoever was handy – Peggy, Niamh or Aisling herself – would run to fill the needs. He never made these little signs at Mam. It was like a pantomime and Aisling had caught it very well. She reddened thinking how cross they would be if ever they knew how she had parodied the nightly routine. But she didn't feel disloyal spending most of the summer in the Murrays' house. It was so sunny and it had a big garden that went down to the river. If you wanted to sit in the sun you took out a deck-chair, not a folded rug or one of the kitchen cushions to put on the step of the yard like at home. There were always cakes and biscuits in the Murrays' house that went back into tins after meals, not like at home where once a thing was out it was eaten and that was that.

Joannie's romance with David Gray came to a head when school started. He didn't have anything to do until October and he begged her to skip school, so they could go off for the whole day together. Joannie, tempted and almost weakening, realised the dangers, even though Aisling agreed to cover for her.

'I could say to Sister Catherine that you were taken bad on the way to school, and I had to take you home.'

'She'd not believe the daylight from you,' said Joannie honestly if ungratefully.

'Well anyone she would believe the daylight from wouldn't do it, that's the whole problem,' said Aisling.

David's blandishments proved too much. He was going to pack a picnic hamper he said, and some cider. He had a loan of a car they could have the whole day, go off to some place in the mountains or by the sea. Joannie decided to risk it. She thought her best chance of success was to leave Aisling out of it. Reluctantly Aisling agreed. She was still considered –

grossly unfairly – to be a trouble-maker; there was no point in creating suspicion for Joannie.

It was by great luck a day when the Murray house would be empty. Mrs Murray was going to Dublin, shopping, John would not be back from the seminary; nobody was likely to call; Tony, the other brother, was in Limerick learning the trade in a wine merchant's, he would not be back. Noreen, the Murrays' maid, was on holiday, she had gone to her people in Wexford. It was the one day in the whole year that Joannie would have an alibi.

Twenty minutes into the first lesson, which was Christian doctrine, Joannie stood up and said she felt sick; after some time in the cloakroom she came back and said she felt awful, and could she go home? Sister Catherine looked round the class for a girl to accompany her; her eye didn't rest for a second on Aisling, who was amongst those waving an enthusiastic hand to be the companion. 'Mary Brady, you go with Joannie, and when you have her safely delivered there, come straight back.' Sister Catherine had chosen the class goody-goody, the Child of Mary, the most reliable and honest girl in the school, whose intention of becoming a nun and joining the order the day she left school was known to everyone. Wistfully Aisling looked out of the window and saw Joannie Murray setting off on her adventure. She found it very hard to concentrate on the Acts of the Apostles.

When Mary Brady came back, eyes virtuously downcast, Sister Catherine asked was everything all right.

The innocent accomplice explained that Joannie had seen her mother and waved to her at the window and she had gone in and was fine. Sister Catherine thanked Mary for her help, Mary smiled, and Aisling O'Connor sighed a sigh of pure envy.

A mystery always hung over the details of that day. Like how the whole idea of the picnic came to be abandoned so early and what the cider had tasted like, and why they decided to drink it in Mrs Murray's bedroom. And it was never clearly explained why Tony, who lived with cousins in Limerick, had come home unexpectedly, and why he had been so upset. The combination of all these things had been a confusion Aisling had never known.

David Gray was forbidden to come near the house again by Tony. There had been great threats about how the Grays would react if they had been told the circumstances. Joannie spent what she always called the worst hours of her life begging Tony to believe that it would not help if Mummy were informed. Mummy went mad over things, and she would never go to Dublin for the day and shop again if she was given a confused account. Tony had said, 'In Mummy's bedroom, of all places, of all places. On Mummy's bed.'

Aisling only heard it in fits and starts. She had called round to the Murrays' as arranged at seven that evening when the picnic should have been finished and shortly before Joannie's mother was meant to return from Dublin. Instead of exciting details and perhaps a glimpse of David fleeing into the distance . . . Joannie sat red-faced at the kitchen table with Tony. Lord, he must have seem them coming back from the picnic. Oh Lord, what a desperate bit of luck. Joannie sounded funny and distant.

'Oh Aisling, it's not such a good time, I'm having this sort of chat with Tony. . . .'

'Sure. . . .' Aisling was puzzled. But she took the message. 'Hallo Tony, you back for a holiday?'

'Sort of,' Tony grunted. He was the one of the family she knew least. He was the eldest, nearly twenty-eight now. He seemed to have got good-looking since she had seen him some months ago, or maybe he was good-looking because he was obviously in a very bad temper. People got good-looking when their eyes flashed and their jaws got grim. Aisling had discovered this from reading and from the films.

'Right, I'll be off, will you come round to my place later or . . . what?' she asked Joannie.

'Aren't you going to ask her how she feels, or was the whole school in on this?' Tony enquired.

'Yeah, sure, that's what I came round for, to know are you all right? Maybe it's flu, Sister Catherine was. . . .'

'I'll see you tomorrow,' Joannie said.

'Right,' Aisling said huffily, and swung out. Next day at school, Joannie, still red-eyed, had given substance to the belief that she hadn't been well. In fact, Sister Catherine was moved to wonder should she have taken another day to make sure she had recovered. Apparently she was saved by the skin of her teeth; Tony had seen sense, she had promised not to get involved with anyone, least of all the Grays. She had tried to explain to Tony that they were doing nothing only fooling around, but he had got into a worse humour at everything she said.

'And were you only fooling around?' Aisling asked eagerly. Joannie was distant.

'That's not the point, the point is that he came back.' She had a look of such disappointment on her face that Aisling decided not to pursue the technical details, they could wait.

'Why did he come back anyway?' she asked.

'He's got fed up of Limerick, he came back to ask Mummy could he start working in our business here, you know take over himself sort of. He says he knows everything, and he got restless yesterday and drove back to talk to Mummy about it. Oh dear God, why couldn't he have got restless today instead of yesterday? Tell me God, why did you let him get restless yesterday?'

'I suppose to prevent you from committing a mortal sin,' Aisling said seriously. When you thought about it, God was very devious.

Tony Murray moved back to Kilgarret that autumn. It seemed to take him a long time to forget what he regarded as a great transgression, and a sign of his little sister's weak moral character. Since Aisling had cunningly been freed from any complicity in what had happened, she was not regarded with suspicion and she could come and go as she wished. Aisling wondered would Sean have felt the same and been so difficult about it if he had been alive. But then the thought of being with anyone on Mam and Dad's bed was so unlikely, and the house being empty ever was so unlikely, you couldn't really compare it. Anyway, the thought of going all the way seemed even less likely than ever now that Joannie, who would have been her only companion in that field, was virtually under lock and key.

The nuns had given Mam and Dad the depressing opinion that Aisling was not of a scholarly frame of mind. Like Maureen, she would probably be more successful in work where no great further study was required.

'Don't ever let Maureen know they said that about it not being a studying kind of a life,' Mam had said. 'The poor girl is demented by all those books on anatomy and physiology. She'd go up to the school and go for them if she were to know that. . . .'

Aisling didn't mind one way or the other. The school suggested that she went to the local commercial college also run by their nuns. Here she could learn shorthand, typing, commercial English and book-keeping. It sounded better than going back to do the sixth year and study for her Leaving Certificate. Joannie was leaving anyway and going to a school in France for a year. It wasn't a finishing school, it was a French convent where they would learn to speak French perfectly, and do sewing and cooking. Tony had been very keen on the idea and Mrs Murray thought it seemed sensible too. It would make a lady out of her. Mam had smiled when Aisling had told her that.

'That's why I was sent to the convent in Liverpool, and look what happened to me. And that's why poor Violet was sent there too. Ladies indeed.'

'You're much more of a lady than Elizabeth's mother,' said Aisling loyally.

Mam was pleased but she pretended not to be. 'We don't know what's going on in Violet's mind,' she said.

'Well, at least you didn't break up your marriage and go off and live with someone in sin and pretend it was all Dad's fault.'

'No,' Mam said thoughtfully, 'at least I didn't do that.'

Dad wasn't pleased that the nuns had said Aisling was not academic. He had been in a bad humour anyway and the news made him worse. While the door was still open Aisling heard him complaining bitterly.

'Fine lot of children we reared. The one couldn't wait to

go and throw his life away for the British, another is meant to be in a job that doesn't need much brain work. We were told at the time that it was the devil and all getting her into that hospital.'

'Will you stop that . . .' Mam interrupted.

'I will not stop. I've Eamonn standing like a corner boy in the shop with a crowd of thick louts in and out looking for him, Donal is so sickly the Lord knows what we'll make out of him, Niamh is a spoiled madam and the only one we had any hopes for, those bloody nuns say, "she's not academic, she's not the studying type". Well what was she with them all those bloody years for . . . ?'

'Sean.' Mam's voice was stronger.

'Now, what are you putting on that face for? Things are not all right. What are you and I breaking our backsides working for, what's the whole thing for, Eileen, if the children aren't going to get on, and do better than we did and . . . ?' Dad's voice was a bit shaky but he shouted. 'I mean if there's any purpose in the whole thing isn't it that the children will do well . . . ?' Aisling didn't hear what Mam said because Mam had banged the door shut very firmly.

Elizabeth wrote when she heard that Aisling was going to the commercial college. She said she had a memory of it being a second-best sort of place.

> . . . I know I sound preachy, but is there any point in going there if it's not the place that will give you the qualifications? Yes, I can hear Sister Catherine's voice too, but they're right. It's something like having the right clothes and implements to climb a mountain. And isn't life like a rotten mountain most of the time? I think you should go back to the convent and do the awful old stuff and get your Leaving Certificate, and then go to the commercial college, because once you had the exam, you'd be safe. Or that's what I think.

Aisling had thought about it. In a way Elizabeth was right.

153

In a way it would be marvellous to cock a snook at the nuns, to put her finger to her nose and say, I got my Leaving and you told my Dad I was an ignoramus. . . . Yes, in a way. But it would be so hard, and she was miles behind, miles. And she couldn't bear being with all those creepy ones who were brainy and who would think she had ideas above her station. And she'd look so silly crawling back and saying that she had been wrong not to have worked harder. It would be admitting that all her antics up to now had only been an act. No. She was going to go to the commercial school. She would get a good job from there, she'd do the kind of work she liked doing, not learning rivers and kinds of soil and trade winds in geography, and all the terms of the treaties and the lists of the penal laws, and all the endless, endless things in history.

At least typing and book-keeping would be new, and shorthand, and she would start equal to everyone else, and this time she would work and come out top of the whole year . . . then she'd get herself a great job with maybe a bank manager or open an insurance office. And then that yellow-faced Sister Catherine with her thin whining voice wouldn't be able to make sarcastic remarks, and Dad wouldn't feel that it hadn't been worthwhile to have her, and Mam would be delighted and say that Aisling had great spirit, and Elizabeth would write one of her letters and say she had been all wrong, that Aisling had done the right thing.

Aisling wished that Elizabeth were here. It was silly to have a best friend miles away in England studying in a blue bedroom instead of here in Kilgarret where she should be.

There were bridge classes two nights a week in the old WVS Hall. The fee of one and sixpence a night meant that only respectable people would attend, and it included tea and biscuits. Elizabeth enrolled Father and herself as soon as she saw the poster.

'I don't want to learn to play bridge,' said Father.

'Neither do I, but we'd better. Let's look on it as some kind of survival raft.' After four lessons, they began to enjoy it.

One night as they walked home together, he said, 'Once you realise that none of it means what it says, it's quite interesting.'

'How do you mean?' Elizabeth was thinking about Aunt Eileen. She hadn't told her about the proposed bridge classes when last she wrote. Aunt Eileen would have approved of her being kind to Father but only wealthy Protestant people like the Grays played it in Kilgarret.

'Well when you say two spades, it doesn't mean that you have two spades. In fact it needn't mean any spades at all. It's just a code. It's a way of telling your partner you have a fairly reasonable hand in most things. . . .' Father was what might even be called animated. Elizabeth was about to tuck her hand into his arm, but she held back. If she did it once, then Father would expect her to be that kind of person always. They didn't touch each other. They were managing very well on this formal level. Better keep it like that.

'I know what you mean,' she said seriously, 'but then I think a lot of conversations become like that as you get older. Sort of code, not saying what you mean, and hoping everyone else knows the rules.'

Mother did write quite a lot as it turned out. Elizabeth had expected the rare and rushed notes which had come with a leaden sense of duty around them all the time she had been in Kilgarret. She didn't write much about life now with Harry, nor did she enquire about life in Clarence Gardens. Instead she talked of the old days, as if Elizabeth was a contemporary who might remember them with her. She talked about how they had been to tennis parties when she was young, parties where sometimes ten servants stood around with glasses of home-made lemonade which were poured from big glass jugs. Ten servants, standing all afternoon in the heat, while little madams and little masters flung their racquets on the ground or their sweaters and expected them to be picked up.

Elizabeth read these letters carefully. She didn't know whether Mother sounded wistful for those days, or if she was condemning their selfishness. Eventually she decided that Mother was belatedly trying to tell her something about her life, so perhaps the best thing to do was to reply in the same way, in generalities, telling little anecdotes. Elizabeth discussed the school and compared it to the convent in Ireland; she wrote about the odd people they met at bridge evenings; she sometimes enquired whether there was some way she didn't know of to make a cake without the fruit all sinking to the bottom, or how to let down a skirt without the hem looking awful. Mother sent her a cookery book eagerly and told her about putting a ribbon or a braid around the edge of the skirt and seemed very pleased to have been asked. Elizabeth tried to think of some household query each week.

She thought that Mother was lonely, she knew that Father was lonely, she felt that Aisling would have nothing to say to her these days and only wrote when Aunt Eileen wrote. She worried that Aunt Eileen was too busy and was only making up nice things to ask like she made up for Mother. She knew that Monica Hart thought she was a boring swot nowadays, no fun, and no use as a decoy for the various young men, since she insisted on staying at home and studying.

And she didn't even have the satisfaction of being a brilliant scholar after all this work. She just managed to keep at the top section of her form. Nobody considered her an outstanding pupil, it took her longer than it took the bright girls to understand what was being explained, but she worried at it like a dog at a bone. She would stand shyly beside the mathematics teacher who would look at her with exasperation.

'I've been explaining this all week and you kept nodding, why didn't you say you didn't understand . . . ?' Then the explanation, quick and often impatient, but usually kind. It wasn't usual to find a sixteen-year-old who would stand humbly after school, hair falling over her face, and admit that she wanted to understand complicated things but couldn't. The teachers usually had the world neatly divided: either they understood and could do it and were a reward to you, or they didn't and never would and idled their way through the school years. Elizabeth fell into neither category.

The art master, Mr Brace, had a lot of time for her. She had been taught nothing at that school in Ireland, he told the other teachers in the staff room. He had asked her what she had done in art class and apparently it had only been pictures of the Virgin Mary, or scenes illustrating the mysteries of the rosary. The other teachers shook their heads absently. Irish convents were indeed full of all kinds of mysteries, but then Mr Brace with his liking for beer at lunchtime was not to be relied on for a factual description. The girls in the school called him Beer-Belly-Brace behind his back and complained to each other that he had smelly breath, but Elizabeth liked him. He explained things to her easily, as if she were on his own level. He used to ask her more and more questions about the convent school. His first wife had been a Roman Catholic but she had never mentioned the mysteries of the rosary. She, in turn, had never thought of perspective before Mr Brace explained it to her, and she flushed happily when he held up her still life as the best in the group. She even enjoyed his history of art classes, which none of the others even listened to. When he held up reproductions of the Old Masters, partly obscured by his dirty thumb-nail, she would look with interest at the picture rather than at Mr Brace's stomach or finger-nails and she would try to imagine a world of castles and palaces and people with strange closed faces because they were princes. She was very familiar with the Madonna pictures but wondered why they hadn't painted any of Our Lady of Lourdes; the school in Kilgarret had been full of Lourdes pictures.

'What was that?' Mr Brace had asked. 'I don't know about it.'

'Oh, it was maybe a hundred years ago, you know St Bernadette and all the miracles and the people being cured and all,' said Elizabeth.

'Well Raphael could hardly have known that in advance,' said Mr Brace. 'He wasn't around to know about the miracles, was he?'

Elizabeth reddened and determined not to speak again. Mr Brace was sorry for her and lent her some books on art history, and one of his precious books of reproductions.

157

'I get bad-tempered, and shout at people in class,' he said. 'Some day you'll be in front of a lot of kids and you'll be the same.'

'Oh, I won't be a teacher,' Elizabeth said definitely.

'What will you be?' he asked with interest.

Elizabeth looked at him blankly. 'I have no idea, but I suppose I'll think of something when the time comes.' Her face looked troubled. He was the first person who had asked her that question. Mother had never wondered what she would do and neither had Father. But perhaps a lot of people had to face this kind of decision alone. She tried to remind herself of what Aunt Eileen had always said to Aisling whenever there was a crisis or a cry that things were unfair. 'Self-pity brings tears to the eyes quicker than anything else.' Aunt Eileen would be proud of me, she thought from time to time as she walked by herself back to Clarence Gardens, her books under her arm, glad to be out of the big, tiled corridors in the school but not anxious to get back into the empty house.

Often she delayed and walked by the library. They had little exhibitions from time to time and it was nice to stroll around and examine their tables full of model buildings, or ancient Greek reconstructions. The librarian, Mr Clarke, was a kind man. He was an albino and he had very poor sight. He told Elizabeth that in fact he could see much better than people had thought, it just looked worse because he peered so much. He had got the job during the war and had built up the library so well, now nobody could take it away from him. He found art books for Elizabeth to read and, even more helpfully, he got her the prospectus and application forms from the local art college.

'I don't think I could really study art, could I?' Elizabeth asked him doubtfully. 'I mean, I don't know anything about it.'

'That's why people study things,' Mr Clarke said, his white head bobbing up and down excitedly. 'That's the point.'

Walking back from the library, she often stopped and examined the window of Worsky's second-hand shop, or rather, antique shop. There were lovely things in the window. She used to tell Mr Clarke about the funny little screens and wondered where they were made. Mr Clarke said she should go in and ask, the owner would be glad to tell her.

'But I don't have any money to buy anything, I can't go in can I?' Elizabeth was hesitant.

'Of course you can, that's what people like, even more than making a sale, to chat about beautiful things. . . .'

And of course he was right. Mr Worsky showed her the panelling in the screens, explained how lacquering was done, and it was all so much more interesting than anything she had ever heard at school. She looked up more books in the library and told Mr Brace about it after art classes.

If only Aisling were here, she thought a hundred times. She would make such fun of her three friends. Beer-Belly-Brace, the albino in the library and the old Polish refugee, Mr Worsky in the antique shop. But it was good to have three friends. And she was able to go to the cinema too, a lot of girls had no money for that, at least once a week she went to the balcony by herself, to the four-thirty show. She saw *Gone with the Wind* four times, and she quite understood why Ashley loved Melanie and not Scarlett. She had written that to Aisling and, as she expected, Aisling had disagreed. Aisling thought that Melanie was a wet, mopey, old baggage and she spoiled the story by being so good.

Other people sang songs about being sweet sixteen and just sixteen and the joys of being seventeen. But Elizabeth didn't join in much. She thought it was a long lonely apprenticeship, and the day she got the news of her scholarship to the art college, she hoped that the weary business of growing up was now over. Father said he hoped it would lead to a secure job; Mother wrote and said that a lot of Honourables were going to art school now and she might meet some. Aisling said she couldn't understand it, Elizabeth had been no good at drawing at school, but Sister Martin who taught drawing was pleased. Mr Brace said she was the first of his pupils to do so well, Mr Clarke in the library gave her four old art books which were considered surplus stock and inscribed them all for her. And Mr Worsky in the antique shop said that now she was an official art student she might even like to come and work in the shop sometimes.

She did get the job in Worsky's antique shop. She called in one Saturday, shortly after she had started at the art college and felt she was a *bona fide* artistic person. At the back of the shop, lost in a catalogue, stood a much younger man than Mr Worsky. Elizabeth's heart lurched, in case the shop had been sold. She hadn't been in for a few weeks.

'What can I get you?' he asked pleasantly. 'Or would you like to browse around a bit?'

He was very very handsome, he had a sharp face – that's what Elizabeth thought was the word you would use to describe it – sort of pointed features, and a lot of black hair falling over his forehead. He looked like a film star.

'Oh, I wanted to see Mr Worsky. He is still here isn't he?'

The young man smiled. 'Oh yes, of course he is, he's having something he hasn't had for a long time. A day off. I'm Johnny Stone, his assistant.'

'Oh yes, of course, he told me about you.' Elizabeth smiled with relief. 'But he described you as an old man, or I mean I thought you were much older. . . .'

'He didn't describe you to me at all . . . but you are very young and very attractive, if I may say so.'

Elizabeth smiled and blushed a bit. 'Thank you very much,' she said. 'You're very kind. I'm Elizabeth White and he once sort of, half-said that if there was extra work here on a Saturday morning he might consider me.'

'If he doesn't, he is a very foolish man, and Stefan Worsky is not that.'

'Oh good, then you're on my side,' said Elizabeth earnestly. 'Can you tell him that I've started now, up at the art college, and I'm doing design courses, as well as history of art, and if it's all right I might call in one afternoon during the week and ask him if he'd really like me to help out on Saturdays. . . .' She looked around. The place was empty. 'It's not very busy, do you think he'd really need help?'

'It's early still,' said Johnny Stone. 'In half an hour the place will be humming. I could ask you to start this morning but that would be a bit pushy. I bet I'll see you next Saturday. I certainly hope so. . . .'

'I hope so too, Mr Stone,' Elizabeth said solemnly.

'Oh come on,' he said.

'I hope so too, Johnny,' she said, shaking his hand.

'That's better,' he said.

The engagement between Maureen O'Connor and Brendan Daly was announced in spring, and a September wedding was planned. It certainly came as no surprise to anyone; the surprise had been that they had waited so long. Their walking-out period had been considered long even by Kilgarret standards. Eamonn had heard a joke about them; he heard that Brendan had finally plucked up courage to ask Maureen and he had said, 'Would you like to be buried with my people?' He had thought it was great, and he kept telling everyone, until his father had told him to shut his big ignorant mouth.

'Isn't it bad enough having the girl being made a fool of by that brood of tinkers without having you laughing like a horse?'

Eamonn was stunned. He had no idea anyone was being made a fool of; he checked it out with Aisling.

'Apparently, by being seen with him or something, she was saying that she was willing; by his not naming the day it looks as if he was taking a bit of time to make up his mind. They're all cracked in this town,' Aisling said absently. 'But what's the worry? She wanted him, she's getting him. That's the system.'

Maureen had been talking about the clothes for the wedding non-stop. Aisling and Sheila Daly were to wear pink. Pink was the right colour for bridesmaids' dresses. It was a pity about Aisling's hair, and the clash, but it couldn't be helped, Maureen wasn't going to change her whole wedding just because her younger sister had such extra-ordinary red hair. Aisling shrugged. She could always have Niamh. No, that wouldn't do, it would look as if there had been a row, it would give cause for gossip. Anyway Aisling and Sheila Daly were around the same height.

Occasionally, Aisling tried to ask Mam was Maureen being normal about this wedding, or was she a bit disturbed; but Mam wasn't giving any sensible answers. She said that a wedding day was something so special that people should be allowed to have any kinds of fancies they wanted. After the wedding day, being married soon settled down to ordinary things again, so that's why people let brides go into such states of excitement. No, Mam hadn't been able to go into a state of excitement herself because things were difficult in those days, there was less money, things were more chancy, people had to concentrate so hard on having a living, a stake in somewhere. Mam's family had lost any bit of money they ever thought they had; Dad's family had nothing. But this was now; things were far better than the terrible twenties. . . .

'But Mam, she's daft altogether, it's only old Brendan Daly. I mean it's only the Dalys she's marrying, you'd think it was the royal family. Do you know she asked me to get thinner for the day! To lose a bit of weight for the ceremony. I couldn't believe it.'

Mam laughed. 'Will you wear a corset and tighten it up a bit and tell her you've lost weight? That's what I'm going to do.'

'She asked you to lose weight too?' Aisling could hardly believe it.

'Yes, but I'm getting on for fifty years of age. I should lose a bit and anyway I've more sense than you'll ever have in your whole life.'

Aisling said she couldn't study her awful grammalogues and do her shorthand preparation after such a shocking discovery about her mother's lack of honesty.

'Go off and write to your friend then,' said Mam. 'Give Elizabeth my love, and ask her whether she might come over for the Great Wedding. . . .'

'That's an idea.' Aisling's face lit up. 'Will I tell Joannie about it too, she'll be home from France in September . . . ?'

'No, better do nothing until the love birds have sorted out whether the Murrays are on their list or not,' Mam smiled.

'You are laughing at them,' Aisling said.

'I am not,' said Mam.

Elizabeth sent a beautiful present for Maureen's wedding. It arrived a good three weeks before the day, so there was plenty of time to admire it. It was a small, oval silver dish.

'It's what they call a bon-bon dish,' Elizabeth had written. 'But I don't think anyone has bon-bons to put in them, we certainly don't here. It would do for anything I suppose, maybe biscuits when you have your friends to tea, or bread even, if you were having people to lunch. It's extraordinary to think of you as a married lady. You're the first of my friends to become Mrs. I've sent a book on hallmarks too, so that you can work out what year it comes from and where it was made. It's quite interesting. I'm always turning bits of silver upside down and looking up their history. If they don't have these four marks then it isn't silver. It's a nice thing to know. I hope you'll be very happy, and if I get good grades next June, perhaps I could come to Kilgarret for a visit and see everyone, and you could have me to tea.'

Maureen was childlike in her enthusiasm. Elizabeth was the first person to have called her a married lady, she was the only one to make something special about being married.

'She's so educated, and interested in things,' said Maureen, busy learning all the hallmarks to blind the Dalys with this new sophistication. 'I wish you were more like Elizabeth, Aisling.'

'Oh people have always been wishing that,' said Aisling cheerfully, 'but it never does them any good.'

Secretly she thought it was a bit wet of Elizabeth to have written such a gooey letter to Maureen and she thought that looking up all these ridiculous names of towns and marks of sterling and makers was just *typical*.

Dear Elizabeth,

You said to write about the wedding, honestly I don't know what to write. The main thing is that it went without any disasters. Father O'Mara was drunk, but people stopped him making a fool of himself, and

Brendan Daly was a bit drunk. He's my brother-in-law you know. I'll be able to say things I heard from *my brother-in-law*, but I don't think I heard anything from him. His sister Sheila, do you remember her at school? I'm not surprised if you don't, she was mousy then and she is mousy now. She normally wears glasses but she didn't for the wedding and she fell over everything, and her eyes were all screwed up trying to peer out. I told her she was better with them, but that was the wrong thing to say apparently. The speeches were endless, I looked really dreadful. I know I've thought I looked dreadful in the past but that was actual beauty compared to the bridesmaid dress. If ever you get over here I'll show it to you. Maureen said it could be changed and used as a dance dress. I said I wanted to keep it for the rest of my life as fancy dress. Another wrong thing to say.

I told you, didn't I, about sort of going with Ned Barrett? There's nothing to it, we go for walks by the river, and a bit of messing about, but nothing great. We go to the pictures and meet inside too. I don't think they'd forbid me to meet him but I couldn't bear all the fuss, and people saying 'You're next'. I don't want to marry Ned Barrett, I just want to practise on him. I was practising a bit down by the river on the corner near the boathouse when who came by but Tony Murray, you know, Joannie's brother. He gave me a desperate look. I think he thinks Joannie and I are sex maniacs, because of the incident. Joannie's gone to learn a year's domestic science in a place where nearly everyone else is a lady or an Hon. That's how posh they've become. She says it's awful and she'd prefer to be at home. I've got an interview soon for a job, a *real* job, in Murray's. Mam says that if Joannie and I are friends then I'm stupid to go and work in the office for them and get a salary. It will change the relationship. I don't agree. Everyone's got to work somewhere. What are you doing? You never tell me properly.
   Love,
   Aisling

164

Dear Aisling,

I never tell properly! I tell you *everything*, you tell *nothing*! *What* incident makes Joannie's brother think you're sex maniacs? *Why* did you look so awful in the dress? What was it like? How is Donal's chest? Is Peggy still there – you never mention her? What's Maureen's new house like? Is Uncle Sean's business going well, does Aunt Eileen still work so hard? Are you really fat or was that just a remark of Maureen's? There's so much I don't know. It makes Kilgarret all seem like a book I read ages ago about a place that's not there any more.

Anyway, to tell you properly about me. Well it's hard because you don't know what life here is like. If I said that Father looks much smarter these days and plays bridge three times a week, you wouldn't know what a change that is. It's as if Uncle Sean suddenly started going to tea parties or something. I get a letter from Mother every week. She and Harry have a shop. She keeps asking me to go and visit them and I'm going to go in November. Term has started in the art college. I didn't realise how lucky I was to have got a place. They made about a dozen speeches telling us we were the *crème de la crème* and that we must fight to keep our places, because there are hundreds outside waiting for one of us to be thrown out.

The others in the class are very nice. It's a bit different to the convent, there are hardly any girls. Imagine. I think Aunt Eileen is right about not working for the Murrays. Suppose you wanted more salary, suppose they wanted to sack you? Won't the other people who work for them feel a bit annoyed when you can go to their house and they can't? Anyway I don't suppose I know anything about it, it just doesn't sound too easy.

I've got a job too, on Saturdays. I work in the antique shop I told you about. It's terrific. I dust the china and the small pieces of furniture, and I fill in stock lists and help when customers come in. It's run by a super old man called Mr Worsky. He's Polish, he came over here just before the war. He has two full-time people. His old lady friend, who is sweet but she's almost blind, and an assistant called Johnny Stone. It sounds like a cowboy's name doesn't it? He's rather like a cowboy too. Very handsome. But not in the shop a lot, alas. He's prowling the country looking for antiques. Love to everyone. Do they remember me? Do they talk much about what became of me?

Elizabeth

VIII

Aisling did not get the job in Murray's. In fact her interview lasted three minutes. She had dressed up exactly as they had told the girls to do in the commercial college; neat grey suit, grey short-sleeved jumper and white collar. No jewellery, very little make-up.

With her gloved hand, she handed copies of her typewriting, shorthand and book-keeping certificates to Mr Meade, who had been running Murray's since Joannie's father had died. As long as most people could remember.

Mr Meade had left the room to study the certificates as if there was a possibility they might be forgeries. Aisling looked around the office. It had a high ceiling and a lot of book-shelves and cabinets of different sizes and shapes. Their pigeon-holes were bursting with envelopes and files, with loosely tied together bunches of documents. It was very untidy and dusty, she thought disapprovingly. Even Mam's little eyrie back in the shop was better than this. At no stage of their secretarial training had anyone told them about an office which seemed to have no proper filing cabinets, no spacious tables and desks for working at. There was one corner of the room which had great boxes with hundreds of labels spilling on to the floor; many of the labels were stained and probably unusable. Aisling's fingers itched to get at them.

The room smelled funny too, of spices, or teas or coffees, she wasn't sure which, because there was another waft coming in on top. A smell of drink . . . a bit like Maher's on a Thursday night. This must be from the wine downstairs, she thought. She wondered how they could be so successful when they were so disorganised. At secretarial college they had stressed that an untidy office was an inefficient office.

But then Maureen had said that they spent months learning how to make perfect corners on beds when she was training as a nurse, and mainly they never did them unless there was a fear that someone would inspect them.

Mr Meade came back, and to his annoyance and to Aisling's surprise, Tony Murray followed close behind him. Mr Meade seemed nervous in the presence of Mr Tony. Mr Tony seemed irritated to extremes by Mr Meade. The typing certificates were handed over.

'These seem to be in order, Mr Tony,' said Mr Meade. He had examined each piece of paper carefully.

'Yes, well she's been there a year, they must have taught her to type,' said Tony ungraciously.

Mr Meade looked put out.

'What makes you think you would like to work here?' he asked precisely.

Aisling was ready for that one. 'I've always thought it would be most interesting to work in a company that offers such variety,' she said, as if reciting lines from a play. 'Murray's is an old-established firm with a long history of business with continental Europe. There would be an opportunity for me to know about the wine trade, the tea blending, the whiskey bonding as well as high-class grocery trade.'

'You would be sitting in an office typing out bills and stocks lists. How the hell will you learn the wine business there?' interrupted Tony.

'Well I will be close to it, connected with it sort of . . .' Aisling stammered. Tony had always been nice to her, courteous, even joky she thought. Why had he turned into this kind of hectoring figure?

It seemed to puzzle Mr Meade too. 'I'm sure that . . . er, Miss O'Connor, realises . . .' he began.

'Quit talking like a parrot, Aisling, what on earth do you want to work here for? It's the same work you could do for your mother over in the square. Why aren't you in there typing bills and stock lists instead of wanting to come here?'

Aisling's eyes blazed back at him in rage. If he was going to break the rules and make a mockery out of the interview, then so was she. She had played fair, worn gloves, kept her eyes down, answered politely. Now she'd answer him as he wanted.

'I'll tell you, Tony Murray,' she said, conscious of the shock on Mr Meade's face without even looking. 'I'll tell you exactly why I want to work here. Here I work in my own twin-set and skirt, in Mam's shop I'd wear an overall; here I'd get money from your family and I'd spend it as I bloody pleased, in Ma and Da's shop they'd be giving me money like pocket money and complaining and saying sit up, and stop fidgeting, and why aren't these done, like they say to Eamonn. In Murray's I'd be someone, I'd be that new Miss O'Connor in the accounts office, I'd meet people, I'd have a bit of class because I was good enough to be hired by the great almighty Murrays, and a friend of the family. That's why I thought I'd like to work here. Now you tell me why you don't want me. . . .'

'Because you're a friend of Joannie, and we like you coming up to the house, and you're a splash of colour around the place, and I don't want to be paying you a wage packet every week. You stupid thick girl. That's why.' He slammed out of the room.

Aisling shrugged. 'Well give me those back, Mr Meade, I gather I haven't got the job.' She picked up her certificates, put them back in her envelope, peeled off her gloves and put them into her handbag. 'Thanks all the same,' she said shaking hands in a totally over-familiar way for a job applicant.

Mr Meade watched her swinging out through the shop. He had no idea why Mr Tony had behaved in that extraordinary way, but in his heart he was quite relieved. That little O'Connor girl, with her mane of red hair, could have been trouble. She might have been quite a disruptive force in Murray's, and they didn't need that.

Mr Worsky was delighted with Elizabeth White. She was exactly the kind of child he would have liked, solemn and alert. His two sons had been interested only in kicking a ball round the yard back in Poland, and wherever they were today they would never have been thoughtful and interested in beautiful things. She was polite and attentive, she had a little notebook where she wrote down what he told her about furniture. Once she had said that it was she who should pay him for his training rather than take money for her Saturday help in the shop. When she left art school she would love to work as a picture restorer, she thought, or an expert adviser on furniture. They spent happy Saturdays and sometimes both of them would sigh with impatience when a customer came in.

Johnny Stone liked the girl too. Mr Worsky could see that. Johnny would speak flirtatiously to her when they were examining porcelain or the inlaid work on some desk. Elizabeth never responded coquettishly, since she had never seen the remarks as admiration. In a kind fatherly way, Mr Worsky made a few tentative efforts to warn Elizabeth about Johnny Stone's charms and how successful they were.

'For a boy of barely twenty-one he has amazing *succès* with the ladies.'

'Oh does he?' Elizabeth sounded interested, rather than hurt.

Mr Worsky went on then, sure that he was treading on no hurt young love. 'Oh a proper Prince Charming . . . that is why he finds such wonderful things when he goes to people's houses. They let him in, they let him come and rummage in their back rooms and their attics. They let Johnny Stone do what he likes.'

'Marvellous for us that they do, isn't it?' said Elizabeth enthusiastically, and Mr Worsky was touched that she thought herself part of his little shop and relieved that she did not seem to have become a victim of the famous Johnny line of chat.

Elizabeth was too busy to think of romance. She envied other students at college who had less complicated lives to lead. She had to organise the food for the week, she had to balance books like Dora in *David Copperfield* – except that she did it swiftly. Father felt that money was trickling down a drain unless he could see neat columns of figures. The cleaning lady sometimes didn't clean too thoroughly since she felt it was infra-dig to be working for a chit of a girl in a house where the mother had hopped it. Why didn't the girl do the cleaning herself, she wondered. Elizabeth had to tread the careful path which would ensure a higher standard of work without the cleaning lady's dignity being offended to the degree of her putting on her coat and leaving them.

Then there was Father. His bridge playing had been so successful it meant that he had to play host to his group every two weeks or so. On these occasions Elizabeth made sandwiches, served tea and emptied ashtrays. She thought it was worth it because it paid dividends. Father was out at other people's houses almost every second night. She didn't have to feel guilty about him, she didn't have to talk to him, except to ask him about his game when he came home. His face would light up as he helped himself to a small tot of ginger wine, and he became almost animated describing how he had finessed a queen, or his partner had gone for a grand slam on no evidence whatsoever.

Father cared nothing about the Saturdays at the antique shop. He had warned her to be sure to see that Mr Worsky paid her on the nail, foreigners could be very decent but many of them could be highly unreliable. But Father never asked her how much she got, nor did it affect her allowance. Girls need their pin money, he was apt to say from time to time. Father didn't realise either how well Elizabeth ran his house for him. But by encouraging him earnestly to grow his own vegetables, she saved them a great deal of money, as well as using up Father's copious spare time at weekends. Elizabeth also gave drawing lessons to two little girls who came to the house and sat with their drawing books at the kitchen table while she did her weekly bake. She made bread, pastry, cake, a casserole and peeled all the potatoes that would be needed for the week, leaving them in water which she changed every day. She topped and tailed fruit, she pressed every left-over into something else. It was a three-hour session; and all the while she overlooked the two children, correcting their perspective, lightening their shading and neatening their calligraphy. Their mother, who had artistic hopes and no money, gave Elizabeth jams, bottled plums, chutneys and even candied peel, for their lessons. It worked very well, and Elizabeth ran Father's home very comfortably while keeping a good quarter of the money it should have taken, in her own little tin box upstairs. Even Aunt Eileen, with all her religion, could hardly have disapproved, Elizabeth thought. . . . She really did earn the money and if Father had anyone else, even Mother, it would have been spent in areas where Elizabeth was able to save.

She didn't know why she was saving. Perhaps it was for flight like Mother, perhaps it was to set herself up in business, like Mr Worsky. It might even be for a velvet dress. Johnny Stone had told her about a singer he had seen who wore a rose-coloured velvet dress and it had made her seem like a flower. She had blonde hair and a rose velvet dress; Johnny had said it was like heaven.

Aisling had been mystified by the whole afternoon in Murray's, when she had gone along confidently expecting to get a job. She was at a loss to explain it to anyone. Mam had been right of course, and so, at long distance, had Elizabeth. Joannie wasn't there so there was nobody to ask, nobody to discuss it with. From nowhere Aisling remembered a line from one of Elizabeth's letters saying the hardest thing about growing up is not having anyone to ask. Aisling had thought it was only because the White family had more or less disappeared, leaving Elizabeth on her own; but now she realised that it was more than that. There are some things you can't just throw on somebody's else's life. This was one of them. She decided that since she was all dressed up she would get another job instead.

She called first at the chemist and spoke to Mr Moriarty. She made her voice light and cheerful, she showed him her commercial college certificates, she thought she would enquire around some of the nicer places in town, she said. The Moriartys said that there was hardly any work that they and the young man who worked there couldn't do. She went to the insurance broker, the solicitor and the jeweller's. None of them needed anyone. They all complimented Aisling on how well she looked and said she was a sensible girl to want to work in her own town, and that something would turn up. The bank she knew didn't hire people from the town; they had to come from far away so that they wouldn't know people's business and gossip about it. The hotel had a receptionist, the two doctors had receptionists. The grain merchants were Protestants, and it would be too common to work anywhere else. Weary and depressed she came into the shop ten minutes before closing time.

'Mam can I have a word with you up in the eyrie,' she called.

'What is it?' Eileen lifted her glasses to see Aisling properly. She saw a tired and disappointed-looking child, very different from the bouncy figure who had set out just after lunch. 'Come on up here,' she called.

Aisling made the little flight of stairs and flopped on to a stool.

'Mam, I've been thinking,' she said.

'Yes, and what have you thought?'

'I've been thinking that you'd be nearing the end of your work here.'

'Oh really?'

'Yes, a woman of nearly fifty as you were saying. . . .'

'A woman of forty-eight so I am. . . .'

'Yes, but I'm a woman of eighteen and honestly, if this place is ever to be a success, the whole family had better try to pull together you know and. . . .'

'Oh I see. . . .'

'No, you don't, you work too hard, everyone says so. When anyone says to you why don't you get someone to help, you always list the problems. Why can't I do it Mam? I'm trained, I have all my certificates . . . what do you think Mam?'

'Well, it's a bit sudden, child, I mean you never wanted to help out here when we were busy, or you never thought of working here before, so far as your father and I ever thought anyway. . . .'

'I didn't want to help out, Mam, that's the whole point. I wanted to work like a real person. You know, hours and wages and pulling my weight . . . you know?'

'Well, I'll have to talk to your father . . . it's a bit of a surprise.'

'Sure, Da will do what you say Mam, you know he will.'

'I know nothing of the sort. This is your father's business, he's very particular about who he hires. Maybe he might think you'd be a bit. . . .'

'A bit what, Mam?'

'Well, young.'

'You mean flighty,' said Aisling mulishly.

'Yes, I mean flighty,' said Mam, simply.

'I'm not flighty any more, not if I'm getting a real salary, and could be sacked and all,' Aisling said.

'You changed your mind about Murray's, then?' Mam asked quietly.

'Oh yes, I went and had a chat, it was more of a chat, not a normal interview. Tony Murray and I agreed it wasn't such a great idea. . . .'

'And you wouldn't rather work, say in the hotel or the chemist where you'd meet more people . . . ?' Mam was gentle.

'No, the Moriartys would only have a living for themselves and the hotel has Judy Lynch.'

'And the insurance, or the bank . . . ?'

'No, they have their own people. Now what I had in mind was building up this place, Mam, like a real big family business. You know, you and Da and Eamonn and myself all talking about the future, and maybe when Donal gets older, some not too tiring job for him. . . .'

Mam was smiling. She seemed to find something funny.

'Well, it's what people do,' Aisling said crossly.

Mam reached over and took her hand. 'And what about Niamh, will we find her a job in this new enlarged family business?'

'I think Niamh had better marry some money and get us the cash to expand. Build on out the back,' said Aisling.

'I'll suggest it to her at supper,' said Mam.

Aisling snatched back her hand. 'You're not taking me seriously,' she snapped.

'I am, child, I am indeed . . . I'll have a word with your Da.
If he says yes, when would you like to start?'

Aisling threw her arms around Eileen, knocking off the
glasses which had been perched on her forehead. 'On
Monday, Mam, and could I not have to wear a shop-coat
like you. Could I wear my own clothes?'

'They'd get very dirty, love, that's why we all wear coats,
the dust.'

'But Mam, I'd keep my clothes clean, I promise.'

'They'd be destroyed, you'd spend your whole salary
replacing them. I'm telling you from experience. We'll get
you a nice shop-coat, whatever colour you like.'

'But Mam, it doesn't look right, not after all that course
and learning all the shorthand and the rest. A shop-coat.'

'You'd look beautiful in green; suppose we got you a
couple of emerald green coats to wear over your clothes?'

'Would it look . . . .?'

'It would look unusual, special, you'd be the most eye-
catching woman in Kilgarret. You're a beautiful-looking
girl, Aisling.'

Aisling didn't know what to say.

'For goodness' sake, go on, Mam,' she said eventually.

'You are. Don't you know it? With all the titivating you
do on yourself?'

'Am I nice-looking?' Aisling asked shyly.

'You're lovely, far too good for that Ned Barrett, but
that's your own choice, I suppose.'

'Mam, how on earth do you know about Ned Barrett?'
Aisling was stunned. 'Not that there's anything to know,'
she added quickly.

'No, of course not,' said Mam. 'But when you're nearly
fifty like me you have to go round imagining things . . . it
passes the time.'

'I don't think I'm going to be one of those people who get
seriously interested in men. I really don't.'

'Oh, I'm sure you're right, Aisling, one has a feeling about
that sort of thing.'

'Mam?'

'Yes love.'

'If Da says yes, can people call me Miss O'Connor, can some people call me Miss O'Connor anyway?'

'I'll insist on it . . . from the start.'

Johnny Stone said that he would be very happy to take Elizabeth up to Preston. He was going to make a journey into the dark north for Mr Worsky anyway with the van, so why not have Elizabeth along for company? She could make calls with him, learn a bit more about the real and the fake, the kind of things that were beautiful and things that only looked good. What did Mr Worsky think?

Mr Worsky thought it was up to Elizabeth and her father. If they had no objection, then he would be delighted of course. To have two staff on the road for him was coming up in the world. He did not foresee any awkward entanglement, where the little solemn face of Elizabeth might become hurt and bewildered. The child was grown-up beyond her years already. She could handle a Romeo like Mr Johnny Stone.

Elizabeth did not discuss her transport with Father. She simply told him that she would use the half-term break from college to pay Mother the long-promised visit. Harry had sent money for her; no, she did not need anything extra, just the normal allowance was fine. She carefully arranged that the first night of her absence, Father's meal would be there. But after that for five days he would have to manage on his own. Then he might appreciate more how smoothly and efficently she ran his house. She also left that week's housekeeping money for him in an envelope, knowing that it would not stretch in any way to meet his needs. She did not think that this was cruel. She thought it was sensible. Father was living a strange life between the bank and the bridge table, far far away from reality. It would be no harm to bring him down to a few basics.

Dearest Elizabeth,
Harry and I are so pleased, so very pleased that you are really coming. I wake up every morning and I say to myself it's only nine more days now. Harry wanted to

know whether it was like this during the war, whether I counted all the days when you were in Ireland? I don't think it was the same. I knew you were safe and well and happy. I read those letters every week and I couldn't think what to write back, there was so little to say about our empty house and about the long, weary hours in the munitions factory.

Here it's different. I think of you at home in Clarence Gardens. I think of the kitchen, and of your father . . . I can't imagine what it's like for you there now. I wish . . . in a foolish sort of way that I was there, because you and I could talk. You could tell me all about Mr Worsky's shop, and I could go in and see it; I am sure that George doesn't even know where it is. At least I did buy some fire irons there once.

I hope you like our place. Harry has worked until after midnight for over two weeks 'to have things right for Elizabeth'. I don't think I'm telling you this so that you will be prepared to make a lot of admiring noises. But perhaps I am. We never made many admiring noises when you were younger, and I remember that week when you came back from Kilgarret you said that everyone reacted more in the O'Connors' house and in school. I'm just rambling on darling.

Only eight and a half days.

Love,
Violet

'Why does she call herself Violet?' Johnny Stone asked Elizabeth the day they set off. It was to be a two-day journey.

'When she went away with Harry she started signing Violet. It's funny but it seemed quite right somehow. I suppose she thought that if she wasn't doing the job of being mother, then she shouldn't call herself Mother.'

'My mother never did the job of being mother but she still calls herself that: ever your loving mother. I think I'll have to tell her that she should call herself Martha. You're younger than I am, I'll use you as an example. Listen, Martha old bean, I'll say, my friend Elizabeth's only eighteen and she and her mother use first names. The world's changing, old dear, I'll say.'

Elizabeth laughed. 'It's not as easy as that. I still think of her as Mother. I'm going to feel out the ground a bit when I meet her. She may like to be called Mother still. She may prefer not. I cheat in letters you see. Dear Both. I worked it out, it was affectionate but not specific if you see.'

Johnny saw. The signposts flashed by, the miles disappeared under the wheels of the old van. Elizabeth unpacked a picnic which they had to eat in the car, since April torrents and winds were howling around them.

They had two calls to make that day. Johnny and Elizabeth crawled around a disused summer-house and collected forty old pictures, some cracked, some so gaudy that Elizabeth couldn't see for the life of her what Mr Worsky would do with them. 'The frames, you silly,' hissed Johnny as they pulled wicker chairs and old cricket bats and croquet mallets out in their search.

The lady who owned the frames, and the summer-house, offered them tea and biscuits and was overjoyed at the small sum that Johnny gave her. Before they left she asked Johnny whether his young lady would like to use the bathroom. Elizabeth flushed, not at the mention of bathrooms but at the woman's mistaking her for Johnny's young lady.

'She's more my colleague than my young lady,' Johnny grinned. 'But seeing you blush like that, Elizabeth, maybe I'll change my mind.'

Elizabeth fled to the bathroom and tried to hide her red cheeks by rubbing in some of the talcum powder that was beside the handbasin.

Back in the van she launched an immediate attack.

'If those are really mahogany and really silver frames, you didn't give her nearly enough,' she complained.

'Dear girl. She was delighted with what we gave her. Delighted. She pressed my hand in thanks, she's going to have the roof mended. She's going to ask the local handyman to come in and paint her living room. Now is that happy or not happy? What do you want me to do, throw poor Stefan's money down the drain. . . ?'

'But Mr Worsky wouldn't want to cheat. . . .'

'Seriously Elizabeth, that woman had those pictures rotting in her tool shed or whatever it was for years. Her husband had always meant to clean up. He never did. He never came back from the war either. Now what happens? We come down, we spend two hours cleaning up, tidying her old shed. You got a broom for heaven's sake. She has a tidy place to put her deck-chair, if it's ever going to stop raining in the next few years, she's got cash in hand to have a new roof, a new-coloured sitting room and a new hat. Now what's that but happiness?'

'It's tricking her. We'll get thirty or forty times what you paid. You gave her thirty-three pounds. The big gilt frame alone will fetch that. More even, if we do it up. And there's twenty-nine others. It's downright dishonest!'

'It's business, you stupid girl, and you look terrific when your face is all red like that. It's really peaches and cream. Typical English rose, you should do it more often.'

'Does it really look nice, or is that a cruel joke?' Elizabeth asked.

'Of course it's nice, whole fortunes are spent by women trying to get their faces to look like that,' said Johnny.

'I was afraid it looked a bit consumptive, you know, too much contrast,' Elizabeth said seriously.

Johnny laughed so much he had to pull the van up on the side of the road. 'You are totally beautiful,' he said affectionately. 'I wish the old bird back there was right and you were my young lady.'

'I'd be no good at being someone's young lady, I'm not ready for it yet. Life's too complicated, there are too many things to sort out.' Elizabeth was utterly sincere. There was no way that she was hoping to be contradicted.

'When do you imagine things will be sorted out?' asked Johnny.

'I expect when I've finished college and get a job, and when Father's learned to live on his own, or have a housekeeper or something . . . about three years I expect.'

'I'll have to come and apply to be your young man then,' Johnny said. 'If I'm not too old that is . . . I'll be nearly a quarter of a century.'

'Yes,' said Elizabeth consideredly. 'You'll probably have given up playing around by then. But I expect I'll find somebody.'

They stayed in the guesthouse that was owned by Mr Worsky's cousin outside Liverpool. The second call had been equally contentious. Johnny had offered an old man twenty pounds for three mirrors and a table. According to Elizabeth they would fetch over one hundred pounds in the shop. Johnny had walked down the steps to the van with her before he clinched the deal. The little old man peered anxiously out the window, terrified they would leave without buying the pieces.

'Once again, Stefan Worsky pays for a shop, he pays me a salary, he pays you something, he puts the petrol in the bloody van, he pays for me to stay with his cousin, he spends hours of his time and his skill – don't forget his skill and training, which took years to come by – in doing up these tables and mirrors. Then, and only then, will he get one hundred pounds for them. Now that's what the world calls business. It's not a well-kept secret. It's what people know happens. Have I your permission to offer this poor bugger twenty pounds before he has a heart attack, or should we cancel the whole thing, break his heart, mine and Stefan's just because Madam White here thinks she knows how to run the world?'

Elizabeth burst into tears. Johnny paid the perplexed man twenty-five pounds instead of the twenty he had been quite willing to accept. In confusion, they bundled the furniture into the van while Elizabeth sobbed in the front seat. In silence they headed for Mr Worsky's cousin's house.

'Do you think we might have a half pint somewhere while the storms abate?' Johnny asked. It was the first thing he had said in eleven miles. Elizabeth nodded. She wasn't able to speak.

They sat in a pub and, red-eyed, she drank a brandy and ginger wine which Johnny said might be just the thing. He made no attempt to cheer her up, to apologise for his loss of temper or to enquire why she cried so long and so deeply.

The brandy warmed her and she had another.

Then, in a small voice, she asked him about Liverpool. Was it a big place, suppose she wanted to find a small place called Jubilee Terrace, would that be possible? Was it idiotic? During her second brandy she told Johnny about Sean O'Connor and how Aunt Eileen had always said that if ever she got anywhere near Liverpool, could she say hallo to Amy Sparks. It was such ages ago, five years. Of course, Mrs Amy Sparks and her son Gerry might be dead. But just because Aunt Eileen had once said ... no, it was silly. Johnny mustn't listen to her, she was just being silly.

'We're far too early for Stefan's cousin, why don't we see if we can find it?' said Johnny.

Gerry Sparks had had a stroke of luck, he said, in that he was good with his hands. He was a watchmaker and he could do a lot of work at home. They fixed a tray on his wheelchair, and he could spread all the bits and bobs out on it and look through his magnifying glass at them. It was a real bit of luck that they discovered his skill in the therapy classes, because the legs hadn't taken. Not enough for them to grab on to, didn't manage to use the muscles from the hips.

Mrs Sparks was now Mrs Benson. She had remarried, as a sensible thing to do; she was able to look after Mr Benson, and cook his meals, keep his shirts nice and clean, he could give her his pension. They had sold his little house and made a tidy profit. They were so pleased to meet Elizabeth and her young man; they knew all about her. Eileen O'Connor, a wonderful woman, wrote a long letter every Christmas and she sent money to the church in Liverpool where they had held this mass for Sean.

They talked about Sean. Gerry said he had been a great mate, he'd never had a mate like Sean before. Elizabeth said he had always been restless when she knew him in Kilgarret. But then she was very young and maybe she hadn't really been able to talk to him.

'I never knew a mate like him,' Gerry Sparks said again. 'Certainly never knew one since then.'

He looked down at his rug on the wheelchair.

'Of course, like this it stands to reason I don't make many mates these days.'

'Yeah, that's the trouble when you work on your own,' Johnny agreed, having deliberately misunderstood him. 'You don't have mates at work, you miss that. Of course, there are advantages working on your own. If you feel like knocking off an hour earlier or taking a long lunch you can do it.'

Gerry brightened up. Together they talked about working on your own, piece-work rate for the hour. Johnny even went out to the car and asked Gerry's advice about an old clock that he had picked up at a sale of work. 'I only bought it for the face, but I think the insides are like scrambled egg.' Gerry had his eyeglass out, and in minutes it was ticking. The small kitchen filled with pride until it burst. Elizabeth couldn't have imagined anything that would have brought more pleasure. Addresses were exchanged, if ever any work came the way of Mr Worsky which needed the touch of a craftsman it would be sent to Gerry Sparks.

In the firelight and under the dim centre-bulb the peaky face and bent back of Gerry Sparks was joined with the handsome young Johnny Stone. If they had met in Italy they might have been mates too. But of course Johnny Stone wasn't old enough to put on a uniform, and the year that he was just old enough they stopped fighting. Elizabeth and Mr and Mrs Benson seemed to exchange innocent, pleased looks about the conversation at the fire. But it was something that could never have been put into words.

Mr Worsky's cousin was not at all interested in their visit to a house in Jubilee Terrace, a small, poor little place. She was very interested in Elizabeth, a lovely young woman, just right for Mr Stone, and very right for Mr Stone to settle down, too, no more of the romancing.

'It's just as well I'm not your young lady,' said Elizabeth wearily as she climbed the stairs to her bedroom. 'Since we left London this morning, everyone has assumed I am and that I have a dreadful time with you.'

Could it really only have been this morning that she had said goodbye to Father? She hadn't given him a thought all day. Perhaps that's what happened to Mother. But then they were married, which was different. She wondered whether Mother would like to be called Violet tomorrow. She wondered whether Johnny would come in and call like he had at the Sparks's house. She wondered how Gerry Sparks got out of his wheelchair when he wanted to go to the bathroom, and whether she should try to stay awake and write to Aunt Eileen about the visit. . . .

There were three more calls on the way to Preston. Elizabeth said nothing about the prices offered to and accepted by a war widow, a clergyman and an elderly doctor. She helped willingly and cooperatively, she wrote things down in her little notebook and she scrambled under a bed in a loft with Johny where their hands touched over some old silver-backed brushes. When they took them downstairs the old doctor said that he vaguely remembered them from his childhood.

'I'll buy them if you like,' Johnny said.

'Oh, they're filthy now, and the hair's all rotting. I'd be ashamed to sell them, I'll throw them out,' said the old man.

'They could be nice if we got them done up, polished you know, and new bristles,' said Johnny.

He caught Elizabeth's eye before she looked away.

'And valuable, Doctor,' he went on. 'We might be able to sell them for a lot more than we give you.'

The old doctor smiled.

'Well, I should hope so my boy,' he said agreeably. 'Otherwise what's the whole business about?'

Johnny celebrated his triumph by avoiding Elizabeth's eye.

When the signposts said that Preston was only five miles away Elizabeth turned to Johnny almost shyly.

'I hope you'll come and stay for supper. . . . I don't think they'd have a bed for the night. Not if Harry's been making all this palaver over doing up the guest room for me, you know. But supper would be super.'

'Why don't I just see you in the door, say Hi to Harry and Vi and push off, arrange what time to pick you up on Tuesday and let the family get together as nature intended?'

'It's not the family, you know that.' Elizabeth sounded troubled.

'I know but it's enough strain on everyone without having a total stranger there sitting in on it.'

'But you're . . . you're very good at making chat and sort of helping things along. Please come and stay.'

'Listen, I'll come in and see what I think. If I think it's better for me to go I'll toddle off, if I think I'm helping I'll hang around a bit. Will that do?'

Elizabeth nodded. He took her hand and patted it. 'You don't have, you didn't have any awkwardnesses in your family, you know with your mum who calls herself your-ever-loving-mother?'

'Awkwardnesses? No. Not really.' He negotiated the wet, slippy road. 'What do you mean exactly?'

'You know, like them being too loving or not loving enough. You know. Like them being not what you expected or wanted.'

'Oh no, heavens, no,' Johnny laughed. 'My mother would like me to live with her and have a small car and drive her to see her friends . . . but I don't like that as a way of life so I have no intention of doing it. None at all. My mother's father wanted her to stay at home and look after him, but she didn't, she ran away with my father. People do what they want to do. Once you know that and accept it you don't have any problems.'

'And your father?'

'He ran off with someone else, with two someone elses. He ran off with people every ten years or so, my mother was the second. He's frightfully keen on running off with people. . . .'

'And you don't see him?'

'Why on earth should I? He doesn't want to see me. Look, it's not like your case, these folk have been painting a room for you for ages. They want you to come, you wanted to come . . . where's the awkwardness? There's no lies or demands or emotions.'

'You hate that sort of thing, don't you?' said Elizabeth.

'Doesn't everyone?'

'I think you do more than most, you were very annoyed when I was crying yesterday. I could see it.'

'No, my dear, honestly, I wasn't annoyed. It's just, I don't know, I don't want to get involved in dramas and tears and heightened scenes. So I never do.'

'It's not a bad philosophy I suppose.'

'It has its drawbacks. People think I'm a bit cold or selfish or too flippant . . . but perhaps all these things are true . . . Heigh ho, Preston, jewel of the North, here we come.'

'Do stay to supper,' she said.

'If they ask me,' he promised.

The bedroom almost brought tears to Elizabeth's eyes. Only the thought of having Johnny see her once more with a red, puffy face held them back. Harry had bought expensive and hideous ornaments which stood on a shelf. 'Girls like pretty things,' he said proudly as he looked at them. The utility furniture had all been painted white and so had rather a nice little bookcase which used to have doors. Elizabeth could see the hinges but they were painted over too. The bed had a flouncy blue and white spread; pictures in what she would now think of as the most awful chocolate-box tradition in shiny new frames covered the walls. In those days of shortages Harry had painted everything in sight. The blue carpet went wall to wall and you could see that he had stitched scraps together to get it to fit properly. His face beamed with achievement.

Johnny spoke first. He was marvelling at the things that should be marvelled at, how perfect the paint surface was . . . were three? three . . . yes, he had thought there must be three coats. Johnny marvelled too at how cleverly the electricity work had been done, a light over the bed, another over the wash-hand basin. He praised the bright, clear colours which made it look so cheery even in winter. As he spoke, Elizabeth found her tongue to praise and thank and marvel. She left her bag on the bed and looked around her with gratitude that nearly made Harry crack apart, so broad was his smile. Spontaneously she hugged him, and when she saw the delight in Mother's eyes she hugged Mother too. It had been a peck on the cheek as she had come in the front door of the shabby little corner shop.

'Oh Mother, this is great,' she cried. Mother hugged her back. Over Mother's shoulder she saw Johnny nodding slightly and she knew she had been right to decide not to say Violet.

Johnny stayed to supper, the atmosphere growing more and more cordial. Harry was like a big child, he had grown fatter and more genial in the two years. Mother had become even thinner, if that were possible; she seemed nervy, she smoked a lot and her eyes looked huge in her thin face. She jumped up half a dozen times, nervous, anxious to please.

They both seemed pleased, in a childish and obvious way, that Johnny did not know Father, Elizabeth thought, in fact Harry went so far as to say, 'That's good, lad, we're the first to have a look at you, eh?' as if Elizabeth had taken Johnny there on some kind of tour of approval.

Elizabeth answered that one without any embarrassment.

'The reason that Johnny doesn't know Father is that Johnny is in Mr Worsky's and Father, as you said in your letter, Mother, hardly knows where the antique shop is.' She paused and, lest it appear to leave an opportunity for Father to be criticised, she spoke again. 'You would be amazed at Father really, both of you. He is such a bridge addict now. No worries about what to get him for Christmas, new cards or scoring pads, or little bridge ashtrays. And he meets people all the time. As soon as somebody new comes to the area, if they can play bridge he's met them in a week.'

'Fancy George having a whole circle of friends.' Mother was mildly amazed, as if it were a story about someone she knew a long time ago.

'They're not exactly friends.' Elizabeth was thoughtful.

'Of course they're friends,' interrupted Johnny, 'if he goes to their houses and they come to Clarence Gardens, what are they? Enemies? Honestly, Elizabeth, you want people to exchange blood from their arms like Red Indians.'

Everyone laughed.

'We did that in Ireland once, Aisling and I,' said Elizabeth suddenly. 'I'd quite forgotten.'

'Yes, well you see,' said Harry meaninglessly. He was trying to say something that would make that Johnny realise he was on his side.

It worked. Johnny put his arm around Harry's shoulder. 'Let the girls talk a bit, Harry, and you show me this workshop of yours, and if you come across any of those old weighing scales on your travels, you know the old-fashioned ones with brass weights. . . .'

Mother lit another cigarette and leaned across to clutch Elizabeth's arm.

'Oh, my dear, he's so nice, he's such a nice young man. I'm simply delighted for you. I worried about that too . . . you know, as well as anything else. I worried that you mightn't have a boyfriend or a social life. You mention so little about it in your letters.'

Elizabeth sighed. 'I suppose it's useless my telling you that he isn't my boyfriend. Really, until today and yesterday we've hardly even had a proper conversation. He's someone I work with on Saturdays. But I agree, he is very nice, isn't he? He's been great company, simply smashing on the trip. The time just flew by.'

'I know,' said Mother. 'That's what's wonderful about being with the right person.'

They spoke of him a lot during the weekend, which was a good thing as it kept them off the topic of Father.

Mother felt guilty about Father, she felt guilty about walking out with no proper explanations.

'I don't think explanations would have done much good,' Elizabeth said several times, feeling years older than she had felt the day Mother left Clarence Gardens. 'Father doesn't listen much, I've come to think.'

Sometimes Harry spoke about Father too, in a worried tone. 'You're a grown-up young woman, Elizabeth, and I don't want to sound like an adult talking to a child . . . but your mother and I worry about you down in that house, it's not healthy for a child to live alone with a . . . well with such a remote man as your father. Now Violet won't hear a word against him, and I wouldn't speak one word either against a person's father but you have to agree that he's an odd fish, a cold person. He has no blood. A real cold fish. There's an art college in Preston. . . .'

'I know, Harry, but. . . .'

'And we'd be no interference, I mean you've been having your own way, you could have whoever you liked into your own room . . . that's a fair offer. We'd give you a key, you could come and go. Violet's eyes light up now that you're here . . . and mine too. I think it's champion, as they say here, to have you in and out. . . .'

'You're very kind, Harry,' sighed Elizabeth, and meant it. And she also meant it when she said that Mother was marvellous to her and had been like the kind of elder sister you read about in books. But no, she must really stay where she was. And no, really, she wouldn't join the general outcry against Father. He had a life to live just like everyone else, and he lived it. If he didn't have much joy that was bad luck and circumstance.

They eventually stopped trying to change her mind. In her shiny new bedroom, Elizabeth lay awake at night listening to the strange sounds of a different city and wondered whether everyone else had to keep being kind to people and talking down to them. She wished that someone would make all the decisions for her, and consult her views and take her moods into consideration.

In what seemed like a totally separate part of her mind she wondered how Johnny was getting on, and whether he would come back with a rabbit for dinner as he had promised Harry he would.

The rabbit was a great success. Johnny had arrived when the shop was very busy. Mother and Harry were both dealing with children who spent thirty minutes trying to decide how to spend their tuppences and their sweet points. Tired women buying thin slices of pressed meat and packets of semolina, old men shuffling in for tobacco. Elizabeth had been reading in the kitchen when she heard the cries of welcome for Johnny in the shop. Harry rushed back in beaming like an idiot.

'He's here, he's here, and he didn't forget, he's got the rabbit. Hurry Elizabeth, there's a dear, get out the pot. Your mother will be in in a minute. . . .'

Elizabeth wondered how she could have ever feared Harry, or Mr Elton as she had called him then. How could she have thought him a sophisticated dangerous man, he was a big baby. She wished that he could be more cool, less excited, Johnny might think they were all very simple and overimpressed by him.

But no, Johnny seemed just as excited. 'I'm going to spend the night here, and we'll leave early tomorrow. Your mother's invited me. We'll have the best rabbit pie ever eaten in this country since before the war.'

It *was* the best rabbit pie that had been eaten in the country since the war. Elizabeth had made pastry, Johnny had gone to the pub for cider. They set a table and Mother made up her face. Johnny told them about how he had got the rabbit. The farmer who had been clearing out his furniture always offered people the chance to shoot a rabbit, because he was too old and arthritic to shoot himself, but he loved to go with another huntsman. Johnny had shot three, one for the farmer, one for his party and one, all wrapped up in wet grass at the back of the van, for Mr Worsky.

And they sang some songs, and Harry recited 'The Green Eye of the Little Yellow God', and Mother did an imitation of how the nuns taught them to curtsey, which was hilarious. Elizabeth was pressed for a party piece. She didn't have any, she said. Mother said that there were always songs in Ireland, that Elizabeth said people used to sing in Maher's. With her hands by her side she began:

'Oh Danny Boy
The pipes, the pipes are calling
From o'er the glens
And down the mountain side

189

The summer's gone and all the leaves are falling
T'is you must go
Must go and I must bide. . . .'

Then they all joined in:

'Oh come you back . . .
When sun shines in the meadow . . .
And when the fields are hushed and white with snow . . .
For I'll be there in sunshine and in shadow . . .
Oh Danny boy, Oh Danny boy, I love you so.'

Every one of them, including Johnny, had tears in their eyes.
Oh God, thought Elizabeth, why do I have to wreck
everything? Why couldn't she have found a cheerful song to
sing, something that would have made people laugh like
everyone else was able to do? Why did she have to pick the
most mournful song in the world? The one party she had
been to since she came back from Kilgarret and now she had
to close it down by singing a sad song.

They were washing-up and scraping chairs and putting
things away. Everyone was saying what a great night it had
been. Mother fussed about sheets and blankets for Johnny,
Harry said better be on the road tomorrow before six
o'clock in order to avoid the worst of the traffic and the big
lorries in the narrow streets.

Elizabeth didn't sleep, she kept jerking awake in the
middle of a bad dream where Gerry Sparks from his
wheelchair was holding her wrist.

'Why did you come to see me if you weren't going to
marry me?' he cried over and over again. Elizabeth felt
herself running away while his mother Mrs Benson and
Harry shouted after her, 'You're always the same, you start
things without thinking and you hurt people. . . .'

After their last afternoon call at an orphange, where Johnny
bought four boxes full of old cutlery, the rain became so
heavy that they had to pull in to the side of the road. The

windscreen wipers couldn't cope with the torrents hurtling at them. As they sat waiting for it to ease a policeman with a flashing torch came to the window.

'Road's flooded ahead, you'll never get past. We're turning back traffic already. You take your missus back to the town there, only a mile or two, you'll not get to London tonight.'

'Well, you're my witness. I did try to get you home!' Johnny laughed goodnaturedly as he reversed the car and was waved on by the policeman in the sheets of rain.

'What will we do?' Elizabeth asked. She wished she could take everything as casually and cheerfully as Johnny did. Already her mind was racing with problems. What would Father say when she didn't turn up? Should she telephone him now before he left the bank? What time would she get back tomorrow? How could she explain about missing her lectures? Might Mr Worsky think that she and Johnny were just having a good time flitting about the country in his van?

'Have a meal and find somewhere to stay I suppose,' Johnny said.

The small hotel had a fire and a bar. Johnny carried in their two bags and talked to the receptionist while Elizabeth warmed her hands over the flames. He came back and put his arm around her.

'We're in luck, they have a room.'

The woman with the large key in her hand looked at Elizabeth's gloveless and ringless hands.

'Do you and your wife care to go up now and see the room?' she asked with a smirk that made Elizabeth feel so angry she didn't even care about the red flush she felt creeping over her face.

'No, I'm sure it's fine,' Johnny said lightly, 'we'll have a drink if we may, seeing that we're residents, and Elizabeth wants to use the telephone.'

In a few minutes of merciful privacy, Elizabeth got through to the bank. Her father hated being disturbed at work for what he considered trivia. Brusque and irritated, he said that he understood, fine, fine, he'd see her tomorrow then. Goodbye. No regrets, no sympathy at her being caught by flooding, no enquiries about her visit to Preston, no hint that he might have missed her.

No way of knowing that his daughter had one of the major decisions in her life ahead of her in the next few minutes.

She stood longer than she needed, clutching the receiver in the dark little box, wondering what to do now. It must be her own fault, she must have given Johnny the impression that she slept with men and that it would be in order to book them a double room. If she was going to be adamant and refuse his suggestion, then the grown-up thing would be to do it immediately ... the longer she left it the more awkward it would become.

Johnny was sitting at a table with a beer, and a shandy.

'I thought this is what you'd like,' he said, smiling up at her, hoping that he had made the right choice.

'Yes,' Elizabeth said. They were in a corner away from everyone. The chintzy little lounge bar of the hotel might fill up later with local ladies drinking port and lemon; through the door the bar with its dartboard stood dark and empty in the afternoon of winter. Nobody could hear them. There would be no public scene.

'Yes,' Elizabeth said again. 'A shandy's fine, but Johnny about the room. I must tell you. . . .'

'Oh sweet Elizabeth, I was just going to tell *you*. It's got two beds, and it's half the price of two rooms, and she doesn't have two rooms. She said she had just one room left before I said anything so. . . .'

'Yes, but. . . .'

'So there wasn't a chance for me to say "May I consult the lady?" ' He looked not at all upset, just as if he had to explain something that was self-evident. 'And I'll turn my back when you're putting on your nightie and you promise not to peek at me.'

'But. . . .'

'We'll be yards away from each other – we were only a few yards away from each other last night and neither of us got carried away.'

Elizabeth laughed in spite of herself.

'No, that's true,' she agreed.

'Well.' The problem was solved for Johnny.

Elizabeth looked into her glass. If she were to make further protests it would appear as if she thought that Johnny was hopelessly besotted by her and was planning to seduce her. Since he said this wasn't on his mind, it would be arrogant and even pathetic of her to keep up this insistence on a room of her own. But suppose, suppose that there was actually a game involved, and that her agreeing to go to the same room meant agreeing much more. . . .

Johnny said he had to telephone Mr Worsky, he'd be back in a moment. Did Elizabeth want to change? There was a bathroom at the end of the corridor apparently but if a bath was needed you had to ask the lady at the desk and she would get someone to turn on the geyser.

He was gone.

Elizabeth ran upstairs, and changed her blouse. She gave herself an icy wash and examined her face nervously at the bathroom mirror, which was speckled where the bits of mercury or silver had peeled off. She wasn't at all pleased with what she saw. Her hair was so straight, and so pale and colourless. It wasn't blonde like real blondes are blonde yellow-and-gold, it was white, almost as if she were an old woman or an albino. And her face. Oh Lord, why were some people's faces the same colour all over when her face was patchy with great pools of red and valleys of white?

With her hands on her waist she looked critically at what she could see of her figure. It was very awkwardly shaped, she decided. Her breasts were small and pointy, she didn't have that nice swell, that sort of 'S' shape that made people raise their eyebrows at each other. In fact she looked like a tall schoolgirl instead of a woman.

With a mixture of relief and disappointment she realised that Johnny couldn't possibly have had any designs on her. Thank heavens she hadn't made a silly fuss.

They had fish and chips in the fish shop up the street. It had looked much more inviting than the hotel dining room even though they did have to run to it through the sheets of rain.

193

They talked about what Mr Worsky would say to each item they had got, and what Elizabeth would do next Saturday in the shop, and why Harry and Violet didn't have any nice furniture, why it was all modern and new and cheap. They talked about Johnny's mother who *did* have nice furniture, but who wasn't warm and welcoming. She'd never put herself out to have a visitor to the house, she just expected her son to be there all the time and sniffed disappointedly when he was not.

Elizabeth told him about Monica and *her* mother, and the complicated lies she had to tell when she went off with chaps. Monica had to keep a small notebook so that she did not get caught out. Johnny said that he thought Monica was very silly; she should tell her mother straight out that she was going to live her own life and she hoped that they could all be friends while she was living it. Then all she would have to put up with was a few sniffs.

'It's different for girls, you see,' Elizabeth said.

'Yes . . . so they keep saying,' Johnny agreed.

They ran back in the rain, and because they had had an early start decided that they should go to bed. Or go *to sleep*, as they kept calling it.

'Do you think we should go back and let you get to sleep, you've a long day tomorrow, the drive back, and unpacking, then college?' Johnny said.

'Yes, I think I will sleep now,' Elizabeth said.

She sat on the side of her bed, the one where she had already put her blue nightdress under the pillow. There was heavy, purple-flocked wallpaper and a huge, ugly dressing table. A small, narrow wardrobe with no room for clothes stood filled with extra blankets and smelling of moth balls. There was one small, white chair; they would both have to put their clothes on that. Elizabeth examined her feet ruefully.

'They got awfully wet, I'll have to go and wash them.' They felt like two little blocks of ice after the cold water, and she had splashed herself all over as well just in case Johnny did . . . well, it would be awful to smell of fish and chips.

She put on her nightie in the bathroom and, peering left

and right before she emerged, she decided it was safe to scamper back to their room. Johnny hadn't used the tactful opportunity to get undressed, he was sitting reading the paper on the ugly white chair.

Elizabeth hopped quickly into bed and held the sheets around her chin in an exaggerated imitation of someone shivering.

'I knew you'd try to have your way with me and make me come in and warm you up,' Johnny laughed pleasantly, still turning the pages of the paper.

Elizabeth felt her neck and face go scarlet. 'No, of course I didn't, I wasn't. . . .'

He stood up and yawned. 'I'm only teasing you, sweetheart,' he said. He bent and gave her a kiss on the cheek. 'Here, have a look at this and become informed about the world.'

Grateful to have something to do while her embarrassed flushes died down, Elizabeth turned on her side away from him and tried to take in something, anything, on the sports page which was what she had opened. . . .

She heard the creak of his bed, and again, relief mixed with a curious sense of defeat swept over her. Naturally, of course, it would be ridiculous to *want* to make love, suppose she became pregnant, suppose it hurt and she were to bleed all over the hotel bed, suppose she wasn't able to do it, suppose he then turned aside and refused to have anything to do with her, which is what the nuns had told them in Kilgarret? If a man is allowed to have his way with a girl he will not respect her, he will have nothing more to do with her, he would not like his own sisters to behave in this way. . . .

'Shall I put the light out or do you want to finish the paper?'

She looked at him and smiled.

'No, I'm so tired, I can't really understand it, I think I'll stop fighting it and go to sleep. . . .'

He put his hand out of his bed and reached for hers. She gave it to him.

'You're a great little companion, it's been a smashing trip.

Night love.' He turned out the light and turned over in his bed. Elizabeth heard eleven o'clock strike, and midnight, on the town hall clock, and some time before one the storm rattled against the windows so much that it woke Johnny from his even sleep.

'Hey, are you awake?' he asked.

'Yes, it's a horrible storm.'

'Are you frightened of it?'

'No, not at all. No. Of course not.'

'Pity,' he yawned. 'I hoped you were. I'm terrified of it, of course.'

'Silly,' she giggled.

He lit a match to look at his watch. 'Oh, that's great, hours more sleep.'

'Yes,' said Elizabeth. She could hear him sitting up, and swinging his legs out of bed. He leaned over and held her hand.

'Are you all right?' he asked.

'Oh yes,' she said in a little squeak. In the dark he stood up; she felt him sit on her bed. Her heart was nearly coming through her rib cage.

'Give me a little hug,' he said. She reached up and found him without seeing him. He held her very tightly.

'I'm very fond of you, you're a lovely little girl,' he said. She said nothing. 'Very fond of you.' He was stroking her hair and her back, in long strokes. She felt very safe. 'And you're very very lovely.' She clung to him even more tightly, he was moving her gently back on the pillow; soon she would be lying down.

'I'm not very. . . .'

'We won't do anything unless you want to . . . if you want to we can do anything. . . .'

'You see. . . .'

'You're very, very lovely.' He stroked on and on and she couldn't really find the right words. 'I'd like to be very, very close to you.'

'But you see. . . .'

'There'll be no problem about that, I'll take great care. . . .'

196

'But I never. . . .'

'I know, I know, I'll be very gentle . . . but only if you want to.' Silence. He stroked her and held her to him. 'Do you want to love me, Elizabeth, do you want to be very close to me . . . ?'

'Yes,' she said.

He was gentle, and it didn't matter that she didn't know what to do, he knew enough it seemed. It didn't hurt so much as it was uncomfortable. It wasn't all those piercing pains you heard about in giggled conversations, and it certainly wasn't all that soaring joy either, but Johnny seemed very happy. He lay on her, his head on her breasts and his arms around her.

'You're a lovely little girl, Elizabeth, you made me very happy.'

She held him in the dark, she pulled the covers over him and she heard the town hall clock strike two. She must have missed three, but she heard it again at four o'clock, and she thought of Aisling and how they had wondered which of them would be the first to Do It, and now Elizabeth had won. Or perhaps she hadn't won. After all, she didn't think she was going to write and describe this. It was too important, you couldn't put it on paper, it would sound disloyal and cheap. Instead of love, which is what it was.

IX

Dear Elizabeth,

That was a great book altogether, you always find marvellous presents, you have so much imagination. I'm sending you this scarf ... it's awful I know, but Kilgarret's a far cry from London and you know there's nothing to buy here. Mam and Daddy loved the book too, they said you were very clever to find all those old pictures of Ireland in one book. I love the old ones, when Dunlaoghaire was still Kingstown ... a lot of people, like the Grays and those, still call it Kingstown of course.

Honestly, there's not much to say about the way things are. You'd have to come over yourself and see. I don't *feel* nineteen. I always thought that when I'd be nineteen I'd be different, I'd be a different shape, my face would be thinner and more knowing. I thought I'd have a different life ... and know a lot different people than when I was young. But it all seems to be more of the same thing.

Well, I suppose I have changed a bit. I can't stand that Ned Barrett near me. I think I've practised all he knows anyway and I'll have to find someone who knows a bit more. From my desk here in the office I can see the bus come in, and twice a day I look at it hopefully in case somebody exciting will step off and book into the hotel. Isn't that pathetic for a grown-up woman in the middle of the twentieth century? Do you remember this time five years ago when we were fourteen and I got my period on my birthday and you didn't, and we thought you were abnormal and Mam had to sort us out? I don't know that being over-normal has done me any good. I wish you'd tell me something about your own life and who you practise on and everything. I feel it would be hard to talk to you. Mam says that's ridiculous, it would take five minutes and we'd be cackling like young geese the way we used to.

It all seems a long time ago. Thanks again for the book. Joannie says the plates in it are so nice I could have them framed but I don't think so, it's nicer as a book. I hope it didn't cost a lot of money. The scarf seems a mean kind of present.

Love from Aisling

Dear Aisling,
I loved the scarf. No, I'm not being polite. Mr Worsky said it made me look very glamorous when I wore it this morning in the shop. I never thought of getting anything red because my face gets so red when I blush I thought the two would clash. Perhaps I blush less nowadays. Anyway it looks super, and I wore it under a cream coloured blouse and I thought I looked *très snob*.

Yes, it is hard isn't it, the letters? I don't suppose either of us really believes that the other would be interested in long details of what goes on each day. I am interested because I know Kilgarret and even though it's so long I can still remember it . . . and whose shop was next to whose shop. I don't know where your office is. Is it in the eyrie beside Aunt Eileen? It can't be, you wouldn't be able to see the bus from there, so where is it? I didn't know your friend Joannie Murray was back. I thought she was at a finishing school abroad. You don't mention Donal. Does that mean he's well again? You don't tell me anything about Maureen's baby, you just said it was a boy. You're an aunt.

Really, I'd tell you about things here, but you don't know Mr Worsky or his lady friend, who now asks me to call her Anna, even though she's about seventy, or Johnny Stone who's the nice partner now of Mr Worsky. He's wonderful fun. And since you never even met Father, I can't tell you about this simply awful woman who has designs on him. I'd love Father to get married of course, but this woman is the end. Father can't bear her and he doesn't know how to get her out of the bridge circle.

And Mother's letters sound a bit funny from time to time. She writes a lot, but odd kinds of things, all about the past. She even forgot my birthday. I'm not complaining, but it does seem odd, I mean, she has only one daughter. Aunt Eileen never forgets and she has five children and a grandchild.

College is smashing at the moment too. We have a lot of classes out in the open because of the weather . . . and it's so marvellous to go into a park, twelve of us with easels and all our stuff and set up like real artists to paint a view or a clump of trees. The others are very easy-going. I do have friends, like Kate and Edward and Lionel . . . I'm sure I've mentioned them to you in letters. Sometimes they have parties in Kate's flat. She has a whole three-room flat of her own, because her parents are dead and her guardian thinks that this is what people should have. Imagine!

But I don't go to many of the things people organise in college. I find the dances a bit dreary. I prefer just talking to people and about things I'm interested in, I suppose. I remember Aunt Eileen once told me that we have to pretend to be interested in some things out of kindness to other people. I do that with Father and Mother so I'm not going to do it in my own life as well.

I spend a lot of time in Mr Worsky's shop I suppose. I drop in after college, or I go down there on my bike after Father's supper. Now that Johnny is a partner there's a lot of changes and little improvements, and sometimes there are four of us because Mr Worsky's friend Anna (aged seventy I swear) joins in. It's a bit like a family I should imagine, and yet none of us is related to any of the others. Isn't that odd?

Love and thank you again for the scarf. It makes me look jaunty. That's what Johnny Stone said.

Elizabeth

Eileen always reminded the family of Elizabeth's birthday each May. She even organised separate birthday cards so that Eamonn, Donal and Niamh could sign them. This year Eamonn had mutinied.

'Mam, I'm far too old now to be sending silly cards with flowers and horseshoes on them to some woman in England that I can hardly remember.'

'Elizabeth White was reared in this house with you for five years like a sister, and you'll remember her as long as I say so,' said Eileen sharply.

'But Mam, she's gone for years and years. I was only a child when she was here. I'm grown-up now, she'll think I'm sweet on her or something. It's ludicrous.'

'I buy the card, I post it. I remember the date. I'm asking you to put your great ham hand around a pen and write two lines and your thick, ignorant signature,' snapped Eileen.

'It's just sentimentality,' grumbled Eamonn. 'If anyone knew this here, I'd be the laughing stock of the town.'

Donal wrote a long piece about how much he had liked the book of watercolours that Elizabeth had sent. He wrote so much that Eileen had to get him an extra piece of paper to add to the card. Niamh wrote a long garbled and almost unfathomable account of school life, studded with characters of whom Elizabeth would never have heard, nuns who were new to the school, friends who had been toddlers when Elizabeth left. Maureen wrote a lengthy description of Baby Brendan, or Brendan Og as he was called in that household to distinguish him from his dadda. Peggy put her name on a card and Eileen wrote a long letter describing the changes and the happenings in the small town. It was Eileen who told Elizabeth about Aisling's new office – just inside the door, a smart raised area where she was away from the herd but still part of it enough to join in if she wanted to. Eileen explained that Joannie Murray had come back from her finishing school and was waiting to go to Dublin for this marvellous job in a wine importer's. Because she was a lady of leisure, she used to come into O'Connor's Hardware and try to distract Aisling. But Eileen wrote with pride that Elizabeth would be glad to know that Miss O'Connor, as she was now called in the shop, had explained that work was work, and indeed young Joannie Murray's brother Tony had come into the shop one day and said the very same thing.

It was Eileen who explained that they didn't see too much of Maureen and Brendan and little Brendan Og because the Daly family were very possessive and liked to be in charge. Eileen said that this would sort itself out later . . . there were a lot of old women in that family, aunts and cousins, and the trouble was they hadn't half enough to do just looking after hens and turkeys so they wanted to own the new arrival body and soul. It would all change when Brendan Daly's other brothers and sisters married and had children, which would take the pressure off Maureen.

Eileen wrote that Donal's chest was still weak, that he had to be very careful of himself, not to get overtired or to catch a chill, but that thank God he was far better than they could ever have hoped at times and he was a grand, handsome fifteen-year-old. He was tall too, nearly as tall as Elizabeth had been when she had gone back to England when she was fifteen. He could reach to the top shelf of the bookcase in the sitting room without standing on his toes. Eileen wrote that Peggy was walking out with a very nice fellow called Christy O'Brien. He worked on a farm out near Brendan Daly's father's place. Eileen half hoped for Peggy's sake that a match would be made – Peggy was in her thirties and hadn't had any great chances – but selfishly she hoped that the Christy fellow would tire of her which would mean that Peggy would stay.

Elizabeth thought to herself sometimes that if she had to rely on Aisling as an informant about Kilgarret she might well believe that all life had ceased there the day she left.

The nuns had been wrong, Elizabeth discovered to her great relief. Johnny *did* still respect her afterwards. Not only did he respect her, he seemed to like her a lot more, and she felt grown-up and proud and confident with him. When they had driven back to London, still through sheets of rain, he seemed more cheerful and happy than ever. Watching his face as he drove, Elizabeth wondered how he could talk so easily and lightly about the funny old farmer who had let him shoot the rabbits, about the way they were going to have a bandage up the inside of the van to stop it leaking, and what Mr Worsky would say about the treasures they had ferried back. Elizabeth knew he must be thinking all the time about their making love and thought he was very cool and calm to be able to talk about other things. She was relieved at this too and talked cheerfully in return rather than dwelling on the events of the night before. This pleased him she could see, and from time to time he pattered her hand and said, 'You are a little darling, you know?'

Nobody at college noticed that she had lost her virginity. Kate asked her had she had a nice weekend, and told her about an awful party where somebody had stolen neat alcohol from a laboratory and everyone had drunk it in lemonade and been very ill.

Father hadn't noticed any change in her either. He had been fussed and anxious because that tiresome Mrs Ellis had wanted to come around and help with the preparations for the bridge party and he had told her his daughter would be there. Now his daughter had turned out to be late home from the North, late back from college and was doing only the most perfunctory of suppers.

'But this is my night for entertaining. You always arrange sandwiches and . . . savouries,' Father began to whine.

'Father, this is indeed your night, and you can make your own savouries and sandwiches. I have biscuits, and a small amount of cheese there. There's bread in that tin, and butter in the larder. It's your night to do it.'

'But that's not what we agreed. . . .'

'How could anyone agree anything with you Father? Answer me that. How could anyone make any possible kind of bargain about anything? I have just come back from my first visit to your wife. Your ex-wife. The woman you married twenty years ago . . . and presumably you loved her then and she loved you. But what have you asked me about her? Not one thing. Mother could be lying in a fever hospital breathing her last for all you care. Mother could be wretchedly unhappy. She could be a million things. But no

203

enquiry from you. At least she asked how you were, and Harry did, and they wanted to know how your life went on. But you don't have it in your cold heart to ask one question about them.'

She was near tears.

Father sat down. 'This is uncalled for,' he said, looking like a schoolboy who is forced to accept a punishment without knowing what the crime was.

'Give me the bloody bread and I'll butter it for you. I'll cut off the crusts, and I'll leave the tray ready. . . .'

'But you are going to serve it aren't you . . . ?'

'You really are the limit. I never understood what Mother meant by a cold fish until now. I really didn't.'

'I knew that Violet and that man would turn you against me. I knew that's what they had in their minds when they made all that fuss about inviting you to stay.'

Elizabeth looked at him in disbelief and unexpectedly she began to cry. Through her fingers she tried not to see Father moving the bread away lest it become damp with her tears and unsuitable for sandwiches.

Mr Worsky noticed. He was the only one. He saw a change in Elizabeth and felt sure he knew the reason. She talked as if she were part of a family with himself and Anna Strepovsky at the head of it, and Johnny as the heir-apparent. Elizabeth talked as if she were marrying into a royal house. Stefan Worsky laughed to himself at his fanciful imagery but really that is what it was like.

'Mr Worsky, I wonder if you thought about having a new sign painted for the shop? You know we do lettering at the college and the teachers are always looking for a real job to do. . . . I was saying to Johnny last night that something in gold leaf might be nice . . . did he tell you? No? Well I don't want to be intrusive with my ideas. . . .'

And another time.

'Johnny and I were going to paint the name of your shop on the car. Would you like that or do you prefer to be more discreet? Johnny bet me two shillings one way, but I won't tell you which he said.'

He had confided his suspicions to Anna Strepovsky but she had snorted at him and said he was full of imagination.

'It's typical of a man to think that because a woman looks happy it can only be because she has been pleasured by a man.'

Mr Worsky wasn't prepared to argue about principles and beliefs but he was prepared to wager any money that he was right about Elizabeth.

Elizabeth was full of worries about what would happen next. Whether Johnny might want to try it again, and if so where and when? And should she appear enthusiastic, or should she try to go along with the theory that the one night in the hotel had been an isolated happening? She wondered too about contraception. Johnny had said that he had looked after that side of it and there would be no danger. She wasn't experienced enough to know quite what he meant but presumably it meant that there were no little sperms inside her which might prove fertile, because he had organised it so that they would be on the hotel sheet instead. Her face still burned at the thought of whoever had to make that bed next day, but it would have been so unromantic and wrong to have tried to wash the sheet herself at the time.

He had said to her that night that next time he would 'get something' and she had nodded peacefully, yet there had been no talk of a next time. But Johnny had been utterly delightful and had seemed overjoyed when she called in on her way home from lectures and even skipped the whole of Friday afternoon's classes to see how the new acquisitions looked once they had been polished and arranged for the Saturday business.

'I'll take you out to the cinema tomorrow night if you're free,' Johnny had said. 'And then you can come back to my place and I'll cook you a Johnny Stone special.'

She smiled back at him.

'I'd love that. Will it be rabbit?'

'No sweetheart, nothing as good, but it might be a Spam special. Will that be all right?'

She nodded happily.

'Oh, Tom and Nick won't be there. They'll be going away for the weekend,' he added casually, 'so we'll have the place to ourselves and we won't be interrupted by their larking about.'

'I see.' Elizabeth saw. And was happy at what she saw. She used her savings to buy a very pretty slip the following morning, she put a toothbrush, toothpaste and talcum powder in her handbag and told her father that she was going to the cinema and to a party afterwards. She would possibly be very late. He accepted it with the same air of defeat that he seemed to accept everything. She had her own key so there would be no problems. Oh, and could Father leave the kitchen nice and tidy in case someone drove her home from the party and she invited them in for cocoa?

Father didn't even say he hoped she would have a good time.

Tom and Nick didn't go away nearly often enough. Tom worked in a motor salesroom and Nick in a travel agency. They were both flattering to Elizabeth and considered her to be Johnny's latest. A phrase which was beginning to annoy her. When it changed to Johnny's girl she began to feel more secure. They were forever making mockingly gallant remarks in front of her.

'If ever you grow tired of this lady, Johnny, be sure to let me know. I could sure step into your shoes. . . .'

Each of the boys had their own bedroom in the big Earls Court flat. But even though it would have been perfectly feasible, it was never suggested that Elizabeth should stay when the other flatmates were there. It was something to do with treating her as a lady and protecting her reputation, Elizabeth thought. She knew she could have a great laugh with Aunt Eileen about such a double standard . . . but then remembering with a shock that of course she could have no such thing. Aunt Eileen would have disapproved strongly. Her wise tolerance, her almost boundless understanding for every kind of situation would not have included this. Elizabeth realised that Aunt Eileen would have spoken very directly.

'What you are doing is wrong. It's silly, irresponsible and wrong. God invented marriage for a very good reason. So that two people could work out the best kind of life possible together, protected by rules . . . by laws, by what the people around you agree is right. You and this boy are being very silly and playing dangerous games. If he really likes you as much as you think he does, and as much as you like him, then why doesn't he do the normal thing . . . why doesn't he tell you this, and tell your mother and father, and propose that you get married? Why does he sneak you in and out of his flat like a criminal, like a common girl . . . ?'

Aunt Eileen never said these words, but they were as clear to Elizabeth as if she had. They were an amalgam of attitudes and other warnings and chastisements and all that had gone before.

But she shook herself firmly. She was a grown-up woman of nineteen. She lived in London, not a backwater like Kilgarret. She didn't have all the Roman Catholic fears about sin and modesty and immodesty and purity and impurity. People didn't think like that in the real world. Aunt Eileen was just old-fashioned. She was a great person but old-fashioned.

Sometimes Elizabeth was able to invite Johnny to Clarence Gardens, not that Father ever went away for the night. But there were always the afternoons. Johnny often did deliveries and had the van at his disposal during the daytime. Elizabeth was often able to sneak away from a lecture or a practical class. They surrounded it with excitement . . . a picnic lunch in the kitchen, a double bolt drawn across the front door just in case the impossible happened and Father came home from the bank before twenty-three minutes past six in the evening. Up to Elizabeth's bedroom where the bed was small but the light was romantic and some of the harsher blues had been replaced by a style of her own choosing.

Johnny had once made a gesture towards the more comfortable main bedroom by an inclination of his head, but Elizabeth without words was able to convey that this was not to be considered. She loved him so utterly now she felt that she could talk to him and understand him without either of them having to speak in sentences. He too was delighted with her warmth and responsiveness. She was a little darling in every way, he told her over and over.

Sometimes as they lay in her tiny bed on an afternoon with the curtains drawn and the companionably shared cigarette passed between them, she felt as if she had never known such happiness; but always she knew that there was a step over which she must not cross. She must not ask him to swear love to her, she mustn't ask him to tell her that he was going to be forever faithful. She must hint at nothing more permanent than what they had. That way he was happy and loving, that way no shadow crossed his face.

Sometimes he spoke of people who had broken the rules.

Tom had a girlfriend, a nice little poppet she had been, but an engagement ring had been high on her list of priorities, and she kept taking him home to meet Mother.

'Oh dear, I took you home to meet Mother,' said Elizabeth archly.

'Ah yes, but you didn't do it with a gleam in your eye,' Johnny had laughed.

He had bought awful contraceptives in little packets, things which looked totally unsuitable until they were actually put on, which seemed to be an irritation and a nuisance to him. Elizabeth wondered what she could do to circumvent this. She didn't want to rely on the safe period which she knew only too well was the method of contraception which had ensured such enormous families all over Ireland. Kate and some of the other girls at college had said that the safe period was a dangerous period. It didn't exist.

'But isn't there anything a woman can do?' she asked Kate, feeling foolish.

Kate said there were a lot of things and described them all very graphically but they seemed much worse to Elizabeth than the rubber contraceptives so she left things as they were. Johnny never seemed to think that there was anything else she should do so she supposed it was just what everyone else had to put up with.

He told her little more about himself in those intimate

times. His mother he spoke of jokingly, he wasn't close to his brother either, he had not even the mildest wonder as to where his father might be, and whether any step-brothers or sisters existed.

When his mother wrote cheerful, inconsequential letters he seemed pleased and told Elizabeth some of the things she said. When she wrote about how lonely she felt and how hard it was to have two ungrateful sons, he just dismissed her.

'Querulous old demon,' he said without the slightest concern.

'Shall I ever meet her? Will you take me to see her?' Elizabeth asked once. It had been a mistake.

'What for?' Johnny began to frown.

'Oh I don't know, to tell her to stop being a querulous old demon and irritating her handsome son,' she laughed, trying to retrieve things.

It worked.

'Yeah, why not? We'll go some time,' said Johnny.

Father had given Elizabeth a jewellery box for her nineteenth birthday. He had actually gone to Mr Worsky's shop and asked Johnny's advice about a gift. He had met Johnny half a dozen times and believed him to be a nicely spoken young chap who was now a partner in Mr Worsky's business which-must-under-no-circumstances-be-called-a-second-hand-shop.

He said he would like a surprise gift and wanted to pay about thirty shillings or two pounds at the most. Johnny steered him towards an antique box saying it was a snip at thirty shillings. Father grunted that it seemed a lot to pay for an empty box but took it. Johnny put the extra nine pounds into the till so that Mr Worsky should not be cheated on the lovely carved casket, and he bought a little marcasite clip with a bluebird in it as his own gift.

Elizabeth, knowing the value of the casket, was touched and amazed that Father had spent so much on her present. In no way did Johnny diminish the gift for her. Johnny had helped her to find the book of watercolours for Aisling also.

Together they had looked through them and she had told him about the Wicklow mountains, and the river Slaney in Wexford and the old houses half falling down but beautiful with perfect Georgian doors, and covered with creeper.

'Perhaps you and I should go over and take a van each. Stefan would have to buy a new showroom when we came back. Hey, that's not a bad idea. Maybe we'll do that in the summer. We could take the van to the boat and then hire another van when we're there. What do you think? And we could go to see your friends, these O'Connors, you're always saying you wanted to go back. Hey? Why not?'

'Oh yes.'

'You're not enthusiastic, you've always said you'd love to go back.'

'Yes, no, I am.'

'Well then?'

'Sure, maybe in the summer some time.'

She was hesitant. She didn't want to say that she didn't want to go back like this. Back as a hustler going into people's houses and taking away their old treasures, into homes where she had been welcomed as a little refugee during the war. She didn't want to go now all grown-up and hard and sophisticated and knowing the price of things and making a profit. She could never say to Johnny that it looked shabby somehow to go back to Kilgarret with a chap but no Understanding . . . when Maureen had been having an Understanding with Brendan Daly, and the hopes that Peggy would have an Understanding with her Christy. But that's exactly what Elizabeth would like to have now . . . an Understanding. She would like to know where she stood with Johnny and unless she did she would not like to present him to her other home in Kilgarret.

Everyone agreed that Aisling was making a totally un-expected success of her new job in O'Connor's Hardware. Much of it was due to the way that Eileen had paved the way for her . . . but Aisling never realised that. She assumed it had all been due to her own strength of character. Before she began as an employee, Eileen had insisted that there should be special quarters in the shop for both the children. Sean thought that this was ridiculous nonsense and told her so forcefully.

'But can't you see that they want to believe there is a real place for them there, that it's proper work? If Eamonn just thinks he's your dogsbody and Aisling thinks she's helping me out . . . what pride will they have in it?'

'What pride will they have? Won't they have the pride and satisfaction of having a business built up for them? That's what they will have. They won't be like half the children around here taking the emigrant ship. That's pride enough. No one asked you or me what pride we needed when we worked like dogs. . . .'

'Pride is the wrong word,' Eileen agreed. 'What I'm trying to do is let them think of home and work as separate, so that they won't cheek you, or answer me back like they would if we gave them an order here in the house.'

Gradually she won her way, a corner was cleared, painted and a door put on it and it became Eamonn's office; it was explained over and over that it was important for local farmers to know where they could find Eamonn, and that he should always be called by his first name since farmers didn't go for the 'Mr' bit. Look at the way they all called Sean 'Sean'; but Eileen was 'Mrs O'Connor', similarly Aisling would be 'Miss O'Connor'.

Aisling's office had a brand new typewriter, a real office chair and proper filing cabinet for the ledgers, the dockets and the paperwork. It wasn't like Eileen's eyrie where paper poked from every corner. It was modern and efficient just as she had been taught in the commercial school. In fact one of the commercial college teachers even took her own class of girls to see Aisling's work place as a model of efficient filing, which delighted Aisling and annoyed every other past pupil deeply.

Her smart green coats and her bustling air of importance gave her the necessary authority. Poor Jemmy, whose wits had grown no stronger and whose strength had grown less, called her Miss O'Connor.

'I don't mind Jemmy calling me Aisling, he's known

me since I was a baby,' Aisling confided to Mam on the first day.

'No, he's quite happy calling you Miss.'

'But Mam, you know with him being not all there, I don't want to be putting on airs for poor Jemmy.'

'No child, you're not. He's happy to do what everyone else does. Just be polite to him always, and especially in front of people. That's what really pleases him.'

Aisling remembered her mother always consulting Jemmy.

'Where do you think we might have put those new lampshades, Jemmy? You remember, the ones that came in last week.' Jemmy would stop sweeping the floor and say,

'Gor, I don't know Mam, maybe they're in the back.'

'I think you're right Jemmy, thanks a lot, that's where they must be.'

For years Aisling had been aware of conversations like these, mildly irritating, mildly mystifying. Why ask poor Jemmy? Now she knew why. Mam was much cleverer than she gave the impression of being.

For the first few weeks Eileen explained the complicated workings of their credit arrangements. She showed Aisling the wages book, the bank pass book, the ledger for supplies and the income tax arrangements. She listened attentively while Aisling worked out neater, clearer and more efficient ways of recording their daily administration.

Sometimes the errors, the gaps and the confusions seemed pathetic and elementary to Aisling.

'Oh Mam, can't you see, you've been doubling the work by not having an alphabetical index? It'll only take half the time to look them up now. I can't see why you didn't set one up. It'll only take a couple of days.'

Eileen agreed that it had been a serious lapse. She didn't say that she had little time to set up alphabetical indexes while she was running the shop with Sean, keeping an eye on customers, deciding who to give credit to and who to hurry for bills, pleading with bank managers for further overdrafts, running a house with a wayward maid and six children. Instead of listing all that she had to do, while any fool could have been working out an alphabetical system, she praised Aisling to the skies and said that maybe they should send to Dublin for a proper ledger book with alphabetical indentations.

'Why would we do that, can't I do one myself at home this evening?' Aisling said.

'No work home from the office. If you worked in Murray's or in the hotel we'd be mad with them if they got you to do work at home.'

'Mam you're great, but sure what else would I be doing?'

'You could be going out and casting a cool eye over the men of this town to see if there's any of them good enough for you.'

'Mam I've told you a dozen times, I'm not cut out for men, and even if I were, there's nothing in this town, it's the end of the barrel as regards men.'

'So you say.'

'Honestly Mam, if I think the time has come, I'll go up to Dublin and make an assault on the place, but there's nobody here you'd be seen dead with.'

Joannie said that there were great men altogether in Dublin. But it was hard to know what Joannie meant these days by great men. She said that they had cars and they wore suits and had coffee in places on Grafton Street and sat in Stephen's Green and went to the races.

'And what do they do for a living, like where do they go to work?'

'I don't know that they do,' Joannie admitted, the thought not having come to her before.

'But how have they got the money? Are they rich men or what?'

'I think a lot of them are students, or they work for their fathers or something.'

'I work for my father,' said Aisling proudly. 'And you wouldn't find me sitting around in coffee shops talking to people all day.'

'That's because there are no coffee shops and nobody to talk to here,' said Joannie.

'I suppose you're right.'

Joannie was very unsatisfactory at explaining what she was up to. The days when they could giggle and find interest in the most trivial encounters seemed to have gone. Aisling thought it must all be all Joannie's fault because she was being so deliberately vague and concealing about her activities. But then she thought Elizabeth too was being distant and wasn't willing to write openly in the way that they used to talk when she was here in Kilgarret. Perhaps that's what happened as you got older, you stopped giggling. Mam didn't have any real friends to talk to. Perhaps when you grew up you had to stop telling people things and begin play-acting. Look at Maureen, for example, stuck out with all those desperate Dalys. She couldn't really like it. She must hate all Brendan's awful sisters and aunts and the whole tribe. Friendships must only be for young people. Niamh had a friend now and they'd drive you mad, Niamh and Sheila Moriarty, screaming with laughter at nothing.

Look at Mam's friendship with Elizabeth's mother . . . that hadn't lasted and Mam said they were the best of pals for years at school. It was probably a sign of being grown-up to realise that friendships weren't important.

'You don't see so much of Joannie these days. You didn't fall out?' Tony Murray asked when he came into the shop to buy a length of flex one day.

'No, heavens no, but she's busy. She's got her friends in Dublin you know, and she'll be going there. I'm tied up here all day working and there's so little to do at night. It's a terrible town, isn't it Tony?'

'You used to come up to our house and make us laugh with your tall stories,' Tony said.

'I suppose I've got a bit more sense than to be telling tall stories now,' Aisling said.

'That'd be a pity.'

He dropped in a lot, and always a few words but no dallying with Aisling. Eamonn said one night that he thought Tony Murray must be going half-cracked because he used to come in for lengths of flex or boxes of nails and not care what he got, or remember that he might have got the same thing the day before.

'He's in a kind of dream half the time I think,' said Eamonn.

'I think he's keen on Aisling' said Donal.

Aisling put down her fork and screamed with laughter.

'Tony *Murray* keen on *me*? Have a heart, he's as old as a bush. He couldn't be fancying me surely.'

Sean was reading the paper. 'Quit making fun of the customers and don't start getting stupid ideas,' he said without letting his eyes leave the pages.

'I'm not getting any ideas Dad, it's Donal. Hey come on, what makes you think that, Donal?'

'I saw him looking at you on Sunday at mass, and he looked like people look when they're keen on someone.'

'What kind of look is that?' asked Eileen, amused.

'Like a sick bullock,' suggested Eamonn. . . .

'Like this,' said Niamh, clasping her hands and closing her eyes in a position of suppliance. 'Be mine, fair Aisling, be mine.'

'Or just pale and sick with internal anguish,' proposed Aisling.

'No,' said Donal. 'More looking at you during the sermon, and then afterwards when we were all talking outside, laughing at things you said and being over-interested in them.'

'You couldn't be over-interested in what I say!' said Aisling. 'In fact, most people are utterly fascinated by everything I say.'

'Jaysus,' said Eamonn.

'Stop that blaspheming at the table,' said Sean.

'And do you see anyone over-interested in what Eamonn's saying? Maybe you could spot a romance there too?' teased Aisling.

Donal took her seriously. 'No, but I wasn't really looking. I think some of the shop girls giggle and snatch his cap and run off with it after devotions on a Sunday.'

'Oh, is that why you're all so keen to go to devotions?' Eileen said. 'I thought it was for the love of the Sacred Heart.'

'It is a bit,' said Aisling, who liked dressing up and going to devotions herself. It was a social occasion, everyone hung around the church and talked afterwards.

'I see I'm demoted to shop girls, but Princess Aisling here has the eye of the merchant prince.'

Eamonn sounded mock gloomy, and everyone laughed.

'Wouldn't it be smashing if Tony Murray did fancy Aisling and they got married? We'd have lots more money and a gardener like the Murrays,' said Niamh.

'What would you want a gardener for? We've no garden, you eejit,' asked Eamonn.

'What do you want fixing me up with Tony Murray of all people?' wailed Aisling. 'Isn't he an old man, he's nearly thirty for God's sake. It's Mam and Dad's generation.'

But of course when she saw Tony Murray next night at the pictures she flounced and giggled and gave him come-on glances just to test whether Donal might have a grain of truth in his suspicions. To her surprise Tony Murray seemed to love it.

'Are you going to be here tomorrow night?' he asked.

'Is that a piece of general conversation, or is it a request?' she giggled.

'It's a request,' he said simply.

'You mean you're asking me?'

'I'm asking would you like to come to the pictures,' he said, having been manoeuvred into it.

'Well now, I accept,' she said.

'I'll meet you here then?'

They looked at the poster . . . *National Velvet*.

'That's great.' There was a silence.

'It should be good,' Tony said.

'Oh yes, it should indeed.'

'Lucky the programme changed.'

'Well it always does on Thursdays.'

'So it does,' said Tony Murray and they parted.

Aisling giggled the whole way home, when she had caught up on Judy Lynch and Annie Fitzpatrick.

216

'I've got a date tomorrow night. Tony Murray's going to pay for me going in to the pictures.'

They were very impressed.

Aisling wondered why he didn't have friends of his own age, and hoped that he wasn't abnormal or anything.

She told Mam about it and said wasn't it a scream that Donal was right?

'Just because he asked you to the pictures doesn't mean he's keen on you, and from the sound of what you said to him it seems to me that it was you who suggested the whole thing,' said Eileen in an unexpectedly stern voice.

'Mam, what is it? What are you so cross for? I was only having a bit of a laugh.'

'I'm sorry.' Eileen very rarely apologised even if she had been sharp. Aisling was amazed by this. 'Yes, you're right, I did sound a bit weaselish.' She took off her glasses. She had been reading when Aisling came in, Sean had gone to bed already. Mam looked tired.

'I don't know. I suppose I think that sometimes you don't realise how attractive you are, Aisling my love. You really are a lovely girl. You could well turn a man's head, and you're too silly still, you'd get your name up with his and then make a mess of it all.'

'But Mam, I tell you, it's only a joke. He's ancient, he could be my father.'

'Love, he's eleven years older than you if that. He's a single man. He's looking to settle down. He's not interested in going to balls and dances up in Dublin, he's drinking with the lads. His mother is very keen indeed for him to be settled – he's just the right age for it. Now do you see what I mean? For him it may not be a joke, so I'm annoyed with you getting your name up with his, all to no avail.'

'But what's getting my name up? It's like as if the banns were being read, Mam. You're making a mountain out of a molehill.'

'It's such a small town Kilgarret, you don't know how people love a chance to gloat.'

'But Mam, what's there to gloat over? They can't say I've

217

been thrown over by him can they, if I'm not the one who's serious about him?'

'No child. Of course they can't. Come on, let's turn out the lights and off to bed and stop all this nonsensical chatter.'

Dear Aisling,
Tell me more about Tony Murray. The last time he was mentioned in despatches was some incident where he found Joannie up to something which was never clearly explained either . . . but I thought he was very old, you know, like an uncle. But you've been to the pictures with him twice for six weeks. Is it a romance? Does he Make Suggestions as we used to say? I wish you'd tell me, I can keep a secret anyway, can't I? I'm miles away in a different country.

Mrs Ellis, the dreadful woman who has designs on Father, is really doing her best. It's Father's fiftieth birthday and she keeps saying that she'd like to organise a little party for 'your papa's half century'. In order to put her off, I said that I was organising a quiet family dinner at home and she had to be satisfied with that. Is Uncle Sean fifty? Did you have any do for that? A family dinner isn't much fun if Father and I are the only family, but maybe when he knows I've chased Mrs Ellis away from him he'll cheer up.

I see a lot of Johnny. It's hard to tell you about it really. I did try but I tore up the page, it sounded a bit like the pages of a mushy love story . . . when it's not like that in real life. I just like him a lot and he me . . . but we don't say I love you or anything. I could explain it more clearly if we met. You asked what he looks like. I think he looks a bit like Clark Gable but thinner and without the moustache. That sounds ridiculous but what I'm trying to say is that he's dark and very handsome, and people look at him a lot, but he doesn't seem to notice them. I'll tell you what happens about the party for Father. Love to everyone. I write to Aunt Eileen sometimes as you know, not secrets just ordinary letters . . . but I haven't for a while, everything's been so busy and complicated here. I hope she understands.

Love, Elizabeth

Dear Elizabeth,

Like Clarke Gable, I don't believe it! No wonder you're being quiet about him, you don't want to share him. I don't know why it's hard to tell what it's like. I know we're not good at writing, but now I'll change all that. I'll try to tell you what Tony is like. He's very old, he's thirty and he'll be thirty-one soon. He's been at university but he didn't do his degree. He's been in Limerick learning the business and now he runs Murray's here. He seems very keen on me. I don't know why. He puts his hand on the back of my neck and squeezes it, which is awful and he kisses me in the car and tries to put his tongue between my teeth but I don't encourage it. I let it happen by accident a bit. I don't like it much anyway.

He tells me I'm beautiful which I like to hear, and he comes and talks to Mam and Dad a lot too, so now everyone knows that he's Interested as they say. Dad doesn't know what to do, he's out of his depth. It wasn't like this with Brendan Daly because Brendan and all the Dalys are all old eejits as everyone knows. Tony Murray is what they call a catch here. Mam is very tight-lipped. She thinks I'm playing with his affections. Me! Aisling O'Connor playing with the affections of a catch who is as old as the hills. Anyway I don't feel much about him one way or the other. I'd like him better if he didn't look so silly, and pant and huff and puff so much in the car.

He certainly doesn't look like Clark Gable. He's fatter for a start. He's got black curly hair and he's sort of square-built. He's not bad-looking but he's certainly not like Clark Gable. Now I've told you everything, can't you sit down and tell me everything? I didn't tear up pages even though that bit about kissing looks a bit yucky.

Love, Aisling

Dear Aisling,
I will, I promise. In about two weeks' time. I'll write
everything. It's just that there's so much happening here.
I'm very taken up. Two weeks. Everything. Gory details,
nothing spared.
    Watch out for it.
Love Elizabeth

P.S. Do you love Tony Murray in any sort of way?

Father said that he didn't really want any celebrations for
his half century. Nothing much to celebrate, he said. This
annoyed Elizabeth greatly.

'You're the only father I've got and you're going to be half
a hundred. I think we should make a little fuss. Now here are
the options: I can take you out to a hotel and buy a bottle of
wine. I have a tiny savings account. I would be very glad to
do that, Father. Or we can have all your bridge people here
and make a party with some people from the bank too and
one or two neighbours. . . .'

'No, no, the bridge people wouldn't enjoy a party if we
didn't play bridge,' said Father.

'Right, it's just us,' said Elizabeth.

'But a hotel is very dear,' complained Father.

'Right, it's Saturday week. I'll ask Johnny to dinner here,
and we'll have wine and high-class food.'

'That would be very nice,' said Father, relieved that there
would be no need for him to do anything now except accept
what was put in front of him. He was mightily pleased that
he had managed to escape anything too festive.

'He's a nice chap, that Johnny Stone. He's good company.
I'd enjoy him coming to dinner,' he said.

Yes, thought Elizabeth, everyone enjoys Johnny Stone's
company. Now the hard part – asking him to dinner.

'You won't think I'm trying to cast a matrimonial net over
you if I ask you to do me a favour?'

They lay wrapped in sheets on the floor of Johnny's flat,
reading the Sunday papers and drinking milk with straws.

'Mm what . . . making noises like a woman trying to pin
me down?' he asked, still reading the paper.

'No, far from it, it's just that one night Father's going to be fifty, and there's nobody he really likes . . . so I thought I'd cook a special dinner . . . a White special . . . and would you come to keep the conversation going?'

Johnny looked up. 'Aw, no love, I'd be butting in. It's a family thing, a birthday.'

'Hell, you know how family Father and I are . . . very little traditional family love in our house. And we'd look silly the two of us. No, we need an outsider to make it festive. Do come sweetheart. Please.'

Johnny shook his head. 'No, honestly, I'd only be in the way. I'm no good on the formal sentimental thing . . . you know that I even hate going home for Christmas with the Old Lady because she wants ceremonies and everything.'

'But you were super with Mother and Harry.'

'But that's different, honeybunch. That was just a nice evening that developed. Not being asked formally or anything, you know, making a big thing.'

'Please Johnny. Please.'

He was reading the paper again. 'No, heart. I'd be out of place. I wouldn't like it.'

'Do you never do things you don't like?' Her voice sounded rather sharp.

He looked up, surprised, 'No, not often. Why?'

'I do, a lot of the time, so do most people. Please Johnny, just one night to please me, and to make Father happy.'

'No, dearest, ask another of your friends. Ask someone else.'

It was settled. He was not coming. He would not do her the favour, he wouldn't even consider it or discuss it. He assumed she had other friends, people as close as he was. He assumed that Kate and Edward and Lionel were on visiting terms.

She had to accept this in Johnny or demand more. But she had just been shown the door had been closed. There was no more being offered. If she asked for more, she would get nothing, and what she had already would be withdrawn. She had seen Lily, a one-time girlfriend, come into the shop. She still liked Johnny, and Johnny was unfailingly charming but Lily had failed the examination at an earlier time and could not take it again. Lily had made scenes when Johnny refused to come to her end-of-term dance in college . . . let Elizabeth be warned.

'Right ho,' she said cheerfully. 'Selfish bastard. Well, you'll miss a good dinner, that's for sure.'

She looked sunny and uncaring. There was no way he would know the hurt and rejection she felt. No way he could see from her laughing face that she had come to a depressing conclusion about her love for him. She knew now that it would have to be one-sided and full of pretence if it were to continue. Johnny wasn't going to meet anyone half-way or even a quarter of the way. You played the game in his territory and according to his rules.

She forced herself to read the paper with a smile fixed on her face. She knew he was looking at her.

'Come here, gorgeous,' he said, unwrapping the sheet. 'You're much too attractive a girl to be reading papers. You should be giving pleasure to a passing gentleman, so you should.'

She lay there happily and looked at the ceiling as his head lay peacefully on her bosom. He was dozing in the morning sun coming in the window. Soon they would get dressed and wander off to a pub on the river where he would get her a glass of shandy and they would eat their sandwiches.

She had passed the examination. She could have flounced off in tears, she could have begged still more and annoyed him, and she could have sulked, but he would have taken no notice and eventually he would have wandered off to lunch alone.

But no. Elizabeth had done none of these things and she had her reward here in her arms. He still loved her and wanted her. It was worth a few little sacrifices.

Tony Murray told Aisling that he would like her to think seriously about him one summer night when the car had steamed up with passion and pushing and advances and rejections and squirmings.

'I want you to know that I haven't ever met anyone else who attracts me as much as you do.'

222

'That's nice Tony, but I'm still not going to take off my bra,' said Aisling.

'I'm glad you're not. I know you aren't the kind of girl who would go with anyone, and I respect you for it,' he said, red-faced with exertion.

'Well, that's the way I am.'

She was puzzled because she had let him go much further than what she considered wise. Surely there had been times when she had gone far beyond the level that someone should go before marriage. After all, it was quite obvious even to someone as inexperienced as Aisling sadly agreed that she was that Tony was satisfying his base desires in all these grapplings . . . and the nuns had said that to be the instrument of that was leading a man into mortal sin.

Still, it would appear that Tony respected her.

'I'm finding it very hard to go on with these kind of . . . outings,' Tony said.

'Oh, I like going out with you,' Aisling said, deliberately misunderstanding him.

'No, I don't mean that. You know what I mean. I mean I like you so much I want to have you all to myself all the time. . . .'

Aisling decided that this was very near to a proposal of marriage. She looked at Tony's face for a moment, as if she and he were strangers.

He was attractive enough looking, she supposed. He had this thick-set neck, and nice dark eyes. Other girls had told her that he was handsome, she heard people refer to him as a fine man. She knew that Daddy would approve. . . . 'You'd be doing well if you married into the Murrays, girl,' he used to say half-jokingly, but she thought he meant it. Mam had her reservations, but only because she thought Aisling was too giddy.

Well I am too giddy, Aisling thought to herself with sudden conviction. And I'm not going to be railroaded into something I'm not sure about. I'm not going to let him ask me and have to say yes or no. I'm going to put it off, I'm going to be clever for once in my life.

She kissed him lightly on the forehead.

'You're a very attractive man, Tony Murray, and you say such nice things you nearly sweep me off my feet. But you're a grown-up, you know what you're doing. I don't, I'm only silly and young and I've never been anywhere.'

He began to speak but she interrupted him.

'I'm going to see a bit more of the world before I let myself fall for you . . . otherwise it would be pathetic. Look, you've been to university, you've lived away from home in Limerick and Dublin. You've been to France and to Rome. The furthest I've been is Dublin and spent a night in Dunlaoghaire . . . and that was with the whole family.

'No, if I want you to think anything of me, I'll have to grow up a bit, not just be the silly provincial Kilgarret girl. Then you'll be mad about me.'

'I fancy you now,' mumbled Tony.

Aisling had manoeuvred them to a sitting position as if by accident. This would mean that the fumbling and grappling could be considered at an end. . . .

'Yes, but wait until I'm sophisticated, then I'll be a magnificent prize,' she tinkled.

'I don't want you sophisticated.' He sounded mulish.

'You want me with a bit more sense and a bit more polish don't you? Come on. You'd love to have me a bit smart, not just plain ignorant like I am.'

'Where are you going to learn all this sophistication and to be smart and polished?' Tony grumbled.

And indeed Aisling wasn't sure how to answer that even though her brain was working feverishly on an answer that would satisfy him.

'Well, I haven't it all settled yet, but I'm thinking of doing a little travelling. Not going away permanently or anything, just broadening my mind, and seeing a bit of the world. I'm not even twenty yet, Tony. I may seem all right now but I could turn into one of those awful dreary women you see up at the church with nothing on their minds except what the priest said to them and what Mrs So and So was wearing.'

'You'd never . . .'

'Oh but I might, I can see the signs of it in me already.'

Aisling had warmed to her cause now and felt she had the upper hand. It was time to leave the subject.

'But listen, I'll tell you next week where and when I'll be going off to see the world.'

He agreed with a grunt, and reluctantly drove her back to the house in the square.

Mother was up as usual.

'You're a bit late,' she said mildly and without much sense of disapproval.

'I know. We went for a drive after the pictures and he spent a lot of time talking.'

Aisling looked at herself hastily in the mirror to make sure her lipstick wasn't all over her face and that her blouse was buttoned correctly.

But Mam didn't seem to be inspecting her. 'I just waited till you came in,' she said, folding her knitting and starting to turn off lights.

'Well Mam, there's no need. You know I'm all right, and that nothing . . . that I wouldn't . . . that I'd always come home.'

'Of course I do, child, but in a way you're my oldest, aren't you? Maureen was away in Dublin at your age, and well, boys are different. It would never matter what time Sean or Eamonn came in.'

'I'm no trouble to you now am I? Nice, reliable assistant in the shop, walking out decorously with the town's best catch . . . and Mam honestly, I'm not such an eejit. I told him tonight that I was too young to be serious about anything. That I'd have to see the world first.'

Mam laughed. 'And where are you going to go to first in the world? Wicklow Town, maybe as far as Wexford?'

'I'll go somewhere Mam. It's just to let him know that I know my limitations in a way.'

Mam ruffled her hair and laughed again. 'You're an entertainment in yourself. No wonder Tony Murray's delighted with you.'

On the hall table was a letter from London. Aisling snatched it eagerly and took it up to bed. This was the promised letter from Elizabeth which was going to tell her everything. It seemed quite thick as well.

She took a glass of milk and a piece of cake from the kitchen first and sat down to enjoy the story.

But when she opened the envelope the letter was very short. What made the bulkiness was a parcel of four five-pound notes, English ones with pictures of the King of England on them wrapped in tissue paper.

The letter was certainly not telling at all.

Dear Aisling,
Is it silly to remember things we did as children, or is it not? Do you remember, when we became blood sisters by mixing our blood in the bottle, we swore to help each other if one was in trouble?

I need your help now. Please, please come to England. I'm sending you the money for the fare. Please come now. You must be here for Saturday. It's Father's fiftieth birthday and I can't cope with it by myself Please come. I'll tell you everything when you get here. Don't let Aunt Eileen know how urgent it is. Pretend that you just want a holiday. Please.

Elizabeth

Well, thought Aisling, isn't that the best bit of luck ever? A chance to see the world and broaden my mind not ten minutes after I started looking for one. It's fate.

Elizabeth hadn't noticed that her breasts were getting bigger but she had noticed that her period was very late. It was now three weeks overdue. It had never been more than four days late. She had deliberately put it out of her mind in the hope that it might have been nervousness, tension or any of the reasons which she had read in a medical magazine.

But on the Sunday night after Johnny had driven her home to Clarence Gardens and sped off again, she could no longer dismiss it. Twenty-one days. She checked the calendar again and even smiled ruefully since she knew that this is what so many nervous girls all over the world must be doing at that minute. Saying to themselves that it couldn't possibly be true, and it couldn't happen to them, and trying to get rid of the hard knot of fear and disbelief that was forming in their chests.

Elizabeth looked out the window and saw Father in the garden. For some reason his ineffectual pottering, his unsuccessful attempts to trail the honeysuckle over the wall, and his sense of bafflement because it lay on the ground and got tangled, seemed to her unbearably sad. He could be seventy she thought, not fifty. He looked so dull and beaten and as if he had always known he would never amount to anything.

If Johnny had been in that garden there would have been life and laughter. There would have been movement and experiment and sudden flashes of inspiration, and determined hammering of stakes into the ground. If Mother was here in one of her good moods she would laugh too and go at it with interest, and Harry would bluster and laugh and make some fun out of it. But Father looked as if he were already dead and as if everything he did were some kind of sad duty forced on him beyond the grave.

Poor dead Father, nothing to live for, nothing to hope for; even bridge had revealed untoward dangers with that terrible widow Ellis in pursuit of him. Elizabeth decided to put away the calendar and its message of despair and go down to the garden to help him.

He was surprised to see her.

'Oh hallo. Didn't know you were in.'

'Yes, I came in about an hour ago.'

'Did you have tea?'

'No, I'd have called you if I had made tea. No, I went upstairs to my room for a bit.'

'Oh I see.'

'What are you doing, Father?'

'My dear, what do you think I'm doing? I'm trying to do something with this wilderness of a garden.'

'Yes, but what in particular? If you tell me what it is, perhaps I can help.'

'Well . . . I don't think it would be any use . . .' He stood looking like an old bewildered bird.

'Are you weeding this bed?' she asked through gritted teeth.

'Well . . . it's so overgrown . . . you see.' He waved at it.

'Yes so it is. Shall we start weeding it now, then, Father? You start at that end, and I'll start here . . . and we'll meet in the middle.'

'I don't know if that would work.'

She controlled her voice with a great effort, by taking it down an octave from where she had been about to speak.

'Why would it not work, Father?' Each word equal emphasis, no sign of rage on her face.

'You know, knowing which are the weeds . . . and which are flowers . . . it's so difficult to see . . . it's so overgrown you see.'

'We could take this kind of grass out, *that's* obviously weed. Then we could look at it again and have a reassessment.'

She stood there looking at him hopefully. Could he not catch a little enthusiasm from her?

He shook his head. 'I don't know,' he said.

Elizabeth went purposefully to the little shed, and took out some cardboard. She folded it into a kneeling mat. She went to her end of the big flower bed and started to wrench big tufts of grass out. 'Hey, look, this is beginning to look better already,' she called out. But he stood there, unsure, unwilling to go along with this sudden outburst.

'Come on, Father,' she called. 'In half an hour we'll have made it look like Kew Gardens.'

He bent over and fiddled again with the honeysuckle.

'This isn't a weed, don't dig up this, this is honeysuckle.'

'I know Father, we're just taking grass. Come on. I'll be catching up on you if you don't start.'

'It's such a wilderness,' he sighed. 'No one person could do a garden like this. Not anyone who has a full-time job like I do. Nobody could do a big garden like this without help.'

'You've GOT help,' called Elizabeth on all fours from the back of the flower bed. 'I'm helping you.'

'You see,' he said. 'It was allowed to get into this state, and now you need a man twice a week in it.'

Elizabeth worked on. It took her forty-five minutes. The sweat was rolling down her forehead and her clothes were sticking to her. She gathered up a mound of coarse grass, and packed it tightly wrapped in old newspapers into the bottom of the dustbin.

'The bin-men don't like grass clippings,' said Father who had fiddled for forty-five minutes with fronds of honey-suckle.

She sighed. 'They won't know what's in it Father, that's why I used newspapers. It could be dismembered bodies for all they know.'

He didn't laugh.

She cleared everything away and had a bath. A hot bath was meant to bring on a period if it was late. There were even stories of a hot bath bringing on even more than a period. Elizabeth felt almost faint when she allowed herself to think that. She patted her stomach, it was still flat. She must be imagining it. She really must have been fancying it. People's periods were always late. The world was filled with false alarms, all the time.

Father had set the table for their supper. It was sardines and tomatoes on toast. Elizabeth was determined to cheer Father up. It became a game almost, like not walking on cracks in the pavement. 'If I don't walk on any lines then I will get an A for my essay.' Just like that, exactly the same reasoning. 'If I make Father cheerful and happy then it will turn out that I'm not pregnant.'

The garden was obviously the wrong area. His depression about the unmanageable jungle outside the door was not going to be lifted, no matter how much Elizabeth praised what had been done and agreed to do an hour every day . . . his head still shook ruefully as if there were things in that garden that Elizabeth could not understand, forces fighting back against amateur part-time gardening. She couldn't really discuss bridge in case Mrs Ellis was remembered. Elizabeth tried but it didn't work.

'Do you think she has hopes of coming to live here

Father?' she asked as she trimmed the toast neatly and shook some dried herbs on the tomatoes.

'I have no idea what that woman thinks or hopes. She is a very common woman. It was a great mistake of Mr Woods to introduce her to the club. He was very badly advised, and utterly misled.'

'Why don't you tell her to get lost then if she's such a nuisance?'

'Oh you can't do that. You can't tell someone not to come.'

'Why don't you start up different games then, without her? You know, just drop her casually if she's so coarse and common? I mean you shouldn't be forced to play bridge with someone you don't like. People don't have to do things they don't want to.' Johnny's attitudes and words tripped lightly and effortlessly from her, but Father didn't agree.

'But of course you have to do things you don't want to. That's obvious. Everyone has to do things they don't want to do all the time . . . Oh Elizabeth dear, don't put any of those herbs and spices on my tomatoes . . . I don't like them with that taste . . . thank you . . . no of course people can't please themselves all the time.'

'But if none of you like her, Father, and she got in by mistake, does that mean you have to put up with her forever?'

'Yes, unfortunately it does.'

Elizabeth had scraped the dusting of dried herbs off Father's tomatoes and when he wasn't looking put them back on again. She set the plates on the table.

'Tell me about when you were my age or a little older, like say in your twenties. Did people never do what they felt like then?'

'I don't know what you mean?'

'*You* know, when you were starting at the bank, Father. Was the world full of people doing what they wanted to do or is it a sense of duty . . . one must do this, one must do that?'

'I don't really know. . . .'

'But you MUST know Father, you must remember. You can't have forgotten what it's like to be twenty.'

'No of course not. . . .'

'Well what was it like?'

'It was very depressing, that's what it was. Everyone was just back from the war, so many wounded and maimed. Others swaggering, just like they were after the last show. Always making you feel that you had a featherbed life because you didn't get accepted for the call-up.'

'It wasn't your fault.'

'I know, but tell that to the boys in uniform, practically accusing you of hiding under the bed. All blow and bluster. I went on my eighteenth birthday down to the town centre. My mother didn't want me to, but I went, I didn't wait.'

'Some people went even before they were eighteen, didn't they Father? Aisling's brother Sean, the one that got killed, he told me that.'

'I don't know whether they did or they didn't. I hope you're not saying I should have gone before the age. . . .'

'No, Father, I was only remembering something. . . .'

'Well, I went the very day, and volunteered for my country but they put me in a reserve because I wasn't strong enough. My spine was weak even then, that's why I still can't do that gardening. It's impossible you know to keep a place this size with one. . . .'

'Did you go out with a lot of other girls Father, before you met Mother . . . ?'

'What? What do you mean?'

'I just wanted to know did you have a lot of social life, and much going out when you were young?'

'I told you, it was just after the Great War.'

'Yes, but we hear about the twenties, and the flappers, and all the fun. You know, people doing the Charleston and having *thé dansants* and wearing those amazing hats looking like buckets. . . .'

'What . . . ?'

'Oh Father, you know, you know the sort of image everyone has of the twenties.'

'Well I assure you that wasn't the image I had of it. That

may have been for a few idle, irresponsible rich people born with silver spoons in their mouths. It wasn't for me or for the people I worked with.'

'But Mother was a sort of flapper girl wasn't she? She used to wear clothes like that. I've seen the old pictures, and she went to *thé dansants* she told me. In fact she often writes about them still, and how she used to go and dance to the Savoy Orpheans. . . .'

'But why all these questions . . . what are you asking me all this for?'

'Father, I'm only trying to get to know a bit more about you . . . we live in the same house and I hardly know anything about you. . . .'

'Oh my dear, don't be so sily. This is utter nonsense.'

'No it's not. We live here together for years and years without my even knowing what makes you happy and what makes you sad.'

'I can tell you that these silly questions . . . what was it like all those years ago . . . make me sad rather than happy. . . .'

'But why Father, why? You must have had happy bits when you were young?'

'Naturally.'

'Weren't you happy when you and Mother were in love, and everything?'

'Now I really don't think. . . .'

'But seriously Father, when you and Mother were expecting me, you know, when Mother went to the doctor and got it all confirmed. What did you do? What did you say, did you celebrate or what . . . ?'

'Please. . . .'

'No, it's interesting to me to know, I'd like to know. Did she come back and say, "It's confirmed, I am pregnant. It will be born in May" or what?'

'I don't remember. . . .'

'Father I'm your only child, you MUST remember!' Her voice was becoming shrill. She remembered to lower it.

'Try to think Father. It would please me.' He looked at her.

'I remember your being born,' he said eventually. 'But I don't remember the day I knew.'

'And were you pleased, or did you think it was a worry and a problem?'

'Of course I was pleased. . . .'

'No, you might have thought it was just another thing to worry about. Why were you pleased? Did you look forward to my being born, being a small thing in a pram . . . ?'

'Yes, well of course I didn't know about what a baby would be like in the house . . . but I was pleased . . . .'

'Can you remember why you were pleased . . . ?'

'Well I think I thought it would make Violet . . . make your mother more content. She seemed restless.'

'Even as long ago as then . . . ?'

'Oh yes.'

'And did it make her more content?'

'Did what. . . .'

'Did I make her more content . . . ?'

'In a way, yes.'

'And what were your happiest times in those days, Father?'

'Really my dear, I don't enjoy this conversation. It's probing and it's too personal, and in a way it's impertinent. People don't ask other people those kind of questions.'

'But how are people ever going to know what people feel . . . ?'

'They know enough my dear. It's not necessary to know everything about people.'

'You're not right Father. It's necessary to know much more than you want to know. You wouldn't mind if you knew nothing about anyone just so long as people behaved correctly.'

'That's not true.'

'Oh but it is true. I'm begging you. I'm reaching out and begging you to tell me about yourself so that I can tell you about me . . . and make you involved in what I'm doing and feeling. . . .'

'But I am very interested in what you do, and very proud of you. You mustn't accuse me of. . . .'

233

'Did you ever talk to Mother about feelings, you know, and what you thought and what you wanted and how much you loved her . . . ?'

'Elizabeth, really.'

'Because honestly, if you didn't, then I know why she went away. It was nothing to do with your not being good enough, or Harry being better. She probably went because she was lonely. . . .'

'And do you think that her fancy Harry Elton is a great philosopher? Do you seriously think he sits down and debates about the meaning of life like you want . . . ? Huh, what a thought.'

'No I don't suppose for a moment he does. But he makes up for it by laughing and joking. The ideal thing would be to have someone who could do both, but I'm beginning to think there's no way you can have the best of both worlds. And Father, if you won't laugh and you won't talk then you're the very worst of both worlds. . . .'

Father stood up and his face was hurt and red. His face muscles were working and his hands were clenched at his sides. He had never looked more wretched and humiliated.

'Well,' he stammered eventually. 'Well, I must say. I don't know what I did to deserve this, I really don't. I was out there in the garden minding my own business, and you come home in a state. You come home and criticise the way I'm doing the garden, even though you never came out to give me a hand in it before . . . you criticise the way I spent my youth. You attack me for not being able to recall every second of your own life before and after you were born. . . .' His voice gathered into a sob. 'And then, as if that isn't enough, you hurl accusations at me about hurtful things and upsetting times . . . and blame me for your mother walking out on her duty and running away.'

He had such pain in his voice that he could hardly get the words out.

'I really don't know what brought all this on. I can only hope that you had a tiff with your young man, and that I needn't expect this kind of performance again.'

Father had never before acknowledged that Johnny was

her young man. His brain would never now take in the intelligence that she and this young man had been rolling around naked on a floor in Earls Court a few hours previously and that she was very probably carrying the young man's child, and that there had been no tiff and nor would there be one.

But the spell hadn't worked. Father was not cheered up, Father was far from cheered up. This must mean that she was indeed pregnant.

She stood up.

'You are quite right. I *had* a silly tiff. It is unforgivable of me to have taken it out on you. Quite unforgivable. I really apologise.'

Then she went upstairs, took some five-pound notes out of her savings box and wrote to Aisling.

X

Aisling had more adventures on her journey to London than she had ever been through in her life. She felt that she had been quite right to tell Tony Murray that she must go out and see the world.

On the boat to Holyhead, an extremely handsome man with his shirt open at the neck had bought her a brandy and lemonade, not heeding her protests that she wouldn't like it. Then he had taken her for a walk on deck, told her she was the most beautiful girl in the world, tried to kiss her, apologised, proposed marriage to her, and finally went into a corner and got very sick. Aisling, who had not realised that he was drunk, had her eyes wide and round in horror at it all, but was rescued by two university students who were going to get a holiday job canning vegetables and tried to persuade her to join them.

On the train going down to London she met a young Welsh school teacher who told her that he was going to live in London because he couldn't stand his village any longer. Everyone was trying to pressurise him to get married. He felt that he should see the world first. Aisling eagerly told him of her own tale and how she was determined to see as much of the world as she could in two weeks, which was the holiday she had wrung from Daddy with difficulty. The Welshman was very scathing about the two-week element of it, he said it wasn't nearly enough. She should go for much longer. Perhaps they should even go to France on a boat. But that was too wild for Aisling, she explained she was coming to see her friend because of a crisis. Her friend wanted someone to help her on her father's birthday. The Welshman said that the friend sounded like someone from a madhouse. Sending money over to Ireland for someone to come to her father's birthday. After four years too. He put his finger to his forehead and turned it around in further explanation of how loopy he thought the friend must be. Aisling then felt resentful of him and returned to her book.

Even at Euston station a middle-aged man asked her if she was lost and said he would be happy to share a taxi with her. But Aisling was looking out for Elizabeth.

She had telephoned Elizabeth early the morning after she got the letter and said of course, she would come that very night. Elizabeth's accent sounded very English like the people in the films who said 'frightfully' and 'jolly'. She said that Euston was a huge place but there were no problems because if Aisling just stayed there at the barrier when she came off the train they would have no trouble finding each other.

'When I came over four years ago, I thought I'd been abandoned,' Elizabeth had said.

'Sure, weren't we only children then,' said Aisling, dismissing it.

Still Aisling's eyes roamed anxiously through the crowds and she paused to comb her hair so that she would make a good impression. She wished she had a smarter suitcase. This one which Mother had used years ago was far too shabby for her nice new turquoise summer coat. But it had been a matter of buying new shoes or a new suitcase and the shoes seemed more important.

She must have walked right past Elizabeth, eyes still roaming the crowd, darting here and there looking for the pale blonde fifteen-year-old but with a few grown-up clothes on nowadays. Then Elizabeth pulled at her sleeve. . . .

'Aisling?' she said, almost hesitantly.

Aisling spun round.

They looked at each other for a moment . . . as if the words and greetings and reactions had been blown out of them like air after a punch in the solar plexus.

They spoke at the same instant.

'Elizabeth, you saved my life by inviting me to come over. . . .'

'Oh, Aisling, you've literally saved my life. . . .'

Then they burst out laughing. And Aisling linked arms.

'Maybe we're Siamese twins that should never have been separated. Maybe we're going to go on saying the same thing at the same time always.'

'Maybe, maybe,' laughed Elizabeth. She tried to lift up the suitcase but it was heavy.

'What on earth have you in this, rocks?' she asked.

Aisling took it back. 'No, food from the land of plenty. They all went mad: cake for your dad's birthday, side of bacon smoked, oh and butter, all wrapped up in newspapers ten times and in a tin. I hope to God it's not running all over the case and destroying every rag I've got in it.'

Elizabeth squeezed her arm and Aisling saw with surprise that in Elizabeth's pale attractive face there were tears in the big blue eyes.

'In a million years you'll never know how glad I am to see you.'

'And me to see you. On the bus to Dublin I began to worry in case you'd have got all different, but you're not. You're thinner though. It is the fashion or is it this country full of shortages?' She patted Elizabeth's flat stomach admiringly. 'There's none of you there. You're what they'd call a rake, in Kilgarret. I'm dead jealous.'

'Oh there's more than you think,' said Elizabeth and got a fit of helpless giggles which were so infectious that Aisling started to laugh too though she couldn't see why.

They stood under the big arch at Euston, unaware of the admiring and interested glances which were directed at the redhead and blonde, both of them wiping their eyes and clutching on to each other with a mirth that had quite a lot of hysteria in it.

From the start Aisling got on well with Father. Elizabeth could hardly believe how well she handled him. Father had been only mildly interested to hear that the visitor was arriving and had helped to take some of the boxes and other bits of lumber from the spare room to stack them in the garden shed. Elizabeth had gone to great trouble to make the guest room look nice. She had picked flowers and even bought a mirror from Johnny in the shop.

'Staff discount,' he had said, halving the price.

'Hey, come on, we're not going to cheat Mr Worsky. . . .'

'When oh when will anyone realise that this is Worsky and Stone. . . . I am a partner here, cherub, I am trusted and loved. I cheat myself if I give it to you cheap. . . .'

'I'm a worker here, Mr Stone. . . . I don't want to see the business I have pride in go down the drain. . . .'

They laughed. Johnny was in great form this week. He was disappointed that they couldn't meet because of her preparations for the friend from Ireland, but he took it lightly.

'Is she pretty, the colleen?' he asked.

'She used to be super. I think I'm going to keep her well hidden from you.'

'Perhaps she wants a chap to show her the sights of London,' he teased.

'Perhaps, but I don't think so. The local lord or squire wants to marry her. She's coming over here to have a think about it.'

'Marry? What does she want to get married at her age for? She's only the same age as you,' said Johnny.

'I know, it's ridiculous,' said Elizabeth, lifting her voice right up with almost a physical effort. 'Perhaps she'll change her mind about it when she sees the delights of London.'

Aisling had loved the room, the flowers, the pretty mirror. She had marvelled at everything: the red buses, the red pillar boxes. The neat gardens, the rows and rows of houses – she couldn't believe so many people must live in one place.

They were having tea at the kitchen table when Father came in. At once Aisling went into the attack.

'You're never a man who's going to be fifty years, Mr White, are you?' she said before any ridiculous introductions were made.

'Well . . . er . . . how do you do . . . that's right I . . . er. . . .'

'Father, this is Aisling,' said Elizabeth unnecessarily.

'Well, it's some kind of mistake I think. I tell you Mr

White, my father is fifty-one and he looks ten, fifteen years older than you. I mean that now, not a word of a lie.'

Elizabeth thought Father would recoil from such over-familiarity but to her amazement she saw him almost preening.

'I'm sure that your father. . . .'

'I don't have a picture of him or I'd prove it to you. Come on now and sit down Mr White. You must be tired after your day's work. Isn't this an astonishing country?'

Hiding a smile, Elizabeth poured a cup of tea for Father.

'Why is it astonishing?'

Aisling burbled happily on, telling of all the marvels she had seen from the train. Huge cities and big factory chimneys and miles and miles of fields. Nobody in Ireland knew that there was any countryside in England, they thought it was all cities.

Then she leaped up and unwrapped some of the foods. She brushed aside Father's worries about how she got them through customs.

'Don't you see this tin has "dinner service" written on it?' The butter had kept, the chicken was perfect, the side of bacon was put in the larder.

'But my dear, we must recompense you for all this. . . .' Father began.

Elizabeth ground her teeth in rage. Trust him, trust him not to understand friendship and generosity and presents. Trust him to think that this was something you paid for. But Aisling didn't seem a bit put out.

'Not at all. These are presents from Mam and Dad. Now of course there is a chance that I might go into the black market seriously now that I've discovered how easy it is to get things in. Then it would be a matter of payment.'

She threw her head back and laughed. Elizabeth thought she looked so lively and bright, she was like a coloured picture when everyone else was in black and white.

'Now, Mr White, what are we going to do for this birthday of yours? That's why I'm here.'

Father looked up in alarm. 'No, not seriously. . . .'

Aisling was quick to see the alarm reflected on Elizabeth's

face. 'Heavens no, I'm only pulling your leg, but it is a coincidence that when I wanted to come and see Elizabeth. . . .' She looked over his shoulder for confirmation. Elizabeth nodded enthusiastically. 'When I asked if I could come for a visit . . . that I also heard it was your birthday.'

His face cleared. 'Oh, it's silly for a man of my age. . . .'

'Not at all, when Dad was fifty we had a great party, and Mam will be fifty next year and so we'll have a massive celebration altogether.'

'What did you do when your father was fifty?' asked poor Father. Elizabeth felt a wave of pity for him, he was like a lonely child.

But Aisling seemed to see none of this. She leant across the table, chatting as if she'd known him all her life.

'Well, it was a Thursday so we went to Maher's. We still do that you know, Elizabeth, and they often ask for you there. It's a pub. . . .'

'A public house, and you all went . . . ?'

'Well, yes, we always go.'

'They're not like pubs here Father. They're half pubs and half shops. They sell groceries at one end and drink at the other.'

'Well I never,' said Father. 'You never told me that.'

Aisling told the story of an evening when Peggy came down to Maher's four times to say that the dinner was stuck to the roof of the oven but Dad wouldn't go home because everyone in the place had to buy a drink to celebrate Sean O'Connor being fifty. Eventually Mam had taken Donal and Niamh home and put them to bed, and they woke up again at eleven o'clock when Father and Eamonn had come in singing, and Mam said that was the last time they'd ever go along with this nonsense of having a dinner in the evening like the gentry, it only led to trouble.

Father actually laughed at the descriptions instead of wrinkling up his lip as Elizabeth had feared. Normally Father spent three minutes having a cup of tea before shuffling off. Today he seemed ready to sit in the kitchen forever.

'It's your bridge evening,' Elizabeth reminded him. 'Mr Woods isn't it?'

Reluctantly Father went off to change his shirt and spruce himself up.

'He's grand altogether,' said Aisling when he was out of earshot. 'You never told me he was a fine handsome man. I don't know what you go on about for in your letters, he seems a very peaceable sort of man to me.'

'You bring out the best in him. I only make him more miserable,' said Elizabeth.

'Oh I know what I'll do. Why don't I marry him? He's not much older than Tony Murray, and to tell you the truth I think he's a finer-looking man. Then I'll be your stepmother and you and I'll be related after all.'

Elizabeth laughed, delighted with the whole fantasy.

'Great, we could have the wedding from this house and the honeymoon in Kilgarret and I could come with you.'

'Yes, Westminster Abbey, no that's Protestant, what's the Catholic one called?'

'I think you're forgetting about the d-i-v-o-r-c-e,' Elizabeth spelled out. 'It might have to be a registry office job.'

'Oh it's off then. Forget it,' said Aisling.

'You must tell me all about Tony Murray, every detail, every single thing.'

'I will of course. But what about Clark Gable, where is he? I thought you'd have him on a padlock and chain at the station. It's not all over or anything is it? Not when I've come the whole way to have a look at him. . . .'

'No, it's not all over. But wait until Father's gone. I'll tell you the whole thing then, I don't want to be interrupted . . . and I don't want to have to break off if he comes in to say goodbye. . . .'

'Does he know about Clark Gable then?'

'Oh he does in a way . . . but it's too complicated. Now tell me about Squire Murray.'

'That's a good name for him. Well, he's a bit of a cock of the walk you know, big fellow with the lads in the hotel. Wouldn't drink in Maher's or anything, but in the bar of the hotel of an evening. He's got a car, a Packard. Well, he runs Murray's, Eamonn says actually that he doesn't do much in it, and that it's their awful little pickaheen Mr Meade that runs it. But you wouldn't mind Eamonn, you see he and his friends would call Tony's lot the High and Mightys – not as high and mighty as the Grays and all, but that's different they're sort of Protestants with big houses. . . .'

'Does that still matter?' asked Elizabeth.

'It doesn't matter, it's just still there. Anyway what else about Tony? Well he started to try and pin me down on Tuesday night last, and I told him a pack of lies. I said I was going to have to see the world before I said anything like yes or no. I'd no idea on God's earth how I was going to travel, and didn't I come home that night and find your letter? Wasn't it like an act of God?'

Elizabeth laughed. 'In a way I suppose.'

'So after I rang you yesterday morning, and after I had an hour-long barney with Dad about the time off, Mam supported me of course . . . I went up to Murray's and asked to speak to him. Ten o'clock and he wasn't there, and prissy-prunes Meade said that Mr Tony might be in around eleven. Oh, the life for some! I was going to write him a note but I thought I'd express it wrong, so I got a lift from the hotel out to his house. His Ma was there. "I'm afraid Tony's in bed," she said. "At a quarter past ten in the morning!" I said. That didn't please her. "He was out late and he's tired," she said. I got an awful urge to tell her why he was tired. Anyway, to cut a long story short, he came down in his dressing-gown. His Ma was sort of hovering around in case we fell on each other. But she went off eventually, and I told him that I was going off that evening.'

'Was he upset?'

'He was outraged. Why hadn't I told him? Why was I springing it on him? Why was I so juvenile? Why this, why that . . . but I was able for him, I really was. I spoke in a low throaty voice like they do in the pictures. I said that I was young and I thought I knew my own mind, but I had to be sure. I reminded him that nothing had been asked or answered and that it was better that way. He listened, a bit mournful, but he didn't interrupt. So I said I'd look forward to seeing him when I got back.'

'It was very good timing for you then?' Elizabeth said.

'It couldn't have been better. It really did save my life as I said at the station. I couldn't have said to you that I wanted to come over and I really didn't have the fare together. Hey, Elizabeth, I can't take the fare from you. Why did you send it anyway? I'll pay you back.'

'Idiot, look at all the food you brought. That's twice the fare.'

'Oh, okay, well anyway, to end up – I told him I couldn't stay any longer, the delivery man from the hotel was waiting for me and that I'd see him later.

'He came out to the steps of the house, you remember it don't you? The big one on the river about a mile out of town.'

' "When is later?" he shouted.

' "Later is later," I shouted back. I don't know what I meant but it sounded great. And then I got myself together and here I am.'

'And what do you really think of him? Do you really like him?'

'I don't know. Honestly and truthfully I don't know. I'm flattered by him, and I'm becoming a bit of a cock of the walk myself with others in the town thinking more of me for going out with him. But. . . .'

'But what . . . I mean when the two of you are on your own. . . .'

'I like it when he tells me I'm attractive-looking, and I like it when he says what he'd like to do with me . . . if you know what I mean, but I don't like all the grunting when he's trying to do it . . . if you know what I mean.'

'Trying, what do you mean trying?'

'You know, him struggling in the car to get my clothes off and me struggling to keep them on, the usual sort of thing.'

'Oh,' said Elizabeth. 'Oh of course.'

Father came in to say goodbye.

'You'll knock them sideways at that bridge party, Mr White. Don't let them run off with you now.'

Father looked ridiculously pleased. They watched him from the window, fixing his tie and smiling to himself.

'Now he's gone, will you take out some kind of an alcoholic drink and tell me what it's all about. Tell me what happened.'

'What do you mean?'

'Oh anything at all, a sherry, a whisky. . . . I even had a brandy on the boat. I'm not particular.'

'I didn't mean what drink. I meant what do you mean tell you what happened? Why, do you think something happened?'

Aisling was on her knees in front of a cupboard. 'This is the kind of a place you'd keep the drink.'

'No, silly, it's in the other room.' They walked in and in the corner cabinet there was a bottle of sherry with three quarters of its contents left. A half bottle of whisky seemed to be untouched.

'I think we'll start on the sherry,' said Aisling firmly. 'If it's bad enough we may get to the whisky.'

'It's bad enough,' said Elizabeth. 'Let's take the whisky with us as well.'

They poured the sherry into two ordinary glasses, great dollops of it.

'Cheers,' said Elizabeth.

'*Slainte,*' said Aisling.

'It's as bad as it could be,' said Elizabeth.

'Johnny Stone threw you over . . . ?' suggested Aisling.

'No.'

'He turned out to have a wife and children?'

'No.'

'Well is it about him at all?'

'Oh yes, yes it's all about him.'

'I can't think Elizabeth, really. What is it? You sounded desperate in your letter, even though you look quite all right now. What is it?'

'I'm pregnant.'

'WHAT?'

'I'm pregnant. My period was three weeks late. I went to have a test and it's positive. I'm going to have a baby.'

'No.'

'Oh Aisling, what am I going to do? What on earth am I going to do?'

'You mean. . . .'

Elizabeth had begun to cry now and there was no stopping her. Aisling moved over and put her arm around the shaking shoulder.

'What am I going to do, you've got to help me.'

'Shush, shush. You mean, you mean you had sexual intercourse with him?'

Elizabeth's hands came from her amazed face.

'Of course I had. How else would I be pregnant?'

'You mean lots of times? For ages or just once?'

'For ages. Oh since last spring.

'And what was it like?'

'What was it like?'

'Sexual intercourse, what was it like?'

'Aisling O'Connor, I can't believe you. I've told you the most terrible tragedy, I've told you the worst bit of bad news anyone could have, and you ask me what it's like having sex. . . .'

'I just didn't know you did, like that you had done it.'

'Listen to me, doing it is no problem, that's easy, it's what to do about it . . . that's the problem.'

Aisling recovered. 'Yes, I'm sorry. I got side-tracked. It just seems to put you on a different side of the fence from me, the ones who know what it's like and the ones who don't. I feel so stupid telling you all about the silly things I was up to and assuming. . . .'

'No, why should you feel stupid? I would never have either if it hadn't been for Johnny. With him it's normal, it's part of the way we go on. He never thinks of it as anything special, or people who Do or people who Don't. I would have been like you otherwise, it's just that I take my line from him.'

'I know.'

'But now it's true, Aisling. I can't pretend any more. I

knew really for days, but I wouldn't let myself admit it. Then on Monday I went off to a doctor miles and miles away. I bought a ring in Woolworth's and I told him I was a visitor and I just wanted it confirmed.'

'And what did you have to do?'

'I took along a specimen of urine, I knew that, I had heard you had to bring what you did first thing in the morning for them to do a test.'

'Yes, I see.'

'So I put it in a jam jar, I didn't know what else to put it in. And he said that was fine. And he asked me to come back on Wednesday. So while you were driving round Kilgarret giving ultimatums to people, I was lying in a chair like a dentist's chair and there were stirrups in it where you put your feet and he felt inside me and examined my breasts and said that there was no doubt.'

'Oh God. Poor Elizabeth.'

'He was very nice actually. He said, "Congratulations Mrs Stone," and I tried to put on a pleased smile. But I bet he knew anyway. I said to him that my husband would be pleased, and I gave him his money, thirty shillings it was, in an envelope. But I bet he knew. He sort of patted me on the shoulder as I was leaving. He said, "These things often work out better than you think." I said I didn't know what he meant. He said, "Just remember that things often work out better than you think." So I said I would. And here we are.'

'Oh Elizabeth. Poor, poor Elizabeth. What a thing to have to go through.'

'Yes, but that's nothing to what other things I'll have to go through.'

'What did Johnny say?'

'I haven't told him.'

'When are you telling him?'

'I'm not going to tell him.'

'But you'll have to tell him some time.'

'No I won't.'

'You're not making sense. When you get married, when it's obvious that you're going to have a baby — you can't

247

keep it a secret until it arrives can you?' Aisling looked puzzled. 'I think you're in shock over it all, I really do.'

'We won't be getting married.'

'Well of course you will, once he knows. Won't you?'

'No. He won't know.'

'But he's fond of you. He still fancies you doesn't he?'

'Oh yes.'

'And you fancy him.'

'Oh I do.'

'And there's no awful secret like him being tied up with anyone else?'

'No.'

'So all you have to do is to screw yourself up to tell him. Isn't that it? And he'll be a bit annoyed because maybe he didn't want to settle down yet. But he'll realise it might as well be now as later. And count your blessings you're in a place like this where people aren't looking at you and whispering and gossiping about you. Nobody's going to count the months you were married before Little Stone junior is born. . . . Elizabeth why are you crying so much? It isn't that bad. All he can do is curse and swear a bit about the timing . . . isn't that all? I mean it's not as if it were your fault is it? You're not trying to trap him or anything. You both did it, so it's the concern of both of you.'

'No, no, it's my decision,' Elizabeth mumbled into her handkerchief. Her eyes were red now and her face streaked. Aisling was very concerned.

'Here, have another dose of this.' She poured some sherry into the glass with a slurp. 'How do you mean it was your decision? You didn't want to get caught did you?'

'No, now, it's my decision now,' snuffled Elizabeth. 'You see I want him so desperately. I'll die if I can't have him. I don't want to go on living if I can't have Johnny. . . .'

'Yes, well.' Aisling was startled at such strong words from Elizabeth. 'Well, you will have him, won't you? He's not going to say that he doesn't want to have anything to do with you. I mean if you work together and like each other, and you've been going out with him and . . . er . . . sleeping with him and everything. It's not just a casual thing that he's going to get out of . . . is it?'

Elizabeth had stopped her crying suddenly. 'Now, this is what I'm going to have to explain to you, and it may take all night. This is why I begged you to come over and why you are the best friend I have in the world. I'm going to have to get rid of it. No, please let me finish. I've decided that's what I must do, but I'm afraid. I really am, I suppose, afraid I'll bleed to death. I'm afraid I'll get an infection and die. I'm afraid it will hurt so desperately that I'll scream and scream and she'll stop. . . .'

'Who will stop?' Aisling's voice was a whisper.

'Mrs Norris. She's a nurse and a midwife and everything, and the place is scrupulously clean. That's what I heard.'

Aisling's glass of sherry remained poised in the air. 'You never mean . . . you can't possibly mean that you're going to a woman to have an abortion? To have her do an abortion on you?'

'It's the only solution.'

'And what does Johnny say about this? Does he approve?'

'Listen, he must never know. I know, I knew it would be like this. I've had to explain it aloud even to myself, and I can't understand it logically . . . but what I've got to do is make you believe that Johnny doesn't get involved in people's lives, in fusses, in things he doesn't want to . . . that's not his style. . . .'

'So you're going to get rid of his child in an abortionist's because it mightn't be his style. . . . Come on, out of that.'

'Pass the sherry, it's going to be a long night,' said Elizabeth.

It was a very long night. They transferred upstairs to Elizabeth's room, lest Father should come in and want to continue the easy-going conversation he had enjoyed earlier on. They heard him come in and go to his room. Later they moved downstairs again and made soup and sandwiches. This was at four a.m.

By now Aisling's eyes were as red as Elizabeth's. And when

dawn came in the kitchen window, she had made the following promises. . . .

— that she would never mention to Johnny anything of this occurrence;

— that she would try to maintain a cheerful and non-curious atmosphere in Clarence Gardens;

— that she would accompany Elizabeth to Mrs Norris's house and stay as long as was permitted.

'I've given in on everything,' she said to Elizabeth blearily just before they traipsed upstairs again to bed. 'I used to think I was a strong character, but now I've gone along with all these things I don't agree with. I can't see why you won't have the baby, I am utterly certain he would marry you. . . . I can't see why you wouldn't have it even if he doesn't marry you . . . if he sees you living happily and cheerfully here with the baby he'll admire you all the more . . . no matter how happy-go-lucky he is. If you are going through with this thing . . . then it's brave and courageous and I really can't see why you won't let him praise you and congratulate you for that. . . .

'But no, you're going to meet him next week as if nothing had happened. I think you're out of your bloody mind, and I think he sounds the most cruel, selfish bum who ever walked. . . .'

Elizabeth smiled weakly. 'No, he's just very honest, he says he only does what he wants, and now I'm learning from him. I'm doing what I want. The unselfish one is you, because you're going to help me even though you think it's wrong. You probably even think it's a mortal sin.'

'God, I've almost forgotten about mortal sin with all the rest of the drama, but you can bet your life that's exactly what it is, a desperate mortal sin on top of everything else.'

The days passed in a blur for both of them. There was the visit to the shop, the meeting with Mr Worsky, how delighted he was with Aisling and her hair, and her name. He made her write it down . . . a fairy dream . . . how beautiful. He called Anna from the back room. She marvelled too. They had both heard of Elizabeth's wonderful years in Ireland. Aisling's heart softened again when she saw how much the old couple did indeed know about Kilgarret, and her big family, and how her brother had been killed in the war.

Then there was the meeting with Monica Hart, who worked in a dress shop now. She wasn't a close friend of Elizabeth's these days but she was delighted to meet Aisling.

'You called a cat after me didn't you?' she said. Aisling looked at the rather scrawny girl in her black shop-dress, her frizzy hair and very orange lipstick and nail polish.

'Yes we did, it's there still. It's a big cat now and it's old and it belongs to Niamh my younger sister. When Elizabeth went back here it sort of was passed on to Niamh like old clothes are.'

Monica came and had a cup of coffee with them in her lunch hour.

'I never see Elizabeth nowadays because of Romeo in the antique shop. Have you met him yet?'

'No,' said Aisling, 'I haven't met him yet. He's away until this afternoon. I am looking forward to seeing him though.'

She spoke jokingly as if Elizabeth weren't there.

'Come on, Monica, tell me, is he as handsome as they say? Is he really as good as he's made out to be?'

'Yes, he's every bit as glamorous . . . he's a real heart-breaker. . . . He's the kind of man that would have slaves if he were in a film.'

'Well, thank heavens life isn't a film,' said Aisling, looking meaningfully at Elizabeth who looked away.

They did the shopping for Father's celebration meal on the following night. Aisling bought him a bright tie and handkerchief to match. Elizabeth got him a smart tiepin and cufflinks. Then they wandered back to the shop where a big van was now parked.

'Remember you promised,' whispered Elizabeth hoarsely.

'I remember,' said Aisling.

Johnny Stone bounded down the shop to meet them. He was so warm and welcoming that Aisling was totally taken aback. From the hours and hours of description last night she had assumed that he would be distant and superior, that he would talk in clipped tones like lords and aristocrats talked in the countless films they saw in the cinema in Kilgarret.

'Well, let me have a look at you. Stefan and Anna . . . those two were meant to be working on cataloguing the last lot of stuff I brought in . . . but no, oohing and aahing over the lovely copper hair. Come here, let me see it in the light. It's good, I grant you, it's real but it's not blonde. I like blondes. You know where you are with a blonde I always say.' He had an arm around each of them affectionately.

He had a beautiful strong face, not at all like Clark Gable, but much longer and leaner. He was a very attractive man indeed. Aisling thought that it would be very dangerous and exciting to have sexual intercourse with a man like that and tried to imagine Elizabeth doing so, but failed.

'Enough playing about, Aisling, you are very welcome to London. What can we do to make your visit a good one . . . what shall we do to make you remember us here when you go back to the Emerald Isle?'

Aisling bit down her nervous giggle. She felt an urge to say that since she was going to take part in a conspiracy, an illegal operation and the Lord knew what else she had plenty to make the visit memorable. But she remembered her promise.

'You'd be appalled altogether to know what I really want to do. . . . I want to sit down and catch up on the last four years with Elizabeth. Everyone in Kilgarret wants to know what she's been doing, and I want to tell her all my adventures. . . .'

'I'm sure there are plenty of them,' said Johnny.

'There's hours of them, thank God,' said Aisling. 'They'll have us entertained night and day. . . .'

She liked him. He wasn't flirting with her. He was being charming, as he would have been to any new acquaintance. He was possibly the most charming and relaxed man she had ever met. She didn't envy Elizabeth, she couldn't understand a selfless, slavish love like that . . . but she did see that if you wanted Johnny Stone to stick around in your life then you would need to be fairly high on charm yourself. You wouldn't want to be unlucky or depressing or to get dragged down, nor to let any of these things rub off on him.

But she gave no hint of this as she smiled delightedly when he said he was going to take them both for coffee and cakes to celebrate her arrival.

The appointment with Mrs Norris was not until Monday morning, so the whole weekend had to be got through.

'Do you feel any morning sickness?' Aisling enquired on Saturday morning when she had brought Elizabeth a cup of tea in bed.

'Heavens no, I've read all about it. That wouldn't happen for ages yet. There's nothing really there you know, inside me I mean, nothing to make me sick. It's only a speck.'

'I see,' said Aisling.

'Not a person, a baby or anything.'

'No, of course.'

'Anyway,' Elizabeth changed the subject, 'you've no idea what a treat this is . . . I don't know when I had a cup of tea brought to me in bed. Let me see. Not in Mother's, no Harry did offer, but I got up. Not anywhere . . . the last time I remember was when we had measles in Kilgarret.'

'Lord yes, we were awful weren't we, and with my hair I looked like a mad thing. Imagine how poor Mam had to cope with all of us, and Peggy being in bed. Sometimes I don't know where she got the energy. . . .'

'You seem to get on much better with her now. . . .'

Elizabeth sat up in bed and drank her tea.

'Yes, I suppose it's normal in a way, I used to be very jealous of the way she could talk to you, but since I've gone to work in the shop, it's been different . . . and she's been very grateful when I do any little bit extra . . . she does ask about you you know, she sent all her love and said that if you had any worries to say she'd say a prayer for you. . . .'

'That was nice,' Elizabeth said with a note of regret.

'I could say it was special intention,' Aisling said. 'Then Mam could pray and Our Lord would channel the prayers somewhere else for you. It wouldn't be right of course for

253

her to pray that you'd get over an abortion or anything. It would be flying in the eyes of God.'

'Oh my goodness, I know,' said Elizabeth apologetically. There was a little silence.

'You couldn't discuss it with your own mother? You said that you were getting along much better with her nowadays, like I am . . . would she be able to help?'

'No, I think it would frighten her . . . confuse her. She's not really able to cope . . . look, there's her last letter, have a look at it. . . .'

'There's no beginning . . . this isn't the start.'

'Yes it is. That's the way she writes nowadays. . . .'

And you would find it very hard in this ugly world, this modern ugly world, to know what it was like when I was a girl. We wore long flowing dresses . . . very tight waists, and flowers in our hair. Always fresh flowers, perhaps four or five different gardenias a day . . . just a little sign of a flower wilting and it was thrown lightly away . . . what we had Elizabeth that has been snatched away from you was beauty . . . so much beauty . . . the lawns where we had spread out the thick white cloths and napkins were green velvet lawns . . . not scrubland . . . the men . . . the young men going off to the war were so gallant and so brave. Their eyes used to dance . . . they were light-hearted about their lives. 'It will be worth it, Violet, if you send me away with a kiss . . .'

Aisling stopped reading.

'Oh God, but none of this is true is it? She wasn't old enough to send people away to the first war was she?'

'No of course she wasn't. It's all imagination . . . there weren't dresses like that, there were no flowers . . . no picnics on lawns. She lived in a house a bit like this and went to a couple of twenties parties and married Father. You see she's got it all mixed up with those romances and books she reads. It looks a bit as if her mind is going doesn't it? Isn't that the way it seems to you?'

'Well a bit, but it might only be for a while. You know, it could only be temporary.'

'Oh Aisling, what *would* I do without you?'

Then there was the birthday party, that stood out in fairly sharp relief. They must have worked hard to prepare a festive meal, though Aisling could not really remember the day whenever she tried to go back over the sequence of events. They must have gone shopping, they must have cooked, and set the table with paper they coloured themselves.

They put on their best dresses, Aisling in a cream colour which she was afraid looked dull and dreary, but everyone else said it did wonders for her hair so she believed them. Elizabeth wore a rose-coloured velvet. She had never forgotten Johnny saying that he remembered this blonde in rose velvet, but in fact she wondered whether the colour suited her. Sometimes she feared she looked wishy-washy.

Father had dressed up too, they heard him humming and even whistling in the bathroom while he was shaving.

'He never does that,' Elizabeth said wonderingly.

'Poor old devil, he's just dead lonely, that's all that's wrong with him. He needs a bit of attention.'

'But when I try to give him some attention and ask him about things and what he feels and what he used to feel . . . he turns purple.'

'Ah yes, but that's the wrong kind of attention . . . he only needs a superficial kind of attention . . . nothing too deep.'

'You've got awfully good at handling men,' said Elizabeth.

'Indeed I have not. If I'm so good at handling them why am I such an eejit with that Tony Murray? Anyone who could handle men would have him like an adoring lap dog. I'm just in a tizzy in case I lose him on the one hand, or in case I'm tied to him on the other. . . .'

'You're better than I am,' Elizabeth said mournfully.

'You're a different class of person altogether, you're prepared to put other people before yourself . . . I never was and never will be. That's what Mam always said when I was young, and honestly I think it's the truth. . . . I *say* Mr White, don't you look the real birthday boy . . . look at him Elizabeth . . . isn't he gorgeous?'

'You look smashing Father.'

'Thank you my dear, and so do both of you. Very attractive young ladies to share the festive day with. . . .'

He offered them a sherry, and they exchanged glances of relief that they had replaced the bottle which had been finished on the night of Aisling's arrival. . . .

They gave him their presents. He seemed very pleased and in a rare mood of participation he decided that he would put them on. It took a time for him to adjust the tie and handkerchief, and place the tiepin and replace his old cufflinks with the new ones.

There was a card from Mother. Elizabeth had censored it to make sure it had not contained anything fanciful or unstable which would upset everyone. But no, it said: 'I wish you happy years ahead and happy memories of the years that have gone before.' He was pleased with it and put it on the mantelpiece. There was a card from Mrs Ellis which was flowery and vulgar and they all laughed at it in a guilty way. There was a small packet which had an ounce of tobacco and a note from Johnny. 'Happy Birthday wishes from Johnny Stone to Elizabeth's father. I'm sorry it's so small but perhaps when you reach your full century rationing will have gone forever.'

'He's a nice young man,' he said, pleased. 'Have you met him Aisling?'

'Oh yes, I met him at the shop, but he and Madam here are having some kind of silly tiff so I didn't get to know him.' Aisling followed the rehearsed line.

Everything was defined as excellent. Home-made bread from Ireland, soda bread, wrapped up in butter-paper to keep it fresh, spread thick with butter, slice after slice of it with the soup.

'Hey, don't let's forget the main course. We must leave room.'

They ran backwards and forwards from oven to table. Flashes of rose and cream, giggles when they bumped into each other. Oohs and aahs at the smell of the bacon . . . every plate cleaned to shining because nobody had eaten anything at midday in order to prepare for the feast.

Then there was the cake. One candle not fifty, that was more reasonable.

They lit it and looked at him expectantly.

'Oh no, I'm not a child . . . this is a bit too . . . it's not really. . . .'

'Come on Mr White. A birthday's not a birthday unless you blow out a candle.'

'No, no that's for children . . . no.'

'Oh do blow it out Father, it's a celebration.' Elizabeth almost trembled as she spoke . . . her lower lip looked a lot like someone about to cry.

'Mr White, if you don't blow it out how can we sing "Happy Birthday", how can we do it?' Aisling looked so eager and excited in the candlelight.

'Well, it's a bit silly.' Father stood up and took a great breath like a child and blew out the candle. They clapped and sang 'Happy Birthday' and 'For He's A Jolly Good Fellow'.

'Right.' Aisling pushed back her chair a bit. It was as if the signal for entertainment had been given. 'Right, what are you going to sing for us? Mr White, you must have a fund of songs.'

Elizabeth looked alarmed. Didn't Aisling realise how little singing went on in this household? They weren't like the O'Connors, who would burst into 'Believe Me If All Those Endearing Young Charms' as soon as there was the slightest encouragement.

Father didn't sing. Flushing, she remembered how she had practically closed down the party that night in Preston by singing 'Danny Boy'.

'No, I'm not a singer personally.' He was clearing his throat.

'You surprise me,' said Aisling. 'I heard great sounds coming from the bathroom there. It wasn't a gramophone you had in with you?'

'Yes, you're trapped now Father,' cried Elizabeth, joining in the game.

'No, no, no,' but he was laughing, not irritated.

'Let me see, what would be your forte . . . music-hall songs? Light opera . . . Gilbert and Sullivan maybe . . . ?'

'Yes, you do know some Gilbert and Sullivan Father. . . .'

'Not really . . . not to sing.'

Aisling had stood up already . . . 'Come on, I'll start you off –

'Take a pair of sparkling eyes,
Hidden ever and anon . . .'

She made gestures as if she were conducting a choir 'Come on can't you . . . don't leave me on my own. . . .'

Elizabeth and Father joined in. . . .

'No, no, we'll start again, do it properly.'

'Take a pair of sparkling eyes,
Hidden ever and anon
In a merciful eclipse
Do not heed their mild surprise
Having passed the Rubicon
Take a pair of rosy lips . . .

Take a figure firmly planned . . .'

Elizabeth watched open-mouthed as Father's voice soared on and on with Aisling, who couldn't really remember the words, humming and encouraging and joining in on last lines. . . .

'I'm not sure if I had the right key, I think I went through about three keys altogether,' he laughed apologetically.

'Nonsense, it was beautiful,' Aisling insisted.

'Now come on Elizabeth, what have you learned since you left Kilgarret?'

'I don't sing much really.'

'Come on, of course you do. Weren't we always singing on our bicycles back home?'

'That was different.'

'All right, wait.' Aisling ran out the kitchen door and came in wheeling Elizabeth's bicycle.

Everyone laughed. The bicycle looked cumbersome and out of place at the table which was full of dirty dishes and the birthday cake. . . .

'Now you have your bicycle, get up on it and sing.'

Elizabeth looked nervously at Father to see how he was taking it. It was all so silly, so irresponsible and childish. All the things he said he detested and there he was grinning like an idiot.

She leaped up and sat on the saddle . . . and pretending it was a horse she started. . . .

'As I was going over the Cork and Kerry Mountain
I met with Captain Farrell and his money he was
    counting
I first produced my pistol, and then produced my rapier
Saying stand and deliver for you are my bold
    deceiver. . . .'

And because it was done with such gusto, she managed to get Father and Aisling standing up and shouting the chorus. . . .

'Whack fol de daddy o
There's whisky in the jar. . . .'

Elizabeth remembered all the verses and they sang louder and louder until the last chorus was almost bellowed.

Nobody cleared the table, the night went on and on. Elizabeth remembered 'Bold Robert Emmet the Darling of Ireland'. Aisling remembered 'Greensleeves' . . . and as his fiftieth birthday was coming to an end Elizabeth's father remembered

'On the road to Mandalay
Where the flyin'-fishes play
An' the dawn comes up like thunder
Outer China 'crost the bay. . . .'

'That's a great one, I don't know that,' called Aisling, and Elizabeth saw Father throw his chest out and sing like she had never known him to sing before. For an instant she wished that Mother could see it and then she was glad that these things weren't possible. . . .

Father even sang it twice, so well did it seem to be going down. . . .

> '. . . An' the temple-bells they say
> Come you back, you British soldier
> Come you back to Mandalay. . . .'

It finished off the birthday on a high and excited note. . . .

Sunday seemed a blur. They must have talked, but their minds were on Monday. And most of Monday was a blur too. Bits of it were only too clear, like the explanation of where they were going. Mythical friends of the O'Connors had been invented, people who lived now in Romford. Elizabeth and Aisling were going to spend three days with them. The warmth and bonds of the Saturday night had to be cooled and disengaged again. Elizabeth had to remind her father by her voice that he and she led separate lives. Aisling had to become distant instead of engaging. They left him confused and bewildered. But that was a small problem.

The guesthouse was very cheerful. It was run by a young woman who believed in plain speaking as she told them at the start.

'Now listen to me good. I don't know why you're here. I have no idea what you are doing in the area. I gather you want to stay and have a little peace and quiet because one of you has to have some kind of job done. Right, none of my business, I never asked, I don't even want to know your names.'

They looked at her fearfully.

She relaxed a bit. 'Well, just your first names, eh? And it's a nice big room and it's got a wash-basin, and there's lots of towels and a rubber sheet and anything else you might need to make you feel comfortable and I'm leaving you in a wireless too for company. There's only a couple of other people staying in the house, a couple of residents, you know, people who live here all the time. They keep themselves to themselves, and a nice couple of gents, travellers. They stay Monday and Tuesday. You won't be disturbed.'

'Thank you,' said Aisling.

'And I'll leave you a kettle, and there's a gas ring, so if you want to do for yourselves, you'll be on your own.'

'Do people often want to be on their own? I mean not able to face people, you know, feeling awful afterwards.' Elizabeth stuttered a bit.

The woman softened still more at Elizabeth's white face.

'No love, I tell you Mrs Norris is really nice. I've been to her three times. Well, don't look surprised my dear, it happens, life is life I say. . . . No, of course you won't have to stay in your room ducks, it's just nice to know that you have privacy if you do need it.'

'Thank you Mrs. . . .'

'I'm Maureen dear, just Maureen. You're . . . ?'

'Aisling and Elizabeth.'

'Ashley, like in *Gone with the Wind?* I thought it was a man's name . . . it's nice though.'

'Yes.'

'I'll show you the room now. Come and go as you like. Listen Ashley, I'll tell you a bit of advice, now take it from Maureen here. I'm in the know. Don't talk about it all too much, no need to talk about things, only makes them a lot worse. That's what Mrs Norris said to me first time and I always remembered it. "Don't talk and talk Maureen, what's done is done." Anyway this kind of thing's been happening to women since the beginning of time. Nature organised life in a very funny way, it seems to me. Even the ancient Egyptians used to have to cope with it and here we are in the twentieth century . . . so you take my advice, don't let her chat too much, brood, wonder is it right is it wrong, was it wrong was it right. No good comes of it.'

'No, that's true,' said Aisling.

'Good girl, she's lucky she has a friend with her. Lots of them come on their own.'

Maureen was speaking as if Elizabeth didn't exist.

They went upstairs.

'Let's not even look at this room properly so that we won't remember it,' Elizabeth said.

'The room isn't important, nothing's important except that you're all right.'

'Do you wish I'd turn back even now? Be honest Aisling. Do you want me to change my mind?'

Silence.

'Answer me, I know that's what you want, I know that's what you think is right. Go on admit it. It's what you hope will happen. You're glad this place is so awful, you're glad that woman's so dreadful and sordid and . . . ugh . . . three times . . . you're thrilled because it makes it all the more squalid. You think it's weakening my resolve don't you?'

'Elizabeth stop it, for God's sake.'

'No, for God's sake you stop it. Stop sitting there with that prissy disapproving look like an early Christian martyr forced to go through something unpleasant . . . I won't have it. Say it straight out – you want me to cancel everything at this late stage and go ahead and have this child, and get it adopted, or look after it. That's what you really want isn't it?'

Aisling took a notebook out of her handbag and began to write in it. She kept her head down as she sat on one of the beds writing.

Elizabeth paced around. 'But you do see don't you . . . that honestly a lot of your attitudes come from Kilgarret. I mean you've said yourself that everyone lives their lives in the shadow of the church. You are full of the notion of sin about it, and you believe all this stuff about souls and heaven and limbo. Well if it has a soul it will go to limbo and on the last day limbo souls might well get into heaven. And maybe we could baptise it while it's still in me. Had we thought of that? Aisling don't be so cruel . . . why won't you speak to me? Why won't you answer me?'

Aisling handed her the notebook. 'At the end of an eight-hour conversation on Thursday night, we agreed that if you had doubts or worries at the last minute that I was to say

NOTHING. That was your greatest fear, that I would talk you out of it, or that you would look for an excuse. You made me swear that no matter what the provocation I would say nothing. Now for Christ's sake will you belt up.'

Elizabeth closed her eyes, and laughed until the tears came through her eyelids.

'You are marvellous, absolutely marvellous,' she said. 'How have I managed to live without you for all this time?'

'I don't know, you seem to be going to pieces all right,' Aisling said, and magically it made them both laugh.

Aisling remembered that going up the steps of the house where Mrs Norris lived was worse than going to confession after her first experiences with Ned Barrett. Elizabeth said that it had the same unreal feeling as had hung around the place when Mother and Father had decided to separate.

Aisling said that she didn't pray and that Mrs Norris was a liar to say that she was on her knees in the parlour of the house when Elizabeth had gone upstairs. She said that Mrs Norris was a dishonest old cow to say that she had been crying and holding her rosary beads when she had been told it was all over. Elizabeth said that Mrs Norris must have heard some praying because otherwise how would she have heard the words 'Hail Holy Queen'? Mrs Norris wasn't a Roman Catholic. She would not have been able to make up a prayer like that unless she heard Aisling say it.

Maureen said that she was sorry she had mentioned rubber sheets if it frightened them. Usually she only said it just to reassure people, of course there would be no need for rubber sheets. It was all over wasn't it? And there, it hadn't been too bad now had it? And there was the rest of her life before Elizabeth wasn't there? She talked to Aisling as if Elizabeth was deaf and dumb.

And Elizabeth felt so well on Wednesday that they went to the pictures. The film was about a woman who had a child but had to pretend that the child belonged to her sister. Bette

Davis played the part of the woman and together Aisling and Elizabeth watched her agony as she saw her daughter grow up but could never admit to being her mother. The film was called *The Old Maid*. It was a great weepie and the two girls blew their noses, wiped their eyes and ate liquorice allsorts like any two young girls on an afternoon out.

'You'd never think we had even more adventures than that would you?' said Elizabeth, and Aisling gripped on to her hand and held it tight.

'You would not. We're great, the pair of us,' she said.

The house in Clarence Gardens looked a bit dusty and unwelcoming when they came back. It needed the windows opened and fresh air to come through it. Elizabeth said that it was an oddly-shaped house. It seemed to trap a lot of dead heavy air all the year round. In winter it was cold and musty and in summer it was hot and musty. She wondered whether it had anything to do with the walls. Aisling said she wondered were they going to talk about the weather for the rest of her visit or could they have a normal conversation again? Elizabeth's father came in just then and said he was delighted to see them back, the place had been very empty without them. Elizabeth said to Aisling later that Father was even more of a trial when he was being interested in things than when he was not, and Aisling said that the divil wouldn't please someone as crotchety as Elizabeth.

Johnny too was pleased to see them back. He said that London had been very dull without them, nobody laughed, people retired early to bed. He hoped that the whole problem had been sorted out and everything was all right now. What problem, they had wanted to know, alarmed. Well, the whole question of marriage and whether it was a good idea or a bad idea or the only solution or the last refuge. They looked at him blankly. But Johnny had thought that was one of the main reasons that Aisling had come over in order to sort out her complicated love life. Heavens above it can't have been very serious or pressing if she'd forgotten all about it already. In his innocence he thought that this was what they had gone off to discuss.

Elizabeth took Aisling to see the college of art. It was the summer holidays but some vacation courses were under way so they could wander about. She pointed out the classrooms, the studios, the workshops. In one of the classrooms a boy stood posing for the life class naked. They could see him through the door. Aisling was astounded. Did Elizabeth have to draw naked fellows like that? Never! And put in everything? Go on. And girls too? Absolutely naked? But couldn't you learn how a person was made and their muscles and all even if he wore underpants? Wasn't everyone's mickey more or less the same?

Around this part of the visit things began to get clearer for Aisling and she remembered that everyone at home would want to know all she had been doing in London. She had better see some sights. She thought too that she had better try to integrate Elizabeth back into the life she was leading before all this drama. She assumed that it revolved around Johnny and this is what Elizabeth wanted to return to. Aisling could ask Johnny take her on a spin in the van the next time he was going somewhere exciting. He thought this was a great idea and said they must all go off to the Tower of London just in case he decided to move Stefan's business down there! He invented a ridiculous reason why they should go everywhere a visitor might want to see. He found a real reason to go to Brighton and Aisling clapped her hands with excitement to see a huge beach. They went for a swim and splashed each other for hours in the water.

'People won't believe that there's real beaches in England,' she screamed happily.

'Oh Aisling stop making the Irish out to be ridiculous. Of course they know there are beaches here.'

'No, they don't. They really don't. I never heard anyone tell of an English seaside before. It's great so it is.'

Elizabeth and Johnny exchanged affectionate glances

265

about her, and Johnny put out his hand to touch Elizabeth as Aisling swam off on her own.

'I miss you. I don't suppose that you could slip away for a bit, Nick and Tom won't be . . . ?'

Elizabeth smiled regretfully. 'Oh no, not while Aisling's here. . . .'

'She wouldn't mind.'

'No, out of the question. It's not the kind of thing that I'd do, that anyone would do, when they have a friend to stay. . . .'

She made herself seem both firm and light-hearted about it. And Johnny understood, he laughed goodnaturedly.

'You're a good hostess, you keep all the rules. "The perfect hostess does not abandon the guest in order to satisfy carnal desires with a Loved One." '

Elizabeth laughed happily. 'That's it, it's Rule Three.'

'Whatever you say, but when the guest has gone back to the Emerald Isle. . . . I warn you I'll be insatiable.'

'Oh good,' said Elizabeth.

Mrs Norris had explained that no relations must take place for two weeks. By then, she said, things could proceed as normal.

'You know you really broke your promise about telling me what it was like . . . sex . . . making love . . . doing it,' Aisling said.

'Funny, I knew I was breaking my promise. The very first night I lay there and wondered had you in fact made love a long time ago and not told me, because there really is something very . . . I don't know . . . something so personal it would be upsetting really to try to describe it.'

'Now you're making it more mysterious than ever. I'll never know. You were my only hope.'

'But I told you, I was sure you knew and everything and weren't telling me for the same kind of reason. . . .'

'Holy God, Elizabeth, how would I know in Kilgarret? How on earth would I find out about having sex the whole way with someone?'

'Well, I didn't expect to either . . . you make this sound

like Paris or something. This is a London suburb . . . there's not much sin going on here either.'

'Have you forgotten what Kilgarret is like? Everyone knows where everyone is all day and all night. It's like being in a goldfish bowl. I mean, without even being like policemen or suspicious, people know what you're doing twenty-four hours a day . . . "I saw you down at the river the other night" . . . "Josy Lynch says she saw you in Moriarty's chemist". The whole town would know when you were having your period.'

'Or I suppose when you weren't,' said Elizabeth.

'Certainly. I don't know how I'd have organised what you had to do. There's nobody that would know.'

'But what do they do?'

Aisling said nothing.

'They must do something, it must happen.'

'Yes, but. . . .'

'Oh go on. Tell me.'

'Well, either a fellow would marry them and talk would die down in a year or two, or in a dire case the girl might go off to the nuns.'

'Up in the school? Never?'

'Oh Lord, no, not those nuns. Nuns in some country place. They run homes for unmarried mothers, and the girls sort of work there and earn their keep, then when the baby is born it's given for adoption and the girl comes back. She usually says she's been to her granny's. It's a known expression, going to your granny.'

'It must be a very lonely sort of thing to have to do.'

'Yes, it's not great certainly. The whole fear of it would put you off going the whole way, even if you weren't afraid of losing the boy anyway.'

'Are people still afraid of losing people by sleeping with them?'

'Yes, definitely. I wouldn't sleep with anyone if I had serious designs on them, because if I was serious about some fellow and did sleep with him, he might think I was a tramp. I'm not saying he's right, but that's Kilgarret law.'

'And would you think he was a tramp, or a male tramp . . . or whatever we'd call it . . . ?'

'No, that's different. You know about men not being able to control themselves, having this urge implanted in them by God. Yes, I do think it's true actually. You know the way they want to do it with everyone. That's God's plan . . . or nature's plan if you want to call it that, of seeing that the human race goes on. Men are mad to do it everywhere and women have to take control of them and insist that they only do it within matrimony and that's society. . . .'

Elizabeth was rocking with laughter.

'You'd be marvellous as a nun, honestly you would, telling all the girls about the facts of life like that. They'd never recover.'

'But honestly isn't they what they told us, in different words?'

'Yes, very different words.'

'I know it sounds ridiculous and complicated but that is the way things seem to work in Kilgarret anyway if not in the rest of the world.'

'Do you blame all those nuns becoming nuns? I think I'd become a nun if I thought all those men were rampaging the town, made to do it everywhere.'

'Spiking their seed all round the place . . . waiting for unwary females. . . .'

'Aisling *honestly*.'

'But that's it, it's just a game, and it's like bridge or poker or whatever, people who know the rules and only take the right risks.'

Aisling was distressed to see Elizabeth cooking the books.

'It's very hard for you to understand,' Elizabeth had explained. 'Uncle Sean wouldn't in a million years question what you spent or what Aunt Eileen spent . . . there's no question of having to account for this and that. Father has the mind of a bank official who has to balance the books at the end of the day. He wants to balance the housekeeping too.'

'But you're cheating him. You're keeping money. If he finds out . . . he'd be upset. Why don't you just ask him for more?'

268

'He's got a small mind, he thinks in small terms and small sums and petty accounts. He never checks whether a tin of Spam costs three shillings or it doesn't, but he does add the total up in front of me. Anything I save I earn, I don't steal his money, I just think of ways of saving it and then I keep what I save. That's all.'

Aisling studied the accounts. 'Yes, I see. But it's a bit petty on your side isn't it? It's not very generous . . . or the way people go on in a family.'

'This isn't a family, Father has never been generous. A big open heart like yours or Uncle Sean's or Johnny's he'd find frightening. He'd think that your household was on the brink of chaos because nobody knows exactly to the last penny how much it costs to feed and clothe you all. He'd never take into consideration that your mother feeds half the beggars that come to the door, and that she dressed and fed me for nothing for five years, and that she sends presents and gifts and has pence always in her handbag for anyone she thinks might need one. No, Father would be alarmed by that. He's alarmed by all the marvellous food you brought from Ireland. Three times he asked me should we pay you. I think I should have said yes, it would have calmed him down.'

'You talk about him very coldly, don't you? You used to want him to be nicer and happier and everything. You used to want him to change?'

'Oh yes I did. I used to think I could change him, that we could become like a picture of a Happy Family. "Mr George White, banker, and his only daughter Elizabeth, estranged wife in North of England but isn't it wonderful how well they all manage in their ways." But it didn't work. You can't change people, they go their own way. . . . Johnny says there's more unhappiness caused in the world by people trying to change other people than anything else.'

"Does Johnny say that? Why?"

'Oh he gives examples. His friend Nick loves football, Nick's girlfriend Shirley wants to settle down, go and look at furniture in the shops. Shirley wants to change Nick, make him stop playing football; Nick wants to change Shirley and make her come and watch football. They fight about it all the time. . . .'

'Well, if old Shirley's got to pound around buying all the furniture on her own, and let loverboy Nick play football . . . is that Johnny's solution . . . ?'

'Something like that, yes, then they wouldn't fight. . . .'

'God, he's more selfish than I thought,' said Aisling. 'I'm sorry, I'm sorry it slipped out. I didn't mean it.'

Elizabeth's eyes filled with tears. 'He's not selfish. He didn't come to Mrs Norris with me because he didn't know, he'll never know. He didn't stop me going there because he wasn't told the situation. Now you can't say he's selfish not to have been divinely inspired, can you?'

Aisling apologised. 'I'm always saying the wrong thing, because I don't think before I speak. I don't understand things either . . . but that never stops me interfering. When I think of all those years you stayed with us and you never interfered or hurt anyone. You only patched up quarrels instead of causing them. I feel very thick and stupid coming in here . . . telling you how to behave to your father, telling you what your boyfriend should and shouldn't think.'

'Oh, but if you knew how I hate your going back. I don't know how I'm going to carry on without you. It's so lovely talking and sharing and knowing that you're interested in everything . . . I've missed that so much, I've had a big hole in my life. . . .'

'So have I. . . .'

'But you've a whole family . . . Aunt Eileen. . . .'

'Yes, but not about the things we talk about, you and I.'

'I know.'

There was a silence.

'Letters aren't really any good are they? They don't explain much. I can't see Kilgarret through your letters, but maybe it will be better now that you know how interested I am in even little things. . . .'

'Yes, and now that I know all the cast over here . . . maybe you'll write about them properly . . . and not all this "nice" and "super". . . .'

'And you must cut out all that "nothing much has happened in the last six months" bit.'

'Oh I will, I'll keep you informed of every groan and grunt in the back seat of the car. . . .'

'Aisling, I'll be so lonely without you.'

'Of course you won't. Haven't you got Johnny?'

Johnny took them both to the pictures on Aisling's last night. And to a fish supper afterwards in a big noisy place with marble tables and high ceilings and a great smell of vinegar and batter. No, he wouldn't hear of any contribution, this was his treat. Elizabeth beamed, glad to see his generosity and big-heartedness shown so obviously to Aisling.

'Anyway,' said Johnny. 'It's a goodbye present.'

'Gosh, I'll have to keep coming and going if I get goodbye presents like this all the time.'

'It's not only for you,' said Johnny easily. 'I'm off too. I'm going to take a train to the Mediterranean Sea . . . so it's a joint goodbye.'

'You're going to what . . . ?' Elizabeth's face was red and then white, just like it used to be when she was new at the school and the nun had asked her a question she couldn't understand.

'We only arranged it today . . . Nick's got a few weeks off. He works in a car firm, Aisling . . . and his boss says business is slow if he wants to go now, he can have half-pay for five weeks and then a guarantee of his job back. He's jumping at it.'

'And you . . . ?' Elizabeth looked horrified. She looked so shocked that Aisling knew instinctively that it was going to irritate Johnny.

'So you're going to jump at it with him, Johnny?' Aisling said hurriedly. 'What a marvellous idea. Can you take time off from work too?'

'Yes.' Johnny was eager. 'Stefan keeps asking me to take a break and now this seems too good to miss. Nick's getting the tickets.'

'When are you going?' Elizabeth's voice was a whisper.

'Saturday, or Friday if he gets a sleeper on the train before.'

'How great.' Aisling had to speak at the top of her voice to try to cover the look of hurt and the stony silence from Elizabeth. 'Is it the south of France or is it Spain . . . or where?'

'It's France, apparently there's a village that a friend of Shirley's was talking about . . . where you can hire a chalet or a tent . . . and you don't need much food in this weather. Shirley said it was meant to be smashing.'

'Is Shirley going with you?' asked Aisling, before Elizabeth could ask the same question in a hurt little voice.

'No, between ourselves, that's part of the reason for the sudden hop. Shirl has been very wearying about everything, and Nick wants a bit of a breather. Too much domesticity and the dangerous clanking sound of wedding bells being yearned for.'

'Oh, he's quite right to run then,' said Aisling. 'That's why I ran from Ireland. You need to put space between yourself and that sort of thing. Thank the Lord none of us have those kind of inclinations.'

She looked sideways at Elizabeth, praying that she would have recovered. She was amazed at what she saw. Elizabeth's face was back to normal and she was smiling broadly.

'Poor Shirl,' she said. 'I suppose I'll have to comfort her when you've gone. I'll try to get her interested in someone else.'

'Oh, I think he quite likes her, it's just that she's such a hanger-on. . . .'

'She's rather pretty. I'm sure she'd find it easy to get another chap. Perhaps we'll go on the prowl together when you're off in *La Belle France*.'

'Ah, but *you're* not to have another chap. You're not to be lost. Do you hear me?'

'Um yes, well I'll probably still be here. I'll be rather too busy to go out prowling, so we'll have to hope that I'm not swept away accidentally. No? I'll work with Mr Worsky and Anna, I might even be a partner when you come back.'

Aisling looked in amazement at Elizabeth's bright face. She was playing it so utterly right. Johnny was almost wavering. He was regretting slightly his decision to go, he was looking at her with enthusiasm and interest.

With a wave of understanding, Aisling realised that if Elizabeth was going to play the game by these rules it was going to be one long act from now to the very end. There could be no normal behaviour, no real reactions, no chance of saying what you felt, what you meant. It would be watching your step, planning your moves.

Elizabeth didn't cry when they got home, she would not admit her shock and upset. She was calm and measured.

'No, I refuse to get upset. I told you before he's what I want. I'll do anything to have him, anything. I've done so much already. I'm not going to lose it all by behaving like silly Shirley and whinging and whining because I'm not being taken along. . . .'

'But for God's sake, I know I'm not going to interfere, but wouldn't it be reasonable to say. . . .'

'I'm not talking about being reasonable. I really am much more like Mother than I thought. Mother wanted something more open and outgoing than Father and so do I. Mother wanted Harry, everyone would have said that it was an unreasonable thing to want . . . but Mother went ahead and she did what was necessary to get Harry and she got him and that's it. That's what I'm going to do. . . .'

'It's different.'

'Of course it's different because Mother was dreadfully odd by the time she did it . . . but the principle is the same. . . .'

Aisling said, 'I suppose I don't know what it's like to be so fond of someone that I'd do . . . well, do all you've done.'

'Oh, you will Aisling. Honestly you will some day be as fond of someone as I am. It sounds a bit . . . as if I were an old woman giving you old wives' advice . . . but you will find someone. And then just like they say in all the songs and the films . . . you'll know.'

273

'Yes, but once you do know, that's when the troubles seem to begin,' Aisling said doubtfully.

Elizabeth's father said that Aisling's visit had been like a breath of fresh air. Mr Worsky and Anna Strepovsky gave her a picture of a fairy woman in a forest and said she should have it framed back in Ireland, perhaps it had to do with her name. . . . Monica gave her staff discount on a blouse she bought for Mam, and Johnny Stone kissed her goodbye on the cheek and said that some time next year he was going to take the van and Elizabeth to Ireland and do a tour of all the old houses which might sell their contents to him.

'I'll come with you if I'm not married to the Squire.'

'Oh, don't dream of marrying the Squire,' said Johnny.

Elizabeth clung to her at the barrier in Euston.

'I keep trying to fight down this awful feeling that I'll never see you again, and that you'll go home and think of everything that happened here and you'll become revolted by it all. You'll cut me out of your life.'

'I'll never cut you out of my life, I couldn't, you're part of it you silly old thing,' said Aisling. 'If it weren't so soppy I'd say I love you.'

'Well I love you too, I'll never be able to thank you. Never.'

The crowds on the platform swallowed up Aisling in her turquoise summer coat as she walked down the length of the long train. And when she looked back at the barrier there were too many people and she couldn't see Elizabeth in her grey dress waving and wiping her eyes with the corner of the red scarf which was meant to make her look jaunty.

XI

Elizabeth thought that it would be much easier to write to Aisling after the visit ... but she found to her great disappointment that it was just as hard to explain, just as difficult to describe things. One set of restrictions had been replaced by another. It made her uneasy since she realised that she must assume Aisling was critical of Johnny. And yet Aisling had hardly said a word that could be interpreted as criticism. But then what she kept forgetting was that Johnny didn't *know* there was any reason for him to feel especially protective and loving and grateful to Elizabeth at that time. Johnny didn't know anything about the visit to Romford and the encounter with Mrs Norris, and he never would.

So the letters seemed strained, again. Elizabeth tried to write cheerful things about Father, but Father had never again been so cheerful since his fiftieth birthday. In fact at times Elizabeth wondered whether she had imagined Father singing all those songs. He never sang since, and she hadn't mentioned the night to him.

It was odd that Aisling was able to write without restraint. Sometimes she would urge Elizabeth to burn the letters once they were read in case they would both be hanged or Aisling put in gaol for pornography. Her descriptions of the ever-frustrated passions of Tony Murray were hilarious, and often apologised for by the phrase, 'But of course to a woman of the world like yourself all this must seem very amateur'. She asked questions too about Father and whether the awful woman who was after him was getting anywhere. She told Elizabeth to tell Stefan and Anna that she had enquired about old houses in Ireland and whether they might be bursting with antiques. The answer was yes, they might, but if anyone came over from England in a van to buy them from them they would immediately assume they were being robbed blind and would hold on to whatever they had.

She touched so lightly and so unsurely on the subject of Johnny, compared to everything else. The references to him were half-joking, guarded almost as if she had reread the sentence before allowing it to go. The rest of the letter was pure Aisling, sentences falling over each other . . . enthusiastic and maddening. Exactly the way she talked.

Aunt Eileen still wrote, cheery newsy letters, half-joking references to the handsome young man whom Aisling had described as being the best-looking man she had ever laid eyes on. Elizabeth found it hard to write about Johnny in any normal way so she wrote in an exaggerated style saying that the Lord and Master had gone off to Scotland, or the Answer to Hollywood had put up a new sign on the shop saying 'Worsky and Stone' and spent most of his day out on the pavement admiring it. She couldn't write to anyone that she loved Johnny Stone so much that her heart was hurting from jumping up and down in her rib cage. That's the kind of thing Aisling would have been able to say but then of course Elizabeth remembered ruefully, Aisling's heart wasn't jumping up and down at all. It was staying exactly where it was, stationary and deliberating whether or not to lock itself permanently into Tony Murray's heart.

Tony thought that Aisling looked even better when she came back from England than she had done before. He had found the days very long because he had no idea when they were going to end. His mother, disapproving and hard to please about this as well as everything else, became a severe trial to him. She had suggested that he might invite one of the Grays to the tennis club dance. Heedless of his protests that he didn't even know the Gray girl and didn't want to go to the dance with anyone, and would like to be allowed to mind his own business, she spoke on in a firm monologue which she believed was reaching him because of its constant repetition. Not that she had a thing against the little O'Connor girl, a charming child. Had she not always been made welcome at their house when she was a friend of Joannie's but such a child, and so nice and so limited, and so young, and what a pity Tony didn't extend his friends a little more. Why, Mrs Gray had been saying only last week. . . . Tony turned off his mind. He would often get up without excusing himself and leave the table, or walk from the sitting room with its view down towards the river. No explanation, no apologies, just one swinging movement into the car and a bold sweep down the drive.

Eileen O'Connor felt that the whole teasing game with Tony was going on too long. True, Aisling was an attractive girl, true there were more ways of getting your man than being available. And indeed it was a great relief after the Maureen and Brendan Daly situation to realise that this time the boot was on the other foot. Eileen and Sean had felt humiliated by the delay in Brendan Daly's proposal. It was as if they had decided to keep the O'Connors on a string. Now Aisling was doing the whole thing in reverse and it was the Murrays who were dangling in uncertainty.

Any attempts now to know what Aisling's intentions might be were skilfully diverted.

'Do you think it's worth painting your office? Will you still be with us next year?'

'Of course I'll be with you Mam. Were you thinking of firing me?'

'No, but you know if you marry into the gentry you wouldn't want to go on working here . . . you wouldn't have to work for a living.'

'Aw, Mam, the Murrays aren't gentry, they're as ignorant as we are. Anyway I'd like to see someone stopping me from doing what I want to do and I want to work here. What colour will we get it painted?'

'Tony Murray wouldn't want his wife working in a shop Aisling, you must know that.'

'Then he can go and take a flying jump at himself. Listen, what about that bright orange paint that came in a while ago? With the doors white and me in my green coat I'd look like the Irish flag!'

She didn't seem to be the slightest bit serious about him, yet she did see him almost every evening. What on earth was going to happen? Time would tell.

Maureen thought that Aisling had become unbearable since her visit to London. She had become more cocky and more of a show-off than ever. All these stories beginning: 'When we were in Piccadilly Circus' . . . and 'Elizabeth and I went for a fish supper in the Elephant and Castle' . . . just plain showing off. Not a present bought for the babies. A feeble excuse about rationing in England, that was nonsense of course. Hadn't the war been over for years now? Aisling was turning out to be quite poisonous, she even managed to make a jeer and a mock of things when she did deign to come to the house. Poor Brendan was most put out by her, and Brendan's mother had said she was in danger of becoming quite fast with all this careering around the place with Tony Murray and no intentions made clear on any side.

Joannie Murray came back to Kilgarret from time to time, full of the great life she lived in Dublin. She found things increasingly fraught at Riverside House on every visit. People were constantly taking her aside to explain the truth of the situation as if her time spent working in the capital city had given her a new sophistication and insight into the big issues of a Kilgarret day. As far as Joannie could see they all revolved around her friend Aisling O'Connor. Mummy used to walk up and down the drawing room clenching and unclenching her hands and saying that she had nothing against Aisling.

From Aisling she got no joy either. Aisling said there was no mystery. She was very fond of Tony and he seemed to be fond of her. No, neither of them had the slightest intention of doing anything drastic like getting engaged. They were young for heaven's sake. Tony wasn't young, Joannie reminded her, Tony was very old, he was over thirty. Aisling would only giggle and say that thirty was like a spring chicken these days. Then Joannie would repeat this kind of conversation to Mummy, and Mummy would become bad-tempered and accuse Joannie of holding things back. It was really very wearying to come home to Riverside House for weekends. Joannie did it less and less.

Sean was getting tired of people asking him when they would see the great merger of the Murrays and O'Connors. One of these conglomerates, they were calling it with wheezy laughs, it could take over half the business in the east of Ireland, a firm that size. They were joking about a possible merger but they weren't joking about Aisling. People wanted to know. Sean was irritated both with the curiosity of the people who came in to him in the shop or drank pints with him at Maher's. He was even more irritated with Aisling.

From time to time he said she was making them all into a laughing stock with her carry-on. Aisling put on huge innocent eyes and said she didn't know what he meant.

Sean would fluff Aisling's hair roughly with his hand and say that the most atrocious thing in the world was to live in a small Irish town and be at the mercy of a lot of small-town gossips.

Elizabeth wrote about Mother. She had been right in her reading of the letters. Mother's nerves were indeed under a strain.

She was in hospital now, and half of the time she didn't know where she was. Harry had been distraught. He begged Elizabeth to come up and see them and to bring that nice young man Johnny who had been such a great fellow the last time. Naturally the nice young man had no intention of going to a house where illness, insanity and confusion would reign, so Elizabeth didn't even try to persuade him. She went by train.

Harry did not look the same Harry when he met her at Preston. He had big worried runnels in his face.

'I did my best for her, Elizabeth love,' he began to bluster as if there was a possibility that he might be blamed for what

279

had happened to Mother. 'I never treated her badly. I tried to go along with whatever she said and wanted. There wasn't all that much money of course, you see there wasn't all that much business. . . .'

To her amazement Elizabeth found herself hugging Harry there and then in the station with passers-by looking at them. Hugging the man she had called that dreadful Mr Elton, the man who had come to steal Mother away all those years ago.

'Harry you old fool,' she said over his big shaking shoulder. 'Harry, you did everything for her. She loves you, she's crazy about you, what are you apologising for? Think what it would be like if her poor nerves had gone when she was in Clarence Gardens. Think how lonely that would have been for her.'

Harry's face was wet too.

'You're a great girl, Elizabeth,' he said. 'Really champion. I don't know how any of us would get along without you. . . .'

Mother was pleased to see Elizabeth, but only pleased in the same way as she was pleased when it was teatime in the war or when it was time to go to the basket-work section in Occupational Therapy. She looked tired and pale. She had very little interest in anything. Elizabeth searched for some subject to bring a spark back to her dead face. She remembered when she had thought that Mother had been overexcited, when she seemed twitchy and nervy, and responded and reacted like a little bird to everything, spreading unease and restlessness around her.

Elizabeth tried to summon up that uneasy life with no success. 'I often read your letters, Mother, about the wonderful times you had back in the roaring twenties. It must have been great, all those *thé dansants*. . . .'

'All the what, dear?'

'Well maybe I'm not pronouncing them right – dancing teatimes, I suppose. Remember you wrote to me about them, you used to go in a lilac dress, you told me, and there were orchestras, small five- or six-piece orchestras . . . ?'

She paused. Mother smiled back gently and vaguely.

'Weren't there people coming over to the table you were sitting at, and saying they would be honoured if you would while away a weary afternoon, you know, fancy exaggerated talk . . . .'

Violet looked at her, nodding politely as if she were being told something that she didn't understand.

'And remember the man who asked you your name and you said Violet, and he said violet dress, violet eyes and now named Violet, and he ran away and brought back six bunches of violets from a woman in the street, he had given her a whole ten-shilling note. You must remember, you often told me about it even when I was little, and you wrote about it again this year. It *did* happen didn't it?'

'Oh yes, dear, if you say so.' Mother was looking around for the nurse. In her eyes was the hope that she would be rescued.

'But Mother,' Elizabeth shouted, 'Mother you're so young, and so lovely and your hair is all matted, why don't you let me wash your hair and comb it for you, let me give you some lipstick, you have such a lovely face, Mother. . . ?'

'Nurse . . .' called Mother in a rising tone. An older woman with a face so lined it looked like a dried mud puddle cracking in the sunlight, said to Elizabeth, 'Don't excite her dear, don't try to take her out of here, she feels comfortable here, you'll see. She doesn't want to be upset and confused.'

Elizabeth turned on her. 'She only needs to be reminded of what she's like. She's forgotten what kind of person she is, *that's* what's wrong.'

'I know,' said the old woman. 'But she's happy forgetting.'

Back in the shop Harry put a closed sign on the door as soon as he saw Elizabeth coming around the corner.

'There's not all that much business,' he said. 'How was she, was she pleased to see you?'

'Harry, take down that closed sign. People who want to buy their half pound of margarine must be able to do it.' She reversed the sign on the door, took off her coat and picked up the beige shop-coat that was hanging on a hook; it wouldn't fasten around her. It must have been the one Mother had worn.

'No, I want to hear, I want to know.' Harry was upset and red-faced.

'There's nothing *to* hear, Harry, I swear it. She didn't know what I was talking about. She seemed happy, the other old crones in the ward say she's happy, the nurse says she's happy. She doesn't remember who she is, that's the problem. She's forgotten how to be lively and it's as if the life drained away.'

Harry's eyes were swimming. 'Do you think it will come back, could she change again?'

'The doctor will talk to me tomorrow. He said he hadn't time today and he would only talk if I promised not to ask for miracle cures. I thought he was arrogant and patronising but I didn't say so. I put on a humble face. . . .'

'But what caused it? Why did Vi lose all the life in her?'

'I don't know, Mother doesn't know, and I'm very sure that pompous doctor doesn't know. But Harry, if you're going to be able to afford the bus fare up to the hospital, we'd better keep open. Now, here we go, who's this . . . ?'

'Mrs Park, the widow, meanest woman north of Manchester, buys one cigarette at a time and two ounces of butter.' The small woman in black came in. 'Hallo there Mrs Park. What can we do for you, do you know my step-daughter Elizabeth?'

'How are you Mrs Park, Harry was just mentioning you were a good customer.'

Mrs Park looked from one to another. 'Aye, well I'm regular, I come here to support local business. Mr Elton, can I have an ounce of that hard cheese, please, more from the middle, not the outside mind, and two Woodbines.'

'Having a party, Mrs Park?' said Harry and Elizabeth had to stuff the hem of Mother's shop-coat into her mouth to stop her laughing aloud.

The doctor sat opposite Elizabeth and explained about illnesses which were psychotic and illnesses which were schizophrenic. He said that Violet's was almost certainly the latter. It was a latent schizophrenia. Normally such a disorder would show itself much earlier. It was a young person's illness. Elizabeth nodded. She kept her scorn for the doctor's posturings out of her face. The self-important way he held his fingertips together and emphasised the words as he spoke to the twenty-year-old daughter of one of his patients. She wondered whether he ever stopped showing off and acting.

'Excuse me, does that mean a split personality? Is it a question of Mother having two sides to her personality like you read about in the novels . . . ?'

This gave the doctor time and opportunity for a peal of laughter. 'Heavens no, my dear. That's a very silly lay person's idea. Dr Jekyll and Mr Hyde. No, it means the person is out of touch with reality, their grip on what is reality has gone. The imaginary, the non-real is just as living to them.'

'And how are you trying to cure Mother?' Elizabeth asked, her cool young voice cutting across the plummy tones.

'As we think best.' His own voice was sharper now. 'With sedation, with giving her a life of order and control where she can be observed and calmed when the forces of unreality become too much. There are new drugs. Largactyl has been in use now for two years and we are trying this on many of our patients.'

Elizabeth forced her voice to be polite and deferential. 'Oh, are you *experimenting* with this new drug on Mother? Let's hope it's a good one.'

'No, I am not experimenting. It is being used all over Britain. We are reporting our findings. In your mother's case the best we can hope for is, well, to be frank, that her life will be as tranquil as possible.'

'You mean it would be foolish for me to hope that she will ever come out of here? She's only forty-nine, doctor. Do I have to tell my step-father that he should regard her as here permanently?'

'You seem a much more adult person than . . .' He looked

at his notes. 'Than Mr Elton. I feel I can speak to you frankly. His reaction is to promise me that he will give her more time and more attention. And making me assurances that he will offer a better lifestyle. In fact from what I understand, she was quite content with him. He was an adequate provider and husband.'

'She adored him.'

'Quite. Well it's no avail making this kind of statement. What we have to do is to hope that she may occasionally be able to go home for visits for the afternoon, or even for a weekend. These drugs have been known to create very surprising respites, you know. Nothing is impossible.'

'Except to believe that Mother will be as she was.'

'Quite. That would be the folly and a road to disappointment.'

Elizabeth looked at him carefully. Perhaps he was not such a phony and a fraud. He was, after all, warning her and had tried to warn Harry against false hopes. She stood up. 'I'll go to see Mother again. I'm very grateful to you Doctor, I will explain all this to my step-father, and I will try to make him see.'

'Thank you, Miss White, it's . . . er . . . a pleasure to talk to somebody so calm. It's a great help in this profession, as you must imagine.'

'Yes Doctor, I'm not really calm, but I am practical.'

'Quite. Oh, there's no point in your own father, her first husband, coming to see her. I mean you do realise that she doesn't actually take into account much of that section of her life?'

'No indeed, I wasn't going to suggest it, I'll explain it all to him too in case he thinks that there's anything he should do.'

'Good, good, well goodbye, Miss White.'

He went along his corridor, importance emanating from him. Elizabeth was glad she had controlled herself, and not behaved like many of the distraught relatives of his disturbed patients must have. She braced herself and knocked on the door of Mother's ward.

Mother had slept for eight and a half hours last night, the nurse told Elizabeth, but it was still a tired face that looked up and gave its gentle smile. Mother was sitting in a chair beside her bed with her hands folded in her lap. Her hair had been combed and tied behind her neck with a piece of ribbon. It made her look thinner than ever. She wore a cardigan over her nightdress.

Elizabeth sat down. She held one of mother's thin hands in hers for a bit and said nothing. Violet looked at her anxiously. She seemed to be waiting in case Elizabeth was going to start some unfamiliar pattern of behaviour, some tirade. It was hard to know if she remembered yesterday's upset or not. Nurse was hovering nearby arranging the flowers that Elizabeth had brought in a small vase.

'Oh Mother, wait until I tell you how funny Harry was in the shop yesterday,' Elizabeth began, and she gave a reassuring monologue of trivia. Violet looked less at Nurse. Nurse moved away. Mother left her hand in Elizabeth's, she smiled at the funny bits.

'So, anyway, I have to go back down to London tonight,' Elizabeth said in the same cheery voice. 'I have my final exams soon. Then I'll have to go out and earn a living, but I'll come back and see you in a month maybe, all right?'

'London?' Mother said wonderingly.

'Yes, to Clarence Gardens, and Father.'

'Father?'

'George, your old man, he sends you his best regards, says he hopes they're looking after you here.'

Mother smiled. 'That was nice of him, thank him, tell him I'm fine.'

Elizabeth gulped. 'Sure I will, and Harry's great too, he'll be in later today. He's a smasher, Harry. You picked a great one there, didn't you Mother?'

'Oh yes, Elizabeth, you see there was no question of it right from the start, I simply had to have Harry Elton. He was the only man I ever wanted.'

'Right, and you have him and he has you.'

'Yes.' Mother was beginning to withdraw into herself again.

'So I'll be off now, I'll write a long letter every week and if

285

you ever want me, you only have to get someone to telephone and I'll come back on the next train.'

'Thank you.'

Elizabeth stood up. She was wearing a grey flannel skirt and a dark grey twin set. To liven it up she had pinned on a big artificial flower. It was a bunch of violets in purple velvet with leaves made from taffeta. It was all wound around wire and attached to a pin. Suddenly she took it off and pinned it to Mother's cardigan. It looked lopsided and out of place.

'Thank you,' said Mother.

'You're a good girl, you're a good daughter,' said the lined old woman in the next bed, the woman who had spoken to her yesterday.

'They'll take it away from her, it's got a pin in it, she may do herself some mischief,' said another with her hair in an Eton crop and a puffy face.

'It doesn't matter,' Elizabeth said. 'I'd like to think she had it for a bit anyway.'

Father listened impassively as Elizabeth explained about Mother's illness. He shook his head when it was suggested that the whole thing had begun long ago and had only come to the surface now.

'There was absolutely nothing wrong with your mother when she was here in this house. Nothing at all. Her mind got disturbed when she went up to that place with that Harry Elton and lived in poverty. She had everything she ever wanted in this house. I'm not going to hear stories that her nerves got bad in this house.'

Elizabeth sighed. 'You're probably right, Father, I just thought I'd explain what the doctor said.'

'We'll say nothing about it to anyone here. I'm a fair man and I'm also a compassionate man,' Father said.

Elizabeth didn't get the drift of his thinking.

'I could easily tell people here, people in the bank and in the bridge club that Violet had become disturbed. I could tell them that she ended up in a home for the insane. But I won't do that. I'll let them remember her the way she was, I won't give them the chance to say she got her just desserts.'

286

'Her just desserts?'

'Oh yes, people here would say that she could have expected no better luck when she upped and left her home and her child without a care, that no good would come of it. But no, I won't tell them.'

'That's good of you, Father,' said Elizabeth, closing her eyes so that she would not betray her utter disgust at his petty, old-womanish, told-you-so thinking.

'No, it's just a fair attitude, that's all, it's letting bygones be bygones. Your mother caused us trouble, now she's having her own troubles. That's life, no point in having her punished further by telling all the people she knew here what befell her. Just let it be, I say.'

Sometimes Mr Worsky would read to Elizabeth from some German magazine articles and essays on designs. He translated them as he went along and she politely sat in the shop, leaning against some well-cared-for piece like the sideboard he would never sell or on the little piano stools that Anna had covered lovingly but in the wrong fabric so they were now completely useless.

Elizabeth sat in the sunlight and listened or half listened. Part of her mind took in his words, she heard enough to be able to smile at the little jokes, and to nod thoughtfully as he explained and elaborated.

Her heart seemed like a big piece of ice that had detached itself from an iceberg and was flowing slowly downstream. She thought of Johnny. She thought over and over that she had been right to keep any bad news from him and she wondered did everyone else keep bad news from him like she did? She wondered had anyone else aborted his child rather than lose him? And if they had . . . if some other young woman had gone up the stairs of a house like the house of Mrs Norris . . . then the poor girl had been through all that for no avail. Because whoever she was she hadn't kept Johnny.

She knew it was fanciful and foolish but she felt some silly comfort in thinking that other girls must have made similar decisions. She couldn't be the only person in the world who had done such a thing for love.

There was this fear growing in her that it had all been a waste of time. Johnny had somebody else. Well, he hadn't really got somebody else, but there was a woman . . . the girl . . . the one that he spoke of, talked of. The one who came into the shop a lot. The high society woman they called her. He couldn't love her. He couldn't. He couldn't touch her and whisper to her . . . he couldn't share with her what he shared with Elizabeth. It was impossible.

Right, it was impossible. She would not believe it. She had been so sensible about everything so far. She must continue, she must close the awful holes in her mind which let these suspicions in. She must try to warm up her heart again and stop it becoming this cold, dead, frightened thing. Everything was fine, Johnny was fine, he loved her dearly, he always went on about it. And Stefan loved her. She tuned in again to his voice. She listened and half listened as he fought for words, and stumbled for translations of theses which would be utterly useless to her in her examination. From time to time, Anna would remonstrate.

'Stefan, seriously . . . the child will not need to know that. . . .'

'Anna, you know nothing about what the child will need to know or will not need to know. She is studying design. I tell her about design, I tell her about European design, otherwise she will think that all Germans made were horrid, horrid steel tubes and hideous modern furniture. I tell her about Meissen china and of the pottery and porcelain of Furstenberg, of Nymphenberg, of Ludwigsberg. . . .'

'Berg, berg, berg,' muttered Anna. 'Why care about these bergs and what they made and what they did? They destroyed your country and mine, the people from Furstenberg and Ludwigsberg, and you sit here in the sun and tell the child about what beautiful porcelain they made.' She stamped off back to her little quarters, face red, full of good will, fearful that Stefan Worsky should be thought to be foolish or a bore.

'Sometimes I think your mind does wander, my Elizabeth. Perhaps it is a boring thing I tell you.'

She lifted a Meissen plate and traced her finger over the

mark. 'If it weren't for you, Mr Worsky, I wouldn't know whether this plate was a new batch from Woolworth's. Now I can read its history, I can read the story of everything here. It's like a new language you've taught me. And I always wanted someone to care about what I'm doing, you know, Mr Worsky, I have so many people I know and not one of them knows what examination I will be doing on Tuesday. Only you and Anna. My father just knows the end is in sight, the great day when all this ridiculous, affected studying of art will be over and I can get a job. That's all he knows. And my mother has lost her mind. I didn't tell you that because Father has this notion that we are to tell nobody in London. She is in a mental ward now of a big hospital in Preston up in Lancashire, and she doesn't really know where she is. I went to see her, remember? But I didn't tell you.'

'Oh, my poor child.'

'And Harry, my big, simple, foolish step-father is up there doing deals with all kinds of people, the vicar, I think, and the doctors and the ward sister, saying that if she gets better he'll look after her better. He looked after her perfectly. She loved every minute with him.'

'Oh my dear. . . .'

'And Monica Hart has just got engaged to a Scotsman who wears a kilt, and she couldn't care if I was doing an examination in design or in plumbing. Aisling O'Connor is waltzing around her home town playing some kind of I'm-the-king-of-the-castle game with all the local gentry, so far as I know. She barely reads my letters, she barely writes any. Her mother, Aunt Eileen, knows it's an examination, but she thinks it's like school. She thinks everyone does the same, she asks how many of them are going in for the exam, as if it was some huge thing that half the country was doing. . . .' Elizabeth was walking around pacing through the furniture. She was more distressed than Mr Worsky had ever seen her. She came back and put her hand on his shoulder. 'So you see how much I appreciate you, and thank you and could never be bored by you in all my life. . . .'

'It is I who thank you, for putting all kinds of happy things into an old man's life and work. Sometimes I am long-winded and boring and I talk too much and I read you long-winded things. Anna is right. I am not sensitive.'

She knelt beside him and took both his hands in hers.

'*You*, not sensitive? Dear Mr Worsky, you are beautifully sensitive. Just now when I'm full of self-pity and listing off all my friends and saying how they don't know and care what I'm doing, you didn't ask me what about Johnny? You didn't say, what about your lover? Surely your young man knows? You didn't say that.'

'But child, Johnny is Johnny, we know that.'

'We do. Johnny is Johnny, and nowadays Johnny is being driven around London in a smart sports car by that woman from high society.'

'She will not last long, the woman from high society.'

'No, you are right, she will want more than Johnny will give her. One of these days she will say to Johnny that they are all going to a house party to meet Princess Margaret, and Johnny will say he's not coming, with no explanation. And the high society woman will sulk and throw him out of her sports car, and she will wait until Johnny telephones to apologise or sends her flowers and then she will forgive him. But what she doesn't know is that he will make no telephone call and send no flowers, there will be no apology.'

'Don't distress yourself.'

'No, that's what will happen, and she will burn with rage for a week and she will call around here, and she will buy something very expensive and she will enquire about Johnny. And we will tell Johnny and he will roll his eyes up to heaven and say Good Lord, and we'll all laugh.' She was still sitting like a child at his knee. He said nothing, but he stroked her hair very lightly. 'So Johnny doesn't know that it's Design Finals and you're the only one in the world outside the college.'

'And I know you'll do very well. If you do not do well there is no fairness in this world.'

'Well there isn't much, is there?' She looked up at him. He said nothing. 'Is there? Your wife dead, your sons lost, your country gone.'

'I have been more lucky than many Polish people. It is you who have had a share of hard times my child. There will be good times to come.'

'Will there? Johnny won't change, you know that.'

'Yes, I know it, what is good is that *you* know it. Now you have two very simple roads to go down. To take him as he is. Or to leave him and to find somebody else. Two clear roads with signposts. You are not lost with a false map.' She stood up and held out her arms. He made an uncertain step towards her. 'Now I give you one big hug and then we go back to preparing for these examinations. If I am the only person who knows you are taking them then I have all the more interest in seeing that you come through with waving colours.'

'Flying colours.'

'I only made a mistake to make you feel superior.'

'I believe you did.'

In July Elizabeth got distinction in her examination results. The dean of the art college congratulated her, and offered her a part-time job teaching and she could do a teacher's training course at the same time.

Johnny had finished with the debutante. Not that it was ever admitted or acknowledged that there had been any-thing to finish. He agreed enthusiastically with Stefan that Elizabeth should be put on the payroll as an adviser and consultant and special buyer.

Father took a very dim view of all this. 'Does it mean that there is no end to the college after all? More time at a training college and back in those art rooms with students and still working in the antique shop? It doesn't seem that you've got very far.'

'I've got as far as I want to get, Father,' she said in a clipped tone.

'And is there any sign of this young man of yours asking you to get married? He's been around for long enough,' Father complained.

'There is no sign of either of us wanting to get married, Father, when and if there is, I will tell you.' Her tone was even more clipped, and she thought ruefully that for the first time for a long time she and Aisling were probably saying the same thing at the same time.

The summer went on. Harry wrote to say that Mother was no better and wondered if Elizabeth might come back again, just to cheer them all up. Aisling wrote to say that Tony Murray had got very drunk and almost had his way with her. In her engagingly explicit prose she explained that she was almost certain that penetration had not taken place, but was dead relieved when she got the curse a week later just in case something had gone wrong. Monica Hart wrote from Scotland. She had eloped with Andrew Furlong because his mother and her mother had been so ridiculous and they had got married at Gretna Green, which wasn't a bit romantic, but wet and miserable, and Scotland was worse. Shirley wrote from Penzance to say that she was going to get married to a very nice fellow she had met in a hotel where he worked as a barman, could Elizabeth please make sure that Nick knew all about it? Elizabeth was to enthuse about how excited and happy Shirley was and if possible to imply that Guy, her fiancé, was actually a hotel manager rather than the barman. He would be some day, of course, so it wasn't really a fib.

And Johnny's mother died suddenly, and he went off to the funeral by himself. Mr Worsky and Anna sent one wreath, and Elizabeth sent another. He didn't want any of them to come. He returned in his usual form, brushing aside expressions of sympathy graciously and easily. Yes, it was all for the best, his mother had been old, she had dreaded the thought of living beyond her time, she hated being on her own, her best was behind her. He and his brother thought it was all for the best.

He took Elizabeth out to a restaurant for dinner on the night he came back and the waiter brought them a free drink.

'It's to celebrate the birth of the new little princess,' the waiter said. Princess Elizabeth had had a baby girl that day.

'I'm sure she's delighted,' said Elizabeth. 'First a boy and then a girl. Just right.'

'Just right for Princess Elizabeth, who has a fleet of

servants and all the money in the world, but not right for my Elizabeth who has no money and no time.'

'Absolutely not,' said Elizabeth, raising her glass to drink to the health of the baby with a brave smile and a defiant wave of the blonde hairs out of her eyes.

Elizabeth enjoyed the teachers' training course. She thought it had very little to do with real life, since the high principles of education were not nearly as important as being able to think on your feet and cope with children and students. She taught two mornings a week in the college, and two afternoons a week in a local primary school. She felt she could write a book herself, and she would say that it was exactly the same problem with seven-year-olds as it was with seventeen-year-olds – keeping their interest and keeping them quiet. Johnny suggested a whiff of ether in the classroom.

Elizabeth had paid two visits to Preston during the summer. Both had been very gloomy. Harry's spirit seemed to have collapsed, and he was wallowing in guilt.

'You used to be the life and soul of things before, you used to be great fun always, she said so,' Elizabeth said to him eventually in desperation. 'Can't you capture any of that back for yourself? I mean it's not as if it was all that long ago, it's only six or seven years. . . .'

'I can't remember anything except how much I wanted to do the best for Violet,' he said, looking like a big, sad baby.

'It's no use, that kind of love, you've got to be cheerful. Suppose she were to get better and come out, what would she have to come out to? She won't want to come here and see the place run down and you like an old sad sack.'

It worked. He didn't become his old self, but he became something more like it than he had been for months. Elizabeth explained to the nurses and the doctor that she thought it might be a sort of therapy to give Harry some hope that things could return to normal, and they agreed. Without telling him any lies they encouraged him to think that a home visit would be likely.

Elizabeth sat and watched Harry telling her silent,

abstracted mother about his plans for her return, and saw
Mother pat his hand from time to time. The hospital had
removed the pins and wires from the artificial violet and had
sewn it to her cardigan. It must have been washed each time
the cardigan was washed because it had faded from its hard
purple to wishy-washy mauve.

Johnny was distressed about Mother. She only mentioned it
to him after her third visit.

'Why didn't you tell me? That's awful for you going up
there to all that. It's not like you to run off like that. You did
tell Stefan some time ago. I asked him.'

'Oh, well, no point in telling you.'

He looked hurt and a little annoyed.

'What are you playing at?'

'I swear I'm not playing at anything. I mean it, my love.
Why tell you sad things? You've often told me that you
don't want to hear gloomy things, or problems, or low, bad
things that depress you.'

'But darling, if your mother, if Violet's been taken into a
mental home, that's big. Why didn't you. . . ?'

'Because there was nothing you could do.'

She looked at him clearly. It was obvious she was indeed
playing no games with him. He put his arms around her.

'You're very dear to me, funny face. You know you are
the only woman I'll ever love properly.'

Elizabeth smiled at him. 'And I love you, Johnny,' she
said.

XII

'Would you say that your romance with Tony Murray was passionate?' Niamh asked Aisling one evening as she sat at Aisling's dressing table and tried on bits of costume jewellery.

'No, more an animal attraction I think,' said Aisling without looking up from her letter.

Niamh giggled. 'Seriously, some of the girls at school were wondering, Anna Barry said it was more a question of a suitable match. Not passion.'

'Jaysus, it's far from a suitable match, it's about the most unsuitable match in Kilgarret from all the buzzing that's going on,' said Aisling.

'Mam would kill you if she heard you take the Lord's name,' said Niamh prissily.

Aisling looked up. 'And she certainly wouldn't like *you* putting on lipstick. Take it off at once and leave that stuff alone. It's mine. I work hard and I spend long hours earning the money to pay for it.'

'If you married Tony Murray, you wouldn't have to work any long hours. You could go to Dublin like his Mam and buy clothes there and three lipsticks at a time.'

Aisling didn't answer.

'I don't know why you don't marry him, you could lose him you know. Even though everyone says he's keener on you than you are on him.'

Aisling still read her letter.

'But they say you'd better not push your luck too far. He was seen with one of the Gray girls, you know, the one who was at school in England. She had a face like a horse once, but it's got a different shape now. Anthea or Althea, you know. He was having coffee with her in the hotel. Honestly.

So I thought I'd mark your card, you know, if ever there's a chance of me being a bridesmaid I don't want to lose it.'

Aisling looked up. Her face was very pale. 'What? What are you saying?'

Niamh was shocked. 'No, nothing, I don't know if he was really with her or not, you know, it's just Anna Barry and all those, their sisters tell them gossip. I'm sure it's all made up. . . .'

'Oh my God.'

Niamh was frightened now. She scrambled off the chair where she had been kneeling. 'Listen, I said there was nothing in it, I was only repeating eejity old things, Aisling, it's all *right* . . . sure don't you know he fancies you like mad? Aisling answer me . . . don't you know . . . ?'

'It's Elizabeth's mother, she's . . . she's tried to kill herself and Harry . . . my God isn't that desperate. . . .'

Niamh was open-mouthed.

'She's in a mental home . . . oh, I don't know whether Mam told you or not, she doesn't tell you things sometimes . . . anyway, Harry . . . he was sitting talking to her quite normally, and she said she wanted him to cut off a trailing string from her cardigan with a penknife and when he took it out of his pocket she grabbed it and stuck it into him first and then her. Oh God, isn't that terrible.'

'And did she kill him . . . ?'

'No, but he had to have eleven stitches, and now she's in a different ward, almost a cell I think, and she can't have normal visitors and she thinks there's going to be another war . . . and she says she couldn't live through another one. Oh why do all these bloody things happen to Elizabeth . . . ? It's so unfair.'

'Did Elizabeth go to see her?'

'Oh yes, she's been up there in the north of England for a week. She's written from there, but she's probably back in London by now. There's nothing anyone can do, and she's spent a week on her own going from the one hospital to the other and back to the little shop on her own at night. Did you ever hear of anything so awful?'

'But her boyfriend . . . would he go up and help her? Why isn't he there . . . ?'

'Because he's a real beaut, that's why, he's the cat's pyjamas, that fellow, there'll be a good reason why he could never be involved in any trouble. . . .'

'I thought you liked him, you said he was smashing-looking. . . .'

'He looks like a Greek god. That doesn't make him any help though.'

'If these kind of things happened to you, I bet Tony Murray would stick by you . . . God forbid, if Mam went mad and stabbed Dad.'

'Niamh will you shut your stupid face and go away?'

'I'm just telling you to count your blessings that's all . . . that's all. I'm being sensible, I'm being grown-up. It's you, you're the one with the silly face. . . .' Niamh left the room in confusion.

Aisling sat down and tried to decide, would Tony Murray be any use in a crisis? Well, there was no point in pretending that he would be a tower of strength but he would certainly be there. He might not know the solution or even be able to suggest a plan, but he would be standing there solidly with his face cross and scowling, which was the way it got when he had to cope with something unpleasant. He was definitely sympathetic rather than unsympathetic too. Aisling sat and thought it all out. Whenever she had been upset about Donal's bad chest he had patted her on her back and let her cry. She had sobbed that she thought Donal might not be able to breathe during the night and might die, and Tony had considered this with a cross face and said no, it wasn't likely. Tony wouldn't run away to Dublin or back to Limerick or over to England if there was any crisis.

Very deliberately, Aisling combed her hair, and put on a little green eyeshadow. She drew a line behind her eyelashes which she normally only did when she was going to a dance. She put on her best blouse and her new shoes, she got out the pale turquoise suit that she had only worn once to mass. Then she scribbled a note to Mam who had gone on one of her rare visits to Maureen and Brendan.

Mam,
I'm leaving you Elizabeth's letter to read, isn't it really desperate news? Maybe we might ask her to come over here for a bit of a rest. I'm going up to Murrays' for a bit now. I'll be home later, before ten. If you haven't gone to bed we might have a bit of a chat. I hope all the Daly Ogs weren't too exhausting. By the way I gave out to Niamh and she'll probably be sulking. She's too pushy for twelve in my view, but then I suppose I was too.
    Love,
    Aisling

Dear Aisling,
You're right, it's like acting a part in a play, isn't it? Writing to congratulate you and wish you every happiness. But I mean it, I mean it so much. I hope that you will be happy every day and every night and always. I am so looking forward to meeting him, but I know, and presumably Tony knows, that it's never going to be as you hope. You've probably bored him to death about me, and all our adventures, and he will be disappointed. And I of course can't see and won't see in him all the things you love, so I too will be acting a bit. But isn't it marvellous? You are so good in the middle of all your excitements to write so long about my problems, but why should you feel guilty about all your good news coinciding with Mother's decline? That's what it is now, there's not any real hope, and even Harry knows it. He's fine again, and there's an awfully nice social worker who cheers him up. He's so very very kind; that's the one good thing that's come out of all this, at least I've uncovered the sheer kindness of Harry Elton. Remember how terrified of him I used to be? Stefan Worsky sends you his love and so does Anna. They are utterly delighted, they want photographs and long descriptions. Johnny sends you a card, I'll put it in the envelope. And of course I'll come to the wedding, try to keep me away. Of course I don't want to be a bridesmaid, I understand all the business about Protestants officiating at sacraments. I bet

298

your explanation is not at all sound, but I know the thinking of Rome so there's no panic. It's nice of you to ask if Johnny would like to come too but I think I'll just refuse for him without saying anything. I'd prefer to come back to Kilgarret on my own. Only three months now, and you'll be a Mrs, but for me, the most exciting thing is that I'll see you all again. My accent is not posh by the way, over here it's considered very middle class.

I'm so pleased, Aisling, and so very very happy and hopeful for you:
    Love,
    Elizabeth

Hi Aisling,
Elizabeth tells me you settled for the Squire. If he turns out to be a mistake come back here and we'll show you a good time. Happy days.
    Johnny Stone

Mam had told her to try to pay a bit more attention to Maureen.

'But why should I pay her any attention?' wailed Aisling. 'She's never done criticising me, I'm too forward, I'm too backward, I've shocked Brendan's aunt, I've scandalised them all, I've stood on Patrick's toys. It's a catalogue of complaints as soon as you get in the door of that place, why should I give her a bit more attention?'

'Well, she's feeling a bit in the shadow. There's more fuss about your wedding than there was about hers, she's tied down with three small children miles out of the town and all she hears is the excitement of your big day, your wedding dress . . . .'

'Well, she doesn't hear it from me, I'm never blowing about things now am I?'

'Of course you're not child, but can't you be generous, try to put yourself in her position? She's feeling a bit matronly and it would be nice if you brought her back into things. Just a bit.'

'It's a long old cycle Mam, and for nothing at the end of it.'

'In a few months you can drive your husband's car up there, so don't pity yourself too much. Take her a pot of gooseberry jam from the kitchen. And tell her I'll be over tomorrow.'

Mam was right, Maureen did seem in a very low spirit. She was surprised to see Aisling sailing up to the door on the bicycle.

'Well now, to what do we owe the honour of this?' she asked sourly. Brendan Og had jam all around his face and his feet were filthy from waddling around the yard. The twins in their pram set up a great wailing at the arrival of a new distraction. Aisling thought they all looked revolting and the worst advertisement for marriage that you could find, but she knew by now that you could criticise everything except children.

'Hallo, pets,' she cooed insincerely. She still didn't know which one was which. 'Patrick and Peggy, say hallo to your old Auntie Aisling, will you? Of course you will.' She turned to Maureen. 'Aren't they gorgeous?' she said, hoping that God wouldn't strike her dead.

'Oh, they're gorgeous to you passing by once in a blue moon,' said Maureen. 'They're not so gorgeous when you have to live with them morning noon and night. Here, Brendan Og, come back at once. Don't *dare* to walk into the house with all that mud on you. Did you want something, Aisling, or were you just passing by?'

Aisling gritted her teeth. How could she be passing by? Once you had cycled the three miles to Daly's, where else was there to go? Wasn't Maureen becoming an old sourpuss? But she remembered Mam.

'No, I thought I'd come out and have a bit of a chat with you. You know, married woman and all. Maybe you could set me straight on a few things.'

Maureen looked at her suspiciously. 'I thought you knew more than any of us about how life is lived,' she sniffed.

'Come on, Maureen, come on, I show off like we all show off but what do I know, living at home with Mam to deal with everything?'

'True, you've had it nice and sheltered. Still it's into a sheltered life you'll be going now. I suppose the Murrays are laying on a maid to welcome you back from the honeymoon. . . .'

'You can't be serious, Maureen, you're having me on? Don't you know what kind of a woman my future mother-in-law is . . . ? She'd give you a pain in the bottom. . . .'

Maureen was thawing a bit. 'Oh well, they say that Ethel Murray is a bit grand all right. . . .'

'She's dreadful. You're dead lucky here, I mean Brendan's mother is fine, isn't she? You always have her around the place or you used to.'

'She's not that great shakes either, between ourselves. Come on in, and I'll make you some tea. Brendan Og, I'll give you a belt across the legs if you kick up any more of that dirt against the door. I don't know what we have that great clutch of hens for, they don't lay all winter, I'm sick to death of feeding them, another of Mrs Helpful Daly's ideas. Wait till you hear the half of it. . . .'

Eamonn refused point blank to be an usher.

'I'll have no talk about it, Mam, not a word. If the fancy Murrays think for one minute that I'm going to dress up in a hired fancy dress and ask people we've known all our bloody lives are they for the bride's side or the groom's side of the church . . . they've got another think coming. I'd be the laughing stock of the town . . . there'd be a crowd from Hanrahan's pub crowding the church just to have a laugh at me.'

'They wouldn't get in, it's *my* wedding,' said Aisling with spirit.

'They'd have to get in, it's the House of God . . . everyone gets in,' said Eamonn.

'Just one day, as a favour Eamonn, just four hours, five at most, then you can go back to your friends in Hanrahan's. Please?'

'Crowd of idle layabouts in Hanrahan's pub anyway,' said Sean.

'You weren't ever in there Da,' said Eamonn.

'I wouldn't want to go in there when I see what comes out. Listen here, Eamonn, the wedding is for your mother and your sister, it's got nothing to do with us. One of these days some unfortunate half-witted girl will agree to marry you and her unfortunate brothers and father will have to dress themselves up like buffoons, and what's more, spend a great deal of money on a meal and a lot of nonsense . . . so will you shut up and do it – it's one of those things like cutting your toe-nails, no one likes doing it, but it has to be done. . . .'

'Dad I'll not do it, I'll leave the town, I'll leave home. You can't ask me to do it, not to please anyone. Mam, take it seriously. Suppose I asked you to walk around the square here, seriously now, in your knickers, would you do it to please me, Mam, of course you wouldn't, you'd say it was making a fool of yourself, and making yourself look ridiculous in front of your friends, no matter how much I wanted you to do it. . . .'

'Eamonn keep a clean tongue in your head, don't dream of speaking to your mother like that.'

Suddenly Aisling interrupted. 'No, I think he's right, he'd hate it, he'd not be able to do it. Why ask him to?'

Eamonn looked up nervously, sensing a trap.

'No, I'm serious, Eamonn, I thought you'd look nice in a suit. All kinds of old gobdaws much worse-looking than you, look terrific when they're dolled up, they'd make you look at them twice. But no, what you said is right. If you wanted Mam or me to dress up like Red Indians or something for your wedding we wouldn't. No, forget it. We'll get some friend of Tony's to do it with Donal. The trouble is most of Tony's friends are about a hundred, but that doesn't matter, he must have some youngish friends.'

Eamonn's mouth was open, a combination of relief and disbelief. 'God, Aisling, I won't forget it, I really won't. Mam you understand, don't you?'

'Don't be a baby.' Aisling was very cold. 'You've got your way, don't look for a pat on the back as well. You're off the hook. I have to go and face that battle-axe of a Mrs Murray and explain why we need another usher.'

'What will you say?'

Aisling looked at him innocently. 'Well, what you said, that your friends from Hanrahan's would come into the house of God and make a disruption for some reason, and that four hours is too long, even though poor Donal's going to stick it.'

'Don't tell her that . . . it's making an awful clown out of me . . . don't put it like that.'

'But what other way can I put it? Tell me. I can't say that you're sick, otherwise you'll have to go to bed. I mean I have to tell the truth, don't I?'

'What will she say?'

'She'll be livid, like she is about everything. She'll say that that's all she might have expected, and that's what's so bloody unfair, because she's constantly expecting rotten things and everything else is going marvellously. Daddy's booked a great wedding breakfast, and paid for extra waitresses during the meal, and Mam has got everyone gorgeous clothes and I've behaved like an archangel I'm so good, so the old bag has nothing to complain about. Still, I do think you're right. If it's that awful for you, and if they're going to invade the church, then you're right not to do it.'

'I didn't say they'd invade the church . . . some of them mightn't even hear of it until it was over.'

'No. Eamonn, if it's as bad as that you'd better not. Here Mam, throw me over my jacket, I'll go and talk to the old demon and get it over.'

'Oh I'll do it, I'll do it,' Eamonn shouted. He left the room deaf to the protestations and assurances.

'Oh, you're learning fast,' Mam laughed. 'Go on now . . . you've won that battle, you probably have quite a few more to fight before the big day.'

'You're right, Mam,' sighed Aisling, thinking of Tony. He had been very irritable last night. Since they would be married in five weeks time why couldn't she take her hand away and give over all this modesty bit? What difference did five weeks make one way or the other? Aisling couldn't think but she had a feeling that somehow it would make a difference and she felt it would be like giving up on some game if she were to give in now.

And Maureen had blossomed a lot with Aisling's visits. She, in turn, began to get an unexpected and not at all welcome idea about how lonely Maureen's life must be. Mam was right to have urged her to share the wedding with her sister. Maureen was obviously very short of excitement out in that dreary place. It was neither farm nor private house . . . a big awkward building almost on the side of the road with four acres stretching up behind it. No crops, only a few geese, a donkey, hens, a sheepdog and other farmers using the land as grazing. Maureen's attempts to make a garden had been ridiculed by the Daly clan, but her newfound ally, Aisling, seemed to regard this as a challenge.

'You don't understand, they think in terms of getting value out of the land, they'd think a garden was a stupid town idea, you know, ideas above my station. You can't eat flowers. . . .'

'But act the innocent, the flowers sort of grew . . . don't be telling them that you're planting a garden, do the work when there's no one around. I'll help you, I'll bring out a few plants and seeds, sure Dad has them in the shop, I'll say it's for a present for you. You can blame me.'

'God, Aisling, you're learning fast, you'll be well able for the Murrays.'

'I think I'll need to be.'

Indeed, Mrs Murray had been surprised to discover that the O'Connors were held in much higher esteem than she had believed. An established business in the town and well thought of. All the children bright and able to give account for themselves, except perhaps for the brother who hung about the doorway of Hanrahan's public house on Saturdays or at closing time of an evening. Aisling was well-spoken and would look presentable as a bride. There were even those who described her glowingly and said she was one of the most attractive girls in Kilgarret. It wasn't what she had hoped for, but then Mrs Murray sighed and realised that she hadn't got a lot of the things she had hoped for. Joannie was vague and mysterious about her life in

Dublin and threw tantrums and caused scenes if any criticism was suggested. She invited no friends to stay, and seemed to need an unending allowance to supplement what she earned with the wine importers. She had developed no sense of business and saintly Mr Meade said that he didn't think she had any commercial leaning towards running the family firm.

A priest in the family was a consolation, and John would be ordained next year. But somehow she had hoped that her son might be a short-cut to understanding and help; she had hoped that John would have words of consolation and open up brighter paths for her to believe in when things were bad. But in fact he was still her son, complaining when Tony took all the hot water for the bath, saying that Joannie was loud and on his last visit he had been disappointed with the front of Murray's, saying that it looked shabby and run down. He said that his father would not like to think that the place was being neglected and this had managed to annoy every single person who heard him say it. Mrs Murray had expected a priest in the family to smooth down troubles, not to add to them. But at least John had been helpful about the honeymoon and had said Tony and Aisling should attend a papal audience, where they would get their papal benediction personally from the hands of the Pope. Mrs Murray had told a lot of people about this, it was one of the high spots. She had said to Tony that sometimes she woke up in the middle of the night and thought about it. Her son kissing the ring of Pope Pius XII, actually there in the same room as him. It used to send a shiver down her spine. Tony had said that he agreed, the Pope did look a bit spooky; he'd probably send a shiver down anyone's spine. Mrs Murray had been extremely upset.

Aisling certainly seemed to know how to manage Tony, though. She had said to him quite firmly that his wedding suit was too tight.

'It's all right when I hold myself like this,' Tony had said defiantly.

'But you won't, you'll fall over, you're holding your breath,' she said.

'I'm not going on any diet, I'm not giving up drinking pints just to fit into a wedding jacket better,' he said, scowling at the thought.

Aisling laughed. 'Did anyone suggest you should? What a stupid idea, just to look well on the day. No, I don't think you should dream of losing a stone to fit into it, no, get him to let it out and you can be grand and comfortable.'

Tony gave up drinking pints for a month. Anyone could stay off the beer for a month, a few scoops of gin and soda to keep body and soul together. He lost the stone in three and a half weeks. Mrs Murray marvelled at it. She felt sure that this is what Aisling had intended when she was dismissing the very idea of it. She was a proper little madam that one.

Two weeks before the day Aisling and Tony walked out to see how the new bungalow was getting on. Aisling said she wanted to time the length it took her to walk from home. At a leisurely pace it was ten minutes.

'That's grand,' she laughed. 'If you hit me a belt over something I can be back in town and have a posse rounded up in no time.'

Tony looked hurt. 'That's a stupid thing to say, I'd never hit you . . . you're like a flower,' he said.

Aisling was touched. 'It's only my sense of humour. You're right, it was a stupid thing to say. That's nice of you to say I'm like a flower. Will we grow lots of flowers? I like delphiniums and lupins . . . we never had any room for them back in the yard in the square.'

'You can grow whatever you like,' Tony said expansively.

Aisling felt that Mam was right, Maureen had a lot of things to put up with. Imagine having to hide flowers from those pig-ignorant Dalys. She put her arm in Tony's as they walked through the unfinished house. Tony had been annoyed because the plumbers hadn't completed last week. Aisling wished that there weren't so many windows and opportunities for her mother-in-law to cluck over them and interrogate her about curtains not even ordered, discussed or thought about.

Suddenly he turned to her as they poked disconsolately

into the half-finished kitchen cupboards filled with wood shavings.

'It'll be grand you know.'

'Oh, I know, sure there's ages of time, I mean we'll be four weeks in Rome . . . that's six weeks altogether,' she said, trying to be cheerful.

'No, I don't mean the house, the whole thing, you know, being married?' He looked eager. And pleading.

Aisling felt very old. 'Of course it will be grand. How could it not be, aren't we the best-matched pair in the whole town?'

'I love you, Aisling,' Tony said, without any attempt to touch her.

'Then I'm really very, very lucky,' Aisling said. I am, I really *am*, she told herself.

Johnny was annoyed that he hadn't been invited to the wedding, but Elizabeth was cool and firm. It was tempting, very tempting to take him with her. The handsome Johnny Stone would steal the show, he would be proof that little shy Elizabeth White had done well out in the big world. He would be so charming too . . . even Aunt Eileen would fall for him. She could imagine him sitting on a high stool with Uncle Sean asking about the business and really wanting to know. In a flight of fancy she even saw him in the convent parlour. That he would be a success was never in doubt . . . but she felt it would be wrong. And, anyway, even more important, it was Aisling's day, not hers. Johnny would be a distraction, he would take from the bride and groom.

But she didn't tell him that.

Aisling was jumping up and down outside the glass partition. Elizabeth had to wait until her suitcases came off the plane and it seemed like a very long wait. Aisling kept making mouthing sounds and sign language and pointing her finger in the direction of the door and making a face. Elizabeth resigned herself to understanding nothing. She thought Aisling looked magnificent in her navy blazer and a green kilt. She even flashed her large engagement ring through the glass partition and mimed that the diamonds were too heavy for her hand to support. The prospect of marrying the Squire in a week's time certainly hadn't tamed her, Elizabeth noted with relief.

Eventually the cases arrived and she was out, she was hugging Aisling like a schoolgirl after a hockey match. Within minutes they were away.

They had timed it well. Eileen had just come in and was having her customary cup of tea in the kitchen . . . the tea that divided the working day in the shop from the working day at home. Between mouthfuls she was instructing young Siobhan, the new maid who had replaced Peggy, on how to set out the salad.

'Don't throw it all together in the dish, Siobhan, lay the lettuce leaves out in lines and a bit of ham on top of each one, and then a bit of tomato on each one. No, give it here to me, I'll do it. Niamh, move your school books, they've no business here, they'll get covered with food. Move them do you hear, up to your room. Is Donal back in yet?'

At that, the door opened and Elizabeth entered. Aisling was behind her, laughing and holding a suitcase in each hand.

Eileen put down the cup and stood up. This tall, slim woman, this girl with the beautiful scarf draped around her shoulders, with the elegant gold pin and safety chain pinned on her lovely cream-coloured dress . . . Eileen could hardly believe it was the child with the cut knees, gawky on her bicycle, nervous and anxious to please, flushing and stammering . . . this was a different person altogether.

She stood at the door looking across the big kitchen and then she ran, she ran like a child and threw her arms round Eileen and squeezed her so tightly her breath nearly stopped. She smelled of expensive soap or talcum powder, but she shook and trembled as much as she had ever done when she lived in the house.

'You're just the same, you're just the same,' were the only words that Eileen could hear as she clung to the thin girl who gripped her so tightly. Eventually she pulled away and there were tears pouring down the pale face, she took out a handkerchief with lace on it and blew her nose hard. 'This is terrible. Here am I trying to make a good impression on you and I nearly suffocate both of us and then I start to weep all over my careful make-up. Can I go out and come in all over again?'

'Oh Elizabeth . . . thank God you came back to us . . . thank God you didn't change.' Eileen held her hands almost as if they were about to dance a reel together. They smiled at each other foolishly.

'Mam, you never make that kind of fuss over me,' Aisling complained in a mock-hurt tone, but laughing in order to lighten the intensity.

'Nor me . . .' Niamh said in genuine envy, tongue-tied by the apparition in the cream dress and the scarf . . . she was as open-mouthed with amazement at Mam's welcome as was Siobhan who stood with the lettuce and cooked ham in her hands gaping at the mistress with astonishment.

'The uniform looks much better on you than it did on us,' Elizabeth said hastily, feeling that Niamh needed some attention. 'Has it changed or something?'

Niamh looked pleased. 'No, but we're allowed to wear our own blouses now so long as they're not *loud*, as Sister Margaret would say. . . .'

'She *never* says it still?'

'She never says anything else.'

Elizabeth sat down on a kitchen chair and stretched her arms. 'Oh, if only you knew . . . if you had any idea how marvellous it is to be back. . . .'

The homecoming was even better than she had expected, even in her best dreams. The bedroom was the same, the two beds with their white candlewick bedspreads, one on each side of the white chest of drawers. The same statue stood on the mantelpiece, a bit more chipped around Our Lady's cloak, but the same one, certainly. The Sacred Heart Lamp burned still at the little oratory on the landing, the rooms were a bit smaller and the stairs a little narrower but the place hadn't *shrunk*. Perhaps because it was such a genuinely large house by anyone's standards, she thought.

And shabby. Had the carpet always been so torn, and escaping from the stair rods? Did the wallpaper peel and have big brown damp stains long ago or had all this happened recently? And did any of it matter? The place just welcomed her from every corner, it seemed.

Aunt Eileen and Niamh walked beside Aisling as the house was toured and even Siobhan followed at a distance, dazzled by this girl with the English accent who seemed to be so much part of the house.

And Donal ran up the stairs two at a time to see her. He was tall and thin and so white it was as if someone had rubbed chalk on his face. He had thin and almost blue lips and when he smiled and laughed his face looked like a thin skull. Elizabeth bit back the tears pricking her eyes. She had hoped he would look like his brother Sean but he didn't resemble him in any way.

'Do you think I grew up well, Elizabeth White?' he asked self-mockingly.

'You're terrific, Donal, you always were,' she said.

'Do I look gaunt, though, and bony?' His voice was light but she could hear the pain and worry.

She touched his forehead and melodramatically lifted a lock of hair that was falling in his eyes.

'La, sir, fie, Donal O'Connor you do seek for compliments, but if you must have them then you must. You look like a poet, you look like an artist. You look a bit like that picture of Rupert Brooke or maybe even Byron. Now, will that do you? Or must I flatter you more?'

He smiled a great smile and she knew she had said the right thing before Aunt Eileen squeezed her affectionately.

Uncle Sean came in as they were investigating the new kittens which had been discovered that morning in the bathroom.

'This is Monica's daughter, Melanie, and these are her first kittens.' Niamh was full of pride.

'Oh, a *Gone with the Wind* period, I imagine,' Aisling laughed.

'I wish I'd had a sister,' Elizabeth said suddenly.

'Hadn't you me, wasn't I better than a sister?' Aisling demanded.

'Yes, but you weren't there all the time.'

'I was there when you needed me.'

'Indeed, I'll never forget it.' Their eyes met.

'Where is she, where is she?' Uncle Sean had got older, much older than Aunt Eileen. He seemed to be full of extra hair, sandy hair in his nose and his ears and on the back of his hands; she hadn't remembered that. Or was it because Father had such smooth, hair-free, almost polished skin?

Uncle Sean was almost embarrassed by the elegance of her until she hugged him hard.

'Faith, and I couldn't keep you in pocket money these days by the look of you, isn't she a picture, Eileen, isn't she like a fashion plate?'

'Oh no, Uncle Sean, don't say that, you don't like fashion plates!'

'I love them, I just don't know enough of them. Eileen, give over this notion of having tea here, I think I'll take Miss White down to Maher's for a few quick ones and then maybe dinner in the hotel. Wouldn't that set the town talking? Sure they wouldn't know who this posh young one is and they'd think I was a great old spark. What do you think of that?'

Elizabeth played along. 'Nonsense, they'll remember me well, and they'll say there's that Elizabeth White who spent years and years taking from the O'Connors and now she's doing it again.'

Eileen said seriously, 'Don't ever even say that as a joke, Elizabeth child, you were as much a part of this family as any of them. The pity was that we couldn't have had you longer . . . but you'd not have turned out as well. I used to miss you as much as I missed my Sean.'

That was new too. When Elizabeth had left Kilgarret Sean's name was not spoken aloud in the house.

XIII

Elizabeth sat between Aunt Eileen and Maureen in the front left-hand seat of the church. Eamonn and Donal were at the church door guiding the guests to their seats. Niamh, as bridesmaid, was at home still with Aisling and Uncle Sean; about now they would be getting into the car which was already waiting in the square. Uncle Sean was pacing the sitting room like an animal in a cage and his hair looked odd since he had had too violent a haircut the day before. Nobody had commented on it, but Aisling had whispered to Elizabeth that he managed to make himself look like a convict, which would undoubtedly add to Mrs Murray's pleasure when she saw the wedding pictures.

Elizabeth looked across at Tony as he knelt with his head in his hands, more from a hope of escape than from piety. He had what love-story writers would call a florid charm, Elizabeth thought; he had a high complexion and there always seemed to be sweat on his forehead. He was a big stocky man, and looked older than he was. If Elizabeth had been asked to guess she would have said closer to forty than to thirty. He had seemed uneasy on the three occasions they had met, but she excused him; so was she uneasy. She was very conscious of saying the right thing, the thing that would make her seem like a friend, an ally, rather than a rival. She found herself talking about the weather, and the journey over from England and the journey down from Dublin.

Then, Tony must be nervous, it was a big day for him too. No wonder he had sweat on his brow, no wonder his mind hadn't been on their conversations. No wonder he half-sat, half-knelt, with his hands over his face, while his friend, Shay Ferguson, the best man, roamed the church with his eyes and winked twice at Elizabeth when he caught her eye.

Shay was even older than Tony Murray and much fatter. He was a confirmed bachelor, and Elizabeth remembered that he had been one as far back as her own time in Kilgarret. Shay and his brothers sold agricultural machinery and they had often been in Uncle Sean's shop. She had always thought of him as being Uncle Sean's age; it was a shock to think of him as a friend of Tony's. Odd and uneasy-making. It was as if Aisling were being handed over to older, coarser men in some way. Elizabeth gave a little shiver and pulled herself together.

She whispered to Aunt Eileen.

'Can I say something or are you praying?'

'I'm only pretending to pray. Go on.'

'Are you happy or are you sad? Your face is hard to work out.'

Aunt Eileen smiled. 'I'm happy really. It took Aisling so long to make up her mind, you know that too. She didn't rush into it. He's a good man. I think he'll be able to look after her. No, I'm not sad. I'm mainly happy. There's your answer.'

Aunt Eileen smiled during her conspiratorial whisper. She looked very attractive, Elizabeth thought. Much, much nicer than Mrs Murray. Aunt Eileen had a lovely pink and grey coat and dress that matched. It had been bought in Switzer's in Dublin five weeks ago and tried on a dozen times while shoes and handbag and hat were matched to it. The great thing about Kilgarret was that you could always take home things like shoes and handbags and try them out in comfort and then decide what you wanted to buy. Aunt Eileen had a little rouge on too. Aisling and Elizabeth had tried to get her to wear more, but she said she looked like a Dutch doll. Her hat was a smart grey one and the battle to make her wear a pink rose in it had been lost.

'I'm a woman in her fifties. I'll not wear decorations like a Christmas tree,' she had insisted.

Maureen looked tense and unhappy. In the daylight and in the church she thought her shot taffeta dress looked cheap and flashy. Certainly her mother-in-law had managed to plant the idea in her mind this morning. Mrs Daly had looked at the changing colours that had pleased Maureen so much and sniffed. Wouldn't a nice two-piece have been more suitable? She would have thought that a wedding needed something a little formal. And those little shoes, they looked like slippers. Was Maureen really going to wear them? Oh well. Maureen looked with envy at Elizabeth's outfit. A lemon-coloured skirt and jacket with a coffee lace blouse underneath. It looked so right for a wedding. And on her hat she had coffee and lemon ribbons. Now why hadn't Maureen thought of something like that? Maureen pulled at the wide taffeta skirt and got no more pleasure from watching the colours change when the light changed. She had thought this was its best feature when she had tried it on and had spent ages admiring it secretly in the bedroom. Now she hated it. Even her hair was wrong. It looked flat and drab though she had washed it and pinned it up last night. Why hadn't she insisted to Brendan that she wanted to join the party back at home when Mrs Collins and the little shampooing girl had come up to do Mam's hair and Aisling's and Niamh's and even Elizabeth's? Brendan had said it was mad to waste money and time; why hadn't she been firm?

Mrs Murray smiled over a few times. She looked harsh and sharp, Elizabeth thought; but perhaps that was only because she had heard so many tales about her during the week she half expected the woman to look like the devil incarnate. Her navy outfit seemed to be all points and edges. Sharp revers on the jacket, sharp edges on the handbag, pointed toes on the shoes, peaky brim on the hat. Beside her stood Joannie, who had only come home the night before. Joannie hadn't changed much in nine years, Elizabeth thought. Still stocky, and legs planted wide apart when she stood. She had freckles and a handsome sort of face, like Tony but better-looking. She wore a white dress and coat ... which Elizabeth had always heard was bad taste. Somewhere in her store of knowledge she had the information that you never wore white to a wedding, in case you might upstage the bride.

But of course, Joannie Murray wouldn't have a dog's

chance of upstaging this bride, even if it had been in her mind. Aisling was going to knock them sideways when she came in.

Elizabeth had actually gasped when she saw Aisling in the dress. It did everything that a wedding dress could do, and you got the feeling that Aisling never wore any other kind of clothes. Elizabeth knew that Aunt Eileen said that the wedding dress could cost whatever Aisling wanted to pay for it. When Aunt Eileen got married it had been a drab and poor affair, in a dress borrowed from a cousin. Aunt Eileen's own family, with notions of being genteel, had no money and they were disappointed that she was marrying Uncle Sean, who not only had no money but hadn't even notions of being genteel. The wedding ceremony had not been colourful. Then, although nobody admitted it aloud, the wedding of Maureen and Brendan had been so master-minded by the Dalys and what they would like and what they wouldn't, that the O'Connors seemed to do nothing but pay for it. This time Aunt Eileen dug her heels in, and she knew she had an ally. Aisling was not afraid of the Murrays, Aisling would do it right.

Together they had gone to Dublin on the bus, they had spent a morning looking at materials and an afternoon looking at patterns. Then, armed with ideas they went in to the dress designer in Grafton Street who made dresses for the best. She knew she was not dealing with country hicks here . . . they were informed, this mother and daughter. They were also happy to pay a deposit in advance. The dress designer became enthusiastic about the tall, auburn-haired girl with the bright face. It had been a labour of love. Nobody but Elizabeth knew how much it had cost. Maureen had been told one sum, Uncle Sean had been told another. Mrs Murray had not been told anything, despite her discreet probing about where it was made and what it was like. Only when Elizabeth saw it on Aisling did she realise that it was worth every penny just for the sheer impression that Aisling would make on all their minds. The dress was satin. Heavy white satin, and not sateen which was all they had seen in Kilgarret for many a wedding. It had a full skirt which seemed to billow out and make her waist tiny. The long tight sleeves came down in little points, vees below her wrists and onto her hands making her arms more slender than they could possibly have ever been. The neckline, another vee, had little seed pearls to pick it out.

The satin looked so rich and cold it could have been marble. On any other girl the dress might have been deadening, it would have made another face seem wishy-washy, Elizabeth thought, a thinner paler girl would have looked like a doll in the dress. Aisling looked like a star.

Mrs Moriarty's sister played the organ, and somebody must have nodded to her because the organ stopped its rambling, gentle notes and gave a burst that startled everyone in the church; but they were standing up in a trice and Tony, his face red from the marks of his hands, stood more quickly than any of them. He looked over at the bride's side: both Aunt Eileen and Elizabeth smiled at him encouragingly. He gave a scowl which turned into a sort of smile. It was endearing in a funny way. Eamonn and Donal had slipped back into the O'Connor pew and they all shuffled a little to leave room for Uncle Sean when he had given Aisling away.

He looked sweet, Uncle Sean, Elizabeth thought, staring ahead of him with a rigid glance as if he were going to be executed, watching each foot as it went in front of him in case one of them might escape. Both his elbows were squeezed into his sides as if he were carrying precious documents that might fall. Aisling's arm might well have been squashed flat but there wasn't a sign of it on her face.

Far from the nervous, demure bride, shy because all eyes were on her, she was utterly in control; she smiled left and right seeing the admiration and even the shock of how well she looked. The church in Kilgarret hadn't seen a bride like this in a while. Her hair was the best decoration she could ever have planned; it escaped deliberately in bronze curls and ringlets, a flash of rich colour in the middle of all the white. The walk up the church took forever, Elizabeth thought, and then they were at the altar. Uncle Sean handed her to Tony, and loosening his collar stepped in beside Aunt

Eileen. The bride and groom moved inside the altar rail and up the steps. The dress was so perfect that you could see Aisling's figure to the best advantage without it looking at all revealing. That was the cunning of the thing, that's why the woman in Grafton Street hadn't charged too much.

Aunt Eileen leaned over in front of Elizabeth and caught Maureen's hand. 'Here we go again,' she said. 'Just like your wedding all over again isn't it?'

Maureen's face brightened up a lot. 'Yes, I suppose so,' she whispered eagerly. 'Of course, I couldn't have known, being up there in the altar myself.'

'It was just like this,' Eileen hissed back firmly.

Elizabeth saw Maureen's face relax into a pleased smile as the congregation sat down and watched Anthony James Finbarr Murray take this woman, Mary Aisling as his wedded wife.

'In all the years I never knew Aisling was called Mary,' Elizabeth gasped to Maureen.

'It's a saint's name, you eejit,' Maureen whispered. 'She couldn't have been baptised Aisling, it's not the name of a saint.'

'I never new that,' Elizabeth said, settling down for the rest of the ceremony.

At the hotel, a room had been reserved for the bride's family. This had been regarded as the most ludicrous of a series of ludicrous expenses. The bride's family, after all, lived a thirty-second walk across the square from the hotel. They had all the rooms they wanted there. But no, the management said that it was included in the whole price and he begged them to avail of it. There was no refund if they didn't. And anyway they would find it a great assistance. Maureen was complaining that the light in the shop where she bought the taffeta dress had been faulty. Eileen said that she looked like a very elegant, smartly-dressed young woman and she was to stop whinging and whining. Aisling had taken off her white stockings and had one foot in a handbasin.

'The bloody shoes are too tight, Mam, I knew it.'

317

'Are you doing the right thing, Mrs Murray, bathing them? You might make it harder to get the shoes back on.'

'Janey, Aisling's Mrs Murray,' said Niamh, who was examining what she deeply suspected was a spot on her chin. 'Imagine, my sisters, Mrs Daly and Mrs Murray. . . .'

For some reason this cheered Maureen up. 'You'll be Mrs Somebody too, Niamh, you mustn't worry,' she said kindly.

'Of course I'm not worrying, Maureen you old eejit, I'm only fifteen. I'm not even old enough to get married if they were all after me.'

'Will Mrs Murray want to come in here and powder her nose?' asked Maureen, looking at the door nervously.

'Well if she does she can powder it outside,' Aisling said, drying her feet. 'This is for the bride's family, it says so on Daddy's estimate. It says no wicked mothers-in-law permitted.'

'She looks very well in that navy, doesn't she? Ethel has always had great taste.' Eileen was trying to be just.

'Oh Mam, she looks like the wrath of God, and you know it . . . her face is like a flour-bag, it's so white.'

'Don't blame the woman for her appearance, now Aisling.'

'Listen to me Mam.' Aisling stood in one stocking, hopped over to her mother and put her hands firmly on Eileen's shoulders. 'Now hear this, Mam, you're not talking to bold, difficult Aisling O'Connor any more, since half an hour ago you're talking to young Mrs Tony Murray . . . and by God if I want to call old Mrs Ethel Murray a hideous old bag, which is what she is, I'll call her that all day long.'

'Well you're going to have a fine easy life ahead of you if you go on like that, young Mrs Murray,' said Eileen. 'Here hold on to me and put on your stocking, we should be downstairs already. . . .'

'It's all going awfully well, isn't it?' Elizabeth said. 'Aren't you pleased with it all?'

'I hope so. There's three things I wish were over . . . this reception, all this awful losing virginity thing and bleeding and screaming . . . and I want to have got myself in the position where old bag Mrs Murray is afraid of me rather than the other way round. . . .'

'There won't be bleeding and screaming, you always exaggerate. . . .'

'No, I'm sure there won't. I think the battle over Ma-in-law is going to be worse than sexual intercourse . . . come on, let's hit the reception. Where's Niamh? She's meant to be standing beside me like an acolyte catering for my every whim, but she's picking her spots in front of every mirror she finds.'

Tony was waiting at the bottom of the stairs; Shay Ferguson was there with a large whiskey in each hand.

'Give her a belt, Tony, let her know that your Missus can't keep you waiting.'

'It's a rural witticism,' Aisling said over her shoulder to Elizabeth.

'You look gorgeous, gorgeous,' Tony said.

'You look lovely yourself,' Aisling said to him.

Elizabeth relaxed. She took Niamh by the arm. 'Since they're paying compliments . . . you look lovely too . . . and there are probably more people looking at you than at Aisling. She's out of the race now, you're still available . . . the only glamorous girl in the competition. . . .'

'What about you, Elizabeth . . . you're not married yet?'

'Ah no, but I'm in love,' Elizabeth said in an uncharacteristic burst of information. 'I have the look of a promised woman about me.'

Elizabeth remembered something. She hadn't thought about Johnny for two days. She had thought she would have him in the front of her mind all during the wedding, that every moment she would wish it was the two of them going through the ceremony, with family and friends and all the promising to love and honour and obey and everything. But she had never even thought of him. What did it mean?

The hotel sitting room was transformed. All the chairs and sofas had been pushed back against the wall and four waitresses stood with trays of sherry glasses. There were minerals on the trays too for those who didn't partake.

319

Elizabeth looked with interest at the scene . . . she hadn't been able to stare properly in the church in case she was being disrespectful, but here it was perfectly acceptable. Some of the older women she recognised immediately. Mr and Mrs Moriarty from the chemist . . . how tall she had grown, how elegant she looked . . . any hope of seeing her take the plunge? . . . how well the Moriartys looked, how little they had changed . . . how much Donal liked working in the shop. . . .

Mrs Lynch, Berna's mother . . . oh yes, she remembered Elizabeth well, how pretty she was, ah well, that's what came of a nice life with no cares over there in England, as for herself, nobody knew the troubles she had seen . . . and her poor husband, the doctor, the Lord have mercy on him, did Elizabeth remember him? Well the poor man had gone to his reward five years now this June. Yes, wasn't it dreadful, the best husband and father a family ever had, his poor liver had been weak, a dreadful death he died. No, Berna wasn't married yet, but she worked in Limerick and had a boyfriend. . . .

She was trapped then by Joannie. 'How much did your suit cost?' Joannie said. No word of greeting, no amazement at not having met for nine years, no expression of pleasure at the wedding or of admiration at the bride.

'*They* seem awfully happy,' Elizabeth said on a slightly rising note, to see what Joannie would answer.

She looked over at Aisling and Tony ruminatively for a few moments. 'Well, I don't know what took them so long . . . they've been walking out together for as long as I can remember. I suppose they'll be all right but I don't know what they want to live in this one-horse town for.'

'I don't know, but of course Aisling likes Kilgarret, she likes being near her family. . . .'

'She must be off her head,' said Joannie.

'They're a very nice family. Of course, I was utterly devoted to them when I lived here. I still am.' Elizabeth's voice was slightly sharp but not nearly as sharp as she felt. How dare Joannie Murray dismiss the whole O'Connor clan with one ignorant remark?

320

Joannie noticed the sharpness. 'Oh no, I'm not saying a word against them. I'm just saying I couldn't live here . . . I don't know what I'd do with myself all the time . . . and you know there was murder altogether because Aisling wanted to go on working in the shop . . . did you know that?'

'In whose shop?'

'In her own, in the O'Connors' store. Imagine, a married woman working there with all the farm implements?'

'Aunt Eileen has worked there for thirty years, she's a married woman.'

'It's different for Mrs O'Connor, she's the family.'

'And Aisling's the family, isn't she?' Elizabeth was bewildered.

'Not any more . . . she's a Murray now . . . she can't do what she likes any more. The Ma will see to that.'

'That sounds very depressing I must say.'

Joannie shrugged. 'What did I tell you, this is a depressing, hick town.'

Uncle Sean was looking at his glass of sherry as if it were a glass of poison.

'I don't know how people drink this stuff, Molly,' he said to the waitress, whom he had known since she was a baby.

'Sure, wasn't it what you ordered yourself, Sean . . . two kinds of sherry.'

'I didn't expect to be having to drink it,' he laughed.

'Yerra, why don't you take a glass of the orange instead, it would be more refreshing?'

Elizabeth laughed at him.

'Go on, Uncle Sean, all the best people are drinking orange . . . look, the bridegroom is even drinking it.'

Uncle Sean looked over at Tony. 'Well, by God, that's a turn-up for the books. Your man normally has a fierce thirst on him. I'd say he has a drop of something in it . . . he's looking far too cheerful.'

'Oh Uncle *Sean*, don't be so unromantic. It's his wedding day! No wonder he's looking cheerful.'

'No, he's unnaturally high-spirited. I'll bet you ten shillings he's got something in it.'

'Well I won't take you on, it would be a highly disruptive

thing to go round sniffing people's orange juice. Isn't it all super, Uncle Sean . . . aren't you delighted with it all?'

'I am, child, I am. And if you'll come over here and marry an Irishman I'll give you a wedding like this too . . . but we'll have none of this sherry.'

'That's lovely of you. I bet you would give me a wedding, but rest assured I won't call on you. Save up for Niamh's instead.'

'Sure who'd have Niamh? She's a desperate terror.'

'You used to wonder who'd have Aisling, and now look at her.'

'Men are terrible fools, Elizabeth. I often thank the good Lord that He guided me to make such a sensible choice myself when I was a young lad. I was a lucky man to get so fine a wife as your aunt.'

She walked with him towards Aunt Eileen who had been making faces at them.

'I think it's time to move them in to the dining room. Sean, will we get them going? Ethel Murray's looked at her watch three times.'

With a surprising vehemence Elizabeth said, 'Don't dare to do anything to please Ethel Murray, Aunt Eileen, you're worth twenty of her, a hundred and twenty of her. You move them into the dining room when you're ready, not before!'

The place names had been checked, and double-checked, by Mrs Murray that morning. The seating plan had taken a lot of working out. Who exactly were the Halleys, she had asked Aisling? Were they the kind of people you could place near Father Riordan? But now it had all been finalised. Uncle Sean's pleas that he couldn't talk to Mrs Murray all through the meal had been ignored, as had Joannie's request that she sit at the end of a table where she didn't have to talk to anyone. All the grapefruits were already in place in their little glass dishes, each with a cherry-half on top. There were two glasses beside every plate. The Murray family had contributed a dozen bottles of champagne, and this would be used for the toast. There were teacups at each place too and jugs of milk and bowls of sugar on the table. The wedding cake was on a side table. There had been a lot of discussion about this, too. Mrs Murray said she believed it should be on the main table, Aisling said that if it were on the table the bride and groom wouldn't be able to see anyone. Maureen said that of course a wedding cake must be on the table, it was the tradition, and Aunt Eileen said that if Aisling would like the wedding cake kept in the back yard that was fine. Miss Donnelly in the hotel had said that the side table was a good idea and the whole table could be carried over for the cutting ceremony so that there would be no danger of the cake breaking.

In little hesitant trickles they moved into the dining room. Some of them exclaimed at how nice it all looked, others raked the table for their own place names before saying anything at all. Immediately people discovered their own name they snatched up the name on either side of them. 'There seem to be two women sitting together here,' called Mrs Halley disapprovingly, finding herself beside Brendan Daly's aunt.

'There are more ladies among the guests than gentlemen,' hissed Miss Donnelly, annoyed to hear the complaints beginning before people sat down. The buzz of conversation had died down as people came in to the dining room, a silence almost like the respectful hush of a church came over them. Elizabeth was hoping that she might be between Donal and Eamonn. She knew that neither of them wanted to make conversation with uncles or priests and she herself felt a bit at a loss. But the endless negotiations had put her beside Shay Ferguson on one side and Father Riordan on the other. Half the people had settled into their seats, and some of them, like the Halleys, had already begun to eat the bread and butter when there was a loud cough.

Father Mahony, the elderly parish priest who had married Tony and Aisling, was clearing his throat.

'I think, if we're all settled,' he said looking over his glasses disapprovingly at those who had the daring to sit down, 'I think that it's about time to say grace.'

Red-faced, the unlucky people trapped in their seats shuffled and scrambled to their feet again.

'Bless us, O Lord, and these thy gifts, which of thy bounty we are about to receive. . . .'

'Amen,' they all said and blessed themselves firmly. It was a signal for conversation as well as for eating. The grapefruits were attacked, more sugar was requested across the table. Slowly the buzz rose . . . how well Aisling looked, quite like the pictures you saw of the Honourable Lady this and that in the Dublin papers. And wasn't she lucky to make such a match? Elizabeth could hear some speculation about how strange it was that Aisling had married so well, while Maureen, who had the better education, had only married into the poor Dalys. She hoped that they would change the subject or lower their voices before Maureen stopped her own conversation and might overhear them.

Shay Ferguson was a tireless talker. He swivelled his head left and right, entertaining Elizabeth on his right and Joannie Murray on his left.

'Amn't I well placed now, between two spinsters of this parish? Huh, huh?' he said roaring with laughter.

'Jesus Christ,' said Joannie, and so he looked for a better reaction from Elizabeth.

'I'm not strictly speaking from the parish . . . though I often feel that I am,' she said pleasantly.

'Is that what you feel, is that all you feel?' he said.

'I beg your pardon?' Elizabeth asked politely.

'Never mind,' said Shay. 'When are they pouring the drink? Murrays are providing buckets of drink you know.'

'I think the Murrays are offering champagne for the toast, but the rest is being given by the O'Connors, the red and white wine,' Elizabeth retorted, anxious that this should be understood even by someone as loud and insensitive as Shay Ferguson.

'Yah, well, where is it? They should have it poured by now.'

She turned to Father Riordan.

'You're not a Catholic at all, they tell me,' he said.

'No Father, that's right, my parents were both Church of England.'

'And in all your years here in the convent with the good

nuns, and with a good Catholic woman like Mrs O'Connor you saw nothing to convert you to our faith? Isn't that a sad thing. Isn't that a lack in us all somehow?'

'Oh, I wouldn't say that, Father. I did learn a great respect and admiration for the Catholic faith. . . .'

'Sure, respect and admiration are no use if you're not going to be able to bow the head in humility and say I believe. That's what the church is about you know. Bowing the head in humility.'

'Yes, I suppose it is Father,' said Elizabeth dutifully. To herself she thought that Father Riordan had it all wrong. Whatever the Roman Catholic church was about it seemed to have little to do with bowing the head in humility.

The waitresses must have heard Shay Ferguson's plaintive pleas for wine. They began to dart in and out between people's faces with a, 'Red wine or white wine?'

'I'd prefer a drop of whiskey, just a very small drop,' said Father Riordan.

'I'll go and investigate, Father,' said one of the waitresses.

'Thank you, Deirdre, good girl,' he said.

Deirdre, anxious to please the parish priest, went to whisper a word to Aunt Eileen before filling the wine glasses of Elizabeth and Shay Ferguson. The best man's face was not a pretty sight.

'Mother of Jesus, where has that one gone?' he said to Elizabeth. 'Did you send her off for something or what?'

'You'll survive for a few minutes.' Elizabeth smiled, trying to placate him and thinking what an unpleasant manner he had. She hoped for Aisling's sake that he wasn't a close friend of Tony's. It was hard to know. He must be fairly close if he had been chosen as best man. Tony's friends were spoken of very rarely . . . he was always said to be at the hotel with a crowd, or off with 'the lads' somewhere. Presumably Shay was one of 'the lads'. Elizabeth looked around the room to see if she could identify any of the others.

It was a big horse-shoe table, and people sat close together because the hotel dining room had never been built with the thought of entertaining seventy-three people to a wedding breakfast. The spaces between the guests and the wall were very narrow and the waitresses were now squeezing awkwardly through with their plates of chicken and ham and salad. Elizabeth couldn't see what she might identify as Tony Murray's friends, there didn't seem to be many men of his age in the company. Still, perhaps numbers had to be kept down because it was a family wedding.

'It's all very well for you,' Shay burst into her thoughts. 'You don't have to make a speech. I have to read telegrams . . . and make a witty speech.'

'I'm sure you'll do it frightfully well,' she said.

'Frightfully, frightfully. . . .' he imitated her accent. 'Yeah, that's what it will be, a fright. . . .'

He turned and called over to the bridegroom. 'How are you, Tony me old divil? Eat up! That's right, need all your strength for later. . . .' Mrs Murray looked up from her conversation with Father Mahony and frowned, but Aisling smiled at him. Shay was encouraged. 'That's right, Aisling, feed him up, and plenty of red meat . . . when you get him home not chicken and ham but red meat!' He laughed, delighted with himself, and at that moment the long-awaited wine arrived. He drained the glass in a gulp and before the waitress got to Joannie, he had it out for a refill.

'That's better,' he said to Elizabeth, and belched.

When the jelly and cream was finished, the teapots had been refilled and the wine waiter from the bar had come in to open the champagne, there was much whispering with Uncle Sean, who shuffled to his feet and said, 'I'd like you to know that the Murray family have kindly provided this excellent champagne for you to charge your glasses . . . when the time comes.'

Shay put his hand on his heart and said to Elizabeth, 'God he gave me a fright there, I thought the old clown was about to lose the run of himself and make a speech.'

There was no point, Elizabeth thought to herself, in saying that she didn't like to hear her Uncle Sean called an old clown. Anyway it was nearly time for the speeches. But first Father Mahony had to say grace, so they all shuffled to their feet again before settling back, chairs pushed back a little.

Shay read aloud the seventeen telegrams, stumbling over names, getting some of them so wrong that nobody knew whom he was referring to.

'Who would they be, Jean and Jilly MacPherson,' Father Riordan asked Joannie, leaning over Elizabeth and behind Shay's chair to make himself heard.

'Oh, he means Joan and Jimmy Matterson, you know from the bakery, he just can't read.'

Then he said that the etiquette book told him he must praise the charm of the bridesmaid, so he would like everyone to consider the charm and beauty of the bridesmaid praised. He was sorry to see his old friend Tony Murray get hooked, trapped into the terrible penal servitude of matrimony but if he had to be caught at least his new wife was a fine-looking woman. He said that he hoped it wouldn't be long before the Murrays had another wedding and their lovely daughter Joannie would get married. He said the hotel had done a great job on the wedding breakfast, and that it was grand to see Father Mahony in such good spirits . . . and so many more of the clergy able to attend. It was typical of the Murrays to send over some vintage champagne . . . but they were known as one of the most generous families in Ireland. He told a story about a Kilgarret man who was in Dublin and was walking home . . . he found the road lined with tombstones he said . . . all Dublin men of different ages but from the same family. They were all called Miles from Dublin; there was the Miles from Dublin who was twenty-five and then some way further along the road there was his brother who was thirty. People explained it to each other and the laughter and clapping went on a long time.

Uncle Sean said a few words too, only to introduce Father Mahony he said. It was a privilege and a consolation for Kilgarret people to know that Father Mahony was there to baptise them when they came into the world, to say their mass and give them the sacraments during this life and to see them out of it at the end with his blessing. It was a very happy occasion today that he was here to bless the marriage of Aisling and the fine young Tony Murray . . . he, too, would like to thank Miss Donnelly and everyone in the hotel for serving them so well . . . and now if Father Mahony could say a few words. . . .

Father Mahony said a great many words . . . he remembered Tony when he was at the Brothers' before he went off to the Jesuits, he remembered Tony's brother John . . . soon, thank God and please God, to be Father John . . . a fine, fine young recruit for the priesthood . . . he remembered the daughter of the house Joan, and he felt sure too that any day now he would be joining her in marriage . . . but of course there was all the time in the world. He remembered Mrs Murray, as brave in widowhood as she had been strong in marriage. Father Mahony tal!.ed about Murray's and the place it had as the centre of Kilgarret . . . there could hardly be a town without it. It had employed so many and looked after them so well . . . and been a pillar of what a Catholic community life should have . . . a good family business, run on Christian lines.

He did speak about the O'Connors too. Elizabeth wondered whether she was becoming over-sensitive when she felt that he didn't pay them as many compliments as he had paid to the Murrays. It was the O'Connors who were holding the wedding, it was their daughter who was the bride, they were four hundred per cent better people than the Murrays. . . . But then it was Tony's turn. He stood up, red-faced and perspiring. Elizabeth felt a wave of sympathy for him and a hope that he would make a good speech.

'Good man, Tony,' called Shay. And then in an aside he said to Elizabeth, 'Jesus, he really is a good man, he must have had five gin and oranges before he even got in here . . . and the wine has been flowing up at their end ever since. . . .'

Tony was getting through his speech, but only just. He looked down after every second sentence to his written notes. He thanked Aisling's parents . . . but had to consult his notes to remember their names. He hoped he would make her a good husband. He read a list of relations whom he was glad to see, and he read them even more haltingly than Shay had read the telegrams. He thanked his mother for all the help and encouragement she had been, he said he looked forward to seeing Rome with his new wife and, if possible, if all went well, please God, going there again next year for his brother's ordination. He wanted to thank everyone for their useful gifts. He hoped they would all enjoy the wedding. He sat down abruptly, and when the clapping ceased there was an uneasy silence. Elizabeth saw Mrs Murray looking at her watch yet again, Shay was fidgeting. She noticed Aunt Eileen lean over and say something to Uncle Sean who stood up again.

'Would it be in order to ask Father O'Donnell to sing us a verse of a song . . . we all know what a beautiful voice he has.' This was greeted with great clapping and cheers.

Father O'Donnell had already arranged his face and his hands and he sang 'Bless This House', and then 'I think that I shall never see a poem lovely as a tree', which was not nearly as successful. As if he knew that he had lost his following, Father O'Donnell said that a little bird has asked him to sing one last song which was a special favourite of the bride and groom. His true clear voice soared again into 'Danny Boy', and a strange unexpected pricking at the back of Elizabeth's nose and eyes began. She looked over at Aisling, who smiled out of her veil and red curls. She had told Aisling about the time she had sung 'Danny Boy' for Mother and Harry and Johnny . . . Aisling had said it was only natural . . . everyone cried when they heard 'Danny Boy'.

With a blur in her eyes Elizabeth looked around the room. Everyone's face looked up at the young priest as he sang, and you could see that a lot of effort was going into keeping their expressions unmoved. There was a sense of rescue almost when it came to the last chorus and everyone joined in . . .

'Oh come ye back, when sun shines in the meadow,
Or when the valley's hushed and white with snow,
For I'll be there in sunshine or in shadow
Oh Danny Boy, Oh Danny Boy I love you so. . .'

And they wiped their eyes and they sniffed and they took great slugs of their tea or their wine, and they clapped, and Elizabeth smiled again at Aisling, blinking back the tears, and thought that weddings are quite emotional enough without introducing a song like that into them.

Aunt Eileen said that her feet had grown twice the size and that they were going to have to cut the shoes off her when they got home. Uncle Sean said that his throat was closing over from all that sweet wine and that only a couple of pints would open it again. Eamonn had been formally released by Aisling. He shuffled and said it hadn't been that bad and since he had been here for so long he might as well wait and see the send-off. Around the horse-shoe table, with the name cards scattered around on the floor and the children racing up and down, relatives sat in small groups and discussed other small groups.

Shay Ferguson had scooped up two very large whiskeys which he carried in one hand together with a glass of water held precariously by the little finger. He made a noise like an advancing train. 'Hoo, hoo, out of me way, I've got to get the bridegroom ready for the long journey ahead. . . .' Tony was changing from his wedding finery into a less formal suit in the back of Miss Donnelly's office.

Maureen was annoyed because Brendan wanted to go home.

'Why can't he go on his own and you come later?'

'Oh, it's easy known you're not married, Elizabeth . . . where one goes the other goes, that's the rule in marriage.' Maureen had two red spots on her face, caused by wine and emotion.

'There's no problem in your getting a lift home, go on let him go on his own . . . then you'll both be happy.'

'No, that way neither of us will be happy. If I go at least one of us will be happy. You go and distract him, talk to him about something, anything, will you?' Maureen looked upset. Elizabeth decided not to fight the matter on principle. She went over to Brendan, who was standing fidgeting at the door.

'Where's Maureen? Really and truly she's very selfish. My poor mother's been looking after Brendan Og since the breakfast is over. I can't understand why people want to hang around instead of going back to their own homes. . . .'

There was a noise behind them, and together Aisling and Tony came out into the hall. From the dining room the women converged and out from the bar with pint glasses in their hands the men came. Aisling wore a suit which, she told Elizabeth, must be described as aquamarine, because it was in fact green but a lot of people thought green was unlucky. She had a tiny pill-box hat too which was covered with the same fabric. Her hair was piled up and tied in a chignon.

'She looks like a film star,' said Maureen in naked admiration. Maureen had appeared from around a corner to savour the moment.

'She looks very old, she nearly looks thirty,' said Donal. 'A glamorous thirty,' he added, seeing Maureen's face. That didn't help. 'Not that thirty's really old, you know,' he said.

Eileen walked behind them proudly as they came to the hotel door. She saw Ethel Murray standing on her own and with an effort she went over to stand beside her.

Elizabeth saw Mrs Murray smile quickly with surprise and then arrange her face in its normal, slightly quizzical, expression.

'Ah yes, Eileen, the moment has come.'

'Don't they look very happy, isn't it great to see them setting out like this?' Mrs Murray nodded. 'He's a fine man, Ethel, apart altogether from the grand family that Aisling's marrying into . . . Sean and I are very glad she'll have a good man to look after her. He's a good, kind man.' Aunt Eileen squeezed her arm, and the two of them walked out to the footpath. Elizabeth stood a little withdrawn from the crowd. She looked at the stranger, Aisling, in the pert little hat. Somehow it was much more alien than the beautiful wedding dress which had been hung up carefully in the hotel room under sheets of tissue paper pinned to cellophane. Later Aunt Eileen would collect it and hang it carefully at home until the bungalow was ready to house it.

The crowd was shouting encouragement. Shay Ferguson was hardly able to stand as he banged on the roof of the car. 'Come on with you, come on . . . it's nearly within your grasp, Tony, stop wasting time . . . don't let her ardour die down.'

'Goodbye Aisling . . . good luck,' called Maureen, tears in her eyes.

'Where did she get that suit? It's very well cut,' Joannie was asking around her.

Aisling kissed Uncle Sean goodbye, and Mrs Murray, and then Aunt Eileen. Tony was shaking hands, holding everyone else's hand in both of his.

'Goodbye, thank you, goodbye, thank you,' he said to everyone.

He came to Elizabeth. 'Goodbye, thank you,' he said.

'I hope you'll both be very happy, Tony,' she said. 'Very happy and give each other great . . . great happiness,' she finished lamely.

'Oh, I'm sure we will,' he said awkwardly.

Shay Ferguson was at his elbow. 'Well if you won't, Tony Boy, it's hard to know who else will . . . what? Give her *lots* of happiness, and get on the road huh?'

Elizabeth was crimson with rage at being taken up in such a loud and coarse way when she was trying to be completely sincere . . . she *did* hope that Aisling and Tony would give each other a lot of happiness . . . some people did, like Eileen and Sean, and like Mother and Harry for a while, but some people definitely didn't. Why had that great vulgar Shay Ferguson been there to overhear her?

Aisling seemed to sense her distress from the other side of the crowd. She rushed over and caught her by the arm. 'Tell me it wasn't all too appalling, tell me that there was a bit of style in the way Aisling O'Connor had her nuptials?'

Elizabeth held her and the two stood as if frozen for a moment. 'It was a beautiful wedding, it was simply beautiful. I've been listening to them. Nothing as classy and as . . . well as outright colourful and glamorous in Kilgarret ever before.'

'Elizabeth, will you come back again? Please, when things are more settled down and there isn't all this Twentieth-Century Fox stuff going on?'

'Yes, of course, I'll come back. Go *on*, Aisling, they're calling you.'

'And I'm right, aren't I. . . ?'

'What?'

'I'm doing the right thing? It will be fine. . . ?'

'Not now, Aisling . . . go.'

'You're my best friend. . . .'

'And you're mine. . . . Go.'

The cheer was enormous when she got into the car and Aisling's smile was almost as great. Shay had put a big cardboard notice on the back of the car with the word 'Honeymooners' scrawled on it. Tony had tried to take it off but Eileen had said he should stop when he was outside the town. The car with its badly made notice revved up and drove off . . . but to everyone's delight it did one lap of the square before taking the Dublin road. Total strangers who had just come in on the afternoon bus cheered too. And then they were gone.

PART THREE

1954–1956

XIV

People had told them to be sure to get a hotel on the north side of Dublin so that they would be on the way to the airport when they had to set out in the morning. Aisling had said to Elizabeth that most friends and relations assumed that they were going to be so weak from the night of passion that they could hardly manage to drive to the airport at all. Maureen had said that there was a guesthouse she knew of which was actually only a mile from the airport. Dad had said they could do worse than go to the cousins in Dunlaoghaire. There would be no bad feeling because they had been sent a wedding invitation but business was brisk and they couldn't be gone for a whole day. Dad had said that he heard they had the place much improved now, with carpets in all the bedrooms, wall to wall, and because they were family they'd get a cut.

Aisling took no notice of them and had written to the Shelbourne Hotel in Dublin, booking a night's accommodation in one of the best double rooms for Mr and Mrs Murray. In fact she had paused and reflected for a long time when she reread the words Mr and Mrs Murray. She remembered for no good reason all the whispered plans with Elizabeth years ago, years and years back when Elizabeth lived in Kilgarret. They would only marry for love, they would marry young men who roamed through the town, not awful businessmen who lived there. In those days Aisling had said suddenly that Elizabeth had a wider choice of business families because being a Protestant she could marry the Grays, and Elizabeth had complained and asked what was the point of learning all about contrition and grace and angels if she was still going to be considered a Protestant at the end of it?

Being Mr and Mrs Murray wasn't part of that plan. But then neither was having an abortion because Johnny Stone couldn't be told that his attempts at contraception had failed. Aisling wondered what Elizabeth did nowadays to make sure that it never happened again. Aisling sighed a happy sigh. Thank God she wouldn't have to bother with that. If she got pregnant it would be fine, she'd have the baby, and the next one, and Mam would help her look after them, and maybe Peggy would come and help her a bit. And Tony of course. She sighed again.

Tony looked over at her, and put his hand on her knee.

'Are you happy, Missus?' he said, imitating some of the old shawlies who always called people Missus even though they knew their names as well as their own.

'I'm very happy, Misthur,' she mimicked back.

'Great, so am I, and in no time we'll be in Dublin and we'll have that drink I've been thinking about at the back of my mind.'

'Yeah,' said Aisling absently. She wondered would he have the drink in the bar of the Shelbourne or would they have it sent up to the room? In films drinks came in ice buckets on trolleys. They might even have that.

'It's grand to be back in the old Shelbourne,' Tony said when the car had been safely parked and the porter had taken their cases. 'Now for that drink. Right?'

'Great,' said Aisling. To her surprise they walked right through the hotel and out again once he had signed the book. It had been curiously disappointing – she thought he would hold her hand and they would giggle. But no. And now where were they going?

'You wouldn't want to drink in here, its too posh a bar, people with accents and notions of grandeur. We'll go to a real bar.'

Aisling had peeped into the bar, it looked marvellous. It had mirrors, and waiters in white jackets. There were one or two elegant women there and she thought she looked the match for them in her aquamarine suit and little hat. But no, they were almost running away from Stephen's Green and on Baggot Street. Suddenly they were in a bar which wasn't as nice as Maher's and not quite as seedy as Hanrahan's. But it had that sour smell of beer and stout that you get when a place is full of spilt glasses and barrels not properly cleaned.

'You don't drink in places like this in Kilgarret,' she said, 'you drink in the hotel. Why won't we drink back in the hotel? It's nicer.'

'I can't go into a bar in Kilgarret or I'd have everyone in the town asking me for a loan of ten shillings, or travellers from the business coming up and trying to buy me a drink and tell me how they should be promoted. That's why I have to drink in the hotel. But here it's all right, no one will know who we are.'

Aisling looked around her. Men with caps on barely looked up from their pints, a group of young fellows near the door laughed and jeered about something. The table was covered with dirty glasses and overflowing ashtrays.

'Oh come on back, the bar in the Shelbourne has drink too, it's much nicer,' she begged.

But Tony was at the counter. He indicated one of the tables with a nod of his head.

'Gin?' he asked.

She heard him order a large gin, a large Power's and a pint of Guinness. She looked with distaste at the table and the barman sent a man around to clean it. The man was a bit slow, like Jemmy back in the shop. He kept looking at Aisling as he wiped the ash and rings of beer. His cloth was so greasy the table didn't look much better after his efforts. Aisling saw an evening newspaper and she picked it up smartly. She put two pages on the table and two on the chair. Now she would only get newsprint on her, she thought angrily. At least it would be better than God knows what other dirt.

'That's grand,' said Tony, coming back to the table with the drinks. He saw no criticism in her improvements. 'Well, here's good luck to us,' he said, raising the pint first and then having a swallow of the whiskey before Aisling had even touched her gin. 'As you said we're a fine pair.'

A man with the red nose of a drinker and a shabby,

crumpled suit that might once have been a good one leaned over and said to Tony as he might have addressed a regular in the pub, 'And what has yourself and your lady-friend all dolled up in a Saturday evening?'

Tony was delighted. 'I'd like you to know that's no lady-friend, that's my wife,' he said and roared with laughter.

The man peered at Aisling. 'Aw, well, it doesn't do any harm to take the wife out now and then, I always say. Were you at the races?'

'No, we were at a wedding,' said Tony winking and leering and looking so stupid that Aisling wanted to get up and walk away. With a jolt she realised that she couldn't do that any more.

'Oh, a wedding. Was it near here?' the man wanted to know.

'No, down the country. Two real country bumpkins.'

The man laughed. 'Oh, nothing as bad as a culchie wedding I always say. They can get desperately pretentious down in the country.'

Tony's face was all smiles. 'I could go along with you, I could lead you on and make a fool of you . . . but you look too good a man to do that to. It was our own wedding. Now what do you make of that?' and he sat back beaming.

The man, his eyes dulled with drink, knew something was expected of him. He stood up and shook hands with both of them. 'My sincere congratulations and my warmest felicitations. Under normal circumstances I would be the first to offer you a. . . .'

Tony seemed to understand the man's predicament as if he had been inspired by the Holy Ghost. This was a man who was about to offer them a drink to celebrate their wedding but had no money. This was a drunk, a pathetic shambling drunk, exactly the kind of man who would want to borrow ten shillings from Tony back home, a man with extravagant promises. Maybe a civil servant once, or a clerk somewhere. Aisling raged inside and her gin and tonic tasted like acid. Tony was at the counter. The man, their new friend, wouldn't touch Power's, he was a man who drank Bushmill's, never touched any whiskey only Black Bush, he said. Funny how many good things came out of the North when you stopped to think about it.

Aisling decided to turn her mind off. She blotted Tony and this man out, she fixed a smile on her face and she worked out what she would have for dinner. She planned her menu, she planned the bedroom scene, where she would wear her new cream nightie and lacy dressing-gown which had to be called a negligee – it was never going to be called a dressing-gown when you considered how much it cost. She planned how she was going to come into the room having undressed in the bathroom . . . she had been delighted that they had got a bedroom with a bathroom attached. Otherwise she would have had to walk down the corridor in her negligee. She planned that after it had all happened they would lie there and talk about the future, and Tony would say that he was glad they had waited for their wedding night.

In the middle of all this she heard Tony's voice and felt his elbow nudging her.

'You're very silent, Ash, is everything all right?'

'Oh yes,' she smiled, and he went back to his conversation and she went back into her mind. The next morning they would drive to the airport and she wouldn't be a bit afraid of the plane. After all, a grown-up, married woman who would have had sexual intercourse by that stage . . . naturally she wouldn't be as eejity and gormless as other people.

She got another nudge.

'Gerry knows a great pub altogether, a known pint house, I said we'd go and have the one there.'

'Will we not be a bit late for dinner in the hotel?' she said, the frostiness plain even to the man who drank Bushmill's whiskey.

'Well, maybe old son another night. . . .' he began.

But Tony Murray had felt no frost. 'Nonsense, tonight's the night, we might never find you again in this city, two culchies like ourselves.' He laughed loudly. Aisling got up obediently and Tony put his arm around her shoulder.

'Didn't I get the best girl in Kilgarret, Gerry?' he asked the drunk.

'Tony, you got the very best,' said the drunk firmly.

There was no dinner in the Shelbourne; the time spent planning whether to have melon or grapefruit or soup as a starter had been wasted. At closing time, Gerry had told them where to get chips. He wouldn't have any himself, he had kept his money for the last bus, but anyway, money or no money, he often found that he didn't fancy food after a few scoops of an evening. He shook their hands and wished them the best. He was no drunker than when they had met four hours earlier. He seemed no redder in the nose, no more dulled in the eye. Aisling was hardly changed either. She had accepted no more gin, only glasses of tonic water. And in the last pub they didn't have any so she had just sat there with nothing in front of her and her mind closed. Now, chips finished, and Tony laughing like a schoolboy, they walked back through the city. In her handbag was a key to one of the most expensive hotel rooms in Ireland; they had money and planned to have had a dinner for the two of them. But instead it had been bar after bar. Five of them counting the first place. In the hall the porters looked at each other and smiled behind Tony's back as he fumbled for change.

'There's no need for a tip now, they've not done anything for us,' hissed Aisling.

'I'd like to give them a tip, it's my money, it's my wedding night,' stumbled Tony, swaying. 'It's my bloody wedding night, I'll give as many tips as I please.'

The porters thanked him. He gave one a half crown and the other two shillings.

'Fight it out between you,' he said.

'Goodnight sir, thank you,' they both said, and Aisling tried to support him as he staggered making them a mock courteous bow.

'Leave me be, woman. She's the same as all of them you know, can't wait to get me upstairs.'

The porters smiled, embarrassed for Aisling whom they could see was sobbing. And humiliated. The older porter took pity on her.

'Mam, let me go ahead with the key,' he said. And as Tony

staggered along the corridor the kindly man said to Aisling, 'If you knew how many honeymoon couples we get Madam, and the men are always scared out of their minds. I think we men are definitely the weaker sex. I've always thought it.'

'You're a very kind man,' Aisling said.

'Nonsense, you'll be the happiest couple in the world, never mind.'

Inside the bedroom Tony was all smiles.

'Come on, let me at you,' he said to Aisling.

'Let me get my suit off me first,' said Aisling. It was filthy already but she didn't want it torn.

She hung the jacket on the back of a chair, and folded the skirt, she stood before him in her slip and her blouse.

'You're lovely,' he said.

'Hold on a minute,' she said. 'Can't I get out my lovely new negligee? I want to put that on. Please.'

'All right,' he said. He sat down in a velvet armchair, suddenly, as if the strength had gone from his legs. Aisling opened the suitcase she had packed so carefully with the dinner dress she had intended to wear on top, the negligee and nightie set underneath and the washbag with flowers on it beside that. She slipped into the bathroom and washed quickly. She would love to have soaked in a long bath but she was afraid that he would not want to wait as long as that.

She looked at her face, which seemed to her tired and drawn, pulled her long hair back and tied it loosely with the cream ribbon she had bought specially for the occasion. She put on more perfume . . . and rubbed a little rouge into her cheeks. She looked better now. Oh God, may he not be too drunk. Please God, may he not hurt her. Please. After all God, I did wait until I got married, a lot of people don't, a great many people don't. I kept my part of the bargain God, please let him not be too rough with me. She went into the room and twirled around so that he would get the full view of the negligee.

Tony was asleep in the armchair. His mouth was open and he was snoring.

Aisling took off the negligee and hung it carefully on one

of the hotel hangers. She switched off the light in the bathroom; took the extra blanket which had been left in the wardrobe and put it over Tony. She raised his head slightly and slipped a pillow behind his neck. She loosened his shoes and took them off and she put his feet on another pillow. She had seen someone do that in a film once, where a man had gone out and got drunk over this woman and when he came home she took his army boots off and put his feet on a cushion. It had seemed a lovely thing for her to do in the film. But of course in the film he had been crying and saying he loved her. He hadn't been snoring like Tony Murray. Her husband.

Dublin airport
Just a quick word to thank you for being such a support and help. Don't leave another million years before you come back to Kilgarret. Everything in Dublin super. Roll on Rome.
   love from
   Aisling Murray

Hotel San Martino
Another picture for your collection. This is the Holy City or the Eternal City as we called it at school. It's very very hot, and there are an awful lot of poor people, much poorer than you'd see in Wicklow, and lots of the Italians have no religion. There's a bank called Sancto Spirito. Imagine having your savings in the Holy Ghost Bank! The hotel is beautiful and there's an old-fashioned lift you can see through. Tomorrow we see Il Papa. Tony sends his love, or he would if he knew I was writing to you.
   Love,
   Aisling

Hotel San Martino
There were a hundred people there, and we were introduced to him. Signor e Signora Murray d'Irlanda. It was unbelievable. I still don't believe it happened. Every

344

time I see pictures of him, I keep saying to Tony . . . he met US. Still very hot. I roam about and look at ruins quite a lot, you'd be proud of me. We have meals in restaurants on the side of the street, not inside at all. Just like those pictures you see in Paris. The wine is very cheap and we drink it with every single meal. Except breakfast.
    Love from
    Signora Murray

It's got even hotter. Everyone else in Rome is golden and sun-tanned, but because of my awful colouring I just burn. So I've bought a parasol. Remember we used to have toy parasols once? Tony doesn't want to go out in the heat, so we see a great deal of indoor things. I went to the catacombs. The poor martyrs, didn't they have an awful time for their faith when it's so easy for us? I'm quite looking forward to seeing Kilgarret where it's cool and green . . . and wet, I gather from Mam's letter.
    Love, Aisling.

Mam, thank you very much for writing here. Nobody else did, I expect they didn't think it would arrive. You're an angel to tell me the bungalow is so far ahead. Thank God we won't have to stay with the old Bag . . . I'll have to put this card into an envelope now, won't I? Everything is smashing Ma, and as I said in the other card, thank you and Dad a million times. I hope the wedding didn't exhaust you and leave you broke or anything. I'm so looking forward to being home. I must try to remember I live with Tony now rather than saying goodbye to him in the square and running up to you and Dad like I used to. Tell the boys thanks again too and Niamh. Wasn't it great that Elizabeth came over for the wedding, and didn't she look marvellous? I've sent her a few cards from here. It must be very lonely for her back in London, I was thinking.
    Love from your Married Daughter, Aisling

'She looked utterly enchanting . . . here, I have the pictures.'
Elizabeth sat on a desk with her feet on a chair and opened
the wallet of black and white pictures. She had been given
this camera by Johnny for her twenty-first birthday and it
had never been taken on a serious outing before. Now she
had twelve pictures of Aisling's wedding, ten of them perfect
she thought, and two spoiled. Stefan and Anna pored over
them.

'Hasn't she become slim since she was here?' Stefan said.

'Look at her beautiful dress,' said Anna.

'Is this her mother, a handsome woman. . . .' Stefan
looked at Eileen and somehow Elizabeth felt her two worlds
grow closer.

'And her husband, this Tony, he is handsome is he not?'
Anna had spread the pictures down on the desk. 'And who is
this man, the one who has his hand on your arm?'

'That's his loathsome best man . . . a frightful fool.'

Stefan and Anna laughed.

'No, seriously . . . really dreadful. I hope for Aisling's sake
he's not going to be a family friend.'

'And who is the sad lady?'

'That's Tony's mother. She did smile a bit, but I don't
think anybody caught it. And that's Tony's awfully bad-
mannered sister, Joannie, and that's his rather wishy-washy
brother who's nearly a priest . . . oh, and that's Donal, the
young brother who used to be delicate. Look at his laugh,
isn't he marvellous . . . and that's me looking silly with my
hat. . . .'

'You look beautiful, Elizabeth,' said Anna seriously.

'Oh she does. Quite as beautiful as the little bride,' said
Stefan.

'Oh, that's Tony pulling a face . . . it was just before they
got into the car to go to the hotel. He was still very edgy at
that stage . . . he got better later on. More relaxed.'

'You don't think they are good enough for Aisling, these
people?'

'Oh Stefan. I never said that. No they're the high and
mighty in the town, honestly. Like the squire, as Johnny
used to say.'

'But you do not like them . . . listen, this Tony he is edgy, his brother is wishy-washy, his sister she is bad-mannered, rude, his mother she is weepy, his best friend is frightful . . . of course you don't like them!'

Stefan laughed. Elizabeth looked at him, almost speechless.

'I didn't mean. . . .' she began.

'But it's not a crime not to like the people that your friends marry. I am sure if my sons are married I would not like their wives. Anna here does not like the family that her sister married into. They live in London, she never sees the family, but she meets her sister every month. So. It's not unnatural.'

'I never even said it to myself. I didn't even know I didn't like them,' said Elizabeth, grinning mischievously. 'But you won't tell them, and you'll never tell Aisling if she comes over here again. Because I don't really dislike them . . . Listen, I won't delay you any more. I just collected these from the chemist and I wanted you to be the first to see. I'm off home now.'

'Johnny should be back next week, then it will all be fun and bustle here again,' Anna said with the air of someone trying to introduce a comforting note.

Elizabeth saw Stefan frown at her.

'Now, Anna, Elizabeth knows all Johnny's movements better than we do, in Brighton and Hove, and back on Friday . . . we don't have to tell her what he's doing.'

Darling Stefan, like Aunt Eileen, a diplomat, always wanting people to be given their dignity, never wanting to score over others. How great it had been seeing him looking at Aunt Eileen and saying she was handsome. Wouldn't it be wonderful if Aunt Eileen came over here . . . or was that silly? Oh God, oh God, from Stefan's face it looks as if Johnny has a new woman. Of course she hadn't known that he was away in Brighton, of course she hadn't known that he was coming back on Friday. Thank God for Stefan and his refusal to admit that anything was wrong between Elizabeth and Johnny. Sometimes she thought that if it weren't for Stefan she would have lost Johnny forever.

*

347

Father was politely interested in the photographs.

'Which one is Violet's friend?' he asked first, and Elizabeth thought that this was a good sign. Usually he refused any opportunity to bring Mother's name into the conversation.

'That's Aunt Eileen there,' she said proudly.

'Nice, nice, yes she looks a very presentable woman. Of course, she'll be glad that Aisling has married and married well.'

'Yes, Father, she is glad. I think she's very glad.'

'Well, of course she's pleased, dear. Her daughter married and set up. Safely off her hands, with a home and a future of her own. It's what every parent would want.'

Elizabeth looked up, amazed.

'Is it what you want for me, Father?'

'Of course.'

'What?'

'Of course I want you to marry and settle down. What else can I want for you?'

'And are you not glad that I'm happy as I am? That I have work which interests me, teaching and working in Worsky's, and that I have Johnny around. . . ?'

Father said nothing.'

'Because I am fine. Really. To be utterly honest, I wouldn't like to be marrying someone like Tony Murray, someone sensible. I prefer to be the way I am. I mean it. I'm not just saying it to cover a broken heart. . . .'

'You're your mother's daughter, I'm afraid, Elizabeth, and that's what worries me. She had a fine home here, and a family and a social life and what did she do, she went off with a fly-by-night black-marketeer, a man who made his money out of other people's suffering . . . she went off with him, flighty and thoughtless and ended up losing her mind. So do you wonder that I worry when I see that feckless side of her in you?' Father said all this quite calmly; there was no twitch in his eye, as there used to be when he became upset. It was as if he believed it all now like a story that had happened to someone else. That poor Harry was a black-marketeer. Harry!

She kept her voice as calm as Father's. If she was going to be able to talk to him, she must follow his lead. She must let his own dead objectivity be in control.

'Yes, I do see that, I can see now why you might be worried. But honestly, things have changed. It's the fifties now, not the twenties and thirties. Things change. Women really are interested in their work. And men, some men are simply not interested in settling down.'

'Yes, well. I would of course prefer you to have a proper life and be looked after. I mean, what's the point of having children if you're going to be worried that they don't settle down?'

Elizabeth hid her amazement. She decided it was time to end the conversation lightly.

'Yes, you may be right, and one of these days I might actually surprise you, throw over Johnny Stone and find a suitable husband . . . then we'll have a wedding like this. Here, look at Tony's mother, now she's a widow and you're divorced – what do you say we make a match there . . . ?'

Father looked seriously at Mrs Murray's gloomy face. 'She looks perfectly pleasant. . . .' He peered at the picture. 'But she has other children . . . I don't think I could take on the responsibility of any more. . . .'

This was the nearest thing Father had ever made to a joke that Elizabeth could ever remember. She was still laughing when the telephone rang: it was Johnny.

'How was the poor sacrificial lamb? Did she go through with it?'

'Oh hallo, Johnny, yes, she went through with it. The whole ritualistic sacrifice. Marvellous, it was. Hymns and priests talking forever. I have some smashing pictures . . . your camera was a great success.'

'Oh good. Listen, I'm sorry I wasn't around. I don't know what Stefan said, or if there was any explanation when you got back . . . ?'

'What? No, don't worry, Stefan gave me your message.'

'He what?'

'He said you said you'd be back on Friday. How's it all going?'

349

'Well, plan's changed a bit, I think I'll come back tonight.
I really only rang to know how the land lay . . . if you felt like
coming round to the flat tonight?'

'Oh sure, that would be terrific. About eight all right?'

'Well, I'll be back by six if you could. . . .'

'No, I've a few things to do here . . . see you at eight. Have
you got any food . . . or shall I get some?'

'I'll get a bottle of wine . . . could you rustle up
something? You sound very cheerful I must say . . . the
wedding didn't make you all gooey and broody?'

'Who me? Listen, you're talking to Elizabeth White, my
friend.'

'Yes, I know and I'm looking forward to seeing her
tonight. I missed you, funny face.'

'I missed you too, Johnny.'

Ethel Murray had said that she was going to be in Dublin
anyway on the day that Tony was expected back. She was
half-wondering would she go to the airport to meet him?
Eileen had thought that was a poor idea.

'I suppose you're right, Eileen. You always seem so
sensible about things,' Ethel Murray said grudgingly. They
were talking outside the church where they had both been
delivering flowers for the procession. Already people were
busy decorating the float for the statue of the Sacred Heart.
The women walked to the gate of the church in a companionable silence. 'I never knew you were so business-like,
Eileen. I suppose you didn't know I was so . . . well, so alone
and so dependent of my children, did you?'

'Ah, we're all dependent on our children, we'd be no use
as parents if we could just produce them and forget about
them, would we?'

'But yours are no problem to you. They don't run as far
away from you as they can get, like mine do.'

'Haven't you a big handsome son coming back next week
to live down the road from you, woman? And better still,
hasn't he the eyes in his head to marry my daughter?'

They laughed. And Eileen wondered again why people
thought she had no problems with her children. Eamonn

and his father rowing worse than ever; Maureen expecting yet again, going to be tied down still more to the Dalys; Donal coughing and wheezing and pausing to catch his breath. Niamh was too pert for her own good. And Aisling. Eileen wished she knew why Aisling's cards had upset her. Sean had thought that the child sounded in great form. But she never said anything about being happy.

There had been an arrangement before they left for Rome that Tony would leave the car keys under the seat and Joannie could use the car for the month that they were away. As soon as they got on the plane for the return journey Tony began to regret this.

'It was sheer madness. I don't know how I got talked into it.' His face looked upset and hurt as if it had been a plot which he had recently discovered, instead of his own plan made long, long ago.

'You said it would be a saving, we wouldn't have to pay for a whole month's parking at the airport, and Joannie could have the use of a car while her own is being fixed.'

'Yes, but that's the point, did we ever hear the full story of why hers is being fixed?'

Aisling laughed. 'We probably never will. Stop worrying about it and look at the clouds. Imagine, these are the things that ruin whole crops on people and spoil people's weddings and picnics, and don't they look harmless from up here?'

'Yes, isn't it a mystery all right. You know, if she's burned out the choke on that car . . . or driven it into the ground, I don't know what I'll do to her. God almighty, Aisling, that's a new car. That's a car with only a thousand miles on the clock. I should have had my head examined before I gave in to the lot of you over it.'

'Tony, you suggested it, for God's sake, I'm not going to sit here saying yes dear and no dear. It was your bloody idea so shut up about it will you?'

Tony looked at her and laughed suddenly. 'Very well, I'll shut up about it. No, I can't imagine you saying yes dear and no dear. It doesn't fit into the picture. . . .'

'It didn't fit into the promise. And you won't yes dear me,

like poor Mr Moriarty does to his wife. We must be equals in the yes dearing and no dearing. Or better still abolish it.'

Tony laughed again. 'You look so funny when you get all hot and bothered laying down the law. Fair enough: no yes dearing or no dearing in our house. Ever.'

'Won't it be very exciting to see it? I wonder what it will look like. Mam said that they had the drive down and all. . . .'

'Good, we'll be able to take what's left of the car inside then, rather than leaving it on the road.'

'Tony. Shut up about the car. It will be grand to have our own home. Won't it?'

He took her hand. 'Yes, it will all be fine there, everything will be fine at home. It's only natural that things should be a bit . . . I mean, shouldn't work out exactly right . . . when people are abroad . . . but in our own home . . . In a person's own home it should all be grand.' He was red and embarrassed, his face working as he spoke, moving from a scowl to a pathetic little-boy look. Aisling deliberately misunderstood what he was talking about.

'Yes, of course things will be great when we have our own food . . . I mean, we never promised to eat Italian food until death do us part or live with that kind of traffic screeching around us. No, what we were thinking about was life in Kilgarret. And that's going to be grand. Don't we know that?'

But he had begun, and he was not going to be turned aside. 'No,' he whispered. 'I meant about the other. The other thing. Bed, you know. All that side of things will be fine too when we settle down at home, in our own place. You know?'

Aisling was utterly light-hearted about it. 'You mean about us not doing it right yet? I think nobody does it right for a bit, I think we have to practise like playing tennis or riding a bicycle. I mean, we don't have anyone to teach us. Nobody has. So they all pretend like mad that they know by inspiration. I bet we'll be just as good as anyone at it in a couple of weeks and then we'll imply there was nothing to it!'

'You're a great girl,' he said.

'Isn't it right, though? I mean it makes sense,' Aisling said and they dropped the subject to talk about Tony's mother and how she must not be encouraged to drop in casually into the new house. Then they relapsed into a silence for a while and Tony looked in front of him. Aisling stared out the window, and wondered did Tony think he should go out drinking by himself still like he had before he was married and go to the pictures other nights with her? If so, did he expect her to sit at home and wait for him? Doing what? Doing bloody what? Calm down, she told herself, no point in getting all upset about something that hasn't even happened and may not happen. Think about something else. Aisling looked out at the clouds and thought about the time she had asked Elizabeth what it was like having sex. Poor Elizabeth had been so distressed about the abortion and the whole situation she hadn't been much help but she hadn't said anything about it taking a long time to learn it. She had sort of given the impression that it was something you did. But of course she was so hopelessly loyal and devoted to that Johnny that she wouldn't even admit that he had had to learn how to do it like anyone else. Or perhaps Johnny had practised on other people. Of course, that was it. That was why it had been so easy for them. And probably Maureen and Brendan Daly had been years and years learning, it was amazing that they had managed to have Brendan Og so soon. Very soon in fact. It must have been a mistake. She shrugged. There were obviously secrets in everyone's marriage. She was never going to tell anyone about that awful night in Dublin with the drunk, and making fools of themselves in the Shelbourne Hotel in front of the porters. And she would never tell anyone about the times Tony had cried and she had cried in the Hotel San Martino in Rome. You didn't tell those things any more than you told things like Da hitting Eamonn in the middle of Sunday lunch one day and Mother standing up with a bread knife to keep them apart. It had shocked everyone so much that nobody ever mentioned it again, or even thought about it.

*

Dear Aisling,

I'm so happy that you are home again and settled into the new house. It sounds very exotic to be writing to you as Mrs Murray in San Martino Lodge instead of Aisling O'Connor, 14 The Square. Was it your idea to call it after your honeymoon hotel or was it Tony's? It's so marvellous to have been back to Kilgarret because now I know where everything is all over again. I had thought that the bungalow was on the other side of town completely – for some reason I thought it was on the Dublin road. Now that I can place things you simply must write and tell me all there is to be told.

You won't have the excuse of being busy, a married lady with nothing to do but tend the flowers all day. I know it's not comparing anything with anything, but my earliest memories of Mother before the war, before I came to Kilgarret, were always of her sitting at a writing desk writing letters. And now I can't think who they could have been to. Aunt Eileen said she only heard from her very rarely, so it's another mystery.

Mother, since I spoke to her, is well. By which they mean she is peaceful, she is so heavily tranquillised now and under such sedation that she doesn't know who anyone is, or where she is. I went up to Lancashire last week just to make sure. She is like a baby, a toddler really. Very thin and smiling. It's as if she were a shell. Father won't hear about it. He did mention Mother of his own accord not long ago when I was showing him your wedding pictures – weren't they super – I had hoped he might be beginning to talk more about things, but no. Having scared me to death by saying that he had always hoped I would marry and settle down, he then went back to his normal uncommunicative self.

Oh, the reason he scared me by advocating marriage was that since he had endured such a poor experience of it himself I was surprised he wanted to see others enter into it. It's quite different in your house. I'm not at all surprised your parents are so happy about you getting married, they had so much themselves out of the whole married state. Anyway, I said to Father quite openly that Johnny and marriage were two separate notions and if I wanted one I couldn't have the other.

I was quite surprised to hear myself saying it, and in a way it was quite good for me. Because even to you I never admitted it openly did I? And you and I have talked about everything. I feel suddenly as if I cheated by holding back something. I didn't mean to. I think it was superstitious magic ... if I didn't admit that Johnny is a hopeless passion in the world's sense then maybe it might not be true. Suppose I went on behaving quite normally, maybe Johnny would come around.

But it's a release somehow to know that the little hints, the veiled enquiries, the polite wonderings don't matter any more. I am now able to admit to myself that there isn't going to be a fairy-tale ending. No bells ringing like they rang for you ... well, we wouldn't go anywhere with bells even if Johnny did want to get married. It would be a registry office. No huge happy family smiling, because there isn't one. No wedding presents and honeymoons on the continent. Johnny is the new generation. Or so I have decided to believe. The generation that wants no commitments, no ties, no promises. It won't tell any lies because there will be no need to lie.

It sounds a bit futuristic, but funnily, since I have decided to accept things like that, Johnny and I are much happier. I didn't actually spell it out to Johnny of course, men don't want things spelled out. But really for the past weeks things have never been better. He insisted on coming up to Preston with me. He even came to see Mother. He said she was like a broken doll. He was marvellous with Harry, and when he went out to get a half dozen light ales – Harry lives with a couple of neighbours now – Harry said to me, "When's he going to make an honest woman of you?" I was able to tell Harry truly and without all that awkwardness that it wasn't on the cards.

Listen, you'll never write to me again if I keep pouring my heart out to you. But you used to complain once that I was too buttoned-up in my letter-writing. So here's the full whoosh of the waterfall.

Tell me every single thing abut the honeymoon and I'll burn the letters. Tell me about the Pope, and coming back to the bungalow, how Aunt Eileen and Uncle Sean were . . . they'll miss you a lot, you know – but you do know. And about Mother-in-Law Murray. Things are great here but I would like to be there too sometimes. Oh, for the chance of a private plane and lots of money.

Love to you and to Tony,
    Elizabeth

Dear Elizabeth,
Of course it's all great, it's just as good as I had hoped it would be. The house is very easy to keep clean – no horrible, dark corners. Of course, that means no nice corners to hide the dirt in either. I give it a huge going-over on a Thursday. Ma-in-Law comes for tea on Thursdays. I was very firm. The first week she was dropping in every second day and so I used to pretend I was going out. And I'd leap on my bicycle and say to her why don't we fix a definite day for you to come? Poor old cow, I'm sorry for her in a way, but she's a bore and a snob and one who Does Things for Show. Burn this letter.

And what else? I've got an awful cookery book with things about filleting fish in it and stock and steamed puddings. None of the things I like. I enclose two pounds; could you buy me a nice one and send it to me? You know, something a bit sophisticated. Nothing about cod and nothing about boiled mutton. I can smell them as soon as I read the recipes.

Not that Tony's hard to please. He eats anything. He actually eats very little, I think, considering that he puts on weight easily. No breakfast, just tea. He has lunch at the hotel with Shay and some of the lads, and then home here about eight. He says he has his dinner eaten in the middle of the day so it's only tea and brack really. But at the weekends I'd like to be able to cook something nice.

You said that I'd have all day to be writing letters now. I thought you were right. I was going to write to you twice a week, but it's odd. Nothing much happens to write about and still the nothing that is happening takes up a lot of time. I never find myself at a desk like your mother did writing letters. The time goes. I don't know where. When I think of all I got done in the days I worked with Mam and Dad: a full job, dressed up to kill, books read during my lunch hour, home and helping Niamh with homework, or Mam with making something in the kitchen, then dressing myself up again after tea and out to the pictures with Tony and a bit of a court and home – and maybe in those days sitting down and writing you a long letter before going to bed. But now there's no energy, no activity and no time.

Maybe it happens to married women to keep them sort of weighed down so that they won't run off and do anything foolish.

I've been five months married now and honestly I can hardly list one thing that has happened. I just feel everything's an awful effort. That's why married women are such desperate bores. Stay as you are with your Johnny, you're better off. I don't mean I'm miserable or anything.

Perhaps I'll feel better next week and write some real descriptions of things to you.

Love, Aisling

Dear Aisling, I'm writing this note immediately to you. I got your letter today and something occurred to me. Perhaps you are pregnant! Couldn't that be it? Not that I'm a great expert on the matter but I did read a lot about it in books at that time, and remember that pregnancy brings lethargy. Go on, you might be Momma. I'll write no more, I'll just wait to hear. Do write back, whatever, won't you? Love, E.

Dear Elizabeth. No I'm not. I got the curse the morning your letter arrived. Thanks all the same. It seemed a

reasonable thing to suppose. I'll write next week. Love.
Aisling

Dear Aisling,
Johnny and I are in Cornwall on a holiday. This is the
hotel writing paper. It's simply beautiful here, the sea is
so wild, it's very foreign, like being abroad.

I didn't hear from you for a few weeks. I hope
everything's all right. I become very stupid and over-
sensitive as we all know, and maybe I'm just being silly,
but when I didn't hear from you and when I remember
your last letter, which was a bit curt and short, I
wondered if I'd said anything to offend you. I rushed off
that note about the possibility of your being pregnant.
Perhaps it was crass, I don't know. It seemed to me like an
explanation for you being under par. I always think of
you as being so bouncy and full of life. I always think of
you as writing letters too. Please write and reassure your
   foolish friend Elizabeth

Dearest Foolish Friend,
No, of course I wasn't being curt, of course you weren't
being crass. We're too young to be curt and crass, that's
only for old ladies and not for friends anyway. No, the
problem is that I don't write as well as you. I give all the
wrong impressions. Sister Margaret said I once described
the school picnic as if it were the Pope's funeral. If I try to
describe ordinary everyday things I bring everyone
down. No wonder you thought I was depressed and
unlike myself.

So, the news cheered me. Everything is great, really
great. I'm so happy all the time, Tony is very devoted and
loving and we've struck a bargain. In return for my
entertaining his maternal battle-axe for tea and scones
(made by Mam but pretended made by me) every
Thursday then he'll come home for the end of it, drive her
back up to her house, go in and have a drink there, and
make out it's as if he never left home. She shows him the
cracks and the leaks and the damp and he forgets all

about it. Then he comes back to me. We go to Maher's for a drink with Dad and Mam and then we have dinner at the hotel. Every Thursday. Remember what a treat it was to have a drink there once? Maureen is apparently pea-green again over the hotel business . . . but honestly I can't spend my whole life trying not to make her jealous. I did tell you she's having another baby didn't I? She looks awful most of the time. If she'd cheer up I'd go down and collect her and take her out places, but God, she's so bloody weepy. When I come with the car to see her, isn't it fine for me having a big car under my backside? When I come without it, isn't it a marvel that those who have cars don't drive them? I'm not a bad driver now, but I hate reversing, in fact if I'm in the square I drive the whole way round in order not to have to turn.

Now, foolish friend, do you believe I'm cheerful and not curt – and please write when you come back from your Cornish love nest to
your inarticulate friend,
Aisling

The college principal asked Elizabeth if she would like to give some adult art classes after Christmas. She said she thought that would be nice but wondered whether she would be able to do them.

'You're silly, darling girl,' Johnny had said. 'These poor sods by their very nature know nothing about art. There's no fear of setting a genius on the wrong path as you might do with kids, or running into a bunch of know-alls, among the students. No, the adult–ed people will be a pushover. Lonely old men and women filling in their evening. They'll be dead grateful for anything you teach them.'

Johnny was both wrong and right. Lonely old men and women they were not, but dead grateful they were. It was a new venture, a course of twenty lessons over ten weeks. Elizabeth gave her object-painting classes on Tuesdays, and on Thursdays the principal lectured on the history of art. It was an attempt, he said, to try to share a little culture on a wider level.

359

'We could arrange visits to galleries in the summer if this is a success,' Elizabeth had offered, and the principal had looked at her with new approval.

Some of the adults were young women, often in secretarial and office jobs. They seemed shy and timid and Elizabeth found herself having coffee in the college coffee shop with groups after the class ended at 9.30. Once or twice Johnny had looked in to collect her, flashing a smile of such charm that the entire group felt better for his having been there.

'Do you think you could take them on a tour of the galleries if I set it up next term?' she asked him one night. 'They really do want to know about art, but they're nervous to ask, they feel awkward, they think the world's divided into Arty People and Non-Arty.'

'Well, it is,' said Johnny.

'I don't believe that,' Elizabeth said.

'I am, you are, your Pa is not, my mate Nick is not. It doesn't matter, it's like being English or Greek, or being tall or short. It's just the way things are.'

Elizabeth was silent. She thought of the men and women who came to her Tuesday class. Perhaps it was just a bit of silliness pretending to open doors to them. But she thought that they really were learning something and several of them had said that they knew now what to look for when they saw a painting; before this they had thought it was a closed world.

'You can learn anything,' she said definitely.

'Sure,' Johnny said easily, 'of course you can learn anything – but you can't learn to *be* anything. You can't change yourself. You can add a few facts and bits of information, but it doesn't change the person.'

'You're very dismissive,' Elizabeth said.

'I find them boring, duck, that's all. The job's a nice one for you, it earns you a few more shillings, respect of Big White Chief and it makes you happy ... but a crusade which I'm going to join, it is not.'

But in the summer term the principal said there was too much happening for him to set up another course, so

Elizabeth was to feel free to do one herself. She printed little leaflets and offered a series of eight visits to the art galleries, each to be followed by a short discussion and coffee. She charged enough to pay for the art gallery entrance, and someone to serve tea and pass biscuits. She said it was 'Art for Everybody' and they even interviewed her for a local paper. 'I don't believe that the world is divided into the artistic and the non-artistic,' she was quoted as saying. Stefan put up advertisements for her and so did her friend, Mr Clarke in the library. She told Stefan excitedly that if twenty people registered she would have enough to make it pay; anyone over that would be a bonus. On the day of her first lecture there were fifty-four students. She was ill twice during the afternoon in anticipation of it. But by seven o'clock she was standing talking to the curator at Late Opening Night, assuring him of cooperation, publicity and indeed increased revenue.

Stefan had lent her a wonderful set of little library steps which she carried under her arm and climbed on so that people could see her whenever she stopped at a painting.

The first time she climbed the little steps Elizabeth felt almost weak. Her voice started and it sounded faint and pathetic like a kitten. She had to clear her throat and begin again. This time it was not much better. How could she have assembled all these people, over fifty of them, and set herself up to take their money and make speeches at them? It was monstrous. Then she told herself firmly that it was exactly the same as she had been doing while in the college, they were the same kind of people, anxious to know more . . . anxious to have other eyes show them what to look for in a painting. Their blurred faces sharpened a little and she grabbed at the courage . . . this time she found her voice, firm and strong, this time she knew that she mustn't think of how preposterous it was for Elizabeth White to have such notions about herself. This time she must just get on with it and tell them what had to be told.

Long before she had settled them down with cups of tea for the discussion, she knew it had been a roaring success. She had suggested some books that they might like to read about painters and great paintings before next week. Shyly she had said that when she was a schoolgirl she had been encouraged to read about art by a librarian and an art teacher; and that many people believed it was not the same as being an artist, but it certainly let you know what being an artist was like. She said reluctantly that she could not accept people's friends, husbands, wives or neighbours next week, that the numbers were rather too large already but that perhaps later they might consider having two separate sessions.

Elizabeth was longing to discuss her triumph with someone; but Johnny had said he would be out of town for the night; no explanation, but possibly pique that she had started this scheme in spite of him, Elizabeth had thought. Father would have no interest, Stefan would be in bed and asleep, the keys to his beloved shop under his pillow. Elizabeth began a letter to Aisling telling her all about it. But she stopped after three paragraphs. It was almost the end of April. She hadn't had a letter from Aisling for . . . it must be months now. No, she had written at Christmas, of course, and after it to thank her for the old-fashioned traycloths, saying that Ma Murray went yellow with being impressed when she saw them. There had been a brief mention of Maureen's new baby, and of Donal being in the chest hospital for three weeks for observation, but he was fine again. Elizabeth had heard from Aunt Eileen the usual inconsequential things which Elizabeth loved to read. But there had been no word at all from Aisling since January. Months ago. Elizabeth tore up the letter. Aisling couldn't be interested in hearing all her silly tales, could she? If Aisling were interested she'd have written. Some sort of letter.

'What are you going to do for your birthday?' Mam asked Aisling at the beginning of May. They sat together companionably in the kitchen with a sense of achievement. Mam had said she had been meaning to tidy the drawers in the kitchen dresser for three years and Aisling had said they should do it now and give it an hour – not a minute more. They found old letters which Aisling put in a paper bag marked 'Old letters for Mam to drool over later and to say how sweet we all were when we were young'. They found string and buttons and coins. Aisling had them into string bags and button boxes and money boxes like a flash.

'You're a great little worker,' Mam had said. 'I'm surprised you're not working like a beaver up in that new house.'

'Sure, it's all done there, there's nothing to do,' Aisling had said, lining the drawers with new paper. 'Now, Mam, you can fill them all up again with rubbish and I'll come round next year and tidy them up for you.'

They laughed at the role reversal and opened a tin of shortbread to eat with the tea.

'My birthday, I don't know. I'd forgotten all about it,' Aisling said.

'Well, that's a big change. I remember you and Elizabeth like two little puppies planning birthday treats from April on. I wonder does she still make a fuss of it?'

'We're too old Mam, the quarter of a century . . . not much to be crowing about.'

'You always did before,' Eileen said, letting no anxiety into her voice. 'I remember this time last year in the middle of all the plans for your wedding you suddenly stopped and said that you didn't like your birthday being over-shadowed.'

Aisling laughed. 'Nor did I in those days, I suppose. Very carefree, nothing to worry about. Birthdays were big happy things.'

Eileen knew she was treading very gently. 'And what has made you less carefree may one ask? A car, no less, and able to drive it like a madwoman; a grand man who thinks the world of you and will buy you whatever you set your heart on; a honeymoon where you met the Pope, a house that's the talk of Kilgarret, and in and out of me as if you were never gone . . . and us all delighted to see you. Tell me what's not carefree about that sort of a life?'

'Mam.' Aisling leaned forward, her eyes troubled. Eileen prayed that Niamh wouldn't come bouncing in with screams and shouts about homework and exams.

363

'Yes love?'

'Mam, some things are a bit hard to put, you know?'

'Oh I know, I know.' Eileen gave a mock sign to take some of the tension out of the conversation. 'When I was trying to talk to you and Elizabeth when you were teenagers I remember searching high and low for words . . . but I could never find them. . . .'

'Yes, it's a bit like that. I wanted to ask you something . . . tell you something . . . is it all right?'

Eileen looked at her. She was too old to take in her arms yet her face was just as young as when she came home with a broken schoolbag or a note of complaint from Sister Margaret. Eileen didn't want her to blurt anything out too suddenly . . . something she might regret having told.

'Child, you can ask me anything. Anything, and you can tell me anything too. But I'll tell you something about telling. Often people are sorry they told things, they feel they let an outside person in on some secret and very unfairly. Then they resent the outside person . . . do you know what I mean? I wouldn't want you to grow away from me because you told something that shouldn't have been told. . . .'

'Then you know?' cried Aisling with a face full of horror.

'Know? Know? What do I know, how can I know anything? Aisling, be reasonable. I don't even know what you're talking about. I was only giving you a sort of general rule about confidences.'

'You don't want me to confide in you, is that it?'

'God, girl, you're very prickly. Listen I'll tell you something. When your Dad and I got married, I remember this bit always and I'll never forget it. Well we didn't have a honeymoon or anything, just a weekend in Tramore in a guesthouse, and neither your father nor I were able to talk about the whole business of being in love or making love or anything, you know, we just did things . . . not talked about them.'

'I know,' said Aisling miserably.

'So there were some of the things about making love and all that when your father started them . . . well, I didn't know whether this was all right or not. You see he would only have been told about it from ignorant men working on the farm with him when he was a lad . . . his mother was dead, God rest her, and then he'd only have heard more things from ignorant fellows when he was serving his time in that hardware store. . . .'

'Yes, Mam?' Aisling was sympathetic and sorrowful.

'So I didn't know whether what he wanted to do . . . whether what we were doing was right or whether it was a sin, or what. Now, I had nobody to ask. Nobody in the world. I couldn't ask my mother in one million years. She was as strict then as she had been when I was a child. To her I still was a child. She died five years later . . . and you know, Aisling, I wasn't much older than you . . . but I never had a real conversation with her. Then Aunt Maureen was a nun, and she wouldn't be much use, and your Aunt Peggy and Aunt Niamh were in America and I couldn't write off to them and ask for advice . . . so.

'So I never asked anyone. I just went ahead and did the things I thought were right and a few of the ones I didn't, and didn't do some of the ones I didn't like, and that's the way it always was. Now, some might say I was wrong not to have asked openly something that a girl had a right to know . . . but I was always glad that I never, sort of, betrayed us if you know what I mean. It was very intimate. It may have been silly, but it was between your father and me and to talk about it diminished him and us.'

'I see,' said Aisling.

'So. I'm just saying that if it's something that's really personal it's probably no harm to keep it to yourself for a while in case you could work it out.'

'I have Mam.'

'Yes. I'm sure you have. But love, we're talking about thirty years ago in Old God's time when we're talking about me. Suppose when we're talking about you and it's something like . . . oh, let me see, like is it all right to have the woman on top and the man underneath . . . well, the answer is yes, of course. Do you see what I mean? I'm trying to gauge how personal it is to you.'

'It's more personal that that, Mam.'

365

'I see. I see, child.' Eileen sat still. Then, 'I'll always listen, I'll always be here, but if you tell me don't run away then and be sorry you told me . . . that's what I don't want.'

'I'd never do that.'

'You might. Here, since I'm confiding so much I'll tell you more. I never let Maureen tell me anything bad about Brendan Daly. Never.'

'Then it must be hard to have a conversation with her, she rarely talks of anything else, except when she's giving out to me,' said Aisling.

'No, when she starts I turn it into an attack on the weather, the house, the mother-in-law, anything except Brendan, because, you see, she is very fond of him most of the time . . . and if she was feeling all lovey-dovey with him and then remembered she had told me he was the greatest criminal walking free from gaol, she'd feel she had to be defensive.'

'I don't feel that about Tony, Mam.'

'I know, I'm trying to give you an example, child. I'm not saying it's the same thing. You couldn't dislike Tony, he's a great fellow, and he'd give you the earth.'

'Yes.'

'So I'm still here . . . you can tell me anything. I just pointed out all those things in case . . . well, just in case. . . .'

'You're very good, Mam. I never realised when I was young how good you were.'

'You're still young. And I'm not good. I'm full of self-preservation. Maybe that's what I should teach you instead of how to make scones. Anyone can be a good listener. It's easy. All you say is, "Go on, go on, tell me. Yes. No. Never." That's easy. It's hard to be a wise listener.'

Sean was tired that evening and for once it was only the two of them for supper. Niamh was meant to be doing her homework with her friend Sheila; Donal had gone to his book-keeping classes. Eamonn had announced he wouldn't be home, a few of them were going out for a walk in the country.

'That's nice for him to get a bit of air these nice evenings,' Eileen said.

'Cock fighting, that's what it is, a crowd from Hanrahan's have arranged it. They think the rest of us are blind eejits and don't know. I'd like to ring Sergeant Quinn and tell him where it is and have the lot of them caught. It's a very cruel wrong thing that . . . grown men throwing pound notes and ten-shilling notes on the ground watching two animals tearing each other to bits.'

'I suppose Sergeant Quinn knows well it's on,' Eileen said.

'I suppose he does.' Sean was reading the *Irish Independent*.

She felt very lonely and foolish at the end of the table with nobody there, only a husband behind a paper.

'Aisling was in today, for a long time. There's something troubling her.'

'What right has she to have something troubling her? Hasn't she got all she wants for the rest of her life? Look at me, stuck in that shop with an amadan of a son who's only a laughing stock. She's not stuck in there with people so thick that Jemmy is the brightest of them some days.'

'Oh, Sean, will you stop it, put down that paper, and stop pitying yourself? Stop it now. Haven't we done a lot for ourselves and the children, and really and truly if it's as bad as all that why don't you sell it?'

'Ah, quit talking rubbish, there's no sense in you talking like that.'

'Listen to me, I helped you build it up, I'm nearly fifty-five years of age, I'm tired, I'm very tired too when I come home in the evening. But today I came home early, so I don't have the financial worries and burdens of the shop on my shoulders, I have a new worry about Aisling. That's what I wanted to talk about, not let loose on myself an avalanche of complaints about everything from Eamonn, to tax men, to the rain in the yard, to O'Rourke's bullocks breaking the door. They broke the bloody door two years ago – you were paid for it, can it be dropped from the catalogue now?'

Sean laughed. 'I didn't mention O'Rourke's bullocks this evening.'

Eileen laughed too. 'That's because I didn't give you time to . . . but it's quite reasonable if you want to sell the place, quit. If Eamonn's such a layabout and on his way to the gallows, well he'll go won't he, and he won't need the shop after our time, and Donal will be a chemist, and Niamh will marry . . . so what have we to do it for? I ask you? Why is that rubbish?'

'I'm sorry. You're perfectly right. It's just a manner of speech. I only complain because I'm tired.'

'I really want whatever will make you peaceful, so I'm just pointing out to you that there are alternatives. Don't think you work ten hours in there a day for necessity. It's only because you choose to.'

'That's true, that's true. I must stop flaring up over nothing. It's bad for the blood pressure as well as being unfair on you. What's ailing Aisling?'

'I don't know, she began to tell me and she stopped.'

'Oh, I suppose she had a row with young Murray, she'll get over it.'

'No, it wasn't like that.'

'Ah, she's well able for him, probably gave him a telling off about all the beer he puts away. You know Aisling can be a bit of a boss. I wonder where she can have inherited that?'

Eileen didn't laugh as he had expected.

'Maybe she's starting a child? You remember how cranky you always were when you were carrying them? That must be it.' Sean looked pleased.

'No.' Eileen was definite. 'No, I have a feeling that that may be the very least likely explanation in the whole world.'

Johnny had to take more notice of the course eventually because it had been so successful. Elizabeth had managed to hit just the right note – informative without being above people's heads, simple without being patronising. Already there was talk of another course to follow this one.

'I'll really miss it you know, when it's over,' she said to Stefan. 'Only two more and that's it, then it's the summer and people all go away. It's a bit flat.'

'Why don't you have a party to round it off?' Stefan had said.

'But where? The thought of having any kind of gathering in Father's house. . . .'

'You could have it here,' Stefan said suddenly. 'This is a huge room – you could have a hundred people here, if we pulled back all the furniture. It would be very nice, it would be a very good setting.'

'And it would be an advertisement for your business, Stefan,' cried Anna excitedly. 'Think, all those people who like art to come at once into our shop.'

'Perhaps it looks too commercial . . . perhaps people might think that was behind it,' Stefan said, his face falling.

But Elizabeth was thrilled. 'It's a wonderful idea, I can't think of anything I'd like more. I did make a lot more money than I thought, so if I were to buy some bottles of wine and offer it around . . . it would be a nice gesture. But Stefan, it would be too much trouble . . . moving everything back against the wall. . . .'

'Well, you can help, and Johnny. . . .'

'Oh, Johnny.' Her face was anxious. 'I don't think he would approve. He doesn't think much of the art classes, you know. I think he'd say it was a waste of effort.'

'Well he can say what he likes. I am not dead yet, I am still the senior partner. I say there is to be a party and a party there will be.'

'And my sister, she will come to help pass the glasses of wine,' said Anna.

'But Johnny. . . .'

'Leave Johnny Stone to me.' Stefan smiled encouragingly. 'You are not afraid of Johnny Stone, you are a director of this little company are you not? Johnny borrows things from the store like the chandelier when his posh friends have a party and he brings it back. Do you object? No. Do I object? No. Johnny will be very happy to help. It will be the first time that either of us has done anything for you in all your years of working here. Now go away and plan it all.'

'Oh Stefan, thank you.'

'And no apologies, excuses or anything to Johnny, mind.'

'I understand.'

'I hope you do.'

She had never been directed so firmly by Stefan about how to behave towards Johnny, and she knew he was right. If she were to be full of explanations and excuses, Johnny's irritation and scorn would grow greater. How wise of Stefan to warn her. As she walked home, a fleeting stab of annoyance about Johnny went through her. Why did everyone have to be so careful of him and walk around him as if he were an unexploded mine? Stefan was right, she *was* a director, even though that was only so that the shop could be a business and claim tax relief, and Johnny *did* do whatever he liked with the place and nobody commented, and, true, Stefan was *not* dead yet and if he wanted to give a party for Elizabeth and her art group so he damn well *would* give it.

Laughing aloud at her resolution she turned in the gate of Clarence Gardens and almost bumped into Father.

'Heavens, Elizabeth, you're talking to yourself. You really are,' he said in alarm.

'No, Father, I'm only laughing to myself, that's quite different, it's almost respectable.'

'It's what mad old ladies do coming into the bank. They talk to themselves and mutter. Old spinsters, it's awful to see them. Really Elizabeth, don't be silly about it. It looks quite dreadful.'

'Father, you're going to have to face it. I *am* a mad old spinster, a quarter of a century old . . . why shouldn't I talk to myself? But this time I insist I was only laughing.'

'Well, there's a letter from your mother's friend, on the hall table. I'm sure that will stop you laughing.'

Father went on gloomily out through the gate, head bent and sighing. Oh God, what could be wrong? Harry didn't write letters. Please, please let Mother not be worse, please let Mother not need her this week when she was going to have the party in Stefan's. Please.

. . . I got to thinking I never laughed or had a good time since Violet got unwell, only the time you and young Johnny came up here. And we had such a good night that evening, and I got a pain laughter, that I began to think

370

you both enjoyed it too. So that makes what I am going to ask a bit easier. Could I come and have a holiday in London? And could I stay in Johnny's place? You see, I can't obviously go near George, I know that, fair's fair. And I don't have enough readies for a guesthouse, and I'm not too steady on my pins and I'd be happier with someone I knew. . . .

Dear Harry,
I'm sorry I took two days before replying to your letter, but I had to work things out, and here's what we're going to do. You're to come down next weekend, on the train and I'll meet you at the station with a taxi. It's not possible to stay in Johnny's flat because apparently there are a lot of people there at the moment. It's like Clapham Junction. But you *are* going to stay with Stefan Worsky who is my boss in the antique shop and his lady friend – well, she's about a hundred but she's still a lady and a friend – her name's Anna. They are doing up their room for you. I wish I had a house of my own Harry, and I'd paint a room like you once painted one for me. . . .

She posted the letter grimly and patted the top of the red letter-box as if it had done her some kind good deal by accepting the letter. It wouldn't know any more than Harry would ever know the two days of drama that had preceded its posting.

She had just shown Harry's letter to Johnny without comment and then, without pleading, she had asked coolly, 'Well, what do you think?'

'Oh Jesus, the poor old sod,' Johnny had said.

'So can he come, or can't he? I've got to write back.'

'Oh Eliza, Eliza, a holiday, the daft old fellow wants to come and spend a holiday with me. I can't have him . . . really and truly. . . .'

'Right,' she said, 'I'll tell him that.'

'Put it nicely . . . put it sort of diplomatically, you know.'

'No. I don't know.'

'I mean, don't say it baldly, get round it, and tell him we'll take him up West one night he's here, and he can tell us what it was all like before the war, he'd like that. He's a nice old fellow.'

'Yes he is. And he obviously likes you too.'

'Don't blackmail me, Elizabeth, I'm not having it. I never ask you to take on any lame ducks for me ever, do I?'

'No, no indeed.'

'So, I'll be glad to see him, but there's really too many people passing through here to make it sensible for him to come and stay.'

'Right.'

'So what will you do?'

'Go to hell,' she said calmly. 'What I do has nothing to do with you.'

'Oh dear, dear. A temper. Look, Elizabeth, you're becoming very odd, sneaking behind my back to get Stefan to organise a party for the art lovers . . . trying to make me turn my house into a convalescent home for ailing step-fathers. . . .'

'Why don't you go all the way and say ailing step-fathers stabbed by mad mothers . . . that would round it off neatly.'

Johnny looked stricken. 'Look, I'm selfish and low. I didn't mean it. I'm very very sorry. I say it with all my heart. I am very sorry I lashed out like that.' He looked at her levelly. He was sorry, she could see that.

'That's all right,' Elizabeth said.

'What?'

'You said you were sorry and I accept your apology, I said that's all right.'

'Well. . . .' Johnny was nonplussed, he had expected her to rush into his arms or to continue being upset. The calm reply seemed to bewilder him. 'Well . . . that's generous, and you know you're my lovely funny-face, don't you?'

'Yes, indeed I do.' She gathered up her handbag and gloves. She was leaving.

'Why are you going away? You are still upset, I said I was sorry.'

'I know, my love, and I said that it was all right. I'm not

upset. I just have a lot of things to do. Arrangements to make. I'll see you.'

'When?' he asked.

'Soon.'

Stefan sat silently and listened. She finished the whole tale. 'I won't start apologising and begging and everything. I'll just ask you yet one more favour. Will you have him?'

'Yes, of course,' said Stefan.

Harry walked very slowly and though he pretended his stick was just an ornament, he needed it to lean on.

My mother did that to him, Elizabeth thought. My poor mother who loved him more than anything in the world did that to him. Left his insides so weak that he can't even walk properly down a platform.

She hated Euston. Mother had sent her away from Euston, she had come back as a grown-up and met Mother, the thin stranger, here. She had waited for Aisling to come that time, the time when she was so frightened, and she had seen Aisling off again when it was all over. No, she preferred the airport really. Big stations made her sad. And Harry's face looked pathetic. Nonsense, it didn't look pathetic. It looked fine. It was only because Elizabeth knew all that happened to Harry she thought he was pathetic. To himself and to everyone else he was not, and must never be.

Harry was the life and soul of the party. He suggested that he sit at the door and give people little names to wear on their lapels. He would write these out himself in his funny curly script. Elizabeth thought that this was quite a good idea, but feared that it might look too business-like.

'People are always a bit shy coming into any kind of gathering,' Harry had said. 'By the time I've got their names sorted out for them, they'll be so relaxed they'll be asleep.'

And of course he was right. People were delighted to talk to the cheerful man who hadn't an ounce of shyness or self-consciousness. He hunted for their names happily in the display in front of him, he complimented the ladies, he pointed the gentlemen towards the table where the drink was being dispensed, he answered questions about the place, questions which many of the guests would never have put to Elizabeth.

'No, this is not Miss White's own shop, she does help out as a consultant and I do believe she is on the board of directors. . . .'

'Yes, Miss White is my step-daughter. I'm very proud of her. I am glad you like the art course, I'll certainly pass that on to her. . . .' 'Yes, it is a nice shop, isn't it, and I believe it does very well. It's run by a great friend of mine, Stefan Worsky . . . that is him over there, the elderly gentleman . . . and that's his assistant and manager, Mr Stone. Mr Stone's a card, you'll enjoy talking to him. . . .'

Elizabeth had no idea whether or not Johnny would come to the party. She had been deliberately vague when Harry wanted to know, and Stefan with his sharp old eyes had asked her nothing but obviously knew nothing either. Johnny was busy, she had explained to Harry. But Harry said no matter how busy Johnny was he would be able to come to the night of Elizabeth's triumph.

Johnny had even bought Stefan, Harry and himself buttonholes to wear for the part. Elizabeth couldn't believe it when she arrived, Harry at the door sitting up at a high desk and wearing a huge carnation; Stefan with his flower, examining the glasses to make sure that they were shining. . . . And Johnny – she still felt a tightness in her chest when she looked at him. He was so handsome in his dark suit and a cream shirt and the jaunty flower in his buttonhole. He stood smiling with welcome and she realised with a start that at the end of the gathering perhaps two dozen of these people would go away pleased and warmed by Johnny's personality. They would never know he dismissed them as amateur dabblers, as poseurs who wanted to learn the jargon of artistic conversation, they would only think he was a marvellous man to talk to. And he would never reveal to anyone, man or woman, that he was Elizabeth's lover, or that she was in any way special. That sort of thing didn't come into Johnny's conversation.

She saw him talking to the Clarksons, a middle-aged couple, both short-sighted, eager and intense. Both their faces were a study in concentration as Johnny explained something to them. He made no move to talk to the two attractive-looking girls among the guests, Grace and Susannah. Elizabeth knew Johnny well. He didn't need to make any move to talk to them, he could bide his time talking to the Clarksons, it would not be long before Susannah and Grace managed to find their way to Johnny. That's the way it worked.

Elizabeth looked around and smiled as she saw Henry Mason and Simon Burke. They were so funny, those two. They had been in the art course from the very beginning because their office was near the art college. She had been slightly surprised when they joined, somehow she had thought that they would both have had plenty of things to fill their leisure hours. . . . She imagined they would have gone to lunches with people who had big gardens sloping down to rivers, and they would have passed cocktail sausages and drinks to jolly girls.

They were always the first to laugh if she made any little joke, they had walked her back to her office several times when the coffee evenings were over and it was time for her to put away her notes and pointers and lists. Now tonight they had come early and had been very helpful at the start, making sure that the conversation kept going.

Simon was a big, rather flamboyant man, though how anyone could be flamboyant in his city suits she didn't know, but there was a hint of it waiting to escape. It was as if he had only dressed up in fancy dress for this life . . . but in another world he would have been a troubadour, a sultan, a cowboy. She giggled to herself at the idea . . . and caught Henry's eye. He was nice too, Henry. Tall and pale, his fair hair always seemed to fall into his eyes. He was possibly taller than Simon but he didn't stand in such a shoulders-flung-back way as Simon did. He used to finger his tie a lot when he had talked to Elizabeth in the beginning, but she noticed he didn't do that any more. It was a mannerism she supposed, like the way she used to shake her own hair out of her eyes. She used to do that a lot, the O'Connors used to imitate her, it had irritated Mother even further back than that. And once or twice Johnny said she still did it and it made her look like a schoolgirl again. Henry Mason had a patterned tie on tonight, he must have changed it especially to be more festive for the party. She thought that was nice.

Elizabeth liked them, and particularly Simon who had an endearing streak of self-mockery. He had enquired whether any of her friends could start an Instant Music Appreciation class, and a Learn to Love Literature source; then he would feel ready to face the twentieth century.

Elizabeth had often seen Henry and Simon chatting to Grace and Susannah and had wondered whether or not the class was acting as a lonely hearts club, one of the many things that Johnny had suggested it might be.

'Henry and I would like to take you to dinner, will you come out with us one evening?' Simon was smiling at her.

'With both of you?' Elizabeth asked, amused.

'Yes, I said I'd been thinking of asking you out to say thank you for the marvellous course, and Henry said the same so we agreed to do it together, if you were willing. That way we could take you somewhere splendid. And that way you wouldn't be afraid of our ulterior motives . . . not if there were two of us.'

'That's true, I'd feel safer certainly,' Elizabeth said gravely. Simon smiled. He was a very pleasant young man. Why couldn't she set her sights on him rather than that man with the crinkly smile and the dark hair who was standing there effortlessly delighting both Grace and Susannah, and who now was shaking Henry Mason warmly by the hand and including him in the group. How simple it would be if she didn't have this ridiculous chain attaching her to Johnny. Then she could look at Simon flirtatiously and allow herself to become interested in him and his uncomplicated life.

Harry and Stefan had wondered whether anyone should make a little speech. They consulted Johnny and sought his advice about what should be done.

'It would be nice to mark it for Elizabeth,' Harry had said. 'And the people here obviously think a lot of her.'

'Yes, to round it all off there should be a few words,' Stefan had said.

Johnny looked at Henry Mason. 'Can you do it? It should be someone from the course. I don't want to butt in, you could say something that everyone would relate to, and you know the people. Elizabeth would like that.'

'Oh do, Henry,' squeaked Grace.

'I'm not very good at speaking in public,' Henry began.

'This isn't public, this is your group, friends now more likely, I'd say. Go on, just a few words. I'll call for hush.'

Elizabeth was startled to see Johnny clapping his hands. Her heart leaped in that anxious way it often did when Johnny did things. Oh, he wasn't going to say anything awful about it being time to go home, was he? Please no.

'Ladies and gentlemen, forgive me for interrupting you for a moment, but a lot of you have said that you would like somebody to express on your behalf thanks to Elizabeth White for all she has done to open doors into the world of art for you. . . .'

Elizabeth nearly dropped her glass. Oh Johnny, darling, darling Johnny, he knew how much it meant to her and to everyone there. He was not cruel and dismissive. He stood with the eyes of everyone in the room on him and he was going to make a little speech about her. Her face went red and white and red she could feel the burning come and go. She saw Harry and Stefan looking pleased and proud . . . oh she would never be able to thank Johnny enough for this.

'. . . so on your behalf I have asked one of the long-standing members of your group, Mr Henry Mason, to say these words to Elizabeth from you all. Henry, the floor's yours. . . .'

The red went from Elizabeth's cheeks again. Johnny was smiling and pointing at Henry and everyone took their eyes away from him reluctantly and looked at Henry. But Elizabeth didn't. With a glassy smile she looked at Johnny's face as she heard Henry's stumbling clichés . . . debts of gratitude, never spared herself, interesting and stimulating talks . . . he stuttered and repeated himself and all the time Johnny Stone's face watched him with a pleasant, alert expression and when Henry finally ground to a halt it was Johnny who led the clapping and the cheers for Elizabeth.

Her heart felt like a heavy weight and there was a choking sensation as if she had swallowed a hard crust of bread which would not go down.

Dear Elizabeth,
This is a picture of the beach in Brighton and the pier. But in fact we do not see much of it since play begins at 8.30 in the morning and there is only one hour for lunch. It is very interesting to meet so many bridge players from all over the country. Our club did well on Day One but we were allowed to slip behind yesterday. I find it all a very good change. I am glad you persuaded me to come here.
    Regards, Father

Dear Elizabeth,
I am sending you two pounds ten shillings and an advertisement I cut out of the *Sunday Express*. Can you ever do me a great favour? Can you buy this strapless bra for me and send it to me? Mark the envelope old clothes so that the customs men don't open it, and could you put in an old blouse or cardigan or something you don't want so that I can tell Mam that's what you sent? The bra costs forty-five shillings and the extra five shillings is for postage. I'm size thirty-four and if they have different cup sizes, which they may have, I'm kind of middle cup. About average. Thanks a million, and don't tell anybody.
    Love, Niamh

Dear Elizabeth,
Henry and I wish to take you up on your promise to have dinner with us. Will Saturday week be all right? Can you telephone us, either of us at the office, (telephone number above) to say if this is suitable and where we should collect you? It's probably best not to leave any message in the event of our not being here. Efficient to the point of obsession they are about work matters, but private lives are wisest not entrusted to them.

We look forward to hearing from you.
Simon Burke

Dear Miss White,
Thank you very much for the kind donation you sent to the hospital. I have to inform you that the general opinion was that flowers would not be a suitable gift for your mother, Mrs Violet Elton, to receive considering her present state of health. Accordingly we went along with your alternative suggestion and have bought a floral arrangement for the Day Room of the ward. We would like to express our thanks to you for both the gift and for your understanding of the nature of your mother's illness.
P. Hughes, Hospital Secretary

Hallo Funny-face,
I've arranged to collect no less than six Welsh dressers before I come back! Now how about that for a working holiday? And you thought I was just sunning myself in Bangor. It is super though, I must admit. No cares and a lot of rest. Remember that girl Grace Miller who was one of the people in your art course? She turned up here out of the blue, so we show each other the Mysteries of Wales . . . and wish you were here.
Home soon.
love always, Johnny

Roma. Anno Sancto.
There are millions and millions of people here, which is bad enough but those millions include *Father* John Murray . . . yes, he's made it . . . and Mother-in-Law Murray and Joannie Murray who, between ourselves and the whole postal system, has become almost insane . . . and also the lovely young Mr and Mrs Tony Murray, toast of the continent. I dreamed last night you and I had some awful fight. We didn't, did we?
Love, Aisling

XV

Maureen said several times to Mam that it was unusual for Aisling to be so long in getting pregnant. 'It's not as if she had any reason to wait about, Mam.' No indeed, Eileen had agreed. 'And, Lord knows, there's plenty of money in that house, a nurse could come home with her for three months like the Grays have whenever a child is born. It can't be the money or anything.' She found Mam unresponsive. 'Not of course that it's my business or anything. It's not the sort of thing you feel you should bring up talking to someone . . . even your own sister. You know, you never like to say anything.'

'Oh I'm glad to hear that,' Mam had said.

'It's just that Brendan's mother was asking me yesterday was there no sign of a baby and I didn't know what to say to her.'

Mam had looked up suddenly and with a flash of bad temper she had shouted, 'Why don't you tell old Ma Daly to go and take a running jump at herself all the way down the road to the lake and right into it!'

'Mam!' Maureen had cried in shock.

'I'm sorry, it's the time of life. I'm going through the menopause. Why don't you go past your mother-in-law's house and discuss that with her too?'

Maureen had looked shocked. 'Well, I must say Mam, I don't know what I said to bring all that on me.'

Mam had relented. 'I know you don't. As I said, I'm becoming a bad-tempered old woman. Will you have a cup of tea or would you be afraid that I might pour it over your head?'

Maureen laughed, relieved. 'Oh Mam, you're an awful eejit at times. You're worse than Niamh with your antics.'

Niamh was delighted when the parcel arrived from Elizabeth. It had been waiting on the hall table and she snatched it away and ran up to her bedroom to check the contents. There it was, boned and firm, standing proudly as if it were a part of a woman's body, a waist-length strapless bra in white satin. And with it a lemon chiffon blouse. The letter said nothing about the bra at all, it was the kind of a letter you could show to Mam easily. Wasn't Elizabeth cunning, she must have been accustomed to doing all this kind of thing for years with Aisling, of course. There was a book on the reproductive organs which Aisling had among her other books but with a different cover on it. Perhaps Elizabeth had sent that in the old days. She tried on the bra: it made her stick out very naturally. Now she could wear that dress with the little bootlace straps, as they were called. She had told Mam that the dress was worn with a bolero and Mam had said that was fine. But she had no intention of wearing the bolero. Anna Barry and her brother were going to have a party at the hotel at the end of August. Everyone had been looking forward to it. Niamh had washed her hair every four days with Sta-Blond shampoo. She had this feeling that if she went to quite a lot of trouble secretly she would burst upon an unsuspecting world. That's what Aisling had done at her wedding last year. Nobody had known how good-looking Aisling was until that day, and now even if she hadn't combed her hair and just wore her old gaberdine raincoat streeling open, she still had the name of being beautiful. It was odd but true. Once people decided you were beautiful then you remained beautiful for the rest of your life.

Niamh was going to wear a pony-tail at the start of the evening with a plastic clip on it, and then as the night went on she was going to take off the bolero and let her hair fall loose and when she was dancing people would notice her suddenly. She had thought of nothing else but the party since the school holidays began. She was waiting for the results of her Leaving Certificate and if she got three Honours Dad was going to let her go to university. The first of the O'Connors to go to college. She had prayed herself into a near coma for a while.

Mam had wanted her to work in the shop, but Niamh had been very unwilling. She was afraid that if she once got into O'Connor's she might never get out. She saw herself sitting for years in the little glass office that used to be Aisling's and had been empty for a year since neither of the new assistants had worked out well. She thought that if her Leaving Certificate results were not good she would do typing and book-keeping in the morning in the secretarial college and work in O'Connor's during the afternoon. Aisling had said she would have no need for shorthand in the shop. How dare Aisling interfere, why couldn't she live her own life now and be grateful for it? It was what she had wanted wasn't it? Why was she always down with Mam and filling Mam up with stupid ideas like Niamh working in the shop? What was she going for walks with Donal for? Why couldn't she let Donal find friends of his own? Niamh thought that Aisling was just as mournful as Maureen in a way. God, the whole business would put you off marriage forever.

Donal was disappointed not to get any letters or post-cards from Rome. 'Aisling wrote three letters the first time she went,' he complained.

'Ah but she has the whole family out there now and the ordination and everything, she's on her toes,' said Sean. 'The girl can't be rushing off every minute to write letters home.'

'You'd think she'd send even one, to let us know how she's getting on,' Donal grumbled. 'The place is very dead without her anyway.'

Eamonn was finishing his supper hastily, he thought he saw his mother looking round for rosary beads and the suggestion that since they were all gathered they might say it early tonight.

'Isn't it amazing that she doesn't seem to be gone, not like Maureen? I mean we see as much of her as we ever did. She's getting no value out of being married at all.'

The return from Rome was fretful and exhausting. Father John was full of names of priests in this order and that order,

382

and of those who had come to the ordination and those who hadn't. Aisling thought he sounded like an old woman. Mrs Murray sounded like a very old woman indeed. She seemed twenty years older than when they had left Ireland, the noise and the heat and the crowds had been very wearing. Aisling had felt sorry for her and had fanned her in the evenings beside an open window while Tony and Joannie went out on their regular four-hour search for a restaurant, coming back plastered both of them with the intelligence that the restaurant in the hotel was as good as anything they had seen in their travels.

By the time they arrived in Dublin Aisling had decided that enough was enough and made a clear announcement as they were collecting their luggage. 'Tony and I are staying in Dublin tonight, we'll come down tomorrow.'

'Oh, I'll stay with you and the three of us will go down in the morning,' Joannie said eagerly.

'No, we're getting a lift with friends,' Aisling said firmly.

'You haven't got any friends,' Joannie said.

'Don't be childish,' Aisling snapped. 'Mrs Murray, we'll help you into the car and see you off all three of you. We'll be home tomorrow night, and ready for the first mass on Sunday.'

'Well yes, the least you could do.' John was huffy and annoyed at being taken by surprise. They moved awkwardly towards the car, as disparate a group of five people as ever you saw. Aisling wondered what other people made of them.

Tony, who had slept the whole way home, was now awake and ready for an evening on the town. He went along smoothly with the notion that they had business to do, people to see, arrangements to make, and brushed aside the irritated squeakings of disbelief about why it hadn't been mentioned before, and who they could be meeting on a Saturday morning. . . .

'Where are you staying then?' Joannie asked, hoping to catch them out.

'With my relations in Dunlaoghaire,' Aisling rattled back. 'Tony hasn't met them yet, it will be a nice opportunity.'

'That's right, looking forward to meeting them,' said Tony, and Aisling threw him a grateful look.

'Well then we can drive you there, no point in leaving you to get taxis ten miles into town from here, ten miles out of Dunlaoghaire, is there?' Joannie's voice was silky. She felt sure she had trapped them somehow.

'That's a great idea,' Aisling said sunnily, and somehow the hour and three quarters through rush-hour traffic was endured.

Then they were at the guesthouse. Aisling jumped out first and ran to the door; in case there was going to be confusion she wanted to try to have a head start in sorting it out.

'Aisling child, how grand to see you,' Mam's cousin Gretta Ross greeted her. 'Did you bring your fine husband for me to have a look at?'

'I brought him to stay for a night if that's all right,' she said quickly.

'Honoured we are, and delighted . . . where is he . . . ?'

Gretta went out to the car and shook hands with everyone while Tony was unloading the boot.

'Isn't he as handsome as they all said?' she said. 'I'm delighted you were able to come to me at last.'

The rest of the Murrays went unwillingly, having refused a cup of tea because John said he must drive on and get them home at a reasonable hour. He gave Gretta Ross his blessing which she asked for and Aisling noticed with a vicious delight that Joannie seemed quite put out to find her suspicions unfounded.

'You're very good Gretta, I just wanted to get away from them all for a bit and have an evening on our own, if you get me.'

'I'm delighted to see you child, and very pleased you thought of coming here. Come on now, we'll shift these bags up to the room on the right of the stairs up here, it's nice, it looks out at the harbour. Yes, and have a bit of a wash or a lie down and please yourselves, I've a lot of things to busy me. You might like to go out and have a nice walk, go off up Killiney hill or somewhere and look down at the view. When you get back there'll be a plate of cold chicken – help yourselves. It'll all be there in the dining room for you. I have about twelve in for supper tonight so I'll not be able to entertain you anyway!'

'God, that's great isn't it?' said Tony when he'd shaken out a clean shirt for himself and given himself a wash. 'That was sheer genius on your part getting rid of them all like that. I'd had all I could take and you probably had too.'

'Yes, I was afraid if we went back to Kilgarret we might never get away tonight.'

'You're a genius I say, I can't say it too often. Now will you put on your clothes like a good girl and come on and we'll head off somewhere and have a drink. I'm parched.'

Aisling put on a clean dress and combed her hair. 'I want to talk to you Tony, which is why I kidnapped you.'

He looked hunted. 'All right, all right. We'll talk in the bar.'

'No. It's not about anything that can be talked about in a bar. Take your choice. Here or we'll go for a walk.'

'What is it, what are you playing at?'

'Just what I said. I want to talk to you. We have to talk.'

'Oh God, not now Aisling, not now when we're knackered from the journey . . . huh?' He looked at her appealingly.

She said nothing.

'Well if it's quick say it here, and then we'll go out. Isn't that fair enough?'

'It's not quick,' she said.

'Can't we find a nice quiet bar like two normal human beings and sit in it in a corner and you can tell me then? Wouldn't that do?'

'No.'

'Why in God's name not?'

'Because it's about sitting in bars that I want to talk.'

'I don't know what you mean.'

'Of course you know what I mean Tony. I want to talk about how drunk you've been all the time we were in Rome. There wasn't a day that you didn't get maggoty.'

'Oh, you don't want to talk, you just want to nag. I knew there'd be a catch to it. Now why didn't you say I want to have a nice nag at you, Tony, instead of pretending you want to talk?'

He seemed pleased that he had identified the problem. He even gave a little smile, a nervous smile.

Aisling's lip trembled. She seemed to have difficulty in keeping calm. But if she wasn't careful the whole thing would slip away as it had slipped away before. She forced a smile on to her face.

'No, honestly, it's talk, really.' She smiled brightly, hoping to get some kind of response. She didn't.

'No, seriously it's talk, you know, me saying something, and you saying something and neither of us shouting . . . so that we can. . . .'

'So that you can nag me,' he repeated triumphantly.

'I don't nag you.'

'You don't hell.'

'I don't. When did I last nag at you?'

'You're always nagging at me, sighing and groaning and throwing your eyes up at heaven. If that's not nagging I'd like to know what on earth is.'

'Please Tony, just tonight, just this one night. Not a bar, not a night on the jar, just a conversation. I swear I'll not say one word more about your being jarred. Honestly.'

'Well what do you want to talk about drink for if you're not going to mention getting jarred?' He was puzzled.

'I was going to talk about why you drink so much, and whether this has anything to do with . . . well with us . . . and what we don't have . . . and what we don't do.'

'Ah ha, that's it. Psychology. Analysis. A psychiatrist's couch. Lie down on this bed Tony, and tell me all your deep feelings. Why do you need a pint? I need a pint because I goddamn want a pint and I'm going to go out and have one, now are you coming with me or are you not?'

'An hour. I'll reduce it to an hour. Please.'

'All right. After we've been to the pub.'

'No. Before. Once we get to the pub, you'll start us talking to old hangers-on and fools and there won't be any chance *to* talk.'

'I won't, I promise, I won't draw anyone on us.'

'No. Because when you do it will be too late. The night will be gone.'

'I can't talk in here, it's choking me. . . .' Tony ran his finger around under his collar. 'Come on Aisling, stop playing about like a child.'

'Suppose I were to go and get us some whiskey? Could you talk here then?' She looked pleading.

'What do you want to say? One hour, mind. It's seven o'clock now. By eight we're to be in a bar.'

Aisling slipped downstairs and out the door. She remembered that there was a bar around the corner from when she had last stayed here. Her sense of direction was good. In no time, with the half bottle of Jameson carefully wrapped by a mildly curious barman she was back in the bedroom.

Tony had lain down on the bed again. She poured two large amounts into the toothmugs that stood on the hand-basin.

'Your health,' he said, almost draining his.

'We are afraid to talk to each other about what's worrying both of us,' she said.

'Go on,' Tony said with a mock wave, as if giving her the floor.

'We've been married for fifteen months and we haven't consummated this marriage. That's what we don't talk about.'

'Oh.' Tony looked stricken.

'Now, I don't know anything about anything, really. But I think it's the kind of thing we might have to go and see a specialist or somebody about, and I wanted to discuss it with you.'

'A specialist. . . .' Tony was amazed at the word. 'A specialist in what might we ask? In ramming himself into people? Is that what we're to look for? Would one of those leery Italian waiters have done? Why didn't we think of it then? Wouldn't that have been a great one to ask? He might even have been a free specialist. We mightn't have had to pay him a penny. In fact he might even have paid you. . . .'

'It's very hard for us to talk about this anyway, but, God

Almighty, you're not going to make it any easier by shouting and mocking at me before we even begin. . . .'

'No, I'm very sorry, let me go back, a specialist, have you found one? Is he perhaps waiting outside the door?'

'Tony.'

'No, go on. Go on, let me not interrupt you. You wanted to talk. Talk on.'

'It's not easy for me to talk, it's a hard thing to talk about.'

'Ah yes, but it's a very easy one for me to listen to. . . .'

'We can't go on ignoring it, we've ignored it for months now. It doesn't work for us, I don't know why, maybe it's something I'm not doing right – that's what I mean about advice. I thought all I had to do was lie there. There must be more I should be doing and I don't know. Please can't you see how awful all this is . . . ?'

'But it's you who wants to talk about it, my dear Aisling.'

'And I'm trying to. I was wondering was it the drink?'

'Was what the drink?'

'Could it be because we both drink so much that we don't manage to do it right, that it doesn't happen for us. . . .'

Tony's voice was cold. 'But how could that be a serious suggestion, my dear Aisling, you hardly drink at all?'

'You're making me say it, aren't you? Listen, before we were married, you were mad to . . . you couldn't stop yourself, you said. You told me that it was cruel to you not to let you. Remember? Remember? In the car. In the orchard. Remember? You seemed to think that it was easy . . . like . . . and nothing to it. . . .'

There was a silence.

'And because you used to want to so much in those days and everything . . . I was wondering, I was wondering could it be because you drink a lot more now than you used to then? Perhaps that's what is complicating things and making it all so difficult.'

'Is that your own conclusion or have you discussed it with assorted people and come to this view as a result of a conference . . . ?'

'Oh Tony, may God forgive you . . . who could I have spoken to about it?'

388

'I don't know, you spend a great deal of time out of the house, how do I know where you are and what you're discussing?'

'I only go out when you go out drinking. If you're going to be home I'm always there, and then I only go down to Mam's or over to Maureen's. I'd prefer to be at home with you . . . but you're never there. . . .'

'I thought you weren't going to nag, I remember you saying something about this not being a nagging session.' Tony reached over and filled his tumbler with whiskey.

'Well, what do you think we should do? I mean this seriously, please take it seriously. Do you think we should go along like this trying to pretend it doesn't matter? Isn't it better to face it and discuss it? We're meant to be great friends, you and I, we used to be. Now we can't discuss anything. I feel if we could discuss the bed thing . . . we'd go back to being able to talk about everything else and you wouldn't run off on me down to Shay and the fellows, and I wouldn't be left alone. . . .' She stopped and looked at him, his lower lip was trembling. He said nothing so she went on. 'Because you know how much I like you and love you, and how you're the one I want, and you're my Tony . . . and it's just ridiculous our pretending that nothing's wrong and that it doesn't matter. . . .' She got up and sat down on the floor and laid her head in his lap. He patted her hair and twisted it in his fingers.

'You always say it doesn't matter . . . you know when it happens . . . when it doesn't happen . . . you often tell me that it's not the most important thing in the world . . . so I thought it didn't matter all that much to you, now you say you've been pretending, that it does. . . .'

'Of course it's not the most important thing in the world . . . but not being able to talk about it . . . that's what's so dreadful, and I feel sure that there's something simple we don't know. If we read books, say, together. . . .'

'I've read books,' Tony said.

She raised her head. 'And what do they say?' she asked.

'They say it's nervousness and inexperience, and that people get over it.'

'Well . . .' She tried to smile.

'And they say that the partner should be nice and consoling and say it doesn't matter. I thought maybe you'd read books too.'

'No I hadn't. I meant it, it doesn't matter.'

'Then why are we sitting here agonising over it?'

'Because it matters in a different sense. It doesn't matter in the night at that minute when it matters to you . . . but it matters in long term . . . my not being able to give you all that pleasure, you know, and children. . .' She stopped.

'Yes?' he said.

'Well I suppose we might talk about whether there is any way of making it work . . . and if we decide there isn't, then there's a possibility that we might both be happier if we didn't try, seeing as it upsets us. And we might adopt a baby.'

'Are you serious?' he asked.

'Well, yes. If you're not feeling deprived and missing that whole side of life, and if I didn't feel that we kept on failing to do something then we might both be much happier and we could choose a boy or a girl and carry on from there?' She was kneeling now on the floor smiling up at him, as if she were suggesting they make just trivial plans.

Tony stood up. 'You can't expect this to be a serious discussion can you, when you come up with preposterous ideas like that?'

'But why is it?'

'Utterly ludicrous . . . didn't you hear what I said? If you want the whole thing spelled out, which a more sensitive person might not want, then let's spell it out. I told you the book said it was temporary, get it? And normal? See? And nothing to be ashamed of? Right? And it passes. And it's due to inexperience . . . because unlike all these fast people and sophisticated people you obviously admire so much I am inexperienced. I didn't sleep around with the whole world. I only slept with you. . . .'

He stopped for a swig from the glass.

'And, if I might add, words from your own mouth, there's not much for the woman to do, is there? I mean you said it yourself, just lie there and wait. So I think we've covered most angles now, don't you . . . or would you like to announce in tomorrow's paper that. . . .'

'Please. . . .'

'No, you had your talk, I can have mine . . . you have told me you didn't mind, then you told me you did, now you tell me you don't care if we never do it. . . .'

'Tony. . . .'

'Listen to me . . . you have told me you have read nothing at all on the subject, but you think a specialist might help us; you think that you are doing everything such as there is to do correctly and that I am not; you tell me you would like to abandon the whole purpose for which marriage was invented so that I can bring up some other man's son. There's only one thing you said which is right . . . only one thing. . . .'

'What's that?' she whispered.

'That you're not going to be drunk tonight, and I am. I am going to be very drunk indeed.' He poured the last grain of whisky into the mug and drained it. He turned the bottle upside down in the wastepaper basket. He smiled at her, a very forced, unreal smile.

'So, would you like to join me, Madam? You are my wife after all, and a wife's place is beside her husband . . . as well as underneath him.'

Aisling stood up. 'I suppose this was our only chance of talking about it ever . . . wasn't it? And we messed it up.'

'So shall we sally forth then?' Tony asked.

Aisling decided in two seconds' reflection that it would be less worrying to go with him than to lie there in terror of his lurching home and waking Gretta Ross and her twelve house-guests.

'Let's sally,' she said.

'That's better,' said Tony, and he looked quite happy again.

Simon and Henry had behaved like a parody of the Western Brothers where one would begin a sentence and the other would finish it. Elizabeth thought that they were great company, when they took her to the smart French restaurant. They had even brought her an orchid to wear on her dress. Simon said that Henry knew a great deal about wine so they would have to sit back and listen to a lengthy discussion with the waiter.

Henry laughed. 'Simon is so ignorant about wine that once someone asked him would he like red or white and he said, "Yes please." '

When Henry laughed he looked younger, Elizabeth thought, less stooped, less conscious of himself, less awkward. He was really at his ease tonight . . . mocking himself, letting Simon mock him. Sometimes he had looked rather anxious and . . . yes, awkward. Perhaps it was because he was so tall, his elbows and his knees seemed to stick out a bit at angles. You felt that if he fell he might break into small pieces. Or if he stood up suddenly that he might knock everything over. And yet that was unfair, he wasn't at all clumsy, he only looked as if he might be.

Tonight his fair or light brown hair looked well. He must have washed it before he came out. It was soft and shiny. His sandy face looked eager and enthusiastic. He had pale eyebrows and his eyelashes were very light too. If he had been a girl he would have darkened them, Elizabeth thought. Wasn't it silly the way girls always felt they had to change their faces, and men didn't?

There was nothing wrong with Henry Mason's face, nothing that he should change. It wasn't very definite, that was all, you had to look hard at it to remember it.

They complimented Elizabeth on everything, on the success of the course, on her knowledge of paintings, on the marvellous party. They complimented her on what a nice house Clarence Gardens was, and they both said they liked her hair pulled up in that little pony-tail effect.

'I think it's rather mutton-dressed-as-lamb, I'm much too old to get away with that teenage hair-style,' she had said deliberately.

It worked. They both cried out that she was not too old, she was very young, and it suited her perfectly.

Elizabeth thought that it was all great fun and rather silly

392

and wondered whether other people went on like this all the time.

'I had a postcard from Grace Miller, you know . . .' remarked Simon, 'she's in Bangor. Apparently you're quite a matchmaker, Elizabeth, she met that chap at your party. You know Johnny . . . from the antique shop . . . and he suggested they motor up there. Quite the love of her life he is now, apparently.'

'Yes, fast mover, Grace, isn't she?' Henry said admiringly.

'And so is Johnny Stone,' said Elizabeth. She felt the food sticking in her throat. Motoring up to Bangor with Grace, or turning up out of the blue – which was true? Was Johnny lying . . . he never needed to? Was Grace lying . . . why should she bother to?

Henry was saying something. 'Oh I say, I'm pleased to hear you say that. I was afraid that he was your chap. Something your step-father said that evening. . . .'

Damn Harry to the bottom of hell, how dare he let any information about Johnny out of the net? He should have known it was something you didn't talk about. 'Oh, what on earth did he say?' she asked lightly.

'Nothing specific, I just thought that he was – you know . . . ?'

'Oh heavens, everyone loves Johnny . . . it's like loving fine weather . . . it would be churlish not to be delighted with it, or him. Now enough about that Romeo . . . tell me how you two Romeos escaped all these predatory female clients who must be stalking you through the Inns of Court. . . .'

They both laughed hugely at this and things were back on course. Elizabeth allowed herself a small excursion in her mind back to Johnny. It must be Grace who had told the lie. Johnny did not need to lie, or if he had then it was serious with Grace and that's why the first real untruth had been told.

Mother died in November. She had a massive heart attack, they told Elizabeth on the telephone, very quick and in many ways a merciful relief. It had happened during the night and

393

Mother had known no terror or anxiety about it. The kind voice said it must be thought of as the best solution.

Elizabeth stood in the cold hall of Clarence Gardens. It was Father's bridge night, she had answered the phone. It rarely ever rang for Father anyway. She had been thinking about Mother at the very moment the bell had sounded in the hall, because she had been in the middle of making a Christmas present list. She had paused to think about Mother and how sad it was that all she could now do for Mother was to send a gift to other people in the same hospital. It was very anonymous, it was like sending money for the black babies when they were in the convent back in Kilgarret — you wished you could see the black baby getting a present.

Now there was never going to be any kind of a present for Mother again. Harry had been told apparently and was very emotional but he would telephone later. Perhaps Elizabeth and Harry or one of them could telephone the hospital again in the morning to discuss the funeral arrangements. They were sorry to have to tell her such sad news but hoped she would see it as a very happy release for Mrs Elton.

From the front room came the sound of laughter; she even heard Father's tone in it. Father who had laughed so rarely in that room where his wife had sat at a little desk and written letters was laughing over a game of cards with people that he hardly knew while Mother was lying dead in a mortuary chapel in the North of England. Elizabeth would not now rush into the room and throw herself into Father's arms and they would not weep for her. Once they must have wept or been near to tears over Elizabeth . . . when they knew she was expected, when she was born, when she said something endearing as a toddler. They must have looked at each other and smiled or held hands then. What had happened to make it end like this?

She thought of Mother that day at Euston. She thought of her with her eyes searching through all that grey crowd trying to find her child, and the slow look of disbelief when she saw the grown-up daughter. She thought of Mother throwing her head back laughing that time when Johnny had brought the rabbit to Preston for dinner, she thought of pinning the violets on her cardigan, she remembered Mother shaking her head dismissively about Miss James back in the first school. She remembered Mother crying outside this door the day she went off with Harry, big tears falling down her face as she had said that she wished things were different . . . those were her words . . . she wished things were different.

The Hardcastles had agreed when she asked them not to bring Harry to the telephone. 'Tell him I'll come up overnight. It doesn't matter what time the train gets in, I'll take a taxi to your house. Can you leave the key somewhere for me, I won't want to wake the whole house?'

'Well love, just put your hand in the letter box, it's on a string. There'll be a flask of tea for you, and rugs and you turn on the electric fire as soon as you get in. You're a good lass to come so quickly.'

'Tell him that Mother would like him looking smart and well and he's not to have red eyes when we go up to that hospital tomorrow,' she said. She rang the station. Dear God would something good happen sometimes at Euston? She wrote a note to Henry Mason to explain why she wouldn't be able to meet him the following day. She also asked him to let Stefan, the art college and the school know. Henry was very reliable, he would do that efficiently for her.

Then she wrote a note to Father . . . she left it in his bedroom in case some of the bridge people might help him to wash up. She didn't want him to have to get the news in front of strangers, and she certainly did not want to be there herself when he reacted. She carefully mentioned the name of the hospital again, just in case he wanted to send flowers. She said that she would be gone for a few days. Finally she went into the bridge room and waited courteously until the hand was played.

'Ah, tea?' Father was pleased and surprised.

'No, not yet, it's all ready in the kitchen of course, but, sorry to interrupt you, I have to go away suddenly. It's all a bit complicated. I won't delay everyone here now explaining. I left you a note upstairs. . . .' She smiled brightly around at the four people and left briskly. At the end of Clarence Gardens she saw a taxi and hailed it. She dropped the letter to Henry through the letter box of the big house where he had a flat. It was a methodical house, like Henry himself. They would sort out the letters for the various tenants and leave them in neat rows on a large hall table. He would make all those other calls for her. She had listed the telephone numbers.

She thought she saw him at the window upstairs as she leaped back into the taxi, but it would take too long to explain everything, and the letter did it better. She would see him next week.

She slept in fits and starts on the train, her head lolling awkwardly so that she woke up with an ache in her neck twice. She rubbed it, trying to ease the cramp.

'Would you like me to do that for you?' said a man opposite her. He had been eyeing her since she got into the compartment. Elizabeth was glad that two other men sat in the far corner. She would not like to have been alone with him.

'No thank you,' she replied crisply without any hint of amusement at his suggestion.

A little later the extra coat, the black coat she had brought with her for warmth as well as for mourning, fell from her knees to the floor. The man picked it up and settled it around her lap with a lot of unnecessary patting and fondling.

She opened her eyes coldly and looked at him. 'Get back to your seat and take your hands off me,' she said.

He laughed.

She looked for support to the other end of the carriage. The other passengers were gone. They must have got out when she was asleep.

'Come on now, the way you were sitting, I thought you'd like a little company,' he said. He was confident. He was really awful, Elizabeth thought, a full face and thick lips . . . she could barely look at him he revolted her so much.

'I do not want company,' she stated. 'And if you believe I do you are wrong, and you are attacking me and I shall pull this cord.' She had stood up and placed her hand on the communication cord. . . .

He looked alarmed. 'Don't be such a fool. Sit down. I didn't mean any harm.'

'Get away from me. Go over to the other side of the carriage. Now.'

Fumbling and picking up his attaché case he moved.

'Now stay there. One more move and I'll pull the cord, and you can make your explanations to the train guard and the police.'

'Don't be such a bloody idiot . . . I wasn't doing anything. . . .'

'And you won't do any more,' she retorted.

He picked up his newspaper and in the dim light of the compartment pretended to read. Elizabeth sat down, fixed her clothes around her, so that the coat kept her legs both hidden and warm.

'Are you the nervous type then?' the man asked, relieved to see Elizabeth's hand at a safe distance from the communication cord.

'Will you *shut up*?' she shouted at him.

'I certainly will, crackpot. Cracked prim and prissy old maid.'

'That's it,' Elizabeth said, pleased.

The week passed in a blur. There were only ten people at Mother's funeral, and that meant only seven apart from Henry and Elizabeth and the nice Nurse Flowers. Elizabeth had taken a small bag with Mother's Effects, as the hospital had called them. She thought that they would upset Harry too much, and even she felt she wouldn't be able to look at them yet. The chaplain had been kind, his words were all about Going Home, and Laying Down One's Head, and Peace. Harry snuffled beside her.

'Violet wouldn't want peace, she hated peace, she wanted a bit of a good time,' he whispered to Elizabeth.

'I think these padres have it all wrong,' Elizabeth whispered back to him. 'Perhaps heaven is full of good times, and Mother's having the time of her life.'

'Not yet,' said Harry, picking holes in this idea. 'Not until after the resurrection and all.'

'Sorry,' Elizabeth apologised, 'I keep getting confused with the Catholics, I think they go there immediately, or maybe I've got it mixed up.'

'Poor Violet,' Harry sobbed. 'Poor little Violet. She wanted so little, she wanted so bloody little . . . and she never even got that.'

Elizabeth stood in the rain under Mr Hardcastle's umbrella and wondered about love. Mother had wanted a great deal, she had wanted much more than anyone else of her time had got. It had been impossible to please Mother. Yet when you boiled it all down all she had ever wanted was Harry. He hadn't given her any great wealth or good times, he had given her a hard life in a small shop. And while she still had her mind she had been happy there. No wonder Harry saw her as simple and easy to please. Father saw her as totally selfish and demanding . . . and people like Monica Furlong's mother had always thought that Violet had to have twice what everyone else in the world had, and that included two bites at the cherry in terms of marriage. Aunt Eileen had said that Mother had been such fun at school. Oh Lord, in all the fuss she hadn't written to Aunt Eileen. She must do that as soon as possible. Perhaps Aunt Eileen might even write a letter to Harry. Though strictly speaking she might prefer to write to Father. What the hell, let Aunt Eileen decide.

There were endless cups of tea with the Hardcastles. There were assurances that Harry's allowances and the rent he got from the little shop were more than enough to cover his board. There were plans made for Harry's next visit to London, and telegrams of sympathy from Stefan Worsky, and Anna, from the art college, from the school, from Henry Mason and Simon Burke, from one or two other people on the art course, whom Henry must have alerted. There was no message from George White and there was no message from Johnny Stone.

The night before she went back to London Elizabeth and Harry went out to have a meal. The restaurant was starting to decorate itself for Christmas and it looked far more festive than either of them felt.

'I say it over to myself that it's no different than it has been. But you know I always thought she'd get better, I thought one morning she'd wake up and say, "Harry, how ridiculous," and it would all be all right. Now I can't think that any more. Did you feel that?'

'Yes,' lied Elizabeth. 'Yes, I did.' She wondered why she had explained Mother's illness to Harry so carefully, she marvelled at his inability to accept what he couldn't bear.

'So you're not to worry about me down there in Fun City,' Harry said.

'No, I won't worry. I'll think of you a lot . . . between your visits.'

'And how's my mate Johnny?'

'He's fine. Fine,' she said. The were both subdued anyway, her tone was not out of character with the way they were talking, but he caught the slightest hint.

'I don't want to pry. . .' he began.

'You don't ever pry, Harry,' she said.

'But I was wondering like . . . when he didn't come with you . . . whether anything . . . if it was all like it always was. . . .'

'No, it's not like it always was. You're quite right.' She looked at the table cloth for a long time. Harry said nothing. 'Well, I mean he's like he always was, and always will be. But I don't feel the same.'

'Ah, you've not gone off a fellow like Johnny? One in a million, that Johnny.'

'It's hard to explain. You see he doesn't have any really special feelings towards me . . . you know, like you had for Mother . . . he doesn't see him and me as any sort of unit. I didn't understand it for a long time. . . .'

'But you always said he wasn't the marrying type . . . you knew that. . . .' Harry was clearly very disappointed to see the end of Johnny in his life.

'Yes, but I didn't understand how light his hold on me was. I've been going out for the past few months with that

399

chap Henry, you remember you met him at the party, the solicitor.'

'Oh yes, he made the sort of speech,' said Harry without enthusiasm.

'Yes, he and his friend Simon Burke, they've been very kind to me . . . and I've grown quite fond of Henry actually . . . and we go to the theatre . . . and we go to art galleries, and oh, I don't know where else . . . he's cooked me supper in his flat, and I've even had him to supper in Clarence Gardens when Father's out, and once when he was there . . . and do you see – Johnny doesn't mind a bit. Not a bit. . . .'

'Well, are you only doing it so that Johnny will get jealous? That's a bit silly isn't it . . . ?'

'No, that's not it, it's just that it would never have gone so far if Johnny had showed the slightest annoyance, he hasn't. He's quite happy if I say I can't meet him on Saturday because I'm going to the Old Vic with Henry.'

'What did you expect him to say?'

'I don't know, I didn't expect him to be so indifferent . . . I asked him straight out. . . .'

'And what did he say?'

'He said, "You know me, pussy cat, I don't tie people down," and of course he pointed out to me that I didn't make a fuss when he took other ladies out so he certainly wasn't going to come the jealous lover bit. I told him that I hated him going out with other women and that I wanted him to come the jealous lover bit with me. He said I'd picked the wrong man for those kind of antics.'

'Well,' Harry said, nonplussed. 'He spoke fair and honest, didn't he?'

'Yes, but that's all there is to it, all there'll ever be. The love . . . the hope and all that. It's all on my side, don't you see? There's nothing giving on his . . . he doesn't need me.'

'So do you see him still?' Harry looked fearful in case his friend Johnny was being mislaid in a welter of confused female attitudes.

'Oh, I see him, I see him at Stefan's, I see him sometimes on a Sunday morning . . . we go and get the papers and go to bed for the morning – I've always thought of that as our time. . . .'

'And Henry . . . doesn't he think . . . ?'

'I don't go to bed with Henry. But I'm very fond of him, he's afraid to tell me that he's serious about me in case I tell him I prefer Johnny. I know it sounds ludicrous, but that's the way it is. So we're all walking on tightropes . . . except Johnny.'

'I'm sure it will turn out for the best.' Harry patted her hand.

'Oh yes, I'm sure it will,' Elizabeth said thoughtfully. 'But as in almost every walk of life, it will have to be Elizabeth White who makes the decision, what is for the best. Nobody else will.'

As it happened Aunt Eileen had heard about Mother because Aisling had telephoned Clarence Gardens one night for a chat and Father had told her why Elizabeth was away. Father had not wanted to hear about the funeral. Elizabeth said she would tell him about it if he liked, but he said no, that Mother had died for him a long time ago.

'I got a nice note from our Mother's friend, Aisling's mother,' he said in a surprised tone. 'Very sensible and to the point. There's one there with an Irish stamp for you too, she must have written to us both. Nice note really, not a lot of nonsense.'

Elizabeth wondered what Aunt Eileen had said that had pleased Father, because she knew it could be nothing like the great outpouring which she had received herself. Eileen remembered all the good bits of when Mother was young, and how Mother had written when Elizabeth was born and said they had never seen such a perfect baby in the hospital, and how Eileen had laughed because they had never seen such perfect babies as Sean and Maureen in Kilgarret either. Eileen begged her to remember the good bits of Mother and put aside the sad bits: that's what she did with Sean, she always remembered him laughing and enthusiastic and giving her flowers for a birthday, and being absorbed in a book. She never remembered him fighting with his father, sulking, or worst of all being blown to bits by a mine. Try to think of her mother as someone very like Elizabeth herself, half earnest and practical and half flighty – not as a figure in a mental home. Not that.

Eileen added that Aisling had seemed in very poor form these days, just between themselves. And if there was any possible chance of Elizabeth rushing over for a visit, then it might be a wonderful time to do it. It would cheer Elizabeth up after all the sadness, and certainly Aisling's face was never known to be long when her friend was round. But Elizabeth would be very discreet and not mention this, wouldn't she?

It was tempting but it wasn't possible. Time to make up at the school, at the college, at the shop. No, there was no way that Elizabeth could go to Ireland. As she was thinking that she might telephone Kilgarret the telephone rang. It was Johnny.

Would she like to go and hear a bit of skiffle or was that too loud and cheery after all she'd been through? Elizabeth said she'd love it. She'd meet him at the skiffle club, it would be just what she'd need, take her mind off things.

'Was it dreadful, funny-face?' he asked.

'Very bleak. Yes,' she said.

'I know. I didn't write or send a wire, meaningless really. Just prefer to remember her as a very glamorous doll. That's what she was when I saw her.'

'Right. True,' she said.

'Old Harry all right? Must have been a bit of a relief in the end for him? Seeing as she wasn't going to get better?'

'I'm sure you're right.'

'Well, I'll see you at nine.'

'Great,' she said.

The telephone rang again. It was Henry.

'I know you won't want to go out and be jolly and cheerful, but if you liked I could cook you a meal, and we could just sit and talk about it,' he offered.

'No,' Elizabeth said slowly, 'no, it's lovely of you but there's something I have to do.'

Henry was apologetic at once. He should have realised it

402

was too soon to intrude. He would give her a couple of days.

'I'd like to come tomorrow if you're free,' she asked.

He was delighted, he would come and pick her up. Call for her. That was nice. Johnny didn't call for her. She said she was looking forward to it.

She had a slight headache when she met Johnny at the club. He said he knew how to cure that and he asked for a coffee with some rum and a stick of cinnamon in it. Oddly, her head did feel a little better.

'How does it work?' she asked.

'It burns the headache away,' Johnny said, taking her cold hand and leading her over to a group of people at a table. He seemed to know them all. She was introduced to them by first names and she wondered which woman he fancied now. It was possibly the small giggly one but she was married to the man beside her, surely. He had his hand on her shoulder and she wore a wedding ring. What difference did it make being married? Anyway the romance, if it was one, would not last long. Johnny held her and she leaned against him as she drank her spicy coffee.

'It's nice that you're back, pussy cat,' he said stroking her neck. 'Are we going back to the flat later?'

'Yes, definitely,' she said. She must have imagined the speaking glances between them, Johnny and the small giggly woman.

She lay in his arms, and he sighed happily. She realised that this was the only reference to her sad pilgrimage to Preston – vanishing off to the other end of the country – no soothings, no sorrow, no consolations. Johnny didn't like thinking about sad things, so he never thought of them. He had told her that years and years ago. Simple, wasn't it?

She had a slight headache again the next night when Henry called for her, but she didn't mention it. She was afraid he might want to call off the evening, or that he would suggest an aspirin and some hot milk, which would be so dull compared to what Johnny had thought up. He had come in and talked to Father for five minutes. Just enough to include

Father, but not involve him. As Elizabeth fetched her coat she heard Henry saying, 'I'm afraid I don't know the form, Mr White, about extending condolences on the death of an ex-wife – but I'm very sorry that Elizabeth's mother has passed away.'

Father seemed able to deal with formal kinds of conversation like this, he probably had a lot of it in the bank. 'Thank you, Henry,' he said. 'Elizabeth's mother had a very uneasy and disturbed life. It is to be hoped that she has found peace at last.'

'Indeed, indeed,' Henry said respectfully. Elizabeth allowed them a few seconds of silence before she came in.

'Well, we're off now, I won't keep her out too late, Mr White,' Henry said. Elizabeth felt that this is what other girls must have had, ten years ago. She had missed out on it. She never knew any courtship, boys coming to the house, dates and having to be home at certain times – it made her feel very young and happy for some silly reason.

Henry had everything ready for the meal: a tin of tomato soup in one saucepan, and four scrubbed potatoes in another; on a grill-pan he had two small lamb chops and four halves of tomato. A tray was set with a little jug of mint sauce and bread and butter already arranged on a plate.

'It's just simple, but I thought it would be nice for you not to have to cook for yourself,' he said. He looked innocent and almost afraid that she wouldn't approve of his preparations.

Elizabeth's face broke into a great smile of delight. 'How marvellous to be waited on like this. You *are* thoughtful and kind.'

Henry flushed with pleasure. 'I just wanted you to sit back, after all you've been through. Tell me about it.' He poured her a glass of wine and sat her down in front of his gas fire in the sitting room. He sat on the floor opposite her.

'Tell me what happened . . . you left here on the train. . . .' He looked at her, interested in her and what she had been through. The sympathy on his face was genuine. He really did want to know all about it. Slowly she began to tell him . . . and when she told him how small Mother was, like a little shrivelled doll, and how much Harry had cried, Henry's eyes filled with tears . . . and then Elizabeth's eyes filled with tears and she wept on Henry's chest beside the gas fire for a long long time. They both blew their noses loudly and Elizabeth went into the bathroom to dab her eyes with cold water and Henry began his laborious preparations in the kitchen and guarded the lamb chops against burning with furious concentration.

Henry had a married sister, Jean, who lived in Liverpool, that was where he was heading for Christmas. His parents had died when he was still young. His father had died the night before he was to join up in 1940 and Henry had been only fourteen. His mother had lived a life of terror and constant anxiety over the war. And then, just after VE day, she too had died suddenly. Henry always remembered the war as taking both his parents away – he could never understand why people looked back half-affectionately to all the solidarity and matinées during those years. He had no nostalgia, a schoolboy with a mother whose nerves were on the point of snapping; it was by no standard the best time of his life.

Yes, he was very fond of Jean, she was a nurse and she had been wonderful to him when he was starting to study law, she had helped support him and given him money for his fees and indenture costs, and she had tided him over until they had sold the family house and had some money of their own. Jean had married Derek and they had one small son. He was called Henry too. Henry was going to get him a train for Christmas.

It all sounded very safe. Henry would take the train to Liverpool and Derek would come to meet him: then they would collect the Christmas tree together and take it home. Young Henry would be asleep; the three adults would decorate the tree. Henry didn't seem to know whether he got on very well with his sister and brother-in-law or not. He didn't even understand the question. Jean was his sister, he went there for Christmas. That was that. Elizabeth felt a little foolish about her questions . . . they sounded like an

405

interrogation. She had hoped that he might say that he and Jean had always been great friends, that they had laughed at the same things, and that he liked Derek enormously. Elizabeth had wanted to hear that at Christmas they sat, Jean and Henry, and remembered the good things about their mother and father, that they told each other everything and caught up on the year's happenings as easily as if they had only been separated a week.

If she had brushed with a Christmas like this, it would somehow make her own a little better. She and Father had weathered many a festive season together since Mother had left home, but it was never easy. Father would grow more and more morose as the build-up to Christmas Day continued, and by the time she carved the chicken he would be positively sepulchral. Elizabeth had learned how to cope with this: she just chattered pleasantly and inconsequentially as if she hadn't noticed any gloom or lack of reciprocal chatter. Then the dishes were washed, and they built up the fire and listened to the radio. She did not even know what Johnny had planned for Christmas; it had never included helping her to enjoy herself and it never would. Johnny had no family — many people might think it normal that he should come for his Christmas feast to Elizabeth and her father. But Johnny didn't do things that depressed him. He would let her know casually; it might be Scotland like it was last year. Six of them had rented an old crofter's cottage and had spent four glorious days, walking and exploring the Highlands, and eating and drinking in front of a log fire. Elizabeth was wan with envy when she heard about it.

As it turned out Johnny went nowhere for Christmas because he got a bad attack of flu; it coincided with one of his little dalliances, and an Italian girl, who fancied herself as a Florence Nightingale, patted his brow and handed him drinks of water. Elizabeth called at the flat on Christmas Eve. In no way did she let the bewildered Francesca know that she was a long-standing love of Johnny's. She behaved calmly and kindly as if she were visiting a friend. She ignored the long white dressing-gown on the back of the bedroom door, she never let her eyes fall on the clothes thrown over the bedroom chair, the make-up on the dressing table or the look of embarrassment on Johnny's face.

'I just came to wish you Happy Christmas, and Stefan said you were in bad shape so I did what they do in books – I've brought you some beef tea. . . .' She laughed happily. And after a moment, Francesca laughed too. Johnny managed a smile. 'So, Francesca can you perhaps heat this up . . . it's meant to do magic things . . . but let's not question what. If it's an old wives' tale, let's just believe it.'

Francesca scampered into the kitchen happily to find a saucepan.

From his fevered face Johnny's smile still looked good. 'I didn't know you'd come over, I thought . . . I thought. . . .'

'I know, you thought I'd be discreet. It doesn't matter.'

'What?'

'It doesn't matter. I think the worst has passed now, it will get better after this.'

Johnny reached out for her hand. 'It will change, I promise you, it won't always be like this.'

She patted his hand and stood up. She was very good at misunderstanding conversations, she had been doing it deliberately for years. She insisted on believing they were talking about his bout of flu. 'You're absolutely right, it will change, tomorrow even, it will have lessened. Of course it won't always be like this. . . .' She blew him a kiss from the door. 'Happy Christmas, Johnny, oh, and Francesca . . . ?'

The tousled head appeared from the kitchen. 'Oh . . . you go Eleezabett. So soon?'

'Yes. I just wanted to say *Buon Natale*. That's it, isn't it?'

'*Si, Buon Natale*.' Francesca was delighted. As Elizabeth walked down the familiar stairs she could imagaine Francesca sitting on Johnny's bed spooning him the beef tea, saying how nice Eleezabett was. And she could imagine Johnny impatiently changing the subject.

Henry came back three days after Christmas. It had been very pleasant, very quiet, very seasonal. Why had he come back so soon, Elizabeth wanted to know? If it was so nice there why had he not stayed until the weekend, until New Year's Eve?

'Because I missed you,' Henry said simply. 'I wanted to see you again.'

Henry wondered if Elizabeth would like to go to dinner with him on New Year's Eve.

'Let me cook a dinner for you instead?' she suggested. 'Father will be away, there's a New Year bridge gathering, he's very excited about it.'

Henry had brought a bottle of champagne and Elizabeth had one already cooling, so they decided not to wait until midnight. They could drink one now and one then.

'You know I'm very fond of you, I've become so very, very fond of you,' Henry said at one stage.

'I'm very fond of you too,' Elizabeth said.

'The problem is I don't know quite . . . where I stand . . . you know.'

Elizabeth looked at him, puzzled.

'You know I'm aware, of course, that you are very friendly with Johnny Stone . . . but I don't know how. . . .'

Elizabeth still looked at him and said nothing.

'You see, I don't want to be foolish and hope that you might be interested in me, if this chap, if there's something . . . so I hoped you might tell me what you think.' He looked so hopeful and eager, and almost dreading her reply. Elizabeth had never known such a sense of power in her life, but she did not get any enjoyment from it.

'It's a long story. . . .' she began.

'Oh, I don't want to know about the past . . . that's got nothing to do with me . . . heavens, no. It's just about what you feel now . . . what you want.'

'I don't love Johnny Stone any more,' she said. Her voice echoed in her head. It was true. Henry's face faded from her, she just thought of that fact. She did not love Johnny. It had happened without her knowing, for the love she always carried around for him had gone and she hadn't noticed it disappearing, it was only now that someone asked her where it was that she became aware that it was missing. She smiled at Henry as his face came back into focus. 'That's true,' she said simply.

'Well, is it possible that you might in time love *me*?' He was hesitant, unsure still. 'I don't want you to feel I'm rushing you or demanding you give me an answer, but if you thought that. . . .'

'But I do love you already,' she said.

Henry was so delighted he looked like a big child. He pushed his fair hair until it stood up around his head like a halo. Up to now he had kissed her lightly on the lips when he was leaving her, now he pulled her towards him and kissed her for a long time.

'I think you are the most wonderful person in the whole world. You are such a beautiful girl . . . I can't believe you might love me,' he said happily as he looked at her proudly.

'You're very good to me . . . no wonder I love you,' she said.

'Will you marry me? Can we get married some time in the New Year?'

She sat up from his arms, startled. To Henry love meant marriage, to most people love meant marriage. Henry was anxious to give up all his other chances, close down any alternative options and live with her, Elizabeth White, for the rest of his life. That's what he was aching to do. And she wanted it too. She wanted to be safe and happy and to look after him. She wanted the two of them to be together and plan things and share things. Yes, she would love to marry Henry Mason.

'I'd love to marry you, Henry Mason. Of course I will,' she said.

Sean had never found conversation with Ethel Murray easy: she was one of those women who spoke so firmly that there seemed nothing to add after any of her statements. He would have escaped her this time, only Eileen was in bed. She hadn't been herself over Christmas – she said it was all the rich food. And there had been too much work in the shop coming up to Christmas. She had determined that they would find a good girl in the New Year and pay her a proper wage. Sean had agreed, had said he would enquire around immediately after the break.

Ethel Murray called unannounced. She wore gloves which she fiddled with and she seemed very ill at ease. They talked politely about how they had all got over Christmas, the nice new priest and what a grand voice he had, just what the choir needed. They remarked that the world had come to a bad state when the poor Pope had to spend his Christmas broadcast on the wireless talking about the danger of atom bombs.

Finally Ethel Murray managed to get to the point. She wondered whether Sean and Eileen might have any . . . well, any information about how Tony and Aisling were getting on. It was as simple as that.

Sean was astounded. Weren't they getting on fine? Had there been any trouble? He had heard nothing – what was she talking about? Had there been an incident? Ethel Murray's face revealed that she had talked to the wrong person. She tried to back-track but now Sean was even more upset than she was. Let her say it straight out what was in her mind.

What was in Ethel Murray's mind was Aisling's announcement during the Christmas lunch that she intended to ask her father for a full-time job back in O'Connor's in the New Year. Her Mam was tired and overworked and a woman in her mid-fifties who should have a rest, and Aisling had nothing to do all day so she might as well fill in the time somehow. Tony had said nothing, but then poor Tony had been a bit under the weather. There must be something wrong, and hard though it was for Ethel to broach this to Sean and Eileen she thought she would do so in confidence . . . and ask their advice.

Sean was moved by her distress, and even more so by her bewilderment. It was not often that you found Ethel Murray not knowing what to do. He calmed her down, he insisted they both have a seasonal nip of whiskey, he said he wouldn't disturb Eileen now, but they would talk about it in the near future. He apologised for his own short temper, and she patted him on the knee with her gloved hand. He thought to himself that in her day she mightn't have been a bad-looking woman at all.

Eileen was back on her feet and up at nine o'clock mass on New Year's Day. She met Aisling just as they were coming out the door. Aisling's eyes lit up.

'Oh Mam, isn't that great that you're well again, come on, get into the car and I'll give you a spin back home – or better still, come up to me?'

'I'd like that, give me a bit of peace – but hold on, let me tell one of them where I'm going or they'll have a search party out for me.' Her eyes went through the crowd coming out into the cold morning, calling Happy New Year at each other. She saw Donal, well wrapped up. 'Tell them I've gone up to Mrs Murray's house for breakfast. Let them eat their own without me,' she called.

'Fat lot you'll get to eat up in the Murrays' house, I'll tell them to put yours in the oven,' Donal called back good-naturedly.

'He's only making a joke of you Aisling,' said Eileen, tucking herself into the car.

'He's not far wrong,' Aisling said and she revved up and headed for the bungalow.

Eileen was shocked to the core by the state of things. The sitting room was filled with dirty dishes, there were glasses on the table, crumbs on the floor. The gleaming kitchen which had been such a cause of envy to poor Maureen was a sorry sight. The oven was thick with grease, saucepans half rinsed but not cleaned stood around, cornflakes were scattered, the sink had not been emptied. It looked filthy and uncared for.

'Child, you're mistress in your own house, but in the name of the Lord would you not make an effort to keep the place a bit better?' Eileen was aghast, she had to move a dirty dishcloth from a chair before she could even sit down.

'Oh Mam, sure what's the point, what in God's name is the point?' Aisling looked not the slightest bit contrite. 'If I tidy it all up and clean it, he'll only destroy it again.'

'But Aisling . . . you can't live like this . . . you can't

possibly. Where's Tony now, is he still in bed?' Eileen had lowered her voice.

'He didn't come home, Mam, he'll be home around lunchtime, to change his clothes and go off down to the hotel. . . .'

'But where on earth is he? On New Year's Eve, were you all alone here? What happened to him?'

'Oh, I suppose he slept where he fell, in Shay Ferguson's, or one of those places. He sometimes sleeps in the hotel too, I'd have thought you'd have heard. . . .'

'No, I heard nothing. Nothing.'

'So I sat here last night by myself. And I boiled some potatoes – that's that saucepan – he often feels like a few potatoes when he comes in with a feed of drink . . . then it got later, and I thought, well, he's not coming home, so I'll cook something for myself . . . So there was some bacon there and I began to fry it with onions and it burned, and that accounts for that pan. And that's yesterday morning's scrambled eggs which he didn't touch, and that . . . I don't know, I think it's milk for something.'

Eileen felt a wave of nausea flow over her.

'How long have things been like this . . . ?'

'Oh, I don't know. Let me see, I've been married for one year and seven months . . . or is it seven years and one month . . . ? About that long. . . .'

It was this dreamy self-parodying behaviour that snapped Eileen out of her shock.

'Do you have hot water in the taps?' she asked crisply.

'What?' Aisling was surprised.

'Is the immersion on? They'll expect me back in the square in an hour's time or an hour and a half. This place is to look right by then.'

'Oh Mam, it's not worth the. . . .'

'Shut up whining and complaining – get started. . . .'

'Mam, I'm not going to do it, neither are you.'

'You're not crossing the door of my house again, you little slut, unless you get up off your backside this minute and get your place into order.'

'It's my place Mam, you said so.'

'My God Almighty it is, and when you think of all the people who would love it, would make it into a little palace, but no, Miss High-and-Mighty-Aisling always has to know better than anyone else in the world. What your sister Maureen would give for a kitchen like this – I saw her face, you know. Think of Peggy out in a bothan on the mountain. What would she give for a house like this? But God didn't see fit to give it to people who would appreciate it, he gave it to a self-pitying snivelling slut – yes, Aisling, that's what you are. . . .'

Aisling was shocked. Not a word about Tony, not a speck of comfort, not a motherly arm around her shoulder about the terrible nature of men. Instead a lecture worse than any she had got when she was fourteen. Almost as a reflex action she stood up. Mam had taken off her coat.

'Hang that up somewhere it won't get covered in filth, and get me an apron or an overall . . . oh all right, get me one of your rags of dresses that cost pounds in Grafton Street, and I'll put that on over my good outfit. Hurry up!' She had found trays hidden away somewhere. 'Keep clearing the sitting room, go on, keep them coming.'

'Mam, I don't want you to wear yourself out. . . .'

'I'm not letting any outside person know the way I brought my daughter up. Do you hear me? Move!'

With a hysterical giggle Aisling thought that they must look like one of those old speeded-up films where the cops and robbers were running jerkily in and out doors.

'The sitting room's clear, Mam,' she called.

'I didn't hear the Hoover,' Mam shouted back.

They had it done in an hour and a half. Mam had opened all the windows to air the place.

'We'll get pneumonia,' complained Aisling.

'Better than diphtheria from the dirt there was in the place,' Mam said.

Bins had been filled, floors had been cleared. Mam had left five saucepans soaking in soap powder, with instructions that they were to be scoured in a few hours' time. She had opened the door of the bedroom and closed it with a bang.

'You have about an hour or two before you expect your husband home. Get in there and clean up that room, take the sheets off the bed and make it properly, I'm coming back this afternoon to see you and I want to see the place perfect. Open those windows if you want to before you drive me back home, it might clear the place up a bit.'

'You're coming back, Mam?' Aisling said fearfully.

'Certainly I am, you invited me for a cup of tea, and, I don't know whether you noticed or not, we never had it. So I'm coming for it this afternoon. And I wouldn't like to drink it from a teapot that's all tarnished either. I got no silver teapots for my wedding, but if I had they'd be shining.'

'Tony may not be here Mam, I don't think you realise how bad it is.'

'I don't think you realise how bad it is,' Mam said grimly and put on her coat to leave.

Tony came in at midday. He looked terrible, Aisling thought. His suit was crumpled and had stains all over it as if he had vomited and it had been only superficially cleaned. His eyes were swollen and puffy. He smelled of drink even across the room with the draughts coming through the open windows.

'Happy New Year,' she said.

'Oh Jesus, I knew you'd be sitting here waiting to nag me,' he said.

'No, I'm not actually, I just said Happy New Year, and I've tidied the place up. Did you notice?'

He looked around suspiciously. 'Yes, yes, it's grand,' he said uncertainly. 'You've done a great job. I'd have given you a hand. . . .'

'No, it's fine. And look,' she led him to the kitchen, 'shining isn't it?'

'Yes, great.' He was worried.

'Now look at the bedroom, that's all tidied too.'

'Oh, Ash, you've done a grand job. Is someone coming?' he asked suddenly.

'Well, Mam may come in for an hour this afternoon, that's all.'

414

'Ah yes . . . well, that's grand for you. I may not be back actually. Shay and a couple of the others. . . .'

'I'd like you to be back, Tony.'

'Now, what's this, what is all this? Some kind of court? Is Tony to be paraded in front of the O'Connors and put on trial? Is that it?'

'On trial for what, Tony?'

'I don't know, you tell me?'

'No, you tell me. I mentioned no trials, I just said I'd like you to be here when my mother comes to tea, that's all.'

'She hasn't bothered herself to come up here for a good bit, why should I be at her beck and call?'

'She's been sick in bed for one thing, and she was here this morning for another.'

Tony's eyes narrowed. 'Here already? Did you tell her where I was?'

'How could I have done that, Tony, since I didn't know and still don't know where you were . . . ?'

'There was a session in the hotel, it wasn't sensible to drive back, a few of us stayed. . . .'

'Yes.'

'It was New Year's Eve . . . you know, excuse for a bit of a celebration.'

'Yes I know, I heard the bells in Christ Church, they played them on Radio Eireann at midnight. It was lovely. Smashing celebration, I thought to myself.'

'Oh Ash, I should have . . . but you know, you're not all that keen on the crowd . . . listen, I'll make it up to you.'

'Good, be here at teatime. Around four o'clock.'

'No, that's not fair, stop tricking me. Stop it. I've made my arrangements. I've got to go out. Are there clean shirts?'

'There are nine clean shirts.'

'What do you mean, nine? What are you playing at?'

'You asked me, I'm answering. The laundry comes every Wednesday. I give him seven shirts, he gives me seven shirts, that's the way we work it. It's called the miracle of having money.'

'I really don't know what's wrong with you, Ash, I don't.

You have everything you want here . . . why are you always so bitter?'

'I don't know, I really don't. It must have been part of my nature.'

'So now it's sardonic is it? Sarcasm.'

'Mam isn't well. She's not looking well at all. I'd like to go back to the shop and work there to help for a while.'

'Is this what the confrontation was going to be about? I don't want it. I don't want my wife working back in her parents' shop.'

'I don't want my husband drunk as a fool, falling around the town making eejits of us both. I don't want to live here alone as if I were a widow. Your mother has more company than I do. There are a lot of things I don't want, Tony Murray, and I put up with them.'

'Now, I'm putting my foot down. I'm a married man and I won't be made little of by my wife going back to her job. Through pig-headed stupidity.'

Aisling stood up. 'And I'm a married woman and I won't then be made little of by my husband saying that there's nothing wrong with us. There is plenty wrong with us. We have not managed to have sexual intercourse yet. After a year and seven months, that is not normal, Tony. And for the last six months we haven't even made the effort. It is not acceptable to me that I sit here and take orders from someone who is pig-headedly stupid enough to maintain that everything's fine.'

Tony looked at her, his fists clenched.

'So what about a bargain?'

'What kind of bargain?'

'You get your way over my job. I'll agree not to go back to work. And I get my way over the other business. We go to Dublin and see a specialist. There are specialists. We can be helped.'

'A crowd of Americans, most likely, or worse, Irish fellows who've been in America, asking a lot of personal questions, getting their kicks that way . . . telling you to lay off the drink for a year . . . telling you to describe this and that. You're not getting me up there. I'm telling you that flat.'

Aisling looked cold. 'So, I go back to work in O'Connor's.'

'Yes, you win, you get your way as usual.' Tony looked at her with his face curled into a scornful look. 'That's right. Play dirty. Get your way at all cost. Do what you like.'

Aisling didn't even bother to argue. Her shoulders slumped and she said almost to herself, 'Oh that's totally wrong, I haven't got my own way. I haven't won at all. But I don't suppose anyone on earth will believe that.'

Dearest, dearest Elizabeth,
I can't tell you how pleased I am with your news. You must have thought that Mam and I were drunk yesterday when you phoned, we'd been sitting here talking and it had got dark . . . and when the phone rang it sort of brought us back to reality with a bump. I hope we sounded as happy for you as we are.

I know I was crass when I thought you meant that you were going to marry Johnny. You see I hadn't really heard of Henry, except very briefly. Now you must sit down and write me a long letter about him, give yourself headings like we did at English class back at school – no I'll give them to you: a) why you like him so much; b) what you talk about; c) what you laugh about; d) where you are going to live; e) what kind of wedding and where; f) do you sleep with him and if so is it nice; g) what did Johnny say?
Love from us all,
Aisling

XVI

Everyone seemed eager to know what Johnny would say. Even Father. He wasn't in a position to say anything for some time since Francesca had swept him off to her aunt's restaurant – somewhere – and she and Auntie were feeding him with home-made minestrone and building him up again. Or that was the message that Stefan seemed to gather from the telephone call. Stefan was pleased but slightly fearful at Elizabeth's announcement. He admired the ring, the single diamond which Henry had bought as soon as the jewellery shop opened the next day. He could have got Henry an antique ring at half the price, something much more beautiful but naturally he made no mention of it. Neither did Anna. Their congratulations seemed flat to Elizabeth, it was almost as if they were looking over their shoulders . . . expecting a fully-recovered Johnny to come in and overturn everything.

Father said that he was pleased, he offered his congratulations to Elizabeth as if she were a stranger, a customer at the bank rather than his only child. He said that he liked Henry and hoped they would be happy. Then immediately he asked where Elizabeth would live, and what would happen to him for the rest of his life? He asked it flatly and not at all accusingly. Elizabeth had the answer ready. She thought that they should arrange for someone to rent her room at a low cost and that whoever the tenant was – perhaps a student, or a teacher – she should cook Father a meal each evening. Father said it would have to be looked into. Perhaps in the bank, it might not be thought, well, proper, to have a woman living under the same roof. Elizabeth kept her temper: yes of course it would indeed have to be looked into, but then of course there might be no need for it. Father was still a young man in his fifties, he was well able to look after himself. Elizabeth would be glad to show him how to make simple meals, and even when she was married she could come from time to time and do some baking for him. Father put on his anxious face for a while and said that it all did seem for the best, and he hoped there would be no problems, no trouble.

'What kind of trouble could there possibly be, Father?'

'Well . . . the other young man, Johnny Stone . . . do you not think he may have had expectations? After all you have been seeing him for years and years. It's not unreasonable for him to have expected. . . .'

'Nonsense,' Elizabeth said quickly, 'I know I have been going out with Johnny and I'm very fond of him . . . but that's different – Johnny's not a person who settles down. He had no "expectations" as you call it.'

'What does he say about you going to marry Henry?' Father asked doggedly.

'Nothing, he doesn't know, he's away.'

'Aha,' said Father.

Harry's letter was muted in its warmth. Oh, he had all the right words but there was nothing behind them. There were three pages of Harry's great sweepy handwriting. Elizabeth had a little bet with herself about whether he would mention Johnny on page two or page three. Probably two, she decided. She won her bet. She threw the letter on the floor in a rage and then had to go and pick it up. Damn Johnny Stone, why did he make everyone think he was right? Why did he have to cloud her marriage even now? She knew that Johnny wouldn't mind if she married Henry, but nobody else knew this. Why did everybody take his side?

She told Henry Mason no lies. She said she had been Johnny's lover, that he had been the only one, that she had loved him for a long time but recently, over a period of a year, she had begun to realise that it wasn't any real relationship, it was an elaborate series of pretences and attitudes. Henry found this an entirely satisfactory explanation.

He had had one affair in his life too. It had not been so long-standing. It was with Simon's sister; Barbara Burke was one of the first girls he had ever met, he met her at tennis parties, she was terribly good. She had found him endearing he thought, but she was very impatient with him, if he didn't win the tennis match, catch the waiter's eye quickly, find a taxi in the rain, she sighed and he felt that he was very inadequate.

Henry had become determined to please Barbara . . . and he had succeeded: for a year they had an affair and she did not think he should be patronised and patted on the head. It had been a very happy time, and Henry had wanted them to get married. But Barbara had said they were far too young, they should see the world a little. And oddly Simon had agreed. Henry had been afraid that Simon might have thought it was a poor show having an affair with his sister and not making an honest woman of her.

Anyway, it had all been for the best, because Henry began to realise that he was in fact involved in a complicated business of pretending that he was happy doing things when he certainly was not. He had to make such an effort all the time. Barbara became so impatient when he forgot things that he had a little notebook where he wrote things she said down. She accused him of not being aware of what was happening so he used to note headings in his book of things to talk about. When she was away and he telephoned her he had a whole list of things to say beside the phone. Then it dawned on him that this was no way to live. He explained it to Barbara, and she didn't believe him, she thought it was all a game; but he assured her that the real Henry would bore her to death in two minutes . . . she only liked the rehearsed and constantly-aspiring-to-please Henry. Barbara never really understood what he meant but the romance ended.

What had happened to her? Oh, she married a doctor, a very successful chap called Donaldson. They all met from time to time – there had been no bitterness. In fact Henry would like to invite them to the wedding if that would be all right? Of course it would be all right, after all Johnny Stone would be invited to the wedding as well.

'I wonder what he'll say when he hears we're getting married?' said Henry.

Stefan had obviously decided that it was not up to him to tell Johnny the news. So when Elizabeth came into the shop muffled up against the cold January winds, he still didn't know.

They hugged each other, she exclaimed at how well he looked. Italian soup must put strength into a man certainly, she laughed. Stefan went on polishing a candlestick that didn't need to be polished, looking carefully the other way.

'And what have you been up to?' Johnny said. Johnny never discussed his dalliances, there had been the slightest little frown at Elizabeth's reference to Italian soup.

Stefan had started to polish more earnestly than ever, and began to move unwillingly towards his own little office. Elizabeth had taken off her coat and long woolly scarf, her gloves and her knitted hat.

'Lord, that's better, I was beginning to feel like an Egyptian mummy. What have I been up to? Didn't Stefan tell you? Henry and I decided to get married. Look, here's the ring . . . you must wish us luck. . . .'

'You and Henry decided to do what?' said Johnny, holding her hand with the ring on it; he didn't even notice that Stefan had scuttled off into his office.

'Get married, some time at the end of the summer, if there ever is a summer, so now isn't that a surprise?'

'You can't marry Henry. It's . . . it's ridiculous. . . .'

'What on earth do you mean? Of course I'm going to marry Henry. It's exactly what I want to do, I'm delighted to marry him, he is exactly the right person for me to marry, and I think I'm right for him too.'

'Funny-face, is this some kind of silly joke?'

'Johnny, of course it's not. I wouldn't make a joke about something like this. . . .'

'Well, that's what I thought, but you're not serious?'

Elizabeth sat down on a carved hall chair. 'I don't know why you keep saying that.'

'What the hell did you expect me to say? Well done, how clever, here's to the bride and groom?'

'Something like that, yes.'

'Oh don't be so stupid.'

'But you like Henry, you like me . . . why aren't you pleased?'

'I had this silly idea that you were my woman. That's all.'

'Of course I'm not your woman, you would hate to think of a tie like that. You've never wanted one. Last summer when I asked you if you had any objections if I went out with Simon or Henry you looked surprised. "What objections can I have, pussy cat? You're your own person." Those were your words. . . .'

'Yes and I meant them. But marrying one of them. Marrying Henry when my back was turned. . . . Oh, come on.'

'I didn't marry him, I'm going to. If you were here I'd have told you. It wasn't when your back was turned. He asked me on New Year's Day and you weren't. . . .'

'Oh spare me the sordid blow-by-blow account, for heaven's sake,' pleaded Johnny.

Elizabeth shrugged. 'It's impossible to please you,' she said.

'You don't try very hard to please me, do you sweetness? When my back's turned going off to marry a twitching solicitor.'

'He is not a twitching solicitor. God, how dismissive and cruel you are. Henry never says anything except nice things about you . . . why do you have to be so hurtful about people?'

'He might say less nice things if he knew what I had been up to with his future bride.'

'He knows.'

'You never told prissy Henry about. . . .'

'You are not to call him names. I told him that you and I were lovers for years, since I was eighteen. I know about his past. We're not fools, but we don't go over and over it with relish. . . .'

'You are serious? You are going to marry him?'

422

'Of course I am. Can't you be happy for me, for us, instead of being all bitter and cruel? Can't you?'

'But I'm not happy, I'm not happy to have my lady love going off to marry someone else, let's not be idiotic. Why should I be?'

'I'm not your lady love. I'm one of them.'

'The main one. For me . . . and I was the only one for you wasn't I?'

'Yes.'

'So why can't things be as they were?'

'They can't, it was nonsensical. I was pretending I didn't care that you had other girls and that you didn't want to settle down, but I did care, and I'm sick of pretending.'

'You should have said. . . .'

'If I had said . . . you'd have left me years ago, you left all the others who said, didn't you?'

'It's rather drastic though isn't it? Going off behind my back and getting engaged to someone else.'

'Wish me happiness?'

'You're making the greatest mistake in your life, choosing him rather than me.'

'You wouldn't have me if I chose you. "Free as the air", another of your expressions. . . .'

'Ah yes, but what we had was super. I thought we got the best of each other and none of the tedium – no valleys, all peaks.'

'A bit unnatural though, as a permanent way of going on, wouldn't you say?' Elizabeth spoke without guile; she was even surprised at being able to talk in this way to Johnny. Her heart didn't race any more, she didn't try to find the right phrase, the good approach. She wasn't eyeing him nervously in case his expression might change.

'Dear Lord, homespun philosophy already.' But Johnny was laughing. 'Right, if you've got such a puritan ethic, you want the bad times and the whole business, then you're going to get it. And I wish you well. And I wish you happiness. Of course I do, of course I do.' Johnny took her by the shoulders and pulled her up to face him. He kissed her gently on each cheek. 'All the happiness in the world. You're

423

a lovely, lovely woman. He is a really lucky man. Hey, Stefan, you old humbug, come out here and give me an account of yourself. . . .'

Stefan appeared nervously from the office where he and Anna had been peering through the slit they used in case there was any shoplifting.

'Stefan, you're a fine watch-dog. While I was away getting my strength back, look what you did. You let that solicitor walk off with my lady love behind my back. And now we've got to wish them well. . . .'

Stefan and Anna burst into smiles of relief. So would Henry, Elizabeth realised, so would Father, and so would Harry. Johnny had decided to get over his pique. The wedding could go ahead.

Elizabeth had a letter from Jean, Henry's sister, welcoming her to the family. Simon Burke was so thrilled he had a drinks party at once in his flat, which was much more elegant and stylish than Henry's place. His sister Barbara was there, wearing a small hat made of smooth feathers shaped to fit her hair-style, a fur stole and a very expensive dress. Her husband, the doctor, looked considerably older than her, greying, a little paunchy and very charming.

Barbara embraced her and wished her every happiness. 'Henry tells me you're so kind,' she purred. 'That's what he needs, lots of kindness.'

Simon kept up a witty act about how he was the loser in some contest. It had always been the same, he complained, hand on brow in mock despair. When either of them wanted something it was always Henry who got it first. The flat with a view over the park? Henry got it. The office upstairs in the solicitors' firm, the one with the big desk? Henry had got it. And now Elizabeth, their beautiful art teacher. Henry had got her. Henry flushed with pleasure and disclaimers about his success. Elizabeth thought Simon was a very good friend, because actually neither Henry's flat nor his office were as good as Simon's.

After the party, Henry and Elizabeth walked in the crisp night air arm in arm and chatting companionably.

'Isn't Simon marvellous? I don't know how he does it, just assembles people and pours them drinks, a few little savouries . . . and it's a party. . . .' Henry sounded admiring and envious.

'Wait until we have our own little place, we'll give parties like that all the time,' she said, struck at how quickly he had been echoing her own thoughts.

'I'd love that,' he said, his face lighting up. He stopped under a street light and kissed her. 'We'll have great times,' he said.

'Sensational times,' she said.

'Would you come home with me now?' he asked. He had been about to take her home to Clarence Gardens; she had argued that it would take him too long, the journey there and back, but he insisted always on seeing her to the door.

'But it's in the other direction,' she said, confused. 'If I were to go back with you and go to Clarence Gardens. It would take all night . . . oh, I see.'

'Yes, I want you to stay with me,' he said full of hope.

'Why not?' she said suddenly.

They lay in the narrow single bed sipping mugs of hot chocolate. Henry had got up and made them and brought them back to bed.

'It's not a very comfortable bed.'

'It's fine, it's friendly,' she said, laughing.

'Yes, well, when I was getting furniture for this place, I thought it might be rather overoptimistic to get a double bed, you know. Tempting fate.'

They laughed together.

'I feel I've been with you always,' Henry said.

'So do I,' said Elizabeth.

'It's just right, somehow,' he said.

Elizabeth laid her head on his shoulder. 'You are the dearest and most loving man in the world, I can't tell you how happy I feel.'

'I was afraid . . . I thought that maybe . . . you know, I was worried that. . . .'

'I don't know what complicated process is going through your mind,' said Elizabeth, who thought that Henry might

425

be about to look for some reassuring comparisons, 'but whatever it is I want you to know that I feel safe and happy and loved . . . and you are my man forever and ever.'

Henry sighed with happiness and content.

Johnny and Elizabeth did the books for Stefan once a month. They had always treated themselves to an evening out when the figures were finished. It had become a little ritual.

'I suppose all that is a thing of the past?' Johnny said casually when they had put away the ledgers. 'Home to my gloomy tomato sandwich for me.'

'Well, I'd like to go out to supper, we usually do, don't we?' Elizabeth said.

'But what about Faithful Henry?'

'What about him?'

'Won't he mind?'

'Why should he?'

'Good,' said Johnny. 'Hang on, I'll get the car.'

'Is good to see you Mr Stone,' said the waiter in the little Italian restaurant. 'I was afraid you an' the young lady had a quarrel, you no come here.'

'No quarrel. She's going to marry another man. But we haven't had a quarrel.'

'You make a joke, Meester Stone.' The waiter looked confused; he knew that somehow Johnny was making a fool of him.

'Shut up, stop embarrassing people,' she said. And after that they relaxed and talked about Stefan and the amazing woman with all that old glass who came in to sell it to him bit by bit, and how Anna was jealous because she thought the woman must secretly hanker after Stefan. They laughed over the contents of a house which had been offered to them, where nothing was more than five years old . . . a brand new bungalow with modern furniture, which had, not un-naturally, displeased its owners.

Johnny's flat was nearby.

'Can I presume this eminently reasonable man's tolerance will include your coming home for a nightcap?' he asked elegantly.

'I never checked, but mine doesn't,' she said lightly.

It was cold and windy in the street.

'Well, goodbye then, my little chick,' he said and kissed her on each cheek.

Elizabeth didn't know why she felt so furious as she struggled against the wind and rain to the bus stop. After all, Johnny had very rarely driven her home to Clarence Gardens, nor collected her either. But here was something calculated. You don't come home to bed with me so you are left out in the cold and rain. She caught the last bus and did not feel at all in the mood for a chat.

'Coldest weather we've had for years,' said the conductor.

'Yes,' said Elizabeth, telling herself she had no right to feel so angry with Johnny. He was sticking to his rules, it was she who had changed the pattern.

'Not been a day as bad since 1895, did you know that?'

She smiled at him, it didn't hurt to be pleasant, she told herself. 'Where did you hear that?'

'It was in the papers, you must have been up in the moon, or in love, if you didn't see it. Was it in love?'

'That's right,' she laughed.

'Well, he shouldn't let you come home on buses alone at this time of night. Next time you see him, tell him that from me, won't you?'

'Yes I will,' said Elizabeth wondering how it appeared that almost everyone in the world, including strange bus conductors, thought that she was in love with Johnny.

. . . If I stop once I'll never start again and you are right, you make all the running, you tell me everything and I'm the one who is buttoned up. So. What do I do all day? Now I work back in O'Connor's again, and I'm happy. What used I to do all day? Cry, wander around the house, cry more. Wash my face, go in and see Mam. Come home. Wait for Tony.

What do we do when Tony gets home? Well that depends. If he comes home before midnight we usually have words. That's not often. He is drunk, and bad-tempered, and the reason he has come home is because

427

no better alternative presented itself. No party with Shay, no session at the hotel. He says I am nagging and I am, I say he is a drunk and he is. Then we go to bed. But most nights he does not come home while I am awake, I go to bed at midnight usually. Or he doesn't come home at all. We do not entertain people. I used to have his mother to tea but the pretences are over now, even with her. We are not invited to other people's houses. Tony may be invited to other people's houses, at two a.m., but if so he doesn't tell me, and I don't think he remembers.

What's next now, sex. I think Catholics are allowed to talk about it, that is if they have it. I haven't even known what it is like so I'm in a poor position to discuss it. Our marriage has not been consummated. We have never done it. Not once. I don't know why I think it's because Tony is impotent. It may not be that, it may be that we just didn't get round to learning about it properly at the start, and then Tony became such a drunkard that he couldn't manage it anyway. But there it is. You ask me do I enjoy sex, I don't know, I'm sure I might. Everyone else seems to. Do I intend to have children? Well there's no rule saying that a star couldn't appear over Kilgarret and another miracle happen, but so far the Holy Ghost hasn't arrived with any messages for me.

Mam isn't at all well. She won't admit it, but she has some very bad days where she looks very yellow and not well. She says it's the weather, or the change of life or indigestion. But I wish she'd see a doctor. I want everyone to see doctors, as you can see. Dad's fine, overworked, he's glad to have me back. He picks rows with Eamonn over nothing; I wish I could tell him what real causes there are for rows but I begin to breathe a word against Tony and they all shut up. Maureen's looking like a woman of seventy — she's not thirty-two yet, and honestly she's like an old woman. The Dalys are a crowd of devils really. Niamh is home about every second weekend with a college scarf and a smirk on her that would drive you up the wall. She and that friend of hers, Anna Barry, think they're the cat's pyjamas just because they're at UCD. I said to her very cattily that we could all have gone to UCD if we'd wanted to and that she was making herself foolish going round pretending she was an intellectual and a genius. She said, truthfully of course, that none of us had the brains to get in there, and I must say it's very galling that snotty little Niamh is the one who's going to be a graduate. You were right all those years ago, I should have, I should have – but then there are so many things that I should have, and more important, things that I should not have done. And Donal's fine. Did I tell you that the Moriartys are terribly pleased with him, and he's almost like a medicine man in there behind the counter? I heard a woman coming to consult him about ointments the other day – wouldn't have Mr Moriarty at all, had to speak to the young gentleman in the white coat who cured her baby the last time. Donal loved it, of course.

Things will not get better. They will only get worse. I am expected to cover up for Tony's drinking. If he doesn't look well in public, people blame me, I swear it. I'm not being a good wife to him, not looking after him. Do you remember that Doctor Lynch years ago? I honestly do remember people said that it was his wife's fault because she was a sour-puss and she didn't give him a good home. She's dead now but I'd like to go up to the churchyard and dig her up and apologise to her for ever having thought such a thing.

I'll certainly come to your wedding. I hope Tony won't, I don't think Mam would be able for it, or Dad to give the time, I think it would fuss Maureen to death, but she might like to be asked to show off to the Dalys. I'd hate Niamh to go, she's had far too much in life already without being invited to a smart London wedding. Donal would adore to go, he would love it. So please make sure to ask him.

I'll post this before I reread it and decide that I am mad –

love, Aisling

They found the dream flat. It was on the top floor but that didn't matter. They were young and strong, they told each other, and if ever the funny little lift did break down, they could manage the climb. It had big rooms with high ceilings, a huge living room and dining room opening into each other. 'For our elegant dinner parties, Mr Mason,' Elizabeth had laughed. A huge bedroom with bathroom attached. 'For endless weekends without getting out of bed, Mrs Mason,' Henry had said, putting on a music-hall leer. There was a big kitchen, and three other rooms. A study, they agreed, a guest room and a nursery. When the regulation boy was followed by the regulation girl they would think again: either change the study or move to a house with a garden.

'By that time you'll be the senior partner . . . we can probably have a weekend cottage as well,' Elizabeth said teasingly.

They held hands in the spring afternoon and walked around their new home. Henry had been opening and closing doors happily. 'I do hope so,' he replied soberly.

'We are going to be ridiculously happy here, you and I,' she said.

After the terrible letter from Aisling Elizabeth had held herself back with an effort. She wanted to telephone, she wanted to write back an outpouring of sympathy. She was even tempted to find an excuse for a visit. But something made her feel that Aisling should have a cooling-off period. So she replied with a mildly sympathetic note about things seeming to be bad, but perhaps they were not quite as bad as they sounded. Elizabeth said she would wait to hear more news before agreeing that life was as black as Aisling seemed to think.

This appeared to have been the right course. A few weeks later there was a very cheerful letter. Tony had taken the pledge. He had gone to some priest in Waterford who was a marvellous man for getting poeple off the drink. This priest had been a two-bottle-a-day man himself once and now he was marvellous. He even offered Tony a drink while he was talking to him, and Tony had taken one but refused the second. He had agreed that it was ruining his life. He had come back to Aisling like a lamb. There had been no plans to have the other matter investigated, but now that the drink problem was over perhaps that would sort itself out. Aisling sounded very happy. She said that Tony had been paying far more attention to his work and that there were a lot of things that needed to be done to Murray's. They were both happy and busy again, and looking forward to coming to London for the Wedding of the Year.

'I brought that girl up very nicely. Look at the fine letter she's written.' Eileen showed it to Sean with a pleased smile.

'It's from Elizabeth, I thought it was from Niamh.'

'Niamh!' Eileen snorted. 'That one, it's very few letters we get from her unless she wants something . . . no, this is about her wedding.'

'You're not suggesting we go across the whole way to England for it now are you? Holy God, Eileen you get tired enough coming back up here from the shop, and there's no way I could find the time, no it's not possible.'

'Read it you clown,' she said affectionately. 'She knows all that, that's what I mean, didn't I bring her up nicely, she's a credit to me.'

Elizabeth had written that she and Henry were so looking forward to a good representation from the O'Connor clan, but she wasn't going to insist that the grown-ups came. They'd have to talk to Father all the time for one thing and that would simply not be worth coming over to London for; whatever virtues Father had, small talk was not amongst them. She said she didn't want to interrupt Niamh from her studies, she knew Eamonn would hate it, but perhaps Donal and Maureen might like to come . . . she was looking for their views on this.

'Well, that's very sensible of the girl,' Sean said. 'Maybe Maureen would like to go, would Brendan go with her? It might cheer the pair of them up. I don't know whether Donal would have much interest though. . . .'

'Donal would give his eyes to go . . . we'll see about

Maureen. I hope the child has a nice day for herself. I would go, I would really, but I get that tired if I do anything. . . .'

'Ah, stay where you are Eileen, and don't worry about the tiredness, it's been a divil of a summer, everyone's exhausted with the heat.'

It had been a divil of a winter too. Eileen had been tired for over a year.

Maureen thought about the invitation for a long time. Brendan didn't want to go, but there was nothing to stop her going on her own, he said. No, of course it wouldn't be too expensive, she must go if she really wanted to. No, they could easily find the money. Yes, he had been putting a bit by – what for? Well for a bit of a holiday for them all next year. Maybe a house in Tramore for two weeks.

Now a house in Tramore wasn't really a holiday, it would mean that Maureen would have to cook and clean and clear up for the family plus Brendan's mother and his aunt. That wasn't exactly what Maureen thought of as a holiday. A slightly rebellious streak came to the surface.

'Yes. It would have been nice, but if you're sure you don't mind me having the money I think I would like to go to London. It's the rest, you see, as well as the change, no four children to look after for a few days.'

Brendan did some rapid thinking. 'Oh you must go, that's definite. I hadn't fixed it about a house in Tramore. We could consult of course, maybe if we all went to a guesthouse for a week instead . . . what would that be like? There'd be no cooking or anything for you in a guesthouse. But if you're dead set on going to London. . . .'

A week in a guesthouse, now that was a proper trade-in. That was worth losing the wedding over. Maureen wrote a long letter to Elizabeth and thanked her warmly. She said that Elizabeth had always been very generous to her, and she still had the beautiful bon-bon dish which she had sent her for her wedding all those years ago. She said that another reason why she was sorry to miss it all was that she would love to have seen what an atheist wedding was like. Now she would never know.

*

Elizabeth had booked a restaurant room for the reception. It would have been far nicer to have had the group to lunch at home, but so many things were against it. Clarence Gardens, Father, Father and Harry. Neutral ground was far better.

Mrs Noble in the restaurant had never met a bride as composed and business-like as Elizabeth. Here was a young woman with whom it was a pleasure to do business, she said several times. She had suggested a charge of thirty shillings a head. Elizabeth had pointed out that through this wedding she would be introducing a lot of possible clients, her husband's guests would include lawyers and businessmen, and on her own side she would have the artistic world. Mrs Noble might see fit to reduce the price in the hope of making new contacts.

Mrs Noble thought not, she thought that thirty shillings was a good price.

Elizabeth pointed out that Mrs Noble might take into account the bottles of sparkling wine which would be ordered on top of the regular rate; on each of these bottles Mrs Noble would make a profit.

Mrs Noble said that she might just make a small profit on the whole undertaking if she were to charge a guinea a head. At this stage both women smiled and shook hands, and Mrs Noble threw herself whole-heartedly into making the occasion a success.

Elizabeth confided that she was paying for this herself: there would be thirty guests, and she paid in advance. She did not want a sit-down meal, she wanted people to pass through constantly, offering drinks and the hot sausage rolls, the plates of chicken and ham, the wedding cake and the coffee. Mrs Noble seemed to understand.

'Will it be a bit difficult?' she asked sympathetically.

'A bit.'

'Second marriage is it? Divorces and exes and so on?'

'No, only one divorce, my Father, my step-father will be here . . . but there's not an easy mix . . . or maybe everyone thinks that.'

'Everyone thinks it dear, but hardly anybody says it,

433

that's why you're streets ahead.' Mrs Noble was positively motherly. 'We'll give you a great day dear, just you see.'

'I'm looking forward to meeting Aisling, I've met all the other people you like ... Harry, Stefan, Johnny, Anna. Aisling's a funny name though.'

'It means a dream or a fairy woman in a dream. I forget now, I just think of her as that name. I never heard anyone else have it. I hope you'll like her. But it really won't matter if you don't.'

'What on earth do you mean? Of course I'll like her. I'm sure I will.'

'No, I wasn't trying to be hurtful, I mean that before she got married, she said she hoped and hoped I would like Tony and that he would like me. And, well, to be truthful we didn't all that much.'

'Well that's not your fault. Tony's a drunk isn't he?'

'Yes, but Henry can I ask you, however excited and relaxed and friendly we all become, let's not say anything about that. . . .'

'Darling girl, of course I wouldn't. . . .'

'I know, I know. It's just that I've told things to Aisling that she has never told to a soul, and I want her to think that I've respected all she said too.'

'But telling me doesn't count.'

'Not to me it doesn't. I tell you everything, my love, but it would hurt Aisling if she knew I'd breathed a word. Anyway he's cured now, he doesn't touch a drop she says, we'll have to get Mrs Noble to serve some lemonade.'

'An Irishman who doesn't drink. There's a turn-up for the books!'

'Henry that's *exactly* the kind of remark I'm afraid you might make!'

'Oh, don't be an idiot darling, of course I won't. I tell you I'm looking forward to meeting them.'

'Aisling will know Father, and Stefan and Anna – and Johnny of course. From her last visit.'

'Oh did you know Johnny all that time ago?'

'Yes, I knew Johnny when Aisling was over here last.'

434

'What are you going to wear to the wedding?' Maureen asked Aisling.

'Do you know, I'd never given it a thought,' Aisling said. 'I'm very glad you reminded me. We might stop in Dublin and get something. And I'd better get Tony respectable.'

'Isn't Tony always respectable?' Maureen sounded envious of the ability to buy clothes if they were needed.

'He is not. When he was on the jar he used to look like a pig when he came home sometimes, half his suits are ruined, you know.'

'Aisling, don't talk like that about your husband.'

'Maureen, you know Tony used to be pissed six nights out of seven, I know it, why pretend it didn't happen?'

'Oh I don't know. It sounds very coarse the way you put it.'

'It's a lot more coarse taking it all for granted that he should come home maggoty drunk. No, he's fine now, thank God, and please God, while we're at it, it will last. But I'd be very hypocritical pretending to my own sister that my husband wasn't in the horrors of drink until a few months ago.'

Maureen was uneasy. She didn't like this way that Tony was being discussed. 'He's very good to you Aisling, don't ruin it by being too high and mighty. He lets you go on working in Mam and Dad's, though what you want to for I'll never know.'

'I love it, it's something to do, I earn good money which I put in the post office. Elizabeth taught me about saving. She was always very good, you know. That time I went over to London to see her she told me I was mad not to save. Do you know, all the years she lived with us in the square, she used to be mortified because Mam and Dad gave her pocket money . . . ? They never gave it a thought, but she was embarrassed every week, she told me that. And she was only a kid of ten or eleven or whatever.'

'She's very nice, I hope she'll be happy. I do wish I could go to the wedding, I really do. . . .'

'You know I'd give you the money,' Aisling said eagerly.

'Go on, what else am I saving for except things like this? I'll give you the fare. Please take it.'

'I can't, it's not really the money, it's the fact of going . . . you don't know Brendan.'

'He keeps saying you can go.'

'Yes but. . . .'

'Why not tell him you won the money on a horse . . . ? Then he wouldn't mind you having it, he won't be able to say that your sister gave it to you. Let's look up a race and see what won and say you had five pounds on it.'

Maureen screamed with laughter. 'I had five *pounds* on a horse . . . oh, Aisling, will you stop! He'd have me taken off to the county home in five minutes!'

Simon said that it looked as though they had timed their wedding to coincide with a war – things looked very dicey in the Middle East. Elizabeth told him to stop being a scaremonger. Henry began to look anxious when Simon spoke like this.

'Well, it makes sense, Henry, Nasser knows what he's at, and the French troops aren't all sitting in Cyprus for the good of their suntans are they?'

'But there's not going to be a war. I mean, they wouldn't – or if they did, we wouldn't – would we?'

'We need the Suez canal, it's as simple as that. Britain didn't stand by in 1939 and let people walk over Europe, it's not going to stand by now. Mark my words, everyone's ready for it. . . .'

'Oh I don't think. . . .' Henry looked so distressed that Elizabeth decided it was time to interrupt.

'No I don't think either, and I read the newspapers just as thoroughly as Simon. Neither of us has confidential chats with Anthony Eden, but nothing is going to happen. People are not ready for it. It's only ten years since there's been a war, nobody wants another one. Come off it Simon, just because you want to remain a gloriously free bachelor there's no need to start rumours of wars once any other bachelor is wise enough to go and get himself married. . . .'

'Were you always so sharp and witty, even when you were a little girl?' asked Simon, teasing.

'No,' said Elizabeth. 'No I was very mousy actually.'

'Oh, come on, we'd never believe that,' Simon said.

'I can't imagine you mousy, a beautiful blonde like you,' Henry said.

'Really I was so timid and shy. I was for ages, I got a bit less mousy at Kilgarret, I think. But it was only when Mother left home that I stopped being . . . so . . . well, so much part of the wallpaper.'

'I suppose we should all be pleased that she did leave home in a way,' said Simon.

Henry frowned, that might be going a bit too far. But Elizabeth didn't seem to think so.

'Yes, it's odd, I do think that more people benefited by Mother leaving home. Even Father. They wouldn't have become any happier, only more miserable had she stayed. I never thought that I would hear myself saying that, I cried so much when she left I thought my eyes would fall out of their sockets . . . my face ached with crying.'

'Oh Elizabeth, my poor Elizabeth,' Henry said, reaching for her hand. 'What a terrible thing to do to a child . . . poor Elizabeth.'

Simon looked upset too.

Elizabeth wondered what she had said that sounded so sad. It had all been true.

Ethel Murray had sent a hundred pounds to the priest in Waterford in order that his good work could be continued. She thanked him warmly and said that her son's cure had been miraculous. To her great annoyance the priest had sent back the hundred pounds. 'It's very kind of you and I know you meant well,' he had said in his letter, 'but I would prefer you to give this money to some charity in your own town. I didn't cure your son, your son isn't cured any more than I am, he has only agreed to stop drinking if he can. Please realise that if he does go back to drink again it's not because he is an evil man or uncaring, it is because the lure of it is too strong to resist. I am afraid every day when I wake up that I may be drunk by night time.'

Mrs Murray was very piqued; she showed the letter to Aisling. 'He'd have done better to have kept it, I suppose, and just sent you a thank you note. He's being too honest.'

'But he's being far too pessimistic. Tony's marvellous — he's totally cured now. It's a miracle. I'm not afraid to say to you Aisling that I thought one time that he was really dependent on the bottle.'

'Well, he was,' Aisling said, surprised that Mrs Murray seemed to think that it could have been otherwise.

'Oh no dear, he was not. Doesn't the fact that he hasn't touched a drop for over six months prove that he couldn't have been dependent on it?' She smiled triumphantly.

Mam had been pleased when Tony gave up drinking; pleased but not surprised.

'I always told you that you were exaggerating your problems, child. Now that he has a nice clean house and a civilised wife to come back to, isn't he grand?'

'I don't think it had to do with the nice clean house, Mam, though I am grateful to you for all your help that day.'

'I was doing it for myself, not for you. Do you think I wanted Ethel Murray going around the town saying I'd reared a tinker?'

'He's not looking forward to the wedding at all, he's said, oh, a whole lot of times, that it's nonsensical going to a wedding when you can't drink. . . .'

'Well, can't you go on your own . . . ?'

'I could and in many ways I'd prefer to, but you know that priest said I shouldn't let Tony slip out of normal life. There wasn't any help for him in just turning into a hermit.'

'And he'll enjoy it when he gets there.' Mam sounded hopeful.

'He doesn't enjoy anything much, he sits there, you know, and he's not a reader, Mam, he wouldn't sit in a room peaceably and read like you and I would do, he doesn't even read the paper with energy the way Dad does. He sits there looking in front of him.'

'Well, I suppose you talk to him, presumably you don't sit in silence.' Eileen sounded a little anxious.

'Oh I talk, it seems a bit empty though, he's thinking of Shay and the lads and the laughs. There's no centre to his days now.'

'With the help of the Lord when you have children that will all change. If you knew what it does to a man – your father, now, when Sean was born, I remember it well back in 1923 – he was like an eejit running round with him in his arms and playing games. He'd got a bit used to it when you came along and the others but he was thrilled with the lot of you. Tony will be just the same.'

'Mam, I've tried to talk to you about this, but you always change the subject. There won't be any children.'

'Now, you are not to say that, Mrs Moriarty was ten years married before she. . . .'

'I could be married a hundred and ten years. Mam. . . .'

'I tell you . . . you don't *know* . . . now you'll say I'm just being a Holy Mary about all this, but the Lord does take an interest in every single one of us . . . and He knows when the time is right. Look now at the way Tony doesn't drink any more, it could be that the Lord was waiting until all that had been sorted out. . . .'

'Mam, I beg of you, don't talk to me about what the Lord is waiting for or not waiting for, what I am waiting for is to have a normal sexual life with Tony. We don't have one.'

'Dear, dear, dear, now what is a normal sexual life, as you call it? There's far too much written in books and magazines nowadays, it's only making people uneasy . . . is mine normal, is hers normal? What's normal in the name of the Lord?'

'I suppose having sexual intercourse is normal, Mam?'

'Yes, well, that's what we're talking about.'

'Not in my case we're not.'

'Well, maybe all this drink and giving it up took a greater toll.'

'Not ever, Mam, not once, not once since we got married.'

'Ah no, no Aisling, you're not telling me that?'

'Yes, very simply that's it.'

'But why ever not . . . what . . . ?'

439

Aisling said nothing.

'I don't know what to say.' Mam stopped.

'Nobody does.'

'You haven't been discussing it with people, surely?'

'No, I mean Tony won't talk about it, I don't know what to do. I did write once, oh ages ago, and told Elizabeth about it, but she didn't refer to it again, except to say it would probably work out all right.'

'And it will.' Eileen grabbed at this slender thread. 'She's quite right, it will. You're a sensible girl, and you won't be the type to take this . . . well, take it wrong, you know.'

'Were you going to say I'm not the type to take this lying down?' Aisling laughed mischievously.

'I was, as a matter of fact,' Eileen said and they both laughed for a moment.

It was the moment that Dad came into the kitchen. 'Well, that's cheerful. Will you share it with me? I need a laugh after dealing with that thick brother of yours.'

'Dad if I told you what we were laughing about you'd drop down dead on the floor, so I won't,' said Aisling. 'Listen, I'm off home, Mam can I take that cake of soda bread for our tea?'

'You cannot. Make your own.'

'Oh Mam.'

'Take a quarter of it. Easy now, that's a big quarter.'

'Oh, there's nothing as hungry as a man that's given up the drink.'

'Go *home*, Aisling.'

'All *right*, Mam. I'm going.'

Aisling sat between them on the plane. Every pocket of air, every little lurch seemed to go through her like an electric wire. She had Donal trembling on one side and Tony shaking on the other.

'Nothing to worry about,' said the air hostess. 'Just a little turbulence. Captain says it will only last for a few minutes.'

'Yes,' said Tony, 'but will we last for the few minutes?'

The air hostess smiled. 'Of course we will. Can I get you anything, a drink?'

'No thank you,' said Aisling.

'Yes, can you get me a large Power's?' said Tony.

'Tony, no please . . .' she began, but the air hostess had gone.

'Just for the journey, God Almighty what kind of gaoler are you? Just to steady my nerves until we're on the ground.'

'Please, Tony, anything, an aspirin, I've got a sleeping pill, you have that, and a cup of tea, please. . . .'

'Oh shut up, Ash, shut up for God's sake. . . .'

The hostess had brought a little tray with the miniature bottle on it and a glass of water; she smiled at the three of them.

'Only one of you having a drink? Nothing for the rest of you?'

'Please take it away, please,' Aisling said to her. 'My husband isn't well, he's not supposed to drink.'

The girl looked bewildered, she looked from the man to his wife and back again, not knowing what to do. She looked at Donal for some kind of middle road. Donal was embarrassed. He knew that Tony didn't drink these days and he had heard tales of his drinking in the past. But really, Aisling was behaving disgracefully in public. Imagine saying that Tony couldn't have a drink.

'Aisling,' he hissed, 'stop making a scene, for heaven's sake — let Tony have a drink, one isn't going to kill him.'

Tony had his hand out; he took the drink and paid for it. Aisling said nothing. She didn't speak at all to either of them for the rest of the journey, not even when Tony pressed his little bell and asked for the same again.

As they came through the customs at Heathrow, Donal said sadly, 'Are you going to keep this up the whole time, Aisling? It's going to spoil the visit for all of us.'

'Too right,' said Tony.

'It's my first time abroad, please Aisling, get back into a good humour otherwise it'll all be desperate.'

Aisling's eyes filled with tears. 'I am a selfish cow. You're quite right. Tony I'm sorry I made a scene on the plane. I really am.'

Tony was surprised.

'No, you're both right. I behaved badly. You said you only wanted a drink because of flying and I had to be so rigid I said no. I'm very sorry. It's over now, is it?'

'Yes, well of course,' Tony said.

Donal relaxed. 'I'll say one thing about the pair of you, when you have a row you make it up handsomely.'

Aisling gave Tony a peck on the cheek. 'Now that's to prove it's over.' She picked up a case purposefully. 'Now, which way to the bus? We've got to show Donal O'Connor London.'

Tony and Donal followed after her as she walked with her little case in one hand and over the other arm, wrapped in cellophane paper, her wedding outfit, the wild silk dress and coat in the striking lilac colour that everyone in the shop in Grafton Street said was sensational. Please God may he not have another. Lord if you *are* looking after us, as Mam seems to think, will you look after us very carefully just at the moment? I have the feeling that we need a lot of attention.

The papers were full of Suez, much more so than at home. Donal said they seemed to be taking it very seriously. 'Do you think they will send a force out there?' he asked Tony.

'Who?' said Tony.

'The English, the British?'

'Out where?' said Tony.

Oh God, thought Aisling, oh God. I know this, I know this path, I've been down it before.

People stared as they ran across the room to embrace each other. The girl with the glorious red hair and the green dress had leapt up from the table where she was sitting; she and the pale, blonde girl in a kilt and a black polo neck jumper, who had left the man she was with, held each other away for a moment and looked with delight, then hugged again.

Only then did they remember the introductions. 'Aisling this is the man, this is the lucky fellow, Henry Mason.' He was tall and fair; he wore a very formal, dark grey suit, a nice sober tie, a nervous look in his eyes and a big smile waiting to break out.

'Henry!' Aisling said. 'You're beautiful. You're quite perfect, I'm delighted with you.'

Henry's smile did come out and it was a happy one. He seemed quite oblivious of all the people watching them and laughing at Aisling's over-effusive Irish greeting.

'And Tony . . . ?' he said courteously, looking at the man standing behind Aisling.

'Oh Tony had to go off somewhere, this is my brother Donal. Donal, salute Henry like a Christian now, before you wrap yourself around your beloved Elizabeth.'

'How do you do, and may I offer you my warmest congratulations,' Donal said shaking Henry's hand, then, as Aisling had encouraged him, he did throw his arms around Elizabeth.

'I'm so glad to see you, I'm so glad to see you. And if you wouldn't wait to marry me, well I'm glad you're marrying Henry.' It was very touching and bound them all together for an instant.

Then Henry asked, 'Will Tony be back or shall we go ahead and order a drink?'

'Oh let's go ahead,' Aisling said lightly. 'Tony Murray's movements are very difficult to plot.'

Henry busied himself with a waiter and when he had ordered the drinks Donal asked him what he thought was going to happen in the Near East. 'Well, I think we should stay a million miles away from it all myself,' he began.

Elizabeth and Aisling sighed with happiness. They were free to talk, for hours if they needed.

'You must tell me what's expected of me at this pagan ceremony tomorrow. Do I have to deny God or anything?'

'Aisling, where's Tony?'

'On the piss, I don't know where. Forget it, forget him. Tell me what I have to do, do I have to answer responses? Imagine me as a witness at an atheist wedding!'

'Aisling, do stop calling it pagan and atheist, everyone there thinks they're Christians of a sort . . . but look, about Tony, do you think we should . . . ?'

'I'll tell you this about Tony, if we can drop the subject afterwards. When we checked in here around five o'clock he said he had to go out and do a bit of business. There *is* no business – we both know that. So I said, can you just take ten pounds with you, so if you decide to spend everything then only ten pounds goes. . . .'

'And what did he say?' Elizabeth was horrified.

'He said I was mean-minded, low and suspicious and that I never gave anyone a chance, I always believed the worst of him and never the best. He deliberately took all his money and gave it to me except what he said was a tenner, but I could see was two tenners. Then he bowed and said, "Permission to leave, Major?" to me, and went out. That was just after five and it's eight now. No word, no message. There won't be. At best he'll come home after closing time, maggoty drunk; at worst tomorrow morning maggoty drunk. But I'll have him in shape for your nuptials. Now, please can we leave him and talk about tomorrow? Who's going to be there?'

Elizabeth looked at Henry who was eagerly explaining why he was a Labour voter, and why Gaitskell was right and Eden was wrong. 'But you're a professional man, I thought you'd be a Conservative?' Donal was saying. Elizabeth smiled affectionately at them. 'Right, I'll make a list. . . .'

There wasn't nearly enough time, not nearly, but it did seem sensible that Elizabeth should go home and get some sleep.

'Tell Tony I'm sorry we missed him, but we look forward to seeing him tomorrow,' said Henry courteously.

'Yes indeed.' They waved goodbye from the foyer.

'Let's go to Soho, and I'll point out dens of iniquity to you,' Aisling suggested.

'But aren't you tired?'

'I wouldn't sleep anyway.'

'Suppose Tony comes back.'

'Let him come back.'

They wandered around in the bright lights and the cosmopolitan crowds and the young men standing at the top of stairways that led down to strip shows. There were book-shops open late and at the back they had sections which had filthy books.

444

'How do you know all this?' Donal's eyes were out on sticks.

'Years ago, years and years – I was much younger than you – I came down here with Elizabeth and her boyfriend that time, Johnny. Johnny told us all these things, we couldn't believe him. But it's all true.'

'What happened to Johnny?'

'He's still a friend, you'll meet him tomorrow.'

Tony came in at one a.m. and the porter helped him to his room.

'I'm afraid there's a pound owing on the taxi,' he said apologetically.

'Thank you so much.' Aisling was icy calm. 'Can you give him twenty-five shillings, and can I ask you to have ten shillings please for a couple of drinks yourself tomorrow? Thank you very much for helping my husband home.'

'Thank you, lady.' The porter was pleased there had been no embarrassing scene. 'I'll give you a hand getting him on the bed if you like.'

Aisling accepted this willingly, and she took off one of Tony's shoes while the porter removed the other.

'Should we try to get him undressed?' he asked doubtfully.

'No, I have his good suit hanging up. You are kind.'

'You're a great little trooper lady,' said the porter.

Aisling got up early on the morning of Elizabeth's wedding. She went to the chemist and bought mouthwash, a bottle of eye lotion, some witch hazel and cotton wool. She ordered a pot of black coffee to be sent up to their room and then from the foyer she rang Elizabeth to wish her luck. She went up to the room and arrived at the same time as the coffee. She took it from the waiter before he could see the spectacle of a man in bed with a suit jacket, shirt and tie still on him. She ran the bath with lukewarm water and wearily pulled back the clothes on the bed.

'Up,' she said crisply.

'What? What?'

'Up. You can get as pissed as you like after the wedding, I

445

don't give a damn, but for the wedding you will look right. Up.'

Tony tried to move. His head hurt him and he swallowed hard. 'How did . . . what happened?'

'You went out at five o'clock to do some business, the business took somewhat longer than you thought. It also seemed to cost you twenty pounds plus a pound for a taxi from Kilburn, which is where the business seemed to end up.' She was moving his feet, still in their socks, towards the floor.

'Ash, will you stop, let me rest.'

'No, I will not. Get up now and walk towards the bathroom, then start peeling off your clothes one by one and throwing them to me.'

He did it, like a slowly moving clockwork toy. When he was naked she handed him the first cup of coffee and kept them coming even though he gagged and said he could drink no more. She sat on the bathroom chair while he made feeble attempts to wash himself then she put a towel behind his head and told him to lean back.

'What're you going to do?' he asked fearfully.

'I'm going to mend your eyes,' she said. As he lay almost drifting off to sleep, she dabbed and soothed and patted his eyes, she soaked the cotton wool in cold water and, after half an hour, the swelling and blotchiness had improved greatly.

'Ash, I feel dreadful,' he said pathetically. 'It's just going to be this weekend, when we get back home again I swear I. . . . Just let me have a couple to get me on target again?'

'As many as you like. After the wedding. . . .' She handed him his clothes, garment by garment, and with a hotel clothes brush she dusted his shoulders.

'You're a fine-looking man, that's the pity of it.'

'Ash, stop horsing about, get dressed yourself. . . .'

'I'm not horsing about, I'm saying the truth, you are handsome and now that you've lost all that weight you look very well. Very well indeed. Can't you take a compliment?'

'I feel dreadful, I'm not in the mood for play-acting.'

'Isn't that funny, neither am I? Now you still stink of

446

drink – I don't know why, God knows you should have washed it out of you. Drink this.'

'For God's sake. . . .'

'Now.' She went into the bathroom to wash and she heard him frantically trying to open the bedroom door.

'Shit, the door's stuck,' she heard him say.

'No, Tony dearest, it's not stuck, I locked it,' she said from the bathroom as she shook on some expensive talcum powder. She had bought it at the chemist at the same time as all the medicaments; it had made the trip less depressing.

In the taxi on the way to the wedding Donal found them curiously relaxed. If he had been Aisling he would have been very cross indeed that Tony had disappeared last night. Aisling was very peculiar in some ways, here she was laughing in a very friendly way.

'So that's the bargain. Three drinks of your choice at the reception, and when we've waved them goodbye then you're on your own . . . you get miles away from the wedding party and do as you like, for as long as you like.'

'Why am I being sent away from the wedding party? That's a bit high-handed.'

'No, it's the bargain, you can drink yourself into a pig's mess like you did last night, you can slobber and pee in your trousers, as you also did last night, I noticed, but not with Elizabeth's friends, you don't.'

'Jesus Christ, what a boss.'

'Good, now that's settled. Donal, we're nearly there, that's Westminster . . . we'll come back here and see it when we've time tomorrow maybe, or Monday. Do you see Big Ben, now we know we must get the right time. It's a quarter to eleven, perfect timing.'

They got out at Caxton Hall, where the sightseers who came to look at weddings brightened up when they saw Aisling's fiery hair, her lilac outfit and her lilac and white hat. It looked like something glamorous.

'Is it a film star's wedding?' a woman said, pulling at Aisling's sleeve.

'No, I'm afraid not, it's a solicitor and an art teacher.' The woman was disappointed. 'But it will be full of glamour, stay around,' she said.

'I will,' said the woman, pleased.

Father looked very smart, he was wearing the buttonhole that Henry had brought the night before.

'Are you sure there won't be any call for me to make a speech?' he asked.

'None, Father, I told you over and over. Simon will make a speech, and that's it. Henry may say a few words, thank you for giving me to him, and for the reception.'

'Well, that's not right, I mean you paid for the reception. . . .'

'Yes, Father, but that's not the point. Anyway, you gave me board and lodging here, and educated me and everything, so in a way any money I saved came because of you and that's you paying for it indirectly, isn't it?'

'I suppose that's right.' Father was doubtful.

'Of course it's right.' She straightened his tie. 'How do I look Father, do you think I'll do?'

He stood away from her and looked her up and down approvingly. 'Oh yes, my dear, you look . . .' He paused. Would he say she looked lovely, or beautiful, or neat? What kind of things had he said to Mother when she was all dressed up? 'You look very . . . *presentable*,' and he gave a little laugh to show that the word was a little joke.

She looked around the hall of Clarence Gardens and in the small mirror caught sight of herself in the cream wool dress and jacket, with the big orchid pinned to the lapel. She pulled the brim of her hat forward and fixed four hairpins in the ends of her hair so that they were guarded against the wind; the hair was meant to flick out not run wild, so she sprayed on a little lacquer. She would take them out when the car stopped at Caxton Hall. Henry was meeting her there with Simon. They had decided to go separately, to make it more formal in a way. And she wanted to have this last journey with Father so that he would realise that he was still special. He had been very silent about Harry coming to the wedding, so travelling to the ceremony with him alone might be some kind of gesture. Elizabeth gave herself a final check and had a last look at the house. In twenty years she had put very little of her own personality into it. It had always been Father's house. She hoped that the flat in Battersea would be different. Already she and Henry had found furniture and rugs and knick-knacks. All her clothes were there in the old-fashioned wardrobe they had bought, and Henry had moved his things in too. He left his own flat officially today.

Superstitiously they decided not to spend a night there until they were married. It would make it more significant they agreed, and laughed at themselves and each other for their silliness.

In under an hour she would be Mrs Henry Mason. Did every woman who got married go through this sort of unreality bit just at the last moment? She thought of Henry's face eager and expectant, and she smiled happily. After all the lonely times in this house, after all the upsets and uncertainties she was finally being rewarded. She was going to marry a man who was goodness itself. That was a phrase Aunt Eileen had used about people who were very kind. What a pity she hadn't been able to come, and she had forgotten to ask what was actually wrong with her. They had had too many other things to talk about. Aisling was so strong about everything; most women would collapse if their husband had disappeared on the rampage in some strange city. But Aisling took everything in her stride.

'My dear, I think we should . . . the taxi has been here for five minutes.' Father hated waste even though Henry had paid for the taxi.

'Right, come on, let's go and get me married and off your hands.'

'You were never any trouble to us. Your mother and I had no problems with you. Ever.' He said it with his back to her as he was double locking the door. Possibly the only compliment he had ever given her. She couldn't answer him because she was afraid she might start to cry, and anyway the people across the road, the rather prim and proper Kentons, were waving like anything. They had come out to see her go, and other neighbours had too. Elizabeth waved to them all, delighted, and Father smiled as they got into the taxi and went off to get her married.

It was much nicer and much more like a real wedding than Aisling had expected. The nuns had said that registry office weddings were mere formalities at the desk of a clerk or a lawyer – they had only been invented because British people had turned away from all religion, even their own. But this was very impressive, and the registrar was almost as good as a priest when he was asking them did they take each other for lawful wedded husband and wife. Aisling had thought that it was all a matter of mumbling and writings things down in a book.

Simon, the handsome best man, was utterly charming. In a different way to Johnny, he was flowery in his speech, he paid extravagant compliments and told her that her loveliness had not been conveyed in any adequate manner, although to be fair, attempts had been made. Aisling thought this was great fun.

'You're the smooth elegant colleague,' she said triumphantly. 'Have you met my husband, Tony Murray?'

'I wish that you had met Tony Murray long after you had met me,' he said over-gallantly, bowing and shaking hands with Tony who looked very pale and not at all able to cope with such flamboyance at this time of the morning.

The ceremony passed in a flash and as they came out, and Stefan and Harry and Johnny organised the confetti, there was another wedding party waiting to go in.

Henry was smiling so broadly that it looked as if his face would break. Donal was busy taking photographs. Elizabeth looked so lovely, Aisling was amazed. She had always thought that Elizabeth was gentle and pale and blonde and pretty in a pastel way, but today she looked different; even though her outfit was pale she looked colourful. Her face was strong, her lipstick was bright, her orchid was dark purple, her hair looked bouncy, not wispy, her eyes were sparkling. Thank God she's having a nice day, thank God, after all the awful things that happened to her, Aisling felt. Who would ever have expected a day like this, with her stepfather cheering as well as her father, and Johnny Stone apparently delighted for her too? If anyone deserved a great wedding day it was Elizabeth.

Mrs Noble was waiting for them, a high-necked blouse, a cameo brooch; she almost made herself the unofficial hostess. In one minute she had decided that Harry and Johnny were her best allies and singled them out whenever anything needed to be done.

'Mr Elton, might I ask you to move that little group near the door down here towards the main body of the room, they seem to be a little left out. . . .'

And Harry was off like a terrier dog. 'Hallo. Might I introduce myself? I'm Harry Elton, on the bride's side. . . .'

Jean and Derek were shy at gatherings and were delighted with Harry; he introduced them to Stefan and Anna and only when a conversation about old folding draught screens seemed under way did he leave them.

Mrs Noble was vigilant. 'Mr Stone, can I suggest that you direct the waitress with the wine over there towards the rather sad-looking man?'

'That's the father of the bride, you couldn't cheer him up,' Johnny said.

'Oh dear, I see.' Mrs Noble felt she might have said the wrong thing.

'He's a widower, Mrs Noble. Now if you were un-attached I'd say you might be able to cheer him up!' Johnny winked at her. Mrs Noble was delighted.

'You are dreadful, Mr Stone,' she said, patting her hair.

Johnny got the message though. Elizabeth's father did look like a wet week. Johnny went over to him and refilled his glass.

'Elizabeth looks lovely,' Johnny said.

'Yes, yes.'

'Very nice, this reception, very generous of you, Mr White.'

'Yes, well, indirectly, only indirectly.'

In desperation Johnny looked for someone to rope in. Tony Murray was nearby. Johnny filled his glass. He was a handsome fellow, this husband of Aisling's. 'Have you met Aisling O'Connor's husband, Mr White?' They had, and obviously hadn't found much to talk about then either. Johnny battled on, and filled Tony Murray's glass again. With relief he saw that Mrs Noble was organising the food on the tables at the end of the room and he was able to direct them both towards it. Tony Murray said he had to slip downstairs to make a phone call. Fine-looking fellow, but a bit restless, Johnny thought.

Aisling had taken down Harry's address and promised to visit him in Preston. She was stunned to find herself laughing so heartily with the terrible Mr Elton who had come to take Elizabeth's mother away. After a while she even felt bold enough to tell him that.

'I know.' Harry was solemn for a moment. 'I think Elizabeth sometimes feels the same. She's such a good friend to me, but I think she stops now and then and puzzles over it all.'

'No, she always talks of you with great love,' Aisling said.

'Does she now? That's good to know, she's a great lass, I think of her as my own daughter. She always loved being over in your place too, mind. She said it was the best time of her life.'

'We are being polite to each other.' Aisling looked around for Tony; she couldn't see him, but he must be in that group which was moving to the food. 'Elizabeth's very happy today, she's delighted with Henry and the whole thing. . . .'

'Yes.' Harry nodded, but his earlier enthusiasm didn't seem so marked now. 'Yes, I hope she made the right choice, she says she has, she says she has. I always thought she'd marry Johnny Stone.'

'Yes, well they both took long enough to consider that one, and it didn't work out at marrying each other did it?'

Harry laughed. Aisling was a great girl, he thought, a corker to look at too. 'Yes, but you see Elizabeth's her mother's daughter, there's a flash of Violet in her all the time. I hope this fellow will be enough for her.'

'Well, if he's not, let's hope that history won't repeat itself, and we won't see another wicked Mr Elton coming to carry her off in the future.' They moved towards the table and Aisling saw that Donal was having an animated chat with an attractive blonde, and she noticed with some relief that Tony had come in the door; he must have been to the toilet. He looked a bit better now, less pale and sickly.

Mrs Noble could whisper without even appearing to move her mouth. 'Mr Elton, do you think we should discourage the waitress from passing any more wine to that rather stocky, well-built man near the door? An Irishman I think.'

'Thank you,' said Harry, 'I'll see she passes him no more.'

A little later: 'Mr Stone, just before the speeches begin can I call your attention to that dark-haired Irishman? Over there.'

'The Squire,' Johnny smiled.

'Well, I don't want to say anything to Miss White, or indeed Mrs Mason as she must be called now, but he does seem to have a half bottle of spirits in his hip pocket. It may be unimportant but I felt you should know.'

Johnny stood behind Tony Murray for a while. Twice he saw the wine glass which had contained white wine until Harry had motioned the waitress away being refilled from a half bottle of vodka which now only had a third of the contents left. He did it very cleverly, with one hand, glass on the table, bottle out, cap off, filling down and bottle replaced in a moment; all the while Tony was looking innocently ahead of him, and with his other hand he was taking little puffs from his cigarette and waving across the room – but there was nobody returning his wave.

Simon was courteous, wordy, flowery, and urbane. Those were the words that Aisling thought she would have used to describe him. He didn't say anything real about either Elizabeth or Henry, it was all little witticisms but people liked them – and indeed he said them very well.

The cake was cut, the champagne was produced, and toasts were drunk.

'Are you going to make a speech?' Aisling asked Elizabeth's Father.

'Oh heavens no, no, she promised, she said I didn't have to.' He looked worried.

'Go on out of that, she'd love you to say a few words . . . just a word or two, it would mean a lot.'

'I don't think . . .' He looked flustered.

'Tell them she was a smashing daughter, and she'll be a good wife and you're glad that everyone is here enjoying themselves and it's a happy occasion.'

'Is that all I'd have to say?'

'Certainly that's all. Go on now, slay them, knock them sideways.'

Father cleared his throat. Elizabeth looked up, startled. It had all been going so well, Father wasn't going to do anything absurd like saying it was over now? There were still five more bottles of champagne to be passed around.

'I'd like to tell you all that I am not a good speaker, but I cannot let the moment pass without expressing my gratitude to you all for coming, my hope that you are enjoying the reception. . . .' A lot of hear-hears at this. 'And I would mainly like to say that I am very happy that my daughter, Elizabeth, is marrying such a splendid man as Henry Mason, I am sure he will make her very happy and I can tell him that if she is as good a wife as she has been a daughter, he will be a lucky man. Thank you very much.' It was so simple and unflowery, after all Simon's complicated and convoluted phrases, that it touched everyone. Glasses were raised again to the bride and Elizabeth had to concentrate very hard on the table cloth to stop the tears coming into her eyes. Fancy poor Father steeling himself to do that, he must have been practising it all the time. Who would ever have thought Father could have thought of just the right thing to say?

Harry had asked Mrs Noble if they could use the piano. She was most enthusiastic, so before Elizabeth was even aware that Harry was on the piano stool he had struck up, 'For They Are Jolly Good Fellows', and everyone in the room including Father was joining in. Harry was in his element, he got them singing 'On Ilkley Moor Baht 'at', and to the cries of more, he had 'My Old Man Said Follow The Van'.

He played 'It's A Long Way To Tipperary', specially for

the contingent from Ireland, and then that turned into 'Pack up Your Troubles In Your Old Kit Bag'.

'Another Irish song,' Stefan called. 'The Irish have the best songs.'

'I'll sing one,' Tony said.

'Oh my God.' Aisling turned round to see who could come to her aid. She saw Johnny not far away. 'He doesn't sing, stop him,' she said desperately.

Tony said, 'Do you know Kevin Barry?'

'No,' said Harry good-naturedly. 'But you start and I'll pick it up.'

'In Mount Joy gaol one Monday morning,
High above the gallows tree
Kevin Barry gave his young life
For the cause of Liberty. . . .'

'Please Johnny,' Aisling begged.

'Hey what about some song we all know?' Johnny called out.

'No, let me finish,' Tony said.

'Let him finish,' Simon said. 'Can't cut a man off midsong.'

'Just before he faced the hangman
In his lonely prison cell.
British soldiers tortured Kevin
Just because he would not tell. . .
The names of those . . .
The names of those . . .'

Tony looked around irritated. 'What comes next? Come on, someone must know?' Everyone looked blank.

'The names of those . . .
His something comrades . . .
And other things they wished to know . . .
Tell us now or we will kill you . . .
Barry proudly answered no.

455

'Ash you know the words, come on, you can hold the tune, join in.'

Aisling spoke clearly across the room. 'I can't remember them, I think you've skipped a verse, but, honestly, it's not a song for a wedding. Hangmen, prison cells, can't you sing something more cheerful and we'll all join in . . . ?'

'It's important that we finish it,' Tony said doggedly. 'There's another verse:

'Kevin Barry you must leave us,
On the gallows you must die,
Wept his broken-hearted mother
As she kissed her son goodbye. . . .'

Harry did a loud crescendo at that point, by way of ending, Johnny started to clap; so did a couple of others and then everyone joined in.

Tony was very obviously not finished, but Harry had a louder voice. 'Right, we've had Ireland's turn . . . anyone from Wales . . . ? Come on, there must be someone from a Welsh choir . . . ? Or Scotland . . . ?' With the heaviest chords he introduced 'I belong to Glasgow', and Mrs Noble made sure that the remaining champagne was being poured among the guests.

Aisling said to Donal, 'Get him out, Johnny Stone will help you.'

'Aisling, I don't know. . . .'

'Right out of the room. If you want to do something to help I want him right out of here.' She saw Donal talking to Johnny and Johnny walking over to Tony. Tony was pointing back at the piano; Johnny was making a sign with his hand of a person who had a glass in his hand – he was asking Tony out for a drink. Tony gesticulated towards the bottle of champagne which he could see circulating. Johnny was shaking his head. He was indicating the stairs. Mrs Noble was with them. Whatever they were saying Tony was going like a lamb.

Harry in his role as compère was saying that as the humble pianist he had been informed that the bride and groom would leave shortly so could everyone join in a chorus of 'My Dear Old Dutch'? He had his arm tightly around Elizabeth's shoulder and she was smiling at him, Stefan was patting Anna on the hand, and everyone was joining in because Harry had a way of roaming around and catching your eye if you didn't sing.

Donal put his arm into Aisling's, and they sang together as Harry swept them back to the beginning of the song again.

'We've been together now for forty years
And it don't seem a day too much. . . .'

Aisling looked at the door; Mrs Noble and Johnny were standing there singing too. There was no sign of Tony. The goodbyes were being shouted. Elizabeth came over and held on to Aisling.

'Bless you for coming. It wouldn't have been a wedding without you.'

Aisling said, 'I remember saying the same thing to you in Kilgarret. Oh, Elizabeth I'm sorry, I'm so sorry.'

'What about?' Elizabeth's clear expression meant she didn't know what Aisling was apologising for.

'Tony. I'm so sorry, I don't know how he got that drunk, I watched him like a hawk. I'm so sorry he stood up like that and disgraced himself and us. . . .'

'Goodbye, Aisling,' Henry interrupted. 'Goodbye, thank you so much for being our bridesmaid, witness. You are good to have come all this way.'

'Thank you Henry.' Aisling fingered the little brooch with the pearl in it that Henry had given her. 'It's beautiful, I'll never forget the day.'

'Oh and say goodbye to Tony for me. I can't see him,' Henry said.

'I spend my time saying goodbye to Tony for people, I think I should say goodbye to him myself. . . .'

They all went downstairs in a happy troop, and clustered around the car. Elizabeth pecked at Father's cheek; she had given Harry a hug on the stairs. She was kissed by everyone and when Johnny kissed her very tenderly he said, 'You're the loveliest lady I ever met, I always said it and I always meant it. Be very very happy.'

Mrs Noble saw Tony and two men coming out of the bar where she had directed him, he had an arm around each of them. She blocked him from view by pretending great surprise. 'Hallo, Mr Murray. Fancy seeing you here,' she said, while she could hear the taxi revving up.

'How do you know who I am?' Tony growled suspiciously; he felt he was being prevented from doing something he wanted to do, but wasn't sure what it was.

The two men who were being dragged with him said, 'Come on back in the pub mate, they close soon.'

'Yes, we'll all be in then, everyone's coming in, in a moment,' Mrs Noble said.

'Great,' said Tony, and re-entered just as the final cheer saw the taxi off. The crowd were dispersing on the pavement.

Mrs Noble drew Aisling aside. 'I thought I'd mention that he is in that establishment across the road Madam, if you wanted to know.'

'You're a brick,' said Aisling, 'I don't want to know. I'm going to take my brother off to the pictures. But thank you for telling me, and thank you for getting him there.'

'Not at all – a very high-spirited man, your husband.'

'Very,' said Aisling. 'Listen, what will you do when the pub closes if he tries to get back into your place?'

'I'll tell him the crowd moved on, I'll point him off towards . . . where would you like him to head . . . ?'

'I'd say the River Thames but that would sound a bit strong. Anywhere at all, he knows the hotel we're staying at so he'll end up there.'

'Poor Aisling, this must be so awful for you, and the last time you saw Elizabeth was your own wedding,' said Donal as they set off.

'That's right.'

'It must be sad for you . . . you know your wedding day turning out so great and now this so awful. . . .'

'Actually, Donal, my own wedding day turned out pretty awful for me too, but that's a long story and let's not tell it now.' She smiled at him and slowly his white, anxious face broke into a sort of a smile too, and they went off to buy an evening paper and see what film they would go to.

458

XVII

Donal told everyone that the very same day they came home from London on the plane the British started their war, they went off to Suez.

'It wasn't a real war, stop going on as if you were out in the front line,' Eamonn said. 'Sorry Mam,' he added suddenly when he saw Eileen's face.

'I wonder, when I'm dead and gone, will any of you remember you had an elder brother?' Eileen said.

'Oh Mam, of course we will.'

'Go on about the wedding.' Niamh was home for the weekend; she felt slighted that Elizabeth had not invited her, but Elizabeth was awfully stuffy and English in some ways. Fancy thinking that it might interfere with her studies.

'I've told you everything, it was like a service only no altars, no music and he wasn't a priest. And it was all in English of course, like Protestants anyway.'

'No, the bit after.'

Eileen sighed. 'Donal, show her the photographs. He took lovely pictures, and they got them developed for cost in the chemist. He's going to send copies to Elizabeth like she did at Aisling's wedding.'

'Janey, isn't her father a small little man,' remarked Niamh.

'That's not her father, that's Harry.'

'The husband?' screamed Niamh, in disbelief.

'No, her step-father.'

'God, it must have been very awkward having both of them there. Were there any scenes?'

Donal paused for a moment. 'No,' he said. 'There were no scenes.'

*

459

Aisling called on Mrs Murray a week after their return. 'Mother-in-Law, I think you'd better get in touch with that priest in Waterford again, sonny boy has broken out.'

'I wish you wouldn't speak in that flippant way, Aisling. We know it's not Tony's fault, the priest wrote it down in a letter. Try to be less . . . well, less joky about it.'

'I think joky is the only way to be about it. What should I do – sit down and weep over it?'

'No my dear, but if you tried to talk to him. . . .'

'I have tried, I try morning noon and night. I went down to Shay Ferguson and I said to him that Tony would actually prefer to be off the drink, and perhaps he could help him by not encouraging him. He laughed and said that Tony liked his pint and his jar like any other man, and wasn't it a pity that he was so hen-pecked. . . .'

Mrs Murray sighed. 'Oh my dear, I don't know what to do, I really don't. Will you stay and have some lunch with me . . . ?'

'No thanks, I'm on my way back to the shop. I only just ran up to you so that you'd know from me before anyone else. He's only been in to work twice, and that's just to get cash. Old Mother Meade is like a wet hen he's so upset.'

'Oh yes. Well, thank you Aisling, thank you. We'll just have to hope it passes over. Is it as bad as . . . before . . . ?'

'Worse, Mother-in-Law. Worse. When I gave him his dinner yesterday he threw one plate on the floor and the other plate at me. That's a new little refinement.'

'Oh Aisling, how can you talk about it like that?'

'Right, give me one other way of talking about it. Should I offer it up to the Holy Souls? Mrs M, the way I'm going I could get so many souls out of purgatory they'd have to close the place down. . . .'

Eileen announced that she was going to Dublin for a day or two. She had to do quite a few things and it seemed more sensible to stay the night, or even two nights. She had to get all the material for the curtains; no point in paying out that money unless you saw the actual stuff; she was getting a new winter coat, doing early shopping for Christmas, getting her hair cut in that good place where she went for Aisling's wedding.

Niamh asked her to stay. 'The flat isn't what you'd call posh Mam, or even tidy, but it's desperately handy for everything, you just have to walk along Baggot Street and Stephen's Green and you're in Grafton Street. . . .'

'No, no, thank you child. I won't settle in on top of you and your friends. I'll go to Gretta in Dunlaoghaire. It's nice to give her the turn.'

'Would you like me to come up to Dublin with you?' Aisling asked.

'What, and have the two of us away on the same day from the shop, are you off your head?' Eileen asked.

Aisling noticed that they were coming to the end of those nice efficient ledger books which she had installed in the shop. You could only buy them in Dublin in that stationer's in Nassau Street. Why wait and get them posted? Mam could easily put two of them in her suitcase. She decided to ring Gretta in Dunlaoghaire.

'Your Mam here? Not at all, never heard a word that she was coming. I wish she'd let me know. Do you think she'll be turning up tonight?' Gretta sounded fussed and bewildered.

Aisling thought fast. 'No, it's all my fault, I looked at the wrong date on the calendar – it was next week she was going to go up. I'm very sorry, Gretta.'

'Well I hope she'll let me know, I'm very full around Christmas.'

'Oh, I'm sure she will. I'm sorry for getting it wrong. Goodbye.'

Dad had said that Mam rang last night, she was settled into Gretta's and everything was fine; she'd stay an extra day and be home on Friday.

'Mam, you're going to have to ring Gretta and talk to her,' Aisling said when she was sure she had the office to herself.

'What on earth do you mean?'

'I rang her when you were meant to be staying with her, and I caused all kinds of confusion. You'll have to put her

461

straight, say you got it all confused and you'll be up after Christmas or something.'

Mam's face reddened. 'She said I wasn't there?'

'Where were you Mam, is everything all right?'

'Did you think I'd run off like poor Violet? Did you tell your father?'

'Mam, what do you take me for? If you'd rung from Dublin I'd have known you were safe; if you weren't with Gretta, well, there must have been a reason. Were you in hospital?'

'How did you know?'

'I couldn't think what else it might have been. Are you all right Mam?'

Eileen looked at her, smiling. 'I am thank God, I'm absolutely fine. I'm all clear, and as sound as a bell, that's what they said.'

'But why didn't you tell us, Mam, why didn't you let me go with you . . . ?'

'And leave the shop?'

'Oh, to hell with the shop, Mam, when you weren't well.'

'But I'm grand now, I promise you, there were cysts, and I was afraid, and Doctor Murphy wondered . . . and we thought the best thing was to be whipped in and out just like that.'

'But why didn't you say Mam, why drag yourself round getting coats and curtains . . . ?'

'I didn't spend much time, just an hour, I picked the first coat I saw, and the curtains are fine, I knew that anyway.' Eileen laughed at her own cleverness.

'But you can't do that, keeping things to yourself.'

'Yes I can, and I'm not even going to mention it to anyone now.'

'Even though you're fine.'

'No, because every time I go out of the room people will think I'm off secretly to a specialist. . . .'

'What did they do to you, Mam?'

'I had an examination under anaesthetic, you know probing around, and just two cysts, both benign, removed easily. . . .'

'Poor Mam, poor Mam.' Aisling was hardly able to speak, she was so distressed to think of Mam all by herself in that hospital.

'But I'm fine, isn't that good news?'

'Are you sure, Mam, are you sure you're not being brave about that too?'

'No, that's different. I wouldn't be brave about that. If I was told that my days were going to be cut short I'd have to make plans for everyone. But they told me I was the healthiest fifty-six-year-old they'd dealt with for a long time.'

'And you really are fine?'

'Yes, my love, and I feel that years are taken off me now that I know that. You're a very good girl not to raise a hue and cry about it all. If ever there was anything else, I would tell you. I mean it.'

'Well, if that's a promise?'

'It is. Now I'd better go and calm Gretta down before she has the whole country alerted.'

Brendan Daly told Maureen that he had seen Tony Murray driving that car of his when he was in no fit condition. Maureen said that she had heard something about it herself.

'Well you'd better say something about it to Aisling, hadn't you?'

'What good will it do? It isn't Aisling who's driving dangerously.'

'I know, but she should be told, in case something were to happen.'

'I suppose she knows already, but I'll tell her.'

'Right. Now I feel I've done my duty. I heard in the creamery that he nearly lifted two people off the bridge the other afternoon.'

'Oh God, isn't he a maniac, wouldn't you think with all that money he could get someone to take him home, or stay in the hotel if he's had a few too many . . . ?'

Mrs Moriarty said to Donal that poor Tony Murray had been looking a bit under the weather recently; was anything the matter with him?

'I don't think so, Mrs Moriarty,' Donal had said, his face as white as his coat. He hated any implied criticism of Aisling.

'I don't like poking my nose into other people's business,' she began.

'I know you don't.' Donal smiled at her. 'You're a grand woman, you're not like all the old gossips in this town. People's characters are safe with you.'

Mrs Moriarty felt slightly disappointed, but she thanked Donal for the compliment.

'Anyway, it would be much worse if he was chasing the women,' she said out of the blue, and went back into her little room behind the shop.

Mrs Murray said that she had been wondering what was best to do for Christmas.

'Cancel it,' Aisling had suggested.

'Not very helpful, dear.' Mrs Murray was worried too, it was not fair to torment her with slick remarks.

'What would you like us to do, Mother-in-Law?'

'What do you think is best?'

'Will we have Christmas dinner at your place? I'll come and help you cook it. It might be more cheerful up there than in the bungalow, with all your family around. . . .'

'I don't know who will be here, Father John is helping with a Christmas liturgy in. . . .'

'Wouldn't it be more Christian if he were to help with his own brother?'

'That's not the point, he won't be able to get away, two bishops and ten priests have been chosen, it's an honour.'

'All right, it's an honour. But we'll have Joannie, won't we?'

'I don't think so. I had a letter. I don't know where I put it, but she's not sure. She thinks that some of the girls in her flat. . . .'

'They're not girls, they're grown-up women, like Joannie, like me.'

'Yes, well, she calls them the girls, they were thinking of going to a house party they saw advertised in Scotland. . . .'

'Were they thinking that, by God? Isn't she a selfish cow?'

'Aisling please.'

'She is, Mrs Murray, a cow, a selfish cow. And what do that group of clowns want going to house parties for? Haven't they their own homes . . . ?'

'You're not going to change things by calling them names.' Mrs Murray looked hurt and upset.

Aisling agreed that she was right. 'All right, Mother-in-Law, it's you and me for Christmas. Let's try to make it a good day.'

'And Tony, of course. . . .' Tony's mother said.

'Oh, and Tony of course.'

Niamh looked very down at the mouth when she came back to Kilgarret for the Christmas holidays.

'It's Tim, this fellow, he's gone off with a really dreadful girl – she has nothing to recommend her, Aisling, she's a real Holy Joe, and she wears awful, long, straggly knitted cardigans.'

'Oh yes. Well do you think he's serious about your one in the cardigan or do you think it's just a passing fancy?'

'I don't know, but you know the *real* thing . . . I can't tell this to Mam, obviously . . . but I'm afraid he'll tell people about us . . . and you know, I don't want them to get the wrong impression. . . .'

'Tell what?'

'Oh, you know, about us, him and me, I wouldn't want people to think that I'd, well . . . with anyone. Tim was special. I'm not indiscriminate, and I wouldn't want him to tell people I was.'

'Do you mean you went to bed with him?' Aisling's face was round with disbelief.

'Well yes, he *is* my boyfriend. *Was* my boyfriend.'

'I don't believe you.'

'Well, suit yourself, Aisling, but don't go blabbing to Mam, she'd murder me.'

'It's very hard to know when Aisling's joking and when she's deadly earnest.' Elizabeth was reading the letter to Henry, who was pinning holly and ivy around the room.

465

'What does she say?'

'Oh, you know it's all about the horrific Christmas, three of them rolling around a huge empty house.'

'I thought she had a big family.'

'Yes, but she's going to be with Tony's mother for some reason, alone. And Tony, she thinks, may have some difficulty in lasting the day with them.'

'Dear me, is he still very drinky?'

'What a marvellous word. Drinky. Yes, he is *very* drinky. It started at our wedding weekend and seems to have gone on since. Oh well, maybe another priest will cure him. Aisling is amazing, she never seems to be as upset as she should be.'

'Would you be upset if I was drinky and didn't come home?' Henry smiled down at her from the chair he was standing on.

'I'd be very upset indeed. So don't try it. And if you were very drinky indeed, which is what I think Tony is, then I'd leave you. I'd just go.'

'Why doesn't she do that? Leave Tony?'

'Oh, they don't do that in Ireland.'

Father managed very well without her. Elizabeth was pleased but slightly annoyed to notice this. Just as he had settled into a routine of life without Mother, so he did in a life without Elizabeth. He kept a little notebook in the kitchen with the words 'Ask Elizabeth' on it. When the queries had been answered they were ticked, and sometimes the answers written down.

'Tea-cup stains,' he had written, and then beside it, 'I am only rinsing them. E says I should rub them with scourer inside and if stain bad try soaking in salt or soda.' 'Sour smell in sink.' 'E thinks it could be dishcloths not properly washed and left to air.'

What a narrow and organised life he liked to lead. Everything in its little box, neatly ticked and docketed and filed away. He had been pleasantly surprised when she had invited him for Christmas, and suggested that he come and spend three days.

'That's very nice of you my dear. But stay? At night?'

'Well, why not Father? Henry would be very happy for you to come. And it would be nicer than flogging home all the way to Clarence Gardens.'

'That's very generous of Henry and of you. Shall I pack a suitcase?'

Sometimes she wanted to shake him until he fell limp from the shaking. He agreed eventually to spend Christmas night itself, but he would return home on Boxing Day.

'Nicer, really, to be in my own place,' he said.

Elizabeth had arranged a little holly for him and put the few cards he had received on the mantelpiece rather than leaving them on the table still in their envelopes.

It was good to work for a school and a college, Elizabeth told Stefan, they kept nice civilised hours, closing down well ahead of Christmas. Shops were a millstone, since people always wanted to buy at the last moment. She was arranging a table with a selection of items they had not sold. She made a card with beautiful lettering suggesting that people regard them as Christmas presents. Stefan had thought she was wasting her time; Johnny had said that people didn't come into antique shops to buy gifts at the last minute.

On Christmas Eve however they were all sold.

'I take my hat off to you,' Johnny said, generous as usual with praise. 'I never thought we would do it. Look Stefan, even those salad servers, we've had those for months. It was clever of you to think of doing those gift cards with the name of the shop. Not only is it good advertising but people will not feel so much that they're giving somebody something used or second-hand. With one of these little cards it becomes an antique. You could have been a great business-woman.'

'I *am* a great businesswoman,' Elizabeth said.

'No, no, you're a wife, and before we know where we are you'll be a mother.'

Elizabeth looked at him in amazement. Not even Henry knew yet, she had only had it confirmed yesterday, and she wanted to tell Henry tonight as a Christmas surprise. She was indeed pregnant. She and the doctor had worked out that the baby must have been conceived on her honeymoon and would be born in June.

Trust Johnny Stone to have guessed.

There were Christmas drinks at the office. It was all very informal, the senior partner had said, but of course it was nothing of the sort. Everybody examined the wives critically, Elizabeth had known this without having to be told. She knew that she would be under a microscope. She was going to do him credit.

The hairdresser brushed Elizabeth's shoulders and together they admired the handiwork. She looked exactly right, she thought: white frilly blouse, cameo brooch, smart grey jacket, and grey and blue check skirt.

'Going somewhere nice?' asked the hairdresser who would be working until 7.30, she told Elizabeth, then after an hour's journey home she would start to stuff the turkey for her Mum.

'Yes, my husband's office are having a little party,' Elizabeth said.

'I'd love a husband and an office party,' the girl said.

'That's funny,' Elizabeth said, 'I used to think there was something safe about having a husband and office party too. It sort of lets you know where you are in the world.'

'You have a nice time, Madam, you look very well.'

She spoke when she was spoken to, she didn't want to seem pushy, but she answered clearly and directly. She told the senior partner about her art classes and how she also worked in an antique shop. When he said that he had a very old picture which had been in his family for years she expressed polite interest and murmured appreciation.

She parried Simon's flowery compliments very skilfully, she talked to other wives in a sunny way. From time to time she saw Henry straightening his tie and glancing at her proudly; he looked less tense and worried as the time passed – she even saw him laughing at one stage. How dreadful to have jobs like Father and Henry did where nervous people become more nervous. And no one could relax.

The senior partner was speaking to her again: 'Are your own family in the law, Mrs Mason?' he asked silkily. Around him people waited for her reply. Would she apologise, would she claim distant cousins who were barristers or solicitors?

'No, far from it, banking is my background. I've had to learn a whole new language. I never heard of precedents and injunctions and indentures . . . you may find this hard to believe, but a great deal of the world hasn't heard of them either!'

The senior partner laughed, and then so did everyone else. Some test had been given, and Elizabeth had passed. Soon she whispered to Henry that she thought it might be time to leave. They didn't want to look like hangers-on.

Simon asked them whether they would like a Christmassy nightcap, before he set out to Barbara's house for the festivities. Elizabeth steered them away from it. She wanted to tell Henry the news.

They sat for hours by the fire and talked about the baby. Henry said that he had to pinch himself to make sure he was awake. This time last year he had been on the train to Liverpool to stay with Jean, now he was a married man, and an expectant father. He put cushions behind Elizabeth, he insisted that she do no work next day, he would do all the cooking. They planned the nursery, the schools . . . they talked of the holidays they would all have together.

Names. They could have written a dictionary between them. Richard Mason, Susan Mason, Margaret Mason, Terence Mason. Henry's father had been called George, too, so that settled it: George Mason if it was a boy.

'Would you like to call it Violet if it's a girl?' Henry was solicitous and courteous.

'No, I think not. I think Father would be upset, you know, every time we mentioned her name. No, your mother's name . . . you told me, but I've forgotten?'

'Eileen,' he said.

Father was embarrassed, and delighted at the news. He

seemed reluctant to hear about dates and missed periods and doctors' tests proving positive, but he was quite pleased with the notion of himself as a grandfather.

He had arrived bearing a bottle of sherry for their Christmas tree. He didn't even *know* it was mean, Elizabeth told herself as she unwrapped it and noticed that it was almost as cheap a brand as you could buy. They had bought him presents – nice playing cards in a fancy leather case, and a thick cardigan with leather bits on the elbows. But Father hadn't chosen anything for them.

'We should look on the sherry as an advance on last year. He never gave me any presents at all,' Elizabeth whispered when they were in the kitchen.

'Oh he must have. Surely?'

'I can't remember anything. No, he wasn't that kind of father.'

'I'm going to be a doting father, I'm going to buy everything in the shops for Little Eileen.'

'Or Little George. And I'll be a doting mother too. I won't run away from Little Eileen. . . .'

'Or Little George.'

'If they're all going to go off like prize eejits to some house party then let them go, Ma-in-Law,' Aisling said. 'There's no use in being martyred over it. Tell them you hope they'll have a great time.'

Mrs Murray agreed that it was better not to appear too dependent. So well did she follow these instructions that Joannie was moved to telephone and wish them a Happy Christmas. Aisling was in the house and answered the phone.

'I feel a bit of a heel, letting you cope with Mummy but, well, there is Tony, and the two of you can share it.'

'Oh heavens no, you mustn't look at it that way, we're going to have loads of fun here,' Aisling said.

'Yes, well, sure. Is Tony there?'

'Tony?'

'Tony.'

'Tony Murray? Your brother?'

470

'Oh, Aisling, don't be tiresome, what are you playing at?'

'Nothing, I just wondered why on earth you thought Tony might be here?'

'It is his mother's house and you're there, and it's coming up to Christmas. . . .'

'Ah no, none of these are reasons. No, no Tony, might be in the hotel. Or I believe he even drinks in Hanrahan's now, he's barred from Maher's, politely, of course, but barred nonetheless.'

'Oh, do stop this nonsense.'

'Nonsense is what it is, but there we are. Some people like to live like that, drinking what's left of their brains away. I don't, and you don't but your brother – and my husband – seems to want it like that.'

'Can I talk to Mummy?'

'Of course you can, and listen, thanks a million for ringing up to say Happy Christmas, and have a great time at the house party. It's in Scotland, I believe.'

'Yes, anything to get out of this dump.'

'But you got out of this dump, you went to Dublin.'

'I meant Ireland.'

'I'm sure you're right, I'm sure Scotland's much less dumpish. Hold on till I get your ma . . . Mother-in-Law, it's glittering Joannie just off to her house party, giving a little tinkle to wish Mama compliments of the season.'

Mrs Murray laughed at Aisling's affected accent. 'Well, it was nice of her to ring anyway, wasn't it?' she said later.

Aisling said nothing.

'It was,' Mrs Murray answered her own question.

Aisling said, 'I was just thinking of all those years when Joannie and I were inseparable . . . and I thought you were remote and sort of untouchable . . . and here we are, neither of us with a word left to say to Joannie but thrown together for Christmas. . . .'

'Not thrown together. . . .'

'We'll be spending Christmas on our own.'

'We won't be on our own.'

'We will if we're lucky.'

*

471

There was a do in the hotel on Christmas Eve. Aisling came for an hour.

'Your mother expects us for supper,' she said to Tony.

'Sure who wants supper on Christmas Eve, won't we be eating like pigs all day tomorrow?'

'Yes, but she still expects us.'

People were beginning to look at them. Tony's face got red. 'Well, you go on up there if it's making you fidgety. I'll come up later.'

'How much later? When will you come?'

'When I'm good and ready, in my own good time. She's *my* mother, it's *my* house. I'll go to it when and if *I* please.'

'Well said, spoken like a man,' said Shay Ferguson.

'Well said, spoken like an arse-licker,' Aisling said to Shay. People thought they must have mis-heard, Aisling Murray looked so innocent and unmoved, could she possibly have said that? No, it must have been something else.

Shay was a dull red. 'Well, I suppose you'll be off now, Tony, this is the last we'll see of you this evening. . . .'

Aisling smiled at Shay. 'Heavens, you must be deaf, Shay, didn't you hear what Tony said? He's going to leave when he's good and ready, not before.'

Shay looked even more put out. He laughed nervously. 'Right, Tony, old stock, what'll it be?'

Tony turned round to say something to Aisling but she was gone.

She went to the bathroom in the middle of the night: it was four o'clock. Tony had not come back. On her way back to bed she passed Mrs Murray's door; it was ajar and the landing light was on.

'I'm awake, Aisling,' the voice said.

Aisling went in. 'Go back to sleep Mother-in-Law, being awake doesn't make any difference. The best thing is trying to sleep . . . because then you have less time to think of it.' She took the woman's thin hand and stroked it.

Mrs Murray's eyes were troubled. 'Of course, they may be back yet, maybe someone gave them a lift and they called into someone else's house.'

'Yes, that could be it.' Aisling was soothing.

'But on Christmas Eve . . . you'd think. . . .'

'Maybe he went to the bungalow, maybe he forgot we were here; perhaps at this minute he's fast asleep in the bungalow, and he'll wake up in the morning feeling a right fool.'

Mrs Murray looked at her hopefully. 'Do you think that might be it?' she asked.

Aisling gazed at her, a thin, gaunt woman in her sixties: a widow; a son in the priesthood gone from her at Christmas; a daughter, half-crazed, gone looking for adventure on a package tour to a gathering of equally restless, lonely souls; and her pride and joy drunk in her home town, out doing the Lord knows what on the most sacred night of the year. Let her have an hour or two.

'I'd say that's exactly it, you know that car, it turns like a donkey automatically into its own yard. That's where he is.' She was about to leave.

'But when he sees you're not there . . . won't he . . . can't he . . . ?'

'He'll probably get into bed without turning on the light so as not to disturb me.' She didn't tell anyone that she slept on the small divan bed, the one that everyone else thought was a sofa. The lurch of Tony into the bed beside her, waking her and smelling of drink and sweat, was more than she could take. He had said nothing the first night she had slept there, when they came back from Elizabeth's wedding, so she had slept there ever since.

Aisling remembered from somewhere deep down in her mind something that Elizabeth's mother had once said. When things are worst, that's when you should spend a lot of time dressing yourself up. I wonder does it work? She thought as she got up in the Murrays' cold guest bedroom. She had not slept since she returned to her room. She had read instead. She had hoped it would distract her but it didn't succeed. It wasn't the author's fault, she thought, trying to be fair. No book could take her away from the never-ending whirlpool. Tony needed help; how could he be helped if he wouldn't listen? How could she get other people to help her to know what to do if *they* wouldn't listen? There had been no answer at four a.m. There was none now as she dressed for mass.

She wore her good dark coat, and she spent time shining up her shoes and her handbag with face cream. Elizabeth's Mother had thought that if you looked all right to yourself at least you didn't have that additional worry about looking like a tramp. . . . It saved you from self-disgust. She arranged her hair carefully, put on plenty of make-up and laid a mantilla on top of her red curls.

'Will we be late?' Mrs Murray fussed with her gloves: she too had dark circles under her eyes, but unlike Aisling she hadn't shaded them away with liquid foundation and pressed powder.

'No, plenty of time, and we'll go by the bungalow in case sonny boy's there. . . .' Aisling spoke cheerfully.

He was not there, but she prattled so ceaselessly Mrs Murray had no time to speculate on what could possibly have happened, and soon they were at the church.

'Aisling, you'd think you were going to a dress-dance with all the pan stick you have on,' Maureen hissed as they met in the porch.

'Happy Christmas, sweet sister, to you also,' said Aisling.

The sermon was about love; Christmas was the season of love – Father said they must put some love in their lives, not enough to talk about it, not enough to buy gifts, but give kindness and understanding. Let everyone look into his or her heart and see where they could give more love today.

I suppose I could decide not to kick him to kingdom come when he does get home, Aisling thought. That would be an act of love. But possibly superhuman. She looked at Mrs Murray's hands clenched in prayer, her eyes closed. Oh God, send him back sober just for today. Please. Not for my sake, I don't care any more, for his mother's. Please. God, you were nice to mothers, can't you give them a better deal? Look at Mam, all that business with Sean running away and being killed and all. And look at poor Mrs Murray, she's really praying. Now if that's not praying, God, what is? And

I'll put half a crown in the poor-box. Five shillings. Please God, because it can't matter to you one way or the other where Tony is, so why can't you send him home?

On the way out of the church Donal sided up to Aisling.

'Listen, Eamonn said that Tony was in some kind of a fight down in Hanrahan's last night.'

'Well, he's not home yet, so maybe he's still in it.'

'Not home, on Christmas Day?'

'I know. Did Eamonn say any more?'

'He said there was a matter of the barman taking away his car keys and Tony wanting them back.'

'He must have been bad if they took away his keys in Hanrahan's, usually they wouldn't notice there if you hanged yourself in the back snug.'

'I don't know any more, I thought I'd tell you myself, you know, rather than your hearing it from someone else.'

'You're very good, Donal.'

'Will you do something for me, Aisling?'

'Sure, what?'

'Can you lend me a fiver? A five-pound note?'

'Of course I can, more if you want. I've twenty pounds in my bag.'

'No, five is plenty.'

'Here you are.' Only her eyes asked the question.

'You see, there's this dance tomorrow night, Niamh's friend Tim is coming up from Cork, and he's always got loads of cash, and Anna Barry . . . just in case I ran out. . . .'

'Sure of course. Take another and buy champagne.'

'No, I have a bit already, it's just that I seemed to spend all my money on Christmas presents.'

'You did too, you're too generous.

Donal shook his head. 'What's Christmas without presents?'

His car was at the bungalow when they drove there.

'Please, Mother, don't lose your temper or be cross with him.'

'No, of course I. . . .'

475

'It's just that I know how to deal with Tony when he's been out all night. He needs to feel that we haven't noticed, honestly.'

'All right, dear,' said Mrs Murray nervously.

Shay Ferguson was there too; he had a folded table napkin dipped in a water jug and was making ineffectual dabs at a cut on Tony's eye.

'Happy Christmas Shay, Happy Christmas Tony,' said Aisling, holding Mrs Murray who was about to run forward and see the extent of the injury.

'Oh, play-acting again, are you,' Shay said.

'No, just a seasonal greeting. What happened, Tony?'

'He had a bit of an accident with the car, he stayed up in my place last night.'

'Are you all right, Tony?' Mrs Murray couldn't be stopped.

'Oh, stop fussing will you,' Tony said.

'Tell us about the accident, was it someone's wall sticking out, or someone's dangerous parked car?'

'I'm trying to tell you. The young Coghlan boy was out on his new bicycle wobbling and teetering over the road . . . he nearly ran straight into the car with Tony and myself in it. Lord almighty. . . .'

'Is he hurt?' Aisling said.

'It's only a cut, I've been cleaning it, it was the mirror, the corner got him over the eye.'

'Not Tony, the child, the Coghlan boy?'

'He's all right, they shouldn't give kids bicycles, you know, silly kids who can't ride them. . . .'

'They shouldn't give cars to drunks, either, silly drunks who can't drive them.'

Tony tried to stand up.

'Take that back.'

'I will not, it's the truth.'

Shay said, 'Aisling, for God's sake, the man's hurt, stop picking on him.'

'I was not drunk. I'd been asleep in Shay's, I had nothing to drink today.'

'It's only nine forty-five, Tony, I wouldn't go round boasting about that.'

476

'He was trying to get back for Christmas Day with you and his mother, quit attacking him.'

'Just tell me what injuries the Coghlan boy got.'

'His leg is . . . well, I don't know if it's broken, they were getting Doctor Murphy when we left. . . .'

'You left? You didn't wait to see how the boy was?'

'Look here, get this straight. Tony did not hit the boy. You can look at the front of the car, there isn't a scratch. He swerved and braked in order to avoid him.'

'Where was this?'

'Outside Coghlan's.'

'Coming up the hill?'

'Of course coming up the hill.'

'But Coghlan's is on the right, if the boy was at his own gate he was on the right, *why was Tony on that side of the road*?'

'The child was all over the road. . . .'

'It's me that should get compensation, look at the cut on me.' Tony had got up to examine his face in the mirror.

'Does he need any stitches do you think?'

'Was the child cut?'

'Only his hands and his forehead, grazes like kids get falling off a bike.'

'We'd better go down and see if he's all right.'

'Don't be silly, going back would be admitting liability, you know, the way people take up things.'

'So what are you going to do?'

'We explained to Dinny Coghlan, that the child had been staggering on the bicycle but that we'd not make a fuss about it since no one was too badly damaged.'

'And what did Dinny Coghlan say?'

'What could he say? He was pleased to see the sense of it.'

'The sense of it being that he works in Murray's.'

'Ash, what have you that sneer on your face for?'

'If you'd run over the child backwards and forwards you'd have made poor Dinny see the sense of something . . . if the boy's leg is twisted I suppose he'll see the sense of it for the rest of his life.'

'You're making a mountain out of a molehill, the boy's all right and so is Tony.'

'So as I said, Happy Christmas Shay. Are you off now?'

'I've no car. I came up with Tony in his to see him home right.'

'Yes, for a man who was stone cold sober, it was nice that his friend should escort him back.' Aisling's face was cold. 'I'll drive you home Shay, no, no, it's no trouble. I'll take my car. Ma-in-Law, why don't you and Tony go on up to your house and I'll come back when I've dropped Shay at his place?'

There seemed to be no fault in these arrangements, even thought they pleased nobody.

Shay smelled of drink as he got into the car beside her. Pointedly Aisling wound down the window.

'You can be a cold, catty bitch,' Shay said.

'Yes.' Aisling concentrated on the road.

'He's the best in the world, Tony, you shouldn't be picking on him.'

'No.'

'Seriously. There's no reason for you and me to fall out. He's the best pal I ever had. I like him, you like him, why do we have to have all these barneys over nothing at all?'

'I don't know,' Aisling said.

'Well, you're very mute, you're singing very low compared to up at the house.'

'Oh Christ God, you are a stupid man.'

'No no no, for the New Year, now will we agree to differ and not be doing each other down, not fighting like enemies?' He looked at her, his big face foolish in the hope that she was going to shake hands and make friends. That the Christmas Spirit was going to soften her.

She stopped the car. They were nearly at the Fergusons' garage, where Shay lived with his father, his uncle and aunt. A big untidy house sprawling behind the garage as if nobody gave any heed or care to it.

'Tony is an alcoholic. He is drinking himself to death. He had almost eight months on the dry. Things weren't perfect but they were a hell of a lot better than they are now. He was lonely for the fun and crack with you. What kind of a friend were you to him then? Did you ever come up to the house when he asked you? Did you ever go out fishing with him, or taking a spin down to the sea during the summer?'

'It's not that easy to get off just at a moment's notice.'

'It's always easy to get off for a drink. But not for the best pal you ever had. You couldn't go for a bit of a walk with him.'

'I'd have felt silly.'

'He felt silly, he felt silly ordering red lemonade, or ginger beer. He felt silly in the long nights when he hadn't got you and the lads. But nobody would come and feel silly with him. That's friendship.'

'Ah, Tony's not an alcoholic. He takes a bit much, don't we all? He'll cut down on it, in the New Year, we all will. And lose a bit of weight at the same time, two birds with one stone.'

'Great, Shay. Great.'

'I mean it.'

'I know you do.'

'Pals then?' He held out a big hand before he got out of the car.

She drove home up the hill past Dinny Coghlan's house. Doctor Murphy's car was still outside the gate.

Mrs Murray had let Kathleen, the maid, go home for Christmas. 'In the old days we always had a girl, it's going to be hard coping,' she complained. But Aisling could see that she was pleased to have Tony to fuss over. All the hard bit, the long cleaning and chopping of vegetables, had been done by Aisling, and she had drawn the turkey and made the stuffing. She had got a plum pudding from Mam, one of the seven that had been made in the square, and she told Mrs Murray that it was her own making. The Christmas table was set for the three of them; Aisling had arranged crackers crossed at each place. She had sliced the bread very thinly and she had prepared half grapefruits expertly and put a glacé cherry on top of each.

'It's very festive,' said Tony, nodding towards the table.

'I suppose it is.' She didn't even look up. They sat opposite each other at Mrs Murray's well-banked fire. From the kitchen they could hear the clatter of dishes and the busy happy hum of preparations. There would have been no heart in the feast without the Prodigal's return.

Aisling couldn't think of one thing she wanted to say to Tony. She was weary of the time-filling tactics. The delaying moves which would put off his first drink of the day. Let him take it, let him swallow it. All she could do anyway was put it off by half an hour. She didn't want to talk any more about young Lionel Coghlan; if it was a boy old enough to have a bike it must be Lionel, Matty was too small. Her words with Shay Ferguson would soon get back to him anyway, changed, bent and slanted. No point in telling him of the conversation now.

And what point in recriminations, or investigation into the row in Hanrahan's? None of it would do any good.

'I got you a Christmas present, but I lost it,' he said.

'That's all right, Tony,' she said. 'It doesn't matter.'

'It does matter. I've said I'm sorry.'

'Okay.' Out of the corner of her eye she saw him stand up and move to the sideboard.

'Well, seeing the day that's in it,' he said, and poured a quarter of a tumbler of whiskey out. His mother came into the room at that moment. She saw the whiskey and gave one alarmed glance in Aisling's direction.

Aisling shrugged. 'Are you right, Mother-in-Law, will we sit down to the festive board?' She sat down and they said grace. And Aisling thought of all the Christmases she had had not a mile away from here. When the gathering around the table had been as exciting as the presents earlier in the morning, when everyone was in good humour and Dad would tell jokes, and Mam would say thank God to have had so many blessings during the year. She always said that – except the year Sean had been killed.

Two years ago it had felt funny not to be having Christmas with the family, but she had cooked for all the Murrays and it had been such a flurry she had hardly noticed the time come and go. Last year Tony had come in drunk at ten p.m. and slept in the chair all night. He had been bad-tempered at his mother's lunch, but at least Father John and Joannie were there to share the burden.

This is the way it's going to be from now on. John won't come home. Joannie won't come back.

This is Christmas.

She smiled up at her mother-in-law and said that the turkey smelled smashing out in the kitchen; she was trying to finish her silly grapefruit so that they could carve it. And she held out her Waterford goblet while Tony filled it with wine.

Eileen said that they had a lot of blessings to thank the Lord for during the year. She closed her eyes for a moment, thinking to herself of the blessing that she alone knew. The fear that had been groundless. She thought of Sean and the shop. He had resigned himself to Eamonn now. He didn't come home with his forehead bulging over some small confrontation. She thought of Maureen, who had been there this morning with the four children, the baby looking like a Christmas card with all his white fluffy wrappings, and Brendan Og turning into a lovely little boy. Eamonn was Eamonn, neither more nor less; at least the year had passed without his leaving the shop or abusing his father in public. Aisling, well she had her hands full with that Tony — and maybe she was exaggerating about the other business. Maybe she only meant that she hadn't had any pleasure from sex — that would be a normal thing to happen. And Donal, God bless him, didn't he look better this Christmas than any gone before? A grown-up man of twenty-two with a career and, as far as she could see, a girlfriend. It was Anna this and Anna that. And then Niamh, as pretty as Aisling without the striking hair, ten times more confident than Aisling at that age, happy as Larry now that she had her Tim back again. And she always included Elizabeth in her children; ten pages of a letter saying how happy she was and how their flat was like a little palace and it would always be a home for Uncle Sean and Aunt Eileen to visit though she could never make them a home as great as she had been given in Kilgarret. Wasn't it a wonder that Violet's child had turned out to be a closer friend than Violet had ever been?

Eileen thanked God for the blessings of the year.

They listened to the wireless after the meal, sitting around the fire eating the Christmas boxes of chocolates, some listening to the variety show, some doing the quiz in the paper.

Eileen dropped off now and then, after the big meal the heat of the room made her sleepy. Sean slept too, until the children laughed at him, with his glasses on, the paper clenched firmly in his hands and his mouth open giving loud snores.

'What's Christmas,' he said crossly, 'without a bit of a sleep?'

Mrs Murray's eyes closed too. Aisling slipped out to the kitchen and did the washing-up. She set a tea tray too and cut some of the Christmas cake. Mrs Murray was going to send squares of it to Father John and to Joannie.

Could it be still only five o'clock? It felt like ten. She came in quietly, it was too soon to wake Mrs Murray. Let the woman sleep, she didn't sleep much last night. Tony can't have slept much either, in Fergusons'. His mouth was open, and he lay out in the chair by the fire. Aisling sat between them and looked at the flames making pictures and houses and palaces as she used to do when she was a child. A log fell out. It woke Tony. He reached out and poured himself a quarter glass of whiskey. 'What's Christmas without a little drink?' he said.

Mrs Murray thought the clock must be wrong; how could she have slept all that time? Heavens, she must do the washing-up, oh dear, weren't they a marvellous pair, to do that, they shouldn't have. No, really, they shouldn't have done it.

A cup of tea was always nice after a big meal, the cake was moist, wasn't it? Was it as good as last year? It was hard to remember last year's but she thought this one was a bit dryer. Maybe not.

Tony was restless; he said he would prefer to spend the night in his own bed. 'I'd like to go back to the bungalow,

Ash,' he said. 'If we're going to the races tomorrow I'll have to have a good sleep. I like to be in my own bed, my own room.'

His mother looked stricken. 'But that is your own room, your own bed, Tony, for years and years. If you can't sleep here where can you sleep?'

Aisling said nothing.

'Come on, Ash, you explain to her, I don't sleep well, I get headaches.'

'Not one night under your mother's roof.' Mrs Murray was becoming tremulous. 'You were the Lord knows where last night, and now tonight you won't even. . . .'

'I was not the Lord knows where, I was *you* know where, Ash knows where, I was with the Fergusons. God all-bloody-mighty will you stop making it a mystery, as if I was in Mongolia? I sensibly didn't drive home when I had a couple too many. Aren't you always asking me to do that? Well, aren't you?' He looked more upset than Aisling had ever seen him.

'Maybe tonight Tony's right in a way, Mother-in-Law, that we should go back and sort ourselves out. Listen I'll be up tomorrow to see you and thank you for a marvellous day. That was a feast, a feast is the only word for it. Wasn't it Tony?'

'Very good, grand, grand,' Tony muttered.

'So we'll be off. It was a great Christmas, Mother,' she said, kissing the thin, tense face.

Mrs Murray squeezed Aisling's hand.

'Well, if you think . . . I don't know, rear a family and still it's a lonely day.'

'Well, they were fools not to be here for that spread, going to their monasteries and their house parties. Wait till I tell them what they missed.'

They waved goodbye and drove in silence through the dark wet countryside. One way back would pass the Coghlans' cottage. Aisling decided not to take it. Tony's face was set and hard.

The bungalow was cold and dark. She plugged in an electric fire and started to clear up some of the blood-stained

483

table napkins which had been used by Shay for dabbing the wound.

'Will I light a fire?' she asked.

'What for?' he said.

'It might be cheery, were you going to sit down? For the evening like?'

'Ash will you stop *interrogating* me? It's like living with a prison warder. Do I ask you all the time where you're going, what you're doing?'

'I only asked you. . . .'

'You only asked, you only asked. . . . I can't bear this constant asking. I'm going out.'

'But where on earth are you going? Listen, Tony, there's drink here, plenty of it. Invite who you want in. Don't go out on Christmas night, please. There's nowhere open.'

'There's friends with houses open, friends who won't nag, nag, question, question.'

'Listen, Shay's not at home, you know he said they were going up to Dublin tonight, you're going to meet him at the races tomorrow. Won't that do?'

Tony had his coat on.

'Look, your eye has that terrible scab on it, if you knock it against anything it will open up and bleed, will you not have sense? I'll light a fire and we'll have a bottle of brandy. We'll sit by the fire like the old times.'

'What old times?'

'When we got married first. It's only a waste going out.'

'I won't be late, I'll be back tonight.'

'But where . . . ?'

Aisling went to bed eventually. It was cold, despite the electric fire. She wore a cardigan over her nightdress. She slipped into the small divan and took a book she had loved as a child, *The Turf Cutter's Donkey* by Patricia Lynch. She read it slowly, like she and Elizabeth had done, she remembered explaining the bits that Elizabeth didn't understand about cutting turf in the bogs. She thought of Elizabeth and Henry and their nice flat in London and Mr White going to stay with them. She remembered the way Henry had looked at Elizabeth during the wedding reception. Tony had never

484

looked at her like that. Why had he wanted to marry her? Or anyone? Had his drinking pattern been started then, only she just didn't see it? Why had she thought that he loved her? She had never thought that she loved him. Not like people love in books. Not like Elizabeth had loved Johnny, or even Niamh was crazy about this medical student. She had never felt that for Tony. Maybe this was the punishment for marrying someone you didn't love. But how the hell were you supposed to know in Kilgarret what was love and what wasn't?

'I must have been mad to marry him. Quite, quite mad,' she said aloud. And somehow when she had said it, she felt a bit better. At least the situation had been defined. Aisling O'Connor married Tony Murray because she was quite mad.

Eileen was surprised that Aisling didn't go to Leopardstown to the races.

'You used to love going up there on St Stephen's Day,' she said, when Aisling came in to pick at bits of the cold turkey around lunchtime. 'Leave that alone, there'll be no lunch if you keep taking the best bits.'

'I didn't feel like it, Tony thinks I'm eyeing him and watching him . . . which I am, I suppose. He keeps saying "It's only my second", when it's his seventh. I only annoy him and everyone else.'

'But shouldn't you be with him? Maureen told me she saw him this morning and he had a terrible cut on his eye. I'm not repeating things, now, to make trouble, it's just because you brought the subject up.'

'He braked hard in the car yesterday morning, just avoided killing young Lionel Coghlan, from what I can understand. The child was on a new bike. Lionel has bruises and two cracked ribs, Tony has a cut on his eyebrow which probably needs attention but he won't go near a doctor or a hospital.'

'Merciful Lord.' Eileen was shocked.

'Oh yes, the Coghlans keep saying, thank the Lord Tony

485

.didn't do himself any serious injury, and wasn't he marvellous to swerve and avoid Lionel, and Lionel is white-faced, in the bed there trying to say he was only playing with his new bike when this drunk maniac came round the corner at a hundred miles an hour. Well, Lionel's not saying that because he doesn't know how, but that's what he should be saying.'

'But Tony wasn't drunk in the morning, yesterday, was he?'

'He was filled with the night before's drink, he had no coordination, he was drunk.'

'Well, thank God that nothing worse happened.'

'Mam, what am I to do, will it be like this always?'

'You know he took the pledge before, a lot of people take it after Christmas.'

'Mam do I have to stay with him? Couldn't I get . . . well . . . an annulment or something?'

'What?'

'You know, I told you about the other business, I'd have no trouble proving that to any court.'

'Are you mad? Are you stark raving mad?'

'But I *can't* spend the rest of my life, Mam, I'm only twenty-six, I can't. . . .'

'Just tell me, what did you promise?'

'What do you mean, promise?'

'Up in that church, in front of all of us, what did you promise?'

'At the wedding, do you mean?'

'At the sacrament of matrimony, tell me some of the things you said. . . .'

'The words of the ceremony. . . .'

'Not words, Aisling, a promise, a bargain, a solemn promise . . . what did you agree to do?'

'You mean better or worse, sickness or health. . . .'

'I mean that, and you meant it too, didn't you?'

'Yes, well. But I didn't know it was different. . . . It can't be counted.'

'Do you know what you are trying to do? Put aside the whole sacrament of matrimony. Oh dear, I didn't know it

486

wouldn't all be sweetness and light. Sorry, let me start all over again. Is that what you think people should do? Is it?'

'Mam, I don't care what people do. I can't be expected to stay married to a man who doesn't want me in any way, who doesn't care whether I'm here or not. I cannot be expected to stand like an eejit beside him for the next fifty years, which is what you seem to think.'

'I do think. I certainly think that's what you should do, and will do.' Eileen looked at the stricken face, eyes dark-ringed and troubled. 'Everything seems worse than it is this time of the year, there's too much fluster and too many expectations. . . . Don't be so dramatic, it will all work out.'

'So you think, Mam, that no matter what happens, the only thing to do is to stay with Tony and hope that things will get better and will all work out?'

'Of course I do, that's the only thing *to* think, child. Will you come on up to the fire with me and have a cup of tea? I was making a sandwich for your father and myself – we'll all have a bit of lunch together. Will you do that, he'll be delighted to see you.' Eileen was coaxing.

'No Mam, I think I'll go back to the bungalow.'

'No, stay here, you're cross with me now. You're in a kind of a sulk, aren't you?'

'No, Mam, I'm not sulking. I asked you what you thought and you told me.'

'But child, you can't have expected me to say anything except what I did.'

'I expected you to say that there was a case for annulment. I think that's what I expected, but you didn't.'

'We're not talking about technicalities. We're talking. . . .'

Mrs Murray was surprised too that she hadn't gone to the races. They had a cup of tea in the kitchen.

'That was a great meal you cooked, can I have a bit of the turkey?'

Ethel Murray bustled around happily getting plates and knives, though Aisling only wanted to taste the skin and to please her by praising it all.

'I suppose he'll be all right at the races,' she said.

'Oh, I hope so . . . he's a hard man to fathom. Can I ask you something seriously? Not wanting a polite answer, you know?'

'Certainly you can.' But Mrs Murray looked worried.

'Would he have been better if he hadn't married? You know, he didn't drink all that much when he lived with you, do you think if he were single again, it might be . . . you know, like it was?'

'But how can he be single again, isn't he married now?'

'Yes, but try to think, suppose he wasn't, he hadn't. . . .'

'I don't know, I really don't. I don't think it would have made any difference, he does drink too much, he drank before he got married and even more after, but I don't think the marriage is the cause of it.' She took Aisling's hand. 'You're not to reproach yourself, you do everything that can be done, you're a grand little wife, if only he had the sense. . . .'

'No, you misunderstand me, I wasn't asking was I a good or a bad wife, I was wondering did you think that Tony was really a bachelor at heart?'

Mrs Murray looked bewildered. 'Well, I suppose there's a bit of the boy in every man. Is that what you mean?'

Aisling gave up. 'That's what I meant. Hold on, don't give me all that much. I'm going over to Maureen's, I'll have to eat something there too.'

Maureen's house looked inviting and homely. Aisling wondered why she had always thought it was so bleak and dreadful. There was a big crib covered with cotton wool, the baby slept in a pram peacefully, Patrick and Peggy played with toys on the floor and Brendan Og read his new book.

'I'd have thought you were at the races, no ties, nothing to keep you at home.'

'Well I didn't go, I came to see you instead.'

Maureen said she would heat up some mince pies.

'I hear you saw Tony's face,' Aisling said.

'I didn't mean to go blabbing to Mam, oh God, now you think I'm talking about you all the time. Wouldn't you think Mam would have had the sense . . . ?'

488

'No, I'm not picking a row, I just wanted to ask you . . . do you think people talk about Tony a lot?'

'What do you mean?'

'You know, his drinking, fights down in Hanrahan's, him neglecting the business and all.'

'Oh Aisling, I never hear anything, I mean what would people say . . . ?'

'I don't know, I was asking you. I wonder do they think he's in a bad way . . . do people think he's the kind of man that . . . you know . . . should be . . . ought to be . . . ?'

'Aisling, what are you on about?'

'I don't think I'm the right person for Tony to live with.'

'But who on earth else would he live with?'

'I don't know, he could go back to his mother, or he could take a room in the hotel, or in Fergusons', they have rooms there, they were going to do them up once, I remember. Maybe they could do them up for Tony.'

'Are you feeling all right? What's this, some sort of game or joke?'

'No. I was just looking at alternatives.'

'And what would you do?'

'I could go back to Mam and Dad.'

'Aisling, you could *not*.'

'Why couldn't I?' Aisling looked genuinely interested. 'Just why not? That way everyone would be happy.'

'That way nobody would be happy. Stop behaving like a spoiled child just because you had a row with Tony and he went off to the races without you.'

'It's not like that.'

'Well, it's something like it. When I think of all the things you have to be grateful for, it makes my blood boil. . . .'

'Like a drunken husband falling around the town?'

'So he drinks too much, you should look after him more, and anyway, look at how much worse it could be. Suppose he was after women, suppose he was like Sheila Moore's husband, or Brian Burns, look at him with a woman up in Dublin as well.' Maureen stopped: Aisling's face looked very grave. 'Listen, you're only talking rubbish, you're not married as long as I am, you're new to it.'

'I've been married two and a half years.'

'When you have a child it will all change. . . .'

'If I were to tell you that side of it, you wouldn't believe me.'

'No, I know, Brendan's a bit the same, he says we can't afford another one, but when they're born he's delighted. He's mad about the new fellow altogether. It would be the same with Tony.'

'I'm sure you're right. Let's not talk about it any more,' said Aisling.

'You're the one who brought it up,' Maureen said huffily.

'I know I did. I'm in a bad mood today.'

'I knew you were.' Maureen was triumphant. 'When he comes back from the races, make it all up with him, have a bit of a cuddle and forget whatever the fight was about. That's what people do.'

When Tony came home from the races it was one o'clock in the morning and he was in a blazing temper.

'How dare you go down to Coghlan's sympathising behind my back. How *dare* you go to that house. . . .'

Aisling had been asleep, she woke with a start. 'Tony, you're drunk, go to bed, we'll talk about it in the morning. . . .'

'We'll talk about it here and now. I was in the hotel. I met Marty O'Brien, a brother-in-law of Dinny Coghlan. He told me you'd been down at the house asking after the boy. . . .'

'Common politeness and a bit of humanity. Of course I did.'

'Behind my back.'

'Oh shut up, you stupid fool, you were propping up the bar in Leopardstown, how could I tell you I was going?'

'Don't call me a fool.'

'You *are* a fool.'

'And you're a thief, where's my money? I had a big roll of notes in my pocket. I didn't have it when I got to the races, only a couple of fivers.'

'It's in the drawer, Tony, you know it is, I often do it when you're going out. It's in the top drawer where it always is. It's to save you spending foolishly or being pick-pocketed.'

'I don't want a bloody keeper looking after me like an animal in the zoo. Don't you *ever* do that again.'

'All right.'

'And another thing.'

'Look, whatever it is will it wait till the morning? I've got to get up and do a day's work. Dad's opening tomorrow, so is Murray's by the way, in case it's of any interest to you. I'm going to our shop. I don't know whether you intend to go to yours or not . . . but I'm having my sleep.'

'What's that supposed to mean?'

'What?'

'If it's of any interest to me. Murray's opening. Of course it's of interest to me. I own it, don't I? It's my shop.'

'That's right. People keep forgetting.'

'What do you mean?'

'You're in it so rarely, and when you are it's to sign for fifty pounds. They see you coming and they say . . . here's Mr Tony, he'll need some cash . . . I've heard them.'

'Are you implying that I neglect my work?'

'Shut up and go to bed.'

'Are you suggesting . . . ?'

Aisling got out of her divan bed and began to strip off the blankets.

'If you won't let me go to sleep here, I'm going into the other room, let me pass.'

'Get back there, or back into the proper bed where you belong. Do you hear me?'

'Oh not tonight, Tony, I couldn't bear it, not tonight.'

He looked at her, his eyes blazing. 'What could you not bear?'

'Don't make me say it. I don't want to try tonight. Please, Tony, let me past you.'

'You're a vicious woman,' he said. His hand came out so quickly, Aisling didn't see it; it caught her by surprise, across her jaw. The sting and the hurt jarred her whole body. He hit out again, this time harder. The blood came immediately from her lip or gums. She could feel it on her chin and falling

491

on to her nightdress. She touched it and looked at her red hand in disbelief.

'Ash, oh, Jesus, Ash, I'm sorry.'

She walked slowly back into the room and looked at her face in the mirror. It seemed to be her lip that was bleeding but a tooth felt loose in her mouth so it could be that that was causing the blood.

'I could kill myself. Ash I didn't mean to, I don't know why I did it, Ash are you all right? Let me see – God let me see. Oh my God. . . .'

She said nothing.

'What will I do, will I get a doctor? Ash I'm so sorry. Tell me what to do and I'll do it. I'll do anything you say. . . .'

The blood was trickling on to her lap.

'Here, Ash, don't just sit there, you have to do something. Will I call someone?'

She stood up slowly and walked towards him. 'Go into the other room and go to bed. Go on. Now. Take these blankets.'

He didn't want to go. 'I'm so ashamed Ash, I didn't mean it, I wouldn't hit you for the world, you know that.'

She handed him the blankets and shamefacedly he went. She took the suitcase very deliberately from the top of the cupboard and began to pack. She wrapped a towel around her neck to catch the little drops of blood that fell from her lip. Very precisely and neatly she packed winter clothes and shoes. Underwear and jewellery. She took off her rings and left them in a conspicuous place on top of the dressing table. She took down a second suitcase, and she put in two blankets and two sheets. She collected letters and photographs and packed those too. After an hour she thought it was safe to open the bedroom door . . . from their spare room came the sound of Tony's heavy breathing. He had split her lip but he could still sleep. She collected a few small things from around the house; a silver sugar bowl that Mam had given her, a teacup and saucer with huge roses on them that Peggy had come to deliver as a wedding gift.

She wrote a very short note to Tony. She told him that she was going to the hospital to have her lip stitched; she would say it was the result of a fall. Then she would leave in her own car and would not come back. There would be no point in asking any other family where she was because they would not know. She wrote a long letter to Mam; she said that she had tried every avenue, sounded out every opinion and nobody seemed to think that she could turn the clock back, so she was going to abandon the clock instead. She said that she didn't mind *what* cover story Mam used, whatever they wanted to say would be fine with her. Sickness, a new job, gone to visit a friend. . . . But she thought it might be better just to say straight out that Aisling had not been able to live with Tony any more and had gone away. That way there could be no speculation and wondering about it. It would be out in the open.

She told Mam about her lip. 'I'm only telling you so that you'll know it wasn't idle fancy and selfish wishing for a happier lifestyle. I know too that there are women in this town whose husbands beat them, and women in every town. *But I will not be one of them.* I will not, and that's as definite as I ever was about anything.'

She said to Mam that she would ring her in a couple of days, and the kindest thing of Mam to do was not to try to organise a reconciliation because there wouldn't be one. Only if Ethel Murray became difficult and began to cause trouble was Mam to tell her about Tony's violence. Otherwise better leave the woman a few illusions.

Her lip only needed one stitch. It was done by a young house surgeon whom she didn't know.

'Are you a student?' she asked him.

'No.' He was shocked at the thought, but she hadn't intended to insult him, she was thinking that she would never know about the dance that Niamh had gone to with Tim the medical student, and whether Donal and Anna Barry had fallen in love, and if Donal had been able to buy rounds of drinks with the fiver she had given him.

She knew two of the nurses and saw by their faces that they didn't believe her story of a fall.

'Come back during the week and I'll have a look at it,' the young doctor said.

'Sure, thank you very much.' Aisling put on her coat again and got into the car. She dropped the note for Mam into the shop, not into the house, she wanted Mam to read it in the peace of her eyrie when she got there early in the morning.

She took one last look back and drove out of Kilgarret on the Dublin road.

PART FOUR

1956–1960

XVIII

It had been the happiest Christmas that Elizabeth had ever known. Even in Kilgarret long ago she had felt a little separate, it wasn't quite her Christmas, she was comparing it with the ones she had known before and would go back to. This was her Christmas. Her husband, her father, and her baby starting to take shape. And in her home. It was as if she were being rewarded for all those other Christmas days, trying to console Father, trying not to worry about Johnny finding somebody new. Now it was all safe and as it should be.

Father had been happy to leave on Boxing Day; he wasn't at ease as a house guest. She had seen him nervously pacing in his dressing-gown with his sponge bag over his wrist.

'What's the matter?' she had enquired, he looked lost.

'I didn't know whether to go in or not, someone might have gone in the other door.'

'Father, I've told you a dozen times, if we go in one door we lock the other one so that no one comes in.'

'Very complicated way of having a bathroom,' he said.

Henry was looking over some papers in the dining room. Father and Elizabeth lingered over breakfast in the kitchen.

'Was Mother ill much when she was expecting me?' Elizabeth asked.

'What? Oh. Oh, I don't know.'

'But you must have known, I mean, did she tell you that she felt groggy or what?'

'I'm sorry, I have no recall for all those details. I could never write a book – I wouldn't remember the interesting bits. . . .' That was Father making a little joke. Or trying to.

She felt a wave of sadness that he regarded the birth of his only child as a *detail*, but perhaps that was too harsh, maybe the whole memory of Mother was painful. She would ask no more.

'Imagine poor Henry taking work home for Christmas, I think he's too dedicated . . . I can't see the others doing it.'

'I think he's very sensible.' Father had a view! Elizabeth was surprised, she had expected a monosyllable.

'He's very sensible, the most important thing for a man to do is to get on top of his work. Once a man feels able for his work everything else falls into place.'

Elizabeth looked thoughtfully at him. 'It's not the most important thing, is it, Father? The most important thing is to get the most out of life, and give to people, you know, not just getting on in work.'

'I didn't say getting on, I said getting in control of it.' Father looked quite animated. 'You know in your world, in the art business it's not the same, there aren't the same pressures, not like law or the bank.' (Of course, it was all men together in the big, stress-filled business world, while silly women just dabbled in art.) Elizabeth didn't care very much about the argument, she was just glad to see Father lively, almost spirited for once.

'Do you wish you had taken work home at Henry's age?' she asked almost playfully. She wasn't prepared for Father's face.

'I tried to, my dear, I tried to advance myself, or even just keep up with my colleagues. I wanted to do evening classes when I first got married. I wanted to buy banking magazines and study them, I could even have sat for examinations in the Institute of Bankers if I had wanted to. But Violet never wanted me to do it. It was, let me see, *stuffy*, and *pathetic*, I think those were her objections. . . .'

'Surely not, Father? Mother would have been eager for you to do well.'

'But I wasn't doing well, I was just doing it to keep up, she knew that. *Petty little clerk* she called me sometimes. Once she asked me was I the office dunce that I had to have help to do a job that a child could do. Your mother could be very cruel sometimes.'

'But you could have gone on studying, couldn't you?'

'No, not really, not if it irritated your mother so much and made her so scornful . . . there was no point in making her angry. . . .'

Elizabeth hated the defeated tone in his voice. It was the voice of a weak man in a film – the coward who blamed other people for his own mistakes. She tutted sympathetically.

'You see, things come easily to you, Elizabeth, you're like Violet in that way. She was very quick, and inclined to be impatient with those who were not so quick. A lot of the world are not so quick . . . remember that.'

Was Father warning her, was he actually going so far, interesting himself enough in her well-being as to offer her some kind of advice? Far from resenting it Elizabeth was pleased. She regarded what he had said as nonsense, but the very fact that he said it gladdened her soul. She didn't want to break his mood, but he changed the subject himself.

'We were thinking of having a nice brisk walk in the park, Henry and I, and a beer and a sandwich at the pub afterwards. And then I'll push off back to Clarence Gardens.'

'You're very welcome to stay here, Father.'

'I'd like to have my things right for tomorrow,' Father said.

What possible things could he mean? He had been working in the bank for thirty-four years. What on earth could he have to get ready for the morning?

Henry came back from the pub glowing with the frosty weather, the brisk walk and the unaccustomed midday pints.

'Your father's got on a bus,' he said. 'He asked me to say goodbye and thank you again. I think he really enjoyed himself.'

'So did I,' Elizabeth said. 'And next year we shall have a six-and-a-half-month-old baby with us, isn't it unbelievable?'

Henry sat down by the fire and warmed his hands. 'I'll have to do a lot of hard work to provide for us all. But I'll enjoy it.'

'But sweetheart, I'm not going to give up work, not all of it. I'll keep on Stefan and the college, I'll give up the school.'

'Well, we don't know darling, we don't know.' Henry looked worried. 'We mightn't be able to get anyone to look after the baby, you may have to give up work altogether.'

'No. It's not necessary. We went over all this.'

'But whatever we do it will mean a cut in our income and you already earn more than I do.'

'Henry, I do not earn more than you do.'

'Count it up, the salary from the college, the salary from the school, the fee from Stefan, the art courses, of course you earn more than my salary.'

'I don't think it is more . . . anyway, it's not mine or yours, it's ours, isn't it?'

'Yes, but I worry, I'm not as light-hearted as you are, I'm not a believer in things turning up, I'm more of a plodder really.'

She tousled his hair and laughed at him and made faces at him and eventually she made him laugh at himself. But there had been a note of warning there in something he had said, it was uncannily an echo of what Father had said a couple of hours before.

How odd that she had never noticed before that Henry and Father very often thought alike about things.

'I'm not going to tell the whole world yet, but just a few friends,' Elizabeth had said when Stefan and Anna had kissed her and examined her complexion and said it was true that pregnant women did look more beautiful.

Johnny came in during the hugging and kissing, so he had to be told too.

'Well, isn't that fantastic? The new generation for Worsky's, eh? Make sure he grows up with a keen business sense . . . that's all we need in this firm. We've got flair and taste and bright ideas, but nobody who knows how to make real money. When young Mason goes to school impress on him that he's to be a financier. Do you hear me?'

They laughed. 'What if young Mason turns out to be a girl?'

'We'll wait for the boy,' Johnny joked. Later he spoke less lightly. 'I'm very happy for you, honey lamb, it's what you want, isn't it? This is really what you wanted all the time. Home, husband, kids. . . .'

'I am happy. I don't know whether I wanted it all the time, but I certainly want it now.'

'A little person no less. I'd quite like that.'

'You would?' She looked at him, surprised, and with a catch in her throat like the old days.

'Yes, I often thought I'd like a kid, without all the marriage bit. Difficult though, some would say impossible.'

'Tucked away somewhere quietly with his mother, and you could call now and then and teach him things and take him for walks.'

'Yes, that sort of thing. Can't find the partners for such an endeavour.'

'Oh, I don't know, look harder, suggest it to people, it might work.' She thought to herself that he could have had it, exactly that, and the child would have been nearly eight by now.

Harry was delighted when she rang and told him the news. He said he would make a cradle, he used to be good at woodwork – but perhaps Elizabeth would have a fine cradle ordered already? On the spur of the moment Elizabeth invited him to come and stay for the weekend. She said she would send him his fare too because she said she wanted him as a consultant for the nursery.

Henry said he was delighted that Harry was coming, but was it not a bit much for Elizabeth's father to know that Harry would be a house-guest?

'Of course it's not a bit much, Father knows well that Harry is a great friend of mine.'

'But coming to stay,' protested Henry. 'It's almost saying that we don't think he was the villain of the piece, to put it very dramatically.'

'Well, I don't think he's the villain of the piece, I haven't thought that about him for ages. Remember we decided that it may have been the best thing for everyone? Remember?'

'Yes, I remember,' said Henry, 'but I never thought it was the best thing for George.' Henry always called Father George when he talked about him. But when he was actually speaking to him he called him Mr White.

Simon had not been told about the baby because, well, that would be telling the whole office and it was all too soon to do that, wasn't it? Henry agreed readily. Elizabeth was marvellous at knowing exactly what things were like in there he said, she always knew little nuances and subtleties without being told.

'I think it's a bit like the staff room at school,' Elizabeth said.

'You say they're a lot of old women, in the staff room,' Henry protested.

'That's exactly what I mean,' Elizabeth said and laughed.

Simon called around on the evening after Boxing Day. Their office was closed until Monday, so in theory they had no work to do, but Henry had been working so much at home that there was little difference between this and a normal day.

Simon was full of his wonderful Christmas, Barbara had been a great hostess, people had dropped in all day, there had been a permanent buffet. Barbara sent everyone lots of love and hoped that the little nest in Battersea was superb.

'I hope you told her it was,' Elizabeth said, jokingly. Henry still looked slightly foolish when Barbara was mentioned to him, she wanted to relax him.

'Yes, I said you had transformed Henry, that he was relaxed and languid these days. Barbara always thought Henry worried too much about little things, and fussed about minutiae.'

'What rubbish, he's practically a beach boy,' said Elizabeth.

Henry laughed, almost an easy laugh. 'I certainly do think I've unwound a lot,' he agreed.

'You're perfect for me,' Elizabeth said, 'why don't you get another drink for Simon while I go and tidy up all my old papers that I have strewn in the other room?'

'Oh, was that your work?' Simon said. 'I thought old Henry had been doing his eager beaver bit again.'

'At Christmas time? You must be joking,' Elizabeth said as she went and tidied Henry's papers neatly into her own briefcase.

Father telephoned that night to say that there had been a message from Ireland, it was from Violet's friend, Eileen. She had been very specific, could Elizabeth please ring her at ten o'clock in the shop. Yes, that's what the woman had said. Yes, he agreed, it seemed an odd time to telephone anyone at business, but that's what she had said. Ten p.m. in the shop, Kilgarret 67, and to tell Elizabeth that there was no accident, nobody had died or was ill or anything.

'Whatever can it be about?' Elizabeth wondered.

'My dear, how on earth should I know, they are your friends. The most important thing I was to tell you was not to ring her at home, not to ring Aisling and to make sure you got the shop.'

'But why doesn't she ring me here? Did you give her my telephone number?'

'I tried to, but the woman kept repeating to me that she couldn't make any more calls, she was in a friend's house and was using the telephone secretly. It's all a very odd business I must say.'

'So must I say, a very odd business,' Elizabeth said. 'Never mind, I'm sure there's some innocent explanation, shall I ring you and tell you about it?'

'No, no dear. Ten o'clock is somewhat late to disturb me. No, tell me about it when I see you.'

Father hung up. Elizabeth realised that he had very little curiosity about people. He didn't like many people enough to be curious about them. She felt a horrible sense of panic. There must be something very wrong indeed if she was not to telephone the house on the square, nor Aisling, but to go through with this charade. Oh dear it was only seven-thirty now, she would have to wait two and a half hours. Better persuade Simon to stay to supper, it would distract them.

*

503

'Hallo, is that you Eileen, Eileen can you hear me?' Elizabeth's voice sounded high and nervous after the endless clicks and spelling Kilgarret and talking to the exchange. It was now ten past ten and she had begun making the call ten minutes ago.

'Yes, child, are you all right?' Aunt Eileen's voice sounded just as usual.

'I'm fine, we're fine, but what is it, what's happened?'

'Have you heard from Aisling?'

'I had a letter from her just before Christmas. Why, what's happened to her?'

'No, she's fine, there's nothing wrong with her – she hasn't telephoned you?'

'Telephoned me, no, not for ages. No, I rang her when we got back from our honeymoon. What is it, Aunt Eileen? Please?'

'I'm trying to be discreet,' Aunt Eileen said.

'But aren't you in the shop, isn't this why I'm ringing you there?'

'Yes, but, you know. . . .' Eileen's voice stopped.

'No, what . . . ? Oh, I see, yes, yes, of course, I see.' Elizabeth remembered the legendary curiosity of the Kilgarret postmistress, Miss Mayes. She listened in to the beginnings of conversations that she thought might be interesting and did spot checks on others until she got a good one to settle down with.

'I know what you mean,' Elizabeth said. She could hear the sigh of relief.

'Well, you know the problem that Aisling had, you know the problems like say your Henry?'

'Yes, I know what you mean.'

'It's over.'

'Dead?' gasped Elizabeth, shocked.

'No, no, wound up, like a business, you know.'

'Can't you tell me properly?'

'That's right, the line is very bad. So I was wondering if you had heard anything at your end. . . .'

'No, no, nothing.'

'You see I got notification of this, today, this morning in the office and naturally I would like to discuss it more.'

'Of course.'

'So if you are contacted you will urge that contact be made here, won't you?'

'Oh obviously, at home or at work?'

'At the shop around this time is good. Less questions asked, less people around.'

'I see, and does Uncle Sean . . . ?'

'Not yet. . . .'

'Who else . . . ?'

'Nobody . . . apparently.'

'And the . . . er . . . problem itself?'

'No word from there, no word at all. There's a car outside the home but that's all I know.'

'And do you know why, why now, and so suddenly?'

'An injury. . . '

'Oh God. . . .'

'No, not serious.'

'But if it's done, it's done, you know what I mean, the contract broken, the business wound up. Why not, well acknowledge that publicly, as it were, it will all have to be sooner or later won't it?'

'That's what she said in her letter, but I'm hoping not.'

'But if it's as final as that, you know . . . ?'

'Child, business in this country is very different to business in your country . . . Violet and Harry's solution isn't open to people here.'

'But is there another . . . another? Lord, I'm so confused about the words, don't know which one I want. Does she have another problem like Mother having Harry?'

Aunt Eileen laughed. 'No, no, that's not it. But you see here there's no way of ending the problem, she'll have to come back.'

'I see.'

'You're very good, child. Do you have people there as you're talking to me?'

'Yes, Henry's here obviously and Simon, our friend . . .' She smiled at Simon.

'They must be mystified altogether . . . I'll write to you

tonight, and remember, when she gets in touch, what she's to do. . . .'

'But surely there must be a better way than all the code . . . ?'

'I'll arrange to go and talk to her – anywhere, in England if needs be, but she must ring me first to tell me that she wants me to.'

'You can't come over here the whole way for that kind of thing. You wouldn't even come for my wedding.'

'I know, and the last time I was there was to bury young Sean. I don't seem to have much luck with my trips to England these days.'

'Perhaps she won't contact me.'

'She will, that's the only thing I'm certain of.'

Aisling rang the next day.

'Where are you?' Elizabeth said.

'In Brompton Road, just opposite the Catholic church, at the terminal.'

'Are there taxis outside passing up and down?'

'Yes. I saw some.'

'Get into one fast and come here.'

'Will it cost a fortune?'

'Whatever it costs I'll pay it. Come here at once.'

'I look awful, you'll be shocked.'

'No I won't.'

'Is Henry there?'

'No, he's gone out to the library.'

'Thank you, Elizabeth, thank you, I don't know what I'd do.'

'Just get into the taxi . . . tell me when you get here.'

She asked Henry if he would go to the library. 'That's a bit steep,' he said. 'Driven out of my own home.' He was irritated at being asked so sharply.

'I'm sorry, but it's important, if it was Simon coming here in a crisis I would do the same – clear out and let you have the place to yourselves.'

'Simon wouldn't do that, men don't,' grumbled Henry, packing his things obediently.

'I'm very grateful, very very grateful.'

506

'Well,' he said, not really mollified.

She went into the guest room and made up the bed. She laid out fresh towels. She thought that she hadn't told Aisling about the baby but she would have to, of course, when she came to stay. What a bit of bad timing, she wished she had told her and got it over with.

She heard the lift coming up to their floor and she knew it was Aisling. Both Mr and Mrs Solomons across the landing went out to work. They would not be home at this time. Elizabeth steeled herself for Aisling's injuries. Aisling had her head down as she struggled out of the lift with her two suitcases. Then she looked up.

The whole side of her face had a black and purple bruise, at the corner of her mouth was a dressing held on with Elastoplast.

'Oh my God,' Elizabeth said. 'Poor Aisling. Poor Aisling.' They stood at the top of the huge curved marble stairway with the ornate little lift behind them; the door of the lift was still open but they didn't even hear the buzzing from below. They stood with their arms around each other and the cases on the floor, Aisling with her good cheek laid against Elizabeth's and they both kept saying over and over, 'It's all right . . . It's all right.'

They kept making tea, pot after pot of it. The telling was not a litany of Tony's wrongs, rather a higgledy-piggledy kaleidoscope of life in Kilgarret. There were no plans, no strategies, no working out of the future. No regrets, or if onlys . . . Tony emerged as a man who should never have married anyone. Nothing was spared, but nothing was lurid in the telling. Aisling seemed to regard Tony's impotence as just one more reason why he was unsuited to marriage.

'He should have been a priest like his brother. Yes, I mean it.'

'But with his taste for drink, well, it wouldn't have worked.'

'I'm not being anti-clerical, but I think it would,' Aisling said. 'Look at the priest in Waterford that cured him that time, the two-bottles-a-day man, isn't he grand now? Priests

507

are able to look after each other, if one of them goes on the jar the others help him, take over some of his duties, don't lead him into bad ways. They have no families to break up, drunken priests don't. . . . It's drunken married men that are the real pity.'

Elizabeth told of Eileen's phone call.

'I'm not going to do it, I won't meet her and have her lay the whole reasons out in front of me again. I'm not going to do it.'

'But you will ring her, won't you?' Elizabeth hated to see Aisling wince when she made some facial gesture as she was doing now. She was trying to put on a cheerful smile and it hurt her lip.

'Of course I'll ring her. I can't have Mam sitting there waiting in an empty shop – but it's not going to do any good.'

Henry came home at six o'clock.

'Is she here?' he whispered in the hall.

'Yes, she's having a sleep, I said I'd wake her again at ten o'clock to ring her mother. . . .'

'Is she badly beaten up?' Henry was concerned.

'Just her face, it looks awful but she says it's only bruising and one cut lip which is swollen. It's a dreadful mess.'

'Her face?'

'Yes, that is a mess too but I meant the whole thing. Everyone seems to think she should have gone along with him, you know, living with him. It's madness, he should have been locked up, for his own good.'

'So why didn't the family have him put away?'

'The family could see nothing wrong with him. I don't know, it's a mystery, but the desperate thing is that she had to run away.'

'In case he'd come after her and be even more violent, do you mean?'

'No, it would cause too much upheaval her going back to her own home, or so she says.'

'Perhaps it will all settle down again, when the first shock is over, maybe she'll go back?'

'She'll never go back to Tony, I know that, the question is can she go back to Kilgarret and not live with him? I think she can, the place isn't half as medieval as she makes out, but she's terribly upset . . . I said she could stay here for as long as she likes, was that all right?'

'Of course it was, you're very good to your friends.'

'She was always very good to me, very very good.'

'You mean having you as an evacuee in the family?'

'Yes, and a lot more.'

Elizabeth spoke to Eileen first.

'The injury isn't too bad at all, it looks very bad but it's definitely not serious and won't last.'

'Thank you very much child, and is there any problem about telephoning . . . ?' Eileen sounded weary.

'No, not at all, I'll hand you over in a moment, she's just having a cup of tea to wake her up, she's slept four and a half hours. But the meeting might be difficult – anyway I'll get her for you.'

Elizabeth and Henry went into the kitchen and closed the door when Aisling went to the telephone. Henry had said to her that she was to talk for as long as she liked. He had been uneasy talking to a girl with such a battered face. He tried to avoid looking at her as he spoke – which made Aisling hang her head even more.

'It will pass, Henry, today and tomorrow will be the worst. It will be gone by New Year's Eve.'

Now she stood speaking to her mother in the softly-lit hallway of the Battersea flat. Neither of them knew where Tony was.

'I haven't asked you to ring so that I can give out to you,' Mam said.

'I know, I know, Mam.'

'And I hear that, bad though it all was, it will go and leave no scar.'

'No, no, so the man said. I told him about the fall I had hitting the chair.'

'I see. I wish I could talk to you.'

'Well I rang you, Mam, when you said.' There was a

509

muffled sound. 'Mam, are you crying, you're not crying, Mam?'

'No, of course not, of course not. I was blowing my nose.'

'Oh good.'

'Will you be able to come back?'

'To work and live with you?'

'No, you know what I mean.'

'Then the answer's no.'

'You could stay with me for a bit.'

'Permanently, or not at all.'

'But nothing's permanent, you know. Is Niamh permanent? Is Donal, is Eamonn? What's permanent?'

'It's longer than you want me for.'

'I'd have you forever, you know that, and so would your Dad. But. . . .'

'But. . . .'

'But it's not reasonable. You'd have to try to make a go of the other.'

'I have tried.'

'Not enough.'

'How much do they want? I could have lost an eye!'

'There's no "they", Aisling . . . it's only you I'm thinking about.'

'There is a "they", Mam there must be, otherwise why are we speaking this kind of pidgin English?'

'You know why, and that's different.'

'Leave me be, Mam, leave me. I'll ring you and I'll write to you. I'll write to the shop and it'll look like a bill. I'll put it in a brown envelope.'

'Child, don't start making arrangements as if it's going to be for a long time.'

'It is, Mam, it's going to be forever as far as . . . as far as the former situaton was concerned.'

'If you'd let me talk to you, to both of you . . . I blame myself, I didn't know how bad things had got.'

'No, Mam, no, I won't sit around while short-term miracle cures are worked from Waterford, and the danger and threat of . . . of falling over another chair hangs over me. I won't do it.'

510

'I'll come anywhere.'

'I know, but you mustn't.'

'What can I do to help you, then?'

'I'm feeling better here, and calmer – but tomorrow night I'll be in a position to tell you more, or maybe the next day. It's a question of writing to people. I'll have to write to Jimmy Farrelly, for one thing.'

'Who?'

'Jimmy, about arrangements, finance and all – no, don't worry I only want very little, far less than I'm entitled to, but I'll work it out. Elizabeth's husband is a solicitor, he'll help me.'

'*No*, nothing like that, it's far too soon, too final.'

'I keep telling you, the sooner it's done the better. And I'll write to his Ma, she's very nice. Mam, I changed my mind about her a lot over the time, you know.'

'I know.'

'That's where you could really help, by being nice to her. She's kind of easy to distract, if you know what I mean . . . you can veer her away from the main point.'

'Yes.'

'And then do what's best for yourselves, you know . . . whatever causes you the least problems.'

'Yes.'

'And that's all, really.'

'*Are you not forgetting anything?*' Eileen's voice was cold.

'No, what?'

'The other half of the bargain and the promise and the agreement.' Aisling said nothing. 'Did you hear me?'

'Yes. I'm trying to forget that part. I hope I will, but it's not going to be easy. Perhaps when my face is better I'll start trying seriously.'

'But. . . .'

'The best thing I could do is to forget all that. If I remember it I'd have to do something about it.'

'Will you be all right there?'

'Yes, Elizabeth's marvellous, Mam, marvellous altogether, and Henry too, they're so welcoming. They've got a grand room for me. I was able to sleep there like a baby. It was great. I really feel much better.'

'I'm glad, child. I'm glad you're with Elizabeth. I feel safe while you're with her.'

'Yes, well, I won't stay long, I'll get myself a place.'

'Not yet, not yet.'

'No, not this week. Will I ring you tomorrow, Mam, or the next night?'

'The next night. I'll ring you, I don't want Elizabeth's phone bill to be enormous.'

'What do you tell Dad you're doing in the shop at this hour?'

'I tell him the truth. I tell him I want to do a bit of ledger work when it's nice and quiet, and I do it too.'

'I wish things were different, Mam.'

'Goodnight, Aisling, God bless you. Go back to bed now. . . .'

Before Aisling spoke to Mam again Simon called; he was horrified to see the injury that Aisling had got when she had fallen over a chair. He was sad, too, to hear the unconnected fact that she had left her husband.

'He was the rather jolly bloke who sang at the wedding, wasn't he?' Simon asked.

'That was the bloke,' Aisling had agreed.

Johnny had called too, with a huge plant-holder for Elizabeth.

'Did the Squire beat you up?' he said sympathetically to Aisling.

'Yes,' said Aisling, 'but we say I fell over a chair.'

'Oh, definitely, that's what we'll say,' said Johnny. 'But I'd like to go and punch his fat stupid mouth in. I could see at the wedding he was a bundle of trouble.'

'Yes, he's a bundle of trouble,' said Aisling.

Elizabeth had been available all the time. 'You can cry, and I'll cry too, if you like,' she had said, 'but I think it hurts your face so try not to. We'll go on living a normal life around you, but any time you want me tell me and I'll slip away from it.'

Shortly before Mam was to ring Elizabeth said to Aisling in the kitchen, 'I'm awfully afraid Father is about to enlist Henry as a bridge player. I can't bear the game, and Henry is so polite he might just go and learn it, to be courteous.'

'They get on very well, that's great, isn't it?'

'Yes, it surprises me all the time. Father was even saying tonight that he was flatterd to think the baby might be called George . . . *Oh God*.'

'No, no, not really, why didn't you tell me? Why didn't you tell me? Isn't that wonderful! Oh, Elizabeth I'm so pleased. Isn't that marvellous? When, when did you find out?'

'Just before Christmas, I was going to tell you when things settled down a bit.'

The phone rang.

'It's a trunk call,' shouted Henry.

Mam told her that Ethel Murray had spent the entire day in the square, and Mam couldn't go to work. Donal was out all day at work and so were Eamonn and Sean. Niamh had gone to Cork with Tim. Ethel Murray had contacted the priest in Waterford, who had come to Kilgarret. Tony hadn't touched a drop of drink for twenty-four hours, he had told his mother, and the priest, and eventually told Mam that he had struck Aisling in drunkenness and he was extremely sorry. Everyone was delighted that he had taken all the blame so firmly upon himself. He acknowledged that the fault was all his. He begged Aisling to come back. He said that things would be different from now on. Mam sounded delighted as she regaled all this news.

'Isn't that great child, you were right all along,' Mam said. 'Now you can come home.'

Aisling waited until her face looked less frightening before she set out to look for a job and a home. It took ten days before the bruising had died down and the scar on her lip had become less vivid. During this time she scoured the Jobs Vacant, and Apartments Vacant advertisements with eager eyes. It seemed to her that most of what she would earn in a

Sit. Vac. would have to go on an Apart. Vac. She had never appreciated the advantage of living at home in the square and putting a couple of pounds a week into the post office for Mam, she hadn't thought about the advantages of living in the bungalow bought by the Murrays' money. She couldn't remember any advantages living there. She had a year and a half's wages in her own post office book, all in her own name so there was no trouble filling in the forms which were sent off to the GPO in Dublin to withdraw the money. She was touched to the point of tears by all the offers of help she got. However had she thought that the English were cold? Stefan and Anna had offered her a room and part-time work if she was stuck. They invited her to a meal one evening and served her a funny strong liqueur that made her cough.

'You could become addicted to this stuff, you'll have me as bad as my husband,' she said.

'It is good that you can talk about it like that,' Stefan had said approvingly.

Elizabeth's father had been kind, too, even though Aisling felt there had been an undertone of disapproval. Mr White must see in her an echo of his wife's behaviour. In fact he seemed amazed that there was no man at the root of Aisling's flight. He offered her Elizabeth's old bedroom at a token rent until she got herself settled.

'I'm afraid I would not be much company for you,' he said. 'I'm a very private sort of person you know.'

Simon and Henry said they would ask a barrister friend of theirs to look up the legal situation for her. There would be knotty problems because of there being no divorce in Ireland for one thing, and the interpretation of the law of domicile for another. A wife's domicile was always judged as being in the country where her husband lived. But they were sure they could iron it out so that he would have to pay her maintenance. They seemed to enjoy discussing it as a technical problem as well as doing it on her behalf.

It was Johnny Stone who seemed to understand better than anyone that she really wanted to be finished with the whole business.

'Don't take anything from the Squire. You're a bright strong woman, you can make a living better than the Squire. If you go about fighting and haggling for his money this way and that way you'll never be shut of him. Wipe him out, start again.'

That's what she really wanted to do, but it was only Elizabeth who realised that wiping out Tony seemed to mean wiping out her whole life in Kilgarret as well.

Aisling went for long winter walks in Battersea Park with Elizabeth, talking about the baby; they read baby books to see what shape it was now. They said that they wouldn't make the mistakes with the baby that everyone else had made with them.

'I'll never make him feel awkward and stupid,' Elizabeth said. 'That's what Mother made me feel when I was little. I remember being so afraid of her when I came home from school, and so afraid of her fighting with Father.'

'I wasn't afraid of that,' Aisling remembered. 'No, we weren't made to feel stupid, and she didn't fight with Dad, but Mam was very set in her ways, what was right was right, what was wrong was wrong. She's still like that in a way. It makes things very sure and certain. It makes them too damn rigid. If Mam had been a bit more flexible. . . .'

Elizabeth didn't fully agree. 'I don't want to keep praising her out of some politeness, but she was utterly reliable. If you knew how important that sort of thing is . . . Mother was difficult, and then flighty, and then disappeared. Father was moody and weak and so much the underdog. Even before I came to Kilgarret and learned about prayer and sin I used to pray that they would be like a mother and father in a children's story book, yours were like that.'

'Well young George or young Eileen will be lucky. I'm becoming silly about the baby myself, and I'm falling in love with Henry, too, so you'd better move me out soon.'

Henry had indeed decided to learn bridge. 'It's only one evening a week,' he had pleaded to Elizabeth, 'I can go on the evening that you do the accounts with Johnny and Stefan. They have a lesson first and then a game, and then a discussion and then tea. . . .'

'But it's so awful there, remember, I went to one. Full of awful lonely people staring at the teacher thinking that if they learn this awful points system their lives will be transformed. I only took Father to one because he was lonely and had no social life. You're not lonely and you do have a social life.'

'I'd like to be able to play a hand of bridge with your father from time to time,' he said mutinously.

'If that's all it was, a hand with Father, it would be great. I'd encourage you like anything. But it's not a game for two, it's a game for four. Awful, awful people come to the house and they talk about nothing except the game and they demand teas with dainty sandwiches. . . .'

'Why don't you take it up again, and Aisling could learn, too? It would be super in the winter evenings.'

'Henry, we have each other for the winter evenings. Stop preparing for some long lonely session. We don't need to play bloody bridge.'

'Don't be so doctrinaire, Elizabeth,' Aisling said. 'I think he's right, and I will learn with him. I'm not a total beginner, Henry, I used to play a bit with Mrs Murray and Joannie and John, when her children deigned to come home and see her. But they were all so busy talking about other things I don't think I concentrated properly. . . .'

Later, Aisling said, 'I hope you don't mind, but he was so eager, and it would be nice for me to play bridge if I'm going to live on my own in London. Better than shove ha'penny, I think, as a social skill.'

'Aisling, you are ridiculous, of course I don't mind, I'm delighted. I was just afraid Henry would become a fuddy-duddy. You know, like Father.'

'We'll make that bridge class go with a swing, Henry and I. Watch out for lively bridge players!'

Elizabeth laughed.

'It's great to see you laughing again, I thought you never would. Why can't you live on here when you get a job, instead of spending all that money on a flat? It would be marvellous.'

'No, it would ruin things. I'd feel dependent and you'd

feel crowded. Where's Manchester Street? Is it on the way to Manchester?'

'No, it's not, it's very central – near Baker Street. You could never afford a flat in Manchester Street, could you?'

'It sounds nice, small and central. They have a minimum let of two years. Is that normal to you, or does it sound fishy?'

'I think people do it, but Aisling, you can't possibly sign a lease for two years. You'll be gone back long before then.'

'How many times do I have to tell everyone? *I'm not going back.*'

She got the flat and the same week she got a job, receptionist to three doctors in Harley Street. She was able to give Henry Mason and Elizabeth's father as references, and she told the doctor who interviewed her absolutely directly that she had recently left her husband in Ireland, and recently signed a lease for two years for a flat in Manchester Street. One act seemed to cancel out the other in terms of suitability.

'Am I to take it that the marriage is irretrievably broken down?' the doctor asked. 'I ask simply to ensure that you might not wish to disappear should a reconciliation take place.'

'No. It is completely over. I am reverting to my maiden name, O'Connor, and whatever else we can be sure of in this life we can be sure that I will not resume my marriage.' Unconsciously her hand went to the small scar on her lip.

The doctor smiled. She was an engaging girl and had perfectly adequate office experience.

'Will you be getting a divorce, Miss O'Connor?'

'There's no divorce in Ireland, doctor,' she said.

'I forgot,' he said. 'What do people do?'

'If they're lucky, they come over here and get themselves a fine job in a doctors' practice,' she said laughing.

They told her she could start next week.

Johnny said he would help her settle in. She said she could afford fifty pounds out of her savings to make the place look nice. That was plenty, Johnny said. They would hunt for some nice bookcases in second-hand furniture shops, and he knew already where they could get her a pair of armchairs . . . She spent most of the weekend with Johnny dragging her away from the windows of department stores where she was eyeing modern furniture with envy. She wrinkled up her nose at the kind of things Johnny was pointing out.

'We have old rubbish like that, rooms of it above the shop, and no one would touch it.'

'Have you really?' Johnny was eager.

'Oh yes, Mam would give it to you in order to get the place cleared out.'

'I always meant to go to Ireland and investigate that side of things. Elizabeth didn't want to go in the old days.'

'Didn't want to go?'

'I mean, not on business, she thought it would look a bit too sharp, a bit profiteering.'

'Why didn't you come? You could have come to my wedding.'

'I wasn't asked,' said Johnny.

Aisling thought quickly. 'No, that's right, you weren't – we were worried about numbers. You didn't miss much.'

'Elizabeth enjoyed it.'

'Yes, I enjoyed it too, to be truthful, as a wedding it was fine. It's just the marriage that was so rotten.'

'Yes, well, we won't talk about that any more. Look at this cane rocking chair. Do you think you could clean it up? And put a funny cushion on it here and another there? It would look super beside the window, and you could sit and watch the world of West One go by below.'

'It seems a disgrace to be buying this kind of thing when it's rotting at home.'

'OK. I'll drive you back to Kilgarret in the van and we'll fill up with second-hand furniture and leave. How does that suit you?'

'Oh stop that nonsense and let's buy this ridiculous thing.'

'If the Squire saw you carrying this up the stairs he'd have a fit,' Johnny said when they got it back to her flat and he was puffing behind with a table and an old tea trolley.

'If the Squire saw me now he'd probably find it difficult to remember my name. I gather his little burst on the dry didn't last very long. . . .'

Aisling wrote a long letter to Mam every week for five weeks, pages and pages going over all the reasons why she could not start again, and why it was unfair to expect her to do so just in order to please public opinion. Mam wrote spirited letters back explaining that public opinion was the last thing she was trying to please. If she had been trying to make an impression on Kilgarret, she wrote, she would have forbidden Eamonn to get in with that crowd living out in a wilderness with the Dalys; she would have forced Aisling to study and go to university and she would have had a coat of paint on the house in the square every five years. She did none of these things because they would all have been for show. What she did want was for Aisling to see that she had broken a promise made to another human being, and that the human being was making every effort; and all she had to do was to meet him half-way, or even a quarter of the way.

Then there was the letter saying that Ethel Murray had been taken into hospital suffering from high blood pressure, strain and her nerves.

Then there was the letter saying that Tony had gone back on the drink after three and a half weeks. His letters to Aisling had been returned unopened which was bad enough; but when Jimmy Farrelly called in to him and suggested that they organise some kind of settlement for Aisling that was the last straw.

Then there was the letter saying Ethel Murray was much better and sitting up with some colour in her face again . . . but she couldn't be told about Tony having broken his pledge until she was stronger.

And one day there was a letter in a typed envelope which Aisling opened because she thought it was from the solicitor.

It was from Tony.

Please Ash, please come back. It's only now I realise what it must have been like for you. I'll go to a clinic and get myself cured properly from the drink. I'll go to a hospital too in Dublin or in London and let them examine me all over to see why I can't do the sex act. I'll drive you to and from work every day,and buy a new record player that you once asked for. If you don't come back I will kill myself and for the rest of your days you will know that you could have saved me from doing that.

I love you and I realise I was a terrible husband but all that is over now and when all is said and done you are still my wife. And if you come home soon it will be better than it ever was.

Love, Tony

Dear Tony,
This is the last letter I am ever going to write to you so I urge you to believe what it says. I am never coming back to live with you. Never. I have no further recriminations, you know them all. I have every possible ground for an annulment of our marriage; if you would like this we can start proceedings. I understand there is a priest in the Archbishop's House in Dublin that we write to with the full details. However, at the moment I don't even feel that I want to do that. I have no intention of remarrying so we could leave the annulment side until one or other of us does wish to marry again.

I do not want you to write again making promises that you could or would not keep. I am not a higher person than you, there is no need to humble yourself. I am just as selfish – I left because I couldn't take the unhappiness any more. I am going to give you some advice, just as I would give advice to someone I only knew for a short time. For your own sake cut out drink because I think it's affecting your liver already. You have had pains that I think are the beginning of liver damage. I would try to take more interest in your firm, because very shortly firms like Murray's are going to be hard put to it to fight supermarkets and big chain stores. It would be wise to examine very carefully what you are doing and where you are going.

And lastly: mothers. Both your mother and my mother are worried sick about us. Yours is in hospital thinking that you've given up drink forever, mine is working in our shop thinking every time she looks across the square she will see me getting off the bus, coming back to start everything all over again. I'm writing to both of them, nice cheerful letters, but this is not a cause for hope, they are not to be allowed to think that I will come back, because I will not. I have started a new life. But they are both so good and have given up so much of themselves to think about their children it would be good if you could make it a bit easier for them by not threatening suicide or saying that your life is over. Because it is not. You have plenty of talents and when I remember all the times we used to laugh and go to the pictures and go for drives . . . you had a lot of happiness then. Maybe it will come back.

I am not going to discuss money or settlements or dividing up the contents of the house. I just want to wish you well genuinely, and to tell you that no promises, threats or entreaties will make me change my mind. Our marriage is over as definitely as if the annulment had arrived from Rome.

I wish things had been different for both of us.

Aisling.

Bit by bit they realised in Kilgarret that Aisling had left Tony. Mam had been so vague and non-commital that Maureen thought Aisling must have gone to hospital with a miscarriage. As the time passed she suspected that Aisling was having fertility treatment.

Tony had been grumpy when people asked where Aisling was. 'Oh, wouldn't you know, gone off to Dublin and London to her friends,' was all he would say.

Donal, anxious to return the five pounds after the night out, had even called to the bungalow. He had met a wild-eyed Tony asking had he any message from Aisling. In the bungalow itself he had seen all the blood-stained towels and cloths which had been thrown into a basket in a corner of the kitchen. 'What on earth happened?' Donal asked, his voice in a screech with fear.

Haltingly and unconvincingly, a tale of a row and provocation and a slight cuff on the ear was told. Donal stood up unsteadily.

'You're a great ignorant lout, Tony,' he said. 'Aisling's much too good for you, I hope she's begun to realise that at last.' Donal went back to Mam and saw by her face that she knew already. 'I won't ask questions, Mam,' Donal had said, 'but if there's anything I can do I will.'

'When we try to get them back together, maybe you'd talk to Aisling about how upset he is,' Mam had suggested.

'Oh, I wouldn't do anything to get them back together,' Donal said surprisingly. 'No, Mam, I've seen this coming for a long time. He behaved like a drunken bum in London, but we all closed our eyes to it.'

Eamonn said, 'The talk in Hanrahan's is that Aisling's run out on Tony – could that be true, Mam?'

'No, there's a bit of trouble but it'll sort itself out,' Mam said. But as the weeks went on Eileen's mouth became a thinner line and the sunny hopes that it was a matter of no consequence began to fade. When people asked about Aisling she shrugged and said, 'You know what young people are like these days, there's no knowing what they'll be up to next.'

The night that Tony came up to the shop and broke the window with a big stone he had carried from Hanrahan's back yard, Eileen was actually sitting in her eyrie. If she had been nearer to the window she would have been badly injured and possibly killed. A crowd gathered and the sergeant took Tony down to the station. Eileen said that it was to be overlooked; Tony was sent home in a squad car to the bungalow which was dark and cold. Eileen begged the sergeant not to tell his mother, it would upset her so much. Mr Meade arranged for a glazier to come first thing in the morning and fit a new window. Father John heard about it and wrote Eileen a letter which was meant to be soothing but in fact turned out to be an attack on Aisling for having deserted her marital duties. But apart from these happenings, life in Kilgarret was able to absorb the scandal of Aisling's flight. And a lot of people wagged their heads comfortably to each other and said that it just went to show that money and good looks don't necessarily bring you happiness.

The spring came to London and Elizabeth became much bigger. She said it was now impossible for anyone to get into the little lift with her and that when she and Henry came back from any outing he had to walk up the stairs. This was not quite true but her protruding stomach was very noticeable. She left the school at Easter and came home tearfully with a huge teddy bear the children had given. She had promised to return and show them the baby in September, she said that if it was a beautiful baby she might prop it up in the art room and they could all paint it. The children loved this idea but she knew it would never happen. Next September there would be a new art teacher who would hate this doting mother returning and looking for the limelight.

In the last weeks she felt she would never have been able to cope without Aisling. She had taught Aisling to cook more adventurously, surprised that she knew only the very basics.

'What would I have had to cook for? At home Mam always had a girl to cook for us, and when I entered married bliss it wasn't long before my husband decided he would prefer to drink his breakfast, dinner and tea rather than eat them.' Aisling shopped, and chopped vegetables and set tables while Elizabeth had rests and put her feet up. She found her legs swelling if she stood around too much. 'You do too much entertaining, what are you having Simon and his yukky sister and brother-in-law for?' She chopped bits of pork expertly and threw them into a casserole as she talked.

Elizabeth sat in the kitchen with her feet on a little beaded footstool that Johnny had found for her. 'You've no idea how much pleasure it gives Henry. He feels somehow that he's their equal if he can have them to dine at his home . . . What are you *doing*?'

'The recipe says a little cider. . . .'

'But that's half a bottle you've put in.'

'That's a little, isn't it? A lot would be a full bottle.'

The baby was two weeks overdue.

'I feel unreasonably annoyed,' Aisling said as they sat in the flat looking out at the park one July day.

'Funny, I don't mind, I feel sort of dreamy and as if it's borrowed time . . . oh I do hope that there won't be anything wrong with it.'

'You'd have just as much love . . . or more, they say. But let's not start preparing for that sort of thing . . . Mam sent you her love by the way, in today's letter. And I got one from Dad, too.'

'What did he want?'

'That's what I wondered, but in fact it was just a chatty letter: your mother tells me that since we're not going to see you at home in Kilgarret the only way I can keep in touch with you is to write to you . . . I think he always felt guilty when Mam did all the writing to poor Sean in the army and he didn't.' Aisling looked suddenly at Elizabeth, whose face was contorted in a kind of grimace. 'What is it?'

'That's the second time . . . oh, oh. . . .'

'Right, get your coat, the case is in the hall.'

'Henry, what about . . . ?'

'I'll telephone him from the hospital, come on.'

'Suppose we don't get a taxi . . . ?'

'Put on that smart summer coat. It was bought for great occasions like this. . . .' Aisling ran to the window and leaned out. Four stories below a taxi was passing by. The taxi driver heard the piercing whistle and saw the redhead waving from the window. 'We'll be right down,' she shouted.

He had pulled in outside the main door of the building when they emerged. Taking one look at Elizabeth, he groaned, 'Blimey, just my luck. Another mad dash to the maternity ward, and I thought I was going to have this gorgeous dolly all to myself.' He drove very quickly and Aisling held Elizabeth's hand and said babies were never born in taxis, first babies were always slow in delivering – people always thought that the contractions were faster than they were. 'You must admit,' she said to Elizabeth as they turned in the gate of the hospital, 'you really must admit that I'm very knowledgeable about childbirth for someone who has not even known the delights of sexual intercourse.'

Elizabeth was still laughing when they came to meet her in the corridor.

Henry arrived at the hospital, white-faced. In the waiting room he and Aisling hugged each other.

'They say it will only be a few minutes now. You're in time. You'll see the baby first. I was afraid I would.'

'It wouldn't have mattered.' Henry was stuttering with excitement.

The nurse opened the door.

'Mr Mason . . . ?'

'Yes, yes, is she all right?'

'She's fine, she's perfect, she wants to show you your beautiful daughter. . . .'

'Eileen,' said Henry.

'Eileen,' said Aisling.

Eileen was the most beautiful baby in the world. Anyone could see that. She was also the best-tempered.

'Did all those Brendan Ogs and Patrick Ogs look like this?' Elizabeth asked as she stared with adoration at the sleeping bundle in her arms.

'Nothing at all like this. They had red, bad-tempered Daly faces looking for notice and attention, and pushing their way on in the world at the age of one day. Eileen is gentle and well bred. You can see that. Look at her expression.'

They looked at the perfect little face and Aisling traced her finger lightly over the tiny hands with their little nails.

'It's impossible to think of her ever doing anything remotely bad, isn't it?'

'I suppose they thought that about us too when we were born.'

'Well, we didn't do much bad did we? We had a bit of bad luck along the way and we coped with it. That's all we did.'

'Yes, that's all we did. Are you listening Eileen? That is all your mother and your Aunt Aisling did.'

'I can't understand what you're having her christened for if you don't believe any of it.'

'It's so hard to explain. It doesn't mean that people want to believe all of it, it's just a nice tradition.'

'But it's a real thing, you know, baptism opening the floodgates of grace.'

'I thought you believed Protestant baptisms didn't count,' Elizabeth laughed.

'They do and they don't. They do if you can't have the real thing, though maybe in your case you have a duty to get her the real thing. After all you were brought up in the Catholic faith by me for five years.'

'I know, and it terrified me to death.'

'So this is only a social affair, is it?'

'Social and ceremony really. Ceremony and tradition – I think that sums it up.'

'Right. What kind of eats will we serve for ceremony and tradition? Roast beef of Olde England?'

'No, you idiot. Elegant hors d'oeuvres, things that can be eaten in one hand while champagne is clenched in the other.'

'Who will be there?'

'Most of the wedding crowd.'

'Will Harry come?'

'Certainly he will, I'm not going to put up with a lot of old-womanish nonsense from Henry and Father. Certainly he'll come. He can stay at Stefan's if that makes everyone feel better. No, he can't, he can stay here like he did the last time. And I won't have Father being brave about it, and noble.'

'You are marvellous Elizabeth ... I wish there were somebody in Kilgarret who would smooth my path home like you smooth Harry's.'

'I've told you a dozen times ... there's nobody keeping you away from Kilgarret except yourself.'

'So you say. Now let's think about food. Will we do it ourselves and say we got caterers?'

'Or shall we get caterers and say we did it ourselves?'

Dear Aisling,
I know, I know, I'm the one that didn't write to you. But I didn't know what to say. Apparently even Eamonn sent you a birthday card. I didn't know. I thought you were in disgrace. Anyway it turns out that you write more letters than St Paul. So I'm sorry, I've been away so much and so involved in other things that people didn't tell me things. Eamonn knows nothing. Donal's like a lovesick calf, Maureen spends her whole time giving out to me for even existing so she's not any help, Mam always thinks of you as her pet and she won't talk about you at all.

Anyway, I didn't write to apologise or to whinge and whine, I wrote because I think Mam looks *awful*. Nobody else will tell you that in their letters because they don't notice. I only come home now and then so I've seen an awful change in her. She's got very thin, and looks kind of sallow. She doesn't eat much and sometimes sits down suddenly as if she had a pain. I may be exaggerating it, but I suddenly thought last night if it was me that upped and left and nobody told me that Mam was looking badly, I'd feel very cross.

I don't know what to say about the whole other thing, I really don't. I suppose it's like when a love affair ends only worse because there's all the fuss and bother. Don't tell Mam I wrote, she'd be very annoyed, she gets sharp with me if I tell her she's looking badly. And I'm not saying it to make you feel guilty so that you'll come home. If things were bad you were quite right to go, and Donal thinks that too. But you might be the one to persuade her to go to a doctor . . . she listens to you.

Imagine Elizabeth having a child so quickly, she must be disgusted. I thought that there were no unplanned babies born in England these days, she must still have her Kilgarret training rooted in her.

Love, Niamh

527

'Just enough to worry us to death and not enough to tell us what might be wrong,' fumed Aisling when she read the letter. 'Ten months of silence and then this. Isn't she really unspeakable?'

'If it's such a village,' Johnny said, 'why can't you ask someone you know and trust to go and have a look at her and tell you honestly?'

'That's harder than you think, rumours start. . . . It's probably nothing, Niamh sounds as if she just got the idea into her head and wrote it while she was still thinking about it.' They were sitting in the Manchester Street flat having little cups of china tea which Johnny said was an elegant thing to do: he had shown her what kind of cups to serve it in and she had now quite taken to the notion of sipping tea that smelled of perfume and which you put no milk in.

'Yes, I'm sure it's all a bit overdramatic.' Johnny got up and stretched. Aisling remembered that Elizabeth had always said that about him. He didn't like to talk about unpleasant things.

'I'm sure you're right,' she said putting away Niamh's letter.

Johnny smiled, stretched again like a cat and sat down. 'What will we do tonight?' he asked.

'It's my bridge night,' she said.

'Oh tell them you can't go . . . ?'

It was a big decision. She telephoned Henry and said she had to go out suddenly. Someone had turned up out of the blue.

'Why didn't you say you were going out with me?' Johnny asked.

'I don't know,' said Aisling honestly. 'I just didn't.'

Mrs Moriarty wrote to Aisling a long reassuring letter; she had been into the shop, and though Eileen looked a bit wishy-washy the light there was never good at the best of times. She had made an excuse and called to the house in the square too. Eileen had been in fine form, full of chat about young Donal and Anna Barry. Not a complaint out of her. Mrs Moriarty had asked quite specifically how Eileen had been feeling and had discovered that she had been feeling in top form. Mrs Moriarty said that Aisling was a good daughter to be so concerned but she really mustn't worry. Mrs Moriarty said she would tell no one of the enquiry, not even Donal, who had become like a son to them. She ended by saying that she was praying that Aisling's problems and worries would be sorted out satisfactorily, and in the meantime, Aisling should rest assured that the Good Lord always looked after people in His Own Way.

Niamh wrote a short letter and said that Mam said she had been feeling a bit under the weather but she was much better now. She had been to Doctor Murphy and got some good tablets. And she did look a lot better.

I'm writing to tell you all this because it's silly to write and tell you the alarming news without writing back when the news stops being alarming. Thanks for not upsetting everyone about it. Or maybe you were too busy over there to be able to get in touch. I hear you work as a receptionist in some specialist's place. Tim and I will be going to London some time before Christmas for a weekend. Could we have a bit of the floor in your place? We've got sheepskin jackets so we won't need much in the way of bedclothes. I'll let you know nearer the time.

I hear Tony has gone off to England to learn more about the business. Diversification, is what Mrs Murray told Anna Barry's mother. Whatever that means. But of course you probably know all this already. I suppose you know that Donal and Anna are thinking of buying the ring. Or so I hear from other people. I find that the older I grow the less people tell you. Or maybe it's just Kilgarret. Or maybe it's just me. Look after yourself and see you in December for two nights, if that's all right.

Love, Niamh.

Johnny took her to the ballet one night and to a little Greek restaurant another night.

'I never knew people had wines like this,' said Aisling happily. 'What's it called again?'

'Retsina. It's a special way they have of making wine.'

'Have you been to Greece?'

'Yes, it's terrific, I'm going to go again next summer. You should come with me. You'd love it, I thought the Squire would have taken you to the Greek islands. I thought that was the kind of thing squires did.'

'This squire took me to the pubs of Rome twice and that was it. So Greece is still to come.'

'It's a date,' Johnny said lightly.

'Can I pay for the meal tonight, you've spent a lot?'

'No, no, heavens no.'

'What can I do to repay you?'

'Ask me to supper in that tasteful flat that I practically furnished for you.'

'Of course. When?'

'Tomorrow?'

'Tomorrow.'

'Hallo, Elizabeth, is it a bad time?'

'No, no of course not. I'm just putting her into the cot, Conchita has arrived.'

'Oh yes, you're off to the college.'

'I hate leaving her actually, very boring and Mumsy suddenly. I thought wouldn't it be great if I could put her in a sling over my arm?'

'I don't see why not, in the art college they should be nice and Bohemian now. They'd accept it.'

'*They* might, but it's pouring with rain, she might drown on the way there. How are you?'

'I wanted to ask you something. It's a bit awkward. . . .'

'Go on, what is it?'

'Well, it's a bit childish, but Johnny asked himself to supper in my flat tonight.'

'Yes?'

'And I was wondering . . . I wondered did you mind?'

'Mind what?'

'His coming to the flat.'

'Heavens above, hasn't he been going to the flat since the day you found it, haven't we all? Why should I mind?'

'Well, just him and me, in case . . . God, this sounds silly, in case there was any lingering anything, you know?'

'I *see*,' Elizabeth said, emphatically. 'Oh, I *see*. No, Guide's honour, and cross my heart and hope to die, the coast is clear. . . .'

'And I'm not . . . ?'

'Treading on any broken hearts? No, not at all. Go ahead. With all the usual warnings.'

'It's nothing like that, it's just that. . . .'

'I know, and you don't have to tell me, but if you do I won't mind.'

'There'll be nothing to tell.'

'Enjoy yourself.'

'I hope you don't mind my taking this extraordinary attitude.' Aisling was almost purple with embarrassment.

'Heavens, no, my dear girl, it's entirely up to you.'

'It's just I feel that by asking you to supper I sort of implied that the other was also . . . on the menu.'

'No no, shall we have another little drink instead?'

'Johnny, you're far too smooth, and like the hero of the film . . . why aren't you flustered like I am?'

'Darling girl, what is there to be flustered about? We were kissing each other very delightfully and I suggested that we might go to your bed and kiss further there, and you said you didn't want to, I said fine, let's have a little drink instead.'

'Yes, that's right, it's not a matter for getting flustered about.'

'You're very pretty flustered.'

'No, I'm not, my red face clashes with my hair. I'm best when I'm pale with anxiety. I once saw my face in a mirror when I was so anxious about something or other that Tony had done – I can't remember now – but I looked quite ravishing.'

They had a companionable drink and Johnny left before midnight.

'It was a lovely meal and a lovely evening.'

'I'm sorry about the other thing.'

531

'Don't worry about it, I'll suggest it from time to time – or better still, you do if it occurs to you. Otherwise we won't worry about it.'

'Are you going to get the tube back to Earls Court?' she asked.

He had his address book out. 'No, love, I think I'll go and call on a friend, it's early still.' He waved at a taxi and was gone.

She went up to her flat which smelled of food and cursed herself for being so stupid. Why could she not have said yes, she would like to have kissed him in her bedroom. Why could she not have learned about making love from a smashing lover like Johnny Stone?

'Nothing happened,' she told Elizabeth next day on the phone.

'You forgot to cook dinner?' Elizabeth asked.

'No I forgot to go to bed with him,' she said.

'He'll ask you again.'

Ethel Murray had never written a full reply to any of Aisling's long warm letters. But she did reply when Aisling said she had heard Tony was in England, what possible course could he be doing in 'diversification'?

I had to say something, Aisling, when people asked me where he was, but in fact Father John was able to use his connections and get Tony into this very nice nursing home. They have a special Catholic chaplain there and mass and confession for all the Catholic patients; others have their own services. I know I've pleaded with you long and often to see him, and I understand in a way some of your reasons for not coming back to Kilgarret, but now that he's in England, over in the same country, could you not go and see him? Make no promises, just go to see him. He's very bad, Aisling. Doctor Murphy here sent him for some medical tests and he definitely has a liver infection. So this is being treated as well as his craving for drink. That wonderful priest in Waterford has been a great support; he told me, and I believe him, that Tony did not mean to hit you that night, that they often do the very reverse of what they would do when sober. It's just their illness. I enclose the address in hope and prayer that you may find it in your heart to visit him. It's not near London, it's more in the North of England. It's near Preston.

Your loving mother-in-law Ethel Mary Murray

Johnny telephoned and asked her if he could cook supper for her one night the following week.

'That would be great. What time?'

'Come earlyish, about seven say. That will give you plenty of time to catch a tube back home – if you want to.' It couldn't have been more straightforward, he could hardly have made it more plain.

She wore not only her best dress, but her good slip, and the only panties with lace on them. She even bought a new bra because she thought the one she had was grubby. She put a mouth-freshener and a small talcum powder in her handbag. Then she remembered having made all those preparations for her honeymoon and her heart became like a stone.

Johnny cooked some dish with rice: she couldn't identify what it was, it tasted like sawdust. The wine was bitter, yet she knew this was all in her mind. After dinner they sipped brandy by his fire and he played 'Unchained Melody' over and over on the radiogram. He kissed her several times . . . and said that they would be more comfortable in the other room.

'That would be nice,' she said weakly.

He helped her take off her clothes and kissed her again as she stood in her slip.

'You won't believe this, but I've never done it before.'

'I know, I know.' He was very soothing.

'No, you don't know. I've never done it at all. Not even when we were married. . . .' She didn't dare look at him. 'That was part of the problem. He didn't, he couldn't . . . so I never. . . .'

533

Johnny folded her in his arms very tightly and stroked her hair. 'Poor Aisling, stop trembling, it's all right, it's all right.'

'I'm very sorry, I should have told you before . . . at my age it's ridiculous.'

'Poor Aisling.' He stroked her hair and held her to him. He was so nice and kind she could hardly believe it.

'So if you'd prefer us to get dressed and forget it, if it would all be a lot of work for you. . . .'

'Stop burbling, Aisling.' He stroked her hair still, she felt safe and happy in his arms. 'Whatever you like my sweetheart,' he said. 'If you'd like to stay with me, that's wonderful. If you want to go home, of course home you go.'

'I'd like to stay with you,' she said in a small voice.

'Then we'll just take it very easily, very gently,' he said. 'You're so beautiful Aisling, you're so lovely – I'm very glad to be the first.' He held her tight to him and she could feel his heart beating.

She was glad he was the first too.

She lay and looked at him as he slept.

It had been so gentle and natural and as if it had been meant to be like that always. In fact it seemed ridiculous to kiss and stroke someone without fitting exactly together with them like that. It had been so lovely to think she was giving pleasure only by welcoming him towards her.

To think how worried she had always been about this. She must have been very silly and immature. There was nothing awkward. No shame, no awful moment of when you did and when you didn't.

Suppose she had met Johnny years ago, years and years ago when it had all been groping and shoving and awkward and rough? Suppose she had always known this kind of loving, that it was there at the back of her mind? Then surely she would have been less hopeless. How great to have been able to love somebody properly, to have been part of this lovely man. If only it had happened to her long long ago, when she was a young girl.

Like it had happened to Elizabeth, she remembered suddenly. Then she looked at the sleeping Johnny and put that very firmly out of her mind.

XIX

Aisling found that being a doctors' receptionist was not very challenging. She welcomed the patients as they came in, settling them in the elegant waiting room with its highly-polished furniture and copies of *Country Life* and *The Field* on the huge table. She kept three immaculate appointment books, the card indexes and a detailed day by day book in three different-coloured pens, so that any of the doctors could look back and see what had related to him on any given day.

They were very pleased with her and each one of them told her separately that when she had taken two weeks' holiday at Christmas there had been utter chaos. The temporary girl had confused everything, and had not been able to follow Aisling's simple system.

'Maybe I've become an old retainer, a treasure . . . wonderful Old Miss O'Connor,' Aisling smiled.

They hastily assured her that she didn't seem at all old to them.

'They have absolutely no sense of humour, that's what's wrong with them,' Aisling said to Elizabeth and Henry as she was doing one of her impersonations. 'But I suppose if I was raking in all the money they are, I wouldn't have time for a giggle either, I'd be too busy counting it and gloating over it.'

'Do they make a lot?' Henry was interested.

'A fortune,' Aisling said firmly. 'I don't write it up, of course, they have a book-keeper – as well they might. I leave all the information there in the files: who came, what was wrong, what happened, what was prescribed . . . then they work out some enormous fees. They have two sets of books, one for the income tax and one for themselves. I know that because I saw the book-keeper working once. Funny little woman – she looks like someone's granny, not a fiddler.'

'That's very unfair of them,' Henry said. 'It's most unjust – if they make so much anyway why are they unwilling to pay taxes on it?' Henry was getting quite worked up about the doctors now.

'Henry, we're not going to cure the corruption in Harley Street – or any other street. As Aisling, said, everyone's doing it. Just because we don't, it doesn't mean the world is like us. Here, take your beautiful daughter from me for a while; I must go and do some work on this year's art course or we'll not earn enough money to pay taxes on.' She smiled and handed Eileen over.

Henry took the baby absently, still looking upset. 'We earn enough money, I've had a rise. We manage. You don't need to do the art course this year.'

'But I *do*. We discussed it. Apart from liking it and wanting to do it, it really does bring in a nice little sum. . . .' She turned to Aisling apologetically. 'Why don't you and your chap Johnny join up, then I'd know I had two pupils anyway?'

Elizabeth had meant it as a joke, but Aisling answered her seriously. 'I was going to do just that, I thought it might educate me a little . . . but Johnny said I would only confuse myself and tie my already garbled brain up into more knots.'

Elizabeth laughed easily. 'Oh yes, I know, pathetic once-weekly culture-seekers . . . middle-class aspirations . . . *Readers' Digest* condensed art lessons. . . .'

Aisling burst out laughing. 'He told you he said all that to me?'

'Aisling, Johnny has been saying that for years. He has always been wrong but he never changes his tune. Still, suit yourself. You're missing the chance of a lifetime, isn't she, Henry.'

'What?' Henry was still annoyed. 'I'm sorry I wasn't listening.'

Elizabeth kissed Henry suddenly. 'If I hadn't had my art course,' she said, 'I'd never have found you, think about that.'

536

'Yes, but if you keep on having art courses, maybe you'll find another one.' Henry was almost good-humoured.

'That's the only reason I keep holding them, you know that!'

Aisling and Elizabeth pushed the pram through Battersea Park. Eileen was so wrapped up it was hard to see how she could get any benefit from the spring sunshine. Still, Aisling said, it was doing the grown-ups no harm to have a bit of exercise. As usual, they stopped at a bench for a cigarette.

'Undoing the good of the healthy walk,' Aisling would say, lighting up happily.

'Does Johnny not try to get you to give them up?'

'Oh, I smoke very little with him, one after a meal, and I'm forever brushing my teeth. He doesn't go on at me so much now. Anyway, it's only a phase, he'll go back on them.'

'No,' said Elizabeth, 'it's not a phase, everything he does he means. He won't go back on them.'

'It hasn't made any difference, between us, my being with Johnny?' Aisling asked.

'No, no, of course it hasn't. I mean that.'

'Yes, I know you said from the start . . . and I know you don't have regrets or anything. After all, it was you that gave him up.'

'Yes, in a way. . . .'

'Does it bring it all back, you know, the good bits, the start, when you see me with him, when I talk about it all? You see . . . it's the only thing I'm not sure about. . . .'

'About what, about me?'

'Yes, I know how you feel for Henry and Eileen and I know almost every corner of your life as you do mine . . . but I don't know about Johnny. If you cared for him so much once how had it turned into a sort of joky friendship by the time I came over here?'

'Because that was the only way it could be. . . .'

'That's what I'm getting at. Do you regret it all, and wish that. . . . I don't know, wish that you and he were married and that it was all great?'

Elizabeth blew out a long breath of smoke. 'I'm being as

537

honest as I know how, I'm not playing with words. But for me to wish that is a nonsense. It's like wishing for a square circle, or wishing that grass was blue instead of green. It's a nonsense because it could never have happened.'

There was a silence.

Then, 'And after all that time, all that involvement, you still don't feel jealous or envious . . . or think that if you were free . . . ?'

'No. No, I do mean that and I want you to believe it.'

'I don't think I'll ever understand it,' Aisling said as they stood up to move on. 'But then you've been in love twice and I've never been in love at all.'

'Not even with Johnny?'

'No. I'm fascinated with him, but I'm not in love, not the way people are who would do anything for the loved one. I don't put him before me. . . .'

'You will,' Elizabeth said.

Dear Elizabeth,
I did what you asked and it wasn't a nice thing to do. The place is a real posh place for a start, very very pricey and they all speak with marbles in their mouths, the staff that is.

I said I was enquiring about Mr Murray on behalf of an intermediary who wondered whether his wife should come to see him. Oh, they wanted to give no information away. I gave details on the understanding that his family in Ireland were not to be told. I said I had met him at a wedding in London and would like to resume the acquaintance.

He was sitting in the garden, and a male nurse was beside him. He looked terrible. He's both fatter and thinner than on your wedding day, his face seems swollen and yet his neck looks thin and hangs in folds of skin.

He didn't remember me, I said we'd all met at your wedding. He didn't seem to recall that either.

So I said that I lived nearby and maybe I might call in once or twice, and he more or less said suit yourself. Then the old biddy who runs the place sort of warmed a bit to me when she saw I really had met him. Anyway, she said he'd never come out of there. She didn't put it like that, Elizabeth, but that's what she said really. It's worse than where your poor mother was because it pretends to be normal, yet they have these male nurses padding round beside the patients trying to look invisible. It gave me the creeps, and if it's all the same to you I won't go again. He's not a man, he's a shell.

Love to you, Henry and my lovely Eileen,
From Harry

'I asked Harry to go and look at Tony for you,' Elizabeth said.

Aisling was startled. 'Why?'

'He's too big a part of your life to cut off and forget.'

'Surely you don't want me to try and go . . . after all you know and heard. . . .'

'No, no indeed, but I . . . we should know how he was.'

'And how does Harry say he is?'

'Like a shell.'

'Oh God. Like a shell.'

Johnny said they should go to Greece. He said she should ask for a month.

'Nobody gets a month off in my kind of job. I'm lucky they're going to give me three weeks. I had the two weeks at Christmas, remember, when we went to Cornwall.'

'That was last year's holiday, this is this year's.'

'Oh, but I couldn't take a whole month. . . .'

'September is beautiful in Greece. . . .'

'I'll ask, but I don't know . . . I don't want to annoy them either.'

'Look, I'll go for a month, you come for as long as you can. Right? That way there's no fuss.'

He was right, of course, but somehow it annoyed Aisling. She felt that she wasn't the whole reason for the holiday in Greece. She felt that Johnny would have been going anyway.

Father said that it was a pity Aisling had dropped out of the bridge classes, she had been very quick and would have made a good player. Elizabeth explained that she was going about with Johnny Stone.

'No!' said Father. 'Your chap Johnny Stone?'

'Yes, he used to be my chap, but not now, obviously.'

'Well, well,' Father said, 'I hope he treats her better than he treated you.'

Elizabeth felt a wave of resentment and irritation. She would like to have screamed at him. Yet she knew that to an outsider, it *was* treating a girl shabbily to have an affair with her for seven years and make no suggestion of marriage. And possibly, in many ways, it was shabby.

'Do you tell Aunt Eileen anything about Johnny in your letters?' Elizabeth asked.

'What could I tell her in the name of God?'

'You know, that you're happy, that you're seeing him – I didn't mean saying you were sleeping with him.'

'But Mam would be horrified to know I was seeing a man. I'm a married woman to Mam, still, you know. I couldn't tell her a thing about Johnny. Mam only sees romance as leading to the altar and while Tony's around there would be no way of going to the altar with Johnny, so Mam can't be told.'

Elizabeth felt that whether Tony were around or not there would be no way to the altar with Johnny, but said nothing. I might not even be right, she thought to herself suddenly. Perhaps he is thinking of settling down, maybe he's had enough flings. Perhaps he might want to marry Aisling and have a child.

The thought disturbed her, and she was annoyed at herself for being disturbed.

But Aisling had told Donal about the affair. Donal after all had met Johnny at Elizabeth's wedding and had liked him. He also knew vaguely that he was the long-standing lover in Elizabeth's past. Donal was flattered to be told the secret, but his words of encouragement and enthusiasm were tinged with a caution that Aisling didn't like to read.

540

Donal was now engaged to Anna Barry; she would do her B.A. Honours in September and they would marry in October. He would so much like Aisling to be at the wedding – but if she couldn't he'd understand. He was glad she was happy and having a romance with Johnny Stone, but he hoped she wouldn't get hurt. After all it was easy for Johnny to take advantage of her, new in London, fresh from a broken marriage. He hoped she wasn't being foolish. After all, he had used Elizabeth for a long time, and she had to throw him over in the end. He was sure it would all turn out for the best. Mam had been much better and was looking forward to the wedding, because the Barrys would have to organise it. Aisling and Tony's bungalow had been sold to a cousin of Mr Moriarty's who said that it was a marvellous labour-saving house. But Aisling probably knew that already. He hoped that she would make a lot of new friends in London as well as Johnny. Anna sent her love.

Patronising little sod, Aisling thought in a fury. Then she softened. It wasn't his fault, he was still a lovely gentle boy; he had just been steeped through and through with the values of Kilgarret. He was a little provincial; her smashing brother Donal had become a small-minded little provincial chemist.

Johnny said they should go to Greece by train and ship. It would take nearly five days to get there and five days back. That was why they needed at least a month. Aisling hadn't asked the doctors yet, in fact she thought that she might send them a telegram from Greece with an imaginary ailment. She wondered would they travel as man and wife . . . it hadn't occurred before. That cottage in Cornwall had belonged to friends of Johnny, so there had been no need for deception. Aisling had been lonely last Christmas. It was the anniversary of all her troubles and she was lucky to have found a marvellous man to whisk her off to the wild seas and peace of the countryside. But she had been lonely for earlier Christmases, the ones in the square.

But a real summer holiday was something different. She could hardly wait for it. Elizabeth had been envious.

'I'm bright green, that's what I am. No, never did I go off to Greece with Johnny, or anyone. . . .'

'But he said he was always travelling. . . .'

'So he was, but without me. I couldn't go, there was Father, or there was Mother, or there was work . . . no wild roamings around Europe like you.'

'Perhaps you should have gone.'

'Perhaps.' Elizabeth cuddled Eileen, who always smiled at exactly the right time, as if on cue. 'Anyway, if I had gone, everything might have been different, and I mightn't have you . . . and that would have been *dweadful*, wouldn't it?'

'Elizabeth, you swore no baby talk!'

'So I did, but I forget. Anyway, I heard you cooing at her yesterday.'

'Ah, that was different. It's coming up to her birthday, everyone's allowed a few coos at a birthday.'

They had a cake with one candle, and they sang to her: Henry, Elizabeth, Johnny and Aisling, Simon and Father. Eileen put both her fat little arms in the air and waved. They were having a slice of cake when the telephone rang.

'It's for you, Aisling. It's your father,' Henry said.

Elizabeth stood up at the same time.

'My God,' said Aisling. 'It must be Mam.'

'It could be anything, don't panic,' said Elizabeth.

Side by side they went into the hall.

'What will we do?' Aisling asked.

'Talk to him, it may be nothing.' Elizabeth took Aisling's other hand as she picked up the receiver.

From the sitting room the birthday party saw them standing together in a shaft of sunlight. Both of them rigid as if waiting for a blow.

'Yes Dad. Of course you were right to ring, Dad. . . .

'And when did they tell you?

'And did they tell her, does she know?

'Oh God. Oh dear God.

'And how long do they say . . . ?

'Oh no, surely not, surely they must say more than that . . . ?

'And does she have pain Dad . . . ?

'Of course, Dad. Tomorrow. No, don't worry about that. I'll sort it out at this end. Tomorrow.'

The doctors had been very understanding. Aisling thanked her lucky stars that she hadn't asked them for the month's holiday; that would have marked her down as flighty. They might not even have believed the tale of a dying mother. She spent two hours writing out a very clear set of instructions for whoever would come from the secretarial agency to do her job.

'Choose an auld one like myself, don't get a flighty little thing,' she said to Doctor Steiner.

'How old are you?' he said laughing.

'Oh, it's in my file, you know well enough, twenty-eight.'

'You had your mother a long time, compared to some,' he said gently.

'Yes, but I ran away from her . . . that's what's hard.'

'Still, you're going back now, when she needs you.'

'Yes, and Elizabeth's coming with me, that's the best bit.'

Henry had been amazed when Elizabeth announced that she wanted to go to Ireland.

'You can't possibily go, what will we do with Eileen?'

'I'll take her with me.'

'You must be mad. Listen, darling, you're just upset by everything. You can't possibly take a year-old baby across the sea to Ireland to look at a dying woman.'

'That's not the way I see it. I want to go.'

'But work and everything. . . .'

'There's no work. The course has only one more lecture. One of the others will give it and tidy up. No college. No, it's all fine. We've booked the plane. . . .'

'You're going to take Eileen on the plane?'

'Henry, you come too if you like, you look as if we're all running away and abandoning you. . . .'

'No, no, of course you must go, I'm sorry, it's all come as a shock. I suppose I didn't realise how much she meant to you . . . to both of you. . . . Aisling has been here for a year and more, and, not going back to see her, well, it's a bit sudden, everyone flying off at the drop of a hat.'

'It's not the drop of a hat. Eileen has cancer, everywhere, all over her. They opened her up and closed her immediately. She only has a couple of weeks to live.'

The air hostess said she had never seen such a beautiful baby and Eileen had smiled, and Aisling and Elizabeth smiled wanly too. They were both very tired. Aisling had organised her work and her flat. And her social life.

'So I can't possibly go to Greece.'

'But when it's all over, you'll need a holiday – that's the very time to go to Greece,' Johnny had said.

'No. And anyway I'll have used up more than my holidays by then.'

'Oh, stop talking about holidays as if you were a schoolgirl, this is compassionate leave.'

'I'm sorry, you'll have to go to Greece on your own – unless you'd like to put it off until next year?'

'Well, you know best.'

There was a silence.

'I'm very very sorry, you know. You know how sorry I am.'

'Yes, I know,' Aisling had said. But he wasn't sorry enough to come to Ireland, or even to the airport.

'Never mind,' Elizabeth had said, reading her thoughts. 'He didn't go to my mother's funeral either.'

They hired a car at the airport and drove into Dublin. The city was filled with tourists, Americans and foreigners of every description. They blinked in the sunlight in the crowded streets.

'I don't know what they want to gather here for . . . full of noise and traffic. Why don't they go off down the country?'

'They like souvenirs and shops,' Elizabeth said. 'It's some kind of human weakness. When I used to take those tours to the National Gallery or the Tate, people wanted to slip away from the group and see the shops. I ask you. Often the same kind of shops they had in Dulwich or wherever.'

'Shay Ferguson was going to do up rooms near his awful garage, and let them to tourists. I wonder did he ever do it, now that his playmate Tony was taken from him?'

'It's going to be hard for you going back, you'll be an object of interest to them, won't you?'

'Honestly, Elizabeth, I couldn't give a damn. If they're such gossips and so low as to be more interested in me and my doings than in poor Mam, well let them.'

'I wasn't saying that, I was only saying that you'll have to be prepared for a lot of emotion. Worse than if you had been at home.'

'I know, I know. Thank God you came with me, you're so good.'

'She's nearly as important to me as she is to you.'

'I know, she'll be so pleased.' Aisling suddenly broke down. 'Oh, isn't it ridiculous that she's going to die, she's not old, she's not sixty, it's so unfair. . . .'

'Stop it Aisling, stop it now, you can't see where you're going, you'll kill us all, is that going to help?'

'No, you're right. I'm sorry.'

'We must be full of bravery when we meet her. That's what she'd want, isn't it?'

'Yes, that's what she'd want, to see us back in Kilgarret behaving very well and keeping everyone else's spirits up. That's what we'll have to do.'

They hadn't told anyone what time they would arrive and Dad didn't recognise the hired car as it came past the shop. But they saw him locking up; he looked old and stooped, his hair was straggly and his face was lined.

'Stop it, Aisling, remember why we came,' Elizabeth said, and the trembling in Aisling's lip stopped.

She got out of the car just as Sean was walking wearily towards the house in the square, and Elizabeth got out the other side holding little Eileen, who was fast asleep.

'Dad,' Aisling began. 'Dad.'

Elizabeth stepped in front of her. 'Uncle Sean,' she said, 'we've come back to show Eileen her namesake. We thought she'd like to see the baby and know that her name lives on. . . .'

That was when Sean broke down and right out in the square, where anyone could see, he sobbed like a child. They patted him and they blew their own noses and they offered him a big handkerchief which Elizabeth had seen sticking out of his pocket. Then he firmed up his shoulders and they went into the house.

'Can we have our old room?' Aisling asked.

'You can have what you like,' Dad said.

They went up and left their cases on the same beds that they had occupied as children, one on each side of the white chest of drawers.

They put the baby, fed and changed in her carry-cot, on the floor between them and sat down.

'Did we ever think in the years gone by. . . .' Aisling said.

'No, but we never thought anything . . . it was all going to be so different, and everyone was going to stay the same age . . . we were just going to catch up with them.'

'And treat them like equals. . . .'

'And stay up as late as them . . . .'

'She's still asleep, Dad says . . . should we . . . ?'

'Yes,' said Elizabeth, 'let's go in now.'

'Take the baby?'

'All right. Brave, remember.'

'I'll remember. There's no point in coming home to weep, she doesn't want that, she wants . . . she wants. . . .'

'That's right. Come on.'

She looked tiny, or they had given her huge pillows. Mam was a big woman but everything, her head, her shoulders and her arms seemed to have been scaled down. The room was darkened, but you could still see the light through the flowery curtains, and you could hear the noises of the town, the bus revving up, children calling across the square, the clip-clop of a horse and cart.

Mam wore a cardigan, a pale blue one that Aisling remembered as one of her better ones. It had become a bed cardigan now. There was a missal, and rosary beads, on the bedside table beside all the glasses of water and bottles and medicines.

Her smile was without tears, her voice matter-of-fact. 'Well, I was right, I was right. Sean told me he had to make a phone call from the shop yesterday. A Sunday. He said it had to do with business. I knew he was ringing you, and he didn't want to tell me in case you didn't come. Let me have a look at you.'

'Oh Mam.'

'Merciful Lord, is that Elizabeth you have with you? The room's so dark. Come here, the pair of you, let me look at you.'

'It's the three of us. I brought her to see you. . . .'

'What do you mean, what are you saying? Who . . . ?'

'I brought Eileen to see her adoped granny . . . you're the only one she has. I thought she should have a look at you. . . .' Elizabeth put the baby on the bed and little Eileen put up her hands towards the sick woman as if she wanted to be lifted. Elizabeth and Aisling stood motionless. The two frail arms reached out and lifted the baby with effort, and laid it against her breast.

'Wasn't that a beautiful thing to do, to bring her to see me? Oh, Elizabeth, I've always said you had more class than any of my own children. And much more than this rascal, who I love more than all of them put together.'

Then they moved to the bed and kissed her and they sat down beside each other so that she wouldn't have to keep turning her head to look from one to another. And sometimes she took Aisling's hand with her own thin ones, and sometime she took Elizabeth's. She told them she was not afraid, and she knew that Our Lord was waiting for her. And that she would see Sean, and Violet and everyone, and she would watch down and pray for them all. She said that she worried about Eamonn and his father, and what would happen when she wasn't there to keep the peace. She said it was a terrible pity that she wouldn't live to see Donal and that nice Anna Barry married, and what a tragedy for them, with all the plans made, and now a bereavement to hang over the wedding festivities. She said that Niamh was as bright as a button and would come to no harm, because she was able to look after herself better than any of them. It

547

came from being the youngest of the family. She didn't worry much about Maureen either. Maureen was a Daly now, and she had settled down; the children were a great delight to her. She would always be a complainer: it was in her nature.

She told them that it was a great grace to be given a warning of your death, not to be killed in an accident or in a war. It meant you had time to take stock and to tell people things you hadn't wanted to tell them before, and set things right. She had even made a little will; not that she had much to leave, but a few personal possessions she wanted people to have. It was a comfortable feeling. She said nothing about Tony or Aisling's departure from Kilgarret. She said there was plenty of time. Doctor Murphy had said she would be well able to talk for a week or two. The trouble was she got tired easily.

She kissed the baby's forehead and let them scoop her up off the bed. Elizabeth held her child in one arm and held out her hand to touch Aunt Eileen's.

'I'll let Aisling come to you on her own . . . we don't have to be like Siamese twins,' she smiled.

Aunt Eileen smiled back. 'But you always were like Siamese twins, that was what was so wonderful about the whole thing, when you came here. Thank God it didn't die, when you grew up. I'm so glad you came back full of strength for me, you two fine girls. It's a great great help. You do know that.'

'Yes, Mam, it's the devil to try and keep cheerful but if it's what you want . . . well, you always get your own way.'

'No, I don't, you bold rossie, I never had my way over you . . . go on now, and let me sleep.'

She was still smiling as they closed the door.

It was very hard indeed to visit Mrs Murray. Aisling rang first to know if she would be welcome.

'Well, of course, you must come, if you want to,' was the reply.

It had been awkward, even when Mrs Murray tried to be warm. Aisling could not apologise for her own behaviour and Mrs Murray could not forgive it. They were two women bound by a wish to be understood but a failure to understand.

'I believe that the home where Tony is staying is very comfortable.'

'How do you believe that, Aisling, if you haven't seen it?'

'A friend of Elizabeth's saw it.'

'Oh I see. Elizabeth brought her baby over, I hear.'

'Yes, they called her Eileen, Henry's mother was Eileen too.'

'That was nice.'

'How is Joannie?'

'About the same, the same really.'

And in the end when the conversation became almost too heavy to hand backwards and forwards to each other, Aisling said, 'I'm so sorry, about everything, Mrs Murray.'

'Yes. I'm sorry about everything too. Truly sorry.'

'I'll go back to my mother now.'

'And I'm truly sorry about your mother too,' said Mrs Murray. 'It's a very hard life that the Lord gives us here on earth.'

'And I gave it a lot of thought. It's not just a foolish dying woman's fancy, now.'

'No, Mam, I know that.'

'What could be better, you could live here and be mistress of this house, you'd have a girl to do all the work? You'd run the shop with your father, keep the peace between himself and Eamonn.'

'But Mam. . . .'

'There's no cause for you to be over in London working as a doctor's receptionist to people we don't know at all, and living in a poky little flat with second-hand furniture, and learning bridge, and going out to eat in foreign restaurants. That's no life, Aisling, no life at all.'

'But I'd be no good here. . . .'

'You'd be great, and I've come round to thinking that all the things you told me about your marriage mean you should ask for an annulment. You should try. Here you are, a fine young woman, and Tony, the Lord be good to him, hasn't his full senses. . . . The Church has to be understanding in cases like this.'

'I don't know if it's worth it, Mam.'

'You were the one who said it was worth it, and I didn't listen to you. After all, if you can prove that you never consummated your marriage, they'd have to say it wasn't a real marriage.'

'That's right.' Aisling looked down at the floor. Mam knew nothing of Johnny, nothing of any other love and interest in her life. Poor, kind, good Mam was trying to see that fate didn't deal her out of her entitlements. 'I'll be fine, Mam, I've . . . sort of settled into new ways, and I'm very happy. I'll be fine. I'd be better there than here.'

'I'll talk to you again about it, girl, I get tired so easily. Today I feel a puff of wind would blow me away.'

'Don't go away, Mam, please, please.'

'What good are you, Aisling, if you start to cry? Aren't we all worn out with weeping, my shoulders and chest are weary with crying.'

'It's only because we love you.'

'If you loved me, wouldn't you help me by being practical? Your father in here on his knees beside the bed . . . "I'll never live without you, Eileen, you keep us all going, don't die, don't die." Aisling, what kind of help is that for a dying woman? I want to know that he'll be all right, that he'll be able to look after everything, that he'll go on to an old age and let you and Eamonn run the business and give all the others their due out of it. I'd like your father to get the ground floor turned into a place for himself, with a bedroom and all, to save him all those stairs. Could you get Kearneys, the builders, in . . . ?'

Aisling stood up, eyes blazing. 'Right, Mam, would you like them to come this afternoon, or will we wait until the day after the funeral . . . ?'

Eileen laughed and her face looked years younger. 'That's more like it, my girl, that's it. That's the Aisling I used to know.'

*

'I don't know how I can be so calm with you, Eileen, we English are terrified to talk about death, and I sit with you casually talking about it all the time. . . .'

'I've always told you you're more Irish than we are. . . .'

'That's a great compliment, from you.'

'It's a compliment from anyone . . . will you send Aisling back? She's better off here. She'll become restless in England, it's not her place. . . .'

'She's settling there though, Eileen. I mean it, if you saw her place, she's made a little home out of it, much more than she ever bothered in the bungalow with Tony. . . .'

'Ah, it was all a very sad mistake, that, wasn't it?'

'Yes, but she did the only thing she could have done when she left.'

'I don't know. I'm more of your opinion now than I used to be, but I'd like her to come home. Not only for Sean's sake and everything; I think she'll find that this is her place. In the end.'

'Maybe eventually, but I think she feels more free. . . .'

'My love, I know well she has a man in London. I've been that girl's mother for nearly thirty years, I don't have to be told. . . .'

'Well, of course, I'm not sure . . . I don't really. . . .'

'Of course you don't, you don't know a thing. Now, tell me one thing – and this is the only thing – I don't want you to tell her that I asked. Is he a good man? Will he be reliable? Will he make her happy?'

Elizabeth looked her straight in the eye. 'He'll make her very happy for a while. He is not reliable and it's hard to know whether he's a good man or not. In some ways he is very good, very good indeed. . . .'

Aunt Eileen sighed. 'So, it's your own young man is it . . . ah, well, well.'

'You have second sight.'

'When it's over, will you send her back here?'

'I'll encourage her to think seriously about it.'

'You are the only person who tells me the truth – everyone else tells me what they think I want to hear.'

'I wish my daughter had time to get to know you.'

551

'She'll do fine now with her own mother. God bless you child. I feel very very weary. . . .'

The next day the family were asked to come to the bedside. Father Riordan gave out the rosary and even Sean gave the responses. *Holy Mary, Mother of God . . . Holy Mary, Mother of God . . .* Maureen was crying and had her hands over her face; so was Niamh. Eamonn and Donal stood by the door with their heads bowed. Brendan Daly stood beside them. The woman breathed hoarsely, the sound and the drone of the prayers seemed to go together. Then her breathing got softer. The prayers went on and on.

Holy Mary, Mother of God, Pray for us sinners. . . .

Holy Mary, Mother of God, Pray for us sinners now and in the hour of our death.

'Goodbye, Eileen, thank you, thank you very much,' Elizabeth said softly. It didn't matter if Eileen heard or not. She knew.

Peggy insisted on coming in to organise the house for the funeral.

'The mistress liked everything done right, the girl you have now wouldn't know what dishes to have out, and how things should be served.'

The kitchen was soon a hive of activity. Chicken boiling in a huge pot, bacon in another . . . Elizabeth looked on in amazement.

'How many people are they going to invite?' she asked.

'You don't invite people, they come. Surely you must have been at some funerals when you lived here?'

'I don't remember anything like this.' Elizabeth stared as more and more people called with mass cards, and sympathy.

'I'll have to go and help Dad cope with it all,' Aisling said. They had been sitting in their bedroom, as always, with the door open, aware of the activity of the house.

'Good, I'll settle the baby down and I'll come down too. Tell me what to do that would help.'

'Oh you'll know, talk, laugh, keep people's spirits up.'

'*Laugh?*'

'A bit, it's always a great help if it's not too solemn, it's unnatural with people making formal speeches.'

The undertakers took Eileen's coffin out at five o'clock that evening. The family followed slowly, heads down. All around the square people stood respectfully. Men had taken their hats and caps off. People blessed themselves as the coffin passed, carried by the four undertakers. People getting off the bus stopped to let the procession pass by and blessed themselves also. It wound up the hill to the church, where the bell was tolling in the most unsuitable way for a warm summer day.

They stood around the coffin at the back of the church for what seemed like hours and hours. The whole town of Kilgarret filed by one by one and shook their hands.

'She was a great woman.'

'She was a marvellous wife and mother.'

'You'll all miss her, she was a fine woman.'

'She never had a hard word to say for anyone.'

'And this isn't the funeral you say?' Elizabeth whispered in amazement to Aisling.

'Of course it's not. Tomorrow's the funeral. This is just the bringing to the church.'

Cousins and customers came back to sympathise with Sean; tea and sandwiches and whiskey for the men were served. People stayed until eleven o'clock.

The room where Eileen had slept and died had been cleaned and aired and the signs of illness had been taken away.

'Do you think Dad should sleep in that room tonight? What do you think?' Maureen asked Aisling.

Already she was in charge. Maureen was the eldest after all, but you'd never know it.

'Yes, of course, he will. Didn't he sleep there all the time Mam was ill, in the little bed? And won't he have to sleep there for the rest of his life? Peggy has all the signs of Mam's illness gone, she's got a grand fresh bed, of course Dad'll sleep there. That's his room.' She went and took Dad by the shoulders and brought him upstairs.

'It's very hard to believe,' he said.

'I know Dad.'

'There's not much point in doing anything, you know, in going on. I can't see any reason for doing anything, getting up, going to work. . . .'

Aisling looked at him, bent and much older than his sixty-odd years. 'Well, I must say, Mam would love to hear that kind of talk and her not a day dead, and not even buried yet. She'd be thrilled to hear that kind of attitude. What did she work for all those years?'

'You're right child.' He straightened up. 'I'll go to bed now.'

'I'll look in, in ten minutes, to see are you all right.' When she came back he lay, a lonely figure, in the big bed, with his pink and grey pyjamas buttoned up to his neck. There were tears on his face and he was looking straight ahead of him.

'She was a very good wife.'

Aisling sat on the bed and patted his hand. 'Weren't the two of you lucky that you had such a marriage for thirty-six years? Not many have that much Dad, try to see it that way.'

'I will, I will, I'll try.'

'What was the worst bit, do you think?' Aisling's eyes were red and sore. They sat in the bedroom with a large glass of whiskey each beside them.

'I think that old woman saying that Eileen used to give her food for the children when they were babies. I can see Eileen doing that so easily, with no fuss.'

'Yes, and poor Jemmy from the shop, I thought that was terrible. He kept wiping his nose with his sleeve and saying the poor mistress won't be back, she won't be back.' They both took a big gulp.

'If you think that's bad, Elizabeth, wait till tomorrow. That'll be terrible altogether.'

Elizabeth dreamed that Johnny came to Kilgarret and told them that Eileen wasn't dead, it had all been a mistake.

Aisling dreamed that Mam had said she should marry Johnny and bring him back to Kilgarret to help Dad in the shop. They both woke up tired and slightly hung over. And now the funeral.

More flowers had arrived for the coffin, and this time there was a choir in the church. The family sat in the front right-hand pew. Elizabeth kept studying the little plaque in brass which was screwed on to the back of the seat that she leaned against. *Pray for the Friends and Relations of Rose McCarthy departed this life January 2nd 1925 R.I.P.* She wondered would they arrange a plaque for Aunt Eileen and in years to come would some holy people kneel there in the church and pray for the friends and relations of Eileen O'Connor? She kept thinking about the plaque: it took her mind off the coffin with all the flowers on it which was only a few yards away at the altar steps.

Aisling had often wondered how people could bear the sadness of seeing a body go down into the ground. Why didn't they say goodbye at the gates of the cemetery and let the undertakers do the rest? But when Mam's body came to the churchyard she knew why. You had to go the whole way, and finish off the life with the person. She watched, drained now of all emotion, while they took the flowers from the coffin and laid them gently on each side of the grave. Then, tenderly and softly, as if Mam might still feel the pain, they lowered the coffin down. Then Dad took the first clay and threw it down. It was filled in and the flowers were put back on top and the people moved away, to Maher's or to Hanrahan's or to the hotel for a drink. And a lot of them came back to the square where, this time, there were plates of cold ham and cold chicken and salad, presided over from the kitchen by Peggy, who never stopped crying all the time. Her tears even fell into the milk jug and she sniffed and said that if the mistress were alive, the Lord have mercy on her, she'd drop stone dead to see such carry-on in her kitchen.

*

They had been fifteen days away. Eileen had only lived ten days of the two weeks she had been given. Henry came to the airport to meet them. He was overjoyed to see little Eileen and swore that she had got bigger in the time she had been away. Henry was very sympathetic and when Elizabeth and Aisling told him about some of the scenes in Kilgarret his eyes filled with tears.

'Come home and stay with us,' Elizabeth said. 'Don't go home to an empty flat. It would be much better if you came back to us.'

'Yes, do,' said Henry kindly. 'It's too soon, you'll only fret.'

'No, honestly I'd prefer it. I think I'd like to get myself settled in. Anyway, Johnny will probably be around, I'll let him know I'm back.'

'Oh, Johnny's gone to Greece,' said Henry. 'He told me last Friday, there was a chance of a group going on the Sunday so he went with them. He sends you both his love.'

'She seemed very upset that Johnny had gone to Greece without letting her know,' Henry said later.

'Yes, well, she's upset anyway for a start . . . and he's very callous, Johnny, for another thing. Once you realise that, it doesn't affect you, but Aisling doesn't realise it yet.'

'When did you realise it about him?' Henry was diffident in asking, he didn't want to pry.

'Oh, I think I knew from very early on. But I agreed to live with it. Aisling has more spirit than I have. I don't think she'll accept things so easily. . . .'

'So what will happen?'

'The affair will end, and then I promised her mother that I would try to persuade her to go back to Kilgarret.'

'How precise women are,' said Henry.

Later still, when they had put Eileen back into her own cradle, Elizabeth said, 'You're worried about something. What is it?'

'I didn't mean to burden you the moment you came home.'

'I'm well home now. What is it.'

'It's so unfair, that's what it is. I don't mind the act itself, it's the sheer injustice I can't stand.' Henry looked very upset and Elizabeth was alarmed. 'I could see it happening, I told you, I told you, I said, I don't believe a word they say. I was right. I knew they were never going to hire a junior, it was too pat.' It was a complicated and troubled tale of office politics. There had been a vacancy, the most natural thing would have been to hire a young solicitor, somebody just qualified who would come in at the bottom and be trained in the general work of the practice. But that was not what had happened. Instead, a man of Henry's age had been appointed, a man who had come from Scotland specially – and you don't come all the way from Scotland without some promises, some understandings. He and Henry were going to share an office, he and Henry would deal with the conveyancing work – together.

Oh, the senior partner had made fine speeches about the work having grown, the need having doubled. But anyone with half an eye could see what had happened.

Elizabeth listened with her heart heavy. She had heard this kind of story before. Often. From Father.

XX

Johnny had a marvellous sun-tan when he got back from Greece, and his hair had grown longer. Stefan told him he looked like a proper teddy boy, but Elizabeth, who was in the shop, said it suited him.

'Tell me all about it . . . was the sea really as blue as it was on all those postcards you sent?'

'I'm awful, I didn't send any cards at all,' Johnny laughed, sounding not at all repentant. He told her some light-hearted tales of a minibus which had taken them all precariously to Greece and back; of Susie, who had driven it most of the way and who could speak Greek and catch fish with her hands. Susie. Elizabeth thought about the name. *Susie*. She wondered if it would send little knife-stabs of pain into Aisling the way it used to do to her.

'How did it all go over there?' Johnny jerked his head. 'Was it harrowing?'

'It was terribly sad, really heartbreaking, but harrowing — no. They make much more of a thing of funerals than we do.'

'Oh, Irish wakes and all that.'

'No.' Elizabeth was annoyed.

'Sorry.' Johnny was puzzled. 'I don't seem to please anyone today, I telephoned Aisling to tell her I was back and she was very bad-tempered.'

'Well her mother *has* just died.'

'I know, but I said, would you like it if I come around and cook you some Greek food tonight?'

'And?'

'And she told me what to do with my Greek cooking, frying pan and all. I wonder if they were all listening in Harley Street.'

Elizabeth gave a scream of laughter. 'Did she really? Isn't she marvellous?'

'Bloody hell, marvellous? She's a madwoman.'

'What are you going to do about it?'

'I'll rethink my position.'

Perhaps that's what she should have done all those yeas ago? But then, thank heavens she hadn't. It would be far too exhausting to cope with Johnny's moods by having equally dramatic moods in return. No, it was just as well she hadn't been as fiery as Aisling.

Aisling refused an offer of dinner in a French restaurant, and a weekend trip to Brighton; she tore up his single rose with its fern and threw it out the window of her flat. After two days he waylaid her on the street going to work.

'Might I ask what all these tantrums are about?'

'Will you let me pass, please?'

'Aisling, I just want to have dinner with you. What's all the melodrama for?'

'Excuse me, you're getting in my way.'

'What did I do, tell me, tell me?'

'You went to Greece without me, you mean bum.'

'You wouldn't come with me . . . you couldn't. . . .'

'And so you went off on your own.'

'Well of course I did. We've no hold on each other, no tie. . . .'

'No tie? We've no tie? We're *lovers*, for Christ's sake, surely that's some kind of tie . . . ?'

People were beginning to look at them, amused. The handsome, tanned man and the angry redhead shouting at each other before nine o'clock in the morning – it brightened the day for passers-by.

'Aisling, do shut up. You do what you want and I do what I want . . . that's always been the way. . . .'

'Good, what I want is to go to work, let me pass, let me pass, or I'll get a policeman.'

'Don't be so childish. . . .'

'*Officer!*' Aisling called at the top of her voice and a startled young policeman looked around anxiously.

'This man is preventing me going about my lawful business,' said Aisling pompously.

'Oh go to hell!' shouted Johnny.

'I feel so stupid, Elizabeth,' wept Aisling in the kitchen of the Battersea flat. 'I feel such a big hypocritical fool. Mam isn't dead ten days and here I am roaring and bawling over your ex-boyfriend and asking you ways to get him back.'

'Oh, it's easy to get him back,' Eizabeth said.

'What will I do? I'll do anything, anything.'

'It's easy, but it's unfair, you can have him back and play by his rules. He'll come back if you write him a jolly little note saying sorry for the prima donna act, have now recovered scattered wits. Why don't I serve you a delicious meal of Irish stew and Guinness, and you can tell me all about your holiday?'

'And will it all be all right then?' Aisling was drying her tears.

'Well, it depends on what you mean by all right. He may have to leave early, because he's had to see some friend he met in Greece . . . that would be the pattern.'

'So I wouldn't have him back at all.'

'Well, if you play your cards right you will, the holiday romance will fade, or she'll want more than he can give . . . and then if you're nice and sunny and not making demands he'll come back to you.'

'It's ridiculous, it's intolerable. Who could put up with that sort of behaviour . . . ?'

'Well, I did for about seven years. For a quarter of my life, when you come to think of it.'

Simon called on Tuesday night when Henry had gone to a bridge class.

'You've just missed him,' Elizabeth said.

'I know, that's why I came.' Simon looked so relaxed and urbane that Elizabeth decided to play his little game with him.

'Now am I to take this as a frightfully indiscreet revelation of a forbidden passion for me, or are you arranging a surprise birthday party for Henry in the office?'

'Neither my dear, I wouldn't dare to aspire to the first, and as for the second, our stuffy office doesn't go in for birthdays. No, simply a lonely bachelor wonders where he could possibly find a welcoming cup of coffee and a charming hostess. Thought comes unbidden to brain, wife of colleague, the lovely Elizabeth, and here I am.'

She made him coffee, he admired the sleeping Eileen, he made small talk about Aisling, about Father, about the Worsky shop. Then he said, 'I'm rather worried about Henry at the office, this is really what I wanted to talk to you about.'

Every antenna was quivering. She did *not* want to hear this conversation, she did not like the way it was being done. 'Oh, anything about the office, don't you think you should discuss that with Henry himself?' She spoke lightly but firmly. A lesser man might have got the message and retreated.

But Simon was insistent. 'No, it's not telling tales, and tittle-tattle just for the sake of gossip, I'm worried about his work. He takes too much time and gets himself into knots. . . .'

'Listen, Simon, I'm very serious, I know you mean well and that your motives are utterly honest . . . but you must understand that I cannot, I *will* not be drawn into a discussion about my husband's work in your firm. You and he are old enough friends. You've known each other forever. You can tell him far more easily than me what's wrong.'

'But this is just it – he won't listen to me.'

'Well, I do not want to hear whatever it is and to be put in the position of having to decide whether to pass it on or not. No, it is not fair, and you will not do it to me. If I have a problem at work I speak about it to the person involved not to their husbands or wives. So should you.'

'I tell you, I have tried, I do this as a last. . . .'

'Or if I find people not able to listen to a conversation I write them a letter . . . it's easier to list things in a letter.'

'Some people are so sensitive and thin-skinned, imagining insult and rebuff, that they would think a letter was a worse way of doing it.'

She smiled thinly. 'Well, I suppose if I were in that position I would do my best to find another way out, one that involved no conniving or disloyalty.'

'You are a magnificent person,' Simon said.

'So you really did come here to seduce me . . .' She tinkled a laugh she did not feel, the conversation had given her a cold fear in her heart.

'Alas no, I don't dare risk further rejection – but if you had married me, what a pair we would have been! Together we would have conquered the world! Why didn't you marry me?'

'Let me think. Oh I know, you didn't ask me.'

Simon hit his forehead in a theatrical gesture. 'Oh, of course!' he said.

'And also because I love Henry very dearly, so I married him,' she said with a note of warning.

He took the warning, they talked a little more. Should they have a television? Simon was afraid that if he did he would stay in all night and forget to go prowling around in search of adventure. Elizabeth was afraid that she would sit glued to it all the time. He asked her if Aisling had any views on the new Pope, and Elizabeth said that Aisling's only comment had been that if he was a man of seventy-six there was no way he was going to be eager to annul her marriage for her. That was her only interest in popes these days.

'Has she given up her faith?' asked Simon, imitating Aisling's intonation.

'It's hard to know, you never know with Catholics. It seems to be much more part of them than you think. Even when they don't believe, they have something inside them that makes them think they do.'

'That's very deep, too Jesuitical for me. I must leave.' He left graciously, joking, waving flamboyantly as he ran lightly down the big marble stairs . . . never mentioning again the subject he had come to discuss.

*

Donal and Anna had put off their wedding until the spring. They thought it would be too overshadowed by Mam's funeral. Anna had come to work in the shop.

'What's a graduate doing in the shop?' muttered Aisling when she heard. 'She's a BA, for heaven's sake, what's she doing rabbiting about with Mam's ledgers and my ledgers?'

'Why don't you go over and sort her out?' Elizabeth laughed.

'I might just do that.' Aisling was undecided.

'Will you go home for Christmas do you think?'

'I don't know, Johnny hasn't said anything, he may have a plan like last year.'

Elizabeth knew he had a plan but it wasn't like last year, it involved Susie. Still, it wasn't up to her, of course, to smooth the path for Aisling but she couldn't bear to see the naked disappointment.

'I'd say they'd love to have you back in Kilgarret, it's going to be a rotten Christmas for your Dad.'

'I know, but I don't want to arrange to go and then Johnny suddenly say that we're meant to be off to Spain or wherever. He's been talking a lot more about Spain recently.'

Elizabeth knew that was right, she had heard him booking the holiday in Majorca for himself and Susie. 'You should ask him outright what his plans are, not just wait about, there's no point in everyone being messed around.' Her voice was sharper than usual. Aisling wondered should she talk less about Johnny to Elizabeth, it was impossible to fathom what her real feelings towards him were.

Aisling went home to Kilgarret, where she heard to her great relief that Mrs Murray had gone to spend Christmas in Dublin with Joannie.

'Do you know that your car is still there?' Eamonn said to her. 'I'm surprised to see you coming off the bus. I'd have thought you'd have used your car. Had it in Dublin, you know.'

'My *car?*' It seemed like a different world: the cream-coloured Ford Anglia that she had been given by Tony to celebrate her learning how to drive. 'Where on earth is it?'

'It's back up behind the yard. Oh ages ago, the guards told Murray's it had been abandoned at the airport, and eventually someone drove it back down here, and Mr Meade said it should be left up here. Mam said none of us were to drive it. I could have done with it, but that was an absolute. *Aisling's car, the O'Connors will not drive round Kilgarret in the car Tony Murray bought for Aisling.*'

'Do you drink a lot Eamonn?' she asked him suddenly.

'What do you mean?' he was annoyed and bewildered.

'Well you used to, not like Tony but you used to get fairly pissed in Hanrahan's a lot.'

'No, I don't drink so much since you ask. I was getting a desperate beer belly on me, and, well, I'll be thirty this year. I thought I could get into the way of it, and after . . . after. . . .'

'After the Tony business?'

'Yes, after that a few of us drew in our horns.'

'Okay, you can have the car.'

'What? You can't just say that, you can't give me your car.'

'I didn't know I even had it until two minutes ago, of course I can. But trade it in, will you, get something else. Everyone will remember it too well. I'll have the papers somewhere, I might even have them with me, I brought out a whole lot of papers to sort out. I'll give them to you tonight.'

'I'll never be able to thank you, God, a car, me.'

'It's all right, Mam would like you to have a car. I have a feeling that she would. It would make you more independent.'

'A car all of my own, I don't believe it.'

Aisling had to look away so that he wouldn't see how moved she was at his pleasure.

It was a strange, lonely Christmas; she felt she had grown away from them even in the few short months since Mam's death. They had all been bound together by the sadness and tension of Mam's funeral. Now it was different.

Donal was in Barrys' most of the time. Anna had been most successful at work. She sat in Mam's eyrie at first but had the sense to realise that this upset people.

'My Lord, I thought it was Mrs O'Connor,' they would say.

'Of course, you soon will be Mrs O'Connor,' they might add. Anna organised her own office, she decided to call Dad Mr O'C. Aisling smiled at that. She had thought Mrs M was more affectionate than 'Mrs Murray' too. It was odd, this whole in-law bit.

'It will be nice for you to have Anna as a sister-in-law,' she said to Niamh.

'Yes, though it didn't work for you and Joannie Murray. You were great friends before you married her brother and then you didn't get on with her at all.'

'I didn't get on with either of them at all,' said Aisling and they giggled.

Dad was low and sunk into himself, it was hard to see what would cheer him up. She took him for a walk on St Stephen's Day. They walked out on to the Dublin road, a lot of cars passing them going to the races in Dublin and people they knew tooting their horns. 'I wonder are they thinking that it's two years today since that bold strap ran out of the place and here she is bold as brass back again? But maybe they're not thinking about me at all. I might have to face that fact.' Dad's face looked gloomy; she felt he was only walking to please her, as she was to please him. 'Maybe we'll turn back now will we?'

He turned obediently and they faced down into the town. 'You're not to worry about us, Aisling, you know,' he said out of the blue. 'We'll all be fine, and you have your own life to lead.'

'I do worry.'

'Well, it's not going to do any good. Your mam is gone but she said to me before she went that nobody was to try to drag Aisling back from London, she'd come when she was good and ready.'

Aisling's eyes filled with tears. How well Mam had understood.

'But maybe I should come back, Dad.'

'No, not until you're good and ready. Your home is always here for you, but don't come back to look after us, we'll be fine.'

'I know, Dad.'

'And haven't you contributed to the peace of nations already by giving that lout a car for under his backside so that he can drive himself off out of my sight?'

'Dad, what a way to talk about Eamonn.' They both laughed.

'You know that I'd prefer to say a lot more, but seeing as it's Christmas, and I was at communion, there's no point in cursing and swearing.'

She did a lot of walking during her visit home. It was easier to think, walking. People nodded at her or stopped for a few words. Mainly they told her that her father was managing well enough and that young Anna Barry was being a great support. Nobody mentioned Tony or the Murrays. It was as if her marriage had never taken place.

She walked past the bungalow one day. It had bright new curtains. She wondered idly what had happened to all the furniture and what they had done with the fawn curtains when they put up these orange and white ones. The orange and white ones were nicer. They had done the garden too, the new people, cousins of Mr Moriarty, she remembered. She hoped they would be happy there. There was nothing wrong with the bungalow. She wondered who had wiped up all the blood in the end.

She walked to Maureen's house. Maureen was surprised and not altogether pleased to see her.

'What are you doing, lady of leisure?' she asked.

'I was calling to see you,' said Aisling, feeling she had had this conversation with Maureen a million times. She was tired of it. She remembered Mam saying that Maureen had been born a moaner and would be one for the rest of her days. Aisling turned to go.

'Oh, don't be so huffy, come on in and have tea. It's just that nobody knows what to make of you, that's the problem. Nobody knows what you're at.'

That was the problem all right.

*

Back in London after the holiday she discovered that Johnny had just come back from Majorca; it had only been a week's visit. Susie was not in sight. Elizabeth had been right about that. She found that the three doctors were so happy to see her back – they realised that nobody could do their work like Miss O'Connor, she had indeed become indispensable – they said they would like to raise her wages and suggest that she have extra holidays if she would agree to stay with them for at least a year. Johnny had been right about that. She heard from Elizabeth that there had been some very awkward and embarrassing scene at Henry's office because he had not got the expected New Year rise. Henry had become hysterical, and did what nobody ever did: he made his disappointment known in public. He had been slightly overexcited and caused great alarm to everyone. Simon had been right about that.

'I don't know what more I can say. I can't tell you more clearly that we have enough, Henry, you and I and Eileen, we have plenty. We have more than almost anyone we know, can you not stop talking about the damn rise? It couldn't matter one fig.'

'Not to you, but to me it does. What have I been doing all those years? Why have I been slaving away and taking work home? Who has been more attentive to their work than I have, what other member of staff can honestly say that he has been as conscientious as I have?'

'But that's not the point. . . .'

'It *is* the point, that's what this office system is based on. It's not marks for being brilliant. *God dammit*, Elizabeth, it's not an American movie about lawyers, we're not getting a bonus or rise for dramatic appearances in courts. It's just a system, when the work is done well and reliably, everyone gets a rise. Well, not everyone, but anyone who has done their part. . . .'

'Henry you're upsetting yourself for. . . .'

'Of course, I'm upset, I didn't *get* a rise . . . can't you see what that means?'

'It means nothing, you're becoming hysterical. Last year

you got one, your work was not out of the ordinary; this year you didn't, your work was not out of the ordinary for you. So what? We don't need their money. We have plenty.'

'You'll *never* understand. . . .'

'Apparently not, but I'd have some hope of understanding if you didn't shout.'

'I'm only upsetting you. I'll go out. . . .'

'Darling love, it's Sunday lunchtime. We're just about to have lunch. Why are you going out?'

'I'm upset, as you said, very upset, there's no point in upsetting you and Eileen.'

'I love you. I love you so much, I wish you wouldn't go out. You're not upsetting me, you're not upsetting Eileen. Look, she's smiling at you . . . why don't you take your coat off? Come back and sit down. . . .' She had followed him to the door. He pressed the button for the lift. 'Please Henry, stay and have lunch, this is the way we always thought it would be, you know, when neither of us had a proper home, the two of us and a baby and whatever we wanted for lunch, not what somebody else wanted. . . .' The lift was coming up. 'And I want you, I don't want you wandering down to the embankment and getting your death of cold, that would upset me much more.'

He came back and took her in his arms. 'You have a fool for a husband.'

'No, I don't, I have the man I love.'

'Eileen,' he called and she crawled from the sitting room, 'Eileen, you have a very foolish father, remember this always. But your mother, she's worth a million pounds.' Eileen smiled happily at them both.

'Will we have a joint birthday party? It'll be the last one before we're thirty?' Aisling examined her face as minutely for lines these days as she had done for spots long ago.

'That's a great idea. I'd like that. Any excuse is good enough for me.'

'Right, will we have it in your place, it's bigger?'

'No, the neighbours, they're difficult, and the stairs.'

Aisling looked up in surprise from examining her eyes.

'Yes,' Elizabeth said. 'Why do I think I can fool you? It's Henry, he's very unrelaxed these days, I think a party would fuss him.'

'Great, we'll have it here. Let's make a list ... Old faithfuls, Johnny, Simon, Stefan, Anna, your Pa?'

'No, for God's sake, let's not ask Father, not to something that's meant to be a bit of fun.'

'Elizabeth, you said he was much better. . . .'

'He is, but he's not jolly . . . let's not. . . .'

'Fine. Johnny's friend Nick is back living with him again.'

'Oh, Nick from the travel agency . . . ?'

'Yes, he's getting a divorce, his marriage went up the spout, he keeps saying . . . he's quite nice. And I can ask the girl in the flat below, Julia. . . .'

'Oh, I remember . . . the one that. . . .'

'Yes, the one that Johnny was ogling. Well, if he does he does. I learned that from you. No point in trying to hide all the competition from him.'

'You learned pretty fast.'

'I was much older and sadder than you.'

'You're never really sad, Aisling, that's your magic . . . that's why Johnny likes you so much. I think he probably likes you more than anyone he ever met. I've never said it before because it seemed . . . well, intrusive, and maybe even giving you a false hope. But I've seen him and he listens to everything you say, and throws his head back, laughing. And he is delighted with all your bright ways. . . .'

Aisling looked embarrassed.

'Yes, I know, it does sound a bit flowery, but I know what I'm talking about. With me it was different. I was so young and so silly but I put on this great mask of independence for years. He admired my sort of gutsiness I think. But with you it's different. I think he'll stick with you. . . .'

Aisling stood up and stretched out her arms wide. 'Yippee. That's the best news I've heard yet. I'm never sure of him, not for one moment. Is that the only reason he's so important – just because people can't be sure of him?'

'I don't think it could be. Not unless he were really

something to begin with. If he were empty and silly, half the world wouldn't be breaking their hearts over him so regularly.'

'Quite right. Now that you've told me this I think we'll strike Julia off the list. Why let her come up two floors just to break her heart over Johnny Stone when you and I know she's only wasting her time?'

Ethel Murray spent an hour sitting at the dining-room table and reading and rereading the letter she had written to Aisling. She would not send it, the girl would misunderstand it. The solicitor had told her she must make no remarks that could be taken up in any way and she must make no offers or promises. Did the letter give anything away or make any concessions? Who could be sure? She had wanted to write to the girl. But maybe it was wiser not. She was wracked with indecision. Why was there never anyone to advise her?

Eventually she tore it up and sent Aisling a telegram instead.

Regret inform you Tony Murray died peacefully today
Requiescat in Pace.
Ethel Murray

'She couldn't go to the funeral. What on earth could she do? Standing up there at a dreadful little ceremony and from a hospital. I know what they're like, Mother died in a hospital. It was terrible, terrible. Just the Murrays there, not speaking to her. Standing in widow's weeds. Of course she couldn't go. It would be ridiculous.'

'All right, don't go on so, I just said that I would have expected her to go. You said yourself that the Irish were very conscious of attending people's funerals. That's all.'

'It's the way you said it, you were criticising her.'

'No I was not, but there are plenty of things I could criticise if I had a mind to. . . .'

'Oh, let's stop, Henry,' Elizabeth said wearily. They seemed to be rowing all the time these days. About nothing. Once she saw Eileen looking at her. She wondered had she looked at Mother and Father like that when she was nearly two? And had they worried about her or each other?

'I don't know what to say to you.' Johnny sat across the room. 'I don't know what I should do, sympathise or not.'

'They don't have a section on this in an etiquette book,' Aisling said. She looked pale and tired. She had been awake all night. The telegram had been so cold. They were cutting her out, keeping her away, when she never had any quarrel with them. Tears of self-pity had come in the night. What would have been the right course, wait until he fell down from drink or his liver gave out in Kilgarret? Perhaps she should have done so earlier. He could never have lived two and a half years drinking the way he had been when she left him. Perhaps Mam was right, she should have stayed. Now she had enemies, hostile people who sent her bitter telegrams, she had people who didn't know what to say to her. In Kilgarret and even here.

'He was very nice, years ago, Johnny,' she said. 'I'm not going to become all maudlin and start crying for what could have been. But when he was much younger, when he used to come round and take me to the pictures, and talk to Mam and Dad, he was nice then. And we used to laugh at the pictures, and even that first time in Rome . . . he was very, very nice. He wasn't always a bastard. . . .'

'I know.' Johnny was soothing.

'He hadn't a happy life, he never really liked working in the business, he didn't get on with his mother – they rubbed each other up the wrong way. And then I wasn't what he hoped either.'

'Well, he was a bit of a disappointment to you too, chicken, don't forget that.'

'No, I don't ever forget that. It's just, well, it's just such a waste, isn't it? Here he is, dead in Lancashire, and nobody loved him and he never had any real happiness – dead from drink before he's forty.'

'He was a loser, the poor old Squire,' said Johnny, and changed the subject.

571

At no time in the next months was it ever mentioned that Aisling was now a widow. She was now free to marry again. Aisling thought about it quite a lot. She thought that Johnny must have thought about it too, but it wasn't something you said soon after a husband died. Any husband, even an estranged one. Elizabeth believed that Johnny had never given it a single thought. If Tony Murray were alive or dead, good or bad, present or absent, Johnny Stone would still have paid the same attention to Aisling. Aisling was certainly Johnny's longest-lasting and brightest-burning romance apart from herself. In fact there were even fewer Susies and Julias than there had been. But marriage? Elizabeth was quite sure that this was never in Johnny's plans.

Simon got engaged, out of the blue, to a very pretty Welsh girl called Bethan. They announced it quite unexpectedly at a gathering in the Battersea flat. Aisling and Johnny were there as well. It was going to be a very quiet wedding, they feared. Bethan's parents were chapel, and very funny about drink and things, so the sooner and the quieter, the better.

In three weeks' time actually.

'Bet you she's pregnant,' Aisling whispered to Elizabeth when they were bringing things in from the kitchen.

'Obviously, but how cunning to snatch Simon just at the right time of his professional life. He needs to settle down now, she's nicely spoken. It could have been any of a dozen of them. Clever little Bethan.'

'I wonder is Johnny at the right time?' Aisling mused, with a gleam in her eye.

'I don't think it would be wise to find out,' Elizabeth smiled. 'Johnny doesn't marry his pregnant ladies.'

'Some of them didn't give him a chance to decide whether he would or not. . . .'

In ten years that was the first time that the abortion had been mentioned.

Jimmy Farrelly, the solicitor from Kilgarret, had written to say that the Murrays had instructed a firm of solicitors in Dublin to handle the inheritance of Tony Murray. His letter was firm and to the point. There had been enough shilly-shallying during Tony's lifetime, Aisling must now decide to claim what was rightfully hers. The law said she was entitled to a one-third share in the business, Murray's Provisions and Vintners; the other two shares were owned by Joannie and Mrs Murray. She owned the bungalow completely — it had not been sold, as she had heard, it had been let to the present inhabitants. She might wish to come to some arrangement about being bought out of the firm, but it was only sensible for her own future to come to a realistic decision soon. The longer the whole thing was held in abeyance, the less likely it was she would get her fair share. Mrs Murray and Joannie had instructed their solicitors to disinherit Aisling on the ground of deserting her husband.

'I don't mind what you do, child, your mother would have known more about such things than I do. Do what you think is fair. That woman has had a lot of trouble, if she can be pleased in some fair way try to see to it. You'll always have your share of this business, such as it is, after my time.'

'Oh Dad, stop talking about *your time*, and *after your time*,' she cried and hung up the phone.

Maureen said she should take them for everything she could. Otherwise they'd all be laughing stocks, everyone knew that Tony Murray was a drunk and a wife-beater. She had put up with a great deal too much. Take what she could. And to hell with their feelings.

Dónal said it was hard to know, but living in a small town he felt sure that things should be worked out in a way that everyone could live peaceably together. It wasn't his affair, but he would urge Aisling to think of the future when she might want to live back in Kilgarret, and it was better not to have too many old sores to reopen.

Eamonn said that if she had to give back the car there'd be a problem because he had done a trade-in, and given fifty pounds of his own money to get a Cortina. But he could work it out.'

Niamh wrote and said that since Aisling had asked their views she would be happy to give hers. If the law said the property belonged to his wife, take it. If she felt like making an act of great generosity to the dreadful Murrays, make it with part of the property, but one of these days Aisling would not be a dynamic twenty-nine-year-old, she would be a rich old bag.

Aisling asked Johnny what he thought she should do.
    'What would the Squire have wanted?' he said.
    'At what stage?'
    'When he was still sane.'
    'I have no idea.'
    'You must.'
    'No, I haven't, in the lovey-dovey bit, of course, he'd have wanted me to have the moon.'
    'Then take the moon, chicken,' said Johnny.

Jimmy Farrelly said it was very simple; he explained that Aisling was prepared to go into open court with a description of her life with Tony Murray and her reasons and justification for leaving him. She could produce witnesses from hospitals, and his own letters received almost three years ago. He said she was not unwilling to be generous about the business once any opposition to her right to inherit was withdrawn. Off the record he had told Mrs Murray that she would not press her share for the third of the firm, new deeds of association could be drawn up, dividing it between the two women, Joannie and Ethel Murray.
    He said it had been electrifying; once they had heard she was prepared to fight it, all opposition fizzled out. Probate was granted, and Aisling inherited everything that had belonged to Tony Murray. His stocks and shares were

transferred to her, the house was sold at a reasonable price to the cousins of the Moriartys, and that money was lodged to her account in England. She abdicated any right to a share in the business of Murray's, and she directed that Tony's car should be given to Mr Meade in the shop.

'God, I never knew anything happen so quickly,' Jimmy Farrelly said to his wife. 'Once those Murrays knew that Aisling O'Connor was prepared to fight it and tell about Tony they went down like a pack of cards. He must have had something desperate to hide, and he was the nicest fellow you could meet, when he was sober.'

It was all completed shortly before Christmas . . . and Aisling pointed out to Johnny that she was now a wealthy widow. 'You shouldn't pass me over, men like you are always on the lookout for wealthy widows.'

'But I haven't passed you over, I've found you and you're mine,' Johnny said, slightly puzzled.

'And when will you make an honest woman of me?' she asked, lightly teasing but in deadly earnest.

He stood up. They had been sitting on the end of her bed. He walked to the window and looked out. There was a light snowfall. 'You mean it, chicken, don't you?'

'Well, don't you want to?' She sat on the bed, her beautiful red hair falling down her back, and her turquoise dressing-gown making her look like a stab of colour against the white bedclothes.

'We *are* together, you *are* an honest woman, you've always been an honest woman.' He looked beseeching.

'I'd like to be your wife.'

'You are in every way, every possible way. This is better than being married.'

'How do we know, we haven't tried being married?'

'You have,' he said.

'To each other,' she said.

'It doesn't mean I don't love you. I do, very, very much, but I don't feel . . . I'm sorry — don't think me very weak. . . .'

'No, not weak.'

575

'What then?'

'I don't know. Mean, I suppose. Afraid to try it, afraid to take me on.'

'Ah, heavens above, Aisling, that's not true. I've taken you on. I'm besotted with you.'

'Why don't you marry me then?' She was begging. God, why had the script gone so wrong? She would lose him altogether. Elizabeth had warned her. It was too late. She was doing it all wrong.

'I've told you,' he said. 'Let's not change everything. Let's leave it.'

To her horror she began to cry; huge tears fell down on her dressing-gown. She couldn't stop. He didn't come over to comfort her. He looked embarrassed, at the window. 'It wouldn't be hard,' she pleaded. 'Nothing will change, we'll be the same as we are now. I promise. . . .'

'Well, why risk it? Why change something that's going so swimmingly? What's the point if nothing's going to change? People only make big decisions in their life if things are going to be better. . . .'

She couldn't laugh. 'Why could it spoil things? Lots of unlikely people are very happy when they're married. It doesn't have to ruin things.'

'Name me one or two,' he said.

'Elizabeth and Henry, just to pick our closest friends.'

'You must be joking,' said Johnny.

'They are, they are happy, aren't they?'

'Sweetheart, they are tearing each other to bits – if you haven't noticed that you are blind. Now, stop all this women's magazine stuff, clean up your face, get your butt into some nice clothes and I'll take you for a drink. . . .'

'Go to hell.'

'Why? I'm being agreeable, pleasant and defusing a dangerous situation.'

'I've asked you to marry me, I won't be palmed off with a drink. . . .'

Johnny laughed. 'That's better.'

She managed a watery smile. And somewhere at the back of her head the humiliation of being refused in her proposal of marriage didn't seem so bad when she remembered what he said about Elizabeth's marriage. Maybe he was right. Perhaps marriage did destroy everyone. It could be nature's way of preventing people from enjoying themselves too much while on earth.

'But you have to come!' wailed Elizabeth, 'I really can't stand it on my own. I can't stand it. Not Father complaining and Henry complaining and Eileen grizzling. I'm in very poor shape these days. . . .'

'Oh, all right, I wanted to stay in bed all day. . . .'

'You can't, it's immoral to stay in bed all of Sunday.'

'Yes, you're right, what about Simon and Bethan . . . ?'

'Oh, they won't come, too busy feathering the nest. You should see the place they've bought. Henry spends hours with a slide rule trying to work out how he pays for it on what he earns. . . .'

'What about Johnny?'

'Well, you should know more about him than I do, where is he?'

'No idea. He went off a week ago, no word.'

'Stefan thinks he's gone to Dover.'

'Quite possibly.'

'Tiff?'

'No, misunderstanding really. I'll tell you later. Why must I get up – I'm nice and warm here in bed?'

'You *must* get up, because you're my friend, and my husband, father and daughter will drive me mad. I don't need relations around me, I need a friend. . . .'

Johnny was right, they were tearing each other to pieces. Not the kind of rows she used to have with Tony, much worse. At least the rows with Tony ended fairly smartly with his flinging himself out of the house. Here they disagreed over words. And what the other had said, or the other had meant.

'Henry thinks that you were mad to give back that share in the Murrays' business to them.'

'I didn't say she was mad, I said that Aisling might have done better to wait a while, that in law the word "gift" is very precisely defined.'

'I'm sorry, I thought you said, "Tell her she was mad". Those are the words you used.'

'You totally misunderstood me. . . .'

Elizabeth's father said nothing. He just ate his food, looking at the plate.

Elizabeth burst into tears and ran out.

'You are picking on him, you know you are,' Aisling said. The lunch had ended by Elizabeth's apologising and a very grudging acceptance by Henry who wanted the whole subject re-examined. Henry and father had gone into the study, and Aisling and Elizabeth remained at the table picking at the apple tart bit by bit.

'I know. I can't help it.'

'It's very bad, you usen't to be like that, neither of you. I'm very uneasy when I'm with you now, I used to love it. I used to feel that I was part of something nice and cheery. Not now.'

'Don't be so dramatic. It's just . . . it's just . . . well, a phase, I suppose. I'll tell you what kills me. I work hard, I go out and earn a living, I find a baby sitter, I teach her and train her to look after Eileen. After September there'll be a pre-school group. I set these things up, I entertain all his godawful friends. I make myself pleasant to people like the ludicrous senior partner and Simon's inane wife, Bethan, for him, and I wouldn't mind any of it, I'd do it all and more if there was any joy in him. There's no life or spirit or happiness. It's all as if we're going round with a great black cloud hanging over us.'

'Well, he is, obviously.'

'But how do I get rid of it? I've tried, Lord knows, I've tried. Am I supposed to get under it as well, make both of us wretched? Invite Eileen in too, depress her, let her think the world is full of insurmountable problems . . . ?'

'But you must have known . . . ?'

'I did not know, and you're a fine one to tell me about what people must know and must not know, you married a violent alcoholic and thought he was the nice boy next door who would be a suitable match.'

'That's true enough.'

'Christ, Aisling, I'm sorry, why am I talking like that to you? You got up and came over here to help me, and I end up upsetting everyone and attacking you.'

'It doesn't matter,' Aisling grinned.

'I'm in such a foul mood. You see they're waiting for the senior partner to retire, and then it will all be fine. Simon and Henry move up to some other level. Both sort of heads of sections, but separate from each other. That's all in the pipeline. Then this interminable bitching and complaining about people doing him down will end. Honestly, I know I sound as if I hate him, I don't, but there's such a wall of hedgehog spikes around him, I can't even see the Henry I love. It's as if he put on a suit of armour.'

'I know, I think I see.'

'Anyway, the light at the end of the tunnel is there. I'm only dragging you down with me, that's not fair.'

Aisling lit a cigarette. 'I'm fairly down anyway. I wasn't going to tell you but I will now. I asked Johnny to marry me.'

'You what? Oh no!' Elizabeth laughed. 'You're joking?'

'No. I'm not.' She sat silent for a moment.

'What did he say?' asked Elizabeth.

'You tell me.'

'He said, "Why spoil a good thing, we're fine as we are?" '

'That's what he said.'

'Well, you are fine as you are.'

'Except that he's gone, another Susie, I think, to punish me for being so foolish as to propose to him.'

'Oh dear me, Aisling.' Elizabeth's laugh had a slightly hysterical tinge. 'We really are a credit to our mothers and our upbringing, aren't we . . . ? I wonder if Eileen will make such a dog's dinner of her life? I wonder what we should do to stop her.'

'I don't suppose anything will stop her if she's as stupid as we are,' Aisling said, and they both were laughing when Father and Henry came huffily from the study and wondered if they might clear the table and have a hand of bridge.

*

Simon called once or twice at Manchester Street. Aisling was quite pleased to see him; Johnny had not returned from his dalliance and she was becoming increasingly humiliated at the memory of her own foolishness. She had made several weak and not very serious decisions not to see him again when he did return. Simon always brought a bottle of wine. The third time he called, he gave Aisling a very warm kiss, and she responded.

'Tut, tut,' she laughed. 'I mustn't play the merry widow while your poor wife struggles with a home and a nearly-born baby.'

'This is the time a man needs consolation most. In ancient Greece, young women and widows always thought it an honour to console expectant fathers, who were obviously anxious and uneasy and unable to find release with their wives.'

'I don't believe you,' Aisling said.

'I made it up, but it sounds good.'

Aisling giggled. It had been lonely without Johnny; she did not have the same draw towards visiting the flat in Battersea since Elizabeth's revelations about her problems with Henry. It was nice to be flirted with, and flattered. On his next visit he brought a bottle of sparkling wine and made an elegant pass at her.

'Heavens, I can't be had for false champagne!' Aisling said laughing. 'What do you think I am?' The next night he brought a bottle of Moët et Chandon, and they drank it very quickly. Then they went to bed.

What does it matter, Aisling said next morning, he loved it, I didn't mind it and nobody's going to tell anyone else so nobody gets hurt.

Stefan told Elizabeth that he was going to retire. From now on he would only come in once a week. He and Anna would get a small place with a garden, they both loved flowers. His eyesight was failing, he no longer could see what he bought or what he sold. He wanted to know whether Elizabeth thought she would like to buy the business.

'But where on earth would I get the money, darling Stefan? We have hardly enough for ourselves. I need everything I earn.'

'I thought, with a rich lawyer for a husband, and a beautiful flat in Battersea, you were on the up and up.'

'No. You couldn't be more wrong. But, anyway, Johnny . . . won't he want . . . ?'

'I talked to Johnny. That's why I am talking to you. I had another idea, a different idea before I talked to Johnny. I thought perhaps Johnny and Aisling might now get married. Aisling has much money since her husband died. I thought that perhaps the three of you together could buy it and give Anna and me money for our last years. That's all we need. But I couldn't abide to have it go to people who would not love it.'

'I know. I know.'

'But Johnny tells me no, on no account must this be mentioned. He does not want to marry . . . I must never never say it to Aisling, it must not be brought up. Yet to me, whether they marry or not, it seems a good idea . . . Anna says so. She says Johnny is wriggling out of one more romance, and that I must talk to you, you and your husband, because Johnny has saved nothing.'

'Stefan, it's impossible. Don't retire yet. Leave it a little while. Things may change. Seriously, Henry is getting a new position in the firm at the end of the month. Next month Father retires from the bank. He may sell Clarence Gardens, we may all buy a different house and go and live together, Father with us. There may be more money. Can you hold on for a couple of months? Things will be better then.'

'I will hold on for a couple of months. I hope things will be better for you, dear Elizabeth, they are not well with you now.'

Bethan had a baby boy. It was born at two a.m. on a Thursday. His father, Simon, was in bed with Aisling at the time, but he was delighted when he heard the next day. Everyone had said it was amazing for a first baby to be born prematurely. Usually they were late.

Henry said that he was not going to consider having a party to celebrate the changes at the firm. It would look as if they were always finding an excuse for eating and drinking.

'I'm sorry,' said Elizabeth. 'When we got married we both said that it was super to be able to have people round to our own home. It was one of the things we loved.'

Henry's eyes filled with tears. 'I know darling, I'm sorry, I wish I could see the world as easily and lightly as you do, but I can't, I worry about things. *Somebody* has to worry. . . .'

'I don't see why,' she said.

Johnny called to Aisling's flat and saw Simon's car outside. He bounded up the stairs cheerfully. 'Hey, you two, let me in, I've got a bottle of pliska. It's a plum brandy, you'll love it!' There was no reply, which was funny because there was a light on – he could see it under the door, and he had seen it through the curtain from the street. 'Come on, are you up to no good?' he shouted. Still no reply. Johnny shrugged and went downstairs. Out on the street he looked up at the window and saw that the curtain had moved.

'I don't know why he can't know about me if I can know about him,' Simon said.

'Ah, but he's a serious contender for my favours, you're not,' Aisling laughed, not that her heart had calmed down again after Johnny had run down the stairs.

'You can't think Johnny Stone is a serious contender as a *husband*, can you?' Simon said.

'He has begged me to marry him, sitting on the end of this bed,' she said.

'And what did you say?' Simon laughed with her, not knowing whether to believe her or not.

'I said, why spoil what we have, it's good now, let's not ruin it.'

'Very wise, my dear, how sensible,' said Simon, putting his arm around her again.

'Won't Bethan . . . ?'

'She'll be busy with the baby,' said Simon.

'Things will be much better when I have the new job, there will be clear lines of demarcation in the office, people won't get on top of each other. . . .'

'If it's going to make all that much difference why wasn't it done ages ago?'

'Because the senior partner has always liked to keep the reins firmly in his own hands and leave the rest of us worrying and jockeying for position,' Henry said.

'Do you think there's any fear that your friend Aisling is two-timing me with your husband's colleague, Simon Burke?' Johnny asked Elizabeth at the antique shop.

'I never heard anything so ludicrous,' Elizabeth said.

'You'll never guess what Johnny came up with . . . he thinks you're having it off with Simon,' Elizabeth said on the phone to Aisling at work.

'Oh shit,' said Aisling.

'God, I'll be relieved when all that big fuss at your office is over. Elizabeth and Henry are like cats on a hot tin roof waiting for his new post, whatever it is.'

'What new post?' asked Simon.

'It's very good of you, and I know you mean well, Lord above, to use your own expression, I know you're doing it for the best, Aisling, but you must have got it wrong. . . .'

'I beg you, I beg you, come in today and have lunch with me. Bring Eileen. We'll go anywhere you say. I have to talk to you about it. I can't explain it on the phone. I can't keep saying how I know and what was said, it's too bitty. . . .'

'I've got the drift, and as I say, Simon's wrong.'

'Elizabeth, darling, he explained the whole thing to me, he's *not* wrong, Henry's got it wrong. . . . I'm only warning you for your own sake, I don't want to be one-up or anything. Christ, I didn't want to be told all this stuff in the middle of the night did I?'

'I know, and you are a good friend to pass it on.'

'I'm not a good friend if you don't take me seriously! Look, there's a queue forming here, I have to go. Please, please. One o'clock. Debenham's? Selfridge's? Where . . . ?'

'I can't come. Not today. I'll talk to you tonight.'

'Tonight he'll know.'

'You're exaggerating things, Aisling, you haven't heard every in and every out of all of this, I know, that's all there is to it.'

'I have to go. I'll ring again.'

'I may have to go out to meet Stefan. I'll talk to you tonight.'

Father telephoned Elizabeth – which was highly unusual of him. She wondered whether he'd thought of some little celebration for Henry, but Father never dreamed up little celebrations.

'Do you know if Henry is insistent on south of the river . . . ?' he asked without making any real greeting.

'What on earth do you mean, Father?'

'I'm looking for houses for us, as you know . . . but two likely ones are north of the river and I think he has his heart set on south.'

'Oh, I think you should look at the north of the river ones, too, Father.'

Elizabeth put her head down on her arms and cried. To be nearly thirty and to have all this to cope with. A father who couldn't make up his own mind about what side of the cornflake bowl he should face towards him; a husband who had managed to frighten himself into a panic all of his own making . . . when had things last been easy? When and where? And why would they never be easy again?

'Why you cry, Mama?' said Eileen.

'Mama's tired,' said Elizabeth.

'Mama go to bed,' said Eileen.

'Mama too busy,' she said.

The telephone rang again.

'Hallo, is that my step-daughter or my step-grand-daughter?'

'Harry.' She had totally forgotten that today was the day

he was arriving. Could she be having some kind of nervous trouble, she wondered suddenly? There was a time when she had held down three jobs, looked after Mother, Father and Harry at varying distances. Now she was hardly able to remember what day of the week it was.

'Harry, where are you?'

'I'm at Euston, you couldn't make it. . . .'

'No, couldn't do it, couldn't get a baby sitter. . . .'

'Never mind, darling, I hung around a bit, shall I come over now, or what? Do you want a spot of lunch out?'

She considered lunch with Aisling at a smart Oxford Street store. . . . That would be fun, Harry would like it, Eileen would giggle and get a lot of attention from people at their tables. . . . But no, it was too much effort, she'd never get Eileen ready. Let him come here. . . .

'Lunch here when you arrive,' she said.

'That's my girl, everything all right is it?'

'Why shouldn't it be?'

'You sound a bit fussed.'

'Can I speak to Aisling O'Connor, please?'

'I'm afraid she's gone to lunch, this is the book-keeper here – can I help you?'

'No, go back to the books.'

'I beg your pardon?'

Elizabeth hung up.

'Henry, can I beseech you not to make a scene in the office? Henry I am your oldest friend, you nearly married my sister. Will you listen to me? Listen to me. This must be discussed somewhere else. Every time a voice is raised, more office excitement is generated. We have to walk out of here calmly, do you hear me, *calmly*. As soon as we are out of reach of the office we will take a taxi to wherever we like, wherever you like. . . .'

'But. . . .'

'I'm going to open this door as soon as I have your promise that you will be quiet. . . .'

'Yes. . . .'

They walked like marionettes out of the office. The eyes of everyone in the office followed them as they walked woodenly to the stairs.

Henry tried to think of somewhere to go but he couldn't remember the names of any bars. Or anywhere at all that he could go.

Simon tried to remember the names of places where they might not want to go again, because he knew they might never be able to. Just before he left he spoke to his secretary. 'Ring our wives, tell mine everything, tell his nothing.'

'Yes, Mr Burke,' she said.

Elizabeth never liked the women who worked in the office with Henry; there was a slightly know-all air about them. None more so than Jessica, Simon's secretary.

'Mr Burke said to telephone you, Mrs Mason, to say that he and Mr Mason have just gone for a drink.'

'No, he didn't say why.'

'Or where. . . .'

'Just to let you know, I suppose, in case you were expecting Mr Mason home earlier or something.'

Aisling and Johnny went to the pictures, and he said he would say goodbye to her at the cinema because he was going to have an early night.

She telephoned him an hour later and there was no reply from his flat.

Harry said that he found it a bit more tiring than he expected, the long journey, so he might turn in early. He went to bed sadly. Elizabeth was in poor health. Not like Violet or anything, dear me, no, but she was under a great strain, the poor girl.

He hoped that Henry was going to come home with good news about the job soon. But better leave the two of them to it. She hadn't stopped looking at the clock all evening: she was worried sick.

They were eventually refused any more drink at the pub and

they went to have fish and chips. It helped. Or it helped Simon. It didn't really help Henry. He was still crying. At one stage he had taken a menu and listed all the good things he had done in his life. His conscientiousness, his honesty, his fairness, his refusal to do another man down, were all added up and set against the list of wrongs that had been done him.

'Where did I go wrong?' he whimpered. 'I did all the right things, I've done nothing wrong. Honestly, I've thought and thought. It's not my fault if. . . .'

Simon was by now losing patience. Glancing at his watch he interrupted. 'Look, Henry, it's getting very late — oughtn't you to be going home? Elizabeth will be. . . .'

'Elizabeth!' snapped Henry. 'That *was* a mistake. She's so busy with her arty job — far too busy to take any notice of my problems, she's no time for. . . .'

'Henry, you're being ridiculous. For the last time, there is *no* conspiracy, Elizabeth is not. . . .'

'No time for Eileen, even. Only ever has time for Aisling. Irish tart. I know. Anything that moves. I know, I heard them talking. Not just Johnny. . . .'

'Go home, Henry. You'll feel much better tomorrow.'

'I'm not going home . . . I know where I'm going.' Henry smiled drunkenly.

'Where? Shouldn't you go home? Will Elizabeth . . . ?'

'To hell with Elizabeth . . . she doesn't understand. She snaps at me for nothing. I don't want to. . . .'

'Well if you're sure you can manage old chap . . . I must be going. . . .'

'I'm much better now Simon, I see what you mean — the whole thing needs to be handled with cunning, not scenes in the office, it's behind the scenes . . . isn't it . . . ?' He laughed foolishly.

'That's it,' said Simon anxiously, 'so you want a taxi. . . .'

'No, you head home . . . I'll go and dally . . . dilly-dally . . . I'll dilly-dally on the way.'

'See you tomorrow, Henry, bright and unemotional.'

'Bright and unemotional,' Henry muttered.

*

'Oh God, I seem to have a genius for attracting drunks. Henry Mason, I have never seen you drunk in your whole life . . . why tonight and why me . . . ?'

'I want to talk to you. . . .'

'Sure, you can talk to me, don't wake the house though. . . .' Aisling struggled into her dressing-gown, and let him into the flat.

'You're undressed very early. Do you always go to bed before ten?'

'It's long after ten actually, but let's not worry about that, and I was tired. Right, will you have a coffee?'

'I'll have a drink. I gather you have a lot of drink here. You're a rich woman now, you can have as much drink as you like. . . .'

'I have one bottle of vermouth here, and it would make you as sick as a dog, but if you must, you must.'

'Why don't you have a drinks cabinet like rich people have . . . ?'

'Henry, you're very funny when you're pissed, because I had a husband who died a screaming alcoholic and I don't feel that I should indulge too much myself. . . .'

'That's what I came here for, to indulge. . . .'

'Well, if you want vermouth, but it's very sickly, I warn you.'

'Not vermouth.'

'Thank God, will we both have a cup of coffee then, and will I ring Elizabeth? Does she know you're headed to me?'

'How could she know I was here? You don't tell your wife when you go to see a whore. . . .'

Elizabeth rang Bethan. 'I hate disturbing you so late – but is Simon there . . . ?'

Simon shook his head from the chair, his mother and father-in-law were there, and he was doing an imitation of a family man.

'No, sorry Elizabeth, I believe he's out with Henry. They must be out celebrating.'

'That must be it.'

'I hate telling her lies and making a fool of her,' Bethan said.

'It's easier for her not to think we all know that he's gone out on a bender,' Simon said.

'But where is he?' Bethan wondered.

'Who knows? It's early still.' It was eleven o'clock. Simon poured another drink for himself quietly, and his in-laws drank their cups of tea.

Johnny said that Virginia could certainly stay the night – he agreed that it would be silly for her to look for a taxi at this late hour. He put on the record player in his sitting room, and turned back the bed neatly in the bedroom so that it looked inviting but not too obvious.

Harry had a bad dream and woke up; he looked at the clock. It was only midnight, and he had been asleep for two hours. Oh well, a man of sixty-two must expect to feel a bit weary after the journey down from the North.

'Let's just say that you were very drunk, and why don't you go now, and I'll forget what you said?'

'What did I say?'

'You said I was a whore, but you didn't mean it.'

'I do mean it, I just want to know if I can join the group.'

'Oh, Henry, go home. You can't hold your drink . . . don't be silly.'

'Don't you dare call me silly.'

Aisling looked alarmed. She had a feeling that he was going to hit her, he was so like Tony that last night, yet he wasn't nearly as drunk.

'Come here. . . .' He reached for her. 'Come here. If you do it with everyone else, why not with me . . . ?'

She leapt up and ran around to the other side of the room. 'I'm just asking you once more. I have not led you on, encouraged you in any way, to believe . . . I am your wife's best friend . . . this is idiotic, it is . . . what can I say it is . . . it's grotesque.'

'You like it with everyone else. . . .'

'Please, Henry, get it into your head . . . I have . . . I'm a lover, or whatever, of one person. Johnny Stone . . . nobody else . . .' She faltered. Damn Simon Burke to the pit of hell, and her own stupidity – it must have been Simon who suggested he come here. . . . 'He's a good friend of yours, of all of us.'

'Oh yes, he is a good friend of yours, all right. I know that.'

'Henry, of course you know that – we all know that. Now, can you stop all this nonsense and go home?'

'A *friend* of yours, and a *friend* of Elizabeth's – how many other *friends* have you two had?'

'Henry, you know quite well that Elizabeth's affair with Johnny was over when she met you. It's you she loves, you great lump. . . .'

'But you met him years ago when you came to London first, you told me.'

She was becoming very tired of him indeed. How could she shift him? 'I met him when he was Elizabeth's boyfriend that time . . . the time of the trouble . . . the business. . . .'

'The business?'

'Henry, go away, you're being very tiresome, go home and talk to Elizabeth about it.'

'The business?'

'You know, Elizabeth told you everything, the time she had the abortion, that was when I met him first. But he. . . .'

'Elizabeth had an abortion . . . ?'

'But you *know* about all that Henry. Elizabeth told you. . . .'

'You are a filthy bitch. You are not fit to. . . . You whore. . . . I do not want you to. . . . Neither. . . .'

'Get out. You know all this. Elizabeth said you know about each other's pasts. That's grand, I thought then, and that's grand I still think. But you're determined to pick a fight and you won't with me. I'm an expert in handling drunks.'

He got up and went out without saying a word. He went too quietly. She called down the stairs after him, he said nothing.

Johnny and Virginia were in bed when the phone rang.
Johnny leaned over to answer it. It was a public call box.

'You're a murdering bastard,' a drunk's voice said.

'Who is that?' Johnny didn't recognise the voice, but the
speaker was obviously drunk or upset or both.

'You let her murder the child. I know all about it now.'

'Who? What are you talking about?'

'Elizabeth,' the voice said and hung up.

Harry woke again. He wondered whether to see the doctor
and ask for some sleeping pills. But no, this time there was a
reason, there were voices outside his door.

'I don't care about the job, I don't care about it, if you
were bloody sacked I wouldn't care. Why didn't you ring
me . . . ?'

'You are a murderer . . . you murdered a child, I know
about it.'

'What on earth are you talking about? Henry, come in
and shut up. You'll wake Harry. . . .'

'You and he murdered a child. I know, everyone knows
. . . you did, and you didn't tell me. I would never have
married you if I had known, never.'

'Henry, keep your voice down. You'll wake Eileen. There,
she's awake already. Now, come in from that door, stop
swaying there, and tell me where you heard this ridiculous
story. . . .'

'From your friend and helpmate, the Irish whore. . . .'

'I don't believe you are speaking like this. You've lost
your reason.'

'Aisling the tart. I've had her, Johnny's had her, Simon's
had her. I suppose if Harry wasn't so old he'd have her. By
God, she's made up for her unconsummated marriage,
hasn't she . . . ?'

'You were with Aisling tonight?'

'I was with precious Aisling.'

'You and Aisling . . . I don't believe you. . . .'

'Oh, I'm sure you'll discuss it in the morning, you talk
about everything . . . I've heard you.'

'Aisling did not sleep with you. That I know. . . .'
'Why not? She sees fit to sleep with Johnny Bloody Stone. I rang him and told him.'
'You told him what?'
'I told him I knew he had murdered a child, with you.'

Harry tried to decide what to do. In a pub if people's voices got to this stage, it was time to step in. Interference was poorly regarded, however, between married couples. But he couldn't believe that this was happening. Henry must be mad. Murdering a child? With Johnny? Perhaps he should try not to listen. Impossible. He had to know what was happening. He had to be ready in case Elizabeth needed help. Perhaps he should call out. If he said, 'Hey up, what's all this?' maybe Henry would straighten his tie, and calm down, and come in or go away. Anything would be better than this business at the door. He could bear it no longer. He opened his bedroom door, just a crack, and then a little further.

The door out on to the landing was wide open, the light streaming in in a harsh triangle, Henry's face was working uncontrollably. 'You whore . . . you murderess . . . you're not fit to be a mother . . . I'm taking Eileen . . . now . . . you bitch. . . .'

'You're mad. . . . No, get out, leave me alone, God damn you. . . .'

'I'm taking my daughter away from you, you murdering . . . get out of my way. . . .'

Harry had to stop them. He didn't care how embarrassed they were all going to be in the morning. He didn't mind admitting that he knew of their row, he pulled the door open. 'Hey, now. . . .' he began, but the words were barely formed when he heard the muffled shout.

Aisling told herself that Henry *must* have known about . . . everything. Of course Elizabeth had told him about the whole dreadful business. She must have done. You do tell people things in intimate moments. She had even told Tony about her early necking sessions with Ned at the cinema. He was just plastered, and half-crazed from not getting the job. That was all. He'd get over it.

Johnny told himself that there were lots of people in London called Elizabeth. He and Elizabeth had murdered no child. Certainly not.

Then there was silence. Nobody seemed to have heard. Elizabeth had closed the front door and bolted it. She remained frozen for a moment. Then she walked unseeing past Harry.

Harry stood breathless. But almost immediately he heard Elizabeth's voice soothing little Eileen.

'It's all right, shush, shush. Don't worry. Daddy will be home soon. Daddy's out late, Daddy's out getting a big job. He'll be home soon. He'll be home soon. Everything will be fine.'

'Oh my God,' Harry said aloud.

The ambulance men left quietly. There was no need to rush to the hospital with sirens blaring. Henry Mason was dead. It was the porter who had gone up to the top floor to tell young Mrs Mason the news. She came to the door in her dressing-gown looking confused and carrying her little girl in her arms.

'What is it? You can't mean it . . . not possible . . . how did it happen? How could it have happened . . . ? He wasn't home. Did he fall? How could he have fallen? Can I see him? Henry? Henry? Henry?'

And there were cups of tea and the police as well. No, Henry hadn't come home, he was out having a few drinks. One of the secretaries had rung to say he would be late. He must have had too many. He wasn't used to drinking. Oh God.

'Elizabeth?'
  'Aisling?'
  'Don't move, stay where you are, I'll sit down beside you. . . .' Aisling sat down on the side of the bed. She took

593

Elizabeth's thin cold hand in hers. Elizabeth said nothing. Aisling rubbed the hand a little as if to bring back the circulation. The clock was ticking very loudly. Outside there was a faint noise of traffic, and almost as faint was the hum of conversation from the sitting room. Harry was talking to the callers in a low voice, discouraging anyone from trying to see Elizabeth, noting all the offers of help. Eileen had gone to stay with friends who had a small child. Elizabeth's father had been and gone. Elizabeth had refused an injection to sedate her. She said she would be all right.

Elizabeth's eyes were not still, not for a moment; they darted all around, into Aisling's face and out of it. . . . Her head never moved, it lay on the pillow as if it was too heavy to raise.

'Can you walk? I think we should go out,' Aisling said.

'Yes, yes, that's what we'll do.' Elizabeth pulled her hand away and pushed back the covers. She was half-dressed. She moved to the chair and pulled on a blue polo necked sweater and a plaid skirt. She found a jacket in the wardrobe. She looked frail and ill.

'Are you sure . . . ?'

'Yes, you're right, it's just what I want to do. . . .' She slipped her feet into shoes and looked at Aisling trustingly like a child.

Aisling murmured to Harry, and in a moment they were out on the landing. Neither of them looked at the floor or at each other. They got into the lift and stood almost rigid as it went down. They walked, heads down and hands in pockets, out the door and across the road. Their steps seemed urgent and anxious until they got into the park, then unconsciously they seemed to change their stride, into the stroll of park walkers, the slow gait of Londoners enjoying the grass and the flower beds instead of the traffic and the noise.

'What am I going to do?' Elizabeth asked eventually. There was a long silence, but Aisling had slipped her arm through Elizabeth's and they walked without looking at each other. 'I mean, what's going to happen?' her voice was very thin.

Aisling spoke slowly. 'You'll make a life for Eileen. You'll remember all the good bits and put the bad bits away. I think that's what people do.'

'Yes.'

They walked on, arms linked.

'It didn't turn out all that well for us . . . what was wrong with us . . . ?' Aisling said.

'What do you mean?'

'Well, here we are, Elizabeth . . . widows, both of us . . . only your Eileen left to show for it all . . . for all the hope and the . . . dreams . . . you know.'

Elizabeth's voice had become stronger. 'Your Mam wouldn't like us talking like that . . . going over the past. . . .'

'No, she wouldn't.' Aisling was quiet for a moment. Then she spoke again. 'Mam always knew what to say . . . she used to say what I thought was the wrong thing . . . but it turned out to be the right one . . . I don't know how she found the right words . . . it was a kind of skill. . . .'

Elizabeth said, 'No, I don't think she even tried, I think the words were just there.'

'Yes,' said Aisling.

They sat down on a seat where they had often stopped when they had taken Eileen out in a pram . . . and even before that, when Aisling had come to London first . . . in those days when she had just run away.

'It must have been very quick for him,' Aisling said.

'The policeman said that it would have been over in a few seconds.' Elizabeth put her face in her hands.

'Stop, stop.'

'No, I'm not crying, I'm just thinking about the few seconds. They must have seemed very long . . . it . . .'

'No, no, think of it like a dream, you know the frightening bit . . . then it's over. . . .'

'But in a dream you wake up.'

'Well, it was over for Henry . . . he felt no more then.'

Elizabeth stood up. 'Yes, I know.'

'It took Tony much longer to die,' Aisling said.

Elizabeth looked at her. 'I suppose it did,' she said.

'And look at all you did for Henry . . . look at it and remember all the good. You gave him a home, he always wanted one . . . you gave him confidence . . . all those things . . . he would never have got them from anyone else. . . .' Aisling looked at the ground as she spoke. Elizabeth looked across the park.

'You made Tony happy too . . .' she said.

'No, I didn't, nobody could have, and I certainly didn't. I made him worse.'

'Don't look at it that way. . . .' Elizabeth's voice was clear now, and strong as ever. 'You were what he wanted and he got you. . . . That's the only thing that gives us any hope out of all this. . . . If people got what they wanted. . . .'

'What can I do for you, Elizabeth? I'll do anything, anything, you know that. . . .'

'I know. I know. You always have . . . you've always rescued me. . . .'

'No, you rescued me . . . you did the rescuing years ago . . . if I hadn't a friend like you all my life what would I have had . . . Maureen, Niamh . . . Joannie Murray . . . some friends . . . they would have been, for all that happened. . . .'

'And we never fought . . . in all those years we never had a real row. . . .'

'I know, sometimes I think when you left Kilgarret first, when you came back here, I used to get annoyed because you were so distant . . . I didn't know. . . .'

'And I didn't know . . . when you and Tony were married at first and you sent these brittle letters . . . I was annoyed. But I didn't know.'

'What can I do for you Elizabeth, please . . .' she asked again.

'Tell me what happens next. . . .'

'There'll be the inquest . . . and the coroner will say. . . .'

'Yes?'

'He'll say how he heard that Henry became upset and . . . and . . . went on a sort of drunken . . . well . . . batter . . . and then came home and then about the accident . . . and how he fell. . . .'

'And what will the coroner say?'

596

'I don't know. . . . I suppose he'll pass a vote of sympathy . . . isn't that what they do when you read about inquests? They say that they would like to extend their sympathy to the relatives and friends of the deceased. . . .'

'Like a sort of obituary?'

'I suppose so . . . something like that.'

'Oh.'

'And then it will all be over . . . and you'll have to start to. . . .'

'Yes. . . .'

'Oh God, Elizabeth, I'm so sorry, I'm so very sorry. . . .'

'I know . . . I know . . . I'm sorry, I'm very sorry too. . . .'

The coroner's inquest was brief and formal.

Aisling had read about inquests in the local papers back in Kilgarret. Mam had said that it was only a scourge and a torture to poor families to have the press reporters there, writing down every word and making it a thousand times worse . . . whatever awful sadness the people had already.

She looked around the small dusty courtroom. Two men were writing in notebooks, they might be press. They didn't look much like journalists. But nobody looked much like anything today. Everyone looked very odd as if they were playing a part in some play they hadn't rehearsed properly. That's what she felt anyway, and she felt sure Elizabeth must be thinking the same thing. It was odd, but for once it was hard to know what Elizabeth was thinking. Her face was like a mask.

Elizabeth's face was very still, but her thoughts were darting all over the place, she felt that she must run after them as if she were collecting marbles that had spilled from a box. She remembered there had been an inquest in the hospital where Mother had died. Yes, dreadful fuss and anxiety all over the place, doctors and nurses very upset. The patient had been in a room near Mother, of very unsound mind, nobody doubted that, she had managed to get the glass to cut her wrists through great cunning that nobody could have foreseen, nobody doubted that either and there could have been no blame attached to any member of staff. But they had hated the inquest. She remembered them telling her that. What good did it do they had asked, upset everybody and didn't bring back the poor old soul who had done herself in. She wondered had she ever told Aisling about that? Aisling looked very strong sitting there opposite her, her hands for once still on her lap.

What an extraordinary place for them both to be. A coroner's court. Harry Elton thought that the room was so small and shabby it must be only a temporary court. This wasn't like courts you saw in films, or the Old Bailey. This was just a dusty room. But of course it wasn't a trial, he told himself for the twentieth time, so there was no need to have a real court. It was only a tidying up of the bits and bobs of papers, that's all it was. If it had been necessary there would have been a real court. But not unless there had been a crime.

Simon Burke looked around, he could tell the titles of familiar law books just by their bindings. The place was a bit dusty. If he had been in charge of the place he'd have seen that it got a good going over each week. It never did any harm to give the Law some trappings, not make it seem like a storage depot in the back of some second-hand bookshop. He wondered what the others made of it. Aisling and Elizabeth so still, so pale both of them. He remembered the first time he had seen Elizabeth, he and Henry had seen her when they went to register for the little art course. Oh God. Henry. Poor bloody Henry.

Johnny thought he saw Aisling smile at him and he smiled back. But she hadn't been looking at him, she had only turned her head his way, her eyes didn't meet his. Lord, Lord, what a business all this was. It was unbelievable that they should all be caught up in an inquest. Henry's inquest no less. It was bloody ridiculous. Henry should be alive and well and going his own way, hitting the sauce a bit less. Incredible to look at both those girls . . . well women . . . Aisling and Elizabeth, and to think that both their husbands had more or less died from drink. The odds against that must be overwhelming. Poor old Henry, Lord this was a bloody awful business. Sooner it was all shut of the better.

Elizabeth thought, Aisling said it would all be very quick and formal. Please make it quick and formal. I can't stand sitting here. I can't stand it one minute more.

Aisling thought, if they don't start soon I'm going to crack. This is desperate, sitting here while he fusses about moving papers from one side of his bloody desk to the other. God Almighty, get on with it can't you, it's meant to be a formality, a formal taking of evidence. Can't you get on with it you stupid old bumbler? Stop making yourself into a little tin God.

The coroner was now ready, everything on his desk was to his satisfaction. He was ready to hear the evidence. . . .

Evidence was given by the police, by the ambulance men, by the porter. Everyone spoke in flat, measured tones about what had happened, and what times it had happened. Only Harry Elton and Simon Burke were called to speak. Harry Elton, step-father of Mrs Mason . . . guest in the house. Heard absolutely nothing until the huge knocking on the door and the porter and the terrible news. Poor Elizabeth shattered. Dreadful tragedy . . . happy family life. . . .

Simon had left him in an intoxicated condition at the corner of Great Portland Street and Mortimer Street. No, he hadn't said where he was going to go. Simon Burke had advised him to get a taxi home, and he had said he would do that. No, Simon Burke had no idea where he might have gone after that.

Nobody called Aisling O'Connor, friend of Mrs Mason, to give any evidence.

Nobody asked Johnny Stone, friend and colleague of Mrs Mason, to describe the telephone call. Because no mention of a visit or a telephone call had ever been made.

*

So they sat in the coroner's court and said nothing until the verdict of misadventure and accidental death by falling down an internal staircase, after excessive alcoholic consumption, was recorded by the coroner.

And then they all came out into the sun.

ECHOES

For dearest Gordon with all my love

PROLOGUE

People seemed to know without being told. They came out of their houses and began to run down the main street. The murmur became louder, and almost without knowing they were doing it they started to check where their own families were. It was still just a figure, face down in the water. They didn't know for sure whether it was a man or a woman.

'Perhaps it's a sailor from a ship,' they said. But they knew it wasn't anyone who had gone overboard. No nice anonymous death of someone they didn't know. No informing the authorities and saying a few prayers for the deceased unknown sailor. This was someone from Castlebay.

They stood in silent groups on the cliff top and watched the first people getting to the water's edge: the boy who had first seen the waves leaving something frightening on the shore; other men too; people from the shops nearby and young men who were quick to run down the path. Then they saw the figures coming down the other path near the doctor's house, kneeling by the body in case, just in case there was something in a black bag that could bring it back to life.

By the time Father O'Dwyer arrived with his soutane flapping in the wind the murmur had turned into a unified sound. The people of Castlebay were saying a decade of the rosary for the repose of the soul which had left the body that lay face down on their beach.

PART ONE

1950–1952

It was sometimes called Brigid's Cave, the echo cave, and if you shouted your question loud enough in the right direction you got an answer instead of an echo. In the summer it was full of girls calling out questions, girls who had come for the summer to Castlebay. Girls who wanted to know would they get a fellow, or if Gerry Doyle would have eyes for them this summer. Clare thought they were mad to tell the cave their secrets. Specially since people like her sister Chrissie and that crowd would go and listen for private things being asked and then they'd scream with laughter about them and tell everyone. Clare said she'd never ask the echo anything no matter how desperate she was, because it wouldn't be a secret any more. But she did go in to ask about the history prize. That was different.

It was different because it was winter anyway, and there was hardly anyone except themselves in Castlebay in winter; and it was different because it had nothing to do with love. And it was a nice way to come home from school that way down the cliff road: you didn't have to talk to everyone in the town, you could look at the sea instead. And suppose she did go down that crooked path with all the Danger notices on it, then she could go into the cave for a quick word, walk along the beach and up the real steps and be home in the same time as if she had come down the street talking to this person and that. In winter there was hardly any business so people waved you into shops and gave you a biscuit or asked you to do a message for them. She'd be just as quick going by Brigid's cave and the beach.

It had been dry, so the Danger bits weren't so dangerous. Clare slid easily down the cliff on to the sand. It was firm and hard, the tide had not long gone out. The mouth of the cave

3

looked black and a bit frightening. But she squared her shoulders; it looked just the same in summer yet people went in there in droves. She shifted her schoolbag to her back so that she could have both hands free to guide herself and once she got used to the light there was no difficulty seeing the little ridge where you were meant to stand.

Clare took a deep breath: 'Will I win the history prize?' she called.

'Ize ize ize ize,' called the echo.

'It's saying yes,' said a voice just beside her. Clare jumped with the fright. It was David Power.

'You shouldn't listen to anyone else, it's like listening in to confession,' Clare said crossly.

'I thought you saw me,' David said simply. 'I wasn't hiding.'

'How could I see you, didn't I come in out of the light, you were lurking in here.' She was full of indignation.

'It's not a private cave, you don't have to keep shouting Cave Occupied,' David retorted loudly.

'Pied pied pied pied,' said the cave.

They both laughed.

He was nice, really, David Power, he was the same age as her brother Ned – fifteen. They had been in Mixed Infants together, she remembered Ned telling someone proudly, wanting to share some experience with the doctor's son.

He wore a tie and suit when he came home from school, all the time, not just when he went to Mass on Sundays. He was tall and he had freckles on his nose. His hair was a bit spiky and used to stick up in funny directions, one big bit of it fell over his forehead. He had a nice smile and he always looked as if he were ready to talk except that something was dragging him away. Sometimes he wore a blazer with a badge on it, and he looked very smart in that. He used to wrinkle his nose and tell people that it only looked smart when you didn't see a hundred and eighty blazers like that every day at his school. He'd been at a boarding school for over a year but now it was closed because of scarlet fever. Only the Dillon girls from the hotel went to boarding school and of course the Wests and the Greens, but they were

4

Protestants and they had to go to a boarding school because there wasn't one of their own.

'I didn't think it would answer really, I only tried it as a joke,' she said.

'I know, I tried it once as a joke too,' he confessed.

'What did you ask it as a joke?' she inquired.

'I forget now,' he said.

'That's not fair – you heard mine.'

'I didn't, I only heard eyes eyes eyes.' He shouted it and it called back the three words to him over and over.

Clare was satisfied. 'Well I'd best be off now, I have homework. I don't suppose you've had homework for weeks.' She was envious and inquiring.

'I do. Miss O'Hara comes every day to give me lessons. She's coming . . . oh soon now.' They walked out on to the wet hard sand.

'Lessons all by yourself with Miss O'Hara – isn't that great?'

'It is, she's great at explaining things, isn't she, for a woman teacher I mean.'

'Yes, well we only have women teachers and nuns,' Clare explained.

'I forgot,' David said sympathetically. 'Still she's terrific, and she's very easy to talk to, like a real person.'

Clare agreed. They walked companionably along to the main steps up from the beach. It would have been quicker for David to climb the path with Danger written on it, it led almost into his own garden, but he said he wanted to buy some sweets at Clare's shop anyway. They talked about things the other had never heard of. David told her about the sanitorium being fumigated after the two pupils got scarlet fever; but all the time she thought that he was talking about the big hospital on the hill where people went when they had TB. She didn't know it was a room in his school. She told him a long and complicated tale about Mother Immaculata asking one of the girls to leave the exercise books in one place and she thought that it was somewhere else and the girl went by accident into the nuns' side of the convent. This was all lost on David, who didn't know that you never under

5

pain of *terrible* things went to the nuns' side of the convent. It didn't really matter to either of them, they were no strain on each other, and life in Castlebay could be full of strains so this was a nice change. He came into the shop and, as there was nobody serving, she took off her coat, hung it up and found the jar of Clove Rock. She counted out the six for a penny that he was buying and before she put the lid on the jar she offered him one courteously and took one herself.

He looked at her enviously. It was great power to be able to stand up on a chair in a sweetshop, take down a jar and be free to offer one to a customer. David sighed as he went home. He'd have loved to live in a shop like Clare O'Brien, he'd have loved brothers and sisters, and to be allowed to go up to the yard and collect milk in a can when the cows were being milked, or gather seaweed to sell to the hot sea baths in bundles. It was very dull going back to his own house now to his mother saying he should really have some sense of what was what. It was the most irritating thing he had ever heard, especially since it seemed to mean anything and everything and never the same thing twice. Still, Miss O'Hara was coming tonight, and Miss O'Hara made lessons much more interesting than at school, he had once been unwise enough to explain to his mother. He thought she would be pleased but she said that Miss O'Hara was fine for a country primary school but did not compare with the Jesuits who were on a different level entirely.

Clare was sighing too, she thought it must be great altogether to go back to a house like David Power's where there were bookcases of books in the house, and a fire on in that front room whether there was anyone sitting in it or not. And there was no wireless on, and nobody making noise. You could do your homework there for hours without anyone coming in and telling you to move. She remembered the inside of the house from when she had been up to Dr Power for the stitches the time she had caught her leg on the rusty bit of machinery. To distract her Dr Power had asked her to count the volumes of the encyclopedia up on the shelf and Clare had been so startled to see all those books in one house for one family that she had forgotten about the stitches and Dr Power had told her mother she was as brave as a lion. They had walked home after the stitches with Clare leaning on her mother. They stopped at the church to thank St Anne that there hadn't been any infection in the leg and as Clare saw her mother bent in prayer and gratitude in front of the St Anne grotto she let her mind wander on how great it would be to have a big peaceful house full of books like that instead of being on top of each other and no room for anything – no time for anything either. She thought about it again tonight as David Power went up the street home to that house where the carpet went right into the window, not stopping in a square like ordinary carpets. There would be a fire and there'd be peace. His mother might be in the kitchen and Dr Power would be curing people and later Miss O'Hara would be coming to give him lessons all on his own without the rest of a class to distract her. What could be better than that? She wished for a moment that she had been his sister, but then she felt guilty. To wish that would be to want to lose Mammy and Daddy and Tommy and Ned and Ben and Jimmy. Oh and Chrissie. But she didn't care how wrong it was, she wouldn't mind losing Chrissie any day of the week.

The calm of the shop was only temporary. Daddy had been painting out in the back and he came in holding his hands up in front of him and asking someone to reach out a bottle of white spirit and open it up this minute. There was an awful lot of painting going on in the wintertime in Castlebay, the sea air just ripped the coats off again and the place looked very shabby unless it was touched up all the time. Mammy came in at the same moment; she had been up to the post office and she had discovered terrible things. Chrissie and her two tinkers of friends had climbed on the roof of Miss O'Flaherty's shop and poked a long wet piece of seaweed through to frighten Miss O'Flaherty. They could have given the unfortunate woman a heart attack; she could, God save us all, have dropped stone dead on the floor of her own shop and then Chrissie O'Brien and her two fine friends would have the sin of murder on their souls until the Last Day and after. Chrissie had been dragged home by the shoulder, the plait and the ear. She was red-faced and annoyed. Clare thought that it was a good thing to have frightened Miss O'Flaherty who was horrible, and sold copy books and school supplies but hated schoolchildren. Clare thought it was real bad luck that Mammy happened to be passing. She smiled sympathetically at Chrissie but it was not well received.

'Stop looking so superior,' Chrissie cried out. 'Look at Clare gloating at it all. Goody-goody Clare, stupid boring Clare.'

She got a cuff on the side of her head for this performance and it made her madder still.

'Look, she's delighted,' Chrissie went on, 'delighted to see anyone in trouble. That's all that ever makes Clare happy, to see others brought down.'

'There'll be no tea for you, Chrissie O'Brien, and that's not the end of it either. Get up to your room this minute, do you hear. This *minute*.' Agnes O'Brien's thin voice was like a whistle with anger, as she banished the bold Chrissie, wiped the worst paint off her husband's hands with a rag that she had wet with white spirit, and managed at the same time to point to Clare's coat on the hook.

'This isn't a hand-me-down shop,' she said. 'Take that coat and put it where it's meant to be.'

The unfairness of this stung Clare deeply. 'We always leave our coats there. That *is* where it's meant to be.'

'Do you hear her?' Agnes looked in appeal to her husband, did not wait for an answer but headed for the stairs. Chrissie up there was for it.

'Can't you stop tormenting your mother and move your coat?' he asked. 'Is it too much to ask for a bit of peace?'

Clare took her coat down from the hook. She couldn't go up to the bedroom she shared with Chrissie because that would be like stepping straight into the battlefield. She stayed idling in the shop.

Her father's face was weary. It was so *wrong* of him to say she was tormenting Mammy, she wasn't, but you couldn't explain that to him. He was bent over in a kind of a stoop and he looked very old, like someone's grandfather, not a father. Daddy was all grey, his face and his hair and his cardigan. Only his hands were white from the paint. Daddy had grown more stooped since her First Communion three years ago, Clare thought; then he had seemed very tall. His face had grown hairy too – there were bits of hair in his nose and his ears. He always looked a bit harassed as if there wasn't enough time or space or money. And, indeed, there usually wasn't enough of any of these things. The O'Brien household lived on the profits of the summer season which was short and unpredictable. It could be killed by rain, by the popularity of some new resort, by people overcharging for houses along the cliff road. There was no steady living to be gained over the winter months, it was merely a matter of keeping afloat.

The shop was oddly-shaped when you came in: there were corners and nooks in it which should have been shelved or walled off but nobody had ever got round to it, the ceiling was low and even with three customers the place looked crowded. Nobody could see any order on the shelves but the O'Briens knew where everything was. They didn't change it for fear they wouldn't find things, even though there were many more logical ways of stocking the small grocery-confectioner's. It all looked cramped and awkward and though the customers couldn't see behind the door into the living quarters it was exactly the same in there. The kitchen had a range, with a clothes line over it, and the table took up most of the space in the room. A small scullery at the back was so poky and dark that it was almost impossible to see the dishes you washed. There was one light in the middle of the room with a yellow light shade which had a crack in it. Recently Tom O'Brien had been holding his paper up nearer to the light in order to read it.

Agnes came downstairs with the air of someone who has just finished an unpleasant task satisfactorily. 'That girl will end on the gallows,' she said.

She was a thin small woman, who used to smile a lot once; but now she seemed set in the face of the cold Castlebay wind, and even when she was indoors she seemed to be grimacing against the icy blast, eyes narrow and mouth in a hard line. In the shop she wore a yellow overall to protect her clothes, she said, but in fact there were hardly any clothes to protect. She had four outfits for going to Mass, and otherwise it had been the same old cardigans and frocks and skirts for years. There were always medals and relics pinned inside the cardigan; they had to be taken off before it was washed. Once she had forgotten, and a relic of the Little Flower which had been in a red satin covering had become all pink and the pale blue cardigan was tinged pink too. Agnes O'Brien had her hair in a bun which was made by pulling it through a thing that looked like a doughnut, a squashy round device, and then the hair was clipped in. They never saw her doing this, but once they had seen the bun by itself and it had alarmed Clare greatly because she hadn't known what it was.

The dark and very angry eyes of her mother landed on her. 'Have you decided that you would like to belong to this family and do what's required of you? Would it be too much to ask you to take that coat out of my way before I open the range and burn it down to its buttons?'

She would never do that, Clare knew. She had hoped her mother might have forgotten it during the sojourn upstairs. But the coat was still going to be a cause of war.

'I told her, Agnes, my God I told her, but children nowadays . . .' Tom sounded defeated and apologetic.

Clare stuffed her school coat into a crowded cupboard under the stairs and took a few potatoes out of the big sack on the floor. Each evening she and Chrissie had to get the potatoes ready for tea, and tonight, thanks to Chrissie's disgrace, it looked as if Clare was going to have to do it on her own. In the kitchen sat her younger brothers Ben and Jim; they were reading a comic. The older boys Tommy and Ned would be in from the Brothers shortly, but none of this would be any help. Boys didn't help with the food or the washing up. Everyone knew that.

Clare had a lot to do after tea. She wanted to iron her yellow ribbons for tomorrow. Just in case she won the history essay she'd better be looking smart. She would polish her indoor shoes, she had brought them home specially, and she would make another attempt to get the two stains off her tunic. Mother Immaculata might make a comment about smartening yourself up for the good name of the school. She must be sure not to let them down. Miss O'Hara had said that she had never been so pleased in all her years teaching as when she read Clare's essay, it gave her the strength to go on. Those were her very words. She would never have stopped Clare in the corridor and said that, if she hadn't won the prize. Imagine beating all the ones of fifteen. All those Bernie Conways and Anna Murphys. They'd look at Clare with new interest from now on. And indeed they'd have to think a bit differently at home too. She longed to tell them tonight, but decided it was better to wait. Tonight they were all like weasels and anyway it might look worse for Chrissie; after all she was two years and a half older. Chrissie would murder her too if she chose to reveal it tonight. She took upstairs a big thick sandwich of cheese, a bit of cold cooked bacon and a cup of cocoa.

Chrissie was sitting on her bed, examining her face in a mirror. She had two very thick plaits in her hair; the bits at the ends after the rubber bands were bushy and didn't just hang there like other people's, they looked as if they were trying to escape. She had a fringe which she cut herself so badly that she had to be taken to the hairdresser to get a proper job done on it, and at night she put pipe cleaners into the fringe so that it would curl properly.

She was fatter than Clare, much, and she had a real bust that you could see even in her school tunic.

Chrissie was very interested in her nose, Clare couldn't understand why but she was always examining it. Even now in all the disgrace and no meal and the sheer fury over what she had done to Miss O'Flaherty she was still peering at it looking for spots to squeeze. She had a round face and always looked surprised. Not happily surprised, not even when someone was delivering her an unexpected supper.

'I don't want it,' she said.

'Don't eat it then,' Clare returned with some spirit.

She went back downstairs and tried to find a corner where she could learn the poem for tomorrow; and she had to do four sums. She often asked herself how was it that with six people living in that house who were all going to school, why was she the only one who ever needed to do any homework?

Gerry Doyle came in as she was ironing her yellow ribbons.

'Where's Chrissie?' he asked Clare in a whisper.

'She's upstairs, there was murder here, she gave Miss O'Flaherty some desperate fright with seaweed. Don't ask for her, they'll all go mad if you even mention her name.'

'Listen, would you tell her . . .' He stopped, deciding against it. 'No, you're too young.'

'I'm not too young,' Clare said, stung by the unfairness of it. 'But young or old, I don't care, I'm not giving your soppy messages to Chrissie, she'll only be annoyed with me, and you'll be annoyed with me, and Mammy will beat the legs off me, so I'd much prefer you kept them to yourself.' She went back to the ribbons with vigour. They were flat gleaming bands now, they would fluff up gorgeously tomorrow. She couldn't get herself up to the neck in Chrissie's doings because there would be trouble at every turn. She must keep nice and quiet and get ready for tomorrow, for the look of surprise on Mother Immaculata's face, and the horror on Bernie Conway's and Anna Murphy's.

Gerry Doyle laughed good-naturedly. 'You're quite right, let people do their own dirty work,' he said.

The words 'dirty work' somehow cut through all the rest of the noise in the O'Brien kitchen and reached Agnes O'Brien as she pulled the entire contents of the dresser's bottom cupboard on to the floor. Tom had said that she must have thrown out the length of flex he was going to use to put up a light outside the back door. She was sure she had seen it somewhere and was determined that the project should not be postponed.

Tommy and Ned were going through the paper for jobs as they did every week, marking things with a stubby purple pencil; Ben and Jimmy were playing a game that began quietly every few minutes until it became a slapping match and one of them would start to cry. Tom was busy mending the wireless which crackled over all the activity.

'What dirty work?' Agnes called: a grand fellow, that Gerry Doyle, but you had to watch him like a hawk. Whatever devilment was planned he had a hand in it.

'I was saying to Clare that I'm no good at any housework, or anything that needs a lot of care. I'm only good at dirty work.' He smiled across, and the woman on her knees in front of a pile of tins, boxes, paper bags, knitting wool, toasting forks and rusted baking trays, smiled back.

Clare looked up at him with surprise. Imagine being able to tell a lie as quickly and as well as that. And over nothing.

Gerry had gone over to the job consultation, saying he heard there was going to be a man from a big employment agency in England coming round and holding interviews in the hotel.

'Wouldn't that be for big kind of jobs, for people with qualifications?' Ned asked, unwilling to think anyone would come to Castlebay to seek out him or his like.

'Have sense Ned, who is there in this place with any qualifications? Won't it save you shoe leather and the cost of writing off to these places if you wait till this fellow arrives and he'll tell all there's to be told?'

'It's easy on you to say that.' Tommy, the eldest, was troubled. '*You* don't have to go away for a job. You've got your business.'

'So have you,' Gerry pointed to the shop.

But it wasn't the same. Gerry's father was the photographer; during the winter he survived on dances, and the odd function that was held. In summer, he walked the length of the beach three times a day taking family groups and then out again at night into the dance hall where the holiday business was brisk and where there would be a great demand to buy prints of the romantic twosomes that he would snap. Girls were his biggest customers, they loved to bring back holiday memories in the form of something that they could pass around the office and sigh over when the

13

dance was long over. Gerry's mother and sister did the developing and printing, or they helped with it, which was the way it was described. Gerry's father expected the only son to take an active part, and since he had been a youngster, Gerry had tagged along learning the psychology as well as the mechanics of the camera.

You must never annoy people, his father had taught him, be polite and a little distant even, click the camera when they aren't at all posed or prepared and then if they show interest and start to pose take a proper snap. The first plate was only a blank to get their attention. Remind them gently that there's no need to buy, the proofs will be available for inspection in twenty-four hours. Move on and don't waste any time chatting when the picture is taken, have a pleasant smile but not a greasy sort of a one. Never plead with people to pose, and when gaggles of girls want six or seven shots taken of them remember they're only going to buy one at the most so pretend to take the snap more often than taking it.

Gerry's beautiful sister Fiona had long dark ringlets; when she wasn't working in the darkroom in their house during the summer she sat in the wooden shack up over the beach selling the snaps. Gerry's father had said that a town like Castlebay was so small you could never have a business if you tried to get big and expand and hire people. But keep it small and run it just with the family and there would be a great inheritance for Gerard Anthony Doyle.

But Gerry never had the air of a boy about to step into a secure future. He examined the paper with the O'Brien boys as eagerly as if he would be having to take the emigrant ship with them.

How did he know whether there'd be a living for him here? His father was always saying that all it needed was a smart-alec firm to come in for the summer and they'd be ruined. Who knew what the future would bring? Maybe people would want coloured photography, there could be newfangled cameras, it was living on a cliff edge his father always said. At least in O'Brien's they could be sure that people would always want bread and butter and milk. They'd want groceries until the end of the world and as long

14

as the trippers kept coming wouldn't they be selling ice creams and sweets and oranges until the Last Day as well?

Gerry always made everything sound more exciting than it was. He saw a future for Tommy and Ned where they'd work in England and then, just when all the English would be wondering what to do and where to go for the summer holidays, Ned and Tommy would come back home to Castlebay, get behind the counter, help out with the shop and have a great holiday as well. And they'd be fine fellows at the dance because they'd be so well up in everything after being in England. Tommy complained that it wouldn't be much of a holiday coming home to work like dogs in the really tough part of the year when O'Brien's was open from eight o'clock in the morning until midnight. But Gerry just laughed and said that would be their investment, that was the only time of the year that there'd be work for all hands. The rest of the year they'd be falling over each other with no one to serve, but in the summer the whole family should be there to make sure that everyone got a bit of sleep anyway and to keep the thing going. It was like that in all seaside towns. Gerry was very convincing. Tommy and Ned saw it all very rosily, and really and truly Gerry was right, shouldn't they wait till the man came and had a list of jobs for them instead of scanning all the ads which told them nothing when all was said and done?

Clare had turned the iron on its end by the range; she was folding the blanket and the scorch sheet and wondering where to replace them since everything from the dresser seemed to be on the floor. Gerry Doyle was sitting on the table swinging his legs and she got a sudden feeling that he was giving her brothers wrong advice. They weren't capable and sure like he was, they were the kind of people who agreed with everyone else.

'Would this man who came offering jobs in the hotel, would he be offering the kind of jobs where you could get on or jobs you'd just have to work hard at?'

They were surprised that she spoke. Her father took his head out of the shell of the wireless.

'It's the same thing, Clare girl, if you work hard you get on. If you don't, you don't.'

15

'But trained like, that's what I mean,' Clare said. 'You remember when that Order came and the girls were all going to be taken off to do their Leaving Certificate and learn a skill if they became postulant nuns.'

Ned roared with scorn. 'A postulant nun! Is that what you'd like us to be, wouldn't we look fine in the habit and the veil?'

'No that's not what I meant . . .' she began.

'I don't think the Reverend Mother would take us,' Tommy said.

'Sister Thomas, I really think we're going to have to do something about your voice in the choir,' Ned said in mincing tones.

'Oh I'm doing my best, Sister Edward, but what about your hobnailed boots?'

'Sister Thomas, you can talk, what about your hairy legs?'

Benny and Jimmy were interested now.

'And you've got to give up kicking football round the convent,' said Ben.

'Nuns kicking football,' screamed Jimmy with enthusiasm. Even Mammy on her knees and having triumphantly found the bit of flex was laughing and Dad was smiling too. Clare was rescued unexpectedly.

'Very funny, ha ha,' Gerry Doyle said. 'Very funny Mother Edward and Mother Thomas, but Clare's right. What's the point of getting a job on a building site without any training as a brickie or a carpenter? No, the real thing to ask this fellow is nothing to do with how much, but what kind of a job.'

Clare flushed with pleasure. They were all nodding now.

'I nearly forgot why I came,' Gerry said. 'The father asked me to have a look at the view from different places, he's half thinking of making a postcard of Castlebay, and he wondered where's the best angle to take the picture from. He wondered would there be a good view from your upstairs. Do you mind if I run up and have a look?'

'At night?' Clare's father asked.

'You'd get a good idea of the outlines at night,' Gerry said, his foot on the stairs.

'Go on up lad.'

They were all back at their activities and nobody except Clare had the slightest idea that Gerry Doyle aged fifteen and a half had gone upstairs to see Chrissie O'Brien aged thirteen.

Nellie was on her knees with the bellows when David came in. 'I'm building up a nice fire for your lessons,' she told him.

Her face was red with the exertion and her hair was escaping from the cap she wore. She never seemed comfortable in the cap, it was always at the wrong angle somehow on her hair and her head seemed to be full of hairpins. Nellie was old, not as old as Mummy but about thirty, and she was fat and cheerful and she had been there always. She had a lot of married brothers and an old father. When David was a young fellow she used to tell him that she was better off than any of them, in a nice clean house and great comfort and all the food she could eat. David used to think it was lonely for her in the kitchen when they were all inside but Nellie's round face would crack into a smile and she assured him that she was as well off as if she'd married a Guard, or even better off. Her money was her own, she had the best of everything and every Thursday afternoon and every second Sunday afternoon off.

David started to help with the fire but Nellie stood up, creaking, and said it was going fine and wasn't that his teacher coming in the gate.

Angela O'Hara's red bicycle was indeed coming up the gravel path. She was tall and slim, and she always wore belts on her coats as if it were the only way they'd stay on. Other people had buttons, but of course other people didn't fly around on the bike so much. She had red-brown hair that was sort of tied back but with such a loose ribbon or piece of cord that it might as well not be tied back at all. She had big greenish eyes and she used to throw her head back when she laughed.

Miss O'Hara wasn't at all like other grown-ups. She wanted to know did they all get a refund of fees because the school had to close for the scarlet fever. David didn't know, he said he'd ask, but Miss O'Hara said it didn't matter, and not to ask because it might seem as if she was looking for more money, which she wasn't. David had forgotten that she was being paid to teach him, it wasn't the kind of thing you'd think about, he sort of believed that Miss O'Hara did it for interest. She had found that very funny. She said in many ways she would well do it for interest but the labourer was worthy of his hire as it said somewhere in the gospels, and if she were to do it for free what about the fancy order of priests he was with – they certainly didn't do it for free. David said he thought the main cost was the food and the beds in the dormitories, he couldn't imagine that the actual lessons would cost anything.

She came for an hour every evening, after she had finished up at the school and called in on her mother. Mrs O'Hara was all crooked from arthritis and David thought that she looked like an illustration of an old tree in one of the children's books he used to read. A book probably tidied away neatly by his mother for when it would be needed again. Miss O'Hara had two sisters married in England and a brother, a priest, in the Far East. She was the only one who had never travelled, she told him. He asked what would have happened if she had travelled and her mother had got all crippled living by herself.

'Then I'd have come back,' Miss O'Hara had said cheerfully. Since her sisters were married and her brother was a priest she would have been the one to look after her mother anyway.

The O'Hara house was out a bit on the road towards the golf course, and Miss O'Hara cycled everywhere on her big red bicycle with the basket of exercise books in the front. There were always copy books and when it rained she had them covered with a waterproof sheet. She wore a long scarf wound round her in winter and if there was a wind sometimes her long hair stood out behind her in a straight line. David's mother once said she looked like a witch heading for the cliffroad and you'd expect her and the bicycle to take flight over the seas. But his father had refused to let a word of criticism be spoken of her. He said that nobody knew how much she did for that crippled mother of hers, morning noon and night, and wasn't it proof to note that when poor Angela O'Hara went on her two weeks holiday a year somewhere they had to have three people in and out of that house to mind the mother and it was never done satisfactorily even then. His mother didn't like Miss O'Hara, it had something to do with her not admiring things or not being excited enough about his mother going to Dublin for outings. It had never been said, it was just a feeling he had.

The table with his books on it was near the fire and Nellie would bring in a pot of tea and a slice of cake or apple tart.

Miss O'Hara always talked to Nellie more than she talked to his mother, she'd ask about Nellie's old father out in the country and the row with the brothers and had they heard from the sister in Canada. She'd giggle with Nellie about something new that Father O'Dwyer's housekeeper had said. The woman's name was Miss McCormack, but everyone called her Sergeant McCormack because she tried to run not only Father O'Dwyer and the church but the whole of Castlebay too.

Miss O'Hara came in now, her hands cold from clenching the handlebars in the wind, and she held them out to the fire.

'God, Nellie, isn't it a sin having a great fire like this banked up just for David and myself. We could work in the kitchen, you know, beside the range.'

'Oh, that wouldn't do at all!' Nellie was horrified.

'You wouldn't mind, David?' she began . . . and then suddenly changed her mind. 'No, don't take any notice of me, I always want to change the world, that's my problem. Aren't we lucky to have this grand place in here, let's make the most of it. Nellie, tell me what are they building on the side of Dillon's? It looks like an aerodrome.'

'Oh, that's going to be a sun lounge, I hear,' Nellie said, full of importance. 'They're going to have chairs and card tables maybe in the summer, and tea served there too.'

'They'd need to have rugs and hot-water bottles if it turns out anything like last summer. Come on, college boy, get out your geography book, we're going to make you a world expert on trade winds, you're going to make them green and yellow striped with jealousy when you get back to that palace of a school of yours. We'll show them what a real scholar is, the way we breed them in Castlebay.'

Paddy Power was tall and thick-set, with a weather-beaten face. His face was beaten by weather of all kinds, but mainly the sharp wind that came in from the sea as he walked up lanes to people's houses, lanes where his big battered car wouldn't go. He had a shock of hair that grew in all directions as if he had three crowns on his head; it had been brown and then it was speckled but now it was mainly grey. Because of his bulk and his alarming hair he sometimes looked fierce, but that was before people got to know him. He had a great way of talking, a kind of good-natured bantering until he could see what was wrong; his talk was merely to relax the patient until he could see where the piece of grit in the eyes was, or the splinter in the hand, the glass in the sole of the foot or feel for the pain in the base of the stomach without too much tensing and alarm.

He was a burly man who never found clothes to fit him and never cared about them either. Life was far too short, he said, to spend time in a tailor's talking rubbish about lines and cuts and lapels. But for all his bulk and his haphazard attitude to his appearance, he was a healthy man and he was able to go down the path from his own garden to the sea and swim for nearly six months of the year and to get a game of golf a week as well. But Paddy Power was tired today; it had been a very long day and he had driven seventeen miles out to see a young woman who would be dead by Christmas but who talked cheerfully of how she knew she'd be better when the fine weather came. Her five children had played noisily and unconcerned around the feet of the doctor and the pale young husband just sat looking emptily into the fire. He had also had to have an unpleasing chat with one of the Dillon brothers from the hotel and speak seriously about liver damage. No matter how carefully he tried to phrase it, he had ended up with a blank wall and a great deal of resentment. Today it had ended with Dick Dillon telling him to mind his own bloody business, and that Paddy Power was a fine one to talk, half the county could tell you that he was drunk as a lord three years ago at the races, so he was in a poor position to cast stones. There were two bad cases of flu in old people, where it was settling in on chests that were never strong, he could see both of them turning into pneumonia before long. People talked about the *good seaside air*, and the *bracing breezes*. They should be here in a doctor's surgery in winter, Paddy Power thought gloomily, there'd be less of the folksy chat then.

Molly said that David was getting on like a house on fire with his lessons, and that he did two hours on his own each morning.

'She's a fine scholar Angela, isn't it a pity that she never got the recognition for it,' Paddy said, wearily taking off his boots and putting on his slippers.

'Never got any recognition? Isn't she a teacher above in the school with a big salary, hasn't she all her qualifications, that's not bad for Dinny O'Hara's daughter.' Molly sniffed.

'You miss the point, Moll. That's a bright girl and she's stuck here in Castlebay teaching children to be waitresses and to serve their time in shops. And what kind of a life does she have in that house? I mean the Little Sisters wouldn't do as much for their flock as Angela does for her mother.'

'Oh I know, I know.' Molly was anxious to leave it now.

'Still, a man on a white horse may ride into town one day for her yet.' He smiled at the thought.

'I'd say she's a bit past that now,' Molly said.

'She's only twenty-eight years of age, a year older than you were when we got married, that's what she is.'

Molly hated when he spoke about things like that in front of Nellie. Molly hadn't grown up here, she came from a big town and she had been at school in Dublin. She didn't like anyone knowing her business nor indeed her age.

She looked at herself in the mirror, no longer young but not too bad. She had made a friend of the buyer in that shop in Dublin and now there was no problem in getting clothes. Nice wool two-pieces, loose enough so that you could wear a warm vest and maybe even a thin jumper under them. You needed a lot of layers in Castlebay. And Paddy had given her nice brooches over the years so that she always looked smart. No matter who came to the house, Molly Power looked well-dressed and ready to receive them, her hair was always neat and well-groomed (she had a perm every three months in the town) and she always used a little make-up.

She examined her face. She had been afraid that the climate in this place might have made her lined or leathery like a lot of the women, but then they probably didn't use any face cream even.

She smiled at herself, turning her head slightly so that she'd see the nice clip-on earrings she had got recently to match the green brooch on her green and grey wool two-piece. Paddy saw her smiling and came and stood behind her with his hands on her shoulders.

'You're right about yourself, you're gorgeous,' he said.

'I wasn't thinking that,' she said indignantly.

'Well, you should have been,' he said. 'A glamorous thing, not like a mother and wife.'

She thought about being a mother for a moment. She had believed it would be impossible. So many false alarms. The weeks of delight followed by the miscarriages at three months. Three times. Then two babies born dead. And then when she hardly dared to believe it, David. Exactly the child she wanted. Exactly.

Angela thought David was a grand little fellow. He looked like an illustration from those Just William books, with his hair sticking up, his shoelaces undone and his tie crooked. When he worked he sort of came apart.

Wouldn't it be lovely to teach bright children all the time without having to pause for ever for the others to catch up. She looked at him as he worked out a chart of the winds and gave it to her triumphantly.

'Why are you smiling?' he asked suspiciously.

'I don't know. I could be losing my mind. I've noticed myself smiling nowadays whenever any child gets anything right, it's such a shock you see.'

He laughed. 'Are they all hopeless at the school here?'

'No, not all, some are as smart as paint. But what's the point? Where will it get them?'

'Won't it get them their exams?'

'Yes, yes it will.' She stood up a bit like a grown-up who wasn't going to follow the conversation on with him. He was disappointed.

Angela cycled home from Dr Power's house into the wind. Her face was whipped by it and the salt of the sea stung her eyes. Any journey in winter seemed like a voyage to the South Pole, and she wondered for the millionth time would they be better if she moved her mother to a town. Surely this wet wind coming in through every crack in the cottage must be hard on her, surely it couldn't be healthy living in a place that was only right for seals and gulls for three quarters of the year. But then she mustn't fool herself: if they moved to a town it would be for herself, so that she could have some life. Let's not pretend it would be for her mother's poor old misshapen bones. And anyway what more life would there be for her in a town? She'd come in as a schoolmarm with an ailing mother, that's if she were to get a job at all. A schoolmarm who was freewheeling down to thirty. Not something that was going to light many fireworks. Stop dreaming, Angela, head down, foot down, pedal on, only a few more minutes now, the worst bit is over, you're past the blasts of wind from the gap in the cliff. You can see the light in the window.

People called it a cottage because it looked small from the front but in fact there was an upstairs. It was whitewashed and had the formal little garden with its boxed hedge and tiny path up to the door.

She wondered how they had all fitted there when her father was alive, when they were children, they must have been crowded. But then her parents had slept in one room upstairs, the three girls in another and Sean, the only boy, in the third. And downstairs the room which she had now made into a bedroom for her mother had been a kind of sitting room she supposed. There had been no books in it in those days, there had been no shining brass ornaments, no

23

little bunches of flowers or bowls of heather and gorse like she had nowadays. But of course in those times the small house had been home for a drunk, an overworked and weary mother and four youngsters all determined to get away from it as soon as possible. How could there have been time for the luxury of books and flowers?

Her mother was sitting on the commode where Angela had put her before going up to the Powers'. She had dropped her stick and the other chair was too far away so she had nothing to support her and couldn't get up. She was uncomplaining, and apologetic. Angela emptied the chamberpot and put Dettol in it, she got a basin of soapy water and a cloth for her mother and helped her to wash herself and put on powder. Then she slipped the flannel nightdress that had been warming on the fireguard over her mother's small bent head and helped her to the bed in the room adjoining the kitchen. She handed her the rosary beads, her glass of water and put the clock where she could see it. She didn't kiss her mother, they weren't a kissing family. She patted her on the folded hands instead. Then Angela O'Hara went back into the kitchen and took out the essays which would be handed back next day. There was no doubt about the winner, that had been obvious all along, but she wanted to write a little paragraph on the end of all the others. They had done the essay in their free time to enter for the prize that she had provided. She wanted to give them some encouragement, some visible proof that she had read them, even the illiterate ones.

She wet a pot of tea and settled down with the wind howling outside and very shortly the sound of her mother's gentle snores about ten feet away.

Clare O'Brien had arrived early at school. The back of her neck was almost washed away, such a scrubbing had it got. The stain on her school tunic was almost impossible to see now, it had been attacked severely with a nail brush. Her indoor shoes were gleaming, she had even polished the soles, and the yellow ribbons were beautiful. She turned her head a few times to see them reflected in the school window, she looked as smart as any of the others, as good as the farmers' daughters who had plenty of money and got new uniforms when they grew too big for their old ones, instead of all the letting down and letting out and false hems that Clare and Chrissie had to put up with.

She thought the day would never start. It was going to be such an excitement going up there in front of the whole school. And there would be gasps because she was so young. Years and years younger than some of them who had entered.

Chrissie would be furious of course, but that didn't matter, Chrissie was furious about everything, she'd get over it.

Clare walked to the end of the corridor to read the notice board. There was nothing new on it, maybe after this morning there might be a notice about the history prize. There was the timetable, the list of holidays of obligation during the year, the details of the educational tour to Dublin and also the price of it, which made it outside Clare's hopes. There was the letter from Father O'Hara, Miss O'Hara's brother who was a missionary. He was thanking the school for the silver paper and stamp collecting. He said he was very proud that the girls in his own home town had done so much to aid the great work of spreading Our Lord's word to all the poor people who had never heard of Him.

Clare couldn't remember Father O'Hara, but everyone said he was marvellous. He was very tall, taller than Miss O'Hara, and very handsome. Clare's mother had said that it would do your heart good to see him when he came back to say Mass in the church, and he was a wonderful son too, she said. He wrote to his mother from the missions, she often showed his letters to people – well, when she had been able to get out a bit she had.

Father O'Hara made the missions sound great fun altogether. Clare wished he would write a letter every week. She wondered what did Miss O'Hara write to him. Would she tell him about the history prize this week?

There was Miss O'Hara now, coming in the gate on her bicycle. Mother Immaculata had a face like the nib of a pen.

25

'Could I have a word, Miss O'Hara, a little word please. That's if you can spare the time.'

One day, Angela promised herself, she would tell Mother Immaculata that she couldn't spare the time, she was too busy helping the seniors to run the potin still and preparing the third years for the white-slave traffic. But not yet. Not while she still had to work here. She put her bicycle in the shed and swept up the armful of essays wrapped in their sheet against the elements.

'Certainly Mother,' she said with a false smile.

Mother Immaculata didn't speak until they were in her office. She closed the door and sat down at her desk; the only other chair in the room was covered in books so Angela had to stand.

She decided she would fight back. If the nun was going to treat her as a disobedient child over some trivial thing as yet unknown, and let her stand there worrying, Angela was going to draw herself up so high that Mother Immaculata would get a crick in her neck looking up. Angela raised herself unobtrusively on to her toes, and stretched her neck upwards like a giraffe. It worked. Mother Immaculata had to stand up too.

'What is all this about a money prize for an essay competition, Miss O'Hara? Can you explain to me how it came up and when it was discussed with me?'

'Oh, I've given them an essay to do and I'm awarding a prize for the best one.' Angela smiled like a simpleton.

'But when was this discussed?' The thin pointed face quivered at the lack of respect, or anxiety at discovery.

'Sure, there'd be no need to discuss every single thing we did in class Mother, would there? I mean, would you ever get anything done if we came to you over what homework we were going to give them and all?'

'I do *not* mean that. I mean I need an explanation. Since when have we been paying the children to study?'

Angela felt a sudden weariness. It was going to be like this for ever. Any bit of enthusiasm and excitement sat on immediately. Fight for every single thing including the privilege of putting your hand into your own very meagre salary and giving some of it as a heady excitement which had even the dullards reading the history books.

It was like a slow and ponderous dance. A series of steps had to be gone through, a fake bewilderment. Angela would now say that she was terribly sorry, she had thought Mother Immaculata would be delighted, which was lies of course since she knew well that Immaculata would have stopped it had she got wind of it earlier. Then a fake display of helplessness, what should they do now, she had all the essays corrected, look here they were, and the children were expecting the results today. Then the fake supplication, could Mother Immaculata ever be kind enough to present the prize? Angela had it here in an envelope. It was twenty-one shillings, a whole guinea. Oh and there was a subsidiary prize for another child who had done well, a book all wrapped up. And finally the fake gratitude and the even more fake promise that it would *never* happen again.

Mother Immaculata was being gracious now, which was even more sickening than when she was being hostile.

'And who has won this ill-advised competition?' she asked.

'Bernie Conway,' said Angela. 'It was the best, there's no doubt about that. But you know young Clare O'Brien, she did a terrific one altogether, the poor child must have slaved over it. I would like to have given her the guinea but I thought the others would pick on her, she's too young. So that's why I got her a book, could you perhaps say something Mother about her being . . .'

Mother Immaculata would agree to nothing of the sort. Clare O'Brien from the little shop down by the steps, wasn't she only one of the youngest to enter for it? Not at all, it would be highly unsuitable. Imagine putting her in the same league as Bernie Conway from the post office, to think of singling out Chrissie O'Brien's younger sister. Not at all.

'But she's nothing like Chrissie, she's totally different,' wailed Angela. But she had lost. The children were filing into the school hall for their prayers and hymn. Mother Immaculata had put her hand out and taken the envelope containing the guinea and the card saying that Bernadette

Mary Conway had been awarded the Prize for Best History Essay. Mother Immaculata left on her desk the neatly wrapped copy of Palgreave's *Golden Treasury* for Clare O'Brien for Excellence in History Essay Writing.

Angela picked it up and reminded herself that it was childish to believe that you could win everything.

Mother Immaculata made the announcements after prayers. Clare thought the words were never going to come out of the nun's thin mouth.

There were announcements about how the school was going to learn to answer Mass with Father O'Dwyer, not serve it of course, only boys could do that, but to answer it, and there must be great attention paid so that it would be done beautifully. And there was a complaint that those girls in charge of school altars were very lacking in diligence about putting clean water in the vases. What hope was there for a child who couldn't manage to prepare a clean vase for Our Lady? It was a very simple thing surely to do for the Mother of God. Then there was the business about outdoor shoes being worn in the classroom. Finally she came to it. Mother Immaculata's voice changed slightly. Clare couldn't quite understand – it was as if she didn't *want* to give the history prize.

'It has come to my notice, only this morning, that there is some kind of history competition. I am glad of course to see industry in the school. However, that being said, it gives me great pleasure to present the prize on behalf of the school.'

She paused and her eyes went up and down the rows of girls who stood in front of her. Clare smoothed the sides of her tunic nervously. She must remember to walk slowly and not to run, she could easily fall on the steps leading up to the stage where Mother Immaculata, the other nuns and lay teachers stood. She would be very calm and she would thank Miss O'Hara and remember to thank Mother Immaculata as well.

'So I won't keep you in any further suspense . . .' Mother Immaculata managed to draw another few seconds out of it.

28

'The prize is awarded to Bernadette Mary Conway. Congratulations Bernadette. Come up here, child, and receive your prize.'

Clare told herself she must keep smiling. She must not let her face change. Just think about that and nothing else and she'd be all right. She concentrated fiercely on the smile; it sort of pushed her eyes up a bit and if there were any tears in them people wouldn't notice.

She kept the smile on as stupid Bernie Conway put her hand to her mouth over and over, and then put her hand on her chest. Her friends had to nudge her to get her to her feet. As she gasped and said it couldn't be true, Clare clenched her top teeth firmly on top of her lower teeth and smiled on. She saw Miss O'Hara looking round at the school and even looking hard at her. She smiled back hard. Very hard. She would never let Miss O'Hara know how much she hated her. She must be the meanest and most horrible teacher in the world – much meaner than Mother Immaculata – to tell Clare that she had won the prize, to say all those lies about it being the best thing she had read in all her years teaching. Clare kept the smile up until it was time to file out of the hall and into their classrooms. Then she dropped it; it didn't matter now. She felt one of her ribbons falling off; that didn't matter now either.

The girls brought sandwiches to eat in the classroom at lunch, and they had to be very careful about crumbs for fear of mice. Clare had made big doorsteps for herself and Chrissie since her big sister was still in disgrace. But she hadn't the appetite for anything at all. She unwrapped the paper, looked at them and just wrapped them up again. Josie Dillon, who sat beside her, looked at them enviously.

'If you're sure?' she said as Clare passed them over wordlessly.

'I'm sure,' Clare said.

It was raining, so they couldn't go out in the yard. Lunchtimes indoors were awful, the windows were all steamed up and there was the smell of food everywhere. The nuns and teachers prowled from classroom to classroom seeing that the high jinks were not too high; the level of noise fell dramatically as soon as a figure of authority appeared and then rose slowly to a crescendo once more when the figure moved on.

Josie was the youngest of the Dillons, the others were away at a boarding school but it was said that they wouldn't bother sending Josie, she wasn't too bright. A big pasty girl with a discontented face – only when someone suggested food was there any animation at all.

'These are lovely,' she said with a full mouth to Clare. 'You're cracked not to want them yourself.'

Clare smiled a watery smile.

'Are you feeling all right?' Josie showed concern. 'You look a bit green.'

'No, I'm fine,' Clare said. 'I'm fine.' She was saying it to herself rather than to Josie Dillon who was busy opening up the second sandwich and looking into it with pleasure.

Miss O'Hara came into the classroom and the noise receded. She gave a few orders: pick up those crusts at once, open the window to let in some fresh air, no it didn't matter how cold and wet it was, open it. How many times did she have to say put the books away *before you* start to eat. And suddenly, 'Clare, can you come out here to me a minute.'

Clare didn't want to go, she didn't want to talk to her ever again. She hated Miss O'Hara for making such a fool of her, telling her that she'd won the prize and building up her hopes. But Miss O'Hara had said it again. 'Clare. Now, please.'

Unwillingly she went out into the corridor which was full of people going to and from the cloakrooms getting ready for afternoon classes. The bell would ring any moment now.

Miss O'Hara put her books on a window sill right on top of the Sacred Heart altar. There were altars on nearly every window sill and each class was responsible for one of them.

'I got you another prize, because yours was so good. It was really good and if you had been competing with people nearer your own age you'd have won hands down. So anyway I got this for you.' Miss O'Hara handed her a small parcel. She was smiling and eager for Clare to open it. But Clare would not be bought off with a secret prize.

'Thank you very much, Miss O'Hara,' she said and made no attempt to untie the string.

'Well, aren't you going to look at it?'

'I'll open it later,' she said. It was as near to being rude as she dared to go, and in case it had been just that bit too much she added, 'Thank you very much.'

'Stop sulking, Clare, and open it.' Miss O'Hara's voice was firm.

'I'm not sulking.'

'Of course you are, and it's a horrible habit. Stop it this minute and open up the present I bought you so generously out of my own money.' It was an order. It also made Clare feel mean. Whatever it was she would be very polite.

It was a book of poetry, a book with a soft leather cover that had fancy flowers painted on it with gold-leaf paint. It was called *The Golden Treasury Verse*. It was beautiful.

Some of the sparkle had come back into the small face with the big eyes. 'Open the book now and see what I wrote.' Angela was still very teacherish.

Clare read the inscription aloud.

'That's the first book for your library. One day when you have a big library of books you'll remember this one, and you'll take it out and show it to someone, and you'll say it was your first book, and you won it when you were ten.'

'Will I have a library?' Clare asked excitedly.

'You will if you want to. You can have anything if you want to.'

'Is that true?' Clare felt Miss O'Hara was being a bit jokey, her voice had a tinny ring to it.

'No, not really. I wanted to give you this in front of the whole school, I wanted Immaculata to give it to you, but she wouldn't. Make you too uppity or something. No, there's a lot of things I want and don't get, but that's not the point, the point is you must go out and try for it, if you don't try you can't get anything.'

'It's beautiful.' Clare stroked the book.

31

'It's a grand collection, much nicer than your poetry book in class.'

Clare felt very grown up: Miss O'Hara saying 'Immaculata' without 'Mother' before it. Miss O'Hara saying their poetry textbook wasn't great! 'I'd have bought a book anyway if I'd won the guinea,' she said forgivingly.

'I know you would, and that eejit of a Bernie Conway will probably buy a handbag or a whole lot of hairbands. What happened to those nice yellow ribbons you were wearing this morning?'

'I took them off, and put them in my schoolbag. They seemed wrong.'

'Yes, well maybe they'll seem right later on, you know.'

'Oh they will, Miss O'Hara. Thank you for the beautiful book. Thank you, *really*.'

Miss O'Hara seemed to understand. Then she said suddenly, 'You *could* get anywhere you wanted, Clare, you know, if you didn't give up and say it's all hopeless. You don't have to turn out like the rest of them.'

'I'd love to . . . well, to get on you know,' Clare admitted. It was out, this thing that had been inside for so long and never said in case it would be laughed at. 'But it would be very hard, wouldn't it?'

'Of course it would, but that's what makes it worth doing, if it were easy then every divil and dirt could do it. It's because it's hard it's special.'

'Like being a saint,' Clare said, eyes shining.

'Yes, but that's a different road to go down. Let's see if you can get you an education first. Be a mature saint not a child saint, will you?'

The bell rang, deafening them for a moment.

'I'd prefer not to be a child saint all right, they're usually martyred for their faith, aren't they?'

'Almost invariably,' Miss O'Hara said, nearly sweeping the statue of the Sacred Heart with her as she gathered her books for class.

Chrissie and her two desperate friends Peggy and Kath had planned a visit to Miss O'Flaherty's to apologize. Gerry

Doyle had apparently told Chrissie last night that this was the best thing to do by far. After all, she knew it was them, they'd all been caught and punished by their parents, why not go in and say sorry, then Miss O'Flaherty would have to forgive them or else everyone would say she was a mean old bag who held a grudge. Chrissie hadn't gone along with this in the beginning but Gerry had been very persuasive. What could they lose, he argued? They didn't need to *mean* they were sorry, they only needed to say it, and then it would take the heat off them all so that they could get on with the plans for the party in the cave, otherwise they would all be under house arrest. Do it soon, and put your heart and soul into it, had been Gerry's advice. Grown-ups loved what they thought were reformed characters. Lay it on good and thick.

Clare was surprised to see the threesome stop outside Miss O'Flaherty's shop. She was sure they'd have scurried past but they were marching in bold as brass. She pretended to be looking at the flyblown window display that had never changed as long as she knew it, but she wanted to hear what was coming from inside the shop.

The bits that she heard were astonishing. Chrissie was saying something about not being able to sleep last night on account of it all, Peg was hanging her head and saying she thought it was a joke at the time but the more she thought of it, it wasn't a bit funny to frighten anyone. And Kath said that she'd be happy to do any messages for Miss O'Flaherty to make up for it.

Miss O'Flaherty was a big confused woman with hair like a bird's nest. She was flabbergasted by the apology and had no idea how to cope.

'So anyway, there it is,' Chrissie had said, trying to finish it up. 'We're all as sorry as can be.'

'And of course we're well punished at home,' added Kath. 'But that's no help to you, Miss O'Flaherty.'

'And maybe if our mothers come in you might say that we . . .'

Miss O'Flaherty had a jar of biscuits out. There would be no more said about it. They were harmless skitters of girls when all was said and done, and they had the good grace to come and admit their wrongdoing. They were totally forgiven. She would tell all their mothers. They skipped out of the shop free souls again. Clare was disgusted with them. Miss O'Flaherty was horrible and she deserved to be terrified with bits of seaweed. Why were they saying sorry now at this late stage? It was a mystery.

She didn't get much enlightenment from Chrissie, who was annoyed to see her.

'I'm sorry, Peg and Kath, but my boring sister seems to be following us around.'

'I'm not following you, I'm coming home from school,' Clare said. 'I have to come home this way, it's too windy to walk on the cliff road.'

'Huh,' said Kath.

'Listening,' said Peg.

'You're so *lucky* that you don't have any sisters younger than you,' Chrissie said. 'It's like having a knife stuck into you to have a younger sister.'

. 'I don't see why. We don't think Ben and Jimmy are like knives,' Clare argued.

'They're normal,' Chrissie said. 'Not following you round with whinges and whines day in day out.' The other two nodded sympathetically.

Clare dawdled and looked into the drapery. She knew everything off by heart in that window too. The green cardigan on the bust had been there for ever, and the boxes of hankies slightly faded from the summer sun were still on show. Clare waited there until the others had rounded the corner. Then she walked slowly on down the street towards the big gap in the cliffs where the steps went down to the beach, back home to O'Brien's shop which everyone said should be a little gold mine since it was perched on the road going down to the sea. It was the last shop you saw before you got to the beach so people bought their oranges and sweets there, it was the first shop you met on the way back with your tongue hanging out for an ice cream or a fizzy drink. It was the nearest place if you sent a child back up the cliff for reinforcements on a sunny day. Tom O'Brien should be making a small fortune there people said, nodding their heads. Clare wondered why people thought that. The summer was the same length for the O'Briens as for everyone else. Eleven weeks. And the winter was even longer and colder because they were so exposed to the wind and weren't as sheltered as people all along Church Street.

Molly Power said that it was lonely for David having no friends of his own and perhaps they should let him ask a friend to stay. The doctor thought that there were plenty of young lads in the town, boys he had played with before he went off to boarding school. But Molly said it wasn't the same at all, and shouldn't they let him ring his friend James Nolan in Dublin and invite him for a few days. His family could put him on the train and they could meet him. David was delighted, it would be great to have Nolan to stay, Nolan had sounded very pleased on the phone. He said it would be good to get away from home, he hadn't realized how mad his relations were. They must have got worse since he'd gone to boarding school and he hadn't noticed. David told him it would be very quiet after the bright lights of Dublin. Nolan said the lights of Dublin weren't as bright as that, and his mother wouldn't let him go to the pictures in case he got fleas. He couldn't wait to get to the seaside.

'And will my class increase by a hundred per cent?' Angela O'Hara asked him when she heard that Nolan was coming to stay.

David hadn't thought of that. He didn't know. It was something he hadn't given any thought to.

'Never mind.' Angela had been brisk. 'I'll sort it out with your parents. But we had a plan for twenty days' work to cover the time you were at home, if Mr Nolan arrives that will cut six days out of it. What are you going to do? Abandon it or try to do the work anyway?'

He was awkward and she rescued him.

'I think you'd rather not have Nolan seeing you taught lessons by a woman. It's a bit like a governess, a country schoolteacher coming to the house.'

'Oh no, heavens, nothing like that.' David's open face was distressed. 'Honestly, if you knew how much I've learned

35

since working with you, I'd be afraid to let on in case they'd never send me back to the school again, they'd put me into the convent here.'

He was a mixture of charm and awkwardness. It was very appealing. The image of his bluff kind father and yet with a bit of polish that must have come from his mother thrown in.

'Why don't I set out a bit of work for you and Mr Nolan to do each day. Say an hour and a half or two hours. I'll correct it, without coming in on top of you at all, and that way there's no embarrassment.'

The relief flooded his face.

'Is Mr Nolan as bad at Latin as you are?' she asked.

'A bit better, I think. He's going to need it too you see, he's going to do Law.'

'Is his father a barrister?'

'A solicitor,' David said.

'That makes it nice and easy,' she said with a bitter little laugh.

David was puzzled, but she changed the subject. It wasn't David Power's fault that the system was the way it was. A system that made it natural that David Power should be a doctor like *his* father, and James Nolan of Dublin a solicitor like his father, but made it very hard for Clare O'Brien to be anything at all. Angela squared her shoulders: hard, but not impossible. Hadn't Clare the best example in the land sitting teaching her? Angela, youngest daughter of Dinny O'Hara, the drunk, the ne'er-do-well, the man looking for every handout in Castlebay. And she had got the Call to Training, and higher marks in the college than any other student, and they had scrimped to send her brother to the missions, and she had nieces and nephews in comfortable homes in England. Nobody in the town could pity them when they walked behind her father's coffin five years ago. If Angela could do it with a drunken father and a crippled mother, then Clare could do it. If she cared enough, and today it looked as if she cared almost too much.

'So, College Boy,' she said to David, 'let's get on with the hedge school before the gentry come down from Dublin and catch us with our love for books!'

'You're great, Miss O'Hara,' David said admiringly. 'Wasn't it a pity you weren't a man, you could have been a priest and taught us properly.'

Molly Power was very anxious that things should be done right for David's young friend, and there were endless instructions to Nellie about breakfast on trays and getting out the best silverware until David begged that they just come downstairs as usual. Then they'd have to do their homework for Miss O'Hara before they felt free, but what a long day stretched ahead. Nolan loved the beach being so near, it was almost like having your own private swimming place, he said enviously, to be able to climb over a stile at the end of the garden and have a path going down to the sand and the caves. A path with *Danger* written all over it. Nolan tried out the Echo Cave and the other smaller caves. He wore wellington boots and slid and scrambled over the rock pools, he picked up unusual shells, he walked out to the end of the cliff road to see if the Puffing Hole was blowing. He walked the course on the golf links and planned that he and David should take lessons next summer. He couldn't believe they were allowed to go to the cinema at night. In Dublin he had only been to matinees and that was before his mother had heard of all the fleas.

Nolan was very popular in Castlebay. He was so handsome for one thing, small, with pointed features and hair that didn't stick out in angles like David's but fell in a sort of wave across the front of his forehead. He had very sharp eyes which seemed to see everything, and he wore his clothes with style, turning up his collars and striding round with his hands buried deep in his pockets. He used to joke about being short and said that he suffered from a small-man complex like Napoleon and Hitler.

He was polite to Mrs Power and insatiable for medical details from Dr Power. He praised Nellie's cooking and he said that he thought Castlebay was the most beautiful place in Ireland. In no time he was an honoured guest. Even

Angela O'Hara liked him. He wrote out his preparation dutifully in small neat writing, and Angela had immediately sent him a note on the first batch of corrected work: 'Kindly make your writing much less fancy and much more clear. I have no idea whether or not you have written the correct ending on the cases of the nouns. I will not be mocked.'

'She must be quite a character, why don't we meet her?' he asked David.

David wasn't really sure, but he knew that it somehow reflected discredit on him. 'She's shy,' he lied, and felt worse.

Next day they saw a figure like a dervish flying past on a red bicycle. The machine did a dangerous turn and an envelope of papers was thrown from the basket to David.

'Here you are, College Boy, save me facing the winds over your way.'

David caught them neatly.

'This is the man who doesn't know the neuter plural from a hole in the ground,' she shouted cheerfully. 'You've got to make the adjectives plural too, my friend. No use just throwing them there and hoping they'll decline themselves.'

'Can't you come and teach us up at the house?' Nolan called out flirtatiously.

'Ah, too much to do, but aren't we doing fine by correspondence course?' Her hair stretched out behind her in the wind, blowing like someone in an open car in a film. She wore a grey coat and a grey and white scarf.

'She's gorgeous,' breathed Nolan.

'Miss O'Hara?' David said in disbelief. 'She's as old as the hills.'

They were still laughing over what age Miss O'Hara would be when Nolan was twenty-five, the age he thought he might take a bride, when they met Gerry Doyle. He had wellingtons and a fisherman's jersey and somehow he seemed much more suitable for the place than they were. Gerry was about the only one who would ever ask him what his boarding school was like, and what they had to eat and what kind of cars fellows' parents had.

'I was thinking they might burn that school of yours down if it has the plague,' Gerry said agreeably. He thought it was all more serious than they were being told, plague and pestilence and scarlet fever, otherwise why would they close down a big important school? He suggested too that they should look out for germs when they got back, in stagnant pools or in the curtains.

David made a mental note to talk to his father about it when he got home.

'Do you want to come to a midnight feast, isn't that the kind of thing you have in your place all the time, before the plague and all?'

'I was at one and we were caught,' David said sadly.

'I was at that and another, the other wasn't caught,' Nolan said as a matter of record.

'Yes well, tomorrow night in the Seal Cave starting at eleven-thirty. If you could bring a few sausages and your own bottle of orange or even beer.'

'Can we?' Nolan's eyes were shining.

'Why not? This is Castlebay, this isn't a backwater like Dublin,' David said bravely, and Gerry Doyle told them that there'd be girls and tins of beans and sausages . . .

Gerry Doyle had told Chrissie not to say a word to Tommy and Ned about the party in the cave. It wasn't that he had anything against them but they were the kind who could accidentally let something slip. He wasn't even telling his own sister, he said, because she was the same. Chrissie was pleased that Fiona wasn't coming and so were Peggy and Kath. Fiona looked a bit too attractive for their taste; she was fourteen of course, which would make her look a lot better, just automatically, than the rest of them but still they all felt a bit second best when Fiona was there. And of course Chrissie wouldn't think for a moment that Tommy and Ned should be invited, they were far too uncertain – they'd wonder aloud for days and in the end they'd all be found out and the picnic in the cave would be stopped. Gerry had said that there'd be about a dozen of them or so, no point in alerting the whole town. They were to meet there at eleven-thirty, and everyone was to try to make their own way in twos and threes at most. So as not to be noticed.

Clare stirred in her bed when she saw Chrissie's legs swing

to the floor on the other side of the room. To her surprise, Chrissie was fully dressed. She was moving very quietly and feeling round for her shoes. The light of the Sacred Heart lamp fell on her as she was picking up what looked like a great lump of sausages and rashers from the shop! Chrissie was actually wrapping these stealthily in white paper and darting nervous glances at Clare's bed.

In a flash Clare understood she was running away. In a way this was great. She would have a bedroom to herself, she wouldn't be tortured by Chrissie morning noon and night any more. There would be less rows at home. But in another way it wasn't great. Mammy and Daddy were going to be very upset and the Guards would be here in the morning and Father O'Dwyer and people would walk along the cliffs when the tide came in looking for a body as they always did whenever anything happened in Castlebay. And there would be prayers for her and Mammy would cry and cry and wonder where she was and how she was faring. No, Clare sighed reluctantly, better not to let her run away, it was going to be more trouble than it was worth.

Chrissie looked at her suspiciously when she heard the sigh.

'Are you running away?' Clare asked casually.

'Oh God in heaven, what a sorrow it is to have such a stupid sister. I'm going to the toilet, you thick turnip you.' But there was fear in her voice.

'Why are you dressed up in your clothes and taking sausages and bacon if you're just going to the toilet?' Clare asked mildly.

Chrissie sat down on the bed, defeated. 'Oh, there's an awful lot of things I'd like to do to you, you're a spy, you were born a spy, it was written on you plainly, you'll never do anything else except follow people round and make their lives a misery. You hate me and so you destroy everything I do.'

'I don't hate you, not really hate,' Clare said. 'If I hated you properly wouldn't I let you run away.'

Chrissie was silent.

'But Mammy would be desperately upset and Dad too, I

mean they're going to be crying and everything. It's not that I'm spying, I just thought I'd ask where you were going in case they think you're dead or something.'

'I'm not running away. I'm going out for a walk,' Chrissie said.

Clare sat up in her small iron bed. 'A *walk?*' she said.

'Shush. Yes, a walk, and we're going to have a bit of a meal on it.'

Clare raised herself up and looked out the window behind the Sacred Heart statue and the little red lamp. It was pitch dark outside. Not a thing stirred in Castlebay. 'Are Peggy and Kath going too?'

'Shush. Yes. And Clare . . .'

'Is it a picnic?'

'Yes, but you're not coming, you're not going to spoil every single thing I'm doing, you're not going to ruin it for me.'

'Oh, that's all right if it's only a picnic.' Clare had snuggled down under the blankets again. 'I just didn't want the fuss if you ran away. That's all.'

There was a small red travelling clock on the kitchen mantelpiece. David took it to bed with him. Nolan said that he'd wake all right in the spare room but David didn't want to take any chances. The clock was under David's pillow and its alarm was muted but it woke him from a deep sleep. For a while he couldn't think what was happening, and then he remembered. He had the bottle of cider and the sausages packed neatly in his school gym and games bag. Nolan had bought four bottles of stout and two packets of marsh-mallow biscuits which he said were great if you toasted them over a fire. Gerry Doyle had said there would be a bonfire in the back of the Seal Cave and that they knew it would work because they had tried it out already. There was a part of the cave which was perfect for it.

The only problem was Bones, the dog. David's father said that Bones would go up and lick the paws of any intruder or assassin but he'd bark the house down if you went in or out yourself. He was more of a liability than a watchdog. David and Nolan had decided to bring Bones with them to the midnight feast. It was either that or drug him and though Nolan preferred the notion of knocking him out for a few hours David had been too strictly brought up, in a house where even aspirins were locked away, to think that this was remotely possible.

He crept into the spare room and Nolan was indeed dead asleep but woke eagerly.

'I was only thinking with my eyes shut,' he said.

'Sure, and snoring with them shut too,' David said.

They shushed each other and crept down the stairs. Bones jumped up in delight and David closed his hand around the dog's jaw while stroking his ear at the same time. This usually reduced Bones to a state of foolish happiness and by the time Nolan had eased open the door they were safe. Bones trotted down the garden to the back wall ahead of them, finding nothing unusual in the hour. David and Nolan with their torches in their pockets stumbled. They couldn't shine a light until they were over the stile, it would surely be the one moment that David's mother was going to the bathroom and would look out the window and then waken the neighbourhood.

But down the path which said Danger they used their torches, and slipped and slid more than they walked. It was dry now but it had been raining earlier and the twisty path had a lot of mud.

'This is fantastic,' Nolan said, and David swelled with pride. When they got back to school Nolan would tell everyone of the terrific time he had in Power's place and the others would look at him with respect. He had always been slow to tell people about Castlebay, it sounded like such a backwater compared to the great places they all came from, but looking at it through Nolan's eyes he realized there was much more to it than he had thought.

Down on the beach Bones ran round like a mad thing, up to the edge of the sea and back again, barking excitedly, but he could bark for ever down here, the sound of the waves crashing and the wind whistling would carry it far away. Dr and Mrs Power wouldn't even hear it in their dreams.

The Seal Cave was dark and mysterious-looking. David was quite glad he wasn't on his own. There was a big fire at the back; Gerry was right, there *was* a part of it that was dry and not dripping with slime. They had begun the cooking and rashers dangled dangerously on long sticks and a couple of toasting forks. There were at least a dozen people around the fire. There were giggling girls nudging each other and breaking into loud laughter. That was Peg and Kath, he knew them to see; and Chrissie O'Brien from the shop. David looked around for Clare but she was too young probably. Chrissie couldn't be more different to Clare, he thought. Screeching with laughter and knocking the food off other people's forks. Clare was solemn and much gentler somehow.

David had never had stout before, but the others were drinking it. It almost made him throw up, it didn't taste like a drink should taste. Manfully he finished one bottle and began another. Nolan seemed to like it and he didn't want to look a sissy. Gerry Doyle seemed to notice though.

'You could have some champagne cider if you liked, it's a different taste, nice sort of drink,' he suggested.

David sipped some: now this was more like it. Sweet and fizzy, very nice indeed.

Gerry, small and eager, was hunched up over the fire. He looked very knowledgeable.

David held his glass up to the light. 'It's good stuff this,' he said appreciatively.

Later when he was getting nowhere after the groping had begun, Gerry marked his card again. No use trying anything with that one, she just laughed all the time. There was the one who would be more co-operative. A manly wink which David returned unsteadily. Gerry Doyle was a good friend to steer you in the right direction.

There were mystery ailments all over Castlebay next day, but against all the odds nobody broke ranks and the midnight feast was never discovered. Chrissie O'Brien had come back home covered in mud with cuts all down her legs where she had fallen coming up the steps from the strand,

and she was sick twice into a chamberpot in the bedroom. Clare said grumpily she hoped that these midnight feasts weren't going to be going on all the time. Chrissie was too busy plotting the morrow and how she would explain her ripped and mud-covered coat, to answer Clare. In the end she decided she would go out early before anyone saw the state she was in and then she could fall again and be considered too sick to go to school. It worked too, nobody noticed that half the mud had dried and the scabs on her legs had started to heal. Chrissie's friend Peggy managed to get to school and stick the day but Kath had been sick in the classroom and had to be sent home.

Up in Power's house there seemed to be no explanation for the burn that had appeared as if by magic on James Nolan's mouth. In fact it had come from his eating a sausage directly from the long bit of skewer it was cooked on, but it was announced as being something that had come upon him unexpectedly during the night. Molly Power worried endlessly what his parents would say when he got back and fussed interminably about it when she wasn't fussing about David who was as white as a sheet and had to go to the bathroom every few minutes. The third peculiar thing in the house was Bones. He had apparently let himself out in the night and was found asleep in the garage with a cooked sausage in his paws. Dr Power told her that in the long run it was often better not to think too hard and try too earnestly to solve all problems. Sometimes it was better for the brain to let things pass.

Gerry Doyle's father told him at breakfast that there had been terrible caterwauling in the middle of the night and did he know anything about it? It sounded like a whole lot of women or girls crying on the doorstep. Gerry looked at him across the table and said that he thought he had heard that mad dog of the doctor's wailing and baying around the town during the night – could that have been it? It could, his father thought doubtfully and sniffed around him. 'This place smells like Craig's Bar,' he said to his wife and stamped off to what they all called his office, the front room beside the main bedroom. Gerry's mother got annoyed and started to slam out the breakfast dishes in a temper.

44

'Brush your teeth for heaven's sake, Gerry, and eat an orange or something before you go to school.' Fiona was not only kind she was practical.

Gerry looked at her gratefully. 'I had a feeling there might be a bit of a trace,' he grinned.

'Trace?' said Fiona. 'You nearly knocked us all out. Was it great fun?'

'It was in a way.'

'I wish you'd have let me . . .'

'No.' He was very firm.

'But I'm older even than some of them who were there.'

'That's not the point. You're not that type. No one must ever say that anyone was messing around with *you*. You are all I've got, I've to look after you.'

He was serious. Fiona looked taken aback.

'You've got all of us . . . like we all have . . .' she said uncertainly.

'What have we got? We've got Dad, who lives in his own world. When did Dad say anything that wasn't about the business?'

'He just mentioned Craig's Bar, didn't he?' Fiona laughed.

'Yes.' Absent-mindedly he took a peppermint out of his pocket and unwrapped it.

'What's wrong?' she asked, her big dark eyes troubled.

'I don't know. It's just he's so dull and unadventurous. How are we ever going to get on if we stay as timid as he is? And Mam . . . Well, honestly.'

'She's a bit better, I think,' Fiona said softly. They had not talked about this before.

'She's not. You say that because she went out to the garden and hung out the clothes. You think that's some kind of success. She hasn't been out of the house for six months. Six months. Tell me if that's normal or not normal.'

'I know. But what can we do? They don't want to tell Dr Power.'

'It's all his fault, he thinks that if we tell Dr Power there's going to be some kind of trouble.'

At that moment, Mr Doyle reappeared, small and dark

like his son, with the same quick smile and almost elfin face.
'I'm only wondering does anyone in this house intend to go
to school or have we all graduated without my knowing
about it?'

'I'm just off. Dad, I may be going past David Power's
house, will I ask his father to come and have a word
with . . .?'

'If anyone needs a doctor they'll go and see Dr Power and
if they're not able to go, Dr Power will be brought to them,'
said his father sternly. That was that. Gerry went to brush
his teeth as had been suggested, and met his mother creeping
along by the wall, alarmed by the word 'doctor'.

'Don't worry, Mary, go back into the kitchen, there's no
need for a doctor,' his father said.

He called at the surgery that evening.

'Well, Gerry?'

'I don't know, Dr Power.'

'It can't be too serious an ailment if you've forgotten it
already.' The old doctor was cheerful.

'It wasn't an ailment at all.'

'Good, good. Was it something wrong with someone
else?' The man's eyes were sharp.

Gerry seemed to hesitate. 'No, I suppose people have to
look after their own illnesses, don't they?'

'It depends. If you saw a wounded man lying on the road
you wouldn't say he'd better look after his own illness.'

'No, it's not like that.'

'Would you like to tell me what it is like?'

Gerry made up his mind. 'No, no. Not now. I came to
know if David and James Nolan would like to go out this
evening? For a bit of a laugh like?'

Dr Power was thoughtful. 'I think there's been enough
laughs for the moment. I think it's time the laughing died
down for those two and they got a bit of work done.'

Gerry looked him in the eye. 'Does that mean they can't
come out? Is that what you're saying?'

'You're as bright as the next man, Gerry, you know what
I'm saying, and not saying.'

46

'Right. Tell them I called and was sorry they weren't allowed out.'

'No, I won't, because that's not the message. Tell them yourself if you want to.'

Gerry Doyle's great skill was knowing when not to push it any further. 'You're a hard man, Dr Power,' he said with a grin, and he was off.

Paddy Power wondered whether he had been going to ask about his anxiety-ridden father or his withdrawn, possibly phobic mother. Maybe the boy hadn't noticed anything wrong with either of them. He was a funny lad.

A parcel arrived for Angela, a small flat box. It was a beautiful headscarf from the parents of James Nolan. 'Thank you so very much for all the help with tuition, your pupils in Castlebay must be very lucky to have such a gifted teacher.' It was a square with a very rich-looking pattern on it, the kind of thing a much classier woman would wear. Angela was delighted with it. She showed it and the letter to her mother but it was a bad day and the old woman's joints were aching all over.

'Why shouldn't they be grateful to you, why shouldn't they send you something? It's money they should have sent. Doesn't the postman get paid for delivering letters?'

Angela sighed. She told David about it that evening. 'Wasn't it very thoughtful of them?' she said.

'They have great polite ways up in Dublin,' David said wistfully. 'We'd never have thought of giving you a thing like that, and we should have.'

'Don't be silly, College Boy. I was only telling you so that you'd know your friend appreciated the lessons and all that.'

'He thought you were very good-looking,' David said suddenly.

'I thought he wasn't bad himself, but a bit small for me. How old is he, about fifteen?'

'Yes, just.'

'Oh well, that's no difference at all, tell him I'll see him when he's about twenty-five, I'll be coming into my prime about then.'

'I think that would suit him fine,' David laughed.

It was shortly before the school re-opened that David met Gerry Doyle again.

'Have you had any good drinking nights since the cave?' Gerry asked.

'I think I'm going to be a Pioneer. I was never so sick. I was sick eleven times the next day,' David said truthfully.

'Well at least you held on to it until you got home,' Gerry said. 'Which was more than some people managed. Still, it was a bit of a laugh.'

'Great altogether. Nolan said he'd never had such a night.'

'He was telling me you've got a record player of your own, a radiogram in your own bedroom, is that right?'

'Not a radiogram with doors on it, but a record player yes, you plug it in.'

'How much would they be?' Gerry was envious.

'I'm afraid I don't know, it was a present, but I could ask.'

'I'd love to see it,' Gerry Doyle said.

David's hesitation was only for a second. His mother had never *said* he wasn't to have Gerry Doyle into the house but he knew she wouldn't approve. 'Come on, I'll show you,' he said.

Any other lad in Castlebay might have held back but not Gerry Doyle. He swung along the cliff road companionably with David as if he had been a lifetime calling on the doctor's house socially.

The summer houses looked dead, as they passed, like ghost houses and it was hard to imagine them full of families with children racing in and out carrying buckets and spades, and people putting deckchairs up in the front gardens.

'Wouldn't you need to be cracked to rent one of those for the summer?' Gerry nodded his head at the higgledy-piggledy line of homes.

'I don't know. Suppose you didn't live beside the sea?' David was being more tolerant.

'But if you had the money to rent one of those for a couple of months what would you spend it on that for, why wouldn't you go abroad to Spain or to far places like Greece even?' Gerry was beyond believing that anyone could pay good money for a place in his own Castlebay.

'But if you were married with children you wouldn't be able to take all of them abroad,' David argued reasonably.

'Ah well, I wouldn't be married, so I suppose that's the difference.'

'Not now, but later.'

'Not ever. Do you want to?'

'I thought I would,' David said.

'You're off your head, David Power,' said Gerry Doyle agreeably.

Mrs Power was in the hall arranging some winter branches in a vase.

'Hallo,' she said when the hall door opened. 'Oh hallo, Gerry, do you want to see the doctor?' She looked slightly quizzical. Her head had inclined towards the surgery entrance. Patients didn't come in the front door, they went in by the porch on the side.

'No thanks, Mrs Power, I'm coming to look at David's record player,' he said confidently.

'I beg your pardon?' She was polite, but frosty.

'Oh, I'm going to show Gerry the record player . . . how much was it, by the way?' David didn't feel as brave as he sounded.

'It was a present, David dear,' his mother said with a smile that wasn't in her eyes. 'We don't ask how much a present cost.'

'No, but maybe you could tell Gerry then, he was wondering if he might buy one.'

'I think it's a little beyond Gerry,' said David's mother in that tone he really hated. But Gerry didn't seem to notice in the slightest.

'You might well be right,' he said cheerfully. 'It wouldn't be until the end of the summer anyway, I work for pocket money but there's nothing really for me to do that's useful until the trippers come. Still it'll be nice to see it anyway.' He smiled straight into the disapproving face of David's mother and with his arm on the banisters and his foot on the first step he called to David. 'Is it up here?'

David followed him without looking back to see the grim expression that he knew had settled on his mother's face.

At lunch Mrs Power waited until Nellie had left the room. 'Paddy, could you ask David not to bring Gerry Doyle back here to the house.'

Dr Power looked up mildly from his newspaper. 'Well, he's sitting beside you, Molly, can't you ask him yourself?' he said.

'You know what I mean.'

'Is this some kind of row?' The doctor looked from his wife to his son.

'Not on my part,' David said.

'See what I mean,' said Molly Power.

'Well, it seems you are being off-hand with your mother. Don't be like that.' Dr Power went back into the paper.

'*Paddy*. Please. Explain to David that Gerry Doyle's perfectly all right but he is not a guest in this house.'

Wearily he put down the paper. 'What's it about?' he said, looking from one to another.

There was no reply.

'Well, what did young Doyle do that caused the upset?' Again he looked from his wife's flushed face to his son's mutinous one.

'Nothing,' David shrugged. 'He came upstairs. I showed him my record player. He admired it. He went home.'

'Molly?'

'That's not the point, as you know very well. You're not an infant David, you know well what I'm talking about.'

David looked blank.

'Your mother is saying that she goes to a lot of trouble to keep this house nice and she doesn't want people tramping all over it. That's a reasonable request, isn't it?'

David paused, deciding whether or not to buy this explanation. Then he saw its flaws. 'Oh sure, sorry Mummy, I didn't know that was what it was about. I thought you had something against Gerry Doyle himself.

You know, like Nolan's mother went through that bit of thinking everyone had fleas. No, that's fine, of course I won't ask people back without asking you first.'

Molly smiled uneasily. She wasn't at all sure that she had won.

'And I'll be going down to his house later on today, he said he'd show me the darkroom and let me help to develop some of the pictures his father took at a wedding.'

He smiled brightly from one parent to the other and helped himself to a glass of orange squash.

Gerry Doyle's sister was gorgeous-looking. She wore an overall, which was like an artist's smock, and she looked like an illustration in a book. She seemed a bit shy and answered yes and no when David asked her about anything. But she was very polite and helpful. She offered to go and make cocoa and said she'd run over to O'Brien's for a quarter of a pound of broken biscuits as well.

'Why didn't you ask her to the Seal Cave?' David wanted to know.

'Oh, you couldn't ask your *sister* to a thing like that. It's all right for Chrissie and Kath and Peggy and those, they're the kind of girls you'd expect to have at a thing like that, but not Fiona.'

David felt he had overstepped some limit he didn't know about. He felt awkward. He felt too that it was hard on the girls who had been there. They had all had great fun and played spin the bottle; and the boys had given them cider and beer and encouraged them like mad. Then the girls had got a bit silly and one or two of them were crying and Kath had been sick and they had fallen and everything. But it was all part of the night. It was a bit cruel somehow to think that Fiona was a different type of girl, one you wouldn't bring to a party like that, but it was true. When she came back with the tray of cocoa and biscuits David knew that he would not like Fiona to have been to a party like that either.

He would have liked to ask her to write to him at school. Nolan had a girl who wrote him long letters. But he thought it was too complicated to set it all up. Firstly if Fiona had said yes he would have had to explain the whole system where the letters were read by the priests and so the girl who was writing had to pretend to be another boy. Nolan's friend who was called Alice used to sign her name Anthony. She had to remember not to talk about hockey matches but say rugby instead, in fact the letter was in so heavy a code or disguise none of them could really work out what it meant. Still it was nice for Nolan to be able to get the letter and tell everyone how good-looking Alice was. It would be nice to do the same with Fiona. But if Gerry wouldn't let her come to a party in a cave down the road he would almost certainly be very much against her writing letters in code to a boy in a boarding school. That would be fast, and Fiona Doyle was not going to be thought of as fast. David noticed that he kept thinking of them as orphans even though they lived with their mother and father. That was odd.

'Your parents don't take much part in things, do they?' he said enviously.

'They work too hard,' Gerry said. 'It was always like that. It's a dog's life, and Mam hates the work but what else is there?'

'What would she prefer to be doing?'

'Arranging flowers on a hall table in a house like yours,' Gerry laughed. 'But isn't that what every woman would want?'

The roof didn't fall in and the skies didn't flash with lightning when David got back home that evening. He sensed that his parents had had a little chat. His mother was sewing the Cash's name tapes on some new socks and pyjamas for him. She seemed to have forgotten the row at lunchtime totally.

'I suppose in a way it will be hard to settle into all that studying again,' she said.

David was determined to be equally pleasant. 'Yes, but I'm very glad that I had Miss O'Hara, very glad. Nolan said we were dead lucky down here to be able to get someone like that, up in Dublin teachers are sharks, he said, they ask for a fortune for grinds and they smell of drink.'

David's father laughed from the other side of the fire. 'Your friend James is full of nonsense. You can't make generalizations about any job no more than you can about mine or his father's. Dear dear.'

'You know the way Nolan goes on,' David said.

'Of course I do, he's a very bright young fellow, we liked him, your mother and I did. Ask him down any time, or any of your other friends, the house is big and there's plenty of room. And it's nice to hear a bit of noise around the place.'

That's a different tune to the one they were playing at lunch, David thought to himself. Then I was invading the privacy of the house. He heard himself saying that he'd love to ask Nolan again, and he was very grateful to be allowed to invite people home. Nolan's mother was still fussing apparently and when she wasn't worrying about fleas she was worrying about ceilings falling down. Nolan said she was having a tonic for her nerves but it didn't seem to be doing much good.

On the last evening before he went back he said he'd like to go and say a proper thank you to Miss O'Hara, and maybe give her a small present. David's mother said that Angela O'Hara wouldn't like that at all, she had been paid adequately, but Dr Power said no, David was right, why not give her a book of some kind from the shelf, she always admired the books when she came to the house.

'You don't need to go up to Dinny O'Hara's cottage,' Molly Power said.

'Dinny O'Hara has been in the churchyard for five years, he's unlikely to come out and corrupt the boy now,' said Paddy Power, and David saw his mother's face get that tight-lipped look again.

Nellie helped him to wrap up a book about Irish place names. They took the torn paper cover off it and it was lovely underneath. Nellie looked at the small print in admiration.

'Imagine Angela O'Hara being able to read all this and understand it. Ah well, that's what comes of keeping to your books.' She had been at school up at the convent with

Angela herself, and had been there the day the news came of Angela's scholarship to the big town. In those days the nuns had been so proud that one of their girls had won the scholarship they used to make the uniform themselves with their own hands. They had kitted out the young Angela for her secondary school because they knew that anything Dinny O'Hara would get into his hand went straight across a bar counter and he wouldn't do much to help his little girl get on.

'She deserved to do well,' Nellie said unexpectedly, as she was making a nice neat corner on the parcel and tying the string tightly. 'She never crowed about all her successes and her high marks and all. Nobody could say that it all went to her head.'

David didn't think that Miss O'Hara had all that much to crow about. To be teaching in that awful convent, to be here in Castlebay with her old mother – when she must have wanted to get far away. Why else did she go in for all those scholarships? He didn't think she had the huge success that Nellie seemed to think. But of course compared to Nellie it must be fine, she didn't have to clear out grates and ranges and scrub floors and make beds and cook meals and wash up and wash clothes and go out in the cold and see they weren't bashed down by the wind. Being a teacher must seem like a nice cushy job to Nellie.

He turned left outside the gate and went along the road towards the golf course. It was longer than he remembered, no wonder Miss O Hara always flew round the place on her bicycle. There was a light downstairs in the O'Hara cottage: he hoped that her old mother wouldn't answer the door bent over the two sticks.

But the door was opened by Clare O'Brien. Clare was thin and alert, big brown eyes and fair hair tied in bunches. She always looked as if she was about to ask a question. He remembered meeting her in the Echo Cave and she had said that it would be like heaven on earth to have lessons from Miss O'Hara without the rest of the class. Maybe that's what she was doing now.

Clare seemed pleased to see him. 'She's putting her

mother to bed, she's got awful pains altogether today, she can neither sit nor stand. Miss O'Hara said she'd be back in a few minutes. Will you come in and sit down?'

David was a bit put out that she was there; he had wanted to make a flowery speech to Miss O'Hara without an audience. But he could hardly order the O'Brien girl to go home or say that his conversation was private. He looked around the kitchen.

'Isn't it like Aladdin's Cave?' whispered Clare in awe.

It was a typical kitchen for a cottage in this area. The fire had been replaced by a small range. That must have come from Angela O'Hara's salary – it never came when Dinny O'Hara was alive nor from the widow's pension that the arthritic old woman got every week. Perhaps the brother and sisters abroad sent money, David wouldn't know. Miss O'Hara was very private, she never told you all about herself and her family like everyone else in Castlebay did all the time, that's why you were interested to know more. David looked up at the walls. Everywhere there were shelves. Each alcove had shelves from ceiling to floor, and there were ornaments and books and biscuit boxes and more books and sewing baskets and statues. Clare was right. Almost like a toyshop on a Christmas card. There was no inch of wall without a shelf, and no inch of shelf without an object. Most of the objects were books.

'She knows where every single thing is, would you credit that?' Clare's big brown eyes looked larger than ever in the semi dark of the room. There was a table with writing paper and a bottle of Quink ink and blotting paper. Miss O'Hara must have been writing letters with Clare when her mother took a turn.

'Are you getting lessons?' he asked. There was a touch of envy in his voice. He would have preferred to learn in this funny enclosed place where everything had a story and every item was known in its little place. It was a much better place to study than his mother's sitting room with the copies of *Tatler and Sketch*, and *Social and Personal* laid out beside *The Housewife* which came every month by post from England. When the copies were a couple of months old they

55

went to the surgery, and of course there were all the encylopedias and big leather-bound books. But they weren't read and touched and loved like things were here.

'Oh no, I wish I could, no I'd like that more than anything. I'd be a genius if I had Miss O'Hara to teach me on her own.' She spoke with no intention of making him laugh. She was utterly serious.

He was sorry for her. It must be desperate not to have enough money for education. You always felt that came automatically.

'Maybe you could do things for her, you know, do the messages or cook or something in exchange.'

'I thought of that,' Clare said solemnly. 'But I think it's a bit unfair, she'd have to be looking round for things for me to do. It would be like asking for charity.'

'I see.' He did see.

'But I came up tonight because Miss O'Hara *is* going to help me, I'm to write to the convent in the town, a kind of letter that would make them think well of me, and inquiring about their scholarships in two years' time.' Her eyes were shining over the very thought of it.

'Miss O'Hara got a scholarship there herself, years and years ago. She says you have to be dead cunning, and look on it as a war.'

Angela O'Hara came into the room then. 'Don't give away all our secrets, Clare, maybe College Boy here might be disguising himself and trying to get into the convent ahead of you.'

Nolan would have made a witty remark. David couldn't think of one, he just laughed. 'I'm in your way, you're writing letters,' he said awkwardly.

'Don't worry about that, David, Clare's writing her own letter actually, and I am meant to be writing one to my brother. I find it so hard to know what will interest him about here. You know: got up, went to school, did not strangle Immaculata ... every day it becomes a bit repetitive.'

'What does he write? I suppose his days are a bit samey too,' David said.

Angela took out an airmail envelope with the stamp neatly removed for the school collection. 'I was just thinking that very thing . . . My mother keeps all Sean's letters, every single one of them – look at the boxes of them – and he does seem to be saying the same thing over and over. But it's nice to hear.'

'When you get older I expect there's not much to write about,' Clare said helpfully.

'Or more when you don't really share the same kind of life,' David said. 'That's why I never had a penfriend in India or anything, once you'd described your life and he'd described his that would be it.'

'It is a bit like that,' Angela agreed. She picked up a thin piece of airmail paper and read to them:

Dear Mother and dear Angela,

Thank you so much for your letter which arrived here yesterday. We are in the middle of a rainy season which makes things very difficult but still it is thanks to all the great and good support that we get from home that God's work can be done.

I wish you could see the little Japanese children, they are really beautiful. I suppose I didn't have all that much to do with children before I came out here, on the missions. Perhaps little Irish children are even more beautiful . . .

Angela broke off and said it was easy known that he never had to pass one day of his lifetime teaching little Irish children in a convent or he would think otherwise.

'It's a bit like the letter he wrote to the school, isn't it?' Clare said.

'It's a bit like every letter he writes,' Angela said, putting it back in the envelope. 'There's nothing for him to say, I suppose, that we'd understand. I do ask him things myself sometimes, like do they ordain many Japanese priests out there, and what happened to all the Chinese they had converted before they left China, did they go back to their old religion or what. But he never answers those kind of things.'

She was silent in thought for a while. David coughed.

'I came to say goodbye and thank you,' he said. 'And to give you this book to tell you how grateful I am.'

Angela sat down and reached for her cigarettes without saying anything. When she spoke it was with a softer voice than either Clare or David had ever heard her use. 'That's very good of you,' she said and bent her head over the twine, fiddling with the knots.

'It's only old twine, you can cut it if you like,' David said helpfully and Clare found a knife. Miss O'Hara sawed through the string, and they all bent over the book. Time passed easily as they read why places they knew were called what they were called, and they were all enraged that Castlebay wasn't in it and said that the man who wrote the book hadn't travelled at all if he couldn't include a fine place like this. From the other room there were sounds of moaning but Miss O'Hara said not to take any notice, it was her mother trying to get into a comfortable position to settle for the night, it wasn't really sharp pain. They had a cup of tea and a bit of soda bread and eventually Miss O'Hara shooed them out into the night lest people think they had been kidnapped.

Angela told herself not to be so sentimental over David's present. It was very thoughtful of the boy certainly, but he came from a nice peaceful home where there was time to be thoughtful and there was ease and comfort. And his father was one of the most generous men that ever walked. It was in the boy's nature to be bright and generous. But it was so different to what she could expect from the children she taught up in the convent. Half of them would never do any kind of an exam, almost none of them would ever open a book again after they left her, except a novel or a magazine.

Not Clare of course. She was the one that would keep you going. Imagine teaching a class full of Clare O'Briens or of David Powers for that matter. She sighed. It was a pity as David had said that she hadn't been born a man. She could have become a priest and taught bright boys in a school where the principal would not go into shock if she asked for a globe.

She wondered did Sean ever regret his choice in teaching the children of Chinese and Japanese workers in pidgin English. Would he have liked the days spent in an ivy-covered college like the one that David and young Nolan went to? Would Sean have liked the evenings in study and chapel and walking reading a breviary in cloisters or discussing philosophy in a dining hall? It was a question that couldn't really make sense, since her brother Sean had never shown interest in any other life except the missions. He had followed the road that got him there without pausing to think or to wonder did people miss him. She missed him from time to time, his letters were no way of knowing him, and recently they had become very static.

You couldn't even hint at that to her mother. Every letter was kept in a box with the date it was received written laboriously on the envelope. As if someone was going to check them some time. The stamps were neatly cut off to add to the school stamp collection, they were never re-read but Mrs O'Hara knew almost by heart the names of the villages and the settlements and the places up country and down country. She knew them better than she knew the countryside around Castlebay, for it had been a long time since she could walk and see it. Angela wondered sometimes what her mother would think about all day if she hadn't a fine son who was a missionary priest to fill her mind.

Back at school Nolan told everyone that Power was a dark horse. They should see the great place he lived in, a big house on a cliff with its own private way down to the sea. They had a maid and a labrador and every single person in the place knew them by name and saluted them. David felt it was going a bit far to call Bones a labrador, but he agreed that the rest was mainly true. He also found himself the centre of attention because of having taken Nolan to a party where real sex games were played. This was the cause of a lot of questioning and David wished he knew how much Nolan had elaborated on the innocent kissing games they had played by the firelight before the drink had taken over and everyone had been too dizzy and confused to play any games at all. But it was good to be a hero, and he laughed knowingly about it all.

He was pleased too when Father Kelly said that he was an exemplary pupil and had kept up meticulously with the suggested course of study which had been handed out to all pupils on the day the school had closed because of the scarlet fever. The essays had been written, the poems had been learned, history questions had been written out and illustrated with neat maps and family trees, the maths and geography were completed, and the Irish and Latin exercises done in full.

'You got private tuition? Well, he was a good man whoever he was,' Father Kelly said in one of his rare moments of approval.

'It was a she actually, Father,' David said apologetically.

Father Kelly's brow darkened: he had been too swift with his praise. 'Ah, some of them are competent enough I suppose,' he said, struggling to be fair, but losing interest.

David told Nolan that Gerry Doyle had a smashing-looking sister, really beautiful, but that he wouldn't take her to the cave that night.

Nolan was very positive about this, as he was about everything. 'Of course he couldn't bring his *sister,*' he said as if it were obvious to a blind fool, 'I mean I wouldn't have let *my* sister go. We couldn't have taken Caroline to a party like *that,* where people would be ... well you couldn't take Caroline there. Gerry Doyle was quite right. Is she going to write to you?'

'I didn't ask her.'

'Right, Power, you've got the technique, don't be too easy to get, don't be a pushover. Leave them wondering, that's what I always do.'

'Will Alice be writing again this term?'

'No, I think I've grown out of Alice,' said Nolan in a voice which revealed that Alice had grown out of him.

Nolan said his mother had got a bit better about things and that she had agreed to go away next summer for a holiday by the sea. Nolan's whole family had been wanting to do this for ages but his mother had always said the seaside was full of rats and beetles and sea snakes. St Patrick had only got rid of the land snakes according to Nolan's mother, but he had no power over the huge snakes calling themselves eels which came in on beaches all over the country. But now the tablets she was taking had made her forget, and they were going to inquire about renting one of those cliffhouses in Castlebay. Because Nolan had come home with such glowing reports they were going to try there first. David was delighted: the summer would be full of adventure if Nolan and his family came to Castlebay.

Angela said that Clare must write the letter herself, it was no use putting grown-up words into a ten-year-old head. But she would monitor it for spelling, and style. She found Clare a writing pad that had no lines on it, but with a heavily-lined sheet you put under the page you were writing on. Clare should ask the convent whether there was any particular course of study she should concentrate on, since she was very anxious to prepare herself as diligently as possible for the open scholarship in 1952. Clare tried to remember the words diligent, concentrate, but Angela said no, she must use her own words, and she must sound like a real person, someone they would remember when the time came. She said to tell the nuns that her parents were business people. Clare wondered was that true; but Angela said, years ago she had told them her father was a substantial farmer who had fallen on hard times because of the Troubles, and since that was way back in 1932 it sounded reasonable. It would have done her no good to say she was the daughter of the town drunk and she was burning to get herself on in the world.

'Do you think there's any hope I might get it? You see I don't want to get myself all excited like I did . . . well . . .'

'Over the history essay.' Miss O'Hara nodded. 'No, I think you have a chance, a good chance if you work like the hammers of hell. Oh and don't tell anyone, it's easier somehow if you don't.'

'But David Power knows.'

That didn't matter, Miss O'Hara thought, he'd have it

long forgotten. But Clare shouldn't mention it at school, or at home, it only got people into a state. Clare had thought there was too much going on at home without letting them get into another state over a scholarship in the distant future.

Tommy and Ned had been for interviews and they couldn't wait to go to England. They had heard that there was massive reconstruction being done over there since the war, the place was full of bombed sites only waiting to be built up again, and roads from one place to another planned for, and housing for all those who lost their places during the raids.

The man who had come to Dillon's Hotel for two hours had taken their names and addresses. He had asked them very little but said they should report to him when they got there; they should wait till the fine weather until they came over. There'd be no trouble at all finding digs; the roads around Kilburn and Cricklewood were filled with Irish households only delighted to have lads from home in to stay. They'd be like mothers to them, they wouldn't need to go near English strangers at all. The man said he was a businessman who could get a good deal for his own countrymen; he didn't like to see Irish lads being made fools of, he'd see them right when they came over.

Clare's father wondered could the man be a chancer. Why would he be doing all this for love? Why wasn't he an agency like any other agency that took fees? That way made sense, a person could understand that, but this way was hard to fathom. A man with an open shirt coming to Dillon's Hotel and giving them all a piece of paper with his name on it and saying he could be found any Friday night in one of two pubs in Kilburn – it sounded a bit suspicious.

But Tommy and Ned would have none of it. What had they to lose? If, after one week, he turned out not to be getting them their full wages, they could leave him and go on to one of these agencies that Da was talking about. They weren't bound to him. He had said he wanted nothing in writing, no complications of any sort. They should be delighted to have his name, and have him as a friendly contact over there instead of making such a fuss about everything.

Tommy had left school. He had no exams, no certificates and, after all his years in the Brothers, he could barely read and write. Clare thought wistfully of David Power that night up in Miss O'Hara's kitchen and the book he had given to her as a present. Tommy would have thrown it aside. He couldn't even read what was written on a packet in the shop, if someone asked him. He didn't read the paper and he never opened a book of any sort now that he had been released from the classroom. He was meant to be helping his father get the shop to rights before he went off to London to seek his fortune. A lot of the time he spent just hanging around.

Clare's father was rearranging the shop, and that was hard to do while people were still being served. It meant that a lot of it was done in the evening when they were meant to be closed. Of course a place like O'Brien's could never close properly: if Mrs Conway came for a pound of sugar, or Miss O'Flaherty decided that she wanted some biscuits with her late night tea, there was no refusing them.

But there was less of a flow after six o'clock, less of the sound of the ping when the door opened and a figure stood letting in the cold sea winds until the door swung closed.

Last summer it had been so crowded trying to sell ice-cream in the middle of everything else, that this year he was going to move the ice-cream cabinet down to one side of the little shop. Chocolate and sweets would be high up over it, and fruit beside it, so the beach people could be served all in one area; while the people who had rented houses on the cliffroad could ponder and deliberate and finally settle for cooked ham and tomatoes as they always did, on a less cluttered side of the shop. It was all fine in theory but it was hard to do and still keep track of where everything was. Each evening they scrubbed shelves and tacked on new oilcloth. The floor was a constant disappointment to them; the lino needed to be replaced but of course there wouldn't be funds for that, so instead new bits were nailed down near the door where the wear and tear was most obvious. Boxes

63

that only contained a few things were emptied out and stored neatly in the storeroom. In the summer, visitors were mad for boxes and lots of the suppliers didn't leave any behind. It was best to have a pile of them ready.

It was worthy work but it ate into homework time. Miss O'Hara had drawn everyone in the class a map of Ireland, a blank map. They were to trace it or copy it and reproduce it every fourth page of their history exercise book. Then, when they learned of the battles and the treaties and the marches and the plantations, they could fill them in on their own maps and they would know what happened where. Clare was lost in the Battle of Kinsale, drawing little Spanish ships and Red Hugh's army on its way down from the north when she heard the voice calling. Perhaps if she pretended she didn't hear . . . This was the wrong thing to do. The door was thrown open and her mother stood quivering with annoyance.

'Aren't you a fine lady thrown on the bed when you're needed?'

'I'm not thrown, I'm filling in this map, look.'

'I've looked at enough of that childish nonsense, you're a grown girl, get downstairs and help your father at once. We've been calling and calling and not a word out of you.'

'It's my homework.'

'Don't be ridiculous, nobody has homework drawing ships and little men, stop that act and come down *at once*. Your father wants a hand to clean those top shelves before we put things up there.'

'But how will we reach them – what's the point of putting things up there?'

'Are you going to debate this from up here or come down like you're told!'

'Where are you off to, Chrissie? We'll be taking down all those old notices stuck to the windows this evening . . .'

'Oh, I can't stay, Mam, I'm going up to Peggy . . . she's going to teach me how to make a frock.'

'A frock?'

'Yes, she's got a pattern, she says it's easy to cut around it. Soon we'll be able to make all our own clothes.'

'Well, all right, but don't be late home.'

'No, I won't. Bye Mam.'

'Clare, what are you doing?'

'The trade winds. We've got to know all about where they come from and why they blew the fleets of . . .'

'Right, get a bowl of hot soapy water, will you, and come with me. These windows are a disgrace, you can't see through them in or out.'

'Clare, child, I know you work hard at your books but couldn't you give your mother a hand with the washing? She's got very thin on us altogether.'

'The washing, Dad?'

'Washing the clothes. I asked her to sit down and have a cup of tea and she said she couldn't, there was a pile of washing to do. You'll have to do washing when you have a home of your own, why don't you take a turn now and learn how to do it properly? There's a good girl.'

'What about Chrissie, Dad, could she do it tonight, and I'll do it the next time, I've this legend to learn. There's all kinds of desperate names in it.'

'Chrissie's gone to do her homework with Kath.'

'Uh,' Clare said.

'You could go on saying the names to yourself as you did the washing,' her father said.

'No, the book would get wet. Do I *have* to, Dad?'

'You don't *have* to. I thought you'd be glad to help your mother.'

'Tommy or Ned?' She asked without much hope.

'Well, if that's the kind of thing you're going to be saying . . .' he turned away in disgust. To suggest that *boys* would do the washing! Clare was being very difficult altogether.

'Oh, all *right!*' Clare slammed closed the story of Jason and the Golden Fleece. She only knew Jason, his father, his two wicked step-uncles and the name of the ship. There was a huge cast still to master, so it would mean waking up early . . . again.

'Clare, come here till I teach you to darn.'

'No, Mammy, I don't want to learn to darn.'

'You that wants to learn everything? Look, it's very simple. Do you see this hole, what we have to do is to make a criss cross . . .'

'No, Mam, I'd like not to know how to do it. Ever.'

'Why, child? When you have a home of your own you'll want to know.'

'But if I know now, I'll be darning Tommy's socks, and Ned's, and Dad's, and Jim's, and Ben's, and maybe even Chrissie's.'

Agnes put her arm round the thin little figure, and smiled. 'Aren't you the funny little thing.'

'No, Mammy, I'm the sensible little thing. I'll never learn to darn, never.'

Agnes was annoyed to see her affection rejected. 'Have it your own way, and you can go and do the washing up if you're not going to take advantage of the lessons I was going to give you.'

'But . . .'

'Chrissie won't be in, their class have a special extra class today.'

'That's right,' Clare said glumly. 'Of course they do.'

'Have you a cold, Clare?'

'No, it's just a cough, Mam. Dust or something in my throat, I think.'

'Have a drink of water then.'

'Right.'

'Clare, don't spend all day in the kitchen, come back and help me with these boxes, and put a scarf or something round your mouth if you're breathing in all the dust.'

'Mam, when we've finished this lot, can I go and do . . .'

'Do your homework, do your homework. Why is it that you're the only one in this family who has to make the excuse of doing your homework? Look at the rest of them.'

'I know. Look at them, Mam.'

'What's that supposed to mean?'

'Nothing.'

*

Often Clare had to do her homework in bed, there was literally no other place and no other time. This made Chrissie very cross. She grumbled loudly if Clare turned on the torch.

'You're spoiling my sleep and ruining your own eyes. You'll be blind soon and we'll have to take you round by the hand and you'll have a white stick,' Chrissie said with satisfaction.

'Shut up, Chrissie, I'm learning something. I can't get it into my head if you keep distracting me.'

Chrissie was surprised at the strength of the reply. 'I'll tell on you, if you don't stop that mumbling and learning and having a light on, I'll tell. *That* will put a stop to it.'

There was no reply. With her hands in her ears and eyes closed Clare was repeating under her breath the words, '*Do Ghealadh mo chroi nuair chinn Loch Greinne*,' over and over.

'You're as thick as the wall,' said Chrissie. 'You mean you don't even know one line after all that saying of it?'

'I don't know what *Ghealadh* means. It's hard to learn when you don't know what something means.'

'Ah will you come on out of that, you don't know what *any* of it means. How would people know what Irish poetry meant? It's just words.'

'It means something happened to my heart when I saw Loch Greinne, but I don't know what happened. *Ghealadh*, what would that mean?'

'It might mean Stop. My heart stopped dead when I saw Loch Greinne.' Chrissie laughed at her own wit.

'Didn't you learn it when you were in our class?'

Chrissie shrugged. 'We might have, I forget, I forget all of it. What's the point?'

Clare had gone back to her book.

'I mean it, I'll tell, and you'll be in right trouble then. I'll say you kept me awake with your caterwauling of poetry pretending you understand it. Wait and see. You'll suffer for it.'

'No I won't,' Clare said. 'I won't suffer from it at all, *you* are the one who'll suffer. It will be wondered why you do no

67

homework, why you don't know anything. It might even be wondered what you and Kath and Peggy get up to. You're not going to say anything, and you know it so will you shut up and let me get this learned so that I can go to sleep.'

Angela waited in the surgery. There was only one other patient, old Mrs Dillon from the hotel. Angela would have thought that the doctor would have visited her privately, but Mrs Dillon whispered that she had come to see him secretly. She had pretended to her family that she was going to say the thirty days prayer in the church, but in fact she had come to explain that her daughter-in-law was poisoning her. Angela sighed. Poor Dr Power. He probably got as much of this as Father O'Dwyer did in the confessional. Angela settled down with an old copy of *Tatler and Sketch* and began to read about the happenings up in Dublin. She was in for a long wait. But in a few moments, Dr Power was ushering old Mrs Dillon out the door, and the woman was smiling ear to ear.

'You'll have time for the thirty days prayer after all, and say a few Hail Marys for me,' he called out after her.

'Sure you don't need them, Doctor, aren't you a walking saint,' called Mrs Dillon.

'She's only saying what's true.' Angela stood up and walked across the corridor with him.

'No. I'm a walking liar, that's all.'

'What did you tell her?'

'I told her I was in there during the week inspecting the place for hygiene and I have instruments that could detect poison a mile off. But there wasn't a trace of it in Dillon's Hotel. I said that the cold weather often made people think the taste of food had changed, that it was a common belief, then I gave her a bottle of rose-hip syrup and she's delighted with herself.'

Angela laughed: he looked like a bold boy who'd been found out telling a fib.

'And who's poisoning *you*, Angela, Mother Immaculata up at the convent, maybe?'

'Not a bad guess, I think she'd like to a lot of the time. No, it's not poison. It's sleep.'

'Too much of it or too little of it?'

'Hardly any of it.'

'Since when?'

'Three weeks, now.'

'Do you know what's causing it? A worry, a problem?'

'Yes, I do.'

'And is there anything that can be done about it?'

She shook her head wordlessly.

He waited, but nothing came. He reached for a prescription pad, shaking his head. 'I won't have you lying awake at night, of course you can have something. But Angela, child, it's no use just knocking yourself out with these.'

'I know. Thank you, Doctor.'

'And I'm not always such a blabbermouth, like I was there about old Mrs Dillon. If it would help to talk about it at all, I *could* keep it to myself. In fact I usually do.'

'You don't have to tell me that, Dr Power. Don't I remember always how good you were about my father.' But she was resolute. She thanked him and said she would go straight to the chemist now before they closed. She smiled a tired smile at him and he noticed she did indeed have the dark circles of sleeplessness under her eyes. As far as he knew it wasn't a man, he'd have heard in a small place like this. It was even more unlikely to be a casual sexual encounter resulting in a pregnancy – and anyway, Angela O'Hara wouldn't lie awake sleepless over something like that. She had been a Trojan in all that business of the child up in the convent who was pregnant: she had been so practical and down-to-earth when everyone else had been flying about in the air. It was Angela who thought of explaining to the girl how the infant would be born, and it was Angela who suggested that the girl's uncle should be shipped off to England with a warning delivered from enough tough people to make him believe that his life would not be safe if he were ever to return to Castlebay. That had been about four years ago; surely Angela herself couldn't have brought such a disaster on herself? He sighed and went in to the sitting room. Molly was reading by the fire.

'Nothing changes, nothing gets much better,' he sighed.

She looked up surprised. Usually he was an optimistic man, seeing hope where there was any kind of life. 'Is anybody dying?' she asked.

'No, nothing like that. Wasn't it a pity I wasn't a ship's doctor.'

'Paddy, don't be ridiculous, you can't dance well enough to be a ship's doctor. That's all they do. They don't have anything to do with sickness or curing people.'

She looked nice, he thought, when she was being enthusiastic and cheering him up, she looked young herself. It was when her face was discontented that she developed the pouting, double-chinned look of her mother – a woman who had been born disagreeable and lived to make life disagreeable for everyone round her until last year when she got a coronary right in the middle of complaining that she hadn't got enough presents for her seventieth birthday.

'I'm very ignorant all right,' he said and went over to the drinks cupboard. His hand hovered for a moment over the sherry but settled round the bottle of Irish. What could be so bad that Angela O'Hara couldn't tell him?

Angela got the sleeping tablets in the chemist and didn't correct Mr Murphy there who thought the pills were for her mother.

'It's a terrible curse, that arthritis, and you know there's no cure for it. Years ago people didn't know what it was; now they know what it is but they can't cure it. Not a great advance, when you come to think of it. These will give her a good night's sleep, anyway,' he said.

'Oh yes,' Angela said.

'You're not looking all that well yourself, Angela, you want to get a bit of rest too you know. Up in that school all day with the voices of those children, I don't know how you stick it. When we come up to see Anna and Nan in the concert we're nearly deaf from the shrieking of them all round the school, and then you have the poor mother . . .'

'I'm as strong as a horse, Mr Murphy,' said Angela and she dragged herself out of the chemist and into the post office. She had her foot on the doorstep when she realized she couldn't take Mrs Conway this evening – the bright artificial voice, the inquiries about how well Bernie was doing, the mention once more of the history prize. Angela would never get an answer to the question she wanted to ask, and today she wasn't strong enough to take Mrs Conway head on. Some days she'd be able to deal with ten Mrs Conways before breakfast. But that was all before she had got the letter.

The letter had arrived three weeks ago, with all the beautiful stamps which she usually cut off and put in the envelope on the mantelpiece at once. They saved stamps for the missions, foreign ones in one section and Irish ones in another. Once a year they got a letter at the school thanking them for their great Missionary Effort. Angela would always pin this up on the wall, knowing that somehow it annoyed Immaculata but there was no way she could fault it. She hadn't noticed that this letter was different to the others, that it had been addressed to her alone and not to her mother. She hadn't seen the word *Confidential* all over it. She could easily have opened it as she sat beside her mother.

The letter began: 'Angela, I beg you read this alone. I was going to send it to the school but I thought that would cause more fuss. You'll think of some reason why I put confidential on it. You'll think of something, Angela. Please.'

And it went on to tell her how Sean had left the religious house three years ago; how he was married to a Japanese girl; and how Father Sean had one child of fourteen months and another on the way.

Sean O'Hara had told the Brothers from an early age that he was going to be a missionary priest. They were pleased with this: it was far preferable to the other ambitions in the school, which seemed to be to drive the Dublin train or to own a sweetshop. Occasionally the Brothers tried to divert Sean to their own order; but firmly he said that what he wanted was not the job of teaching schoolboys who were already Catholics in Castlebay, he wanted to go out and meet savages and convert them to Christianity.

He was never a holy kind of boy, and none of his schoolmates thought that there was anything remotely pious in his vocation. They were slightly envious in fact to think that Sean would go off to all these exotic places. It was never firmly decided whether it would be Africa, or India or China. The Brother who taught geography was quite grateful to young Sean, as the boy was always sending off to Missionary Orders asking for details of their work; and in return for magazines and pamphlets Sean organized the silver-paper collection for them too.

He had even managed to get a missionary priest to come and give a talk at their school when he was around thirteen. The priest told him to slave hard at his books and maybe he would be taken into a seminary; but for everything in this life it was essential to be good at the books.

Sean was three years older than Angela but he found her a willing ally. She borrowed books for him from the convent; she shared the task of going round to look for their father each evening and finding a neighbour willing to help carry him home. It was she who insisted that a corner of their kitchen be made into a sort of study for them, and had the oil lamp fixed firmly to a shelf so that it couldn't be taken away from them. Their two sisters, Geraldine and Maire, were already planning to leave the nest. Geraldine had been in touch with a hospital in Wales where she could train as a nurse, and Maire had a friend who worked in a very nice store in London which was so smart that it wasn't like being a shop girl at all. Fifteen and sixteen, and their futures were certain. Within months they were gone. Holidays at home very rarely, letters from time to time, pictures of grandchildren never seen, never known, growing up with English accents and a promise to come home some day.

Geraldine and Maire had come home for their father's funeral. Grown-up, distant, wearing-black coats and hats, startled that everyone else wore raincoats and headscarves. They had borrowed the black outfits specially. They had looked around with restless eyes at the wet cold churchyard, and at the entire population of Castlebay standing with bent heads against the wind. It was so unfamiliar to them after thirteen years in another country. They had looked pityingly at the small house that had been their home for over half their lives and shaken their heads sadly. Angela had been enraged. *They* didn't know how hard she had worked during her father's last illness to try to make the place look respectable, so that her mother would have some dignity at the end. So that she could give the neighbours tea and cake and whiskey without feeling ashamed of their home.

But of course the best consolation at the funeral had been Father Sean. He had been due back later in the spring but when Angela wrote to him and to the Superior of the Order – a measured letter explaining that her father would not be alive in spring, the liver damage was irreversible – the Order had acted swiftly and humanely. Of course young Father O'Hara could be spared from the mission fields a little earlier.

And home he came, stepping from the bus to a buzz of excitement; children ran ahead up to O'Hara's cottage to give the news that he had arrived. The long skirts of his habits he raised slightly to avoid the mud of Castlebay, the way they were used to avoiding the swamps of the Far East. Father O'Hara, home to give his father Extreme Unction and to say his Funeral Mass.

Father Sean had a word for everyone in Castlebay. His eyes didn't cloud with pity for the people, he didn't look sadly at his old home, his bent mother, nor did he close his ears from the life his father had lived. 'He was an unhappy man in this world, let us pray he finds that happiness he was always seeking in the next.' It was generous and forgiving and loving, people said. He had been away for most of his father's spectacular unhappiness, away in the seminary in the novitiate and eventually in the mission fields. But still, the principle was the same, and if he was able to forgive his father for all that neglect and trouble, people thought it was big-hearted of him in the extreme.

Angela's mother's bones ached less when Father Sean was around, and on the very last morning, before he went away

73

again for five years, he said a little Mass at a side altar in the church just for the two of them. They didn't even have an altar boy; Angela answered the responses in Latin from her missal. Geraldine and Maire had gone back to their families in England with promises to return regularly.

When the Mass was over, Mrs O'Hara pressed eighty pounds into her son's hands for the missions; she had been saving it and hiding it for years waiting for his visit.

He had gone that day. The tears of goodbye were in the house, and the brave faces were at the bus stop opposite Conway's post office; there was a waving of handkerchiefs, and the pride of the widow that everyone in the town should see how her fine tall son had turned out.

And the letters never failed: thanks for the cuttings from the local paper, or for the news that their stamp collection had been the biggest in the county; sympathy to the Dillons when old Mr Dillon died, a holy picture to be given to the family with a few words of blessing written by Father O'Hara himself; less and less about what he did himself and more and more in response to their own tittle-tattle in the fortnightly letter which Angela now wrote for her mother since the arthritis had reached the old woman's hands.

Not long ago, Angela had written on her own behalf a little request: 'Sean, you're so good to be interested in all our petty goings-on here, but tell us more about you. In the beginning you used to tell us about the House and the various fathers who lived there, and the schools you all started. And I remember the day a bishop came to confirm everyone and there was a monsoon and they all ran off into their huts and no one got confirmed that year. It's *interesting* to us to know what it's like for you every day, and what you do all the time. If you were a priest here with Father O'Dwyer we'd know, but it's so different out there we find it hard to visualize . . .'

Why had she written that? If she had said nothing maybe she would never have had the letter that burned a hole through her handbag; the letter that told of the end of the vocation for father Sean but would spell the end of any kind of life at all for his mother.

74

Sean had written that he couldn't bear the deception any more, he said that Shuya and he found the letters from home unbearable now; they referred to a life long past. And when money arrived for Masses, it was spent on rent and food. Sean taught English in Tokyo. There had never been a religious house of his order there at all; the address on letters from Castlebay was in fact the house of Shuya's brother. Sean collected any mail from him.

The family spoke English, and were puzzled to know why he was still addressed as 'Father' on the envelope, and why their house was described as a religious foundation.

The other fellows had been terrific about it all, even his Superior. They had tried to change his mind at first and said that, even though Shuya was pregnant, surely Sean could come back to the House, and a provision be made for the child. They didn't understand that he loved her and wanted to have a family with her, and that long before he had met her, the conversion of the Far East had lost all sense for him. He could only see that they were fine with their own beliefs and he didn't think the Lord wanted them changed at all.

Eventually, when everything got more settled, he was going to send his plea to Rome to be laicized and released from his priestly vows. It happened much more than people thought. Then he would be free to remarry Shuya in a Catholic church, and their children could be baptized. Shuya said she had no objection to the children being Catholics.

There was a finality about it that was chilling. The letter left no hope that Shuya was a dalliance, a shameful thing which you often heard whispered about when priests went abroad – something like that or two bottles of the local liquor a day. This woman was in his mind his wife. His fellow priests *knew* about her, they had been kind and supportive. His Superior knew. And Sean found the letters from home 'unbearable'. He couldn't 'bear' to read them now because they referred to a life that no longer existed. *To hell with him*, she thought in fury. He can bloody bear to read them for as long as we send them. I shall never tell that woman about the Japanese Shuya, I shall *never* tell her about the half-Jap grandson, called Denis after his grandfather. How could poor Mammy take it in and cope with it, if even Angela who was young and meant to be modern and intelligent couldn't take it in herself? And then there were other moods: poor, poor Sean, how desperate, with only one life to lead, and finding it empty. Led on and seduced by this Japanese woman with no religion and no morals. To her, a priest was the same as anyone else; she would have no idea what a sin it was, and what a terrible decision Sean had to make. At other times still she had moments of calm: it's not so bad, we'll say nothing, Mammy doesn't read my letters, I'll write him ordinary letters referring to his new life, and ask him to write the old-style letters referring to his old life. That way nobody will be hurt.

But in the night, when she had been asleep for about an hour and would wake with that start which she knew meant no more sleep for the rest of the dark hours, Angela knew that she was fooling herself. A lot of people had been hurt already. And in her moments of real self-pity she got up and lit a cigarette and looked out of the window: *she* had been hurt most of all. Struggling all that time, scrimping to send him money, even during her teacher-training when she was penniless from start to finish and wore away her legs walking because she had neither bicycle nor bus fares. She had come back for a one-year appointment to the convent here, the year her father was dying. She had decided that she owed her mother that support and that the woman should have at least one of her children around for the bad months that lay ahead. She had been loath to leave the big, cheerful school in Dublin; but the Reverend Mother there had said she would certainly keep her job open for a year – Miss O'Hara was too good a prize to lose. She had walked the cliffs with her brother Sean when he was back for the death and the funeral. They had talked as naturally as they always had, the bond hadn't been shaken in the slightest. They had stopped at stiles and leaned on grassy banks looking out to sea where the gulls swooped and cried; and Sean had talked gently about ties, and duty, and doing what you felt you had to do. And she knew then that she wasn't going back to her job in Dublin, she was going to stay and look after her mother. She felt no resentment, then or later. She didn't hate Geraldine for not shipping her English husband and children over to Castlebay, nor Maire. How could they do anything of the sort? Sean was a missionary priest who had already given up his life to good, and anyway what use would a boy be around the house, even suppose he had been able to come home?

But somehow, now, in the dark sleepless hours where her heart was caught with a permanent sense of alarm and dread, she felt little love for him. How dare he talk to her about duty? How *dare* he? Where was his duty, she might ask. The first temptation and he leaves his priesthood, he closes his ears to what he had known since he was old enough to learn his catechism: that once a priest always a priest. He had slept with a Japanese woman, over and over, she was about to have his second child. Angela had never slept with anybody, and she was more entitled to try it than was a priest of God.

In his letter he said that he had told Shuya all about Angela, and Shuya had said it sounded as if she were strong enough to sort out the whole thing. Thank you very much Shuya, Angela thought in the night. Nice, helpful, Japanese sister, thank you. Shovel it all on to Angela, as usual. Oh, you're becoming an O'Hara all right, Shuya, don't doubt it.

Clare received a letter from the nun in the secondary school enclosing the syllabus for the 1950 open scholarship. It arrived with the usual crop of bills, receipts and advertisements from suppliers which made up the O'Brien family post.

Agnes was sitting near the range so that she could supervise the lifting over of the big teapot and the spooning out of the porridge. The older boys and Chrissie sat on one side of the big kitchen table with its torn oilcloth; Clare and the two younger boys had their backs to the door. In winter, breakfast was one meal where they were unlikely to be disturbed. The ping of the shop bell never went before the family was off to school.

The kitchen was warm and not really uncomfortable, but it was so cluttered that it was almost impossible to move once any of them stood up from the table. There were clothes and schoolbooks scattered around on the dilapidated couch, there were bags that hadn't yet been sorted for the shop heaped up against the wall. The washing hung perilously from the ceiling and the dresser bulged with so many things that had been 'just put there for the moment' that it was impossible to see the plates and dishes.

Tom O'Brien groaned and sighed as usual over the brown envelopes, the ones with windows in them and the ones without. Then he gave a start. 'Well now, Clare, there's a letter here for *you*!'

Clare had never had a letter before, so it created a lot of interest in the O'Brien household.

'I suppose she's got some awful, ugly, scabby lover,' Chrissie said.

'Don't talk like that, don't be such a loud-mouth always,' said Agnes O'Brien crossly to her troublesome daughter.

'Well who is it from? Why don't you ask her? You always ask me everything, where I was, who I talked to. Why can't Saint Clare be asked anything?'

'Don't speak to your mother like that,' said Tom O'Brien, who was already in a bad humour. 'Come on, Clare. Tell us who the letter is from and stop all this mystery.'

'It's a list of books for exams,' Clare said simply, producing the roneoed sheet of paper that the nun had sent. She left the letter in the envelope.

'What do you want that for?' Chrissie scoffed.

'So there won't be any mistakes in what I have to study.'

Chrissie looked at the list. 'We did all those last year,' she said.

'Good.' Clare was calm. 'Then maybe you'd have the books for me to use later.' She knew that Chrissie's books were long torn up, or scribbled on, or lost. It was not a subject her sister would discuss for much longer.

Agnes O'Brien had more on her mind than book lists. She was preparing to send her two first-born sons to England, where they were going to live in a strange woman's house and go out to work with grown men of every nationality each day. It was a terrible worry. But what was there for them here in Castlebay? If they only had a few fields of land it would have been different, but a small shop like this one, there was hardly a living in it at all.

Clare decided to show the letter to Miss O'Hara after school, but she was careful not to be seen hobnobbing with the teacher in case anyone should suspect that she was favoured, getting extra help and advice all the way. She would go to the O'Hara cottage instead. Miss O'Hara never seemed to mind her dropping in, and surely she would be interested in the letter.

Mrs O'Hara answered the door slowly and painfully. Clare had been tempted to run off again when she heard the scraping of the chair that meant the old woman was beginning her long, aching journey to the door, but that would be worse.

'I'm sorry for getting you up.'

'That's nothing,' the old woman said. 'I may have to be getting up to answer the door myself in a short time, that's the way things look.'

'Are you getting better?' Clare was pleased.

'No. But I may be on my own, that's the way the wind is blowing.'

'Miss O'Hara going to move out of the house?' It was incredible.

'And out of Castlebay, by the looks of things.'

'She can't!' Clare was stung with the unfairness of it. Miss O'Hara *had* to stay, until she got her scholarship. She *couldn't* leave now.

'Is she getting married or something?' she asked, full of hostility to the whole notion of it.

'Married? Who'd have that big long string of misery? Of course she's not getting married. Restless, that's what she's getting, restless. Her own words. She's up pacing the house all night long, you couldn't get a wink of sleep with her. What's wrong you ask her. Restless, she says. Ah well, nobody has any time for you when you're old. Remember that, Clare.'

Miss O'Hara returned just then. She looked very tired. She had been short-tempered at school too for some time, though not with Clare. So Clare didn't expect sharp words.

'*God Almighty*, am I to get no peace, at school, on the street and now at home?'

Clare was shocked.

'You give people an inch and they take a bloody mile. What is it tonight, Clare, is it the long division or is it the Long Cathechism? Tell me quickly and let's be done with it.'

Clare stood up and placed the letter from the distant convent on the O'Hara kitchen table. 'I thought you'd like to see the reply they sent me, since you helped me write the letter.' She was at the door now, her face red and furious. 'Goodnight, Mrs O'Hara,' she called, and was gone.

She marched down the long golf-course road, where more and more people were doing bed and breakfast in the season. Down towards the top of Church Street and straight into the town. She didn't even see Chrissie and Kath sitting on a wall swinging their legs and talking to Gerry Doyle and two of his friends. She didn't notice all the excitement in Dwyers' the butchers, when the mad dog belonging to Dr Power had run off down the street with a leg of mutton.

At home two suitcases were being packed even though the boys wouldn't leave for a few days yet. It was a rare thing to go on a journey; the packing was always taken very seriously.

Clare's father had found a good leather strap that would hold one case together – the locks had long rusted and wouldn't catch any more. They would probably use several layers of thick cord to hold the other.

Mam could hardly be seen in the kitchen behind the lines of washing. There were five bars – long wooden slats, and they went up and down over the range on a dangerous pulley system that only Mam could work, everyone else reached up by standing on a chair. But today there seemed to be a crisis of enormous proportions. The range was out. And Mam was standing on it at the back fixing what must

80

have been a row of washing that had fallen, judging by the rage and the pile of ash-covered clothes in the corner of the kitchen.

Mam looked as if nothing would please her, and indeed nothing did.

'Can I do anything to help?' Clare asked after a moment, thinking that was a better approach that asking what had happened.

'It would be nice if *someone* did something to help,' Mam cried. 'It would be very nice if *anyone* in this house did something to help. That would be very nice. And very surprising.'

'Well, tell me what you want, and I'll do it, do you want me to make the tea?' Clare asked.

'How can you make the tea for eight people, don't be stupid, child.'

'Well, what do you want me to do?' Clare's voice was becoming querulous. What was the point of being nice to Mam if she was going to be so bad-tempered? Clare wished she hadn't come into the kitchen at all but just gone upstairs to the bedroom.

'Why don't you go and stick your nose in a book, isn't that all you ever want to do?' Mam shouted and at that moment the rest of the clothes from the line, all of them damp and some of them almost dripping, fell on top of Clare's head.

There was a silence and then Mam was down ripping the shirts and sheets off Clare and flinging them regardless to the floor. 'Are you all right, child, are you hurt?' Mam was near to tears with the shock. Her hands tore at the clothes until she could see Clare's face. When she found it, it was laughing, from shock more than anything. Mam hugged her, with the damp clothes between them. Then she hugged her again. Normally any thought of pressing wet clothes would make Mam start talking fearfully about rheumatic fever. But not now.

'You poor little thing, are you all right, are you all right? That was God punishing me for being cross with you over nothing.'

Clare was bewildered and delighted. The accident seemed to have put Mam into a great temper for some reason.

'Now let me get you out of all this wet swaddling clothes . . . or we'll both have rheumatic fever. And I'll put the kettle on and you and I'll have a cup of tea, just the two of us with some biscuits, then we'll throw the whole bloody lot of this into the bath, it'll all have to be done again anyway. And then we'll get one of those useless men of ours to mend the line.'

Mam looked happier than she had done for a long time.

David Power was in great trouble, and because of him so were the rest of the school. Father Kelly had read the letter out to Assembly not once but three times as a living example of how deceitful boys could be.

The letter was from a girl who was called Angela O'Hara and who apparently came from Power's home town. The letter was now almost known by heart throughout the school:

Dear David,

I have no objection to sending you the family tree of the Tudor monarchs with notes on how each one treated Ireland. I would have thought after all the money you pay in that great ugly castle up there, one of those priests who doesn't even have to make his own bed or cook his own breakfast could find time to do it for you, however. But I do not intend to join in your silly games of calling myself 'Andrew' when I write to you and filling the letter up with details of fictitious rugby matches. If that is the kind of hot-house nonsense that is encouraged in your school I am sorry for you, and for the men who are supposed to be in charge of you.

I wish you continued success and also to your friend James Nolan.

Regards Angela O'Hara

The grossness of this letter had never been equalled in the memory of every single member of the Order. Imagine a boy writing to *anyone* else for a teaching aid, when it was known that this was the best school in Ireland and one of the best in the whole of Europe. Imagine describing it as, letting it be believed to be, 'a great ugly castle'.

To allow, nay encourage, such slurs on men who were the anointed priests of God, to make remarks about these priests not cooking their own breakfast – as if this is what they had been ordained to do! Worse still, to encourage deception, to ask this girl whoever she was to pretend to be a boy, to sign herself with a false name, to invent details of rugby matches to deceive the innocent guardians in whose care they had been placed. And more, to suggest that this was a common practice. That this had been going on undiscovered in the school before this sickening letter had been exposed. There would be thorough investigations and in the meantime those boys who knew anything were expected to come forward.

David apologized to everyone as best he could. He couldn't have known she would do a thing like this. She had been great altogether before, he appealed to Nolan, who in all honesty had to admit that this was so.

'She must have gone mad, that's the only explanation,' David said.

'Yes, that must be it,' said Nolan who was familiar with madness, if extremely annoyed to have been mentioned by name in the letter that shook the school.

The sleeping tablets were very odd. You could feel your legs getting heavy first, then your arms, and your head wouldn't lift from the pillow and suddenly it was eight o'clock in the morning. Angela felt that it took her until noon to wake up properly. Then she felt fine for the afternoon. So at least they bought her some good hours, hours when she could correct exercises, mark tests and try to undo some of the harm she appeared to have done during the first weeks after the letter from Sean, the weeks when she had hardly ever closed her eyes.

Mother Immaculata had said she was looking her old self again, which was irritating beyond words, and Sergeant

McCormack, the priest's housekeeper, said she was glad that Angela seemed to have got over whatever it was that had made her so disagreeable. Mrs Conway asked was there anything in particular that Angela wanted — she kept coming into the post office and leaving again without making any purchase at all. And her mother said she was glad the pacing had stopped and added mysteriously that whenever Angela had any definite plans the fair thing to do was to tell them immediately.

But Clare O'Brien was not won back so easily, not in those alert hours of the afternoon. Angela looked at the small white face and the large dark eyes. It was only a few months ago that there had been those bright yellow ribbons and the big bright hope that she had won a history prize. Now there was nothing of that. There was the watchful look of a dog that has been struck once and won't let it happen again.

Angela had tried to put it right.

'Here's that letter back from Sister Consuelo. It's very encouraging really, isn't it?'

Clare took it with thanks.

'I was a bit hasty that day you came to the house, I had a lot on my mind.'

'Yes, Miss O'Hara.'

'So I'm sorry if I appeared a bit short-tempered, it had nothing to do with you, you know that.'

'Yes, yes indeed.'

'So why won't you come on back again, and we'll get a bit of work done, any evening you like.'

'No thank you, Miss O'Hara.'

'*God dammit*, Clare O'Brien, what do you want me to do, go down on my bended knees?' There was a silence. 'I'm going to tell you something now for your own good. You're a bright child. I would *love* to see you get the bloody scholarship. I don't mind working till midnight every night to help you get it. What better way could I spend my time? But you have a really *sickening* habit of sulking. Oh yes, you have. I remember you were just the same when you didn't win the history prize. *Nobody* likes a sulker, Clare, it's a

84

form of blackmail. I didn't get what I wanted so I'm not going to speak to people. It's about the most objectionable vice anyone could have, so my advice is to get rid of it if you want to have any friends.'

'I haven't many friends,' Clare said.

'Think about it. That might be why.'

'Anyway, you're leaving, so why tell me you'll help me?' She was still mutinous.

'I'm leaving, am I? That's the first I heard of it. Where am I going?'

'Your mother said . . .'

'My mother doesn't know what time of day it is.'

'She said you paced round the house all night planning to leave.'

'Oh, Christ Almighty, is that what she's on about?'

'So you're not?' Clare had brightened a little.

'I'm not, but unless I see a marked change in your attitude, I might as well have left as far as you're concerned. Come up to me this evening and we'll make a start. I need a bit of distraction to tell you the truth.'

'It'll soon be the bright weather and the long nights will be over.'

'Why do you say that?' Angela sounded startled.

'My mother always says it to cheer people up. I thought it was a nice thing to say.'

'I think it is.'

She decided not to send him a telegram, and it took her five weeks from the day she got the letter before she was able to reply. Only the thought of him waiting and watching for a Japanese postman to bring a letter made her put pen to paper at all. She began the letter a dozen times. The words didn't ring true. She couldn't say she was glad he had confided in her, she would prefer never to have known a thing about it. She couldn't say she sympathized with him because she didn't. She could find no words of welcome for her sister-in-law Shuya, her new nephew Denis, nor any enthusiasm about the arrival of the next child. Instead, her mind was full of snakes and worries slithering around.

85

Would her mother have a stroke if she heard the news? Was there a possibility that the family might have to pay back some of the money spent educating Sean to be a priest, now that he had abandoned it all? Was it something that he might be excommunicated for, and the excommunication made public? Would all the priests in Ireland hear about it? Would Father O'Dwyer get to know through some clerical bulletin? She knew she should think kinder thoughts and treat him as a lonely frail human being; those were the words he used about himself, but then in the next sentence he said that he now knew perfect happiness, and understood for the first time why man and woman were put on this earth.

Several times she had her foot on the doorstep of Mrs Conway's post office prepared to send the wire telling him that his news had been received and urging him to communicate no further. But what would the town make of *that* piece of intelligence. The houses and shops up and down Church Street and up the golf-course road and across on the far cliffroad would buzz happily with speculation. If Angela wanted to send a telegram like that it would have to be sent from the next town. And it might provoke Sean into doing something really foolish. After all he had talked fondly, and insanely, in his letter of the day when he could come back to Castlebay and show it to his wife and children. *Father* Sean O'Hara show Castlebay to his wife and children! He must be raving mad! Not just *mad,* but sheer raving *lunatic* mad!

She tried to imagine what she would advise if it were somebody else. Her friend Emer back in Dublin, whom she had taught with and prowled the likely places with looking for husbands. Suppose it were Emer's brother. What would she say? She would probably urge a noncommittal kind of letter to tide things over. Fine. But once you started to write to your own brother about something like this you couldn't remain uncommitted. It was ridiculous to expect that you could behave like an outsider. So eventually she wrote from the heart.

She wrote that she was shocked that he had given up his vocation, and that he must realize everyone in Ireland would be shocked too, no matter how good and supportive his fellow priests in the mission field had been. She said that if he was absolutely certain that this was not a temporary loss of faith, then she was glad that he had found happiness in his relationship with his Japanese friend, and pleased that the birth of their son had given them both so much pleasure. She begged him to realize that Castlebay in 1950 was a place where understanding and casual attitudes towards married priests simply did not exist. She wrote that, as she sat in the dark room with the rain outside the window, and with her mother poking at the open door of the range with a rough old poker that she held in two hands, it became more and more obvious that their mother should never know. After her time, then they might all think again; but it would destroy the woman's life, and they had all agreed that when lives were being handed out Mam had had a very poor one given to her. She said she knew it was hard; but could he as a higher kindness write letters that assumed he was still in the Order. And because Mrs Conway looked at every envelope that went through her post office, Angela had decided she was going to address hers in the way she always had done. Could he imagine the excitement if she were to drop the Father bit? She said she knew this was not the warm, all-embracing letter he had hoped for, but at least it was honest and it was practical and for the moment that was the best he could have.

It was on the dresser for two days before she could put it in the postbox. It was sealed and there was no fear that her mother would open it – the old woman thought that it contained the usual letter and the four folded pound notes for Masses. She half hoped it would blow away or fall down and be lost so it would never be sent.

Clare O'Brien, looking around her with wonder as she always did, spotted it. 'Can I post that to Father O'Hara?' she asked eagerly. 'It would make me feel very important posting a letter to Japan.'

'Yes, you post it,' Miss O'Hara said in a strange voice.

'Will we look at the globe to see how many countries it

will go over before it gets to him?' Clare asked. She loved getting out the old globe which creaked when it spun round.

'Yes.' Miss O'Hara made no move to pass the globe which was near her.

'Will I get it?' Clare was hesitant.

'What? Oh yes. Let's see.' Angela lifted the globe on to the table. But she didn't start to move it yet.

'Well, it will leave Castlebay . . .' Clare prompted.

Angela O'Hara shook herself. 'That's the hardest part of its journey,' she said, like her old self again. 'If it gets out of Mrs Conway's sticky hands without being steamed open for Madam in there to read it, then the worst's over.'

Clare was delighted to be made party to such outrageous accusations about awful Mrs Conway, the awful mother of really awful Bernie Conway. She decided to take the letter to Japan by the westward route and brought it over the Atlantic to Nova Scotia where they said all Irish planes stopped first, and then she took it slowly across all the United States, going to Hawaii and then on to Japan. That's probably the way they'd take it, Clare thought, less land, less places to stop in. Could you choose whether it went one way or the other? Miss O'Hara shook her head. Clare supposed it depended on which way the planes were going first; she looked at Miss O'Hara for confirmation and to her surprise she thought she saw tears in her eyes.

'Will he be home soon at all?' she asked sympathetically. She realized that poor Miss O'Hara must miss her brother and maybe she shouldn't go on and on about how far away he was and how huge the world was. Maybe it wasn't tactful.

Chrissie said that Clare wasn't normal because her big toe was bigger than her second toe. This was discovered when Chrissie was painting her toenails and the bedroom smelled so much of lacquer that Clare had wanted to open the door.

'You can't do that,' Chrissie hissed. 'Everyone will smell it.'

'But nobody can *see* it under your socks. What's the point of it?' Clare had wanted to know.

88

'It's the difference between being grown-up and being a stupid eejit like you are,' Chrissie had explained.

Clare had shrugged. There was no use in trying to talk to Chrissie about anything, it always ended up with an explanation that Clare was *boring* and that seemed to be the root cause of everything. Chrissie taunted her about every aspect of her life.

'Your hair is awful. It's like a paper bag, it's so flat.'

'I don't put pipe cleaners in mine like you do,' Clare said.

'Well, that's it. You're so stupid you can't even put curlers in.' And then on another tack: 'You've no friends at all at school. I see you in the playground on your own, you walk to and from school all by yourself – even your awful stupid class must have sense, they know not to be friends with you.'

'*I do* have friends,' Clare cried.

'Who? Name me one friend. Whose house do you go to in the evening, who comes here? Answer me that! Nobody!'

Clare wished devoutly that Kath and Peggy didn't come so often – it meant that she couldn't go to the bedroom, and downstairs she was always being asked to do something.

'I've lots of friends, different friends for different things you know, like I'm friendly with Marian in domestic science because we're at the same table and then I'm friendly with Josie Dillon because I sit beside her in class.'

'Ugh, Josie Dillon, she's so fat, she's disgusting.'

'That's not her fault.'

'It is too, she's never without something in her fat hand eating it.'

Clare didn't like Josie all that much: she was very dull, she couldn't seem to get enthusiastic about anything. But she was harmless and kind and she was lonely. Clare didn't like all the faces that Chrissie was making.

'Ugh, Josie Dillon, well if you had to have a friend I might have guessed that it would be someone like that big white slug.'

'She's not a slug, and anyway your friend Kath had nits in her hair, everyone in the school knows that.'

'Aren't you *horrible*!' screamed Chrissie. 'What a

desperate thing to say about anyone. When I think how nice Kath always is about you.'

'She was never nice about me, all she said ever was shut up and go away, like *you* say.'

Chrissie was looking at Clare's feet. 'Put your foot out.'

'Why? I won't,' Clare said.

'Go on, just for a moment.'

'You'll put that awful red paint on it.'

'No I won't, I wouldn't waste it. Go on, let's see.'

Suspiciously Clare put her leg out of her bed and Chrissie examined her foot.

'Show me the other one,' she said after a while. Nervously it was produced. Then Chrissie pronounced that Clare was deformed. Her second toe should be longer than the big toe, Kath's was, Peggy's was, Chrissie's was, anyone you saw on the beach had feet like that. Clare fought back. Why was it called the big toe if it wasn't the biggest one?

Chrissie shook her head. 'Oh well,' she said.

Clare was frightened now. 'I think I'll go and ask Mam,' she said scrambling off the bed. A hand thrust her back.

'You'll do nothing of the sort, Mam will want to know why we were talking about toes, she'll want to see mine maybe, keep your awful complaints to yourself, and don't be seen in your bare feet.'

Clare crawled back on to her bed.

Chrissie looked at her and decided to be sympathetic. That was worse than anything else that Chrissie had ever done.

'Listen, nobody'll notice, and I tell you, I won't give you away.'

Clare looked miserable still.

'And Josie Dillon's not *too* bad. It's better than having no friend, isn't it?'

'Did you have a friend at school, Miss O'Hara?' Clare wanted to know.

'Yes, several. Why?'

'I just wondered, what happened to them?'

'Well, Nellie Burke is working up in Dr Power's house,

she was a friend when I was about your age, and Margaret Rooney, she went to England and got married, she lives near my sister. And Cissy O'Connor became a nun God bless her, she's praying for all of us in a convent up in the North.'

'They weren't working like a demon like you were, like I am?'

'Oh no, they weren't working like demons at all, they thought I was mad.'

Clare was pleased with this, it made her path seem less odd.

'But when I got to the big convent, to the secondary school, it was different because there were lots of people there with the same interests, you didn't have to hide your work or anything. And when I went to the training college I had great friends altogether, still have in a way, but of course it's not the same now that I'm away, most of them teach in Dublin you see. But there'll be plenty of time for you to make friends, don't worry.'

Angela was being reassuring. Someone must have been getting at the child. Wouldn't you think they'd be delighted to see someone try to get on? Give some encouragement and support. But it had never been the way.

'I do worry a bit, I don't want to be abnormal.' Clare was solemn.

'Well, I hope you're not big-headed enough to think that you're something special. That would be a sin of Pride you know.'

'I suppose so.'

'You can *know* it, not suppose it. It's there in black and white in the catechism. The two great sins against Hope are Pride and Despair. You mustn't get drawn towards either of them.'

'Were you ever tempted a bit to either of them?' Clare was an odd mixture. She could be quite familiar and probing sometimes as if she were the equal of the teacher sitting opposite her, yet she could also be totally respectful, and up at the convent she never gave a glimmer of the intimacy they shared in the O'Hara cottage.

'If I was, I suppose it was a bit more towards Despair,'

Angela said. 'Sometimes I used to think I'd never make it and what was it all for anyway. But I did and here I am, and I'm teaching the second great genius to come out of Castlebay, so will you open your books and not have us here all night talking about sins against Hope and friendships long gone.'

Clare giggled and got out the special copy books she had bought in Miss O'Flaherty's shop, a different colour to the school ones so that she would never get confused. They both knew that nobody at school would be pleased if they knew that Miss O'Hara was giving hours and hours of private tuition free to a ten-year-old. It was never mentioned. And at home Mam thought that Clare was getting help because she had fallen behind a bit. It was a devious business studying your books in Castlebay.

When the summer came David began to wish heartily that Nolan's family had never decided to rent the house on the cliff. First there had been the letters, they wanted the Very Best house, and could the Powers send them a list of accommodation. Castlebay wasn't like that, there were twenty houses on the Cliff Road that people let for the summer, usually a month at a time. And up towards the golf course there were other kinds of houses, smaller maybe but great for people who played golf all day. And then at the other side of the bay there was a jumble of houses, some owned by people who lived twenty miles away but who came out to stay there for the summer. People just knew the houses and knew what they wanted, it was very hard to explain all this to the Nolans. Molly Power was worn out from trying to explain.

She settled on Crest View and arranged the letting with Mrs Conway's sister who owned the house. She spoke of the professional people from Dublin, who would arrive with the three children and their maid and she insulted the Conways and all their relatives by suggesting that a coat of paint be put on the porch which was peeling somewhat under the constant wind and spray. But huffed though they were the Conways arranged that the porch be painted. They weren't going to have any professional family from Dublin casting aspersions on the house they were renting by the sea.

David was worn out inspecting Crest View with his mother and being forced to face unanswerable questions about where the Nolan parents would sleep, in this front room or that. And would Caroline Nolan share a room with the friend she was inviting? And did David think the room on the stairs was big enough for the maid? Dublin maids might have notions about themselves.

Nearer the time Mrs Power arranged to have a box of groceries delivered from the town to the kitchen of Crest View to welcome them. David had watched his mother while she dithered over the list.

'I don't think she'll notice really what you order,' he had said helpfully. 'Nolan says his mother is mad most of the time.'

'David will you *stop* that silly kind of talk!' his mother had cried out in rage. 'Here am I wearing my fingers to the bone trying to see that you have nice friends for the summer, and that they are comfortable when they get here and all the help I get from you is to say that some poor woman you've never met is mad. Honestly.'

'I did meet her when she came to see Nolan at half term,' David said.

'And . . .?'

'And it was one of her good days apparently.' He was unconcerned.

O'Brien's shop looked well, he thought, it had a new sign over it, and one of the ice-cream firms had put up a big tin sign as well so it looked much more modern than last year. He supposed they'd all be working in the shop: all the O'Brien family, cutting ice-creams, counting out sweets, putting oranges in white paper bags, giving change, getting greaseproof paper for the slices of cooked ham or the half-pounds of rashers. Wasn't it nice for Tommy and Ned to have that to do as a way of getting pocket money in the summer.

There was no sign of either of them. He asked Chrissie

93

where they were and heard they had gone to England months ago. What for? To work on the buildings of course. It gave him a start.

Chrissie didn't know if they liked it or not. They only wrote very little on a Friday. They wrote every Friday? Well they sent something home of course. Of course. He'd forgotten. Mrs O'Brien was serving another family, young Clare was cutting ice-creams carefully and watched equally carefully by those who were buying them. It would be a disaster if a twopenny ice-cream were ever the teeniest bit smaller than the allotted ridge. Only Chrissie had time to talk.

'James Nolan and his family are coming to stay up in Crest View.'

'Oh, the fellow who burned his mouth.' Chrissie giggled.

'The very one.'

'Well he's in great time, Gerry's going to be organizing a picnic way down the sandhills of the golf links soon, he'll tell you all about it,' she hissed conspiratorially.

That was good news. David had been wondering whether this visit would live up to the last. A secret picnic in the sand dunes – that would be great.

'Does he have any sisters or anything? Gerry was saying there aren't enough girls. Though I think there are,' Chrissie said.

'He has a sister, Caroline, and she's bringing a friend but I don't think . . .' He stopped suddenly. It mightn't be polite to say that he didn't think *they* were the kind of girls you invited to somewhere that there was going to be messing.

Molly hadn't been so excited for a long time. To think that a Dublin family who were quite well known were coming to stay in Castlebay just on the word of a boy who had been a visitor in her house. She was very flattered. She hoped that young James Nolan hadn't exaggerated the style of their living.

The letters from Sheila Nolan had been courteous and warm, but alarmingly had given the impression that Castlebay was a little like Monte Carlo. She had said she so

94

looked forward to going to the Spa each day with Molly. The Spa? She must mean the seaweed baths, but they were old and shabby and rusty, and only priests or cranky sorts of people went to bathe there. Molly could hardly have them transformed with a coat of paint as she had done with the house.

But wouldn't it be great to talk with Dublin people again, and laugh over Robert's at the top of Grafton Street, and wonder was that nice Miss so-and-so still in Switzer's and had Brown Thomas changed their displays. It was such a pity that there were so few people she could ask to meet the Nolans. The Dillons at the hotel were a very mixed bunch, and it was hard to think who else they could ask. The Nolans would think them very dull sticks.

Paddy had told her to relax, but men never understood anything. He said that he had seen the high and mighty of the land coming on holidays to Castlebay over the years and it was funny but they never seemed to want the comfort and style of home, there was something in the big bay, the cliffs and the sunshine that made up for everything else. He was certain it would be the same with the Nolans.

Yes maybe, but Molly wished they had the kind of life where friends dropped in for a sherry or they had a group of people to meet in the hotel. The danger of going out with Paddy was that every drunk and hopeless poor creature in the place would attach themselves with details of their symptoms. Molly also wished they had a conservatory. Wouldn't it be lovely to say to the Nolans, 'Do come into our conservatory with your coffee, we always sit here in the evenings.' Why hadn't she pushed Paddy more about it? Bumper Byrne who did most of the building in the town said that it wouldn't be hard to do but Molly had wanted someone with a little more style than Bumper. Now she had no conservatory at all.

Her heart fell when she remembered Sheila Nolan writing about where to shop. Shop? In Castlebay? Imagine a woman from Dublin who was used to going to places like Smith's on the Green having to stand in O'Brien's little shop and wait while those children laughed and skittered. That coarse

Chrissie with the frizzy hair, and the thin worried-looking one, Clare, who often had a book in her hand if the shop was quiet. And they had nothing nice, nothing at all.

As she thought of O'Brien's with no pleasure she remembered that she hadn't put any flour or indeed any baking things at all on the list. The Nolans were bringing a maid after all, she might want to make scones or bread the first evening, they wouldn't know where to shop. Molly should have thought of a pack of brown flour, white flour, bread soda, it would show she understood that they didn't need to live off shop food all the time like people who knew no better.

Better do it now, she'd have so much on her mind tomorrow when they arrived and anyway she'd be getting her hair done and making the last-minute arrangements. A walk would do her good, it was a lovely day. She set off down the Cliff Road trying to look at Crest View quickly as if she were a stranger who hadn't seen it before. It certainly looked the smartest of the houses with its newly painted look. And Molly had seen to it that the grass was cut too, unlike some of the other places along the road. Down on the beach there was already great sign of activity, the season had begun, Paddy was surely right, the Nolans would love it.

She had hit a quiet time in O'Brien's, only Clare was serving, and she was deep in a book.

'Whenever you're ready,' Molly said.

Clare looked up, unaware that she should be paying attention to the customer. 'Did you do clouds at school, Mrs Power?' she asked.

'Clouds?'

'Clouds. Mam and Dad didn't and I was wondering about the cumulus. There seem to be lots of different kinds of them, I thought it was one name for one cloud.'

'I haven't time to talk about clouds now, I want to buy some flour, that's if you are serving. Perhaps I should wait for your mother . . .'

'No, no.' Clare put down the book guiltily. 'What did you want, Mrs Power?'

The child got the flour and the bread soda, she even

suggested lard and then she added the items up carefully on
the back of a white paper bag. She looked so intense that
Molly felt a pang of guilt about having put her down so
strongly. She was very young and after all it was good to see
a child trying to study. But she looked so streelish in that
faded dress which was much too short for her and too wide
around the shoulders. Why couldn't Agnes O'Brien dress
the child properly when she was on show for the summer, it
gave such a bad impression of Castlebay. Molly's irritation
returned.

'It's one pound four shillings altogether, Mrs Power.'
Clare proffered the list but Molly waved it away and rooted
for notes in her handbag.

At that moment a group of English visitors came in to be
served and Tom O'Brien, hearing the ping of the door and
the voices, came out to serve them. They were nicely spoken
people staying at Dillon's Hotel and Molly looked at them
with interest in case they might be possible company when
the Nolans arrived.

Tom O'Brien stood like a landlord in an inn, pleased to
see the civilized chat between Mrs Power and the visitors. It
was only when the door pinged again to admit further
customers that he thought he should speed up the process
and serve someone.

'Well I hope I'll see you while you're here,' Molly said,
pleased to discover that the two English couples had
brought a car and a dog each on their vacation. This alone
made them into people of standing.

She turned to Clare. 'I'll take my change now and rush
along home,' she said.

'It's twenty-four shillings, Mrs Power.'

'I know, I gave you five pounds.' Molly was impatient.
'Hurry up, Clare, give Mrs Power her change. Come on
now.'

Clare hesitated. 'You haven't . . . um given . . . me the
money yet,' she said despairingly.

'*Clare!* Mrs Power said she gave you a five-pound note.'
Tom O'Brien was horrified. 'Give her the change this
minute. What did it come to? Twenty-four shillings. Give

Mrs Power three pounds sixteen shillings and stop dreaming.'

'Mrs Power, you put the five pounds back in your handbag,' Clare said.

'I'm very sorry, Mrs Power.' Tom pushed his daughter away from the drawer where they kept the money. He started rummaging for notes and coins.

'Look, Daddy, there isn't a five-pound note there. Mrs Power took it out but she put it back in her bag when she was talking to those people . . .'

Everyone in the shop was looking on with interest.

Two spots of red appeared on Molly's face. 'In all my life . . .' she began.

'Please forgive this, Mrs Power . . .' Tom O'Brien was mortified, he kicked the door into the back open so that Agnes could come out and help with the ever-growing group of spectators.

Molly had opened her bag and there on top of it for anyone to see was a five-pound note, hastily stuffed back there. She wouldn't have hidden it anyway, she told herself, but now there was no opportunity to do so. It was far too obvious to everyone. The flush deepened on her face.

'It's *perfectly* all right, Mr O'Brien, your daughter is totally correct, I did indeed put it back into my bag in error. How good that you have such a watchdog.' Graciously she handed over the note, waving Tom away and giving it deliberately to Clare.

Clare took it calmly and gave the change. She joined in none of the mumblings of her father, nor the assurances of how it could happen to anyone.

'Thank you, Mrs Power,' Clare said.

'Thank you, Clare,' said Molly Power.

The door pinged behind her.

'She'll never shop here again,' Tom O'Brien said to his wife.

It was a long day. Clare never got back to the chapter on clouds in her geography book. There was never a moment for her parents to speak alone with her or for her to explain

98

the misunderstanding with Mrs Power. As the hours went by she became less repentant and more angry with Mrs Power. It was *her* fault after all, and she hadn't apologized, not in the smallest way. Clare hated her father for having humbled himself, she could have killed him for being all upset and sorry over something which was that woman's fault, not hers, not his.

The shop was empty for a couple of lovely minutes. Clare reached her hand out to her geography book and took it back. She looked across at her mother.

'It's all right, he'll forget it, it will all be forgiven and forgotten by tomorrow,' Agnes said soothingly.

'There's nothing to forgive! She didn't give me the money. Was I meant to give her three pounds sixteen shillings *and* her shopping? Was I?'

'Hush Clare, don't be difficult.'

'I'm not being difficult. I just want to know. If I am meant to do that, then tell me and I'll do it. I just didn't know.'

Agnes looked at her affectionately. 'I don't know where we got you, you're brighter than the lot of us put together.'

Clare still looked mutinous.

'There are some things that are neither right nor wrong, you can't have rules laid down for. Would you understand that?'

'Yes,' Clare said immediately, 'I would. Like the Holy Ghost.'

'Like what?'

'Like the Holy Ghost, we have to believe in Him without understanding Him, He's not a bird and He's not a great wind. He's something though, and that should be enough without understanding it.'

'I don't think that's the same at all,' said Agnes, troubled. 'But if it helps you to understand the problems of trade in a small town then for heaven's sake use it.'

It was eleven o'clock before they closed the door in O'Brien's. Tom O'Brien had a pain across his back from bending and stretching and lifting. He had forgotten the summer pain and the constant tiredness. This was just the first week: there would be another ten like it, please God, if they were to make a living at all. He was behind in paying one of the creameries and the bacon factory always allowed people a bit of credit until the summer pickings were in. He sighed deeply, it was so hard to know about things. Last year everyone had wanted those shop cakes with the hard icing, this year he had only sold two of them and the rest were growing stale under his eyes.

Everything was so precarious nowadays, and a man with a wife and six children had nothing but worries morning noon and night.

He worried about the two lads gone to England; particularly Tommy, he was so easily led, so slow to work things out. How would he survive at all in England where people were so smart and knew everything? And Ned, though he was a brighter boy, he was still very young, not sixteen until the summer. Tom O'Brien wished that he had a big business, one where his boys could have come in to work with him, gone to other towns and served their time in big groceries and then come home to Castlebay. But it was only a dream. This was an outpost and it wouldn't be here at all, the community would have broken up and scattered long ago if it weren't for the yearly influx of visitors that began in the first week of June and ended sharply on September first. Eleven weeks to make sense of the other forty-one weeks in the year. He called out to Agnes, wanting to know if there was any hot water.

'What do you want with hot water at this time of night?'

'There's these bath salts we sell and there's a picture of a man with an aching back on the front and it says he gets great relief by putting these in his bath,' he said simply.

Agnes read the packet too. 'We'll boil up some. Clare child, before you go to bed will you fill a couple of saucepans, and Chrissie. Chrissie?'

'I think she was doing some holiday work with Kath and Peggy,' Clare said automatically. She knew that the amusements had started for the summer and the three were dolled up to the nines with their painted toenails freed from summer socks.

'That one should be running the country with all the homework and holiday work she does,' grumbled Tom O'Brien. 'Why is it that she gets these bad reports every term, I might ask.'

'They're fierce strict up in the convent now, it's not like the Brothers. They say awful things about everyone.' Clare was struggling with the saucepans. One way to buy an easy life was to keep Chrissie's cover, that way she got to stay out later and she tortured Clare a bit less.

Clare's mother was opening the packet of bath salts. 'It's hard to think that it would work,' she said doubtfully. 'Go on into the bathroom, Tom, and we'll see if it's any good.'

Clare was still there; the youngsters were asleep a long time; Chrissie would come home when the amusements had closed down, when she had won something on the roll a halfpenny table and maybe had a ride on the bumpers. Tommy and Ned were asleep in their digs in Kilburn.

'Go on up to bed, Clare child. You've been a great help today,' her mother said. 'I've got to fire a bit of energy into your father, we can't have him getting pains and aches in the first week of the summer season.'

Clare heard them laughing in the bathroom and it sounded comforting to Clare as she got ready for bed. She looked out the window and saw Gerry Doyle walking down towards the beach with a very pretty girl, a visitor. *That* would annoy Chrissie if she were to hear of it. She saw a crowd who had been in Craig's Bar carrying brown bags of bottles with them, they were heading off the Far Cliff Road on the other side of the bay; they had probably rented a house there. In the distance the music of the dance could be heard. That's where everyone was. Chrissie was dying to go, but not until she was sixteen; it was two years and five months away. The moon made a pointed path out over the sea, Castlebay was coming alive for the summer.

The Nolans arrived on the train from Dublin and the Powers had driven to the station in the town twenty miles from Castlebay to meet them. Dr Power called a porter immediately when he saw the amount of luggage that was assembling beside them. There would be two cars, the Powers' own Ford and a taxi. Sheila and Jim Nolan looked around them with interest and then spotted David running towards them. There were a lot of handshakes and much giggling from Caroline Nolan and her schoolfriend Hilary.

Mrs Nolan wore a very flowing sort of dress with huge red and green flowers on it as if she were going to a garden party of some type. She glanced around, sniffing the air as if suspecting it might be germ laden.

Dr Power took both of her hands in his and his face was wide with welcome, then he shook the hands of Jim and said what a pleasure it had been having their son to stay, and how everyone in Castlebay was waiting to welcome the whole family; he said his wife was organizing tea in the rented house for them, otherwise she would be here too.

Jim Nolan was a thin, fair-haired man of a slightly distracted appearance. He also had a role in watching out for the eccentricities of his wife. Sheila had a face which must have been that of a beauty when she was younger. Even now approaching her late forties she was handsome, with pale eyes and a disconcerting stare. She looked long and hard at Paddy Power.

'You are a good man, you are a man we could trust,' she said after a pause.

Dr Power was well used to intense stares like this. In his line of work he came across them regularly.

'I very much hope so, because you'll need to rely on me, on us for a bit until you get used to the ways of our strange country parts.'

With that he shooed them gently into his car with most of the luggage. David was to organize the taxi for the young people and Breeda, the Nolans' maid. There was a lot of waving and goodbyeing, until they would meet again in twenty miles' time in Castlebay.

It seemed to David that Caroline and Hilary seemed a bit scornful of everything they saw. They wanted to know where was the nearest big town to Castlebay, and giggled when they were told that they were in it. They asked when would they be on the main road and giggled even more when they learned they had been on it for three miles. They asked about tennis and were very disappointed to know that there wasn't a proper club, but they could play at the hotel. How did you meet people if there wasn't a club they wondered, and David found himself apologizing almost. Eventually, the taxi driver who also drove a hearse and had a half share in a pub, took over from him and explained Castlebay in much more attractive terms, talking about the quality who came every year and how the place was much sought after. English couples came too, often middle-aged people with a car and a dog and golf clubs. Fancy them coming all the way to Castlebay when they had the whole of their own country and Scotland and Wales to choose from. David realized that this was a much better way to go than his own style of excusing things. He brightened up and told them about the golf club and how this year he and Nolan were thinking of learning. You could hire clubs there.

Caroline and Hilary giggled and thought this was great, they might learn too.

You didn't really get a good view of the sea until you came over Bennett's Hill and David looked at them eagerly to see if it pleased them. Their faces seemed to say it all, so he sat back happily and exchanged conspiratorial winks with the taxi driver.

The girls were silenced for once as the whole coast spread before them . . . the tide was out so the beach spread out like a huge silver carpet, the headlands at each end looked a sharp purple and as they came to where the roads divided there was no need to explain any more, Castlebay explained itself. They drove down the main street – Church Street – with the big church on the right, past all the shops, well-painted and decorated for the summer, some of them with low whitewashed walls where holidaymakers sat and chatted in the sun. People were eating ice-creams and carrying beach balls and children had rubber rings and fishing nets. You could smell the sea. It was like paradise.

The taxi driver drove slowly down Church Street so that they could savour it all; the girls looked excitedly from the front of the big dance hall, to the entrance of Dillon's Hotel.

They saw Dwyer's the butchers with a big notice saying 'Get your holiday meat here'. Everyone seemed to be talking to each other or waving or calling, it was as if all the people on the street going down to the sea knew each other.

Majestically the taxi turned right at the Cliff Road so that they could have a good view of the beach.

'There's Gerry Doyle!' cried Nolan, delighted to recognize him. 'Who is that he's with?'

'That's his sister, I told you about her, Fiona,' David said.

The Doyles waved and James Nolan let out all his breath in a great rush. 'She's *gorgeous*,' he said.

The girls in the back were annoyed. They didn't have to say anything, you could just sense it in the way they rustled.

'How are we going to become great golfers if you're going to sigh like that over the first girl you see in Castlebay?' David said.

'Quite right.' Caroline was approving. 'We don't want the holiday spoiled by silliness and falling in love.'

'No indeed,' said Hilary very vehemently.

It was totally unconvincing but there wasn't time to debate it because everyone was getting out of the taxi and there was a joyous reunion on the lawn. David noticed that his mother had had her hair done, and was wearing her best dress. Bones was not there; he must be tied up at home on the very accurate assumption that he would not lend any tone to the gathering. The sun was shining down on the garden and Molly had brought Nellie with her in order to help serve a welcoming tea. There were canvas chairs and stools out in the garden, the cups were arranged on a tray in the porch and there were sandwiches and bridge rolls cut in half with egg on some and ham on others. There was apple tart too, on two large plates. Nellie had a small white hat on as well as her apron. James introduced her to Breeda who immediately took off her hat and coat and went into the kitchen to help.

Mrs Nolan was sitting back in her chair, eyes closed with pleasure. 'What a *wonderful* welcome,' she said. 'What a beautiful place. James, we are lucky that you have marvellous friends like these to make it all possible.' Molly Power reddened with pleasure.

'Heavens it's very small and simple after Dublin,' she said in a tinkly voice that David didn't often hear.

'It's heavenly,' said Mrs Nolan. 'And the flies are going to be quite manageable I do believe.'

'The flies?' Molly was startled.

'Yes, but one has to expect them, I've been watching, you get about one bluebottle to eight flies, that's not too bad is it?'

'No, I suppose not.' Molly was puzzled.

'We brought quite a lot of muslin with us of course, but in the end we have to realize this is holidays, this is the great outdoors and . . . well they can't kill us?'

'Er . . . no?'

'The flies. They can't *kill us*. And I think this place is heavenly.'

And that put the seal on the summer. Dr Power had told her that it was one of the healthiest places in the world because of the sea and the ozone and the gulf stream, and goodness knows what else he had added for good measure; so now Nolan's mother need have no fear of fleas or damp or anyone catching anything. Mrs Conway's sister had come down to inspect the professional people from Dublin and had been slightly overawed to see eight people on the lawn of Crest View being served tea by two maids. But her curiosity got the better of her so she came in. She was given a chair, a cup of tea and fulsome thanks from Mrs Nolan as having provided the best house in Castlebay. Mrs Conway's sister took everything in, asked about eight searching questions and left to go to the post office and fill them in on the new arrivals. Dr Power had given his lecture about drowning. Every year he said for the past fourteen years there had been a death in the summer. All except one of them had been people who had just arrived; the accident had happened in the first few days, before they got used to the terrible undercurrent that pulled you out and sideways after a big wave. There were notices all round the beach but people didn't believe them. There was a lifeguard – but there was only so much he could do and if a bather was swept out by huge waves, the call often didn't go up until it was too late. Dr Power was very grave. Caroline was enraged by the warning; she pointed out that she had had swimming lessons in the baths in Dunlaoghaire. Dr Power said that some of the people whose purple bodies he had seen had been swimming in other places for thirty years. Castlebay had a very very strong undertow and he would be a poor man to welcome them to the place if he didn't tell them that. He was solemn and they all fell quiet for a moment. It was enough to make it sink in. Dr Power turned his attention to the golf club then, and the chance of a game with Mr Nolan and whether they should make the boys junior members for the summer and get them lessons from Jimmy the Pro. Mrs Nolan wondered was there a nice hairdresser in the place, since Mrs Power looked so elegant there must be. Nellie and Breeda were in the kitchen having a chat about the dance, the amusements and the pictures.

Caroline stretched and said she felt filthy after the journey, would anyone mind if she changed? She and Hilary dragged cases upstairs and settled into their room. They came down not long after; Caroline had her hair loose now, not tied back behind her neck. It was curly a bit like Fiona Doyle's, but not as luxuriant. She wore a yellow shirt and white shorts. She looked really smashing.

'Will you show me the town of Castlebay?' she asked David.

It would be very nice to be seen with this lovely thing in white shorts and yellow shoes to match her shirt. He would love people to look as he took her for a tour. But it would have been bad manners.

'Sure I will,' he said, deliberately misunderstanding her. 'Let's all get our swimming things and meet here in ten minutes and I'll take the conducted tour to the beach.'

David thought that Caroline was a little put out. Great, he thought, she fancies me.

It *must* have rained some days. There had to be clouds and a wind would definitely have come up at high tide. But none of them remembered it. Hilary said it was the best holiday she ever had in her life and since she and Caroline had a fight the following term and were not best friends any more, it was her first and last time in Castlebay. Mrs Nolan grew stronger and got browner every day; she and Molly Power became firm friends and even took tennis lessons at the hotel in the early mornings when there weren't many people about. It was something they both wished they had done in their youth, but it didn't matter, they were catching up now. Nolan's father stayed for two weeks, then had to go back to work, but he came down every weekend.

They had their lunch outside almost every day and David usually ate with them. On Sundays they came to lunch at the Powers', a proper lunch with roast beef or two chickens, and soup first and pudding afterwards. And when the trippers had to eat oranges or try to boil cups of tea for themselves on the beach, the Powers and the Nolans could just walk up the cliff either to the doctor's house or to Crest View, and Nellie or Breeda would serve a real tea with sandwiches and biscuits and apple tart. It was heaven.

They went for picnics too, and because the Nolans had a primus stove they often cooked sausages which tasted much better in the open air. Mrs Nolan couldn't be told that they fried sausages on their own – she was afraid of conflagrations – but they kept the primus in the Powers' garage so that there was never any fuss.

It was the first summer for a long time that nobody drowned in Castlebay. One child did get into difficulties but Dr Power made him vomit up all the sea water and in an hour the incident was almost forgotten. A woman fell and broke her hip on the path going down to the beach and Dr Power went out in his shirtsleeves and hammered in a board nailed to a stick saying *Very very dangerous path*. The Committee didn't like it at all, and wanted it removed. Dr Power said he was the one who had to pick up the pieces when people got injured and that if anyone removed his sign he would call the Guards. Eventually the Committee arranged a neater sign, properly painted and agreed to spend some money next year in making the path and steps less perilous.

Clare watched it all from the shop. It was like a different

world to her, these carefree people with different clothes every day. Caroline Nolan, who had brown legs and white shorts, must have had seven different-coloured blouses. She was like a rainbow, and her friend Hilary was the same, and they were always laughing and the boys all stood round and laughed too when they were there. There were the Dillon boys from the hotel, and Bernie Conway's brother Frank, and David Power and James Nolan, and of course Gerry Doyle. Normally Gerry didn't join anyone's crowd, but he often seemed to be passing by, or perched on his bike leaning against the wall chatting to them.

They seemed to have endless money too, Clare noticed. Hilary bought ice-creams three or four times a day, and that Caroline thought nothing of buying a bottle of shampoo one day and Nivea Creme the next and three fancy hair slides the day after. Imagine having so much pocket money that you didn't even have to think before you bought things like that.

David Power was the nicest of them all, but then he always had been nice and he was from here. He didn't change because of his new crowd.

'Can you do me a favour?' he asked one day.

'Sure.'

'Nolan and I want to buy some things, but we . . . um don't . . . want to bring them home with us, can we pay for them and leave them here?'

'Do you want them delivered?' she said eagerly. Her father had been right – Mrs Power did not visit the shop any more. This might be the breakthrough.

'Oh heavens, no,' David said. 'You see we don't want them to know at home or at Nolan's, if you know what I mean.'

Clare made up the order for sausages, and bottles of orange and red lemonade, for bread and butter and biscuits. She even suggested tomato ketchup and when David wondered about a cake with hard icing on it, she said she'd put one of their own knives in the bag as well so that they could cut it.

'Is it a picnic in a cave again?' she whispered, eyes round with excitement.

'No, not a cave, down the sandhills,' David whispered.

'Oh great. When will you be collecting the food?'

'That's what I was wondering, could you sort of hide it outside somewhere, where nobody could find it except us? We'll be going about two o'clock in the morning.'

They debated putting it in the doorway behind the big potted palm. But suppose a dog got at it? Or if they put it anywhere too near the shop, Clare's father might think it was burglars coming to rob the place and raise an alarm.

'Is Chrissie going to the picnic?' Clare asked.

'Well yes, yes she is.'

'Then that's fine, I'll tell her it's in the press under the stairs and she can bring it with her.' Clare was satisfied she had sorted it out so well. She took David's money and gave him the change. Also a list of what he had bought so that he knew how the money had been spent.

'I'm sorry that you . . . I mean, I think it would be a bit . . .'

'I'm too young for picnics,' Clare said simply. 'Too young and too boring. In a few years I'll be old enough, I hope.'

David seemed relieved that she was being so philosophical.

'You will, definitely. Definitely,' he said, full of encouragement.

At that moment the floating, flowery prints of Mrs Nolan appeared at the door of O'Brien's.

'Do let's have an ice-cream Molly, in Dublin you couldn't be seen dead licking a fourpenny wafer. So full of *germs*, too. Isn't it marvellous to be here?'

There was no way that Molly could refuse to come in now. Clare acted quickly. 'I'm sorry, we don't have any of those Scots Clan left,' she said to David in a clear voice. 'We'll be getting deliveries this afternoon.' She turned politely to the two ladies. 'Can I get you an ice-cream?' she asked.

'Is it all kept nice and *fresh*?' Mrs Nolan wanted to know.

'Oh yes, indeed. Look inside if you like, but why don't I open a fresh pack just in front of you?'

Mrs Nolan was pleased. David scurried out, unnoticed.

Clare went to the kitchen and got a clean jug of hot water, and a clean sharp knife. She dipped the knife in the water and slit open the carton of ice-cream. She made the indentations on it firmly and cut two fourpenny wafers which she handed over gravely.

'This *is* a nice shop, Molly,' said Mrs Nolan.

'Oh yes, yes indeed,' said Mrs Power uneasily.

'I think it's a better place than where you told us to shop.'

'It's very good, all right,' Molly agreed, looking at the ceiling.

Clare prayed her father wouldn't come in and start fawning. She bade them farewell.

'Nice little girl,' she heard Mrs Nolan say. 'Very undernourished looking, but a bright little thing.'

Chrissie said that Clare had a horrible gloating smirk on her that was terrible to look at, and that Clare would be unbearable now she knew about the picnic in the sandhills.

Clare sighed. She said that David's bag was in the press behind the coats, and there was one knife of theirs as well.

'Did he say whether Caroline and Hilary were coming or not?'

He hadn't, but Clare presumed they would be. Weren't they old enough?

'Oh they're old enough, but Gerry Doyle seemed to think they weren't.'

Chrissie was *hoping* they weren't. Gerry Doyle had too many eyes for Caroline Nolan altogether. She had seen him laughing too much with her – over nothing. She didn't explain this to Clare but Clare seemed to understand somehow.

'They'll all be gone back at the end of the summer, and you'll still be here,' she said comfortingly.

'I know that, stupid,' Chrissie said, examining her face in the mirror. 'That's both good and bad.'

Nolan was very disappointed that Fiona Doyle wasn't in the number that giggled their way up the sandhills in the moonlight. He had decided that Caroline and Hilary could come – thereby making it respectable – and he was very annoyed with Gerry for putting it out of bounds to *his* sister.

'It's not as if there was going to be all that messing like we had in the cave,' he said to Gerry.

'I know, but she's just not going to come with us, not at night. Not in the sandhills.'

'You sound like as if you're talking about a nun, not about Fiona,' James Nolan grumbled.

Gerry gave him a smile that took all the harm out of it. 'Listen, I know what you mean, but Fiona *lives* here, you know. It's not just a holiday night out like it is for your sister, and for Hilary. If you live in a place, it's different. There's places in Dublin you wouldn't want Caroline to go, even though there might be nothing wrong with them in themselves.'

Nolan was impressed.

They had a wind-up gramophone and they had walked so far that nobody, not even the seagulls, could hear it.

They lit the primus and cooked the supper; and David had his arm round Caroline for a while, and Chrissie was snuggling up to Gerry Doyle – but he had to disengage himself a lot to open cans or to see to the stove and turn the sausages. Nolan found himself with Kath, who had improved a lot since last winter, he thought. Nobody paired off and disappeared, but as the light from the primus flickered and died and people didn't bother to wind up the gramophone it became obvious that it had all worked out nice and neatly.

It was Gerry Doyle not Chrissie who decided when the party was over, and with a little laugh managed to get them all on their feet again, blouses being hastily rearranged and a few little giggles here and there. They walked back along the beach which was silvery and magic, stopped chattering when they reached the foot of the steps and then whispered and giggled their way home.

They weren't drunk this time, Kath and Chrissie giggled, but more experienced. Hilary and Caroline raced along the beach in the moonlight, putting their fingers to their lips and giggling. Hilary had been heavily romanced by one of the Dillon boys who had buck teeth but wasn't bad.

James and David walked at a more leisurely pace, James telling David he had put his tongue in Kath's mouth and it had been *horrible*. It was all full of spit. There *must* be some other way of doing it. David nodded with interest and said there must; he didn't reveal that Caroline Nolan's mouth had not been full of spit at all, but had been very nice indeed.

Caroline and Hilary were lying on the cliff top when Gerry passed by the next day.

'You didn't get caught?'

'Not a bit of it. Mummy takes so many sleeping pills she wouldn't know if we had had the picnic in the garden,' Caroline said.

'So does my mother, and pills to keep her awake and pills to calm her down.'

'Like Smarties,' Caroline giggled.

'It was a nice night,' Hilary said.

'Yeah, could have been better though.' Gerry seemed to be looking directly at Caroline.

'Yes. Well,' she said, flustered.

'I came to take your pictures for my wall,' he said,

'Oh we've lots of pictures already, nearly an album,' Caroline said.

'No, I don't mean the ones you bought, these are for me, as souvenirs of the most gorgeous girls to come to Castlebay. Ever.'

They protested. They hadn't the right clothes, no make-up, nothing. He soothed them and they agreed. Hilary first, joking at first, making faces, then posing in silly ways then smiling, then looking straight at the camera. 'You must have a hundred there,' she said.

'At least. Now Caroline.'

There was less joking this time. Caroline seemed to relax immediately. 'I feel very foolish,' she said once. 'This isn't the kind of thing I do.'

'You're not doing anything,' Gerry said. 'You're just being yourself, you're fine. I think you look lovely through this, very nice indeed.'

She basked in his approval and smiled and leaned towards

the camera. Without even realizing that she was doing it she ran her tongue across her lower lip and opened her eyes wider. It seemed quite natural to look at the camera as if hypnotized while Gerry clicked and clicked and talked on naturally too. He spoke about her skin and how it was very soft and tanned and he hoped that somehow by light and shade this would show up on a black and white film. She didn't feel embarrassed at these compliments in front of Hilary, and Hilary didn't giggle or feel embarrassed either. In fact she just wished she had put more into the whole thing the way Caroline was doing, then Gerry Doyle might have said something nice about her skin and her hair too.

He put his camera away.

'That's what I love, taking pictures of beautiful women. That's what I'd love to do all day, not sweating couples at the dance and hopeless family groups on the beach.' His voice sounded bitter. That was unusual for Gerry Doyle who was always so carefree.

'Why don't you do that then? You always seem to do what you want.' Caroline's eyes met his and she was saying more than the actual words.

'I do usually,' he grinned.

It seemed to Angela that more people than ever asked her about Sean that summer. People who had never asked about him before. Mother Immaculata wondered was he going to Rome for the Holy Year, so many fathers from all over the world were going to go to the Holy City. Angela thought he couldn't be spared from the mission fields. Young Mrs Dillon from the hotel told her excitedly that there were two guests who were actually going to Japan in September. Maybe they could take something to Father Sean for her, or go to see him. Angela said that by ill chance she thought September was the very month he had said he would be away touring the Philippines.

Sometimes she surprised herself with the way she could talk about vocations and missions, when she knew all that she did. What was the Lord thinking of all those years ago when he hovered over O'Hara's cottage and picked Sean?

Didn't God *know* what was going to happen in the future? Why did He let Himself be mocked and bring such unhappiness on everyone? She was leaning the bicycle up against the wall of O'Brien's when she realized with a sudden shock that *everyone* had not been made unhappy, in fact very few people had. There was a possibility that only she was unhappy about it all. Her brother was totally content, learning as he said for the first time the meaning of true content. Her sisters Geraldine and Maire were quite content about it too. They sent him letters at Christmas and on his birthday and their children added bits in round unformed writing. And back up in the O'Hara house her mother who was sitting out in a chair watching the people walk up and down to the golf course, saluting and smiling and nodding at everyone who passed, she was happy too. Secure in the knowledge that she had a son a priest, interceding for her directly to God, making ready her place in heaven.

Angela didn't know whether to be pleased or outraged that she was the only one who suffered over Sean's predicament. She should be pleased, she supposed, that it meant that the sum of human misery was less. But the sheer *unfairness* of it all seemed huge when you began to think of it like that. Mouth set hard she marched in, and saw young Clare working away. Her face wasn't tanned golden like the girls who sat on the wall up in Cliff Road. She didn't wear a bright pink blouse that would have given her life and definition. Instead she looked shabby and wan, in a dress with faded yellow and pink flowers that must have been Chrissie's. She was furrowed with concentration, getting somebody change.

'I'm quite quick at change usually,' Angela heard her telling the woman. 'But when the shop is crowded and we are all at the drawer of money together it's easy to get flustered, that's why I'm being a bit slow.'

The woman smiled at the earnest child who didn't even have time to see Angela at the other side of the shop. Mrs O'Brien asked about Angela's mother, whether the weather was good for her bones, if there was any word of Geraldine or Maire coming home this summer, and how soon would his Reverence be back – wasn't it a pity he hadn't been able to come this year, he could have gone to Rome for the Holy Year. The Dillons were going to go there in October when the season was well over. Imagine going to Rome and being able to see the Holy Father. There had been talk of making a collection to send Father O'Dwyer, but nothing had come of it, the idea had come too late and everyone was working so hard now there'd be little time for meeting about it. Angela responded with a series of automatic grunts and replies. Often she felt that if you had been born dumb and never known the gift of speech you could converse quite happily with most of Castlebay. All you had to do was to listen and nod and smile and shake your head and make a sound. She knew she was right when she was packing her shopping in the basket of her bicycle and she overheard Mrs O'Brien saying to Miss O'Flaherty that Angela O'Hara was a very nice girl and it was no wonder the children were all mad about her. Angela smiled with pleasure at this and was only slightly taken down when Miss O'Flaherty's complaining tone which saw very little right with the world said that was all very fine but when was Angela O'Hara going to get a husband for herself.

That was indeed the question, Angela said to herself wryly. Suppose, just suppose she did herself up and went to the dance and found a nice fellow here for the summer holidays, he'd live in Dublin or Cork or Limerick, or Dagenham like the fellow she met three years ago did. What then? There was no point in thinking about it. If she had stayed with her mother this long she was going to have to stay the distance. There was a time five years ago when she might have left, but she couldn't leave now. She couldn't trust her brother not to blow the whole thing apart. Miss O'Flaherty, who was in a poor position to throw stones, would have to wait a long time before she saw Angela O'Hara getting a husband for herself.

Weeks later she met Dr Power. He slowed down his car to drive beside her along the golf-course road.

'I was thinking of dropping in to have a look at your mother.'

'Do that but for God's sake let me get in five minutes before you and put a clean blouse on her otherwise she'll be complaining all night that you saw her shabby.'

'I have to go up and see someone in the club first. I'll call on my way back.'

Wouldn't *he* be a lovely person to be married to, Angela thought. Old as the hills of course, but so calm and kind. That fusspot towny wife of his was very lucky; Angela wondered did she know how lucky she was or did she sit there restlessly examining her rings and her lightly painted nails and wish for a life of more sophistication. Was she grateful for that bright son of hers, did she love the big white house that looked straight out to sea on two sides and was she pleased every morning when she woke up to hear Nellie cleaning out the fires and making the breakfast? Nice laughing Nellie Burke who had wanted to be a fiim star when they were at school. Dr Power wasn't a saint exactly. Sometimes he was bad-tempered and impatient with people, But he was very kind and Mr Murphy in the chemist said that you'd travel far to find such a good doctor. If he was above in Dublin with a brass plate on the door of somewhere in Fitzwilliam Square he would be called a consultant physician and people would pay him a fortune. Angela hoped that Mrs Molly Power was never given this piece of information, for deep down Paddy Power was like herself, he wouldn't leave. He had been born on a big farm outside Castlebay and it had been his life since he could remember. He wasn't going to any square for any plaque on his door or any fees in his bank account.

She smartened her mother up, giving her a quick wash and a dusting of talcum powder. A clean slip in case Dr Power decided to feel her poor knee joints, and clean stockings of course.

She looked well when she was smartened up, Angela thought, the fine handsome face of Father Sean O'Hara got its good cheekbones from the mother's side, and her hair was curly and soft. Everyone looked a bit better when they were smartened up, Angela said to herself firmly, and changed her own dress and put on a little lipstick.

'Now we're like two tarts on a night out,' she said to her mother.

Mrs O'Hara looked round the room nervously in case anyone might have heard. 'You say terribly stupid things sometimes, I'm sure people get the wrong idea of you.'

'I bet they do, mother dear,' Angela said, as the doctor arrived.

It had been some visitor who played too much golf, no exercise at all, at home fifty weeks of the year, and then thirty-six holes of golf over a hilly course here, five days in succession. No wonder he had collapsed. There should be Danger notices on the golf course as well as on the beach.

'Will he be all right?' Angela asked.

'Oh, the worst he has to recover from is all the abuse from me. He'll be fine. I might have done him a good turn even, warned him about his way of life. He may live to a hundred and thank me every day. Enough about him, how are you, Mrs O'Hara?'

Angela watched him as he felt the swollen joints of her mother's legs. And then he took the twisted lumpy hands in his own.

'It hasn't got much worse to the outside eye,' he said cheerfully, 'but I know that's not much help inside where it's all aches and pains.' He made it easy for them to complain a bit; Dr Power's patients didn't have to bite back their fears and their telling the tale of their illness. He had all the time in the world.

She walked him back to the car.

'Mind you, I think you put on a clean blouse and a clean face for me yourself,' he said, teasing her. 'Did you want to consult me too?'

'No, I'm fine,' she laughed.

'If you were fine you'd sleep at night,' he said.

'I nearly do now. I only take half one, not a whole tablet like I did in the beginning.'

'Is it any better whatever it is that's worrying you?' He

was on one side of his car. She leaned over with her elbows on the roof of the car.

'It is a bit better, I suppose. It hasn't gone away but I've got used to it.'

'It's not any kind of sickness or health worry. You needn't tell me: I could tell you the name of a very nice doctor, someone strange to you?'

'No. It's not that, thank you all the same.'

'And if it's a man, we're not worth it. Not one of us is worth a woman staying awake one hour over us.'

'Stop fishing.' She laughed. 'You're fishing for information, *and* for compliments, half the town is sleepless over you Dr Power. I was only thinking that this evening in the house there, wasn't it an awful pity I wasn't around ten years earlier and I might have caught you.'

'Oh, you'd have had to be around long before that, I'm an old dog. A dull old dog.'

He got into the car and wound down the window. 'If you find a fellow you want to go off with, go now. Do you hear me, don't be thinking you have to grow old in that house there. I'll sort your mother out, I'll see she gets looked after. You live your life.'

'No, it's not that, honestly.' She smiled at him affectionately.

'Or a nun or anything,' he said suddenly.

'Oh it's *definitely* not that.' She pealed with laughter.

'No, well I suppose one in the family's enough,' he said and he was gone.

One was more than enough, Angela thought as she went back into the house.

Gerry Doyle had taken two smashing photographs during the summer. One was of David and Caroline playing with a beach ball and the big waves rolling in behind them. David thought it looked great, like an advertisement for Come to Sunny Somewhere, like you saw for English seaside resorts. The other picture was of Nolan sitting eating an ice-cream on the wall outside O'Brien's shop. He was surrounded by girls: Hilary was sitting on one side, and Gerry's own sister

Fiona on the other, and at his feet sat Chrissie O'Brien and her two henchwomen Kath and Peggy. He looked like a sultan, tanned and powerful and surrounded by women, all he needed was the headgear. These pictures did Nolan and Power a great deal of good at school. In fact David began to wonder if half the pupils and their parents might turn up there next summer. The Seal Cave had become a legend for night adventures, the sand dunes for even more excitement, Brigid's Cave where you shouted a question and the echo answered. The tennis in the hotel and up on high stools at the bar afterwards for a lemonade, the lessons up at the golf club and the junior tournaments. Not only did they have the stories, they had the proof in these photographs. David kept the picture of Caroline under a piece of paper in the back of his atlas. It was awkward being in love with your friend's sister because you couldn't talk to him about it freely. You couldn't say that you had kissed her at the pictures and she hadn't asked you to stop. He couldn't tell Nolan that he had kissed Caroline in the sea and in the Echo Cave. He did tell Nolan that Caroline was going to write to him at school and call herself Charles, but Nolan was only mildly interested. Fiona Doyle, Gerry's sister, was going to write to Nolan calling herself Fred and Hilary was going to sign herself Henry. If Chrissie O'Brien could write she would probably have written too and signed herself Christopher, but it was deeply suspected however, that Chrissie was illiterate and so the question didn't arise. David Power and James Nolan decided that since she had Gerry Doyle right there in Castlebay she would be too occupied even to consider writing to people in boarding school. Gerry Doyle seemed to win all the girls without ever making the slightest effort.

They didn't know that Chrissie was growing more sure every day that Gerry Doyle didn't fancy her as much as he had at one time. She discussed it at length with Kath and Peggy, but they reached no conclusion. She had gone as far as she could go without going the whole way, or without even doing things that would embarrass them seriously in the broad daylight when they remembered it. What else were you supposed to do? Her spots had gone, her hair had got blonder, and, thanks to the pipe cleaners, was much curlier. She had a big bust and a tight red belt around her waist. She never plagued Gerry or bothered him or asked him to go steady. And still he seemed to have gone off her. It was a mystery. Kath and Peggy agreed, all fellows were a mystery.

'We must take up photography seriously, it seems to make you very popular,' Nolan suggested to David one day.

'I've a feeling it's more than that,' David said. He liked Gerry but he wished that Caroline didn't think he was so great. It was irritating to be in the middle of saying something to her and then to see her face light up and her hand go up waving. He knew that could only mean Gerry Doyle had been spotted again. And Gerry would just wave back with a friendly smile, he never came panting up eagerly like Bones did, shaking with enthusiasm and pleasure to be noticed. Less like Bones, more like Gerry Doyle, that seemed to be the motto as far as success with women was concerned.

Success at school was easier. David came first in the class at the Christmas tests and Nolan came second. Nolan hated being second and the following Easter it was Nolan first and Power second. They made a pact not to work hard during the summer term and to spend all the time getting really good at tennis. Tennis was about the only game that Gerry Doyle didn't play and excel at. And that's because it was the only one he hadn't tried.

Chrissie said she wanted to leave school and learn something useful. Like what, they had asked her. She shrugged, anything, anything except boring school lessons. Nobody knew how time was wasted up in that convent she assured them, the nuns had no control and the children just sat there doing nothing all day. It was pointed out that Clare seemed to get on all right, but Chrissie said that proved nothing, Clare was distinctly odd, she had no friends, she was driven to study her books out of sheer despair that the rest of her life was so awful. This line of argument did not go down as well as Chrissie had hoped, there was no question of her leaving school at fourteen she was told, she would stay on another year and·mind her manners too. Anyway it was wrong to say Clare hadn't a friend, hadn't she Josie Dillon?

Miss O'Hara had been very pleased with Clare's work over the months, she said that by any standards she would have to win the scholarship. She'd nearly get it this year while she was eleven, so next year she should have no problems at all.

'Sometimes I feel guilty teaching you, Clare,' Miss O'Hara had said one evening. 'You are able to read on your own now, and you actually enjoy it, all I'm really doing is sitting here praising you.'

'You won't stop?' Clare was terrified.

'No, of course not, I just meant that people like Josie Dillon or the young Murphy girl might benefit more, at least they might leave school knowing how to read. That would be nice for them.'

'Josie *can* read,' Clare said. 'Of course she can.'

'But she doesn't, does she? I can't ask her to read aloud from the history book in class or the English book, she can't take any part in the plays we read aloud or we'd be all day and all night in the classroom. You know that.'

'She's not very interested, that's all.'

'What *is* she interested in? Her sisters were all right you know, not genius standard but reasonable. Josie'll never get a chance to go away to school like they did, it just won't be worth it.'

'Yes, she knows that.'

'Is it settled? I was only guessing. Does she mind?'

'No, I think she's quite glad, you know she doesn't really want to leave home, she's nervous, she doesn't want things to change.'

'You should give her a hand if you're a friend of hers, why don't you help her to get on a bit? And it would be good practice for you too.'

'Practice for what?'

'Practice for being a teacher. Hey, have you forgotten that's what all this is about? We're making a teacher out of you, Clare O'Brien.'

'Oh yes, yes of course.'

She hadn't realized that this is what Miss O'Hara saw as the end of the road. Being a teacher in a convent, either here in Castlebay and cycling home every afternoon, or somewhere else somewhere like this. She didn't know that Clare wanted to see the world, she wanted to be an ambassador or the head of a big company or an interpreter, not just a teacher. But of course it would be very tactless to say anything like that. It would be saying that Miss O'Hara hadn't done well enough for herself.

'So? Are you going to give her a bit of help? Not doing it *for* her, you know, explaining it a bit.'

'She'd wonder what was the point.'

'Well if she likes staying here, why not tell her that she should work hard enough to get herself into some kind of commercial college, then she could learn book keeping and typing and shorthand and she could work in the office of the hotel when that old dragon of a grandmother of hers dies and lets any of them into the office.'

Clare was never so happy as when she was allowed in on grown-up viciousness like this. It made her feel very important. 'I'll see what I can do,' she said.

'It's better coming from you,' Miss O'Hara said. 'Most people think that any advice given by a teacher is bound to work out to their doom in the end.'

Josie had her twelfth birthday when all her sisters and brothers were away at school. Her mother, who was always called Young Mrs Dillon, said that they should put off the celebrations until the rest of the family came home on their holidays. Surprisingly Josie didn't agree, that's what had been said when she was ten and when she was eleven she said, it was not happening this year. This year she would like to invite Clare O'Brien to tea and then for them both to go to the pictures.

The pictures! At night, and during the week. It was unheard of.

Clare O'Brien said that her mother said it would be all right if Josie's mother said it was all right. Young Mrs Dillon looked at the large pasty face of her youngest daughter and was moved. It would be all right, she said. At least from what she could see the young Clare wasn't as much of a tinker as her sister Chrissie was, and perhaps it was good that poor Josie should have some friend even if it was a child from a huckster's shop.

While they were waiting for the picture to start Clare told Josie that she was so lucky to have a bedroom of her own and that was something Clare would like almost more than anything in the world.

'It's all right for you,' Josie said. 'You *like* studying.'

'I don't really *like* it, nobody could like learning things off by heart and nobody could like long division and fractions and problems. I just do them so that I'll get what I want afterwards.'

'What do you want?' Josie looked at her with a dull face.

Clare wondered whether to risk it. 'Well, I sort of hoped that since we don't have any money or anything, not for secondary school, I wondered if I worked hard maybe they'd take me on free like, to encourage other people to work hard.'

'Who would?'

'Some secondary school.'

'I don't see why not, they should be glad to have hard-working people like you instead of lazy people who pay.'

Clare was heartened. 'So that's why I do it, you should too.'

'But we have money to send me to a school, there's no point. I don't want to go to one.'

'What *do* you want to do?'

'Stay here.'

'In the hotel?'

'Of course, where else would I go?'

'But you'd better learn to do something Josie, otherwise you'll be making beds and serving on tables there. The boys will all serve the time as hoteliers, won't they?'

'I suppose so.' Josie had never thought about it.

'And Rose and Emily, they'll do something I bet like a hotel management course or something.'

'Yes, well they might.'

'So to make sure they don't push you out of it, *you* should do something.'

'What could I do, Clare?' Josie looked at her pathetically.

Clare didn't want to come up with a solution too quickly. 'You could get trained for something they haven't done, so that you'd always be needed.'

'Like what?'

'Well suppose you did a commercial course, would you have anyone to stay with in the town so that you could live with them and come back home at weekends?' She knew that the Dillons had at least three sets of cousins in the town.

Josie remembered that slowly too. Yes, it was possible. 'But I'd be all on my own there.'

'Isn't it attached to the convent, the secondary school?'

It turned out that it was, and after all if Clare's plans went right she would be in the secondary school herself. They could barely concentrate on the film when it came on, real-life plans were more exciting.

'They'd only laugh at me. I'm no good at spelling and everything, I'd never learn all that stuff.'

'I could give you a hand if you like.'

'Why would you do that?' Josie was almost ungracious in her disbelief.

'Because you're my friend,' said Clare awkwardly, and Josie smiled from ear to ear.

It began then: the working in Dillon's Hotel rather than at home. It was much easier, and nobody seemed to mind. Clare wasn't one to be up to any devilment, not like Chrissie. If you passed the hotel you could even see the two of them working at an upper window with their books out. Clare helped her with the spellings first and Josie thought that it was a marvellous coincidence that Miss O'Hara announced a spelling bee at the very same time. The handwriting became neater, the exercise books were clean and orderly, and Josie even stooped less and seemed more alert. She once asked a question in class and Mother Brendan had nearly fainted. Clare frowned across at Josie, they had agreed the improvement must be gradual, and that she mustn't look so smart that they would decide to send her off to her boarding school and spoil everything.

The nuns had a rule that they never walked anywhere outside the convent alone, so it was common practice for a nun to ask a lay teacher or an older girl to accompany her to the post office, to Miss O'Flaherty's stationery shop or whatever errand it was. So Angela was not surprised when Mother Immaculata asked if she would accompany her down the town.

Together they walked out the convent gates and down the hill. It was never easy to find idle chat for Mother Immaculata at the best of times, and this was not the best of times for Angela. She had slept very badly despite the half pill taken with warm milk. She had a letter from Emer in Dublin with the great news for Emer that the engagement ring was being bought on the following Saturday. She wanted to know if Angela would come to Dublin and be her bridesmaid. Angela's mother had been very very stiff this morning and dressing her had been like bending painful wood to pull on stockings and to twist aching arms into garments. The children's voices had been shrill all morning, a child had been sick during religious instruction in First Year and despite open windows and Dettol the smell seemed to permeate the school. Now when she had been hoping for a cigarette and a look at the paper she had to waltz this ridiculous nun down town to buy a post card or whatever it was she wanted.

'Why don't they allow you out on your own, Mother? I'm delighted to accompany you of course, but I've often wondered.'

'It's part of our Rule,' Immaculata said smugly. Angela felt like punching her in the face.

'Are they afraid you'll make a run for it?' she asked.

'*Hardly*, Miss O'Hara.'

'Well there must be some reason but I suppose we'll never know.'

'We rarely question the Rule.'

'No, I suppose you don't, that's where you have my wholehearted admiration. I'd question it from morning to night.'

The nun gave a tinny little laugh. 'Oh, I'm sure you would, Miss O'Hara.'

Angela wondered again how old she was – possibly only ten years older than herself. This white-faced, superior woman was quite likely to be below forty. Wasn't it extraordinary. The children probably thought she was ninety, but on the other hand the children thought every teacher was ninety, so that was no guideline.

'I wanted to talk to you actually – that's why I seized this opportunity.'

'Oh yes?' Angela was wary. What was so urgent it couldn't be discussed within the confines of school? Could Immaculata possibly have heard Angela talking about the stink of the school being quite bad enough without having the children puking all over the place?

'It's about your brother, Father O'Hara.'

Hot bile in her throat and a feeling like a hen's wing of feathers in her chest.

'Oh yes?' She said it again, willing her face to look normal, reminding herself that this stupid, mannered nun paused for effect after every single phrase she uttered. There was nothing sinister in the way she waited.

'There's a sort of mystery, you see,' Mother Immaculata said.

'Mystery, Mother?' Angela played the game by the rules: the more quickly she spoke the quicker would be the response.

'Yes. I was wondering is he . . . well is he all right, you know? If everything is all right.'

'Well I sincerely hope so. It was when I last heard. How do you mean?' Angela could hear her own voice speaking briskly and marvelled at it. How great of it to come out with just the right responses when her brain had frozen solid and seemed to be unable to control it.

'You see there's this sister in our Community, she is not in this house but she was staying with us last year. You may not have met her – she was hardly ever in the school, she was mainly in the nuns' quarters. It was more or less a holiday that brought her to us.'

Angela kept a bright interested face in the monologue and swallowed the cry urging the nun to get on with it.

'And Sister has a brother who is in a seminary and he is about to go to their foundation house, and he hopes to go to the foreign missions, and you see this is why Sister came to me.'

She paused. The smile from Miss O'Hara was as polite as that of any child who thought that favours were to be bought by courtesy.

'And Sister is in this predicament, because alas her family, far from being delighted that a second child had been called by God are standing in this boy's way. They say they want to know what kind of life it is out there and can they talk to any of the priests who have come back from the missions so that they can know what their son will be doing in his new life.' Mother Immaculata paused to tinkle an unsatisfactory little laugh. 'As if any of us could know what our lives in Religion were going to be like.'

Angela swallowed and nodded.

'So I told Sister about our Father O'Hara here from Castlebay, and I gave her the address. And Sister got this very strange letter back from him. Very strange.'

'She was writing so that he could tell her parents about the daily life out there, was that it?' Surprisingly strong and unfussed.

'Yes indeed, and Sister says that *her* letter was very clear, which I am sure it was, because she does express herself very well. Of course it's not easy to explain to an ordained priest that your family is not totally committed to the vocation of your brother, but I told Sister that she could write in freedom on that score. I told her that although I wasn't here at the time, I felt that Father O'Hara's own path to the ordination was not entirely spread with roses, that he had his own difficulties.' She smiled at Angela.

Bitch, Angela thought with a ferocity that frightened her, she told this blithering Sister all about drunken Dinny O'Hara and his outbursts.

'No indeed,' said the voice of Angela O'Hara, 'far from being spread with roses I can tell you.'

'Anyway, Sister had this very strange letter.'

'He couldn't help her?'

'Not that exactly, he *did* give a very detailed account of the daily life, and how they had to regroup after the expulsion from China, and he wrote about Christianity in Formosa and in Macao and the Philippines, and of how they hope local people will train as priests and help in all this work.'

'So?'

'But it was strange, two things were strange, he said nothing at all about Japan, where he is himself, he said nothing of the work that the Foundation does there, and he also said . . . I think these were his very words, "I feel sure my sister will have told the community of some of my own problems here, so I am hardly the man to write to your parents on your brother's behalf." That was more or less it. I think those were his exact words.'

Oh, Angela thought, we can be sure those were his exact words. Immaculata, you must have them by heart now and the rest of the letter, but there's no mileage in quoting the bits that don't sound strange, that don't sound as if there might be the trace of scandal or trouble in them. No no, don't learn by heart and remember his words where he was helpful to this garrulous fool of a nun and her indecisive brother. Just the bit that might yield some gossip.

'Well well, what could he mean?'

'That's what we wondered, Miss O'Hara?'

'Oh, does Sister's family want him to explain himself more?' She was just within the bounds of manners but only just.

'Of course not, it's just that it's worrying.'

'What is?'

'The problems he has, his own problems, that he told you about that he expected you had told the community about. All that. And why he is hardly the man to help in this matter.'

'Because he's such a rotten letter writer.' Angela was amazed that Mother Immaculata didn't see it too.

'But the rest of his letter was very clear.'

'That's it, he can be marvellous describing the climate and the soil, I told him we should have him in the geography class. But he's useless about describing what he feels, and thinks. I think it's not just him, really. I believe that all men are hopeless at telling you what you want to know. My mother and I are always criticizing him for not giving us his feelings about it all . . .'

'But there must be more to it.'

'Exactly, Mother, that's what I always say, and what Mam says. There *must* be more to it. What's it like when he finishes a day in Tokyo, does he walk home through the crowded streets and look at the people's faces and think that he and the other fathers made progress today, that the Lord's word was spread among the people? Do the young Japanese children understand what it was like in Bethlehem, it's hard enough for us but what about them?' Angela was burning with indignation at this brother of hers who couldn't describe the everyday business of being a missionary to everyone's satisfaction.

In the end Immaculata gave up. They were at the top of Church Street.

'Where did you want to go?' Angela asked innocently.

'Nowhere.' Immaculata's mouth snapped like a mouse-trap. 'I just wanted to talk to you about all this.'

Angela was sunny-tempered about it. 'Well never mind Mother, I wanted to get some cigs anyway so you can accompany me into a shop for them. I'd go down to the end of the street to O'Brien's to give them the turn, but we might be late for class.'

She smiled like an angel, wrapped the scarf round her neck flamboyantly and went into a shop which was half a pub and stank of stout, so that Immaculata had to hover in a fury at the door.

She wrote to him that night as she had never been able to write before. She said that he had broken the agreement and broken it shabbily. How else might he have done this in ways that she didn't know? Must she live a tormented life wondering where would be the next weak link, the next confession of something wrong, something irregular? She said that she would prefer that he came home and asked Father O'Dwyer to allow him to announce it from the altar rails, rather than have any more of this. They had been through it a dozen times by letter and reluctantly he had agreed; now he was going behind their backs and allowing the worst, the most powerful thing that a place like Castlebay could ever know to run riot. Rumour, speculation, suspicion. She must have his word that this would happen no more. Why couldn't he have ended his letter to the mad nun where any normal person would have ended it? What was the need for this confused breast-beating, and to a community of nuns of all people on the face of the earth?

She added that she *knew* it must be hard, she did realize that. She knew he was trying to keep faith with people and she had managed to stop silver paper and sales of work for him, saying that the money was coming in different ways from the mother house. She really and truly *did* know that he was so transparently honest and generous that he hated hypocrisy, but surely he must know how everyone's hearts would crack in two if any of this were known. Since he must remember his home town it was only fair that he should keep faith with it and not hurt the people he claimed to love so much.

She put extra stamps on it, and for the first time she left out the word 'Father' on the envelope. She laughed at her silliness when she was buying the stamp from Mrs Conway.

'Heavens above, I forgot to put Father. Still I'll leave it rather than write it in a different ink. It's so hard to remember when it's your own brother.'

It was the right line to take. Mrs Conway laughed too, and said imagine what it must be like being the Pope's sister, you'd probably forget to call him Your Holiness as well. Mrs Conway wondered when he'd be home and Angela said that she hoped soon.

She got a letter from him three weeks later. He had read what she said but none of it was important now. He had wonderful news. He had sent all the details of his situation to Rome, and he and Shuya were going to go to Rome themselves, together with Denis and little Laki, who was such a beautiful girl and so like her mother. They were all going to Rome.

He was going to plead his case; there was every belief that he would be heard favourably, that he would be released from his vows, that he would be laicized. Then everything would be perfect. He could come home to Castlebay and bring his family.

The mills of Rome grind slowly. Another summer came and went and Angela learned to sleep at night without the tablets. Sometimes during that summer she took herself with a book out far to the rocks, but she rarely read. She stared at the sea.

At the beginning of term Fiona Doyle shyly presented her with an envelope: it was a picture of Angela, sitting on a rock looking at the sea. Taken completely unawares.

'Gerry's very pleased with it, he says it's a bit artistic,' Fiona said.

'Tell him it's very artistic and I'm very grateful, I'll put it on my wall at home,' Angela said. She looked at it again; it looked like a picture to illustrate The Lonely or The Mad or The Outcast.

That was the summer when Father O'Dwyer went out on a sick call one night and unfortunately passed a lot of parked cars on the Far Cliff Road over the other side of town. He was surprised to notice that there seemed to be people in all of them. Precisely two people, one male and one female. Father O'Dwyer was horrified by what he saw, and he wished he could think it had only been the trippers, the people from big towns whose morals might already have been in danger, but there was ample evidence to convince him that some of his own flock might have been involved.

At the beginning of September when the visitors had gone home he preached his horror and warnings and his threats about what would happen if any of this was noticed in winter time. Parents and guardians were urged to be for ever vigilant, young people were teetering on the edge of an abyss, and alas the world we lived in had lowered its standards and debased its values. Next year there might be a radical change in the leisure pursuits, the whole ethos of the Dance would have to be looked at again. Father O'Dwyer was purple in the face about it for three weeks and his housekeeper the Sergeant McCormack went round with her mouth in a thin line of disapproval that His Reverence should have been vexed so severely.

That was the summer when Josie Dillon and Clare O'Brien learned to play tennis at the hotel. They used to go to the courts early in the morning when Mrs Power and Mrs Nolan were having lessons; they would act as ball boys, and then afterwards because of their help and because Josie was a daughter of the house they got a short lesson as well. Chrissie was disgusted with this, especially since she and Kath and Peggy had been asked formally by Young Mrs Dillon not to come into the bar again. Barred from the hotel at the age of fourteen. It was so unfair, and there was goody goody Clare who was only eleven and the awful white slug Josie playing tennis as if they were somebodies. Clare had a pair of white shorts that Miss O'Hara had found at home, and she unearthed an old pair of Ned's games shoes which she whitened up every night. Josie had got her an old racquet from the hotel, and with her white school blouse she was the equal of any of them. Angela saw her one morning as she ran earnestly up to the net to return a difficult shot and she paused, pleased that she had bought the child a pair of shorts in the Misses Duffy's shop. Angela had washed them once or twice and turned up the hem on the legs in order that Clare wouldn't think they were new. It was well worth it to see the child looking so confident, and was it her imagination or had Josie Dillon lost some weight? Certainly she was able to move around the court better than Angela would have expected.

That was the summer when David Power seemed very disconsolate. Angela had met him once or twice on his own, mooching around hands in pockets. Nolan was with Fiona Doyle morning noon and night, and Nolan's sister? Oh she seemed to have developed an interest in photography. Ha

Ha. David laughed bitterly at the poor joke and the poorer situation. Maybe they could all have a double wedding, you saw that sometimes, didn't you, brother and sister marrying sister and brother. Angela said you didn't see it all that much actually; and that the Doyles were like summer lightning; they were different to everyone else. They weren't *real* like everyone else, they didn't get involved in anything, they just floated around on the outside. David didn't understand, the Doyles had got pretty involved with the Nolans as far as he could see. No, Angela insisted, Fiona just goes her way and James follows along carrying the milk can, carrying the shopping, paying for the bumpers rides or whatever. Gerry goes around the beach with the camera, and Caroline trots behind him. Their father Johnny Doyle was the same years ago, everyone was fascinated with him, he was like a gypsy. David said he didn't think Angela understood, Angela said she was willing to have a bet with him, but it was unfair to take money off minors.

That was the summer Tommy and Ned O'Brien stopped sending home money from England. Mrs Conway noticed of course, almost before Agnes and Tom O'Brien did.

'Not helping out are they nowadays?' she asked with a show of great concern.

'Oh, we told them to keep that, they had to set themselves up a bit better over there, give themselves a bit of comfort, a start you know,' said Agnes O'Brien with a big smile that didn't manage to cover the hurt and worry.

It was also the summer when Angela got a letter from her friend Emer every week. Emer would just about forgive Angela for saying that she was too old to be a bridesmaid at the age of twenty-nine, she would overlook the insensitivity that was involved. After all didn't that make Emer a little bit old to be a bride at thirty? But what Emer would not forgive, or even countenance, was for Angela not to be at the wedding. They would be getting married next Easter; since Kevin and she were both teachers this was a very suitable time for them. The problem was that everyone seemed to be taking over the wedding on them. Emer's mother hadn't spoken to her for four weeks, her two married sisters were in and out of the house at all hours with advice that nobody wanted. Her father had said more than once in Kevin's hearing that he wasn't going to finance a great extravagant do for a third time. He had thought that all that was behind him now and since Emer wasn't exactly in the first flush of youth, he had thought it should be done quietly. Kevin's family were all religious maniacs; there were old nuns who were getting permission to leave convents for the ceremony, and war to the knife among various priestly cousins as to who was going to do the marrying. Emer said it was like a three-ring circus with a Greek tragedy going on in the wings. Angela was to miss it at her peril.

The letters were light relief compared to everything else. Angela said that she would be there, of course. Nothing would stop her. She had to force herself to remember that these were indeed all real disasters and crises for Emer; the letters were so funny and full of ridicule they hid the hurt and the humiliation. Well so did Angela's own letters, perhaps. Wry accounts of life in a one-horse town with the demon Immaculata and the horrific Mrs Conway of the post offfice. Not a word about what it felt like to be trapped here for ever with the shadow of a mad brother – who had left the priesthood, taken up with a Japanese woman and produced two children – hovering on the horizon.

Dunne was to be Head Boy in their last year. David and James had agreed not to compete for the honour because they had been too busy keeping up their postal romances and working for their exams. They explained this to Dunne at the beginning of term so that he wouldn't get any notions about himself. Dunne however had become very authoritarian. He said they were talking nonsense and the Community wouldn't have dreamed of appointing either Nolan or Power to any position of trust since they were both unreliable and dishonest, and were known to carry on illicit relationships with the opposite sex. Nolan said that Dunne was showing all the signs of becoming a roaring homosexual. People who got all steamed up and purple in the face over other people's relationships, illicit or licit with the opposite sex, were queers, and that was widely known. David said that he heard Dunne had been called Daisy as a child and maybe they should revive the name. Dunne waged a war on them and saw to it that their every activity was monitored, their letters scrutinized, and even if they were going for a quick cigarette they were sure to be caught and reported.

In a way it was no harm, it gave them time to study, for what else was there to do? And for Nolan it was particularly helpful because it took his mind off the faithlessness of Fiona. David was mightily pleased to hear that Caroline was suffering the same kind of deprivation at her school. She had been expecting to hear from Gerry Doyle but a similar lack of communication seemed to be occurring there also. Nolan said that Caroline had been pretty annoyed when they had been home at half term. He had been in a very poor temper indeed on his return; he had telephoned the Doyles in Castlebay and spoken to Gerry. When he had asked to speak to Fiona, he was told that she was studying. Where? Upstairs. Well could she come downstairs? No, not during term time, she had to work. As cool as a cucumber. The rat, and not a word about Caroline either, Nolan had mentioned that she was home for half term, and Gerry Doyle had just said that was nice.

A few weeks later David got a letter signed Charles. The letter in its heavy code seemed to be saying that she was sorry the summer had been a bit complicated and she saw things more clearly now. He read it several times and the message definitely was one of reconciliation. He wrote back a short letter, saying he was too busy to get into correspondence at the moment, with the Leaving and Matric coming up, but he looked forward to seeing her next summer. A distant letter, and he signed himself David not Deirdre, just so that she'd get into trouble in her convent. She needed a little punishment for all she had done to him.

Gerry and Fiona Doyle's father was taken off to hospital in the town, and it became known that he would not come back. For a while there was a lot of talk that Mrs Doyle didn't go in to see him like you'd think she would have done. Then Dr Power let it be known that the poor woman had a kind of temporary condition, something to do with blood pressure, which meant that she found it very oppressive to go out of the house at all. Dr Power also suggested that poor Johnny Doyle was better not to be troubled with too many visitors since he found it hard to speak. Gerry drove his father's van everywhere now, and acted as an unoffficial taxi service for anyone wanting to go into the town. The nurses said Gerry was an extraordinary visitor. He calmed not only his father but the three other men in the ward.

The screens were put around while Johnny Doyle hissed with what was left of his voice that Gerry mustn't expand, he must listen to nobody telling him that Castlebay was a boom town, there was a living, a small living, nothing more. It wasn't something like a dance hall or a hotel or even like an ice-cream shop that you could make bigger. There were just so many people and so many snaps of themselves they would buy. Gerry agreed, he nodded, he promised.

The old man died more peacefully because Gerry was there easing away his worries. Gerry told him that the business was doing fine, which it was, that Gerry would never expand it, which he would, and that Mam was getting much better, which she was not. Her agoraphobia was so bad now that she didn't even go to answer the door. Gerry had eased her guilt about not going to see her husband by saying that Dad was too tired to talk. He only took Fiona three times because it was too distressing.

Gerry was there when they closed his father's eyes. He didn't cry, he asked the nun was it always as peaceful as this, and the nun said no, Mr Doyle had been lucky, he had died with few worries, his son was reliable, his wife was cured and his business was in good hands. Not everyone had such peace at the end.

One of the old men in the ward asked Gerry Doyle to come and see them even though his father was gone. Gerry said he would come every week or so, but not regularly because he didn't want the men waiting on him. One of the young nurses who thought that Gerry Doyle was an extraordinarily attractive young fellow told him that he was quite right, and she congratulated him even more when another old man wanted to know if Gerry would take his picture. Gerry looked at the wasted face and the thin neck coming up out of the pyjamas and decided against it, but he explained that it was very hard to take pictures indoors with these white walls and he would wait till the weather was better. The weather became better but there were no old men left to take pictures of.

Gerry put all his efforts into his work, his mother got a bit better sometimes and at other times she got worse. He never let Fiona come home from the pictures in the dark by herself, and he helped her to do the housework, especially cleaning the windows and polishing the brass knocker on the door so that the place looked well on the outside. Since nobody much came in, the inside wasn't so important.

But if you saw Fiona Doyle with her shiny ringlets and her well ironed dresses, or Gerry Doyle with his elfin smile and easy ways, you would never know that there was a thing wrong in that house; or that their father had died from cancer, their mother was in the grip of her nerves and that the bank manager had offered to give them a big loan to expand the business. Gerry told his mother that Dad had told him to go ahead with any plans and his mother fretted and worried about that, but since she worried about everything it didn't make any difference to him.

Fiona must have understood that her father's wishes did not include any kind of expanding, but she said nothing. She was quiet and smiled gently but said very little. That's the way Gerry thought it was best to be for a girl. Otherwise you got your name up with people and you got talked about, and people misunderstood. He didn't want any of that for Fiona.

The letter from Sean had an Italian stamp. He had been five weeks in Rome, he said, and had wanted to get settled in before he wrote. Things were progressing but very slowly. He had no idea that there would be such an endless form-filling and waiting about and answering the same questions twenty times for some underling and trying forty times to see the person one step up but not being able to. Still the process was underway. He and Shuya had got here pretty exhausted after such a long journey and he was working now as a tutor to a very ancient family, real nobility. They had a house in Ostia which was at the mouth of the river Tiber and on the sea. It was a huge villa, and Sean taught the boys for three hours a day, which gave him time to go up to the Vatican to see how things were getting on. Shuya helped in the linen room because she was a wonderful seamstress. The children loved the place, they had a little lodge of their own to live in, they were well established there. It was torturing to be so near and yet so far. Last week he had seen a group of Irish pilgrims; they had all carried Aer Lingus bags with the name of the travel agency added to it. He had been dying to talk to them, but he was keeping his word. If Angela said it was so desperately important that nobody must know until after the laicization then she must have her reasons, he had held himself back from chatting to his compatriots. Sometimes when little Denis said the sea was beautiful Sean got an urge to carry him in his arms right back to the beach at Castlebay. He was longing to hear from her, and of course letters would travel much quicker to Italy than to Japan.

They would. Angela addressed the envelope to Mr and Mrs S. O'Hara and she changed her writing so that Mrs Conway wouldn't guess. Lord Almighty, was she becoming paranoid? There *must* be other O'Haras in the world, mustn't there?

Clare said that there was a typewriter in the hotel and Josie had got a book called *Teach Yourself Typewriting*. It didn't look too hard, but the bits with your little finger were crucifying, you had to keep typing Qs and As and Zs with your little finger so that you could do it without looking. Josie was full of confidence now. She had gone on a diet too, and she had her hair cut. She had also begun the process of convincing her parents that it would be a good idea to take this course. Angela had managed to manoeuvre Immaculata into a position where the nun had thought she had dreamed up the whole idea of Josie's future career herself, so they would be able to rely on her for support. Now the only real thing was Clare's scholarship. It would be held in the Easter holidays. Angela would be in Dublin at Emer's wedding, but that didn't matter. Clare could cope on her own now. In February she had asked Mother Immaculata if she thought she should enter, and once Immaculata began to think of it as her own project all was well. Nothing had changed, Angela had noticed, in nearly twenty years. The nuns were still enthusiastic that one of their pupils might win a place, they offered extra tuition here and there, all of which Clare accepted gratefully. She surprised them all with how much she knew already.

Funny little dark horse, they said in the Community room, you wouldn't believe she was Chrissie O'Brien's sister; remarkable little face with those big dark eyes and fair hair, you didn't usually get that mixture. The nuns were kind. They made her gifts – a lace handkerchief to bring with her, numerous holy pictures all mounted on bits of satin with sequins and decorations. One old nun gave her a fountain pen which had been sent for a feast day and another gave her a bright-coloured carved pencil box. Immaculata bathed in the glory of it and Angela O'Hara watched entertained from the sidelines.

'What have they said at home?' Angela asked her.

'I haven't said. You said not to say.'

'You'd better say now, otherwise they'll think you're holding out on them.'

'Right,' said Clare, 'I'll tell them this evening.'

Agnes O'Brien was looking into the big saucepan with no pleasure. 'This thing about getting cheap meat because Chrissie works in Dwyers' is a mixed blessing,' she said. 'This is a pile of bones when all's said and done.'

'It'll make soup,' Tom O'Brien said, peering in at it.

'Yes. Again!' Agnes said. 'Still there's few enough mercies to be thankful for these days, I suppose I mustn't turn up my nose at meat got for half nothing.'

Clare took her books out of her schoolbag and covered them immediately with a paper bag. Any schoolbook left casually round that kitchen could well be covered in soup, spattered fat, dust from the range or a variety of stains.

'Something nice happened at school,' she said. She rarely spoke of school now. It had raised such scant interest. The very fact she announced it like that claimed their attention.

'What was that?' Agnes asked, transferring her glance from the big saucepan.

'Mother Immaculata and the other nuns think I should enter for the scholarship to the secondary school. In the Easter holidays.'

'Secondary school?' Tom O'Brien was astounded.

'I know Dad, I mightn't get it, there'll be people from all over going in for it. But isn't it great that the school think I should try?'

'A scholarship. That means they'd take you without paying, as a boarder and everything?' Agnes said.

'Yes, if I won it.'

'How do you win it, is it a competition?' Ben was interested.

'Sort of,' Clare said. 'Well yes, really. A lot of girls come and sit an exam, on one day, and the best one gets to go to the school.'

'For ever?' Jim wanted to know.

'Well for ever until school's finished, you know, sixteen or seventeen.'

'Would you stay at school *that* long?' Ben's eyes were round with interest.

'That's very good,' Agnes said slowly. 'Tom, what do you think of that, Clare going to the secondary school?'

'With the daughters of everybody,' Tom said happily.

'I haven't won it yet,' Clare said.

'Ah, but they wouldn't be putting you up for it if they didn't think you were in with a chance.' Tom O'Brien rubbed his hands delightedly. 'Mother Immaculata is a very intelligent woman, she knows what she's doing.'

Clare smiled to herself: it had all been kept from intelligent Mother Immaculata for nearly two years.

'I'll need to study very hard for the next few weeks. I'm not saying that to get out of things, you know that?' She looked from one to another.

'We know that, child, weren't we always anxious that you should be at your books?' Clare's mother really seemed to believe that she had been.

'Wait till everyone hears that,' Tom O'Brien said happily. 'There'll be very few who'll look at us crooked then.'

'Only if I get it.'

'You'll get it. Agnes, see to it that this child doesn't do one hand's turn of housework, do you hear me?'

'I was just going to tell you, don't have her out there lining shelves and running messages for you.'

They argued happily over the saucepan of mutton bones while Jim and Ben looked on.

The door opened and Chrissie arrived in her blood-spattered apron. 'God it's freezing out, and in the shop too with the door open. I nearly cut off my arm to give to Miss McCormack with the chops for the parish priest.'

'Clare's going to the secondary school,' shouted Jim.

'For years and years and it's all free,' said Ben.

'I'm *not* going,' Clare cried. 'I'm only entering a competition to go, you wouldn't say you'd won the crossword in the paper if you just did it, would you?'

But she was unheard.

'What do you think of that, your young sister has been chosen to go and enter for a scholarship in the school in the town,' Agnes said triumphantly.

'Look at that now,' said Tom O'Brien.

It was too much for Chrissie. A long hard day's work in a cold shop, home for her tea and they're all praising Clare, horrible sneaky little Clare, going behind everyone's backs.

'Will you be a boarder?' Chrissie asked.

'*If* I win it, but I mightn't have a chance, I might never get there.'

'Oh, you'll get there, you get everything you want,' Chrissie said bitterly.

'I don't, I don't!' Clare cried. 'I hardly ever do.'

'Oho no, it's Saint Clare this and Saint Clare that. Well I

hope you *do* get to your boarding school, then I'd have my room to myself for a bit without Saint Clare spying on me and making my life a misery.'

'Chrissie, stop that.' Her mother looked at the angry girl with the red face in the filthy butcher's coat. 'You should be delighted that Clare's doing so well.'

'They'll think all the more of you up in Dwyers' if your sister's in secondary school,' said Tom excitedly.

'Oh they wouldn't care there if she was in the county gaol,' Chrissie scoffed. 'But I'm glad all right, I really am, a bit of peace in this house at last.' She slammed out and upstairs, so Clare's hopes of taking her homework there vanished.

'Don't mind her,' said her mother, 'she's delighted really.'

Chrissie went upstairs and threw herself on the bed. It was too much, coming today of all days, today when Gerry had come in for a half-pound of minced meat. Chrissie had joked with him like she always did, how was it that he was doing the shopping, a man in a house with two women? He had said nothing, just smiled. Then she had asked, out of politeness, out of *niceness,* how was his mother, did she still feel she couldn't leave the house? Gerry had turned on her. In a low voice that the others couldn't hear he had called her a big-mouth. He had said the word several times. Big-mouth Chrissie, can never leave well alone, never knows when to say things and when not to. Big-mouth. She had stammered, what had she said wrong, wasn't she only inquiring after his mother? But Gerry hadn't smiled. Chrissie should not use her big mouth to air other people's business in public, he had said.

Frightened, she had asked him would she see him at the pictures that night, a crowd of them usually went on a Friday evening.

'You may see me, you may not,' Gerry had said. His anger was over. He was distant now. She knew that just from a civil inquiry about his stupid old mother, whom she hadn't seen for months come to think of it, she was going to see no more of Gerry Doyle.

And now there was going to be a God Almighty fuss

about Clare. Wasn't it desperate the way things never come singly. There was all that fuss about Tommy and Ned having left their digs in London, and when Mam wrote to the landlady to know why they weren't replying, the landlady wrote back this real snotty letter saying they had disappeared, owing her three weeks' rent. Dad had been very upset and nearly cried. They sent a postal order to the woman in England and their apologies.

The O'Brien boys had left their jobs: they were working with a different gang now. The landlady, who had become more friendly since the sudden and unexpected appearance of three weeks' rent, which she had said goodbye to a long time ago, told the O'Briens that the fellows their sons had joined were rough and not what they'd want. She said that everyone was paid on a Friday night in this pub so if they wrote a letter there it would reach them. And then of course there was a letter. Ned was sorry they hadn't written, but times were hard. They had changed jobs and changed where they lived; there wasn't much to spare at the moment and he hoped that Mam and Dad understood. Mam and Dad wanted no money – only please keep in touch. So the odd postcard arrived. Nobody in Castlebay liked getting postcards: it gave Mrs Conway a perfect right to comment on all your business. Agnes O'Brien sent Ned a pound note in an envelope addressed to the pub, asking him to buy proper envelopes and stamps: she didn't want the whole of Castlebay to know their business. And why was there never a word from Tommy?

Well, Tommy wasn't much for writing as they all knew but he was fine, getting on great.

Tom O'Brien wondered would the scholarship cover everything, supposing Clare did win it. Everything, Clare said firmly. She didn't know but she wasn't going to have it all debated now. Miss O'Hara had said that she should assume she was going to win and that when she won she was going to go, otherwise she would waste precious time worrying about things over which she had no control.

Dr Power said that he would drive her into the town on the day of the scholarship. He said he had to go once a month anyway so it might as well be that day. No, of course it wasn't too early. Angela had asked him this favour since the bus would have the child too late. He would pick her up in the evening, he said, and it would be a privilege. He hoped that he would have some part in bringing honours to Castlebay. When he said that Clare's parents were almost overcome, they hadn't realized that it would be an actual honour, they thought it might be just one more problem.

There were still six weeks to go. Clare came steadily to Miss O'Hara's house twice a week. Sometimes Miss O'Hara just gave her an essay title while she busied herself making her mother's meal or setting the place to rights. Then she would go over the essay, praising and correcting, discussing and debating. Clare never felt she wrote a bad essay, but she learned how to write one that would win her even more praise. She was to consider this day as an audition, her one chance. There would be no other.

She was writing an essay on the 'Rural Life versus the Urban Life' which had been one of the topics a few years ago on the scholarship paper, when Miss O'Hara gave a sudden start. Clare looked up and saw that the teacher was reading a letter. Old Mrs O'Hara looked up too, and they waited for some explanation.

'It's Emer,' Angela cried. 'She and Kevin are so sick of the whole fuss about the wedding, do you know what they're going to do? They're going to get married in Rome. They have it all arranged, they're going to get married in a side chapel in St Peter's basilica in Rome on Easter Monday. A friend of Kevin's is a priest who's doing some postgraduate work . . .' Angela was reading from the letter now '. . . He has said there is no problem, we've sent all the documents and we will be married in the Holy City. Now nobody can object to that, can they? Even Kevin's awful cousins are struck dumb because they can't fault us, it would be like criticizing the Pope or something. And it's too dear for anyone to come, and it's too far. And I can wear what I like not what my sisters say, and we can have a honeymoon there as well. I can't think why we didn't think of it sooner.'

Angela hugged herself with pleasure. 'Isn't that magnificent?' she said to the old woman and the young girl who looked at her, dumbfounded.

'But that means you can't go,' her mother said.

'It does not. I was going to Dublin, now I'll go to Rome instead.' Angela threw herself into a chair and spoke to the ceiling. 'Now I do believe in miracles,' she said, smiling up at it.

Emer couldn't believe it. 'And you'll be my bridesmaid?'

'Why not? They've seen lions eating Christians in Rome, they must have seen ageing bridesmaids as well.' Angela was phoning from Dillon's Hotel – that way Mrs Conway would have had to tune in deliberately to hear her.

'We'll have a great time, and you can be round for the honeymoon bit too, can't you? You don't have to rush off home the next day.'

'No, I'll bring my best nighties and a frilly dressing gown and I'll get into the bed with yourself and Kevin. It'll be great.'

'Oh Angela, it's the very best news in the world that you're going to be there. Imagine you coming all the way to Rome. What a friend you are. I'll never be able to thank you.'

'When I get married I'll have the ceremony in Jerusalem, then we'll put you to the test.'

Emer laughed. 'I don't think there's much chance of a romance between you and the best man, but you never know.'

'Oh you never know, Italian music and wine, it could be highly romantic. '

'Angela, isn't it *marvellous*. I feel like a young girl again.'

'So do I, truly,' Angela said.

Everyone seemed to know she was going to Rome. Dick Dillon who had given up drink and was as bad-tempered as a weasel called her into the hotel one day and showed her a lot of brochures. Apparently, because of the pilgrimages, the best way to go to Rome would be on an all-inclusive tour.

That way she'd have a hotel booked already, and she'd be with people while she needed them. Angela was very grateful to him: she had feared the plane would be too expensive, but of course Dick Dillon was right. It turned out too that all Emer's party were going on a similar kind of arrangement.

Dick Dillon said he had been in Rome once and he had thrown coins into the fountain which meant you would come back again but he never had. He shook his head gloomily.

Angela said there was nothing stopping him going back any time he wanted to. He said that she didn't understand: now that he had given up the jar there was no point in going anywhere. Being in Italy and not being able to drink that wine? And the grappa, oh God, the grappa gave a fierce kick to the back of the throat, it was marvellous stuff. No, there would be neither rhyme nor reason going somewhere like Rome and drinking milk.

They got on to less heartbreaking subjects: Angela said she was glad that Josie was going to the commercial college next year, and hadn't she come on a lot lately? Dick Dillon agreed – she had been a terrible pudding of a poor thing but she seemed to have brightened up all right. Good for her anyway, *she* wouldn't be left on the side while the bright brothers and sisters got the pickings of the hotel; she wouldn't be left in a corner with no position, no status, just drinking her liver to bits like he was.

'But you're all right now, Dick,' said Angela a bit impatiently. 'Why can't you wrest your share back for yourself, or take control, or get in there and fight, or whatever you want to do?'

'I suppose I don't know *what* I want to do. That's the problem.' Dick Dillon was morose.

'Come to Rome with me as my escort,' she said.

'I could, I suppose, but I'd be no company and we wouldn't be able to go on anywhere they served drink,' he said, taking her seriously.

'You'd better stay where you are then, I'll send you a postcard of your fountain.'

*

David Power was furious that she was going to Rome.

'I was going to bribe you to go over my whole history course with me. You make it all sound so reasonable, as if they were normal people.'

'Then I must be getting it wrong, because most of them weren't.'

He was wrapped up in himself, his worries, his future.

'You'll be fine, David, you're very bright, you've worked hard, it's only nerves now after all the years. Anyway you've got weeks yet to cover the things you aren't sure of. Look at Clare O'Brien – she's really the one to pity, one shot, only one chance for a proper education. Your father's a very kind man, he's going out of his way to drive her to that scholarship next week. If she doesn't get it, that's it. And she's mad to learn.'

'I bet she's a bit fed up with you going off to Rome when she needs you.' He was still mutinous: it had never occurred to him that Miss O'Hara would be doing anything except waiting for chances to teach.

'No, oddly enough, she's very pleased for me, but then of course females are much more considerate than males, and generous, it's known.'

David smiled, his good humour restored.

'I hope she gets it.'

'I hope she gets it too. I remember this time seventeen years ago, it must have been the year you were born, I went over to the town to do the scholarship too, and I had no idea how many farmers' daughters there might be up against me. To be the brightest in Castlebay wasn't much, it was the rest of the county all around.'

'And when you got it, was it great?'

'No. Not really. My father was very drunk that day and very abusive. It had nothing to do with the scholarship. Well, not at first. Then he got upset about that and said that people were giving Dinny O'Hara's child their charity. No, the day wasn't great.' She brightened up. 'But it was great afterwards . . . How's James Nolan?'

'Languishing over Fiona Doyle – not over his revision I'm afraid.'

'And his sister? Languishing too?'   .

'She's got over her miseries. Much more fickle females are than males.'

'Has she transferred her attentions back to you?' Angela ignored his barb.

'There was a tentative move in that direction, but I discouraged it, until my exams were over.' He was as proud as punch. 'I'll play a bit hard to get.'

'Oh, I'm glad I'm not your age, you'd have my heart broken in bits.'

'Will you pray for me in Rome, Miss O'Hara?'

'Of course I will, Clare, in St Peter's itself on Easter Sunday, and again at the wedding on the Monday, and I'll go to Mass somewhere specially for you on the Tuesday, on the day.'

'That should work.' Clare was adding it up in her mind. 'Nobody will have that many prayers for them. I wish you were going to be here.'

'No, in a way it might be worse for you, might make you too anxious. You're probably better on your own.'

She was doubtful. 'There'll be no one to tell.'

'Yes there will, there'll be Dr Power in the car coming back; there'll be Josie, she'll be dying to know. And your mother and father. Now be sure to tell them all about it, they mightn't *sound* as interested as you hope, but in their own way they are.' Angela sought more people that Clare could talk to. It wasn't easy to find them, she would be wise to keep away from the convent: Mother Immaculata would depress her into the ground, with the Answers She Should Have Given and the Things She Ought To Have Said.

'You could always talk about it to David Power?'

'I wouldn't tell him about it, Miss O'Hara. He's a bit snobby.'

'No, he's not. His mother is, but he isn't, not at all. But suit yourself. Hold on till I get back. I'll be back on the Saturday night late, too late for you, but leave a note up in the house about how you got on, and come round after early Mass. We'll have breakfast together and you'll tell me step by step how you went in there, flags waving for Castlebay.'

Suddenly Clare threw her arms round Miss O'Hara, on the side of the road where it divided in three to go to the golf club, to the Cliff Road or down Church Street. There was nobody but a man on a bicycle and his dog passing by to see.

'You're so kind, you're the best help anyone in the world could have. I'll never be able to thank you.'

Angela was embarrassed but she hugged her back quickly and released her. 'That's all right, child, wait for the long weeks until we know, that's going to be the hard bit.'

Kevin was a lovely fellow, Angela thought. He was waiting with Emer at Kingsbridge station to meet her the night she arrived in Dublin. He ran up to take her suitcase and welcome her. He had freckles and reddish hair and he was as delighted with Emer as if she were a present that had been handed down to him from a Christmas tree.

Emer hadn't changed at all in the seven years since they had met. She had a brown corduroy pinafore dress and a white blouse; with her shoulderbag she could have been a student still. Angela touched her own face in some kind of reflex, she wondered had the years of living in wind, rain and sea spray with an invalid woman and teaching in a very narrow school taken their toll? She must look much, much older than Emer, when she was in fact over a year younger. And her clothes. They were drab and old. Though she had ironed them all and folded them with care in Castlebay now she wished she could lose the suitcase that Kevin was carrying as they swung along the platform to the bus. Emer had her arm linked and the years rolled away.

'I'll never be able to thank you for this, you know,' Emer said, looking at her with a shining face. 'It makes it all more normal, less odd if you know what I mean.'

Kevin was nodding too, eagerly: 'You're a very good friend, Angela, I can't tell you how pleased we both were, Emer danced round the room when you rang that day. It was terrific of you.'

'I couldn't wait for the post,' said Angela.

'My mother is pleased too, and Lord God nothing has pleased her since I don't know when. She remembers you coming to the house and she thinks you're much more reliable than any other friend I have.'

'Why on earth does she think I'm reliable, I'd hate to be reliable,' Angela said indignantly.

'Well you went and looked after your mother, didn't you? I mean how more reliable could another mother think one could be? You get all the points in the world for that.'

They laughed as if they had never been separated, and as if they had both known Kevin always. As they climbed on the bus and ran lightly upstairs so that they could smoke, Angela felt the first pang of envy for Emer. Wouldn't it be great to be on the verge of spending your life with this easygoing, happy man. They talked on the bus about the house they had bought, and how it needed a lot of doing up but it would be terrific in the end. They took her to the kind of a restaurant that hadn't existed when she was in Dublin. It had candles in wine bottles, and a foreign man serving them – it was like being abroad already.

Mrs Kelly was at the door waiting for them.

'Here you are at last, Angela,' she said crossly. 'What has she been up to, keeping you out till this hour? Why on earth were you not brought back here straight from the station, there were sandwiches made and all.'

'Isn't it wonderful news about the wedding! Imagine being married in Rome! Could you ever have believed it?' Angela was an expert at changing subjects and getting old women to talk about more cheerful things. And you didn't always do it in one step either.

'Well yes it is of course, but it's so far away, and the family . . . and I'm not altogether sure whether . . .'

Angela clapped her hands like a gleeful schoolgirl. 'I think you're all marvellous, Mrs Kelly, but I'd do the same if it were my daughter, if there were a chance of her seeing the Holy Father and having all the Easter ceremonies in Rome. *Anyone* can get married in Dublin but if it were my choice I'd much prefer to think a child of mine was able to have all this experience and there'll be the photos and everything.'

It was the right thing to say. An element that had not yet been introduced, that it was one up on everyone else. Mrs Kelly liked it. She liked it so much that she offered them both a sherry as a nightcap.

Emer was about to refuse and Angela hissed, 'Last night under this roof.'

So they all sat down and talked about how impressed people would be when they saw the pictures. Mrs Kelly asked Angela what kind of a hat she was going to wear. Angela had never worn a hat in her life and was momentarily stuck.

'We're going to choose it tomorrow morning,' Emer said.

On the way upstairs Emer said that it would be a great excuse to get out of the house for an hour or two, before the family came to wave goodbye and annoy them all.

There was a divan bed in Emer's room which was used as a settee when she was on her own but could be made into a spare bed. That was where Angela was to sleep, but they both sat on it and talked for two hours. In the end they remembered that they would still have days and days in Rome, and that from now on Angela was to come to Dublin every year and stay with Kevin and Emer in a house where nobody would interrogate you the moment you came in the door.

'I never spoke to you about money,' Emer said as she got into bed. 'Kevin asked me to say that the groom gives the bridesmaid a present, and he wanted me to find out tactfully if you'd like some of the money towards the fare instead of a gift. He said I wasn't to say it straight out but I can't think of how else to say it.'

'Isn't he very kind. You are so lucky, Emer.'

'I know.' She hugged her knees in bed, a schoolgirlish gesture. 'I can hardly believe how lucky I am. Well, what will I tell him?'

'Tell him I was touched to the heart but I'd prefer a present. I don't spend much in Castlebay you know, I live at home. I don't go anywhere much, I save a bit each week in the post office and I save that much again at home like a mad old lady in a box under my bed.'

'Why on earth do you not put it all in the post offfice?' Emer was amused.

'Because I wouldn't give it to that demon Mrs Conway to know how much I *have* managed to put by over the years. No honestly, Emer, I really do have the money, thank you and Kevin very much, and I don't spend much on clothes so I'm fine. I was always hoping that I'd have a great opportunity like this.'

Emer blinked away tears. Angela looked so sad lying on her elbow in the divan bed, her long brown hair brushed and tied loosely back with a rubber band, her face pale and worried looking. Emer felt guilty that her friend had such a sad life and was now spending her savings coming to Rome. Yet Angela seemed absolutely determined to be there, from the very first moment too. It was almost as if she had been looking for an excuse to go there and this was it. It was marvellous to have such enthusiasm as that, compared to everyone else moping and complaining. Emer drifted off to sleep happily, and didn't know that Angela smoked five cigarettes hoping that sleep would come, and when it didn't she took half a sleeping tablet with a sip of water.

They were meeting the best man in Rome, and so the party that set out on the plane were Kevin's cousin Marie who worked for Aer Lingus and could get a reduction, and Emer's Uncle David who was an artist of some kind and who went to the continent once a year to paint. It had all been balanced with great care. One relative from each side but no mothers or fathers, no clerics or nuns from either side and no sisters or brothers. Emer provided a bridesmaid and the best man who was working his way there by train was a friend of Kevin's and a teacher in the same school.

There had been a full day of discussion about whether the parents should come, but Kevin and Emer while pretending a certain enthusiasm had marshalled every possible argument against their making the journey. It worked. They were through the barrier at Colinstown airport in Dublin, with Angela, Uncle David and Kevin's cousin Marie. The wedding had begun.

*

He was waiting outside her hotel. She had *told* him not to come in person – it was a hotel where Irish pilgrims stayed, but he should leave a note for her saying where they should meet.

The taxi that Father Flynn had organized for Uncle David, Cousin Marie and Angela stopped outside the door. Sean jumped eagerly but Angela motioned him angrily away. Her first shock was that he was wearing a blue suit with a pale blue shirt open at the neck. It had never occurred to her that he didn't dress like a priest any more.

David and Marie spent ages being assured that she was fine, that she had her passport which she would need, that they knew of her at the desk, and then they all repeated to each other where they were going to meet for lunch the next day. At the foot of the Spanish Steps, on the bottom step, that way nobody could get lost.

Angela stiffened as she was aware of Sean listening eagerly to the arrangements. She wanted to keep him out of it, she wanted the two lives separate. She *hated* him for standing there mute and dying to join in. She hated herself too for keeping him at such a distance with a wave of her hand. Eventually, finally they went, back into the taxi and on to the hotel where Father Flynn and the happy couple had gone. Where the best man should be arriving tonight if all went well. Emer had been upset that Angela couldn't change her arrangements and stay at their hotel too, and that she wouldn't even try. But Angela had insisted that the booking remain the way it was. They would see plenty of each other, the hotels were only ten minutes' walk apart.

She was given the key to her room and pointed towards a very dangerous-looking lift. Sean came towards her.

'Are they gone?' he asked fearfully.

'Yes.'

'Oh Angela. *Angela*. Thank you, bless you for coming, bless you, and thank you from the bottom of my heart, Shuya says I must begin by giving you her thanks, she wants you to know that very specially.' He had his hands on her shoulders and his face was working uncontrollably.

'Don't . . .' she began.

'If you had any idea what this means to me.' He shook his head from side to side. There *were* tears in his eyes, she hadn't been mistaken.

'Please . . . I'll just go and . . .' She wanted to give him time to pull himself together, to stop this fawning tearful act, so unlike her confident brother the priest who was always so right and who knew what people should do and what they shouldn't do, and who knew about duty and staying with one's mother in Castlebay for all of one's life.

'I'll come with you.' He lifted the suitcase.

'No, you can't, what would they think?' She hissed this furiously at him.

In easy Italian he explained to the small fat man behind the desk. The man nodded, si si. Father Sean could still charm them, Angela thought bitterly.

There was barely room to breathe in the perilous lift. Angela held her breath as it groaned up the flights. Sean opened the door of the small room. There was a single bed, a dressing table and a chair. On the wall were five hooks with hangers on them. Single rooms didn't have luxuries like wardrobes or washbasins. They had passed rooms called *Il Bagno* and *Il Gabinetto* on the corridor. Angela looked around her, this wasn't how she had wanted to meet her brother. She had wanted to come in and lie down and gather her thoughts. She had wanted to have a bath and change her clothes, hanging up her wedding finery and the new hat bought in Clery's this morning. Was it only *this* morning they had been in O'Connell Street with all those crowds? She had wanted Sean to leave her a letter suggesting a nearby café. She could have strolled there in the cool of the evening and they could have talked at a quiet table. Talked for hours if need be. She hated this hot, emotional, awkward meeting.

He had put her case on the floor and laid the big bag carrying her wedding hat carefully on the dressing table beside the big room key. And as she stood not knowing what was going to happen now, totally out of control on her first time staying in a hotel, her first time out of Ireland and her first time meeting her only brother since he had left the priesthood, Sean put his arms around her and with his head on her shoulder he cried like a baby. She stood there dry-eyed, wondering how could anything be as bad as this. He wasn't stammering how sorry he was that it had all happened, he wasn't saying that he had made a mess of everyone's lives. No, he was stumbling out words about the laicization and how long it was taking, and how glad he was to see Angela because he had been so afraid from her letters that she meant he was never to come back to Castlebay again.

They all found the Spanish Steps with no problem. Marie, the girl who worked in Aer Lingus, had been in Rome several times, and David the middle-aged artist had been there years ago. Emer and Kevin would have found the planet Mars if that had been the rendezvous point, so excited and full of energy did they seem. Father Flynn was excited too – this was *his* show, his town now, and he loved every minute of the role of organizer. Angela was the last to arrive but she was only minutes after the others. She had paused to buy dark glasses and had found herself always in the kind of shop where these glasses cost a fortune. In the end she paid a fortune, and the woman in the shop admired them and said that now she had a *bella figura*.

The others laughed when they saw the new Angela. They told her that it had not taken her long to go native and they joked about overindulgence in wine the night before. As they debated where to eat Emer asked Angela in some concern what she *had* done the night before.

'Wandered,' Angela said. 'You know me, wander and only half absorb where I am and what I'm doing. It's a beautiful place, isn't it?' Emer was satisfied. Years and years ago in Dublin Angela used to wander like that, for ages along the canal, or in the Dublin mountains, walking around for miles. It figured she would do the same in Rome. Emer went back to the argument about lunch, they dismissed the very notion of Babbington's Tea Rooms, an English-style place just beside them. They hadn't been in Rome for a full day yet, it wasn't long enough for them to start hankering over good old tea and scones.

They walked companionably to a place that Father Flynn knew. 'I haven't completely wasted my time here praying and studying,' he said happily. 'I've done some useful things like discovering where to eat and drink.'

A man in a cream-coloured jacket and a very showy handkerchief in his pocket made a play for Angela in the restaurant, jumping up from his table to ensure she had an ashtray and trying out his few lamentable words of English on her.

'I think these glasses suit me, I might wear them all the time,' Angela said when the man had backed out of the restaurant bowing and smiling and ogling. She hadn't seen that much attention in years.

Then they left her alone. Once she had made a little joke they thought she was all right, she could opt out for a while and run the whole night over for herself as if it were a film. She had got Sean out of her room eventually, and he had written down the name of a café. She said she only needed an hour to calm herself and unpack; but as it turned out she did neither, her clothes remained in their suitcase and her anxiety grew ever more. She kept looking at the travelling clock and wondering why she had sent her brother, red-eyed, away. She was going to have to talk to him anyway, why hadn't she left the oppressive bedroom with him and gone to one of those picturesque squares?

They did walk to a square, the Piazza Navona. There were restaurants all around and the centre was full of people selling things and doing tricks as if it was a carnival. Not a person seemed to have a care except the O'Haras, she thought. They sat and ordered tiny coffees.

He had recovered himself fully. 'Let me tell you all about my family,' he began. She listened. She heard of Shuya and how he had met her almost immediately after they had gone to Japan to regroup after the expulsion from China; she heard of Denis who was three and the brightest child that had ever been known. And of Laki who was a baby of eighteen months, so beautiful it would make your eyes prickle when you saw her. And of the life they lived in Japan in Shuya's brother's house, and what they did here in the strange villa in Ostia, and how they would get married here in Rome as soon as the laicization came through. He talked like someone possessed: he had always been a great one to hold the floor, but that was because he was the only one who could, at home. He had been away to seminary and then on the missions, he was a priest of God who had more right to tell tales and get a hearing, who had better tales to tell. She listened. Nothing had changed much except the content. He was sure of his audience, sure that she was glad to know details of Laki's birth which had been a complicated one, sure that she was as absorbed as he was in the minutiae of the laicization process and his dealings with the Congregation for the Clergy.

Once or twice she tried to interject, but he raised his hand slightly in that clerical gesture which was only slightly a courteous request for permission to speak further – it was mainly a statement that he was *going* to speak further.

He wasn't going to go back tonight: it was too far, it would be too late. He would stay in Rome. Shuya had insisted, said it would be less tiring because surely he would want to talk to his sister again in the morning. As the monologue went on Angela became grateful that he was going to stay in Rome. Since she was obviously not going to get any innings at all, she would *need* the morning to try to explain to him some of the things that stood in the way of his sunny view of the future. But where would he stay? Much of his chat had included how short of money they were and how even fares were a big consideration. But he was fine for a bed. A friend of his, an English priest who was staying at the English College, said there would always be a bed there for Sean. It was nearby.

He talked of the priests he had met and the ex-priests, and of the spirit of change and questioning in the Church. He was prepared to talk for ever about such things. Angela nodded and made the necessary sounds as he spoke but all the time her mind was racing. It was just like getting his letters; he ignored every point she had made in her own letters, and had written as if Angela had addressed no thoughts, pleas or words to him at all. She had written to say that she was coming to meet him to explain to him face to face how impossible it would be – laicization or not – to return to Castlebay with a Japanese or any wife and two children. He seemed to have ignored the main part of her letter, and acknowledged only the first sentence, that she was coming to Rome to see him.

She hoped that a change of venue might change the tack of the conversation, so she suggested they have a meal. He hesitated. Angela said she would be glad to pay. He agreed. It was just that he felt so guilty spending anything on himself instead of on Shuya and the children. But nothing changed, he ordered for them in perfect Italian, bottles of mineral water as well as wine; told her he could make spaghetti thirty-four different ways now, and he made a salad every evening at home, often with leaves they plucked from the garden. You can actually eat *all* kinds of things like the leaves of flowers. Did Angela know that?

She didn't, but by the end of the evening she knew a lot of things like that. She could have gone into Radio Eireann at home and asked to be a panelist on *Information Please* after all she learned in the Piazza Navona, as the lights came on and the musicians played, and other people had beautiful Roman evenings. From her handbag she took a piece of paper and wrote down four words. Then she handed the list to him.

'What's this?' he asked, surprised and even a little amused.

'It's our agenda for tomorrow morning. When we meet in the daylight. I want to discuss the subjects written down there and nothing else.' She smiled pleasantly; she took a sheaf of huge Italian notes in almighty denominations and signalled for the bill.

Sean was reading aloud. 'Hypocrisy and Betrayal. Family and Community. What is this Angela? It looks very like the title of some sermon or a pamphlet in the Catholic Truth Society.'

She was still easy and relaxed. 'Let's leave it till tomorrow, will we? It's been a lovely evening and it's too late to start on these things now.'

He was genuinely bewildered; he wasn't acting. He sought to placate her. 'Right, sure, whatever you like. And we'll arrange for you to come to Ostia.'

She shuddered at that. She felt a slow sweat form on her shoulders and back at the thought of meeting this Japanese woman who shared a bed with her brother the priest, and a dread of meeting these two children.

'Not until after Emer's wedding, not until next Tuesday.'

She was firm: he was disappointed.

'But we were *sure* you'd come for Easter itself.'

'I'm going to go to the Holy Week Ceremonies tomorrow and all of the weekend with my friends. When that's all over I'll come to Ostia.' If it's too awful to face, she thought, I can always pretend to be sick. To have a fever or something.

Sean was downcast. 'I had thought that . . .'

'It's all fixed.'

'No, I mean I thought that maybe you were going to ask us to the wedding. To Emer's wedding.'

She looked at him, stunned.

'I've met Emer, remember, I met her when you were in Dublin, and she came to Daddy's funeral.'

'Yes, she knows you as a priest.'

'But surely you've told her?' He was amazed.

A headache was beginning right across her eyes. 'Don't be ridiculous, Sean, of course I haven't told her, I haven't told *anyone*.'

'This is much more complicated than I thought,' Sean said, shaking his head. 'I thought it was only Mam you were keeping it from until the time was right. I didn't know that you had such old-fashioned views, and hard attitudes. I'm still a Catholic for God's sake, I haven't given up my Faith or anything. I still go to Mass and Communion.'

It was far too late to debate it now. The bill was paid and they walked amicably back to her hotel. All the time he pointed out places to her as if she were an ordinary tourist and he were her ordinary brother. He kissed her on each cheek and walked away into the night to his friend who was still a priest and who would not lie awake all night anguishing about what had happened to Father Sean O'Hara, and what course his life would take now.

She was businesslike in the morning. She said that she would prefer him to listen to her and only speak when she asked his view: otherwise her visit would have been wasted. He was startled but agreed. She examined the possibility of his coming back to Castlebay once more, once only and pretending to be still a priest. He was so horrified, he leaped up from the table. But she persisted. Examine it: technically, what would be the flaws, did he still have any clerical clothes, could he get away with it or would someone from the Mother House hear of it? No, don't ask *why* was this necessary at the moment, just see could it be done? According to Sean, even if he wanted to do an insane thing like this he couldn't do it. He would be found out in days, and as he wouldn't say Mass in Father O'Dwyer's church, he would be an object of suspicion at once.

Could he say that since the Order had left China there had been a change in the Rule and priests had become workers and teachers and were working among the community more? Could he imply that *all* priests had been downgraded, not only Father Sean? No that was ludicrous too. You only had to read the papers to know that this was untrue, it wouldn't hold good for five minutes.

Could they pretend that he had died, been kidnapped? Sean looked at Angela as if she weren't all there. Why on earth should anyone begin such a tissue of hypocritical lies and bungling?

Angela's eyes flashed. She would tell him why, because if he told their mother the truth it would break her, literally *break* her. The only thing of value she had done was produce a priest for God, it was the only constant and hope in her soul and it was her only standing in the community. That's what Angela meant about Betrayal. To tell the old woman with the enlarged joints and crooked limbs that her priest wasn't a priest – that would be betrayal of a high order. Angela had come to Rome to beg her brother not to do this.

He was patient with her, he began to explain that once the

process of making him a layman was completed, he had as much right before God to marry as anyone had, so he had anticipated it but it would then be regularized, post hoc. Angela silenced him with a word, this was *her* time: last night had been his. He was to decide between hypocrisy and betrayal. She would listen to no more speeches about breaths of fresh air blowing through the dusty corridors of the Vatican and new thinking and the Congregation of the Clergy. There was no fresh air blowing through Father O'Dwyer's church in Castlebay except what came in the windows on the day of the east wind. There was no radical rethinking in the O'Hara cottage, there was no spirit of brotherly love and understanding among people like Sergeant McCormack. Sean must decide between *hypocrisy* and *betrayal*. He must decide on the old principle of the greatest happiness of the greatest number. Which way would less people get hurt.

But, Sean protested, there could be no question of that, the truth was the truth, it was absolute. It couldn't be tinkered with and played with like plasticine, deciding who should believe what.

Their coffee cups were refilled over and over. Angela banged on the table to get him to stop talking and listen to her account of daily life in Castlebay. She didn't intend it to be humorous, but sometimes she said things that made him smile and she smiled herself to acknowledge that she did exaggerate in some areas. But not in the general picture.

She swore that it wouldn't matter all that much for her; to be frank she would prefer not to have the pitying and patronizing stance of Immaculata for the rest of her working life, and she would like not to have the knowledge that they had just stopped talking about it all every time she appeared. But she could live with it, she had lived with her father's reputation after all. She'd survive, but she was going to fight with every breath in her body for her mother not to have to try to survive it.

'When Mam dies, Sean, then I'll walk with you down Church Street in Castlebay. Don't come to her funeral, but six months later you can come back and I'll stand beside you.'

'That's the wrong way to do things,' Sean said. 'To wait till someone dies before you can bring your children home. How do you tell your son and daughter that you have to wait until their grandmother has been buried before they can come home, come home to where they belong?'

Angela's heart lurched again. He really and truly thought that these half-Japanese children and their mother *belonged* in Castlebay. She looked at her watch, and stood up to call for the bill again. It was time to go to lunch with the wedding party. He looked confused and unsettled.

'You will come, you will still come and see us?'

'Yes,' she promised.

'On Tuesday, and you'll stay a few days.'

'No, I won't stay the night, I might come again, but I'll just come for the day. Thank you all the same.'

'But why not? There's a bed there.'

'There's a bed in the hotel too, I'd prefer to come back.'

'Shuya will want to know do you send her a greeting.'

'Yes, yes of course.'

'What is it? What is the greeting?'

'Say I am happy to meet her.'

'It's not very warm,' he grumbled.

'It's all I've got. And you think about what I've said, because we have to sort it out. Will you discuss it with Shuya?'

'Yes, I suppose so, but it's hard, her family were so good, so welcoming, I don't want her to think mine are like a row of stones.'

'No. I understand.'

'Thanks anyway Angela. You're doing your best,' he said.

That's what did it, that's when the tears started, she threw some money on the table and stumbled away. *Doing her best!* God, wasn't she doing her bloody best! The ingratitude and lack of understanding were no longer possible to take. She ran almost blindly away. She heard him calling that he would collect her at the hotel on Tuesday and she nodded, not able to look back. She ran until she was well away, then she began asking directions and from the concerned looks people gave her she realized she needed dark glasses if not a full veil to cover her red-blotched face.

Father Flynn was a treasure, there was nothing he didn't know the answer to. He said it was going to be as dull as ditchwater when he got back to Dublin after all this, and the place was so gorgeous too. Dublin was so grey and gritty. Kevin's Uncle David, considered a little eccentric by the rest of Kevin's very straight-laced family, didn't usually go a bundle on priests: he said that normally they gave him a pain in the top of the stomach. But this little Druid was an exception. He wore a soutane which didn't at all suit his small round figure. Once when they were passing a lingerie shop which sold frilly waspie-waist corsets he asked Emer and Angela should he get something like that for himself to wear so that he would look good in wedding photographs. Father Flynn was full of stories about everyone and everything, all very ridiculous but not hurtful. And best of all, he could laugh at himself. He seemed to be well known everywhere they went. Italian shopkeepers setting out their cheeses on display would shout greetings to Fazzer Fleen.

But he had his serious side too and he told them that it was an honour to be married in St Peter's, and that obviously they would remember it all their lives. Nobody was so forgetful as not to recall where they got married, but this was something special. He took them down to the crypt chapel and they looked at it in awe on Holy Thursday afternoon just as the huge basilica was getting ready for its Holy Week ceremonies. Emer and Kevin were to be married here – it was almost too much to take in.

And the man seemed to know about clothes. He was fascinated by what they should wear at the wedding and thought that they would look absolutely great – apart from the shoes. There was something about Irish shoes that didn't look quite *right* in Rome. Late on Thursday evening the strange party wandered along the Via Condotti, and Angela and Emer tried on different footwear and paraded them for Father Flynn, Kevin, Marie and David. Marie became so excited that she started trying them on too, and Father Flynn said if his soutane didn't hide them he would be sorely tempted by those grey suede ones. Everyone in the shop was nearly hysterical, and when they settled on the fiercely elegant ones that all three had decided to buy, Father Flynn began to haggle like a fishwife about the price and brought the cost down enormously.

He stopped them at a flower stall where he was well known too. He did great gesticulations and explanations about the colour of dresses, Emer's white with a blue trim, her hat blue with a white ribbon. Angela's dress was beige and her hat was white with beige and brown flowers. The family who ran the flower stall became highly excited over the wedding and fought amongst each other about what the bouquets should be. Soon they were all shouting at each other while the Irish group looked on amazed. Flowers were being held up to Emer first, then to Angela, heads were shaking, arms were waving and in the end a satisfactory combination of flowers and timings and delivery to the hotel and prices was arrived at. The family gave everyone a buttonhole there and then as a gift. There was hand-kissing and good wishes, and they seemed as pleased as if it were one of their own family.

'Could you imagine my mother being as pleased as that over anyone's wedding?' Emer said wistfully. 'Is it any wonder people would love to come here to get married, total strangers are delighted with us and at home there's been nothing but fuss.'

'My family would have half the geriatric priests and nuns on the move by now, all of them complaining,' Kevin said.

'Less of that attitude,' Father Flynn demanded. 'I'll be a geriatric priest some day, and when your children are getting married in about thirty or thirty-five years from now, I want someone to come for *me* in a wheelchair and take me to the party.'

He was *so* nice, Angela thought with a rush of affection. Despite all his joky going on he was one of the kindest people she had ever met. What a sensitive little man he was; wouldn't he be a great priest to have in a parish instead of dull old Father O'Dwyer; instead of people who couldn't even stay *in* the priesthood. *Stop.* She was not going to think about Sean until Tuesday: that was her little treat to herself. She hoped she would be able to keep to that promise and enjoy herself.

There had been a bit of a problem about the best man. He hadn't turned up. But Father Flynn had that sorted out too. If the best man wasn't there, couldn't David stand in? David was doubtful, he wasn't actually in the State of Grace, he said, he wasn't what you would call a conventional person to take part in the ceremony, as one of the performers, that was. Father Flynn seemed to regard a public announcement of being in a state of sin as the most normal thing in the world.

'There's no question of being a performer,' he said. 'You're only a witness, you could be alive with mortal sin, reserved sins and all, it wouldn't make a whit of difference to the ceremony. Of course, now that you're here in Rome, if you wanted someone to hammer a good confession job on you, I know plenty that would see you right.'

'Well, now I don't think . . .'

'No need at all, just letting you know it's there if you want it. I know a priest who's almost stone deaf, there's a queue a mile long outside his box but I could get you up to the top of the line by shameless pull and influence.'

It was hard to know if Father Flynn was joking or not. But in any event by the time they got back to the hotel after the wonderful warm afternoon wandering around Rome, the best man was there. His name was Martin Walsh. He was about six foot two tall and forty years old. He was painfully shy and he had got on the wrong train. He looked as if he was about to burst into tears. Father Flynn had it under control in minutes.

He couldn't have arrived at a better time the little priest said, because they were all going to split up now and meet again at nine o'clock. Martin would have *hours* to get over the shock of it all, and have a bath and a few cold beers and a chat with Kevin. Everyone else was perfectly capable of looking after himself or herself. He said this because Martin had kept babbling his apologies about not being there to organize the flowers and the bridesmaids. He had bought a handbook on the best man's duties and he seemed to have fallen down.

Father Flynn told him to throw away the book on the role of the best man. Everything was much simpler in Rome. Martin's big sad face started to look human. Up to now he had looked like a thin wretched bloodhound.

The little wedding party walked with faltering steps into the huge basilica which they had visited every day since they came to Rome. Today it was different. There was a mixture of formality and casualness. People shouted good luck in different languages and a group of Germans took their picture. The walk seemed endless, but then they were in and down the marble stairs to the little chapels beneath. Father Flynn disappeared to robe himself, and the others knelt silently, heads down.

Angela prayed hard. She forced words to come into her head and she mouthed them to herself. She asked God to be kind to Emer and Kevin, and to make it a nice life. She explained to God that Emer had kept the rules and that it would be a good idea to reward her. Emer deserved to be happy. With her gloved hand she squeezed the white-gloved hand beside her and Emer grinned gratefully.

Father Flynn shone in his gold and white vestments. He was smiling at them all. The words began and Angela felt her eyes water when she heard Kevin's and Emer's uncertain voices. Then it was done. They were man and wife. They pecked at each other chastely and went to sign the huge register. The photographer was anxious to get them outside and grouped – on the steps first, then down to the centre of the square beside the big column, a great place to stand because you got a view of St Peter's in the background.

Sean was in the foyer when she came downstairs.

'Tell them you mightn't be coming back tonight, just in case, and in case they worry about you.'

'I'm coming back here tonight,' she said.

'It's so dear going up and down on the train,' he pleaded. 'Shall we go now?'

He shrugged; but soon he was in high good humour. Young Denis knew his Aunt Angela was coming. Angela shuddered and hoped he hadn't noticed the revulsion she felt coursing through her. She asked what language he spoke. Apparently he spoke Japanese and English and now because they were in Italy they were using a lot of that. *Mia Zia*, Sean said dotingly.

'What?'

'*Zia*, the Italian for aunt. *Zio* is uncle. *Mia Zia*, my aunt.'

Angela wondered could this possibly be happening? Was she really having a language lesson as they walked? It had all the qualities of a dream where the wrong people are in the wrong places saying idiotic things. But this had been going on too long for it to be a dream. She wasn't going to wake up and find Father Sean still sending for stamps and silver paper from the Far East. That was long gone now.

She tried to tell him about the wedding – anything, rather than fall into the normality of his life with him. She didn't want to hear that this was the platform he normally sat on to wait for the cheaper train, she didn't want to become part of his ridiculous pattern of commuting from this new home and family to try to get audiences and hearings and advance his documents further with the Congregation of the Clergy. She wanted this *over*. She looked at the station, at the monument to Mussolini, who made the trains run on time for the first and only period in Italy's history. By the time she came back here tonight she would have met them. Sean's family. It wouldn't make her feel any different, she knew that.

'What would you like best to happen now?' he asked her suddenly as they sat on the train opposite each other.

'I don't know.'

'What would be the very best thing that could happen as far as you are concerned? Best for everybody.'

She looked out the window at the buildings with all the washing hanging from sticks and poles that jutted through windows.

'I don't know, Sean, I really don't. I suppose I'd like you to reconsider and to ask to go back to your Order, for Shuya to see that this is your vocation, and for her to return to Japan with the children. I know it's not possible and it's not going to happen, but you did ask me what I would like.'

'Shuya must be a mind-reader,' he said happily. 'She said this is what you want.'

'I'm coming to see them, I'm doing that much – stop getting at me!'

'I know, and I'm so happy, soon you'll know them. A normal way of life is beginning for all of us.' He was like a child who thinks he's getting a bike for his birthday. Angela closed her eyes and kept them closed to discourage further conversation.

They waited in a hot noisy line of people for a bus and they didn't get a seat. Sean was smiling, blinking into the sunlight and bending down to look out, squinting for landmarks to point out to her.

After the bus ride, they walked for ten minutes. The gates of the villa were huge and wide, like the big gates of ruined Castlebay House at home. But the villa couldn't be more different: it was yellow-coloured with white shutters and there were flowers tumbling all over the walls. Sean looked through the gates with pride. Wasn't it beautiful? The Italians knew how to do things with style. The Signor and Signora didn't spend a great deal of time here of course, but they kept it up fairly well didn't they, when you considered everything. Angela wondered why they weren't going in. Maybe at this last moment he was getting some nerves, beginning to doubt the sense of the mad enterprise. It was only eleven o'clock in the morning and she felt she had put a whole day over her.

They moved away, to her surprise. It must have shown in her face.

'Our entrance is round here,' Sean explained easily. They went in a much narrower entrance a few hundred yards down the wall. It didn't need to say 'servants' entrance', that was so obviously what it was. Here the flowerbeds were overgrown and the walls of the out-houses were peeling in the sun. But there were flowers too, and as Angela walked beside Sean, she saw some small, dark-eyed Italian children playing in and out of the open doors. It would be a good place for a child to grow up in some ways, a bit in the shadow of the Big House of course but it was safe and friendly and there would be plenty of other children to play with. She was walking warily now: she must keep her wits about her.

'There they are . . . we're home . . . Shuya! Shuya, she's here! Denis, come here . . .!'

The little boy had his hand up to his face, shy, not wanting to be the first to make the move, hanging back. Behind him came waddling a small fat baby with nappies hanging down underneath its knitted knickers. And leaning against the door was Shuya. Not in Japanese clothes as Angela had thought she would be, not wearing a bun with two sticks coming out of it, no big wide belt with a rose attached to it, no tiny pointed feet.

Shuya looked like an old, old woman. She had an Eastern face, like the face of a poor Chinese or Filipino woman holding out a begging bowl, the kind of face you saw in the missionary annals. Her skin was muddy grey, her hair was lank and tied back like Angela's own. She wore a shapeless dress and over it a long, faded cardigan. This could not be Shuya. Shuya must be inside waiting to come out, this was somebody else minding the children for her, an older friend. The thin tired figure smiled at them both. 'Welcome Anjayla . . . wel-come. It is so good of you to come all this way to meet your family.'

Shuya's smile moved from brother to sister as she walked out of the shadow into the sunlight. Her smile was bright and it made her old thin face look less beaten, less resigned. Sean was staring at her with delight. In a flash Angela thought she understood it all. He was *lonely*. The poor stupid fool was *lonely* out there and she was kind to him, she was the first person to be kind and warm. That's what it's all about. It didn't make it any better, but it was some explanation.

169

'Hallo Shuya,' she said. Every word seemed leaden, but she forced them out. 'I'm very glad to meet you. Will you introduce me to the children?'

There was a pause. She must say something a bit warmer, Sean had probably built her up to the skies, described her as beautiful and generous and brilliant, just as he had built this sad creature up when he had spoken of her to Angela.

'This is Laki,' Shuya said. The toddler was whirling her two fat little arms round like a windmill in the effort to keep upright.

'Hallo Laki O'Hara.'

When the limelight was off Denis he realized it was safe to approach. 'I am Denis,' he said.

'I knew you were, I knew it the minute I saw you.'

There was no sending this lot back. Better banish the dream of Father Sean rediscovering his vocation, and his instant family being absorbed somewhere back in Japan. These were here to stay.

She went back on the train every day. Sean had been right, it would have been much easier to have stayed the night, but she had to stay true to her earlier words, and not let it appear that her first visit had been an inspection, and that she would stay if they passed the test. She brought them toys, she bought ridiculous over-decorated boxes of sweets. Laki sat on her lap and Denis wanted to know why she couldn't speak Japanese or even Italian. Shuya said little.

On Thursday, Sean had to see two priests who knew better routes than the ones he had been following. There was great hope they would steer him in the right direction. Angela said she would still come to Ostia, as usual. This was only her third visit but already it seemed natural. In fact she was glad that Sean would be away. Perhaps Shuya might talk more, might say the things that Sean reported her as saying. The woman was so quiet that Angela could hardly believe that she was the author of such philosophical announcements as Sean had always claimed. Shuya said little or nothing in her presence, and served the simple salads and pasta as if she were a maid, sitting a little away from the others as they ate. But when Sean wasn't there she would have to speak.

At first she was content to let young Denis talk to his aunt, but Angela put a stop to that. She asked Denis to go and collect her ten different kinds of leaves, each one different, from the grounds, and lay them all out on a sheet of paper; then they would try to put names on them. Denis went off happily; Laki was playing with a fat Italian baby about her own age. The women were on their own. Shuya seemed to recognize it too: she sat with her hands folded, waiting for Angela to begin.

It was hard because Angela had to be in the role of questioner for such a long time. Shuya replied dutifully. She had three brothers, and two sisters. Her mother was dead and her father had married again. Yes, they did like his new wife, but now he lived with his new wife's people and they did not see much of him. Her family liked Sean. No, they didn't really think anything about his having been a priest. Or being a priest still, as Angela said. No, you see it was just a job to them – he had been teaching when he was a priest, he was still teaching. He had not been married before, now he was married to Shuya. It was so simple.

On close questioning Shuya proved to see some complications. She said that it was a very big thing, it was like being married to the Church and the Church would release you if you found a higher happiness. But there were a lot of formalities. That is why they were here, that is why Sean had gone to the Vatican again this day as he did so many days.

No, of course it didn't matter to her, not even a little bit, about whether this laicization happened or not. But since it mattered so much to Sean it had become important to her too. She wished it to happen to please him. Then they could get on with their lives.

This was a minefield. Angela had to tread carefully. Where did they see the rest of their lives? Shuya didn't really know. They did love Italy of course, and anyone with children would love to be here, the people adored all children. But after? Sean would want to teach in a school, possibly. He was so clever, and he could teach so well. He would want to teach and live in a school at the same time. Then Denis could go to the same school and there would be a school nearby for Laki.

And where would this school be? In Italy or Japan or where? Shuya didn't know exactly where, but it would be somewhere in Ireland. She wasn't sure if Sean knew himself, but of course it would be Ireland.

She began to explain to Shuya about Ireland, and about Castlebay. She was never interrupted as she had been by Sean. Shuya came out with no roaring denials and assurances that things had changed now. Shuya listened as if she were being told a tale from a far country. She listened as if Angela knew what it was like because that was her land. She was passive during the recounting of the struggle to get the money for Sean's ordination, and the moment of glory at his first Mass and then his first Mass in Castlebay, and even his return seven years ago for his father's funeral. So passive that Angela wondered if she understood any of it. Angela tried to explain that despite what all the clergy in Rome said to each other, it made not a bit of difference back home, whether a priest had been laicized or not. Even if his marriage was as white as the driven snow in the eyes of God and state, in the eyes of the community it could never be accepted.

She begged Shuya to ask her questions, to challenge what she said. Shuya said there was no reason to challenge anything. Obviously Angela must be telling the truth, but did this mean that Sean should never go back to Ireland? Was this what Angela was trying to explain?

Yes. That was it. That's what she had been trying to say to Sean in her letters, and again when she had met him in Rome. Had he not told her this? Oh he had told her, but then when Angela had agreed to come to see the family on Tuesday, and come back again Wednesday and today, he realized that he had been forgiven and that it would all be all right. He had hoped that this would happen and now it had.

Denis came back with his leaves. He was about to lay them out for discussion and identification. Angela passed a hand wearily over her forehead, she was in deeper than ever now. Her visit had been the positive green light that Sean had been waiting for. Was she ever going to get out of this mire of misunderstanding or was she walking everybody further into it?

For the first time Shuya seemed to take some action of her own. She suggested that Denis and Laki have their lunch and siesta in the house across the courtyard. Denis felt short-changed.

'Your Aunt Angela will be here when you come back,' Shuya soothed, marching them over the cobblestones, bringing some of Angela's sweets as a bribe. It was the house of a gardener and his wife, who also helped with the sewing in the linen room. When the gardener went to market his wife had a young lover in and on those occasions Shuya took her children: so it was a fair exchange. Angela was taken aback by the racy life in the servants' quarters and the casual way that Shuya had accepted it. But it worked in her favour and she was not going to criticize.

She seemed younger, stronger, when she came back and sat down. It was as if her listening had a different quality. She scented a problem where she had thought there was none, she wanted to hear, to learn and to see what could be done. This time she talked back, she asked questions, mainly unanswerable ones. Like why, if these people were very religious, would they not recognize and believe in a document signed by the Pope saying that Sean was released from his vows? Or why would people who say they follow a rule which is based on love for each other not give that love? Angela was helpless. But because she didn't bluster, because she didn't defend and make excuses, the conversation never became angry. In the end Angela asked about Japan: wasn't there some code of honour that they had too, some kind of thing that an outsider might think was odd? Shuya paused. They had *ko* which was a sort of filial piety, but it wasn't the same as what was being asked for here. With *ko* you had to be docile to your parents and for a woman in particular docile to your mother-in-law. But they didn't have anything which meant hiding the truth, and no notion that hiding the truth could ever be a good thing in itself.

173

The sun came in through the slats in the shutters and Angela felt a great sadness and tiredness. In Rome, Sean was bent over still more documents with still more clerics. In Castlebay the neighbours would have cleared away her mother's lunch things. It would still be cold and windy. Up at the convent Mother Immaculata would be getting the timetable ready for the summer term. In Amalfi, Kevin and Emer would possibly be holding hands after lunch in a restaurant by the harbour or be on a boat to Capri. In O'Brien's shop Clare would have told them about the scholarship exam and how she couldn't wait until Miss O'Hara got back to hear the details. And here she was with this woman discussing *honesty* and *truth* and *hypocrisy*. She felt as if she would like to curl up and go to sleep for a month, waking up only when everything else was sorted out. She was thinking about this so wistfully that she almost missed Shuya's words.

'I suppose then that the best thing is for us not to go to Ireland at this time. It is best for Sean to alter some parts of his dream?'

'What?'

'For him to change his hopes about going to Ireland at this time.'

'Do you think he will? He's so set in his belief that it will be all right. I wore myself out and he didn't change an inch, not an inch.'

'Well, I will explain to him.'

'Shuya, how can you explain, he will only think that I tried to browbeat you or go behind his back or something.'

'But that is not so.'

'I know it's not so. I'd have said every word in front of him, but he'd have interrupted me a thousand times, I don't understand *this*, I haven't understood the *other*, Moral Law, Canon Law . . .'

'I know.'

She didn't dare to hope that this strange ugly woman with the lined face and the clothes of a beggar should be able to convince her big handsome brother of anything. 'Could you . . .? I think it would make everyone happier. Not just my mother, Sean's mother. But other people as well. They would be happier not to have to face it. I find that hard to say, especially since I know you and I know the children. I don't think it's fair or it's right, but I do think it's the way it is.'

Shuya nodded. 'I think it's the way it is,' she said.

There was a silence.

Could it be possible?

'What would you do if you didn't come to Ireland?' It was tentative.

'Stay here I suppose until the laicization, and after that . . .' she shrugged. 'I feel that may be a long time anyway, if it ever happens.'

'I suppose he'll keep trying.'

'He says it was like an official contract with his God. It was made formally, it must be ended formally. Like a business deal. His God wouldn't wriggle out of it, neither must he.'

'But in a way God *did* wriggle out of it, if He took Sean's vocation away.' Angela was trying desperately to be fair.

'The hardest bit is going to be the letters from your mother.'

'I know. I know. What should I do? Should I not post them, should I not write them? Will I just write a sort of account of her instead?'

'It's hard,' Shuya said. 'And on you it is most hard of all.'

Angela looked up, surprised and touched at this sympathy. Her brother had not sounded so soft and so understanding.

'I manage,' she said with a weak grin.

'Yes, but you manage alone, you manage without your sisters in England. Nobody has mentioned them because obviously there is nothing they can or will do to help. You manage without the help of anyone in your town, your priest or your friends. And you do not complain, you spend your teacher's salary to come to see us even though you think that we should not be here, and that Sean should still be a priest.'

Angela couldn't find words, she stammered. 'It's not . . . it's not that easy on you, you have nothing either.'

Shuya's plain face smiled, a smile of disbelief. 'But I have everything, I have everything in the world,' she said. And on cue two figures started staggering across the yard, Denis weighed down under still more leaves and Laki, her face a red rim of pleasure from the tomato sauce she had eaten on her spaghetti lunch.

She came again on the Friday. Sean was still high with hope – the two priests he had met yesterday were really helpful. They had shown him how things could be simplified. Go for the direct route always, they had said. Don't be misled, don't go up side alleys. Angela's heart fell when she listened to him. She had been foolish to get buoyed up with hope that Shuya would change his mind. Then he said, 'Shuya and I were talking last night. She was saying something very interesting. She has the most extraordinary insights, you know.'

Shuya was up in the Signora's linen room at the time having insights about hemming frayed pillowcases and darning perfect small darns in white silk.

'What did she say?'

'It was about the difference between country and town. It's the same in Japan, it's the same here. In the country people are slower to see what's happening in the world, they resist change. It takes so much longer to persuade people in the country of anything. It's not their fault of course.'

She listened with a new patience. Perhaps she even looked like Shuya now, her hands folded, waiting for him to get to the point.

'Things will change of course, but in their own time. You can't rush people and expect them to go at your pace. In terms of absolutes you might be wise to hold off until the growth of acceptance is sufficient . . . until the ground swell of opinion has become so strong that there will be no doubt and no confusion. That way the hurt is lessened, the debate is less sharp and the lines of love rather than the letter of the law would mould people's attitudes . . .'

She closed her eyes with relief. In his convoluted way he was telling her that he wasn't going back to Castlebay.

176

They were all sad to be leaving Rome on the Saturday, and Father Flynn was at the airport to wave them off as he had welcomed them ten days before.

'It worked out all right, did it?' he said to Angela when there was no one else around – the others wer   ling with luggage.

'What?'

'What you had to do, sort out?'

She looked at him hard. Another Irish priest in Rome. Sean talking his head off everywhere he went about it all. It was only too possible that Father Flynn knew, and had known from the start. But she was going to admit nothing.

'Oh, I sorted myself out a great few days. I really love Italy. I'm heartbroken to leave, like they all are.'

'You might come back?'

'It would cost a fortune.'

'I'm sure it would be appreciated,' he said and let it drop. He was laughing and smiling and wondering what he would do next Tuesday when he had no big important wedding to officiate at.

The journey home was something she forgot. She must have talked to people, she must have said her goodbyes and gone to the station to get the train home. She caught the bus to Castlebay: Clare was waiting at the stop. At a hundred yards away Angela knew she had won the scholarship and she started to cry.

She was crying as she got off the bus, but Clare put a finger to her lips.

'Don't say anything, Miss O'Hara, don't say anything, only you and I know. Not Mother Immaculata yet, not Mam or Dad. I wanted to tell you first.'

'I can't tell you how happy I am, I can't tell you how glad.'

Clare picked up the teacher's bag. 'I'll walk you home. We can talk when there aren't people looking at us.'

She was right. It would only take half an hour for it to be known everywhere that the two of them were crying and embracing.

They walked up the golf-course road, Clare bubbling about how the nun, the very nice nun in the town convent, had asked her to telephone the day before the official results, just in case there was any news. And Clare had telephoned this morning and yes, the nun had said it was definite, her Mother Superior was going to ring Mother Immaculata tomorrow. It was absolutely definite.

They had got to the O'Hara house and Angela let herself in.

'Do you want to be on your own . . . a bit?' Clare held back.

'Of course I don't. Mother! Mother, I'm back.'

The old woman was sitting in the chair and her face lit up. 'I was hoping you'd get the bus, was the plane very frightening? Did you have holy water with you?'

'I was laden down with it. Mother, I've got great news for you. The best, the best.' She had both her hands on her mother's shoulders as she spoke, and suddenly she remembered that for her mother the best news might be the imminent return of Father Sean from the mission fields. Hastily she jumped in. 'Clare's done it, Mother, she's won it. Isn't that bloody marvellous!'

Angela threw herself down at the table and sobbed as if her heart would break. The tears that had never come in Rome came in a torrent. Her shoulders shook.

Clare and Mrs O'Hara looked at each other in alarm. Nothing could be heard but the heavy sobs from the table. Mrs O'Hara reached out but was too far away to comfort Angela. Clare didn't know whether she should move towards the teacher or not. Tentatively she touched her on the arm and patted it awkwardly.

'Don't cry,' she said. 'Please.'

From the chair came support. 'Oh Angela, please stop that crying, we should be delighted for Clare, there was no crying in this house when *you* got the scholarship.'

Angela raised her head and saw the two stricken faces. Her own face was blotched and stained. But she found what they were both looking for, her good humour and her strength.

178

'It's the journey, and the shock and the pleasure, the sheer sheer pleasure of it. Well done, Clare, well done, may this be the first of many triumphs for you.' Her smile blazed out through the tears and suddenly Clare wanted to cry. But that would be ridiculous. Instead she did something much more ridiculous, she ran into Miss O'Hara's arms and together they swung around the room shouting with excitement. Mrs O'Hara clapped her hands in her chair and they laughed like people who had long forgotten what they were laughing at.

PART TWO

1957–1960

Clare hated sharing the room with Chrissie when she came home from school during the holidays. Chrissie's clothes smelled of sweat, she always had stockings rolled up and stuffed into shoes, the dressing table was covered with spilled powder and hair clips and combs with tufts of Chrissie's curly hair caught in the teeth. She used Clare's bed as a place to store her clothes and only very grudgingly removed them when the occupant returned from boarding school at the end of term.

Clare thought almost nostalgically of her small clean white bed in the dormitory, of the chair where her uniform lay neatly waiting for the morrow, with the stockings folded on top like a cross. It was always nice and airy in the dormitory, freezing sometimes, actually, but there was never that close smell of bodies that you had sharing a room with Chrissie. Worst of all were the blood-spattered white coats. It had never been defined who was to wash these coats and where the washing was to be done, but while it was in dispute two or more of them often festered on the floor. Clare would hide them under other garments so that she didn't have to speculate what part of what dead animal had bled over Chrissie's middle. She looked around her in disgust.

She *should* feel sorry for Chrissie, she knew this, but it didn't make it any easier. It was a desperate life standing up in Dwyers' butcher's shop and having to hack great bits off carcasses of dead sheep and cows. It wasn't a glamorous job, and it couldn't do her any good at the dance when fellows asked where she worked. Clare had suggested more than once that she try to work somewhere else. The chemist maybe? And be with that old bore Mr Murphy, Mr

183

Murphy, a daily communicant who kept his own daughters under lock and key? No thank you very much. Or the hotel even? And be a skivvy passing round dinner plates or washing up for Young Mrs Dillon and her mad old mother-in-law, no thank you, not even if Clare was friendly with them. Thank you, Chrissie would prefer to earn her own wages and be done with the place as soon as she left it in the evening.

There had been a hope that she could have used the room they had called the Boys' Room, the downstairs room where Tommy and Ned used to sleep all those years ago when they lived at home. But Mam and Dad said that room had to be used as a storeroom now, and since the business was far better than ever before a storeroom was needed. The new caravan park up on the Far Cliff Road meant a great deal of trade. People in caravans had to buy everything; they didn't do much cooking so it was mainly cold ham and tins of things. When they trekked across from the caravan field O'Brien's was the first shop they met, perched as it was at the top of the steps going down to the sea. Very few of them went any further, and then the caravan people came back again to stock up for the day on the beach, and on the way home they would buy things for their tea. It was all great but it did mean that the Boys' Room was gone as a possible place to sleep, and Clare felt she must keep the rows to a minimum, only fight over things that are really important.

Miss O'Hara and Clare had another secret, another scholarship, another over-ambitious project. Clare O'Brien was going to go for the county scholarship. One student in the entire county would be offered a place in University College, Dublin, to study Arts, to do a B.A. degree. It was called the Murray Prize. A Mr Murray long dead had left his money for this, and the competition was fierce. Usually a bright boy from one of the seminaries won it, but three years ago it had been a girl, a very brainy girl whose father was professor already. Clare and Miss O'Hara had decided to take it on.

The prize was awarded on the strength of marks received in the leaving certificate together with a personal interview.

184

Those candidates with a sizeable number of Honours Papers and who had already announced their participation would be called to appear before a committee. Even to be called to interview by the Murray committee was an honour. But it was an honour that wouldn't happen until the end of August. The examination results had to come in first. Miss O'Hara had begged Clare to enjoy the summer, it might be her last summer of freedom. If she *did* get to university there would always be the need to study, and she would have to work for extra money – the Murray scholarship was not princely. If she did *not* get to university then she would be working during the rest of her summers, so there was even more reason to enjoy this last one. Have a bit of a fling, Miss O'Hara had advised her, and Miss O'Hara had said embarrassingly that Clare was turning into a fine-looking girl and she should make the most of it.

Clare looked at herself in the mirror. She wanted to lighten the colour of her hair: she used Sta-Blonde shampoo, which claimed to bring out the blonde highlights, but it didn't or else there were no highlights to bring out. She would have used some peroxide in the rinsing water like some of the girls at school did but, really, one look at Chrissie's peroxided fuzz would be enough to turn you against the stuff even if the smell of it didn't. Clare had grown tall, all of a sudden, when she was fourteen. Nobody had expected it, least of all Clare, and it was highly irritating. School uniforms had to have false hems and be let down to the last possible thread. She wore her hair in a pony tail with one of those nice plastic clips. Chrissie had said it made her look like a horse, but Clare had taken no notice. The great thing about going away to school was meeting so many other people and being able to compare Chrissie with them. Now she no longer believed her elder sister and didn't feel put down by the scathing insults heaped on her all the time.

Clare would like to have had blue eyes. Brown eyes were wrong in her face she thought, her complexion wasn't right for them. If she were like Ava Gardner, or had a dark smouldering face, then big brown eyes would be good; but she thought they looked out of place with her light hair and fair skin. Still. There was nothing she could do about them. Josie told her they were fine, and what's more they were unusual, so there. She should be delighted with them and stop complaining.

Josie was going from strength to strength these days. She was already in the office of the hotel, wearing a frilly white blouse and a cameo brooch. She had lost a great deal of weight in the two years she spent living in her aunt's house while she went to the commercial college. Her aunt was the meanest woman in Ireland and the meals that were served were extremely sparse. But it was all to the good and Josie's two sisters looked at her with shock each time they came home from their boarding school, and, eventually, the Hotel and Catering College. Slow, fat Josie could type letters like the wind, had understood book keeping and simple accountancy. She was helping Father and Uncle Dick and Mother with far more confidence than they seemed to be able to drum up. In fact Rose and Emily were quite jealous of the sister they used to call poor Josie. They even complained when they saw her change into whites and play tennis with that Clare O'Brien from the shop. But Josie was calm. She and Clare played tennis every morning from eight to nine; then they went to work, Josie in her family business, Clare in hers. They played again at seven in the evening. Rose and Emily had all day to play if they wanted to. It was unanswerable. Which was why Rose and Emily hated it; it was even further irritating to see that Josie and Clare played well and often played a mixed doubles with guests from the hotel.

Clare and Josie had more fun at the dance than Rose and Emily who thought, wrongly, that they would be exotic and a treat coming home as they had from Dublin. But the visitors didn't know where they had come from and the locals all knew the two girls who were around all the time; they were never without a partner.

Leaning over the balcony and watching Josie rocking enthusiastically to 'See You Later Alligator', Emily complained loudly one evening that the young ones had it very easy, didn't they? Nice cushy job ready made for them in the hotel, no studying hotel management, all plain sailing and life one long holiday. Chrissie O'Brien, another wallflower, watched her younger sister with equal rage and said that there was no justice in life. Rose and Emily had to disassociate themselves. Annoyed they might be, but they weren't going to ally themselves with terrible Chrissie O'Brien.

The Nolans still came to Castlebay, they were part and parcel of the place now. At least, Mr and Mrs Nolan did. Of James, there was no sign, Josie sighed.

'Maybe he'll come down this summer, and you'll dazzle him,' Clare said.

'No, I interrogated his mother, he's in France picking grapes with David Power. Can you imagine anything more stupid, those two picking grapes? They don't need the money, why aren't they here where they *are* needed?'

'It's a funny time of year to be picking grapes,' Clare said thoughtfully. 'I thought all that was much later on.'

'Maybe they're up to no good. They could have French mistresses.' Josie was deliberately making herself miserable.

'They should be working for their exams,' Clare said primly. David Power was about Fourth Med by now; and James Nolan had a B.A. in Economics, but he still had to do his Bar Final. Josie was right; they were much too grown-up and sophisticated to pick grapes or whatever in France, but they were much too grown-up and sophisticated to come to Castlebay as well.

Molly Power was delighted with the letter. It said she was to let the Nolans know too. David and James would be arriving next Thursday week. Things hadn't worked out exactly as they had hoped in France, long explanations later, but meanwhile they thought they would come back to Castlebay. Waving the letter Molly ran out on to the drive as she heard her husband's car on the gravel.

'Great news, David's coming home next week.'

His face lit up with pleasure. 'David's coming back, Bones,' he said and the animal did three circuits of the car, barking delightedly.

Paddy Power took his wife's arm and they sat on the garden seat, looking straight out to sea. On a day like this it was paradise.

Nellie called from the kitchen window. 'You look very comfortable out there, stay as you are. I'll bring out your dinner.'

A polite protest.

'Sure why don't you act like the quality,' Nellie said and closed the window.

They smiled at each other, pleased greatly that their son was coming home.

'I arranged for old Mrs O'Hara to go into the County Hospital for a couple of weeks today. Observation, I call it.'

'And what is it? What has she got?'

'Nothing, as far as I can see. Nothing she hasn't had for years. But I want to give Angela a holiday, that's what it's really about. Angela hardly ever gets a break. I want her to enjoy a bit of this summer. Lord, she's living in a place that half of Ireland and indeed half of England as well seems to be descending on . . . but she never gets out to enjoy it.'

'You're very thoughtful.' Molly touched his knee affectionately.

'I've always liked her, always, she's got such pluck, I know it's a funny word, it's not a word for people like us, but that's it. Pluck. Do you know I often think young Clare O'Brien from the shop has it too. I always see her as sort of an echo of Angela O'Hara.'

'Do you?' Molly frowned.

'Same way of sticking their chins up and getting on with things, no matter what.' Dr Power smiled at the thought.

'I don't think so.' Molly was shaking her head. 'Angela had spirit certainly, and it's wonderful she got so far, considering . . .' She left unsaid the ripples of disapproval over Dinny O'Hara's behaviour, and her own remoteness towards the life looking after an old woman.

Dr Power hid his impatience. He hated Molly in that *grande dame* mood. 'Well the child Clare O'Brien has nobody to be apologizing for, just the fact that she was born poor and triumphed over it.'

'She was born sneaky, Paddy, you're too kind, you don't see these things. A woman would notice. She has deceitful eyes.'

'*Molly.*'

'Well, you say what you think, I say what I think.'

'But it's silly. Silly, to say such a thing about a child.'

'To me some of the things *you* do and say are silly. I don't pass remarks about them.'

'All right, Moll, all right. Life's short, let's leave it.' The day seemed less shiny somehow for him.

Gerry Doyle arrived at the O'Haras' cottage later in the afternoon. He was to give them a lift to the hospital. 'Take as much time as you like,' he told them. 'I'm in no hurry, so don't be rushing.'

But they were ready: Mrs O'Hara tremulous and afraid of a bumpy journey in that young tearaway's van, Angela pale and anxious. The little suitcase had been packed.

'Well will we head off then?' Gerry was a great person to drive them. He didn't care enough about Mrs O'Hara to be making inquiries about how she felt, and he had plenty of good casual chat to keep Angela distracted. Dr Power had said that since he went into the town every Tuesday to get equipment and supplies, he'd be the very man to give them a lift. Dr Power had even gone and called on Doyle's Photographics himself to save Angela the business of asking him for a lift.

He was kind and practical about getting the old woman into his van. 'Tell me first what movements hurt you most, and I won't drag you the wrong way,' he said.

Mrs O'Hara had to pause and think. The worst bit was having to bend her legs. Right, that was easily organized, Gerry got a box for her to stand on then she sat into the front seat of his van and Angela eased her legs in as straight as it was possible to do. Mrs O'Hara settled in fairly cheerfully. Angela climbed into the back.

'You're very agile for a woman of your age,' Gerry said, smiling at her in the driver's mirror.

'Will you stop that nonsense, I could run rings round you.

189

Your generation have no stamina.' She grinned back at him through the mirror. He was a handsome lad. She had always liked him. Much more than his sister, and she had often asked herself why she didn't take to Fiona Doyle, without ever coming to a satisfactory conclusion.

They were good youngsters both of them. Since their father's death, they had not only kept the business going, they had made it boom. The big increase in visitors had meant a huge demand for snaps. During the summer the Doyles hired another photographer to help out. They had smartened up their little booth on the cliff with bright paint, and they had been doing great business calling to the houses along the Cliff Road and the Far Cliff Road taking family pictures, which they enlarged and presented in a little cardboard frame. Nearly every family wanted to have a souvenir like that, something to show at home, the family in their own place. Messages used to be sent urgently to get young Jimmy back from the amusements, or call young Eddie up from the beach; Mother would change into her best dress and the milk bottle would be hidden away while the picture was being taken.

'I see your star pupil is home from school,' Gerry said.

'She is a star pupil,' Angela said proudly. 'I have great hopes for her, I really do.'

'So do I,' said Gerry, smiling roguishly. 'Great hopes altogether.'

'Stop sounding like the villain in a pantomime,' Angela said crossly. *Please,* she thought, don't let Gerry Doyle distract Clare before the interview. Don't let him get his hands on her until she's won the Murray Prize.

They were very nice to Mrs O'Hara in the hospital, and the change suited her. Everything was new and interesting: the Little Flower ward with the big statue of St Theresa and the roses falling around the crucifix in her arms. Mrs O'Hara had always had a great devotion to the Little Flower. The woman in the next bed was some distant relative by marriage so they spent hours tracing people long dead and lowering their voices about people whose careers had not been too glorious. Angela felt nothing but relief that her mother was being well looked after. Dr Power had been right: the change would do Mam good. She spent the first few days after her mother left doing a kind of spring-clean. She never liked to paint the place while the housebound woman was there; the smell would be hard to bear. She pulled all the furniture into the middle of the floor, and began to take down the books and ornaments. It was a much longer job than she would have believed but it was a very peaceful one. She sat on a ladder dusting books and reading them at the same time, polishing ornaments and remembering who had given them or where they had come from. It was days before she actually began to paint. She had gone in twice and been reassured that her mother was happy and well looked after. This was a good break for her, house-painting in the morning, a stroll down to the hotel, a sandwich sometimes with Dick Dillon, still mourning the fact that he had been put off drink and pushed sideways in the chain of command in the hotel. Then she would go down to the beach, and swim. She would know at least twenty people that she passed, pupils present and past, people from Castlebay sunning themselves. But usually she took a book and sat on the grassy cliff base. Then when it got very hot she would run down into the sea and battle with the breakers. Once she came across a small child who was being constantly buffeted by the waves and knocked down every time she got to her feet. Angela swooped her up and carried her out of the water. She was just the kind of child who could be one of Dr Power's casualties. The kind of thing he was always worrying about, visitors who didn't know the pull of the current, the strength of the waves. She found herself telling the family tearfully that they must pay more attention to a child of that age or she would be swept out to sea. The child's parents were grateful and startled, and she overheard them saying as she left that possibly she had a child that was drowned herself and that's what had unsettled her so much. Angela didn't *feel* unsettled. She felt fine. But she realized that it was the first summer she had ever got a tan, been to the pictures regularly and gone to the dance.

She hadn't intended going to the dance. She thought women of thirty-five were pathetic in their summer dresses, their white cardigans and their newly lacquered hair queueing up at the ticket desk with the hope of a starry and glittery night ahead. Even when she heard that the Castlebay Committee were having a special dance to raise funds she didn't think of going. The Committee was going to charge a big price for the ticket, but there were going to be enormous spot prizes. Every business in the place was giving something. Gerry Doyle was going to take a family or group portrait free, Mrs Conway in the post offfice was offering a set of a dozen views of Castlebay on postcards with a small frame as well. Dwyers' were giving a leg of lamb. Miss O'Flaherty was offering a writing case with pad and envelopes. The O'Briens were giving two big tins of Afternoon Tea assortment, the best biscuits there were. The money they raised would go to make the place look more attractive, to build a proper car park possibly and prevent the road being cluttered with cars making it impossible to get in or out of Castlebay. Or maybe plant a big flowerbed on the way into town where the three roads met. Some people wanted to put up fairy lights down Church Street, and others wanted to have public lavatories built on the beach. It would all be debated long and excitedly during the winter, and the money raised would sit in Mrs Conway's post offfice for ages. Angela, as a teacher and respected member of the community, had been on the Castlebay Committee but it never occurred to her that she was expected to go to the dance. Dick Dillon said that this is what always happened when you had a bunch of old meddlers and busybodies running things, now they were all nicely stuck and had to go to the wretched dance or their lives wouldn't be worth living.

'Will you come as my partner?' he asked Angela in a voice filled with such doom he might as well have been asking her to leap off the cliff with him in a suicide mission.

'Certainly,' Angela said.

He looked at her suspiciously. 'You can collect me at the hotel then,' he said.

'No Dick, a gentleman collects a lady at *her* house,' Angela said in a parody of every Doris Day film she had seen. If Dick had seen the films he didn't recognize the parody.

'Very well,' he said. 'Seeing as how I don't drink any more I might as well get value out of the car by driving it.'

She hardly thought about the dance again, she was so busy painting the house. She decided that the only way to do it was to divide the big downstairs room into two halves, and when the first half was painted she would put back the books and knick-knacks before starting the other side. It did look much brighter and more awake. She was standing in a paint-spattered smock and her hair in an old scarf admiring it, when a car stopped at the door. James Nolan and David Power had come to call. Better than that, they had brought a bottle of champagne cider.

She was delighted to see them. She had followed their careers with delight and when nobody else remembered what exams they were doing, Miss O'Hara always did. She used to know the names of their professors too and she never asked embarrassing questions like did they have girlfriends, did they spend much money on drink, and what exactly were they doing in France?

They picked chairs and stools out of the heap of furniture and sat happily telling her about everything. David was tall and fair-haired with a peeling nose, and James small and dark-looking like a little Italian, so tanned was he after whatever they had been up to in France. They were full of plans for the summer. It was going to be two hours' work every morning and then free as the air all day and all night. They wanted to know was there any talent in town. Any gorgeous blondes or redheads with tiny waists and huge bosoms. Angela said she wouldn't have noticed if the town was full of them, but they'd have to look sharp before Gerry Doyle grabbed everything that was going.

'That fellow, is he still at it?' James Nolan said. 'I know I'm a small runt of a thing myself, but he's a dwarf. What *do* they see in him?'

'I can't believe he's *still* the Romeo,' David complained.

'He was always getting the girls without having to lift a finger. I'd have thought they'd have seen through him by now.'

'Different crop every year of course,' Angela said.

'But seriously, Miss O'Hara, seriously.' David looked lovely when he was trying to be serious. He pushed the long lick of hair on his forehead back so that it stood up like a fan. 'Now would you as a *woman* . . . well, as a *female* – would you tell us what's so attractive about him.'

'As a *female*, I would find it very hard to explain. He's good company, he has a nice smile, he smiles a lot. He doesn't try too hard to please, but he does seem to *like* women, without exactly flirting with them. Is that any help?'

She looked from one handsome student to the other as they sat in her upside-down house. They were both thoughtful.

'That's a great help, actually,' David said earnestly. 'Not trying too hard to please. I think that's where I fall down.'

'I don't think I *like* women like he does. I think I like the idea of women more than I like them as people,' said James Nolan.

'I'm sorry I don't have a couch free,' Angela laughed. 'You could lie down one by one and I could psychoanalyse you, maybe I could psychoanalyse half of Castlebay, and I'd make a fortune. Your father could send me a few patients, David, and maybe Father O'Dwyer could too. Oh and anyone left roaring and bawling after the dance could always come here for a midnight session, I'd straighten them out.'

She was great at knocking down their pomposity. David had been glad to hear from his father that the old woman was in hospital for the summer; he didn't like calling to see Miss O'Hara when her mother was there, you felt you should talk to both of them. He remembered why he had come.

'I really wanted to know if you'd like to come with us to the Castlebay Committee dance next week. Mummy and Daddy are going too and the Nolans and we were all going to have a drink in our house first and go together.'

Angela was flattered to have been asked; but she regretted that she had a date already.

They were excited when they learned it was Dick Dillon. A romance? A local love affair possibly? A slow-flowering friendship blossoming into a late romance? Would there be wedding bells pealing out from the church before long?

She said they shouldn't be so cruel and heartless and tease an old maid, a poor spinster of the parish. David said it was just because she wasn't an old maid they could tease her. It was the best compliment she had ever got, even though anyone else hearing it might have thought it inexplicable.

Clare came twice a week to rehearse the interview for the Murray Prize. They had found out who sat on the board: an uncle of Josie Dillon on her mother's side was one of them. He was a bank manager and the Murray money was in his bank so that gave him some kind of right to be there when it was being handed out. According to Josie he was mad and snobbish, and thought that Dillon's Hotel in Castlebay was rather beneath him. Angela and Clare were still working on their strategy for him. Clare arrived shortly after the boys had gone.

'The place stinks of drink,' she said accusingly.

'It's my age, at the change of life we women become all funny, we start shifting the furniture around and drinking on our own.'

Clare laughed. 'You're never at the change of life yet, Miss O'Hara?'

'*Of course I'm not!* God, remind me never to make jokes talking to children. Please Lord, let me never be ironic again. The drink was a gift from two young gentlemen callers. They came and brought champagne cider and invited me to the Castlebay Committee dance. How about that for a poor, old, decrepit, barren geriatric?'

'Who was it?'

'David Power and James Nolan.'

'And are you going?'

'No, I thought I'd leave the field free for younger, plainer women. I'm going with Josie's uncle. He did ask me first. Are you going?'

'I suppose I will, Josie and I'll go together. You don't need a partner. I think she'd rather like it if James Nolan was around, she fancies him a lot.'

'Tell her to pretend she doesn't even notice him, that will work. Come on now, do something to help me, lift one end of this contraption with me, I'm going to paint it out in the back. If I paint it here I'll stick to it every time I pass by. It's not going to rain they say on the wireless, so that should mean we'll have a nice fine evening . . .'

She broke off suddenly. Clare hadn't moved, she was sitting troubled and hadn't even been listening.

'What is it?' she said. 'You surely haven't got the results yet?'

The only thing that could make Clare's face so downcast must have to do with the Leaving Certificate results, but they weren't due for two more weeks.

'Tommy's in gaol,' Clare said simply.

'Tommy. Tommy?' It was so long since she had seen the O'Brien boys she had forgotten their names. It came to her a couple of seconds later. 'In gaol? In England? What did he do?'

'Housebreaking.'

Angela sat down. 'When did you hear? Who told you?'

'Just now. The afternoon post. I'm afraid I came up to you straight away. I couldn't bear to stand in the shop thinking about it. Mam will be furious. Still. I'll cope with that.'

'God Almighty, isn't that desperate? How do you know?'

'A letter from Ned. So as not to worry Mam and Dad immediately, but so as I could forewarn them in case it gets back to them. What *does* he want me to do? Tell them or not to tell them? It might appear in a paper he said, then again it might not. Thomas O'Brien is a very ordinary name he says, but Thomas O'Brien from Castlebay would place him pretty clearly. Here, you can read the letter . . . see if you know what he wants. See if you know what I'm meant to do.'

Angela didn't reach out to take the ill-written pages on their lined paper. She sat with her elbows on her knees and her head in her hands. There was a silence for a while. 'I don't need to read the letter, I know what he wants,' Angela said eventually. 'He wants *you* to make the decisions. He wants *you* to take on the responsibility.'

Clare was surprised. 'Why?'

'Because you're not Chrissie who wouldn't know what day it was, and you're not your mother who would cry her eyes out, and you're not your father who would get into a temper and you're not Ben and Jim who are too young to be taken into account. And because you're bright and got a scholarship, that's going to fit you and make you ready for any burden from now on.'

Clare was very startled at her tone. 'Miss O'Hara . . .' she began.

'What sentence did he get?' Angela asked crisply.

'Ned says two years.'

'That was more than ordinary housebreaking. He must have had a weapon. The great thick fool.'

'No wonder he never wrote home.'

'Tommy was hardly able to write if I remember rightly. What do you think you'll do?'

'I don't know. I've no information. If I thought it was going to get into the papers here I'd tell Ma and Da, but if not what's the point in hurting them?'

'I know, what we need is information as you say.'

'But I've no way of finding out . . .'

'I have. See can you find a writing pad under those newspapers there, I'll write it now and you can get it into the six o'clock post.'

'Who? What will you say?'

'I have a friend in London. He's a priest – but not like Father O'Dwyer here or anything. He'd find out for us.'

'But could you ask him? Wouldn't he . . .?'

'No, he wouldn't be shocked, and he's one of the best men in the world to keep a secret. Have you the paper? I'll start straight away.'

Clare's eyes filled quickly with tears of gratitude as Miss O'Hara wrote her address across the top of the paper and then wrote: 'Dear Father Flynn, I wonder can you help me. Yet again . . .'

Father Flynn was magnificent. There was a reply in eight days. He had been to see Ned, who was working in a pub now, washing up. It was a rough sort of place, Father Flynn had got him a new job where he was better off – he could live in and the landlord would keep an eye on him. He had heard the details. Tommy had been in with a gang. They had done several jobs and six months ago, Tommy had got probation for his part in the theft of building supplies from a site. This time it had been a smash and grab raid on a small jeweller's shop. What they hadn't realized was that the jeweller was still in his shop when the windows were broken with crowbars and the goods seized. The jeweller's mistake had been to stand up. He had been hit on the side of the head by one of the gang – he could not identify it as being Tommy. But the rest of them escaped and were gone well to ground when the police came looking. Only Tommy was there still with some of the jewellery.

Tommy had said he didn't know who the others were, and couldn't give descriptions. He insisted that he had only met them that night and they didn't give their names. So, according to Ned, the gang were pleased with him and they would make sure he got his share when he came out. He would be out in eighteen months. Father Flynn had visited him in Wormwood Scrubs and reported that he was very pleased to have some contact with home. Since he had been asked to be totally frank, Father Flynn had to report Tommy O'Brien in poor shape, he was missing most of his teeth; he asked for nothing but comics to read from the prison library and he had all the appearance of a loser. Since it was hardly helpful to make such comments without offering anything more positive as well, Father Flynn wondered was there a way Tommy could be brought back to Castlebay when he was released. He did not seem a strong enough character to survive on either side of the tracks in the life he had found for himself in London. If Castlebay was not a realistic solution Father Flynn would try to keep an eye on him, but it would be hard. As soon as Tommy was released he would be given money to show approval that he hadn't squealed; and within three months he would be inside again, for he would loyally go along with the next job suggested to him, and be the patsy there as well. As regards publicity there would be none. The name T. O'Brien had appeared in a local evening paper in London; it would not be taken up by the Irish newspapers. Unfortunately, the arrest and imprisonment of people with Irish names was only too commonplace now. It didn't rate as news.

Angela and Clare read this glumly. He had certainly been as frank as they had asked him to be. But he had been exactly the right person to go and see what was happening. He made no judgements and expressed no shock or disapproval.

'I wonder how Tommy lost his teeth. A fight maybe?' Angela said.

'Maybe they just rotted away,' Clare said. 'He was very nervous of everything, Tommy. He wouldn't ever go to the dentist. I can't think how he was brave enough to get in with a gang of robbers, I'd have thought he would have run a hundred miles in the opposite direction.'

Her face was sad even though her voice was calm. She hadn't cried or shown any great shock when she read the priest's letter. She sat very still with her elbows on the table and her chin in her hands. Clare had the ability to be very still, Angela had noticed. When she was reading only the turning of the pages showed she was awake. When she listened it was the same. Now she heard of her brother's disgrace without expostulating, or making excuses.

'I don't suppose he had to be very brave to get in with a gang. Probably need to be brave *not* to get in with one. Will you write to him in gaol?'

Clare hadn't thought of this. 'Is there any point if he can't read the letters? Would we be better to pretend we didn't know he was there at all? I think that's what he'd like best,' she said without conviction.

'Too late for that. Ned wrote to you, remember? You can't pretend you don't know. You can keep it from your parents and the rest of them but you can't go back on what you know.'

'Yes.'

'So, will you write to him?'

'He never wrote to me, not in six years, nor to any of us, it would only be hypocritical, wouldn't it? And maybe even boasting. Look at me, how well I'm doing, I even have my sights on being a college girl, a graduate, and where are you? You're a gaol bird.'

'I don't suppose you'd write a letter like that.'

Her immobility had gone, her eyes flashed. 'You think I ought to, don't you? If it were you, you'd be sunny and forgiving and like a saint, the way you are about everything. But the world isn't full of saints, it's full of ordinary selfish people like Tommy who go stealing, and me who doesn't want to write him pious letters.'

Angela said nothing.

'I know I shouldn't say it's all right for you, I *know* you had your share of awful things years ago when your father was . . . but that's all long past you, people have forgotten that, you've no shames and no secrets now. You're where you want to be, and you're nice and safe as a teacher here, and your family are all respectable, and you've got a brother, a priest, for God's sake. I've got a brother with no teeth who can't read and who's in Wormwood Scrubs.'

'Clare,' Angela said sharply.

She looked up.

Angela paused. No, not now. It wasn't bad enough, it was only a fit of annoyance and self-pity. She wouldn't tell her.

'Nothing.'

Clare was surprised.

'If you don't get the Murray Prize remind me that I was going to tell you something this afternoon and I changed my mind.'

'Why won't you tell me?'

'I won't, that's all. Now are we going to waste any more time listening to how sorry you are for yourself? You asked me to find out about Tommy, I have. He's your brother, write to him if you want to, don't if you don't want to. I'm not spending one more minute discussing it. If you haven't the generosity to give some bit of hope and optimism to that poor eejit in there, then you haven't. I'm not involved in making you a nice person, nobody can do that for you. I'm only helping you to get on academically. Let's see, where were we?' She took out a notebook and checked the items they'd covered last time. 'Now we've been over a lot of current affairs and you're fine on Eisenhower and the Middle East and the end of Anthony Eden, and King Hussein of Jordan, but there's a good chance that none of the committee will have ever heard of them. Maybe we should concentrate on what they really know about, the Pope and de Valera. When was Plus XII consecrated as Pope . . . ?'

'I'm sorry. Of course I'll write to him.'

'Write to who you like. Plus XII. And what was his name?'

'Pacelli, Eugenio Pacelli, he's eighty-one, he was elected in 1939, the year the war started, he was Papal representative in Germany.'

'*Nuncio, nuncio,* say it.'

'Nuncio.'

'And don't come out with it too cocky. Try not to sound as if you know everything. They won't like that.'

They laughed. Clare wanted to say more about Tommy, but she was headed off.

'De Valera . . . now this is a tricky one, they'll be bound to love him or hate him, but you're not expected to have any views . . . just facts. Born?'

'In New York in 1882, of a Spanish father and Irish mother, brought up in Bruree, County Limerick . . . but I do have views . . .'

'Of course you do, but when you are being tested for the Murray Prize is not the time to express them. If any of this lot are in their fifties or over they'll remember the Civil War. Not just remember hearing about it, they'll bloody remember it themselves, so will you go carefully and don't throw the whole thing away. We could concentrate on what Dev did in the last war, that shouldn't offend many of them, but if there's anyone with an Anglo-Irish accent there watch it, the English never forgave Dev over our staying neutral. No point in waving a red rag to a bull.'

'Thank you, Miss O'Hara.'

'Stop simpering and keep learning. Talking of simpering, did Gerry Doyle ask you to the Castlebay Committee dance?'

'Yes he did. I said no, Josie and I were going on our own, we'd see him in there.'

'It's you who should be teaching me,' sighed Angela.

Dick Dillon looked very cross when he came to collect Angela. She invited him in and offered him a cup of tea or a glass of orange. He looked around in surprise.

'You have it very nice, considering.'

'Considering *what*?'

'I don't know, just considering,' he said. Angela wondered why couldn't she have said to Dick Dillon that she'd see him inside? Why did she have to put up with this groaning and grousing?

'I painted it recently, while mother's in hospital. Dr Power said she should go in for observation. She'll be back soon.'

She heard her own voice, boring, talking trivia to this old man. What did young Clare mean the other day when she said that Angela had got all she wanted? She did not want to be talking to a reformed alcoholic sitting there patronizing her little house. In as grouchy a manner as his own she flung his orange squash in front of him and very deliberately took a bottle of gin out of the press.

'Since I haven't been put off it yet, I am going to have a drink to get us through this night, Dick Dillon. So will almost everyone around you, so you might as well get used to it now.'

A slow smile of admiration came over his face. 'That's the first time anyone has treated me as a normal human being for seven years,' and he raised his own glass to her. 'Good luck,' he said beaming all over his face.

Molly Power had laid out little plates of biscuits with cheese on some and mashed-up eggs on others. The eggs ones had been a mistake. She had forgotten how quickly they would go soggy. She had nuts in little bowls and that afternoon she had gone and collected masses of gorse, which looked gorgeous in bowls and jugs all around the room. Their sitting room had yellow curtains and the chintz covers had a lot of yellow in them too. One day Nellie had brought in gorse and Molly had been about to throw it out but Mrs Nolan had admired it. So now Molly had adopted it as her own idea.

David was rubbing Nivea Creme into his nose. 'I think all the peeling's gone now,' he said, looking at himself in the mirror over the mantelpiece.

'I told you to stop pulling at it and picking at it, it would have gone much sooner if you'd left it alone,' his mother said.

David sighed. There was never anything that Mother didn't know or wasn't right about.

'I know, I know,' he said wearily.

'Well it stands to reason. You're fair-skinned. You get burned. You must wait until the dead skin falls off. Don't pull at it.'

'I won't,' David said, exasperated.

'I don't know why you're getting into a mood.' Molly was annoyed. 'Here we are, having a party for all your friends before you go to the dance. You will have a marvellous evening and all you can do is snap at anyone who tries to help you.' She sounded aggrieved.

David said nothing.

'It's not as if your father and I ever interfere in your life or ask you what you get up to. When the dance is over, do we ever say you must come straight home? No we don't. We let you live your own life.'

'Ah, come on now,' David, trying to hide his anger without much success, laughed insincerely. 'Come on, Mother, I'm a grown-up man, not a little boy with a fishing net. I live my own life in Dublin – naturally I live my own life here too.'

'*Naturally*,' she said in her pouting voice.

He chose not to hear the sulk.

'Good, then we're both saying the same thing.' He squared his shoulders in his new jacket and gave himself one last look.

'Well, that will have to do. If I don't get the lovely Caroline away from Gerry Doyle tonight, I never will.'

'Gerry Doyle? Don't be ridiculous. He'll be there taking snaps.'

'Oh no he won't, he'll have a minion doing that. Gerry will be there on his own terms, making no effort and they'll all come crawling to him.'

'That's disgusting and all in your mind.'

'See for yourself tonight. Caroline's only one of a queue.'

'I never heard such nonsense . . . oh there you are Paddy, don't you look nice and clean?'

'Clean?' Dr Power roared. 'Is that all you have to say to me?'

'I meant dressed up and smart,' Molly laughed.

'Clean,' he snorted. 'What were you saying was nonsense, when I came in?'

'This belief that Gerry Doyle is some kind of ladykiller. Even Caroline Nolan. Caroline, with the whole of the university to choose from . . .'

'Caroline's here,' Dr Power said. 'There was a great tooting of cars and I saw her arriving up at the crossroads. She has a Morris Minor all of her own now. Anyway, she said she took it into her head to come to Castlebay, and I told her she picked a good night and that she was to come up here for a drink first. She got into a great fluster and said she'd have to wash her hair. I don't know why women go on so much about their hair. They're always washing it or having it done at the hairdresser's, and complaining if you don't know every rib of it that's been changed.'

'Well now we'll see if she's interested in that Gerry Doyle,' Molly said to David. 'And stop eating the cheese ones. If you want to eat anything, eat the ones with egg on them.'

Chrissie had given the dance a lot of thought. At one stage she was fully prepared to abandon it. A snobs' dance, an old people's dance. Catch Chrissie O'Brien dead at that? Then she saw that the feeling of the town was not the same as her own. In Dwyers' they discussed endlessly whether they should give mutton, beef or pork as a spot prize, and Kath and Peggy had even bought new dresses. Chrissie decided that she didn't want to be humbled watching Gerry Doyle ignore her. He only gave her the coolest of nods these days. She couldn't bear him to see her standing there as he whirled by with whatever new glamorous piece who had come to town. Even if he danced with her once or twice like he used to, that would be fine, but he had lost all interest. He didn't need Chrissie.

She sighed a lot when people asked her was she going to the Committee dance. 'Only if someone asks me,' she said. 'I'm too old to go to a dance without a partner.'

Kath and Peggy couldn't understand it. The *point* was to go without a partner and find a partner there. But Chrissie was adamant. Bumper Byrne the builder was buying meat and heard Chrissie O'Brien talking like this. He told his younger brother Maurice, or Mogsy as he had been called ever since anyone could remember. Mogsy came down to the shop.

'Will you be my partner for the Committee dance please?' he said across the counter. Mr Dwyer the butcher sighed with relief.

'What do you mean by being a partner exactly?'

'I mean I'll pay for you, I'll dance with you when you're not asked up by other people. I won't stand in your way if some fellow you want a spin around the floor with comes along, and I'll buy you minerals at the bar,' said Mogsy who wore his hat back to front and wasn't too bright.

Chrissie considered it. 'And what would you get out of it?' she asked ungraciously.

'I don't know.' Mogsy hadn't thought of it like that. 'I suppose I'd get the right to dance with you and put my arm around you and say you were my date for the night. Aren't you the best-looking girl in Castlebay?'

Chrissie smiled across the marble counter. 'Thank you very much, Mogsy, I'd be glad to come to the dance as your partner,' she said.

Best-looking girl in Castlebay. Well now. Not that anyone was saying Mogsy Byrne was bright or anything, but he wasn't *too* bad, and she would never be left standing, and she'd go in on his arm. That would show Gerry Doyle not everyone had to sit around and wait for him.

'Good, that's fixed then.' Mogsy was off.

'Have you a suit and everything?' she asked.

'I've a gorgeous suit,' he said.

'We'll show them, Mogsy,' she said.

Josie and Clare were putting on their make-up.

'It must be something to do with the colour of your lips to start with,' Josie said. 'Sari Peach looks quite a different colour on you than on me.'

They had bought one lipstick between them in Murphy's chemist. Mrs Murphy had said it was very unhygienic to share a lipstick, it could pass on germs. They had laughed the whole way home remembering how the whole school would share one lipstick at times and nobody had come out in a rash.

Clare wore a red corduroy skirt and a white frilly blouse: she had a red velvet ribbon on her hair. She dressed up in Josie's room because Chrissie had the bedroom at home commandeered. Josie had a lemon-coloured dress with a square neck back and front, trimmed with white broderie anglaise.

'Are you sure I don't look like a tank?' she asked for the tenth time.

'What am I going to do with you?' Clare wailed. 'You *don't* look like a tank, you haven't looked like a tank since you were twelve and you're nearly eighteen now. That's a third of your life you haven't looked like a tank and you still think you do!'

Josie laughed. 'I'm thinner than Emily and Rose. They hate it.'

'They hate everything. They're like posh versions of Chrissie. She says that I'm thin because of all the badness in me, it eats up the food from within, and you're thin because you've got worms.'

They fell about the room laughing. Which was worse, to have worms or inner badness?

'I don't think he has anyone else this summer, anyone serious that is,' Josie said, pouting at herself in the mirror.

'James?'

'Who else?'

'Not a sign of it. He and David have been playing golf a lot. Miss O'Hara told me. They call into her sometimes on the way there or back. No sign of women at all. His sister's arrived. Lady Caroline. I saw her rushing into reception downstairs asking for a loan of a hairdryer. '

'Did they give her one?' Josie wanted to befriend the beloved's sister.

'I think so, there was a great fuss – you know the way Lady Caroline talks, she expects things done.'

'I hope they got her one.'

'I don't, I'd like her to have rats' tails for once instead of looking like an advertisement.'

'I think she fancies Gerry Doyle.'

'Tell her to join the queue,' Clare said, applying more Vaseline to her eyelashes to get them to curl.

'I was just thinking,' Josie said. 'Suppose I won the spot prize we gave, you know the one the hotel gave.'

'Well, what would be so funny?'

'It's a weekend, all expenses paid, staying here. I could have a room with a sea view and have Emily bring me my breakfast in bed.'

Chrissie was just ahead of them at the ticket box. She was arm in arm with Mogsy Byrne who was in charge of the churns when the farmers brought the milk in. Tonight, he wore a suit. He looked a bit drunk already.

'I would have thought that the elegant Miss Clare O'Brien and her friend Miss Josie Dillon wouldn't be seen paying for their own tickets to the dance,' Chrissie said loudly.

She looked awful, Clare thought. After all that work and all that flinging of clothes and make-up around the bedroom. The pink satin dress was much too tight, the white cardigan was grubby and the glittery diamante jewellery looked flashy, like the bright red lipstick and heavy white powder. Still, other fellows were giving her admiring glances. Maybe she was more suitably dressed than Clare, perhaps the blouse and skirt were a bit dowdy, a bit schoolgirlish.

They were playing 'The Yellow Rose of Texas'; the ballroom was festive, with balloons and decorations all around, and a big banner saying that the Castlebay Committee welcomed everyone and thanked them for their support. There was a huge table, groaning with gifts, on the stage near the band, and a spotlight going around picking out lucky couples who would then be given a gift. The instructions were that not too many should be given early, and only the inferior ones. As Clare and Josie came in they saw a couple in the spotlight being presented with a small talcum powder and bath cubes in a presentation box. There were much greater things to come. They were heading across to a corner which they thought was a good vantage point when they were both asked to dance at once. This was a good omen, they thought, as they were whirled out on to the floor.

Dick Dillon said he was great at the waltz but he wasn't going to make a public display of himself over this jiving, and rock and roll.

Angela said the waltz was her forte too, just so long as they didn't twirl too fast. As luck would have it the band had announced 'Tales from the Vienna Woods' just as they came in.

'I suppose you'll want to go to the ladies' cloakroom,' Dick grumbled.

'Why would I?' Angela asked and they were off, round and round, bending and swooping, Dick looking over his left shoulder and Angela looking to her left. He held her firmly in the small of the back and didn't slip, even though the floor had been treated to make it shine. Angela's beige silk dress, the one she had bought for Emer's wedding, swirled round. If Emer could see this! It is *ridiculous,* she thought, I am a ludicrous figure. And she smiled to herself as she saw admiring glances, not laughter. She saw Dr Power pointing her out to Mr Nolan. That would have been her party if she hadn't agreed to come with this madman.

The madman in question spoke out of the side of his mouth. 'I think we're showing them a thing or two,' he hissed.

'I'd say they'll clear the floor any minute for the two of us to do a demonstration,' Angela said, and at that moment the spotlight landed on them and the band leader announced that they had won a leg of lamb kindly presented by Messrs Dwyer, the premier butcher in Castlebay.

Everybody was in good humour, and suntanned and cheerful. Simon, the handsome lifeguard, who wore a pullover tied casually round his shoulders, was talking to Frank Conway who was a guard, and very tall with a back like a ramrod. A lot of the girls were eyeing them with interest. Frank Conway kept glancing at the door. 'I was watching to see if I could see Fiona Doyle coming in,' he explained.

Simon smiled. 'I bet a lot of people are. But I wouldn't be surprised if the guard dog hasn't let her out.'

'The what?'

'Her brother. He is like a guard dog. He barks if anyone comes near. It's fine for him to do what he likes, but she can have no fun.'

Frank was disappointed but he wanted to stand up for Fiona. 'In a way, Gerry's right, you can't have *girls* doing what they like – it wouldn't be right.'

'You're not like that with your sister Bernie. She's a free agent.' Simon glanced at Bernie Conway, smooching with one of the visitors.

'Yes, well.' Frank was irritated now on every score. When the dance was over he went up to Bernie and invited her for the next waltz.

'This *is* a surprise,' she said, not altogether pleased.

'I think you should behave in a more ladylike way in public.'

'I think you should go and stick your fat head in a bucket,' said Bernie, and walked off the floor. Simon saw her free, and asked her back to dance.

'My brother is mad. Stark staring mad,' she said.

'Let's not talk about your brother,' said Simon, holding her very close to him and running his hand up and down her back.

Gerry Doyle never *asked* anyone to dance. He always seemed to be beside the girl that he wanted when the music started, and he would smile and hold out his hand. He asked Josie Dillon first, and she was glad to be seen out on the floor by James Nolan, who had just come in. Josie had noticed that Caroline's dark hair looked nicely set, so the hotel must have been able to find her a hair dryer all right. Gerry was a terrific dancer of course, and she was glad that she and Clare had spent some time learning the Twist at the beginning of the summer. The world was divided between those who could and couldn't do it. Gerry had probably been *born* . knowing how to do it.

He admired her dress, he said it was a lovely sunny colour, that she and Clare O'Brien looked the classiest girls in the whole ballroom. She asked would Fiona be here, but he said she had a summer flu. They both agreed that Uncle Dick had turned out to be a demon dancer. He hadn't been off the floor since he came in and insisted on doing formal quicksteps to the rock and roll numbers.

James and Caroline Nolan had arrived, and Gerry had seen them. He escorted Josie back to where he had found her with a big smile. 'I wish they all danced like you, Josie Dillon, the Ginger Rogers of Castlebay.' Josie was pink with delight. She was about to tell Clare, but at that moment Clare was whisked off by Uncle Dick. Josie could have died of mortification. Why couldn't Uncle Dick just sit down like other old people, or venture gently into a foxtrot or something? Why did he have to make a fool of her by asking her friend to dance? The band announced a series of Latin American numbers beginning with the 'Blue Tango'.

'I'm not great at it, not a semi-professional like yourself,' Clare had confessed.

'Listen to me once, you're meant to be a bright girl. It's one step rock back, two steps rock back, three steps rock back. Repeat that.'

They hadn't started to dance yet. Clare repeated it.

'Right, hold on tight and follow me, none of this independent doing fandangos on your own.'

He stood beside her but facing in a different direction, he stretched their arms out as if they were pretending to be scarecrows in a field. He waited for thè beat and they were off. The man was a wizard. She began to enjoy it and relaxed when it came to the turns. She noticed other people admiring them too, and saw from one part of the room Miss O'Hara, doing a very amateurish version of the same thing with Dr Power, smiling proudly towards her . . . Gerry Doyle – dancing with Bernie Conway – was looking at her in delight. David Power, dancing with Caroline Nolan, called her attention to the spectacular couple. Clare would have preferred it to have been a younger and more dashing man but she forgot about that after a while. Especially when they went into the cha cha '. . . rock forward, rock backward, side close side . . .' he said and after a few bars she had all the confidence in the world. They won a spot prize too. A bottle of Jameson Ten Year Old.

'You can have that, my drinking days are over,' Dick Dillon said.

'Your dancing days sure aren't,' Clare said and went, flushed with success, to leave the bottle in the ladies' cloakroom and get a ticket for it.

The Committee were very pleased. They had charged a slightly higher price for admission, which was justified by the many gifts which would be given away, but it also kept out some of the riff-raff. Not *all* the riff-raff, they noticed, as they saw Mogsy Byrne throwing Chrissie O'Brien around in the way most calculated to show her knickers to the crowd. Still.

There was a brisk trade at the mineral bar. Oranges and lemons and ginger beers were passing with speed across the counter, and there was a percentage on all that for the Committee, too. No real drink could be served in the dance hall, on this night any more than any other. Dancers wanting a break to visit a pub applied for a pass-out card, and a good few had small bottles in hip pockets.

The band, which was there for the season, had dressed itself up to mark the special nature of the night. The men wore rosettes in their buttonholes, and Lovely Helena, the vocalist, wore a big rose at the waist of her tulle and net dress.

Out in the street, youngsters who were considered well below the age tried to peer in and every time the inner door swung open they caught a glimpse of the glitter inside. Through the ventilators the sound of the singing and the clapping of the announcement of yet another prize being delivered were heard, and then blasts from the band again. During the summer people became used to the sound of the dance hall. It was as familiar as the waves crashing on the shore, background music.

Sometimes people shook their heads with amazement and said wasn't it extraordinary that Lionel Donelly of all people would have had the foresight to build a dance hall, to borrow the money and build a big monstrosity that everyone said would be a white elephant. Now there were people driving to it from far and wide. Lionel, who never passed an exam in his life, had gone to England to learn the building trade and learned that people were building dance halls.

Clare went back to the dance floor. She thought she saw David Power coming towards her, but before he was near enough Gerry Doyle reached out his hand for her. It was a slow smoochy dance and he didn't bother holding her at arm's length for a few bars, he put his arms around her at once and she laid her cheek against his. They were the same height. She had worn her flat shoes.

The lights were dimmer for this number, the sparkles of the glittering globe cast a thousand little shines on people. 'Once I had a secret love,' sang the girl in the miles of net dress at the microphone. People sang the words softly to each other, oddly assorted people like David Power who sang them into Josie's ear because he hadn't got to Clare O'Brien before Romeo. James Nolan sang them into Bernie Conway's ear, because when he saw Gerry Doyle dancing with her, he thought she must be something special. Dick

Dillon and Angela didn't sing them at all because they were concentrating on the curly bits and side chassis. Gerry didn't sing them because he didn't need to, and Clare had her eyes tightly closed.

At the last dance Josie was happy because finally James had seen her and flung her into a spirited version of 'California Here I Come'; and a great many other people were happy too. The Committee had made a great deal of money, the dance had been a social success, and all the people who had given spot prizes were pleased with the advertising.

'I have a caravan,' Gerry Doyle told Clare. They had danced together three times, almost enough to be considered a lifetime commitment for Gerry.

'A what?'

'A caravan. All of my own. I'm looking after it for people. They only come at the weekend.'

'Really, that's nice,' Clare said innocently.

'So?'

'So what?'

'Will we go there? You and me?'

'Now?' she asked, her heart beginning to beat faster.

'Sure.'

There was a pause. He was looking straight at her. She must say yes or no. She was not going to make any blustering excuses.

'No,' she said. 'Thanks all the same.'

His eyes showed nothing, there wasn't a hint of persuading her to change her mind.

'Right,' he said. 'Goodnight sweetheart.'

Before her eyes, he went over to Caroline Nolan. She heard him sound surprised to see her, as if he hadn't known she was in the dance hall all night.

Clare watched Caroline smiling delightedly as Gerry suggested something. It was too far away to hear, but when he put his arm around Caroline's shoulder and they walked off together, she knew it had to do with his having a caravan.

Dr Power said he would give Angela a lift in to collect her

213

mother. He never made that journey into the town without driving people in one direction or the other; he was the kindest man that ever lived.

'I saw you leaping about in great style with Dick Dillon,' he teased her.

'Well would you have believed it? The man could have medals for it. I never got such a surprise.'

'He's a very nice fellow, Dick. Never got a proper chance in that hotel. The old mother always preferred his brother. Still, he consoled himself fairly spectacularly during his day.'

Angela smiled, that was one way of describing a man who had been as heavy a drinker as her own father. Of course, Dick Dillon had been able to have the money to do it in comfort, and the trips to Dublin to be dried out, and now he had stopped. He had seen her home and come in after the dance; she had made tea and bacon sandwiches, and they had talked long into the night.

'What he needs is a steadying hand, Angela,' Dr Power said.

'Am I going to be hearing this for the rest of my life?'

'Probably. They'll say you could do worse. He's not a bad catch, sensible too nowadays, all the wild oats sown. Oh, they'll say that.'

'But it's not a question of catching, sure it's not? I always thought that if it happened it would be two people suddenly discovering they were more interested in each other than anything else. Not a *catch*.'

'It *should* be like that,' Dr Power said, negotiating a herd of cows and the boy who was halfheartedly moving them along the road.

'How about you?' She felt impertinent, but he could always laugh it off if he didn't want to answer.

'I met Molly at a dance in Dublin on my twenty-fifth birthday. She had a red dress on and she had her head back laughing and I thought to myself that I'd love her to be laughing like that at things I said. And that was it, I suppose. I went after her relentlessly. It was nothing to do with her being a catch, or me being one.'

'And she did go on laughing, didn't she?'

'Yes, mainly. Sometimes it's a bit quiet and dull here in the winter, and I wish she had more people to meet that would entertain her. Or that we had more children. If you have only one you concentrate on him too much. I'm always thinking about his medical studies and Molly's always wondering about his meals and damp clothes and what he does with himself in Dublin. If we had half a dozen it would be more spread out.'

'But David's sensible, isn't he, and he's as bright as paint.'

'He is, and we've managed to move very successfully from the notion of you and Dick Dillon.'

'He's an old man, with nothing on his mind except his long-lost days of drinking and sometimes the thought of an olde tyme waltz.'

'He's not ten years older than you. He's a fine man and he's lonely. Don't throw the idea aside too easily, Angela, girl.'

He was being serious. She decided not to make any more jokes.

'It was funny Fiona Doyle going off to London in the middle of the busy season to do that photography course.'

'It was bad timing, but I suppose she had to go when the opportunity came up.' Dr Power looked straight ahead of him at the road and the small white houses which broke the monotony of the hedges as they went along. Sometimes it was hard to be a country doctor and to hold the heartbeats and consciences of everyone in the parish. He knew only too well what bad timing it was for Fiona Doyle to have to go to London.

There had been a haze over the sea when Clare got up at six-thirty. It would be another hot day. A scorcher. Well, that's what they all wanted: eighty hot days with a little rain at night just to keep the farmers happy. Clare picked up all the litter from the corner of the shop which they had cleared for people to stand around having lemonades and fizzy orange, ham sandwiches and chocolate biscuits after the dance. It was good business: there was nowhere else to go

215

except the chip van. But it was wearying clearing up in the morning. She put the returnable bottles all together in a crate, and stuffed the others into the rubbish bin. She opened the doors to let the fresh air in and glanced up the street with its white and coloured houses all still asleep. The winter painting done in Castlebay always looked at its best on an early summer morning; the town looked so clean, like sugared almonds. The pink of Conway's post offfice and the lime-green walls of Miss O'Flaherty's looked just right.

Clare went back to put on the kettle; her mother would be up soon, and not long after that her father would be down moving boxes, worrying over supplies and only just remembering to pause and shave before the early morning caravan people came in looking for their breakfast materials.

The kettle was boiling as Agnes came downstairs. Before she could reach for her shop coat which hung on the back of the kitchen door, Clare saw with a start how thin she had grown, and how tired.

'Why don't you have a bit of a rest today? I can cope with it.'

'*Rest?* On a day like today – it's going to be one of the busiest yet. Are you mad?' her mother wanted to know.

'You look very tired, that's all.'

'Of course I look tired, and Tommy Craig looks tired up in the bar and Young Mrs Dillon looks tired. Lord God, Clare, when would we not look tired if not in the middle of the season?'

'Shush shush, I'm not attacking you, Mam, I wanted to know if you could have a couple of hours more rest that's all.'

Agnes softened. 'No, I'll be all right when I've had a cup of tea, nobody looks anything until they've had a cup of tea.' Her thin face smiled a bit, but she wouldn't even sit down to drink it. She was hurrying into the shop and sure enough as soon as she was behind the counter the door pinged and the first customer arrived.

It was non-stop all day. A lot of people seemed to take advantage of the clear blue skies to plan picnics, and Clare was busy cutting sandwiches and wrapping up ice-creams in several layers of newspapers.

Caroline Nolan was early. She ran in from her little Morris Minor, which spluttered and made noises outside.

'Picnic things,' she said to Clare, barely politely.

'For how many?' Clare asked.

'I don't know. Can I take things and if we don't need them bring them back?'

'No,' Clare said.

'What?'

'I said you can't. Suppose you brought back tomatoes or bananas that had been out in the sun all day – who else would want them?'

'I meant tins, or things that wouldn't spoil.'

'Why don't you just work out how many might be going?' Clare was impatient with this glowing girl, all fresh and summery in a white dress with big red spots; she looked so clean and awake and lively compared to Clare in her faded dress and her tired thin mother in the yellow shop coat.

'Maybe you can help me?' Caroline had decided to be charming. 'You see, a friend suggested we take a drive out to this place where you see seals, and I'm to provide a picnic. He, my friend, would bring a bottle of wine. And I'm not sure whether he meant us plural, like my brother and David, or whether he meant us singular, just me. You see my problem?'

'No,' said Clare. 'Ask him. Ask him did he mean you singular or you plural, then you'll know.'

Caroline left the shop.

Half an hour later she was back. 'He said he meant you plural,' she announced.

'Bad luck,' Clare said, and without being asked made a selection of the freshly made ham sandwiches and cheese sandwiches, apples, bananas, oranges, a packet of chocolate biscuits and four bottles of fizzy orange.

Caroline took it in silence and packed it into the boot of her car.

Gerry came in for cigarettes a bit later.

'I thought you'd be off on your picnic,' Clare said.

'I'm going to join them later, I gave them directions to get to the seals. Why don't you come with us?'

'How can I? I have to work here. Anyway, I'm not asked.'

'You are, I'm asking you.'

Clare laughed. 'No thanks. How can any of us take a day like today off? How can *you* take today off, come to think of it?'

'Why do I pay someone to take pictures for me, if it's not to give me a day off. Come on, be a devil.'

'Stop it, you know I can't.' She was annoyed now, she wished he'd go.

'One day out of the summer? One sunny day?' He wasn't joking.

'Go away Gerry, go away.' Clare was laughing but her voice had a steely ring. 'We are going to take care of our business, even if others we wouldn't mention are letting theirs go down the plug-hole.' And anyway, Clare told herself, there was no point in going out with that gang without the proper ammunition. Clare had no crisp cotton dress with big red dots on it, Clare had no golden suntan, she had a faded mauve dress and long white legs in old- fashioned sandals. Hell, she wasn't going to compete with Caroline unless she had a chance of winning, and if she wanted the attentions of Gerry Doyle she wouldn't look for them now.

The good spell was set to last. In the days after the picnic, Clare decided that she hated sunshine. For other people it meant that the holiday dream was coming true, it meant a healthy out-of-doors life. For the young couples in their tents it was pure magic, for the Nolans and their friends just more long days lost in sandhills on seal beaches, on golf courses, and racing in and out of the waves. For children it meant rushing into the shop asking for a bottle of fizzy orange, open please and with three straws. But for Clare the sun just meant it was time to take the cakes and things that might melt from the window, and to make sure the stocks of ice cream were ready for Jim and Ben to cope with.

Gerry came in. 'I've a message for you, come on, up to the post office, now! Old Ma Conway said there was a phone message, they're going to ring again in fifteen minutes, well ten now, come on.'

Clare's heart was thumping as she ran up Church Street

with Gerry. The hotel and the chemist and the dance-hall and the hardware shop passed in a blur. And then they were in Conway's.

'Oh you found her?' Mrs Conway looked disapprovingly over her glasses.

Please may it not be about Tommy. Oh Please God, I'll say the thirty days prayer, please Our Lady, I'll begin the thirty days prayer *today* if it's not some awful thing about Tommy.

'You must be very nervous,' Gerry said sympathetically.

Her heart gave another jump. 'How do you know, I mean what do you mean?'

'Your results,' he said simply. 'That's what it is, isn't it?'

It was. It was the convent, incoherent with delight – in all their years they had never been so proud. Clare had done nine subjects on her Leaving Certificate and she had got honours in *all* of them except mathematics; but of course she had passed that safely. And now wasn't there every chance that she would be called for the Murray Prize interview? Three of the sisters were starting a special novena today and Clare could be assured that the whole Community would remember her every day at Mass. She could hardly see Mrs Conway's pinched face, forcing itself to be congratulatory, having heard every word. Gerry lifted her off her feet and swung her round three times.

'Eight honours, eight honours, hell's bells and spiders' ankles!' he shouted.

'*Eight honours!*' Clare screamed. '*Eight!*'

'Well I must say I think congratulations are in order . . .' Mrs Conway said, her face pursed at the horseplay.

'I must tell Miss O'Hara, now,' Clare said. 'Now, this minute.'

'I'll drive you up in the van.'

She hesitated for a moment.

'I won't come in, I know you want to tell her on your own.'

Angela was out in front of the cottage, watering the scarlet geraniums. The sun shone in her eyes and she had to put up her hand to shield them as the van screeched to a halt. Clare tumbled out the door before it had properly stopped.

'Eight, Miss O'Hara, *eight!*' she shouted excitedly, and Angela put down the water jug and ran towards her. She clutched the thin body – trembling with excitement – to her in a big awkward hug of delight.

They had both forgotten Gerry, who sat motionless in his van watching them with his dark handsome eyes.

The whole town knew by evening. Josie had been so excited when she heard that she put the lid on her typewriter and said she was taking some time off to celebrate. Agnes and Tom O'Brien were bewildered with pleasure and worn out shaking people's hands across the counter and taking praise on behalf of their bright, hard-working daughter. Dr Power was going past on his way to the caravan site and stopped to pay his respects. Sergeant McCormack had got wind of it, and it wasn't long before Father O'Dwyer's little car stopped outside O'Brien's as well. It was a miracle that anything was bought or sold, or money taken or change given in that shop all day with the comings and goings.

'Will you come to the dance to celebrate tonight?' Gerry said.

'Ah, there'd be too much of a crowd there, all the Caroline Nolans and all,' she said, smiling at him.

'We could go somewhere where there wouldn't be,' he grinned back.

'I don't think so, don't change any of your own plans.'

'There are eighty nights in the summer,' Gerry said. 'If you don't come tonight you'll come another night.'

She had a lovely night. She had a drink with Dick Dillon who taught her how to make a drink called a Pussyfoot which had no alcohol in it but sort of fooled you into thinking it had. Josie gave her a yellow blouse and a yellow ribbon to match it for her hair – she had been saving it as a surprise. Josie had a date with James Nolan and was in seventh heaven herself: they were going to the pictures and he had said he would meet her in the queue. She swore to tell Clare everything that happened and had worn a dress with a high collar in case he might start to fumble and she would have to decide whether to let him or not.

Clare walked down the Cliff Road. It was sunset and people could be seen indoors, finishing their supper or just sitting around with the dishes still on the table before heading off for the night's entertainment. It had been so long in arriving, this day. She was going to savour every minute of it.

It was getting dark now and she shivered a little in her new yellow blouse. Josie and James Nolan were well into the Main Feature and who knew what else at the cinema. Chrissie and Mogsy Byrne had gone down the sandhills, she knew that because she had seen Chrissie changing her slip and getting out her good knickers, the ones with lace on them. Gerry Doyle was in his caravan. No, she was *not* going to the caravan park. She would go up to the anmusements and have two rides on the bumpers and then if she didn't meet anyone she would come home and pitch Chrissie's things to the other side of the room and go to bed. She would *not* go to the caravan park tonight.

There was never a greater demand for space than this summer. Somehow the word had spread that there was fun galore in Castlebay. Not all the visitors were desirable of course; this would be discussed by the Castlebay Committee during the winter. There had been a very noisy element with tents, and the dirt of the caravan people had to be seen to be believed. Dr Power said they weren't to be blamed until somebody put up lavatories and washbasins for them, and arranged proper bins and a rubbish collection.

There was hardly a day that Angela and her mother weren't approached by passing visitors asking for a night's lodging.

To her surprise her mother had said they should do it. Everyone else in the town made a profit out of the summer, why shouldn't they?

Angela washed sheets and tidied up the back room. Why not? It would be a few quid, and people were so grateful. She would point out that she had a mother who wasn't well and couldn't have anyone noisy. But it had been fine. First a couple of girls who had crept in like mice after the dance, stayed four days and had both said that Gerry Doyle was the most gorgeous thing they had ever seen in real life. Up to now they had only seen his likes on the cinema screen. Then there had been a married couple, a quiet pair in their forties, dull, nothing to say to anyone or each other, Angela pitied them, and was puzzled when they said it had been a lovely visit and they would come back next year. Then two lads from Dublin, with accents you could cut, roaring laughing at nothing and saying it was the best fun they'd had in years. The night they had got very drunk they had the decency to sleep in the shed rather than trying to find their room. Angela told them they were marvellous and refused to charge them for the night's accommodation.

'You won't suffer for that, Missus,' one of them said. 'We'll send you our mates.'

And indeed there was a never-ending supply of Dubliners, lads from building sites, from factories, and then the two housepainters, Paddy and Con. God, they'd never seen the like of the place, they were going to have a swim immediately, they were sticking to themselves with the sweat after the train and the bus, and the sea looked a treat.

'Be careful,' Angela called automatically. 'There's a very high tide, it's treacherous at the end of August. They call it a spring tide.'

'Oh, you couldn't drown us,' called Paddy and Con.

She heard the cry about half an hour later. It was like a wail growing and fading, louder and softer. And she knew there was someone drowning down on the strand. She had been buying the bacon and eggs for their tea in O'Brien's. She had her bicycle with its carrier basket parked outside. Automatically she found her feet heading for the cliff top and there saw everyone clustered and pointing out beyond the caves and the fishing rocks. The waves were enormous.

On the edge of the water there was a commotion. Five or six men were trying to hold back the struggling figure of Simon. Ropes and lifebelts had been thrown, to no avail. Angela's stomach lurched when she saw a hand raised desperately, far, far out, and beside it the head of someone else. There were two of them. She dropped the bacon out of her hands, and she knew that it was her lodgers, Paddy and Con.

They were shouting at Simon on the beach. 'You've been out twice, you've been battered, you can't do any more, it's suicide. You've done all you can. Simon, have sense.'

Simon's side was bleeding from where he had been scratched against the rocks.

'Let me go! Let me go!' His face was working and his eyes were full of tears. Gerry Doyle was gripping him, holding his arm behind him in a lock.

'What's the point in getting you killed? Look at your back, you've been thrown on the rocks twice. What are you trying to prove? You've done all you can, for Christ's sake, you warned them – you went out after them once and brought them back in.'

'They're new, they were all white,' Simon wailed, 'let me go.'

There was a great cry from the people who could see the figures.

'One's holding onto a rock, he'll be all right. Look! Look!'

But in seconds a huge wave pulled the small figure, its white arms flailing, down into the sea.

Helplessly the crowd watched. There was no boat, no swimmer, no throw of a lifebelt that would reach Paddy and Con. They would die in front of a thousand people.

Father O'Dwyer had been sent for, and as if by reflex, the people standing near him went down on their knees.

Father O'Dwyer called out the rosary and the swell of Holy Marys increased. Simon stopped struggling eventually and sat with his head in his hands, sobbing. Gerry Doyle sat beside him with an arm protectively around his shoulder.

There was no sign of the figures now, the waves kept crashing as if they were unaware of what they had done. Men went for strong drinks, women gathered up their children and issued useless, angry warnings about the need to stay in shallow waters.

Clare had come out too. She felt a hand reaching for hers and to her surprise, it was David Power.

'Would it have been quick do you think?' she asked.

David shook his head.

'Oh,' she said in a small voice.

'I don't know. Not the first bit, not the being swept out, they'd have known what was going to happen.'

'I suppose so.'

'I have to go down there,' he said. 'With my father.'

'When?'

'When the tide comes in tonight, they'll be washed up.'

She was full of pity, and warmth, and she squeezed his hand.

'I don't *have* to, but I will. He just said that he'd like me to, and anyway I'll be a doctor soon myself. I'll have to then. It's just . . . it's just . . .'

'I know, it's just when its your own beach.'

He smiled at her gratefully. 'They might come in sooner.' He was full of dread.

'Would that mean they'd get battered up more?'

'I don't know.'

There was a great sound from the beach again and people were shouting and pointing. On the side of the beach near the caves, where it seemed calm, there was something that looked like a person. And near it was something similar. There was no movement, no waving or swimming. Then you could see they were face down. Bobbing on the water like the airbeds that they sold up at the top of Church Street. They didn't look like people: they looked like a bad joke.

Clare turned away, suddenly feeling a bit faint. This is what being dead looked like. She had almost forgotten she was still holding David Power's hand and when she turned it was towards him. She put her head on his chest. He put his arm round her shoulder. Then she pulled away a little.

'You've got to go down,' she said.

Gerry Doyle and two other fellows passed, helping Simon up the steps. The lifeguard's side had been examined on the beach by Dr Power, who had asked Gerry to get him away as soon as possible. Dr Power didn't want Simon there when the bodies came in. They would float in with the last minutes of the incoming tide.

Gerry Doyle looked at Clare evenly. 'If you've finished canoodling, you might go to your friend, Miss O'Hara – she's the one who's going to have to cope with it all and go through their things.'

'Why?' Clare cried, shocked. 'Why on earth will she have to do that?'

'Because they were staying with her, they're from her house, that's why.' Gerry put his arm under Simon's and continued to shove and push him along the street.

Clare saw Angela, standing by herself with her hands over her mouth in disbelief. Her hair blowing loose behind her, she was looking down on the beach while the crowds stepped into the shallow water and pulled the bodies of Paddy and Con on to the sand. Father O'Dwyer was there with his holy water, and his soutane, his long black skirt flapping in the breeze. Dr Power was urging people to keep the children well away and leaning on the chests of the dead men in the futile hope that there would be any life left in them. And in a minute beside him was his tall fair-haired son, helping too, looking calm and in control; not the trembling boy who had been standing moments earlier with his hand in Clare's.

Clare turned away from the scene on the beach. Gerry was quite right. If she was to do anything to help it should be for Miss O'Hara.

They talked about nothing else for days. The dance was cancelled that night as a mark of respect, and so was the cinema. They didn't know what to do at the amusements so they compromised by not playing the juke box. Clare and Angela had found an address amongst the few shabby belongings of Paddy and Con, and the Guards in Dublin were asked to go around and inform the families.

It had been strangely unreal for everyone and the greatest sympathy in the place was given to Simon. Nobody knew the families of Paddy and Con, any more than anyone had really met the lads in the short couple of hours they had spent in Castlebay between getting off the bus and being taken out of the sea. Simon's easy laughter had disappeared

225

now. He was a very serious young man. He didn't go to the dance in the evenings and he had little time for high jinks on the beach. He sat nervously on a high stool that he had made himself from boxes, and he shouted angrily at children who played ball in his line of vision. One night in Craig's Bar he lost his temper and said that the Castlebay Committee were totally irresponsible encouraging people to come there with their plans for fairy lights and big car parks. They should build a pier and breakwater, they should enclose a swimming pool and only permit people who were known to be strong swimmers to venture beyond it. You wouldn't let people play with matches and jump through bonfires would you, he had said in a high nervous voice. They forgave him over and over, they told him of the children he had saved, of the cramp victim he had rescued, of the artificial respiration to the girl who swallowed so much water. They praised him for the countless others he had made safe by his daily parades up and down the beach edge. But his eyes got darker and they knew they would never see him again when the summer was over.

Angela and Clare didn't talk about it, not after the first night when they had found the address and folded all the clothes neatly into the two shabby grip bags. Talking about it only made things worse. Instead they rehearsed feverishly the kind of questions that Clare might face on the first Thursday in September when she had to meet the Murray Prize Committee.

They planned her appearance down to the last detail. She must look in need of their gift but not too needy. She must look quiet enough to be studious but not so quiet that she looked dull. Neat enough to be thought respectable but not so drab as to be thought dreary. Her good marks would impress them automatically, her grasp of current affairs was masterly, her simple direct explanation about coming from a family which was anxious for her success but not in itself academic was so patently honest it would have to convince them. She was not a fly-by-night either, she had always been ambitious, hadn't she got the scholarship to secondary school at the age of twelve?

In the end Angela said she was satisfied. There was literally no more they could do to prepare for this event. They would end up making her so nervous that she would not be able to speak at all.

Angela lent her a navy jumper and the good silk scarf that James Nolan's mother had given her all those years ago. It had lain idly in a drawer and this was an ideal opportunity to give it an outing. She wore her good blue skirt and a pair of Josie's shoes. Her hair was to be shining and in a pony tail, only the barest hint of make-up, like a trace of Sari Peach lipstick, rubbed on and rubbed off again.

If school hadn't started, Angela said, she would have gone into the town and waited nearby until Clare came out. It would have made it better for both of them.

But term would have started. Angela's twelfth year in the convent. For a woman who was going to stay twelve months, things had escalated. She felt no bitterness towards Sean about that now. It had been her own decision for a long, long time. She didn't even rebel at the thought of his unctuously clerical tones when he gave that advice. She had no more hate for Sean and the differences between what he preached and what he did. It had been a long time, teaching beside Mother Immaculata, certainly. But it had been a longer time for Sean in waiting for a laicization that never came.

Gerry Doyle called to the O'Brien house the night before.

'I have a job tomorrow, so I'll be going to town. I can give you a lift.'

'That's very nice, but I was getting the bus. The timing's all right for once and even if it's a bit late I'll be fine.'

'I'm going to the door,' he said. 'The Committee have asked me to photograph them and the shortlist of candidates. So go on the bus if you like but the lift is there.'

There were two girls and five boys. Gerry arranged them according to height and took several shots. He was able to relax them without having to clown around. It was a gift, Clare thought as she watched him. He never called her by

227

her name. He was professional. It mightn't look good for her to know him, he was making sure she had nothing special about her one way or the other. He left her free to examine the competition. The girl was taller than Clare; she looked older and very studious. She had bushy, badly-combed hair and glasses. She could have been quite nice-looking but she had made no effort at all. There was a tear in her tunic – she wore a school uniform, for heaven's sake – and her shoes were down at heel. Anxiously Clare looked down at Josie's smart shoes and the neat cuffs of Miss O'Hara's good cardigan. Maybe she looked cheap and superficial?

'Makes us feel a bit like cattle,' said a small boy, who didn't look old enough to have done his Intermediate Certificate let alone his Leaving. But Clare was not deceived: this was the most dangerous one, she felt sure. Two of the others were clerical students: they wore black jerseys and were more reserved. There was a nervy boy who would irritate the committee and one who spoke after such a long pause each time, the interview would surely be over by the time he had answered anything.

The girl was nice. She had been at a convent about fifty miles away. She asked Clare how many honours she had got in her Leaving. Angela had prepared her for that and told her not to boast, and if at all possible to keep her great score to herself.

'I don't think they go on that any more,' she said. 'That's what I've heard, anyway. Nowadays it's not the number you have it's what they think of you.'

The boy who kept drumming his fingers looked up startled at this. 'Is that right? Then I'll be lost. I got six honours, I thought that was what was going to sail me through.' He laughed nervously, showing some broken teeth.

Clare thanked Miss O'Hara again and again in her mind. Miss O'Hara had beaten this nervous laugh out of her long ago.

They talked easily enough until the lady chairman came to address them. She was a self-important woman in a tweed suit; she had a huge chest and looked so like a pigeon, Clare was not arraid of her resounding voice. They were to be taken in alphabetical order. Clare was second last; the nervy boy was O'Sullivan, and he would be last.

She kept her mind calm. She refused to get up and go to the lavatory even when the others did suddenly. She knew she had eaten or drunk nothing that would make her need to go; she had eaten barley sugar sweets just as she had done when she was twelve and Miss O'Hara had been training her to get the scholarship to school. That had not been terrifying neither would this. She had eight honours in her Leaving Certificate. She was the equal of any child in Ireland.

Gerry Doyle was told he would be needed in two hours. They would have come to their decision then. That surprised him. He'd thought they wouldn't decide there and then on the day. But it was better that she knew today. He didn't think she'd make it. Just from looking at them he thought the big untidy girl or the small boy who looked like a child prodigy were the most likely. Those were the kind of faces you saw in a newspaper with a paragraph underneath saying what they had won.

He came back in good time and sat in his van reading the local paper. There were three of his pictures in it this week: a wedding, a sand-castle competition and the foundation stone for the new wing of the Brothers' school in Castlebay.

The awful bossy woman with the big chest rapped on the window for him as if he were the gardener and called him in to photograph the winner of the Murray Scholarship to University College, Dublin, Clare O'Brien.

Angela O'Hara asked Dr Power if she could have a word with him in his car. He was practically home and suggested she come into the surgery. She didn't want to. The house then, and have a sherry? No. It was something a bit unethical she wanted to ask, better to ask him on neutral ground. Unethical? His big bushy eyebrows rose. Angela? Nothing desperately unethical, she assured him, a fake doctor's cert, that was all.

'Get into the car,' he said. 'This is serious. If I'm going to be struck off we'd better make sure it's worth while.'

She laughed at his kind, worried face and told him what she wanted. She'd like to go to Dublin for a few days. Her best friend Emer had just had a baby, and now they wanted her to be godmother to the baby. Young Clare was going up to Dublin to start life at university, and it was a great opportunity to show her round a bit – not be a mother hen but just show her a few things so that she wasn't a total gobdaw when term started. It would be lovely to have a few days off school, but she couldn't ask for it. It was unheard of. Immaculata would have a blue fit. Was it possible that Dr Power could say she had something which meant going to Dublin?

He looked at her over his glasses, doubtfully.

'I never asked you before. I never in all my years up in that place asked for one day off.'

'You misunderstand me. Of course I'll do it. I think you should have a fortnight in Dublin . . . I'm only trying to think what you might have.'

She gave him a look full of gratitude. 'Would we say it was in my womb? That should embarrass Immaculata so much she'd shut up about it.'

'Yes, but there's no reason why you wouldn't go into the County Hospital if it were just a D and C,' he objected. 'It would have to be something that needed going to a specialist for or some kind of specialist hospital. A skin disease?' he suggested brightly.

Angela was doubtful. 'She might keep moving away from me and telling people not to use the same cups at our tea break.'

'Blood tests, you're a bit anaemic and I want it checked further.'

'You're a great sport,' she said. 'I was hoping I could rely on you.'

'I'm not doing it because I'm a sport. I'm doing it because you *do* need a break. I'd feel quite justified signing a certificate saying you are under great pressure and you need a change and a rest, but of course, if you wrote that to any of that lot of beauties up in the convent, they'd think you were having a nervous breakdown and they wouldn't let you back again. Blood tests it will have to be.'

Emer and Kevin were delighted to see them.

They had to fight the nuns and nurses off to get baby Daniel home from the nursing home without having him baptized. They explained that the godmother had to come from the country but there had been terror that the baby's immortal soul would be lost during the delay. Anyway it was all settled now. Martin, the shy best man, was going to be the godfather, and best surprise of all, Father Flynn was going to perform the baptism. Wasn't that something! To gather the cast of the wedding in another city five years later!

They hadn't noticed the colour go from Clare's face when the priest's name was mentioned. She sat silently. She had been pleased to be invited to this warm, friendly house, to meet the laughing, undemanding friends of Miss O'Hara's. She had been delighted to be included in the christening party the next day, but she didn't want to meet this priest who knew all about her family and had been to see Tommy in prison. She would ask Miss O'Hara could she get out of it.

As they got the house ready on the evening before the christening Angela felt wistful as she often did in the presence of Emer and Kevin, they were so utterly complete as a pair, they hardly needed the rest of the world at all. And their delight in this funny, creased, red-faced baby was so touching it would bring tears to your eyes. When they peered at him in his cot Angela thought she had never seen anything so happy.

She wished them so well that she didn't like the little feelings of envy that came to her unwillingly when she was with them. Nowhere else did she wish so strongly that *she* had found a Kevin of her own, someone she could share everything with. Someone she could laugh with about Dr Power and his kindness. Someone she could talk to at night about Sean and Shuya. She remembered, returning from her last visit to her brother's family: she had longed to take off her shoes and sit down by the fire and tell Emer and Kevin all

231

about it. But it wasn't the same telling a story to a couple. When the evening was over they would go to bed, she in the neat guest bedroom with the gingham curtains and bed-spread, they in their big double bed where they would lie in each other's arms and whisper low how terrible it was for Angela. She didn't want that sympathy, however loving and generous. She wanted a sharing. It was lonely holding Sean's secret for seven years.

She looked over at Clare, who was on a chair helping to put up the silver and white decorations they had organized for the sitting room. She had been rather short with the child there earlier on. She had no business being short with her; after all, she refused to talk to Father Flynn about Sean even though it was Father Flynn who had found the school in England for Sean to teach in.

She was just as much an ostrich as Clare, burying her head in the sand, refusing to accept someone's help and thank them for it in a simple straightforward way. It was uncanny how alike their lives had been. Scholarships, first to the convent and then to college; neither of them came from scholarly families, and both of them had brothers in trouble. And Father Flynn was being a lifeline to both brothers – one despairing in an English school and waiting for a voice from Rome that would never come, the other reading comics in an English gaol.

The day was winding down, and Clare found herself near Father Flynn. 'Thank you very much for all you do for my brother, Tommy,' she said, forcing the words out. 'And for Ned too, getting him a job and seeing that he writes home. It's very good of you.'

Father Flynn looked at her. 'Oh, then you're Clare O'Brien, of course, that writes the letters to Tommy. He looks forward to them, and sometimes I read them to him – so don't say anything bad about me in the next one or I might find myself reading it aloud!'

Clare warmed to him. He hadn't shaken his head sadly and said it was a Dreadful Situation; Miss O'Hara was right.

'There's not really anything for him in Castlebay, you know, Father. I was thinking about it, he'd only be hanging around.'

'There's plenty of time to think yet, maybe he'd be better hanging round there than where he was hanging around.'

'Yes, that's probably true. Maybe I was just trying to keep him away, out of sight, out of mind.'

'But that's not true of you,' he smiled. 'He's not out of your mind. You're a generous girl. I hope you have a very successful career at university and that you meet a lot of people and read a great deal and have years that you'll always remember.'

Nobody had wished her well in such terms. Nobody had spoken aloud all her own hopes and dreams. She did want to read a great deal, and have time to read, and she wanted people to talk to, people who would talk about the things they read. This funny, fat little priest with the beady eyes knew just what she wanted.

She went to see Miss O'Hara off at the station. They had inspected the hostel where she was going to live, and Angela had said it wouldn't be bad at all because in a week it would be filled with girls from all over the country, united in their hatred of the nuns who ran the place and all as nervous as Clare, but none of them as clever. Miss O'Hara had walked the legs off her round the city, and they now knew which side of Stephen's Green was which, and where the Physics Theatre was, which oddly was where a lot of the first Arts lectures would be held. She had registered and got her student's card.

Clare felt very experienced, catching a bus back from the station to O'Connell Bridge, she looked out eagerly at the city which was to be her home for three years. It was so bright – that was what she was going to find most hard to get used to. In Castlebay in winter there were hardly any lights on Church Street, none at all on Cliff Road or the golf-course road, but in Dublin even side streets, even lanes were lit up. And shops had their lights on in windows all night so that you could go and look at what they had for sale any hour at all. As the bus went up the Quays to the centre of Dublin the buildings were reflected in the river Liffey: the Four Courts, the big churches and the rows of tall buildings shimmered in the dark water. It was all so enormous, after home.

She had walked through the grand stores with Angela O'Hara, and looked at the rings and bracelets in the windows of jewellers'. She had been to the second-hand bookshops and bought all her texts for the first year. Angela had even climbed up on ladders in order to get better or cheaper editions for her. She had made herself known at the big red-brick hostel where she would stay. Angela had come with her and informed the nuns that this was no ordinary pupil, it was a Murray Prizewinner, and that her fees would be paid by the committee. The nuns were impressed. It reminded Clare a little of her secondary school, and she was disappointed that it had no garden or cloisters. It was part of a big terrace of Georgian houses, and the convent was in fact four of them all joined together. Angela had said she wouldn't have time for gardens. There was always Stephen's Green in the summer, and the fact that the hostel was so near the university meant it was worth its weight in gold. She could get out of bed literally minutes before lectures while other students had to cross the city.

Clare got off the bus at O'Connell Bridge and leaned across the parapet looking below to where two swans went by. They looked confident, even arrogant. They felt no unease about being swans in a place where everyone else seemed to be human beings. Clare smiled at the thought. She owed Miss O'Hara so much – or Angela as she must now call her. She owed her everything, including these last days, this great preparation.

She knew which bus would take her back to the hostel but she decided to walk. She would walk almost everywhere anyway, why not start now? She went up Grafton Street, pausing to look at fur coats, at household equipment, at pictures and frames, at a chemist's window full of perfumes and soaps and talcum powders. She saw books on display and furniture, big deep leather chairs in shops. She read the tariffs in hairdressers', she saw the sign to the little church in Clarendon Street. At the top of Grafton Street she wouldn't need to pause like so many new students, she knew to walk on along a side of Stephen's Green and on to her hostel. She had left her luggage there earlier, and they said the young ladies would be arriving after six p.m. She had discovered that there wouldn't be supper, so she was that much ahead of all the rest who thought that there would. She looked up at its slightly forbidding outside, took a deep breath and walked into her new home.

There were going to be three in a room. She was the first so she could choose her bed. It was unlikely that there would be much study done here: it was too small, there wasn't much light, and anyway the libraries were meant for study. Clare took the bed by the window. It was the one where she would get most fresh air and she had checked, there didn't seem to be draughts. She thought of Chrissie alone in the bedroom at home, puzzling out her relationship with Mogsy Byrne.

The first room mate arrived. Mary Catherine was American, her father wanted her to have an Irish education, she had never been so cold in her whole life, she couldn't believe that they didn't have a bathroom attached to the room, she couldn't understand why there hadn't been a reception down there to welcome them, she was going to study English, she had majored in English Literature at her college, she was very confused, and where were the closets? Clare sat on the bed wondering how she was going to live with this voice for a year, when the door opened and in came a girl with short curly hair and tears streaming down her face.

'Isn't it *awful*,' she sobbed. 'It smells just like school, there's no supper or dinner or anything tonight, there's a list of rules as long as your arm, *how* are we going to survive it?'

She threw herself on the empty bed and sobbed into her pillow. Her luggage had the name Valerie painted on the end of each case.

Clare decided to take control. 'Of course it's awful Valerie – if that's your name – it smells even worse than school. I'm Clare and this is Mary Catherine and she's from America and she hates it because it's cold and it's not got a bath each and no closets, whatever they are. And of course there's no supper and no welcoming party because they don't know we're all expecting a bit of a fuss of it, but for God Almighty's sake let's not start moaning and groaning before we even start. Why don't we go out and have some chips and think what could make the place better?'

She could hardly believe that it was Clare O'Brien, the scholarship girl from Castlebay, speaking. She'd never really shouted at two totally strange girls, had she? But it had worked like magic.

The chips cheered them up so much they had apple pie and ice cream. Clare told them about the Murray scholarship. Mary Catherine said that her father was a mailman in the States, but he had told her to tell everyone in Ireland he was in government work – which in a sense was vaguely true. She was the only child. He had dreams of her marrying someone who owned a castle in Ireland. Valerie said her parents were separated. Her father lived in England with a fancy woman, and he had to pay for her education. Valerie didn't want to go to university but her mother said she must, and she must stay there for years in order to get as much out of that rat as possible.

They were immensely cheered by each other's life stories, and they learned what they would have expected: that none of them had any experience with men. Mary Catherine knew a girl in the States who went the whole way with four boys before she left school. No, amazingly, she didn't have a baby, but she didn't have a friend either. A girl in Valerie's school left hurriedly in the middle of Fifth Year but it had been a great mystery because she didn't have a boyfriend. There was a whisper round the school that it was someone in her family, her father or her brother. Clare offered some tales from Castlebay of things that had happened down the sandhills, but they were all second-hand and third-hand. She was going to say that she had her doubts about Chrissie and Mogsy at times; but Mogsy and Chrissie were such non-glamorous people she decided she wouldn't embark on it.

Full of food and confidences and friendship they stood up to go back to the room they were going to transform. They were going to buy a second-hand bookshelf on the Quays, they were going to buy coat hooks and screw them into the wall so that there would be more space for their clothes. They were going to price cheap reading lamps and buy one between them.

Just as they were leaving the restaurant, someone called from a crowded table. 'Hey it's Clare, Clare O'Brien!'

She was startled. All she could see was a sea of young men in duffle coats and scarves. One was waving. It was James Nolan. He stood up and came over to them.

'Well, well, well,' he said.

It seemed to be very little to say after coming all the way across the restaurant.

She introduced him to Mary Catherine and Valerie, smiling at him politely as if to assure him that she wasn't claiming any friendship.

'Well, well,' he said again. 'Is the rest of Castlebay up in Dublin too?' His eyes roamed over Mary Catherine and Valerie, assessing them.

'Josie Dillon might be coming up for a few days,' Clare said eagerly.

Josie had begged her to find out James Nolan's haunts, and said that she would love to come to Dublin if Clare could track him down. Imagine meeting him on the very first night!

'Josie?' He looked blank.

'Josie Dillon from the hotel.'

James Nolan shook his head absently.

'You must remember her, you were often with her in the summer,' Clare blurted out, and could have kicked herself.

'I don't think I do.' James was polite but bored by the subject. Clare would have liked to hit him hard.

'It's my mistake. I'm sure she doesn't remember you either.' Her eyes flashed a bit and he looked at her with surprise.

'No. Well. Listen, it's nice to see you girls. Oh, and there's a party on Saturday. All three of you of course. Here, I'll

237

write it down.' He scribbled an address and time on a piece of paper.

'Ten o'clock! We have to be *back* at that place we're staying by eleven o'clock,' Valerie said, disappointed.

'Late pass, ask them for a late pass, cousin invited all three of you to twenty-first. The nuns love cousins, they think they're safe, sign of a big united family. They love twenty-firsts, it gives them a sense of continuity.'

They promised to be there and they linked arms, giggling as they went down the dark unfamiliar streets, and said that they'd all be lost if it had not been for Clare to guide them and tell them where they were and get them invited to a party on their very very first night in Dublin.

It was a great alliance. When other girls were lonely and self-conscious, they often looked with envy at the three girls; the tall fair one from the back of beyond with the dark brown eyes, the American with her outlandish clothes, and Valerie, the curlyheaded terror. It was Valerie who made friends with a workman doing some building work on the outside of the hostel wall. She pointed out that if he were to put three very sturdy bars jutting at intervals they could climb back into their room at night.

He was very nervous about it. 'You might get fellas climbing in to attack you,' he had protested. Nonsense; Valerie explained that there were three of them in the room, and any fellow climbing in uninvited would meet his match. She supervised the placing of the rungs carefully, and also their disguise. No passing nun could see them and realize what they were, a stairway to freedom. Valerie very cunningly asked that one or two extra rungs leading nowhere be hammered in as well. That way the purpose would never be discovered. And indeed it wasn't. They allowed very good friends to know the route, and regularly the light step of a girl was heard to fall into their room and someone, shoes in hand, would creep through, whispering a sorry or a thank you, but giving no explanations.

Clare and Mary Catherine didn't really use their escape route all that often but it kept them sane just knowing it was there. Only Valerie got real value from the contraption. She went dancing and to parties, and needed the footholds she had so cleverly organized at least three or four times a week. Valerie usually lay with her curls barely peeping from above the sheets when Clare and Mary Catherine were heading off to lectures. It was always kept as a polite fiction in front of nuns and other girls that Valerie was very lucky to have late lectures. Valerie rarely attended any of them anyway, no matter what time of the day they were held. As she told Clare and Mary Catherine, her mother had said nothing about passing any exams, only about using up the money for fees at university.

At Christmas, Valerie went home to her mother who was going to sit and curse her father all the time; Mary Catherine went to stay with American friends. Clare caught the train home. Her mother had asked Gerry Doyle to pick her up; he sent her a postcard, saying, 'Passion waggon will be parked in darkest side of yard outside station. See you then. Love, Gerry.' The other girls were intrigued. Even more when they heard that he was the heartbreaker of the country who had twice invited Clare to his caravan.

She felt cheerful going home. There was no guilt – she had written to her mother every single Friday, and to Tommy as well. She had written less to Angela. She had thought she would write more to her than anyone but it was very hard to describe it all: the National Library every afternoon, where it was peaceful and studious – you felt that everyone there was a real scholar, not just learning things with their hands in their ears for exams. She had read a great deal around the courses and everything on the course. She could meet every member of the Murray Committee, look each one in the eye and say truthfully that their money had not been wasted. Funny that she couldn't seem to write this to Angela.

She saw David Power on the train, and put her head back into her book so that he wouldn't notice her as he came along the corridor. It wasn't that she didn't want to talk to him, but it was silly, there she had been three months in the same city and never laid eyes on him, only to meet on the way home – it would be very forced.

He saw her only as they were getting out of the train and his face broke into a great smile. He thought she looked very nice, in her navy duffle coat, knitted navy and white scarf and her hair in a jaunty pony tail with a white bow on it. It was only the other day that she had been a kid. But then, his mother kept saying it was only the twinkling of an eye since he was in rompers.

He saw his father waving from the other side of the gate. 'Can we drive you home?' he said. 'I'm delighted I saw you in time.'

'I have a lift actually, but thank you very much,' and as they came to the barrier he saw Gerry Doyle leaning casually against the machine that wrote your name in metal.

Gerry wasn't bothering to move and wave and position himself as everyone else was doing, as David's own father was doing. Gerry knew he would be seen when the time came. Clare raised her hand in salute.

'Second fiddle to Gerry Doyle, winter and summer, it's the story of our lives,' David said and went over to his father.

'Your mother's in the car, it's very cold. I didn't want her waiting in the draught.'

'Quite right,' David said. For some reason he couldn't explain to himself he was glad Clare hadn't accepted the lift. His mother didn't really get along with her. All right in her place of course, but David felt that his mother thought her place was behind the counter in O'Briens, not as a university student and certainly not as a passenger in the doctor's car.

She had forgotten it would be so quiet, that it had always been so quiet at this time of year. There were no lights or Christmas trees in the windows, there was no traffic bustling up and down the street. She had forgotten how few people there were there, and how the wet spray stung your face when you went outside the door.

She had forgotten too how handsome Gerry Doyle was. He wore a leather jacket and his hair was long and shiny. In the station he had looked like a film star. He had brought a rug for her to wrap around her knees.

'Is there anything wrong?' Clare asked suddenly.

240

'Your mother had a fall. But she's fine. Fine,' he said.

'How fine?' Her voice was clipped.

'She nearly came to meet you with me, that's how fine.'

'Why didn't they tell me? Why did no one tell me? Where did she fall?'

'She fell on the cliff path. She broke her ankle. She wasn't even kept in hospital more than one night.'

Clare's eyes filled with tears.

'No, it's not bad, honestly, she hobbles a bit and that's all. Your dad's being very nice to her and he brings her tea in the morning.'

'She must be bad then. When did it happen?'

'About three weeks ago. Listen Clare, will you stop, I was going to tell you just as we came into Castlebay so that you'd have no time to be going through all this useless kind of nonsense. So as you'd see her in five minutes and know she was all right.'

'She could have been killed.'

'She couldn't. Don't make it so dramatic. She's been through all that now, it will only make it worse if you start attacking them for not telling you and saying what could have happened.'

He was right. She admitted it grudgingly.

'Very well, tell me about other things. I'll see Mam soon enough.'

He told her that business was changing, as he had always suspected it would. More and more people were bringing their own cheap cameras to the beach, Murphy's chemist was demented with visitors wanting their holiday snaps developed. The demand for beach photographs was growing less.

But then he had always known it would, so the thing to do was to change direction, to expand. He was in portrait photography now, and doing special commissions for hotels and new buildings which wanted prestige pictures of their premises. It meant of course that he would have to improve his own premises. Big important places only came to you if they thought you looked big and important too.

Wasn't that risky, Clare had wondered. No, it was business, Gerry assured her.

241

He told her that Josie Dillon had managed to get a whole lot of people to come to the hotel for a bridge weekend, and it was such a success that bridge people from all over were going to come there regularly. Josie's Uncle Dick had learned to play bridge when he'd been ordered off the drink apparently, and he had been saying for years that they should do this but he'd done nothing about it. Now he and Josie were as pleased as punch. Josie's sisters were hopping mad and her grandmother claimed that it was all *her* idea in the first place.

She told Gerry about the size of the university and about the Annexe where they had coffee every morning and how there were hundreds and hundreds of nuns and priests studying too, which she had never expected.

Was Fiona back yet for Christmas, she wanted to know. It would be interesting to compare notes with her about what her polytechnic was like.

No, she wasn't coming home apparently, in fact Gerry thought he might go over and see her.

'Not coming home for *Christmas?*' It was unheard of.

Gerry kept looking at the road.

'But what's she doing that she's not coming home?'

He sighed, almost his whole body went into the sigh. 'Jesus, Clare, you're not an old biddy, why do you sound so amazed? She wants to stay there, that's all. Do I have to build up a story for you too, an explanation? Will everyone in Castlebay want a full account of what everyone else from Castlebay is doing for the rest of their lives?'

'I'm sorry, you're quite right,' she said contritely. 'I don't talk like this in Dublin, it must be coming home that makes me do it.'

'Yeah, well some of us never left home, don't forget that, but we grow up too in our own way.'

She wasn't sure what he meant but it sounded like a criticism. She nodded apologetically. They drove on in silence for a while.

'I'm going tomorrow in fact,' he said. 'I haven't told anyone else, I'll just go.'

'Sure,' she said, 'that's a good idea.'

'I might go to see Tommy and Ned while I'm in London,' he said unexpectedly. 'I haven't laid eyes on them in years.'

She jumped a little but he couldn't have noticed.

'Do you have their address to give me?'

'No,' she said. 'No, I don't.'

'Would your mother . . .'

'I think not.' Her mouth closed like a trap. She too stared ahead of her.

'Right,' he said eventually. 'As we were saying there's no reason why being brought up in Castlebay means you've got to be at everyone's beck and call the whole time.'

She smiled, biting her lip. She had as good as told him now, hadn't she? She might as well have said the whole thing. It would have been easier in the long run.

Chrissie had got the ring for Christmas, she and Mogsy – whom she would now like to be referred to as Maurice – would be married next June. Mogsy – or Maurice – was building a house for them, a small place up near the creamery. Dwyers' had said Chrissie could go on working until there was a sign of a little Byrne coming along. They couldn't do fairer than that.

Clare's mother looked tired. 'Aren't you going to hare up and see your friend Miss O'Hara before you even sit down to talk to us?' she said the first night.

'Don't be giving out to me. I'm only just home.'

'Home! It's not much we'll see of you. Up there with the books, hardly a word to your own flesh and blood.'

'Mammy, why are you saying all this? I'm only in the door! I'm not going up to Miss O'Hara's, I'll go and see her tomorrow or the day after maybe, but you never minded that, you were always grateful to her too.'

'I know, don't mind me, I'm cranky these days.'

'What is it?' They were on their own.

'A bit of everything.'

'It's not Chrissie's wedding, you're not upset about that?'

'Not at all, for every shoe God made a stocking. I tell you those two were matched in heaven.'

'Well what then?'

'I suppose I get to thinking, I wonder about Tommy.' Clare's heart jumped. 'You'll know this yourself in years to come, there's something about the eldest one, I don't know what it is. But he never writes, he never comes back. Wouldn't it be great if he walked in this Christmas, that's what I was thinking I suppose.'

'Tommy never wrote more than his name in his life, you know that.'

'Yes, but I'm not settled about Ned's letters, he's hiding something. I'm going to ask Gerry Doyle when he comes in here will he go and see him, he's going to England tomorrow.'

'When did he tell you that? He said he was going to tell no one.'

'I asked him if he'd pick up some supplies for us before Christmas and he said he wouldn't be around, he just told me now, a few minutes ago when you were getting your stuff out of his van and being surprised at the sound of the sea all over again.'

'Gerry'd not have time to go finding Tommy and Ned.'

'Ah he will, he's a good boy for all that they give him a bad name around here. I'll have a word with him tomorrow.'

Clare left a note into Gerry Doyle's house that night. She said she wanted to stroll out to see the cliffs, her mother said she was stark raving mad but you might as well talk to a stone wall as to any of her children.

Gerry was sitting on the wall next morning as she had asked him. It was dark grey and threatening but it wasn't raining. They were both wrapped up well.

'There's a bit of a problem about Tommy,' she said.

'I thought there was from the sound of you.' He didn't sound triumphant or curious.

'Wormwood Scrubs to be exact,' she said.

'That's a bit of a problem all right.' He grinned at her comfortingly. 'And your ma doesn't know?'

'Nobody knows except Ned and me.'

'That's hard.'

'No, it's worse on him in the gaol, and the old man

they beat up doing the robbery, those are the people it's hard on.'

'Sure, well what will I do, say I can't find him?'

'No, could you just ring Ned, I've his phone number here written out, and talk away to him and then tell Ma that Tommy's fine. Would that be all right?' She looked very young and very anxious in the cold morning air.

'That's fine, I'll look after it.'

'Thanks Gerry.'

She hadn't asked him to keep it to himself, she didn't need to.

'About Fiona,' he said.

'It's none of my business,' she said suddenly.

'No, but anyway, she's having a baby this week. A Christmas baby of all bloody things.'

Clare nearly fell off the wall with shock. But for Gerry's sake she hid it. 'She's lucky to have you,' she said.

'We're a great pair,' he said and leaped lightly off the wall. He helped her down.

'Happy Christmas anyway,' he said.

She looked at him gratefully. His small pointed face was cold in the chilly dawn. He had said as little as could possibly be said, offered little sympathy when there was nothing to say. He had told Fiona's secret just so that she would have something in return, so that the pain and shame of her telling could be written off in a balance on some kind of scales.

'Happy Christmas, Gerry,' she said. 'You're very very nice.'

'I've always been telling you that, you're the one that didn't realize it,' he joked.

'I don't mean *that* sort of nice,' Clare said, but she wondered as she said it was she being truthful. He was so handsome and kind, he had this great sense of being in charge, nothing could go really wrong if you told Gerry. Fiona had been very lucky to have a brother like that. Fine help poor Tommy or Ned would have been in such a predicament. She felt sorry that he wouldn't be around for the Christmas holidays. She felt this odd kind of wish to hold on to him. Not to let him go.

245

'I'd better head for foreign parts,' he said. He was still holding her hands since he had helped her down from the wall.

'Safe journey. I hope . . . I hope Fiona'll be all right.'

'I'm sure she will, she's going to give the baby for adoption, and then I suppose I'll have to teach her something about photography.'

'About *what*?'

'Photography.' He gave his familiar crooked grin. 'That's what the whole place thinks she's been studying for the past six months.'

Angela was delighted to see her, no of course she wasn't too early, come on in and have breakfast like the old days.

'When I'm properly grown up and have my own place, I'll have exactly the same breakfast as you do,' Clare said, tucking in.

'What do I have that's special?'

'You have white shop bread and you have nice thin shop marmalade and you don't have thick homemade bread and awful homemade marmalade like people buy at sales of work.'

'Is this all your university education has done for you, made you whinge and whine about shop bread? Tell me about it all there, tell me about Emer and Kevin. Why don't you write to me, great long letters like you did when you were at school?'

'I don't know, I really don't know.'

'That's very honest of you.' Angela smiled, not at all put out. 'Anyway you're very busy up there.'

'It's not that.' Clare struggled to be honest. 'I write to my Mam, and to Josie and to Tommy. I *do* have time.'

'It might be easier in a while,' Angela seemed untroubled by it. 'Let me tell you about the place above. You won't credit this. Immaculata has gone totally and completely mad this term, the men with white coats will be stepping out of a van for her before Easter, mark my words.'

Mrs O'Hara frowned. 'You're very foolish and wrong, Angela, to say such things in front of a child. For all Clare's great marks she's only a child.'

'It's all right, Mrs O'Hara,' Clare said. 'I've heard it all, I say nothing, I keep my mouth closed.'

'You're the only one in this county who does then,' grumbled Angela's mother.

There was a long and insane story about Mother Immaculata having a Christmas pageant where everyone had to bring a toy for a poor child, they would all be gathered by the crib. Then one child had asked where they would go.

'To the *poor*,' Mother Immaculata had shrilled.

'But aren't we the poor?' the child had asked. 'There isn't anyone poorer than us.'

Clare laughed and while more tea was being poured she wrote Angela a note. 'I want to talk to you about Tommy, but not in front of your mother.'

Angela suggested that Clare come upstairs to see some new books that she had bought, and Clare sat for the first time in her teacher's bedroom. She was surprised at how sparse it was, with the very very white bedspread and the crucifix hanging over the bed head. There was a small press, Mary Catherine would have wept over the lack of closets. And a white chair. No carpet but a nice rug on the floor. Somehow it was a bit sad.

'I had to tell Gerry Doyle about Tommy,' she explained. She told everything except Gerry's secret.

'I had to tell him,' she said eventually when she saw Angela's troubled face. 'What else could I have done?'

'I suppose you could have let him find out and hoped he wouldn't tell your mother.'

'But it would have been so devious, such a long way round.'

'You might be right. I'm sure you are, it's just that now you've told him you're sort of in his power.'

'That's very dramatic.' Clare tried to laugh.

'He's a very dramatic young man. I've always thought that. Far too handsome and smart for Castlebay, he's dangerous almost.'

'I won't be in his power, honestly.' She looked straight into Angela's eyes. 'As much as I know anything, I know that. I'll never be in his control.'

David came into O'Brien's shop on Christmas Eve. Bones sat obediently outside the door.

'You can bring him in, everyone else brings their hounds in,' Clare's father said. 'In fact Mogsy Byrne brought in two cows a month ago.'

'I'd thank you to remember his name is Maurice, Dad, and he did not bring them in, they came in because the young fellow who was meant to be minding them wasn't.'

'Congratulations Chrissie, I heard you are engaged.' David was polite.

Chrissie simpered and showed him the ring. David said it looked terrific.

'No sign of you making a move in that direction yourself?' she said, arch woman of the world now, trying to encourage those who were hanging back.

'Oh, I think I'd better wait till I'm qualified. It's bad enough asking someone to take on a doctor but a medical student would be a fate worse than death, and we'd have nothing to live on.'

'Have you lost your heart up in Dublin?' Chrissie wondered.

'Chrissie, stop it, you're very forward,' Agnes said.

'No, I've been working too hard really to have any time for romance.' He smiled easily at them all. 'Is Clare here?'

'No, no sign of Clare – where would she be but up in Miss O'Hara's or in the hotel with Josie Dillon, there's no sign of her round here, I can assure you that.' Chrissie's voice was resentful. 'Sorry your visit was in vain,' she said spitefully.

'Not at all, I came for cigarettes,' he said easily. 'And for a tin of those nice biscuits as well for Nellie, and some black pudding.'

'Your mother got black pudding this morning,' Tom O'Brien said – it would be no use alienating a customer by selling the same thing twice.

'I'm sure she did but I bet she didn't get enough, I want six bits on my plate when we come back from Mass tomorrow morning. You've no idea how I miss black pudding in Dublin, they only have mean little slivers of it, and it doesn't taste the same at all.'

He wished them happy Christmas and they found a piece off the end of some cooked ham for Bones, and Bones gobbled it up and raised his paw in the air even though nobody had been offering to shake hands with him at all.

Clare was lying on Josie's bed telling her all about the hostel and the rungs up the wall and the laughs with Mary Catherine and Valerie. She told her about the lectures and the debating society on Saturday nights, and the hops, and how each Society had dances which were meant to make money.

Josie was disappointed that she had only met James Nolan on two occasions – in the café and at the very hot crowded party in somebody's flat. Clare revealed that he had danced with Mary Catherine twice, if you could call it dancing in those dark rooms; but he hadn't asked Mary Catherine out on a date or anything. Clare *didn't* tell her that James Nolan had forgotten her, she didn't think that was useful information; instead she said that she got the impression he was a bit fickle and faithless. But Josie said that was only when you didn't know him well.

Josie was thrilled about how she was building up the winter business in the hotel; and Uncle Dick had become really nice, not mad and grouchy like he used to be. Granny was totally gaga now; she had told Josie that Josie's mother had been putting arsenic in all their food for years now, and had even poisoned some of the guests, which was why they hadn't come back since. Her sisters Rose and Emily were home for Christmas and weren't a bit pleased about the bridge weekends; and they had almost told her to her face not to interfere. Clare didn't know how awfully quiet the place was in winter. When they were young they hadn't noticed it so much, but it was really so quiet you wouldn't believe it. She had learned to play bridge herself with Uncle Dick and sometimes the two of them went up to the Powers' and played a few rubbers with Mrs Power and Mr Harris, that auctioneer man who lived in a big house halfway

249

between the town and Castlebay. He was *eligible*, Uncle Dick said, but he was also a hundred and ten. Well he was thirty-seven, eighteen and a half years older than Josie, twice their age. Uncle Dick must be mad. Clare agreed and told Josie not to dream of trapping the eligible Mr Harris.

They speculated about Chrissie and Mogsy and wondered what either of them could see in the other. Would their children be as awful as both of them, or twice as awful?

Father O'Dwyer went round to the houses of the sick on the night of Christmas Eve and brought them Holy Communion. He came to the O'Hara cottage as his last visit. Angela had prepared the place for his visit and had a little candle-lighting in front of the crib.

She had gone upstairs while the old woman's confession was heard and then when the Priest called her she came down to kneel while her mother received Communion. They were all silent for a few minutes, but after that Father O'Dwyer had a cup of tea and a tomato sandwich from which the crusts had been cut off.

'Isn't it a pity that Father Sean didn't make it over to see you this Christmas?' he said conversationally.

'Oh well, you know the way it is,' Angela said meaninglessly.

'You see he's in a part now where they don't even have proper postal services,' Mrs O'Hara said. 'That's why we have to write to their house in England in order that priests there can forward them or deliver them when they're going out.'

'Yes, yes,' Father O'Dwyer was soothing the way he listened to all old people, not taking in very deeply what they were saying.

'But maybe he'll come back next year,' he said.

'Please God, Father, please God. Still the way I look at it is that it's better that he's there doing the Lord's work with savages and people who never heard of God than here coming to see me.'

Her face was radiant in the firelight and the aftermath of receiving Communion.

Angela bit her lip hard.

Father O'Dwyer patted Mrs O'Hara on the hand and said, 'That's right, that's right, that's the spirit that sends the labourers into the vineyard.'

Dr Power had asked Nellie would she like to go home for Christmas. 'You ask me that every year and the answer's always no sir, thank you very much, I have a nicer time in this house, and a better meal and more peace. And I can go down to see them all in the evening.'

'If you're sure . . .' he said.

'Anyway sir, the mistress wouldn't like you playing fast and loose with the arrangements. I'd like to see her face, if I said I wouldn't be here for Christmas Day.'

'Stop trying to stir up a row, Nellie,' he said affectionately. 'This is a happy house now, do you hear me?'

'It is and all sir,' said Nellie goodnaturedly. 'I've been here since I was sixteen, that will be twenty years next year, and there's hardly a cross word ever said under this roof.'

'You've been here too long, Nellie. Why don't you go and marry someone?'

'And have a lout asking me to cook his dinner and polish his shoes for nothing for him, aren't I like a king here, with my own wireless that I can take upstairs and plug in in the bedroom if I want to, and a big chair beside the range. What would I want with marriage?'

'Will you sit with us and have your Christmas dinner at our table tomorrow?'

'God love you sir, you ask me that every year too, and I won't. The mistress would be annoyed for one thing, and for another I'd be dropping the food off my fork.'

'You're a very obstinate woman.'

'I've no brains but I'm not a fool, that's all.'

Clare had bought bright Christmas decorations while she was in Dublin. It had been marvellous going down Moore Street and Henry Street with Mary Catherine and Valerie listening to the women shouting their wares, and the last of this and the last of that in order to whip people up into a frenzy thinking things were running out. Clare had bought the last of the shiny chains, only to see dozens more coming from under the stall. She had also bought the last of the Christmas sparklers which were like low-key fireworks giving off little tinselly sparks. Jim and Ben had loved them and they were a treat in Castlebay so she felt it was a good buy. She had gone without lunches for three weeks in order to buy the gifts, and had stocked up on bread and butter from breakfast to keep her going through the day.

It was bright and cold on Christmas morning. The O'Briens went to early Mass from habit. There was no need to be back in case anyone would call to the shop. Nobody would admit that they had forgotten anything for Christmas, the family would be able to eat their meal undisturbed.

Clare had wrapped up all her presents and Chrissie eyed this pile of gifts with some suspicion.

'I hope you realize that being engaged and everything we have to put all our savings towards our future,' she said to Clare. 'We can't be wasting everything on silly gifts.'

'Sure,' Clare had said and resisted the temptation to pull out every hair of Chrissie's permed, frizzy head.

After their breakfast there was an endless amount of preparation for the main meal. Agnes, still frail and unable to move about, sat with her leg on a stool and gave instructions, lift the ham carefully from the water where it had been soaking. Carefully, don't drown the whole kitchen. Set the table properly. Properly, Chrissie, it *was* Christmas Day, take that dirty cloth off and find a cleaner one. And peel the potatoes Ben, not with your finger, with a knife, and move that holly Jim, before it sticks into people.

Tom O'Brien sat beside her, repeated her orders with increasing impatience, and added little asides of his own about how you'd think people would be glad to help when their unfortunate mother had been injured in a fall.

Clare did most of the work and when the meal was ready she was nearly exhausted. She couldn't understand why a lot of this work hadn't been divided up and done the night before, but a word of criticism would open the floodgates, and she kept her thoughts to herself.

After the plum pudding, she distributed her gifts. Mam thought the scarf was very nice, a bit light for this kind of weather, but very nice for warmer weather, that is of course if you would wear a scarf at all in warmer weather. Her father looked with interest at the map of the county she had found with such trouble in a second-hand shop in Dublin, and then framed. It was very generous he thought; of course it would be a poor man who didn't know his own county, but maybe strangers might look at it. Jim and Ben genuinely *were* pleased with the puzzles and games she had got them. Chrissie looked at the manicure set with dulled eyes.

Clare had been so sure that Chrissie would love a manicure set, for as far back as she could remember Chrissie had been filing and painting her nails, her fingernails and her toenails, surely the set in the little red case would be exactly what she would like. But Clare must have been remembering a time too far back. Chrissie opened the parcel with her stubby fingers and Clare noticed that her hands were calloused and her nails were bitten short. Still, she thought hopefully, maybe.

Chrissie turned it over and said it was very nice, especially of course if you were a student and had time to be doing your nails. She put it aside and never looked at it again during the day.

Clare got a box of sweets taken from one of the shelves from her mother, and a tinsel card from Jim and Ben. Her father gave her £1 peeled from the notes in his pocket. She fought the stinging of the tears in her eyes. They were her family for heaven's sake, they didn't need to be going on with too much ritual. It was silly to get upset because of the lack of trappings.

Angela had warned her long ago that one of the dangers of going away to be educated was that you expected too much when you came back, and you built up a whole wall of disappointment that was unnecessary. It had been a bit like that when she came home from the scrupulously clean convent boarding school and had to share a room with Chrissie, it was the same now. After knowing people like Emer and Kevin with their politeness and consideration towards each other and everyone they came in contact with . . . this seemed a dull, leaden sort of day.

She remembered Mary Catherine reading somewhere that more people wanted to commit suicide on Christmas Day than any other day. She would not join them. Putting her elbows on the table full of dirty dishes and the wrappings of the presents that only she had given, Clare managed a big smile.

'Will we tell a ghost story?' she said.

'Who knows one?' asked her father.

'We could make one up as we went along, each person adding a bit. You start, Chrissie.'

'I don't know how to make up ghost stories.' Chrissie was not going to join in.

'Yes you do. Just start.'

The others looked eager.

'Once upon a time there was a ghost that had this desperate sister,' Chrissie began. 'It had four brothers who were all right but it had a really terrible sister . . .'

There was always a Christmas tree in the window of Dr Power's house. On the side where it could be seen from the road. There were presents which had arrived by post from the Nolans in Dublin and from cousins and friends all over the place. David placed his own gifts there on Christmas Eve night, wrapped in red crêpe paper and each one with a cut-out Santa Claus.

David looked at all the neatly labelled parcels. He glanced through at the dining room already set with gleaming glass and shining silver, decorated with holly and criss-crossed crackers. Why did it feel so empty and hollow? He hated Nellie being in the kitchen, although he knew she would never come and join them; he hated the games-playing, where he and his mother and father would pull crackers and read jokes and exclaim over gifts. If they only knew about some of the homes he visited in Dublin when he had been doing his practical work, then they'd find this kind of playing at Christmas very shabby. But his father must know.

They walked across in the cold Christmas air to Mass;

everyone was good-humoured and cheerful despite the wind. Dr Power dealt with a young woman who had fainted, and reassured her it was just the result of a three-mile walk fasting on a cold morning. 'But I'd have to fast and go to Holy Communion on Christmas morning, wouldn't I?' the woman said, detecting some criticism in the doctor's voice as he bent her head down.

'Of course you would, that's just what the Lord likes on His birthday – people nearly killing themselves,' Dr Power muttered.

All though the day, David felt as if he were under some kind of spotlight. They were all anxious to know what David thought, what David wanted. Did David think they should eat now? Have a sherry? Would David like to open the presents? Was he sure he liked the sweater? If it wasn't big enough, if it wasn't the right colour it could be changed.

They had soup first, and little fingers of toast; and then the turkey was carved – was David sure he wanted the leg? There was plenty of breast.

They clapped when the flame lit on the plum pudding, and they raised their glasses to another good year and to the year that lay ahead. Molly Power wondered whether the Nolans were at this moment having their Christmas lunch in Dublin, and they drank a toast to them too.

'James' mother gets very odd at Christmas,' David said, to make conversation. 'Apparently last year she had a handkerchief on her head all through the meal.'

Dr Power burst out laughing. 'Did she say why?' he asked.

'Well, she did when Caroline asked her, she said you never knew with ceilings – then I don't think they asked any more.' David grinned back, thinking of the story.

'I don't like you telling stories like that about Sheila, she's different, she's unusual, that's all, you make her sound batty when you talk like that.'

'She is a *bit* batty, I think,' David said apologetically. 'You know, not dangerous or anything but definitely not firing on all cylinders.'

Dr Power frowned slightly and David understood.

'Sorry, I was just joking – unusual is more the word for it.'

Molly smiled, pleased. She didn't like her friend being defined as insane. She passed round the liqueur chocolates, exclaiming with delight as each centre was read out. Would she have kirsch or would she try cherry brandy? Which was more alcoholic? David fought down his wish to say that since there was less than half an eggspoonful of alcohol in each it was immaterial.

'*Do* you see a lot of Caroline?' Molly's voice was over-casual.

'A fair bit, but I'm working hard, very hard. People never believe this of students. We went to a party just before I came down here, she sent you both her love.'

'I think she likes it here, I think she's a Castlebay person at heart, she wrote a very nice note in her Christmas card saying it must be lovely in the winter.' Mrs Power was still fishing.

'Oh, I think just for holidays,' David said.

'You'd never know. A lot of people thought they'd come here for holidays and changed their minds, ended up staying here altogether.' Dr Power patted his wife's hand as he said this. David felt a sense of overpowering claustrophobia. Not only were they wrapping him in cotton wool while he was here; they were planning the day when he came back full time as a doctor to help his father; and they were now planning his wife for him.

'I think I'll go for a bit of a walk . . . all that food . . .' he stammered.

He stood up, anxious to be out of the warm room, the smell of mince pies and the beam of their attention.

But it was no use. They both thought that would be a great idea: Dr Power went to get his stick and Molly ran upstairs for her coat and gloves. David carried the tray of coffee cups out to the kitchen. Nellie was nodding off to sleep beside the big range with the wireless on, and Bones was fast asleep due to a surfeit of turkey.

He left the tray quietly on the kitchen table and wrapped his scarf round his neck.

He knew he was a selfish, selfish ungrateful so and so, but he wished that he had fourteen brothers and sisters to share the responsibility with him; or that he had no parents at all like one of the students in his year, who was going to spend the festive season with a lot of English people in Belgium. Everyone knew that English girls were outrageous and this fellow was going to have a really great time.

'Ready, David,' called Molly and everyone in the house woke up in confusion: David from his dream of permissive coach travellers, and Nellie and Bones from their kitchen sleeps.

The family walk was underway and soon it would be the family tea, and then tomorrow it would be the family Stephen's Day. David sighed heavily and hated himself for the sigh.

On New Year's Day Clare went for a walk on the beach to collect shells and make New Year's resolutions.

'I will not expect too much of my family.

'I will work out a better revision system, not just big pencil marks saying *must revise later*.

'I will get a job in a café one night a week in Dublin.

'I will have my hair cut in an interesting style.

'I will find a person to take me out on a date.

'I will write a proper letter to Angela O'Hara every single week.'

She found some nice cowries and put them in the box she had in her pocket. She heard a shout and there was David.

'I hoped I'd find you here. You and I are the only people who use the amenities out of season.'

'Or in season, they're all too busy to come down on the beach, my father can't even swim.'

'Anyway, here you are.' He looked pleased to see her, she felt suddenly a little embarrassed.

'Where's Bones, you don't look fully dressed without him.'

'Poor Bones, he has a cough. Believe it or not, he's coughing like an old man. My father has him dosed better than if he were the president but Bones is whooping and hacking away. Nellie has an old jumper tied round his neck, you never saw the cut of him.'

Clare laughed at the idea of it but said it was rotten to think of Bones not being well.

'Will you do me a favour?' he asked.

'Sure.'

'I want to go back the day after tomorrow . . .'

'But term doesn't start until . . .'

'Exactly. That's the point. I have to say it does, will you back me up?'

'Certainly, but I can't go back the day after tomorrow.'

His face fell. 'No, I suppose you can't.'

'No, I don't mean leaving here or anything, they wouldn't mind. It's just I've nowhere to stay. The hostel doesn't open for us till the first day of term.'

'Oh.'

'We could say medical school opens earlier, I could say that to anyone, but anyway what does it matter what I say? I don't meet your parents.'

'No, but if you'd gone back they'd know, everyone knows everything here, every single thing.' He sounded annoyed.

'I'm sorry,' Clare said. 'I know what you feel, and I wouldn't mind at all going back myself, but you do see . . .'

'You could always stay in our flat, my flat,' he said.

'No I could *not*.'

'I don't mean any funny business, you'd have your own room, one of the fellows won't be back until term starts.'

'We'd be killed if I was caught, and I'm damn well not going to risk getting caught for something I haven't done, or putting myself in danger unless I'm getting value out of it.' She was full of conviction and quite unaware how vehement she looked.

'All right, calm down. I see your point of view.'

'Did you have a nice Christmas?' she asked suddenly.

'Not very. Did you?'

'Not very.'

'Are you missing lover boy Gerry Doyle? I hear he went off to the bright lights of London.'

'No, I'm not missing him. I don't suppose I gave him a thought. I must be the only woman in the western hemisphere that isn't.'

'Aha then he'll go after you all the more,' David said.

'Have *you* a lover girl in Dublin that you want to be back to meet?' she asked.

'Yes and no. Yes there is a girl, but it's not only that. I feel a bit too *important* in the house. I'm all they've got. Do you know what I mean? I think they pay too much attention to me.'

'It's the reverse in my house. They don't pay enough attention to me. I'm not nearly important enough.'

He laughed. 'Nobody ever gets what they want, do they? Will I see you at all in Dublin? I could ring you in the hostel some evening.'

'Great,' she said.

He never rang, but that was no surprise.

Clare thought about it, and decided that David had never meant it, it was just the way the Powers had of saying goodbye. They couldn't actually say the word, it seemed too final, so they said something insincere instead, like promising to ring you at the hostel.

Perhaps it was just as well, she thought, making the best of it. There were thousands and thousands of men in UCD; she shouldn't try to get a date with someone from Castlebay who was on the other side of the cliffs so to speak.

Valerie had had a fairly uneventful Christmas, all things considered. She had nearly come to blows with her mother when they were playing Scrabble: her mother said Quorn was a word, and Valerie had claimed it was a proper noun and the name of a hunt somewhere. Her mother had flung things on the ground and said she wouldn't be patronized. They had an adventurous time with a cook book, each taking it in turns to make a dish, one more exotic than the other; apparently Valerie's father in England had refused to pay any actual money but would pay bills in the local grocery so they only chose dishes with very highly priced ingredients.

Mary Catherine had an adventurous Christmas too; James Nolan invited her to his house three times. She had thought Caroline was a *pain*. Caroline was finishing her thesis for her M.A. about Spencer and Ireland and thought almost everyone in the world was illiterate and that Americans were more illiterate than most. James Nolan showed a very unhealthy desire to go to the States in the summer: he said he would be sure to look up Mary Catherine and her family, and perhaps he could come to stay? She had agreed, and made sure not to give him her home address. Her mailman father told her when she married a man who owned a castle to keep her American side of things under wraps until the deal was done. James Nolan wasn't exactly a castle owner but he was an attorney almost, and that couldn't be bad. No, of course she didn't love him. But she wasn't going to pitch him overboard yet. Clare thought of Josie back home typing away in the hotel, organizing bridge conferences with Uncle Dick, fighting off her two jealous sisters Rosie and Emily. She sighed. It wouldn't be reasonable to tell Mary Catherine to hold her horses, because James Nolan couldn't remember Josie Dillon from a hole in the ground.

Mary Catherine came running up the stairs two at a time. 'There is a *dee-vine* young man downstairs asking for you, Clare. I said I would see if I could find you.'

'You mean thing! Why didn't you say I'd be down in two ticks?'

'Because I'm your friend. I wanted you to put on something good and to comb your hair and put on some make-up. I'm *too* good a friend, that's what I am.'

'Oh, it must be Gerry Doyle, he's the one who always gets that reaction.' Still, she did put on a little lipstick.

She picked up her dufffle coat.

'Very confident he's going to ask you out,' Mary Catherine said.

'You should play hard to get,' Valerie suggested. 'He'll think it's too eager if you go down ready for the off.'

'That fellow only knows people who are too eager, that's the style he's used to. Anyway, we'll just go out for coffee, I imagine.'

'I think we should leave the window unlocked. You may

need to climb the rungs tonight from the sound of it.' Valerie was pleased.

'He's not strictly good-looking. He's got an *aura*,' said Mary Catherine.

'You and your auras, you learned that word a week ago, everything has an *aura*.' Clare was gone before they could retaliate. She ran lightly down the stairs. Gerry was standing in the hall as relaxed as if he had been a regular visitor.

'This is a great surprise,' she said with genuine and unaffected pleasure. 'I didn't know you were in Dublin.'

'I'm not. I mean not in Dublin itself if you know what I mean, I'm passing through, on my way back from London. I got a longing to talk to you.'

She was going to say something joky – but his face looked tired.

'Great,' she said simply. 'Let me take you away from here before they devour you.' She tucked her arm companionably in his and they went out of the hostel and down the steps. 'Coffee or a drink?'

'A drink would be very nice. Do you know a pub?'

'There's two here, just round the corner. Shows you my virtuous life, though, I don't know what they're like. Have a look into the first one and tell me what you think.'

He came back in seconds, grinning. 'How many people are there in Dublin – half a million maybe?'

'More, much more, I think. Why?'

'In that pub, who do I see but David Power and Caroline Nolan looking into each other's eyes.'

'Go on. Well, we could have a Castlebay reunion, if you'd like that.'

'No. I wouldn't like that. I'd like to talk to you, that's why I came to find you.'

They went into the second pub. There was a mixed collection of drinkers: students in college scarves, workmen from a building site nearby, a few red-nosed old regulars.

'This is Paradise,' Gerry said. 'No one from home. Is it still bitter lemon or have you got more adventurous?'

'Still bitter lemon,' she said, pleased that he had remembered.

He told her about Fiona. The baby was a boy, born the day after Christmas. She called him Stephen. The old nuns had been very kind – disapproving of course, and thought Fiona was a great sinner – but kind in the end; and they had arranged the adoption when the baby was three weeks old. Fiona had a sort of depression apparently. That's why he had gone over again, to cheer her up, to reassure her that she had done the right thing. There was no other course open to her if she wanted to live her life in Castlebay. She had to pretend it had never happened. She *had* to keep it a secret.

Clare didn't want to hear about the baby's father, but Gerry wanted to tell her. He was a married man. Wouldn't you know? One of the crowd that came down golfing last year. He had told Fiona he was single; he had also told her when she wrote to him about the pregnancy that there was no question of his becoming involved; and that if she made any trouble all his friends had agreed to say that *they* had had her too. What options did she have? If this were known at home she would be a slut *and* a fool – what a combination . . .

He talked on about the business. Times were hard and getting harder. It hadn't been as easy as he had thought: there were all the expenses. If Clare could only see what he had to lash out on equipment – the new modern machines were so expensive, and of course they would eventually pay for themselves, but the trouble was *when*.

Even doing the place up had cost a lot of money. There had been some good commissions, but not enough.

'What are you going to do?' she asked sympathetically.

'Survive. Isn't that the only thing to do? What you and I have always been doing.'

He looked as if it might be quite an effort to survive. Shadows under his eyes, and his face pale. She felt very protective towards him suddenly, almost as if she would like to put her arm round his shoulder and draw him towards her soothingly. She had never felt like that about Gerry Doyle before, and had been rather relieved. It was as if she were the only girl in town who hadn't caught the measles. But this was different. This wasn't being keen on him like

Chrissie and everyone else. This was wanting to look after him, he seemed defenceless and vulnerable sitting there in front of his pint glass.

She reached out and took his hand.

'So I thought I'd come and tell you about it. If there's anyone who'd understand, it's you.'

Pleased and surprised she asked, 'Why me?'

'Lord, it hasn't been easy for you to get where you've got. No one to help you on, just Clare do this do that, iron that shirt Clare, sort those potatoes Clare, when they should be so proud of you and helping you to study.'

He had noticed, all those years. He understood.

She was trying to lessen the intensity of his stare: he was looking at her as if his eyes were boring through her.

'You're different, Clare. I've always said that to you. You and I are the same type. We're the only two they produced in Castlebay. We belong together.'

She was startled now and not quite sure how to handle it.

'Look at that couple over there,' she said suddenly as a girl student, somewhat the worse for drink, started climbing on the lap of her companion. 'That's *belonging together* in a rather public way. How long before they're thrown out?'

She turned her bright smile back to him but his glance hadn't changed.

He grasped her hand. 'Stop talking about things that don't matter. It's true. We *are* the same. And I know every thought you have, as you know mine.'

'I don't know yours, Gerry. Really I don't.'

'Well you will.'

'When will I? I have so much work to do here in this university I'll never have time to get round to reading people's thoughts.'

'Not *people's* thoughts. *Mine*. I'll wait for you.'

'It will be a long wait. I'm going to get a list of letters after my name, you know.'

'Stop trying to avoid it. I'll wait for you, no matter how long I have to wait. In your heart you know that.'

She looked at his troubled face, never so handsome as now, and wondered what he meant by all this. It had a very solemn air about it. Like a vow.

She met David Power not at all during the term, and got over her pique that he had promised to ring her. She went on one date to the Abbey Theatre. The serious history student who had asked her said he hoped she didn't mind being in the gods. By the time they got there they were nearly ready for a hospital bed. He told her that he didn't believe in spending money foolishly; and when they had a cup of coffee afterwards and he said, 'You *don't* want anything to eat, do you?' Clare agreed in her mind that indeed he was *not* someone to spend money foolishly. Or even at all. He asked her to go to the National Gallery with him on the following Saturday afternoon. But she didn't like him enough; and she preferred going there on her own anyway. And it was honestly *too* mean to ask someone on a date to a place that was free. She wrote about it to Josie, deliberately making it worse than it was. She didn't want Josie to know how much fun it was in Dublin. She didn't want Josie to know that she had met James Nolan either.

James always looked deliberately well-dressed, as if he were posing as a very elegant man at the races.

'Is your nice American friend Mary Catherine loaded?' James had asked her unexpectedly in the Annexe one morning when she was having coffee and reading an article in *History Today* at the same time.

'Loaded?' She pretended she hadn't understood.

'Loaded with money, weighed down with wealth.'

'I have no idea,' Clare said, looking at him with her big dark eyes opened wide in innocence. 'What a strange thing to ask.'

'Well I can hardly ask *her*,' he complained.

'But why not? If you want to know, isn't she the one you should ask?'

'It looks odd. And anyway women are so apt to take things the wrong way.'

'I know,' Clare said sympathetically. 'Isn't it sickening?'

'You're laughing at me.'

'I am not. I'm horrified by you if you must know.'

'It's just that I was half thinking of going to the States this summer – see how American I've become? I don't say "going to America" I say "going to the States" – and if I could stay with Mary Catherine's family for a bit it would cut down the cost.'

'Sure, but why would it matter if they were loaded or not? Couldn't you stay with them, if she asked you, even if they were just ordinary, and not wealthy? Wouldn't it be a bed wherever it was?'

James looked down into his coffee cup. 'Yes, but it is my last summer holiday before I settle down to work. I'd like to go somewhere where they have a bit of *style*. A swimming pool, a ranch or a big apartment on Fifth Avenue . . . She's very secretive about where she lives. That's why I asked you.'

'Why don't you just come back to Castlebay as usual? I think the complications about America are wearing you out.'

'You don't understand anything Clare, that's your problem.'

'I know,' Clare grinned at him. 'It's always been my problem. I'm as thick as the wall.'

They parted friends, and yet Clare felt guilty. This pompous man was being a real heel towards two of her friends. It was disloyal sitting in the Annexe and giggling with him.

Emer and Kevin said they would be delighted if Clare came to stay for Easter. She had offered them a deal: she would babysit, wash up every single thing that went into the sink and do two hours a day digging the garden. In return could she have a place to stay and a little food? She had written to Angela and said she couldn't bear to go back to Castlebay: this was just the period when she had to revise and prepare for her First Arts. She'd try to square David Power too. She left a note for him at the medical faculty. He rang her that night at the hostel.

'Why should I help you?' he asked in a mock temper. 'You never helped me at Christmas.'

'Your romance didn't suffer as a result of it,' she said sharply.

'Do you have a fleet of detectives?' he inquired.

'Please, David, it's just that I really do have to work, I'm the scholarship girl don't forget, I don't get chances to repeat things. And I don't get any time at home. It's not like your house.'

'OK. *I'll* go along with *your* lies.'

It annoyed her. 'Thanks very much, David. I'll see you in the summer, I'm sure,' she said curtly.

'Oh, I'm sure you'll have thought up something else by then,' he said.

She hung up immediately before she could lose her temper with him. *Spoiled, self-important pig.*

'They *don't* resent it.'

'They do, Clare. They mightn't even realize it, but you've grown in ways that they never will. You speak better than they do, than you used to. You look better. It's not just the book learning.'

Clare twisted her glass in her hand. She and Angela were having a drink in the corner of Dillon's Hotel lounge. There was a beautiful view of the beach. Shortly, Josie would be putting her cover on the typewriter and would come for the game of tennis. Some things hadn't changed over the years. But Clare realized that Angela was right. She did have much more confidence. Her own mother would never dream of coming into the hotel and sitting down in the cushioned chair looking out over Castlebay. That wasn't for the likes of them, she would say. Her father wouldn't stand at the bar and drink his pint in the hotel either, it would be Craig's or nowhere. Jim and Ben would be tongue-tied and shoving at each other. And as for Chrissie! She and Mogsy wouldn't be caught dead inside a stuffy place like that, she had said on more than one occasion. Clare sighed. Lord knew that Dillon's Hotel was hardly the sophisticated capital of the world, but wasn't it maddening to think that she was the only member of her family who would feel comfortable there having a glass of shandy.

'I'll be very nice at the wedding. All day,' she smiled at Angela.

'Good, I don't want to sound like a sermon on charity but you have had so much more than Chrissie and you always will have. Make it as nice a day for her as possible.'

'All I'll get for my pains is Chrissie giving out to me all day, and if I'm *nice*, that will be further cause for complaint.'

'You promised.'

'Yes. What about your brother, when he was being ordained? Was that a hard sort of day?'

'No.' Angela's voice seemed distant. She was looking out to sea. 'My father didn't have a drop to drink. Dr Power gave him some tablets and told him it was dangerous to drink with them. I don't know whether it was or not. And my poor mother had a hat with a veil. I'll never forget it — and gloves. No, that day was no trouble at all.'

'You don't talk about him much nowadays.'

'I'll tell you some time.'

'Sure. I'm sorry.'

'Here's Josie and Dick.' Angela looked up brightly. 'You're looking very well, Josie. Very pretty.'

'Thank you. I've been on another diet. The summer visitors will be here at the end of the week. I'm trying to ensnare one of them.'

'One in particular, or just anyone?'

'Well, I have my eye on one. But he's a bit hard to get.'

Clare didn't catch Angela's eye. She had told her about Josie, and James Nolan going to the States for the summer; and debated whether or not she should tell Josie this.

Angela had said she should have let it fall casually ages ago, but Clare said it was very hard to let things *fall casually* when Josie sat up on her bed and hugged her knees and made plans for the summer.

'This is the last night we'll sleep together,' Clare said to Chrissie.

'I'm sure neither of us are sorry about that,' Chrissie

sniffed. She was examining her face in the mirror with dissatisfaction. There was a definite spot on her chin.

'Well, it's the end of one part of your life. It must be exciting,' Clare soldiered on.

'Well, I'm twenty-one. It's time I was married.' Chrissie was defensive.

'It'll be a grand day.'

'Yes, it will. It'll be grand without any pats on the head from you, either.'

'I'm not patting you on the head. I'm just trying to say I'm pleased. That it's great. That it's the first wedding in the family. That's all.'

Her face was angry. Chrissie softened.

'Yes, well. All right. Sorry. I suppose I'm a bit jumpy and everything.'

'You're going to look terrific. The dress is fabulous.'

It was hanging on their wardrobe with an old sheet draped over it to keep it clean.

Chrissie looked at it mournfully.

'And your hair, it's super. I've never seen it so nice.'

'Yes, well. Peg's coming round in the morning to give it a comb out. You know, get it right for the veil.'

'Maurice will be delighted with you.'

'I don't know. Look at this spot. It's going to be desperate in the morning.

'Listen. I tell you what to do. I'll dab a bit of Dettol on it. And don't touch it, do you hear? The Dettol won't work if you touch it, and then in the morning if it's not gone we can put some extra make-up on it. But it will have flattened a bit if you don't touch it.'

'Why were you never like this before?' Chrissie asked suspiciously.

'Like what?'

'Interested in spots, and ordinary things.'

'I always was, but you used to say I was mad, remember?'

Fiona Doyle said she'd be happy to look after the shop for them while they went to the wedding. She asked how thick she should cut the bacon and was there anyone she should or should not give credit to. Tom said she was a model shop girl and that if ever the photographic business folded, there'd be a job for her in O'Brien's ten minutes later. Agnes said that Fiona was a brick to come down so early because it gave them time to get ready themselves without rushing out into the shop every time the door opened.

There had been a pink card with 'All Good Wishes on Your Wedding Day' from Tommy, and a nicely wrapped tablecloth from Ned with a small greetings card wishing them every happiness, and regretting that he wasn't able to be there. Clare saw the fine hand of Father Flynn in both of these gestures.

Chrissie had been pleased. It hadn't struck her as remotely odd that neither of her brothers would return for her big day. Agnes was pleased too. She had somehow resigned herself to the thought that the boys weren't coming home again. Gerry Doyle had assured her they were well settled there, and wasn't it better in this day and age, when half the country were down taking the mailboat to England looking for jobs, that her two sons had got there first and got themselves established. In fact Agnes O'Brien was more cheerful than she had been for a long time. Her ankle had recovered now, everyone said that it was her accident which had finally been responsible for the Committee putting up the new steps and railings, so she was regarded as a bit of a heroine.

She dabbed unaccustomed powder on her nose and looked affectionately at Tom as he struggled into the new suit he had bought. He had needed one anyway, and this was the perfect opportunity. He struggled with the unfamiliar fabric which seemed hard and full of pointy bits and corners.

'I'm just so relieved,' said Agnes. 'Glad that she's settling down.'

'Mogsy Byrne isn't the worst, I suppose,' Tom O'Brien said – reluctantly.

'No, when you think the way Chrissie *could* have gone.' They'd never spoken of it before, but they had been through their worries. Was Chrissie getting a name as being fast? Did she hang round with the girls who were known to be up to no good in the caravan park? They were lucky that poor Mogsy, not the brightest man in Castlebay, but the brother of Bumper Byrne who was certainly the sharpest, was going to take Chrissie on for life.

There had been a time when Chrissie had held out for Dillon's Hotel; but after a look at the menus, the rates and whole set-up she listened more carefully to her future brother-in-law's advice. Bumper and his wife Bid had advised Chrissie not to throw away her money just making the Dillons rich. Why pour out all that money so that Young Mrs Dillon could have a new fur coat? Chrissie had wanted the day to be very splendid, but she and Mogsy listened obediently and heard that it could still be splendid without paying out a fortune. And this way they could invite more people; which was always good for business, and it didn't insult people and cause grievances.

In fact Chrissie and her Mogsy had come round to the view that Dillon's Hotel would be a very stuffy place to have a wedding anyway.

So they were having it in the big room behind Father O'Dwyer's house. It had been a storeroom once, but Dr Power and Miss O'Hara had somehow managed to persuade Miss McCormack that it should be used for the parish. Father O'Dwyer took very careful note of what she said. Now it was used for fetes, and sales of work. They had the Irish dancing competitions there too, and recently it had been used for weddings or christening parties. There were long trestle tables covered with cloths, and there was a big tea urn. There would be plates of sandwiches, and bridge rolls, and sausage rolls. There would be jelly and cream as well as the wedding cake. Gerry Doyle was going to take the photographs, and cousins were coming from three separate towns for the occasion.

Chrissie and Mogsy had said they were keeping it small, but that still meant forty-five people. Just enough, Agnes thought, pleased for it to look respectable. There was no question of a rushed job. Nobody could say it was a hole-in-the-corner affair.

Clare was being very good over all the arrangements, Agnes noticed with surprise. And she was keeping Chrissie calm this morning; she had even bought some bath oil at Murphy's chemist and said that Chrissie should be allowed to have the bathroom to herself for half an hour so everyone else should wash quickly or else wash at the kitchen sink. Agnes hadn't expected Clare to be so helpful. Usually she and Chrissie had nothing but harsh words.

The young couple were going on a week's honeymoon to Bray: which was just another seaside resort, but still it would be miles away from Castlebay and that was the main thing. Then they would be back, a married couple living in the new house, and Mogsy would be organizing the churns and the milk collection; and Chrissie would be back in the butcher's shop, but with a new respect now. There would be two rings on her finger, she would be 'Mrs Byrne', and she could talk about 'my husband'. Agnes felt a great surge of sympathy for her large, brassy, argumentative daughter.

She could hear laughter coming from the bathroom. Clare was scrubbing the bride's back.

'You'll be next, Fiona,' she said to the beautiful dark-haired girl standing quietly in the shop.

'Oh, I don't know, Mrs O'Brien, who'd have me?'

'Tut tut child, aren't you the most beautiful girl in Castlebay?'

'I haven't got much life in me though. Fellows like someone with life in them. I'm like that advertisement up there on the wall: *Do you wake tired?* I seem to wake tired all the time.'

Agnes O'Brien had never heard the young Doyle girl utter a sentence as long as that in her whole life. She wasn't at all sure what to do. She wished Fiona had chosen a better time to confide in her.

'If I were you I'd go and have a chat with Dr Power, it might be tablets you need. Dr Power has great iron tonics in bottles too, they'd make you feel strong. Maybe it's a lack of iron.'

The thin, kind face of Agnes O'Brien under her unaccustomed hat and dotted with unfamiliar powder was concerned. Fiona shook herself.

'That's what I'll do, Mrs O'Brien. I'll go up to him the next chance I have. It could well be lack of iron.'

Agnes beamed; and then decided to hurry on the bride and her sister.

Peggy had now arrived dressed in her bridesmaid's gear and carrying a hairbrush and a can of lacquer. She pounded up the stairs.

'Your room looks different,' Peggy said, looking around. Clare said nothing. She didn't mention that she had put all Chrissie's clothes in the wash, everything that she wasn't taking on the honeymoon. Clare would personally transfer these to the new home. Chrissie had an alarming habit of saying that she'd 'leave this here' or 'leave that here for the moment'. She couldn't grasp the fact that she was actually moving residence. Clare had taken all the old shoes and put them in a box marked 'Chrissie's Shoes'. For the first time in years there was actually room to move.

Peggy began the back-combing and the teasing of the hair, expertly and with great intensity.

'Are you sure you're not in a huff because I asked Peggy to be the bridesmaid instead of you?' Chrissie asked for the twentieth time.

'No. I think you're quite right. I told you,' Clare said.

Chrissie examined her miraculously cured spot. 'It was just that we didn't know if you'd come or not. You see?'

Clare bit back her rage. There had never been any question of her not coming. 'I know,' she said sympathetically. 'I'll try not to be *too* jealous of Peg,' she added cheerfully, and Chrissie laughed.

Peggy shrugged her shoulders. Chrissie *hated* Clare! What on earth were they laughing like old friends for? Oh well. It was her wedding day. She was entitled to laugh if she wanted to. Not that marrying Mogsy Byrne was anything much to laugh about, Peggy thought sourly. She'd prefer to be a spinster of twenty-two than marry Mogsy.

Father O'Dwyer was waiting at the gate of the church when the wedding party arrived. The Byrne family were all installed. The O'Briens arrived together – it was only a five-minute walk from their shop up Church Street and this was the triumphal journey. Chrissie walked on her father's arm. She wore a white dress, which the dressmaker had said was far more suitable as a dance dress. Chrissie had giggled, and said why not, one day it would be a dance dress. Her veil was short and held in place by a headdress of wax flowers.

It was a sunny Saturday morning in June. The season hadn't really begun; the people would start arriving in the next few days. But the whole town saw Chrissie O'Brien go to her wedding. They waved and shouted from shops and houses. Josie Dillon waved out from the hotel. Miss O'Flaherty at her stationery shop; the Murphys were in the street in front of the chemist's shop. Dwyers' had a big sheet of paper with *Good Luck Chrissie* written on it. She was very excited when she saw it, and kept drawing people's attention to it.

Behind Tom O'Brien and his daughter walked Peggy in a very bright yellow which didn't suit her.

Clare and her mother walked next, with Jim and Ben. Clare wondered would she ever walk like this with her father, as she had seen so many other girls walk to the church. It was nice because everyone had a chance to see the wedding party without having to go up to the church uninvited and peer. But Clare couldn't imagine it. She could not see herself going through this kind of parade for anyone. It would have to be somebody quite extraordinary waiting up there in the church if she could endure this pantomime for him.

Just as she was wondering what kind of person it could be, Gerry Doyle appeared at her elbow.

'Stop dreaming about me and listen,' he said.

'You arrogant thing!' she laughed.

'I'll run on ahead. Make sure Chrissie stops yapping enough for me to get a proper picture of you all coming into the church. Do you hear me?'

'Just her and Daddy? Or all of us?'

'I'll want both, but she's so excited now she'll have half the town in the picture. I'm relying on you to calm her down.'

273

Clare smiled at him affectionately. Gerry Doyle understood how this album would be treasured for years, when Chrissie and Mogsy had few ceremonies to entertain them.

Yes, she'd calm Chrissie down for him. Even if it meant being bossy, superior Clare again.

Chrissie became very quiet in the church, and you could hardly hear her responses. Maurice Byrne resplendent in a blue suit, was almost as mute. Only the firm unchanging voice of Father O'Dwyer could be heard properly. Then it was over and it was into the room that was too small to call a hall.

There were photos cutting the cake; and then the going away photograph of Chrissie with one foot on the ground and one foot in the car, the big Cortina that her brother-in-law was letting them drive to the station. There was confetti too – the understanding being that the family would clear it up before nightfall. Then Mr and Mrs Maurice Byrne had gone.

Nobody worked hard in Second Arts. It was a year off in a way because there was no serious examination at the end of it.

Valerie had had an eventful summer; her father had gone to hospital in England and had written from his hospital bed a long apology for his life. What had her mother done? Instead of laughing hysterically and opening another bottle to give her further fluency to curse him, didn't she up and off to England? Her father had got better; and promised to abandon the fancy woman and come home. But not immediately. These things needed time, he had said. Valerie's mother, however, had become a different person. No more morning cocktails. In fact, no cocktails at all. There was now no question of wasting as much money as possible and making-that-bastard-pay-up. Now it was different. Valerie must work hard in UCD, and make full use of the generous fees her father paid for her; she must remember that money didn't grow on trees; and what's more, they had to spend the whole summer doing up their house and getting it in order for the return of the Prodigal Father. Since Valerie had only scraped First Arts this was going to be a hard year. She was full of gloom.

Mary Catherine had been very off-putting when James had asked if he could come and call. She had said that the family would be moving around a lot during the summer; and, really, it wouldn't be a good idea, because they were sure to be vacationing with friends whenever he arrived. James had tried to pin her down by giving her definite dates; but she had been adamant. James seemed much more interested in her this year; he had asked her to a dress dance. Mary Catherine had spent the entire summer working in a soda fountain making milkshakes. It was very wearying trying to explain Ireland to people – they thought it was full of cottages and leprechauns. Her mother worked in the garment district and her two younger brothers did paper deliveries all summer. She hardly saw any of them until the big Labor Day picnic that the parish organized. Mary Catherine said it was nearly as difficult to explain America to the Irish as it was the other way round. She said she was hopeless at being an ambassador and that is exactly what her father thought that she was going to be when she graduated. Why else should she be so highly educated if it weren't to get herself a big job like that? Obviously he had decided that she wasn't going to marry an Irish nobleman with a castle if she hadn't nabbed one the first year and he was pinning his hopes on her becoming a career woman instead.

Clare said she hated anyone being secretive but she had very little to tell. It was a summer like any other in Castlebay. Chrissie's wedding had been exciting, and the weather had been good. Which was smashing, because that meant business was good and everyone was happy. Yes, she had met Gerry Doyle a bit. But he had been followed around by a very glamorous piece who had been meant to stay for three weeks. Her name was Sandra. And when the three weeks were up, Sandra decided that there was plenty to keep her in Castlebay, so she stayed the whole summer. Gerry Doyle had found her a caravan that wasn't being used. They were the talk of the town, but Gerry didn't take the blindest bit of notice. Apparently she was a student in Queen's University up in Belfast, and she had a red bathing suit which she wore all summer long, with open shirts of pink and purple and orange, all the colours that are meant to clash with red. She had a big mane of hair and she used to wash it in public with a shampoo, using the new shower that Dr Power had got the Committee to put up near the bottom of the steps to the beach. Valerie and Mary Catherine were rather sorry to think that the handsome Gerry had been so spoken for during the whole summer.

'Didn't you have any adventures and romances at the dance or anything?' Valerie asked interestedly.

'No. I hardly went to dances. I went to the Committee dance, because I had to, like everyone else, but I had no romances. I worked in the shop from morn to night, it was bloody exhausting. Do you know I find myself apologizing to Josie that I don't have romances in Dublin and to you that I don't have romances in Castlebay.'

It wasn't a light year for David. This was the year of his finals. He told James that he was going to put his head down and study, and he must be counted out of any socializing. James was affronted: it was his final year too, he insisted, and the Law was every bit as sacred as medicine. Wouldn't David come to this dance and make up a party? He had invited the American heiress who had played so hard to get during the summer.

David was resolute. He was going to work.

He found Caroline less than understanding these days. She had been very moody down in Castlebay, and had fought with her mother on every possible occasion. She had been obsessed with a rather trampish-looking girl called Sandra from Northern Ireland who seemed to be Gerry Doyle's choice for parading around the town. Caroline had even worn her own shirts loose over her bathing suit and had bitten the head off her mother when Mrs Nolan had complained mildly that Caroline seemed to have forgotten her skirt.

'Do you *still* find Gerry attractive?' David had asked her in exasperation. 'I thought you got over all that as a child.'

'Oh, don't be so patronizing,' she had snapped. '*Nobody* gets over Gerry Doyle. He's just there driving everyone mad all the time, isn't he?' She said it as if it were as obvious as night following day. He felt very irritated.

Or maybe he had just lost his way with girls. That could be it. He had taken Bones for long walks down the Far Cliff Road. Bones was nice and simple. He just wanted walks and for people to throw things which he would bring back. Bones imagined rabbits for himself and went happily in useless pursuit of them. It would be easier to have been a dog. Bones felt no guilt, no uncertainties. If he didn't get what he wanted he sat panting and smiling with his foolish face, and sooner or later, someone took him for a walk, threw him a stick or gave him a bone. Bones didn't sit smoking in his kennel at night and wondering what to do. Like David did. Well, his bedroom, but the principle was the same.

For the first time in his life he had not enjoyed the summer in Castlebay. He had grown away from Caroline so much that there was hardly any pleasure in being with her. She seemed to find him plodding, and yet she didn't really know what she wanted either. She was restless and impatient, she wouldn't talk about her career and her future. It was all too silly, she said, there she was with an M.A. degree and no chance of a job, she had to learn shorthand and typing like that patronizing halfwit Josie Dillon in the hotel who kept hanging on to her and giving her advice for some reason. *A nice commercial course* indeed! She had mocked Josie's accent. David had always liked Josie: she was far more pleasant than her two older sisters. And she had been such an ugly duckling when she was young – but Caroline wouldn't have known any of that. Anyway, David knew Josie was trying to cultivate Caroline from a deep interest in Caroline's brother. It was very transparent; and futile.

But that hadn't been the main problem of the summer: the main problem had been at home.

His mother had talked happily about his coming back to Castlebay to help his father in the practice. The way she put it reminded him of the times he used to help Nellie make

277

shortbread, or help old Martin in the garden. She didn't understand that he was almost a fully qualified doctor. You didn't go round *helping* people if you were qualified, you practised medicine. He had his intern year to do first in a hospital before he was even allowed to practise; then he was going to do a year in paediatrics and a year of obstetrics and . . . but his mother had said in that really *irritating* voice, that it really wasn't necessary to do all that extra work. The best training was on the ground. His father needed all the help he could get. He even employed a young doctor to come and help in the surgery as a locum during the summer season – there was always something happening to the visitors. He had a heavy enough caseload with the people of Castlebay themselves . . .

David knew from Nellie all about the miscarriages and the two stillbirths that had gone before. He knew from unasked-for confidences from people like Mrs Conway or Miss McCormack, what a precious child he had been. 'To have come the full term, to have survived birth, to grow up strong and handsome.' To be nearly a doctor. It was a dream come true, people said. In his disgruntled moments, David had wondered how you got out of someone else's dream and started dreaming your own.

Clare had a very satisfactory second year. She set herself a very disciplined plan of work, and kept to it. Since nobody else seemed to be doing any work at all her efforts brought her to the attention of the tutors, and this is what she needed. Her plan was to do an M.A. thesis in history, and she would need the enthusiasm and support of the various members of the History faculty, she would also need their advice about how to get money to survive. The Murray Prize was for a primary degree. Once she got her B.A., that was it, she would be on her own.

But she was determined to have a social life as well. Every Friday was late pass night and Clare made the most of it.

Living in such cramped discomfort – three in a bedroom that should really only have housed one – Mary Catherine and Valerie were also involved by necessity in everything she did. They were all more or less the same size; which was both good and bad. Good, because it meant that in dire need one good blouse could be worn by any of them. And they had even bought a black polo-necked jumper between them and insisted that anyone who wore it had to use dress shields, and it had to be washed after the third wear.

But it was *bad* when they were looking for a favourite garment and realized that it must already be on the body of one of the other two. They learned to dress for their dances and their hops and their social outings of various sorts, each sitting on her own bed: if they all stood up it was like the bear cage in the zoo.

The dressing table was an area of war. Valerie didn't buy make-up. She claimed she didn't use make-up, but she wore a great deal of heavy black eyeliner (Mary Catherine's); she made heavy inroads into the Sari Peach lipstick (Clare's); she was loud in complaint about spilled face powder but her own nose was suspiciously unshiny so she must have used it fairly regularly. Mary Catherine had a habit of leaving bits of cotton wool all over the room. Wool that had removed eye make-up, lipstick or the painted pancake which she sometimes spread on face, throat and shoulders.

Clare was accused of leaving combs filled with hair around the place. Just because she had long hair, they said, this was no reason why most of it should be distributed round the room.

But despite this, they never had a tiff that lasted longer than a few minutes – except the time that Mary Catherine discovered Clare had gone out wearing Mary Catherine's only smart shoes, and that Valerie had not only broken her mascara box but what was left of it was swimming in water and was a revolting grey puddle. *That* argument lasted a long time, and included three threats on Mary Catherine's part that she would go back to the United States where people were normal.

They would go to Bective, or Palmerston, or Belvedere or Landsdowne; they were the names of rugby clubs which held dances every weekend. It was funny to go to a rugby club; nobody in Castlebay knew anyone who played rugby.

Possibly David Power's school had, but even the school the Dillon boys had gone to played proper football and hurling; and anyone from Castlebay who ever came to Dublin to see a match would come for the All-Ireland finals at Croke Park; they wouldn't dream of coming for rugby international at Landsdowne Road.

Clare went to a rugby match at Landsdowne Road, one cold afternoon, to cheer on UCD. It was called the Colours Match, played every year between Trinity College and University College. The Trinity students were very upper class; and in order to pinpoint the difference even more all the UCD supporters would chant, 'Come on COLLIDGE, C-O-L-L-I-D-G-E, college.' It got a laugh no matter how often they did it.

Clare had a date for the match, a law student called Ian. She had met him at one of her Friday outings; and he had taken her to the pictures twice, and once out to a *bona fide*, which was a pub three miles outside the city. If you were a *bona fide* traveller you could go there and drink late. Clare didn't really like Ian – he seemed a bit pompous and superior. He didn't talk about normal things, it was all 'making an impression' and 'how things sounded', or 'how they looked'. But she had been having discussions with the girls; both Valerie and Mary Catherine united against her saying that Clare was becoming the devil to please, and you'd expect a law student to go on a bit and show off. That's what they were studying, for heaven's sake, that's what they'd be doing for the rest of their life in courtroom.

Ian had borrowed his parents' car and they went to a pub after the Colours Match. Then he took her for bacon and eggs in one of the big cinemas and to the film. They did a bit of necking during the film, but Clare kept lifting her head away from him, which annoyed him greatly.

'Later then?' he asked.

'Later,' she said staring at the screen.

They drove back to the hostel an odd way, through a lot of back streets. And then there was a bit of waste ground, where cars sometime parked during the day. Ian stopped the car.

It was all very embarrassing. Clare wept later, in the bedroom, while Valerie produced some vermouth to calm them all down. It wasn't a bit like the films, where people were able to say no without offending. It was *awful*. It was like the rugby tackles they'd been looking at during the match. And worse it was all *her* fault. She had *said* later, according to Ian. He called her all kinds of names. He had said she was a tease, and that it was physically bad for a male to be put into this state of excitement without being able to relieve it. That had worried her too. It was all her own silly fault. That's why everyone said you shouldn't go in for necking and groping and all. It just encouraged boys and made them sick if they couldn't go the whole way.

Valerie said it was ludicrous that you couldn't say yes or no, as you felt like it, like having sugar in your tea or not. But Mary Catherine said it was much more important than having sugar in your tea, and that it was so complicated because there were these limits. You were allowed to go so far, and it was all fine, you were a warm sweet responsive person; and then there was some line which, if you crossed it, meant you were going the whole way, and if you didn't boys got this awful thing about being in distress.

Though they discussed it in great technical detail, they couldn't agree from their limited experience where this line was, and how you crossed it. It had been different for all three of them. Maybe it was different for everyone, which was why there was always such an almighty fuss about the whole thing.

Clare said it had been a lesson to her. She was a scholarship girl, and the Murray committee had meant her to study, not to go round in people's parents' cars groping them and being groped and then being driven home in a black fury with accusations coming at her thick and fast. From now on, there was going to be no messing with men.

She had it all planned out. She would get her B.A. in Autumn 1960, then she would study for two years for her M.A. That would bring her up to 1962. Yes, fine. Then she would go to Oxford or Cambridge to do a doctorate, her Ph.D. She would tutor, of course, while she was there. That would get her to 1964. Then she would go to America, to Vassar or Bryn Mawr, for three years as a visiting fellow. In 1967, she would return and she would take a position as Professor of Modern History in either Trinity College or UCD wherever the History professor died first. To make her mark on the place she should serve a seven-year term, writing, of course, all the time. Then, at the age of thirty-four, she would marry. It would be just in time for her to have two children, and no more. She would marry a don in some other field, and they would have a small unpretentious house covered with ivy, and lined with books. They would live near a café and they would eat out most evenings, all of them, including the babies as soon as they were old enough to get their hands around chips.

Valerie and Mary Catherine rocked with laughter at the long-term plan, it was so detailed – the names of the most prestigious universities in the world, the age at which everything would happen, and the need for chips nearby.

'It's not a joke,' Clare said, her brown eyes full of determination. 'I will *not* teach children in a school. I'm not going to have all this open to me and end up teaching rotten, stupid children who don't want to learn. I will not teach. And I will not get married until I'm good and ready. If I wanted to get married, I could have stayed at home in Castlebay and picked my nose like Chrissie.'

'She feels very strongly about it.' Valerie spoke as if Clare weren't in the room.

'I tell you, when she's settled down with a nice job, and a nice engagement to a nice young man, she'll remember this and laugh,' Mary Catherine said.

'You're nearly as stupid as boys, the pair of you,' Clare said, and drank some more vermouth.

Clare had a phone call from Dr Power next morning. She caught her throat in alarm, but he came quickly to the point.

'Mrs O'Hara died, Lord rest her, and since you and Angela were such friends, I thought you'd like to know.'

'When is the funeral, Doctor?'

'On Sunday, but don't you go spending all your money

coming back now, it was just in case you wanted to send a Mass card.'

She rang Emer, who said she would send a telegram at once. Then Clare walked up to University Church.

The priest wrote Mrs O'Hara's name down in his notebook so that he would remember to include it in his prayers at Mass. Clare had two half-crowns in her hand. He shook his head.

'Isn't it five shillings, Father? I thought that's what it was for students?'

'It's nothing, child. I'll be glad to say a Mass for the repose of the woman's soul. Was she a friend of yours? A relation?'

'No, she wasn't really a friend. She was my teacher's mother, she used to sit there while this teacher used to give me extra lessons. She has a son a priest, and that used to give her a lot of happiness even though she was a sort of cripple.'

The priest was pleased to hear that. 'Well, she'll have a lot of Masses said for her soul by her own son, but don't you worry, I'll say a Mass for her as well. He wrote his name on a Mass card, on the dotted line beside the word 'celebrant', and Clare thanked him for his generosity. She wouldn't have minded paying five shillings for Angela's mother's Mass, but it did make things a lot easier now that she didn't have to. Guiltily she bought a stamp, and stood in the post office, writing a letter of sympathy. She wondered what would Angela do now.

It took a long time to answer all the letters of sympathy and to send notes of thanks for the Mass cards and the flowers. Angela did it methodically each night. She changed the position of the furniture in the cottage and put her mother's chair upstairs so that she wouldn't find herself looking over at it.

People had been so generous – even Immaculata had been human and offered her more days off than she was entitled to. Angela had said no, thank you, she would prefer to take a couple of days at the end of term. Immaculata hadn't liked that. Christmas, and the concert, and everything. That was it, Angela said. She would find it hard to put her soul into the Christmas concert this year. So Immaculata had to agree.

Geraldine and Maire had been more helpful than she could have hoped during the whole time of the funeral. And they distracted people, in their black coats and their English accents, and their innocent and transparently honest concern that Father Sean hadn't been able to come home for his mother's funeral. Guiltily they admitted to each other that they hadn't written to him much and that they never got more than a Christmas card from him these times. Geraldine even went so far as to wonder was he happy in the priesthood; he had been so full of it all in the early days.

But Angela was never in the position where she had to answer a direct question about him, only mumble a regret that he wasn't there to say the Mass.

There was so much to organize: food for the people who would call, beds for Geraldine and Maire, dividing Mother's things so as to give the girls something to remember her by. They even had to talk about the cottage itself. It had been very hard to sit down with her two sisters who were almost foreign to her with their talk of shops and towns and seaside resorts she had never heard of in England. But it had to be done, they were entitled to a share of what small amount their mother left.

She showed them their mother's post office book: there was just over £100. She also had a burial policy so her funeral was paid for. Angela said they would divide the £100 into four. Maire wondered should they send it all to Sean for the missions: that was what their mother was most concerned about always.

For a short minute Angela was tempted to tell them. It was late: there would be no more callers to interrupt them. It would take it from her shoulders a little if she could lay it on theirs too. They lived in England, for God's sake, they could go to see him, decide for themselves about his plight and what their attitude should be. But something about Sean and Shuya seemed too vulnerable to let them be exposed to Maire and Geraldine and their strange, enclosed worlds. She wouldn't tell them yet.

Would her mother's soul think she was right to have told Sean nothing about the death? Was that the right thing to have done in terms of real and genuine acting for the best? She was very much afraid that a lot of her protestations to Sean had been hypocritical. Why did she not let him come home now and declare himself? His mother was no longer there to feel the shame and the hurt. Was there a possibility that Angela was becoming a settled schoolteacher who didn't want things upset for herself?

Angela wondered why she had never told Clare about Sean. In ways she had been closer to Clare than to anyone. Clare had her own secret and disgrace with poor Tommy in gaol over in London. But there had never been the right time. And now it was almost too late.

Angela looked at Clare's letter of sympathy, and the Mass Card signed by a priest at University Church. The girl was very good to have written so soon and to have spent what little pocket money she had on having a Mass said. Angela knew what a sacrifice that would have been. Clare had written that Angela must have some consolation in knowing that she had always been there to provide a safe and happy background for her mother to live in; and that she had done it with no sense of grudging, but with humour and happiness; that it was a great gift to give a parent. And Clare said that she would never be able to do anything as positive herself. It was possibly the only letter that didn't say what a great consolation it must be to have Father Sean praying at this time and how sad it was that he hadn't been able to get back for the funeral.

Angela went to England during the last week of term. She told the children that she would like no Christmas cards this year and that she might stay away for Christmas with her sisters or with friends in Dublin. Everyone seemed to think this was a very sensible thing to do. No point in trying to celebrate Christmas in an empty house, although there were plenty of people who would ask her for the day.

It was cold and wet on the mailboat; and stuffy and uncomfortable on the train journey to London. She was puffy-eyed from lack of sleep as she got on yet another train to take her to Sean's school.

She walked a mile from the station, and remembered the day she had come with Sean to see the big house in Ostia where his wife and babies were tucked away in the courtyard. She recalled the sense of dread she had felt then at meeting them, and how it had been replaced by sadness.

She had been here to this school before, when Father Flynn had arranged the job, in the days when the cause at Rome had not been deemed lost. Sean had still been enthusiastic, and as busy in his letters to the Vatican as he had once been in his visits.

There had been little mention of it recently in his letters. He had written that Shuya had taken in a lot of work; and that Denis was doing very well in the Junior School; Laki was getting on famously at the nearby convent, and they both had lots of friends. It wasn't really permanent or anything, but it was a very good, expensive education for Denis that they wouldn't have been able to afford.

Angela wondered what kind of work Shuya was doing: surely in a school like this they wouldn't go along with her doing mending and sewing as she had been doing in Rome? But perhaps they were less hidebound in England: maybe a Latin master's wife might well take in sewing or even washing.

Angela arrived at the small gate lodge. The garden was much more cared for than when she was last here, even though it was midwinter. There were nice silver trees and golden bushes giving colour. The door was painted a bright, sunny yellow. It was a much more cheerful house than when she had seen it first.

She knew that Sean would be at school and she intended to meet him as he left his classes and came home for lunch. He had said that one of his greatest joys was to walk across the playing fields just for half an hour's peace in the cottage with Shuya, and then walk back. Angela understood only too well how welcome that break from the shrill little voices would be. She didn't have such luxury herself: Immaculata saw to that.

She tapped on the yellow door. Shuya. A smiling, delighted Shuya, arms outstretched.

'I saw you from upstairs. I ran down. Welcome, welcome. I can hardly believe it. I am so very happy. We are all so happy. And you have a suitcase, this time you will stay with us.'

'This time I'll stay with you, Shuya.'

They had tea, and Angela looked around. Shuya was *different* somehow. Younger-looking, smarter. She had her hair up in a chignon; she wore a light-green jumper and skirt, and a big white collar pinned with a brooch of Connemara marble.

Angela had brought it the last time she came to visit, and her heart was touched to think that this might be the only piece of jewellery that Shuya had. Shuya talked about the work she took in. It was far from washing and sewing. It was typing for theses; it was translations for Japanese businesses in London; it was roneoing and duplicating for anyone that needed it – one of her biggest customers was the school itself. They found it far better to pay Mrs O'Hara for neatly done examination papers, or notices, or leaflets, than to work a machine themselves and ruin reams of paper. She had quite a cottage industry going, she told Angela proudly; and she even employed a girl to come three afternoons a week to help her.

On the piano there were pictures of the children; grown now so much that Angela realized she would hardly know them. Denis, over ten years old and Laki eight. In another frame was a picture of her mother, the only nice one that had ever been taken. Young David Power and James Nolan had taken it years ago when they got a camera first and were busy snapping everyone in the town, to try to set up as some kind of rivals to Gerry Doyle. It had been a rare thing to catch her mother smiling, without the lines of pain on her face.

Her eyes rested on it. And Shuya noticed.

Very quietly she said, 'Have you come to tell Sean about his mother?'

287

'Yes,' Angela whispered.

'Is she very ill? Does she ask for him?'

'No. It's not that.'

'Because if it helps, he must go, go alone, dressed as a priest. If it is best. I will persuade him, if it is best.'

'No Shuya, no. She's dead. She died a month ago.'

'One month ago?'

'I know. I know. I had to make up my mind on my own. It seemed best.'

There was a silence.

'Please Shuya, wasn't it best? It took the decision away from him. Sean didn't have to decide.'

'Maybe he should have decided. Maybe he can't be protected all the time from having to make a decision.'

'I don't know anything any more,' Angela said sadly.

'Forgive me. Please, what am I thinking about? Your mother has died, and I give you no sympathy. I must be so cruel and thoughtless. Tell me about her death. Was it sudden?'

'Yes. Yes, she had a heart attack, you see. If it had been something slow then I would have let Sean know. But it would have been too late for him and I didn't want . . .'

'Please. Please. I think you did what was going to be the most painless for Sean. As always you acted for his good.'

Shuya stood up and put her arm around Angela's shoulders. 'You did what was best. I thank you for not having to go through all that with him. All the agonies. I thank you for giving us all this peace. He will become resigned to his mother's death. She has only been a dream to him, for thirteen years, since he last saw her. It is not a real person he will mourn. It is an idea.'

'You are wise, Shuya.'

'I think I shall be a teacher. I am doing examinations that will qualify me to teach typewriting and shorthand. I suppose they will recognize these examinations in Ireland.'

'Well, yes. But are you going to Ireland?'

'Sean talks of little else.'

Shuya pointed out the path she should walk to meet Sean.

She said she would leave them alone in the house to talk. The lunch was all ready.

He wore a heavy overcoat with the collar turned up and his hands were in his pockets. He looked younger than a man of almost forty. His face split open into a big foolish smile . . . he started to run towards her and then stopped.

'Is it bad news?' he asked suddenly.

'Mam died very peacefully. She died without fear. It's all over.'

He blessed himself. 'The Lord have mercy on her soul.'

'I came when it was all over to tell you.'

'You're very very good to us.' He took her and hugged her to him.

'I hope I did right. It was all so quick and so sudden. I could have telephoned you. I rang people to tell Geraldine and Maire. But I just didn't, Sean. I thought that if Mam can see you she'll understand everything and it would have been too much on you, and, to be honest, on us.'

She felt better having admitted her own selfishness. He had his arm around her shoulder as she walked back to the gate lodge with him.

'Does Shuya know? Have you told her?'

'Yes.'

'What does she think? Does she think it was for the best that Mam is dead and buried without my being there?'

In a flash Angela understood what Shuya had meant. People *protected* Sean. They kept the world away from him. If she were to say now that Shuya gave her approval there would be the quick smile of relief and everything would be fine.

'Yes. Shuya said it was the right thing. She thanked me for giving you all a gift of peace, that was the way she put it.'

Sean smiled as she knew he would. 'I would like to have been there to hold my mother's hand. But if it all happened so suddenly, then thank you again for shouldering everything, Angela.' His arm was around her companionably still. 'Was it all very sad, very harrowing?'

'No. You know the way people say it was a blessing. It was, Sean. She was in *such* pain, all the time. Every movement was an ache or a stab to her. She couldn't dress herself, or move without help.'

His face was pained. He wouldn't want this to be part of his idea of his mother.

'Dr Power said that she had the worst arthritis he had ever known. And she was incontinent too, not because she really was, but because she couldn't get up in time.'

He closed his eyes with distress.

'It wasn't much of a life. She wasn't really happy from the time she woke up in the morning. It is peace for her. I look at the corner of the room where she used to sit and I think that all the time.'

'How long ago?'

'A month. I couldn't come any sooner, because of school. You know the way it is.' She smiled at him the resigned conspiratorial smile of one teacher to another.

They had reached the house. He looked anxious that Shuya wasn't there when they went in.

'She's gone into town. She said she'd leave us to talk, I told her there was no need.'

Angela found herself pouring the soup for her brother, even though this was not her house. She put on a kettle to make tea afterwards. She cut the bread. She had been in the door only a minute and already she was mothering him.

'I wish the children had seen their grandmother. They have no grandmother,' he said.

'Well neither did we, Sean, not to speak of. Dad's mother was dead before we were born, and Mam's mother died when I was a baby. You don't remember her, do you?'

'No. But Denis and Laki will have a better life than we did, things are different now. And they know that one day they'll go to Ireland. I have books, look, here . . . Lots of books about Ireland, so that they'll know. And we have books about Japan too. They're not going to grow up confused, and not knowing who they are like we did.'

'You want very much to come to Ireland, then?'

'But I've always said that.'

'I know. I know.'

Sean thought about his mother being dead and put his head in his hands. It didn't seem real to him, he said, he thought of her cheerful and full of chat and bursting with information about things and the centre of everything. She *had* been a bit like that perhaps in 1945, when Sean had last been home, when the glory of the priest son in full regalia very largely compensated for the loss of the drunken troublesome husband who had been a heart scald to her for her whole married life. Yes, Mother was bright in her spirit then, even if she had pains in her joints. And Sean hadn't seen her since. He could be excused for thinking that she had been a woman with as clear a glance and a smile as she had in the photograph frame on the piano.

She played with her cheese salad while he talked about times gone by.

'We'll say the rosary for her tonight, all of us,' he said. 'That will make it important for the children.'

She wished she could get it out of her head that her brother was living in mortal sin and that it was quite incongruous for him to be organizing rosaries. And yet he seemed to see nothing out of character in it.

'Will the new Pope make any difference do you think?' she asked suddenly, reaching out and touching his hand. 'He looks kind.'

'It hasn't got anything to do with kindness. It's just as complicated and tedious as the civil service,' Sean said sadly. 'If I could *get* the papers to John XXIII then it would be a matter of days but if I could have got them to Plus XII it would have been the same.'

'Does the fact that it's gone on so long mean there's more hope or less?'

'I don't honestly know. It means that there's more red tape, I suppose. If something has already been looked at by one person then other people are slow to take the file themselves.'

'Do they know here?' She nodded her head up to the school.

'At the very top yes. Otherwise no. I was very lucky to get in here.'

He was much less confident than he was before. There was a time when he would never admit that he was lucky to have got anywhere. It was all open to him, the whole world, whatever life he wanted. This whole business with Rome had changed his thinking.

But before they had the children with them, before they were all kneeling and saying a rosary for the dead grandmother the children didn't know and wouldn't have understood, she had to go back to his plans for Ireland.

'So you think you'd like to come back to Castlebay.'

'You wouldn't mind?'

'No. Of course not,' she lied.

'Well I know you said that, long ago in Rome. You did say that the only reason for me to stay away was because it would break Mam's heart.'

'That's what I said. I'm not going back on it.' She couldn't be any warmer. It just wouldn't come out as more welcoming. It would be lunacy. It would upset everyone, the enormity of the deception for all those years. Denis, a big boy of ten. How could he not see it?

'No, no, I know you're not going back on it. You've always been straight as a die, Angela. No one could have a better sister or friend.'

She made the tea, and poured a cup for herself. Her hand was shaking.

'It's been awful for you, all of it. What will you do now, will you live on in the house on your own?' His voice was full of concern.

'I don't know yet. I will for the moment.'

'Yes, yes.'

'Maybe you'll want the house? If you come back that is?'

Now she had said it, brought it right out in the open. This nonsensical idea of the priest going back to live in his native town with his Japanese wife and grown-up children.

To her relief he didn't seem to think that this was automatically the way things would go.

'Oh, I don't think we'd want to *live* in Castlebay. Where would I work? Where would they go to school?'

Angela fumed inside for a quick moment. What was so wrong with the convent where she taught? Or the Brothers, which had been good enough to educate Sean O'Hara. Still, this was all to the good.

'True, I suppose. But you do want to go back do you, and meet everyone – talk to Mrs Conway in the post office, Sergeant McCormack, the Murphys, the Dillons.' She had deliberately chosen awful ones to mix in with ordinary people. She had to tread carefully.

'Well, it's my home. It's where I came from.' He was defensive. She didn't want that at any cost.

'Don't I know it's your home – I'm offering you Mam's house to live in. Of course it's your home. I just asked what sort of way you'll be coming home. Will it be in the summer? Do you want me to let people know you're coming, or will you explain it all when you get there?'

'I thought that you'd . . . I don't know. That's something that can all be arranged later.'

'Of course it can.'

She went to see Father Flynn on her way back through London. He said they must go out and have dinner.

'I know now why people become priests. It's a licence to eat dinners out in restaurants for the rest of your life. I never ate in so many restaurants before or since as when we were in Rome.

'Ah, those were the days all right. But this is half-work. Young Ned O'Brien asked me to the place he's working in. The landlord's just opened a dining room off the pub, and the bold Ned no less is running it. Wait till I turn up with his ex-school marm.'

'I don't think he'll be a bit delighted. Not that I ever taught him anything. I don't think we can lay his educational deficiencies at my door. And Tommy, he's out isn't he?'

'For the moment. That was something I was going to ask tonight.'

'I'll make myself scarce.'

'You don't need to. He knows you're in on it.'

'You're grand and easy about things, Father Flynn. Is it something that goes with the job, like deafness goes with teaching?'

They saw Ned, important and nervous at the same time. Father Flynn pretending ignorance of everything so that Ned could put him at ease. In the midst of doing this Ned lost a lot of his own nerves. He explained that there were three things you could have: steak, chicken or fish. And you got soup before and ice cream after, no matter what you chose. But the price depended on the main course. He could have Father Flynn as his guest but, to be honest, he wasn't sure about Miss O'Hara. Angela said that there was no question of her being a guest, she was going to have steak, the dearest, and was going to love it.

'I'm very sorry to hear about your mother, Miss O'Hara,' said the head waiter of the new dining area in which they were, as yet, the only guests.

'How did you know about it?'

'Clare writes to Tommy every week, regular as anything. She told him. I sort of . . . well, I read the letters to him. I'm very sorry.'

'Thanks Ned. She was old and in awful pain, it was for the best.'

'I don't think Tommy'll stay long with your friends, Father,' Ned hissed out of the side of his mouth.

'A pity. Why?'

'He keeps thinking these other lads will be looking for him. I don't think they want to see hair nor hide of him, but he has had a message that they're leaving him some money next week, his share like.

'But if they don't want him in on whatever they're doing, then maybe he *might* stay with the Carrolls?' Father Flynn had got Tommy a live-in job with an Irish family who owned a small greengrocery. Tommy would be sweeping and helping at first, but they'd keep an eye on him; and if he was any way helpful at all, they'd give him a shop coat and let him serve the public.

'You know Tommy, Father. He's just a big baby.'

Angela sighed and wondered were all brothers big babies.

'What will I do, if Sean comes back to Castlebay?' she asked, later.

'You'll survive it, like you've survived everything else,' said Father Flynn.

She went back to Dublin in time to spend Christmas with

Emer and Kevin. The boat was filled with returning emigrants, singing and happy to be on the way back to small villages or towns all over Ireland.

The house was full of holly and ivy and long paper chains across the hall. Emer hoped they weren't too cheerful. After all Angela had been recently bereaved. No, she assured her, they were exactly what she wanted to see. Clare would be dropping by that evening on her way to the station. She had a Christmas present for Daniel and Emer had invited her to supper.

Clare looked thin and tired, Angela thought, but was very cheerful. She told them she was hopeless with men and that once she felt her academic work was under control she was going to take lessons from someone who knew. It was apparently like bridge and driving a car: even stupid people could be good at it if they learned the technique.

Clare wished that she could stay here in this pleasant, easygoing household for Christmas, but shook the idea away. She was looking forward to seeing home again. There would be no Chrissie, and she had painted her bedroom before the summer ended. There was good news about Ned from London and no bad news about Tommy. Angela had been full of detail, and had even written a letter to Clare's mother to describe the elegance of Ned in his new job. Compared to everyone else's Christmas hers would be fine.

Valerie was going to have to face the return of the long-lost father, and *Mary Catherine* had been invited to the Nolans and was wishing every minute of the day that she had refused. Clare thought about them both as she stood on the cold platform of Kingsbridge station waiting for the train.

On an impulse she went to the phone box and rang Val, who was still at the hostel.

'I'm in a great hurry. The train's nearly going. Tell him what you think, don't go along with all your mother's lovey-dovey bits. *You're* not in love with him. He's your father and he walked out on you. Tell him that you were greatly upset and that it might take a bit of time to be sure he's back for good.'

'What?' Val was stunned.

'There's no need to pretend that nothing happened. That's pretending that he's a madman. He left when you were thirteen and needed him. Don't just gloss over that, or he'll think it was a perfectly reasonable thing to do.'

'Then we'll spend the whole of Christmas fighting, and my mother'll come after me with a cleaver,' Val said.

'Nonsense, you can do it without a fight. Happy Christmas.'

She looked the Nolans up in the book and rang. James was surprised to hear her on the phone. 'Nothing wrong is there?' he asked.

'Heavens no, James. You're far too young to think a telephone call means bad news.'

He was annoyed – as she meant him to be – and went to find Mary Catherine.

'Tell them your father's a postman. Immediately,' Clare said.

'What?'

'The only reason you're not going to enjoy Christmas is because you're going to be up to your ears in pretence. Tell them, for heaven's sake, the moment they ask, or *before*. They're not going to throw you out in the street.'

Mary Catherine started to laugh.

'Well will you?' Clare said impatiently. 'I have to go for my train in a minute.'

'I guess I will,' Mary Catherine said. 'When you put it that way, there's no sense in not.'

The porters started shouting excitedly that the train was now backing into the platform and would be ready for boarding.

Clare wondered what would someone say to her if they were to give her good advice for Christmas just as she had been dispensing to others. She decided that Angela's age-old advice had always been the best. She must be *positive* and *cheerful,* and never let them think her education and her hopes were a threat to them.

She did all of that as if it were a Christmas homework she

had been set to do. She helped her mother make a last-minute Christmas cake. She called to see her married sister's new house. She went with Jim and Ben on the back of a cart to a farm where they had a lot of holly and ivy and were glad to see people thinning it out. They decorated the shop and the house.

She went for long walks with her father down the Far Cliff Road, and discussed with him seriously the possibility of buying a soft ice-cream machine. There was little to discuss, really, except whether her father had the courage to borrow the money to buy one or not. It would obviously be a huge draw; sooner or later someone else in Castlebay would get one and a lot of trade would move to the place where the delicious whipped-cream cones were on offer. But Clare's father hunched his back and worried over and over about the wisdom of getting into debt for something that would only be used eleven weeks of the year. Clare said that people bought those soft ice-creams in Dublin even in the winter. You often saw people eating them in cinema queues. But her father puzzled and wondered . . .

Dad looked old and tired; and though he said he liked to get out in the fresh air to walk with her the wind seemed to hurt his eyes and make him seem frail. She debated telling him about Tommy; but the debate with herself did not take long. A man who couldn't decide whether or not to get an ice-cream machine couldn't possibly cope with having a criminal son.

Josie was cheerful, but busy. She had decided all on her own to inquire whether there might be a demand for a Christmas programme, as it was called in hotels. And there was; they were going to have twenty-nine guests over Christmas and everyone was in a fever of excitement. There was bad blood between the family about it, and her sister Rose, who was meant to be coming into the hotel full time, said that since *Josie* seemed to make all the decisions nowadays, what was the point, and she was going to go to another hotel.

David Power came into the hotel that night for a drink and

to wish them well in the Christmas programme. The guests were assembling and the Dillons were at their wits' end. They had never thought of finding someone who could play the piano. In the summer they always gave bed and breakfast free to any student who would play the piano in the lounge in the evenings.

Josie's mother looked at David appealingly. 'Just for about an hour, David? You would be helping us better than you could ever believe.'

'But I'm no good,' David protested. 'Clare, can't you play?' he beseeched.

'No. In my education, there was never time for it. But a renaissance man like yourself now. Every social skill . . .'

'I *hate* you, Clare O'Brien,' he said good-naturedly.

Josie thanked him profusely and led him to the piano. Haltingly, he got into a version of 'There Is a Tavern in the Town'. Dick Dillon, who was planted amongst the guests, began to sing and in no time they were all joining in. It was obvious after about three songs that he would be there all night. Dick got him a pint and left it on the piano. Bones, who had been sitting patiently in the hall, hoping that the music would stop soon, was taken into the kitchen and given a plate of soup. He fell asleep beside the Aga and dreamed of sandhills full of rabbits and big firm beaches when the tide was out, where people would throw sticks for him hour after hour.

In the summer of 1959 some people said that the world was going to end: it was the hottest weather ever known. Tom O'Brien cursed his cowardice as he saw people troop past his door to go to Fergus Murphy's soft ice-cream machine. Fergus built up a lot of business because people bought sweets and magazines and groceries while they waited for the ice cream queue to file by. The Castlebay Committee congratulated themselves on their foresight in organizing a booking register so that visitors could be directed to the available rooms in the resort rather than having to knock on doors. There were two full-time lifeguards and when the tides were high people had to bathe between two flags.

Nobody drowned that summer in Castlebay, and nobody fell and hurt themselves on the paths up the cliffs because they were all finally built properly with rails to hold on to. People still went into the Echo Cave and asked it questions. The Dillons were very distressed to hear of plans for a new and huge hotel but were subsequently overjoyed to discover that two of the five businessmen who were going to start it were undisclosed bankrupts at the time, so that plan never got off the ground. Dr Power said he was getting old and slow and he was so proud that his big handsome son had passed Final Med with flying colours. He would do an intern year in Dublin and then who knew what would happen.

James Nolan was called to the Bar and did his first case in court. He said he thought he was never going to get another brief but he carried a great many papers tied with pink tape.

Fiona Doyle announced her engagement to Frank Conway, the pride and joy of Mrs Conway. Mrs Conway had never been anxious for her Frank to marry anyone, and she had her doubts about the Doyles in general. Gerry was as wild as anything and should be kept in a zoo if half of what you heard about him was true. And the mother was odd – some kind of phobia they said. She hardly ever went out. But you couldn't say a word against Fiona – a good-looking girl, great self-respect. She'd never let a man near her, even in the days when a girl was silly and could have her head turned. Mrs Conway sighed. Frank could have done a lot worse, she supposed. She gave them her blessing. And then that pup Gerry Doyle had the impudence to say he'd like a *talk* with Frank, since Fiona had no father. Mrs Conway never found out what the chat was about, but it had impressed Frank no end.

Chrissie Byrne discovered on her second visit to Dr Power that she was indeed pregnant, and bought a maternity smock on the way back from the surgery to the butcher's shop. Ned O'Hara came back for a flying visit to Castlebay with his fiancée, Dorothy. Dorothy thought everything in Castlebay was terrif. When she and her Neddy got old, like about thirty, they would come back here and start a restaurant. Dorothy thought the O'Briens' house was terrif.

299

Dorothy's mother was Irish, and she wished that her mum had taken her to Ireland before – it was simply gorgeous.

That summer, a registered envelope arrived for Agnes O'Brien. There were twenty-five ten-pound notes in it and an ill-written note from Tommy saying he had been saving for years to get a present for his ma, and now he had.

Tom said immediately that they must tell nobody outside the house about it. They discussed long and secretly that summer what Mammy would do with the money. Chrissie was left out of the discussion because she was a Byrne now and if Bumper, Bid and Mogsy knew about it they'd be down like a flash.

In the end it was spent on a new coat for Agnes and the long and often discussed extension on the side of the shop. It was Tom O'Brien's one concession to the magnificent site of his business: he wanted a Perspex roof on an extra room where they could put a couple of tables and chairs. This way they could serve those who wanted to sit down for their Club Orange or their tub of ice-cream. And they were even going to add sandwiches and tea next summer. Tommy's gift made it possible.

In the summer of 1959, Mother Immaculata asked Angela O'Hara whether she intended to stay on in the school or, now that she was free to see the world, if she planned to travel. Angela, seeing that Immaculata would love Miss O'Hara to roam off around the world, said firmly that she was going to stay in Castlebay. It was also the summer that Dick Dillon asked Angela O'Hara to marry him and she said very gently that she thought they would drive each other mad within months, and the ambulance would be arriving from the town and they'd both be locked up in the asylum on the hill. Dick had smiled bravely and she had patted his knee and invited him to the Committee dance so that he would know she liked him greatly.

Clare's professors said she would get a First: they were all in agreement. *Clare O'Brien to get a First* – she said it to herself, not caring to believe it. Any student with a First was worth looking at. From then on she would never have to apologize again. Clare went off into one of her rare little daydreams in the National Library. Imagine it. Never would she have to tell people she was only a scholarship girl or she had to do this because of some Committee or other, she would be her own person. And a scholar. She tore a page from her ring file and decided to write to Angela O'Hara there and then. She wrote as she hadn't been able to write before, she said that somehow for the very first time she believed that it was actually happening. Only now did she feel it had worked, all that praying up in the church, and all the shouting in the Echo Cave and all the learning and learning, the disciplines that Angela had taught her.

Angela replied by return of post. She said that it was the most wonderful letter she had ever received in her life. It made everything – and everything included the seagull-faced Immaculata – all worth while. She said it was a letter written on the crest of happiness, and from that heady standpoint the world was there for the taking. She hoped that that would last for ever.

It was a warm and generous letter. Clare folded it in four and put it in the little flap at the back of her big, black leather notebook. The book, which she carried every-where, had been a gift from the nuns in the secondary school when she won the Murray Prize. Immaculata had sent her a picture of Maria Goretti, with a big padded frame of coral-pink velvet. Fortunately her mother had liked it, and it hung in the back of the shop getting grimier and dirtier as the years went by. Gerry Doyle had given her a fountain pen. He had insisted. He had only been asked to do the pictures he said because there was a candidate from Castlebay. She knew this wasn't true but it was nice of him to say it. She still had the pen. She never lent it to anyone and she always put the cap on very carefully, clipped it to her notebook and then put a rubber band around the whole thing. She had so few possessions that she valued them all. She thought about Gerry. She could never write to him like she did to Angela but somehow she did want to talk to him. It would be nice if he came to Dublin again and they could walk by the canal maybe, or she could show him off to the girls. She sighed. She'd never get any kind of degree if she spend time daydreaming like this.

Still, she bought a postcard of O'Connell Street and sent it to him; a cheerful card saying it would be nice to see him if ever he passed through Dublin.

She heard nothing for ages.

She was annoyed.

Thank God she wasn't in love with him.

It was neither one thing nor another, being an intern; David discovered that very early on. Some people thought he was a fully-fledged doctor, who knew *everything;* others thought he was a schoolboy dressing up in a white coat and wouldn't ask him the time of day in case he got it wrong. And the hours! There was the solidarity of a prisoner-of-war camp in the Res, where bewildered young doctors coped with the unfamiliar and the frightening without any sustained sleep. They told each other that they would never sleep again. That their metabolisms would never recover from the strange hours and speeds at which they had to grab food. And even more immediate and urgent – their social lives were now finished for ever.

James Nolan, handsome, well-dressed young barrister, carrying his black bag that contained wig and gown casually slung over his shoulder, said he despaired ever of seeing David any more.

David was paged urgently, and rushed to the phone. 'Dr Power speaking.'

'Dr Power, this is Mr Nolan, barrister at law. I wondered if you would like to come and have a long boozy lunch with me. I got a cheque for seven guineas.'

'A lunch?' said David in disbelief.

'You *know*. You've heard of them. They're what people have in the middle of the day. Food and wine. You sit at tables.'

'You bloody don't do that here,' David said.

'Well, can you come? It's a gorgeous autumn day, walk a bit towards me and I'll walk a bit towards you.'

A wave of impatience came over David. How could James

be so insensitive? He had no idea of what David's life was like. He had been up all through the night – but that made no difference to today's schedule. The ward round went ahead as usual. Blood tests here, a drip there, organizing an X-ray for another. The ward Sister – a poisonous woman – never gave him any information about the patients: she confided all that only to the consultants. The housemen were made to look fools as a result.

This morning a difficult patient had pulled the drip out three times, and so three times it had to be set up again. Then there was the teaching round with the consultant. And now he was in outpatients. He had been examining a man's swollen foot when James had rung.

As politely as he could, David told James that he would have to find someone else to celebrate the seven guineas and to lunch with. David's own lunch would be something very quick and not very nice. If he ate at all. Then it would be dealing with admissions, seeing the patients, getting the preliminaries sorted out before greater men came to deal with them. And he was on call after that. Barristers? Lunches? Guineas? Bloody parasites.

He returned to the man with the swollen foot. 'I don't know,' he said honestly. 'I'd like to see the other foot. Can you take off your shoe and sock?'

The man was hesitant.

'So that I'll be able to compare,' David explained.

Reluctantly the man took off the other shoe and sock. The foot that he knew would be examined was nice and clean. The foot that he hadn't expected to be asked to bare was filthy. It was a foot that had not been washed in a long time. David stood slightly back from it to see if there was a similar swelling. His eyes met the eyes of the foot's owner.

'I didn't think, you see . . .' the man said.

'I know,' David said sadly. 'That's the trouble. We hardly ever do.'

He was on his own. He had never felt that Dublin was lonely when he was in the medical school, but now, isolated in hospital, it was different. That was your life. You didn't escape from it – or if you could you found nobody to escape with.

Full of self-pity in the darkening evening air, he walked up Kildare Street. People were going in and out of the National Library and the College of Art. The Dail had its guards at the gate, and that seemed to be bustling too. Everyone except David Power had something to do.

Suddenly he saw Clare leaving the library with her bunch of books. She looked lovely in the evening light.

'Clare! Clare, I was hoping to catch you,' he lied.

She was pleased to see him. He tucked his arm into hers. 'Will we go and have a coffee?'

'Sure. What were you hoping to see me for?'

'To ask you if you'd come out tonight. I know it's ridiculous short notice and everything but we never know in the hospital when we'll be on or off.'

She didn't seem put out by the shortness of notice. She'd love to. But first she had to go back to the hostel and see was there a message. Someone had said he was going to be in Dublin, possibly tonight, and if so she and her two friends were going to go out with him. If not then she'd go with David.

'I can't say fairer than that,' she said.

He grumbled as they walked towards the hostel: why three girls and one man? What kind of superman was this?

'It's Gerry Doyle,' she said simply, as if that explained everything.

A great and unexpected surge of annoyance swept over David. Gerry was so *cheap*. His line was so *obvious*. When he was a kid he had thought Gerry was good company, there was always a touch of the dangerous, the daredevil about him. But not now. Gerry was too slick. And too *much*.

'I thought you'd have outgrown him,' he said in a very superior voice.

Clare was surprised. David Power didn't usually talk like this. 'Nobody outgrows Gerry,' she said. It was an echo of what Caroline Nolan had said to him. A flash of anger came over him.

'What's so great about him? Has he some new technique as a lover or something?'

'I wouldn't know.' Clare was cool.

'Well, what *is* it then? It's not his intellectual conversation is it? Surely Gerry Doyle isn't a rough diamond concealing a poetic soul?' His face was twisted in a way she had never seen before.

'Why are you so cross?'

'I'm not cross. I'm just disappointed with you for making yourself so cheap. You've always been different. Why be so bloody predictable? Following as soon as Gerry Doyle raises his little finger. Gerry's a nobody, Clare. He's just *trashy*, you deserve better.'

She was unaware of the crowds moving up and down the street and even the people who had to move off the footpath because they couldn't get past the angry young couple.

'You keep your disappointment to yourself, David Power. Don't come bleating it out to me. You can take yourself off with your insults and your jeers. *You're* the one that's cheap, not me. I've been working here all day, and now I've finished. I'm going back to my friends and if Gerry's around he'll cheer us all up and make us laugh. He'll make no comments about whether we're predictable or not. He'll be nice to us. That's what you'll never understand in a million years. Gerry is *nice* to people. He's *glad* to see them. He smiles and he asks them questions and he listens. He *likes* people. And I'm *glad* he's coming to Dublin tonight, and Val will be glad, and Mary Catherine will be glad.'

'I didn't mean . . .'

'Oh, go away and leave me alone. I'm tired.'

'I'm tired too. I've been on duty since I don't know how long. I'm cross-eyed with tiredness.'

'Yes,' she said briefly. 'I see that.'

'Can I still come along with you, if he's there, or . . .'

'No. You cannot. I'm not going on an outing with you both knowing that you've said he's cheap and flashy and what was it . . . trashy. I'm not going to sit in a pub with you and know that you mocked at him and his lack of education, and made fun of his intellectual conversation. You can find your own company tonight. And whoever it is, she has my sympathy.'

Clare turned away. David watched her as she walked in a rage along Stephen's Green.

Clare had a letter from David a week later.

People often make jokes about medics being illiterate and now I see why. It's so long since I wrote anything that wasn't an examination answer, a report on a case, or notes at a lecture, I'm not sure how to begin. But I want to say I was in an extremely bad mood the other day when we met and I am very sorry indeed for taking it out on you. I really do apologize. You were minding your own business, you were loyal to a friend. I just behaved like a boor. I don't know why I said all those things about Gerry Doyle. Reluctantly, I have to put it down to simple, unattractive jealousy. I've always envied him his easy charm. I envied his reputation as a ladies' man. And that night in particular I envied him because he was going to go out with you when I wanted to. It's hard to say all this, and I'm sure I'm saying it very badly but I want you to know I regret it all very much. There's a Halloween dance in the hospital. I'd love you to come as my partner . . .

Clare sent him a postcard. David turned up at the hostel, in James Nolan's car, to collect her. She wore the same yellow and red dress that Mary Catherine had worn to the dance with James. 'Same dress, same car, only the cast has changed,' Mary Catherine said as she looked out the window.

'Don't they breed them handsome in Castlebay,' said Valerie watching David in his dark overcoat and white silk scarf, tucking Clare into the car.

They had decorated the Res up with funny faces cut into turnips and little nightlights burning inside. There were pictures of witches on the wall, and the lights were covered in red or black paper. They had apples hanging from a string and you had to bob for apples too. Everywhere there were basins and baths and the fronts of shirts were wet as heads were pushed far into the water. The hilarity was more important than the actual trapping of the apple. They had a big selection of records; and a lively nurse with her leg in a plaster cast was responsible for playing them three at a time, saying after the third, 'Thank you very much, end of dance, thank you.'

David was very popular, and much in demand for the Ladies' Choice. Clare was nearly knocked down in the rush of nurses towards Dr Power. It was funny to hear him called that. She kept expecting to see his father.

He introduced her to other doctors, interns and even registrars. 'Who's looking after the sick tonight?' she asked.

There was a system of call, and about a third of the people there couldn't drink in case they were needed.

'Those are the ones to watch out for,' a bearded doctor told Clare. 'If they can't drink, their minds are very definitely set in other directions.'

'I'd better stay with the winos then, if I want to keep my virtue,' she laughed. David seemed proud of her, and she saw him with new eyes. In this world he was relaxed and funny. She never thought of David Power as someone you laughed with. In fact, when his face came to her mind, she used to think of him as being a bit solemn. Either with his parents when he was young, or walking with Bones along the beach in winter.

Of course when the Nolans had come to Castlebay he had been fairly excited and laughing during those summers when she had been stuck behind the counter in the shop . . .

'What are you thinking about?' He was dancing close to her.

'About you,' she said truthfully.

'Good. Were they happy positive thoughts?'

'Yes, I suppose they were. I was thinking how well you fit in here, how happy you seem.'

'I think that about you too. You always disapproved of me in Castlebay.' He was half teasing.

'Jealous, I suppose. You had more freedom. You could have such a good time.'

David smiled. 'I used to envy all of you. A sweetshop, you could come and go as you liked, they weren't sitting waiting for you to come in, hanging on your every word . . .'

'No one's ever satisfied with what they have. I told you that. Do you remember?'

'I remember. I didn't think you would,' he said. 'I remember it because I thought it was a sad sort of thing to say and to mean.' His smile said he wanted her to cheer up.

She laughed at him, and at that point the music changed to a faster beat, and Mary Catherine's red and yellow dress was swung into a very energetic version of 'Down by the Riverside'. It was actually a Ladies' Choice but David and Clare hadn't noticed. Several nurses retreated in defeat.

The supper was magnificent. Real Halloween food: colcannon, mounds of mashed potatoes with chopped-up onion and kale in it as well as threepences and rings. There were plates of sausages, and afterwards huge amounts of toasted barm brack, with extra rings pushed in so that there could be a lot of happy screaming at the thought of a marriage within a year.

Clare got a ring, which she nearly swallowed. 'Lord above, how frightening,' she said.

'Did you nearly choke?' David asked.

'No, the thought that I'd be married in a year.'

They were sitting in an alcove of the big room, a window seat away from the crowd. They had brought their glasses of red wine, and the noise was away in the background.

'Would that be the end of the world?' he asked.

'Yes. It would. The end of *my* world.' She explained her plans, the M.A. the Ph.D. the terms in the United States, in Oxford or Cambridge and finally the history professorship. She felt he was smiling inside.

'I will, you know. I really will. If I got this far I can get to the moon.'

'I know.' He was gentle.

'You don't know, David. You really don't. For all that you were brought up beside me, you don't know how hard it was to get here. I don't want to go on and on about it. But, you see, it's not just like saying I want to be a film star, or I

308

want to be the Pope, for me to say I want to be a professor of history. When I was ten I wanted to be an Honours university student. And who would have believed then that I could?'

'You give me very little credit. I do know. Of course I do. It's you knows nothing about me. What do you think I want for my career? Tell me. Go on.'

She paused. 'I suppose you'll go home and be a doctor with your father,' she said.

'See, you don't know a thing. I'm not going back to Castlebay for ages. If at all. Being a doctor like that in a small place . . . You choose it. You can't have it chosen for you.'

'But everyone thinks . . .'

'Everyone thought when you were a small girl in the convent that you'd leave school and marry someone from up the road. Like Chrissie. But you didn't.'

'It's not the same. If you didn't want to be a doctor why did you become one?'

'I do want to be a doctor. But I haven't become one yet. I have years more to do, at least four or five in different hospitals learning under specialists, seeing the new developments . . . There's much more to being a doctor than saying tut-tut-poor-thing and knowing when to call the ambulance.'

'So will you be a specialist?'

'I don't know. I think I would like to be a GP, like my father. But not yet. And not in Castlebay. Can you see anything so stupid as sitting down with my mummy and daddy, like I did when I was a young boy, coming home from school, and describing How I Spent My Day?'

She giggled. 'I know, it does sound silly. But perhaps you'll marry someone and then it won't be like that. It will be more normal.'

'Not yet. And if I'm going to wait for you to be thirty-four, I'll be nearly forty.'

'Oh, I wouldn't go back to Castlebay even when I'm thirty-four. You'd better not marry me,' Clare said, anxious that there should be no misunderstandings. 'I just said I'd be ready to marry then, not give anything up like my Chair of History.'

'I think you'd be too complicated for me. I think I'd better marry someone else all right.'

'Caroline Nolan? Would she be suitable?'

'Not really.'

'Why not?'

'I don't know. My mother thinks she'd be suitable. Her mother thinks she'd be suitable. Her brother thinks it too. That's probably why.'

'Does she think she'd be suitable?'

'I don't know,' David laughed. 'Let's dance.'

A red-haired doctor with a Cork accent asked David if he would lend him the lovely lady in the red and yellow dress for one dance. He was called Bar. He said most people in Cork were called some form of the name Finbarr, with his being the patron saint. Bar said that he was a registrar and very important in the hospital and that David's whole career would depend on Clare being nice and willing and co-operative and giving herself in every way to Bar. Clare pealed with laughter at this and asked whether this line of chat ever worked.

'Sometimes,' Bar said gloomily. 'But less often than you'd hope. Women seem to be brighter these days. They have minds and things.' Was she David's girlfriend? No. Good. Just a girl next door from Castlebay, that was nice. Clare said it wasn't exactly next door, but this was never a concept you could explain to anyone in Dublin; they all thought that you were rewriting Cinderella if you explained the gulf of difference between the O'Brien and Power families.

Bar was holding her very tight and saying that he was on call so he couldn't have a drink, which made the party a bit of a bore but on the other hand it did sharpen his awareness of who were the best-looking girls.

Diplomatically, Clare released herself in order to help him choose the best-looking girls. Bar found this irritating but he couldn't fault her. They were discussing the attributes of a group of girls in the corner when David rescued her.

'Thank God,' she said as she danced with David again. 'That fellow's like an octopus.'

'I'm disappointed that groping is out,' he said.

'David! You'd never grope. You'd make sophisticated gestures when you knew the feelings were returned. Aren't I right?'

'You are. God you are,' David said, holding her close to him but not allowing his hands to roam like those of Registrar Bar, the octopus as he would be known for evermore.

On the way home he parked the car. Clare looked up in alarm.

'It's all right. I haven't turned into an octopus. I just wanted to talk for a bit. It's one of the few nights I'm not crashing to the ground with sleep. James says I'm the most boring friend to have. I have no time off, and I can't stay awake when I do.'

They talked on easily, happily, like old friends.

'We should go out together, sometimes . . . you know, the pictures or a coffee. What do you think?' He looked enthusiastic and casual at the same time. He didn't sound as if he were asking her for a date, or a commitment, just friendship.

'I'd like that, certainly. Of course I would,' she said.

'There'd be nobody to bother us here,' David said. He didn't need to mention that there would be plenty of people to bother them in Castlebay. He gave her a kiss on the cheek to settle it and drove her back to the hostel. He watched in alarm as she climbed up the iron rungs and disappeared through a window.

'Was he nice?' Mary Catherine asked sleepily as Clare climbed in the window.

'Very.'

'Did he jump on you?'

'No, no. Nothing like that.'

'But it's desperately late, what else were you doing?'

'Talking. Just talking.'

'God, that's serious,' Mary Catherine said, waking up.

'Don't be silly, go back to sleep, I've hung up your dress, it's not too sweaty.'

'What is it?' Valerie was awake now.

'Clare's back. She *talked* to him all night. They're in love.'

'Great,' Valerie snorted and settled down again.

'I'm *not* in love. Even if I wanted to be in love with David Power I couldn't. So there.'

'Why? Is he in fact your long-lost brother? Why not?'

'Because his mother would throw a cordon of Guards around the big house on the cliff if she thought that any of the O'Briens from the huckster's shop had notions about her son. That's why.'

Clare had snuggled down in her bed and pulled the sheets to her chin. Mary Catherine was wide awake and concerned. 'You can't let that kind of crap stand in your way! You're not going to tell me that . . .'

'I'm not going to tell you anything till tomorrow. *Goodnight* Mary Catherine.'

Ned's letter was short. Tommy had left Mr Carroll's greengrocery shop on a Friday. He had said that he wouldn't take his week's wages. He had got another job and it wasn't fair to ask to be paid for the last week. The Carrolls had telephoned Father Flynn, but no one could find Tommy. Until the following Wednesday, when the police found him. In a stolen car which had crashed during a police chase. The car was being chased because it was seen leaving the scene of a robbery with violence. Tommy had ended up with a dislocated shoulder, a broken jaw and a nine-year sentence. Ned just wanted to ask Clare whether someone should tell Mam and Dad now or was the pretence to go on for ever.

Poor, stupid, *stupid* Tommy. She couldn't think of him as bad Tommy, dangerous Tommy, in with a gang of thugs and joining in their violence. She could hardly remember him, but he had seemed nice like Ned was last summer when he came home.

She would tell them. But not by letter. And not making a special visit.

She would tell them when she went home for Christmas.

It was hard to choose the moment to begin. There never

seemed to be any time when they were all together. Mam was thin and tired, but she was always on the move, from range to table, from kitchen out to shop, from shop to storeroom. Dad was always fiddling with things, and Jim and Ben were coming in one door and out another.

After tea, the first night home, she thought she had them all in one room, at least.

'I have some bad news about Tommy,' she said loudly, to get their attention. 'He's not injured, or sick, or anything. But it *is* bad news.'

They all stopped what they were doing. She certainly had their attention.

'So will you sit down, and I'll tell you,' she said.

'Stop acting like a judge and jury. What is it? If you've something to say, say it.' Her father was annoyed.

'I wanted to tell it to you from the start. Jim, why don't you put the sign up on the door?'

'How long is this going to take, for God's sake?' Tom O'Brien was now worried.

'Tommy . . . Tommy . . .' The tears were already starting to form in Mam's eyes.

One by one, they sat down round the table and she could hedge no more.

'I had a letter from Ned. Tommy's in gaol. He's going to be there for . . . for a long time.'

'How long?' Mam's voice was almost steady. She didn't ask what he had done, or why he was there. Just how long.

'This is hard, Mam. Very long. Nine years.'

She looked at the table. She couldn't bear to see the shock round her. They had all thought that Tommy was living an ordinary life until twenty seconds ago. Now they had to try to understand all this at one go. She *should* have told them ages ago.

'You can't mean nine *years*,' Agnes said. 'You can't mean *years*.'

Clare told them what Tommy had done. She told them what he had done before. It seemed like a story about somebody else's brother as she was telling it. She looked at

313

her mother's face, and realized that it certainly sounded like the story of someone else's son.

Gerry Doyle came in while she was telling them.

Mam was crying. Dad was throwing back his head and saying what would you expect. Jim and Ben were round-eyed, and teetering between a grudging admiration of their brother for doing something as brave as running with a gang and a sense of horror about the disgrace that was going to fall on the family.

'I didn't think *Closed* meant me,' Gerry smiled around the kitchen door.

'It does tonight.' Clare gave him a smile that wasn't a smile, and to her relief he understood.

'Sure. It was only a packet of fags. I'll take one and run. Pay you tomorrow. All right?'

He was gone. Clare settled down again for the abuse. How dare she play God and decide to hold the first bit of news back from them? What did she and Ned think they were playing at, telling packs of lies? How could anyone know now if *this* was the whole truth? And who was this priest that none of them knew, fiddling in their affairs? And did Ned's fiancée know all about it too? Was she in on the whole deception?

Clare soldiered on. Already it was getting easier. The more they knew, the less frightening it became. She wished that she had told them ages ago, she admitted this to them, but she said truthfully that since she had hoped that Tommy might have just had that one phase, it would be a pity to damn him in their eyes for ever.

Mam wondered did anyone else in Castlebay know. And Clare looked her straight in the eye and said that nobody knew. She decided that she could trust Angela and Gerry. They had kept it to themselves so far; there was no reason for them to speak now.

The news made them look older. All of them. Clare wondered had it done that to her too when she got the first letter from Ned. Mam's thin shoulders stooped more under the navy cardigan she wore, and Dad's face looked grey and set while he painted the new extension that would never bring him a day's happiness now that he knew it was built with stolen money. Jim and Ben lost a bit of their good spirits. Clare saw that they stayed in the house more than usual, rather than roaming the town looking for divilment with their friends from school.

Chrissie arrived on visits, the size of a mountain now, and said that it was like going to visit a graveyard instead of your own family at Christmas time. If this was the cheer that Clare brought home with her she might as well have stayed in Dublin.

Clare said she was going to spend a day with Angela. They were going to go over a lot of work Clare had to do for her finals.

'Don't be telling her our business now,' Agnes warned.

'Why would I tell her anything of the sort?' asked Clare. She had planned to spend hours discussing it, if Angela had the time.

She lost the sense of time there. They must have had tea, or a meal. There was certainly drink, a bottle of port wine was on the table.

At one stage Dick called, and Angela asked him to go away.

It wasn't all Clare's tale.

The story of Father Sean O'Hara was told too. Not only had he left the priesthood years and years ago, but he had a grown-up family nearly. And they were all coming to Castlebay for the summer. They had booked a caravan. Father Sean O'Hara was coming back to show his home to his Japanese lady friend, and to show his children their roots.

In Dublin Clare could meet David anywhere she liked. He could come to the hostel to collect her, she could take a bus up to his hospital and they could have coffee in the canteen. They could go to the pictures or to have a drink. Nobody took any notice. In Castlebay it was almost impossible to do any such thing. Without even saying it they knew they were going to be further apart for the two weeks they spent in Castlebay than if they were on different sides of the Atlantic.

They didn't have to tell each other that it would be awkward to invite the other home. They knew. Like they knew about spring tides, and about Father O'Dwyer's sermons. Clare would not be invited to the Powers' for supper. David could chat easily with the O'Briens across the counter, but they wouldn't let him in to see their kitchen with its old rusty range, its torn lino and its boxes of supplies all round the place, an inelegant overflowing storeroom for the shop which had never been properly organized.

They couldn't go and sit in Dillon's Hotel for hours on end, or the whole town would know about it. Clare didn't play golf, and Castlebay would have mocked her if she had learned. It wasn't for the likes of Clare O'Brien. That meant the golf course and its rolling dunes were out. If they went to the pictures together there would be talk.

And they didn't want talk. It wasn't worth it. They weren't in love with each other. They were friends. They were great friends. But such a concept didn't exist in Castlebay, and if it were going to exist it was very unlikely it would develop between the handsome, eligible son of the doctor and the bright perky little girl from the store.

They went for a long walk with Bones. David had had a bad row with his mother that morning and was not going to apologize in order to keep the peace. He had said he was going to the pictures that night and he was thinking of asking Clare. Molly had said very sweetly that it wouldn't *do* at all. It would be unfair on the girl. It would give her ideas. Raise her hopes. Furious, he had said this was rubbish, that he often met Clare in Dublin and neither of them had any hopes, just a good friendship. Molly had raised her eyebrows very high and said she thought David could have done better for himself, a professional man, than to be going out with the sister of Mogsy Byrne and Chrissie O'Brien. He had laughed in his mother's face and said that since she couldn't find anything to blame Tom and Agnes for, she had to draw in the least respectable member of the family and her eejit of a husband to complain about. Molly Power, with two bright spots of red on her face, had stormed out of the room and upstairs. His father had already gone out on his rounds but the whole thing would be aired again this evening. He almost told Clare but stopped. She might take it as a slight, even though she was always making jokes herself about confusing the rank and file of Castlebay.

Clare nearly told David about Tommy. He was so nice and understanding, so solid and unshockable, he might well reveal that both his mother's and father's parents had been in gaol for years. But she didn't want him to have more things to apologize for when he met her. Nellie had told Chrissie that there had been an almighty row this morning already about David meeting Clare at all. Better not let him know she was the sister of a criminal in an English prison as well as being one of the poor O'Briens, God help us.

There were New Year's Eve celebrations in Dillon's Hotel but Clare didn't feel any heart for going. She suggested to her mother that they ask Angela O'Hara for supper.

'We're not the kind of people that have people to supper,' her mother said.

'Maybe we should be,' Clare said. Her father said he didn't mind, it was no concern of his what the women did or didn't do.

The evening was a surprising success. Angela taught them to play rummy and even Agnes began to enjoy it. She had been hesitant at the start and wanted to stay out of it. Angela said more than once that it was very nice to spend New Year's Eve with a family.

'Oh, you wouldn't call this much of a family,' Tom said disparagingly.

'Why ever not? One daughter married and going to give a grandchild this spring. Another, the town genius. Two lads in England making their own way, two here, and please God there'll be work for them when they leave school. A good business . . . what more of a family could you want than that?'

Agnes said when you looked at it like that it was true, they had a lot to be thankful for. But she sighed a sigh that went down to her feet almost as she said it.

'Everything isn't as it seems,' Tom O'Brien said darkly, shaking his head.

Angela nodded enthusiastically at him. He was absolutely right, nothing *was* as it seemed, there wasn't a family in Castlebay without its own sadnesses and worries and confusions. She often thought that at Mass on a Sunday, people kneeling there so calm-looking and only the Lord knew what was in their hearts. Every one of them had a worry. She had hit it just right. This gloomy-sounding old soothsaying cheered up the O'Brien family greatly. They weren't alone in their cross. In fact Clare's father was so cheered that he thought it was time for everyone to have a glass of something to see the sixties in. They wished each other Happy New Year and shortly afterwards Angela left: she had promised Dick Dillon to look in on him in the hotel and wish him the compliments of the season.

Clare walked her up the road. She felt very wide awake and restless. She went to the seat that the Committee had put up last summer, the big green seat just at the top of the steps. A perfect vantage point for surveying the beach on a crowded summer day. Tonight you could just sit and look at the stars and the bright clear night. The sea looked navy somehow, and the cliffs like cardboard cut-outs.

Gerry arrived, silently, and sat beside her.

'You pad around like a leopard or a cat,' she said. 'You frightened the life out of me.'

'Happy New Year,' he said taking a half bottle of brandy and two little metal cups out of the pocket of his leather jacket.

Clare clapped her hands in delight.

'Aren't you one of the wonders of the world. Do you go round with mobile picnics and parties in your pocket all the time, or is it only on festivals?'

'It's only when I see you on your own. I was coming out of the hotel. I saw you coming down here, and raced home for the supplies.'

They toasted each other and looked out to sea.

'This is *the* year, isn't it? The finals, the big degree?'

'Yes, Lord I'll have to work when I get back, I'm doing

nothing here. I thought I was going to get lots of reading done, but I haven't opened a book.'

'I'm sorry for intruding the other night. Was it a family conference?'

'It was about Tommy.'

'Don't tell me. It's not my business.'

'Oh no, it's all right. You know anyway. But he did it again, and this time they wounded a man so badly he'll be in a wheelchair and Tommy's gone to gaol for nine years.'

Gerry let out his breath like a whistle. 'Nine years. Lord.'

'So this time I decided I would tell them at home. They have a right to know. They were very low as you can imagine. Angela cheered them up a lot tonight. But they think nobody knows, so I swore that nobody did.'

'Sure.'

He was easy and her restless feeling was fading fast. Or maybe it was the brandy. He had put his jacket around both of them. It kept out the wind, and it was companionable. He kissed her, a long gentle kiss. She didn't pull away. He put his arms inside her duffle coat and held her to him as he kissed her again.

She felt something touch her leg and jumped.

It was Bones looking at her eagerly, waiting for her to disentangle herself from Gerry. Behind Bones, a dozen yards away, was David.

'I was just going to say Happy New Year,' he said. 'I'm sorry. I didn't mean to disturb you.'

He turned very quickly and walked along the Cliff Road home.

Bones looked hopefully at Gerry and Clare, in case there was going to be any fun and games for him. But deciding there wasn't, he cantered off after David who was walking unnaturally quickly through the bright starry night.

His parents were still at the hotel. Nellie had gone to her family. The house was empty. David nearly took the door from its hinges with the bang he gave it.

He was going to sit down in the sitting room where the fire was still warm and have a drink to calm him down but the fear that his parents would come back and that he would have to talk to them civilly was too great. He poured himself a large whiskey and went up to his bedroom. He pulled back the curtains and looked out at the sea. Years ago, when Gerry Doyle had first seen this room, he had said in admiration that it was like a ship. You could see no land unless you turned your head or leaned out to see the garden beneath.

There were two big rooms with bay windows upstairs, and his parents slept in the one next door. David had a window seat running round the three windows of the bay. His toys had been kept inside it when he was young. He looked to see were they still there and indeed, there was a small cricket set, a blackboard and easel, there were boxes of soldiers and boxes of playing bricks. His Meccano set was still there and there was a box which said David's Colouring Things.

It annoyed him to see them still there. And yet what should his mother have done with them? Given them away? They were his after all, and one day he might want them for his children . . .

But anything would annoy him tonight.

It had been a very boring evening. He had made a very tactless mistake with Josie Dillon. Apparently Clare had never mentioned that Mary Catherine had been an off-and-on girlfriend of James Nolan since the Lord knew when. Josie had been distressed by the news but even more by the fact that Clare hadn't told her. She had become quite weepy and had gone off to bed before the singing of 'Auld Lang Syne', so that would have to be sorted out.

But nothing had prepared him for the strength of his feelings when he saw Clare in Gerry Doyle's arms like that. He felt sick all over until he was nearly shaking to think of it again. Him, with his arms around her, inside her coat, fondling her, and kissing her, there on the bench in the dark, with a cheap half-bottle of brandy at their feet. David had walked up to them because he recognized Clare's duffle coat, and the moonlight was shining on her fair hair. It was quite obvious who she was. He hadn't really seen Gerry; it was dark that side of the bench, and they weren't kissing when he started to walk over. If only Bones hadn't rushed across he might have been able to escape without speaking to them.

But even so it was churning his stomach to think of Gerry Doyle's mean, small, dark face pressed on Clare's. To think of *him* giving her brandy and forcing himself on her. And to imagine that bright Clare, lovely, bright, sunny Clare, could be so stupid as to fall for it. Why was she letting him crawl all over her?

David felt so sick he couldn't finish his whiskey. He poured it down the wash basin, and lay back on his bed.

He was pale at breakfast and his mother asked him whether he might be getting flu.

'There are two doctors in this house, Mother. Leave the diagnosis to us,' he snapped.

Dr Power looked up in alarm. 'I heard a kind courteous inquiry after your health from your mother who is concerned about you,' he said quietly.

'Yes. I'm very sorry. That's what I heard too. I apologize, Mother.'

'That's all right.' Molly was gracious. At least he was able to say sorry now, a few days ago when she had said something perfectly harmless about the young O'Brien girl he had leaped down her throat and he had *not* apologized on that occasion.

'I'm in surgery all day, David. Do you want to take the car and drive off somewhere? It might be a nice break for you.'

'That's very nice, Dad.' He paused. He'd better make the offer. 'Would you like to go for a drive, Mother?'

Fortunately it was a bridge afternoon and she had to get ready for it. But it was nice of him to ask her. Honour had been satisfied.

New Year's Day or not, people would have their ailments and Dr Power shuffled off into the other side of the house. Nellie made David a big turkey sandwich with lots of stuffing in it and a flask of tea. He didn't even notice where he was driving until he came to a wild rocky place he had only seen from the road before. He parked the car and got out.

It must have been the same for centuries, he thought. Bleak and unwelcoming, the sea washing on it endlessly, as remote in the summer as in winter. Who would walk for forty minutes as he had through thickets and briars and down stony crumbling paths to get to a place that didn't even have a sandy beach? He threw stones into the water mechanically, one after another in a kind of rhythm. He couldn't be so obsessed with Clare that he shivered at the thought of Gerry touching her. He was only awake last night because he had drunk too much, because he had a stupid quarrel with Josie Dillon, because he was worried, as he was always worried, about this business of coming home to live like a child again in the house with a mummy and a daddy and a doctor's coat.

But her face was there, and her shoulders, and her hair. And her bright smile, and the way she was always so interested in everything and had so many views on any subject. He remembered the day he had felt so annoyed with her outside the National Library in Dublin when she was running back to her hostel to know if Gerry had rung. He remembered the relief that she didn't seem to be at all interested in the amorous Mr Doyle. Her work plans were daunting and over-ambitious, but she was certainly destined for a first-class B.A. and acceptance as an M.A. student. So why was she behaving like a cheap tramp last night? That's what it was. The cheapest way to go on, with a bottle of spirits and right in public. And with Gerry, who had felt up and touched every girl who was any way attractive and quite a few who were not.

His hand throwing the stones into the sea paused and he dropped the stone and clenched his fists. Gerry Doyle would never touch her again. Never. He would keep his hands to himself. He would not go near Clare O'Brien, he wouldn't dare. Last night had just been silly, a New Year silliness, to be excused but never to be repeated.

He would explain this to Clare, and she would understand. They would even laugh about it.

But what would he explain?

He wished he had taken Bones with him. Just looking into

the dog's foolish face helped; but he hadn't known where he was going to go and the dog could have been a liability.

What would he say to Clare?

The wise man would say nothing. The wise man would make a little joke and forget the scene on the cliff top.

But David began to think he was not a wise man. He could not forget the tableau and he couldn't stop a feeling of light sweat forming on the back of his neck at the memory.

He couldn't want Clare that badly for himself. He couldn't. It must be pure bloody jealousy that Gerry struck lucky on New Year's Eve in the cold, while he, David, had a boring evening listening to old-timers singing 'Darling, You Are Growing Old' – which was too painfully true – having a totally ludicrous conversation with a tearful Josie Dillon, and then coming across Love's Young Dream on the bench.

No. It was more. He wanted to see Clare. Now.

He wanted to tell her that she was special. And to ask her to give him a chance to prove himself her lover as well as her friend.

It was highly awkward, but as sure as he knew anything he knew he loved her.

Clare didn't know why she felt so furious all next day. There was no way she could fault David. He hadn't been rude. Under the circumstances he had been polite. His voice hadn't dripped with sarcasm, as it had that time he had unleashed a tirade about Gerry in Dublin when he called him trashy.

But she wished he hadn't come along. It had been nothing, it had only been a couple of kisses, and she didn't think it would have gone any further. It was too public a place for one thing; and she *wouldn't*, for another.

But she had this feeling that David was always on the verge of going on to another level in their friendship. She had never admitted this to the girls. She kept telling them how unsuitable the liaison would be, and they made jokes about the security forces Mrs Power would need to employ and where she should station them around Castlebay. But Clare knew it wasn't just a joke.

323

She felt they talked as she never could with anyone. They didn't just talk gossip or plans. She was always interested to know what he thought about things. He never bored her. And she had the feeling that he was delighted with her. But he had never touched her or kissed her. So she was a bit in the dark about what he really felt. She would like to have been close to him, closer than she was, but she didn't want to push it because she had no idea at all how he felt.

Anyway it might be just hero worship. When she'd been the poor little girl in the shabby cotton dress in the shop, David and James Nolan had been swaggering round Castlebay like gods. Now she was their equal in a way. He sought her out and didn't meet other people at all.

It was all such bad timing. If only she had stayed at home. Or gone straight home. Or said no to Gerry Doyle. Or if only that big idiot of a dog hadn't spotted them and come like a detective to find them out.

She'd never know now what David Power had felt about her, if anything. It would have vanished on that cliff top last night. *Damn* Gerry Doyle, to the pit of hell.

Very few people came in on New Year's Day. It was a holiday of obligation and they had all been to early Mass. Clare hadn't looked round to see if David was in the church. She thought she saw his father, but she didn't want to meet any of them. She hurried home afterwards, down the quiet cold street.

Clare decided that she would invite Josie to supper, too. If only her mother would get out of this servile approach things would be much better. There was no reason why Josie Dillon shouldn't have sausages and beans, and brown bread-and-butter in their kitchen. She would enjoy it.

Clare had tried to catch Josie's eye in the church, but Josie looked away every time. Possibly she hadn't seen her.

The shop doorbell went. Her father was cleaning the paintbrush out in the back. Ben and Jim were reading the funnies in a paper. Chrissie had arrived for a woman-to-woman chat with Mam and was sitting on a hardbacked chair while Mam ironed. Clare had been half reading a very dense account of the differences between common law, equity and statute law, for what she had been hoping would give her a better understanding of the history of the English courts.

'I'll go.' Chrissie quite enjoyed meeting the public and serving them now that she was such an important person in the town. Mrs Maurice Byrne, and seven months pregnant too.

'It's young Dr Power, for Miss O'Brien,' she said scathingly on her return.

Clare went out and pulled the kitchen door a little closed behind her.

'Please come out with me now. Please,' he said as if preparing for a long debate about it.

'Right,' she said and took down her duffle coat from the hook.

She was surprised to see the car outside the door.

He held open the car door for her, and then ran round the other side. 'I wanted us to go for a drive,' he said. His eyes looked very bright but he didn't look upset.

'Yes, of course.'

They drove to that strange rocky place, bleak and dangerous. They got out of the car and looked down at it. Apart from the seagulls, there wasn't a soul around.

'I was down there this morning,' he said.

Clare said nothing.

'I was down there for a long time. Throwing stones in the sea. And I realized something.'

She looked at him.

'I realized I love you,' he said.

'I love you too.'

She didn't know why she was crying, it was ridiculous to cry when this happened. This was the best thing in the whole world that could happen. Why did the tears come down out of the corners of her eyes? She could taste them mixed with the spray, the salty spray which came up and whirled lightly around them as they kissed each other and held on to each other on the cold New Year's Day of 1960.

PART THREE

1960–

David's father and mother drove him to the train; Dick Dillon and Angela drove Clare.

'There's David,' Angela said, pleased, as they stood on the platform.

Clare was casual. She had a book in her hand already. Everyone knew she was going to study all the way to Dublin. David waved cheerily, and his mother nodded, a kind of bow as if she had hurt her neck. Dr Power had gone to the newsagent's stall to buy David a magazine for his long journey.

When the train was half a mile from the town they were in each other's arms in the corridor, each whispering the other's name over and over. They were going back to Dublin. City of freedom. So Clare was in a hostel run by nuns and David was a resident doctor in a big city hospital. Compared to where they came from this was licence and freedom.

The book on the history of law and the magazine just bought at the news stand lay beside each other on the seat of the train unread. The train was not crowded. They had a compartment to themselves for most of the journey, and when they were joined it was by an elderly American who said it was the coldest country he had ever visited in his life and he had visited a few. David encouraged him to wrap something round his feet – it was the extremities that often felt most cold. The American had a huge muffler and they tied it loosely around his ankles. He was asleep in no time and they kissed and held hands and snuggled up to each other happily in the corner without interruption.

They had two whole days in Dublin before anyone knew

they were back. Clare's hostel didn't open till Sunday; and David wasn't expected in the hospital until eight a.m. on the Monday morning. It was only Friday night. They had made no plans, almost as if they both felt it might be unlucky.

Now in the winter evening outside Kingsbridge they walked past the line of taxis and to the bus. Clare had one small case, David two huge ones. She accused him of having brought all his washing home for Nellie to do and he opened his eyes wide. Didn't everyone do that?

She wanted to ask him what they were to do now. Or better, she wanted to tell him all her options: she could stay with Kevin and Emer, if he wanted to go and stay with James for example. She could go to the hostel and throw herself on the mercy of the nuns. They thought she was one of the most reliable girls they ever had, so they would grumble only a bit and let her into her room – even though it hadn't been aired for her and no hot-water bottles had been put in the small iron beds.

She had £18 in her wallet. They could stay in a guest house: there were lots of them in Glasnevin, she knew lots of students who had cheap digs out that way.

But she thought she should wait and see what David had in mind. Her throat closed over once or twice in case he suggested that they sleep together. She hoped and prayed he wouldn't ask her to. Not yet. She had to think. It was all too sudden.

As they got on the bus to O'Connell Bridge, David said easily, 'You know the flat I used to stay in before they locked me up in the hospital?'

'Yes.'

'I still have the key. And I can go there always. There'll be nobody back until Monday. And there's lots of rooms. You could go in the one I used to have, it's one of the nicest. And I could go . . . well anywhere. Far away from you, I think, so that I won't come and break down the door and get at you.'

She smiled at him, relieved that she hadn't spoken, pleased that he felt the need to break down the door, and very grateful that he wasn't going to. He had said absolutely the right thing.

They had a honeymoon without sex. They held hands and she took him on tours of her Dublin. He had never been inside the Bank of Ireland to look from within at what had once been the Irish Parliament. He said he must have known that but somehow he had forgotten. She promised to take him on a weekday.

She crossed the road with him and showed him the book of Kells in Trinity College. He said he had known it was there and he had been going to see it one day.

They climbed Nelson's Pillar to look out over the city. It had a long, dark, windy staircase. There was a lot of pausing to catch breath and to kiss. David embarked on a long tale of a doctor who was married but having an illicit romance with another married lady. They couldn't go anywhere to make love because they were too well known, so they used to meet twice a week inside Nelson's Pillar and make love on the stairway. If any tourist climbing up or down was troublesome enough to interrupt them they just flattened themselves against the wall.

'That's why I brought you here of course.' She laughed and jumped lightly ahead of him so that he'd know she wasn't contemplating it for a moment. She took him down the Quays to St Michan's, an old Protestant Church where they had a totally preserved mummy in the vaults.

In the evenings they made themselves meals. David was rather better at preparing them than Clare.

'I thought you'd be very domesticated, big family, all those brothers to cook for,' he teased.

'I'd be fine throwing a big dinner for eight on the table, lump of bacon, half a ton of spuds. But I've never cooked just for one or two. We get the food handed to us up in the hostel.' She sounded apologetic.

'It's not the end of the world, Clare. Stop looking so mournful!'

'What will we have tonight? Will we go out and get something or what?' She hoped he'd say that they'd get chips from the place down the road.

'Oh, there's lots of eggs there – why don't you just make

an omelette?' He was talking absently, concentrating on clearing out the grate.

Clare looked stricken.

'There's a bit of cheese there, isn't there? We could have a cheese omelette,' he called.

'I'll do the fire, *you* do the omelette.'

'Don't tell me you can't make an . . .' David stopped when he saw her face.

'We never had them at home. If you show me, I'll know then.'

'Listen, it doesn't matter, scrambled eggs, anything . . .'

'Show me how to make an omelette. I want to know.' Her face was set and determined.

'All right then.' David was good-natured. 'It doesn't matter a damn, you know, you *do* know that, don't you?'

They kissed over the frying pan. It didn't matter a damn.

On Sunday night, he asked her. 'What are we going to do?'

'I don't know.'

They sat for a long time on the floor with a bottle of wine between them.

'It's too soon isn't it? We met too soon.'

'We met when we were babies, David.'

'You know what I mean. Now. It's too early.'

'I love you. The other seems unimportant. I wouldn't want to be a history don somewhere without you.'

'I don't want to be anywhere without you.'

'Maybe we can go round the world only taking universities that will have research facilities for both of us.' She smiled nervously.

'But in real life . . .' he said.

'Yes. Real life. Which begins tomorrow.' She looked stricken.

He kissed her and rocked her in his arms. 'Nothing bad can happen now, I was never more sure in my life. I'll love you for ever. I half loved you always and didn't know it.'

'No, nothing bad can happen now,' said Clare.

*

They knew immediately of course. Mary Catherine and Val. There was no point in denying it.

'Do you mind if I don't talk about it,' she said.

'Yes we bloody do,' Valerie said indignantly. 'What kind of nonsense is that? We've told you everything, every pant and groan.'

'It's very unfair to hold out on us now. It's secretive and it's not like you at all. I can't understand it.' Mary Catherine was upset.

'But there's nothing to tell. I beg you, there's no new panting and groaning in it, in fact there's a lot less than there was with Ian that night in the car. So now, will that satisfy you?'

'It will not. How did it happen? Did he say he loved you, did a thousand violins start to play? I *must* know.' Valerie was sitting on her bed, legs crossed like an old-fashioned tailor. She looked very young, Clare thought. They were all young, nobody was twenty, she was too young to feel the way she did. The realization swept over her.

'You see I'm too young,' she said stupidly.

'For what? God Clare, you're very irritating when you put on this dramatic bit. Does he think you're too young for him or what?'

'No, but it's all right for him. He's old, he's twenty-five. His life's nearly over. In terms of studying I mean.'

'This is very tedious,' complained Valerie.

'I *told* you it was tedious,' Clare said defensively.

'It may pass over. Seriously, if you've known the guy all your life and never thought about him in that way until ten days ago, it's bound to blow over.'

'It won't. That's what really is going to be tedious for you. I can't think of any better way to put it than this and it's going to make you vomit.'

'Say it,' said Valerie grimly.

'I feel as if I'd been looking and looking for something I'd lost and now I've found it. It's like going home, except much nicer than going home, it's like you think going home should be.'

'It's a bit soppy,' Val said objectively.

333

'I'm afraid it is.'

'Will you be any fun do you think, ever again?' Mary Catherine asked.

'Oh I hope so, but do you see what I mean, it's no good my talking about it, I can only use these awful, sickening words.' She looked from one to another.

'It's going to be very hard,' said Val. 'In the middle of a perfectly normal conversation about sex or about who we're going to set our sights on at a party we'll remember that you've had this coming home feeling about the boy next door.'

'Will you do me one favour, will you get it into your heads that he is not the boy next door. Whatever he is, he's not that.'

He was hungry for every detail of her, he told her that he used to envy the O'Briens as children going off with their jam jars picking blackberries, or with the same jam jars on strings trying to catch pinkeens. There were always children running in and out of the shop and calling to each other winter and summer while his own house was very big and you could hear the clock ticking in the hall.

She told him about how terrible Chrissie had been and somehow they made her into a comic character. All her cruelty, and pulling Clare's hair, and trying to persuade her she was abnormal didn't matter any more.

He told her about his father and how he tried hard not to drag David back to the practice but he really wanted him there. Tomorrow. David admitted that his mother sometimes drove him mad. She was full of childish nonsenses; but years ago in a man-to-man talk his father had urged him not to be impatient, and said that Molly had given up a lot of bright lights and fun to come to a backwater as a country doctor's wife. It irritated David greatly that his father should be somehow grateful to his mother for this. It was her choice after all. And there was the history of miscarriages and stillbirths so she had to be forgiven her little silliness from time to time.

He told her that his mother came to Dublin every year to

spend a few days with the Nolans; and he used to be ashamed of her carry-on, sitting in the lounge of the Shelbourne, or the Ibernian or the Gresham having afternoon tea. Far too dressed up, and asking at the top of her voice who all the other people were, then trilling with affected laughter when David hissed that he didn't know and saying that really he was quite a recluse. Clare was sympathetic. It was probably because Mrs Power wanted to feel important just for a couple of days; she could go home and remember that so and so had saluted her and so and so had made a fuss of her. It was like a child really. David's father indulged her just like a child. Some people always got that kind of treatment.

After a while she told him about Tommy. She wasn't going to. He didn't need to know and it seemed disloyal to them all at home with this sad secret they hugged to themselves. It seemed somehow indulgent to confess it in the great heat of love. Maybe David shouldn't have to hear it either. But she told him suddenly, when he had been talking so honestly about his own life and hiding nothing. She told him quickly and unemotionally. He reached across the table and held both her hands tight. He was upset but not shocked. If Tommy were such an eejit as to get in with this kind of a crowd, maybe the safest place for him was in gaol. And since he'd always been such a nice fellow he wouldn't get beaten up by the other prisoners or the warders or anything.

'When you and I go to London some time . . . we'll go to see him,' David said expansively. 'And that'll show him that he's not cut off or anything.'

Go to see Tommy? In a prison, on visiting day? She nodded at him, unable to speak.

He reached out and stroked her face. 'I don't think you have any idea of how much I love you, you are part of my soul. I would do anything for you. Going to see Tommy would make me happy if it were to give you some ease and pleasure. I'd go tonight on the mail boat.'

She closed her eyes and held his hand to her face. 'I don't deserve you. I'm so narrow and one-track and self-obsessed. Why do you love me so much?'

'I've no idea. It's just there. Filling all those empty spaces I used to have. There's no more doubt now. I just want you and what's good for you.'

He sat opposite her in the little café, his face tired from lack of sleep, his shirt collar open at the neck, his smile enormous and all over his face, lighting it up.

'You look like a man that's won the Sweep,' she said admiringly.

'Now you're just feeding me lines so I'll say that I *have* won the Sweep when I've won you,' he said.

As they left the café he asked whether anyone else knew where Tommy was.

'Angela. She was the one who insisted I write to him every week. Oh, and Gerry Doyle,' she said.

He frowned. Why had she told Gerry? He tried to keep his voice casual but she knew he hated Gerry knowing the family secret before he did.

'It was a long time ago. Gerry was going to London and my Mam asked him to go and find Tommy. I had to tell him what was happening. I couldn't have him going around investigating it and turning it up for himself, and then not knowing what to say. It was easier to tell him straight out. He never said a word, naturally.'

'Naturally.'

'Why are you studying in bed?' Valerie complained.

'Because I did nothing today. I met David for two hours, I went back to the library and I wrote him a letter. That was another hour. Then I spent an hour thinking about how nice it would be to go to London with him. Then I spent about half an hour working out how he should tell his father he can't possibly go back to Castlebay until he's done three years at least in Dublin hospitals. Then I went to this place where they do your hair cheaply in the afternoons, then I went out to the hospital with my new hairdo and had a cup of tea in the canteen with him, and gave him the letter. Then I came home. That's the work I did today, that's the amount of work the Murray scholar has put in towards getting her first-class honours degree.'

'All right, all right.' Valerie hadn't intended to bring on such an onslaught.

'No. It's not all right. I didn't know this would happen.' Clare looked mournful.

'Christ, you're only having a bit of fun. One day, one day, Clare O'Brien, with this fellow – it's not as if it were something stupid, like me making eyes like a sheep at that fellow who doesn't even know that I am alive, or Mary Catherine going out with James. You've got the real thing, what we all want. Stop *bellyaching*.'

'I know it must *sound* like bellyaching . . .'

'It does.' Valerie was grumpy.

'But if you knew how annoyed I am for doing nothing today. If you knew.'

'I'm *beginning* to know. For God's sake will you get out of bed, put on your coat, sit at the dressing table and work properly. Stop hanging out of the bed and trying to read with the light on the floor. Do it properly. I'll get to sleep. Don't mind me.'

'Valerie, stop making yourself into a tragedy queen,' Clare said.

Val laughed at the scorn; but she said that it was no harm to take Professor Clare O'Brien down a bit. She talked about her studies as if they were a sacred ritual. Clare had to smile as she climbed out of bed and put on clothes so that she wouldn't freeze.

A girl they didn't know tapped on the window, having climbed up the rungs. Clare let her in and she thanked them profusely.

'You three are a legend in this place,' she said breathlessly. 'I mean you're so old, and so settled, and make all your own rules.'

'We're also mad,' Val said from the bed. 'We take it in turns to get up and get fully dressed in the night to keep guard over the others.'

The girl was startled and said she should be off.

'You have to make a cup of tea for us as your payment for going through the room,' Clare said, as a joke – but ten minutes later the girl crept back with two cups of tea.

'I presume your friend is still out,' she said, nervously looking at Mary Catherine's bed.

'Of course she is,' said Val. 'It's only three o'clock in the morning.'

Clare said that Valerie was giving them all a reputation for being stone mad. Val said that she wondered what on earth Mary Catherine and James Nolan could be doing until after three in the morning if they weren't in bed together.

About ten minutes later, Mary Catherine came through the window. She and James Nolan *had* been in bed together, and it had been all right. Not *great*, but *all right,* and she would like them to start a novena this minute because her period was due in exactly nine days' time, so if ever a novena was called for it was now.

Dick Dillon told Angela that he hadn't changed his mind. That he wasn't much of a catch for her, and he wasn't as well read, but at least she knew that he'd never turn into a drunk on her. Then he remembered that a drunk is exactly what Angela's father had been and he apologized so much for the remark that she had to tell him to shut up or she would beat him to death with her bicycle.

But *seriously,* he said. Wouldn't it be a good idea? Angela was lonely in that cottage, he was lonely in a little corner of the hotel, his bedroom and sitting room. He would be agreeable to whatever she wanted – live in her cottage, build a new place, he could get a site easily. Angela could go on teaching if she liked. The ban on married teachers had been lifted now. Or she could take a rest from it. He so enjoyed her company. He was never one for the flowery words, but genuinely he had flowery thoughts in his heart.

Angela was thoughtful. She said that in her heart she still felt it would be the single most foolish act since the partition of the country but she wouldn't think of it now. There was something else to the forefront of her mind. But the thing that was in her mind would be out of it one way or another at the end of the summer.

Then she would sit down with him seriously and discuss his suggestion, without any jokes or smart-alec remarks.

'It's not so much a *suggestion,* it's more a *proposal,*' he said, affronted. 'This . . . thing, this worry in the summer. Is there anything I could do to make it easier for you?' he asked.

She looked at him. He had a very kind face. 'No, Dick. Thank you all the same.'

'It isn't another man?' he asked anxiously. 'You're not making up your mind about another person or anything like that?'

'No. There's no other man in that sense at all.'

'You're not thinking of entering the convent?' He was fearful of all the rival possibilities.

'Immaculata would have the place closed down rather than let me into the community,' she said.

'Well, sure one religious in any family is enough,' said Dick Dillon, unerringly putting his finger on the one thing that was guaranteed to set every nerve end jangling. Father Sean O'Hara. Who still wrote excited letters about how much they were all looking forward to the summer.

Paddy Power said it was a very clear day altogether, you could see cliffs and headlands miles and miles away. Nellie had told him he was back early: it would be half an hour before the lunch was ready, the potatoes were still like bullets. Molly said she'd walk a bit along the cliff with him since it was so bright and fresh out.

'Will you go up to see Sheila? You like going there in January.'

'Yes. I was thinking of it. David was a bit offhand on the phone when I suggested it.'

'Offhand?'

'He said he might find it very hard to get any time off to meet me, he just said that he'd like to warn me in advance.'

'Well that's fair enough. I remember it was like that in my time as well, you don't have a minute of your own.'

'Oh, he has minutes of his own all right.'

'What do you mean?'

'He said to me that he heard the Guards had to be called to Dillon's Hotel, I asked how he heard that – we hadn't told him and he said that he had met Clare O'Brien and she'd told him. Josie Dillon had written to her all about it, apparently.'

'Well?' Dr Power couldn't see where all this was leading.

'Well it shows he gets enough minutes off to meet that Clare O'Brien.'

'Molly, don't be giving out about that child. You've always had a down on her.'

'I've had nothing of the sort. I just mentioned to you in passing that it's odd our son has time to meet her when he's not going to be able to have any time to meet his own mother.'

'Now, now, now. He ran into her – what more natural than they talk about Castlebay?'

'No, he didn't say he ran into her, he said when he met her, as if they met all the time. And stop sounding exasperated with me like that. I *know, I* tell you.'

'If he *is* meeting her, would that be the end of the world?'

Molly looked triumphant. 'A minute ago I was drawing conclusions, I was imagining things. Now all of a sudden I'm right.'

'Yes, Molly . . .'

Valerie said you couldn't do a novena for something like that. God just wouldn't listen. Clare said that if anything had happened it had happened now and no amount of prayers could change it. Mary Catherine said that neither of them had understood the nature of prayer. In her parish back in the States it had been very clearly explained. God knew in advance that you were going to pray later. It was foreknowledge, not predestination. They had endless debates about it, but fortunately events overtook them and on the appointed day the news was good, so there was a great sigh of relief from the bedroom of the three ageing eccentrics.

Mary Catherine said she wouldn't run the risk again, although James had said that he would Look After Things. She said she didn't really want to either. She couldn't think why she had in the first place except that she was so sick of him pestering her about it, and saying no, and finding excuses, and thinking up reasons why not. She said he had nearly dropped dead when she said she would go back with him to this flat. The same one that David had lived in . . . They all brought their girls there, it seemed.

But Mary Catherine said they probably talked much more than they actually seduced. James said he was fairly experienced, but without being too technical Mary Catherine thought he wasn't. No honestly it would be too detailed, she couldn't say any more. And she had asked him very casually if he thought that David Power was a ladies' man, and he had said that David was being terribly secretive and the belief was that he was having it off with a fast nurse up in the hospital otherwise why wouldn't he come out to play with the rest of them?

Mary Catherine said she couldn't see the need for secrecy but if it was so desperately important to Clare and David, she'd go along with it. She didn't care much one way or the other she said, she had a far bigger worry of her own. How to brush off James politely. Far from casting her aside once he had his way with her, he was on the phone morning noon and night, presumably hoping to have his way with her over and over again. She didn't want to turn him down too brusquely and she certainly didn't want him to tell everyone that she was a good thing.

In the safety of daylight and public places Clare and David talked about sex. David told her that he never had it with anyone, he had implied to the lads that he was at it all the time, but he actually never had. There was a sort of a near miss on one occasion but he needn't detain her with that. Anyway that had all to do with drink and nothing to do with love.

They discussed almost abstractly what they would do if they had the opportunity presented to them. Suppose now for example that Clare had her own flat where nobody would bother them. Suppose David had his own place. Would their resolution be so strong?

Clare said that she could never go through the anxiety.

She didn't like to tell tales on Mary Catherine, but it turned out that David knew anyway. This was a bit alarming, but they couldn't fault James really since Valerie and Clare knew all about it as well.

David said that there were probably ways round the anxiety bit, and what with being a doctor and everything he'd have more access to the ways round it than anyone else. Anyway people went to the North of Ireland where you could get contraceptives legally, so there should be no problem there.

'That's *if* we were thinking of it seriously,' Clare said.

'Yes, that's if we were,' David agreed.

Emer rang Clare at the hostel and asked her would she do her a great favour. Kevin had been asked to go and find out about new educational aids in London. For three whole days. And would you believe it, she was going too. Her mother was looking after Daniel. And what she'd really like is if someone were to stay in the house, to keep an eye on it. Would Clare like to? Clare said she'd like to very much.

She contemplated not telling him. For two whole hours.

Then she told him. He asked for his three days' leave at that time.

'I hope we won't have to be doing any more novenas,' Valerie grumbled.

'Suppose I never want to see you again afterwards?' she said as they went to the bedroom.

'Why wouldn't you want to see me again afterwards?'

'Mary Catherine didn't with James.'

'They don't love each other. They're only just pretending to.'

'So being in love would make all the difference?'

'That's what I've always heard.'

David stroked her long fair hair on the pillow afterwards. He kept moving his hand from the top of her head to the end of the hair. He was afraid to speak in case she was hurt or unhappy.

Her eyes were open as she lay there beside him but he

couldn't read her face. Was she frightened? Or disappointed? Had she felt anything like the pleasure that he had, or the peace he felt now?

'David,' she said. Her voice was very small.

He gave a great cry of delight and gathered her up in his arms and held her to him. He couldn't believe that it was possible to be so happy.

James Nolan tracked David down eventually.

'I thought you'd been murdered and the body buried,' he said. 'Nobody knew where you were.'

'Is anything wrong?' David asked quickly.

'Depends how you view it. Your mother's coming to stay with mine tomorrow. Both maternals are a bit shirty that you couldn't be found. I think you'd better ring your own to pat down ruffled feathers. Where were you anyway?'

'Wouldn't it *have* to be this weekend she was looking for me? Wouldn't you bloody know.'

James shrugged. 'I did my best. I thought maybe you'd gone off with a bird. I said there was a match on and that you might have gone to that.'

'A match for three days!'

'I said it was in Northern Ireland.'

'OK, that'll do. Thanks, James.'

'Don't hang up, where *were* you?'

'As you said. At a match.'

'I'll deal with you. You're meant to be coming to lunch with us on Sunday.'

Molly Power was martyred, on the phone.

'Please don't think I'm checking up on you. I don't mind where you go on your time off. Your father's always saying you're a grown man. I agree entirely.'

'I'm glad to know you're coming up to Dublin,' he said, gritting his teeth.

'It's just that the Nolans thought it was so *odd* that you couldn't be found. I mean, David, nobody wants to keep checking up on you, I've told you that, it's just that if anything happened to your father – God forbid that it should – and we were looking for you . . .'

He held the receiver at arm's length. He would like to have smashed it against the wall.

' . . . do you think you'll be able to *tear* yourself away from *whatever* is occupying you so much to come and meet us when I'm in Dublin?'

'I'm really looking forward to Sunday lunch,' he said, willing an eagerness into his voice.

'Am I not going to see you *until* Sunday?'

'No . . . I meant that, in particular . . . of course I'll see you before then.'

He leaned his head against the wall when the three minutes were up. 'Clare,' he whispered to himself. 'Clare, Clare.'

'Are you all right Doctor?' A young nurse with freckles was looking at him. A lot of the young housemen went a bit loopy, she had been told, and she thought it could well be true.

Angela read the letter with great surprise. If Clare had got into a political group, or become very active in a cause, she would not have been so surprised, but David, lovely big nice David Power who was coming back to Castlebay next year to share the work with his father? How had it happened? And what would Clare do if she married him? She would marry him, it seemed, reading between the lines. Clare had said how they both felt as strongly as each other and they couldn't bear to be apart. She said he had it as badly as she did. Angela was bewildered, reading the outpourings. Bewildered because there seemed only one thing to say. So she said it:

I suppose you must work as hard as you possibly can, get your First as you know you can, then relax, and do your Higher Diploma. And then, who knows? I might be put out to grass here and you'd be over-qualified, but I'm sure they'd take you in the school. But as Mrs Power, young

344

Mrs Power, would you *want* to work? Would you want to teach all day . . . ?

Clare read the letter in dismay. She had been *stupid, stupid, stupid,* to tell Angela. The woman understood *nothing.* There was *no* question of going back to Castlebay. That was what all the *agonizing* was about. David didn't want to, she didn't want to. The *root* of the problem was how to explain this to David's father without breaking his heart. In a million *years* Angela wouldn't understand. She had been too long in Castlebay, that was her trouble.

'I'm going to meet your mother-in-law and your intended on Sunday,' Mary Catherine said.

'How on earth . . . ?'

'James has asked me to lunch. He said Mrs Power was coming and that David would be there too. Didn't he tell you?'

'Yes. It slipped my mind.' David hadn't told her. She was furious.

'I didn't want to talk about anything bad, that's all.'

'Your mother coming to Dublin isn't bad.'

'Yes it is. It makes it all more real, it brings that side of things into our life here.'

'She comes every year. You don't have to announce to her at lunch in the Nolans' house that your plans for the future have changed.'

'No. But I'd prefer to be with you on Sunday. Not there.'

'Mary Catherine's going. They must be having a big do.'

'*That's* an idea. Why don't I get James to ask you too?'

'Are you stark staring mad?' she asked.

The ideal thing would have been to find somewhere near the hospital, but the roads were too posh and the prices of flats were too high. If they went far out of the city they could afford somewhere nice but then it would be pointless, David would hardly ever be able to escape to somewhere so far away. They read the small ads in the evening papers and couldn't believe how quickly any reasonable-sounding bedsitter was snapped up. Sometimes they found long queues on the doorstep of a place that had only been advertised that very day. They got to know other young people and exchanged information. Rathmines wasn't too bad, people said. It was about twenty minutes' walk from UCD. Lots of people had bed-sitters there. They went on an expedition, just knocking on every door: that was meant to be as good a way as any. Clare looked around at the area. There was a big main street and a lot of tall houses which had once been family homes but now housed several families. Some were very well kept with well-painted halls, nice half-moon tables where the post for each flat dweller was laid out in neat rows. Others had torn lino, walls badly in need of papering and a faintly unpleasant smell about them. These were the ones they were going to be able to afford.

It was a nice area, they decided. A bit like a village or a place all on its own rather than part of the Dublin they knew. But there were buses constantly back and forth, it was near the canal for walks and, because this was where a lot of young people had flats, the shops stayed open later. There was also a chip shop nearby. Clare looked at it gratefully. This might be very useful indeed.

They looked at the small grimy room up three flights of stairs, in the big house with the uncared-for garden and the peeling paintwork. They looked at each other and said yes. They handed over the first month's rent and moved in on Saturday. The landlord said he hated students usually but seeing that this was a young married couple, that was quite different. He did hope that there was no question of a child yet because they would understand he had to run a quiet house. They shook their heads. No, there would be no question of that and they quite understood.

David had given her a plain ring which cost fifteen shillings; one day it would be a proper one. Like one day it would be a proper place to live. They had an oil stove, and the place smelled of paraffin; the bed was a bit lumpy and the little cooking ring was very dirty after the last tenants.

The bathroom was down two floors. But it was their own. And apart from Valerie and Mary Catherine who had to know everything, nobody else in the world knew where they were.

They went out to buy bacon and sausages and a bottle of red vermouth for their first supper. They bought a bookcase at a second-hand shop because the landlord said he didn't like his walls being mutilated. The walls were so rough and uneven, and had such shaky plaster, they would have been hard put to take a nail let alone a shelf. Clare felt settled when the books were in place.

He kissed her hands and looked up at her face. 'Look, it's all going to be all right. You'll study and I'll come to you every minute I can. You'll get your First and I'll finish my year and start somewhere else, just as if it were the most natural thing in the world. I won't be an intern, we can live together like this, only better. I'll be getting real money.'

'So will I,' Clare said excitedly, 'if I'm tutoring.'

'We haven't a worry in the world. If we can do this . . .' he waved his hand expansively around the small shabby room '. . . if we can do this in a few days, can't we do anything?'

It was a lonely Sunday, but all Sundays could be a bit down in Dublin.

Clare scraped at the cooking ring for a while, then she went out to buy a Sunday paper. A bell was ringing and great crowds were going into the big church in the main street of Rathmines. She hurried past. There had been five Sundays since she was in mortal sin. She had gone to Mass as usual the first Sunday, but it was ridiculous, she couldn't say any prayers, it was hypocritical to kneel there knowing that she was going to commit further mortal sin. For all her brave words to David, it was a sin, and that was that. There was no point in acting the part of a person who was praying. If Clare were the Lord she'd prefer those kind of people not to come to church at all.

Val had gone to a lunch where six people were going to make a curry. It sounded awful, yet Clare would like to have been there. She didn't feel she could ask Emer and Kevin if

347

she could call, it seemed like using them, and anyway she did feel slightly embarrassed going back to their place even though they had no idea why she should be. Mary Catherine was at this Nolan lunch and so was David. Perhaps she should have said yes, and agreed when, in his innocence, he had suggested she should be invited too. It would have been hard to take: Mrs Power's rage and scorn would have communicated itself to everyone there and Clare didn't really like James or Caroline Nolan enough to think they might have supported her. But still this was very hard too, this hanging around and waiting.

It was like being in love with a married man, like that girl who was so depressed in the hostel last year. She had been having a romance with one of the lecturers; she was suicidal at weekends.

'Don't be so silly,' Clare told herself aloud. 'There is no comparison. We have a flat together of our own. He'll be coming back here. It's his *mother* he's seeing, for God's sake, not a wife. Why feel so chilly? Why this awful sense of doom?'

There were five cars parked in the drive in front of the Nolans' house: Mr Nolan's, his wife's, Caroline's and James's. David didn't know who the last one belonged to. He ran lightly up the steps. Breeda opened the door. She took his coat, and put it in the breakfast room, where a lot of other coats were already hanging and draped.

He went up the stairs to the first-floor drawing room. His mother was standing by the fireplace, leaning on the mantelpiece. She looked very made-up and a bit fussy, David thought. Too many frills at her neck and her cuffs. He didn't have time to see who else was there, since Molly gave a scream of welcome.

'The *prodigal*! He's torn himself away!'

He wished she hadn't. It made such a commotion. He should have gone in quietly and greeted James's mother and father. But now because she had called such attention to him, he had to go straight to her.

'You're looking marvellous, Mother,' he said, kissing her on the cheek.

348

'Oh, you're a worse flatterer than your father,' she said, still in this high silly voice that he hated.

He looked around. Mrs Nolan looked vague and sort of fluttery as usual. David wondered yet again why his mother didn't see how strange Sheila Nolan was, how dotty, for want of a more technical word.

'Lovely to be here, Mrs Nolan,' he said dutifully.

'Oh, David.' She looked at him as if she had never seen him before but as if she had learned his name to make him feel welcome. 'How good of you to come to see us. Your mother is here too you know.' Sheila Nolan looked around vaguely.

'Yes, yes. I've just seen her.' David was beginning to feel trapped, to experience the hunted sensation that Mrs Nolan managed to create all around her.

'David – they tell me you love sherry. Sweet or dry?' The woman stared into his eyes as if waiting for the Meaning of Life in his answer.

'Dry would be very nice, Mrs Nolan.' He *hated* sherry of any kind.

He saw James had managed to get a gin and tonic, but it was too late, the sherry glass was in his hand. Caroline was talking to Mary Catherine by the window. Two priests were talking to Mr Nolan. One of them looked familiar, yet David hadn't met him before. Breeda came in and passed round cheese straws and little bits of celery filled with cheese.

The voices of his mother and Mrs Nolan talking archly at him receded, and David wanted Clare and their little room and a tin of tomato soup. He wanted to be miles from this overheated room and babble of chat. He answered the questions automatically: yes, it was pretty hard work, no, he didn't know that specialist, but of course he knew him by name, and how nice of the Nolans to say they'd have a word. He asked his mother about home, and about his father, and had Bones recovered from the terrible paint incident. Molly Power said that Bones had never looked beautiful but nowadays he would actually frighten you to look at him. They had cut off so much of his coat where the spilled paint had all hardened and matted. He looked very odd but had no idea that his appearance had changed. Old as he was, he still ran round in circles barking happily. Molly said you couldn't take him for a walk anywhere because the explanations were so lengthy when you met anyone, and the memory of finding him lying on his back on the kitchen floor in a pool of red paint was not one you wanted to relive.

'Will you be down before Easter to see him? And us indeed,' she asked.

'Not a chance . . . oh and about Easter . . .' he began, but Sheila Nolan had clapped her hands. Lunch was ready.

They moved to another very overheated room with nine places set around a table, two bottles of wine already open and a huge joint of beef on the carving table.

'Isn't this the life,' said Molly Power wistfully as they went into the room with its heavy dark furniture and thick curtains. Her voice was envious for a life which could assemble people around a table like this, far from Castlebay.

David took his mind from the dingy bed-sitter not two miles away, and forced himself to feel some sympathy for his mother. Dad had always said that she needed very little to make her happy. And it was true, there she was, revelling in the showy lunch that Sheila Nolan had organized in her honour. He was not going to be rude to her. He wasn't going to spoil her visit. He'd tell her about Easter later.

David was sitting between Caroline and one of the priests. Caroline was in high form and full of confidences and whispered questions.

'Do you think James is serious about the Yankee lady? Oh go on, he must tell you. I don't believe this strong silent act. Men do tell. I know they do.'

'But you are so wrong, Caroline, men are much too gentle and sensitive to discuss their emotions, would that we had the strength of women, able to bring anything out in the open, air it, examine it and dust it down.'

She laughed. 'Do you think they're *involved,* if you know what I mean? Once upon a time he used to be only interested whether she had money, now he's a bit lovesick, I think.'

They both looked at Mary Catherine, who was battling

with interrogation from Mrs Power and glances of fluttery hostility from Mrs Nolan.

'Why don't you ask her? She'd tell all, the way women do.'

'No, she's like a tin of sardines that one, I wouldn't get to first base, to use her own kind of language.'

'And how about your own romances. Are you the toast of the Incorporated Law Society?'

'You only ask me that to break my heart. You know I think of no other man.' Caroline waved her eyelashes up and down at him jokily.

'What chance would a humble country hick like myself have with a sophisticated girl like you?' David smiled. He had always liked Caroline. He had fancied her of course when he was very young, and in phases ever since, she was so easy to talk to, so joky, and she took nothing too seriously. He remembered with a start that his mother had always regarded them as a likely match, and with some alarm noticed that Mrs Power and Mrs Nolan were looking at them fondly.

Caroline was unaware of it. 'I never tried seriously to capture you, David, I hate failure, I feel that with you I have to bide my time, wait till you're ready for me, and fall into my arms like a ripe plum. Maybe on the rebound from some other female.'

She threw back her head of dark hair and laughed. Clare had once said that Caroline Nolan had too many good, white, even teeth, it was a sign of great money and breeding, rich people didn't rot their children's teeth with sticky things, and rich people took their children to the dentist regularly.

Caroline did look very healthy.

She looked very attractive too: she had a lemon-coloured jumper and a green and gold sort of tartan-type skirt. She wore a big amber necklace. She said that she must have been mad to listen to the nuns who said that a degree was the answer. It wasn't the answer, it was the question. You had to ask yourself what to do then. Fortunately now that she had done the boring secretarial bit she was nicely installed in her father's office as a solicitor's apprentice where she should have been years ago. Before she became old and grey.

She turned to pass the vegetables in their heavy tureens and David found himself talking to the priest with the small buttons of eyes.

'I know your face from somewhere, Father. Would there have been a picture of you in the paper or anything?'

'I hope not. I'm in bad enough books with the archbishop already. No, I don't think I've come across you – I know you're from Castlebay. Your mother was telling me before you arrived.'

'I'm not such a genius as she makes out,' he said.

'She didn't make you out to be a genius at all,' the priest said.

'I don't know if that's good or bad.'

'We do have a mutual friend though. Angela O'Hara. She and I met at a wedding in Rome, oh it must be eight years ago now. A long time. But somehow we all remained great friends. A couple called Quinn got married . . .'

David remembered why the priest was familiar. He was the Father Flynn whose round face shone out of the wedding photos in Kevin and Emer Quinn's bedroom.

The photo that he had looked at for a long time as Clare slept in his arms in the big bed that belonged to Kevin and Emer.

Mary Catherine didn't like David's mother one bit. She thought that Clare was going to have a hard time of it with this one.

'Tell me about Castlebay,' she said brightly, smiling her perfect smile and pretending an interest she didn't feel. 'I hear it's one lively town.'

'You hear wrong,' Mrs Power said definitely. 'It's a small community, very, very small, swollen to about twenty times its size in the summer. A lot of *riff-raff* have been coming recently, and *loud* people. It used to be a wonderful family resort. Remember, Sheila, when you all came down . . . ?'

Molly caught David's eye and realized that she mustn't run down the place she was trying to get him to come home to. ' . . . But I think that's just my age, really. For young people, for young *professional* people, *working* there, for the *doctor* or the young *solicitor,* or the people in the hotel, it's a wonderful life. And a lot of very nice people a few miles back from the coast. Very nice indeed. Wonderful big estates and everything.' She nodded owlishly.

David raged within. She had never been invited to any of the big estates nor did she even know anyone who had. Why did she try to impress people with a line of chat which was just making her pathetic?

'I was thinking of spending a few days there this summer. When I do my degree I'll have to go back to the States, so best see a bit of Ireland while I can.'

Molly was a little nonplussed. On the one hand the girl had been talking about her father being a postman and her mother working in a clothes factory of some sort, hanging garments on rails. On the other hand, the Nolans seemed to think that James was serious about her. Who knew what way to jump?

'Well, that would be very nice, dear,' she said non-committally. 'Be sure to let us know when you arrive, and come to see us.'

'Thank you, Mrs Power.'

'Will you stay in Dillon's Hotel?'

Mary Catherine spoke without thinking. 'I guess Clare will find me a bed . . .'

'Clare?'

It was too late. Clare had asked her not to bring up her name at all, but it was done now.

'Clare O'Brien, I share a room, I've been sharing a room with her.'

Molly Power sniffed. 'I doubt if there's going to be any room for you with the poor O'Briens – but maybe Clare didn't describe it to you properly. It's not a place that anyone could *stay* in.'

David's face flushed a dark red.

Mary Catherine spoke quickly. 'I explained it badly, I meant to say that Clare said she would book me in somewhere. But heavens, who knows if I'll ever get there, there's so much work to do . . . Was your last year full of frights and horrors, Caroline?'

'Dreadful. I didn't know you shared a room with Clare O'Brien.'

'You never asked,' Mary Catherine said with spirit.

'I know Clare O'Brien,' said the small priest. 'A very bright girl. She won that scholarship for three years from your county, didn't she? I always think it must be the most terrible pressure on young people when they get that kind of bursary . . .' He chattered on lightly, knowing there was some tension in the air but not knowing where it came from.

'So you know Clare O'Brien too, Father? My goodness, doesn't she get about?' She turned to Sheila Nolan. 'Remember them, Sheila? Big, straggling family, not a penny to bless themselves with?'

'I don't think so.' Sheila Nolan's vacant blue eyes were vaguer than ever.

'Oh you *must* remember them, we used to go in to buy ice-creams there. Though I never particularly liked dealing there. Not terribly *clean.*'

'Why did we buy ice-creams there, then?' Mrs Nolan was bewildered.

'It was near the beach, that's why, I think.'

'I would never have bought ice-creams there had I known it wasn't clean.' Mrs Nolan's thin hand went to her throat as if regretting the possible germs that might still lurk there.

'No, no. That's not the point. I was just telling you who the family were. One of them put her mind to her books and she's come a long way. Everyone here is on calling terms with her except you and me . . .' Molly Power looked fussed and annoyed. Sheila Nolan looked confused and worried about possibly unhygienic ice-creams eaten in the past.

Father Flynn thought he saw the lie of the land. He asked his colleague, Father Kennedy who was the new curate in the Nolans' parish, to tell them all the story of the archbishop's garden. It was a harmless little tale but it distracted them.

Father Flynn looked at David levelly. 'People often sound much more cruel than they are. In their hearts they're probably very kind.'

'Yes,' David mumbled.

354

'Eat up. That's lovely beef. I bet you don't get food like that in the hospital.'

David didn't respond.

'And there's nothing for concentrating the mind like eating.'

David had to smile. 'I knew the clergy were dangerous,' he laughed.

'That's better. Give Clare my love.'

'Were you the priest who was so helpful about her brother?'

'You must be a *good* friend if she told you all that. Yes. Not that I was all that much help as it turned out.'

'Clare said you were great.'

'Is she going to get a First? She was very eager about that.'

'I think so. I'll keep her at it.'

They spoke low and stopped when Caroline turned to join the conversation.

At the other end of the table Molly whispered behind her hand to Sheila. 'I can't explain it, but I *never* liked that girl. She didn't ever do anything against me, but I don't *trust* her. Do you know the feeling?'

'I do.' Sheila was equally conspiratorial. Her glance rested on Mary Catherine. 'That American girl is going back where she belongs,' she said.

'The pity of it is, that it's hard to say where Clare O'Brien belongs now and where she should go back to,' Molly whispered.

She was lying on the bed reading the verses in the Memoriam column. 'Listen David, listen to this one: "Now every year upon this day/We ask just why you went away." '

Clare pealed with laughter. 'They couldn't could they? Each year on her anniversary, they sit down and say, "What *could* have happened to her?" '

He sat beside her. 'Why aren't you studying? You said you'd have a full day without me what are you doing reading this rubbish? Where are your books?' He looked around, there was no sign of study.

'Don't give out to me. What was it like?'

355

'Oh, very Nolanish, you know.'

'I don't know.'

'Men are hopeless at describing things, you're always saying that. There was too much to eat.'

'I know. You smell of food.' She nuzzled him.

'Oh, and your friend Father Flynn was there. He's over for a few days' holiday.'

Her face was bright at the thought of him; then it looked puzzled. 'How did he know you knew me?'

'Castlebay and everything.'

'Yes.' She looked at him. 'David. Was there any more?'

'I nearly lost my temper with my mother and walked out . . .'

'Tell me the whole thing.'

It wasn't *so* bad. Nothing they hadn't known already: that David's mother did not think the sun and moon and stars shone from Clare. That was all. Why was David so upset?

'I didn't want to be there. I wanted to be here.'

'You're here now.'

Much later they did the boldest thing they had ever done. They ate a tin of pears, with spoons, straight from the tin, and bits of the juice kept falling on their bodies and they had to lick it off their shoulders – or wherever it fell. Towards the end of the tin they were covered in the sweet pear syrup and so was the bed. They laughed until they both ached. They dropped the pear tin down on the floor, and put their sticky arms around each other again.

'Is this squalor? Is this what we live in?' Clare asked.

'It's lovely, whatever it is,' David said.

Father Flynn decided to go to Castlebay to see it for himself. He booked himself into Dillon's Hotel, made a courtesy call on Father O'Dwyer, and told Sergeant McCormack that he had heard her highly spoken of, which inspired her to make scones for his tea. Choosing his time well, he went to O'Brien's shop and told them that Tommy was getting on well, with a prison visitor who was bringing him picture books of wild flowers and he sometimes drew them. They marvelled at some English woman who would take the time to go to visit an Irish boy with no teeth in gaol for robbery with violence. Father Flynn said he knew it was hard, but the odd letter, with no criticism or abuse but just descriptions of what life at home was like, would work wonders. Clare had been unfailing in her letters. Agnes was proud to hear that. Clare had never got uppity despite her great success and advances, she told Father Flynn.

'You must be hoping she'll find a good man and marry him and settle down,' the little priest said.

'That one? Marry and settle down? She's going to be a professor, no less. She never had much of an interest in boys when she was young, and I used to think that was a mercy. Chrissie had far too great an interest in them. But not Clare. I suppose in a few years she might meet a professor somewhere, but she'll be gone from us in Castlebay, I knew that the day she got into the secondary school.'

'Suppose she were to marry and come back here?'

'But who would she marry here, father? Hasn't she more booklearning than anyone in the parish?'

He called on the Powers too, because deep in his heart he was a man filled with curiosity. A big, square house, built to withstand the gales and spray from the sea. Father Flynn noted that it must have to be painted every year. There was a large garden, part of it obviously leading to a cliffpath down to the sea. It wasn't an elegant house; but it was sturdy and substantial.

Inside too it was comfortable. No antiques, nothing very old, but nice furniture and good carpets, big arrangements of flowers and greenery on window sills and surfaces. A pleasant maid with wispy hair and a broad smile showed him into the drawing room while she went to get the mistress. Molly was delighted to meet him again, and flattered that he should have come to call.

Father Flynn liked David's father enormously: a bluff, kind man who was an old-style adviser to his patients. Probably does a lot of the work that dry stick Father O'Dwyer should be doing, Father Flynn thought ruefully.

Over a drink, a lot of admiration for their magnificent view of the sea and some words of sympathy to an elderly mad dog, half-shaved, half-particles of red paint, he talked to the big warm man. He told him about the work with the emigrants in Britain, some of its lighter side as well as its gloomy overtones; that it was often the weakest and the least prepared who were the ones who had to emigrate.

Dr Power told him of the good and bad things in Castlebay. People would never die of loneliness, as they might in a big English city; but attitudes could be cruel, and tolerance was low. In nearly forty years of practice here he had seen a lot of intolerance: families couldn't cope with what they called 'shame and disgrace'. He was sure Father Flynn knew well what he meant. You didn't stamp out young love and young desire by refusing to face up to the consequences.

Dr Power said it was great to have lived through the years that saw TB being wiped out. When he started off, people still hid the fact that they had tuberculosis in the family. It was denied, and if anyone had a spot on the lung it was considered a disgrace and something that would prevent other members of the family being able to marry well.

Father Flynn said he had had the pleasure of meeting Dr Power's son, a fine boy, in Dublin. What were his plans?

Dr Power didn't know, precisely. If the boy were going to work back home then the sooner he came back the better. He would want to find a wife for himself; and it would be wiser for him to be installed here, and choose from here, rather than starting off a life with some girl in a big place with lots of life in it and then asking the poor woman to come back here with him. There was a slight sadness which Father Flynn thought must be hearking back to his own situation.

'And do you think he's met anyone that suits him yet?' he asked.

'Divil a fear of it. He's having too good a time with all those nurses up in the hospital,' said Dr Power with a laugh.

Father Flynn talked about it with Angela too.

'Aren't you a terrible old woman?' she teased him.

'Terrible. That's why I'm so good in confession. I'm never bored and I like to meddle in other people's lives.'

'Are you meddling with David Power and Clare O'Brien?' she asked.

'It worries me a bit, and I only know the fringes of it,' he said. 'I don't know why I feel that it's so doomed. But that's the word that keeps coming to me.'

'It could just be First Love.'

'It could.' He was doubtful. 'But I must get over this tendency to play God. Are you going to let this brother of yours come here and upset everyone?'

'I promised him in Rome. Those were my words. That's how I bought him off from doing it years ago. I can't go back on that now. He's like a child, you can't go back on a promise to a child.'

'Children can do dangerous things. Sometimes promises needn't be kept.'

'Is it dangerous for him to come home? He's had his heart set on it. I don't have children, you don't. We don't know all this about showing them their roots. I mean, I don't think it matters, and you don't. But suppose it's everything? Then he should do it. I'll survive it if I have to.'

There was a silence. He drank his tea, and looked admiringly around the book-lined room. When he spoke, it was with the voice of one introducing an entirely new subject.

'That's a very civilized fellow in the hotel, Dick Dillon, brother of the man running it, I think. Very pleasant sort of a man altogether. Someone you could always rely on, I'd imagine, if there was a crisis.'

'I'm sure you imagine right, Father Flynn. Such a pity that you got over this tendency to play God, isn't it? You could have had a field day there.'

Before he left Castlebay Father Flynn decided to buy a few postcards of the place: not the garish ones which looked like everywhere else, but those nice black and white ones full of outlines which Angela often used to send him.

He asked Josie Dillon where they were on sale.

'We haven't had them for ages. I used to put them up just to please Gerry Doyle – that's the photographer – he took them, you see. But visitors mainly preferred the coloured ones. But now you mention it, he never brought any replacements. You could ask in Doyle's, it's the place with the big bright sign, Doyle's Photographics. You can't miss it.'

You couldn't miss it. Josie Dillon was right.

There was a small, dark-haired man inside.

'Father? What can I do for you?'

He was a likeable fellow, with an easy smile.

'This is a very grand place.' Father Flynn looked round in admiration. 'I'd not have thought Castlebay would have something so fine as this.'

'Don't let my mother hear you, or my sister, or, Lord rest him, my father. They would all agree with you.'

'Well I'm not a businessman – what would I know? Is it too small an order to ask do you have those nice pictures of the place, the black and white ones. They were very good. I kept the ones people sent me.'

Gerry flushed with pleasure. 'Go on, is that a fact?'

'I can't find them in the shops.'

'I didn't bother. Hold on till I see where they are.' He pulled out drawers here and there, and called to an assistant. There was difficulty in finding them.

'It doesn't look as though I'm much of a businessman either,' Gerry grinned.

'If it's too much trouble . . .' Father Flynn began.

'No. It's a matter of honour now.' He found them. 'Here they are.'

'Could I have . . . er a dozen, please, assorted views.' Father Flynn had been going to buy three cards, but after all this trouble on his behalf he felt it would seem piffling.

Gerry had made a bundle and thrust them at him.

'There's more than twelve there.'

'Nobody else ever praised them before. I'd like you to have them. As a present.'

'That's extraordinarily kind of you . . . Mr Doyle,' Father Flynn said in some embarrassment.

'Not at all. You keep sending them to bishops and priests and tell them to get their ordinations and enthronements recorded by me.'

'You're a very fine photographer. I'd be delighted to put any work in your way. But I'm sure you hardly need it.'

Father Flynn looked around again at the big counter, the carpeted floor, the large framed photographs on the wall. It had all the appearances of a studio in a large city. He recognized a picture of Clare on the wall – taken a few years ago, but very recognizable as the same face.

'Is that Clare?' he asked.

'Do you know Clare?' Gerry was pleased. 'That was when she got the Murray Prize, a scholarship to UCD. They sent me to take the winner. I never believed it was going to be Clare. I hadn't enough faith. Fortunately she did.'

'She works very hard, certainly. I met her with friends in Dublin.' Something made him uneasy about the way Gerry was looking at the picture.

'She's very unusual. For Castlebay that is. I don't think she's from here at all. I think she's a changeling. I've always thought that. Like myself.' He laughed to take the oddness away from the statement. 'That's why I'll marry her. When she's ready. When she's got all this studying out of her system.'

'And bring her back here?' Father Flynn sounded politely doubtful: inside he felt a slight tremor of anxiety.

'Oh, no. Clare's grown well beyond Castlebay. And as soon as I get this business organized, so will I.'

'Tell me about Gerry Doyle. The photographer,' Father Flynn asked Dick Dillon.

'Trouble from way back,' said Dick. 'But the women won't hear a word against him. Even a sensible woman like Angela O'Hara says he's got a nice way with him.' Dick Dillon snorted, and Father Flynn shivered a little in the sunshine.

Sometimes they finished at about ten o'clock, and everyone else in the Res went for a few drinks before closing time. But

David never joined them. These days, he would hare out of the hospital down to the bus stop.

'I don't know why you even call it the Residence,' one of the other doctors said to him. 'You barely reside here at all.'

David grinned. 'I had no idea we were going to be on call so much, I thought we'd have far more freedom.'

'No, you didn't. You knew you'd be cooped up here, you just didn't think you'd meet such an available girl.' The red-headed registrar laughed at his own perception.

David Power's face was cold and hard. 'I beg your pardon?' he said.

'It was only a joke . . .'

'I didn't think it was a bit funny.'

'No . . . Well, I'm sorry. I mean I don't know anything about it, I know nothing.'

'That's right, you know nothing, which gives you licence to say everything. That about sums you up.'

He marched, white with anger, out of the Res sitting room, having thrown his white coat over the back of a chair.

'What did I say?' Bar pleaded to the empty room.

It was cold and wet. The bus took for ever to arrive and even longer to get to Rathmines. He burned with rage still. A nice, *available* girl. *Available. Clare.* How dare he?

David was tired and very much on edge when he climbed the stairs. Clare was at the makeshift desk they had rigged up for her with planks of wood and builder's bricks. She was wearing mittens on her hands which made her look so endearing he stopped and stared at her with pleasure.

Her eyes were tired and had circles under them. 'Lord, are you home already? Is that the time?'

He was pleased she called it home, but a little disappointed that she hadn't been waiting for him, looking out for him.

'Did you get a lot done today?'

'I'm back into it again, thank heavens. I didn't notice the time or anything. I heard a man selling oil so I rushed downstairs with the can and got some.' She looked proudly at the glowing little oil heater.

'It's lovely and cosy. What are we having to eat?'

She looked stricken. 'There's nothing. I meant to get something.'

'There must be something. Toast even?'

'No. There's nothing.' She opened the little press. 'Look, real Mother Hubbard stuff. Bare. We'll go out and get chips,' she added when she saw how disappointed he was.

'I only just got in,' he said. 'I'm dog tired.'

Clare got up and reached for her coat. 'Stay here, I'll go out for chips and bring them home.'

'Then I'll be here all on my own,' he grumbled.

She looked at him startled. This wasn't his way of talking.

'Darling Clare, I'm sorry. I'm just desperately overtired, I hardly know what I'm saying.'

She was full of concern. 'What are you apologizing for? Sit there. Rest for ten minutes. I'll be back and we'll have a feast.' She wouldn't hear of him moving.

She took his shoes off and pulled the two pillows into a bundle behind him. She said no to money, she had some. Dinner would be her treat. She was gone down the stairs, and he felt guilty.

What a way to come home. Like a typical husband shouting, 'Where's my tea?' This was a hopeless way to go on. Both of them so tired they could hardly talk. No money, no comfort. If they had more money Clare could have lived in a flat near the hospital: they wouldn't have this smelly stove, and this filthy house with bicycles, and the smell of urine downstairs in the hall.

He felt restless, got up and walked over to her desk. In her big, firm writing with the funny old-fashioned fountain pen and ink, not a ballpoint like everyone else, she had pages of notes.

She had been concentrating on economic history lately. The works of John Maynard Keynes were this week's project . . . she had taken notes in the library, now she had been sorting them out and fitting them into her scheme. She was so bright and hungry to know. He wondered had he lost some of that himself, he used to feel a bit that way at school, and so did James Nolan then. Nowadays James was so languid it was hard to know what he felt, and David was so tired and so used to sleeping with an ear ready to be called to a ward that he would have thought that hunger for information was a luxury.

There was a letter to Clare on the desk in a brown business envelope. The odd thing was that it was addressed here, to this flat. Nobody knew they lived there, *nobody*. And even worse, it was addressed to her as Clare O'Brien. They had told the landlord they were married. It had a Castlebay postmark.

David had never read anyone else's letter in his life. This time he justified it. He wanted to know. If he asked her she would tell him, and there would be an explanation; but he had already been so testy and crotchety tonight he didn't trust himself. He would just have a quick look and then nothing need be said. He pulled the short letter out of the envelope. It was on headed paper which said 'Doyle's Photographics' and it was signed Love Gerry.

Clare had bought them a choc-ice each as a treat. The man in the shop said they must be supermen to eat ice cream in weather like this. She unwrapped the chips and found plates. There was an awful plastic flower in a pot which they always put on their table for meals and made jokes about Doing the Flowers. They had tomato sauce and salt as well as the vinegar that the shop had provided. Clare chattered happily about the advantages of living in bed-sitter land where you could go out any hour of the day and night and get food.

David said nothing.

'Lord, you really are tired. Maybe you should just go to bed a couple of the really bad nights there, so you don't have to drag yourself up here.'

'Maybe,' he said.

'Did anything happen?'

'No.'

'Is anything worrying you, then?'

'That letter.' He pointed to the desk.

'What letter?' She stood up. There were two letters: one

was from her mother addressed to The Ladies' Reading Room at UCD. She had said that this was a quicker way of getting your post and her mother hadn't questioned it.

'This one?' she held up the brown envelope.

'Yes.'

'If you read it, why are you worried?' Her voice was cold now.

'I didn't read it. I swear to you. But I know who it's from. And I was wondering why you gave him our address and told him you lived here. This is our secret. And we're meant to be man and wife. Why the hell is Gerry-bloody-Doyle allowed into anything and everything? And don't tell me what everyone says when his name is mentioned, that *it doesn't count telling Gerry*, or *Gerry knows everything*, or *everyone loves Gerry*, because I find that sickening.'

She had taken the letter out of the envelope and was reading:

Dear Clare,
I did what you asked me, I hope to hell it doesn't get lost in the post or I'll look a nice criminal.

The place is full of activity here, your Chrissie getting ready to produce your nephew or niece, our Fiona getting ready to marry Frank Conway, Josie walking out with a very suitable older man. I suppose you know all the details. Only you and I left around from the old guard.

Send a card or something so that I know it arrived OK.
Love Gerry.

She read this, brushing aside his protestations that he didn't want to hear it. She threw the letter on the bed at him, she reached into a drawer and took out a post office book and threw that too.

'I asked him to get my post office book for me from my room at home in Castlebay. I didn't want Mam asking what I needed my savings for. I need my savings, you bloody, suspicious, mean-minded pig, because now that I live here I have to buy things that I didn't have to buy when I lived in the hostel. Like milk, and bread, and tea, and sugar, and packets of soup and Vim. And I pay a share of the rent here. And it all costs money. And I don't have a penny left. In fact I owe Valerie three pounds. So in order not to appear a kept woman or a hanger-on, or to define even *more* the fact that I am poor Clare O'Brien and you are rich David Power, I sent for my savings account.'

Her eyes blazed with rage. 'I asked him to send it here because I didn't want a valuable thing like a post office book with sixty-three pounds in it, money I've been saving for three years, to get lost in college or get mislaid at the hostel. And Gerry Doyle doesn't give a tuppenny damn if I live here or on the top of the Dublin mountains, so I gave him this address. *And* I was not going to tell him that I am pretending to be your wife, so I gave him my name. *And* the landlord no more thinks we're married than he thinks that he's charging us a fair rent.'

Her hair had fallen over her face as she spoke. She lifted her plate of chips and poured them roughly onto David's plate.

'I have no appetite now, I'd do anything rather than share a meal with such a mean-minded human being.'

'Come back . . . come back!' he called.

'I'll *not* come back. Not tonight. I'll come back tomorrow when you've gone.'

She had grabbed up a few papers and put them into her duffle bag, she had pulled the nighty from under the pillow.

'Clare, you can't go out in that rain . . .'

'I went out once, to get *your* supper, didn't I? To give you time to poke around and make accusations. Go to *hell!*'

She ran faster than he did and jumped on the last bus going towards the city. She got off and slipped round behind the hostel looking left and right. She climbed the rungs, praying that Valerie and Mary Catherine might be out. But it was not a night for prayers to be answered.

They were reading magazines and listening to Chris Barber on their small portable record player. When she came through the window, furious and dripping, they were convulsed with laughter. They laughed as they got one of the younger and more frightened occupants of the hostel to go for tea, and they laughed as they gave her a big bath towel and ran a bath for her in the big old bathroom at the end of the corridor.

They felt that it called for even more than tea, so the brandy was taken out from the drawer. And eventually she laughed too. She laughed as she dried her hair and sipped the tea with brandy in it and told them the outline of the story. And then eventually she went to bed in the third bed.

Valerie and Mary Catherine had fought like tigers not to have a third girl. They said that since Clare had paid until Easter anyway it would be double letting, and the nuns couldn't do anything as dishonest as that, could they? Secretly Mary Catherine had been certain that Clare would be back: she felt that the romance with David was not going to get beyond first base. But she said none of this as Clare sighed happily and settled back into her old familiar place. Neither did Valerie.

'I'm really sorry. It makes me such an eeejit,' Clare said.

'Nonsense, it makes you much nicer,' said Valerie. 'Now we know you're still normal, and not all this awful sickening peace and calm of true love. That was the distressing bit.'

Bar apologized to him formally as they were having coffee the next morning.

'I'm afraid I spoke out of order last night. I meant no disrespect.'

'That's fine. Sure. Thanks,' David mumbled.

'You look a bit rough. I don't want to say anything that you'll take amiss, but are you all right?'

'Sure, I'm fine.' David swallowed his coffee and went back on the wards. He had spent about three hours tidying the flat. He had removed all the rubbish, including the uneaten chips. This morning he had gone out and bought supplies of tea, coffee, milk, sugar, cornflakes, sardines and oranges. He had arranged them as well as he could, and he had bought a vase too. He left the vase on the desk with a note:

This is for the flowers I would like to bring you tonight.

I'll understand if you don't want me. But I will be heartbroken. You are all I ever dreamed of and hoped for. You are much, much more. Please know that I didn't think I was mean-minded. But I realize I am. I don't want you to put your arms around me and say it's all right, that you forgive me. I want you to be *sure* that you do, and to know that my love for you will last as long as I live. I can see no lightness, no humour, no joke to make. I just hope that we will be able to go back to when we had laughter, and the world was coloured, not black and white and grey. I am so sorry for hurting you. I could inflict all kinds of pain on myself, but it would not take back any I gave to you.

He had written it over and over to try to take out the phrases that sounded tired. He tried to make it just himself. But he was in such unaccustomed low form, it didn't end up sounding like him. Perhaps he should have just left a card with a heart on it, or should he have gone round to the hostel after her last night? He had telephoned from a phone box and asked to speak to Mary Catherine. The nun on duty had asked did he know the time, all the young ladies were in bed, he could leave a message in an emergency. He had hung up. Perhaps he should have feigned illness at the hospital and taken a day off. He could have waited at the bottom of those rungs, Clare would have had to come down that way, she wasn't meant to be a resident. Perhaps he should have stood in the hall up at UCD and waited till she came in for lectures.

Most of the morning was spent speculating between beds. The secretary at the front desk handed him a note as he passed. 'This just came for you, Dr Power.'

In her big firm handwriting she had written:

It was just our First Row. That's *all* it was. Of course I love you. I'm hot-headed and impatient and I'm very sorry for that too. I am ashamed I ran out and left you there, tired and depressed. I love you and I'm greatly looking forward to those flowers and whatever else you might think of as a way to spend the evening.

They were often too tired to talk, too tired to make love when they went to their bed, but not irritably tired. They looked forward to David's proper leave days with excitement and planned them down to the last detail. They went to the zoo, which was lovely in the winter because it wasn't crowded, and they went out to Bray on the train one day and climbed Bray Head to look all over County Wicklow and County Dublin.

Sometimes they ate out, and they had gone to the pictures with Mary Catherine and Valerie one night. But they didn't mix much with David's hospital set, and they didn't look up old friends. James had given up on Mary Catherine and he seemed to be in a very social set. David and Clare didn't need James Nolan, they didn't need anyone but each other.

They had decided not to think about the future yet. David was going round doing interviews for hospitals where he would do his Post Intern year once he finished his present post in July. Clare had her mind fixed firmly on her degree.

By next September they would both be earning money, they would afford a better place, they would not get married yet, they just skated over that bit, but neither of them wanted to bring on the storm. Up here in Dublin in their own little world, nothing mattered, nobody bothered them.

They would be all right unless something happened.

Coming up to Easter two things happened.

Dr Power had a mild stroke.

And Clare discovered she was pregnant.

It was Angela who found him when he passed out. He was just getting into his car, which he had parked a quarter of a mile from the golf club in order to give himself a little walk. He had bandaged the finger of the barman, delivered a strong lecture on the danger of sharp knives, and explained that it didn't matter whether a lemon was finely sliced for drinks but it did matter if dangerous knives were left where people could cut their hands on them.

He walked cheerfully down to the car and then felt everything go dark. He realized that he must be about to faint and lowered himself to the ground beside his car. He tried to call out but he could hear a rushing sound and knew that he was losing consciousness.

Angela was hanging up some clothes on the washing line. She saw the car, and just as she was about to turn back into her house, she saw his black bag thrown on the ground. She ran quickly and was at his side when he was recovering consciousness.

'Did you have a fall?' she said.

'No, Jhangelgha,' he said. 'Shmore a vainting . . .' His voice sounded very odd. As if he were drunk. She was practical as he would have expected.

'Tell me what to do in yeses or nos. Can you stand up if I help you?'

'Yesh.'

'Will I open the door and put you sitting in the car?'

'Yesh.'

He started to speak again, she had the door open and the big man seated in the passenger seat.

'Now, do you want me to get your wife, or to go to a phone and call the hospital in the town? Sorry you have to answer yes or no. Will I get Mrs Power?'

'No.'

'Will I phone the hospital?'

'No. Drive.'

'No, Dr Power. I could curse myself to the pit of hell but I can't drive. Let me get someone to drive you . . . is it safe to leave you here?'

'Yesh. Shafe.'

'Very well, I'll get my bike, I'll be back in five minutes . . .'

'Anjheala.' He seemed agitated.

'Trust me, trust me. I'll get the right person. Are you better here or would you like me to help you back to my house?'

'Alrigth.'

She was a blur of bicycle wheels and then he heard a car coming. Dick Dillon and Gerry Doyle stepped out. The two men he would have picked himself in the whole of Castlebay.

They had been marvellous to him in the hospital, masking

their shock that it was the man himself who needed a bed, not one of his patients.

One of his oldest friends Tim Daly was with him in no time. 'That's a light one, Paddy, take more than that to put you in a wheelchair,' he said.

That was what Paddy Power wanted, no fancy chat, no pretending nothing had happened. He knew a stroke when he saw one, and even more so when he had just been through one.

He pointed at his mouth. 'Shpeesh,' he said.

'Sure, that can go on for a day or two even in the slightest of strokes, you know that.'

'Shide,' he said indicating the side of his body.

'Same thing, it's not paralysed in any strict sense, it's just a bit numb.'

'Yesh.' Power's face was sad.

'Will I drive out to Molly myself, and tell her we're keeping you here for a few days, bring her in with me maybe?'

'Itsh far.'

'No it's not. It's no trouble. And would you like me to tell David? There's no need, as you well know. You could stay here and come out and he need never be any the wiser. Is that what you'd like?'

'Yesh.'

'Sleep a bit, Paddy. It's hard I know, but it's what will do you good . . .'

'Tim . . . Tim . . . locum.' He was straining.

'I have it in hand. I've told him three weeks, you're not to get frightened. I said that, so that you can have a real rest, maybe a week away somewhere with Molly.'

Dr Power closed his eyes, secure at last that everything was under control.

Tim Daly was right. It was a very light one. So light that it was never even referred to as a stroke. Dr Power said that it wouldn't give a young mother confidence if she thought that the doctor attending the birth of her first baby might keel over paralysed. It was described as a little turn and it caused

371

hardly any comment in Castlebay. The locum doctor was a nice man too and not a bit put out by people saying that if he didn't mind they'd wait until Dr Power was ready before they'd have their stitches out or go for those blood tests.

Dr Mackey had lived for a long time in the North of England in industrial towns. He thought the peace of Castlebay was something that should be bottled and put on prescription for those who were tense or anxious all over the world.

'Faith and there's a fair few very tense and anxious here all the same,' Paddy Power said to him. He, Dr Mackey, and Dr Tim Daly were all having a progress discussion. Paddy had been out of hospital for a week: Dr Mackey was still booked for another ten days. The speech had fully returned to normal and there was no more trace of numbness. But Paddy agreed that it was a warning, and agreed further that his own advice to anyone in similar circumstances would be cut down drastically. He knew there should be no more night calls. He would in fact have to cut out a lot of his long drives over bad roads on home calls. He needed someone else to help him. Since there would not be a living for two doctors, he would need a younger man as an assistant. That man should be the one who intended to follow him. David.

'I have written to him. It was easier to write than to say.'

'You're not asking him much,' sniffed Dr Mackey. 'To come back to a ready-made practice. You can teach him all he doesn't know already. You won't be a dog in the manger trying to keep the good will – an *ideal* set-up for any young doctor.'

Dr Power sighed. 'Ah yes, but this young doctor was all set to do his paediatrics and then obstetrics and then the Lord knows what . . . he hadn't it in his mind to come back now. That's what I said to him, I said I knew it was bad timing. He's coming home tomorrow. The hospital gave him compassionate leave. He had to tell them I was at death's doors but he'll be here tomorrow.'

Molly came in with Nellie and a tea tray. Molly had surprised them all by being so calm. They had expected hysterics and they had got a very practical woman. She had even agreed that David should not be alerted until they knew the extent of the trouble.

Tim Daly thought that he must have misjudged her. He had often said to his own wife that Paddy Power had deserved someone less feathery and citified than Molly; but maybe he had been wrong. Anyway there was never any doubt about that son of his, a big, square, handsome, bright lad. Tim Daly sighed again thinking of the strange hand of fate that had dealt him five daughters in succession and no boy anywhere along the line.

David knew about his father before he got the letter. He had heard from Angela almost immediately after it happened. She wrote that she was becoming increasingly unable to mind her own business as she grew older and unable to avoid meddling in other people's affairs, but just in case he would need more time to think about it than he would get, his father planned to write to him in a few days and tell him of a mild stroke which was genuinely believed to have been slight and no threat to his life, but which would mean that he might need David much sooner than expected. Angela said that he mustn't acknowledge the letter or anything, it was just sometimes nicer to be forewarned.

She had written to him at his hospital, and without her having to put it in writing he knew she hadn't written to Clare. It was to give him time to think. It was all bad news but he thanked her deep in his heart.

He thought. Three times he was pulled up for not paying attention, and on one occasion a patient said to him that he looked as if he was on another planet.

He went into a cubicle in casualty and sat on the bed. Suppose he did go home? In July, when he finished this intern year? Suppose Clare studied on, back and forth from Castlebay to Dublin? Suppose she took her degree and was accepted for M.A.? It was by thesis. You could write a thesis anywhere, couldn't you? He was desperately vague. Could you do it from Castlebay?

He rang the admissions office of the university, and the voice kept saying he would have to come in and discuss it.

'*God damn it!*' David cried. 'There must be a *rule*. Can people do their M.A. without being in the university or not? *Yes* or *No*? Is that too much to ask?'

It was, or the tone in which he asked was too much to reply to.

He couldn't go back to hide in the cubicle, it was time to go back to work.

He had hidden nothing from Clare up to now and there was no point in pussyfooting around and trying to get non-existent information about her degree. Anyway, their futures were together. She deserved to know anything that he knew.

He would do no special pleading.

He wouldn't try to sell her on the idea of going home. He wouldn't apologize for his father's ill health.

He would tell her no flowery tales about how much she would love his mother once David and Clare were married.

He would gloss over nothing.

But he must tell her.

There was no bus coming so he decided to walk. He saw her coming up the road towards him, hands in pockets, thoughtful.

'You came to meet me,' he cried.

'Yes, I wondered if we could go somewhere just to have a drink maybe?'

'That's great.' He tucked her arm into his. It would be easier to tell her in a pub that their life in Dublin, their freedom, their study, was going to be cut short.

He carried the drinks to the corner table. He would tell her at once.

'David. You're not going to like this. But it's no use putting it off. I'm pregnant.'

There was a long silence.

'I'm very sorry. But it's confirmed. I sent a sample to Holles Street. It's positive, and I . . . well, I know . . .'

'But you *can't* be . . . we took such care.'

'Not enough, it seems.' She looked very small and young and frightened.

'Oh Clare, Clare,' he said. 'What will we do?'

374

'I don't know. I've had two weeks to wonder and worry. And I still don't know.'

'You should have told me.'

'What was the point? Silly, frightening both of us to death unless it was definite.'

'And it's *definitely* definite?'

'It is David. It is.'

He put his head in his hands. 'Oh *Christ*,' he said. 'Christ, God, isn't that so unfair. Isn't that *all* we need.'

His drink was untouched and so was hers. Nobody was near enough to hear them or have any idea what they were talking about.

She sat icy and withdrawn. She had hoped he would touch her, put his arms around her. Now she felt she would kill him if he tried.

He took his head out of his hands, hair tousled, face flushed. 'I'm sorry,' he said.

'What for?'

'For it happening. I'm meant to be a doctor. Some medical knowledge I have.'

'Don't worry about *that*. It's not an exam. Nobody's going to give you marks or take them away for it.'

'Clare!'

'Well? What else is there to say?'

'I don't know. I suppose we should think what we'll do . . .'

She was silent.

'Make plans . . . It's just, just such a shock, and such a bloody shame. Now of all times.'

'Yes,' she said.

Her face looked small, white and hurt. He remembered suddenly that he hadn't told her about his father. She didn't even know that side of it. He remembered too that she was in the most feared condition of any girl from any small town and maybe any big town in Ireland. She was In Trouble.

He reached out for her hand. 'We'll sort it out,' he said.

She pulled her hand away.

'You haven't touched your drink,' he said awkwardly.

'Neither have you.' The pint looked too big and too sour.

'I think I'll have a brandy,' David said. 'Would you like that, for the shock? Doctor's orders.' He tried a watery smile.

'No. Thank you,' Clare said.

When he came back, she leaned across the table. 'I'm terribly, terribly sorry. I can't say any more. I know how frightening this must be for you, David. I'm trying to keep calm and think what on earth we're going to do. But you probably don't know what you feel yet. It's probably still unreal to you.'

'Yes. That's right,' he said, grateful that she understood that much .

There was another silence.

He drained his brandy. 'Will we go home?' he said.

They stood up and left, each afraid to touch the other and walking several paces apart.

Out in the street the yellow light shone down and made their faces look even more strained. They walked in silence towards the bus stop where David had been heading less than an hour before. They sat silent on the bus, too. Once or twice they looked at each other as if to say something but the words didn't come.

About two stops before their own David stood up. 'Will we get out here?' he asked her diffidently.

'Yes. Of course.' She was very polite. Under normal circumstances she would have questioned him and joked and argued.

They were beside the canal. 'Let's walk a little here,' he said.

They walked in silence and both stopped when two swans glided up to them.

'I only have a bit of chewing gum,' Clare said in almost her ordinary voice. 'Do you think they'd like it, or would it stick their beaks together?'

'Will you marry me?' David said.

'What?'

'Will you marry me. Please.'

'David?' her voice was low and unsure.

'*Please*,' he said again.

'David, you don't have to say anything yet. Don't say anything now. I don't expect you to . . . you don't have to. Honestly. We'll talk, we'll make plans, it's not the end of the world.'

'I know. I love you,' he said.

'And I love you. That's never changed, that never will.'

'So,' he said, eyes shining. 'We'll get married. Now rather than later. Won't we? Say yes. Say, "Yes David." '

'You know I'd love to, but there are other things, other possibilities which we should discuss. You know that.'

'Not with our *baby*, our own child. No other possibilities.'

She stared at him, her eyes filling with tears.

'You haven't given me your answer, like they do in stories.' He was eager and still not sure what she would say.

She paused and took his face in her hands. 'If you mean it . . .' she began.

'That's not an answer, that's a conditional clause,' he said.

'I would love to marry you. Yes. Yes, *please*.'

They walked home and bought chips, and wine, and a chocolate cake. They sat down by their oil stove to make plans and to think about the future.

'Can we get married here? In Dublin? I couldn't bear it at home.'

'That's not the way my wife is going to talk about our big day!'

'You know what I mean.'

'Yes. Of course we'll get married here. Wherever you like. London. Paris. Rome.'

'And then we'll come back and get ourselves a bigger flat, and wait till the exam and the baby. There's a month between them. The finals are over at the end of September and the baby arrives in October, the third week.'

He held her hand between his. 'Isn't it marvellous,' he said again.

'I'm so glad you're pleased. I was afraid that when you get your job in the hospital, you wouldn't like coming home at night to a baby.' She smiled at him. He said nothing.

377

'I mean it's not what a young doctor, a junior hospital doctor wants to come back to, a flat of nappies and a wife at her studies . . .' She was worried by his sudden silence. 'But the great thing is that I *will* be able to do a lot of work at home, I was discussing it with one of the postgrad students. She said that as long as they know your circumstances and can see that you're in there and doing the work and consulting every week or so, you don't have to present yourself every day or anything.'

'Oh.'

'What is it?'

Then he told her about his father's stroke, and that they would have to go back to Castlebay.

Because of Angela's letter, they had five days. Five terrible days. Sometimes they raged at each other, sometimes they just clung together. There were times when they were calm and worked out the alternatives. There were no alternatives. Sometimes Clare taunted him and said he was a Mummy's Boy. No other man would throw his whole career away. Sometimes he wounded her and said that her love was meaningless and shallow if it could change because of place. True love survived wherever it lived. They knew of a doctor that Clare could go to – he had been struck off the medical register, but he did a steady practice in terminations. Because he was a doctor, it wouldn't be dangerous. Then they could think again. But they never talked of that seriously. The miracle of a child of their own seemed about the only cheerful thing in the middle of all the tears and confusion. They would solve none of the dilemma if the baby were taken out of the picture. The pregnancy, and having to tell both families, was not the biggest thing.

The biggest thing was going back.

Neither of them wanted to.

David was going to.

That's where it stood when David got the letter from his father.

Clare cried and cried when she read the letter. It was so

generous, so understanding. The old man had put down on paper all the things they had been talking about during the week. He said he regretted so much asking this of David that he barely had the strength to write it. He set out clearly the impossibility of asking another doctor to hold the fort for three or four years until David might feel ready to return. He sympathized almost dispassionately with David.

What is very hard, for both of us, is this emotional blackmail. I hate to ask you back: you hate to give up your plans. But I have to ask and you have to say yes or no. If I had died, then your decision would be much more clear cut. If you had not wanted to take over this practice then it would have been far easier for you not to have done so. Your mother might have moved to Dublin and nobody would have been greatly hurt or let down. This, I am afraid, is the hardest way and I am well aware of it.

All I can do is try to make it as attractive for you as I can. This house is yours, as you know, but you might feel more independent if you had a place of your own. We could do up the Lodge for you so that you could have a private life of your own and not feel like a little boy again. But the other thing of course, David, is that a doctor in a small community like this can't have much excitement in his private life, if you know what I mean. It's all very hard on you, boy, it's a letter I hate having to write to you . . .

The Lodge. It was a small house just within the half-acre garden of the Powers' residence. It needed a new roof. It had about four rooms, David thought. No kitchen, and only an outside lavatory. They had always been intending to get it done up. At the moment it just housed extra furniture.

It would be their new home.

They travelled back on the train together.

This time they were quiet. They looked out as the fields and telephone wires flashed by. At one place where the train slowed down there were children at a gate waving excitedly at the passengers. A six-year-old held up a fat baby who waved like mad with his two fat arms and his face split into a grin showing one tooth. David and Clare automatically reached for each other's hand. By Christmas they would have something like that. Not as big, not with a tooth, but a bit like that. They gave each other encouraging smiles. They weren't silent out of pique, or despair. It was just that they had been over the plans so often they didn't even want to mention them again.

The plans were complicated. Clare was going to stay on the train while David left as one of the first passengers. His mother would meet him and he would hasten her out of the car park as quickly as possible. Clare had asked Angela to arrange for someone to meet her. She had telephoned Angela at school, and could almost see the disapproving face of Immaculata.

Clare had said that for reasons she would explain later she didn't want to be met by Gerry Doyle, but anyone else, and for reasons which she would also explain she would be the last person to leave the train, well after Mrs Power had cleared the car park. Angela said she understood perfectly.

She felt sick when he went through the ticket barrier without a backward glance, as they had arranged.

She waited till a porter walked through the train picking up newspapers before she got out.

The ticket checker was surprised. 'Well, now! I was off to my tea. Fall asleep on the train, did you?'

Clare smiled at him. Lucky man. Just his tea to worry about.

In the car park Dick stood, waving enthusiastically and coming forward to carry her bag.

Molly Power wore driving gloves. She had been told that they gave you a better grip on the wheel. She looked very well, David thought, her hair freshly done, a nice wool two-piece in a soft green — not the fussy, insecure over made-up woman he had met a few short months ago at the Nolans' house.

She was calm and practical about his father too. She understood the nature of his attack and the need not to exert himself. There was no evidence of panic or anxiety. She spoke pleasantly of Dr Mackey the locum, of the great delight that David had returned home so quickly to discuss things, of the conversation she had held with Bumper Byrne about getting the Lodge fixed up.

David raked her face for clues of how she would react in a couple of hours when she knew she was going to have Clare O'Brien as a daughter-in-law.

Dick Dillon was easy to talk to. He talked about things, not people. She asked was it easy to learn to drive, and he said it was very easy. He showed her the pedals at his feet and said he'd have the theory of it taught to her by the time they got back to Castlebay. And indeed he had. A was accelerator, B was brakes and C was clutch.

She studied his big feet in their neatly-laced, shiny brown shoes as he told her what he was doing each time. 'I see, you have your foot heavy on C and lightly on A and as you release C you press A. I have it,' she said excitedly. 'And now you're pressing B because you want to slow down at the crossroads,' she said.

'I want to *Stop* at this crossroads, Madam. Because I see a big sign saying *Stop*.'

'That's great. I have the hang of it. I'll get a licence as soon as I can.' She would need to know how to drive, and to drive far, if she were going to be living in Molly Power's garden.

His father listened attentively. David said they had hoped to marry in a couple of years' time and he had hoped to get further experience in Dublin hospitals. But now, since circumstances said otherwise, they were happy to come back and start both married life and practice all at the same time.

His father looked thoughtful. Weren't they very, very young to settle down? Clare wasn't twenty yet, well, only barely twenty. Still very young.

No. David was firm. Circumstances had changed so they would marry now. In a few weeks' time in Dublin.

'So Clare is pregnant.'

'We're very very pleased,' David said defiantly.

'You may well be. But is it the best start for a marriage, for a young girl like Clare, for the baby?'

'Dad, whether it is or not, it has started. We never thought for a moment of trying to unstart it.'

'No. No. I'm glad of that.'

'So, I suppose what I'm trying to say is, that once we've told Mum and once Clare has told her family, we'll just get on with it.'

'Is Clare home?'

'Yes.'

'You didn't say . . . Molly didn't say she was with you.'

'We thought it best to come separately from the station.'

Dr Power gave a very deep sigh.

'I'm sorry to have to break it to you like this, Dad.'

'You're very irresponsible, really, you know.'

'Well we didn't mean it to happen, obviously. But then, as you know, I'm sure only too well from all your years here, it just does happen.'

'I didn't expect it to happen to my own *son*. You shouldn't have taken advantage of her. It's not *fair*. Just because you knew her from home, because you knew she was going to be timid.'

'There was no taking advantage of her. You don't understand. In Dublin nobody thinks of Clare as poor little Clare O'Brien from the shop. That's only here. And not everyone here. It's mother, and a few people. I didn't think *you'd* be like that.'

'I'm not being like anything, boy. I realize you're upset. I'm just saying it was a pity that this had to happen to you. You, with your whole life ahead of you.'

'Ahead of us now, Dad. That's what I'm trying to tell you.'

'She's only a child, a child herself. She doesn't know what she wants.'

'Oh she does, she very much does. She's going to finish her degree, you know. Her finals are a month before the baby is born. So we want to get married as soon as possible.'

'It won't be soon enough for Castlebay.'

'Well to hell with what they think.'

Dr Power poured himself a very small brandy.

'It's medicinal. I prescribe it for myself now and then.'

'Are you going to drink my health? *Our* health?' David asked.

'Not immediately.'

'You're not shocked, Dad.'

'Not in that sense. I don't know. You're very young, David. You've only got one life. You don't have to marry Clare if you don't want to. You can be very honourable and just without marrying her. You can acknowledge the child and give her maintenance. But there's no shotgun at your head. Not today, not in 1960.'

'You've got it all out of proportion. The fact that Clare is pregnant is only part of a much bigger thing, which is that I love her. I love her desperately, Dad. I'll never want anyone else in the world. I couldn't contemplate anyone else marrying Clare. I didn't explain that properly.'

'I think I'll let you explain that to your mother. You'll have to do a fair bit of explaining there, so there's no point in doing it twice.'

'Do you think I could have a medicinal brandy?'

'No. I don't. I think you can make your explanations without any stimulant.'

'If I'm to be your partner in this practice, then I can prescribe too. I prescribe myself a brandy twice the size of yours.'

Dr Power laughed and poured it for him. 'Go to it, son,' he said.

'Aren't you coming with me?'

'No, I'm a man who mustn't have too much excitement. I'm going into my study.'

Agnes O'Brien had noticed that the tourist trade was beginning to have a bit of a surge at Easter. More and more people who owned their own caravans up in the site thought they should get value from them by coming more than once a year. She wasn't surprised to hear a ping on the door. She was very surprised to see Clare.

'What brings you back? You never said you were coming?'

'I got a chance, suddenly. So I came,' Clare said.

'You never wrote or anything.' Her mother was full of wonder. In her world people wrote letters announcing what they were going to do; *then* they did it.

'No. As I said, I just got the chance.' She must hide her impatience with her mother. 'Will we have a cup of tea or anything?'

'What am I thinking of, I didn't expect you, you see, come on in, give me your bag.'

'You look much better, Mam, how's your leg?'

'Oh, that's long forgotten, now haven't I enough to be worrying about without thinking of old ailments? No, thank God, I walk fine now, not even a bit of a limp.'

'That's great, Mam.'

'Well come on in, and don't stand there staring around as if you'd never seen the place before.'

'Where's everybody?'

'Your father's gone with Ben to get him a job, or we hope he will. There's a new garage opening out at the crossroads. They want two young fellows to work there. They'll have them trained by the summer, when the business will be great. Your father's gone up there with Ben. Ben's not great to give an account of himself.'

'When did they go?'

'They were to meet the man up there at six. Why?'

'I want to talk to you.'

Clare had put the Closed sign on the shop door. Agnes laid down the kettle without filling it.

'Mother of God, you're pregnant,' she said.

It took time for her mother to stop crying. Clare had time to fill the kettle, boil it, make the tea, cut them two slices of fruit cake and find two paper table napkins for her mother to use as a handkerchief.

'How you can sit there, as bold as brass, and tell me this? How you can do it? It's beyond belief!' her mother wept.

'Mam, I've told you nothing. I just nodded when you

384

asked me was I pregnant. Then you started to cry. Now let me tell you what I really came home to tell you . . .'

'Oh! You weren't going to *bother* with this then, were you? This isn't *news* at all. This is something we were meant to expect, along with your high and mighty ways.'

'*Please,* Mam. Let me tell you. I'm getting married.'

'A bit late in the day for that isn't it?'

'No. Listen. I was going to get married anyway, and this just means we get married a bit sooner, that's all. Honestly, that's all. But it was the getting married bit I wanted to tell you about.'

'I'm not stopping you, tell me about it.' Agnes's eyes were red, she hadn't touched her tea and cake.

'It's David, David Power. We're getting married in a few weeks' time in Dublin, and then he's coming back here – I mean we're both coming back here. His father hasn't been well and . . .'

Agnes stood up. 'David Power! You let *David Power,* the doctor's son, make little of you, and get you into trouble? I don't believe it. I can't believe my own ears.'

She knew this was her mother's vocabulary. In advance she had warned herself of words like *disgrace* and *get into trouble.* But it still didn't make them easy to hear.

'I wish you wouldn't put it that way. At this moment he's up in his house telling his parents too. And whether this had happened or not we were going to get married anyway. So don't talk about people *making little* of other people, or of him *disgracing* me. I was just as eager, all the time, as he was.'

'Don't boast of it, you little tramp. Don't stand there like a slut in my kitchen and tell me what you were eager for and what you weren't. You've ruined us all in this family. We'll be the laughing stock of the place – marrying into the Powers no less. Do you think that Mrs Power is going to let the likes of *you* cross her doorstep? Do you think that woman is going to let her son, with the fine education he has, marry a girl from a shop in Castlebay? A girl who is no better than she should be?' Agnes was laughing now, a twisted, ugly laugh. 'Now, I never did even my Primary

385

Certificate. *I'm* not college educated like you. And yet I can see with the two eyes in my head that there'll be no marriage. There'll be an *explanation*. David almighty Power will have to go abroad to finish his education – or some such excuse. Don't be fooling yourself, girl. There's going to be no wedding for you. Only *disgrace* and a child to bring up. And there's going to be nothing for us but jeers.' Agnes started to cry again.

Clare found herself pitying the thin woman with the rolled-up table napkins crying at her kitchen table.

She spoke very gently. 'Mam, listen to me. I know this is hard to believe. But it's true. David is twenty-five years of age. He's a grown man. He doesn't have to ask their permission for anything. We've arranged the marriage, and the priest. It *will* happen. If his mother turns against him, let her turn. She'll turn back eventually. You know the Lodge up in their garden near the cliff edge, well, Bumper Byrne is going to get it done up and that's where we're going to live. *Mam*. And when Chrissie's baby is born, she'll wheel hers down to see you, Mam, and I'll wheel mine along the Cliff Road. And there's no disgrace. No jeers. It's all *grand*. Don't you understand?'

Her mother looked up with tear-stained face. 'It's all very simple for you, Clare. But life isn't like that.'

'It is, Mam. I'm as good as David. In every way. He knows that. And so do I.'

'If you think that you'll be the only two in Castlebay who do,' her mother sniffed.

'Mam, drink your tea. Please, Mam.'

'When is it going to be born?' She looked at Clare's stomach.

'End of October. Just after my exams.'

'You're never going to go on with your exams.'

'But I have to. That's what it was all about, the three years. I've got weeks in hand. They may have to cut a hole in the desk for me to fit into it, but still I'll manage.'

'Don't say things like that.' Her mother had sipped the tea; she was getting back to normal.

'So what I was going to suggest was this: that we say

David and I are getting married in Dublin, not having a big fussy wedding because we're both still studying, and then as soon as the house is done we'll be back. No need to mention anything else at all, is there?'

'But people aren't fools, Clare. They can count to nine like the rest of us. If someone gets married in April and has a baby in October, they'll know.'

'But what will they know that matters?' Clare's impatience was beginning to show.

Her mother sighed deeply. 'You'll never understand. And, Clare, child, if you believe they'll let you be happy here you'll believe anything.'

David decided to say it quickly.

'Mother, I've just had a long chat with Dad and it's all sorted out. I finish my internship, and come back here at the beginning of July.'

Her face brightened. 'I knew there'd be no problems. Paddy kept saying it was a pity to call you home before your time, but I said you'd be happy to come.'

'You were right. And I love the idea of the Lodge. I'll talk to Bumper Byrne myself tomorrow.'

'There's no real hurry with the Lodge, is there? Your room is there . . .'

'Well . . . you see . . . I've other plans too, Mother. This is my big news. I'm getting married.'

'*David!* You can't be *serious*. You've never told us a word . . . we didn't even know you were courting. Paddy, Paddy . . .'

'He's gone to the study. I wanted to tell you myself.'

'But haven't you told him . . .?'

'Yes. He knows.'

She suspected trouble.

'I just thought I'd tell you myself, in my own way. I'm going to marry Clare O'Brien. Very soon. In four weeks' time. In Dublin. And as soon as she has finished her degree she will come back here and we will live in the Lodge.'

The colour had gone from Molly's face. She was standing,

she had jumped up in her first excitement. Now she swayed slightly, and held on to the back of the chair.

'We intended to get married later on, and live in Dublin. But, of course, now, with Dad needing me back at home that's all changed.'

'*Clare O'Brien.*'

'So we're not having any big wedding, or any fuss. But Father Flynn, do you remember him, he's going to be over again, he's going to be based in Dublin now and he's going to marry us . . .'

'I don't believe it.'

He deliberately misunderstood her. 'Oh, but he is. And he's been very helpful about it all.'

'You know what I mean. I cannot believe that you are being forced to marry that girl. No matter what you may have done.'

'Not forced. We want to. I've explained that. We've planned this for a long time.'

'When you discovered she was up the pole.'

David swallowed. He had rehearsed with Clare how they would behave when their parents said the unforgivable things, when the accusations started. Somehow he hadn't thought his mother would use such a coarse expression. 'That's a vulgar way of describing it.'

'She's a *vulgar* girl.'

He was very calm. 'No, that's not true. Clare isn't in the least vulgar. She is gentle and sensitive, she is bright and well educated and considerate. I would never think of her as vulgar. Never. But she is poor. And her family are poor and uneducated. And her sister Chrissie is most definitely vulgar.' He spoke without any anger.

'David. You *mustn't* do this.'

'I'm going to say this very carefully. So please listen to me. Just listen, and then talk later. It's very important. Nothing you say, *nothing,* will make me change my mind. I love Clare. I *will* marry her. And we *will* be happy. And we will have a child in October. And any harsh words you say now will only make things difficult between us, always, so I'm going to beg you not to say anything until you've had some time to think . . .'

She was without words. Looking at him.

He moved towards her. She stiffened as if forbidding him to touch her.

'I don't know what to do, Mummy,' he said, using the form of address he hadn't used for years. 'I really don't. You see I want to talk to you about it all now, and tell you about how happy I am and how much Clare means to me. But I'm afraid . . . I'm afraid you'll say something so hurtful that I'd find it hard to forgive.'

She nodded mutely.

'So I'm going to go out with Bones for a bit. I'll come back in at half-past eight. And then I'm going to meet Clare at nine in the hotel. She will have told her family then too.'

'*David* . . .' It was a sad cry.

He left the room and, pretending he didn't see his father hovering at the study door, called for Bones. He looked back at the end of the drive, and he saw the two silhouettes in the window. He saw his father put his arms around his mother, who was obviously crying on his shoulder.

Ben had been taken on at the garage, so Tom O'Brien returned in a fine good humour.

'What's all this? The Closed sign on the door?' he asked. 'Ben's not going to be able to keep the lot of us with the job he's got. Why are we closed, will you tell me?'

'Clare's home. She came unexpectedly. We were having a chat.'

'Clare's back?'

'She's engaged, Tom. Engaged to be married.'

'Clare? Never! To some college fellow, is it?'

'To David Power.'

'Our David Power? But I thought she hardly knew him in Dublin?'

'That's not the way it would appear.'

'Well that would beat the divil.' He scratched his head, not sure what to make of it, looking at his wife's face for guidance. Agnes's eyes looked a bit too bright, but she showed no signs of crying.

'Isn't that a bit odd?' he searched her expression, but got nothing. 'Isn't the whole thing odd?'

Clare came down the stairs. 'Have you heard my news?'

'You have me stunned,' he said.

'Is that all I get? Where's the congratulations? And the delight? Where's the looking at my ring . . .' She held out a small diamond for admiration. It had been bought with the remains of her savings and the money the pawnbroker gave David for his good sheepskin coat.

She approached her father to give him an unaccustomed hug. He looked at Agnes and, seeing what he considered approval, gave her the hug. Then she hugged her mother.

'Mam says it won't be easy. But nothing's easy, is it?'

'I suppose it isn't, child. But I'd say you've taken on the World Champion when you're taking on Molly Power.'

She didn't mention the baby to her father, and though his eyes seemed to ask many a time, neither she nor her mother took him up on the unspoken questions.

Clare looked at the clock. There was still half an hour before she met David in the hotel.

She had a sudden feeling of fear. Suppose they had talked him out of it? Suppose she had come all this way to meet him, and to agree to going back cheerfully to Castlebay, suppose she had made all those concessions and somehow that mother of his had talked him out of it? Suppose he was at the hotel gate, and said with fallen face that he had agreed to wait until the baby was born before they married? Then she really would feel *cheap,* and *betrayed*.

They were both in the hotel lounge by five to nine. They entered by two different doors. Bones was with David, refusing the polite request to sit in the corridor outside.

They nodded at each other.

The worst was over.

'What will I get you to drink, Mrs Power?' he asked gently.

She smiled at him.

Rose Dillon was behind the counter. She had always tried

to include David in her parties and picnics without success. She smiled at him coquettishly still. 'To what do we owe this honour? We don't see nearly enough of you in Castlebay.'

Clare watched fascinated: Rose Dillon didn't even acknowledge that she existed, sitting in the chair by the window. She only had eyes for David.

'I'll be coming home for good soon.'

'Oh, that will cause a flurry – they'll be dying to marry you off,' she twinkled.

'I'll be married off sooner than you think,' David said.

Rose frowned. She looked over at Clare O'Brien and shook her head. *No*. That would be *ridiculous*.

They walked up to Angela's cottage to tell her. She was the one person they hoped would be totally delighted. She could see that from their faces. She was touched.

'Will you come to the wedding? Please? It's going to be a bit tense.'

'I'm great at tense weddings,' Angela said.

'Father Flynn will be marrying us.'

'He and I could nearly set up a company, awkward weddings catered for. A speciality in fact.'

'Will you though?'

'If Immaculata lets me. I don't want to anger her too much after all, the big guns will be out in the summer when the prodigal returns.'

'What's that?' David asked.

'You didn't tell him about Sean? That was good of you, Clare, but in love and marriage you can tell all. It's allowed.'

David looked bewildered.

'Listen, David. Your marriage, which is going to raise a few eyebrows and the imminent birth of your child – which has not been announced to me but I am sure is a likelihood – will raise a few more. But let me assure you that those eyebrows will have you long forgotten when the other excitement hits the streets of Castlebay. When Father Sean O'Hara, much respected missionary priest, returns to stay in a caravan with his Japanese wife and his two children.' She laughed when she saw David's face. 'I hate to take the limelight away from the pair of you, but prepare to live in obscurity . . .'

Dr Mackey delivered a nine-pound baby to Chrissie Byrne. It was a boy, and Chrissie and Mogsy said he was going to be called John Fitzgerald after the President of America. Clare went to see her. And got little thanks for her visit.

'You were always one to steal someone else's thunder, Clare. You must have announced your engagement just to spite me as soon as you heard that John Fitzgerald had arrived.'

'Don't be a goon.'

'Always the same,' grumbled Chrissie.

'Here, let's see him.' Clare was eager.

'Don't touch him. You'd drop him.'

'I just want to look at him.' Clare peered in at the little bundle in her sister's arms – a red face and lots of black hair.

'He's beautiful,' she breathed, with such admiration that Chrissie was slightly mollified.

Clare decided she had better ask her. Life would be intolerable if she didn't.

'David and I are having a very small wedding, as you know. Just his family and ours, and a couple of friends. Will you and . . . er Maurice . . . be able to come?'

Chrissie looked doubtful. 'It's very soon, altogether. I'd have John Fitzgerald with me. Maurice and I have been discussing it. I think with regret we will have to refuse.'

Clare looked just disappointed enough, but not too upset. Nothing that would make Chrissie go back on her decision. 'I'll keep you some of the wedding cake,' she said.

'Imagine you marrying the gentry,' Chrissie said. 'What I can't understand is why you're going back to college. Haven't you done it now? Haven't you got what you were out to get? A rich husband?'

It wasn't at all as she would have expected. Mrs Conway had been pleased. She made a point of crossing the road to tell Clare that she wished them well. 'I always thought my

Frank could have done worse than marry you,' she said — which was a high accolade.

Josie, oddly, did not seem as pleased as Clare would have thought. She was very formal about the news and only offered the most distant of congratulations.

Josie had been walking out with Mr Martin Harris, the auctioneer. Martin was *mature*, which meant old; and *responsible* which meant dull. Josie, who had never been jealous of anything Clare had done, was now very envious of Clare coming back to Castlebay and snatching the only attractive man, and the only *catch*, from under their noses.

Father O'Dwyer wrote out her letter of freedom. It was an odd thing not to get married in your own parish, but this Father Flynn had been a very decent person and he was sure he would do it right.

Angela had begged her to call on Immaculata. There was great false excitement in the convent over the ring, which was admired by the whole community. There was genuine excitement about how Molly Power would take the new daughter-in-law.

They kept the meetings with the families as brief as possible.

David shook Tom's hand and thanked him for letting him marry Clare.

'Divil much a say I had in it one way or the other,' Clare's father said.

'I know you'll be pleased to have her back in Castlebay,' he said manfully to Clare's mother.

'I suppose it *may* turn out all right,' Agnes O'Brien said.

Up in the big house, Molly waited nervously at her fireplace; she had rearranged everything in the room a dozen times, and shouted at Nellie who was sulking in the kitchen. She had changed her dress twice.

She saw them walking up the drive. Laughing. The girl was *laughing*, instead of shaking in her shoes.

David had his own key.

'Mother, we're here,' he called.

Clare was tall. Molly had forgotten that. She was tall and thin, and her face seemed pale.

'Well.' Molly looked her up and down. It was just on the right side of being a calculated insult. But only just.

'Hallo, Mrs Power,' Clare said. Her voice was steady.

'So,' Mrs Power said.

I won't let her annoy me. I will not rise to her bait, Clare told herself, fists clenched by her sides.

David wasn't saying anything, which was what they agreed.

'David has told you our news, and our plans, Mrs Power.'

'Oh yes.'

'So I just wanted to add that I hope very much that I will make him happy, and that eventually I will make you and Dr Power pleased that we married.' Not too confident. It angered Molly more than anything had ever done in her life.

'I doubt if that will ever be the case,' she said holding back the temper that was threatening to spill out. 'I am here to greet you. Would you like me to ring for tea?'

'Thank you, but no, Mrs Power. If I may, I'll just go and pay my respects to your husband. I have a lot of things to do before going back tomorrow. Thank you for welcoming me to the house, and I'll look forward to seeing you at the wedding.'

I could kill her, Molly thought. I *wish she were dead*. The feeling swept over her and was gone. She felt shock and guilt. It confused her and she didn't make her farewells as she intended to.

'What . . . oh . . . yes. Yes, the wedding day. Yes.'

Clare had smiled and was out of the door.

'Thank you, Mother,' David said. His face was in a pleasant smile but his eyes were cold.

It was much later when she saw him. Sitting on the wall, by the hotel.

'You were going to run out of town without telling me.' He was cold and unsmiling.

'Don't be ridiculous.' She forced a light laugh that she didn't mean. 'Of course I was going to tell you. If I hadn't seen you tonight I'd have left a note for you.'

'You're a liar.'

'Now stop that,' she said, her anger rising. He was not going to upset her, she would not let him, but *hell*, he wasn't going to call her a liar. Especially since he was right.

'You had no intention of telling me,' Gerry said.

'Why wouldn't I tell you? Don't *dramatize* everything so much. I've been telling all my friends that I'm getting married. Why wouldn't I tell you?'

'Because you knew what I'd say.' There was no answering smile on his lips.

'And what would you say? What will you say?'

'That you're mad. You musn't do it.'

One more attempt, thought Clare. Just one more, to get this on to some kind of normal plane and then I abandon it.

'Well, listen to me, just because you and I were the only people left, everyone else getting hitched, that's no reason why I'm going to stay single just to keep you company. I'm delighted with it all. And I won't put up with any nonsense from you.'

'Don't do it. *Clare.*'

'Stop it. Can't you wish me well? Like ordinary people?'

'I do wish you well. But not married to David Power. And you're not ordinary people, I've always told you that. Neither am I.'

'You're certainly not like generous people or mannerly people,' she said.

'You can't marry him. You have to marry me. You always knew that.'

She looked anxiously at his pointed face for the lopsided smile, the grin that made anybody else grin too. There was none of it there. She stared at him, shocked.

'Well, I don't suppose there's anything more to say.' Clare moved towards the entrance gate.

Lithe as a cat, Gerry leapt to the ground. 'Don't go yet.'

'Of course I'm going. I'm not talking to you for one more minute. How dare you upset me and say all these things? How *dare you?* If it were you that had got engaged, I'd be so pleased and wish you well.'

'Got engaged? Got engaged? You and David haven't *got*

engaged. You're getting *married* in three weeks. What does that mean? Well? What does it mean?'

'Go to hell.' She turned and ran past him.

He ran beside her, half jumping, half running. 'It's the wrong thing to do. Girls like you, like Fiona, you shouldn't be just forced to make fools of yourselves. *You're* not tramps. You're too trusting. If something goes wrong then you should work it out properly . . .'

She stopped and looked at him levelly. 'In my case, *nothing* went wrong. *Nothing*. Do you hear me? Everything is fine, as right as can be. Our marriage is a bit sooner than we intended but it's exactly what we wanted. It's going to be perfect.'

Gerry had stopped opposite her. He looked straight into her eyes. 'Your marriage to David Power is not going to be perfect. You foolish, *foolish* girl. Your marriage is doomed.'

The girls had been magnificent. They had been through the entire hostel in search of clothes, and since everyone was so much in awe of Valerie and Mary Catherine, clothes were forthcoming. They had a huge selection for Clare to choose from.

There was a nice pink suit which fitted Clare very well. They took a wine-coloured hat from another girl, and a very expensive black bag. Now all she needed were wine-coloured gloves and good black shoes.

They bought her the gloves between them, and she bought the shoes herself. She was kitted out.

Mary Catherine was to be bridesmaid, and James Nolan the best man. David seemed a little cool with James. Clare didn't know why. Anyway they were all in such a frenzy with study and getting clothes ready and dismantling their flat in Rathmines and finding a better one, that there was little time to speculate.

Clare had received a note from Caroline Nolan wishing her well, expressing surprise at the suddenness of it all, and regret that the Nolan family offer of hosting the wedding hadn't been taken up.

Clare had been adamant about that. It was not going to be

on Nolan territory. It was to be on neutral ground, the hotel near the church. Father Flynn had discussed the menu and suggested one that seemed not too ambitious. David and Clare had opened a bank account: the manager loved young doctors and David, without actually saying it, implied that he was well on the way to being a consultant in Fitzwilliam Square. They had a small overdraft. It would pay for the wedding. There was no way the Nolans could get their hands on Clare's day.

They went through the list. There were the *relaxed* and the *tense*. The relaxed seem to outweigh the tense. David's father, Angela, Father Flynn, Emer and Kevin, Mary Catherine and Valerie. And James and Caroline would be all right, wouldn't they. Snobby, Clare thought, but all right. And what about Ben and Jim? *Tense,* Clare said, and if by any unlucky chance they did become relaxed it would mean that they had become hooligans.

Well, that was a fair number of easy people. On the other side of the scales would be David's mother, who would look like an avenging angel all day long; both Clare's parents, who would be so timid and fearful of doing the wrong thing they would have everyone's teeth on edge; and there would be the Nolan parents, who seemed to regard this marriage as in the same class as the loss of the *Titanic*.

'It's great that we're able to laugh about it,' Clare said.

'That's the only thing that makes me feel it's not doomed,' David agreed.

Clare didn't like the use of that word. It made her shiver.

The O'Briens came up by train the night before. Jim had never been in Dublin before; Ben had been once on a school trip. Clare met them at the station. She was taking them by taxi to the hotel where they would all stay the night. Mr Ryan, the owner, had arranged a very good rate. There were three rooms booked: one for Clare's parents, one for her brothers; and one for herself, where the girls would come tomorrow to help her dress.

Her heart filled with pity for them, for all she was putting them through, as she saw them getting out of the train.

Blinking after the long journey, tired and nervous about what lay ahead ... Their suitcase was enormous and very shabby – surely there were a couple of *small* bags at home? But then, they rarely went anywhere.

Ben and Jim were chastened by the hugeness of Kingsbridge station. The boys were squeezed into the front of the taxi. Clare's parents looked nervously out of the car on each side. She chattered: there would be tea and sandwiches in the hotel, Mr Ryan was going to have it ready. There wasn't a bar as such, but he said that he could get a few bottles of stout for them. Clare's father brightened; and so did Ben, but Ben was told that there was no question of a bottle of stout for him. There wasn't much need for conversation. They were all so tired that the tea and stout were enough to close their eyes.

Ten times Clare's mother asked what time they had to leave. Ten times, without complaining, Clare told her that they would walk across to the church – a distance of fifty yards – at eleven o'clock.

It was a beautiful sunny day. Mary Catherine and Valerie arrived giggling in their finery. They had the hat and the good black bag with them. Those were only borrowed for the day: the owners were so terrified to let them out of their sight, they had promised to return them before nightfall.

'I brought some brandy. In case,' Val said.

'Not now,' Mary Catherine said. 'We have to dress the bride.'

Clare looked pale so they rouged her up. She also looked extremely smart. The outfit was a work of genius and Clare blessed the anonymous donors. She felt that it was taking the Something Borrowed superstition a little too seriously, and they were all laughing at that, when Clare's father arrived beating on the door nervously and saying they had only twenty minutes – should they be on their way?

Clare didn't know there would be music. She was surprised to hear the burbling sounds of a church organ. Her father's arm stiffened in fright.

The altar did seem a mile away, but soon she was near

enough to see them turning round. She saw the admiration in Angela's face first, and it was warming. She saw Angela clutch Emer, and they were both nodding with delight at her. Her unnaturally clean brothers seemed surprised too at how well she looked and this made her hold her head high. She saw Caroline's eyebrows go up, and that was pleasing too, as was the big smile from Dr Power. But best of all was the way Mrs Power's face changed just a fraction. The superior look which seemed to be built into it as she was whispering to Mrs Nolan left it for a moment. And because Clare felt so exhilarated, her smile was sparkling.

By the time David turned round she was glowing with confidence and happiness; transformed, almost, from when she had started to walk up the aisle. He had never known she could look so beautiful. He looked at James standing beside him and smiled. James smiled back encouragingly. The coldness, the tactless words James had spoken, were forgotten. David was stepping out of the pew to take his beautiful, beautiful bride to the altar.

The Powers were not taking any photographs. If the Nolans had brought a camera it was not produced. Kevin Quinn had a camera though; and when Father Flynn saw the sparsity of picture-taking he gave Jim O'Brien some money and sent him off to a nearby chemist to get three more films.

'Keep snapping,' Father Flynn hissed to Kevin. 'You're the official photographer.'

They walked cheerfully enough across to the hotel. Mrs Power looked at it as though it were some kind of museum piece. She was annoyed to hear the Nolans saying they hadn't known it was there, and what nice antiques in the hall. Mr Ryan had taken the decision to serve the drinks out in the conservatory, which opened on to a garden. There were flowers and plants and rays of sun coming through coloured glass.

'It's not bad at all,' hissed Valerie through clenched teeth. 'The way Clare was going on, I thought we were in for a place smelling of cabbage, with sauce bottles on the table.'

'There's nothing wrong with the place,' Mary Catherine said. 'But isn't the mother-in-law a *bitch*.'

'She'll soon see she's outnumbered,' Angela said. They jumped. They had not intended anyone else to hear. 'I agree, she's behaving like a bitch, but she's got no confidence, herself. When she sees the rest of us thinking it's marvellous, she'll come round.'

'I'll go and talk at her for a while,' Val said. 'Blind her with tales of my background.'

Mr Ryan called them in to lunch. There was cream in everyone's tomato soup, and a little chopped parsley on top.

Mrs O'Brien wondered whether it was just a decoration; Father Flynn solved that by spooning his own down noisily the moment grace had been said. Agnes saw what to do, and her family followed her. The rolls were slightly warm; and there were little clusters of bottles on the table: red wine, white wine, orange squash, and stout bottles artistically arranged at intervals.

The seating plan was a miracle of diplomacy. No O'Brien was left without a friendly neighbour. Clare and David felt the breath they had been holding all day begin to slip out naturally. It was too big a number for general conversation, but there was a nice buzz; and by the time Mr Ryan and his two waitresses had cleared the chicken à la crème away and dusted the table for the bringing on of the ice cream and cake, it was far more friendly than anyone could have believed possible.

Molly Power was flanked by Kevin Quinn on one side and Father Flynn on the other. Without being deliberately rude, there was nothing she could do but respond.

Agnes O'Brien was on the other side of Father Flynn, and then there was Valerie. They had dispensed with the traditional order of seating since that would have been a *certain* recipe for disaster.

Father Flynn had instructed James in some of his duties: he asked him to call upon Miss O'Hara to speak, and to ask David's father to say a few words too.

'It's not *traditional*, Father,' James complained.

'Whose side are you on, boy?' Father Flynn had replied sharply.

It worked. Tom O'Brien's bumbling words, the studying of his piece of paper, went almost unnoticed. If it had just been Tom, and the fluent young barrister James Nolan, the difference would have been very marked.

Dr Power was warm and cheerful. Doctors were often apt to say at weddings that they brought the bride or the groom into the world, as if that gave them special standing in the community. In this case he had brought both of them into the world, and had considerable responsibility for the existence of the groom. He wished them long, happy years in Castlebay – which as everyone knew was the centre of the Universe, and would those people who had not yet been to Castlebay please hurry up and go there.

Angela, more hesitant than she ever had been at school, spoke about how sentimental teachers always became once the pupils were out of their hands.

James was flowery. It was very nearly over. David stood up to speak last.

Clare had to fix her eyes firmly on the heap of telegrams so that she would not cry at his words. He was speaking simply and directly about his happiness and his hopes for both of them. He was thanking everyone there by name for all they had done. Nobody could be more happy than he was at this moment.

They all clapped. Molly's gloved hands; Agnes's thin bony hands; Jim's and Ben's scrubbed clean hands – examined before they were allowed out; Father Flynn's plump little white hands and Angela's long artistic hands.

Clare went up to change, to remove the pink suit – on which not a crumb or drop had been spilled – to place the hat and the handbag back in tissue paper. She wore Valerie's good grey dress and a set of cheap wine-coloured glass beads, which matched her gloves. She grabbed up her own shabby bag. She was ready for Going Away. James had said he would give them a proper present later when they were settled into their new home. In the meantime perhaps the car might be useful. David thanked him again warmly as he took the car keys in his hand.

'It's good of you, James. And thanks for all the marvellous support. At the meal. You know.'

They stood awkwardly waiting for Clare to come downstairs. 'It was all great,' James said.

'Yes. Yes, of course.'

'And it will all turn out marvellously well.'

'Yes,' David said.

They were both thinking of the days when they could say anything to each other. A long time ago.

For the three-day honeymoon they had said they were going to a quiet hotel in Wicklow and everyone had nodded sagely. They were in fact going back to their new flat, which was in total chaos. They wanted nobody else. They wanted no gaiety or candlelit dinners, they just wanted each other and the knowledge that the day they had dreaded was over.

James Nolan had left champagne cooling, and when they got back to the Nolan house, Breeda was ready with a tray of glasses.

'This is more like it,' Caroline said.

'It was very nicely done, very nice,' her father said.

Dr Power took his glass of champagne and walked out into the well-kept garden. A man was mowing the lawn. For other people it was an ordinary working day.

Molly saw him standing by himself and went out to him. She stood beside him wordlessly.

'You were very good, Moll,' he said.

'Good?'

'You didn't want it, but you didn't let that spoil their day. Even though your heart wasn't in it.'

'Clare . . .' she paused.

He said nothing.

'She looked very well, I thought. The outfit was smart.'

Inside, the champagne was flowing. Caroline wanted to know why Clare hadn't carried that super handbag away with her when she was leaving. 'There was a fearful coldness between James and David, did you hear? James was nearly not going to be the best man!' She was giggly and conspiratorial.

'I *didn't* know,' Valerie said, giving her the cue to go on.

'*Apparently*, when David told James about the marriage, and the *hurry* and the *dramas* and all, James said, very reasonably I think, but anyway he said *bad luck* or something, and David said what do you mean, and James said that *really* David didn't *have* to marry a *scrubber*, and David poured his glass over James – it was in a hotel bar all this – and walked out, and James had to run after him. Gosh, it was *awful*.'

'Wasn't it?' Valerie said fervently. 'Wasn't it about as *awful* a thing to say as anyone could think of.'

'No, what I mean is . . .' Caroline saw she had put her foot in it.

'Isn't it *quite* extraordinary how James ever managed to make it to being an attorney with a mind like that,' Mary Catherine said in amazement.

June had always been a stifling month, waiting for the end of term.

Angela had written to Sean and Shuya in reply to their excited letter. Yes, indeed, she would be here, she would be in the cottage as always, and once they had decided what they were going to do, they could come and tell her, she would be happy to see them all, as she was always happy to see them.

Sean had said no, he hadn't written to anyone in Castlebay about his changed life, who would he write to? But Angela had been very firm on that one: it was Sean's story to tell, not hers. He must be the one to decide who to talk to and what to say.

No letter with any change of plans came. There was no reprieve. They would be here on Saturday.

On Saturday morning, panic came over her as she was buying meat in Dwyers'. Chrissie, back at work, wanted to know if Miss O'Hara was going to have a party.

'No. Why?' Angela said, alarmed.

'Well you're just after buying enough meat to feed an army.'

Angela looked in horror at the huge lumps of meat. Without thinking she had bought dinner for Sean and his family. She felt dizzy and leaned against the wall.

'Are you all right?' Chrissie asked, frightened. 'Jimmy! Give Miss O'Hara a hand.'

She had steadied herself again.

'I'm very sorry. I've got a bit of summer 'flu, I think.' She paid for the meat, put it in her bicycle basket, and wheeled it home. She didn't dare to get on the bike for fear she might faint. Though in a way it wouldn't be a bad time, if she had to die, to die now. She sat at home glumly all day. Why had she not had the courage to tell people after her mother died? Why had she lied to them, and gone along with their messages of sympathy, their requests for prayers? She had never taken a penny of their money: she had said that it should all be sent to the missionary headquarters. But they wouldn't remember that.

She thought of the nice, honest people who always asked after him, the people she had fooled, rather than the awful people who would crow with horror. She didn't care all that much about the Sergeant McCormacks and the Mother Immaculatas. She thought about Dick Dillon, and her heart went down to her feet.

It was a beautiful day, the kind that they would sigh over, the trippers in for the day, the visitors down for the month, the shopkeepers who had been hoping for weather like this all year.

Shuya and Sean would sigh with pleasure too, and Denis and Laki would be as delighted with the long golden beach and the bright blue sea. She never remembered feeling so sad.

She had shown herself she was a person of no courage. She hadn't the courage to beg them not to come, nor the courage to go to the station and welcome them with open arms. What a useless, spineless friend and sister she had turned out to be.

404

They would have been here three hours at least now. They had taken the overnight boat from England, the morning train to the town, and since there was no one to meet them to take them to Castlebay, they would wait for the bus. They would have been in their caravan for an hour.

Had they taken the children for a swim? Had they gone to O'Brien's shop to buy provisions? Had Sean leaned eagerly across the counter and shaken Tom O'Brien's hand?

'Don't you remember me, Mr O'Brien? I'm Dinny O'Hara's son Sean. And this is my wife, and these are my children. Say hallo to Mr O'Brien, Denis . . .'

Were they on their way up the street now? Had they reached the corner? Were they turning down the golf-course road?

She had said she would be in her cottage. She wanted to run away.

She never remembered the clock ticking so loudly or her heart moving so oddly in her chest.

She sat and waited.

And waited.

By the time the children should be well in bed, there was a knock on the door. She steeled herself and went to it slowly. There was no sound of voices on the step. Perhaps they were upset that she hadn't come to meet them.

She opened the door.

It was Dick Dillon.

'Hallo,' she said faintly. She stood leaning against the door. She made no move to ask him in.

'I was wondering if I might come in at all? Or would that be out of the question? I do come to call here occasionally, you know.'

'Dick, I'm sorry. Come in.'

'I know you said you didn't want to come up this week, and that you'd explain it all later.'

'Well it didn't do much good my telling you that, did it?'

'I knew it was all right to come.'

'That was very arrogant of you.' Her voice was weary.

'No. It wasn't arrogant. I knew I could come. I knew they weren't here.'

'What?'

'I knew I wouldn't be blundering in on top of them. They're sitting down on the seat at the end of the town looking at the sea.'

He had discovered them by complete accident. He had seen them getting off the bus, he had looked because of the foreign woman, and the children being half foreign-looking.

'He didn't recognize me. I was in my drinking mode when he was here last. I'd only have been a blur to him or indeed he to me.'

'So how did you know?'

'The boy said when were they going to see Aunt Angela, and the woman said they were going to their caravan first, and Aunt Angela would be waiting up in her cottage for them later when they got settled in, today or tomorrow.'

'I'm sorry, Dick. I'm very, very sorry.' Angela wept. 'I'm such a coward, I'm so bloody weak, I couldn't tell you.' She put her head on his shoulder and sobbed like a child. His arms went around her, and he patted her comfortingly.

'It's going to be all right,' he said, as if to a very small, very upset toddler. 'Dick is here, he'll look after things.'

They sat in the sunset and watched the red ball disappear down behind a big navy line of horizon. Behind them, the music of the amusements and the cries of laughter, and around them the chitter-chatter of holidaymakers.

Denis and Laki were both fast asleep, exhausted. Already he had pointed out the Brothers' School where he had gone every day, he had shown them the big rock pools where he used to play, and he had taken them into the Echo Cave to shout their questions.

Sean had remembered O'Brien's shop. But it had been much smaller then; he didn't know the boy serving there – it must be one of the young sons. He saw Mrs O'Brien in the background; but he was shy suddenly. It wasn't the place to catch her eye and begin the great comeback. He had bought a colouring book and pencils in Miss O'Flaherty's shop, but she was busy serving someone else and he didn't know the young woman who served them.

On the street, a child of about eight looked at Laki with interest. 'What land do you come from?' she asked.

'I was born in Japan, I am half-Irish, half-Japanese,' Laki said proudly.

'I had a Japanese doll when I was young. It didn't look a bit like you,' the girl said curiously.

They had eaten their meal and made plans for the next day; there would be swimming and a picnic lunch on the beach. But first they would call on Aunt Angela. The children had thought this perfectly satisfactory.

'This is a good place to have as another home,' Laki said. Sean had been talking about Castlebay as their 'other home' for as long as the children could remember. But this time he said nothing.

'I'll show you the town,' he had suggested to Shuya. But when they came to the bottom of the street, he hung back; he didn't want to go to the dance, he was too old to take her to the amusements. A middle-aged couple on the bumpers? It would be idiotic. Then, in the hotel, sitting drinking, and seeing other groups: would he go up to them? If so, would he give his name? He remembered the Dillons vaguely, but he hadn't known any of them well.

He had hesitated as they approached Church Street. It was Shuya who pointed out the nice bench.

'That wasn't here, years ago,' Sean said. 'Probably afraid that people might sit here and cuddle or do something outrageous like that.'

She put her arm around him. She sensed his unease, the flatness about everything.

'It's changed a lot, of course. Everything,' he said.

'It must have. Was that big amusement centre always there?'

'Much smaller, much shabbier. And I don't think the dance hall was like that. Of course, in those days I wasn't likely to be going into it, so I hardly noticed it.'

'It's funny,' Shuya said. 'Most people, when they go back,

find that things have grown smaller. Here you find they have all grown much bigger.'

'You wouldn't know the place in ways,' he said. 'It's very painted and bright and the shops have all got things hanging outside them, buckets, and water wings and sunhats. There was none of that in my day.'

There was a silence.

'Would you like us to walk up to your home, to see it, even if you don't want to go in?'

She was trying hard. It worked.

'Yes, that would be an idea. I don't think we'll go up Church Street, we can go up the Cliff Road, it's longer but it's very nice.'

'Let's go by the Cliff Road,' said Shuya.

They walked on to the golf-course road. Late golfers were coming back from their drinks after the last hole.

It was a warm, balmy evening. They walked on till they saw the house. The curtains were drawn and there was a light in the main room. Angela must be waiting there for them.

'Is it cheating to walk past it, and not go in?' he asked.

'Angela said come any time we were ready. I don't think you're ready now,' Shuya said gently.

'No. I'm not, somehow.'

'Well then, it's not cheating.'

He pointed out where his room had been, and which had been the window he used to climb out of if he wanted to race out and have an early-morning swim. They marvelled at the energy of a boy who could have raced down a half mile to the sea and a half mile back . . . he would run on the road, and there would be cows going for milking . . . he would be back in his room and studying again before anyone in the family got up.

He showed her the little geraniums that his mother had planted in the window boxes and said that it was wonderful they had survived so well. He pointed out the chimney where the birds had made a nest, and the porch where they had to scrape off the snow in winter in case it became too heavy and broke the glass.

Shuya whispered that now she had a very perfect picture of the way he used to live.

They walked together back down the road, arm in arm, to the caravan park; again by the quiet cliff road, not the bustling Church Street with all its lights and the fun of the season getting underway.

Dick Dillon came downstairs; he had been peeping through the dark bedroom window.

'They've gone,' he said.

They had heard whispering outside and he had crept upstairs to have a look. Angela had remained at her post. If they knocked she was to let them in and Dick was to leave the back way. He would not stay and greet them – otherwise they would get the impression that the whole of Castlebay would accept him as willingly. They had to make their decisions according to the facts, not just from meeting Dick.

'What do you think they were at?' she asked.

'We'll probably never know that,' he said.

'Would you stay the night, Dick?' she asked suddenly.

'What?'

'I don't mean in the bed with me, I'm not inflicting that on you. Just in the house.'

'I'd love to stay with you, and since you're on the subject, it would be no infliction at all if you weren't to bother to go to all the trouble of making up another bed.'

'Ah, it's no trouble, Dick,' she laughed.

'I was hoping maybe you might have no bedclothes aired.'

'They're aired, and it's the middle of summer. Will there be a hue and cry for you if you don't go back to the hotel?'

'Angela, my girl, they don't know whether I'm there or gone, whether I live or die in that place.'

'Stop playing on my sympathies, you'll have your own bed here, I'll go and make it for you now.'

'I'd be no trouble to you, that's a grand big bed you have up there. I was just looking at it and speculating.'

'Speculate away. Dick?'

'Yes.'

'Thank you *very* much.'

She thought they would go to late Mass, so she was surprised to see the four of them at First.

When she saw Sean and the two children go to the altar to receive Communion she closed her eyes. Castlebay would forgive a lot but it would never forgive that.

She left before the Last Gospel. She was buying her Sunday paper from Mickey Mack outside the gates when she heard a farmer say to his wife, 'Did you see the Chinese woman at Mass, and the two half-caste children, going to the rails and all?'

'Isn't China full of Catholics?' said Mickey Mack: he wasn't an ignoramus just because he couldn't read the papers he sold.

She had plenty of soda bread, and cornflakes for the children. Dick had gone back to the hotel and he wouldn't come to the house until she sent for him. She could always phone from the golf club if there was an emergency.

She sat down to read the paper, calmer now. Nobody had recognized them.

They must have been having some kind of second thoughts if they had come to look last night but had not come in.

She waited for them with a dread that was much less sharp around the edges. And she didn't feel too bad about herself either. Last night Dick had assured her that she had behaved most honourably. She felt less of a coward today.

Today she could take them.

They arrived excitedly, chattering like starlings. There were hugs and a present for Aunt Angela and delight at the breakfast.

Shuya wandered round the room entranced by the books and objects. 'You never told me it was like this, Sean.'

'It wasn't, when I was here.' He seemed sad. Shuya was praising the one thing that didn't date from his time.

Casually, very casually, Angela asked him had he met any friends to introduce to Shuya.

'No.' He seemed troubled. 'Not yet.'

'Of course, a lot of Sean's friends would have been made through his mother, and through you, Angela. When he came home, she would gather people round and because of his status as priest, people would call.'

Shuya understood.

'I don't seem to know anyone from school.'

Angela clenched her fists. *Know anyone from school?* The man was mad! Thirty years ago, little fellows running in and out of the Brothers? Who in the name of God would he know?

'No, I suppose you've grown away, and they have,' she said cautiously.

'You know, it's very changed, Angela. Do you not find that?' he said.

This was it. If she moved carefully, this might be the lifeline that was being thrown. There would be no point in coming back to a *changed* Castlebay.

'Oh I do,' she sighed. 'I think what it used to be like in the old days, room to walk on the footpaths, only a few families on the beach . . . You knew everyone to say hallo to.'

Shuya was playing the game too. 'Sean told me last night that it has changed too much, become big and what was the word you used . . .?'

'A bit *brash*. Hasn't it? To be honest, Angela, it's getting a bit like those places in England, that used to be so nice, but very noisy and full of trippers.'

'What can you do?' Angela cried. 'I often think of leaving it myself, getting a better job in a bigger school. I don't know why I hang on, but like you, I suppose it's roots.'

Shuya said levelly, 'If *you* left, Angela, you could always come back. To see people. After all, you do have friends here. Sean doesn't have many.'

'I wouldn't say that . . .' He didn't want to appear friendless.

'No, you'd know a lot of people, of course, Sean. But Shuya's right. They're Mam's friends, not our own. Really, the best of ours went away. It's the same in a lot of small places.'

He repeated it. 'The best of ours went away. It's true for you, Angela. True.'

The children came in from the garden: it was scorching, could they go for a swim? Of course they could. Would Angela join them on the beach? No. If they didn't mind. But she'd be here tonight. She had bought a lot of meat, would they come and have a big supper?

'Which is a nice, quiet part of the beach . . . um . . . for the picnic?' Shuya called.

Angela told her the part where there was least chance of Sean O'Hara being unmasked.

'We were thinking, Angela, that it would be a pity not to see a bit of the rest of the countryside around here, now that we're this far.'

Her breathing was short – it was going to happen. 'I think that's a good idea. Take day trips, is it?'

'No. Go on and see a few other places, places they can remember, write about in their projects and scrapbooks.'

Shuya said, 'And I want to see Dublin. I was promised Dublin.'

'Well, of course, that would be nice. But the caravan?'

'There's people queuing up to get into caravans, they'll even let us have the balance back, which is very fair.'

'But you'll come back again? To Castlebay? Before you leave Ireland?'

'No. It wouldn't make sense. We'd be retracing our steps.'

'I see. Yes. You're right, of course.'

Shuya said, 'So we thought we might start out tomorrow. They can let the caravan from lunchtime.'

Angela said nothing. Her heart was too full.

Sean mistook the silence for disappointment. 'I don't want you to think we're running out on you. I'll never be able to thank you for the welcome. It's just . . . it's just . . .'

'I think I understand. Some things have changed a lot.'

'And some things haven't changed at all.'

'The bus leaves early. We must rise very early . . .' Shuya said.

'I have a friend – you won't remember him – Dick Dillon.

He could give you a lift to the town, and you could start out from there . . .'

'Would he mind?'

'Not at all. I'll tell him tonight.'

'Angela . . . there's just one thing . . . about this Dillon man.'

'What's that?'

'You won't tell him who I am? You see I'd prefer in a way if people thought . . .'

'I won't tell him who you are – didn't I say I'd leave it to you to tell who you want.'

She came down the Cliff Road with them all and kissed them goodbye at the corner by the seat that looked out to sea. They walked on up to the caravan park. She told them Dick Dillon would pick them up at the caravan site at a nice civilized time, like ten o'clock.

When she went home she prayed on her knees, long sobbing prayers of thanks to a Lord that she had thought recently had been hard-hearted.

The days fell into a hypnotic routine. They got up early. There was no one on their part of the beach so they went down the steps beside the Lodge to the beach for an early swim. Bones knew about this, and even though he was so old he had to be helped back up the steps again, he always came with them. There was no one to see the swelling of Clare's stomach except David, who patted it lovingly as they went out into the early-morning waves.

Then they ate bacon and tomato, which they loved. David joined his father, and Clare walked down the Cliff Road to her old home. She had a cup of tea in the kitchen, did any shopping that was needed. Then, while it was still early, she would walk back the Cliff Road watching the families getting ready for the day on the beach, and she would let herself into the Lodge. The day would pass in studying. David usually found time to come in at least twice before he was home for the evening. They rarely went out to the hotel, and apart from the Committee dance they had no social outing. It was peaceful in the evenings, the sunset looking

413

like an exaggerated picture from their own window. And sometimes they did a little desultory painting of the upstairs rooms. Bumper Byrne's contract had only gone so far as to get the place habitable and have the downstairs part decorated. 'After all, who'll be looking at the upstairs except the pair of you?' he had said cheerfully. David and Clare were so happy to be into the place they didn't argue.

There were three rooms upstairs: their bedroom, the room they would make into a nursery and the storeroom. Clare had thought of having that made into a study. Wouldn't it be great to have a place you could spread your books and papers and never have to take them up when a meal was needed or when you had to tidy the place up? But, David had said, what was the point of having a study upstairs? Wouldn't it be a bit antisocial, locking herself away there, and when the baby arrived . . .

Clare agreed. She would leave it till later.

They painted the nursery a sunny yellow colour, and as soon as they started murmuring quietly about hoping to start a family around Christmas, Nellie became very excited and made curtains for them with all kinds of nursery-rhyme figures on the fabric.

David took his toys from the window seat of his old bedroom, slowly bit by bit, and always when his mother was out. He wasn't stealing them, he just did not want to have to mention the child. Her face froze over in a mask when the subject was hinted at. David dreaded thinking about how she would react when the baby was born.

'I think she'll come round. Not to me, but to the baby.'

'We should make sure she has some time with him herself. Or her, of course.'

They were convinced that it would be a boy. He was to be christened Patrick Thomas.

As the days went on it seemed impossible they had lived any other kind of life. The hectic, rushed meetings in Dublin, the dirty flat with the smelly hall and the unpainted, uncarpeted stairway in Rathmines seemed from a different life lived by different people. David said he could hardly remember the name of the registrar with the carroty head who was always fighting with everyone in the Res. Clare said that if she were on a torture rack she wouldn't be able to remember anything at all that she and Mary Catherine and Valerie talked about for two and a half years.

Now they talked about David's patients. He delivered three babies that summer. But, actually, Mrs Brennan had done most of the work, she was a marvellous midwife he said, reassuring and practical. The women loved her. That interested Clare, she had always thought Mrs Brennan was an almighty bossy boots but this cast a new light on her. David told Clare the secrets of the town, knowing that she wasn't going to speak of them to anyone. Josie Dillon's grandmother had senile dementia and was in the county home; very quietly, the whole thing was done, but that was where she was. Mrs Conway was going to the town shortly to have a hysterectomy. Father O'Dwyer had such a bad chest David's father had told him that it was an act of suicide to continue smoking and the Lord would look on it very poorly indeed. Father O'Dwyer had told Dr Power to keep his religious pronouncements to himself and concentrate on medicine. 'I am concentrating on medicine, you stupid man,' Dr Power had roared at him, and there had been a slow process of reconciliation in which David had to be the middle man.

She learned that her own brother, Jim, was very hard of hearing – not just slow, and stupid, as they had all thought. He was going to have a hearing aid, and David said that there could well be total hearing loss.

'Maybe you could teach him lip-reading, after finals.'

'Teach him what?' Clare laughed. 'I don't know how to lip-read.'

'But you could learn, couldn't you? It could make all the difference. Otherwise he'll just end up like Mickey Mack or someone.'

Clare was shocked. Yes, of course she could learn. There must be books on the subject, and diagrams. Yes, of course, she would.

David was becoming like his father already, concerned and involved in everything that happened. In a few weeks people had stopped thinking of him as a boy helping his father and holding the fort until the real doctor arrived. The day came when a woman said to David's father that she had begun with young Dr Power and she thought she would continue with him if that was all right, he had been so helpful.

David's father took out a bottle of sherry at lunch that day, and Molly had laughed with pride and told Nellie about it as the meal was being put on the table. And as they smiled about how well David was settling into the practice, no mention was made of his wife sitting fifty yards away, bent over her studies with a cup of soup.

There was no phone in the Lodge yet but there was a buzzer from the house, so that David could be woken for night calls. It was awkward, because it meant he had to go up to his parents' to hear the details before setting out. Still, they had been promised a phone soon, and were at the top of the priority list.

Clare heard the buzzer with surprise one morning; David had long gone on house calls, they must have known she was on her own. Resignedly she walked to the house. Molly was in the hall.

'There's a call from Dublin for you,' she said and held the receiver out as if it might contaminate her.

'I'm sorry for disturbing you,' Clare said.

It was Mary Catherine. She and Val had the most marvellous flat, they were installed now and they would keep it for a year. Val was going to do a Higher Diploma in education and Mary Catherine was going to do a Diploma to be a librarian. Any time Clare wanted to come and stay, there was plenty of room.

A longing so great came over Clare, it almost made her faint.

Miles and miles away from Dracula, who was sighing as if the phone were needed urgently. Molly was just in earshot, fiddling with some flowers that didn't need adjustment.

Clare sighed too.

'Well? Can you come up? Will you?'

'I'll write to you about it.'

'Can't you talk?'

'That's right.'

'Do your best. We'd love you to come. David, too, of course, if he can get away. We've got a big double bed in the spare room.'

'Sounds great.'

'So you'll try?'

'As I said, I'll write.'

She told Mrs Power pleasantly that her friends were inviting David and herself to visit.

Mrs Power gave a tinkling laugh. 'That's very nice of them, Clare dear. But David's never been short of a place to stay in Dublin. Heavens *no*. We've *lots* of friends there, and the Nolans' house has always been a second home to him.'

Clare smiled. And before her face cracked with the effort, she returned to the Lodge and started to bang things, hard, with a ruler. She was so angry she was shaking. She tried to concentrate on her work but *that woman*'s superior voice rang in her ears. She was going out.

She left a note on the table in case David called in, and marched out nearly taking the door from its hinges. She walked first to Bumper Byrne's lean-to shed that he called his office, and spoke to him sharply about their gate. It was meant to be a proper entrance, with a gate, and tar-macadamed path. What was it but a hole in the hedge? No. It was *not* perfectly adequate for the moment. She would like it done. This week. Could he tell her which day? No? Well then, she'd wait here till he *could* tell her which day. No. She didn't mind waiting at all. In desperation Bumper said he'd have someone up there on Thursday, and she thanked him warmly.

Then she went to Peter O'Connor who had a saw and used to cut down trees. He'd be about the only person in Castlebay who could advise her on how to build a hedge.

'I want to plant a hedge that looks small and harmless now but will grow up like a flash and make a big forest,' she said to him.

He knew why she wanted the hedge.

417

'I'm not great on the pronunciation but I think it's called Cupressors that you want.'

'That's the Latin for a cypress tree, is that what you mean?'

'The very thing. I could get you a set of nice young plants . . .'

'Not *too* young, Mr O'Connor.'

'When do you want them in?'

'This afternoon. And I'd like them to grow twenty feet tall by next week.'

'Come on, now. She's not as bad as all that?'

Clare laughed. 'Of course not. Just as long as it's grown fairly soon.'

She called to see her mother. The shop was full.

'Do you want me to get behind the counter and give you a hand?'

'Are you out of your mind? The doctor's wife? Serving? Have some sense.'

She went into the hotel.

'Will you have lunch with me Josie? A real lunch in the dining room? I'll pay . . .'

'I can't, Clare, not in the middle of the season. Mummy'd go mad and Rose would make another scene. We're meant to leave those tables for the paying customers.'

'I would be a paying customer,' Clare said crossly.

'No, real people. Not us. It's ages since I've seen you. How are you, anyway?'

'Like a weasel,' said Clare and left with a wave.

She thought she would go up to Angela's cottage. She bought a bottle of sherry in Costello's, and snapped the head off Teddy Costello who called her Mrs Power.

'God Almighty, Teddy, we were in mixed infants together – you called me Clare until a few months ago. Am I to start calling you Mr Costello?'

He stammered, he thought it was what she'd like, what Mrs Power senior would like. He was sorry.

'You know what they say in the films: "You're beautiful when you're angry, Miss Jones."' It was Gerry. He had been behind her, and she hadn't noticed.

She laughed, in spite of herself. 'No, *really*, Gerry, this Mrs bit is the last straw.'

'Fiona likes it. She says it makes her feel grown-up.'

'It doesn't do that for me. It makes me feel we're all in some school play or other.'

'You see, I told you,' he sighed. 'You should never have married him. Go off and abuse the rest of the town. You've demolished Teddy fairly successfully,' he added good-naturedly, and disappeared.

Just as she was leaving the shop she saw Angela carrying fruit and a big bottle of orange over to the back of Dick Dillon's car.

'Are you going on a picnic?' she asked enviously.

'Just a few miles down the coast. Dick has a day off, we thought we'd explore a bit.'

'Great.'

'Why aren't *you* at your work by the way?'

'I came out for a bit of air.'

'And a something to keep you going?' Angela eyed the bottle-shaped parcel.

'Yes. Well.'

'I hope it helps the studying,' Angela said cheerfully and waved goodbye.

Disconsolately Clare walked back to the Lodge. Her anger with her mother-in-law was gone. But so was a lot of her good spirits. She hoped that David had been in and out while she was on her travels. She didn't feel like talking to him now, she wouldn't be able to get the despondent note out of her voice. There was a note on the table beside her books.

Glad you went out, it's the best day of summer. Why don't we take a day off together and go down the coast a bit? I was in seeing Peter O'Connor's child who got burned and he told me you'd ordered little saplings for the garden. That's a great idea, he's going to look them

419

out for us and bring them tomorrow which is very speedy
for Castlebay!

I love you my darling, and I'll see you this evening.

He wrote his name with a heart round it.

She sat down at her table and cried till the tears showered
down on her big handwriting in all the files of notes.

He was the most generous and loving man in the whole
world and here she was marching around the town trying to
build a drawbridge and moat between him and his family.
She felt wretched and shabby: maybe some of the things that
Dracula believed about her were right? She just wasn't good
enough for David.

They had their picnic down the coast. There were gulls and
two small seals, and a school of porpoises too. They lay in the
sun, happy and rested; they ran in and out of the sea; they
drank their bottle of wine and their flask of coffee and ate their
hard-boiled eggs and brown bread and butter. And the ice
cream, which hadn't melted, wrapped up in six newspapers.

They kissed and laughed, and David accused her of
having given Peter O'Connor unmentionable favours in
order to make him do the hedge so quickly, and even more
favours to Bumper Byrne and his gang, who had suddenly
produced a very presentable entrance, having promised it
since last April.

Clare said all his female patients were in love with him
and that Rose Dillon at the hotel was definitely out to get
him, married man or not. They wished they had taken old
Bones with them; he would have loved this beach but he was
getting a bit creaky now and he might have found the walk
down and back too much for him.

They were as happy as they ever had been.

On September first she went to Dublin on the train. She had
fourteen days before her exams began. David was going to
come up for two weekends, and then to collect her and take
her home when the exams were finished. She said it would
be a waste for him to come with her now.

'I wish you all the luck in the world, my girl,' Dr Power had said, 'but you've never done anything except come in the top league in every examination you ever did. Do you remember my driving you into the town all those years ago, to do your scholarship? I remember it as if it were yesterday . . .' Dr Power beamed at her, and sighed at the way the years had flashed by.

Molly had decided to be charming. 'I hope you get all the questions you're looking for,' she said. 'Maybe that's not a very intellectual way of putting it but you know what I mean . . .'

They drove round by O'Brien's and she went in to kiss her mother goodbye.

'Lord, child, it's not the ends of the earth you're going to,' Agnes said.

'I know, Mam, but this is *it*, this is the B.A., the degree.'

'Well I know, Clare, and we all hope you'll do very well, but that's all behind you now, isn't it?'

Her mother came to the door and waved, puzzled at the exasperation that had come into Clare's face. After all, she had only said what was true. A lot of people didn't think that Clare should have bothered to go back to college to do that exam after getting married.

It was somehow like showing off.

'Will we have to learn first aid?' Val asked fearfully as Clare took off her shoes and eased her back with a cushion.

'What do you mean?'

'In case your man gets born here, what do we do? I know you need a watch to time things.'

'Not a chance. Week beginning October fifteenth. David's father hopes it's going to be the eighteenth, that's the feast of St Luke apparently, and Luke was a doctor in his time. What is it?' she asked suddenly as she saw Mary Catherine looking at a diary.

'Oh dear. You'll miss Conferring,' she said.

'I will *not* miss Conferring. I will bloody not. If Patrick Thomas is three days old, I'd be well enough to travel, wouldn't I? I *can't* miss Conferring. Maybe he'll come early . . .' Clare addressed her stomach. 'Be a good boy now and please your Mammy . . . arrive around the end of September, maybe the twenty-ninth, so that Mammy will be ready to come back up to Dublin and get Conferred.'

Mary Catherine was still looking at her diary. 'That would be quite a good day, actually. Feast of St Michael and all the angels.'

Clare clapped her hands. 'Right! Did you hear that? Be here on September twenty-ninth and we'll add Michael to your names.'

'I thought this yucky mumsy stuff only started *after* they were born,' said Valerie.

It was just as she had dreamed it would be. Plenty of room, books all around the place, cups of coffee being made all day and all night, friends dropping in. Down to the National Library where people noticed her condition and smiled congratulations. In to UCD where people noticed her condition and were surprised. She had been a quiet student, and only the people in her own group knew her well.

She paid her examination fee, and got her number. It made it seem very close when she had the card with her own number.

She went to see Emer and Kevin and she noticed from their faces they were surprised to see how pregnant she now looked. Perhaps she had been holding herself in at home: everyone here seemed more aware of it.

Clare discussed the work she had done with her tutor.

'I didn't think we'd ever hear from you again,' he said.

'Why on *earth* did you think that?' Clare asked furiously.

'Well, married bliss, and a summer in Castlebay, a *summer* there, mind, not a week. I thought you wouldn't open a book again.'

'My only worry is the B.A.' Clare smiled at him. 'I suppose I sound a bit intense, and off my rocker to a lot of people. But when it's so hard, you get a kind of Holy Grail thing about it.'

'I know, I wish they all found it as important as you do.'

'Wish me luck then.'

'You don't need luck, Clare O'Brien . . . or whatever your name is now. You're the grade, everyone in the department knows it.'

They knew. Now all she had to do was prove it to them. She smiled as she went to sleep that night.

She had phoned David. He had just returned home after his second visit to Dublin. The Lodge was lonely without her, but in under ten days she would be back and they would wait. Together.

He wished her courage and energy and confidence. He couldn't say he loved her because he was standing in the hall, but he did say, 'And everything,' which was their code word.

She turned over and went to sleep happily.

Mary Catherine woke up in alarm.

'Come quickly! She's groaning, and shouting!'

'What? Who?'

'Clare. She's doubled over. Jesus, Mary and Joseph, I think she's having the baby. After all our joking about it.'

'Don't be ridiculous. It couldn't be. It's not for weeks yet.'

'Shut up. It could be a miscarriage. No, it couldn't, it's much too late . . . I don't know. Get an ambulance.'

'She keeps saying no.'

Clare was white-faced, with sweat coming down her forehead. 'It's all right,' she gasped. 'I couldn't be having it. I couldn't. These aren't those pains you have. No downward pull or whatever they said.'

'We don't know any doctors here, we're not on anyone's list, we're calling an ambulance, Valerie's phoning it this minute.' Mary Catherine was trying to be calm.

'Please don't. I can't go to hospital. The exam . . . There's nothing wrong.'

'Please, Clare. Just go in and be a false alarm, will you? Just for us? Please. Then you can come out twenty minutes later, and we'll all laugh at it. Please.'

She kicked the door closed with her foot so that Clare couldn't hear Valerie explaining down the phone how bad

423

the patient was. 'Then we'll all go in and do the exams calmly.'

'I don't want you to be up half the night,' Clare cried.

Valerie came in, looking pale. 'We'll get dressed. We'll go with her.'

'*No!*' screamed Clare.

The ambulance was there in ten minutes. The girls had packed Clare's things quietly, and out of her line of vision.

The ambulance men were reassurance itself.

'It's all a false alarm,' Clare said with a tear-stained face. 'I'm so sorry and you see we're all starting our exams tomorrow. Our finals.'

She bent over with pain.

The ambulance men exchanged glances, and the driver leaped smartly into the driving seat and switched on the siren.

The pain was beyond anything she could possibly have imagined; nothing helped; not panting like a dog as they had taught her, nor reciting poetry very fast in an undertone, nor writhing and wriggling into different positions. A lugubrious student midwife kept telling her to relax. Clare wanted to kill her.

She was in labour for two hours before they told her that something was wrong. The midwife, listening for the third time to the foetal heartbeat, straightened up with more than usual gloom.

'The baby's in some distress.'

'Oh my God,' cried Clare wildly. 'What's wrong? Can you tell what's wrong?'

'The heart's not standing up to the contractions.'

'But will it be all right? The baby, I mean?'

'I can't say,' said the midwife, 'I shall have to report it.'

It seemed like hours. Clare felt pure terror; and the most intense longing for David. It had never occurred to her that the birth would be anything but straightforward; now it appeared that the baby was being killed by something uncontrollable inside her own body. Before she had held it, kissed it or even looked upon its face, her baby would die; and there was nothing she could do about it.

She was holding her breath as though that might ease the baby's distress when the door swung open to admit Bar, the red-headed doctor whom David disliked so much. The examination took seconds.

'Cord's dropped,' he said. 'I'm very sorry. I know how disappointed you will be. We shall have to do a Caesarean. We'll also have to ask you to sign a piece of paper giving your consent.'

'A Caesarean,' said Clare, high-voiced with joy. 'Oh thank God. Thank God. I'd forgotten all about Caesareans.'

Later she knew that a dropped cord was the worst emergency after a haemorrhage. Then she was only aware of Bar, now in a white mask and a green overall, giving clipped instructions. His face, which before had seemed rather heartless, now looked blessedly confident and know-it-all. Sister McClusky, summoned because she was an 'expert at cords', was an enormous, jovial woman who stuck her hand inside and gave Clare a running commentary on how well the baby was coping, all the way to the operating theatre.

'I love you,' she said, then they put her under. She felt the first violent pain of the knife, heard someone say it was a beautiful baby girl, before the anaesthetic took effect and she knew no more.

She woke up in the recovery room where the first person she saw was David holding their baby in his arms.

'She grinned,' he said. 'I've been holding her for an hour, waiting for you to come round, and she gave me the biggest grin you've ever seen.'

'She's not normal, is she?' said Clare.

'Darling, she's *perfect*.'

'You're lying to me, she's a mongol.'

'Here, see for yourself, she's beautiful.'

'Babies don't grin until they're six weeks old.'

At this point the baby began to cry, steadily angrily; and Clare, taking her in her arms for the first time, made two extraordinary discoveries. The first was that on contact with

425

her mother the baby instantly stopped crying; and the second was that she was indeed utterly, perfectly, beautiful. True, the nose was a bit squashed, but her eyes were big and clear, and she had masses of hair. Her fingers looked as if they'd been soaked too long in washing-up liquid, but they were slender and graceful with long, pointed nails – almost as if they'd been specially manicured for her debut. Round one minute wrist and one ankle were plastic bands stating that she was Girl Power, and the date and time of birth.

With a flash of insight, Clare suddenly wished that they could all stay here forever, the baby safely cradled in her arms, protected by the hospital staff. For with this new love came also a new and terrible vulnerability, from which there would never be an escape. How shall I endure chicken pox, and tree climbing, and reading about children dying in fires? she thought. Life stretched away in an infinity of dangers and she felt afraid.

PART FOUR

1960–1962

There were all the explanations: nobody got their arithmetic wrong, but it was the strain and the stress of the exam that brought the baby on; or she was genuinely a baby that was kicking and screaming to be born and would not wait the time; or Clare had been eating all the wrong food and not taking enough rest.

She had a very small face, but it wasn't nearly as red as the faces of other babies in the hospital; and her eyelashes were longer than any they had ever seen. She was so delicate and fine, that suddenly John Fitzgerald Byrne became a huge, hulking monster in comparison, and any other baby was crabbed and ugly.

Clare and David looked at each other and back at this magnificent person they had created. They kept saying over and over that they couldn't believe it. They said it so often in front of Father Flynn that he said he thought that's what they wanted her christened.

They decided they would give her a name that nobody else had, nobody else they knew. She wouldn't be Molly or Agnes; nor would she be Chrissie or Caroline or Angela or Emer or Valerie or Mary Catherine. She would not be a Fiona or a Josie or a Bernie. She would be a name that nobody had used before and put a shape into like wearing a jumper.

They didn't know any Victorias, and neither of them knew anyone called Martha; so those two were considered. Then David thought of Olivia, and the more he said it the more the tiny baby seemed to suit it; and the more they liked it. Olivia Power. It was a name that sounded made for her.

'You'll have to have a saint's name as well,' said the nurse who knew everything.

'I don't mind, any saint,' Clare said cheerfully.

'Mary's always nice,' said the nurse.

'What's your mother's name?' Clare asked David suddenly.

'It's Molly, you know that.'

'Yes, but what's it short for?'

'Margaret.'

'Right. We'll call her Olivia Mary. I just didn't want to let poor Saint Agnes feel left out. Da was put out enough about John Fitzgerald Byrne, I'll tell you that . . .'

Olivia Mary Power was ten days old when she left the hospital. Her mother was still pale, and rather shaken-looking. Olivia would need more bottles than a baby which had gone the full nine months, but she was perfectly well and healthy. She had a small christening, with champagne, in the private room which had been found for Clare when they realized she was a doctor's wife and not the hysterical student they had taken her for when she was admitted. There were flowers and cards, and a great deal of admiration.

At no time did anyone say that it was a pity that this of all babies had to be premature since they were going to pretend in Castlebay anyway that it was a premature birth even if it were six weeks late.

And at no time did anyone mention to anyone in the room that it was a pity that Olivia Mary Power could not have delayed her arrival for ten days so that her mother could have sat the examination for the degree she had so much wanted.

There was so much delight about the new baby, it would sound unwelcoming to say anything about bad timing.

'Do you think she minds desperately and isn't saying?' Valerie asked Mary Catherine.

'I have no idea. I know I was about to show her the examination papers and something stopped me. And I never mentioned them again.

'It's funny, I've never been afraid to ask her anything, and even when I was on my own with her and the baby the other day, I couldn't ask.'

'Neither could I. That plausible attorney called me to ask me out, and in the midst of my saying no, he suddenly cut in and asked was she going funny in the head about the exams. He said that since he met her as a kid she's been talking about getting a degree, and now she doesn't mention it.'

'I don't think she minds. I think she's so goddamned pleased about the baby.'

'There's a bit in the New Testament about a woman getting all pleased about a man being born into the world.'

'Spare me your interpretations of the Bible, Val. Nobody in Ireland has ever read the book as far as I can see.'

'Wasn't that the worst luck ever? Poor Clare.'

Dick and Angela were learning to cook from a book, and each week they made something new in Angela's kitchen.

Angela agreed. 'I thought it would be the end of the world, and that we'd hear the tears of her the whole way from Dublin. But it seems she's not taking it badly at all.'

'I suppose, now she has the baby . . .' Dick broke off and frowned into the bowl. 'Is this the pale and light in texture that I should beat it until?'

'The people who write these books should be hanged. It looks pale and light in texture to me, but how would you know? This one says cook till ready. If we knew when "ready" was, we wouldn't need their stupid books.' She banged round the kitchen a bit.

'I suppose she could always sit it again next year.'

'She could. But people don't. It's like that. And with a small child she won't keep up her studies. How could she?'

'You're worried about her.'

'I am, but don't mind me. I worry about everything.'

Agnes read the letter out to Tom: the way the child's hair came forward and sideways from the crown like a little star. How the tiny toes each had a perfect little pink nail on them. How David had to bring all the things for the baby when he came up in such a rush, and he couldn't find half of them so he had packed table cloths and sheets and teatowels instead of the little matinee coats and vests.

'She seems to be delighted with the child,' Agnes said, pleased.

'Didn't it arrive a bit early? Isn't that what people will think?' Tom O'Brien looked at her over his glasses, waiting to see what reaction he would get.

'Wasn't it *miles* too early? Isn't that why she missed her exam?' Agnes said.

'But even if . . .'

'Tom, will you stop that, doesn't everyone know that the child wasn't expected for an age. Clare thought she was going to be doing her B.A., and everything.'

'Yes. Yes.' He saw there was going to be no scolding and complaining on the home side, which was a great blessing. 'Queer sort of name they gave it,' he grumbled.

'Oh you can be sure that's the Powers' doing. Some fancy choice of Molly's. That's what it will turn out to be. But saying nothing, that's always the best.'

Nellie wanted to know when they'd be home. She had been down to the Lodge on her day off in order to have it right for them. She hadn't liked Clare coming in there at first, she was sure there would be airs and graces. But as the months went on Nellie had felt sorry for the girl, stuck in there at her books all day. If ever you passed the window she wouldn't even look up, reading and studying and learning.

Nellie had known from the word go that there was a child on the way, and she knew better than anyone how enraged it had made the Mistress. The trouble was that the Mistress had no real friends she could talk to, and was sore to the bottom of her heart about it. She woke bad-tempered and she went to bed bad-tempered.

Nellie pitied her. She wasn't a bad woman – full of nonsense, of course, but everyone had something a bit wrong with them. Of course she'd have liked David to have got a finer girl than one of the O'Briens from the shop. David Power was the equal of anyone, but if he *had* got the little O'Brien girl into trouble and if he *did* seem happy to marry her, then Nellie thought that the best should be made of it all. There was no point in conducting a war across fifty yards of garden. Maybe it would be better when the baby came back, but you didn't need to be a genius to see that the Mistress was even more livid that the child had arrived so early. Now there was *no* way of covering up.

Molly said that they'd be arriving on Saturday.

'Will I set the tea for all of you in the dining room?' she asked.

Molly was about to say no, then she thought again. 'Yes, that's right, set it for all of us.'

Nellie smiled to herself, at least she had done that much for the young couple, they wouldn't have to be banished to their own little place and wait till the Mistress buzzed for them.

Dr Power was waiting on the platform, eager as a child.

They were in the front of the train, so they passed him, blinking happily into the carriages. Clare felt the tears come to her eyes, and David leaped up to wave out the window. 'Father, father.'

They didn't like Dr Power to drive on his own now, so he had brought Mrs Brennan with him. She had wanted to do a few things in town. She was waiting now in the car. Molly had said she'd prefer to meet them at home and because she had arranged a welcome-home supper, Paddy hadn't argued with her.

He hurried until his steps were a run down the platform and he peered into the white bundle. He took off his glasses and wiped them and put them on again.

'Isn't she perfect, God bless her, perfect little girl,' he said.

Clare was very nervous of anyone else touching the baby; but there she was thrusting it into her father-in-law's arms. He joggled her around expertly. He was so sweet that other people started to look at them.

'We're making a circus of ourselves,' he said. 'Come on, Clare, girl, let's go home.'

They walked to the ticket gate and Dr Power showed off his grandchild. Mrs Brennan in the car admired the baby with all the right words.

'Am I holding her right, do you think, Mrs Brennan?' Clare asked.

433

It was very much the thing to have asked. Mrs Brennan's face softened to the girl she had thought of as a bit of a madam up to now. All the way back to Castlebay they had lessons on supporting the head, and keeping the spine firm and the way to tilt the bottle. Dr Power hid his smile of pleasure when he saw how genuinely interested Clare and David were in what the woman was saying.

Six months ago they would both have crossed the road to avoid talking to Mrs Brennan. Now they hung on her every word.

Dr Power drove to the door of the big house.

'Molly has supper for you all here. Will we go straight in and show her the baby or would you like to go to your own house first?'

There was no doubting which he wanted.

David looked at Clare quickly.

'We'd love to come in and show off the baby,' she said.

Molly had been to the hairdresser, and she was wearing her best knitted two-piece. She was standing in the sitting room as if the gentry were coming.

David ran in and kissed her, and then stood back.

Clare put the baby straight into Molly's arms, which startled her. She had expected to bend over Clare and admire the child that way. Now she was holding her grandchild all on her own.

They couldn't stop admiring the baby. Clare looked at Molly occasionally, when she wasn't looking; Dracula was absorbed in the baby.

Nobody was going to be forgiven for anything, like blighting David's young life, forcing him to marry a girl from the lower classes, a shotgun wedding and an early baby. But given all that, at least Molly liked her grand-daughter. At least she wasn't going to reject the child. Things were looking up.

At Mass next morning they met Gerry. He was full of congratulations.

'Olivia, that's a fine posh name for Castlebay,' he said approvingly.

'Ah, they're sick of these Davids and Clares and Gerrys, the dull old names,' Clare laughed.

'I hope they won't call her Olly,' David said.

'Make your own nickname then,' Gerry said.

'Livy?' Clare suggested.

'Liffey even?' Gerry said. David was buying the papers from Mickey Mack.

'I'm sorry about the exam,' Gerry said in a low voice.

'It doesn't matter,' she said brightly.

'Of course it does.'

'No, really. It sort of faded away. I didn't think it would.'

'You can't fool me. I know that's what you wanted so much, so don't throw my sympathy back at me as if it was worth nothing.' He stamped off

They insisted that Angela come back to the Lodge where Nellie was minding Olivia.

They had coffee and toast, and Angela said she was going to give the baby a book, not a matinee coat, because she couldn't knit for one thing and everyone else gave matinee coats.

'You gave me my first book, remember,' Clare said. 'To console me for not getting the Prize.'

'*A Golden Treasury*. And it turned out better in the end.'

Clare cradled the new infant to her, and her thin white face looked misty remembering all that struggle ten years ago.

Angela wondered, as she saw Clare plant a kiss on the baby's forehead, did she regard this child as a consolation prize for not having got a history degree? And did she think it had all turned out better in the end?

Chrissie was the only one who mentioned that they had only been married five months when the baby was born. 'I'm disgraced in front of the Byrne family,' she said.

Clare sighed. 'Weren't you able to tell them the baby came early?' she asked.

'No baby comes *that* early.'

435

'Is there a chance that you'd like to look at her at all? I brought her to see her cousin. John Fitzgerald seems in great form.' Clare struggled as she felt she had been struggling for years just to get some kind of normal reaction from her sister.

'Oh I have nothing against the child, poor creature, it's none of her doing.'

'Good, then here she is to have a look at.' Clare handed her over. She had found that this was a sure-fire way of making people enthusiastic about the baby, once it was in their arms they felt different.

'She's grand, isn't she?' Chrissie said. 'A bit small of course.'

'That's to do with being born prematurely, I told you,' Clare said.

Chrissie had to laugh then.

'Come here to your Auntie Clare.' Clare picked up John Fitzgerald and gave him a cuddle.

'Well now, you're a big fellow. Six months old. You're a fine big fellow.'

'If you knew all the trouble I had with him being born,' Chrissie said.

'Well I do a bit. It's not a bundle of laughs, is it?'

'What are you talking about? You didn't have to give birth to this little thing at all! Wasn't she lifted out of you?'

'It's a way of describing it, I suppose.' Clare gritted her teeth.

'Sure there'd be no problem, we'd all have a half dozen if that's all there was to it. You wait, Clare, you wait for the next one, and see what it's like. I was in labour for fourteen hours. *Fourteen hours!* But of course that wouldn't be right for the wife of a doctor. They wouldn't leave her pushing and shoving for a whole day and into the night.'

'It must have been desperate all right.' She would have been happy to push Olivia into the world too. But useless to say that to Chrissie.

'Well it was, it wasn't something you forget in a hurry. Still it's more natural, in a way more normal. Imagine, you're only the same as me now, after all the grand plans, all the studying.'

436

'I know, isn't it strange?' Clare said without rancour.

Chrissie felt guilty. 'Well, you'd done enough anyway, hadn't you?'

'Oh definitely.'

All the patients seemed pleased that David was a father. It was nice to have a family man, they said. They sent soft toys for the new baby, they embroidered little dresses. Often the people who had little or no money to pay a doctor were able to give gifts, and they loved an excuse.

A man gave him a pair of hares that had been shot that day. 'Tell your wife to make a nice jugged hare, very good for a baby that is.' Another gave him potin to wet the baby's head and a woman whose house was always thought to be of the illest fame sent a miraculous medal to the little girl and said that this medal would protect her all her life.

Clare became more deft at giving the bottle but it still took a long time. In fact everything about Olivia took a long time. Clare looked with awe at the women trailing six or seven youngsters around with them. How had they managed? Maybe it was only the first that was such a problem, after that you had a team to help you. Now that she came to think of it she remembered giving a bottle to Jim and to Ben, while Mam was in the shop.

Olivia was so sweet you could play with her for hours. Just poking her gently in the tummy made her wave her arms and legs a bit. And she smiled, long before babies smile Olivia was smiling.

'I'm sure everyone must feel a bit like that, but they don't have the time to say it and think about it,' Clare said, looking at the small white bundle in the cradle.

'I don't have all that much more time to say it and think about it, I'm off again.' David finished his cup of tea as he pulled on his coat. 'I don't know how Dad looked after a quarter of this, I really don't, and yet he must have, you don't hear any complaints about him.'

He kissed his wife and daughter and ran through the rain to the car. He was becoming more and more involved in the work and all the patients; he said you'd learn as much in a month in Castlebay as in a year up in the hospital.

In the first few weeks there was no question of doing any studying, and Clare had no intention of beginning it until after Christmas. Everyone said a baby needed your full attention for the first three months. What nobody had said was that a baby took every ounce of your energy for the first three months too. But maybe you were meant to know that.

Olivia was a good baby they said, people who knew, people who had had babies like Mam, and Molly Power and Chrissie and Young Mrs Dillon and Anna Murphy and a dozen more. And the amount she slept was good. But sometimes she cried for long long times. Clare was despairing one morning and just before she took her child up to its grandfather in the surgery she discovered that a nappy pin was open and sticking into the tiny leg.

'How could I have done that to you? How?' Clare wept and held the small baby so close that the howls started again as the child began to feel suffocated.

The bath took a long time. You had to be very careful to hold her properly, she was so slippy, and you had to keep the soap from her eyes and yet make sure she didn't get cold.

And then the bottle. This was a slow day, she kept pushing it away. Finally it was almost finished and she was laid down. But she wouldn't settle. Over and over Clare took her up. It seemed an age before she agreed to sleep, even though her eyes were fighting to stay open.

Then there was the washing. Nellie had offered to help, but unfortunately she had offered when Molly Power was there, raising her eyebrows. So Clare thanked Nellie profusely, and said not at all. It was quite impossible to imagine that a tiny baby like that could provide such a mound of washing. Not to mention David's shirts. At home nobody changed their shirt every day. Dad would wear his shirt for four days maybe. And the boys . . . Lord knew when they changed theirs. But David had a fresh shirt every single day. It took seventeen minutes to iron each bloody shirt in the beginning. Now it took eleven. It was still far too long.

Eleven minutes. That was a whole hour on five shirts one morning, and it was easier to do five at a time because otherwise he used to seem disappointed that he hadn't a choice.

'Ifyou hate it so much I'll do it, it might be quite restful,' he had said once when she protested.

'No you damn well won't, the very first day you do one your mother will call and see you, and I might as well throw my hat at it after that.'

Today she had decided to iron three. But in the middle of the first one Olivia woke up again, and since it was nearly time for her bottle that was the end of the shirts. Then David was home for lunch. Then she had to tidy herself up. This was the day she had been invited for a cup of tea in the big house. Molly talked almost entirely to Olivia, in baby talk, and twice asked the baby, who was not yet three months old, whether she thought that matinee coat was a little bit too tight.

Clare answered, as the baby didn't. It was a fine fit.

'Why then, Olivia, do you have these little red marks on your arm, little sore marks? *Poor* Olivia.'

Clare wanted to hit Molly with one of the big hard uncomfortable cushions on the sofa. Instead she sat back and swallowed her thin tomato sandwich.

David rang her later in the afternoon.

'What's wrong,' she asked, alarmed.

'Nothing's wrong, I'm just celebrating that we have the phone that's all.'

'Yes, it's marvellous. No more buzzing from the Great House.'

'Now, Clare!' he laughed.

'Sorry. Sorry. Will you bring home some chops from Dwyers'?'

'It might be closed when I'm coming back. Why don't you ring them and ask them to deliver?'

'And have Chrissie calling me Lady Muck for a month.'

'Oh well, do what you can. I have to go. I thought I'd just ring.'

'There was nothing you wanted to say?'

'Only that I loved you.'

She hung up, and realized she should have said she loved him too.

She asked Nellie to look after the baby in the kitchen and walked down to Church Street and a confrontation with Chrissie.

Her mother-in-law moved the curtain in the sitting room and watched her go.

She wrote to Valerie that evening but tore up the letter. It was a list of complaints and moans and grouses. It was the kind of letter you would hate to read. Then she put the pieces in the range in case anyone ever found them torn up in the bin and pieced them together. She wondered was she going mad to imagine anyone piecing together one of her letters to Valerie.

David was called out twice in the night.

When the phone went the second time Olivia woke too. Clare went to pick her up. David was putting on his socks and shoes as he talked to the woman on the phone.

'It's no life this, is it?' she said jiggling the crying baby up and down in her arms.

'It's not for that woman.' David nodded at the phone which he had just put down. 'Those bloody dogs they have out there have just eaten the face off her baby.'

'No!'

David had his clothes on by now.

'What will you do?' Clare asked, stricken.

'Hope the baby's dead, properly dead. Hope we can get its mother to agree to go into the hospital. For a couple of days, anyway. She'll need more than just a sedative after that lot.'

He was down the stairs and into the car. It was three hours, and dawn, before he came back. Olivia was asleep again. Clare was in the kitchen, she had a kettle ready and made some tea. He took the mug gratefully.

'Was the baby dead?' she asked.

'Not quite,' he said.

She waited. He said nothing.

'And Mrs Walsh? Is she all right?'

David still said nothing. His shoulders were shaking. He was crying, but he didn't want her near, he went to the window and looked out at the dark sea and the shapes of the cliff heads only becoming visible now. He stood there for a long time and she found no words or gesture to help him.

She went over to the big house to take the paper back. She had read it from cover to cover. There was a voice in the kitchen, talking to Olivia. She thought David must be back, but she didn't see his car. It was Gerry. He was dangling a little woollen ball, a brightly coloured pompom, in front of the baby who was looking at him eagerly.

'Gerry?' She was not pleased. He had given her a fright, and anyway, how dare he come in uninvited?

'I don't remember asking you in,' she said.

'I don't remember a time when friends in Castlebay had to wait to be invited in. Maybe it's different here in the . . . um . . . in the Lodge.' He made the name of the house sound laughable.

'What do you want?'

'I came to see your daughter and ask her would she like her photograph taken. That's all.'

'Don't be childish, Gerry. What do you want?'

'What I said. Would you like a picture of the baby . . . as a wedding present?'

'No,' she said quickly.

'What nice manners they teach up at the Lodge.'

'No thank you. I'm sorry. No thank you very much.'

'Why not? I take nice pictures of babies. They like me.'

Olivia was indeed gurgling up at him and the red, black and yellow ball of wool.

'I'd prefer not, if you don't mind. Thanks, though. Sorry about my manners.' She smiled, hoping he'd go.

He stood up. 'She's beautiful,' he said. 'I sometimes think I'd like one.'

'Well, nothing's stopping you.' She tried to be light. 'You know how to set about it.'

'Ah, but it would be no use if it weren't yours too.'

She flinched.

He put up both his hands in peace. 'I'm off, I'm off. Take that look off your face.'

He did have his camera with him, in its shabby black bag that he had always used. 'Whenever you think she's old enough, I'd love to.'

'Sure. I'll talk about it with David,' she said.

'Do that.' He smiled and was gone.

She felt very uneasy and didn't know why. He only wanted to take a photograph. He had only made those sort of flattering remarks that he made to everyone. Why did she feel so bothered?

She invited her mother-in-law to see the baby being bathed. She spent the whole day tidying the place up first.

Molly came to watch the ritual.

Clare tested the heat of the water with her elbow, feeling very experienced.

'Do you do that? How strange,' Molly said. 'How very strange, with all the thermometers and everything. Ah well.' She sighed as if her granddaughter was being brought up by a thick, ignorant peasant who knew nothing.

One grey morning she heard a timid tapping on the door. It was her mother.

'You haven't been down for a bit. I called to see you.'

'That's great. Come on in.'

Agnes O'Brien looked around as if fearful someone might ask her what she was doing there. 'Have you done up the parlour yet?' she asked.

'You're always asking me that. What would we need a parlour for or a sitting room or drawing room or whatever we'd call it? This is where we live.'

Agnes jerked her head up towards the big house. 'But wouldn't they expect . . .?'

'Let them expect what they like. David and I want to make this a nice bright room that we can live in. Armchairs and bookshelves and the advantage of it being the kitchen as well.'

'And when are you going to start?' her mother asked innocently.

'Will we have a cup of tea?' Wearily she emptied the tealeaves from the pot and put it on the range.

'Are you using a kettle?'

'There's just the two of us, Mam.'

She was wrong.

Molly Power was at the door.

'I thought you might want something from town, I'm going in with Mrs Dillon this afternoon. Hallo, Mrs O'Brien.'

'Good morning, Mrs Power. Good morning.' Agnes stammered a little.

'Come to admire the baby?'

'Yes, well, Clare hasn't shown her to me yet.'

'Clare dear, do show the baby to your mother.'

Clare fumed. Her mother had made it seem that she had never seen her granddaughter at all. Mrs Power made Clare feel like a very unsatisfactory hired help.

She went upstairs for Liffey. She was not only wet, her nappy was filthy. The clean nappies were downstairs.

She went down to get them.

'Oh, don't bother dressing her up specially.'

'I'm not,' Clare hissed.

She did a rapid change job and Liffey, alarmed by the speed and lack of gentleness, cried in fright. Clare handed her first to her mother.

'I don't know whether I should . . .'

Why did Mam have to be so humble?

'You had six of your own, I'm sure you won't drop her.' Her voice was sharp. The teapot was hissing. Trying to shield her actions from her mother-in-law, Clare put four spoons of tea into the boiling water and pulled it aside.

'What a funny way to make tea,' Mrs Power said clearly.

'I've told Clare a dozen times not to do that,' Agnes said. Awkwardly she passed the baby over to Mrs Power. For a few minutes Molly Power cooed at her grandchild, and by magic the child stopped crying.

'There you are,' said Molly triumphantly, as if she alone knew the secret.

443

She refused a cup of tea without actually shuddering, and left.

Clare and her mother were full of gloom.

'You shouldn't let her see the house like this, Clare, really.' Agnes looked at the heap of dirty clothes in a corner, the unwashed saucepans on the draining board.

'It's my house. I'll have it look exactly the way I want to.'

'Oh all right.' Her mother was about to take offence and leave.

'Not you, Mam, sit down. I mean her. Why should we bow down before her? I'm damned if I'll do everything the way Lady Molly wants.'

'No, but you could do a bit of cleaning and cooking, that's not bowing down before her,' Agnes said coldly.

Clare knew that she wouldn't drop in again casually; she would have to go and invite her from now on.

She had been very entertained by Angela's attempts to learn to cook; and decided it wasn't a bad idea. She might well do the same herself. She made shortbread biscuits one morning and took a plate of them up to the house for Molly.

'Won't you come in and have coffee with me?' Molly said.

'I left her there on her own,' Clare said.

'Oh well. Another time then.'

The woman could have said, go back for her, couldn't she?

She lay on her bed resting one morning, and her mind just drifted off. She wasn't asleep for more than a moment. David came in.

'Hey, you worried me. I thought you weren't here.'

'What is it? What's wrong?'

'Clare, what *are* you doing? Olivia's crying her head off downstairs, Bones is sitting looking at her, and there's no lunch.'

'It's not lunchtime.'

'It's half past one, I thought I'd be late.'

'Christ, I'm sorry, David. I must have fallen asleep.' She leaped from the bed and raced down the stairs. With Olivia

444

in one arm she grabbed a saucepan and broke three eggs into it, she reached for some butter.

'What are you doing?'

'David my love, I'm making you a scrambled egg. I'm sorry, I'll make a proper dinner this evening, I tell you I must have drifted off to sleep. I feel so tired sometimes.'

'I know. I know. It's all right.'

'It's not all right, I'm dreadfully sorry.'

'Look, will I make toast or something?'

'No, hold your daughter, I'm quicker.'

She swept the breakfast things away and into the sink.

'I don't want you to feel you have to cook a lunch for me every day, don't think that . . .'

'Darling David – will you stop it. One day, just *one* day I fell asleep. Every other day I love to have lunch with you. I love it. I used to be very lonely when you were up with your mother and father and I was there at the window working.'

They both looked over at the window as she spoke. No books there now, just a big arrangement of dried flowers.

'Aren't you going to start studying again?'

'What for?'

'Clare, please. Don't be like that. For your degree of course.'

'I studied for it once, why should I do it again?'

'Because you didn't take it, you clown. You were happy studying.

'Not all the time I wasn't. A lot of the time I was worried and anxious.'

'Will we go to the pictures tonight?'

'Are you trying to entertain me by any chance?'

'A bit I suppose.' He looked troubled.

Clare asked Angela was there any kind of Christmas present you could make for people, by cooking, something that would look as if you'd gone to a lot of trouble over it.

'I suppose you could make fudge,' Angela said doubtfully, 'and put it in nice coloured boxes. But why do you want to make things? You're worse than me. And I think they'd expect a bit more than fudge from you.'

445

'Who'd expect? I don't care what they expect, I'm so tired, I tell you Angela I can't stay awake these days. It's such an effort to go into town, and there's nothing here . . .'

'Well stay awake long enough to go into town just one day. Make a list of what you want. Come in with Dick and me on Saturday afternoon.'

'Yes, I could do that. I'll ask her Ladyship would she mind Liffey.'

'Liffey. Isn't *that a* name, now. How did you think of it?'

'I just made it up,' Clare said. She didn't want to tell anyone that it was Gerry Doyle's idea.

'Am I going to teach you to drive, Clare? Remember we set it all up. You learned the theory all at once.'

There was a silence at the back of the car.

'I think she's asleep, Dick,' Angela said.

'No, sorry, what was it?'

'Will I give you driving lessons after Christmas?'

'I don't know if I'd have the time. It's very kind of you. If I have the time . . .'

Molly and David were sitting by the fire in the big house when she came back.

'You look exhausted,' David said.

'David, you must get Clare some nice clothes, it's terrible to have her dragging round in all that student-type thing. No wonder the girl looks so dawney.'

Clare let them talk about her.

'Why don't we all have a sherry, you've provided the excuse.' David leaped up.

'A really nice coat in a good bright colour, something that would put some colour in her face.' Molly was thoughtful. 'A cherry red maybe.'

David handed them both a sherry.

'Thank you, my dear,' Molly said.

Clare said nothing.

'Was it exhausting?'

'It was very tiring all right,' Clare said.

'Did you leave your parcels in at the Lodge?'

446

'No. This is all I got.' She had a small shopping bag with a few little things in it.

She sat on a stool looking into the fire and eventually David and his mother went back to talking as they had been before she came in. They didn't even try to bring her into the conversation.

David bought all the Christmas presents in the end. He even wrapped them and wrote the cards. He put the Christmas cards she was to send to Mary Catherine and Valerie in front of her and she wrote Love from Clare on each of them.

When David opened his Christmas present from Clare he said he was delighted with the shirt. It was just what he wanted. You couldn't have enough shirts. He said this one was particularly nice, and he put it away hastily before his mother could see it had been bought in the shop in Castlebay and was exactly the same as half a dozen which he had already.

David had bought Christmas tree decorations when he was in town: he couldn't bear anyone in Castlebay to see him buying them locally. He brought a tree home from one of his country calls, the man whose child had been sick was delighted to give the young doctor a fine green tree.

'Your wife will enjoy decorating that, Doctor,' the man beamed as they fitted the tree into the back of the car.

'Oh, she's going to love it,' David said with a smile he didn't feel.

He looked carefully at his mother's tree that evening and did something a bit similar to their own; Clare looked up at him gratefully as he stood on a chair.

'That's terrific, David, it looks really lovely. I'd do it myself but I'm just worn out.'

It was cold clear weather, from the window David saw his parents warmly dressed and in their comfortable walking shoes setting out with the dog. He knew they would head far along the cliff away from Castlebay and they would point things out to each other, and see the birds swooping low and hares running through the fields. They would come back to

447

a hot lunch. They would sit on either side of a big well made-up fire and read. He looked over at Clare to know if she too would like a walk. She was sitting at the kitchen table. She had been reading, but in fact she had dropped off over her book.

There was a call for the doctor to come quickly. A child. Come quickly. They rang off. A five-year-old had fallen over rusty farm machinery and opened his eye.

David remembered Clare saying that she had cut her leg years ago on the rusty spikes of half-hidden machinery. He felt a surge of anger about people raising children so casually among all these dangers.

Soothing, reassuring, and speaking confident words he didn't mean, David wiped the drying blood from the child's face. It wasn't too bad. Calming and chatting to distract their attention he said it wasn't bad at all, it would all be fine, now now, could someone start to make some tea. Then he took out his bag and put five quick stitches into the small face. He examined it critically. It wasn't bad. The child looked at him trustingly.

'Isn't that fine,' David said.

'I'm Matthew.'

'Of course you are, and you're better now.' David gave him a hug just as the tea tray was being brought in.

'Aren't you the cut of your father, and the same grand ways with you.' Matthew's mother was holding one of his hands between both her own.

'Thank you.'

'We were all delighted when you married a local girl, not getting yourself a fancy wife from Dublin.'

'I'm glad.'

'And how's your own little girl, Doctor?'

'Oh she's beautiful, thank you. Simply beautiful.'

'I'm glad to hear that, you give so much to other people's children, it would be very sad if you didn't find happiness in your own.'

Liffey was crying when he got in. She was wet. Her little legs

448

were red and chapped, and the napkin soaked. As it was cold, she had obviously been lying like that for some time.

Clare was lying in bed reading a recipe book.

'I thought I'd make drop scones, they don't look too hard,' she smiled at him.

'Sure, that would be fine, Liffey's very wet.'

'I'll see to her in a minute.'

'She's been wet for ages, Clare.'

'Oh all right.'

David spoke sharply. 'No, I'll do it, it'll be quicker.'

'Oh good.' She went back to studying the recipe book.

Clare went back to bed early, so she should have had a fair bank of sleep when Liffey woke. But the child cried and cried and Clare never turned over in bed.

David got up. He fed and changed her again, but she still wouldn't settle. He walked her up and down. Eventually, she slept.

About ten minutes before he intended to get up Liffey began again. He poked Clare gently.

'You get her this time, love, will you, I want to grab a few minutes' sleep.'

Clare swung her legs out of bed and put her woolly dressing gown on over her long nighty. She picked up Liffey with a few words of comfort and carried her downstairs.

When David had washed and shaved and come down for his breakfast, Clare was sitting at the table, asleep. The kettle was on the range, hissing and spitting; Liffey was screaming from her cradle.

That was the morning David told his father in halting, broken sentences that he thought Clare was suffering from post-natal depression.

His father said that these things were too easily defined and put into categories. Clare was a bit low. Life was very different and less demanding than it had been last year, and it should never be forgotten that the child had missed her degree. That would be hard enough on any girl but on a little girl who had fought like a tiger to get there it must have been harder still.

David said it was more than that. If it was only that they could talk about it and sort it out, but she was so physically tired, she was drowsy all the time, and without losing any love for Liffey she seemed to have lost interest in her.

David's face was white and his eyes were dark and sleepless-looking. His father was full of pity for him.

'I think you should still try other ways before you say that we should treat it, or send her to someone.'

'I don't want to send her to anyone, but couldn't she be put on Tofranil? Wouldn't that sort her out in a month or two? Dad, that's what we'd say for anyone else. Why can't we say it for Clare?'

'Because it could be a lot of other things, she could be lonely, she could be unsure of herself, Molly might be making her feel inadequate. Talk to her. Talk, and tell her things and maybe you'll see. It's not a question of her being some unfortunate woman who has no one to understand her. She's got a fine husband, a great husband.'

'I can't be all that great if she's changed so much.'

'Do you still love me?' he asked her.

'David, what can you mean? I love you more than ever.'

'That's the third time you've been too tired to make love.'

'I'm sorry, I just felt a bit weary. OK. I don't mind, now I'm awake.'

'It's too late now.'

'Oh David, stop sulking.'

He swung his legs out of bed and plugged in the electric fire. He wanted to talk and he didn't want them to freeze.

'I promise you on my oath I'm not sulking. But when I think the way we were jumping on each other this time last year, it seems as if we were two different people.'

'This time last year we were in Dublin and we hadn't all the responsibilities we have now,' she said.

'This time last year, you were working fourteen hours a day for your exams, I was working fourteen hours a day in that hospital, we had to get round the city on buses, we were up to here in anxiety. Now we have our own house, our own child, our freedom to jump on each other morning, noon

450

and night if we wish to do so, I have a gentle and satisfying amount of work to do rather than the mayhem as an intern, you have no official things to do and we're still too tired.'

'You're not, I am,' she said, correcting the facts.

'But why, Clare, *why*? I'm not just being a raging beast like all men trying to demand my rights, or more rights, or anything. Why are you so tired?'

'There's so much to do,' she said.

'Are you sure you love me, and you know I'm not picking a fight?'

'Yes, of course.'

'Then let me tell you what you did today. You got up and I got breakfast. And I changed Liffey. And I said I'd get a leg of lamb in Dwyers' on the way home and you said no, *you* would. Before I went out I brought in some potatoes from the bag outside. I peeled a few, *you* said leave them. I came home for lunch. You had been asleep all morning. Liffey was wet and bawling . . . you were upset because there was no lunch. Clare . . . this is terrible. This isn't meant to be a row, do you understand, I'm just trying to find out why you could be tired? I made us a tin of soup and we had some of Nellie's bread while you got the bottle for Liffey. This time I insisted on getting the meat. I left it back in the house at three o'clock. You were asleep in the chair. Clare, *I* put the bloody meat into the oven, and that's how we had dinner. I thought we'd go to the pictures but *you* said *you* were too tired. You've been asleep all morning, all afternoon and now you're weary, you say, when you come to bed. I'm your doctor as well as your husband. Of course I'm worried about you.'

'I'm very sorry. When you put it like that, it's indefensible.'

'Darling heart, I'm not blaming you, I'm only asking you as my best and dearest friend, can you tell me what's wrong?'

'I don't know. I didn't think anything was.'

'But we can't live like this. I mean, you can't go on like this – if I weren't a doctor I'd bring you to a doctor.' He smiled and put both his hands on her face.

451

'What do you think?' she looked like a worried child.

'I think it's a depression.'

'I'm not sad.'

'No, a clinical depression.'

'But I swear I'm not depressed.'

'And your exams?'

'Yes, but I've got over that. Honestly I have. I had harder things to fight against ten years ago. Now I'm a nice middle-class married lady, no worry about the fees. If I haven't the guts to do it again it's my own fault, not anybody else's. Not Liffey's fault, not yours, only mine.'

'And will you have the guts to do it again?'

'I think I'm too tired. There, I've said it again.'

'I'd like to give you an anti-depressant.'

'More energy, like?'

'No, I'm not going to talk to you as if you were an ignoramus, they've got nothing to do with iron or energy, they work on the chemicals, on amino acid in the brain, and on the nerve endings. It would take about three weeks to make any difference.'

'What does your dad think?'

'I'll ask him.'

'I'm sure you have asked him, it doesn't matter, you have to ask him things.'

'He thinks you're just lonely and unsure of yourself here.'

'And you think it's a post-natal depression, and I think it's just tiredness.'

'It could be a bit of all of them,' David said.

'Well feed me the medicine, Doctor, and let's hope we see a miracle cure.' She smiled at him, a smile from the old days, and he went to sleep feeling a little better than he had felt for some weeks.

Next day he suggested that they take Liffey to see Mr Kenny, and Clare said that was a great idea: the nice old solicitor had sent them a lovely silver spoon for the baby. But when David got home expecting Liffey and Clare to be ready, the baby hadn't been changed or dressed, and Clare said she felt very tired today.

David said fine, they'd go another day and without

making any big drama out of it he started her on a course of Tofranil.

'I was up this way and I wondered if there was a cup of tea going.'

'Nobody's up this way, but you can have a cup of tea,' she said.

'You never come down town any more,' Gerry said.

'And how would you know whether I do or not?'

'Your mother mentioned it to me, as it happens.'

'Oh Lord. I meant to go to see her this week.'

'This week? Clare, she's only ten *minutes* away. She thinks you've joined the gentry.'

Clare felt very guilty. The days ran into each other, yes, it was a whole week since she had brought the baby over to her mother, it must be three days at least since she had seen her mother-in-law.

'Do you feel all right, Clare?' Gerry asked gently. He was sitting at the kitchen table.

She was pouring the kettle of water into a teapot.

'Thank you very much for all this interest, Dr Doyle. Have you become a medical consultant now as well as a home counsellor, bearing me advice from my family?'

'I'm serious, Clare.'

She brought the tea to the table.

'I'm tired, that's all. It's very exhausting looking after a baby.'

'That one doesn't seem to need much looking after. She's fast asleep.'

'Ah, but they wake up, Gerry, that's a little trick they have.'

They drank their tea.

'And is the handsome young doctor giving you anything for your tiredness?'

'Yes of course he is . . . a course of tablets.'

'Good. I'm glad he noticed.'

'Please don't speak badly of David, Gerry, it makes me very upset.'

'I'm not speaking badly of him. I'm just saying he's wrong for you.'

'Now you really must go.' She stood up, coldly. 'Friend or no friend, Gerry, you are not coming into my house when David is not here and saying that. No you bloody can't.'

'You're only getting upset because it's true.'

'Oh don't be ridiculous. You can win any argument if you say things like that. The truth is I am upset to hear any bad reference made to David at all, and if you ever knew what it was like to love someone rather than just . . . well . . . use them . . . then you'd understand.'

'I love you,' he said.

There was a silence.

Then she threw her head back. 'Don't be idiotic. You only say that because you once or twice made a pass at me and I didn't give in. You feel it's broken the track record for you, it's not one hundred per cent. Bingo! Isn't that it? That's what it's all about. I pity any girl you really say that you love because you don't know what the word means.'

He sipped his tea. 'In this case I suppose it means that I'd do anything to have you, anything.'

She felt frightened.

'Please . . .' she began.

'I saw David one day last week kneeling in the middle of the road. I thought of putting my foot on the accelerator. Nobody would have blamed me. He was in the middle of the street, any court would have let me off. Then I saw he was looking after a puppy someone had run over. I couldn't do it.'

Clare stood up. 'You aren't serious, you're just saying these things to make yourself sound like a villain.'

'No, it's quite true. Quite true.' His voice was calm.

'But *why*?'

'Who knows? Who knows anything about why people love other people? Anyway I decided that it could never be done that way, and even if David had an accident, a genuine accident, and you were a grieving widow, that mightn't work. It might take years for you to get over him. So it has to be a different way entirely.'

'This is a game, is it?'

There was another silence.

454

Clare didn't like him sitting there looking at her. 'I'll tell you something, maybe it's foolish but I'll tell you anyway. I don't feel all that well, I think I have a sort of depression, and honestly I can't take any more upset. I would be sitting here day and night in a panic if I thought that anything you were saying, *any* of it, were true. Can you reassure me that it's not? Please?'

'I thought you had a depression,' he said sympathetically. 'Remember Fiona did too, in England that time. But she got over it, and so will you. Is he giving you proper tablets for it?'

'Yes.'

'You'll be fine, and you'll be back at your books, and madam there will grow up to be a pride and joy to you.'

It was as if he hadn't said any of the other terrible things. Clare felt dizzy.

'So put everything out of your head. I'll just love you quietly from a distance. For ever. You know?'

'Or until summer,' she said.

'No, for ever. But you're right, there's no point in getting you upset, you're to get yourself better now.'

He got up to leave.

'Yes. Yes I will, I'll be fine.'

'And go to see your Mam, eh? And Josie, right?'

'Right. Goodbye, Gerry.'

The baby woke just then and began a little cry.

'Aren't you going to pick her up?'

'Yes, in a minute. I was just seeing you off. Hush, Liffey, I'm just coming.'

'Liffey?' he smiled from the door. 'You call her the name I gave her.'

'I think we're going to have to come to terms with pastry,' Angela said.

'I came to terms with it years ago, I love it.'

'No, I think we should make it. We've been avoiding all these recipes that begin telling you to roll out the crust. Let's make the damn thing tonight.'

'Right,' he said. 'Will I get the ingredients?'

'No, I'll call into O'Brien's on the way back from school, I think it's only flour and lard or something, but I might be wrong.'

'I can't think of any other woman of your age who doesn't know how to make pastry,' he said, teasing her.

'Less of that, you got yourself an intellectual as a girlfriend, you should be delighted with yourself and counting your blessings all the time.'

'Are you my girlfriend?' he said, pleased.

'Of course I am. I didn't mean to be but I am,' she said.

The following night they made the pastry. It was nightmarish. The book had said you could use lard or butter or margarine.

'Why doesn't it tell us what ordinary people use?' Angela fumed.

It had told them to Rub The Fat Into The Flour.

'That actually is not English, you rub something out, or you rub something, you don't *rub in*. God, these people.' They made it look like breadcrumbs which is what it said, but it also said use a Light Hand.

'That's the most stupid thing I ever heard. How can you be light with all this rubbing?' Dick had an apron on over his good suit. Angela had insisted.

'I don't know what you wore a good suit like this for, just to do cooking,' she scolded. But she knew well . . .

It was the same reason that she had worn a smart blouse and washed her hair.

The question had to wait until they worked out what Bake Blind meant. By process of elimination they discovered it meant that you put the pastry into the oven and you cooked it by itself first. Angela wrote a short note to the book's publishers saying that it should be withdrawn for its general misinformation.

Then they sat down and poured themselves a drink. Dick stood up again and said he would like Angela to marry him.

'Dick, are you sure? You've been asking me a long time you know.'

He put his glass of orange squash down on the table and took her hands. 'I thought that maybe when you let slip that

456

you were my girlfriend that we had made a bit of progress,'
he said.

'I'm very difficult,' she said.

'I know,' he said.

'And you're set in your ways of course,' she added.

'I am *not* set in my ways. When I got to know you, which
is not today or yesterday, I was set in my ways. Now I do all
kinds of things I'd never have done before. I read long
books, I cook great meals. I'm cheerful instead of miserable.
What do you mean, set in my ways?'

'Yes, please.'

'What?'

'I said yes please, I'd love to marry you.'

Angela tried the beautiful ruby ring on, the ring that Dick
Dillon had bought long ago hoping for the day it would be
needed. It was perfect.

'I'll make you a good wife – not a peaceable one mind, but
I'll be good to you, and love you and look after you.'

'The love bit is the most important one,' he said shyly.

'It is for me too, I just felt awkward saying it.'

'We don't need to feel awkward any more,' he said, and
they sat in the firelight, as the pastry burned black in the
oven and the red ruby glittered and shone.

'Do you have this funny feeling that it's all over? It's all
happened? Like everything went into the past tense instead
of the future tense?' asked Clare.

David looked at her. He had no feeling like that at all. 'I
know, I know,' he said, his heart heavy.

'Oh good. I was afraid it was just me. I suppose we'll get
used to it, and adapt.'

'I think that's what happens to people,' he said.

'It's not regrets or anything. You know that?'

'Of course.'

'But you must find that too. I mean you don't regret
coming back here, but the kind of work you do, the life we
lead, it sort of happened a bit soon, didn't it?'

He patted her hand. She was much brighter than before,

she was far more aware of Liffey and spent hours playing with her. She had taken driving lessons from Dick Dillon. David had even seen some of her history textbooks out by the window again.

Perhaps Clare was just too young and unprepared to settle down so quickly. Perhaps she would never settle down. It made it all the harder to tell her that he *loved* this life. He liked caring for sick, frightened people, and curing them with medicines from his black bag; or sewing up their wounds; delivering their children sometimes or closing the eyes of their dead. A couple of years ago he might have been mildly tolerant of his father's brand of medicine, preferring instead to think of a more scientific approach. Now he couldn't see anything that would be better for the patients than to see a face they trusted, an old face and his son a newer face. This gave them some confidence and very often that was three-quarters of the battle.

It all made him feel unsettled. He didn't worry about Clare's health any more but he felt that the great closeness they had grown used to, and accepted as if it was their natural right, had disappeared. The words were the same, the interest was there, she was eager to hear about his cases and discuss them. But it was as if she believed that somehow they had been shunted into a siding and forgotten about, and they were trapped in this middle-aged world, so they had better play the role of old people as cheerfully as possible.

Dick and Angela were married in Dublin. There had never been the slightest discussion about it. They knew they wanted nobody from Castlebay, not one of Dick's hotel relations, and Angela said that she certainly didn't want to draw sisters and brothers and the whole of Japan on her either. It was arranged with no fuss, Father Flynn again, of course, and Emer and Kevin.

Just the five of them at a small side altar early one morning.

'It's not festive enough for you,' Father Flynn complained.

'Our life is festive enough, Father, we don't need it on a wedding day. Honest.'

He gave in grudgingly.

They went back to Emer's and Kevin's house and they had scrambled eggs and bacon and a cake that Angela and Dick had made themselves from the section called 'Simple Cake Making' which they said was another example of lies in cookery books. Reluctantly they allowed Father Flynn to take one photograph of the occasion which, when it came out, was so ludicrous that Angela said it could illustrate an article called Christmas Day in the Asylum.

They took the picture out occasionally if they wanted a good laugh, but they didn't need anything to remind them of the best day of their lives. That's just what it was, Dick said, pure and simple. The best day ever. And for once even Father Flynn found himself without a word to say.

It came as a great surprise to hear that the Nolans were going to take a house on the Cliff Road again. Mr Nolan hadn't been well: he had been told to take things easy and get a bit of sea air. Caroline had finished her apprenticeship and was in the throes of looking for a job. She thought she would have a break. James said that he could prepare his few briefs just as well in Castlebay as anywhere else.

That was the way the news was broken to David by letter. He read it to them all with suitable James gestures and Clare was surprised to see how pleased they all were.

Even Nellie was delighted. 'It puts the Mistress into great good humour when that lot comes down, and their Breeda's a very nice girl, I'll be glad to see her again myself.'

Mrs Power started in a mad rush to get the garden done up. There was a nice corner with lupins and she wanted to be able to have afternoon tea served there. She had all the deckchairs of course but they looked a bit shabby.

'I'll paint the deckchairs blue for you, and we'll look like an ocean-going liner. What do you think?' Clare looked at her mother-in-law.

'I don't think so . . .'

'Oh go on, you've got blue and white china, you could get blue paper serviettes. It would be terrific.'

Mrs Power seemed to regret having shown how flustered she was to Clare, she wished she hadn't admitted her wishes to impress the Nolans, she began to take it all back.

'Well, thank you, dear, for the idea anyway,' she said dismissively.

'Are we going to do it?' Clare cried, 'because if we are I'll ring Bumper and ask him to get some cans of paint round here right away.'

'I think not, Clare. Thank you, no.'

Two red spots burned in Clare's cheeks. 'A bit flashy, might it be?'

'Since you say the word, that's just what it might look like, you know, a little . . . well, a little overdone.'

'Common?' Clare asked.

'No, no, heavens what a thing to say about your idea, but you know . . .'

'I know,' Clare said grimly and walked back to the Lodge.

'You've got a common flashy mother,' she said to Liffey, 'a mother who is a little . . . what's the word again . . . overdone.'

Liffey seemed pleased with the attention and the tone of Clare's voice.

'And Liffey, you also have an almighty bitch of a grandmother, I never want you to forget that. She is in the major league of bitchiness as your godmother Mary Catherine would say, she is a Class A bitch.'

Clare felt better when she had defined everything. Liffey was a good listener.

Caroline looked very elegant. Clare remembered when she had come to Castlebay first, and she had been so jealous of all the fun Caroline and her friend Hilary had been having with David, James and Gerry Doyle.

How strangely it had all turned out. She felt uneasy when she thought of Gerry and his strangeness.

She was surprised when Caroline, languidly reclining in a deckchair with Liffey on her lap, said, 'Is Gerry Doyle still the Main Attraction?'

'I think so,' Clare said carefully. 'I'm not as in touch as I used to be. Possibly the younger ones have other heroes, but I think he does very well.'

'Well, I think I'll stroll down later and have a look at him,' Caroline said. 'Now that you've taken the most gorgeous man in Castlebay, I'll have to start looking round at the second bests.'

She laughed, and they all laughed. David too.

Clare was furious. The *bitch* – why did she say that in front of Molly? Clare had seen the look of regret come over Molly's face. Suppose David and Caroline had married, now wouldn't that have been something special? Suppose she and Sheila Nolan had been cooing over Liffey. Molly would have much preferred that than have Liffey also the granddaughter of O'Brien's shop.

Valerie came to stay in the Lodge for a week.

'I can't stand Caroline Nolan,' she said. 'Stop being so nice to her, Clare.'

'I'm only being civil. Not nice. She'll be gone in a couple of weeks.'

'I wouldn't bet on that, she's asking that old man the solicitor friend of David's father . . .'

'Mr Kenny.'

'Yes, she's asking him are there any openings for a solicitor round here, a country practice would be so much more interesting than a city one, you'd see all sides of the law.'

'But she couldn't be a solicitor in Castlebay, there isn't any need for anyone apart from poor old Mr Kenny and most people go to the town.'

'Aha, that's what he told her, she's going into the town today to investigate possibilities. Gerry Doyle's giving her a lift.'

'That's all baloney, as Mary Catherine would say, she's just gone to get a quick feel from Gerry Doyle, she fancies him rotten, she always has. She pretends it was David, but I remember all those years. It was Gerry this and Gerry that.'

'I hope you're right,' Val said.

'I wish you didn't have to go, you make me feel safe,' Clare said.

'You are safe, stupid.'

'Well, normal, then.'

'Come to the dance tonight,' Valerie said suddenly.

'No, I'm too old, too dull. David's going to be out all night, nearly, he rang. Mrs Brennan says there are complications in a confinement.'

'You come anyway, David would like that, I know he would.'

'I don't want to, I feel wrong, somehow.'

'I won't go either and I was so looking forward to it.'

'Damn you, Valerie, now I have to go. I have to wash my hair and go.'

'Yes you do,' said Valerie, pleased.

They all had a drink at the hotel first, Caroline, James, Josie and Martin, Valerie and Clare, then they crossed the road and headed for the dance hall. The sound of the band hit them as soon as the swing doors opened.

'I feel that old excitement, just like when we were young,' Caroline said.

'So do I,' James Nolan said, eyeing Josie Dillon speculatively.

Martin said nothing.

Inside, the familiar smell of sweat and perfume and suntan oil came to them, and the band struck up a Paul Jones.

Clare remembered the excitement of the Paul Jones years ago when you could stop opposite literally anyone, and half the girls in the ballroom wanted to stop in front of Gerry Doyle. She forced herself to relive that sense of excitement.

'Come on girls, get into the ring,' she called.

'Good to see the grass widow enjoying herself for a change,' Caroline said.

Clare refused to wonder what that meant. It probably meant nothing. It was a clever-clever thing that Caroline *would* say.

She stopped opposite a boy of about sixteen, red faced and sweating with nerves. It might even be his first dance.

'Hallo,' she smiled. 'I'm yours, I think, for the dance.'

'Um, thank you, I'm not a great dancer,' he said.

'You couldn't be any worse than I am,' Clare said cheerfully and she made him feel so confident in their gallop around the room that she knew he would come back and claim her over and over, unless she told him.

'That was lovely,' she said. 'I'm married to the local doctor here. We have a little girl. It makes me feel nice and young again to dance like that.'

He was gone like a bow from an arrow. A married woman! Heavens!

Valerie seemed to be happy, Clare thought later as she looked down on it all from the balcony, a freckled man in a check suit had asked her to dance several times over, he looked nice and they were chatting away too. James Nolan, the smooth, two-faced rat, was dancing cheek to cheek with Josie Dillon who was admittedly very foolish indeed to allow and encourage such a thing. Clare didn't approve, but she could have foretold it. She could also have foretold that Caroline and Gerry Doyle would have found each other out too.

She leaned with her elbows on the balcony looking at them. Caroline was taller than Gerry, but who wasn't? Saying not much but smiling a lot, not groping but dancing very close. Very sure of each other. Clare wished that Valerie would leave the check-suited man and come up here for a moment. Then she would get over this silly idea that Caroline Nolan was a troublemaker with eyes for David. Anyone could see that Caroline had eyes only for Gerry Doyle.

Clare remembered the days when she and Josie would come to the dance and be rushed off their feet. Not so for Josie tonight, she never left James Nolan's side. Not so for Mrs Clare Power, the doctor's wife, and mother of the doctor's daughter. None of the boys who used to ask her to dance would approach her now, and it wasn't the Castlebay Committee dance where she would have found older people to dance with. She didn't mind being a wallflower, she didn't really wish David was here, she felt she had grown away from the dance. Not too old for it, just away from it.

Three little things happened before they played the national anthem and the night was over. Martin told Josie in a shaking voice that he was leaving now and would she like to come with him or not. He put a lot into the question, and Josie answered head on. No, she would not, she would like to stay. Thank you.

Then Bernie Conway came up to Clare and said it was marvellous to see her again, she had been such a recluse in the beginning.

'I suppose it was the shock of the baby coming so early.'

'It must have been,' Clare agreed.

'And who's looking after her tonight? David?'

'No, no, if he were free he'd be here, Nellie Burke loves to have her from time to time.'

'Oh, the resident domestic. Nice,' Bernie said.

There was a pause.

'I'd never have expected to see you here on your own . . . after . . . after everything,' Bernie said.

Clare wanted to push her out the window on to Church Street but decided against it. 'I'm not really on my own, I came with about five or six other people, I'm just not being danced with at the moment,' she smiled sweetly. 'Like you.'

And the third thing was that Gerry Doyle and Caroline waved casually and went off into the night towards the caravan park.

Caroline's father said she was very sensible to get experience in a country town, there was nothing as useful as learning the business on the ground at every level. They were all congratulating her on having got a position in the town twenty miles from Castlebay.

James said he hoped she would get the firm to send all the cases to advise to him, he needed a good country contact. Sheila Nolan said she would come down and help to settle Caroline in, and then she could come across to Castlebay and see Molly for a winter weekend. Dr Power said that she'd find it a real change from the summer, in fact some of the Castlebay Committee didn't agree with Josie Dillon that visitors should be allowed in the place in winter at all, let them think it was the land of eternal summer.

Clare was silent. She remembered how she had laughed when Valerie said that Caroline was a schemer and that she was plotting to be down in this part of the country. Was Caroline really a bit keen on David as Valerie had all but said? It couldn't be. Hadn't she taken up her romance with Gerry Doyle exactly as she was planning? Perhaps she was scheming to be near Gerry Doyle. Surely not. Caroline had too much intelligence for that.

They often had tea in the garden at Crest View, Caroline seemed to be able to summon it up with a wave of the hand, while Molly Power would fuss for three days about any entertaining, Sheila Nolan never seemed to think of it, and Clare never suggested it in the Lodge since she thought none of them would want to come there.

But Caroline just knew automatically that what people loved around five o'clock was a huge pot of tea, and plates of nice thin tomato sandwiches. Even Dr Power loved dropping in, for half an hour or so. Caroline had painted all the deckchairs bright red.

'Do they belong to us, strictly?' James asked.

'Of course not, but they were so tatty. The old bat who owns the place will be delighted with us.'

Molly said it was a *very* clever idea. And very *tasteful*.

She took Liffey sometimes but not always. A ten-month-old baby was lively and needed attention, Caroline had limited time for babies. And this summer it seemed as if Caroline was calling the shots. After all she was planning to become a native. Almost.

David did seem to find her good company, but then he always had. They had been friends, and now he seemed to laugh and relax more with Caroline than he did even with James.

Clare sat with her hand on the pram, rocking the sleeping Liffey. Mrs Nolan was describing some dream in elaborate detail; Molly Power listened enthralled. Dr Power and James Nolan were discussing the business of calling doctors as expert witnesses in court cases. Breeda was refilling the teapot and setting out further plates of sandwiches. David and Caroline were sitting on the whitewashed wall of Crest View watching the beach below.

What am I doing here? Clare thought. This isn't *my* place. I'm not meant to *be* here with these people.

It was like an echo of what Gerry Doyle had said.

'I always hated saying goodbye to this place,' Caroline said. 'Now it's not goodbye at all. I am glad about the job.'

'So are we,' David said eagerly. 'But won't it be very dull? Honestly, Caroline, you've no idea how quiet it can be in this area. I know the town is bigger but it's still small after Dublin.'

'How could a town with Gerry Doyle be dull? Answer me that.' Caroline was being light and joky but she saw immediately she had said the wrong thing.

'Oh, him,' David said.

'I was only teasing you, I don't think he'll form part of my winter social life, hardly the suitable escort for the legal profession.'

'You must choose your own friends, I'm only a stick in the mud.'

That wasn't so, and anyway she'd find it hard to make friends at first. 'I'll be relying on you and Clare to introduce me round.'

'We hardly know anyone.' He wasn't apologetic, he was stating a fact.

'We'll have to take up golf again, will we do that, have a game every now and then?'

'I'd *love* that,' David said. 'Yes, that's something I really would like. I'm meant to have an afternoon off in the middle of the week, I hardly ever take it.'

'Well now.' Caroline smiled at the marvellous notion. 'There we'll be, old country doctor, old country solicitor, out for an afternoon's golf.' Her laugh pealed out like a bell. 'Who would have thought it, David, that we'd come to this?'

Clare listened to them from her red-painted deckchair. Old country doctor, old country solicitor, and there was Clare – old country nothing.

The wasps were dying, the seaweed was coming in on the tide, the visitors were packing up. Angela was getting her books and charts ready for school.

Clare came to the door, wheeling Liffey in a push chair.

'She must be nearly a year.'

'Next week. Is Dick here, Angela?'

'No . . . oh hell he is, he said to say he was out if anyone came. But for you. Come on in.'

Dick was at the table with plans spread out all over it. He jumped guiltily.

'It's only Clare, love,' Angela said.

'We were going to tell her anyway.'

They were going to make their cottage into a small hotel. Dick was getting his share out of Dillon's, which would suit everyone there, and they were going to open a small twelve-bedroom hotel of their own. Angela owned the field behind the cottage: they would build a hotel just for golfers, with places to leave their clubs, with early breakfasts if they wanted it, with late suppers. They might not get a licence to serve alcohol; but people could order a bottle of whiskey or whatever and it would be supplied in their room. Their plan was to open it next June, Angela was going to leave the school.

'Is that why you've been doing the cooking?' Clare asked eagerly.

'The one thing we *proved* is that we have to hire a cook before anything else, we'll make the beds and wash up but *not* cook!'

They had tea and looked at the plans. 'That should cost a fair bit of money,' Clare said.

'I'll be owed a fair bit of money out of Dillon's,' Dick said.

'Will your brother be pleased or furious?'

'He'll be delighted I'm out of his hair, but he'll be furious about this, that's why it's a secret you see, the money bit goes through this week. A firm in the town are handling it, in fact that girl – what's her name? – was here.'

'Caroline Nolan?'

'The very one. Nice girl for a Dubliner, very straight-forward.'

'Um,' said Angela.

'Um indeed,' said Clare.

'What did you want Dick for, by the way?' Angela remembered why Clare had called.

'I was wondering would you give me a few secret golf lessons when Angela went back to school, I thought you'd have some time on your hands, but now I see you won't.'

'I'm not the one to give you lessons, I'm very bad.'

'I don't mind only learning a little.'

'No Clare, you don't understand, I'd teach you the wrong grip, the wrong stance, you'd have to unlearn it all over again.'

'Why don't you go up to Jimmy the Pro?' Angela wanted to know.

'I wanted to learn secretly, without anyone else knowing.'

'That's why you can't ask David,' Angela said.

'Right.'

'What about Gerry Doyle, he's a good golfer?' Dick suggested.

'No, I'd probably spend most of the lesson on the flat of my back in the sand dunes,' Clare laughed.

'I'll tell you – that girl Caroline, *she* loves golf, she says she's going to come over here and play as much as she can. *She* might be the one.'

Dick Dillon's face shone with pleasure at having solved a problem.

'I'm sorry, Clare,' Angela said, 'some men are as thick as the wall. But you mustn't worry.'

'I don't know what you're complaining about, you've come up with no suggestions. I've given two, and they've been laughed out of court,' Dick grumbled.

'I'll solve it for you,' Angela said, 'why don't I book lessons with Jimmy and you could so-called come along and watch, and join in, it wouldn't look like you learning.'

'It would really, and anyway you don't want to learn.'

'If I'm to be the genial co-proprietor of a golfing hotel I'd better know how to play the damn game,' Angela said. 'I'll talk to Jimmy and you come up casually like around Lesson Two or Three.'

468

'You're always helping me,' Clare said. 'It's probably very silly.'

'No, I think you're quite right,' Angela said seriously, in a way that let a shiver of cold go through Clare.

Josie was in tears at the Lodge that evening. Martin never wanted to see her again. He said she had made a fool of him over James Nolan. Oh how stupid she had been, Josie could kick herself from here to Dublin and back, she was so annoyed. What should she do? Clare was so good with men.

'I am not good with men, what makes you think that?'

Well hadn't Clare got David Power as her husband, and the town Romeo Gerry Doyle was saying only the other night in the hotel that he wished he had moved in before the young doctor.

'Gerry was saying that. In front of people?'

'Yes, yes.' Josie was much more interested in her own disasters. Should she write to Martin? Did James have any *real* interest in her? What did Clare think . . .

'I can't tell you what I think until I know what you want,' Clare said, exasperated. 'If you tell me straight out what you want, I'll tell you what I think you should do.'

'I want James Nolan, but I don't think he wants me, so if I'm sure of that and that there's no hope there, I want Martin. Now is that honest and truthful enough for you?'

'You wouldn't just like to be on your own for a bit and let life go by, and eventually meet someone else?'

'No thank you.' Josie was firm.

'That's what I think you should do.'

'I told you what I wanted, it's easy for you to say that, and all this bit about being independent, you have a husband, a child, and Gerry Doyle ogling you as well.'

'Right. I'll drive you out to his house, you can put a letter under his door: "Dear Martin, I behaved stupidly, I suppose I wanted to see did you really care about me . . ." that sort of thing. Not too cringeing, not too apologetic, but don't be defensive either, we'll write it now if you like . . .'

'I don't think James Nolan will ever . . .'

'I agree. I don't think James Nolan ever will either . . .'

469

Two weeks later Josie and Martin bought the ring. Three diamonds in a cluster.

'You're a genius, Clare,' Josie breathed to her a few days after the announcement.

'That's what I am,' Clare agreed.

But Clare couldn't be a genius for herself.

She despised women who were coquettish to men, and during those heady days when she and David had been so in love that Dublin just seemed like the backdrop on a stage for them, he and she used to laugh at the posturings of women who thought flirtatiousness was attractive, and the men who were fools enough to be taken in. They had sworn then that they would always be able to tell each other how they felt and say it straight out, the other was allowed ten minutes to be upset but after that he or she was to remember that this was the Love of the Century and that any plain speaking was a part of the very special relationship they had.

Clare wondered would it work if they went back to Dublin and raced round in duffle coats in the rain. In the winter and spring of 1960 it had been easy to talk, in the winter and spring of 1962 they had lost it.

She wrote him a letter one day. A long letter trying to recapture how it had been. But she re-read it and it sounded like a list of complaints so she tore it up.

She even tried to talk to his father about it. Very obliquely. But she realized soon that the old man thought that everything was fine between them. He acknowledged that Clare had been a little low after the birth of the baby, perfectly normal under all the circumstances, he saw no yawning gaps or wide distances now. It would have been cruel as well as pointless to try to tell him about them.

She found it very hard to study again. Almost impossible.

She wrote to the cheerful tutor who had said he never expected to hear from her again. She said that he might have heard what had happened on the day she was ready to sit her finals, but that the baby was now almost a year and a half, and that Clare would like to get back to work again. He wrote back saying that she had to apply formally of course, but he knew there would be no trouble once people knew the facts, the very dramatic facts. He admired her courage for starting again, because in eighteen months she must have got out of practice. He said to be sure to contact him if she were in Dublin.

And that was it. No other way of getting back into the frame of mind she had been in once. She looked at her notes. How had she been so intelligent? How could she have written those paragraphs on the left-hand side of each double page, paragraphs headed 'essentials' and then on the other side quotes, references, details. Was there a possibility that she once knew all this? Did other people up in Dublin know this kind of thing now?

Should she go to Dublin for a few days? Would that make it more real?

She discussed it with David. He said he thought she should go.

She planned to stay with Emer and Kevin and the now monstrous Daniel. They were dying to see Liffey, having met her only at the christening. Would David come too? Just for a couple of days?

No, he said. It was the worst time to leave. Old people got pneumonia at this time of year. But he'd love her to go, really and truly.

'Have you gone off me, David?' she asked him that night without rancour.

'Well really, what nonsense,' he said. 'Are you sulking because I can't get away?'

'Of course not, I meant it much more generally.'

'I haven't gone off you, sweetheart, why should I?'

'I don't know, who knows why people love and they don't?' She was standing in the same spot of the kitchen as she had been when she had heard Gerry Doyle say those words from the kitchen table. She had echoed them unconsciously.

She shivered a little.

'Well I know. I know I love you and I haven't gone off you. So there.'

'Are you happy, David?'

'What's happy?' he asked, shrugging his shoulders.

'This room is beginning to be like the Echo Cave,' Clare said. 'You asked me a year ago was I happy, when you were telling me that I wasn't loopy. You asked me then was I happy.'

'This is very intense. What did you say?'

'Don't you remember?'

'No, and love, don't pick a fight because I can't remember every word of every conversation we have had in two years. If I were to quiz you, there must be many things you've forgotten.'

'That's fair. I'll tell you what I said. I said I was happy. And you said "But . . ." asking a question and I said, well, "But . . . we'd sort of got a bit settled down hadn't we" and you said yes you felt that too.'

'Well, what's the production?'

'The production is that we've changed a lot, you were the one who was beseeching *me* and wanting to know how I was, now I'm the one.'

'I've had a hard day, a really hard day. A woman of forty-four died today. Down the coast. She'd been fine, not a thing wrong with her. Cancer all over her in two months. She had six children and a big stupid husband and I had to stand there and talk about the good side of it. Clare, there was no good side to it, believe you me there was no good side.

'I came back and sewed up the eye of a child of five whose father hit her with a chair, the father is in a worse state than the child. I have to write a report of it all for Frank Conway. Frank Conway asked me how his mother was and I had to tell him she won't come out of hospital.

'Then Dad asked me if I'd mind looking after everything on my own for a week in about a month's time, he's feeling very tired he says, he wakes at night with his heart racing, he'd like a little rest.

'Rest? He's hardly doing a quarter of the load, so if he wants a rest at this level of work the man is really bad. Then I come back here and I'm met with pleas and beggings to come to Dublin which I can *not* do much as I might like to. And now the whole fabric of life has to be analysed.'

There was a silence.

'I'm sorry,' she said.

'There's no reason why you should be. These are the joys and horrors of my day, not yours.'

'What *would* you like from me? What would have been best tonight? Tell me.'

'I suppose a bit of peace, chat about other things, not about us and where we were going and who loved whom more.'

He stood up and put his arm around her. 'It's all right, Clare, it's not magic all the time, but people in jobs like ours, well like mine and when you were studying feverishly you were the same, you understood . . . in the time off you need just to relax, not to have to think of what love is and what it isn't.'

'I see. I do,' she said.

The telephone rang. David answered it.

'Oh hallo.' His face broke into a smile. She knew it was Caroline Nolan, who understood what people wanted in their time off. They didn't want *concepts,* they wanted a nice effortless exchange of words and an arrangement to play golf.

She wrote to Emer and said she wouldn't come just yet, she wanted to stay at home to sort out a few things. Emer said there was no bother, the bed was always there. Mention of the beds in Emer's house always caused Clare to feel a little guilty.

Angela was a very good golfer, Jimmy the Pro said. She had a swing like a man. Angela did not regard this as the high praise which Jimmy intended it to be.

'Your little friend here now isn't too bad either.' Clare made a face at him. 'Try to keep your head still and you wouldn't be a disgrace at all.'

'Great,' Clare said.

'Why don't you come out and play with that husband of yours sometimes? When the solicitor lady isn't around. I bet David would love a good game of a Saturday.'

'I must, but I'd be no match for him.'

'Oh, you'd give him a game, you did quite well there at the second, you were on the green in three and you only took two putts.'

'But it's a par three.'

'It's very respectable, I tell you.'

'Was it good, the golf today?' she asked him when he came home next time.

'No. I couldn't hit a ball out of my way.'

'What did you get on the second?' she asked innocently.

'Don't talk to me about the second, it's a par three, I took seven,' he wailed.

'Never mind, there are days and days, aren't there?'

He looked at her gratefully.

In women's magazines they told you to smarten up your appearance, lose weight and turn back into the girl he married. She tried wearing make-up but rubbed most of it off again, it looked heavy on her and unnatural in this part of the world. Her clothes were all right, she had a few nice jumpers and skirts and she wore smart blouses as well. She didn't need to lose weight. She was almost too thin if anything, and she was better-looking than the girl he had married. So there was no joy there. The women's magazines had never met a wife who was so tense and irritating that she had driven her husband into the arms of a country solicitor. That wasn't one the agony aunts could handle.

But still she would try. She followed every bit of an article in *Woman's Own* about how to do a perfect evening make-up.

She used the shadow and the eyeliner exactly as they directed.

She put on the taffeta skirt she had worn only once at the dance. And a nice top. She got her hair set in big loose ringlets.

Chrissie came over to the hairdresser's and stood in her dirty overall.

'I saw you coming in here, where are you going tonight?'

474

'Nowhere,' Clare hissed from under the dryer.

'You must be going somewhere, why else are you getting your hair done?'

'Oh go away, Chrissie,' she said.

'This is a public place, you can't order me around here.'

Clare knew that everyone would hear of the pleasant sisterly exchange between the young doctor's wife and the assistant in Dwyers' butchers.

She called in to her mother.

'Are you all right, Clare? You look as if you've been crying.'

'It's make-up, Mum.'

'Where's Liffey?'

'Nellie's minding her, I was getting my hair done.'

'Waste of money in this wind, it will be blown out before you get home.'

Jim came into the shop. Clare turned around and spoke to him, moving her lips deliberately.

'I wish you wouldn't speak to Jim like that,' her mother said. 'You make it sound as if he's a halfwit. Jim's not a halfwit, he's only idle, aren't you, Jim?' Her tone was affectionate but she got no reply. Jim hadn't seen her lips move and he hadn't realized that anyone had spoken to him.

She had slaved over a good dinner for David, he was tired and distracted, he didn't notice her hair, her eyes, the food or the way she had made everything look nice.

He said he was exhausted, they went to bed early, and David fell asleep as she was about to move towards his side of the bed.

'Caroline?'

'Oh David, don't tell me you're going to cancel the golf. I've been looking forward to it all morning.'

'So have I, no, of course I'm not cancelling it. Look I was thinking, it's such a long drive back for you after the game, why don't we have a meal before you head off?'

'Oh, that's very nice, but I don't want to put Clare to too much . . .'

'No, I thought we'd go out somewhere, you know.'

A pause.

'Yes, that would be super. Where did you think?'

'Well, I don't know why I said somewhere, there only is one place, the hotel. We can get a nice enough meal there.'

'Great, that's very nice. Give me the strength to drive back here again.'

'Good, good. I'll book us a table then. I'll ring them and reserve a table for the two of us.'

At first it was just a game of golf with Caroline, then it was golf and a couple of drinks at the club. Now it was golf, drinks and dinner. Josie was on the phone next day. Just for a chat.

'I hope the food wasn't too good last night, you'll be setting me impossible standards,' Clare laughed.

'What do you mean?'

'Well, I'm going to ask the golfers to come *here* next week, would you and Martin join us as well?'

Josie thought that would be great. She was relieved to know that Clare was in the picture about David playing golf and being seen with Caroline. Her sister Rose had come in all excited from the dining room last night to say that David Power and Caroline Nolan were holding hands under the table. But that mightn't be true. Rose had always had a soft spot for David, and Rose had been very bitter and odd since Josie had announced her engagement.

Clare asked Molly if she'd like to come to dinner next Thursday.

'It's a bit far in advance to be planning that isn't it?' Molly said. 'But that would be very nice. Do you think you could manage it?'

Angela said that under any other circumstances she would drop everything and come, but the Mother Provincial of the order was visiting the school and the nuns were having a sort of feast for her. In all the years she had worked in that school since 1945 they had never offered them a bit of food and now it was happening. 'It will be horrific, I'll take notes in a jotter and tell you later.'

'In all the years you've known *me* this is the first time I've ever offered you a bite of food, and it would be the same night,' Clare sighed.

'Is it for anything special?'

'Survival or something,' Clare said.

'Oh, you're inviting your mother-in-law?'

'And my husband's golf partner.'

'That's ambitious, what are you giving them to eat?'

'I haven't thought yet.'

'Let me give you a hint, give them something cold to start, like hard-boiled eggs with stuffing in them. Emer said that she went out to a house to dinner in Dublin and they had a whole lot of tins of sardines and lemon juice mashed up and served in a china bowl and people helped themselves and spread it on bread and it was lovely.'

'That might be fine in Dublin, but if you didn't give them soup here they'd have you taken to the county home.'

'Soup's hard to concentrate on and serve if you've got to think of the next bit.'

'Keep your fingers crossed for me, will you?'

'You'll be fine,' said Angela with no confidence in her voice.

Old Mr Kenny said that it was very nice of the young people to think of inviting him to dinner, he was very touched. And that made up her eight.

She asked Nellie to help her bring two chairs from the big house and she went through all her dishes and cutlery to make sure she had enough. She did all her preparations secretly when David wasn't there. Any time he came home she dropped the fussing. He was pleased about the dinner, that meant that he couldn't really have a great deal to hide, she thought. If he and Caroline had been up to anything more than these long relaxed conversations, the quick peck on the cheek as they said goodbye, surely he couldn't bring

477

her into the house and act as if nothing was going on. She had phoned Caroline at work, and she too had been pleased at the idea of dinner after golf.

'What a lovely thing to suggest, Clare. Will you be able to manage?'

'Manage what?' Clare asked pleasantly, seething with rage.

'Oh, dinner and everything.'

'Gosh I hope so,' Clare said and went back to the kitchen in a fury.

She took Liffey out of the pram and spoke to her seriously. 'Listen to me, kid, this world is full of bullshit, as my friend Mary Catherine, who is your Godmother, used to say in her less refined moments. Now you and I aren't going to put up with that, we are not going to be walked on, Liffey Power. And I make you a solemn promise. If you are a good baby on Thursday, if you don't wet anyone or get sick over them or cry, I will give you a great life full of freedom and adventure, and if you want to go up in a Sputnik and your father says no, I'll fight that you can go up in a Sputnik.'

Liffey clapped her hands, pleased with all the concentration.

'So that's it, a deal. Good.'

Bones came into the kitchen.

'And you too, friend, no scratching your bum when they're here, no huge unexpected howls because you've seen a bluebottle or the lighthouse or anything. Just look like a sweet affectionate hound who loves the young mistress. Of course you could take a bite out of Miss Nolan's rear end but make it look as if she attacked you first. What will I give you? I'll tell you, I'll save you from the knacker's yard. David said you might have to be put down, I won't hear of that.'

Bones smiled at her and she went back to the cookery book.

It would have been so easy if she could have had Nellie, and Nellie would love to have helped, but the whole point of it was that she couldn't. She had to do it on her own. She couldn't even let Nellie know how nervous she was. Nellie's first loyalty was to her own household, she could well tell Molly that there was pandemonium out in the Lodge. That would defeat the whole thing. She had phoned Valerie for tips, and Val had said keep it simple and give them so much to drink they won't remember what they had to eat, which might have been fine for Val's people but was not much help here. Val said that she should warm the bread rolls and put cream in the soup, and to have mashed potatoes or roast potatoes because they couldn't let you down.

Chrissie said wasn't it great to be able to afford huge lumps of beef like this.

'Why didn't you ring up and we'd have sent it over to you?'

'I hoped if I came you might give me a nice cut and show me what direction to carve it in,' Clare said humbly.

'Carve it? Just cut a lump off for each person like you always do,' said Chrissie, helpful and sensitive butcher-sister who could be relied on to put your nerves at ease before an occasion.

Thursday was early closing day in the town twenty miles away. It was David's golf day, and it was the day of the dinner.

Clare thought the women's magazines would be proud of her and the way she said to David that he must bring Caroline back to the house whenever he liked, she would want to change for dinner. The others were coming about seven, so after they had a few drinks in the club . . .

'Won't we be in your way?'

'Not at all,' Clare trilled.

He kissed her goodbye on the nose and then kissed Liffey.

'Bones is creaking a lot, isn't he, I wonder is he in pain? The problem is he always seems to be smiling, you wouldn't know.'

'Oh, Bones has plenty of life in him.' She patted the dog's head. A promise is a promise and Bones wasn't going to be sent to sweet dreams while Clare was around.

*

479

Liffey deposited all her carrots and mashed potato on her best hand-smocked dress. Clare snatched it off and washed it. It might just be dry enough to put back on her again. That was the dress Molly had made such a fuss about. It was being worn in her honour. Then when she was cleaning the spoon, the beautiful silver spoon that Mr Kenny had given the baby, Bones thought it was a toy and galloped off with it.

He took it round the garden three times and then buried it in a flowerbed.

The cream was off, of all days in the year, and two of the table napkins had tears in them. In her haste rushing past the table she knocked over a jug of water so she had to put pillow cases under the corner and pray it would dry out in time.

Because Caroline would change in their bedroom Clare deliberately made it look a much more cosy and loving place than it actually was. She bunched the pillows right up close as if this was the way they normally slept, and she took out her black nighty, the one that actually looked awful on, but exotic if draped around the place. She put a bunch of flowers in the room, and a soft romantic lamp.

She had also tidied up the cupboards and drawers in case Caroline would poke around. Any shabby old shoes or things that were not meant to be seen were hidden firmly in the spare room, and she removed the bulb so that no light could be thrown on that confusion, should somebody open the door in error.

They all arrived at once.

David poured sherries and everyone said wasn't this all nice at least three times each.

Caroline looked glowing with health. Her hair looked shiny and smart. Clare had *hoped* it would have become matted and windblown. She said she'd simply *love* a quick wash, and came down in a commendably quick time wearing a long red wool skirt and white lace blouse.

'It was simply marvellous out there today,' she said. 'You really should learn, Clare.'

'Did somebody tell me you were taking lessons, Clare?' Josie asked.

Clare could have smashed her face. 'No no, but they may have seen me once with Angela up there, she's learning.'

'Oh yes.' Angela Dillon was a sore subject in Dillon's Hotel. There was great fear that Uncle Dick and the schoolteacher might well have lifted the entire golfing trade from the old hotel.

'James plays a lot in Dublin, in fact some think that he spends far too much time on the course,' Caroline said. That wasn't a tactful subject either. Martin's hand tightened round his glass at the mention of the perfidious James Nolan.

Clare decided the meal should be served.

Damn the magazines to the very blackest spot of hell.

The rolls had burned black in the oven. Black.

She sliced some of Nellie's soda bread and put it on a plate. Molly said that Nellie had one of the lightest hands with pastry and bread in the country.

'This bread is very nice too,' Mr Kenny said.

'This *is* Nellie's bread,' Clare said in despair.

The beef was tough; the mashed potatoes were dry; the sprouts were soft and the gravy was lumpy.

Clare could see a series of plates with food left and eventually had to admit that no one was having more and that knives and forks had been left together. Burning with embarrassment she cleared the table.

There was no cream for the chocolate pudding. It had been too late to go and get any more. She had cursed her mother and father for not having a phone, because they could have sent someone over with cream or even ice cream. She should have gone herself, she should have put Liffey into the back of the car and raced down, but at the time she had thought it was better to stay at her post, it seemed less flurried.

They waded through the pudding. Nobody had the cheese she had laid out so carefully with biscuits in lines.

She went to make coffee and discovered that the full coffee jar she had seen in the press was not full of coffee, it was the jar she used to keep cowrie shells in, until she found a place to display them.

She said she had to go to Liffey for a moment and crept out of the house in the dark to see could she find coffee in her mother-in-law's kitchen. It was Thursday, Nellie's evening off. She wouldn't be there. She fell over Bones and landed flat on her face. Bones barked joyfully and so loudly that Dr Power came out to see what was happening.

'My God, Molly,' he called, 'there's somebody in our kitchen!'

David was masterful. He picked up a golf club and insisted that his father stand back.

As Clare crept out of the Powers' kitchen with grazed hands, a bruised forehead and a suspicion of a loosened tooth, Bones was baying at the moon with excitement.

'I'll kill you,' she said to the dog. 'You'll go for the chop and I won't lift a finger to help you.'

Suddenly she saw the entire party framed in the light of the Lodge waiting for her, and David advancing slowly with a golf club.

In the distance she heard the familiar sound of Liffey waking and starting a crying jag that was going to last two hours.

Angela laughed till she cried.

Clare *was* crying as she told the story.

'No I *can't* see the funny side. *Stop* all that laughing. I'm so bloody fed up. I made a *fool* of myself. I might as well have got up and danced on the table in my knickers. It was *dreadful*. They pitied me, all of them, even Josie.'

'It's your own fault,' Angela said. 'You were always the one who was great with the advice to Mary Catherine . . . tell them your father's a postman, see do they care. Why couldn't you have told them you had a coffee jar of cowrie shells?'

'Not on top of the burned rolls, the lumpy gravy, the tough meat. I bet Chrissie did it on purpose, gave me some old hindquarters of a donkey.'

'What about David?'

'He patted me down afterwards, he said first dinners are always a trial. *First!* First and last more likely. How was Mother Provincial?'

'Like a hamster, wrinkling her nose, pointed little teeth.'

'What did they talk about?'

'The decline in faith and morals. And we had egg sandwiches and tea, that was the feast.'

'I'd have loved it,' Clare said feelingly. 'Compared to what went on in my house last night it sounds like paradise.'

Gerry Doyle called in on a wet Thursday.

'I'm a bit busy, Gerry.'

'I can see that,' he said, looking at the open newspaper on the kitchen table.

'Well,' she said awkwardly.

'Well, it took some time. But it's happened.'

'What has?' Her heart was full of fear.

'David.' He stood there smiling.

Her hand went to her throat. 'What's happened to him?'

'I think he's found true love, Clare. In a caravan.'

'*What?*'

'Well, it's much too wet to play golf isn't it? Look at that, they'd be soaked through.' He had been sitting down uninvited, but when he had given her the news, he stood up.

'See you,' he said, and left.

David came home quite dry.

'Did you get a game or was it too wet?'

'No, we battled on, quite exhilarating you know in the wind and the rain.'

'I'm sure.'

'Horrible night for Caroline to have to drive all that way back,' he said.

'Isn't it. Should we have asked her to stay or anything do you think?'

'No, no, but I'll tell you she is thinking of getting a caravan here, just in case she wants to stay over. Makes a lot of sense, doesn't it?'

'Gerry Doyle is in a lot of trouble,' Clare's mother said.

'What way?'

'Well he has a big bill here for one thing, you know three months. All his groceries and cigarettes, it mounts up.'

'I'm sure it does.'

'Your father said I should ask him about it, what with my always getting on well with him.'

'And?'

'And he said he was a bit pushed. And Chrissie says he has a bill as long as your arm in Dwyers' too, and he can't get credit in Costello's any more. He over-extended himself with that place, they don't get enough orders for that size of a set-up. They were fine when they had the little hut and the developing in the house. Dick says he'll have to sell up.'

'Gerry's a survivor.'

'That's what I've said always but when I asked him about his bill here and he said he was broke, I said it was all right, pay a little off it here and there to keep Tom happy . . . and he said I wasn't to be nice to him, he wasn't going out with a whimper, when he went it would be with a bang that would be heard all over the county. What can he have meant?'

'I'll take Liffey to Dublin in a week or two, show her the other Liffey, the river.'

'That's a good idea.'

'Will you go and have your dinner with your parents when I'm gone?'

'Yes, some of the time. I'll cook here a bit maybe if I feel up to it. Oh and Caroline will be in her caravan. I'll probably have a meal or two with her to settle her in.'

Gerry came again.

'I have pictures this time,' he said.

'What kind of pictures?' She was feeding Liffey and needed her full concentration.

'Can I have a cup of tea?'

'No, Gerry, you know I don't like you coming here.'

'Here, you're making an awful mess of that. I'll feed her. You put on the kettle.'

'Will you go then?'

He fed Liffey expertly, holding the spoon just long

enough in her mouth for her to have to swallow what was on it.

Clare poured the tea. She had no sense of alarm. He looked vulnerable as he sat feeding Liffey and gurgling at her.

'Oh, the pictures. These ones.' He emptied an envelope on the table. About a dozen black and white prints of David and Caroline making love on the cramped bed of a caravan.

She put her hand over her mouth and went to the sink. She vomited and retched.

He moved her away and turned on the tap. He cleaned the sink and gave her a glass of water.

'Drink that,' he said.

She threw it at him. It missed and shattered all over the floor. She was shaking.

Calmly he took a towel and wet it under the tap, he went up close and wiped her face, as you would wipe a child's face. She was powerless to stop him.

She poured herself another glass of water and drank it.

'What are you going to do?'

'Nothing,' she said.

'OK.' He put his hand on the door.

'Take these.' She gathered them up with a shaking hand.

'Sure,' he said.

She sat for a long time staring into space.

She told David she felt a sort of 'flu coming on, if he didn't mind she'd sleep downstairs.

He was concerned, and felt her forehead. She did seem a bit feverish.

They made up a bed for her. In the kitchen near the fire.

'It looks very cosy,' he said. 'Maybe we should move down here altogether.'

'Remember when we lived in Rathmines? It was so tiny, and the bed, the stove, the dining table were all on top of each other.'

'That's right,' he said, and sighed.

She got into bed and pulled up the sheets like an obedient child.

485

He kissed her forehead.

'David?'

'Yes?' He looked alarmed.

'Nothing, thanks for everything, sleep well.'

She heard him go upstairs, the lavatory flush, and eventually his shoes fall. He was in bed.

She saw the reflection of the bedroom light go off. He was asleep.

She got out of bed, wide awake. What on God's earth was she going to do?

She made a pot of coffee.

She sat up all night and only when she heard the bed creak did she get back into her own.

He tiptoed down and made a pot of tea.

He brought it to her bedside triumphantly.

'Who's a good husband?' he said.

'David's a good husband,' she said mechanically.

She looked very fluey, David thought as he went up to the big house. Funny that she hadn't a temperature – he had taken it automatically. But her eyes were bright, her forehead hot and she was white as a sheet. Or maybe it was just that he felt he could hardly look at her these days without guilt and confusion.

It was so easy to believe when he was with Caroline. Nobody would be hurt, nobody was going to make any demands, there would be no public scenes and at no time would Clare ever be humiliated. It would be discreet and it would be between them. Nobody would know. They would be the first lovers in the history of Castlebay who would get away with it.

Caroline was so relaxed about everything, she never demanded to know what he thought or what he felt. She wanted no promises, no reassurances and certainly no discussion of the future.

After a session with Clare about where they would be in ten years' time and did he really love her and would they ever have got married if it hadn't been for Liffey, it was like a warm bath to come to Caroline.

486

Caroline said that he must of course make love to Clare, why ever not? She wanted no stories about separate beds or lack of relations. David was taking nothing from what he and she had if he and Clare made love any more than she was stealing anything from Clare by having him come to her in the caravan.

Sometimes he asked her what was going to happen. Would they have a great fight and hurt each other or would they just drift apart? She would laugh and say it was nonsensical to think of the future. It was very restful and it took all the guilt away.

Clare was still lying in her made-up kitchen bed when she heard David's car drive off on his rounds.

A minute later Gerry Doyle came in. 'Quite right too,' he said when he saw the bed.

'*Get out!*' she cried.

'Shush shush.'

'Gerry, I'm going to call Mrs Power. *Help!*'

He put his hand over her mouth gently, and his arm around her. Her thin body in the pink brushed-nylon nightdress with its long sleeves trembled. Her eyes were wild.

'What do you owe him? You saw what he's done to you. Clare?'

She wrenched herself free. And out of his grasp. On her way to the door she picked up the carving knife.

'Don't be silly.' He wasn't a bit afraid. 'Put it down, Clare, I won't touch you, put it down, you'll hurt yourself.'

She laid it down.

'I'll go now, I'll come back for you later.'

'Come back for me?'

'I think we should go away, you and I and Liffey, far away.'

'You're mad.'

'No, not at all. We leave the pictures on the table so they know why. And off we go.'

487

'I know you're in trouble, Gerry, I know you have money problems, could I lend you some or get you some or something?'

'We'll get plenty in time. You and I, we'll go to London maybe. I can work there, we'll have a home.'

'This is fantasy . . . you must stop.'

'You're not to use big words like that to me, those are for the Powers. I'll come back tonight.'

'No you mustn't, I'll tell David, I'll tell Dr Power, you can't.'

'You won't tell any of them, I know. You want to come away with me.'

'Stop, don't go, let me explain!'

'Make up your mind, one minute you're telling me to go, with a carving knife – the next you're calling me back.'

'Don't come back tonight. Don't. I won't be here. Or I'll have the Guards here and David and his father and everyone, you must understand now I do *not* want to come away with you, whatever David's done, I am going nowhere with you.'

'See you.'

He was gone.

She sat frightened, teeth chattering.

David phoned about six o'clock. His last call had left him near town, it made more sense to have a meal there than driving home through all this storm. How was her 'flu?

'David, can you *please* come home?'

'What is it?'

'In all the time we've been here I've never asked you to come home, I've never been a clinging person.. Isn't that true?'

'Darling, of course it is, of course. But it's awkward now. I met Caroline, I just made arrangements to have a meal with her, as it happens.'

'You can have three hundred and sixty-five meals a year with Caroline if you just come home *tonight*.'

'I *am* coming home.'

'No, *now*. I'm frightened.'

'I'll make it an early meal,' he said. 'I'll be home then, and you can tell me what's worrying you.'

'I see,' she said, and hung up.

She left a note on the kitchen table which said, 'I feel very edgy and unwell tonight, so I've gone to the main house where there will be a lot of people to keep me company.'

That would do either for Gerry if he came, or for David.

At six-thirty she knocked on her mother-in-law's door.

'You don't have to knock, Clare,' Dr Power said. He was just about to listen to the news.

'Come on in and sit down.'

Molly was darning by the fire, they had finished their supper.

'I hope you don't mind. I've not been feeling well all day, and David's been delayed. He won't be back until about nine or ten. Do you mind if I stay here?'

They exchanged looks.

'Of course not,' Molly said.

'I think it's in bed you should be, David said you have a touch of 'flu.'

'It's not 'flu, it's just jitters, I have this awful sense of something going to happen.'

'Nonsense, it's the storm. You're even nearer the sea than we are. Don't give in to it, child. Stay with us for a bit, then I'll walk back and tuck you up. And tuck her ladyship up too.' Liffey chortled in the basket. She could only make it stretch to an hour and a half. By eight o'clock she was back in the Lodge.

Dr Power glanced at the note. 'Well, you can tear that up now, he'll find you asleep in bed when he gets back.'

He fussed and filled a hot-water bottle for her, then he went up the stairs. She was ashamed that she hadn't made the bed since last night, since David had slept in it.

Dr Power didn't make any comment.

As soon as he was gone she locked the door and put a chair against it, then she made sure the windows were fastened.

She would stay up by the fire. David could only be an hour, couldn't he? There was no way Gerry could get in.

There was a movement behind her. And there he was, in his leather jacket, smiling at her easily.

'Oh my God.'

'I was in the dining room. It's all right, it's all right.'

'You don't *understand*. You've read it all *wrong*. I'm *not* coming away with you.'

'You've always wanted me, we're the same type, Clare I said that to you years ago. We're greedy and we want everything. Well we're going to have it. David's different, he's gentler, born into a gentle life.'

'If I did anything in my whole life that would make you think I was in love with you I swear I can't remember.'

She wasn't frightened, now, that he'd hurt her. She just couldn't bear the great fight when David came in, the producing of the pictures – and David had always thought that she liked Gerry. It was so unjust, so terribly unjust. David was the one who was unfaithful, and here was she locked into the house with Gerry Doyle.

'Will you pack your things? I have the car up the lane.'

'You are talking like a madman. There's no question of it.' Gentler, now. 'I've admired you and liked you, like everyone, but that's all.'

'Very well.'

'What?'

'You know what you are saying. I presume you mean it.'

'I do.'

He went to the door, her body was relaxing by the moment with relief.

'You'll be sorry of course. Sorry you didn't come with me tonight. You'll always be sorry. You'll wake in the bed beside your cheating husband, or in a bed downstairs, and you'll be sorry you didn't leave tonight with me.'

'No, Gerry. I won't. We'll always be able to talk you and I . . . always.'

'No,' he said.

She waited, when he was gone, hoping to hear the sound of the van starting up in the lane. There was no sound. Or the crashing of the sea and the wind drowned it if there was.

*

David cursed himself for having rung home. It was just that he had wanted to know how her 'flu was. *Now* look what he had brought on himself. This was exactly. what he knew would happen despite all Caroline's fine words. Now he was pleasing neither of them. Clare would be fretting at home over whatever was worrying her, and Caroline would be annoyed that he had to leave early, and slightly scornful. She had been like that once or twice recently. More or less taunting him, saying, *of course* he must go home to *poor Clare* if she needed him. Caroline had said more than once that there were no chains around his legs tying him to *her* apron strings. It had been very humiliating and oddly he had also felt like defending Clare. He would feel that way tonight too. The girl had 'flu, he would say, and how defensive and idiotic it would sound.

He parked his car in the little yard of the small house that Caroline rented. He had been looking forward to the evening. Perhaps he would say nothing about his promise to be home early, perhaps he could ring and say that something had happened . . .

Caroline was not in the kitchen. He had let himself in the back door. A saucepan with water was hissing on the back burner of the gas stove. He reached out automatically and pulled it away. The bottom had just begun to burn.

'Caroline,' he called. There was no answer.

That was odd. She must be at home. She still had the city habit of locking the doors when she went out.

'Caroline,' he called again. Perhaps she was in the bathroom upstairs. He didn't want her to get a fright if she came out and saw him unexpectedly. 'I'm here,' he called again.

There was a sound from upstairs.

'Are you all right,' he called, alarmed suddenly and taking the stairs two by two.

Caroline was sitting grey-faced on the bed. Both of her hands were held to her mouth.

'What is it?' Could she have been attacked? Raped even? Why didn't she speak?

'Oh my God, my God,' she said over and over.

David told himself that he was trained to deal with people in shock, but it was no use, he had forgotten what to do if he had ever known. He knelt down opposite Caroline. He stroked her bent head, he unclenched her hands, he tried to get her to look into his eyes. That was the hardest bit. She wouldn't meet his glance.

'Tell me, darling Caroline, tell me.'

'I can't.'

'Did anyone hurt you, touch you?'

She shook her head.

'Please, please, I have to help you. Have you had bad news from home? Your father, mother?'

'No, nothing like that.'

'Did you see something, an accident, what is it Caroline? Tell me and I'll help you.' He went on stroking her hair and looking up as she sat on the bed, her face stricken and her eyes wild.

'David,' she said.

'Has it anything to do with me?'

'He's mad, he's mad enough for a mad home, to be locked away for ever . . .'

'Who? Who are you talking about? *Tell* me.'

'Gerry Doyle.'

'What has he done now?' David stood up in impatience. He followed Caroline's glance to the dressing table and saw what had made her the way she was.

One by one he looked at the dozen pictures, bile rising in his throat at what had been private turning into this. 'It wasn't like that,' he said eventually. 'It was special. You know.'

That cheered her somehow, she reached out a cold hand for his.

'Why did he do this?' David looked through the pictures once more and turned them face down on the dressing table.

'Because he's mad,' Caroline said simply.

David pulled the bedroom chair up beside her and held her hands. 'Did he give them to you?' he asked gently.

'No, they were here when I came home.'

'Did he leave a note or anything?'

492

Caroline reached down and picked up a piece of paper, it had *Doyle's Photographics* on it. In small writing it said:

Delivery three sets of pictures only.
a) Miss Caroline Nolan.
b) Doctor David Power. The surgery, Castlebay.
c) Mrs Clare Power. The Lodge, Castlebay.

'My God.' David stood up. 'That's what Clare wanted. That's why she rang.'

'She's seen those?' Caroline's hand was to her mouth again.

'I don't know. She rang me, very hysterical, I mean I rang her to say I was coming here, she said she wanted me home. I said I'd be home fairly early.'

'She couldn't have, she *couldn't* have seen these?'

'No.' David was slowly going over the conversation. 'No, she couldn't have. She said I could have dinner with you three hundred and sixty-five days a year or something . . .'

'What?'

'She said I *must* come home tonight, I said I was meeting you for dinner, she said you can have dinner every other night of the year but please come back now.'

They looked at each other wildly.

'He couldn't have given them to her, she wouldn't say that if she'd seen them.'

'But why did she want me home?'

'Do you want to go back?' She sounded frightened.

'I can't leave you.'

'But suppose, just suppose he *has*.'

'He couldn't have. I'd have known by her voice.' David stood up and paced the room. 'I'll ring her, that's what I'll do.'

He telephoned the Lodge, there was no reply. They looked at each other: was that good or bad?

'She might have gone in to your mother and father,' Caroline suggested.

'No, however bad she felt she wouldn't do that.' He looked tormented.

'Where could he have been, just at the window of the caravan?' she glanced over at the dressing table.

'That's what he must have done. But why? I mean is it for money? His business is meant to be in a bad way, but he couldn't expect us to pay him.'

'We would, wouldn't we?' Caroline said simply.

'Yes I suppose we would. But he doesn't *ask* for money. Do you think it's because he disapproves, because he wants you and he's jealous?'

She shook her head: 'I don't think that would explain it.'

'But *why*? Why would someone do that, it's so perverted. To peer through a window ... my God. He must be obsessed with you, it's the only explanation, he can't have you himself so he does what he can to ruin the chances of anyone else having you.'

'Oh, he's *had me* himself, many, many times. That's not likely to be the reason. He's actually lost his mind and become a lunatic.'

She had her head in both hands and didn't see the look of shock and pain on David's face. She went on talking.

'The trouble is we can't really tell the Guards or they'll want to know why, but he should be locked up, shouldn't he?' She looked up for confirmation.

'He didn't sleep with you,' David said.

'David, that's neither here nor there. You sleep with Clare, do I mind that, did I mind it? Once?' Her voice was getting shrill and hysterical. 'Christ, this isn't the time to do the Victorian Husband bit, everyone in the county has been with Gerry Doyle in some form or another, the point is what do we do?'

She looked young and frightened and alone.

'I know this is the most unhelpful thing in the world, but I think I should go back to Castlebay. Under the circumstances I don't think you should come with me . . .'

'No.'

'I'll ring you when I get there, I'll ring to know are you all right.'

'Sure.'

'I'll come to see you first thing tomorrow morning, when we're calmer, we'll decide what to do.'

'Great.'

'Is there anyone, have you any friends, anyone who could come in, or someone you could go to?' He looked around, willing himself to find her some support, hating to leave her.

'No.'

He swallowed and couldn't speak.

She turned her head towards the dressing table and the pictures that were turned upside down.

The wind and rain lashed the car, the road was strewn with bits of branches.

A steady drumming beat in David's heart. May Clare be all right, may Clare be all right. May he not have shown her the pictures, may he not have shown her the pictures . . .

Clare stood at the window for a long time. She hadn't heard the car starting up. Perhaps he would come back again. But then he had been very final when he had left.

Please God he had been lying when he said he showed the pictures to David, and to Caroline. Please may David not know about them. It made everything so definite if he knew, if he had seen. She would deny she had ever seen them if David asked her. She couldn't bear to hold any discussion based on what she had seen. It didn't make her retch now, it made her sad. But she had known for months, hadn't she? All Gerry Doyle had done was to make her admit it to herself.

Please may Gerry go away from Castlebay, for ever and ever. Please, please.

Gerry closed the door gently behind him. He had never slammed a door in his life. He would like to have taken it from its hinges.

Clare had looked at him as if he were mad. As if *he* were mad! It was Clare who was mad. To have hoped that she would be accepted in that family for one thing, to have looked at the evidence in black and white and *then* to decide

495

to stay . . . That wasn't the Clare O'Brien he used to know, the Clare he had the plans for. He had been so *forgiving* towards her, so *understanding*. He had said so little when she behaved like a common *tramp* and got into trouble with the boy from the big house. No accusations had come from him. And there she stood tonight, *frightened* of him and *doubting* him.

He hit violently at some gorse that jutted out of the hedge between the Lodge and the cliff. He remembered telling a hundred girls, maybe more, about the old saying, 'When the gorse is out of bloom then the kissing's out of fashion.' They had always been surprised that gorse seemed to bloom all year round, and Gerry would laugh. He hit again and scraped his hand on the prickly branches.

How dare Clare talk to him in that frightened, teeth-chattering way? How *dare* she look up at him as if she were afraid he might strike her? She had more to fear from her big unfaithful husband than from him . . . from Gerry, who had always wanted her, *waited* for her.

He moved angrily to the cliff top and looked out at the sea.

Everything had gone now. *Everything*. Not just the business, he had seen that coming for many a month, but Clare's face tonight . . . He had not foreseen that. She was frightened of him as if he were a stranger who would do her harm, not her soul's other half. Her one true friend and love who would make a home for her and her baby, and accuse her of nothing except bad luck, as he had had.

His breath came in short bursts.

She *would not* do this to him . . . She *would not* back out now . . . Now, after *everything* . . . After all he had planned . . .

Clare! It was too much to take, too much for her to do now at this stage.

She would regret it for the rest of her life.

There would be no drive to England in the van tonight for her.

There would be no new life for her.

What did she mean by throwing back all he offered her?

496

She would want him in a little while, when it was too late. When he had gone. When nobody knew where he was. She would stand on the cliff and wish she had left with him tonight.

He found that he was trembling, shaking with anger. He had never known such a sensation – it was as if a great wind had taken hold of him and borne him up in the air . . .

He was shaking too much to drive. He would walk on the beach. It would clear his head.

He slipped and climbed down the path. The beach looked dark and dangerous, but the bigger waves were dying down; the tide must be going out now. It was on the turn anyway. He walked, his head wet from the salt spray and the rain; but he didn't care.

He had really blown it now.

The business was a shambles. He couldn't meet even one of the bills that were piled neatly on the desk under a paperweight for whoever would have to go through them. He hoped it wouldn't be Fiona but he couldn't think who else it might be. When the staff couldn't get in tomorrow, there would be a hue and cry but he had left no note to say that he was going to England. There would be no Guards looking for him for bounced cheques. He could always get by on credit; that's what he had always done.

There were very few lights up in Castlebay. He looked up at the outlines of the houses clustered together and the dark spire of the church. He would never look at them again from here, or at all. Once he got to London it would be a new life. It would be *exciting*. It would not be exciting to stay to see their sympathy, to work for someone else, to see Clare, lovely, *lovely* Clare put up with that *sod*. He was *glad* he had done it. He was near the rock pools. Since he was a child he had loved walking over them, balancing, teetering on the edge. It was only inches of water if you did trip over and fall in. Tonight the waves were crashing over them . . . but still, it was a temptation.

He walked around them, playing games with himself, his feet and legs wet to the knee. He cried out with hysterical excitement. It was ludicrous, but it was exciting.

The wave knocked him down and he cut his cheek on the jagged rock.

It wasn't funny any more. Here came another one. Then the drag, he felt his leg being scraped across the rocks. Desperately he reached out with his hands.

But the drag was too great.

When the third wave had reared up at him, he knew he was going to drown or be battered to death on the rock pools where he had played since he was old enough to walk.

'Clare.' He rattled the door. It was locked.

'Clare? Are you all right?' She came to the door pale but calm.

He reached out his arms for her but she stepped out of his way.

'I'm very sorry. I was frightened. It's the storm, I'm all right now. I'm sorry I called you home.' She spoke like a stranger.

'I rang, I rang twice about seven, and again at a quarter to eight.'

'I was in your parents' house.'

'Are you all right?'

'Yes I am now, I think. But I don't feel like talking. Do you want tea or food? Were you able to have your dinner?'

'No, no it doesn't matter.' He wasn't concentrating.

'Was the road bad?' Again like a person making conversation.

'Yes, branches, and in one place a tree down, you'd have to drive right up on the ditch to get past.'

'Imagine.'

'Clare.'

'You know I said I'd like to go to Dublin for a few days and you said that would be fine, because you could get looked after . . .?'

'Yes?' His voice was hollow.

'I'd like to go very soon. Tomorrow maybe.'

'You're not all that well, wait a few days.'

'I don't want to wait.'

'It's silly to take Liffey off the whole way across the country when you're not well.'

'It's sillier to stay here on my own hour after hour listening to the sea when I'm not well.'

'You don't have to be on your own here.'

'No. David, will you do me a great favour? Will you not make a scene? I've had as much drama as I can take, and I'm sure you've had a bad day too. But I want to go up to Angela and Dick tonight. Please.'

She must know.

He must have shown her the pictures. David's heart was like a stone.

'Why? What brought this on?'

'I think if I stayed here tonight it might be bad for us. We might say things that would hurt each other.'

He tried a little laugh. 'Heavens, isn't that very fanciful?'

'No,' she said. 'It's not.'

'Do you want to take Liffey with you?'

'Please.'

'I could try to explain . . .' he began.

'And so could I. But we know too well how easily people say things that are unforgivable when they're hurt or annoyed. We've done very little hurting and wounding. Don't let's risk it tonight.'

'Have you packed?' he asked.

'Yes, just things for tonight. I'll come back tomorrow when you've gone out and I'll sort out what we'll need in Dublin.'

'I'm saying yes, not because I'm weak but because I think you're very sure what you want, and I'm not, so we should go along with the one who is sure.'

He grinned at her and she almost took a step towards him.

'Thank you,' she said formally.

'Is Angela expecting you?'

'Yes.'

'Well.' His shoulders drooped.

'She doesn't ask, you know Angela, she doesn't ever ask.'

'I wasn't thinking of that.'

'It's better.'

'I suppose it is.'

So many times they had wished Liffey would sleep rather

499

than struggle and chatter and try to escape. Tonight when they could have done with a bit of distraction she lay in Clare's arms breathing evenly, her long eyelashes making shadows on her cheeks.

David held his daughter tight in his arms and two tears came down his face. 'I'm sorry, Liffey,' he said.

'Why are you sorry?' Clare said gently. 'I have much more to apologize to her for. But it's only like talking to ourselves until she can understand.'

'Goodbye, Clare.'

'Goodbye, David. For a while.'

They didn't touch.

Angela had seen the car drawing up outside the cottage; she had sent Dick scurrying off to bed in case Clare wanted to talk.

Clare stood with Liffey in her arms and watched the car turning and going back down the golf-course road. She gave a little wave but David was looking straight in front of him and didn't see.

'Come in,' Angela said.

'It's very hard to explain.'

'Most things are quite incapable of being explained. I've always thought that,' said Angela.

She showed Clare her bed and made a cup of tea from a kettle which had been boiling in readiness.

'That's to take to bed on your own,' she said. Clare blinked her gratitude at the teacher who knew by magic when people wanted to talk and when there was nothing left to say.

Jim O'Brien ran back into the shop looking frightened.

'Dad, Dad, where are you, where are you?'

'Where would I be but getting out of my bed?' Tom O'Brien grumbled.

'Dad, come here will you.'

The boy looked frightened.

'Dad, come out with me . . . now, come quickly.'

Tom O'Brien pulled his coat over his pyjama top. He had

his day trousers on and his shoes and socks, he had been dressing on the side of the bed when he heard the shouts.

They ran on to the top of the cliff and Jim pointed down on the beach. 'I think it's a person, Dad, it's a body.'

There was wind and spray. Tom O'Brien took off his glasses and wiped them. 'It's a shape, but it couldn't be a body, who'd be in the water in this weather?'

'It is, Dad. It *is*. I'm going down, will you get the Guards and Dr Power?'

Jim O'Brien, almost totally deaf, didn't hear his father warning him to take care. He started down the steps to the big treacherous beach at Castlebay where somebody drowned nearly every summer but where they had never seen a body washed in by a winter tide.

People seemed to know without being told. They came out of their houses and began to run down the main street. The murmur became louder, and almost without knowing they were doing it they started to check where their own families were. It was still just a figure, face down in the water. They didn't know for sure whether it was a man or a woman.

'Perhaps it's a sailor from a ship,' they said. But they knew it wasn't anyone who had gone overboard. No nice anonymous death of someone they didn't know. No informing the authorities and saying a few prayers for the deceased Unknown Sailor. This was someone from Castlebay.

They stood in silent groups on the cliff top and watched the first people getting to the water's edge; the boy who had first seen the waves leaving something frightening on the shore; other men too; people from the shops nearby and young men who were quick to run down the path. Then they saw the figures coming down the other path near the doctor's house, kneeling by the body in case, just in case, there was something in a black bag that could bring it back to life.

By the time Father O'Dwyer arrived with his soutane flapping in the wind the murmur had turned into a unified sound. The people of Castlebay were saying a decade of the rosary for the repose of the soul which had left the body that lay face down on their beach.

David had only had two hours' sleep when he heard the shouting. He thought it was still part of his dream, but it was real. He sat up in bed – Clare wasn't there. He remembered the scene last night, taking her up to Angela's house, and he remembered coming back and taking the house apart looking for any trace of the photographs. He knew Clare hadn't taken them with her – he had looked in her small bag. She had only some things for the baby and a nightdress for herself.

He had put off ringing Caroline until it was too late to ring her. Then he told himself it would be cruel to wake her when he had nothing helpful to say.

He had been dreaming that people were coming after him, waving papers or big envelopes at him, all running down Church Street calling at him in anger. In his dream he didn't know why they were so against him but he was frightened and trying to run away.

Then he realized the shouts were real. It was Bumper Byrne's voice and Mogsy's, and then his father's.

'Come quickly, there's someone on the beach, there's been a drowning.'

His heart nearly burst in fear.

He ran down the stairs in his crumpled shirt and trousers, he hadn't undressed last night.

He caught the unfortunate Mogsy Byrne who was at the doorway by his arms. 'Who is it? God damn you who is it?'

'I don't know ... I don't. I don't ...' Mogsy was stammering at the wild-eyed look of David Power who was always so calm and capable.

'*Tell* me,' David roared at him. 'Tell me or I'll break your neck.'

'He's got his face down, David,' Mogsy managed to get out. 'I left the cliff before they knew, they said to come quickly.'

He had said 'he'. It was a man, it was a man thank God, it was a man. Oh God, thank you for letting it be a man.

David's eyes had cleared. He grabbed a coat and ran to the surgery for his bag, his father was already there.

'Don't come down the steps. Please, Dad. I'll do it. Come down the other way.'

'I've been coming down those steps to take bodies out of the water since before you were born.'

'Who is it, is he dead?'

'They don't know, they think it's Gerry Doyle.'

David put out his hand to steady himself on a desk. Just beside a big brown envelope printed with the words Doyle's Photographics.

His father was already out of the surgery and heading towards the cliff. David steadied himself, put the envelope in a drawer of his own things, down at the bottom of it. And with shaking legs he followed his father to the cliff path.

They saw the group around the body and realized even at this distance that their work would not be needed. Father O'Dwyer had been sent for, he was the only one who might be any help to that body which lay spreadeagled on the beach. Even through the wind and rain and from far away David knew it was Gerry Doyle's lifeless body. He held his arm out to steady his father.

'Young fool,' Dr Power said. 'Bloody young lunatic, his whole life before him. What did he want to do that for? Bloody criminal fool to throw away the one life God gave him.'

David's heart was like stone when they turned the body over and he saw all the lacerations and tears down the side of the face of Gerry Doyle. As if in deference to his father he stood back and let the older man pronounce what everyone knew, that life was extinct.

'Where's Clare, will the pair of you come in and have breakfast with us?'

'She's not here, Dad, she spent the night up at Angela Dillon's.'

'She what?'

'Dad, please. You asked me where she was, I told you.'

'Yes, yes you did. Well, will you come in and have a bit of breakfast? You could do with one after all that.'

503

'No. No thanks, I'll make a cup of tea, that's all I want.'

'And has my grandchild gone to live up with Mr and Mrs Dillon or am I not to ask about that either?'

There was a bit of a smile on his face to take the harm out of the question. But it didn't hide the worry.

'It was only last night, Dad. It'll sort itself out.'

'Clare has some kind of 'flu, she was shivery and very jumpy last night, I'm not interfering, I'm just telling you.'

'Did she say what was wrong?'

'That she was frightened, she had a cup of tea with us, I brought her back. You weren't home.'

'Yes.' Dr Power narrowed his eyes. 'Lord God, is that Gerry's van parked in the lane over there? It is. What on earth is it doing up here? Lord have mercy on him, poor fool. And he could be one of the nicest fellows you'd ever talk to.'

Clare slept, to her great surprise. She slept well in the strange white bed with its clean hard sheets and its hot-water bottle. Liffey slept in a cot. Clare had been surprised when Angela said there was a cot, she had forgotten that Angela kept summer visitors, and had thought it wise to invest in two cots years ago when her mother was still alive.

Liffey too had slept. Maybe it was being away from the roar and crash of the sea, or from all the anxiety.

Clare only woke because Angela had come in with a cup of tea. To her surprise, Angela had drawn up a chair beside the bed and sat down. Surely she wasn't going to give a lecture or want a heart to heart chat at this time in the morning.

Certainly Angela's face looked drawn and strained.

Clare thanked her for the tea and waited.

'Take a big sip.'

This was different, there was bad news of some kind. She put down the cup and looked almost on reflex at Liffey as if to make sure that she was all right. 'What is it?'

'There's been an accident. Gerry Doyle was drowned. They've just carried his body up from the beach.'

Total silence. Only the sounds from Liffey's cot where she played happily with the red satin rabbit whose ears had been torn off long ago.

'Clare?'

'He's dead. Is he dead?'

'Yes, it doesn't seem possible. Gerry of all people. There was no one as full of life.'

Angela broke off as she looked at Clare's face. It was expressionless. She just sat in the white bed with her long hair tied loosely behind her pale face, staring straight ahead of her. Her hands were clasped around her knees.

It wasn't natural to react like that. Angela was alarmed.

Clare *had* been friendly with Gerry of course, very friendly maybe. Perhaps even now when Clare's marriage seemed to be going so disastrously wrong, Gerry had been on hand to give consolation. Could that be the explanation of this sense of shock and disbelief? Angela reached out her hand, hoping that if she patted Clare's arm or did something warm the girl might come out of this trance.

She was totally unprepared for Clare to throw herself into Angela's arms, sobbing and shaking. And the only words she could distinguish over and over were, 'He's really dead, thank God, thank God.'

They said it was accidental death, that had to be said, otherwise he couldn't be buried in consecrated ground. And things were bad enough for the poor Doyles without that.

They said he must have been out for a walk and slipped, his face and side had been very lacerated so he could have been walking on the rock pools, everyone knew that Gerry Doyle loved to balance there. That's what they said but nobody believed it, not for a moment. They knew it was suicide.

It had to be suicide, his business was in ruins, it was a matter of weeks before it would have been taken from him, there was a farmer out in the country who had been making very open threats to come after Gerry on account of the farmer's daughter being pregnant and Gerry Doyle taking no interest in this state of affairs. Fiona Conway, pregnant and heartbroken, told how he had said he wouldn't be in Castlebay for much longer, but she had thought he meant he was going to England. Mary Doyle his mother said that only two days previously he had sent her £20 in an envelope with no explanation, just the words 'From Gerry'. Agnes O'Brien said that she had been saying for months that the boy was in trouble of some kind but nobody had ever listened to her. Josie Dillon said he had cashed two cheques at the hotel which had bounced but they had kept it quiet, and Gerry had thanked her and said when he went to another land and made his fortune he would think of her. She had thought he was going to emigrate, *how* could anyone have thought he would do something like this?

As quickly as they could the formalities were organized and the body was released for burial.

Gerry Doyle would be laid to rest after ten o'clock Mass on Thursday, Father O'Dwyer announced from the pulpit, and blew his nose loudly because he still couldn't take it in.

David went through his work automatically, everywhere he went they talked about the tragedy. A woman with chest pains pointed to the pictures on the walls, framed photographs of the First Communions and Confirmations. He was a lovely boy, always a laugh, never took anything too seriously. In the next house the old man who had hardening of the arteries was more interested in what could have happened to poor young Doyle than he was about his own imminent departure to the county home which David was trying to introduce.

'He was practically born in the water that young lad, which is unusual in these parts, half of Castlebay never takes to the sea at all, but the young Doyle fellow, he swam like a fish.'

In the room of a ten-year-old girl with jaundice they talked as much of Gerry Doyle as of the patient. He told them not to be worried by the colour of her urine, it was quite natural that it would turn the colour of port wine. They nodded and said that they had heard Gerry Doyle's business was in a bad way but surely he wouldn't drown himself over a thing like that? There had to be more to it than that.

'If people drowned themselves when their businesses

went wrong, wouldn't the sea be full of bodies?' asked the child's father.

David agreed absently and looked at the little girl's eyes. They were yellow and he told her that her skin would go a little bit yellow like a Chinese.

'Are the Chinese yellow?' the girl asked. 'Really yellow?'

'Come to think of it they're not, any I saw aren't yellow at all.'

'Have you *seen* a Chinese?' The girl was very excited.

'In Dublin, yes, there were Chinese students at University and there was a Chinese restaurant we went to.'

She could have talked to him for ever about it. He wondered would Liffey want to know things like that too. His heart sank again when he thought of Liffey. And Clare.

The day ended somehow and he went back to the surgery. Quickly David retrieved the envelope and brought it back to the Lodge. He saw his mother pretending not to look through the curtains at him, but he went on as if he hadn't seen.

The kitchen was tidy. He looked around hopefully for a note. Clare had been in during the day, he could see that. The dishes and cups he had left after his breakfast were washed up and put away. He noticed that she had done some shopping: a packet of tea, a pound of butter, a loaf of bread and some sliced rashers of bacon were placed on the table near the range. The bed upstairs was made and although some of her clothes were hanging in the wardrobe she must have taken others. Most of Liffey's things seemed to have gone, and one of their two suitcases had disappeared. He looked around to see if she had taken all her books. It would be good in a way if she had, that would mean she had gone through with her plan of going to Dublin for a while.

Please may she have gone to Dublin. Let her not be here for the funeral. Please.

He sat down in the kitchen, having locked the door first, and he took out the pictures. He looked at them again. Exactly the same as he had seen last night at Caroline's. Last night? Is that all it was? There was the same list in the small handwriting naming the three people to whom they were being sent. He must have given them to Clare. He must have come to this house, that's why his car was there, his big ugly van with the name of the business, parked in the lane beside their house. David's father had phoned the Guards to report it being there, they had come to collect it but it had told them nothing. But it told David everything, he must have called on Clare. That was what had frightened her so much, that was why she had wanted him to come home. But had he come in and spoken to her, shown the pictures to her personally? Or had he just pushed them through the door and said he would be back?

David opened the front of the range and one by one he put them in. There was nothing exciting about these pictures taken through a caravan window. They were not the kind of pictures that would do anything except destroy the three people they were sent to. That was what Gerry Doyle had done before he destroyed himself.

Why? David allowed his brain to start on that again. All day he had pushed the thought out of sight while he attended to his work. But now as the flames burned up the record of his time with Caroline, time that he had convinced himself was not evil because nobody was losing and nobody was being hurt . . . he wondered again why Gerry had bothered. It couldn't have been blackmail. Caroline and David didn't have the kind of money it turned out that was needed by Doyle's Photographics, they would only have been able to pay a few pounds a week at the very most. He didn't hate David, in fact they always got on very well when they were children, and of late, well David had been a bit scathing about how easily women fell for Gerry but he would never have known that. Or if he had, he couldn't have cared enough to hound David in this way.

David had assumed that it must have been Caroline, but she had been adamant, she had said with an unattractive honesty that had revolted him that she was Gerry Doyle's for the asking, and had been – and, no doubt, would be again – so it could not have been unrequited passion that

508

made him take the pictures.

What did that leave?

It only left Clare.

Clare.

He remembered the time he had come across them kissing on the bench over the beach, and how annoyed he had been. He remembered Clare running up from the National Library back to her hostel to see if Gerry Doyle had rung. He remembered the easy way Gerry Doyle danced with Clare in the ballroom with the glittery revolving light sparkling over them as they smiled at each other.

It was Gerry Doyle she had asked to get her post office savings book that time. Then, only weeks ago, he remembered Gerry complaining that Clare wouldn't let him come and photograph Liffey. 'She's afraid that if I take the picture, I somehow steal the child,' he had laughed. And Clare had said nothing.

The photographs were all burned. He poked around and the ashes were gone, mixed into the other ashes of the range. He closed the little gate and looked around. The clock was ticking and below the sea was crashing. Those were the only sounds. Those were the sounds that gifted bright Clare O'Brien heard all day, and all evening. That was the life he had given her.

She was too smart now for Chrissie and her mother to feel easy with her. She wasn't smart enough for her mother-in-law to make her welcome. And Gerry Doyle had loved her and wanted her to come away. He had taken the pictures to prove that there was nothing to keep her any more. He had wanted Liffey as well, she must have sensed that at the time he wanted to photograph the child.

Had he come to the house and asked her to go away?

Did he drown himself because she wouldn't go.

After all, as the father of that sick child had said this afternoon, if everyone whose business was in a bad way swam out to sea then the beach would be littered with bodies. Gerry Doyle didn't kill himself over cheques that bounced and bills that would not be paid. But if he was prepared to go to such lengths and take such photographs to incriminate her husband then he really must have wanted Clare, and wanted her enough to end his life if she wouldn't come with him.

The clock ticked on and the waves crashed on. He walked around the small house restlessly. There was no sign of Clare in this house. No pictures she had chosen on the wall. No books. There were some in the spare room but they had always looked as if they were in transit, not as if they had come to stay. On the window sill was a cookery book and inside in Clare's big bold writing were the instructions for the dinner party that had been such a disaster. That was the only evidence that this woman had lived here.

David Power put his head in his hands at the kitchen table and cried.

For *all* that had happened.

Tuesday evening. It was only twenty-four hours ago that he had come to the house sure that she would pack her things and leave in his van. Would he have killed them all? Would he have driven Liffey and Clare into the sea? Clare didn't know. He might have been sane, and really meant them to go to England as he said. But that in itself wasn't sane. She had been over it a thousand times, there was no way she had led him on. A few kisses years ago, a few dances holding him close. But Gerry Doyle had that and much much more from every girl he met. He couldn't have seen it as some kind of attraction or involvement. So, he knew that she wasn't very happy with David, that her life had not turned out to be the dream she once thought . . . but still.

Angela and Dick had been wonderful, but to say that, to think that was just to let the record go into a groove where it said the same thing over and over. They had always been wonderful. For as long as she could remember.

'Take the car,' Dick had said. 'I don't need it just now. If you want to go and collect anything.'

She took his car, and went back to the Lodge, she knew

that both Molly and Nellie were looking out of different windows trying to see what she was up to. She didn't care. She didn't even know what she was up to herself.

Methodically she went through the house tidying it for David, she made the bed and put all the washing together in a pillowcase, none of her own things, only his. She left the place so that it wouldn't offend anyone if Molly and Nellie came in to look after poor David. She even cleaned out a particularly grubby corner of the food press she had been meaning to do for ages, and lined it with fresh paper.

She made a big rubbish bag out of one of the pillowcases, and into that she threw all the torn stockings, almost-empty marmalade jars. She sat in the unusually tidy kitchen for fifteen minutes trying to think of something to say to David in a note, and then decided there was nothing to say.

He had left her no note, after all. He had been here all night, and then they said he had been called down to the beach when Gerry had been found. Perhaps there had been no time.

With her head in her hands she sat there. Could Gerry really have sent those pictures to David? Could he have left them in the van? No, the Guards had said there was nothing in the van, Angela had told her that, no photographic things even. It had been empty as if he had been clearing out.

Suppose Gerry had dropped the pictures into the surgery. Suppose Dr Power had opened them. Her heart gave a jump thinking of that nice old man seeing such indecent evidence of his son's adultery with a family friend. Then she hardened her feelings. Why should she care now? The pictures were not of Clare. She had been here minding the child and the house while all this was going on. She was not going to let herself feel sympathetic when she was the one who deserved a great great deal of sympathy.

She stood up, arranged the things she had bought for his supper where he could see them, and then loaded the car with the suitcase she had packed. She put the pillowcase of rubbish in the back, she shook more anthracite into the range, and pulled the door behind her.

*

'I won't stay here for ever,' Clare said to Angela.

'You haven't been here two days yet, stop being so dramatic. Aren't you company for us?'

'Not really. Not at the moment.'

Liffey asked to get up on Clare's lap and then she wanted to get down again. She waddled over to Angela with the same request.

'It's a pity Gerry didn't see Fiona's child born.'

'What?'

'Fiona's having a child any time now, you know that.'

'Oh of course, I was thinking of . . . Why do you say that?'

'He loved children. He was very good with them too. He often talked about Liffey here. Did you know that?'

'No.' Clare shivered.

Angela decided to change the subject. 'I was talking to Fiona on my way back from school, I went down Church Street. She was going in to Doyle's Photographics to sort things out . . . Clare? What is it?'

'Oh my God, my God I forgot that entirely. Can I take the car again Angela, please, five minutes.'

'Of course you can but what . . .'

Clare was out the door and into the front seat. The keys were always left in the ignition. Dick Dillon looked out the window upstairs to know who was driving his car off crashing the gears like that.

Fiona wore a grey smock with a big white collar attached to it. She hadn't any mourning clothes in maternity wear. They probably didn't make them, Clare thought.

Fiona was sorting through the brown envelopes with their codes and dates.

'I'm very sorry,' Clare said.

'I know.' Fiona went on sorting. 'It sort of helps to do this, it makes things more normal in a way.'

'Yes.'

There was a silence.

Clare had acted on such an impulse when she remembered the photographs that she hadn't paused to think how she would ask for them. Now she was here and she must speak. She couldn't let anyone discover them, nobody should open an envelope and see what she had seen on Sunday night. Nobody should be allowed to look at what she had to look at.

'Fiona?' she began hesitantly.

The perfect oval face, pale with dark circles under the big dark eyes, looked at her inquiringly.

Clare swallowed and began to speak. 'Do you know the way just when you think there's no way out of something . . . you know there's no way out and when somebody helps you. It can change your life.'

Fiona looked at her, confused.

'Surely in your life, ages ago there must have been some problem, some big worry, and maybe Gerry helped you, just said nothing, asked nothing, but gave help.'

Fiona looked at Clare, trying to read in her face whether she could have known about that first pregnancy, and how Gerry had come to England to look after her. Clare felt she was walking on very thin ice.

'I suppose all of us have something like that in our lives, and if someone agrees to sort it out then it *can* be solved.'

'Yes.' Fiona was still doubtful.

'Well I know Gerry did a lot of that for people, you probably don't know how he helped a lot of people when they were in trouble, and I'd like to help him now.'

'How can you help him now?' Fiona cried.

Clare spoke quickly. 'There are some pictures, here somewhere or in a private file or somewhere, that I don't think he'd want people to see.'

'What sort of pictures?'

'Does it matter what kind of pictures if you believe me? If you believe that Gerry wouldn't have wanted them found.'

'Is it very important?'

'I think it is.'

'But why wouldn't Gerry have sorted it out before he . . . before he . . .'

'He didn't drown himself, Fiona.'

Fiona looked left and right. Nobody had said this aloud in front of her but everyone had thought it.

513

'But . . .'

'He couldn't have Fiona, he wasn't that kind of a person, *you* know that.'

'I didn't think he would but how else . . .?'

'Because he was upset, he must have been upset and just went climbing around the rocks. He was always doing that.' Of course it wasn't possible but it would be good for Fiona to think this, and she was beginning to believe it.

'I suppose . . .'

'And it would give a lot of people a better chance if the pictures weren't seen. I just know this, like I know I got a second chance and you probably did too . . .'

Fiona's big troubled eyes filled with tears. 'Gerry did give me a second chance years ago. I wanted to do one thing and he wanted me to do another, he was quite right as it turned out.' Almost unconsciously she stroked her stomach as if thinking of the other child Stephen, now in somebody else's family.

'Well this is what I mean.' Clare didn't want her to confess. 'If I could just . . .'

Fiona handed her a key. 'If they're anywhere they'll be in his room in that steel cabinet. By the window.'

'Thank you Fiona.'

She found them at once. There was hardly anything else there except the cheerful postcard she had sent him once from Dublin, the letter asking him to find her post office savings book and another note thanking him when he had.

It was the same brown envelope that he had showed her on the kitchen table back in her house. But there was an invoice note on it saying that there were copies being sent to Miss Caroline Nolan and David Power as well. So she was too late after all. With leaden movements she placed the contents of the drawer into her big briefcase, the letters she had written him, harmless little notes. Why had he kept them? She put it in and left the drawer open.

She leaned her head against the window.

Should she tell Fiona there was nothing, or should she say that she had found them? Which would cause less worry?

As it happened she needn't have worried, there was no decision to make. Fiona knocked on the door.

'Can I come in?'

'Yes.' Clare was still looking out the window at Church Street, at the people going about their lives in an ordinary way.

'I'm glad you came,' Fiona said.

'Why?'

'Because now I do believe for the first time that it *was* an accident. If Gerry was going to end it himself, he'd have left nothing to get him into trouble ... or you, Clare. He worshipped you. Now I think it must have been an accident.'

'Yes, it must have been.' Clare's gaze was still on the road.

'And so he'll not have gone to hell. I couldn't bear Gerry to go to hell for taking his own life, that's what I've been thinking since Monday morning.'

Clare put her arms awkwardly around Fiona and looked over her shoulder, out of the window at the view that Gerry Doyle must have seen every day as he sat in this ridiculous, over-decorated office and ran his father's steady little business into the ground.

David was looking at an X-ray with his father.

'That poor hip's worn away a lot on her, hasn't it?' Dr Paddy Power was full of sympathy for an elderly woman out on the Far Cliff Road. 'She must be in great pain with that all right.'

'She doesn't complain very much, but she's limping a lot.'

'Ah well, nothing for it, it's terrible to have to tell them it'll just get worse.'

'But you don't tell them that, do you Dad?'

'No, I tell them they're lucky it isn't malignant or anything, try to look on all the positive side of it, no point in being negative and saying it's arthritis and it just gets worse and worse ... David? What is it?'

David had jumped up as if he were shot.

'I've just remembered something. I have to go.'

'Hey ... come back here, leave me the notes, you've got poor Mrs Connolly's whole life story with you.'

515

'What? Yes. Sorry.'

'Are you all right, son?'

'I have to go out for a bit. I'll be back shortly.'

The *negatives*. Why hadn't he remembered them? They were probably in a drawer in Doyle's Photographics, unless of course the little bastard had sent them to someone else like the solicitor's firm where Caroline worked, or to Clare's parents.

He walked around clenching and unclenching his hands in the dark afternoon.

He would have to do it. He walked determinedly down Church Street.

Fiona was by herself in the shop. She looked very young and innocent. Too young for the great curve under her grey smock with its white collar.

'Oh David,' she said. 'Aren't you nice to call.'

He swallowed a bit. 'I don't have the right words to say. My father seems to know exactly what to say that helps people. I don't. Maybe when I'm older and have seen a lot of awful things I will.'

'At least you came in, that was very kind of you,' she said.

Now it was more difficult than ever.

'I'm sure a lot of people have been to say how shocked they are, how upset.'

'No. It's a bit awkward, you see.'

'Why?'

'I think a lot of them think he may have . . . that he may have meant to do it.'

It was impossible to stand talking to this beautiful serene girl who thought her little monster of a brother might have been swept away by some tide.

'Well I don't suppose we'll ever know . . .' he began.

'But I do know. I know he couldn't have meant to do it, take his own life. I *know* that.'

'No, no.' He was soothing.

'I just know.'

'Of course.'

He couldn't broach it, he couldn't say that he had really come not to express sympathy but to know if he could rummage through her dead brother's private files.

516

'What are you doing here? You should be at home resting,' he said in his professional voice.

Fiona looked at him gratefully. 'No, I'm better to keep busy.'

What an end to the Doyles. The bright glittery Doyles of long ago.

'That's good,' he said uselessly.

This was going to be the last time he would talk to Fiona normally. She was going through the picture orders methodically, she would come across prints or negatives, she would scream when she saw them possibly, or feel faint. She might be so revolted she would show them to someone in authority like Father O'Dwyer and ask him what she should do. She was a simple girl, simple and inexperienced, she would be so shocked by all it would mean, for Gerry as well as for him and Caroline. Could he dare?

'Fiona. I was wondering,' he began.

She raised her eyes and he saw the dark shadows underneath for the first time.

'I was wondering . . .' he began. But he couldn't do it. There weren't the words.

'Nothing,' he said, turning to go.

'Clare left her scarf here earlier, can you give it to her?'

'Clare was here?'

'Yes. About an hour ago.'

'What on earth for?' He said it without thinking.

Fiona looked at him thoughtfully. 'Nothing in particular. She just came in.'

'Of course.'

He left with a stooping walk.

Clare had come for the photographs, she hadn't come just to sympathize. If she had, Fiona would have said so.

David didn't notice anyone who spoke to him as he walked back up Church Street and turned left to go home.

Chrissie shouted something at him out of Dwyers' but he didn't hear it. He didn't notice Rose Dillon from the hotel hooting the horn of her scooter at him. Nor did he see Ben O'Brien his brother-in-law waving at him from a pick-up truck.

517

He turned up his collar and paused at the crossroads. Should he go up to see her now? Should he ask Angela and Dick for a few minutes to talk? What would he say? 'I believe you've got the pictures. I'm sorry.'

No, there was nothing to say. He turned and went back to the big house. He walked past it and on to the Lodge. How had he never noticed how silent the place was? And sad.

Clare sat in the car, motionless. She must burn them. Now. But it was much easier said than done to burn something if you hadn't a house of your own. And at the moment she didn't feel she had a house. She could hardly go to the shop: 'Oh. Hallo Mam, Dad, excuse me, I'm just going in to the range to burn a few things, I like a nice fire . . .'

And she had behaved quite madly enough with Dick Dillon and Angela already to ask them did they mind if she burned a few papers in their range.

What about Josie? Would she be able to accept Clare coming in and saying that she'd like a few moments on her own poking around at the Aga in the hotel kitchen? It was nonsensical. Her mind churned. But she would not leave them somewhere where they could be found. They were so awful, those pictures and their negatives, she wanted the satisfaction of seeing them burn in flames. Only that way could she begin to get them out of her mind.

There should be a public burning place, somewhere that people could go and get rid of the things that depressed them or frightened them. A public burning place in the middle of every town.

She remembered suddenly that Dr Power had made a great fuss once about there being no incinerator up at the caravan park. How were the unfortunate campers meant to keep the place hygienic he had thundered unless there were proper rubbish collections and somewhere for them to burn things? The proper rubbish collections had never been set up but the brick incinerator had. It used to burn during the summer getting rid of the worst of the campers' litter.

The caravan park. That would be a nice bit of irony, go up and burn the evidence at the scene of the crime. There wouldn't be a fire in the incinerator now, but she could make one. She had her matches in her handbag, there was a can of petrol in the back of Dick Dillon's car. The more she thought of it the more she liked the idea. She drove slowly down Church Street, past O'Brien's shop, past the bench that looked out over the cliff to the sea, and turned left down the Far Cliff Road to the caravan park.

David rang Caroline again. He had been so relieved the first time when the woman with the bad cold at the solicitor's office had said she was not there. No other explanation. She wasn't at her house either. Now he had rung her office and her house three times and had found her at neither of them. He was no longer relieved, he was worried. He hadn't wanted to talk to her, and presumably she had felt the same at the beginning. But now it was Wednesday evening – two days after the discovery of the pictures. They should talk.

'If Miss Nolan isn't in do you know when and where I could find her?' he asked the woman with the streaming cold.

'In Dublin,' the voice said.

'Has she gone on holiday?' David asked.

'No, she's gone and left. All of a sudden. Gone for good.' The sniff was full of disapproval for the flashy irresponsible ways of a young solicitor from Dublin who didn't know how things were done.

David didn't know whether he was relieved or upset. Relieved, he thought. At least in Dublin Caroline would have people to look after her, people to talk to. In the town here she had nobody. He clenched the kitchen table as he thought of it.

He seemed to spend a lot of time at this table. Sitting here while the time passed. They had thought it would be nice to have a kitchen which was also a living room, that had been the plan, but they had never really done it up or chosen any furniture for it properly. It must have been a kind of prison for Clare.

He thought of Caroline going back to Dublin, her chin raised with that determined look, driving through rain and fog in her little car. He thought of Caroline saying that Gerry Doyle couldn't have had any hopeless unrequited love for her. 'He had me.' Those were her words. Did Gerry Doyle have Caroline in the caravan park, did he share all the same things? God, God. At least David had been spared pictures of it. He only had his imagination.

It was windy and exposed up in the caravan park. It was impossible to see why so many people headed from all over Ireland and England to come here in the summer. It seemed like a different planet.

Clare knew which was Caroline's caravan. She had listened wordlessly when David had said what a good idea it was to get one, she could always spend the summertime in it fully, or in the winter it provided a place to have a change of clothes or an overnight stop when it was too late to drive back to the town. She had forced it out of her mind then. She had refused to think of it.

The same way that she had refused to think of David and Caroline making love. She had blocked it from her mind. Even on the nights that she knew with every instinct that they had she did not acknowledge it. It made things safer, like not stepping on cracks in the pavement. She had never admitted it to herself until she saw those pictures. God, but Gerry Doyle was clever. In a few more days she might well have thought he was a possible alternative to such a cheating husband. It wasn't likely but she hadn't known just how bitter and resentful she would feel. Those pictures that she had in her hand, had gone a great way towards doing what Gerry, mad insane Gerry, had wanted them to do. She must burn them. Now.

Maybe she would feel a bit better.

The wind whipped her hair as she took the can of petrol out of the boot. You couldn't light a fire on a day like this without a rag soaked in something that would leap up in flames.

The grey anonymous caravan that Caroline Nolan had rented for six months stood like a big menacing shape, not far from where Clare was standing. This was where her husband came when he was meant to be playing golf. Those pictures had been taken on a bright afternoon; Gerry must have followed them, on his light little feet. They hadn't bothered to draw the curtains. Who would look in at them? The caravan looked out to sea . . .

She was drawn to see it. Looking left and right as if anyone else would be in this wild place, she tiptoed up to it. It was stripped bare of any possessions, there were no lamps, rugs, little ornaments in it. She remembered her mother-in-law giving Caroline some cushions, two rather nice ones. They were still there, oddly. But none of the tartan rugs that had figured in the pictures, nothing at all.

Perhaps she had gone. Caroline. Perhaps when she saw the pictures she had run for it. Perhaps she was just trying to hide the evidence. She was so clever that one, you'd never know what she was up to.

She took the big envelope out and laid it down on the cold iron bars of the incinerator, she shook some petrol over a cleaning rag and watched the pictures and the negatives and the letters she had written to Gerry Doyle burn. It was a small fire. She poked and poked, they were gone, there was no way that anyone, not a fleet of detectives, could know what they were.

She breathed in the salty air. She still felt restless and jumpy, somehow she had thought that burning the pictures would help but it hadn't. It was all still here, the memory, the caravan. The knowledge of what they had done and might still do, the caravan. The loneliness, the lies he had told her. The caravan.

Almost without realizing it she was walking towards it. It was set far away from the others. She still had the petrol in her hand, the matches were in her pocket.

She paused for one long moment and acknowledged what she was doing. 'Yes,' Clare said aloud. 'Yes, I bloody will.'

The petrol soaked the bed, she put most of it there, and then more near the door. She lit the rag, threw it in and ran as fast as she could away. By the time she reached Dick Dillon's car, parked on the road outside, the flames were coming from the windows.

She drove excitedly back towards town, and stopped the car not far from her parents' shop. She could see the blaze in the winter evening . . .

She felt better than she had for a long time. She called in to her mother.

'What are you driving Dick's car for?'

'God, you were always great with the greeting Mam, I'll say that for you.'

'I've never been able to understand you Clare, never.'

'You didn't do too badly, Mam. Do you think I might have a cup of tea or is it only abuse I'm going to get?'

'Make it for yourself then. Some of us have work to do.'

'Are you cross over something in particular or what, Mam?'

'I don't know what you're up to, that's all.' Agnes had her mouth in a hard line.

'I don't really know myself, Mam, I'm meant to be going up to Dublin to see about sitting this exam again. I'm sort of on the way there – Liffey and I.'

'You're never taking that baby up to Dublin, away from her home.'

'Not for ever Mam, just to give her a taste of city life, look what it did for me.' Clare's eyes were bright, too bright.

She was still sitting on the counter sipping a mug of tea when the shouts went up that there was a fire in the caravan park.

'What's all the fuss and excitement?' Clare asked giddily.

'Lord God, child, someone might be burned to death.' Agnes was white with anxiety.

'Who'd be up there in the middle of winter?' Clare said.

'How could a caravan catch fire unless some poor unfortunate turned over a stove or an oil lamp on themselves?'

They came for David but he wasn't able to move.

'Ask Dad, take him in your car,' he stammered out to Brian Dillon who had come with the alarm.

David's limbs had stopped co-ordinating, it took him five whole minutes to pick up the phone.

The post office took what seemed like an hour to connect him to Dublin.

James Nolan answered the phone. He made a pretence that David was a long-lost traveller who had just returned to civilization. 'We never thought we'd hear your voice again.'

'Cut that out,' David said roughly.

'What?'

'Is Caroline there? Quickly.'

'Well quickly or slowly I can't tell you. Isn't she meant to live in your neck of the woods?'

'James please. I beg you.'

'Have you two had a lovers' tiff?'

'I said I beg you.'

'Very well, since you beg me so nicely, she is here but I'm not to tell you.'

'Are you sure, have you seen her, is she in your house?'

'I don't know where she is this minute but I spoke to her at breakfast and she rang me at the Law Library to arrange something for this evening. But shush, I didn't tell you.'

'No.'

'David? Are you all right?'

He had hung up.

The burning of the caravan was a mystery. It must have been youngsters playing with petrol, everything had been soaked in it. Poor Caroline Nolan.

The Guard had rung her in the big town but they couldn't find her. Still wasn't it a mercy that nobody had been hurt?

Clare drove in to the garage where her brother Ben worked. She got Dick Dillon's car filled up and also the petrol can he kept at the back. She drove back to the O'Hara house.

'You said only a minute. I was worried,' Angela said.

'Stop sounding like my mother.'

'Are you all right? You look very flushed.' Angela was conerned.

'No. I'm much better now. There was something I had to do.'

Mrs Corrigan from the other side of the road came in with

523

the news that there had been a big fire over on the Far Cliff Road, and a caravan burned to a shell.

Angela wanted to know was anyone hurt.

'Who would be there in the middle of winter?' Clare had said, her eyes still too bright.

'People are sometimes,' Angela said cautiously.

'Well, they're up to no good then.'

Angela looked so frightened then, that Clare took pity on her.

'It's all right, Angela, it's all right, there was nobody in it. I did check.'

Clare picked up Liffey and held her tight, she was so big now it was quite a weight.

'Well Liffey, in a day or two you and I are heading off to the great unknown to seek our fortune — well, to seek Mummy's degree for one thing.'

'I'll never say. You won't, either, I hope.'

'No, of course not, but you're different, you can know everything. The good and the bad.'

'It wasn't all that *very* bad, considering,' Angela said with a smile.

'No it wasn't was it?' Clare seemed recovered now.

'Did you know that Clare's up in Angela Dillon's house?' Agnes asked Tom O'Brien that night.

'Sure hasn't she been living up there since she was ten years of age, what's strange about that?' he asked.

'No that's just it, she *is* living up there, she's been there three days.'

'Nonsense, Agnes, you must have got the wrong end of the stick. Hasn't she a perfectly good house of her own?'

'I know, but that's what I heard, so I asked her straight out.'

'And?'

'You never get a straight answer from Clare, she said she was on her way to Dublin to inquire about exams or some such nonsense.'

'Better say nothing, say nothing at all, you'll get little thanks for what you say.'

Agnes thought that for once he might be right. This could be one occasion when it might pay to take no notice.

People said that Gerry Doyle's poor mother had to take so many tablets now for her nerves that she would hardly realize what was happening at the funeral. Fiona had tried to get her a black coat and she said no, she always hated black, it reminded her of funerals. Gently Fiona had tried to persuade her that this actually was a funeral, and didn't know whether to be pleased or upset that her mother hadn't taken in the fact that Gerry was dead.

Nellie Burke's family asked her was it true that David Power and Clare were living apart. Nellie, stubborn and loyal, said she knew nothing of the sort. Her brother's wives, who were spectacular gossips, were disappointed. They thought she would be the source of all information. So they had to make do with saying that a marriage like that could never work. They had known it from the start. She had been a silly little girl to think that a bit of education made her the equal of the doctor's son.

'Did David tell you that Caroline Nolan's packed up her job and gone back to Dublin?' Paddy Power asked Molly.

'I don't believe you.'

'So Mr Kenny says, remember he got her the job in the first place, very upset he is about it all. Just told them she wasn't suited to country life, worked all day and all night to get her work finished and left. Same in her house. Wrote them a cheque for the rest of the quarter and vanished.'

'I must ring Sheila.'

'Maybe not, Moll. Maybe not. Let it settle down a bit yet.'

'Why do you say that?' She looked anxious.

'We don't know half of what goes on, we might be making it worse.'

'How could we make things worse, we're their friends, we haven't done anything to upset Caroline, to make her run off from here.'

'No Moll, you haven't and I haven't,' he said levelly.

She looked at him in alarm and realized he wasn't going to say any more.

'There'll be so many there they won't miss me. I'm not going,' Clare said.

They could hear the bell tolling on the cold, wet morning.

'You shouldn't hurt the living. Fiona, his mother.'

'I can't stand there and pray for the repose of his soul. It's a mockery.'

'It's what people do, it's a custom, think of it like that.'

'You don't know . . . you don't know . . .'

'Clare, stop it this minute. Of course I don't know, you didn't tell me, and you are not going to tell me now when we have to be in the church in ten minutes' time. I've arranged for us to put Liffey in Mrs Corrigan's, she'll not be going, she's got five babies in that house already.'

'No. I have to stay here and mind Liffey.'

'Clare, stop being a child. Put your coat on. Now.'

'Would you like to walk up to the church with me, son?'

'Dad, I was half thinking I wouldn't go. You know, stay here in case anyone needs one of us.'

'If they need us won't they know where to find us, where would anyone find anyone on the day the bell is ringing for a young man?'

'I know but . . .'

'There's going to be talk if you don't go.'

'That's nonsense, the church will be full, the whole of Castlebay will be there.'

'And you should be there.'

'But there are a lot of things I can't explain . . .'

'And there's no need why you *should* explain, just come up to the church with me now, come on David, it's a small thing to do, but it's a big thing if you don't do it.'

'If you think . . .'

'I do think. Come on now, the bell's ringing, your mother's gone already in the car.'

*

With cold hands they blessed themselves. Almost all of Castlebay went into the familiar church. The only thing that was unfamiliar was the coffin up near the altar rails. It was covered with Mass cards and there were two wreaths, one from his mother arranged by Frank Conway, and one from Fiona and Frank also arranged by Frank Conway. For some odd reason other people hadn't sent flowers. You didn't associate Gerry Doyle with flowers for the dead.

The church always seemed colder at a funeral. In the front row Mrs Mary Doyle knelt in the black coat that had been borrowed for her, her eyes vacant and her hands clasped. Beside her Fiona sat. Face paler than ever, wearing a loose black coat and a mantilla. She looked like a Spanish widow, she had never looked really Irish at all.

David and his father arrived just at the same moment as Angela, Dick and Clare. They exchanged the funeral words people spoke at such times – terrible tragedy, young man, makes you wonder at the sense of anything.

David and Clare let the others go in before them.

'Did you burn the caravan?' he asked.

'Yes. And the pictures. And the negatives.'

'It doesn't matter I suppose,' he said eventually.

'No.'

As if they were a million miles from each other they walked into the church side by side. Angela and Dr Power sat beside each other deliberately. David and Clare joined them. So Castlebay was not treated to the sight of the young doctor and his wife having a public coldness right in the middle of a funeral. They genuflected and knelt down, where they had been manoeuvred to be. Beside each other.

There had never been a Mass as long as this.

When she was certain it must be the communion it was only the offertory. When she was sure it was the last Gospel it was only the post-communion.

Sitting, and standing, and kneeling, beside David; looking at his cold hands clasped in front of him; noticing that he needed a haircut; seeing that his shoes were well-polished and wondering had Nellie done that for him.

And then every time she lifted her glance seeing that coffin which they said held Gerry Doyle.

Where would she go back to? If she could go back . . .?

Before she got pregnant? No, that would mean no Liffey, and the only good thing that had come out of all this was Liffey.

After Liffey was born, had she been really terrible then? It was odd, she couldn't remember much about all that winter and spring. She must have been a poor companion. As drugged and vacant-looking as Gerry's unfortunate mother looked now.

Was that where she would start again?

David wished that she wasn't kneeling beside him, but there was nothing else they could do. She had her elbows on the back of the seat in front and her forehead resting on her clenched hands. He noticed how thin her wrist was, with the watch he had given her hanging slightly loosely on it. When he glanced at her he saw her eyes were open and distant. She wasn't praying, obviously.

There was plenty to think about. He felt a great weariness come over him. He was too tired to make her promises, to beg her to come back to the Lodge, to tell her it would all be all right. It might not be all right, and they had never lied directly to each other, they had lied by omission. He had never denied that he was with Caroline, because she had never asked him what way he was with Caroline. If it hadn't been for those pictures, they would have had a chance. Those pictures. If he could only go back to before the pictures . . .

Had she really burned them? Is that what she had been doing when she went to burn the caravan? He shivered to think of it. Suppose the wind blew the wrong way and had swept the flames towards her? But why should she have gone up to the caravan park to burn the pictures, for God's sake? Couldn't she have burned them anywhere? He turned his head and looked at her, head still leaning on one hand, her dark eyes looking ahead, her shoulders tense and full of hurt. Had he been right when he said that nothing made any difference now? Was it too late?

The priest had walked around the cofffin with the thurible and the sickly sweet smell of incense filled the church as Father O'Dwyer made his circle of the box that contained Gerry Doyle. Then four men, men who had been boys with Gerry and who had watched helplessly while he had taken their girlfriends away, picked up the cofffin as if it were no weight at all. They walked out of the church followed by the whole congregation.

They walked, heads bent in the wind, the quarter of a mile to the graveyard which stood high on a hill. There the grave had been dug and the two gravediggers removed their caps as the funeral procession arrived.

Visitors often looked at this little graveyard and said it would be a beautiful place to come to rest. Surrounded by a stone wall, filled with the celtic crosses of years, its own little ruined church covered with ivy in the corner.

Because it was on a hill you could see the whole beach below, the white flecks of the waves coming in ceaselessly. The sand and stones being pulled out in their wake. Hardly anyone could have looked back down at the beach without remembering that this is why they were here.

The only people who didn't look were Gerry's mother and sister. Mrs Mary Doyle looked vaguely around. It was like a bad dream, everyone seemed to be looking at her she thought, but her sister held one of her arms and her daughter held the other. There was no sign of Gerry but he must be away working somewhere, he'd be here soon.

Fiona's tears were mixed with the salt wind and rain, but she felt much more at peace now, now that she realized Gerry couldn't have done it on purpose. Whatever those pictures were, Gerry would never have left anything behind him, deliberately . . . not anything that would hurt someone or ruin their life.

She listened to Father O'Dwyer, she didn't understand the Latin words, but she knew that they were necessary to set Gerry's soul at peace.

*

Angela looked at Dick. His face always looked very cross when he was upset, and he was greatly upset by all this. Last night he had whispered to her that there was a lot of violence in Castlebay, a sort of passion that was very destructive.

'It might cease now. Now that poor Gerry Doyle is dead,' Angela had said.

'No, it seems to be starting, what could have possessed that young fellow to do a thing like that. What could have been so bad that made him do it? And look at the caravan being burned out. I know that may not have anything to do with it, but it all seems very violent. All of a sudden.'

Angela said nothing. Some day she would know what it was all about.

Molly Power looked across at the O'Briens as they stood together. Agnes thin and frail always, her two sons beside her, Tom standing a bit back. That's all she had now, after rearing that huge family, two boys in England, that Chrissie married into the Byrne family. And Clare. Who knew what to make of Clare? Certainly her parents didn't; and Molly didn't. She looked over to where the girl was standing stiffly, her long hair blowing in the wind. A good dark coat, not that terrible dufffle coat she used to live in at one time. She was a strange girl. No wonder David found it so hard to deal with her.

Father O'Dwyer knew how to bury the dead of his parish. He had been doing it for years. But the dead were never like this. The dead were old men and women who hadn't been able to survive a winter. Or someone who died tragically young leaving a family of small children. Occasionally the dead might be children – that was very hard, but there was something to say, about God taking innocent little souls to himself.

Paddy Power wondered what would Father O'Dwyer say to a congregation who knew what a life Gerry Doyle had lived, and that he had ended up by taking that life himself.

Dr Power had reminded himself only that morning that God was merciful: and if God was, then Father O'Dwyer must be also.

The priest looked around at the cold faces all spattered by the sea spray and whipped by the wind. He would not keep them long but he must keep them long enough to do honour to the dead man. Otherwise why have the ceremony at all?

'You all knew Gerry Doyle, and as we stand here around his grave and pray that his soul is in heaven with the angels we will all remember his love of life, and how he was involved in everything that went on in Castlebay . . .

'I think it's true that since this young man personified life, and youth and energy, his sudden death will make us realize once more what a very slight hold we have on our mortal lives, how easily they can be whipped away. While we pray for Gerry this morning, let us think of the briefness of our own lives. This time next year, not all of us who stand here now may be here, and in ten years' time, many more will have gone to their Maker. But it's not only the old and those who are ready to go, it's the young who are totally unprepared to face the kingdom of heaven, and who still have so much to say to each other and to their families and their friends.

'If Gerry Doyle had been given one more day there might have been many things he would wish to have said, things to put straight, people to reassure. But the Lord doesn't let us know the time He calls us. Everyone here has a cheerful memory of Gerry. Let us keep those memories in our hearts and pray that his soul is in heaven today, and will rise again on the Last Day.'

There were the last three Hail Marys and the glory be to the Father and then Fiona leaned forward to raise the shovel of earth, the first one to fall on the coffin that had been lowered into the ground. She looked down into the big open grave.

'Thank you Gerry,' she said unexpectedly.

People were almost embarrassed, nobody ever spoke at a time like this, certainly nobody expected the quiet dignified Fiona to say anything so emotional. One by one the men shovelled on earth, filling up the dark hollow space.

This was the bleakest part of a funeral. The finishing touches. People huddled closer together almost unconsciously as if they were looking for some warmth from just being in a crowd.

Clare and David moved together. Partly because they were jostled, partly because they wanted to.

It was David's turn to take the spade in his hand. He paused and looked at Clare. Her glance was steady. She didn't turn away.

David dug into the heap of clay that lay beside the grave and heard it fall on to the earth that was already on top of Gerry's coffin. He took three steps back towards Clare, she had her hand out in its little knitted glove.

He took it and they both watched the gravediggers finish off the work that the parish had begun. Two tall bony men, they had it finished in no time. The two wreaths were put on the little mound. In a year they would put up a tombstone to Gerry Doyle, Born 1935, Died 1962, and passersby would shake their heads and say he died very young.

The people began to trickle down the hill, towards Craig's Bar some of them, some to Dillon's Hotel, others to open up their businesses which had been closed to honour Gerry Doyle.

A long time ago, back in Dublin when there had been a simple sort of life, David used to take Clare's hand in its knitted glove and put it into his pocket for further warmth. He wondered did he dare do that now. Very gently he drew her hand towards him and she placed it in his pocket without him having to do anything.

They walked down the twisty road with the loose stones. Down the hill to Castlebay.